ABOUT THE BOOK

This complete collection includes all three books in the trilogy!

A feisty outlaw.
A conniving prince.
A war of magic and shadows.

Wanted by the crown for a murder she didn't commit, Cora dreams of getting revenge on the mage who framed her. In the meantime, she hides in the forest and hones her witch magic. But when she discovers her enemy's violent hunt for faerie creatures, she forms a plan for vengeance.

Prince Teryn, heir to a bankrupt throne, will do anything to keep his country from sinking into ruin. When he meets an outlawed witch wanted by a neighboring kingdom, he gets his chance. The woman has an impressive bounty on her head, one that could pay off his kingdom's debts.

If Teryn can help Cora save a few magical creatures, he can gain her trust, hand her over to her king, and collect the bounty. But Cora has plans of her own, and none of them include being betrayed by her handsome new traveling companion.

The closer Cora and Teryn get to their desires, the harder their tasks become. And it isn't just their budding attraction that's the problem. A secret war is coming, one stemming from ancient feuds and forgotten fae magic. They must work together to stop it, or else both their kingdoms will crumble to ash.

PROPHECY OF THE FORGOTTEN FAE is perfect for fans of *Throne of Glass, Air Awakens,* and *Shadow and Bone.* If you like elemental magic, fierce witches, and slow burn enemies-to-lovers romance, then you'll love this epic fantasy tale.

PROPHECY OF THE FORGOTTEN FAE is an upper YA fantasy that contains moderate violence/gore and adult situations. The romance is slooooow burn, leading to open-door mild spice in the third book.

PROPHECY OF THE FORGOTTEN FAE

COMPLETE SERIES COLLECTION

TESSONJA ODETTE

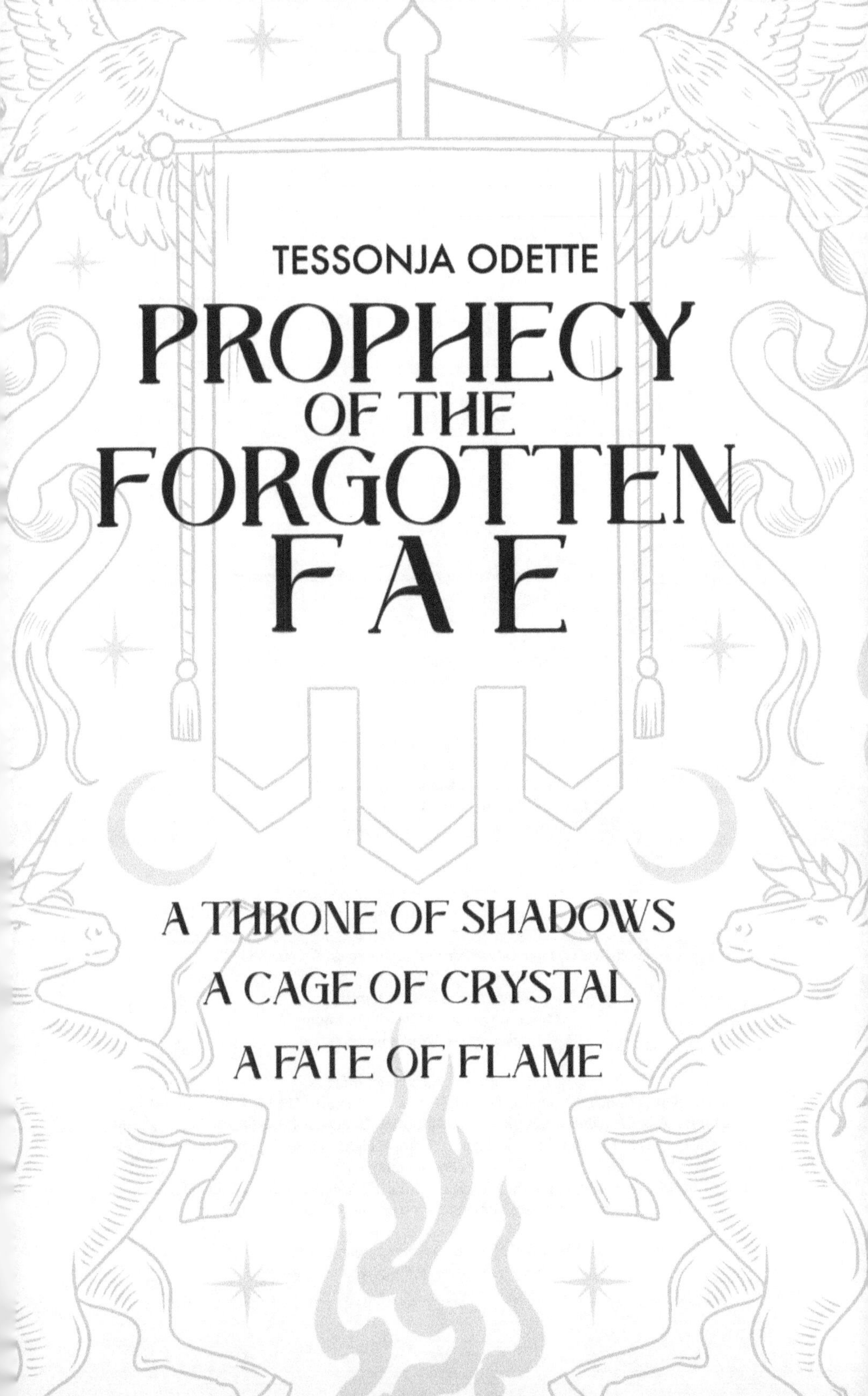

TESSONJA ODETTE

PROPHECY OF THE FORGOTTEN FAE

A THRONE OF SHADOWS

A CAGE OF CRYSTAL

A FATE OF FLAME

Cover and interior illustrations by:
Cover by Bookish Averil
Maps and headers by Tessonja Odette
Cora and Teryn illustration by Alexandra Curte
Four tarot card illustrations by Bon Orthwick

Publisher: Tessonja Odette, Crystal Moon Press, Tacoma, WA USA
Authorized Representative:
Easy Access System Europe
Mustamäe tee 50, 10621 Tallinn, Estonia
gpsr.requests@easproject.com

Printed and bound by IngramSpark.
Australia: Ingram Content Group AU Pty Ltd, Melbourne, Victoria. US: Lightning Source LLC, La
Vergne, Tennessee / Allentown, Pennsylvania / Jackson, Tennessee, United States. UK: Lightning
Source UK Ltd, Milton Keynes, United Kingdom. Europe: Lightning Source UK Ltd, with facilities in
Germany, France, and Spain.
The authorized representative in the European Economic Area is Lightning Source France, 1 Av.
Johannes Gutenberg, 78310 Maurepas, France. compliance@lightningsource.fr

ISBN (paperback) 978-1-955960-31-1
ISBN (hardcover) 978-1-955960-30-4

RISÆ
NORUN
THE WALL
TOMAS
VINIAS
KHERO
SELAY
MENAH
SYRUS
ZARAS
SOUTHERN
ISLANDS
Balma
Sea
CARTHA

LELA
DELANY
CAMBRON PASS
RIDINE CASTLE
Khero
ISHVONN WOODS
CENTERPOINTE ROCK
Selay
DERMAINE PALACE
Menah
VERLOT PALACE
BRUSHWOLD
N
W
E
S

A THRONE OF SHADOWS

BOOK ONE

1

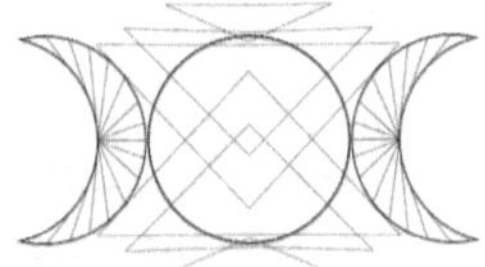

When Cora dreamed, she dreamed of castles. Not the storybook variety with shining turrets and glistening marble columns, but dark towers brimming with even darker magic. These castles held no masked balls, boasted no gilded statues or impressive tapestries. Instead of fancy footmen fluttering about the halls, the corridors were empty, black, and soundless. All that existed was a *feeling*, a deep and hollow knowing that something wasn't quite right.

In her dreams, Cora could do nothing but follow this sense of unease, this wrongness that existed outside of her, calling to her like the mythical sirens of fae lore. It was a silent song, one so chilling it made her hair stand on end. Still, she could do nothing but follow. Follow. Meeting dead end after dead end.

The feeling intensified, growing heavier, tugging her bones until it bore down upon her like a leaden weight. She knew she should stop following the feeling. Knew she should turn around and forget the dark pull. But even when she tried to forget, tried to turn around, the feeling only drew nearer. Soon the halls closed in, inch by inch, until they narrowed down to a single corridor, one that ended in the same door no matter which way she turned.

A rattling sound echoed around her. Glancing down, she found it was coming from the serving tray she carried. A teacup trembled against its saucer. Her hands were shaking even more.

The door loomed ahead of her, gaping like a hungry maw.

Against her will, her feet moved toward it. Too soon she stood in the dreaded doorway. As she saw what lay beyond, she felt as if she'd known all along. There was a bed. And upon that bed...

Blood. So much blood.

A scream shattered the air, piercing her eardrums.

She shook her head, trying to rid her eyes of the sight and her ears of the blaring shout. It grew louder. She blinked several times, but that only brought her closer to the bed. The blood was no longer just in front of her but all around, dripping from her hands. The sharp tang of it filled her nose, seared her throat.

Then a question filled her mind, the voice angry and familiar.

What have you done?

The scream intensified.

It was coming from her.

~

CORA OPENED HER EYES BUT ALL SHE COULD SEE WAS BLACK. TWO WEIGHTS PRESSED down upon her shoulders—hands—and she flailed against them, fighting the unseen assailant who restrained her.

"Cora, quiet, you're safe."

The voice leached the fight from her bones. She went limp beneath her friend's touch, pursing her lips against the screams that still crawled up her throat.

"It's just me," soothed Maiya, stroking the damp hair away from Cora's forehead. "You're home. It was just a bad dream."

Cora gritted her teeth and breathed away the remnants of her terror. In its place, anger grew. Not at her friend but at herself. She was supposed to be stronger than nightmares. She was a witch, after all. Witches were meant to be powerful.

"I'm sorry," Cora muttered, finding her voice far weaker than she liked. Wiping furiously at a few errant tears, she rolled onto her side and buried her face in her blanket. Maiya gave her shoulder a light pat and returned to her cot at the other side of the tent they shared. Even in the darkness, Cora could feel the other girl's eyes burning into her.

"Did you take your sleeping tonic last night?" Maiya asked, caution heavy in her tone.

"Yes." She'd brewed it herself. Stronger than usual.

"Is...is something wrong?"

Cora remained silent because she had no answer. This was the third night in a row she'd woken screaming from this same terrifying nightmare. Such dreams plagued her on occasion but never with such alarming frequency. Her sleeping draught was normally enough to drive them away.

"Would you like to tell me about your dream?" Maiya asked, trying to sound nonchalant but failing miserably. "Perhaps I can help divine its meaning."

Cora ignored her. Not because she didn't trust her friend. Maiya was probably the only person she trusted with her whole heart. She was like a sister to her, one of the very few people Cora had let herself grow close to ever since she was taken in by the Forest People six years ago. But Cora's burdens were hers to bear. Besides, Maiya was a witch too and growing proficient at dream divination. What if her abilities had grown beyond the realm of dreams? Cora couldn't risk her discovering any of her secrets. It was too dangerous for them both.

Without another word, Cora focused on slowing her ragged breathing until it settled into a gentle rhythm. Hoping Maiya would fall for her ruse and think she'd drifted back to sleep, she kept up the act until she heard her friend's soft snores. Only then did she let herself remember the dream.

A dream that felt like a memory.

⁓

CORA WOKE TO MORNING SUN KISSING HER EYELIDS. EVEN WITH JUST A SLIVER OF light peeking in from the open tent flap, it was bright enough to tell her she'd slept in. She pressed a tattooed palm over her eyes, but it was no use. She was already awake. Not even the black symbols inked into her skin could ward away the evils of everyday responsibility. She rolled over and peered at Maiya's cot. Her bedroll was empty, and her wool blankets and furs were neatly folded on top of it. How late in the morning was it? Cora rubbed her eyes to rid them of grit, but nothing seemed to soothe them. Her throat too felt raw, and she was almost of a mind to go back to sleep. However, she knew there was no use lingering in bed all because of a bad dream.

With a stretch, she forced herself to rise from her cot. Her arms prickled with gooseflesh beneath the cool spring air that drifted into the tent. Dressed only in her linen shift, she peeked outside and found her freshly laundered clothes hanging on a line. The smell of lavender wafted on the air, mingling with the earth, woodsmoke, and pine scents of camp. All at once, Cora felt a sense of calm. Of safety. She was protected by the Forest People. With their proficiency at wards and subterfuge, her enemies couldn't find her here.

If only her dreams couldn't either.

She tugged her patchwork petticoats and bodice off the line, then brought them back inside to get dressed. She'd have Maiya to thank for the clean clothes. Her friend had clearly been up working hard while Cora dozed.

Once dressed, she strolled between the tents of varying shapes and sizes, each structure draped with oiled hides, and tried not to look anyone in the eye. Her screams had to have been loud enough to wake half the camp, and she dreaded knowing what everyone thought of her. Did they think she was crazy? Or did they feel pity? Cora wanted neither sentiment and preferred no one thought much of her at all. Luckily, it seemed most of the Forest People were too busy with their daily tasks to pay her any mind, whether they were hunting, cooking, weaving, brewing tinctures and salves, or practicing the Arts—magic, in other words.

Magic was the lifeblood of the Forest People, infusing their way of life. The nomadic commune was once comprised of the last living Faeryn, ancient fae who practiced the Magic of the Soil. Nowadays, there wasn't anyone left of pure Faeryn blood, as most had eventually mated with humans, but some within the commune still bore obvious signs of their heritage—petite stature, the slightest hint of a pointed ear, skin and hair in the richest earth tones.

In recent decades, those with human magic came to live amongst the commune too, making the Forest People an eclectic group. Most citizens in the Kingdom of Khero didn't believe in magic, but they had no qualms about ostracizing anyone who possessed uncanny senses or an unusual fondness for nature. Whenever the Forest People came across these individuals, they welcomed them with open arms. They did the same when they found Cora, an orphaned girl wandering alone in the woods.

Cora nearly fit in with the Faeryn descendants with her dark hair, brown eyes, and warm tan skin, but she wasn't of Faeryn blood. She was a witch. Even though this made her welcome with the Forest People, it didn't make her feel like she belonged. She'd been with the commune for six years, but she didn't think she'd ever stop feeling like an outsider. Probably because her new family might very well revoke their welcome if they knew who she was.

She made her way to the heart of the camp, her stomach growling at the smell of roasting meat and vegetables being heated over the cook fires. Once she reached the common area, a clearing surrounded by brightly painted wagons, she found Chandra on cook duty. The middle-aged woman was of stout build with dark eyes and a bronze complexion. Her hair was black with the faintest hint of dark green— a sign of her Faeryn heritage. Inked designs extended from her palms to her shoulders. Cora stared at the woman's tattoos with longing. Unlike the cook, Cora's ink only marked her palms and forearms, indicating the levels of the Arts she'd proven herself accomplished in. She wished to one day be covered to her neck with ink. Maybe then she'd be strong enough to banish her nightmares.

"Twenty-five years," Chandra said.

She frowned. "Pardon?"

"That's how long I've worked to get my *insigmora*."

Insigmora was the Forest People's name for the tattoos—a tradition passed down from the ancient Faeryn. The thought of spending two more decades honing her Art left a pit in Cora's stomach. She didn't want to wait that long. "They're beautiful," was all she said, forcing a smile to her lips.

Chandra's expression turned wary as she eyed her. Cora held her breath, hoping the cook wouldn't bring up her nightmares. The cook was known for her bluntness, and the last thing Cora wanted was for her to ask about the screaming that shattered the peace of the camp last night. She bit the inside of her cheek, resisting the urge to open her senses to the woman so she could read her feelings.

As a witch, Cora's talent was clairsentience. Every witch had an affinity for at least one of the six senses—feeling, knowing, seeing, hearing, tasting, or smelling. Sensing the feelings of others had been a bane since she was young, but after she was found by the Forest People, they taught her to shield against constant outside stimuli. Now she could use her Art at will, but it didn't always go undetected. Not when used on fellow witches or the descendants of the Faeryn.

"Stew or porridge?" Chandra asked, finally breaking eye contact and nodding toward the cook fires.

Cora let out a sigh of relief and turned her attention to the simmering cauldrons. The smell of root vegetables made her mouth water. "Stew."

Chandra went to the nearest pot and ladled a hearty serving into a clay bowl.

Cora nodded her thanks as the woman handed over her breakfast. As she went to turn away, Chandra spoke. "What are they about?"

Cora paused. "What do you mean?"

"The dreams that make you scream at night. What do you dream of when that happens?"

Cora's muscles tensed at the question, but there was only one answer she could give. "Death."

A bow in Cora's hand always felt like home. And a belted dagger at her waist felt like safety. Strength. Practical defense to fill the many gaps in her magic. There was only so much a clairsentient witch could do. Cora was determined to do more. To *be* more.

She donned her cloak and gathered her weapons from inside her tent, shouldering her bow and quiver of arrows, then securing her belt with its sheathed dagger. There was no doubt Cora had missed the day's hunt, considering she'd slept in so late, but she could at least practice her archery. She rarely missed a day using her bow. Besides, she needed to harvest more valerian root for her sleeping tonic. She knew she could get some from the potions tent, but the Forest People kept up a stringent inventory of their ingredients during harvesting, stocking, and brewing. If Cora asked for yet another pouch of valerian, people would start talking. They'd know just how strong she'd begun to brew it. Which was why it was even more frustrating that her nightmares had become so persistent.

She left the tent but only made it a few steps before she pulled up short. Maiya stood just outside with her arms crossed. She was dressed in her most brightly patterned skirts and had pink cherry blossoms woven through two long black braids. An amused smile danced over her lips as she assessed Cora's much plainer ensemble. "Really, Cora? On Beltane?"

Cora grimaced. "I forgot it's Beltane."

"Some witch you are," Maiya said with a chuckle. She hesitated then, some of the mirth leaving her eyes as she shifted from foot to foot. "So...did you sleep all right?"

"I'm fine, Maiya," Cora said with what she hoped was a reassuring grin. "You can stop looking at me like I'm made of glass."

Maiya gave Cora's shoulder a playful shove. "I just worry about you, that's all.

I'm here if you want to talk. My mother is here for you too. Salinda's an elder. She has more wisdom than anyone."

"I know she does." Cora started off toward the edge of camp. Maiya shadowed her every step, silent although Cora knew she was dying to say more. From the corner of her eye, she could see her friend opening and closing her hands—Maiya's telltale anxious gesture. The girl's palms were inked with only a single tattoo at the center of each, a design made from several overlapping circles and triangles that vaguely resembled a flower. She was a year younger than Cora and only just beginning to explore her talents with the Arts. While Maiya's mother was half witch and half Faeryn, Maiya's magic seemed to favor her witch heritage. She was claircognizant and used her keen knowing to divine meaning from dreams.

"You could let me practice on you," Maiya said, voice brimming with innocence. "It would be good for me. And...and I think it would be good for you too."

Cora halted and faced her friend. She knew Maiya meant well. Knew in her deepest heart that Maiya's prying was done with nothing but love. Still, it had to stop. Maiya didn't understand what she was asking to get involved in. "Just drop it, all right? Please."

Maiya nibbled her lip. "I only want to know that you're really okay. I know something is bothering you."

"It's nothing."

Maiya reached for her hand. As soon as their fingers made contact, Cora was overwhelmed with a sense of worry and desperation—Maiya's feelings. Her breath caught in her throat at the sudden onslaught of emotion. Wrenching her hand away, she took a stumbling step back.

Maiya's eyes turned down at the corners, her sympathy palpable. "Cora—"

"You are not going to believe it!"

Cora startled at the voice, but it was a welcome interruption. It severed her involuntary connection to her friend's feelings. Her breathing eased as she faced the figure darting their way.

Gisele stopped before them, bouncing on the balls of her feet. "It's Roije. He's back!"

Maiya's face went blank, her preoccupation with Cora's wellbeing instantly forgotten. The name Gisele had mentioned was probably the only word in the history of the spoken language that could wipe all prior thought from Maiya's mind. Her voice turned wistful. Anxious. "Roije...he's...he's really back?"

"I thought you'd want to know," Gisele said with a wink. "Come on!"

Before Cora could argue, Gisele linked her arms through both of theirs and dragged them across camp. They came upon a crowd gathering near the picket line where the Forest People's horses were kept. A familiar young man stood at the far end, hitching his horse. Cora's first glimpse at Roije showed he'd grown at least three inches taller since he'd left the Forest People a year ago. His hair had grown too, no longer cropped close to his head but in black waves that fell over his dark eyes. She turned her attention to his clothes and discovered more changes to admire. Instead of the leather britches and wool tunic most of the men wore around camp, he was dressed in a fine linen shirt and black trousers. His sleeves were rolled up to reveal inked forearms—proof of his skill in the Arts. But as Cora drew closer, she noticed something else about his shirt—a haphazard spatter of rusty reddish brown. Blood.

Strange appearance aside, Cora was surprised Roije was back. He'd grown up with the Forest People, but his father was not of their commune. When his mother took ill and died a year ago, he left to find the man who had sired him. His loss was felt by many, especially since his tracking skills were second to none. His Art was the Magic of the Soil, thanks to his Faeryn heritage, and he used it to speak to the earth. Before he left, he was considered the most marriageable bachelor in the commune. Now that he was back, Cora was curious to know why. She wasn't the only one, based on the size of the crowd.

Cora expected to come upon giddy conversation, but the closer she and her two companions drew, the more obvious it was that something was wrong. It was too quiet. Roije had never been a frivolous man by any means, even before he came of age. He was never one of the youths who snuck off to the nearest towns to drink at pubs or steal kisses from farm girls. He took his tracking duties seriously and had gone to great lengths to care for his mother in her dying days. Even so, the look in his eyes was unlike anything she'd seen in them before. They seemed... haunted.

He unsaddled his horse with slow motions, wincing now and then as if he were injured.

"Roije!" Gisele released Cora's arm to wave frantically for his attention, clearly unable to read the mood. "Where did you go? Did you find your father?"

Roije paused his ministrations and ran a hand over his face. He gave a solemn nod. "I found him. Turns out he...he was a butcher in Kubera."

"What's Kubera like?" Gisele asked. "Is it a large village? A wealthy one?"

It took all of Cora's restraint not to stomp on the girl's foot to quiet her. A single word nestled within Roije's answer said everything she needed to know. *Was.* His father *was* a butcher. She held no optimism that his usage of past tense suggested a change in occupation. His emotions were written clearly on his face, in the tilt of his eyes, and the dark circles beneath them.

Even if his expression had been blank, Cora would have known, for his emotions were so strong they slipped past her shields, much like what had happened with Maiya minutes ago. Grief flooded her heart, followed by shame. It made her feel heavy. Dizzy. Disconnected.

Breathing deep, she turned her attention to her own emotions, her own body. She focused on the cool spring air against her skin. The smell of earth and pine. Soon the unwanted emotions began to fade. She breathed deeply again, imagining the air around her growing thicker, gathering roots from the soil beneath her feet, soaking up water from earth, from the molecules in the air, then absorbing the bright light of the sun, the warmth of its fiery rays. Welcoming all four elements, she imagined them dancing, weaving, forming an invisible wall that hummed with energy all around her.

With her mental shields strengthened, she returned her attention to Roije.

"I'm so sorry," Maiya said, her voice barely above a whisper.

His gaze cut to her, and his expression softened. Their eyes held for a heated moment that made Cora want to look away.

Gisele glanced from Maiya to Roije. "What? I don't understand. What happened?"

"My father accepted me into his home," Roije said, his eyes finally leaving Maiya's. "When I tracked him down, I knew there was a chance he'd turn me away, but he didn't. He remembered my mother and was eager to get to know me. Then *they* came."

"Who's they?" asked one of the men in the crowd.

"King Dimetreus' soldiers. They came to Kubera."

Every muscle in Cora's body stiffened at the mention of the King of Khero. A spike of anger burned her blood, but she tried not to let it show on her face. She wasn't the only one who seemed unsettled by the news, however. Some stared with hard looks while others exchanged wary glances. It wasn't hard to understand why. The Forest People may have resided primarily in the Kingdom of Khero, but they served the land, not its king. They owed their allegiance to no monarch and avoided royal politics like a plague.

Roije continued. "They were recruiting young men to join the army by force. Father begged me to hide, said they wouldn't know I'd ever been there. Two soldiers came to the shop while I hid in the cellar. Rumors about me had spread. Father refused to give me up so they...they killed him." His expression hardened, taking the breath from Cora's lungs. She knew that look. Terror meets a thirst for vengeance. It was as familiar to her as her own skin.

"Oh, Roije," Gisele cooed, "that's so terrible. But I'm glad you made it out alive."

"Barely," he muttered. "I had to take the two men out with me." With that, he turned back to his horse and began brushing him down, a silent dismissal of his audience.

The tension was heavy in the air as the crowd dispersed. Gisele remained in place with a pout on her lips, but Maiya tugged her arm. "We should give him some space."

Gisele cast one more longing glance at Roije before obeying. Cora was more than happy to follow, but before she could take a step, Roije's voice called out. "Cora."

With a frown, she turned back to face him, her cheeks burning beneath the sudden scrutiny of her companions. Gisele looked scandalized while Maiya's expression flickered with hurt. Maiya had always held a secret affection for the man while Cora had never been close with him at all. It made little sense why she'd be the one he wanted to speak to after returning. She gave Maiya an apologetic smile and then approached him. Dread filled her stomach as a terrifying possibility occurred to her. Could his summons be romantic in nature? Goddess above, she hoped not. But why else would he single her out? It was Beltane, after all. Then again, why would he harbor romantic thoughts when he was clearly grieving?

Cora sent out a silent prayer that there was a perfectly reasonable explanation for his summons that had nothing to do with courtship. It wasn't because she was unattracted to him. He was without a doubt the handsomest young man in the commune. But she knew how Maiya felt. Besides, romance was something Cora sought to avoid. Love needed to be built on trust and honesty. And for a girl with a past shrouded in blood and secrecy…

"What is it?" she asked, trying to smile but managing only a grimace.

He continued to brush his horse, keeping his voice low as he spoke. "I just wanted to tell you to be careful."

She frowned, not sure how to respond to that. "All right." When he didn't say more, she took a step away. "Welcome back—"

"Avoid the villages."

"Excuse me?"

"I know you normally stay at camp when we trade with the local towns, and… that's smart. You should keep doing that." He paused and met her eyes. The gravity in his expression sent Cora's heart hammering against her ribs.

All she could think was, *He knows. Goddess above, he knows who I am.*

Before he could say anything more, she turned away, once again haunted by dark castles and blood. And a question. The question that haunted her mind, twisted her heart.

What have you done?

Her footsteps quickened until they kicked up into a jog, then a run, as she made a beeline for the edge of camp.

She didn't stop until she disappeared into the shadows beneath the trees.

3

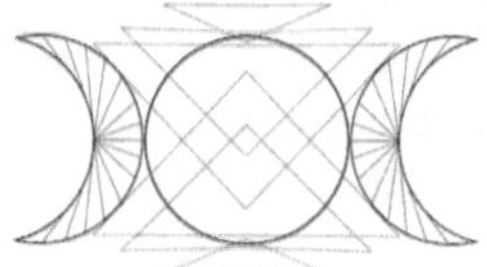

Teryn Alante, Crown Prince of Menah, tried his best not to scowl at his fiancée. It was a difficult task considering the woman he'd been engaged to for three years was publicly courting eight other men before his very eyes. It was under the guise of accord with neighboring kingdoms, but Teryn knew what was truly happening, as did everyone around him.

Princess Mareleau was keeping her options open.

Not that he blamed her. And not that he didn't wish he could do the same. The Princess of Selay was beautiful, but he felt not an ounce of affection for her. How could he when they'd hardly exchanged more than a few letters over the years? Her first letter to him had been uncomfortably ardent while the rest were icy enough to assure Teryn they held each other in the same unfeeling regard.

He stared at Mareleau standing stone-faced upon the balcony two floors up, watching some northern prince spout poetry from the garden courtyard below. Her expression looked more appropriate for someone attending an execution than a Beltane festival. Teryn was grateful his scowl could at least be blamed on the sun beginning its descent behind Verlot Palace—home of his betrothed.

The princess' long hair shone a silvery blonde in the waning sunlight, adorned with pearls and lace flowers, while her dress was a confection of silvery blue brocade trimmed in white fur. Her skirts were so wide, they nearly spanned the length of the balcony floor. Her parents, King Verdian and Queen Helena of Selay, stood just behind, looking equally as ostentatious. Although, come to think of it, pompous was probably a better word. The king wore a powdered wig and an overly ruffled lace shirt beneath his crimson jacket, while the queen bore skirts that were twice as wide as her daughter's, her graying brown hair assembled in an enormously tall updo. Selay was known to be a fashionable kingdom, and if that meant ridiculous clothing ensembles and a hefty dose of snobbery, he could see why.

Teryn gritted his teeth as the prince continued to serenade his fiancée. He was fully aware that his glower was growing deeper by the moment. He'd once hoped his engagement would be dissolved before it could come to fruition, but that was before he knew how badly his kingdom needed the marriage. Back then, he would have felt only relief at seeing his fiancée entertain another suitor, but now it gave him no small amount of anxiety.

One of nine. That was all Teryn was to Mareleau now.

When he'd been invited to Verlot Palace for the Beltane festival, he'd assumed it was to solidify plans for his and the princess' upcoming nuptials. Ever since their betrothal was arranged by their parents three years ago, the plan had been for the two to marry in 171 Year of the Hound, which it was now. So he was quite surprised when he arrived at the palace and found he was one of nine men who held the same marital notions as he. What followed was a week of dinner and dancing—occasions the princess was mind-bogglingly absent from for the most part—and now culminated in a spectacle called the Heart's Hunt. The nine princes would read the princess poetry from under the garden balcony like some idiotic story-book hero. Afterward, Mareleau would select her three champions whom she'd then send on a scavenger hunt. He who returned with her requested prize would win her heart. It made sense for Beltane, he supposed. As for his pride...

"This is humiliating," he muttered under his breath.

His half brother, Larylis, leaned in and whispered, "I told you she was cruel."

Teryn nodded with a shrug. Larylis *had* warned him. Several times. And if anyone knew the princess' true nature, it would be Larylis. His brother had met her a time or two when he'd lived as a ward to Lord Ulrich, Mareleau's uncle.

Teryn's father stood at his other side, posture tense. "Grin and bear it," he said, demonstrating the feat himself. His grin, however, looked more like a snarl.

Teryn knew his father's humiliation must be equal to his own. Mareleau's public defiance of her engagement to Teryn wasn't just a slight on Teryn's behalf. It was a direct affront to his father, King Arlous of Menah. If their kingdom had been in better financial standing, the rulers of Selay would never so blatantly insult an ally, especially not in such a public manner. Wars had been started over far less. Either Mareleau's parents were well aware of Menah's state of financial ruin, or King Arlous' sinful reputation had made the match between Teryn and Mareleau unsuitable in her parents' eyes.

Another thing he couldn't blame them for.

His father had made a mess of his kingdom, all in the name of love. The thought alone made Teryn's blood boil. He respected his father as king, but he didn't think he would ever forgive him for trying to replace his mother—Queen Bethaeny—with the king's mistress. It nearly resulted in war with the queen's home country, a dispute that could only be settled by taking out a hefty loan from the Bank of Cartha to make amends. In the end, Teryn's mother kept her crown and a good portion of his father's finances, not to mention a newly built palace of her own. Teryn applauded her for it, for she had every right to defend her place as queen. But after the attempted-divorce scandal and a year of bad crops, his kingdom now stood on the brink of bankruptcy.

Leaving Teryn to pick up all the pieces.

He *needed* this marriage alliance. To do that, he had to stoop so low as to become a poet.

Larylis must have sensed Teryn's unease, for he grasped him by his shoulder. "You can do this. You only have to read it once."

His only answer was a tightening of his jaw. Why did this farce have to be public? The audience consisted of more than just the nine princes and their families. While the royal guests stood around the courtyard beneath the balcony, there were leagues upon leagues of festival spectators filling the lawn behind them.

The northern prince finished his lengthy poem with a smug grin. Teryn forced himself to bring his hands together in applause along with the rest of the audience, but the gesture felt more violent than friendly. The young man returned to the edge of the courtyard, and the Master of Ceremonies took his place. "Thank you, Prince Nadris of Charsony. Next, please welcome Prince Teryn Alante, son of King Arlous and Queen Bethaeny Alante of the Kingdom of Menah."

The blood left Teryn's face at the sound of his name. He stood frozen for a moment, the loud hammering of his heart drowned out by the new wave of applause. His brother gave his shoulder another encouraging squeeze and his father leaned in close. "Just woo the spoiled brat," he whispered.

His father's voice steadied his nerves and reminded him what was at stake. If Teryn didn't secure a favorable marriage with a wealthy kingdom, he'd have no crown to inherit. The Bank of Cartha had already sent pirates to sabotage Menah's trade routes in warning. Next, they could send war.

With a deep breath, Teryn strolled to the center of the courtyard and lifted his face to the balcony. The sun was now fully behind the palace, casting the princess and her parents in shadow. Good. If he couldn't see her, he could pretend she was someone else. Someone he loved. Someone who deserved the words he'd agonized over for the last week.

He tilted his lips in a crooked grin and relayed the poem with a ridiculous flourish of his hand. He knew he was about to make a complete ass of himself. But it seemed only an ass had a chance at wooing his bride.

> "Oh, what beauty shines from my love fair!
> 'Tis greater and beyond any to compare,
> Her eyes, they glisten like the sea so blue,
> She is as sweet as my love is true,
> Her lips are rosebuds, her skin like a dove,
> Her smile is what my dreams are made of,
> Her voice rings like bells so sweet,
> I ask one thing; will you be my queen?"

It was over both too soon and not soon enough. His poem wasn't nearly as long as Prince Nadris' sonnet, but it was better. Wasn't it? Or had he just royally screwed up? He blinked at the backlit balcony, now wishing he could see the princess' face. A small part of him hoped she'd hate his poem. Hoped his words were enough to sever the tie he'd never wanted.

But a greater part of him knew he needed her to love it. To love him. To choose him and his bankrupt, scandal-ridden kingdom over all the others there today.

Polite applause erupted behind him, snapping him back to attention. Keeping his head held high, he returned to his brother and father while the Master of Ceremonies announced the next prince.

Teryn's stomach turned as he caught a glimpse of the princess. He hoped he'd find her eyes on him, hoped he'd find some sign of her favor. But she seemed as unmoved as ever.

He leaned toward Larylis. "She hated it, didn't she?"

Brow furrowed, his brother hesitated before answering. "No, I don't think she did."

"Seriously?"

Larylis met his eyes then, and there was something pained about his expression. "She smiled."

Teryn tilted his head back in surprise. "She did?" He hadn't seen her smile at anyone yet.

His brother's throat bobbed. Once. Twice. The pained look still heavy on his face. Then, in the blink of an eye, it was gone, replaced with a jovial grin. Larylis slapped Teryn on the back. "Yes, brother, she smiled. It seems you stand a chance with the Thorn Princess after all."

Teryn snorted at the nickname. Thorn Princess. A woman known for her prickly demeanor and even pricklier heart.

A woman who would—hopefully—soon become his bride.

4

Princess Mareleau Harvallis thought her face would crack from the effort it took not to guffaw at the ridiculous spectacle she'd just forced herself to endure. Nine poems she'd pretended to tolerate from nine princes she'd wanted only to sneer at. Thankfully, she could rely on what she liked to think of as her *magic trick*. It was a way to present a carefully curated outer composure no matter how she stewed inside. Only once did it crack, and that was when Prince Teryn, her fiancé, read his awful poem. She'd wanted to glower at him but instead, she'd grinned, knowing she'd soon be free of their engagement. She'd been trying for years to sever it, but this time she was finally close to getting her way.

With the poems read, it was now time to choose her three champions for the Heart's Hunt. Mareleau and her parents left the balcony and strode into the foyer. The low heels of her silk shoes clacked against the white marble floors as she made her way to the tea table and took a seat across from her mother. Their wide skirts fanned out around the table in an array of silk, fur, and lace. Her corset kept her back straight as she leaned forward and took up a freshly poured cup of tea. Her father, meanwhile, took a seat in his favorite wingback chair, a glass of brandy quickly placed in his hand by a servant.

"I'll choose first," King Verdian said, then took a hearty sip of his drink.

Mareleau brought her teacup to her lips to stop herself from releasing an irritated groan. Unfortunately, Mareleau's parents had insisted they choose two of the three champions. She already knew who her father would pick before the words left his mouth.

"Prince Teryn."

"Of course you choose him," she said, setting her cup back down. "Even though you know I don't want to marry him."

"You're already engaged to the man," he said, tone barbed. "You have been for three years despite your every attempt to get out of the arrangement."

She planted a pleasant smile over her lips. "Don't forget to mention *your* every attempt to try and sell me to the next highest bidder."

"And yours to undermine my decisions." He burned her with a sharp look. Despite his powdered wig and elegant white-and-gold silk coat, King Verdian was anything but the pretty monarch he appeared to be. He was fierce. Cold. Calculating.

Probably where Mareleau inherited the same traits herself.

Her father shook his head. "Your marriage to Prince Teryn will give us access to their trade with Brushwold. Additionally, once you inherit my throne, Selay and Menah can merge as one kingdom. Even though this marriage sets you up as the future queen of what could become the greatest seat of power in southern Risa, I've tried to find you an alternate match. All to stop your incessant whining about how much you despise Teryn Alante. So don't act like I've done anything but the best for you. You're too spoiled, Mareleau."

"Spoiled." She scoffed. "Is it spoiled to not want to marry a man from a kingdom that was recently embroiled in a divorce scandal?"

Her father took another drink, unfazed. "You fought me on this engagement long before that came to light."

She opened her mouth but didn't know what to say. He was right. She'd wanted out of her engagement to Teryn the moment she'd learned of it. Not that Teryn had done anything to deserve her scorn. His only crime was not being his half brother, Larylis.

The same was true for Larylis, she supposed. He too suffered from not being his brother. Had he been a prince and not the illegitimate progeny of the king and his mistress, he'd have been an acceptable match for a princess. She would have loved him regardless, of course. She couldn't have cared less about his unfavorable parentage and could even forgive his kingdom's scandal. What mattered was that Larylis was a liar. When it came to acting on pretty words, he'd failed her. Abandoned her. Broke her heart until there was nothing left but brambles and thorns in her hollow cavity of a chest.

Were she a crueler woman, she'd marry Teryn out of spite, if only for the chance at wounding her former paramour. Then again, perhaps he didn't care. She'd seen Larylis in the audience today. While she couldn't handle meeting his eyes for fear of shattering her composure, she'd stolen a few covert glances. She'd seen him smiling with Teryn, laughing, encouraging. As if watching his brother marry the woman he'd once professed to love was nothing.

Nothing.

"Come now, my darlings," her mother said from the other side of the tea table. "Let's not talk of scandals."

"Then speak some sense into her, Helena." Verdian stood from the divan and threw back the rest of his drink. "She doesn't know what's for her own good. She doesn't want to marry Teryn. She doesn't want to marry King Dimetreus. She doesn't want to marry Prince Augustine. She doesn't want to marry Prince Frederick."

Fire burned through her blood at the mention of those names. She stood from her seat, her skirts bumping the table and sending the teacups rattling. "Oh, don't get me started on them! King Dimetreus is a widower—"

"Of six years," her father interjected.

"—who lives in a creepy kingdom where everyone dies. Prince Augustine was twice my age and had his hand up my skirt within minutes of our first meeting alone." She said the last part through her teeth.

Verdian at least had the decency to blanch at that, but he quickly steeled his shock behind a stony mask. "And what of Prince Frederick?"

Mareleau took a few steadying breaths, knowing it was time to utilize her *magic trick* again. She forced her lips into a trembling frown, let her shoulders droop. Her voice came out small and quavering as she brought her hands to her chest. "You know he broke my heart, Papa."

Prince Frederick was the most recent royal her parents had paraded her before. After she'd caught him dallying with her former lady's maid, she'd bullied him into ending their engagement. It served to garner pity from her parents when she pretended to be hurt by his abrupt end to their courtship and softened their ire enough to put her current plan into motion.

Beltane. The Heart's Hunt.

King Verdian huffed, but she could tell she'd drained some of the fight from him.

"We're talking nonsense again," Queen Helena said, rising gracefully from her seat to stand next to Mareleau. "Talk of the past isn't worth our breath. We must speak of the present instead."

"I said my piece," the king grumbled. "I choose Prince Teryn as one of the three champions and I won't change my mind. If the both of you want to dance about selecting the remaining two, have your way. I'd like to get this farce over with." With that, he marched past them and left the foyer.

Queen Helena faced Mareleau with a glowing smile and took her hands. "Don't fret, darling. Just because Teryn is one of the champions doesn't mean he'll win the Heart's Hunt. It could very well be your choice or mine."

Mareleau said nothing. If all went to plan, there wouldn't be a winner.

The queen's voice took on a serious tone. "However, if Teryn wins, you must honor that, just as we've promised to honor the winner as your betrothed. This was your idea, remember?"

She gave a reluctant nod. It had been her idea. After she'd claimed a broken heart following Prince Frederick's rejection, she'd appealed to her mother's romantic side, saying she needed to marry for love. It was almost too good to be true when the queen fell for Mareleau's insistence that the Beltane festival held the perfect solution, that a poetry contest and the Heart's Hunt would prove a suitor's true love. Pathetic. But that was the kind of girl her parents thought she was. A starry-eyed fool who dreamed of storybook romance and epic declarations. That wasn't her at all. She was practical. Sharp. While she'd once entertained notions of love, back before Larylis proved himself unworthy, she now wanted no husband at all.

As her parents' only child, she was set to inherit the throne, something the king and queen thought possible only if she married a king or prince. Otherwise, her uncles would fight for the throne. While she understood the implications of having her right to rule contested, she railed against the assumption that a woman must have a man at her side to be a proper queen. It fueled her rage to no end, but royal succession was a game of well-placed maneuvers. A game she could play. For now. This time, she'd be the one moving the pieces.

"Fine," Mareleau said, forcing her face into an agreeable smile. "Who is your choice of champion, Mother?"

Queen Helena clapped her hands in front of her chest, crystal blue eyes—the same shade as Mareleau's—alight with excitement. "I choose Prince Helios of Norun. He's wealthy, handsome, and...dare I say a perfect match?"

Mareleau nodded along, pretending she had even the slightest inkling whom her mother was referring to. She'd done her best to ignore the visiting princes all week and learn as little about them as she could. That often included their names. "Oh, yes, I'm sure you're right."

The queen beamed at that. "I knew you'd think so. Do you recall his poem? It was quite moving. I particularly liked the part where he compared you to the Goddess of the Sea."

Had he known her, he would have chosen the Goddess of War. Or better yet, the Goddess of Death. But Mareleau kept that to herself. "Yes, that was lovely, wasn't it?"

Queen Helena released a dreamy sigh, eyes distant for a moment. Then, with a shake of her head, she said, "Now, who do you choose, darling? If I haven't already stolen your choice." She said the last part with a wink.

Mareleau opened her mouth, realizing she'd made a grave error in her attempts to keep the princes at a distance. She had no one to select as champion. Not that it mattered. These princes were all the same, bandying about words like *love* to a stranger they knew nothing about save for the fact that she was pretty and had a dowry that rivaled their own kingdoms' wealth. With a simpering smile, she said, "Uh, Prince Thomas, I think it was?"

Her mother's expression hardened. Mareleau knew there hadn't been a Prince Thomas, but she couldn't resist sparking her mother's ire just a little. "Mareleau Harvallis, don't you dare tell me you aren't taking this seriously. It was *your* plan—"

"Pardon, Your Majesty," said a small voice. Lurel, Mareleau's fifteen-year-old cousin and newly appointed lady's maid, approached. Mareleau hadn't noticed when the girl had entered the foyer, but her other three lady's maids followed in her wake, clustered together as they gossiped behind their hands. The three girls stopped their chatter to curtsy for Mareleau and the queen, then went right back to it. Lurel dipped low, bowing her head far longer than necessary. Showoff. When she stood, she lingered, smiling and wringing her hands awkwardly.

Mareleau gave her a pointed look. "What is it?"

"Oh, yes!" Lurel blushed. "I was going to say, could the princess be referring to Prince Lexington of Tomas?"

Mareleau quirked a questioning brow.

"When you said Prince Thomas."

Queen Helena's mouth fell open with a light laugh, her previous irritation gone in a flash. "Darling, is that who you meant?"

"How silly of me," Mareleau said with a forced chuckle. "Yes, that's him. Of course it's him. Prince Lexingbton of Tomas." She said the name slowly, enunciating each word, certain she hadn't heard it uttered even once this week.

Her mother furrowed her brow. "Odd. He doesn't seem your type. And the only line I remember from his poem was, *You are graceful like a deer and smart like a fox.*"

It took all her restraint not to snort a laugh. She kept her expression serious as she said, "Oh, he's exactly my type."

Suspicion flashed in Queen Helena's eyes, but she only said, "Very well. Are you ready to award your champions and announce the object of the Heart's Hunt?"

"I am."

"And you have selected an object for the Hunt, correct?"

"I have."

Another suspicious look. "What have you chosen?"

Mareleau did her best to keep her malicious grin at bay. "You'll see. It's a surprise."

After the queen left to find the king, Lurel spoke again, her voice rich with excitement. "Oh, I can't wait to find out what the object is. Will you give me a clue?"

Mareleau's eyes dipped to the pair of white earrings dangling from her cousin's ears. They were delicately pointed at one end and rounded on the other, with just the hint of a spiral pattern. Mareleau had been bitten with envy the moment she'd spotted them. She'd asked Lurel about them and learned the earrings were a gift from Lurel's father, Lord Kevan. And if Lurel was to be believed, they'd been carved from a piece of bone.

A rare piece of bone.

One belonging to what was a presumed-extinct fae creature.

And if her uncle was to be believed as well, he'd seen it with his own eyes on a hunt up north.

Mareleau's lips pulled into a smirk. "You, cousin. You're the hint."

HALF AN HOUR LATER, MARELEAU STOOD BACK ON THE BALCONY WITH HER MOTHER and father. The nine princes once again surrounded the marble courtyard, their upturned faces alight with hope. A hope she'd soon crush.

The Master of Ceremonies addressed the audience from below. He thanked their guests and the royal families in attendance, then announced the three champions.

Prince Teryn Alante of Menah.

Prince Helios Dorsus of Norun.

Prince Lexington Quill of Tomas.

Mareleau was particularly curious to learn who she'd chosen as champion and was rewarded with a chubby young man with ruddy cheeks and messy blond hair. His elegant silk coat was buttoned askew and his white neckcloth was tied all wrong. As he made his way to the center of the courtyard next to the other two champions, he looked about as thrilled as he'd be at a funeral. That made two of them. She reined in the laughter that bubbled in her throat and settled on trying to appear moderately pleased instead.

The queen stepped closer to Mareleau and whispered in her ear, "Are you certain that's the young man you intended to select?"

Mareleau glanced over her shoulder at her mother. "Of course it is." She caught her father's grunt of disapproval from the other side of her, which made her smile grow wider.

The crowd applauded, and the Master of Ceremonies called for an encore of the poems. Mareleau made no effort to listen—because why torture herself a second time?—and instead compared her three champions. Prince Lexington was the shortest of the three and the only one who wasn't smiling. Prince Helios was the tallest, standing about two inches over Teryn. The former was a brute of a man with a barrel chest, tanned arms roped with muscle, and a smug confidence that made Mareleau want to take him down a peg. His hair was bronze and cropped close to his scalp, the planes of his face hard, his jaw shadowed with stubble. If she were to guess, he was at least five years her senior.

Teryn, on the other hand, was just a year older than she was. She knew this because he and Larylis were the same age, both born by their separate mothers the same year. Despite only sharing a father, they looked almost similar enough to be twins. Both were annoyingly handsome with their father's green eyes, sharp cheekbones, and dark hair. Teryn's tresses were shorter on the sides and wavy on top, lightly touched with gold, while Larylis' hair was overlong, curling at the nape of his neck, and glinting copper when touched by light. Larylis was the leaner of the two, although both were tall and broad of shoulder.

Larylis suddenly met her eyes from across the courtyard, making her breath catch in her throat. Her heart hammered as she averted her gaze. She hadn't realized she'd been staring. It took a few moments longer than she cared to admit to gather her composure, but by the time the last of the three poems were read, she'd replaced her cold countenance.

The Master of Ceremonies congratulated the three champions, then gestured toward the balcony. She knew what came next. His voice took on a dramatic tone. "It is now time for Princess Mareleau to announce the object of her Heart's Hunt."

The crowd went quiet and all eyes focused on her. Despite her outward confidence, sweat began to bead at her neck. She hated attention. Hated crowds. But she knew what had to be done. Better yet, she was glad to do it.

Tapping into her make-believe magic, she took a deep breath, doing her best to settle her nerves. She lifted her chin, her chest, standing tall as she focused her intent on shaping an outer persona that radiated poise. Demanded respect. Inspired awe.

She knew her so-called magic trick wasn't really magic at all. It was only a matter of controlling her demeanor in a way that shifted the perceptions of those around her. Still, people always seemed to respond the way she wanted. Sometimes it curried favor. Garnered sympathy. Won her friends. Other times it brewed hate and discord. The latter was how she'd escaped so many prior engagements. As she took in the audience before her, she saw reflected back that which she intended now. She saw awe, respect, desire, admiration.

She had command of the crowd.

Stepping closer to the rail, she placed her hands on the balustrade and projected her voice out over the garden. "My three champions have been chosen for their love for me," she said with a false smile. "In one week, the three of you will embark on a dangerous mission in search of my heart's desire."

Her mother gasped behind her. "One week? The Hunt was supposed to start tonight," she whispered furiously, but Mareleau ignored her.

"The champion who returns first with what I demand will prove he loves me most and will, in turn, receive my hand in marriage. What I ask for is rare and will put its seeker in grave danger. You must accomplish the Heart's Hunt without the aid of hired help, professional hunters, or the accompaniment of servants and guards. He who has the determination and skill to persevere is the one worth my hand. Listen carefully to what I ask, for you must bring me exactly what I demand."

"Mareleau," King Verdian drew out her name in a whisper laced with warning, but she ignored that too.

"For the Heart's Hunt, you must find me three unicorns. From the first unicorn, I require a horn. From the second, its pelt. And the third will be my pet. No item shall be purchased or traded for. It must be freshly harvested by your own hand. I wish you three the best of luck, and may the worthiest man win."

Stunned silence followed. She assessed the faces of the crowd. Some looked mortified while others bore half smiles, as if they expected her to laugh and take it all back.

She put their hopes to rest with a wave as she said, "Goodnight, and thank you for joining us for Beltane." With a triumphant grin, she turned on her heel, only to find her father's fingers winding around her upper arm.

"Unicorns, Mareleau? Is this all a game to you?" His face burned beet red.

She blinked back at him with an innocent expression. "Of course not. I told you, I'm only marrying for love and this will prove which man loves me most." Lies. Delicious lies.

"I'm of the same mind as your father," Queen Helena said, voice quavering with suppressed anger. "This is ridiculous, not to mention offensive to our guests. You cannot send three suitors on a fruitless quest for creatures that don't exist."

That was precisely the point, of course. Send the three men on a mission that had no expiration, only an impossible goal. And she had the perfect person to blame for her absurd request.

"Oh, they exist. Just ask Uncle Kevan." With that, she brushed past her parents into the foyer. There, she found her cousin staring wide-eyed at the three royals. Mareleau gave a light flick to the girl's dangling unicorn-horn earring, sending it swaying back and forth. "Lurel will tell you all about it."

Her parents burst into a heated argument, which was Mareleau's cue to make a hasty exit. Mirth bubbled in her chest with every step she took, but she swallowed it down. Only when she reached the quiet halls outside the foyer did she finally let herself erupt with victorious laughter.

5

Cora nocked an arrow into her bow and pulled the fletching back to her cheek. Her heart thumped heavy in her chest, her mind still reeling with the echo of Roije's words. It was sundown—several hours since he'd delivered his cryptic warning—yet she still couldn't shake what he'd said.

She released the arrow and heard the beautiful strum of the string snapping forward, a sound that normally settled her nerves. Now it did nothing to calm her, especially when the arrow missed her target and struck an innocent cherry tree standing just behind the pockmarked stump she'd been trying to hit. Pink cherry blossoms rained down to the forest floor in protest.

She cursed under her breath and withdrew another arrow from her quiver. As she nocked it, she replayed Roije's warning for the hundredth time.

Avoid the villages.

What had he meant by that? Was she simply imagining the darker implications of his statement? His warning must have had something to do with what happened to his father...

Murdered by King Dimetreus' men.

But had the warning been given out of general worry? Romantic favor, like she'd first assumed?

Or because he'd learned why she'd really been stumbling through the woods six years ago when the Forest People found her?

Her fingers trembled, sending her aim wildly askew as she shot her arrow. "Damn." She nocked another one, willing her hands to remain steady, her grip easy on her bow as she shot her arrow. This time it struck the rotting half-felled tree, but nowhere close to the circle she'd carved as a target when the Forest People first settled camp at the beginning of spring. This little pocket of isolation was her safe space. Her private training ground. Not that it was doing her any good at the moment. She was normally an adequate archer. But today...

With a grumble, she threw her head back and closed her eyes.

Breathe, she told herself. *Breathe. It was nothing. His warning meant nothing.*

Releasing a slow exhale, she forced her worries aside and tried focusing on her inner sensations instead. As a clairsentient witch, *feeling* was the source of her power. She knew this, and yet it wasn't always easy to remember in practice. But as the Forest People liked to say, magic was strengthened by challenge. Often that meant doing the very thing that felt the hardest. Right now, Cora's greatest challenge was getting out of her head and into her magic. The last thing she wanted to do was abandon her attempts at logic, but she could at least admit her current state was doing her no favors. Not where her sanity was concerned, and certainly not for her archery practice.

She breathed in again, narrowing her attention down to the sensation of air moving through her nose, filling her lungs, then warming her nostrils as she released the breath. Shifting her focus to her skin, she felt it prickle beneath the cool evening breeze, then warming under the blush of the setting sun, diffused beneath the canopy of trees overhead. Next, she brought her attention to her feet, to the feel of solid earth beneath her leather boots, and imagined she could sense the Magic of the Soil the way the Faeryn descendants could.

Calm replaced her racing thoughts, settling her heartbeat into a steady rhythm. She took several moments to relish that calm, to feel it with every fiber of her being, before she opened her eyes. Drawing another arrow from her quiver, she nocked it in place and assessed the stump with its carved target, saw in her mind's eye her arrow soaring straight to it. She drew her arrow to her cheek, felt calm radiate down her arm, her hand, felt her tattooed palms tingle with magic.

Everything inside her felt her next shot wouldn't miss.

She released the arrow and watched the arrowhead strike the center of the circle. Exactly how she'd seen it in her mind. Exactly how she'd *felt* it would hit.

Her lips flicked up at the corners, but her smile faded as soon as she heard the crack of a twig behind her. Nocking a fresh arrow, she whirled around and aimed her weapon.

"Salinda," Cora said, tone full of apology as she quickly let down her bow.

The other woman didn't so much as flinch at having been momentarily targeted. In fact, there was a good chance that snapping the twig had been intentional. A test. Salinda nodded at the stump that still bore Cora's arrow. "You shot that arrow with clairsentience, didn't you?"

"I did," Cora said and went to retrieve her numerous arrows that were scattered around her practice area. It was considered disrespectful to turn one's back on an elder when approached, but Cora had a feeling she knew why Salinda was here and hoped she could end the conversation before it began. Besides, Salinda was Maiya's mother, as close as Cora had to a mother herself, which meant the woman expected less formality from Cora than the others.

"Maiya told me about the nightmares," she said.

Cora sighed as she tore an arrow from the stump and tucked it into her quiver. "Of course she did."

"That's not why I'm here, though."

Cora slung her bow over her shoulder and turned back toward Salinda. "It's not?"

With slow steps, Salinda closed the distance between them, stopping a few feet away. She and Maiya looked similar with their petite stature, dark eyes, brown skin, and warm smiles. Salinda, however, had the slightest point at the top of her ears. Even being half witch, she still might have had the most Faeryn blood of any of the Forest People. Salinda also had more tattoos than most, with black ink trailing from her palms to her inner forearms, disappearing beneath the sleeves of her green linen dress, only to peek up again above her bodice. From there, geometric shapes adorned the sides of her neck, ending in a single tattoo at the tip of her chin—the sign of the triple moon. A symbol only the elders' chins were marked with.

Salinda gave Cora a warm smile, one that made her eyes crinkle abundantly at the corners, and took another step closer. "I think you should take the path of elders."

Cora stared back at her, stunned silent. Taking the path of elders was a high honor, as one could only begin training by invitation of another elder. Thirteen Forest People comprised the council of elders. Aside from Nalia, the High Elder, there were six witches and six Faeryn descendants on the council. The six witches represented the strongest in each of the six senses, while the six Faeryn performed a separate vital task. Unlike Maiya, Salinda's magic favored her Faeryn side, although she understood witch magic just as deeply as the Magic of the Soil. She was so skilled in her Art that she'd earned herself a place as one of the Faeryn elders, tasked as the commune's Keeper of Histories. It wasn't just Faeryn lore she kept either. She also recorded anything relevant to the witches of the commune. With how intermingled the two people had become, the distinctions between the witches and Faeryn were growing less stark. New traditions were being created every day, new spells, tonics, and rituals that combined witch magic with the Magic of the Soil. It made Salinda the perfect candidate for the job of Keeper of Histories.

Cora knew she should feel triumphant. Proud. To be singled out as a witch worthy of one day becoming an elder...it should have been a dream come true. The way her heart raced, cheeks warm under Salinda's kind gaze, made it seem like Cora's body knew exactly what kind of honor it truly was.

But her mind...

Her mind filled with echoes of her nightmare. Echoes of Roije's warning. A reminder that being singled out for anything could be dangerous. And not just for her. For the Forest People.

Reining in the joy that begged to fill her chest, she took a step back. "I don't think I'm the right choice for the path of elders."

Salinda reached for Cora's hand and cradled it in hers, Cora's palm to the sky. "You've only been with us for six years, yet look how your *insigmora* has grown."

Cora's eyes dipped to her inked palm, taking in the pattern of overlapping shapes. The tattoos were a Faeryn tradition, the process itself meant to represent the elements—minerals from the earth to form the pigment, water to turn it to liquid, fire to transmute it into ink, air to aid the tattoo's transformation from a wound to a permanent marking of the flesh. The symbols themselves were thought to help connect one to the elements as well as direct one's magic. Another high honor Cora wasn't sure she was worthy of.

She slid her hand from Salinda's. "There are other witches stronger than me who've earned far more *insigmora* in a shorter time."

"Time isn't everything, Cora. And I promise you, you're stronger than you think. You came to us fully clairsentient."

Cora chuckled. "You mean plagued by it."

Salinda's tone softened. "You didn't understand it. Yet you learned so quickly what your powers meant after we took you in. You learned to put up mental shields within your first three months of being with us. The way you can feel what others feel, sense outside emotion...not all clairsentient witches can do that. Most simply connect to their magic through feeling, bodily sensation, and personal emotion. What you do is no small thing."

It felt like a small thing, but Cora didn't say so. She was grateful she'd learned to control her Art, but even after six years, being clairsentient didn't make her feel powerful. Or safe. Archery, on the other hand, made her feel at least somewhat capable. Strong. That was all she wanted—one thing that could make her feel like she could face the horrors of her past and overcome them.

Instead of being destroyed by them.

Cora's hand went to the bow slung over her shoulder. She closed her fingers around the solid wood wrapped in smooth leather. "I think I'd rather take the path of hunters."

Salinda's smile fell, revealing the full weight of her disappointment.

Before the woman could reply, Cora rushed on to add, "I've been practicing. You saw me use my magic to make that last shot. I've been joining the hunts."

"And do you enjoy them? The hunts? Do you honor the process of taking life from an animal, blessing its spirit and its sacrifice for the good of the commune?"

Cora bit the inside of her cheek, trying to form a proper response. The truth was, she cared little for the hunt itself, only for the opportunity to learn how to use her weapons in a practical manner. She hated the act of killing. Hated skinning rabbits and carving hides. The other hunters didn't relish such acts either, but she could tell they honored the process, held it in high regard. Cora didn't have a sacred connection to hunting. If there was a path of warriors, she'd prefer that.

"Cora, I'm proud that you've learned to use clairsentience with your bow, but your magic has more potential than you've been giving it. If you let it flourish, you could step fully into the role of empath."

Again, Cora knew she should feel honored. An empath was the strongest kind of clairsentient witch, much like a seer was the strongest clairvoyant or an oracle was the strongest claircognizant. An empath had the power to do more than read feelings. According to legends, she could use the power of sensation to accomplish many magical feats, and most were too fantastical to believe—use another's emotions to read their mind, control physical material using touch. Cora wasn't sure she *did* believe any of those things were possible. The commune had one empath, an elder. Her greatest feat of magic was taking on the pain of the ill or wounded so they could be more easily healed. But that would always leave her recovering from the pain she'd taken on, and the actual healing was left to those skilled in brewing tinctures and salves or setting bones.

Salinda released a sigh. "You don't value the role of the empath."

"I'd rather be more useful."

She placed a hand on Cora's cheek. "Magic is so much greater than you know. You don't believe in its power because it leaves very little evidence to the naked eye. That is the way of things. True magic is quiet. Unassuming. Easily explained away through logic. But remember, just because magic is quiet doesn't mean it isn't strong."

Cora wanted to argue. She'd seen magic before that was neither quiet nor unassuming. It was dark. Terrifying. How could she value the gentle power of the empath when she'd witnessed something so much darker?

"Sit with me at the Beltane ceremony tonight," Salinda said. "*Feel* what it's like to be amongst the elders."

Her heart sank. Part of her yearned to make Salinda proud, to be the person Salinda thought she was.

If only she knew the truth…

"I believe in you," Salinda whispered, then took her leave.

Cora watched her go, stomach sinking under Salinda's faith in her. Part of her wanted to run after the woman, take all her doubts back, profess that she really did want to take the path of elders. That same part of her craved the future the opportunity offered.

Prestige.

Respect.

Family.

But it would all be a lie. Cora may have been a witch, but she wasn't truly one of them. No matter how much she wished it, no matter how much she yearned to bury her past, it haunted her.

With the resurgence of her nightmares and Roije's mysterious warning…

She felt more than haunted.

She felt hunted.

6

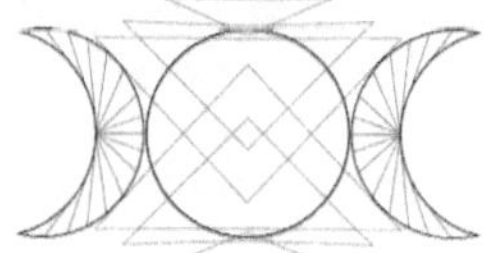

Night had fully fallen and Cora still couldn't bring herself to return to camp. The Beltane ceremony would soon commence, something she dreaded in and of itself. During her first few years with the Forest People, Beltane had become one of her favorite holidays. She loved dressing in her brightest skirts, wearing flowers in her hair, dancing around bonfires, weaving ribbons around the maypole. However, now that she was older, she was acutely aware of the deeper themes that came with the holiday. Fertility, primarily. Or, to put it bluntly, lovemaking.

Not long ago, Cora had entertained the idea of taking a lover from the commune, but it had culminated in nothing more than heated kisses and a few experimental trysts. That was all it took for her to learn what risks came with romantic pairings. Not the usual dangers the young women whispered about during their monthly moon cycles, but ones personal to Cora. Intimacy. Honesty. Questions she couldn't answer. The discomfort of being courted into a deeper relationship than she was capable of having.

And after what happened with Roije earlier today, Cora wasn't sure she was ready to face him. Especially not at Beltane. There was still a chance her first instinct had been correct. That he favored her. Romantically.

Cora shook the thought from her head and collected her latest bunch of arrows from her target. Her aim had significantly improved since her conversation with Salinda, but it was too dark to practice any longer.

As much as she wanted to avoid what came next, she knew it was time to face it. Beltane. Salinda's offer. Roije.

With her quiver full, she made her way back toward camp, her steps purposefully slow. She was only halfway there when a light shone up ahead, revealing two figures behind it. They were too distant to make out, but when Cora opened her senses, extending them until she tapped into a much-familiar energy, she knew who at least one of them was. With a deep breath, she replaced her mental shields and closed the distance between her and her lantern-bearing friend. As she drew near, she realized the second girl was Gisele. Maiya still wore her colorful skirts and flower-laced braids while Gisele was outfitted in her finest floral-patterned dress, her golden-brown hair tied up in a ruby scarf.

"There you are," Maiya said. "Mother told me she found you practicing, but I didn't think you'd still be out here."

Gisele's lips twisted in a wry grin. "Oh, Cora. Always the overachiever. But enough work for the day. We're going to the hot springs."

Maiya gave Gisele a sharp look. "I said I'd only go if Cora does."

Gisele quirked a brow at Cora. "Of course she wants to go."

Cora frowned. "What about Beltane? The ceremony—"

"The ceremony is the same every year," Gisele said with a roll of her eyes. "Besides, the boys are extra ravenous tonight, if you know what I mean. Had I any magic, I'm sure I could smell the desire raging through camp already." Gisele's mother was a clairalient witch, her magic rooted in scent, but unlike Cora and Maiya, Gisele showed neither talent nor interest in the Arts. Not everyone born within the commune did. "And I don't know about you, but I've had enough of *boys*. They can come find me when they're ready to be men."

Cora suppressed a huff of laughter. Gisele had certainly made her rounds when it came to sampling the company of single men within the commune. She'd never complained about it before. Cora turned her attention to Maiya and quirked a suggestive brow. "What about you? Is there any reason you might want to enjoy the ceremony?"

Even under the warm glow of the lantern, Cora saw a blush crawl from Maiya's neck to her cheeks. They both knew Cora was hinting at Roije. "No," she said too quickly, her voice small. "But...but I'd understand if there was a reason *you* wanted to go."

Cora didn't need to let down her shields to understand the meaning behind her words. Maiya must have come to the same conclusion Cora had first entertained regarding Roije's earlier summons. More than that, she was giving her blessing. Giving Cora the go ahead to court the man Maiya had fancied for years. Her friend was always too generous. Too kind. A trait that would probably annoy Cora to no end were it anyone else. But with Maiya...that was just how she was. She was the best of them.

Cora gave her friend a pointed look. "No, Maiya, there's not a *single reason* I'd want to attend tonight's ceremony. I promise you."

Maiya's lips pressed into a shy smile while Gisele looked from one girl to the other, brow furrowed. "Does that mean you're both coming or not?"

Cora didn't immediately answer. Going to the hot springs would provide the perfect distraction both from Salinda's offer and the inevitable romantic overtures she was sure to receive from one source or another. But she didn't want to keep Maiya from enjoying what could potentially be a pleasant night, should she finally get the courage to speak to Roije about her feelings.

As if Maiya knew exactly what Cora was thinking, she lifted her chin in defiance. "I already told you, I don't want to go to the ceremony."

Cora shrugged. "All right. I suppose we're going then."

Gisele bounced on the balls of her feet and hefted a woven basket. "Good, because I already pilfered two bottles of wine."

THE HOT SPRING CAVES WERE LESS THAN AN HOUR'S WALK AWAY. WITH THE AID OF one of the bottles and its intoxicating contents, Cora felt as if the walk went much faster. She and her two companions were a mess of laughter by the time they reached the mouth of the cave. They huddled close together as they proceeded inside, their giggles turning to silence. Entering the cave came with both reverence and a healthy dose of fear. The antechamber was blanketed in a darkness so bleak, their lantern only lit the next few steps. Cora kept her breaths shallow as they made their way slowly forward, deeper into the cave. The antechamber narrowed to a corridor and soon the warmth of steam met her skin, bringing with it the telltale aroma of sulfur. Then light just ahead.

The three women quickened their pace, their steps now fueled with excitement as the corridor took them down a slight decline toward the belly of the cave. The sulfurous aroma grew stronger, and while it wasn't the most pleasant smell, Cora was more than happy to suffer it for the benefits that awaited. Finally, they stepped into the main chamber, the walls of the underground cave glowing with biolumi-nescence, lighting the surface of the three small steaming pools pocking the rocky floor. The heat alone had every muscle in Cora's body loosening, and she couldn't wait to slip beneath the warm waters.

Gisele looked from Cora to Maiya with an inebriated grin. "Ready?"

The three girls darted toward the largest pool, roaring with laughter as they stripped down.

"See, we're celebrating Beltane just fine," Gisele said as she pulled her shift over her head. "Skyclad. Naked as the day we were born."

Cora rolled her eyes as the girl sauntered into the pool without an ounce of inhibition. Still, Cora knew the hot springs were no place to try and maintain modesty. Not when walking home in a sodden shift was far more uncomfortable than the brief moment of nudity she'd endure. Besides, Gisele was right. Going *skyclad*, as the Forest People called ritual nudity, was neither odd nor shameful. And yet, Cora hadn't been born under such freedoms. She was born into a world of strict rules and propriety.

Turning her back to her friends, she unshouldered her bow and quiver, tucking them next to a low boulder before removing the rest of her ensemble.

"Hurry up," Gisele called, sending a splash of water to the hem of Cora's shift. Squealing at the warm spray, she pulled her shift the rest of the way off, then rushed to the pool and plunged shoulder deep. Maiya was up to her chin in the water, the cherry blossoms that had once adorned her braids now floating wilted on the surface. Gisele lounged against the side of the pool, her arms outstretched and propped on the rocky ledge.

Cora tilted her head back and admired the blue-green glow lighting the pool from above. Peace settled over her, mingling with the warmth in her belly leftover from the wine. She felt every last bit of stress she'd picked up from her day dissolve. "This was the right choice," Cora whispered.

"I told you so," Gisele said. She reached for her basket and retrieved their bottle, taking a drink before passing it to Maiya, then she to Cora.

Cora took a hearty sip, finishing the remnants. Gisele was already opening the second bottle.

"Do you think it's true?" Maiya asked, turning her gaze to the glowing ceiling.

"What? The legends about the caves having once hosted dragons?" Gisele said the last part with a sardonic look.

"It sounds silly when you say it like that," Maiya said.

"It is silly." Gisele took a sip from the new bottle. "Do you really think those," she pointed at the ceiling, "were once dragons?"

Maiya dipped a little lower in the water. "Maybe."

Gisele chuckled and passed Maiya the wine. "What do you think, Cora? Historical fact or faerytale?"

Cora shrugged. "Faeryn legends are faerytales, aren't they?"

"I suppose," Gisele said, "but are they true?"

Cora wasn't so sure. When the Forest People had first found the hot spring caves a month prior, Salinda had been adamant that the caverns had been left behind from days when fae still roamed the land, back when pixies, sprites, and unicorns were as common as squirrels and deer. Back before the Elvyn and Faeryn —the two races of High Fae—went all but extinct. No one knew why the fae disappeared, only that a terrible war hundreds of years ago had prompted it. The stories told how all fae creatures turned to regular animals after that. And Salinda was convinced the glowing worms that painted the cave walls in bioluminescence were once dragons. The hot spring caves, according to her, had once been home to the legendary fae creatures. There was no way to know if Salinda was right. She may have been the Keeper of Histories, but that didn't mean the tales of the past hadn't been skewed by the fancies of those who came before her.

"True or not," Maiya said, "this is the best place we've ever found."

"I can agree with that," Gisele said, taking the bottle of wine back. "I hate that we'll have to leave the caves behind soon."

Cora's heart sank. They all knew the Forest People would be gone by Litha— the summer solstice. They traveled to a new camp with every season, both to follow the most favorable weather in Khero and to ensure they never overburdened the land that nourished them. Even after six years with the commune, Cora still wasn't used to constantly moving around.

She'd been in one place the first twelve years of her life.

Before everything changed.

Before she became an outlaw.

Chased by dark magic.

Haunted by blood—

A sound coming from beyond the cave snapped Cora from her thoughts. Maiya, who'd been saying something Cora hadn't been paying attention to, cut off mid-sentence. She and Cora turned their gazes to the corridor from where they'd emerged.

The sound was slow and rhythmic. Footsteps.

"Someone's coming." Cora reflexively reached for her bow, but it was too far.

"Relax, Cora," Gisele said, looking completely unflustered as she took a deep drink of wine.

Cora narrowed her eyes at her friend, suspicion crawling up her spine. The steps drew nearer and nearer.

Gisele's lips curled into a guilty smile. "Don't worry, he's harmless."

"He?" Cora and Maiya said in unison as they both dipped deeper into the waters. "Who the hell is *he*?" Cora said through her teeth.

There was no time for Gisele to reply, for the male figure striding into the cave was answer enough. The bioluminescent glow revealed an unfamiliar man a few years older than Cora. His hair was blond, his face handsome with a short beard covering his jaw. He was dressed in leather trousers, tall boots, and a travel-worn greatcoat.

"Gisele," he said, smiling when his eyes landed on her. "You came."

She batted her lashes. "I said I would."

His gaze briefly darted toward Maiya and Cora. "I wasn't aware you'd be bringing company."

"Neither were we," Cora said, not bothering to hide the bite in her tone.

He paused several feet from the pool, posture hesitant as his eyes strayed from Gisele to the pool's two extra occupants. "Should I..."

"Meet me in that pool," Gisele said, pointing to one of the smaller ones nearby.

His shoulders relaxed a bit as he gave her a nod, then made his way to the pool she'd indicated.

Gisele whirled back to her friends with a grimace. "Don't be mad."

"I'm not mad, I'm seething," Cora said. "I thought you said you wanted nothing to do with boys tonight."

"He isn't a boy," Gisele said, expression all innocence. "He's a man."

"Who is he?"

"His name is James. He's a hunter camped out close by. I met him yesterday when I was foraging for Mother. I promised to meet him here tonight, but I didn't want to meet him alone. He could be a murderer for all I know."

"That isn't comforting," Cora said through her teeth.

Gisele nodded. "Tell me about it."

"You said he was harmless," Maiya said, her tone far gentler than Cora's.

"I'm pretty sure he is."

Cora turned and started to get out of the pool, modesty be damned.

"Please don't leave," Gisele rushed to say.

Maiya tugged her arm before she could heft herself onto the ledge. "We can't leave her with him," she whispered.

Cora clenched her jaw. Of course Maiya would put her own discomfort beneath the safety of others. And if Maiya was staying...

"Fine," she bit out and settled back into the pool, "but you owe me."

"Always. Forever." Gisele's tone was more desperate than convincing. Without another word, she climbed from the pool and hurried to the one the man waited in.

"We should have known better," Maiya said with a sheepish grin.

"Yes, we should have." Had Cora's shields been down, she might have sensed Gisele's duplicitous intentions. But there was nothing to do about it now.

She eyed the two figures in the other pool, watched Gisele melt into the man's arm as she pressed a kiss to his lips. The kiss immediately grew heated, and Cora averted her gaze. It landed on a boulder between the two pools, one strewn with the man's discarded clothing. She was about to turn her back to the pool completely when something caught her eye—a small detail on the man's greatcoat, illuminated by the glowing ceiling. It was a symbol embroidered on his sleeve.

A black crescent moon on an indigo background.

The sigil of Duke Morkai.

The man who'd made her into a murderer.

7

All the relief Cora had felt since entering the pool fled in an instant. Her muscles coiled, stiff with rage, her mind reeling.

This hunter, James, belonged to Duke Morkai. But he was more than just a duke. More than one of the most influential men in Khero, second only to King Dimetreus. He was a mage too. Not merely a witch, working quiet magic or the elements. No, he was something else. Something darker. Stronger. His Art was blood. His spell was death. Only Cora seemed to know the truth.

It brought her back to the dreaded bedroom of her nightmares. To the blood on her hands. To her screams. To the condemning voice, half anguish, half anger.

What have you done?

"Cora. *Cora.*"

She jumped at the arm lighting upon her shoulder. She had to shutter her eyes a few times to clear them of the bloody tableau.

"What is it?" Maiya whispered, casting a quick glance at Gisele and James. "Is it the hunter? Do you feel danger from him?"

Cora didn't know what she felt about the man. Her senses were too clouded with ghosts of the past. That and her shields were still firmly in place. With a slow exhale, she imagined a small window parting the elements that comprised her mental shields. Narrowing her focus to the two figures in the other pool, she extended her senses, let herself feel what they were feeling—she snapped the window shut faster than she'd formed it.

Desire was all she'd sensed. That and...arousal.

It was enough to steal away some of Cora's prior tension and send her cheeks heating.

Maiya snorted a laugh. "Did you just try to read their feelings?"

"I know, I know. It was a bad idea that I should have seen coming."

"Hopefully we won't see anything else coming, if you know what I mean."

It took Cora an extra second to understand what she was referring to. When she did, her mouth fell open and she gently slapped the surface of the water, sending a teasing spray to her friend's face. "Maiya! Did you just make a naughty joke?"

She sank down a little with a bashful grin. "I'm serious though. If they do anything more than kiss, I'll...I'll...throw a rock at them."

"Make sure it's a big one," Cora muttered. She risked another look at the couple, but thankfully they'd parted from their kiss and now chatted side by side. As she pulled her gaze away, her eyes lingered on the boulder where James' greatcoat was draped, that patch of indigo bearing a black crescent moon still watching her like an eye.

"Are you mad I told Mother about the nightmares?" Maiya said in a rush.

Cora wrested her eyes from the hateful sigil.

Maiya's grimace was laced with guilt. "I know she came to talk to you earlier today. Are you mad?"

"Of course I'm not mad, Maiya. I couldn't be angry with you if I tried."

Maiya gave her an apologetic smile. "Did Mother end up...helping at all?"

Cora bit her lip, debating whether she should tell her the truth. "She didn't talk with me about my nightmares."

"She didn't? What did she say?"

Again, Cora considered keeping the facts to herself. But she trusted Maiya. Besides, if she didn't know now, she probably would soon. Maiya and Salinda had an honest relationship. "She wants me to take the path of elders."

Maiya's eyes went wide. "That's amazing! That's the highest honor—"

"I told her I don't think I'm right for the position."

Her friend blinked in disbelief. "Why?"

Cora shrugged. "I'm certain there's someone better suited to the position. Someone who has been with the Forest People far longer than I have."

"Cora, when will you finally accept that you're one of us?"

Cora's eyes darted back to the sigil. She would never truly believe she was one of them. Not when her presence alone could put everyone at risk. Not when there was a chance she'd be banished if they knew the truth. And she'd been tempted to tell the truth. The closer she got to Maiya and Salinda, the more she wished she could be honest with them. But honesty had never proven to be on her side. Not when dark magic and murder were involved.

Maiya's expression fell. "Why do I feel like you're always one step away from leaving us?"

Cora opened her mouth but no words would form.

She was saved from having to reply, however, when Gisele hopped into the pool between them. "What are we talking about?"

Cora gave the girl a wry grin. "Oh, just how we can make you pay us back for subjecting us to your makeout session."

"Do you like him? James?" Gisele asked, a hopeful gleam in her eyes.

Cora glanced at the other pool where the hunter lounged alone, his gaze fixed longingly on Gisele. "What does it matter if we like him? You seem to like him well enough."

"He's sweet, isn't he? Kind. Funny."

"I didn't realize he had a personality, but I'll take your word for it."

Gisele rolled her eyes. "Oh, Cora. You're so droll."

"Who does he think you are, by the way?" Maiya asked, her voice barely above a whisper. "You didn't tell him..."

"About the Forest People?" Gisele's mouth fell open with indignation. "Of course not. What kind of fool do you take me for? I may not be all magical like you two but I know our rules."

"Then where does he think you live? If he's a hunter, he should know the nearest village is hardly a casual stroll away."

Gisele frowned. "Well...he hasn't asked."

Cora gave her a pointed look. "Sweet and kind indeed."

"It's not like I'll see him again after tonight," Giselle said with a casual flip of her sodden hair. "Tomorrow morning he and his companions are leaving their camp and heading north to join the rest of their hunting party."

Cora's stomach knotted for reasons she didn't quite understand. She itched for something she couldn't name. The idea that the duke's men were so close filled her with a frenetic quality, an urge to move, to run. Not *away* either. But toward them.

That was when she realized what the uneasy feeling was. Vengeance.

Thoughts of finding the hunters' camp, sabotaging what she could, knowing whatever she destroyed was indirectly the property of the duke, filled her with the most delicious satisfaction.

But the longer she entertained the fantasy, the more ridiculous it felt. What could a girl like Cora do against a group of trained hunters? And how would it have any impact on Duke Morkai in a way that mattered?

Morkai was second to the king. He was King Dimetreus' most respected councilman. The hunters were likely on an errand to fell some great beast for a royal dinner. And what was Cora dreaming of doing? Breaking their spears like a child throwing a tantrum in hopes that her greatest enemy would be mildly inconvenienced. Gisele had said James and his men were joining the rest of their hunting party. If they too served Morkai, harassing this smaller group would do nothing of import.

She breathed her thirst for vengeance away. It was childish. Silly. Besides, acting on her fantasy went against the Forest People's most important rule—never get involved with royal matters or attract the attention of agents of the crown.

"Gisele," James called, a note of yearning in his voice. "Come back."

She tossed a coy smile over her shoulder at him. "Have a little patience. I came with my friends. You can't have all my attention, you know."

He bit his lower lip. "I'd have all your attention and more if you'd give it to me."

Gisele giggled, but Cora simply rolled her eyes. "Desperate much?" she muttered, earning a warning glare from Gisele. Maiya snorted a laugh.

James narrowed his eyes at Cora, then returned his gaze to Gisele. "Come with me tomorrow."

Gisele chuckled. "He's already in love with me," she whispered to her friends.

Cora had other words to describe him. "He's a creep."

"He knows nothing about you," Maiya added.

Gisele lifted chin. "You two are just jealous."

"I know what would make you want to come with me," James said, drawing their attention back to him. "If I showed you what I have waiting for you back at camp, you'd be impressed. And I promise you, there's more where that comes from at our next stop. It would blow your mind."

"Is that so?" Gisele waggled her brows, her gaze dipping to the surface of the pool that hid his bottom half. "I like having my mind blown by a handsome man."

"It would blow *all* of your minds."

That earned a sharp scowl from Gisele, but Cora gave a dark laugh. "I doubt that very much."

"Have you ever seen a unicorn?"

Gisele's expression turned perplexed as she whispered to her friends, "Is he still talking about what I thought he was? He's referring to his..."

"If so," Cora said, barely able to smother her laugh, "I daresay it's a little lacking in girth."

"I'm being serious," James said, tone affronted. "Have any of you seen a unicorn before?"

"No one's seen a unicorn, James," Gisele said. "They're fae creatures. They went extinct with the dragons and sprites and all the other mythical fae nonsense."

"You're wrong," James said, eyes hard. "If I could show you..." He snapped his mouth shut, then turned his back on the girls with a shake of his head.

"Do you have any clue what he's talking about?" Maiya asked.

"He never mentioned unicorns before." Gisele cast a bewildered glance at her lover. "If he had, I probably wouldn't have agreed to meet him here. He might be out of his mind." The girls fell into a fit of stifled laughter, only to have it broken by a bellowing sound. They went quiet, whirling to face the entrance to the tunnel.

The sound came again, clearer this time. "James!" It was a male voice. Although it was distant, it echoed through the tunnel.

James cursed under his breath and scrambled out of the pool. "I wasn't expecting them to notice I'd left," he muttered. From the corner of Cora's eye, she could see him shoving his legs unceremoniously into his trousers, then hastily donning his shirt and coat.

Again, Cora was reminded of the sigil, and of the fact that James' companions undoubtedly belonged to the duke as well. And they were close. So close. She breathed deeply to reel in that itch for revenge, forcing it to dissipate. In its wake, something far more pressing remained—a sensation that made the skin prickle behind her neck.

A clairsentient warning.

Fully dressed, James raced to their pool and planted a kiss on the side of Gisele's forehead. "I'm sorry our rendezvous is cut short but I must get back. Stay here for a while. Don't...don't come out yet." With that, he stormed into the tunnel and out of sight.

Gisele stared after him. "What was that about?"

"I don't know." Cora rose from the pool and marched over to her clothes, her pulse kicking up. "We should go, though."

"Why?" Gisele pouted. "There's still wine left."

Maiya didn't hesitate to follow after Cora. She pulled her shift over her head. "Is it...a feeling?"

Cora nodded. "I don't know if it means anything, but...I think we need to leave." She was a little ashamed that she couldn't elaborate. With offensive skills taking such a high place in her priorities, she'd neglected training her Art defensively. She knew how to shield, how to extend her senses to read others' emotions, but there was so much more to clairsentience that she hadn't valued enough to train. Ways to analyze feeling and sensation and know exactly what each subtle difference meant. For all she knew, she could be overreacting. Regardless, the skin continued to prickle at the back of her neck, bringing with it a dark and hollow feeling in the pit of her stomach. She at least knew enough to consider it a sign of danger.

"Oh, all right," Gisele said, reluctantly leaving the pool and meandering over to her pile of discarded clothes.

Cora had on her shift and petticoats. She bent down to retrieve her bodice—

That was when the echo of footsteps reached her ears, pounding down the tunnel toward them. She glanced over at Maiya, who was fully dressed aside from the undone laces of her bodice. Gisele quickly threw on her shift.

Just then, three figures entered the cave. James brought up the rear, a frantic look on his face. The men stopped when they noticed Cora and her friends. The tallest stepped forward, a cruel grin twisting his lips. "Well, now, what pretty beasts do we have here?"

8

The three newcomers were dressed in the same style of greatcoat James wore, with Duke Morkai's sigil marking their right sleeves. All but James appeared at least ten years older than Cora. Their appearances were far more rugged too, with mud-splattered boots, bushy beards, and wild, unkempt hair. One carried a spear while another held what looked like a coiled leather whip covered in metal barbs. The tallest—who Cora assumed was their leader—palmed the hilt of one of the daggers sheathed in his bandolier.

James shuffled to the front of the group and faced the three men with raised palms. "Gringe, it isn't what it looks like."

The man named Gringe scoffed. "And what exactly do you think it looks like?" James stammered for words, but Gringe cut him off before he could reply. "You left your post. Not only that, but you left to dally with three women and didn't think to share." His cold eyes wandered from Cora to Maiya, then Gisele. Cora's heart hammered against her ribs, her stomach roiling as the man assessed them like livestock.

"I'm sorry I left my post," James said. "I shouldn't have, but I figured it was safe to come for a quick soak. And they..." He cast a helpless glance over his shoulder at the girls before returning his attention to Gringe. "They were here by coincidence."

"So you don't know them?"

"No."

"Then I suppose you won't mind if we...get to know them ourselves."

James stiffened. The three other hunters erupted with laughter. With their attention on James, Cora took the opportunity to dip down and retrieve her belted dagger. As soon as her fingers met leather, she stood and pulled it behind her back, just as Gringe's eyes shot to her.

His expression hardened. "You. Where are you from? The closest village is miles away."

Cora's mind raced to come up with an answer, but Gisele spoke first. Batting her lashes, she said, "We're from Palovore, sir. We made the trip here just for Beltane. These caves are famous, you know. Everyone comes to the hot springs during the holidays."

"Then why are you the only ones here?"

Cora stepped forward, purposefully edging closer to Maiya. "We're just the first to arrive," she hurried to say. "Dozens more are coming. My...my husband will be here. My brother too." She hated having to use the threat of another male for protection, but right now she was willing to say anything to keep the hunters at bay. Besides, better they thought she was a helpless female who needed a man to fight her battles than a girl with a dagger in her hand. If only she could retrieve her bow without them noticing.

"Dozens," Gringe echoed. His smirk said he wasn't falling for her bluff.

"Please, just leave them be," James said.

Gringe sneered at the man. "Who are you to give me orders?"

James shifted from foot to foot. "It was...more of a suggestion."

"Did you tell them?"

"Tell them?"

"About our...prey?"

James shook his head. "They know nothing, I swear."

Cora stepped closer to Maiya until their shoulders brushed. "Count to thirty," she whispered, "then take Gisele and run for the tunnel."

"What? No! We're not leaving you."

"I'm just giving you a head start."

"Are you crazy?"

"Count to thirty."

"Cora—"

"Just do it!"

Maiya made a pleading sound but took a step toward Gisele.

Gringe's gaze snapped to her friend. "Here's a suggestion," he said with a dark laugh. "Tie them up. We take them back to camp and figure out where they really came from."

With that, the hunters surged forward. Cora's heart leapt into her throat. "Thirty!" she shouted at Maiya, who'd frozen at their approach. Cora took her dagger out from behind her back and threw it at the nearest man. It glanced off his chest hilt first and fell to the ground. She wished she'd actually practiced throwing daggers before attempting that pathetic spectacle. Cora lunged for her bow instead and nocked an arrow. This gave the hunters a moment of pause. "Thirty, Maiya!" she shouted at her friend. Finally, Maiya's feet flew into action and she grabbed Gisele's arm. They darted for the tunnel. One of the hunters lunged at them, but Cora shot an arrow. It skimmed his wrist, making him pull up short.

Her next arrow grazed his neck. It would have hit dead center if not for her erratic breathing, sending her aim wild. This was nothing like practice where targets stood still, where her only threat was being mildly distracted by her own thoughts.

"Go after them," Gringe barked at the man she'd narrowly missed. He obeyed and darted after Cora's friends. Cora nocked another arrow. "You too," he said to James. "Clean up this mess you made and I'll consider not delivering your head to the duke."

Mention of the duke had Cora's blood burning with rage, clearing her mind just enough to remind her to breathe. One more hunter was still approaching—the man with the barbed whip. Gringe remained near the mouth of the tunnel, grinning as if he expected an entertaining display of theatrics. The hunter flicked his whip. She shot her arrow. Just as her fingers left the fletching, searing pain sliced down her arm. One of the barbs had torn her flesh. Her shot went wild.

The man closed in.

She kicked, she flailed, she bit, but it was to no avail as he crushed her in his grip.

BOUND, GAGGED, AND BLINDFOLDED, CORA NO LONGER REGRETTED NEGLECTING HER understanding of defensive magic. Now she wished she'd spent twice as much time honing her skills with weapons. Perhaps then she wouldn't have been in such a position that left her hauled over a hunter's shoulder like a sack of grain. She struggled in vain, wishing she could at least pound her fists against the hunter's back or slam her feet into his chest, but her wrists were tied behind her back, her ankles bound together. No matter how she wriggled, he paid her no heed. She heard the shift in sound as her captor's feet left the stone cave to the forest floor. "I'm going to do horrible things to you," he said, a dark chuckle in his voice.

"We question them first," she heard Gringe say from up ahead. "See if they were lying."

"But after?"

"They won't be leaving alive," Gringe said, "so do what you will."

She shouted into her gag, cursed them both with every vile insult she could think of. None of it reached their ears, as muffled as her words were.

"Gringe!" A new voice came from just ahead.

"What is it, Sam?"

"I saw it."

"Saw what?"

"The white. The one we were tracking earlier. It waltzed right into camp as if it wanted to be caught. I tried to catch it on my own—"

"Damn it. We can't let it get far. Not on our last night here. Erwin, leave her at camp and take the south. Sam, go north. I'll signal James and Velek to head east. I'll take the west."

The hunter carrying her, Erwin, kicked up into a jog, jostling Cora with every step. From behind, she heard a low bellowing sound—a horn being blown—that ended in three sharp bursts. That must have been the signal Gringe had mentioned. Other horn blasts echoed back from farther away. A few minutes later, her momentum shifted. Erwin heaved her off his shoulder, and her back met hard earth as she landed on the ground with a thud. His retreating footsteps followed. Cora held still for a moment, straining her ears for any sign that she wasn't alone.

Nothing but a crackling fire answered. She took a few deep breaths to steady her nerves—as well as she could—and cut a window through her mental shields. Extending her senses, she opened herself to nearby emotion. At first, she felt nothing. Then...*something*. Or was it nothing as well? An unfamiliar sensation filled her bones, bringing with it a quiet sorrow. And yet...it didn't feel like anything human. An animal? The hunters' horses, perhaps?

Another thought came to mind as Cora remembered what James had said about unicorns. He couldn't have been telling the truth, could he? Unicorns hadn't been seen in hundreds of years. Legends stated that all had become horses by now, leaving nothing of their ancient fae origins intact.

Rolling onto her side, she pressed her face to the ground beneath her, feeling dirt grate against her cheek as she worked to lift the cloth from her eyes. Finally, she managed to shove it over her brow.

Blinking, she took in her immediate surroundings. First, she saw the light of a campfire several feet away. Closer and just out of arm's reach—had they not been tied behind her back—laid her bow, her quiver of arrows, and her belt. Her dagger had been returned to its sheath. She glanced around the rest of the camp, seeing no one else in sight.

She wriggled across the ground, making a haphazard line for her belongings. Sweat beaded across her brow with every inch she drew near. Soon the items were within reach. Rolling to her other side so her back faced her weapons, she fumbled for her belt. Her fingers only had the slightest reach beyond their bindings, and she struggled to gain proper leverage. Finally, her pinky looped around her leather belt. She stretched her hands to get a better grip, then moved her fingers down the length of it. One hand met air as she reached the wrong end. Gritting her teeth, she reversed directions until she felt her sheath. Excitement sparked in her chest as she then walked her fingers up the sheath until they came around the hilt—

Footsteps pounded toward the camp. Gripping the dagger, she wriggled a few feet away from her belongings and rolled halfway onto her back, hopefully obscuring her weapon in the folds of her skirt. James came into view, face strained as he hauled a female form over his shoulder. Far more gently than Erwin had been, he laid his burden next to Cora. Her heart lurched as she saw Maiya's profile, her temple marred with blood. Her hands were bound in front of her, but she was neither gagged nor blindfolded.

James glanced around the camp, then met Cora's eyes with a frown. "I let Gisele get away," he whispered. "And don't worry, this one is just knocked out."

Am I supposed to thank you for that? Her words, stifled by the gag, sounded only like a string of mumbles. She cut him with a glare that probably looked anything but threatening in her bound state. Then her eyes landed on a strange marking she hadn't noticed before. Just below his ear was a patch of raised skin in the shape of an *R*.

Cora's blood went cold. She knew what that marking was. It was a brand reserved for criminals set for execution. That *R* stood for one of the most heinous and violating crimes she could imagine.

His gaze turned steely as if he could see the realization in her eyes. "I wasn't going to hurt your friend," he said, tone curt. With that, he darted away, grabbing a spear off the ground before he left the clearing.

Alone again, Cora shifted her attention back to her dagger. Angling it toward the knot between her wrists, she sawed the blade against it. It was painstakingly slow, and for a few moments, Cora thought her efforts were futile. But then she heard a satisfying snap as part of the rope was severed. With some mobility freed, she redoubled her efforts. Another snap. Then freedom. She brought her arms in front of her, wincing at the strain on her muscles. Her forearm still seared from where Erwin had lashed her with his whip. Pulling herself to a seated position, she quickly cut through her ankle bindings and tore off her gag.

Her chest burned with anxiety, lungs contracting as she scrambled over to Maiya. She cut her friend's bonds, setting her hands free. Maiya remained limp. Cora set down her dagger and framed Maiya's face in her hands. She whispered her friend's name. Nothing. She sought her pulse at the base of her neck, relieved when she felt a soft beat. "I'm getting us out of here," she said, then cast her gaze around the camp. She needed a safe way to flee. Steal one of their horses, perhaps. But she saw no sign of one, heard no evidence of a nicker or a neigh.

Subtle movement caught her eye from the opposite side of camp, drawing her attention to two metal cages. Both were composed of six barred panels assembled into a large box, their corners and sides tied together with rope. One stood gaping open, empty, the front of it slightly askew on its roped hinges. The closed one, however, held a single occupant—a male equine creature, brown and nearly skeletal. He wavered on hooves that seemed overlarge for his too-thin body. He blinked sleepily at her, his head dipping low, as if too heavy to hold upright. That was when she noticed the slim, white, spiral-ridged horn protruding from the center of his head, aglow with the light from the fire.

A unicorn.

9

Shock rippled through Cora like a shuddering current, nearly taking her breath away. Without meaning to, she rose to her feet and took a few steps closer to the creature before her, her eyes fixated on the white spiral horn. Her pulse thrummed wildly.

"Mother Goddess," she muttered under her breath.

Before her was a fae creature. A unicorn. It was like he had walked straight from legend. Like the stories had said, he was larger than a regular horse, his neck sinuous, his hooves massive. That was where the comparisons ended between the faerytale descriptions and the creature before her. For his brown coat was dull, not shiny. His body was emaciated, not broad and strong. His eyes seemed more lifeless than keen.

The unicorn wavered on his legs again, head dipping, eyes blinking slowly as he took a swaying step back. His rear came up against the bars of the cage. With a sharp equine cry, the unicorn jolted away, but the movement brought his flank against the other side of the cage. Another piercing sound, one of pain.

Cora stepped closer again, squinting as she studied the cage to identify what could be hurting him. All she saw were plain iron bars bound together with rope. Such an assembly suggested the cages were used for travel, with the ability for the sides to be cut loose and reassembled with ease. The enclosure was obviously too small for a creature of his size, but it seemed otherwise benign. There were no sharp edges, no nails, no barbed corners—

Cora's breath hitched, her eyes narrowing on the seemingly innocuous metal bars.

Iron.

A metal that—if the legends were to be believed—was harmful to the fae. Deadly, even.

Her heart plummeted and with it went her control over her mental shields.

They crumbled around her. Before she could gather her senses enough to replace them, she was struck by an onslaught of emotion, so powerful it made her legs quake. Hunger, pain, fatigue, terror, sorrow. The feelings enveloped her, permeating her blood and bones. It was all-consuming, all-penetrating—

"Cora." Maiya's strained voice startled her. It was enough to help her get control, to breathe, to push back against the unwanted emotions.

Taking a stumbling step back, Cora tore her gaze from the brown unicorn, breathing deeply until she felt the remnants of the emotions fade. In their place her chest was tight, her throat dry. She ignored it and whirled toward her friend, finding Maiya wincing as she tried to push herself to sitting. Cora ran to her and kneeled at her side. "Are you all right?"

"Where are we?" Maiya asked, squinting as she looked around the camp.

"Somewhere dangerous." Cora left her friend's side only to retrieve her belt, bow, and quiver. She sheathed the dagger and shouldered her other weapons. Then she squatted back down next to Maiya and put her arm around her. "We need to get out of here. Can you stand?"

Cora tried to lift her, but Maiya let out a hiss of pain. "My ankle," she said, voice quavering. "I fell. Twisted it. That's how they caught up to me."

Dread filled Cora's stomach. If her friend couldn't run, they'd be at an even greater disadvantage. Their only hope now of making it back to camp was if the hunters remained distracted long enough. "It's all right," Cora said, more to herself than to Maiya. "We're going to make it."

Shifting her stance so she could help Maiya rise on her good leg, she attempted to pull her up again. Finally, they were both on their feet. With one arm secured around Maiya's waist, Cora led them toward the edge of camp. Each step was slow and hobbling, sending a spike of panic through Cora's heart.

"You should leave me," Maiya said, hissing as she nearly tripped with her next step. "I wouldn't blame you."

"I'm not leaving—" Cora's words died on her lips as the sound of thundering steps came tearing through the woods. The hunters. They were coming back.

From the sound of it, they were heading straight for them.

"Goddess above," Cora muttered, part curse, part prayer. She angled them to the side, attempting to flee to the other edge of camp, but they were too slow.

Too late.

The pounding steps tore into the clearing.

But they didn't bring a horde of angry hunters.

The steps belonged to hooves, not feet. The thundering rhythm had belonged to a gallop, not a run. And the creature that now reared up before Cora...

Maiya's hand flew to her lips to cover her gasp. "Is that..."

Cora swallowed hard. "Yes."

Another unicorn stood before them, but he was nothing like the emaciated brown one. This creature was enormous, muscular, his white coat splattered with mud. His russet eyes were wild as he bared his teeth.

They took a staggering step back, one that sent Maiya sprawling to the ground. Cora tried to dive for her friend, but the unicorn darted between them. He stomped his hooves, sidling toward her and shoving her back from Maiya.

A feeling slammed into her. With her shields still down, she had no defense against it. Desperation, rage, fear, struck her one after the other. She froze in place as the feelings grew, rippled, changed. Soon the sensation shifted into a sense of need, bearing a weight she'd never felt before when reading anyone's emotions. The weight undulated, multiplied, divided. Cora could do nothing but feel it unfold inside her until it settled into something new.

A word.

A voice not heard but felt. Understood.

Help.

Cora's eyes went wide. Never before had she experienced anything like this. Never had emotions become thoughts, become words. It felt strange, invasive, and utterly terrifying.

She looked to Maiya on the other side of the white unicorn. Her friend scrambled back on her forearms, struggling to stand. Cora's eyes darted between the creature and Maiya. She dove to the side to skirt behind the unicorn, but he skittered back, blocking her.

Help, came the feeling-turned-to-word again.

"I don't understand what you want from me," she said between her teeth. She tried to outmaneuver him in the opposite direction, but it was no use.

He stomped his hooves, nearly connecting with Cora's feet. She danced back to avoid having her toes crushed, but the unicorn pursued her, sending her backward again and again.

Cora's fingers flew to the hilt of her dagger. She unsheathed it and brandished it before the creature. The unicorn tossed his mane, releasing a frantic whinny.

Help.

Help.

Help.

He stomped toward her again. Cora cast a glance over her shoulder in search of trip hazards, but her gaze settled on something else.

The caged unicorn.

The white beast was forcing her toward the cage.

She faced her pursuer. "You...want my help. As in...you want me to free the other unicorn?"

He tossed his mane again. Her heart raced as she looked at Maiya. They didn't have time for distractions. Not with Maiya's injury. If they didn't get free of the camp before the hunters returned...she didn't want to consider what would happen then.

Still, the memory of what it had felt like when she'd connected with the brown unicorn's emotions made her heart sink. There wasn't a doubt in her mind that the unicorn was being kept in a too-small iron cage on purpose. The hunters *wanted* the creature to hurt. If she had a chance to set him free...

"Fine," she said to the white unicorn. "I'll help release your friend, but after that, you need to get out of my way."

As if in answer, he sidled back and put space between them.

Cora cast another glance at Maiya. Her friend's brows were knitted either with concern or confusion. Then Cora whirled toward the cage and closed the remaining distance. The brown unicorn inside the enclosure only blinked at her, each flutter of his lids slow and heavy. She brought her dagger to the ropes binding the bottom left corner of the cage and cut through them. Then the bottom right. The upper corners were more of a challenge as they were high above her head. Standing on her tiptoes, she extended her arms and cut as much as she could reach, starting with one corner, then moving to the next. The process was slower than it had been with the bottom bindings, but soon the ropes began to fray and snap. She sheathed her dagger and wrapped her hands around the iron bars, tugging at them until the front frame began to tilt on its own, snapping what remained of the ropes. Cora darted back just as it swung down and landed in the dirt with a thud.

"Go," Cora whispered when the unicorn inside made no move to claim his freedom. She pointed to the perimeter of the camp and infused her voice with a warning edge. "Go. Now."

Finally, he took one wavering step. Then another. His bony legs trembled as he left the cage, his hooves trodding quickly over the iron bars as if they burned. As soon as he was fully upon the dirt floor, he kicked up into an uneven trot and darted into the dark woods.

"Cora," came Maiya's voice, quivering with warning.

She turned back to her friend, but the white unicorn reared up before her. A lashing sound shattered the air, followed by a guttural neigh from the unicorn. Cora lurched back as the creature returned to all fours, but she heard the lashing sound again. This time she saw a flick of something slice the unicorn's hide. As it withdrew, a red mark welled up in its place.

Erwin, the hunter who had hauled Cora into camp, stood behind the unicorn, lashing out again with his barbed whip. Only now did Cora understand its true purpose.

The barbs were made of iron.

It was a weapon designed for wounding fae creatures.

"Run and I'll find you," Erwin said. Although he kept his eyes on the unicorn, Cora was certain he was speaking to her. The angle of his head revealed a mark under his ear, just like James' brand. This one was shaped into *TR*. She tried to recall what crime that stood for. *T* represented treason, but the two letters were too close together to stand for two separate charges. "I won't hesitate to use this on human hide. You've only had a taste so far. With another lash, I could cut through your flesh like a knife through butter."

Now she recalled what his brand meant. *TR*. Torture. He slashed at the unicorn again. Again.

The unicorn bared his teeth and tried to dance away, but no matter which direction he tried to flee, the whip found him, sliced him.

Cora jumped with every snap of the whip, but she slowly edged around the fire toward Maiya, trying to put as much distance between herself and Erwin as she could. The hunter continued to pursue the unicorn toward the cages, much like the creature had done with Cora mere minutes ago.

Finally, Cora reached Maiya, who was halfway to standing on her good leg.

Cora helped her the rest of the way up, then shifted toward her bow. She paused as Erwin's eyes locked on hers.

He angled his body to the side so he could keep her in his sights. Watching her from the corner of his eye, he continued to snap his whip at the whinnying creature. "Don't even think about trying anything clever," he growled. "This whip can reach you from here."

She believed it could. The portion he held was still coiled, suggesting its length was far more expansive than it was now.

Without warning, the unicorn charged Erwin. The hunter darted back and lashed out with his whip. The leather circled the unicorn's neck, its barbs digging into the creature's skin. The unicorn tried to rear back, but Erwin tugged, tightening the whip's stranglehold.

Cora lunged for her bow and swiftly nocked an arrow. Her heart pounded a thundering rhythm but she told herself to breathe. Just breathe. She planted her feet firmly beneath her, imagining the soil steadying her, holding her. Then, pulling the fletching to her cheek, she narrowed her focus to Erwin. He continued to struggle with the unicorn, weaving back and forth as he tried to get the creature under control.

The unicorn calmed.

Stood still.

Erwin took a confident step closer.

Cora shot her arrow, felt in her bones that it would hit its mark.

It did. Slamming through the center of his throat, it tore through his flesh.

Erwin's mouth fell open as he staggered back, clutching at his ruined throat as blood poured from the wound.

Cora's stomach bottomed out. A ripple of disgust crawled up her spine.

Disgust in what she was seeing.

Disgust in herself.

She already knew the wound was fatal, knew—as Erwin slid down to the earth, still clutching his neck—that he was going to die.

Her first human kill.

And she wasn't sorry for it.

Disgusted. But not sorry.

She whirled toward Maiya. Her friend's face had gone pale, her eyes locked on the dying man. "We need to go. Now," Cora said.

Maiya nodded, the movement erratic, and let Cora guide her toward the edge of the clearing. A face stared back at her, appearing from behind the trees—it was James. He hesitated, gaze shifting from Cora to the camp, landing an extra beat on something behind her. She had no doubt it was his dead companion.

His lips peeled back from his teeth as his eyes locked back on hers. Then he put a curved horn to his lips and blew. The sound fractured the night. Rage coursed through Cora's blood as James blew the horn again. An echoing blast sounded from not too far away. With a parting, murderous glare, James fled.

Cora cursed, and Maiya let out a cry as she tripped on her injured leg. Maiya's panic seeped into Cora's awareness. Or was it her own panic she felt? Gritting her teeth, she tried to bear more of Maiya's weight to help them quicken their pace.

Four more horn blasts surrounded the camp, coming from every direction. Cora paused, eyes darting about as she tried to discern which way to go. She shifted their course slightly to the left and hefted Maiya forward—

The white unicorn blocked their path.

"I don't have time for this again," Cora said through her teeth.

Danger, came the unsettling invasion of feeling-thought.

"I know."

Danger, he said again. This time, the unicorn lowered his head and sidled closer. *Mount. Safety.*

Her eyes widened at the creature's marred flank. "You want us to...mount you. Like a horse."

He scraped a hoof in the dirt in an agitated gesture. *Safety. Now.*

She exchanged a glance with Maiya, who could only seem to nod. Then, squatting down, she hefted her friend with all her might until Maiya took hold of the unicorn's mane. "Sorry," Maiya said with a wince as she pulled the creature's hair harder to aid her efforts in climbing the rest of the way. Then Maiya extended an arm to Cora. Gripping Maiya's palm with one hand and the unicorn's mane with the other, she hauled herself up. She was hardly seated in front of her friend before the unicorn took off. Maiya encircled her arms around Cora's middle while Cora wrapped the creature's white mane around her fists.

They took off into the night, swallowed by the dark forest.

10

Prince Teryn Alante had witnessed his share of preposterous things in his life. His father's attempt to replace the queen with his mistress topped the list, as did the time Teryn and Larylis snuck out to Dermaine City dressed as palace guards to watch the traveling mummer's troupe. Only to realize he and his kingdom were the subject of their play. It hadn't been flattering. But nothing—absolutely *nothing*—compared to being sent by his fiancée to hunt down mythological faerytale creatures in exchange for her hand.

Even now, hours later as he stood on the balcony outside his guest bedroom at Verlot Palace, he still harbored the hope that it had all been said in jest. This was the Heart's Hunt, after all. The tradition was meant to be symbolic and the quest itself was supposed to be relatively simple. A scavenger hunt that could be solved in a single evening. Of course, Teryn knew nothing about this particular Heart's Hunt was symbolic.

"Where the bloody hell am I going to find a unicorn?" Teryn asked for probably the hundredth time that evening. "And not just a single unicorn, mind you. *Three.* Do you think it was a riddle?"

Two round black eyes stared back at him, but he received no answer. Not that he expected one.

"You don't think so?" Teryn said to his peregrine falcon perched on the balustrade next to him. He slipped her a strip of raw duck he'd had brought up from the palace's kitchens. His hosts hadn't been thrilled that Teryn would be bringing the falcon, but where Teryn went Berol went too. The falcon had bonded to Teryn as a hatchling, injured and nursed back to health by the prince's own hand. Berol obeyed Teryn as much as a bird of prey could. So, to appease his hosts, Teryn promised to keep her from hunting on palace grounds during his stay and would hand-feed her instead. He could tell the bird was a little restless, but at least they'd be heading home by tomorrow. "You're right, Berol. This is absolutely hopeless. Ridiculous. Insane."

"Your choice of words suggests you must be talking about Princess Mareleau again." Teryn glanced over his shoulder and found his half brother standing in the doorway to the balcony. Larylis leaned against the doorframe with a smirk.

"Right you are," Teryn said.

Their father came up just behind Larylis and stormed onto the balcony. "I've talked to Verdian," King Arlous said. His tone alone was evidence enough that he didn't bear good news. Hands on his hips, Arlous shook his head with exasperation. "He suggests his daughter's request is sound."

Larylis frowned and pushed off from the doorframe. "Seriously? Everyone saw his face during Mareleau's speech. He was furious."

Teryn nodded and gave Berol another strip of duck. His brother was right. Anyone with eyes could have seen that King Verdian had been taken by just as much surprise as everyone else when his daughter brought up unicorns. Not to mention the way he stormed after Mareleau when she left the balcony. Or the muffled shouts that slipped beyond the closed glass doors not long after that.

King Arlous ran a hand through his dark hair. "If King Verdian revokes his support of the Heart's Hunt, he'll be admitting he has no control over his daughter."

Larylis threw his hands in the air. "So he's going to let her send our crown prince, Mareleau's legitimate fiancé, on an insane quest. Did he make any apologies? Bring up their marriage contract even once?"

"You know he doesn't have to apologize," the king said through his teeth, cheeks flushing either with rage or shame. "He knows we don't have the funds to fight him. And he knows that *we* know exactly where we stand in his eyes. We're lucky the marriage contract hasn't been torn up entirely. If it weren't for our exclusive trade agreement with Brushwold, it probably would be."

Lucky. Teryn internally scoffed. He had several choice words to explain his pairing with Mareleau and *lucky* certainly wasn't one of them. Still, he knew what his father was getting at. He turned to fully face the king and his brother, propping his back against the rail as he slouched into it. "I have to go through with this farce."

King Arlous nodded. "There's a chance Prince Helios and Prince Lexington will back out. Either way, I'll send informants to gather intel on whether there's any truth to this unicorn nonsense."

Teryn opened his mouth to ask if they could afford informants but stopped himself. While he knew information didn't come cheap, he also knew his father couldn't be persuaded against a course of action when he had his mind to it. Hence his kingdom's current financial state. So instead, he gave a reluctant nod.

"Arlous, my love, there you are." The king's mistress stepped onto the balcony. "I've been looking for you everywhere. You promised we'd attend the Beltane feast tonight."

The king's expression softened although his posture remained tense. He met his lover with a soft kiss to her forehead. "Apologies, Annabel. We were just discussing...important matters."

Her face brightened. "You mean about the Heart's Hunt?" She faced Teryn with a simpering smile. "Unicorns! Aren't you just...so excited?"

Teryn wanted to roll his eyes but he forced himself to mutter a curt, "Thrilled."

As much as Teryn resented Annabel Seralla for nearly usurping his mother, he knew the blame didn't lie entirely with her. His father was the one who'd risked the stability of his kingdom in the name of love...and failed. Lady Annabel had been the king's mistress since before Teryn was born. He'd been raised alongside his half brother, fully aware that their mothers were two different women. They shared the same father but not his surname. It took him nearly thirteen years of life to understand the taboo undercurrents of his familial ties. That was when things got complicated. When his parents' fights grew louder, more frequent. When his mother demanded Teryn's brother—a boy who'd become his best friend —be sent away to be raised out of her sight. For three years, Larylis lived as a ward to Lord Ulrich until, without explanation, Ulrich suddenly sent him back home to Dermaine Palace. Teryn's mother was furious at his return and demanded he be sent away again. What followed was the scandal that nearly bankrupted the Kingdom of Menah.

Lady Annabel turned back to King Arlous. With a pout on her lips, she straightened his lace neckcloth. "Can we go to dinner now? You know Verlot's feasts are far better than ours."

Teryn's father smiled down at his mistress. "Of course, darling." Then, turning back to Teryn, he added, "We will make this work, Teryn, I promise you. If there's a way for you to win the Heart's Hunt, I'll find it."

Teryn tried to give his father what he hoped was a confident smile, but he'd learned years ago not to put much weight in his father's promises. Not that his father didn't try. He did. He was steadfast and tenacious when it came to those he loved. Often, though, love wasn't enough.

No, if Teryn wanted to see this ridiculous Hunt through, he'd have to do it himself. The question was how. He was a skilled hunter, so that wouldn't be an issue. He'd gone on royal hunts since he was old enough to walk. He'd felled his first beast at age ten. It was the same year he not only developed a keen love for the spear—his weapon of choice—but found Berol. Ever since, he'd spent his summers honing his craft, learning to hunt larger and rarer beasts. But never a legendary beast. This wasn't the age of unicorns and dragons. This was the age of reason. Something Princess Mareleau clearly lacked.

Annabel gave Larylis a casual wave as her only acknowledgment of her son before the couple left the balcony. That wasn't unusual behavior for Annabel. She'd borne two more children after Larylis—both boys—and had sent them away to boarding school as early as she could. Teryn could surmise it was to keep them out from under the queen's ire, but he'd always thought Annabel seemed far more interested in being a lover than a mother.

Teryn fed Berol the rest of the duck and stroked a finger over the top of her head.

Larylis came up beside him. "I don't know how you pet that thing without fearing loss of a finger."

"Fear is for the weak," Teryn said in jest. "Besides, you've petted her plenty of times before."

"Yes, with a healthy dose of fear." Larylis reached out to lightly scritch the back of the falcon's neck. Berol extended her wings and ruffled her feathers, making him jump back. Then, stuffing his hands in his pockets, he leaned against the balustrade. "So...how are you really feeling about all of this?"

Teryn ponded his answer. In truth, he was frustrated. Irritated. Absolutely perplexed. And yet he was resigned to do what needed to be done. His kingdom was running out of time to repay their debt to Cartha. If they waited much longer, the bank would escalate their efforts from sending pirates to hiring mercenaries. The latter wouldn't simply raid their trade ships. They'd collect Menah's debt in lives.

The most reasonable solution was to wed Mareleau. Her dowry would be enough to settle their debt with the bank. If his engagement with the princess fell through, well, they'd be left with very few options. Sure, another marriage alliance could be made, but what were the chances another kingdom would be willing to risk allying with them? He knew it could take years to draw up an agreeable contract.

The Kingdom of Menah didn't have years. Not where the Bank of Cartha was concerned.

With his brother's question still hanging unanswered between them, Teryn planted a crooked grin over his lips. "You want to know how I'm really feeling? I feel like today has been the most humiliating spectacle since we visited that mummer's troupe. Remember that? They had us played by literal dogs while Father's impersonator went about humping a woman dressed as a sow."

"I'm serious," Larylis said, although he couldn't hide his laugh. "Hunting fae creatures, competing against two other princes for a woman's hand that you've already been promised...it's a lot to do for someone you don't love."

There was trepidation in his tone, which brought Teryn's attention to his brother's face. That same pained look he'd noticed earlier had returned. "Are you truly concerned about me doing too much for a woman I don't love? Or for her because I don't love her?"

Larylis stiffened.

"Wait." Teryn took a step closer to his brother, startling Berol, who sidled down the balustrade. "Do you...have feelings for her?"

"Of course not," Larylis rushed to say, pushing off from the rail to straighten. Despite his words, there was a sudden flush in his cheeks. "I don't—"

"You knew her. Back when you were a ward to Lord Ulrich. Did the two of you—"

"No, Teryn, it isn't what you think." He shifted from foot to foot, then slouched to the side. "Oh, all right. We kissed."

Teryn's eyes nearly bulged out of his head. "You *kissed*? Are you telling me I'm engaged to someone you've kissed? And that you've never found it pertinent to mention until now?"

"It was three years ago. I was sixteen. It meant nothing." His voice dipped with a note of regret, one that wasn't lost on Teryn.

"Larylis, if you have feelings for her—"

"I don't." This time his tone was firm. Certain. "You know I dislike her."

"Yes, well, I hadn't known you disliked her after having had your tongue in her mouth." Teryn's last word quavered with a chuckle. That was when he realized something. He wasn't mad at his brother. Disturbed, perhaps. A little indignant that Larylis hadn't trusted Teryn enough to tell him the truth until now. But Teryn was neither angry nor jealous.

Which probably wasn't a good thing. Not where his future romantic prospects were concerned. However, Teryn had always known he wouldn't marry for love. Unlike his father, he was determined to do what was right for his kingdom. He'd stay true to his word. His duty.

Unless...

"Promise me you don't have even the slightest feelings for Princess Mareleau. Or...if you do, just...just be honest." Teryn held his breath as Larylis stood frozen, shoulders tense. He didn't know what kind of answer he expected, or what he'd do if Larylis did in fact harbor a secret affection for his fiancée. Part of him wanted to hear his brother proclaim a deep love for the woman, to beg him not to marry her. Teryn knew Larylis couldn't wed Mareleau, though. She was a princess and Larylis was illegitimate. Even so, it would be the one thing that could set Teryn free, the one thing that would fix his heart firmly against the unwanted match for good.

And, as a result, would send their kingdom into further peril than it was already in.

Finally, Larylis' posture relaxed. "I have a lot of feelings about Princess Mareleau, and I guarantee none of them are good." He punched Teryn lightly on the chest. "I feel bad for you. That's all."

Teryn wasn't sure if he believed his brother, but the sense of calm settling in his gut reminded him that any other answer would have brought nothing but turmoil. "I feel bad for me too," he said with a smirk. "She must be a terrible kisser."

Larylis threw his head back with laughter, shattering every last remnant of tension between them. For a moment, Teryn felt like they were boys again, enjoying each other's company without a care in the world. Without knowing the weight of a kingdom would one day fall upon Teryn's shoulders. And that Larylis wouldn't be allowed to share the burden with him.

Once they sobered from their mirth, Larylis took his leave, insisting he wanted to visit Verlot's library before they headed home in the morning. That sounded like his brother, all right. Larylis had never met a library he didn't like.

No sooner than Larylis left did a knock sound at Teryn's door. With a frown, he opened it, finding a palace servant on the other side. The man handed Teryn a small envelope. It bore no emblem, just an unmarked wax seal. "Your Highness," the servant said with a curt bow.

Teryn dismissed him and brought the mysterious envelope inside his room and out onto the balcony. Berol immediately tried to take the envelope from him.

"No, this one isn't for you," Teryn said, pulling it out of her reach. While Berol wasn't a messenger bird, Teryn had trained her to carry letters on occasion. Mostly to his mother or back home to his father while visiting his mother's palace.

Teryn opened the letter and removed its contents—a single sheet of paper with only four sentences scrawled across it. None of them bore the name of the sender.

Meet me in the garden at midnight. Water nymph statue. The busty one with the ample breasts. It will be worth your while.

Teryn read it five times over, then flipped it back to front. Who the hell had sent such a strange missive? And what could they possibly want?

It will be worth your while.

Teryn realized the letter could have been sent by an emboldened chambermaid hoping to get Teryn alone on Beltane. It was almost tempting enough to excite him. He'd entertained numerous liaisons of a similar nature in the past. That is, until he started to feel too much like his father. Breaking hearts. Spending time with women he knew he could never wed. Should he seek pleasure now, he had to do it with predetermined detachment. Not on a whim with someone who very well might expect to become his mistress. Besides, if he were to enjoy a meaningless tryst, it wouldn't be in the home of his betrothed. Still...

He read the letter once more, snorting a laugh over the *ample breasts* line. If the letter wasn't sent in the name of seduction, he hadn't a clue to its purpose.

What he did know was—come midnight—he'd be damned if he didn't find out.

11

Larylis Seralla didn't have his father's name. He wasn't an Alante like Teryn, nor was he a prince. Instead, Larylis went by his mother's surname. Seralla. And yet, it didn't matter whose name he'd been given or whose blood flowed in his veins. For he had neither of his parents' fickle hearts. They'd nearly started a war over their love. Larylis was determined never to be so foolish. To never forget his place.

So when Teryn had asked him if he had feelings for Princess Mareleau, he'd lied. Sort of. While Larylis no longer kept love in his heart for the princess, he hadn't been telling the truth when he'd said their kiss had meant nothing. And there hadn't been just a single kiss, but several. However, only one had felt significant. It was their final kiss. At the time, it had meant the world to Larylis because it had sealed their mutual expressions of love. Of course, that was before he'd learned what it really meant to be the illegitimate son of a king. Mareleau must not have understood it either at the time. Not until they were caught kissing in the stables by her uncle. That was when Larylis had been sent back to Dermaine Palace. By the time he'd arrived, he'd learned Mareleau was already engaged to Teryn. Whether the arrangement had been made before or after they'd been caught kissing, it mattered not. For the letter he'd received from her that day told him everything he needed to know.

I could never love a bastard.

Meanwhile, Teryn had been sent a letter too, one chronicling her excitement over their upcoming nuptials and professing her undying love.

Larylis knew then that Mareleau wasn't who he'd thought she was. Despite the way he still caught his heart lurching at the thought of his former flame, Larylis was determined not to get in the way of her and Teryn's union. Not like his mother had done, driving a wedge between the king and queen until Arlous did the unthinkable—broke vows, severed royal bonds, and nearly drove his country into chaos in an effort to make Lady Annabel his new queen. His father had insisted it was in Larylis' best interest too, for if Annabel was queen, Larylis could be named a prince. His mother had whispered far more devious suggestions—that it could also mean he might have a stronger claim to the throne after Arlous passed.

A claim he never asked for.

Never wanted.

His jaw tightened at the memory. A sour taste lingered in his mouth as he left his brother's door and headed for the library. Seeing Teryn struggle with the burden of having to right their father's wrongs reminded Larylis exactly why being a prince was far less admirable than storybooks made it sound. Sure, were Larylis a prince, he could have wed the girl he'd once loved. Then again, considering how cold and duplicitous she'd proved to be, he was willing to bet he'd dodged a dagger in being born a bastard.

Larylis reached the end of the hall before he realized he'd passed the turn that led to the palace library. After a week of dining and dancing, he craved the quiet solace of books. Besides, the library at his home palace was starting to get out of date, with his father approving fewer purchases to stock it.

He looked back the way he'd come, down the length of polished marble floor, the elegantly papered walls, the gilded frames and oil lamps interspersed every few steps. At this end of the hall, the lamps were dimmer, the bustle of servants far less frequent. He looked to his left, finding an unlit corridor. Even after three years away from the palace, he remembered it. Knew where it led. Perhaps he'd had a subconscious reason for bypassing the library.

His feet began to move before his mind caught up. Soon the corridor opened to a circular alcove. He stood at the center of it, remembering how many times he and Mareleau had met there in secret. A half smile tugged his lips as his eyes roved the four enormous windows, each with a cushioned seat built into the sill with a view that overlooked the garden, perfect for reading on a blustery day. Three of the floor-length velvet curtains remained tied open, while one on the far right was pulled closed, obscuring both the window and its sill. He recognized that window, even with the drape drawn shut. It had once been his and Mareleau's favorite place to hide.

Feeling a nostalgic pull, he approached the curtain and tugged it open.

His heart climbed into his throat.

For a moment, he felt as if he'd stumbled upon a tableau from the past. There sat Mareleau, curled on the cushion with her knees pulled up to her chest, just like how she used to sit when they were younger. She startled and whirled away from the window. If this truly were a scene from memory, Larylis knew what would happen next—she'd give him her secret smile, take his hand, and drag him down next to her. His breath would hitch, his heart would race, and his lips would burn with their desire to claim hers...

"What are you doing here?" she blurted out in a rush, eyes wide.

It was enough to shatter the illusion, to remind Larylis this wasn't a tableau and the woman in the window wasn't the girl he once loved. "Sorry." Larylis dropped the curtain and turned away, but before he could take more than a few steps, he heard her rush out from behind the velvet drape.

"Larylis."

The sound of his name on her lips sent his pulse racing. It was the first time he'd heard her say it since the day he'd been sent back home. That was the last time they'd spoken. The last time they'd stood close enough to touch. Slowly, he turned to face her.

She was still dressed in the same silvery blue gown she'd worn during the poetry competition, but it hung a little looser off her curved frame, as if she'd undone her laces for comfort. Her hair too hung differently, with pearls and flowers dangling haphazardly from the ends. A portion of her pale tresses had been pulled into a crooked braid, one she anxiously fumbled with now.

It was a braid Larylis had seen many times before. She always braided her hair when she was nervous. Or happy. There was a time he'd fantasized about unraveling that braid himself, unraveling the laces of her gown, trailing kisses down her—

He shuttered his eyes, forcing himself back to the present so he could gather his composure. He sketched a stiff bow. "Princess Mareleau."

She stood silent, her fingers winding around the ends of her braid. Her expression flickered with uncertainty, her lips darting between a frown and the barest ghost of a smile. She opened her mouth as if to speak but quickly snapped it shut. Releasing her braid, she folded her hands demurely at her waist. She stood tall, chin lifted, features schooled behind a haughty countenance. "I said, what are you doing here?"

He averted his gaze as if she wasn't worth looking at. If there was one thing he'd learned about being a bastard, oftentimes on the receiving end of insults and mockery, it was how to pretend things didn't bother him. "I certainly wasn't looking for trouble," he drawled, "but it seems I've found it. Good evening, Your Highness." He made to step away, but she only drew closer, forcing him to halt in place. The aroma of jasmine invaded his senses, making his lungs feel tight. It was a scent he'd thought he'd forgotten. He'd been wrong. Now that she stood so close, he found himself unable to keep his eyes off her.

Seven gods, she was beautiful. More so than he remembered.

It was an observation better left forgotten, one he banished before it could breach his lips in the form of a compliment.

"Is there more you wanted from me, Highness?" His words came out far rougher than he'd intended. But when he saw Mareleau stiffen and take a step back, he was grateful for his inadvertent gruffness, if only to place more distance between himself and that intoxicating jasmine.

Her gaze turned cold. "How did you like the poetry competition?"

"You mean the way you publicly insulted my brother by allowing eight other men to compete for your hand?" He pulled his lips into a humorless smile that didn't meet his eyes. "Charming."

Her cheeks reddened, her eyes narrowing as she put her hands on her hips. "You can't blame me for not wanting to marry your brother." Her voice trembled, her chest rising and falling rapidly above the bodice of her gown.

Larylis was surprised at how flustered she was. Finally, he managed to look away from her again, keeping his gaze fixed firmly over her head. "Do you enjoy torturing your suitors?"

She lifted a delicate shoulder. "A girl must take pleasure where she can."

"Because a man's sincere admiration isn't pleasure enough for you."

"Sincere." She scoffed. "I haven't met a sincere man in my life."

Larylis jutted out his bottom lip in a mock pout. "What a shame. At least you can settle for riches and a title, which I'm sure you value far more."

Her mouth fell open in indignation.

That prompted a wicked grin to form on his lips. He knew he shouldn't take any joy in irritating her. It wasn't like he blamed her for rejecting him all those years ago. He understood her position. Her duties. What he couldn't forgive was her treatment of Teryn. Her flagrant mockery of their engagement. The one she'd once insisted by way of letter that she was so excited about.

He brushed a piece of lint off his silk waistcoat, then assessed his nails. "If we're done here, I have far more entertaining matters to attend to."

She crossed her arms. "Oh? Are you going to dinner then?"

"That depends. If you'll be there, I'd rather clean the stables."

She blinked at him, and her lips once again darted between a frown and a smile. He couldn't fathom why she'd consider smiling after such an insult.

Unless...

Did she *enjoy* his teasing? Did it remind her of when they'd first met? How he'd tease her relentlessly and she'd return lighthearted insults just as fiercely? How their first kiss had been sparked after exchanging verbal blows only to wind up tangled in each other's arms? In fact, it had happened in this very alcove...

His heart thudded at the memory, but he shoved it away. Taking a step back, he gave her another bow. "Goodnight, Your Highness."

"Larylis, why did you never—" Her words were cut off by another voice.

"Mareleau Harvallis." Queen Helena's tone rang heavy with reproach as she stormed down the corridor toward them, followed by four young women who he assumed were Mareleau's lady's maids. Three were around the princess' age, while the fourth he knew was a few years younger. It was Lurel, Mareleau's cousin. He'd met her several times when he was their uncle's ward. She gave him a surprised half smile, which he wasn't able to return under Queen Helena's furious scrutiny. "Where have you been? You're supposed to be at the feast."

Mareleau lifted her chin. "I wasn't hungry."

"I don't care if you're hungry. Tonight is the last night your guests are here. You *will* attend." The queen faced the four girls. "Sera, Ann, Lurel. Return to Mareleau's room so you can prepare to make the princess...presentable again."

The three girls ducked into curtsies and quickly scurried away. Larylis quietly edged down the hall, hoping he wouldn't draw the queen's notice.

"Breah," Queen Helena said to the remaining woman. "Escort Lord Seralla back to his room so he doesn't get *lost* again."

He bristled at the queen's unspoken demand—that he was not to attend tonight's feast. It wasn't as if he'd planned on going anyway. Gritting his teeth, he turned back to the queen and offered her a bow. As he let Breah lead the way, he couldn't help but wish he'd gotten to hear what Mareleau had started to say.

~

Mareleau stared after the man she'd once fancied herself in love with, torn between relief over being rid of his aggravating presence and regret that they hadn't been able to speak longer. Their interaction hadn't been even remotely enjoyable. Or—more accurately—it shouldn't have been. And yet, for reasons Mareleau couldn't comprehend, she found herself invigorated by the interaction. Perhaps because, beneath his casual composure and coarse words, she'd sensed something. Maybe it was all in her mind, but she could have sworn Larylis Seralla still had feelings for her.

It shouldn't matter to her. He'd ignored her when she'd needed him the most. Refused her letters. Sent back silence for every tear she'd cried after being forced to part with him. Left her standing alone before the altar in a rundown Godskeep several miles from home, watching the door for hours. He'd never shown up.

She knew now it had all been for the best. A fifteen-year-old girl had no business eloping. Still, he could have at least replied to her letter. It would have saved her many tears and a whole lot of embarrassment.

Queen Helena angled her body so she blocked Mareleau's view of the hall— and Larylis' waning figure. The queen had been in a dark mood ever since Mareleau made her announcement, and she didn't seem anywhere close to being rid of it. Her mother was like that at times, drifting between maternal kindness and cold fury without anything in between. "What were you doing alone with that boy?"

"That boy? You know who *that boy* is, Mother."

"And your father and I have forbidden you from speaking to him, much less being alone with him. He nearly soiled your reputation once before. Had anyone but your uncle caught the two of you in that stable—"

"Reputation," Mareleau said with a cold laugh. "I don't recall you caring much for my reputation when you left me alone with Prince Augustine."

Her mother's expression softened at that, draining some of the fury from her eyes. She put a hand to her forehead, then swept a curl from her brow. When she next met Mareleau's gaze, she wore a sympathetic smile. "I just don't want you to do anything you'd regret."

Mareleau wanted to say that marrying any of her current suitors would lead to more regret than anything else would, but she held her tongue. So long as her mother was trying to control her temper, Mareleau would too.

"Darling, I understand what it's like to be in your position," the queen said. She took Mareleau's arm and linked it with her own. With leisurely steps, she led her out of the alcove and down the dark corridor. "I too had to give up my own desires in the name of duty. However, I held far less responsibility on my shoulders. I wasn't the heir to my father's crown like you are. Even so, I had to relinquish my dreams to marry Verdian."

Mareleau sighed. She'd heard this all before. Whenever the queen wanted to prove just how much she sympathized with her daughter, she'd go on and on about *abandoning her dreams* and how grateful she was to have done so.

Queen Helena's tone turned nostalgic. "I had perfect pitch, you know."

Mareleau *did* know, as she was forced to hear about it again and again. Helena, in her youth, had been a talented musician. She played the harp and piano and had the most pleasant singing voice. She could play any song by ear after hearing it only once and composed new music from thin air.

"The audience used to weep when I'd play. My father nicknamed me his *Little Siren* after the creatures of fae lore."

Mareleau nodded along as if she hadn't heard this a thousand times.

Then, as if coming out of a daze, the queen turned to Mareleau with a warm grin. "Speaking of fae lore, I apologize for not trusting you when you announced the goal of the Heart's Hunt. I'd assumed you hadn't been taking the competition seriously."

Mareleau studied her mother's profile, startled by the unexpected apology. "That means...you've changed your mind? You think I *am* taking it seriously?"

"Your father and I spoke to Lord Kevan. He confirmed he had, in fact, seen a unicorn with his very eyes, as did several of his men. They hunted it for a week before it crossed the border from Selay into Khero."

Mareleau pulled up short, her heart leaping into her throat. "He...he really said that?"

The queen nodded.

"So...Lurel's earrings..."

Queen Helena gave a dismissive shrug and nudged Mareleau to start walking again. "Your uncle purchased those earrings for her, which were only rumored to be made from unicorn horn. Still, it gives added legitimacy to your Hunt."

Mareleau bit the inside of her cheek. While she'd needed her uncle to carry the blame for her ridiculous request, she hadn't expected his tale to be so convincing. Could he have been telling the truth?

The queen's tone turned sharper. "I'd have preferred it if you'd picked something far easier and hadn't delayed the Heart's Hunt for a week. But I can't blame you for being a romantic. You always were."

Mareleau wanted to gag. Seven gods, her parents didn't know her at all. She wasn't a romantic. She simply wanted freedom from cold courtships, from groping hands and loveless declarations. She wanted to be respected as heir to her throne without needing to marry. Was that so much to ask? At the very least, she wanted to avoid marrying Larylis' brother. If it ever came down to a forced alliance, she could handle marrying just about anyone but Teryn.

Despite how much she'd hardened her heart after Larylis had shattered it, she would never be able to reconcile living in the same palace as him, dining at the same table, bearing his brother's children while the boy she preferred—

Fiery rage bubbled inside her, but she forced it down. Right now, there were more pressing concerns to worry over.

If Uncle Kevan hadn't been lying, if unicorns truly had returned from extinction...

That meant her suitors might successfully complete the task she gave them.

And she'd promised to marry whoever did first.

The thought made her want to crawl out of her skin. At least she had one small comfort. For the time being, no matter how short it might be, she was free.

12

Just before midnight, Teryn made his way to the palace garden. The evening's festivities were still underway, so no one paid him much heed as he slipped through the halls, past the bustling ballroom, and out to the garden court-yard. From there, he began navigating the twists and turns of the walking paths flanked by elegantly manicured shrubs and flower beds. He came to the first statue along the path, but it was a marble likeness of King Verdian, not a busty water nymph. He chose another branching path, discovered a few more statues, but none resembling the description in the letter.

The deeper he went into the garden, the more wary he began to feel over the possible intentions behind this meeting. Nearly every twist and turn brought him stumbling upon lovers stealing covert kisses, couples locked in passionate embraces meant only to be witnessed by shadows. He supposed he shouldn't have expected less on Beltane.

Teryn reached a portion of the garden boasting impressive water features—ponds and fountains as well as several artistic arrangements utilizing pumps and pulleys that almost seemed like magic. The sculptures here looked far more like water nymphs than the previous ones had. And yet, there wasn't much to distinguish the characteristics of one statue from another, nor was there any sign of someone waiting for him. Not until he entered a quiet courtyard with an enormous fountain standing at its center. Only now did Teryn understand the emphasis on ample breasts in his letter, for the figure atop the fountain was heavily endowed indeed, plus a rounded swell of belly and curved hips. Even more telling was the hooded figure standing before it, back facing him.

Teryn took a few tentative steps forward, but the figure didn't seem to notice his approach. He stepped closer again and realized the rush of the fountain was likely drowning out the sound of his steps. With a deep breath, he closed the remaining distance and placed his hand on the figure's shoulder.

The figure lurched back and whirled around, revealing a man several inches shorter than himself dressed in plain black clothing and a rather conspicuous cloak.

Teryn blinked a few times to ensure he was seeing whom he thought he was. "Prince...Lexington?"

"Seven gods and demons," the man cursed, clutching his chest. Prince Lexington was one of the three champions Teryn was competing against in the Heart's Hunt. Which meant he couldn't have been the one to send him the letter.

Could he?

Lexington let out a low whistle. "You scared me half to death." His eyes flicked from Teryn's face to his brocade waistcoat and formal jacket. "You don't look incognito."

Wait, did that mean...

Teryn kept his voice neutral as he said, "Your letter didn't say I should."

Lexington shrugged, confirming that he, in fact, was the letter's mysterious sender. "Well, I suppose it doesn't matter, so long as I can say what I came here to say."

Teryn stood tall and crossed his arms, narrowing his eyes with suspicion. If they were to be competitors, he assumed this meeting wasn't going to be a friendly one. "What exactly did you come here to say, Prince Lexington?"

"First of all," he said, raising a finger, "call me Lex. I despise the name Lexington. Second of all..." He cast his gaze around the small courtyard and motioned Teryn closer to the fountain. Lowering his voice to a whisper, he continued. "I'll make this quick. I'm here to offer you an alliance to help you win the Heart's Hunt."

Teryn tilted his head back. "Why the hell would you help me? We're supposed to be adversaries."

"How can we be adversaries when we both want the same thing?"

Teryn narrowed his eyes again. "Are you telling me you want me to win? Why?"

"Because you're going to let my kingdom in on your trade agreement with Brushwold."

"Our trade agreement is exclusive." He did not add that—before the Bank of Cartha had started sending pirates—it was the only thing keeping his kingdom afloat. Brushwold was a small country but had something no one else had— Aromir goats. The animals produced the most coveted wool, famed for both its warmth and softness. Since Teryn's kingdom specialized in clothing manufacture, the trade alliance had been a natural one. Anyone on this side of the Balma Sea who wanted Aromir wool had to purchase it from Menah. It had been just enough for Teryn's kingdom to get by. Until Menah stopped receiving Brushwold's shipments, that is. And if they started sharing that trade...

Teryn nearly blurted out a *no* until he considered an alternate perspective.

If Teryn won the Heart's Hunt and secured his marriage to the Princess of Selay, Menah would have Mareleau's dowry. His kingdom could finally pay off their debts to the Bank of Cartha and turn their financial situation around.

Teryn brought a hand to his chin, considering the man before him. "Why do you want to help me, Prince Lexington?"

"Lex."

He rolled his eyes. "Why do you want to help me, *Prince Lex*?"

The man gave him a bewildered look as if the answer should be obvious. "Because I've no desire to marry that spoiled harpy of a woman."

Teryn pursed his lips to keep them from quirking into a grin. "If you don't want to marry her, then why are you here?"

"My father wants me to marry the princess for Selay's trade with the Southern Islands. However, if I can get us Aromir wool, Father will be satisfied."

"Why me? Why not offer an alliance to Prince Helios?"

Lex's lips pulled into a grimace. "Have you met him? He looks like he strangles puppies for fun. And that's after he's finished drinking the blood of virgins and kindly grandmothers."

Again, Teryn had to force himself not to grin. His own impression of the brutish prince hadn't been much different. He lifted his chin and posed his next question. "How exactly do you propose to help me?"

"By forfeiting to you, obviously."

Teryn expected more to follow, but only silence stretched on. "Wait...are you saying you have no plans to physically aid me in any way?"

Another perplexed look from Lex. "Of course not. I'll stay here, you'll go frolic through the woods in the name of love, and when you return with the princess' gifts, you'll brag about what fierce competition I was."

"Is that so?"

"It's a solid plan."

"I don't see the benefit to me."

"Less competition," Lex said with a shrug. "Better odds."

"I automatically have better odds because you just revealed to me you have no intention of winning."

"Damn. Fine, I'll come with you. I'll help you...kill magical creatures and such." He said the last part with a flourish of his hand. "Then we'll return with the gifts, and you'll spout on and on about my hunting prowess and how you beat me by only the narrowest margin. We'll dine, we'll dance, we'll celebrate your nuptials, and you'll grant the Kingdom of Tomas access to your trade arrangement with Brushwold."

"I'll *try* to include your kingdom in the agreement," Teryn amended, "and if I can't, I'll arrange a special discount on the purchase of Aromir wool. And that's *only* if I win."

Lex's mouth fell open. "Only if you win? That's hardly fair."

"Take it or leave it." Teryn honestly wasn't sure which option he'd prefer. While aid would be welcome, especially since Mareleau's terms forbade her three champions from hiring help or bringing guards, was Lex going to be *that* helpful? Helpful enough to put his kingdom's greatest asset on the line?

If I win, he reminded himself, *Menah won't have to rely so heavily on said asset.*

Lex shook his head as if the whole arrangement were a personal affront. "Fine." With a resigned smile, he extended his hand and took a step toward Teryn—

And halted as a steel blade blocked his path. The sword was held by Prince Helios.

～

LEX STUMBLED BACK FROM THE SWORD, ITS EDGE GLISTENING BENEATH THE moonlight. Prince Helios didn't pursue him. Instead, he grunted, "Dead." He whirled toward Teryn, whose hand was already flying to his hip. It came away empty. Teryn cursed under his breath. Why hadn't he thought to arm himself before meeting a stranger in a shadowed garden? "Dead," Helios said again, pointing his blade at Teryn's heart.

"Very cute," Lex said in a mocking tone. "We're all good and dead. Mind telling us what in the name of the seven gods you're doing here?"

Teryn took a cue from Lex and tried to pretend he wasn't at all intimidated. He forced himself into a casual posture, eying Helios through slitted lids.

Prince Helios sheathed his sword and stared stone-faced at them. "I'm here to join your alliance," he said in a gruff voice.

Lex's face went conspicuously pale. "What alliance?" he uttered too fast.

"The one you invited Prince Teryn to join but not me."

Lex's gaze shifted furtively from Teryn to Helios. "I...don't know what you're talking about."

"At eight this evening, you sent a servant with a message for Prince Teryn. At a quarter to midnight, you left your room and entered the garden. At ten until midnight, Prince Teryn entered the garden. And here you are."

Lex's eyes bulged. "How do you know all that?"

"The servant you paid a single gold *sova* to deliver your message only required two *sovas* to tell me exactly where the message had been sent. The chambermaid who brought your dinner this evening, Lexington, only required five *sovas* to watch your room for the remainder of the evening. Meanwhile, one of the hall servants watched Prince Teryn's room for the cost of six."

Teryn scoffed. "Are we supposed to be impressed?"

"Everyone has a price. Every piece of information can be bought if you know the right currency."

"Do you like speaking in riddles," Teryn said, "or is that just an aspect of your glowing personality?"

Helios' jaw tightened as he slid his gaze to Teryn. "I don't know why the two of you chose to form an alliance, but your terms have now changed. The three of us will be working together."

Lex huffed a laugh. "Why would we agree to work with you?"

"I've already demonstrated my knack for gathering information," Helios said. "It just so happens I already know much about the prey we seek."

"How do you know we don't too?" Lex said, puffing his chest in a way that was not at all convincing.

"You don't."

"How do you *know*—"

"Answer me this," Helios cut in. "How many hunting parties are currently seeking unicorns?"

Teryn and Lex said nothing.

Helios' lips curled into a smug grin. "Who are they hired by? Where are the unicorns most commonly spotted? When did the first sighting occur? How thick is their hide? What's the best weapon to use against them?"

Teryn's fingers curled at his sides when he really wanted to send a fist to the other man's face. It took all his restraint to appear unflustered. "What's the best way to shut you up?"

Helios glared at Teryn. "Have you any clue how to most effectively skin a unicorn?"

"No, because I'm not a complete psychopath," Teryn said dryly.

He turned to Lex. "How does one dehorn a unicorn?"

"You pay someone to do it," Lex said with a nod.

Helios shook his head. "The two of you are clueless. You'll never find the unicorns without my help."

"If we're so clueless, why bother making an alliance with us?" Teryn asked.

"Unicorn hunting is not a solo endeavor. Even with three of us, it would be hard."

"All right," Teryn said, entertaining his line of reasoning. "What are you proposing then? We team up, help each other seek the prizes? Each champion must find three unicorns. One for its pelt, one for its horn, and one as a pet. That's a total of—" He was about to say six, since Lex had already forfeited his place as champion...but what if that was a piece of information Helios didn't have? Even if he'd been spying on them a while, could he have heard their hushed conversation over the rushing fountain?

Teryn watched Helios closely as he continued. "That's nine unicorns total if we agree to help each other complete the Heart's Hunt. How do we know you won't take advantage of our aid to steal the first three unicorns all for yourself and abandon us? And if not, what do we do once we're done helping each other? Make a mad dash back and see who gets here first?"

Helios showed no sign that he knew Teryn was withholding anything. "We aren't going to find nine unicorns. We're going to find two."

Teryn's stomach dropped, but he tried not to let his surprise show. It still didn't mean Helios knew. "Why only two?"

"We'll take the horn and the pelt from the same unicorn. Mareleau will never know the difference. It's impossible to tell. We'll bring back the second unicorn as her pet."

Teryn waited for him to elaborate but he didn't. "That's your plan? We hunt only two unicorns to collect one of every prize...and then what? Are we supposed to duel to the death to see who gets to keep them?"

"We're all keeping them," Helios said. "We find the unicorns together. Gather the pelt, horn, and pet together. We bring them back to her together. Her terms stated that he who returns first with what she demands will prove he loves her most and will, in turn, earn her hand in marriage. This way, all of us return as equal victors."

Teryn frowned. "Then she'll owe her hand to all three of us."

Lex raised his palms in a defensive gesture. "No, thank you. I'm not sharing a bride with the two of you."

"No, you fool," Helios growled, "she'll be forced to *choose* one of us."

"And if she refuses?" Teryn asked.

Helios let out a dark chuckle. "What, afraid your fiancée won't choose you once her hand is forced? I'd be scared too. Rumor has it she's already courted half the continent since your so-called engagement began."

He bristled at that but kept his voice calm. "I'm serious."

"If she refuses to choose, that's when we'll duel to the death."

Teryn waited a beat, expecting his words to have been in jest, but Helios made no attempt to take them back. "This plan is madness."

"Everything about this situation is madness," Helios said. "I don't know about you, but I have neither time nor patience to play the princess' game. I say we beat her at it. Use her own terms against her. Force her to simply choose a husband like a sane person. My kingdom wants the marriage alliance, but not at the cost of me doing the impossible alone. With the three of us working together, we'll be finished in two weeks tops. If the two of you try and attempt this without me, I'll be walking down the aisle before you so much as catch a whiff of a unicorn."

Teryn narrowed his eyes. "Is that a threat?"

"A fact. The things I know..." His smirk widened. "I'm honestly embarrassed just thinking about you attempting the hunt without me."

Lex crossed his arms and squinted at Helios. "Prove it. Give us one reason to believe you know anything about what we're up against."

Helios reached for his belt. Teryn stiffened as he unsheathed a dagger. Lex launched a step back, almost tripping as his calves collided with the lower ledge of the fountain. Helios chuckled at Lex's reaction and aimed the dagger at Teryn.

It took Teryn a moment to realize he was handing it to him hilt first.

He assessed Helios' arrogant expression before taking the weapon from him. As soon as his eyes landed on the blade, his breath caught. It was pale white, its tip sharply pointed, its edges curved in a sharpened spiral. He angled it, studying the strange knife beneath the moonlight. It was unlike anything he'd ever seen before. The blade seemed denser than bone, lighter than steel. He met Helios' eyes. "Is this..."

"Unicorn horn," Helios said, taking the blade from Teryn. He sheathed it, not even bothering to offer it to Lex. "Taken from a unicorn by my own hand."

While there was every chance the prince was lying—the blade could have been a fake, or Helios could have purchased it—Teryn couldn't help but feel a spark of awe.

"What do you say?" Helios asked, his face brimming with confidence. "Do you agree to this alliance, or do we part ways tonight knowing you will fail without me?"

Teryn's blood boiled at the indignity of the situation. He hated to admit Helios could be right. Teryn knew plenty about hunting but nothing about unicorns. He could fell an enraged boar and take down the largest stag in the woods, but what if there was something to what Helios had hinted at—that unicorn hunting had its own nuances Teryn wasn't aware of?

Lex edged closer to Teryn and whispered, "This is probably a good time to inform you that I know nothing about unicorns. Or killing. Or hunting. Or... forests."

Teryn suppressed a groan. If he had any chance at securing his engagement to Mareleau, he had to put his trust in Prince Helios. At least there was one thing Helios didn't know—Lex had already forfeited to Teryn. That had to count for something, right? If he could find a way to use Lex's support to gain the upper hand...he just might be able to win this.

"Fine," Teryn said. "But first—"

"See you in a week then," Helios said, not waiting for Teryn to finish before he turned on his heel and stalked out of the courtyard.

"A week," Teryn called to his back. "Don't we need a plan?"

"I have a plan," Helios said over his shoulder. Then he was gone.

Lex stared straight ahead, eyes unfocused. He blew out a heavy sigh, making his ruddy cheeks puff out. "I'm going to regret every word I've said today." With that, he too walked away.

Teryn was left alone by the fountain, wondering if pirates, financial ruin, and an unfulfilled engagement contract were about to be the least of his worries.

13

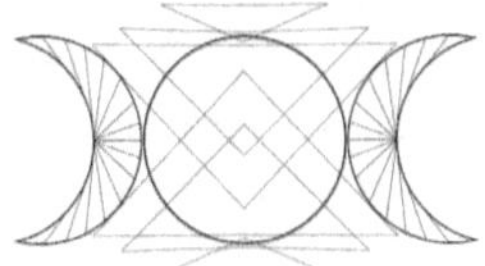

Cora had only gone out riding a few times since coming to live with the Forest People. The commune normally reserved their horses for pulling wagons when moving to a new camp or when going to trade with local villages. A few times, though, Cora and Maiya had been allowed to ride for leisure, to explore the nearby landscape outside a new campsite, or to simply exercise the horses. Before that, she'd ridden many times as a girl.

But never bareback.

Never racing through the night, her cheeks whipped by branches.

And never, of course, on a unicorn.

The ride was equal parts exhilarating and terrifying. She had to fight to keep her seat, and her inner thighs were burning within minutes. Maiya clung to her waist with all her might, her head tucked behind Cora's shoulder. Their speed was a near neck-breaking pace. She'd never ridden so fast, not even on her most daring leisure ride as a girl. She was confident there was no way the hunters could keep pursuit.

Cora was breathless by the time the unicorn slowed his pace to a canter, then a trot. Finally, the unicorn stopped. Cora looked around, seeking signs that they were anywhere familiar. She knew the areas between camp and the hot spring caves, but other than that...

A fresh wave of panic climbed up Cora's throat.

What if she couldn't find her way back to the Forest People?

What if she and Maiya were lost?

The unicorn stomped his hooves in an agitated gesture, telling Cora he was ready for them to dismount. She hated the idea of being lost while the hunters could still be searching for them, but she had no right to expect anything more from a fae creature. She was lucky enough the unicorn had bothered to save their hides at all. Shifting in her seat, she climbed down and nearly fell over in the process. Once she had her feet beneath her, she helped Maiya come down far more gracefully, careful not to let her land on her injured ankle.

The unicorn backed away a few paces.

Cora turned to him with a grateful nod. "Thank you for saving us."

Help, he relayed to her.

"Yes, you helped."

Help, he repeated, the feeling-word tinged with urgency.

Cora shrugged. "What are you trying to tell me?"

"Cora, are you...talking to the unicorn?" Maiya asked, coming up beside her.

"Sort of," she muttered, feeling somewhat self-conscious. "It's more like a feeling of his that I'm picking up, and it...somehow turns to words in my mind. He keeps saying *help*. The same isn't happening to you?"

Maiya wrinkled her brow and closed her eyes. She was silent for a few moments as she breathed deeply. Her eyes flew open, and her expression went slack. Maiya was accessing her Art—claircognizance. After a few moments, she gave a solemn nod.

"Did he speak to you?" Cora asked.

"No," she said softly, "but I did pick up on something. There are more like him."

"Unicorns?"

"Not just that. Caged ones. They're...they're being harmed in a way I don't understand. All I know is they're in danger."

Cora looked back at the unicorn. "You want our help rescuing more of your kind?"

He tossed his mane and Cora felt an approving emotion from the creature.

Cora and Maiya exchanged a look. "We...can't help you," Cora said, feeling her vengeful side rebel at her words. "We barely survived what just happened."

The unicorn's energy turned aggravated as he raked his hoof into the earth.

Maiya sighed and faced Cora. "I wish we *could* help. We were raised on tales about fae like him, raised to believe we'd never see them with our own eyes. Now that we know they aren't extinct, it makes me sick that they're being hunted."

Cora could sense her friend's sorrow, her desperation. Cora felt something similar herself. She remembered Gisele mentioning that James and his companions would be leaving in the morning to join the rest of their hunting party. She recalled how he'd boasted about the impressive *thing* awaiting at camp, and how there were more at his next destination. Cora hadn't taken his words as anything more than a poor attempt at seduction, but now it all made sense.

There were more captive unicorns. More tormented fae.

And they were likely all working for Duke Morkai.

Her enemy.

A spark of fiery vengeance—the same she'd felt when she'd first glimpsed the duke's sigil—roared through her.

She tamped it down. Her conclusion was the same now as it had been then. There was nothing she could do that mattered.

And yet...

"*Maiya.*"

"Cora."

Two voices sounded through the trees, one male, one female. Maiya's hand flew to her heart. "Is that…"

"We're here," Cora called back.

Their names echoed again, not too far away, and they ran toward the sound, Cora and Maiya calling back with every step. Soon two figures emerged from between the trees and bounded forth.

Roije stopped as soon as they came into view, his face slack with relief. Behind him was Gisele, trails of tears marking her cheeks, sparkling beneath the light of the moon. She ran forward, breaking into a sob as she gathered Cora and Maiya in her arms. "It's my fault. It's all my fault," she cried.

While Cora couldn't help but agree, now didn't seem like the time to say so. Instead, she said, "We're safe."

Gisele released them, which in turn made Maiya hobble back before she caught her balance. Roije was at her side in an instant. "You're hurt." He framed her face in his hands, his expression hardening when his eyes landed on the blood at her temple.

Even in the dark, Cora could tell Maiya was blushing. "I'm fine," she said with a bashful smile.

"I can carry you," he said, and was halfway to scooping her up before she put a hand on his chest to still him.

Just as quickly, she snatched her hand away. "It's just a sprain. With help, I can walk."

"You're sure?"

"Yes." She waved at Gisele, who wordlessly obliged, putting her arm around her like Cora had done.

"Come on then." Roije angled his head in the direction he and Gisele had come from. "We're not too far from camp."

They started off, keeping a moderate pace for Maiya.

"Thank you for finding us," Cora said. "How—"

"The Magic of the Soil led me here," Roije explained. "Gisele sprung upon camp looking half dead with a wild tale about getting attacked by hunters. A dozen of us went out looking, and Gisele insisted on coming with me."

"I knew if anyone would find you, it would be Roije," Gisele said. It was a solid bet, considering his renowned magic-aided tracking skills. Gisele's lip quivered. "I'm so, so sorry. I never should have been so reckless."

"Let's just get back to camp," Cora said, still uneasy with the thought that the hunters were still out there. She knew the unicorn's speed had helped them outrun them—

Remembering the creature, she whirled around.

Her heart dropped when she realized he was nowhere to be seen.

Roije turned too. "What is it?"

She looked deep into the dark woods, searching between the trees for any sign of white fur. Nothing. She was surprised at the pang of disappointment that tugged her heart. Releasing a sigh, she caught back up with Roije. Gisele and Maiya were now several paces ahead.

"What happened out there?" he whispered.

She nibbled her lip, uncertain what to say. Would he believe the truth? She remembered the idea that had begun to form before Roije and Gisele had found them.

"Can you track...*anyone*? Even someone you haven't met?"

He considered that and shrugged. "It depends. I'd never met my father, but the Magic of the Soil led me to him. His blood called to mine."

"So, you couldn't track a stranger?"

"If I could track them for a while by usual means, I'd perhaps be able to tune in to their essence enough to utilize magic as well."

"How fresh of tracks do you need?"

He turned to face her, eyes narrowed with suspicion. "What is this about?"

She looked from him to her two friends. Cora returned to walking while keeping a slight distance behind them. Maiya looked over her shoulder with a questioning glance before casting her gaze ahead.

"Gisele told you we were attacked by hunters."

He nodded.

"They weren't just any hunters, Roije. They'd captured..." She gulped a few times, gathering the courage to say what she knew would sound crazy to him. "They had a unicorn in an iron cage. It looked starved. I witnessed one of the hunters lash another unicorn with an iron-barbed whip."

Roije made no outward sign that he was surprised. Or perhaps it was only that he didn't believe her.

"I'm telling the truth, Roije. You can ask Maiya. We both saw it. We—" She almost confessed they'd ridden the unicorn, but that seemed too unbelievable to admit. "I know it sounds crazy, but we have to do something. We need to stop them. We must tell the elders."

He halted in place and faced her. "No." His tone was neither sharp nor unkind. It was more...tired.

"What do you mean, no? This is a matter of the fae. If anyone should care, it's the Faeryn. The Forest People might no longer be of pure Faeryn blood, but their heritage is fae, just like the unicorns. It's a matter of magic—"

"No, Cora," he said, expression sagging with grief. "While it may involve fae creatures, it is a royal matter, not a Faeryn one."

Cora took a step back, taking in his posture, his feelings of defeat that began to seep into her. "You already know."

He nodded. "I spied the hunters on my way to camp. I saw them with their... their prey. I also saw whose sigil they bore on their coat sleeves."

Ice filled Cora's blood, battling the heat of her rage that always sparked when she thought of Morkai.

"Duke Morkai is too powerful. Facing him or his agents would be equal to facing the king. You know why we can't do that."

Cora swallowed back every argument. She knew he was right. The Forest People served no crown, recognized no king. If King Dimetreus—or anyone loyal to him—learned of the commune's existence, knew that a group of nomads lived on the king's soil paying no taxes, no dues...the Forest People would be hunted.

Forced into modern society at best. Exterminated at worst. That was the very reason the commune swore never to get involved with royal matters. Never cross paths with agents of the crown. Never engage in anything that could draw the crown's attention.

"Did you tell anyone?" Cora asked.

"I met with the elders this morning and told them what I'd seen. They won't directly interfere."

Tears pricked Cora's eyes as she remembered the skinny brown unicorn. She could still feel his sorrow. Then there was the white unicorn, who turned his grief into rage, fought against his captors, and risked getting caught just to free one of his kind. Risked his life to save Cora and Maiya. "There must be something we can do."

He shook his head. "You need to forget what you saw. You more than anyone need to stay away from those hunters."

It took a few seconds to feel the weight of his words. Echoes of his earlier warning pounded through her head. "What do you mean by that? Why me more than anyone?"

He started walking again. "You know why."

Cora stared after him. He was halfway back to catching up with the others when Cora tugged his sleeve. "Tell me what you mean."

He rounded on her and stuffed his hand beneath his coat. When he brought it back out, a crumpled piece of paper was crushed in his fist.

"What is that?"

Without a word, he handed it to her.

Cora felt the blood leave her face as she unfolded the paper. Once she'd smoothed it flat, she squinted at what she beheld. It was hard to make out at first, with the night so dark, but soon her eyes followed the lines of black that formed the sketch. It was a female face. Long hair. Lightly rounded jaw. Almond-shaped eyes.

The paper shook violently in her hands as she stared at her own face, the likeness as accurate as her reflection. Above her head, bold letters spelled *Wanted* while the script below the portrait read: *For the murders of Queen Linette and Princess Aveline. Reward: 500,000 gold* sovas.

Sovas were the highest form of currency on the continent. The sum was considered a fortune. Her eyes fell on what was written beneath that. *Wanted alive and turned over to the crown.*

Cora dropped the paper and lurched a step back. "Where did you get that?"

He picked it up and stuffed it back in his coat. "In Kubera. The signs were... everywhere."

"Has anyone else..."

"I don't know, Cora. If these signs are papered around the other villages, I suppose it's only a matter of time."

She took another step back, her heart racing. She felt as if the ground were about to swallow her up.

"It doesn't matter," Roije said, reaching for her. "I don't believe what it says about you. There's a chance the others won't either."

She wanted to take his word for it, but she could feel the weight of everything he left unsaid. They both knew the truth. Once word got out that she was wanted by the crown, she wouldn't be allowed to stay. Sure, Salinda would defend her. Try to protect her. But what of the others? If the Forest People were so determined to stay out of royal affairs that they'd refuse to help captive fae creatures, then they'd certainly refuse to harbor a fugitive. Worse...what if they turned her in? It would go against the Forest People's rules, but the likeness...it was too close. When she'd first been condemned for the crime, she'd been a twelve-year-old child. No one could have guessed her current appearance so accurately. Could someone in the commune be a spy? Could they have discovered Cora's identity and...and...

A far more reasonable explanation came to her, one that filled her with the darkest shade of dread.

No one had spied on Cora. No one had run off telling her enemies of her appearance. For if they had, why not turn her in right away? Why not reveal where to find her? No, this was a matter of magic.

Dark magic.

A mage's magic.

Duke Morkai could somehow *see* her.

And if he could see her...

She glanced at Maiya and Gisele, almost at the edge of her vision. If he could see her, he could see *them*. All of the Forest People. If he didn't know their location yet, he soon could. She could handle the thought of being personally targeted by the duke. In fact, part of her relished the thought. Relished the prospect of getting her chance at revenge. What she could not tolerate was putting the Forest People at risk in turn. Suddenly, her fear over her own fate shifted to that of her friends. Of the few amongst the commune who'd become as close as family.

It wasn't enough to avoid villages. To hope her identity wasn't discovered.

Her throat burned, eyes prickling with unshed tears, even as she forced her heart to harden. To do what she knew she needed to do. "I have to go," she said, voice strained.

"What do you mean?"

"You said it yourself, Roije. The Forest People don't get involved in royal matters. *That*," she pointed at his coat where he'd stuffed the Wanted poster, "shows just what a danger I am. What a danger I've always been."

"It's different with you," he said. His voice held so much conviction she almost believed him. "Salinda—"

"Salinda deserves better. You all do. I can't...I can't endanger you." She took another step back, then glanced at her two friends again. "Tell Maiya I'm sorry."

Before he could say another word, she turned and ran.

~

THE SUN WAS JUST BEGINNING TO RISE BY THE TIME SHE MADE IT BACK TO THE HOT spring caves. Progress had been slow in returning, as every step was haunted by the threat of hunters, not to mention the threat of hope. Every snap of a twig, every hoot of an owl sent her stomach into a roiling mess. Half of her was terrified she'd see one of the duke's hunters, while the other part hoped Roije was just behind the next tree—that he'd tracked her, had come to stop her.

To take her back home.

To comfort.

To safety.

She shook the thought from her head as she took a tentative step inside the cave. The commune was never her home, she reminded herself, no matter how much she'd wanted it to be. She could never be truly welcome, not with a bounty on her head. She'd been naive enough to think her past was only a threat if she confessed her identity, or if someone else was clever enough to figure it out.

She made her way into the tunnel, finding it empty. The hot spring cavern was thankfully empty too. Tension unraveled from her gut as she made her way to the boulder where her discarded belongings remained. With a sigh, she sat on the boulder, resting her feet as she donned her bodice, overskirt, and cloak. She was tempted to curl up right there and sleep, but she had to keep moving. It was already a risk to return here, but she knew she wouldn't get far without her cloak. It had been a mild spring so far, but nights still carried a chill. As to where she'd go next...

Her lack of options nearly overwhelmed her.

She knew how to use her bow. Skin smaller animals. She could survive in the woods and feed herself, but...was survival enough?

The duke's sigil flashed through her mind, heating her core with fiery rage.

This time, she didn't tamp it down, didn't shove her vengeful thoughts away. As she left the hot springs and returned to the mouth of the cave, she let her anger unfurl, let it heat her blood until a reckless, wild idea took root in her mind.

Because now she had nothing left to lose.

So what if she was only one girl against a pack of hunters?

So what if her efforts had to be small?

At least they'd be something.

If Duke Morkai could somehow see her, then it was only a matter of time before he found her. He might as well watch her destroy his machinations. And when he found her, she wouldn't cower. Wouldn't run. She'd send an arrow between his eyes. Show him she was the killer he'd made her out to be.

She walked through the woods, idly seeking shelter. It took her a while to realize she was no longer alone. Glancing to the side, she caught a flash of white between the trees. She stopped in place and the unicorn stopped too. They held each other's stare until the creature emerged and stood before her.

Help, he said.

Terror surged through her, tinged with an unsettling excitement. Both emotions were wholly hers. "Yes," she said to the unicorn. "I will help you."

14

____

King Arlous slumped into the chair behind his desk, posture defeated. "Three more ships have been sacked by pirates. We'll lose our contract with Brushwold by fall at this rate."

Teryn's stomach plummeted at his father's words, although he wasn't sure how much farther it could sink. Today was the official start of the Heart's Hunt. A week had passed since the Beltane festival, and he was now back home at Dermaine Palace. In the week since his meeting with the princes in the garden, he'd exchanged only a few brief correspondences with Prince Helios, the latest of which directed Teryn to meet him and Lex at a certain inn by nightfall. That meant Teryn had but an hour to spare before departing. A prospect that had his nerves pressed in a vise. There was still a chance Helios' offer of alliance had been a ruse. Tonight's meeting could end in sabotage.

Arlous rubbed his brow, as if that were enough to erase his worries. Then, with a forced smile that didn't match the vacant look in his eyes, the king reached for a decanter on his desk. He poured a generous finger of amber liquid into two glasses and handed one to Teryn. "Let's share a drink. You didn't come here to listen to my woes. You came to bid me farewell."

Teryn accepted the glass and took a long pull. The burning warmth of the strong spirit was a welcome distraction from his anxiety. "As heir to the crown, your woes are mine to bear."

His father winced. "I failed you, Teryn. I promised to find information on unicorns and have nothing of value to give." He lifted one of the letters haphazardly strewn upon his desk. "One informant wrote to me with vague rumors about unicorn sightings up north. Like that's supposed to mean anything. North where? Northern Menah? North as in Khero? Northern Risa?" With a huff, he took up another letter. "This one might as well be blank for all it's worth." Another letter. "Same goes for this one." He crumpled it in his hand and tossed it toward his waste bin. It missed by several inches, which made King Arlous throw back the rest of his drink and pour another. "I'm being outbid, that's what's happening. I can't afford my own spies."

Teryn didn't know what to say to that so he took another pull from his drink. His eyes wandered over the king's desk. The letters his father had referred to appeared useless indeed, considering how brief they were. His father's frustration was his own, for that was how every correspondence from Helios had been this week. And Teryn was supposed to trust the man.

King Arlous finished his second drink and began gathering up the discarded letters. He fumbled and lost half the stack to the desk, proving he'd already been well into his cups by the time Teryn had arrived at the king's study to say goodbye.

The topmost sheet caught Teryn's eye. He leaned forward squinting at it. "What's that?"

Arlous lifted the page in question, then handed it to his son.

Teryn assessed it closer, finding a portrait of a beautiful young woman beneath the word *Wanted*. He nearly dropped his drink when his gaze landed on the sum at the bottom of the page. "Five hundred thousand *sovas*?" It was enough to repay the Bank of Cartha and still have money to spare. "Who is she?"

The king left his desk and stood at his window. The morning was gray and heavy with fog, obscuring the view of the palace gates and the rolling hills behind it.

"A wild goose chase," Arlous muttered. "An informant brought me the poster, but no one has been able to deliver anything else on the girl since. Not her name. Not her age. Not her last seen whereabouts. All we know is that she poisoned Queen Linette and Princess Aveline. It is common knowledge that the crimes were committed by one of the queen's maids, but the murders occurred six years ago. If that's what she looked like then, she could look far different now."

Teryn studied the girl again. Her expression had been rendered neutral, her eyes small and slightly angled, her hair dark and lustrous. She didn't look like a murderer. He returned the paper to the desk. "How long have you been seeking her?"

The king shrugged. "A few months now. I've been seeking an alliance with King Dimetreus for far longer, but he responds to nothing. This, I thought, could grant me both a formidable alliance and the funds to repay Cartha. I have nothing else to offer him. Your sisters are too young to marry."

Teryn's heart clenched at the mention of his three younger sisters. His father rarely spoke of them. Teryn only ever saw them anymore if he visited his mother's palace.

"If I could catch this outlaw," King Arlous said, "we'd have everything. Paying back the Bank of Cartha would allow us to set everything else to rights. Our trade with Brushwold would thrive. We'd never again be slighted by Selay. Verdian wouldn't dare put off your marriage to the princess any longer, knowing we had the funds to threaten war."

Teryn shifted in his seat, uneasy at the talk of war. His kingdom had already been on the receiving end of such a threat when Arlous attempted to dissolve his marriage to Teryn's mother. That was enough experience to last Teryn a lifetime.

"Don't worry, Father, we'll have the princess' dowry before the next ship leaves Brushwold's shores." His tone was confident, but he knew his expression didn't match.

King Arlous turned away from the window and frowned at his son. When he spoke, his voice was uncharacteristically soft. Quavering. "I'm so sorry, Teryn. I don't say it to you enough because I can't regret what I tried to do for Annabel. I love her. You must know that."

"I do," Teryn said, although he didn't consider it a virtue on his father's part.

The king returned to his desk and braced his hands on the tabletop, his head slumped with defeat. "This burden you must bear...I fear it will only leave you a younger version of me, trapped in a loveless marriage." Teryn bristled at that, but Arlous rushed to add, "That's nothing on your mother, son. She's a good woman. I respect her."

Teryn pursed his lips to keep from scoffing. How could his father claim to respect the woman he'd once dragged through scandal? Arlous had tried to annul his marriage to the queen by accusing her of infidelity. He'd claimed she'd been intimate with his late brother before his untimely death, which meant his marriage could never be considered valid in the eyes of the seven gods. Teryn had a hunch his father's actions had more to do with the fact that his mother bore only girls after Teryn while Annabel had birthed two more boys after Larylis.

"I can't take it all back," King Arlous said. "Nor can I stop hating myself for what I'm doing to you."

He met his father's eyes, saw the remorse in them, and found his own resentment softening. Even with everything the king had done, Teryn's father did love him. More admirable than that was Arlous' standing with the people of Menah. Teryn wasn't sure how many other monarchs could try to depose their queen without inciting massive rebellion. Instead, King Arlous had the people's sympathies, thanks to Annabel's popularity with the common folk. He was certain, however, that a lot of that support would disappear if Menah's poverty were more apparent in the day-to-day workings of the kingdom. For now, the king put the people first, ensured they had jobs, food, and homes while pirates ate into Menah's profits and sent the crown's coffers deeper into the negatives. Soon, the king wouldn't be able to keep the kingdom afloat without inflicting suffering upon their citizens.

Teryn had to make sure that never happened.

"I wish you didn't have to marry that woman, Teryn. I wish you didn't have to take my failures upon your shoulders."

"It doesn't matter," Teryn said. "I'll win the Heart's Hunt. I'll fulfill my duties."

The king pushed off from his desk with a growl of frustration. "I wish you didn't have to do it alone. That fool girl."

"I won't be alone." He didn't elaborate further than that. Helios' letters may have been brief, but he hadn't failed to stress the importance of keeping their alliance a secret.

Arlous assessed Teryn with a keen gaze. "Good. I don't care what you have to do, what rules of hers you have to break. Hire a hunting party. Buy the pelt and horn. She won't know a difference."

Teryn threw back the rest of his drink and set the empty glass on the desk. "I must leave soon. I should say goodbye to Larylis."

Arlous nodded. "Safe travels, son. Send Berol with word now and then."

"I will." He turned his back on his father, hoping that the next time they saw each other, they'd both have reasons to smile.

~

TERYN KNEW EXACTLY WHERE TO FIND HIS BROTHER. SURE ENOUGH, AS HE OPENED THE doors to the palace library, Larylis was hunched over a stack of books. It wasn't an unusual sight, as Larylis frequented the library as often as his own bedroom, either poring over poetry, historical texts, or the latest novel. But ever since they arrived home from Verlot Palace, Larylis had spent nearly every waking hour in books. Teryn knew what held his brother's fascination. Knew his extra time in the library was spent on Teryn's behalf.

He approached the table his brother occupied. Larylis didn't bother looking up from the paper he was furiously scrawling something on. "Don't get your hopes up," Larylis muttered. "Everything I've written down is rubbish."

Teryn chuckled and looked over his brother's shoulder. Several stacks of books surrounded him, as well as crumpled bits of loose parchment covered in scratched-out notes or angry-looking blotches of black ink. A book lay open at his elbow, which must have been what he was currently taking notes from. Teryn scanned the wall of text in the book. At the bottom was a black-and-white illustration of a unicorn laying next to a young girl with flowers in her hair. The creature's head was in her lap, round eyes staring adoringly up at the girl. Four pixies fluttered around them. Teryn turned his attention to the sheet of paper Larylis was writing on. It contained half a page of brief notations, one which read, *According to one faerytale, unicorns are drawn to virgins. Weird. Why?*

"Virgins?" Teryn said.

"I told you it was all rubbish. You'll see another line about a faerytale where a fae queen had six lovers and two pet unicorns. Obviously, the virgin thing is a myth." He finished writing his latest note and leaned back in his chair with a grumbling sigh. "That's the last book on unicorns I've found."

"I told you that you didn't have to do this."

"And I told you there was nothing you could do to stop me."

Teryn grinned at that. They were similarly stubborn. He supposed they both inherited the trait from their father. "Aside from pure rubbish, did you at least read anything interesting?"

Larylis shrugged. "Faerytales, mostly. The only scientific texts I found on unicorns stated they haven't been seen in over five hundred years. Our scholars are obviously behind on their records."

Teryn's own recent research—albeit far less thorough than his brother's—had revealed the same. It made no sense. How could an entire species come back after almost five hundred years of extinction? There was a part of him that still held doubts that unicorns *were* real. Then he'd recall Helios' strange blade. It had been rather convincing in the moment, but...could he have been fooled? To what end?

"You haven't read anything about hunting them, by any chance, have you? Dehorning them? Skinning them?" Helios had suggested there was some special method only he knew, but Teryn was uncertain how much of that had been posturing. "Found any maps suggesting where they can be found?"

"No," Larylis said as he reached for a book in the middle of one of his stacks, "although, I found a map in a book that mentions unicorns. I don't think it's of here, though. It talks about Lela at the end of the book, but the map says Le'Lana."

That piqued Teryn's curiosity. *Lela* was the original name for the portion of land that was now divided into three kingdoms—Menah, Selay, and Khero. Even though the land was part of the continent of Risa, there was much lore regarding Lela and its origins. Most tales insisted Lela hadn't always been part of the continent, that one day the city of Delany was the southernmost point of Risa, and the next the coast had sprouted an entirely new portion of land. Teryn had always enjoyed tales about how Lela had risen from the ocean or formed from mist. Other stories claimed the land had always been there, hidden behind a magical veil. He didn't believe any of those tales, but they never ceased to fascinate him.

Larylis handed him a book. "The map is in this one."

Teryn gathered it up, assessing the worn brown leather cover embossed with a simple gold title that read: *The Once and Former Magic of Ancient Lela*. He flipped open the cover and thumbed past the title page until he spotted the map Larylis had mentioned. It displayed an enormous land labeled *Le'Lana* and was marked by numerous rivers, forests, mountains, lakes, and streams. As interesting as it was to study, it didn't resemble Lela at all.

"Told you," Larylis said with a crooked grin. "Rubbish. I won't be offended if you'd rather not burden your saddlebags with my useless notes."

Teryn handed the book back and traded it for his brother's notes. "I'll take it. It'll remind me of home while I'm gone."

"You mean, rubbish notes to remind you of our rubbish kingdom that's about to be sunk by pirates?"

Teryn landed a playful punch on his brother's arm. "Exactly."

Larylis laughed but his mirth quickly fell away. "I feel like I should be going with you."

"I feel like you should too, but you heard the princess' terms. She wants her champions working alone. Besides, you're needed here. You'll have to carry the mantle of prince while I'm gone."

Larylis huffed a dark laugh. "You and I both know that isn't true. A bastard cannot be a prince." His expression fell, reminding Teryn of how he'd looked the day of the Beltane festival. That, of course, only served to recall what Larylis had said about having kissed Mareleau. He'd claimed not to have feelings for her, but Teryn couldn't help wondering...

As if Larylis knew exactly who'd sprung to Teryn's mind, he said, "Don't get yourself killed for that thorny harpy, all right?"

Teryn lifted a brow. "You clearly have no faith in my hunting skills."

"Oh, I have faith in your hunting skills," Larylis said as he rose from his seat. "It's sleeping in the dirt for nights on end that will be your downfall."

"Who says I won't be sleeping at an inn every night?" he said in jest.

Larylis squeezed Teryn's shoulder with a mock pout. "Aw, that's adorable. Looks like you'll need my notes after all."

Teryn returned the squeeze and left the library. His conversation with Larylis had momentarily lifted his spirits, but now his stomach was sinking back into its familiar state of dread. There was no denying it any longer.

It was time for the Heart's Hunt to begin.

15

Cora dreamed of blood again.

The stench of it was overwhelming, the cloying tang searing her throat. She stood in the doorway of the room with the bed, a tray of tea and cookies in her trembling hands. She already knew something was wrong, for she'd begun following that tug of unease before she'd picked up the serving tray. But seeing all that blood, those sheets soaked with red, the queen lying limp with sightless eyes that stared at nothing...

Cora's scream shattered the air, and the serving tray tumbled to the ground at her feet. Only then did she notice the figure who stood at the side of the bed. Duke Morkai whipped his head toward her, his hair a slash of black tinged the slightest bit blue where it was struck by the lantern light. His face was all hard lines and sharp edges, making him appear both ancient and ageless at once. Like a statue chiseled to capture a famed faerytale hero. Or a villain, perhaps. Her breath caught when she met his eyes. His pupils were black and so large they swallowed the whites that should have framed his irises. He stood with one hand raised several inches above the body of the queen. Specks of blood rose from the sheets toward his palm. As if he were...hiding the blood. Somehow. It made no sense, but one thing was clear.

He'd done this.

Cora bit back a cry and slowly inched away from the door, hardly daring to blink as Morkai pinned her beneath his unsettling stare. Her foot hit a slick spot on the marble floor.

Blood.

No, tea from the broken teapot she'd let clatter to the floor. She staggered to right her balance, and when she next locked eyes with Morkai, his appearance had changed. His eyes were no longer black but an icy pale blue contained to his irises.

Blood no longer rose to his palm, and his hand was outstretched as if in plea, not... whatever it was Cora had thought she'd seen a second ago.

"Don't just stand there," he said, waving her inside the room. His voice trembled with distress. "Help the queen!"

Cora shook the conflicting images from her mind and rushed across the threshold. Morkai shifted to the side to let her take his place. She assessed Queen Linette. Blood trailed down the woman's cheeks, her nose, her mouth, soaking the collar of her dressing gown. Nausea churned Cora's gut as she gathered the queen's cold hand in hers. "I don't know—"

"What have you done?" The voice was soft. Anguished.

A glance over her shoulder revealed King Dimetreus standing in the doorway, eyes wide with terror. Duke Morkai stood just behind him. When had he left the bedside? The duke leaned close to the king and lowered his voice to a whisper. "You recall what she said to the queen earlier."

Cora blanched. She knew what Morkai was referring to, but...but...she hadn't meant it! She'd regretted what she'd said to Queen Linette the moment the words had left her lips. It had been an outburst, not a threat. The words had sprung from the anger of a twelve-year-old girl, nothing more. Besides, what did *that* have to do with *this*?

King Dimetreus' expression turned hard, jaw set as he burned Cora with a glare. "You did this." He stormed over to her, his voice rising to a growl. A yell. "What have you done?"

~

CORA JOLTED AWAKE, HER SCREAMS CUT OFF BY SOMETHING HEAVY NUDGING HER shoulder. She scrambled onto her side, blinking into the dark. She expected Maiya's comforting words, the feel of her cot, the walls of her tent. Instead, all around her was dirt and the dying embers of a fire.

Where was she?

Where *was* she?

Time to wake. They move.

The words cut through her panic, helping her swallow down the terror of her dream and recall that she was no longer with the Forest People. She'd been away from them for just over a week. That was how long it had been since she'd last taken her sleeping draught, too. Not that it would have helped.

The heavy thing nudged her shoulder again, and this time she knew what it was. She angled her head and looked up at the white unicorn standing behind her. He pawed the dirt with a hoof.

We follow, the unicorn said.

In the week that she'd been traveling with the creature, she'd become better attuned to his feeling-thoughts. So much so that their communications seemed no different from any other kind of conversation. She still didn't quite understand how it was possible. Was it his magic? Or hers?

"All right," Cora said. Urgency propelled her to her feet. If the hunters were on the move, she and the unicorn had to be quick to follow. Not too quick, of course.

Quick enough not to lose their trail but not so fast as to risk crossing paths and getting caught.

The sun was barely beginning to rise by the time Cora and the unicorn started off down the game trail the hunters had been following. She assessed the markings the hunters' feet had left behind. They were perhaps an hour's walk ahead of them. She was pretty sure, at least. She'd learned some tracking with the Forest People, but without much opportunity to practice, her skills were rudimentary. But after a week of following the hunters, she'd begun to understand what it looked like when the tracks they followed were too fresh. That was when the unicorn would get skittish, halting her with warnings of *danger* and *slow down*. Thankfully, his senses were stronger than hers. His scent and hearing far keener.

Or perhaps it was his magic. If that were the case, Cora wondered why he couldn't simply guide her directly to the next party of hunters that held captive unicorns. Then again, he'd nearly been caught the last time he'd approached one of their camps.

Wouldn't have been close to getting caught, came what she'd come to interpret as the unicorn's voice, *if not for freeing brethren*. A wave of indignation rippled off the creature, echoed by Cora's own. Not only could the unicorn understand her spoken words, but now and then he seemed to pick up on her thoughts too, even with her mental shields in place. Likewise, she was always able to glean his emotions and communications, shields or no.

"Oh, and how many of your brethren did you save before I came along?"

Another ripple of affront. His lack of answer told her his grand total before she'd freed the brown unicorn on his behalf must have been zero.

"By the way, it's rude to read people's minds without permission."

Then stop listening.

Cora cut a glare at the unicorn. "I didn't mean *me*."

He gave no indication that he cared whom she'd meant. With a huff, she returned her attention to the markings on the trail before her. She was relieved there were no tracks of any captive unicorns in tow. Her companion had confirmed as much through his own senses.

They continued at a moderate pace well after midday. Cora saw no signs that they were gaining too closely on their prey. But when the unicorn halted suddenly on the trail, ears twitching back and forth, she knew they had.

They've slowed. Left trail.

It wasn't an unusual course of action for the hunters. While they were clearly following a direct path along the game trail, and their pace suggested expediency, they'd still break to hunt now and then.

Cora pulled up short next to the unicorn, and he led her off the path. They backtracked a good ten minutes and waited. Waited. Waited.

The waiting was Cora's least favorite part. Walking felt productive. Tracking busied both her body and her mind. Whenever they were forced to stop outside of evening rest, however, Cora felt caged. Restless. It made her recall James and the other vile hunters, the blood at Maiya's temple, the arrow piercing Erwin's neck. The latter stirred feelings of equal parts disgust and triumph. It made her want to do more, to hurt the hunters more. Based on their behavior and the two brands she'd spotted, she suspected the entire party was comprised of the worst kinds of criminals. With Erwin dead, there were four left. Four men she held a personal vendetta against. Four men she yearned to put down. She remembered all of their names from that night. James, of course. Gringe, the leader. Velek. Sam. All names that made her blood boil.

She wrapped her fingers around her bow, letting its familiar heft steady her. Ground her. Root her in place. She didn't draw her weapon. Didn't nock an arrow. Instead, she reminded herself why she couldn't make a move on them yet.

She needed them alive. Needed a trail to follow.

The party the hunters joined next had more unicorns. That was the reason she was out here to begin with. Once she found *them*, she could do work that mattered. She wasn't sure exactly how she'd free the captive creatures without getting caught herself, but she knew she'd need to keep her head on her shoulders. Exercise patience. Caution.

It made Cora's muscles twitch with frustration just thinking about it.

"Do you have a name?" Cora asked, keeping her voice low. The question was more to distract herself, but it was something she'd been wondering the past week.

The unicorn rippled with confusion. *You know I am unicorn.*

"Yes, but do you have a name unique only to you? You know...like how I am a human but my name is Cora."

I don't remember. His words were tinged with agitation. She got the distinct feeling he was grasping for an answer to her question...but it was lost to him.

Cora furrowed her brow. Could he be such an ancient creature that he no longer remembered his name? If so, where had he been all this time? "Where are you from?"

A pause. Then, *Forest.*

"What forest? These forests? Have you always lived in Khero?"

Again, she got the sense he was straining to find the answer. It was almost painful for him. *Not these forests. Like here but not here. Close, but not close at all.*

Cora wanted him to elaborate but his feelings of frustration were enough to tell her he likely couldn't. Theories began to buzz through her mind. What if the unicorns hadn't been extinct but in some sort of slumber? What if they'd been... trapped in some way? Of course, if unicorns were returning, then perhaps other fae creatures were too. There could be dragons, pixies, kelpies, selkies—

Only my kind, he said, cutting through her thoughts. *Only my kind are here. No others.* A wave of sorrow seeped from the unicorn, sinking Cora's heart.

"What do you think happened to the others? Better yet, what happened to you? Your kind hasn't been seen in hundreds of years."

He scraped the earth with a hoof. *Don't remember. I try. I try and try, but it's... gone. All I remember is...my forest. Then being here. Hunted.*

"How long have you been here?"

Time feels...not what I remember it feeling. Wasn't here long before I met you.

The unicorn's predicament both saddened and fascinated her. Before her very eyes was a myth come to life. A mystery unraveling. Not even the Forest People knew the creatures had returned.

Well, at least they hadn't before Roije informed the elders. And that was only if they hadn't known all along and kept the intel from the rest of the commune.

Cora's heart clenched with a mixture of anger and longing. She missed Maiya. Salinda. The comfort of her daily routine. She missed what it was like when she hadn't known just how great a danger her presence was. But mingled with those feelings was irritation at the elders' unwillingness to intervene with the plight of the unicorns. She understood why the Forest People refused to involve themselves with royal matters, but surely the capture of fae creatures was worth taking a stand against. If she had the support of the commune—even just a handful of their best trackers and hunters—they could overpower the men she followed, keep one alive for the sake of leading them to the next party, and then attack them too. She could free the unicorns and leave no one alive to tell the tale of the mysterious people who'd interfered—

So violent, the unicorn said with disdain.

Cora pursed her lips. The Forest People would likely feel the same about her bloody fantasy. They were a nonviolent people. Even hunting was done with ritual reverence. No life was taken without need. No tree was felled without blessing the soil it belonged to. No hide was skinned without gratitude for the animal that gave its life to provide food and warmth.

Another reason Cora never truly belonged with the Forest People. When she'd killed Erwin, she hadn't bothered to bless his soul or pray for his family. And she still had no desire to.

You can call me something, the unicorn said. The offer was stiff and begrudging, but it came with something that felt like camaraderie. Perhaps he too understood Cora's pent-up rage.

"You mean I can give you a name?"

Better be good.

"All right." She studied his white fur flecked with silver. His wounds left by Erwin's whip were almost fully healed, and his coat looked twice as lustrous as it had been when they'd first met. He was graceful. Quiet. "How about...Ghost?"

Rather not be named after being dead.

"Fair enough. Snowball?"

He gave a derisive whinny. *I am not a snowball.*

"Mister Cuddles?" Cora smirked.

He sidled away from her, bristling with indignation. *You mock me. I am not to be cuddled. I am strong and fearless. I am brave. Hunters tremble at the pound of my hooves.* It was the most descriptive communication she'd ever felt from him. Which meant she really must have gotten under his skin.

"Fine," she said with a soft chuckle. "Something brave then. Thunder Hoof. Rage Mane. Valorous Maximus."

He radiated with a hint of approval. *I sort of like the last one. Want it simpler though.*

"Valor? No, Valorre."

Those were both the same word.

"There was an extra *R* in that last one. And an *E*. It makes it a proper name."

Why? Your alphabet means nothing to me.

"It just does. Trust me." She was mostly teasing for the sake of entertainment, but she did like the way the name looked in her mind's eye. "Valorre. There you have it."

Fine. The word was curt but she could sense that he liked the name.

She grinned at Valorre and realized it was the first time she'd smiled since leaving the Forest People.

Valorre stiffened.

Cora's momentary mirth drained in an instant as she felt the unicorn's trepidation. "What is it?" she whispered.

The hunters. They do not pause to hunt. They pause to join others.

Fear and anxious excitement clashed in her stomach.

They'd found their prey.

16

Every inch of Teryn's body was sore, but nowhere more so than his ass. When he'd imagined the Heart's Hunt, he'd entertained a multitude of ridiculous notions, but mostly he'd imagined, well...hunting. Stalking prey like he was used to. Moving quietly between the trees in search of mythical creatures. What he had not anticipated was five days of hard riding with only an hour or so of scouting the surrounding woods before making camp. No part of their day contained an element of what Teryn would consider *hunting*.

The first day of the Heart's Hunt had gone as he'd imagined it would. He'd ridden north until evening, met his allies at the inn Helios had specified in his letter, and—surprisingly—wasn't betrayed and left with a dagger in his chest by morning. After that, Helios had set them to riding at a brisk pace north into the Kingdom of Khero, leaving the main road on the third day only to maintain the same pace on the hunting trails through the forests. Helios clearly had a predetermined destination in mind. One he showed no intention of sharing with his companions.

Teryn's eyes unfocused on the fire blazing at the center of tonight's camp. They were somewhere in northeastern Khero by now, a prospect that didn't sit well with Teryn. Even though he was a prince, it wasn't exactly fine manners to go hunting in another kingdom without permission from its monarch. That was yet another thing Helios claimed to have under control. Yet another secret he kept to himself.

With a grumbling sigh, Teryn leaned his head against the trunk of a tree. One glance at Prince Lex wincing as he shifted in his seat on the ground was evidence that he too found the excessive riding a bit much. Helios was currently nowhere to be seen, having stalked off wordlessly an hour ago.

"My bum has been flayed raw, I just know it," Lex said, adding a wadded-up shirt beneath his bottom, on top of four other articles of clothing and his bedroll.

Teryn let out a halfhearted chuckle. Berol angled her head at Teryn from her perch on his shoulder. His hunting vest was fitted with extra padding on each shoulder for that exact purpose. He reached into his pocket and retrieved a strip of dried venison. After taking a bite for himself, he fed the rest to Berol, who snatched it from his fingers with relish. "Lazy animal," Teryn said with a grin. "You have the entire forest as your personal buffet and yet you still come to me for treats."

"I cannot believe you have a peregrine falcon as a pet," Lex said, eying her from across the fire with a grimace. "Those talons look sharp enough to rip out my throat. And that beak. I've no idea how you can feed her by hand and still have a full set of fingers. Those are your original fingers, right? They aren't constructed of wood by now?"

"You sound like my brother." Teryn huffed a laugh and gave Berol a light scritch on the side of her neck. "She won't hurt me, though. I've had Berol since she was a hatchling. I found her injured while out on a royal hunt. Father almost didn't let me bring her home with us, but he figured it would be a proper lesson in death and the futility of fixing broken things. In the end, it only served to prove the virtues of stubbornness in the face of great odds."

"Cute," Lex said, though his expression said anything but. He shifted on his seat again, then gave up to recline on his side. "Do you think Helios actually has a plan? Or has he dragged us out here to murder us and steal your bride?"

Mention of Helios had Teryn's mood turning sour. He'd given the prince the benefit of the doubt during the week leading up to the Heart's Hunt, hoping he'd eventually share his plan with them. But after more than five full days together, he was coming to regret ever agreeing to their so-called alliance. "I don't know."

"Where is he, anyway?" Lex glanced around the camp, then shifted slightly closer to Teryn. A mischievous glint sparked in his eyes. "Should we leave him?"

"The prospect is tempting but far from rational."

Lex quirked a brow. "Nothing about our situation is rational."

"Valid point."

Lex glanced around the camp again before saying, "Our original terms still stand. You know that, right?"

Teryn was relieved to hear Lex still held a greater allegiance to him than to Helios. Although, he still couldn't figure out how that would do him much good. First, they had to find those damn unicorns. But how were they going to find a single one by riding all day and hunting so little? What was Helios' plan? Gritting his teeth, he reached into his pocket for another strip of venison, but his hand came away with only a crumpled sheet of parchment. It took him a few moments to sift through his cloud of fatigue before realizing he'd reached into the wrong pocket. Berol nipped at the paper, then gave Teryn a look that conveyed her agitation at finding parchment over treats. To further prove the gravity of such an offense, the falcon launched from Teryn's shoulder and landed on a branch in the tree above him, sending a shower of cherry blossoms to rain upon his head.

"It was an accident," he called to Berol, although he couldn't keep the laughter from his voice. He studied the paper again, smoothing out its crinkled folds until he realized what it was—Larylis' list of notes. His lips tilted into a grin as he scanned his brother's scrawled writing.

Unicorns are found deep in the forests. Obviously. Not helpful, thanks.

According to one faerytale, unicorns are drawn to virgins. Weird. Why?

Never mind the last note. I just read another faerytale that contradicts the virgin thing.

Scholars say unicorns have been extinct for over five hundred years. Why are they back? Where have they been all this time?

Unicorns avoid populated towns and cities. Alright. That might be helpful. Be prepared to spend a lot of time sleeping in the woods, brother.

He felt a pang of homesickness then. Not for the first time, he wished Larylis were with him. Aside from the three years Larylis had lived in Selay, they'd gone on every hunt together. Larylis hadn't enjoyed hunting as much as Teryn did, preferring to admire the flora and fauna, but he had the aptitude to make a clean kill. More so, his company was second to none.

"What's that?" Lex asked, shaking Teryn from his thoughts.

Teryn refolded the paper and returned it to his pocket. "A letter from my brother. He took notes on unicorns for me."

Lex's next question came with a hint of hesitation. "Do you get along with your brother?"

"I do. He's been my best friend my whole life."

"You're lucky," Lex said with a sigh. "I don't get along with mine."

"Why is that?"

Lex's jaw shifted back and forth. When he answered, his words were ground out between his teeth. "Ben is a sniveling little troll who's constantly trying to upstage me. He's three years younger and yet he's the one who secures an engagement alliance first, and to a *proper princess.*" He said the last part with clear mocking. "Well, guess what? His *proper princess* still has baby teeth. She won't be old enough to wed for at least a decade. Oh, and then he takes over *my* project to build the stupid wall between Tomas and Norun—" He cut off suddenly, his cheeks having grown red. "Never mind. I hate Ben. Let us not speak of that brat."

Teryn pursed his lips to hide his smile. "Very well."

"What did your much-less-annoying-than-mine brother's notes say?"

"Nothing helpful. Unless, of course, you're a virgin. If you are, we could test a theory and use you as bait. I saw an illustration in a book once. The virgin princess had flowers in her hair. We could weave you a nice crown of cherry blossoms." He gave Lex a teasing grin.

Lex smirked and rolled onto his back. "Your tone suggests you assume I *am* a virgin. So let me enlighten you and say that I am not."

"Really." Teryn couldn't help the note of surprise.

Lex cut him a glare. "I have a lady back home. Is that so hard to believe?"

"Oh, I imagine you're quite the bodice ripper in Tomas."

"*One* bodice. And quite the bodice it is, let me just say."

"Is that so? If you're so taken with her, why are you competing for another woman's hand?"

Lex scoffed. "You and I both know I'm not competing. Besides, participating in the stupid Heart's Hunt was never *my* idea. It was my father's. If you haven't gleaned as much already, my father wants his sons to marry princesses. Well, my lady isn't one. But once I come back with the trade agreement we spoke of, I think Father will finally approve my request to marry."

Teryn considered that. It seemed like a fair plan. Of course, it all hinged on whether Teryn actually won. "What's her name?"

"Lily," Lex said with a dreamy sigh.

"What's she like?"

Lex waggled his brows. "You recall that water nymph statue? Lily puts her to shame."

"In what way?" Teryn tried to keep a straight face. "Her silent disposition? Her failure to respond to your touch?"

Lex rolled his eyes. "I meant her shapely form."

"Prince Lexington wouldn't know a shapely form if it fell naked onto his lap." The brusque voice silenced Teryn and Lex as Helios stalked into camp. Teryn felt as if the temperature had plummeted with the prince's arrival.

Lex said nothing in reply. It was one thing for Teryn and Lex to tease each other. Their exchange of lighthearted jabs was friendly. But there was nothing lighthearted about the way Helios teased. His every word always held a sinister edge.

Helios took a seat by the fire and set to sharpening a knife. "There are no unicorns here," he said without looking at either of them.

Teryn waited for him to elaborate, but the hope was futile. "What exactly does that mean?"

"It means we ride at dawn. Continue north."

Teryn curled his fingers into fists. It was always the same answer, night after night with nothing else to add. "Helios," he said through his teeth, "tell us the damn plan."

Helios slowly slid his gaze to Teryn. "I'll tell you the plan when I've deemed you worthy of hearing it."

Teryn shot to his feet, chest heaving with rage. "We are in an alliance. We are not your servants. When we agreed to this arrangement, we conceded to work together. Not for you."

"I'll share my intel on a need-to-know basis."

"No." It took all of Teryn's restraint to speak with control. "You will tell us everything you know. Now."

Helios lifted his brows. "Or what?"

Teryn held his gaze. "Or we'll leave."

"You won't."

"I will. I am tired of being—"

"Tired." Helios scoffed. "Of course you're tired. You're too soft. Almost as soft as Lexington."

Lex sat upright. "How many times have I told you not to call me Lexington?"

"I'll stop calling you Lexington when you stop dressing in silk shirts. We're hunting. Not dancing."

Lex's fingers went to the silk collar of his stained shirt. Over it, he wore a brocade waistcoat that had grown equally filthy in the last week. "I like silk. It feels better on my skin than linen or leather."

"Who cares about Lex's wardrobe," Teryn said before Helios could speak again. "What matters is that this alliance has become a joke, one I'll no longer be on the receiving end of. If you need our help so badly, then tell us what you know."

"Why? So the two of you can cut ties with me and run off to finish the Heart's Hunt on your own?" He huffed a dark laugh. "Do you think I don't know? You've been planning on betraying me from the start. I'll not give you the fuel to light my pyre."

Teryn crossed his arms over his chest and watched Helios through slitted lids. He was only partially right. While Teryn hoped he and Lex could eventually outmaneuver Helios, he seemed to think they had a solid plan to do so. "You must give us something," Teryn said, keeping his tone level. "Give us a reason to trust you and we'll return the trust in equal measures."

A tic formed at the corners of Helios' jaw, but he said nothing.

Teryn shook his head at the prince. "Is it all a front then? Are you keeping silent because in truth you know nothing? Have you truly seen a unicorn before? Hunted one? Or did you buy that pretty ridged blade from a toy shop?" Teryn waved a hand at Lex. "Pack up. Let's go."

Lex's eyes went wide. "Seriously? Oh, thank the seven gods—"

"Stop." Helios held out a hand toward Lex, stilling him. Keeping his glower fixed firmly on Teryn, he said, "I'll tell you some...things. But I will not share all my intel for obvious reasons."

"Tell us what you can," Teryn said with a shrug. "If we deem your information worthy, we'll stay."

Helios' jaw continued to tic, his glare darkening with rage as his knuckles went white around the hilt of the knife he'd been sharpening. Teryn's fingers flinched, his hand ready to lunge for his sword—

"Very well," Helios bit out and finally dropped Teryn's gaze. "I'll answer three questions."

Teryn wanted to argue that three questions wouldn't suit. They needed to know more. Still, at least it was something. "Where are we going?" he asked. "And don't just say north. You have a destination in mind, otherwise we wouldn't be traveling at such a pace."

Helios glared at the fire as he spoke. "My destination isn't as clear as you think, but we are heading north, for that is the only place we'll likely find unicorns. I haven't been surprised that we've yet to come across any on our travels, which is why we only hunt briefly before making camp."

"How do you know there are no unicorns south?"

"Because Duke Morkai has hired hunting parties to keep all unicorns contained in a specific area."

Teryn blinked a few times, surprised both by what he said and the fact he'd said it. It was the most detail he'd gotten out of Helios yet. Teryn pondered the information. Duke Morkai was said to be the second most powerful man in Khero, the first being King Dimetreus. While Teryn didn't know the duke personally, he understood that the man had great influence with King Dimetreus. He opened his mouth to ask another question, ask how Helios knew this and what the duke's intentions were, but Teryn was on his third and final question. He'd have to pick something that couldn't be answered by his own reasonable deductions. If he had to guess why the duke was herding the unicorns to a specific area, it would be because he sought to gain a monopoly on them. If unicorns were truly alive and flourishing, it made sense he'd try and capitalize on that. So Teryn chose a different question.

"How did you come by that blade?" Teryn nodded at Helios' hip where the strange dagger was sheathed.

Helios set down his knife and took out the weapon in question. The white blade caught the light of the fire, sending the dagger sparkling. This was only the second time Teryn had seen the dagger, and he wasn't any less awed than he'd been the first time. It served as a reminder of why he'd been immediately convinced of its authenticity. This simply wasn't a normal blade.

"A year ago," Helios said, "my father was gifted a pelt by a hunter claiming it belonged to a unicorn that was found at the southern edge of my kingdom. He claimed he'd tried to gift the horn as well, but it crumbled to ash in his hands when he removed it from the dead creature. Father dismissed the gift as a hoax, but a few months later, our spies learned of rumors about unicorns being spotted in the Kingdom of Vinias. I forged a treaty with the King of Vinias, gaining permission to hunt his lands. The rumors proved true. We caught several of the creatures just north of the border between Vinias and Khero, but like the first hunter had claimed, every attempt at removing the horn rendered it useless. We knew it was possible, for there were unicorn horn items being sold at exorbitant prices by a merchant in eastern Khero. So I sent men to find the merchant, then his supplier, and...*ask nicely* for the information I sought." His lips curled into a smirk as he shifted the dagger this way and that, sending it glittering again. "I took this from the next unicorn I found. It was, unfortunately, the last unicorn I ever saw for Duke Morkai had taken control over the hunt by then."

Teryn stared at the white blade, biting back the flurry of questions that sprang to his lips. He was relieved to finally know *something*, but it still wasn't enough. "I take it you have no intention of telling us how you finally obtained the horn without it turning to ash."

Helios gave Teryn a curt nod. "Right you are. You will know after we find our first unicorn."

Teryn gritted his teeth. "In the meantime, we head north until we hit this *specific area* and hope we find a unicorn?"

"A unicorn," Helios said, sheathing the white blade, "or one of the hunting parties."

"What exactly does that mean?" Lex's voice held a tentative edge, congruent with the skin prickling at the back of Teryn's neck.

"I've already answered four questions. That's one more than I agreed to. I'll tell you more once we enter unicorn territory."

Teryn bit the inside of his cheek and returned to his seat under the tree. What he really wanted to do was pummel the man until he spilled everything else he knew. He wasn't sure that was a fight he'd win, regardless of whether the pummeling in question was verbal or physical. Helios had kept his promise to answer three questions, and he'd given more information than Teryn had expected. He doubted further threats to abandon their alliance would earn him more answers. And as for a physical confrontation, well, Helios was taller than Teryn, something he could say of very few people. He was bigger too. Broader. Longer reach. Teryn was trained in the art of combat and swordsmanship like any proper prince, but he'd had little practice against someone like Helios.

"Satisfied?" Helios stood and began laying out his bedroll. When Teryn and Lex said nothing, he turned a smug grin on them. "I admit, it would have been precious to see you try and leave this alliance. The two of you make the most pitiful pair. Prince Teryn, you do realize your little friend here was raised on a velvet cushion, right? He probably doesn't know how to lift a sword."

"I know how to lift a sword," Lex said, although his expression suggested he strongly preferred not to.

Helios faced Lex, arms crossed over his chest. "I'd like to see it. Come, Lexington. Show me what you can do."

"For the last time, don't call me Lexington—"

"Enough," Teryn spat through his teeth. "Both of you."

Helios rounded on Teryn, but he froze as Berol glided from the branch to Teryn's shoulder. It seemed Berol was ready to forgive Teryn for the parchment mishap. Helios eyed the falcon, some of the smug confidence draining from his expression. Finally, he said, "Get some sleep. You'll need it." With that, Helios turned his back to them and settled onto his bedroll.

Glaring at Helios' back, Teryn reached into his pocket—the correct one, this time—and pulled out an enormous strip of venison. Berol accepted it as well as a hefty dose of scritches. "Good girl," Teryn whispered. "If he tries anything in the middle of the night, scratch his eyes out."

Berol tilted her head, but Teryn had no doubt the falcon would come to his defense if needed. It almost made him wish Helios would try something. If only Teryn could be so lucky. Instead, Teryn knew that when he awoke, Helios would still have both eyes, and he'd have to face yet another day of nonstop riding. At least this time he knew relatively where they were going—and the reasons behind their destination.

17

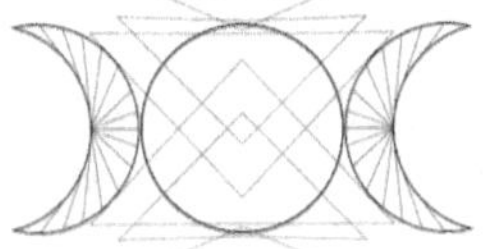

Cora waited impatiently for six days. Six days scouting. Waiting. Hiding. Six days watching. Learning. Listening. Six days of being almost close enough to touch the cages that held starving unicorns without being able to lift a finger to help. There were guards on duty night and day. But that didn't mean she did *nothing*. She took everything she'd learned and put her plan into motion.

Tonight, she would do what she came here for.

She'd set the unicorns free.

The sun was beginning to dip toward the horizon by the time she reached the hunters' camp for the second time that day. She'd laid the groundwork for her plan earlier that morning. Now it was time to act. She crept between the trees, her every move silent. Her skirts were tucked between her legs and into her belt to keep them from swishing around her ankles. By now, she'd discovered the quietest route to her destination—and the one that offered the most cover. She'd learned the lay of the camp, got an idea of their guard rotations, their habits. The company was made up of nine men—the four she'd followed plus five who'd already been here when the newcomers arrived. They always left two men to guard the camp while the rest went on their daily hunt from sunrise to sundown. One man guarded the perimeter while the other protected the cages.

Cora heard the footsteps of the perimeter guard drawing near, several paces away. Her pulse kicked up and she whirled behind a tree, pressing in close to its trunk. She knew which path he'd take, knew he rarely left the thin trail he'd worn through the underbrush circling the clearing. Still, it didn't keep her heart from pounding as his footsteps reached the other side of the tree. She held her breath, assessing the crunch of each step, terrified that she'd hear him pause, shift, turn. But he didn't. She released a slow exhale as the man continued past. Only then did she dare open her eyes.

Angling her body around the tree, she stole a glimpse at the guard, a man she'd learned was named Paul. He was middle-aged. Shrewd. As foul a man as the rest of them. Her suspicions had proved correct. Every member of the hunting party—both from the initial group and the one they'd joined—bore the brand of a criminal. There were no marks of simple thieves, drunks, or adulterers. They were murderers, kidnappers, or slavers. Men convicted of violent assault. Paul bore the *M* for murder. Based on what she'd overheard, his victim had been his wife.

She eyed the two flasks he carried on his hip. One was for water, the other for rum. He never drank from anything but those two flasks. However, Cora knew he refilled his rum flask every night from the bottles kept at camp, always taking his fill from the top before the rest of the men started drinking. And drink they did, night after night while she watched from her hiding place. She'd hoped she'd witness them drink themselves into a stupor, become so deeply inebriated that she could sneak into camp, save the unicorns, and leave only a mystery behind for them to wake to. But she'd had no such luck. While some of the men certainly imbibed enough to lose all mental faculties until morning, others observed moderation. That was where Cora would help them along.

She watched the guard until he was out of sight. Thanks to her observations, she knew he'd stop on the eastern edge and stay for the next half hour. Which meant it was time for Cora to move.

She stepped out from behind the tree, doing her best to ignore the hammering of her heart. She shifted her focus to her mental shields, ensuring they were firmly in place. This time, she only strengthened them in one direction—outward—while leaving herself open to receive, to sense, to pick up energies nearby. Her tattooed palms tingled as she drew on the elements, letting them weave around her like a cocoon. She called on air to muffle her footsteps, asked the earth and trees to warp her image as she approached the camp.

That was how she pictured it in her mind, anyway. She'd learned the theory of shielding and had utilized it for the practical purpose of deflecting unwanted outside stimuli. But she'd also heard tales of advanced shielding, of witches who could turn invisible simply by focusing their intent on not being seen, on merging with the elements. Cora had never seen a lick of proof that it was possible. Whenever she'd ask Salinda why there were so many tantalizing tales of magic but very little visible evidence, she'd remind Cora real magic didn't show off with puffs of purple smoke and glitter. If ever a witch used shielding for invisibility—or, more rationally put, to subtly evade notice—Cora wouldn't know. That was the whole point.

Despite having once scoffed at such a concept, Cora was willing to try it now. She was willing to try anything. Because tonight she'd need all the luck and magic she could get.

Cora crept to the western side of camp opposite from where the perimeter guard stood watch. Once there, she paused several feet back from the clearing, assessing it. She caught movement from the interior guard—James. Her fingers curled into fists at the sight of him. It took no small effort to wrench her gaze away and study the cages instead. There were six enclosures in total, all constructed of the same materials as the ones she'd seen at the previous camp—barred iron frames bound together with rope. Four of the cages were occupied, the latest catch having been brought in the day before. That unicorn was stronger than the other three. He was the only one that shifted restlessly in his too-small enclosure. She could feel the unicorn's rage at being contained, his pain whenever his flank made contact with the iron bars.

Cora itched with her desire to barge into camp and cut the unicorns free at once. She knew she could do it. She could catch James by surprise, send an arrow between his eyes, and another to Paul's heart when he came to check on the source of the commotion. Then she could cut the ropes, open the cages, and that would be the end of it.

But that was precisely the problem. It would be the end of all her efforts.

If she killed the guards, leaving clear evidence of her attack, the remaining hunters would increase their numbers, their defenses. She'd likely never get another chance to infiltrate their camp again. Never save another unicorn. Meanwhile, they'd continue the hunt.

No, she needed a strategy. And she had one. It was why she was here. Why she'd spent days spying followed by nights of stealing. She'd taken a pot here. A flask there. Harvested belladonna—a plant famous for its deadly poison. She wouldn't merely kill a couple guards and leave the rest to do the duke's bidding. She'd put an end to the entire operation in a single night. There'd be no one left to hunt unicorns.

Cora's chest carried a leaden weight, one that formed with the understanding that the Forest People would never approve of her using her knowledge of potions this way. But it didn't stop her. In her days spying, she'd only grown to revile the hunters more. If their crime brands weren't already enough—not to mention their braggery over said crimes—she also saw the way they sneered at the unicorns, how they prodded them with iron rods out of sheer entertainment. They didn't feed the fae creatures. Didn't bring them water. It was clear that these men had been selected for a reason. Not because they were skilled hunters, but because they were heartless. Cruel. Men whose only other option was the executioner's block.

If Cora had to lose a piece of her soul to put them down, so be it. She'd do what needed to be done.

Besides, it was too late to turn back now. She'd already slipped into camp that morning and laced the rum with her deadly decoction.

She crept behind the cages to a cluster of pines. There she waited until James paced to the opposite end, chuckled at something Paul said. Then she reached for the bough above her and pulled herself into the tree.

All that was left to do was wait.

～

Teryn Alante dipped his hands into the rushing waters of the river. The sky was a pink blush overhead, painting the river the colors of sunset. He gathered a handful of cool water and splashed it over his face, scrubbing his stubbled cheeks. Layers of grit and grime were encrusted beneath his palms. He'd need more than a splash of river water to get clean. Still, he doused his face once more, then drenched his hair for good measure.

"What do you think is worse?" Lex asked from farther downstream. Their horses stood between them, drinking their fill after another grueling day of travel. "Riding or Helios' repugnant face?"

"That's a tough choice," Teryn said. He rose from the riverbank and approached Quinne, his golden-brown palfrey. "I might have to choose riding as my least favorite thing right now, considering the repugnant face in question is out of sight for the time being. Which is unfortunate, as I used to love riding. Sorry, old girl." He added the last part for Quinne and patted her neck.

"What do you think is better, then?" Lex asked, "A warm bed or a hot meal?"

Teryn closed his eyes. "Why are you torturing me? Both. Obviously."

"You two are pathetic." Helios appeared behind them, lips curled in a sneer. Just like that, the repugnant face was back.

Lex muttered a string of insults under his breath, then said at proper volume, "I thought you were scouting."

"Unlike you," Helios said, "I don't need all day to make myself useful. Tether your horses. Then follow me."

"Tether your horses then follow me," Lex mimicked in a high-pitched voice. Teryn suppressed a smirk, but Helios gave no indication he'd heard.

"Come on," Teryn said to Lex. "Might as well see what he wants."

They met Helios near a half-visible game trail. Without a word, he led the way through the underbrush until the smaller trail joined a much larger path, this one marked with human and animal footprints alike. A few more minutes down the trail, Helios stopped.

He squatted down and pointed at something in the dirt. "There. This print is larger than the hoof of a normal horse, yet it leaves a lighter indent in the soil." His voice had taken on a reverent tone, one that almost made him not seem like a total ass. "Do you know what this means?"

"Big feet, skinny body." Lex said. "My youngest sister is like that."

Helios turned to them, and Teryn braced himself for the glare that was sure to come. His own lips were laced with venom, ready to intervene should Helios and Lex start verbal sparring like they always did. But when Teryn caught Helios' expression, the other man's eyes were wide, a tight-lipped grin stretched across his face. "It means a unicorn has been here."

That wiped all prior thought from Teryn's mind. "Are you serious?"

"Serious. Certain."

Lex shrank back a little. "You mean a *real* unicorn?"

Helios' expression shuttered, returning his dour countenance. "Why else do you think we're here?"

"What's the plan?" Teryn asked, stealing Helios' attention back to him. "Do you think we can catch it?"

"No." Helios returned his gaze to the hoof print. "This unicorn has already been caught."

"How do you know?"

"See this print next to the unicorn's? It's smaller, probably belongs to a boy. An apprentice, perhaps. These marks are about a week old but consistently show up together. This tells me the creature has been caught and is being towed along behind the main company." He pointed to a cluster of several larger footprints, these ones overlapping. "These belong to the other hunters, also a week old. The prints continue along this trail some ways. I also found fresher tracks about an hour's walk away."

Teryn had to hold his tongue to keep from expressing his shock over the fact that Helios was volunteering useful information for once. The unicorn print must have done a number on his brain.

Helios stood and faced them. "We're going to follow the tracks. The newest ones tell us the hunters have settled into a new base camp by now. The older ones will lead us to it."

"You're so certain," Teryn said, half in awe, half in question.

Helios nodded. "That's how trained unicorn hunters work. Each party is assigned a specific region. They'll hunt a small radius for a few weeks at a time, then move to new grounds once they've cleared an area. We're going to catch up to this party."

Lex grimaced. "Catch up to them and...politely ask to buy their unicorn?"

Helios grinned in a way that was not at all comforting. "Something like that."

Teryn didn't like what Helios was leaving unsaid. He had a feeling there would be no polite anything. Shouldn't that worry him?

His gaze fell on the hoof print. A *unicorn* print. Proof that everything they were doing wasn't crazy. Well, he couldn't say his mission was altogether sane, but for the first time since the Heart's Hunt began, he had hope. And he was determined to do whatever it took to keep that hope alive.

"Come on," Helios said. "We can cover more ground before nightfall."

18

Cora maintained her post as the sun set and dusk turned to night. The hunters returned but not a single drink of rum was taken. She watched. Waited. The mood within the camp was strained, the silence palpable. Hardly a word was exchanged as the men sat idly around the fire hour after hour. It was eerie. Enough to make Cora's skin crawl.

Careful, came Valorre's warning. He sounded quieter than normal, but she shouldn't have been able to hear him at all.

What are you doing so close? she sent back, unsure if her words would make it through her dense shields. Not that she'd ever been so lucky to avoid him reading her thoughts before. Still, it was dangerous for Valorre to come anywhere near camp, even after the company had finished their day's hunt. She and Valorre had made great efforts not to leave tracks where the hunters would likely follow. They kept Valorre well outside their scouting radius whenever they could.

Have a bad feeling, was his reply. *Something isn't right.*

A knot formed in her stomach, but she wasn't sure if it was his anxiety or her own. There was definitely something strange happening. If the silence and solemnity hadn't already been enough, the hunters' rigid postures and darting glances were.

A horn sounded in the distance.

Hammond, a man with yet another *R* brand, who Cora had learned was the leader of this crew, rose to his feet. "Harvest," he said. "You know what to do."

Cora's throat went dry as she watched the men leap into action. Most formed a line in the middle of the camp, hands behind their backs, postures stiff, while Gringe retrieved a small chest. Cora leaned forward, bracing herself against the trunk of the tree as he opened it. Through the pine's boughs, she caught a glimpse of what was inside—two thin, white, spiral-ridged bones.

Unicorn horns.

Cora frowned. She hadn't seen these horns before, nor had she witnessed any of the hunters removing a single horn from the unicorns. So far, all they'd done was keep the creatures in iron cages, letting them grow weaker and weaker from lack of food and their close proximity to iron.

Gringe removed the horns from the chest and placed them on the ground. Hammond shot him a pointed look. "Only two? James said you'd caught three in the Ishvonn Woods."

Gringe glared at James, who already stood in the line, then muttered, "James was mistaken."

Hammond huffed a dark laugh. "If Duke Morkai finds out you left your region while another unicorn was out there—"

"James was mistaken," Gringe repeated, more forcefully this time.

Hammond shook his head and stood at the center of the line, hands behind his back like the rest of the men. Gringe took his place next to him, then barked at James, "Get to the cages."

James' eyes bulged but he made no argument as he unsheathed a knife and approached the cages.

Cora's heart jumped into her throat. She expected him to hack open the nearest cage and slaughter the unicorn or—at best—cut off its horn. But James did no such thing. He simply stood, knife in his trembling hand.

Silence returned for several minutes, broken only by the arrival of Paul. His face was pale. "It's here," he said, then stood at the end of the line.

Anxiety swarmed through Cora. It wasn't just her own. She felt it pouring off the hunters, building and building until it was so strong that her head began to spin. She swayed on the branch and gripped the tree trunk tighter. Then, with a deep breath, she strengthened her shields both ways. The outside emotions fell away, leaving her with the much softer hum of her own worry. A worry that increased with every breath. Especially when she noted what Paul had just said. *It's here.* What did that mean?

Danger. Valorre's warning was laced with panic.

She swayed again. This time, however, it wasn't from an overwhelming surge of emotion. Her lack of foothold was aided by a rumbling in the earth below, one that sent the tree thudding. It was a rhythmic pounding that echoed the riotous pace of her heart.

Run, Cora, Valorre urged. *Run. Beast. Abomination.*

That was when she saw it. A dark form stalked from between the rattling trees a dozen feet away. It was an enormous creature, three times the width of a horse and twice as tall, resembling something between a boar and a wolf. Its head, which seemed too large for its shoulders, had a boar-like snout and tusks, but no visible ears. Its front legs bore hooves while its hind legs ended in enormous paws. It was a hairless thing with raw-looking flesh. Tiny spikes protruded from its body, lining the ridge of its back. It plodded toward the clearing, its immense hooves and paws leaving turned, loose ground in its wake.

Cora was frozen in place, unable to look anywhere but at the creature. She'd seen it before. It used to haunt her nightmares. It still did now and then, lingering just beyond that bloody room, taunting her, clashing in a place between memory and make-believe. In recent years, she'd begun waking before the Beast appeared. It had been her one solace. But seeing it now, outside the realm of slumber...

Run, Cora.

Valorre's words echoed strains of memory, but the voice of the past belonged not to the unicorn. It belonged to her enemy. The man who'd smirked when she was labeled a murderer. A man who'd dragged her to the edge of the woods outside the castle walls, drew blood from her palm, and shoved her out into the night. After that, shadows had come to life, growing paws and hooves and teeth. "Better run," he'd said—

Run, Cora! Get away! Valorre's warning roused her from the haze of memory, but she still couldn't take her eyes from the creature. It plodded into the camp and went straight for the two horns, consuming them in a single bite. Gringe leapt back but Hammond flung out an arm and forced him to be still. Next, it swung its head toward the cages, where James was slicing loose the bindings with trembling hands.

The Beast let out a roar as he dove for the unicorn in the now-open cage. The creature moved too fast for Cora to realize what was happening. Not until she heard the halfhearted, terrified whinny, then a crunch like bones snapping, teeth gnashing. Saw a slash of blood spray the dirt at James' feet.

That was all it took to send her half falling, half climbing down the tree. She had no awareness of whether she'd been seen, whether her shields were up or down, whether the sounds she heard now were her pounding steps, her racing heart, or the crash of another cage coming open.

She knew nothing. Saw nothing through her tears.

She simply ran.

~

VALORRE FOUND CORA HOURS LATER. SHE WAS CROUCHED AT THE BASE OF A BIRCH tree, her shoulders heaving, legs burning from how fast and how far she'd run. He nudged her in the shoulder with his muzzle. When she wouldn't look at him, he blew a warm breath in her face and nudged her cheek. Finally, she glanced up at him with eyes that burned in the wake of her tears.

"They're dead, aren't they? The unicorns?" Her voice came out small and tremulous. Weak. She hated it. Hated that she'd run.

The three older ones, yes. I no longer feel them near.

Cora's stomach turned as she recalled the sound of bones snapping beneath the Beast's jaws. The sight of blood. She shuddered as the vision played over and over in her mind's eye. Followed by her moment of cowardice.

There was nothing you could have done, Valorre conveyed. His sorrow was equal to her own. She could feel it in her bones.

"I could have tried to shoot it."

And get shot back by the hunters? She felt his emotions ripple with something like a disbelieving scoff.

"I could have done something," she said, but even as the words left her lips, she knew they were folly. She'd done the only thing she could have through the haze of her terror.

The haze of memory.

Valorre studied her. *You know the abomination.*

"I've seen it before. When I was twelve. Although..." She swallowed hard as near-forgotten visions surged through her. It had been the middle of the night after the queen was found dead, and Cora was locked in a dungeon cell. She'd spent all evening crying, shouting at the guards to hear her out, begging them to listen to the truth. She wasn't responsible for killing Queen Linette. Morkai was. She'd seen him standing over her dead body. She'd witnessed him doing...*something* with the blood. Something with his hands. Dark magic. It *had* to be dark magic.

But no one listened. No one came.

Only Morkai.

Cora shuddered and stared down at her palm, trying to see beyond the ink, seeking a thin pink line. A scar. But there wasn't one. There hadn't been when she'd received her first tattoo, and it had made her doubt how much of what she remembered from that night had been a fever dream. But now...

Now she knew better.

It had been real. All of it.

She remembered how the duke had pulled her from the dungeon. Bound her, gagged her, dragged her through the sleeping castle, across the lawn, through a secret gap in the castle wall, and out to the edge of the woods. There they paused in darkness, the moon nothing more than a sliver above them. "I'm doing this for you," he'd said as he cut her bindings. "I could have let you rot in that cell. Remember that. The king would see you dead for what you've done."

She bared her teeth and scrambled back from him. "I did nothing wrong. It was *you*. I know it."

He ignored her. "You murdered Queen Linette."

"You lie."

"You killed Princess Aveline."

She froze in place at the name. "What?"

Before she could say a word more, Morkai seized her hand and ran his knife over the center of her palm. Blood welled in a thin red line. She tried to snatch it away, tried to cover the wound, but he held her hand in place. With his other, he trailed a finger through the air. Ribbons of blood appeared out of nowhere, suspended in midair. With another wave of his finger, her own blood rose to meet it, weaving toward the other threads until they merged as one. It was over as quickly as it had begun. One moment, it was as if some gruesome tapestry was forming before her eyes, then the next, it fizzled into air.

That was when she heard the pounding. That was when she saw the dark shadow tearing alongside the castle wall as if it had sprung from shadow.

His lips flicked up then, stretching into a malicious grin. "Better run."

Valorre nudged her in the shoulder, forcing her back to the present. She trembled from head to toe. Her eyes fell to her palms where her fingers had curled inward. Half moons from her nails had formed there, threaded through the ink.

"I...I'd convinced myself the Beast hadn't been real," she said. "After the Forest People found me...I didn't know what to think. I knew what I'd seen, but...surely the Beast had been a nightmare." Her dreams had been vivid back then. Constant. Worse than the new ones were. "Have you seen it before tonight?"

No. Never.

"So, you don't know what it is? It isn't a fae creature? A chimera, perhaps?"

His surge of indignation was answer enough. *No fae creature. Nothing like me or my kind.*

Cora frowned. The Beast was unlike anything she'd ever seen before. If it wasn't fae...what was it?

Vile abomination, Valorre said with a derisive snort. Then, after a pause, he asked, *Will you leave now?*

Her eyes shot up to Valorre. "Leave?"

Because of the monster. Will you stop trying to help my brethren?

Cora considered her answer. She still felt shaken from what she'd witnessed, from the memories she'd unearthed. But she remembered what Valorre had said when she'd asked if the Beast had killed the unicorns.

"You said it only took the three older unicorns."

Yes.

"Then one more is still alive. The newest one they captured."

Yes.

It hadn't eaten all of them. Only the oldest, hungriest, most fatigued unicorns. Would the Beast come back for the other once it reached a similar state? If so... why? And how did the duke tie into all of this?

The questions sharpened her mind, sent her fear scurrying. In its wake, she knew her work was not done. Yes, she was terrified to learn that the Beast was real. The thought of ever having to face it again sent her pulse racing. At least next time she'd be prepared.

Next time, she wouldn't run.

She'd shoot.

She'd shoot it again and again until its blood drenched the earth.

"No, Valorre," she said with a sigh. "I'm not going anywhere." She rose to her feet and brushed her hands on her skirts. They'd come untucked sometime between running and sulking by the tree. "Let's make camp by the stream. We can hide our tracks and I can refill my water skin."

Valorre snorted. *You could use a bath too.*

She recognized the teasing in his words, understood his attempt to lighten her mood. It worked. Her lips curled up at the corners. "Fine, a bath too, first thing in the morning. By evening, I'm going back to the camp. Sooner or later, they'll drink that rum."

19

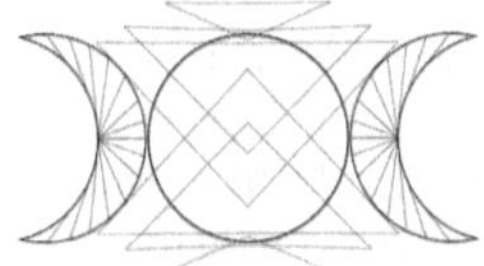

The next morning, Teryn Alante gripped his spear in his right hand, relishing its comfort, its familiarity. With his left foot forward, right foot back, he angled his body to the side. In one fluid movement, he raised his spear, rotated his hips, and brought his right arm down in a smooth arc. He released the shaft and sent the spear soaring straight ahead. It landed with a thud in the dirt. He wiped the sweat from his brow and retrieved his weapon, then returned to his previous spot. Set his feet. Angled his body. Threw the spear. Then again. Again.

"Are you going to do that all day?" Lex asked in a bored tone. He sat in the shade at the base of a tree, a novel in hand. The morning sun was warm with only a mild spring breeze to interrupt the heat of its rays.

"Shouldn't you be practicing as well?" Teryn asked, taking aim for another throw. "We're close. You heard Helios this morning."

"Oh, I heard him," Lex said, then returned his attention to his book. "Mostly, I heard when he told us to wait here because we're—what was it he'd said? That's right. *Bumbling idiots who he wouldn't allow to mess things up now that we're close to our prey.*"

Teryn threw his spear with extra gusto this time. It landed several feet farther than the last. Lex was only slightly exaggerating Helios' parting words when he left them after sunrise. Before that, Helios had spent an hour studying the tracks around the clearing they'd bedded down in for the night. He was certain he'd found additional unicorn tracks, no more than a day old, but was befuddled that they only appeared alongside the smaller set of human footprints, separate from the rest of the hunting party's tracks. Helios wouldn't say more than that, only that he'd spend the day scouting, convinced they were closing in on the hunters' location. That was when he'd told Teryn and Lex to stay put and added some insult over their intelligence and capabilities. It had taken much restraint on Teryn's part not to throw his spear into the other man's back as he walked away. Which was why he'd decided to funnel all that pent-up aggression into throwing practice. Spear was his weapon of choice for hunting. If Helios' observations were correct, he'd have reason to put it to use very soon.

Teryn retrieved his weapon, then stood before Lex. "You do plan on actually helping me, don't you?"

Lex looked up from his novel. "I am helping."

"Are you, though?"

"I already told you I don't hunt."

"Have you any skill with weapons?"

Lex put a hand to his chest, affronted. "Are you questioning my integrity now too?"

Teryn shrugged. "Just curious how much of this alliance benefits me at all."

Lex turned a page in his book. "You'll get your beloved princess."

His stomach turned at the word *beloved*. Planting his spear tip in the dirt, he slouched to the side and propped an arm on the end of the shaft. "Oh? And how do you suggest we do that? So far, our plan is to return with a tie."

"Don't know," Lex said absently. "Maybe we can slit Helios' throat in his sleep."

"Are you offering to do the throat slitting?"

Lex quirked a brow. "Of course not. I'm skilled with a sword, not a dagger. Besides, I'm not going to war with Norun. My kingdom has been avoiding that for a decade."

Teryn frowned. He remembered when the Kingdom of Norun conquered Haldor and Sparda, two smaller kingdoms that had been south of Norun's borders. The other Risan kingdoms, including Teryn's own, feared Norun would seek to conquer other neighboring lands. Thankfully, the conquest never went any further. Menah had the benefit of having two other kingdoms standing between them and Norun. Lex's kingdom, however, shared a border. "Don't you have a wall?"

Lex shifted awkwardly in his seat as if the question annoyed him. "Yes, we have a wall. Don't you have traps to check?"

Teryn held up his palms. "I didn't realize a wall was such a touchy subject." Even as he said it, though, he remembered Lex's rant about his brother stealing the wall-building project from him.

"Yes, well, I'm starving. I get cranky when I haven't eaten."

"You know, you could check the traps yourself."

He turned another page in his book. "And get blood on my shirt? No, thank you."

Teryn rolled his eyes, but there was only amusement in the gesture. Lex was probably the least helpful ally he could ever want, but he was entertaining in his own way. Best of all, he wasn't Helios.

"What are you reading, anyway?"

Lex glanced at the cover. "Some naughty romance. It's about an earl who falls for his sister's lady's maid."

Teryn's grin split his face. "You read naughty romance?" He wasn't even sure

Larylis read such fare, and he tended to devour almost anything of the written word.

Lex lifted a shoulder. "I do now. Stole it from the library at Verlot before I left."

"You stole that. From Verlot Palace."

"Figured I'd want some reading material for the journey."

"You do realize you're a prince, right? You could walk into any bookstore and probably take any book for free."

Lex continued as if he hadn't heard a word Teryn said. "I didn't realize it was the naughty variety, but I daresay, I'm finding it rather informative." He waggled his brows at that.

Teryn shook his head with a chuckle. Then, spear in hand, he left the small clearing and entered the cover of trees. He peered overhead for any sign of Berol, but the falcon was nowhere to be seen. She'd left to hunt half an hour ago. Which was what Teryn now set out to do himself. Well, perhaps not hunt, but fetch lunch just the same. He'd set a few traps nearby for small game and one in a stream for fish. Unfortunately, the first three traps proved empty. Damn. That left the fish trap. He shifted course to the east where he'd found the stream earlier that morning. Walking along the bank, he sought signs of where he'd left the trap. He remembered a boulder that reached about waist high. And a cherry tree standing just above it, pink blossoms clinging to its boughs. It was rare to find trees with that many blossoms still intact this late in the spring, but there was one hardy variety— the Rosa Solara—that carried pink petals almost until summer. That should make it easy to find. Sure enough, a hint of pink caught his eye upstream. He took a step—

And froze.

A flash of movement snagged his attention. He turned, seeking what had fled the opposite side of the stream. There was nothing there, just ripples amongst the rushing current. He held still for several moments, keeping his breaths slow and steady. When he witnessed no further signs of movement, he continued along the bank, slower this time. He kept a more mindful grip on his spear, used his front foot to test the ground ahead before fully taking a step. Teryn should have been doing so all along. Regardless of whether his traps proved successful, any found prey would do for lunch.

The foliage grew denser around the stream the closer he came to the tree. He navigated around it with silent steps, creeping up a slight hill until he found a slim trail that led back to the stream. As he drew close to the cherry tree, it became clear it was not the one he'd been looking for. There was no boulder. No trap. Still, there was something in the music of his surroundings that kept him moving forward. A light cadence punctuated by birdsong. It was the sound of hooves. A deer, perhaps. Too graceful to be a boar. His mouth watered at the thought of venison. He'd fed the rest of the dried strips of meat to Berol last night.

He held his breath and waited for the sound again.

There.

It was coming from near the stream behind the densest patch of foliage. With slow, careful steps, he moved forward, softly prodding the earth with his lead foot to avoid snapping twigs or kicking loose stones. The hoofbeats grew clearer, approaching the stream from the opposite side of the brush. Then it stopped, replaced with a gentle splash. Then another. The creature was likely drinking from the stream. Teryn edged closer and closer until he was finally able to glance around the edge of the brush to the rushing waters on the other side. His breath caught as his eyes took in the animal facing away from him. But it wasn't a deer at all. It was...a horse. An enormous white stallion with hooves the size of—

His foot shifted, caught on a loose rock. He regained purchase, but the sound had already caught the creature's attention. It stopped drinking at once and swiveled its head toward Teryn.

He blinked several times, certain his eyes were deceiving him. Perhaps it was hunger. But no matter how he tried to battle both reason and visual evidence, there was no denying the white horn protruding from the horse's head.

It wasn't a horse after all.

20

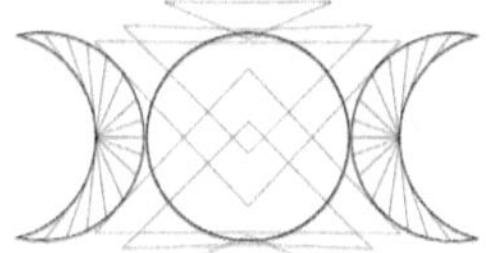

Teryn swallowed hard, feeling as if his throat had turned to sand. His heart hammered against his ribs like it would break free from his chest at any moment. He didn't dare blink. Didn't dare move a muscle as he waited for the unicorn to dart away.

It didn't.

It simply stared back at him, its russet eyes penetrating, probing. That was when Teryn remembered the spear in his hand. And the reason he held it.

Not the reason he'd come to the stream, but what had prompted his practice earlier that morning.

This enormous, impossible creature was the very reason Teryn was in these woods. *This* was his prey.

Sweat slicked his palms. His forearms felt stiff, as if they were rebelling against the command Teryn was trying to give. *Lift. Throw. Kill.* That was what he'd come here to do. With one throw, straight to the lungs or heart, he could win two of Mareleau's prizes. The horn. The pelt. After that, only one live unicorn to serve as the princess' pet would stand between him and victory. He tried to feel emboldened by the thought, but his stomach only clenched tighter. Revulsion crawled up his spine, prickling his skin like tiny knives. He'd hunted before. He was no stranger to killing an animal. But, for some reason, this felt different. Wrong.

Damn it, he cursed silently to himself. *You must do this. You cannot fail now, you sorry fool. Lift. Throw. Kill. Done.*

Steadying his nerves, he took three deep breaths, then slowly angled his body to the side. He paused, waiting to see if the movement would set the creature fleeing. Instead, it took another step closer. There was something defiant in its posture now, the way it lowered its head, the way its lips began to lift from its teeth. Teryn saw its horn in a different light. This wasn't simply a pretty faerytale decoration. It was a razor-sharp weapon. If Teryn missed, he'd be on the receiving end of that horn. Feeling a greater sense of urgency, Teryn lifted the spear. The unicorn stepped forward again, lips flapping with angry breaths. Teryn's muscles tensed. Sweat dripped down his forehead and into his eyes. Another wave of revulsion swept over him, sending his stomach churning. He knew what needed to be done but his body wouldn't respond. Nor would his heart.

Throw, damn it! Throw!

He lowered his arm the briefest increment, not toward the creature but...down.

A sharp pain seared the side of his neck. He flinched back and slapped his palm to the sting. The unicorn hadn't moved, hadn't charged, and yet something wet and warm dripped down Teryn's neck. From the corner of his eye, he could see an arrow protruding from the cherry tree a few yards behind him. Someone had shot at him. Before he could fully register what that meant, he felt the cold tip of a blade press against the underside of his jaw. Without moving, he glanced to the side, but only caught sight of an arm.

"Who are you?" The voice was quavering with rage, and...feminine.

Teryn slowly opened his palm, letting his spear drop at his feet. Then, raising both hands, he carefully shifted to face his opponent. His eyes widened as his gaze took in a petite young woman dressed in a linen shift and unlaced bodice, her skirt tucked between her legs and into a leather belt to form something like pants. She had a quiver of arrows at her back and a bow slung over one shoulder. Her hair was sodden, trailing rivulets down her tan arms—arms that bore black ink from palm to inner elbow.

"Got your fill or would you like to paint my portrait too?" She tapped the underside of his chin with her blade, forcing his gaze back to her face. Her cheeks were tinged pink as if his assessment had embarrassed her. Or enraged her, more like. She scowled. There was something familiar about her dark eyes, but he couldn't place why. Perhaps it was just that she was so unexpectedly stunning. In a wild and terrifying sort of way. Like a wildfire. He had no doubt she was equally as dangerous. "I said who are you?"

"You don't know me?" Too late, he realized the folly of his question. While he expected his face to be well known in his own kingdom, this was Khero. Besides, he didn't quite exude royalty in his current state.

She lifted her chin. "Why should I?"

He assessed her again, studying her grip on the dagger. Her height. Her reach. She was shorter than him by at least a foot. Even though she appeared comfortable enough wielding a blade, his reach was far greater.

She stepped in closer, angling the blade so its edge kissed the skin at the base of his throat. "Answer my question. Who are you?"

"My name is Teryn Alante," he said, keeping his voice level.

She gave no indication she recognized his name. "You hunt unicorns."

He hesitated before answering, which earned him a sharp bite from the dagger's edge. "Yes."

Her eyes roved the side of his neck, then inspected his hunting vest, as if she were searching for...something. Her expression flickered with confusion before she steeled it behind an icy mask. "Who do you work for?"

Teryn frowned. "No one."

"Who sent you to hunt unicorns, then?"

"A spoiled harpy named Princess Mareleau. Do you know her?"

Another flash of confusion crossed the girl's face. Her grip on the dagger slackened, and he took the opportunity to launch a step back. Before she could react, he struck her wrist and twisted it, forcing her to drop the blade. She unsheathed a smaller knife from her belt and slashed out at him. Her blade sliced his forearm, but he closed in on her anyway. Taking her free hand, he twisted her arm at an angle, wrenching it behind her back and spinning her around until she faced away from him. He tugged her arm close to his chest while she continued to try and slash him with her knife.

"Will you stop trying to stab me?" he growled. As she suddenly froze against him, he realized how close his lips were to her ear. He angled his face away from her, caught off guard by that realization.

"No," she said with a grunt and slammed her heel into his instep. He winced but didn't release her. She tried to stomp on him again, but he widened his stance and hooked a foot around her ankle. Her balance gave way, and he assisted her fall to the ground. He pinned her knife hand overhead to keep the weapon's tip from his face.

"Mind telling me why you're accosting a prince?" he said through his teeth as he finally pried the knife from her fingers and tossed it a few feet away.

"Like I care about pretty princes." She lifted her head and slammed it into his nose.

"Seven devils," he cursed, feeling blood streaming over his lips. He sprang back, hand to his nose. She brought the heel of her palm to his sternum and sent him falling on his back. He rolled onto his side, felt his hand come around the shaft of his spear. Rising to his feet, he swept his weapon out in an arc, then lifted it in preparation to throw. His eyes were glazed from the pain of his probably broken nose. It took a moment for his vision to clear. When it did, he found the woman several paces away, bow drawn, arrow nocked.

Their eyes locked, weapons still. Her chest heaved above her bodice while his rose and fell beneath his vest. "I'm not trying to hurt you," he bit out.

"Perhaps not, but you tried to kill my friend."

"Friend?" Realization dawned as he remembered what had happened before the woman had attacked him. "Wait, the unicorn? That's your...friend?" He saw no sign of it now, nor had he any time during their fight.

"How many unicorns have you killed?" she asked.

"None."

"But you were going to kill Valorre."

Valorre. Was that its name? Was this unicorn not a wild creature but a...pet? Teryn recalled Helios' bewilderment over the tracks they'd found. They'd appeared alongside a small set of footprints—this woman's footprints. Not a boy's.

Teryn's spear arm was starting to ache from holding his position. He needed to de-escalate this situation. Quickly. Gritting his teeth, he said, "I'm sorry I tried to kill your friend."

"Sorry isn't enough. Give me one reason why I shouldn't shoot you where you stand."

"If you missed the part where I said I was a prince, then you may not have noticed the spear aimed at your heart either. So allow me to point it out."

"I can shoot faster than you can throw."

"Want to test that theory? Even if your arrow struck true, you'd have the entire Kingdom of Menah hunting you down in recompense."

"Only if you lived to tell about it."

"And only if you survived a spear wound to your most vital organ."

She narrowed her eyes. "Lower your weapon and I'll lower mine."

"Not a chance," Teryn said. "I'll stop waltzing when you stop leading. Lower your bow."

"Count of three, and we both lower our weapons. One. Two. Three."

Neither of them moved.

She released a frustrated groan. "I'll lower my bow if you promise me this. Never come near a unicorn again. If you do, I will kill you. I will not spare your life twice, prince or no."

Teryn almost opened his mouth to make that promise and mean it with his whole heart. He remembered how he'd stood frozen when finally faced with killing his prey. Every inch of his body had rebelled at doing what needed to be done. It was a worrying prospect, but one he didn't have time to address right now. All that mattered was getting on his attacker's better side. "I promise," he said. The words sent something like relief through his body, even as his mind screamed that the vow was a lie. He still had to win the Heart's Hunt.

She kept her arrow trained on him for several more breaths, then finally let it down. Teryn did the same. Neither severed their gaze.

"I'm going to fetch my things now," she said, tilting her head toward the weapons that littered the ground between them.

"Go ahead," Teryn said. They watched each other warily as she stomped over to her dagger, then her knife, sheathing them before striding to the cherry tree. She tugged her arrow from its trunk. Teryn's hand went reflexively to his neck where the blood was already beginning to dry. Had she shot an inch to the left, he might have been dead. "Nice aim," he said.

She tucked the arrow into her quiver and burned him with a glare. "I missed."

His lips curled into a smirk as he watched her walk away. Only when she was out of sight did he let himself skulk over to the tree and lean against its trunk, catching his breath while he pondered the notion that he just escaped death at the hands of a rather frightening girl. He brought a palm to his chest, finding the front of his shirt wet. It must have gotten damp from her sodden hair when he'd pulled her against him. Proof that he hadn't just hallucinated the strange confrontation.

He flinched as one of the boughs trembled overhead. "Berol," he said with a relieved sigh. "You chose the absolute least helpful time to show up. I could have used you a minute ago."

The falcon quirked her head from the branch above.

"You're right. I look a mess." He wiped the skin beneath his nose, finding sticky blood on the back of his palm. With a groan, he pushed off from the tree and headed back the way he'd come from. Berol launched off the tree and landed on his shoulder. He sighed. "Let's hope we don't run into her ever again."

<h1 style="text-align:center">21</h1>

Cora stood in shadow, eyes trained on the man. Fury roared through her blood as she watched him recover from their fight. Part of her wanted to take aim from between the trees and shoot him down before he even knew her arrow was coming. Instead, she remained motionless, silent, waiting until he left the cherry tree—strangely, with a falcon on his shoulder—before she dared leave her hiding place. Once the man was out of sight, she retrieved her cloak from where she'd left it before she'd sprung her attack, and stormed off into the woods. She made it only a few steps before Valorre appeared before her.

"What were you thinking, Valorre?" She halted before him with her hands on her hips. "You should have run before he spotted you. That's what I did. The first time, at least." She'd been in the middle of bathing in the stream when she'd seen the man stalk down the opposite bank. As soon as he'd passed her, she'd scrambled out of the stream and donned her clothing as fast as she could. By the time she was dressed and had located Valorre, the man was about to make his kill.

I would have ended his life. You should have seen how he trembled before my might. His spear was not iron. It would have merely tickled.

She rolled her eyes and started off again. Valorre kept pace at her side. She glanced at him a few times, eyes falling on his flank where he'd been struck by Erwin's whip. The wounds had healed but it didn't stop her from remembering how his skin had split beneath the iron barbs. Her heart sank as she reached out to touch his soft hide. "You're made of flesh like anything else. You may be particularly sensitive to pure iron, but steel can wound just as deep."

I will not cower before a boy.

Cora wanted to argue that he was far from a boy. He may not have been like the men from the duke's hunting parties, but he was tall. Broad. Strong. *Very* strong. The way he'd whirled her around, pulling her against his chest when he'd tried to disarm her. The way he'd pinned her on her back and wrenched the knife from her fingers. Angry heat crawled up her cheeks at the memory. She shook her head and shifted her attention to the name he'd given.

Teryn Alante.

She hadn't realized it then, but she knew that name. Remembered hearing it when she was a child. Teryn Alante was the Crown Prince of Menah. What was he doing out here? He'd admitted to hunting unicorns but also insisted he hadn't killed one. She'd opened her senses to him then, felt the truth of his statement, mingling with conflict over what he'd almost done to Valorre. Then there was that odd bit he'd said about having been sent by Princess Mareleau. He had to have meant Mareleau Harvallis, Princess of Selay. Another name she recalled.

If you're so worried, then you should have killed him instead of letting him go.

Cora cut him a glare, but she had no argument to give. She wasn't entirely sure why she'd let him go. They'd been evenly matched once they'd faced off with spear and bow, but she could have shot him after. He was a unicorn hunter, and that made him her enemy. Sure, he was a prince, and killing him would make her an enemy to his kingdom. But she could have fled the scene and left no one the wiser to what she'd done.

Still, she couldn't fight the feeling that settled in her chest, one that told her that—despite all evidence to the contrary—he didn't deserve to die.

"I miss when I only understood you in one-to-two-word spurts," she muttered.

Valorre rippled with something like laughter. *The boy agitates you. Or interests you.*

"You're the only one agitating me. Next time you come across a human holding a weapon of any kind, you run. Understand? Otherwise, you can rescue your brethren on your own if you're so tough."

Valorre's emotions contracted with something Cora couldn't read. Then he conveyed, *You care.*

Her irritation softened. She reached for Valorre again, stroked his white fur. "Yes, Valorre, I care. You're my...friend." That was what she'd called him when she'd confronted the prince.

Friend. He seemed to take the word and roll it around in his mind before saying it again. *Friend.*

"Friends keep each other safe, no matter how tough the other thinks they are. So no more unnecessary heroics, all right? Save that for our rescue mission."

All right.

Cora's lips curled into a small smile. It had everything to do with Valorre and nothing—*absolutely nothing*—to do with stray thoughts of the aggravating prince she'd met at knifepoint.

~

TERYN, LEX, AND HELIOS RODE ALL AFTERNOON. BY THE TIME THEY SLOWED THEIR pace, night had fallen. The sky was dark, the forest quiet. The only sounds were swooping bats and the pound of their horses' hooves. Teryn glanced up at the canopy of trees, trying to spot Berol flying overhead. If Teryn had to guess, the falcon was certainly making a meal out of the buffet of bats currently on display.

Helios made a clicking sound with his tongue, and his horse slowed to a stop. Teryn and Lex halted behind him as well. They'd left the main trail some time ago, and their current path was narrow, allowing only enough room to ride single file. Helios dismounted and crouched in front of his horse. He studied the path for a few silent moments, then snapped his fingers at Lex. "Lamp."

Lex stared at him. "Seriously?"

"Lamp," he said again, with more force this time.

With a grumble, Lex dismounted and retrieved the oil lamp from Helios' saddle. Handing it to him, he said, "You could have done that yourself."

Helios took it from him wordlessly and continued his study, seeking signs of the hunters they'd been tracking all evening. Teryn had insisted hours ago that they make camp for the night, but Helios refused, stating he had a plan. Like usual, Teryn and Lex were not let in on what exactly this plan entailed. Teryn had only been back at camp for an hour after his encounter with the unicorn girl when Helios returned from scouting. After relentless teasing over Teryn's bloodied state —which Helios attributed to the hare Teryn had been in the process of skinning— Helios ordered them to mount and ride. He'd found the camp. "They have a unicorn," he'd said, revealing some of the excitement Teryn had glimpsed when he'd shown them the first hoof print. He'd also mumbled something about another set of prints. Prints that made no sense because—again—they did not follow the others. He'd trailed these strange tracks. Lost them in a stream.

Teryn had nearly spoken the truth then, almost told him what had happened, why he'd had to set his nose and clean wounds on his neck and forearm.

But he hadn't.

Instead, he'd kept quiet. Not even Lex knew the truth.

Now he smirked at Helios' back. It felt good to know something Helios didn't.

After studying the trail a few minutes longer, Helios gestured for Teryn to dismount as well. As soon as Teryn left the saddle, a dark shape swooped down from the trees, startling the horses. Teryn's horse calmed first, as it was only Berol, coming to perch on Teryn's saddle horn. Quinne was used to the falcon, but that didn't mean the palfrey was immune to being startled by Berol from time to time.

"That thing is terrifying," Lex said, hand clutched to his chest.

"You mean adorable." Teryn reached up to stroke the falcon's feathers. Berol nipped affectionately at his fingers, then set to preening.

"Both of you shut up," Helios muttered.

Lex made a face behind Helios' back.

They continued on foot at a moderate pace, punctuated by Helios' observations. Finally, he seemed to find what he'd been looking for. "Stop here." Helios began to rummage around in one of his saddlebags. As he withdrew his hand from the bag, he held a piece of parchment in his fist.

"Mind telling us what that is?"

Helios faced Teryn and Lex with a smug grin. "We're going to have dinner with friends."

THE SOUND OF VOICES FELL UPON TERYN'S EARS. THAT WAS THE SECOND CLUE THAT told him they were nearing their target. The first had been a plume of smoke wafting over the trees—a campfire. He tightened his grip on his horse's reins as he walked her through the underbrush, his muscles tensing with every step. Helios seemed fully confident in the plan he'd concocted, but Teryn wasn't so sure. Helios had told them to follow his lead. Act cordial. Don't gawk at any captive unicorns as if they'd never seen one before. When Teryn had pressed him to elaborate, Helios said only, "We dine. We sleep. Then in the morning, we take what we came for."

Lex seemed even less comfortable with what they were about to do. Time and again he tried to catch Teryn's eye with a pointed look, as if he hoped he'd intervene. But Teryn wouldn't. He only had a small notion of what it would take to steal the captive unicorn, and he assumed it meant parting camp as friends and returning as foes, perhaps while most of the hunters were off on their hunt. There was no honor in such a ploy, and the prospect made his skin crawl. Still, he wouldn't stop it. Not when he was so close to getting what he needed to save his kingdom from ruin.

Soon the light of the campfire shone through the trees. The conversation coming from inside the clearing was louder now. But as they closed the distance, the talk cut off. Their approach had been noted.

"Seven gods," came Lex's panicked voice.

Helios shot him a glare. "Act natural."

"This is me being natural," Lex whispered back, but he said not a word more as they continued forth.

Teryn's pulse raced as they approached the clearing. Helios halted just outside the perimeter, hands raised. Teryn and Lex pulled up short in turn. Four of the eight men inside the camp already had weapons drawn. Even the unarmed hunters demonstrated threat in their stiff postures, their hands fisted at their sides. Hostile didn't even begin to describe their expressions. It was enough to distract Teryn from the row of cages at the far end—and the gray unicorn inside one of them.

Helios flicked his wrist, a motion that was followed by every set of eyes, but all he held was the piece of parchment he'd taken from his saddlebag. "Easy," Helios said. "We're brothers."

The man at the center of camp, one holding a crossbow, nodded at the figure next to him. The second man approached Helios, sword in one hand, and took the paper with the other. He scanned it before returning it to Helios. Teryn caught sight of a brief letter bearing a seal etched with a crescent moon—an unfamiliar sigil. The hunter stepped back but his posture remained stiff. "Whose company?"

"Drass," Helios said with ease.

"Drass," the man echoed. "He still out in the Dorvish Pass?"

"The Cambron Pass."

The man eyed Helios through slitted lids. "What are you doing out here, then?"

Helios nodded his head back toward Teryn and Lex. "Our contract is up. We were heading to Brocken Village to refill supplies for our trip home when we were waylaid by bandits." Teryn was surprised not only by how well Helios could lie, but by the subtle shift in his tone. It was brimming with camaraderie, devoid of his usual smug brusqueness. Instead, it held a rough edge that masked any hint of royal flair.

The hunter's eyes roved from Helios to Lex, then landed on Teryn, gaze falling on his bruised nose. "Bandits, eh?" He then dragged his eyes over their horses, pausing when he caught sight of Berol, still perched on Teryn's saddle. The falcon stared back at the man just as intently, shifting her stance as if to draw attention to her sharp talons. The man's knuckles went white on the hilt of his sword, and he returned his attention to Helios.

"Aye," Helios said. "They provided us a good chase before we buried their sorry bones. Still, it took us far off course. We saw your fire and hoped for company and a meal to share."

"I'm surprised you deigned to dine with us at all. Drass and his merry band of mercenaries tend to think themselves above our ilk."

"I don't see why. We all work for the same man, don't we?"

The hunter assessed Helios one more time, then looked over his shoulder to exchange a glance with the man holding the crossbow. Teryn held his breath as the camp fell under a tense silence. He sure as hell hoped Helios knew what he was doing. His lies sounded believable to Teryn's ears, but still...

Finally, the hunter lowered his crossbow with a nod. "We'll share a meal."

The other man sheathed his sword and stepped to the side. "Brothers," he said with a nod. Teryn didn't know if he'd imagined the mocking lilt to the man's voice, but he returned the greeting just the same.

"I don't like this," Lex whispered to Teryn as they followed Helios the rest of the way into the clearing.

Teryn ignored him but he couldn't agree more. He could almost feel the dark glares burning into his back as they tethered their horses. He could hear suspicion pitched into every whisper as they approached the campfire. No, they weren't amongst brothers at all, and Teryn wondered if the hunters felt the same. If so, they might as well have stumbled into a nest of vipers.

22

Teryn barely tasted his meal as he ate. Every bite of pheasant settled like ash in his stomach. But he kept on eating. Kept filling his mouth with one slow bite after the next if only to keep from having to talk. Thankfully, Helios took the brunt of that burden, joking with the men and regaling them with hunting tales so convincing, Teryn entertained the possibility that this had been his true identity all along. Whenever a question was directed at Teryn, he kept his answers brief. And when the same happened to Lex, particularly when he was caught staring at the caged unicorn, Helios interjected before he could speak. "This one's mute."

One of the hunters, a man Teryn had learned was named Sam, began to gesture with his hands.

"And dumb," Helios added. "Hunting's the only thing he's keen at."

Lex started to scowl but seemed to think the better of it, adopting a vacant expression instead. Teryn could see evidence of his indignation in the red flush that crawled up his neck.

After dinner, the mood became far more relaxed. Helios' act was so convincing that the man who'd held the crossbow—Hammond—insisted they stay the night. After that, bottles of rum were passed around, and the mood relaxed even further. Lex retired to his bedroll early, stomping the whole way there. Berol too abandoned Teryn, fleeing the incessant chatter and taking a perch in one of the trees. Meanwhile, Teryn remained at the campfire. Listening. Watching. He studied the men, their behavior, their words, trying to glean as much information as he could. He knew better than to rely on Helios alone. The hunters were all in various states of dress, most down to their tunics. Others wore heavily armed bandoliers while a few remained bundled in greatcoats. He caught sight of a sigil on their coat sleeves —a black crescent moon on an indigo background—the same sigil that was on the paper Helios had. He wondered if it belonged to Duke Morkai, the man Helios had mentioned as having a monopoly on the unicorn hunt.

As the night wore on, it was safe to say the men were the most unpleasant company he'd ever kept. Not in their treatment of him, but in the hard looks in their eyes, the sharpness of their words, their unsavory topics of conversation. Blood. Violence. Their treatment of women. It only served to further unsettle the meal in his stomach.

Teryn accepted the rum whenever it passed his way but he did all his drinking in act, determined to keep his focus sharp. Though, time and again, his attention slid to the caged creature. There were six cages in total, but only one was occupied. The unicorn inside was nothing like the enormous white one Teryn had confronted that morning. This one seemed weak, wobbling on its legs. His chest felt tight as he watched it, unable to tear his eyes away—

"I know that look." Teryn startled as the youngest man of the party, James, sat next to him. "That's envy, isn't it? I take it you didn't have the best luck during your contract."

Teryn grunted his response. He was going for a Helios-like persona. Man of few words. Gruff. It was a bit nauseating impersonating a man he so disliked, but if that was what it took to keep a low profile, he'd do it.

James handed him a bottle, and Teryn accepted it. The liquid brushed his closed lips before he handed it back. "Shame," James said. "You should've been out here last year. There were unicorns everywhere. We'd spend a month in one place and catch dozens. Now, we barely last three weeks before deeming an area over-hunted. We had only five horns for harvest last night. *Five*. Can you believe that?"

Teryn gave him a sympathetic look as if he understood the struggle keenly, but his mind snagged on the word *harvest*.

"Only three were live kills because the others had been taken manually and *that one* isn't ready yet." He nodded at the caged unicorn. "Although I hope he makes it long enough for the next harvest. I hate doing it manually, you know?" He glanced at Teryn, a meaningful look in his eyes, but Teryn couldn't fathom what he was trying to convey. Part of him wanted to remain silent, but the other half felt as if he were on the brink of something important.

Infusing his tone with an air of bored disbelief, he asked, "You hate doing it manually?"

James shrank down as if embarrassed. "Yes, don't you? The way they...you know. And the noises they make." He paled and took a deep drink from the bottle.

Teryn lifted a shoulder as if the matter was no bother to him. Inside, he was bothered indeed. What noises? What was he referring to? Was it...removing the unicorn horns? Helios had mentioned a special method but had yet to elaborate.

"I'm always the one holding them down," James said, lowering his voice. "Never the one wielding the knife. I think holding the knife would offer a...I don't know. A distraction."

"A distraction?" Teryn echoed.

"Not like the monster is any better. At least then all I have to do is cut open the cages and try not to get blood on my boots."

A chill ran down Teryn's spine, one that sent his heart thudding. It took all his control to keep his composure. "The monster."

James took a deep drink of rum and handed the bottle to Teryn. Keeping his eyes fixed on the other man, Teryn pretended to drink again. James' eyes went unfocused. "I saw it today," he said, voice barely above a whisper. "No one believes me, but I did. I was checking traps when it plodded by. You know what that means, right?" James leaned in close. "It's claiming our prey outside of the harvest. Which is unfair. If we don't collect, we don't get paid."

Teryn made an indignant noise, nodding along.

James went on. "And if it can do that...why are we even here? Why are we starving these creatures to an inch of their lives if the monster can run amok as it pleases, gobbling up the freshest fare?" He took another long pull of rum, anger written in the set of his jaw. His eyes had become glossy with drink, his pupils so wide they nearly filled the rim of his irises. He ran a hand through his hair which revealed a mark on his neck, just under his ear. It was a brand. An *R*.

Teryn didn't think his blood could go any colder. His kingdom didn't brand their criminals but he knew Khero did. He also knew what that *R* likely stood for. Add to that the way James talked about unicorns—starving them, harvesting them for some monster, holding them down, wielding a knife...

He didn't see the full picture James was painting, but the edges were becoming clear.

Teryn looked across the fire to where Helios was chatting amiably with a hunter named Gringe—the one who had questioned them when they first arrived. Helios caught his stare and narrowed his eyes. He grinned then, and there was something sinister in the curve of his lips. In the way he held Teryn's gaze without falter as he continued to chat. It was a dare of sorts. A silent confession. Teryn's fingers curled into fists, his eyes narrowing right back. He understood then that Helios knew exactly what James had been referring to, whether he'd heard their conversation or not. Helios knew whatever the harvest was, what the monster was, and what it took to manually remove a unicorn's horn.

Teryn suspected Helios had kept the information to himself less out of a need for control and more because—had he told Teryn the truth—perhaps he never would have come.

~

CORA'S ANGER REACHED NEW BOUNDS AS SHE WATCHED THE PRINCE MINGLE WITH THE men he'd sworn he didn't belong to. When she'd confronted him, she'd asked who he worked for. He'd said no one. She'd reached out to him with her senses, felt nothing to suggest he'd been lying. Clearly he had.

She glared at him from her hiding place in her tree, smirking as she watched him press the poisoned bottle to his lips. He'd get his due soon enough.

She'd been waiting in her tree since before dusk, hoping tonight her plan would finally come to fruition. Her relief had been palpable when the hunters were back to their crass, rowdy selves upon returning from the day's hunt. That meant tonight the Beast would not come. However, she nearly gasped out loud when she saw Prince Teryn Alante enter the clearing, his companion bearing a writ marked with Duke Morkai's sigil. Was Teryn Alante even the man's real name? Had he lied about being a prince too? She supposed it didn't matter now. He'd sealed his fate when he drank the rum.

Her heart clenched at the thought. But why? Why did she recoil at the idea of him dying by her clandestine machinations? He may not have borne a brand like the other hunters, but was he any different on the inside? She could admit, he didn't look altogether comfortable. She only wished she could hear what he and James were whispering about. The other men were too loud, too boisterous.

The branch shuddered above her. At first, all she saw was shadow, but her breath caught as she made out the shape of a falcon amongst the pine boughs, its condemning eyes locked on her.

What do you want? she tried to convey, but this animal wasn't like Valorre. It couldn't understand her. Still, she was pretty sure she could understand *it*. The falcon curled her talons around the branch, inched down its length until she was a foot over Cora's head. A silent threat. Cora held her gaze, daring her to try anything. The bird may have had talons, but Cora was armed too. Her bow wouldn't serve her at this range, but her knife or dagger could. Even so, she had no desire to fight off a falcon at all.

"It's too late," she whispered. "I'm sorry." She doubted the bird could understand her, even when speaking out loud. The falcon made no further move. Instead, she turned her head, nestling down as if preparing to nap.

A thud struck the earth at the base of the tree. She startled, as did the bird. But as she peered into the dark, she saw it was Paul, who'd once again been on perimeter duty. Now he lay facedown in the dirt, his flask in his hand.

She didn't need to open her senses to know he was dead. Cold sweat pricked her neck as she stared down at the body. She'd done that. Her hand had brewed the decoction, poisoned the liquor. Her actions and intentions had snuffed out life in an instant.

Killing Erwin was one thing. He'd directly threatened her, attacked Valorre.

But Paul...

He's no better than Erwin, she reminded herself. Perhaps he had no personal qualms with Cora, directed no immediate threat her way. But he was not only a convicted murderer but a willing participant in the hunt. He'd captured fae creatures, trapped them with iron, denied them food and water. He'd stood by while the Beast devoured the unicorns.

Her guilt faded into a cold and deadly calm.

Setting her jaw, she returned her gaze to the camp and waited for the next body to fall.

23

Teryn watched James die. He hadn't realized that was what had happened, at first. When James had begun to slump to the side in the middle of his story—something Teryn was grateful for, considering the repulsive subject matter the man favored—it seemed James had just fallen asleep. It wasn't until another man toppled over. Then another. Teryn glanced at James with renewed interest, saw the blue tinge to his lips, his open eyes that stared sightlessly ahead.

With a jolt, Teryn rose to his feet, just as two more men fell. The camp burst into fits of commotion as the remaining men ran to their comrades, checking their pulses, shouting panicked orders at each other.

Teryn's eyes darted around, then landed on Helios. Suspicion crawled up his spine. Helios, however, looked just as perplexed as Teryn. Heavy brow furrowed, Helios stood frozen as another man collapsed, fingers clawing at his throat as his face turned blue.

"What the hell is going on?" came Lex's voice as he sprang up from his bedroll. His question went unanswered.

Only three of the hunters remained breathing. Gringe, Hammond, and a man named Sam. Gringe and Sam were distracted by their fallen brethren, but Hammond was backing away from the fire. Toward his crossbow.

Teryn palmed the hilt of his belted dagger, edging slowly toward his horse, where he'd left his shortsword and spear with his saddlebags. Lex simply stared at the horror unfolding around them, muttering curses under his breath.

One step. Two steps. The next brought him to his horse—

Hammond cocked his crossbow, loaded a bolt, and aimed at Lex. He swayed slightly on his feet before planting his legs firmly beneath him. "I thought you were supposed to be mute, boy."

Lex's hand flew to his hip, but he too had come to the campfire unarmed.

Hammond squeezed the trigger on his crossbow, but Teryn already had his spear in hand. Hammond swayed again, and his bolt missed Lex by a foot. Teryn's spear, on the other hand, did not miss. It struck the center of Hammond's gut. The man looked down, staggering once more. Gringe and Sam whirled away from their companions. Gringe's sword was drawn, while Sam unsheathed his dagger. Unlike Hammond, neither man seemed affected by whatever had felled their friends.

Helios already had his sword drawn by the time Gringe rounded on him. "Did you poison our meal?" Gringe said as steel met steel. "Or our rum?"

"Neither," Helios said through his teeth as he parried Gringe's attack.

That was all Teryn could witness before Sam sprang at him. Teryn didn't have time to reach for his sword or his spare spear, so his dagger would have to do. Sam was a grizzled man, older than Teryn by at least twenty years, and his stout stature put his reach at a disadvantage to Teryn. But his confident composure was that of a man who had no doubts about who would come out the victor. Teryn dodged a lunge aimed at his stomach, then another angled toward his side. He sidestepped, turned, brought his blade beneath Sam's ribs. The other man blocked him, slicing Teryn's inner elbow. Teryn staggered back, his fingers flying open from around the hilt. Sam lunged for his throat, but Teryn dove to the ground, fighting through the pain in his arm as his hand closed around the hilt of his dagger again. Blood slicked his palm, but he blocked Sam's thrust. With a kick to the gut, Teryn sent him back a few steps. Sam staggered for only a moment before he closed in again. Teryn blinked sweat from his eyes, felt a wave of dizziness rush over him. Was it blood loss, or...

He knew the truth then. It had been the rum. Every man had shared the meal, but not everyone had drunk the rum. Not Helios. Not Lex. He hadn't realized it then, but he'd never witnessed Sam or Gringe accept the bottles either. But Teryn...

He'd let the liquor touch his lips when he'd feigned drinking. Lips that he'd surely moistened at some point during the fight. It wasn't enough to knock him off his feet, but dread filled his bones. He tried to clear the terror from his mind and parry Sam's attack—

The attack didn't come. Sam halted a foot away. Teryn shuttered his eyes, trying to figure out what had happened. In a matter of seconds, a spurt of red caught his attention, trickling down Sam's neck to stain his tunic. That was when Teryn saw the steel tip protruding from his throat. Lex withdrew his sword and they both watched Sam fall to the earth, clutching his throat until he died in a pool of his blood.

"Seven gods," Lex said, voice panicked. His sword fell to his feet. "I...I killed a man. I've...I've never killed a man."

Teryn met Lex's haunted gaze, realizing he could say the same for himself. He glanced beyond Lex at the carnage littering the camp. At Hammond, dead with Teryn's spear protruding from his gut. At the men lying lifeless around the fire. Finally, his eyes settled on Helios, who simply stood with his arms crossed, a smug smirk on his face. Gringe lay motionless against a tree, his tunic punctured with several wounds.

"Turns out Lex is the better man with the blade after all," Helios said, tone mocking. "He just saved your pathetic life."

Teryn stormed over to him. "While you just watched."

Helios shrugged. "I was curious."

Fire raged through Teryn's blood. "You did this. You poisoned them, didn't you?"

"No," Helios said, "but it certainly benefited us, didn't it?" Without another word, he stalked over to the caged unicorn. A dead man was slumped before it, and Helios kicked him to the side. The unicorn trembled within the cage, lips peeling back from his teeth as Helios brought his dagger—the one carved from horn—to the ropes binding the frame.

His conversation with James swarmed his mind, and he recalled the suspicions he'd had right before James fell. Teryn wiped his bloodied hand on his pants and strode over to Hammond. After prying the spear from the man's gut, he raised it. "Stop."

Helios glanced over his shoulder, but only let out a dark chuckle. "You wouldn't dare, princeling. Trust me, you need me for this next part."

"Tell me everything about this *next part* or I will throw this spear. If not to kill, then to maim your leg. You're not keeping any information from me for a second longer."

Finally, Helios stopped cutting the ropes and turned to face Teryn. He spun the unicorn horn blade in his palm, unfazed by Teryn's threats. "I respect your initiative," he said, though his expression revealed anything but respect. "What would you like to know?"

"Tell me what you're planning on doing to that unicorn."

His answer came out smooth. "I'm going to remove its horn."

"*How* are you going to remove its horn?"

"The only way that allows it to remain intact and not turn to dust."

Teryn narrowed his eyes, which earned him a dark chuckle from Helios.

"Very well," Helios said. "Try not to piss yourself. In order to remove a unicorn's horn, one must carve it from the creature's skull while it's still alive."

Bile rose in Teryn's throat, the image James had begun to paint now made fully clear. "And the pelt?"

"As much as possible should be removed while the unicorn breathes, although not all can survive the skinning. Unlike the horn, the pelt won't dissolve if the creature dies. Instead, it loses its texture and sheen. Any part removed while it's alive is worth a pretty fortune."

Another wave of dizziness struck him, but this time he wasn't sure if it was Helios' words or the poisoned rum. He planted his feet, forced himself to keep his spear arm steady. "What of the monster?"

Helios scoffed. "What monster?"

Teryn studied his face, seeking signs that he was lying. "You don't know about the monster?"

Shaking his head, he returned to face the cage.

Teryn took another step forward before Helios could resume cutting the bindings. "Stop, Helios."

"No."

"We aren't taking that unicorn's horn. Or its pelt."

Helios let out an irritated groan and turned back around. He wagged his dagger at Teryn. "This is why I didn't tell you. I knew you'd be too soft."

"We'll take this unicorn as the princess' pet."

"No, we won't. That's only one of the three gifts. We cannot return without all three, or else our plan will mean nothing. Three gifts. Three champions. Equal effort to meet Mareleau's demands in the cleverest, most efficient way. Do you want a chance to marry the princess or not? Is your kingdom not worth one animal's life?"

Teryn felt his resolve weaken. He glanced at the caged unicorn, saw fear in his eyes, hunger in his gaunt form, pain where open wounds marred his hide.

"That's all it will take," Helios said, a placating quality to his voice. "One unicorn, and we'll have the hide and the horn. After that, finding the pet will be easy. We can kill this one before we take its hide, if that is your wish. The horn, however...you know what must be done."

Teryn thought about his father, his kingdom, his duties as heir. The promises he'd made. His heart ached to spare the unicorn, but when had following one's heart ever served the greater good? His father had followed his heart and nearly brought war to the shores of Menah. Mareleau was supposedly following her heart by seeking a better match than Teryn, but her Hunt had now resulted in a massacre. Teryn's duty was to his kingdom. Mareleau may have had no qualms with breaking their contract, but he'd promised to marry her. Promised his father he'd do what needed to be done to secure her hand.

And if it meant killing one unicorn...

He glanced at the creature again and felt his stomach drop. Grief tugged at his bones, dragged his heart over brambles and thorns. The words left his mouth before he realized what he was saying. But they were true. "It's not worth it. It was *never* worth it." If his promised bride was so heartless as to make such a violent request in exchange for her hand, then he wanted nothing to do with her. She'd broken her promise. Teryn would break his too.

Helios' shoulders tensed. "So, you forfeit."

Teryn swallowed hard, his throat dry. "I suppose I do."

"And you, Lexington?"

No answer came.

Teryn cast a quick glance at Lex and found him still standing over Sam's body, his face pale.

Helios moved, bringing Teryn's attention back to him. He now held his sword in addition to the dagger. Teryn prepared to throw his spear, but Helios was quickly closing in. Instead, he held the spear out before him. If he couldn't throw it, he'd fight with it. Helios continued his charge but was suddenly stopped by a flurry of feathers and talons. Berol scratched at his face, forcing Helios to shield his eyes. The falcon raked her talons through the man's forearm, sending his sword clattering to the ground. Helios slashed out blindly with the dagger.

Teryn's heart pounded as he watched Berol carve gouges in the man's flesh. He was torn between aiding Berol's efforts with a spear to the gut, or calling the bird back. Before he could consider what to do, he swayed on his feet. *The poison*, he thought with terror. He swayed again, legs trembling. Berol suddenly took off, heading straight for Teryn. He expected her to land on his shoulder, but the falcon only flapped her wings in his face, forcing Teryn back. Back. Back.

"What are you—"

His words dissolved under the sound of trembling earth. Something enormous barreled past Teryn, directly over the place he'd just stood. He heard Lex cry out, turned to find him curled on his side, cradling his arm. When he looked back at whatever had invaded the camp, he realized *this* was the monster. There was no other name for it. It looked as if two creatures had merged into one, born from flame, its skin raw and red. A ridge of spikes ran down its spine. Teryn scrambled back, but the monster paid him no heed. Its beady eyes were fixed on Helios. In the next moment, it was upon him. The creature opened its giant, salivating maw and closed it over Helios' head and shoulders. Teryn couldn't blink as Helios' muffled screams pierced the air. Blood poured over the monster's lips and dripped to the ground below. Helios clawed, stabbed, but the monster continued to bury its teeth deeper into his flesh. The unicorn horn blade fell to the ground, and Helios' body went still. The monster released him, but Teryn knew he was already gone. He held his breath as the creature ran its nose over the earth, as if seeking something. It inched closer and closer to Helios' discarded blade.

A crash sounded. Teryn's eyes flew to the cage where the unicorn was bucking madly.

With a roar, the monster charged the cage, slamming it with its enormous front hooves. The iron bars dented but didn't break. Still, the monster relentlessly struck the cage again and again.

Suddenly, the monster reared back with a roar. An arrow pierced its neck, and Teryn saw another had already gouged its eye. A figure emerged from the trees, bow raised, arrow nocked. The girl from the stream shot the monster again, blinding its other eye. The creature roared and wailed, trampling the lifeless bodies strewn about camp as it tried to shake the arrows free. The woman shot it again, directly between the eyes. Teryn expected the monster to falter, to slow, but it didn't. Instead, it tore away from its attacker, crashing against tree trunks as it fled into the night.

Teryn's chest heaved as he struggled to catch his breath. His body trembled from head to toe. Something brushed against his temple. Berol. She nipped at him as if to test that he was unharmed. "I'm fine," he muttered, voice strained. He wasn't sure when the falcon had landed on his shoulder. He'd been too distracted by the monster.

His eyes drifted to Helios' maimed body, the blood all around him, the battered earth left in the monster's wake. Movement drew his gaze, reminding him the threat wasn't over.

The woman stormed over to him, an arrow aimed at his heart. "Why aren't you dead?"

24

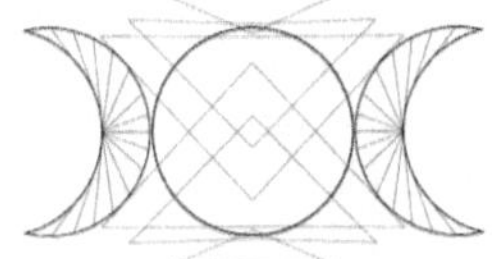

Cora tried to keep her bow steady as she confronted the prince, but her body was racked with tremors. It had been one thing to watch her carefully laid plans end in a bloodbath as Gringe, Hammond, and Sam turned on the prince and his friends. She'd waited in her tree for the fight to end, knowing she'd have to take down the victor. She hadn't expected Teryn Alante to battle his friend over the fate of the unicorn, nor had she anticipated the Beast. As soon as it had threatened the unicorn, she had no choice but to act. Now it was gone, but she didn't know for how long. Her arrows left it wounded. Would that be enough?

Teryn stared at her, his spear still clutched in his hand, forearm stained with blood beneath an open wound at his inner elbow. His falcon watched her with unblinking eyes, daring her to make a single move that would harm the bird's master. Or was the prince—like Cora was to Valorre—the falcon's *friend*?

Teryn's eyes narrowed. "You're the one who poisoned the rum."

"And you drank it. So why aren't you dead?"

She expected terror from him. Or rage. Anything but the weary answer he gave. "I didn't drink. It only touched my lips." He gulped. "Will I die?"

She released a sigh and let down her bow halfway. "No, but do you recall the promise you made?"

He squeezed his eyes shut and rubbed his brow. "That I wouldn't come near another unicorn."

"Or else I'd kill you," she finished for him.

His eyes were unfocused when he opened them. "It seems today is a day for breaking several promises."

She huffed a laugh. "Do you expect me to break mine?"

"I...I didn't know."

"Didn't know what?"

His gaze sharpened and slid to the unicorn. "I didn't know what it took to remove a unicorn's horn."

Cora felt the blood leave her face. Before she'd witnessed Prince Teryn's fight with the man he'd called Helios, she hadn't known either. She'd assumed the horn had to be severed, not...cut from the unicorn while it was still alive. Did Valorre know?

Teryn met her eyes. "I'll never do that," he said, tone laced with conviction. "I'll never take a unicorn's horn."

She considered his words, opened her senses to try and feel if he was lying. Not that she trusted her observations. "You lied when you said you worked for no one."

"I didn't lie."

"I saw the writ your friend had."

Teryn glanced at the dead man, then winced, as if he'd forgotten the carnage. He shook his head. "I don't know what that was, but I can only guess it was a forgery. Why would we work for anyone? I'm the Crown Prince of Menah. Helios was the Prince of Norun. Prince Lex—"

Teryn stiffened. His spear slid from his hand as he whirled around. The motion sent the falcon launching off his shoulder to land in a nearby branch. Cora drew her arrow, following Teryn's every move as he crouched down beside a man Cora hadn't realized was alive until now. "Lex!"

Cora hesitated, watching the two, before letting down her bow.

The man named Lex lay on his side, his arm pressed to his chest. Blood stained his silk shirt, marring the gold brocade of his frayed waistcoat. "What the bloody hell, what the bloody hell..." Lex repeated over and over. Finally, he met Teryn's gaze. "What the bloody hell was that thing?"

"The Beast," Cora said.

Teryn glanced over his shoulder at her. "You know what it was?"

She nodded. "It...works with the hunters. They feed the unicorns to it."

"Why did it..." His voice trailed off as his eyes landed on the body of his dead companion. "Why did it attack Helios? It barely spared me a glance, but it went straight for him."

"I don't know." With slow steps, she approached the body. A few feet away, she found a discarded dagger. Gingerly, she picked it up, noting its white spiral blade. All at once, she sensed a dense, murky energy that buzzed against her palms, burning the ink there. The feeling was so strong, her lungs began to contract. Dropping the blade, she launched a step back.

Hide that, Valorre said. Cora startled at his sudden appearance behind one of the trees outside the camp. There he remained, not daring to take a step within the clearing. *Sheathe it. Cover the blade. The abomination is drawn to our horns.*

Her heart slammed against her ribs. She glanced at the waning campfire. *I could feed it to the flames*, she said in her mind.

It will not burn.

She considered simply leaving it where it lay or burying it in the ground. But the idea that someone else could find it, wield it...

Worse, she imagined the Beast returning, unearthing it, devouring it. She wasn't sure why the Beast was drawn to horns, why the hunters fed it starving unicorns. But there had to be a reason. Whatever it was, Cora needed to do whatever it took to keep the Beast from consuming another horn.

Without a second thought, she reached for the white-bladed dagger again and dropped it into her quiver. As soon as it struck the bottom, she felt its dark energy recede. Relief flooded through her. Now she just had to hope that her inability to sense the horn anymore meant the Beast couldn't either.

She returned her attention to the two men—only to find Teryn removing his shirt. Momentarily shocked by the unexpected sight, she could do nothing but stare at the flex of his shoulder muscles as he drew his tunic over his head and immediately set to tearing it into strips. He tied the first one around the cut on his arm, then crouched by Lex and began to dress his friend's wound.

We must go, Valorre said.

Cora shook her head to clear it and tore her gaze from the two princes. She knew Valorre was right. It was madness to linger. The Beast could be back at any moment. There was but one thing left to do.

She jogged over to the unicorn's cage. The creature within trembled as she brought her knife to the ropes and severed the bindings. The front of the cage fell open, but the unicorn did not move. "Go," Cora said, voice soft. "You're free."

A sharp sound pierced the quiet of the camp. Cora startled at the noise, as did the unicorn. In a flash, it darted out of the camp in a blur of gray. She whirled around, finding Teryn behind her, hands pressed together. That was when she understood the sound had been a clap.

Cora glared at him, keeping her eyes anywhere but below his chin. He'd donned his hunting vest again, but he'd only secured the bottommost closures. Which meant he might as well still be topless. "You didn't have to scare it like that."

He lifted a shoulder in a fatigued shrug. "Perhaps fear will keep it well out of the monster's range." With that, he turned away from her and strode back to his friend.

She watched him walk away, her argument dying on her tongue. As much as she didn't want to admit it, he was right. The unicorn needed to get far away from here, no matter what. And so did she. Casting a final glare at his back, she made her way to Valorre. He remained in shadow at the edge of the clearing.

The stout one is badly wounded, Valorre said.

Cora followed Valorre's line of vision and saw Teryn and Lex walking toward three tethered horses. She noted the way Lex continued to cradle his arm to his chest. "Why should I care? Let's go." She skirted around him but Valorre remained rooted in place.

The tall one tried to save my brethren from the dead man. He radiated with something like awe. Gratitude.

"Weren't you the one telling me I should have killed him at the stream?"

Maybe I was wrong, he said with a touch of indignation. *Maybe he and I both were.*

Cora bit the inside of her cheek, urgency propelling her to leave the men behind. She owed them nothing. If anything, they owed her for warding off the Beast.

Valorre scraped the earth with a hoof.

"Fine," Cora said between her teeth. She crossed the camp, trying to ignore the dead bodies she stepped over, and approached Teryn and Lex. Teryn was trying to aid his friend into his horse's saddle, but Lex kept losing his balance. "Let me see the wound."

Teryn whirled around, brows knitted. "Excuse me?"

She ignored Teryn, addressing Lex directly. "Your arm. Show me."

He eyed her from head to toe. "Like I'd trust you. Did you not just poison an entire camp?"

"They were bad men," she said, swallowing down the guilt that crept up from her heart. "Did you not see the brands on their necks? Besides, I had to stop them from hurting more unicorns. This was the only way I could do so on my own."

Lex scoffed but said nothing more.

"Show me your arm." When he still refused to move, she added, "You'll have a much easier time riding if you don't bleed to death."

"I wrapped it well," Teryn said.

She turned her scowl to him. "You bandaged his wound with your filthy shirt. Did it never cross your mind to use a clean one?"

"Did it ever cross yours that perhaps we don't have any? We've been traveling for—"

"Then I assume you were planning to eventually stop, boil fresh strips of cloth, disinfect the wound, and pack it with a poultice. And that's only if he doesn't also need sutures."

Teryn said nothing, only held her gaze, jaw set. Finally, he relented. "Just let her see it."

Lex eyed her through slitted lids several moments before he too seemed to relent. With a roll of his eyes, Lex extended his arm. Cora stepped close and knew at once it was bad. The bandages were already soaked through over what appeared to be three gouges. She opened her senses to him and discovered just how much pain he was hiding. His arm radiated with the severity of his wound. She could *feel* it darkening her senses, could almost see it in her mind's eye as she took his arm with gentle fingers. Peeling back a corner of the bandage, she caught a glimpse at part of the wound. It only confirmed what she'd already felt. "Is that from..."

"The monster kicked me out of the way with its hind leg," Lex said stiffly.

Again, Cora debated turning her back and leaving them to their own fates, but she could feel Valorre's reproach from here. When did he get so softhearted? She let go of Lex's hand and released a sigh. "The wound needs sutures and a poultice. Come." She turned and waved for the men to follow. "Gather your horses. I'll help you."

"I don't want your help." Lex's tone was laced with venom.

Cora threw a look over her shoulder. "Do either of you know how to stitch a wound? Disinfect it? Do you know which herbs will relieve pain and calm inflammation? Which ones will stave off infection?"

Teryn and Lex exchanged a glance. Of course they didn't. According to Teryn, both men were princes. Royals had no need to learn first aid. The Forest People, however, were well versed in healing, even those whose Art didn't specialize in the craft.

"Have you any particular fondness for that arm?" she asked.

Lex huffed. "Of course I do. What kind of question—"

"Unless you want it amputated after infection sets in, come with me." She left the camp and didn't wait to see if they'd follow.

25

"I'm not drinking that," Lex said, scowling at the clay cup Cora handed him.

Teryn watched their icy standoff with a mixture of amusement and trepidation. They were seated around a modest fire in the middle of a secluded clearing by a stream. He was pretty sure it was the same stream he'd met the woman at the day before, and—from the way Cora brought out cups, flasks, and pots from behind a bush—he assumed it was where she'd made camp for the last several days. They'd trusted her enough to follow her away from the scene of the bloodbath and obeyed her instructions to start a fire, boil water, and soak fresh strips of linen torn from yet another of Teryn's shirts. She'd told them her name, briefly introduced them to her unicorn companion—much to Lex's awe and incomprehensible stammering —but that was to the extent that they knew her. Well, that and the fact that she'd poisoned nearly an entire hunting party. Teryn couldn't blame Lex for his trepidation.

"It will help calm your nerves and ease your pain," Cora said.

"Yes, being dead certainly puts an end to nerves and pain. No, thank you."

Cora rolled her eyes. "It's not poison. It's tea. Lavender, chamomile, and willow bark."

Lex gave Teryn a pointed look, drawing Cora's attention to him as well.

Teryn sighed. "Surely you understand why we wouldn't want to drink anything you offer."

She pursed her lips and held his gaze. He only shrugged. "Fine," she said, setting down the cup and taking Lex's arm. "Suffer through the pain if that is your wish."

Lex blanched a little but made no further argument.

"Are the bandages dry yet?" she asked Teryn.

He ran his fingers over a corner of one of the strips of cloth she'd asked him to dry by the fire. "Yes."

"Bring them here."

"You make demands like a queen," he muttered as he gathered the cloth and brought it to her.

"No," she said as she began untying the blood-soaked bandages from Lex's arm, "just someone who has no reason to help you but is anyway."

The unicorn named Valorre tossed his mane. The creature had maintained his distance from Teryn and Lex, keeping to the opposite side of camp. Even so, Teryn caught the unicorn watching him from time to time, likely holding a grudge over the spear incident. Berol, meanwhile, took up post as far from the unicorn as she could get. Every so often, she'd shift in the branch overhead as if to remind both Cora and Valorre that she was watching.

Cora paused her ministrations and looked at Valorre. Then, resuming her removal of the bandages, she said, "Why should I be nice? I don't see you being warm and cuddly."

Teryn frowned, eyes darting between the girl and the unicorn. "Did you just... talk to Valorre?"

Her face went slack with surprise. Perhaps she hadn't realized she'd spoken out loud. She quickly covered the expression with a look of nonchalance. "Don't you talk to your feathered companion? What's her name? Barrel?"

"Berol," Teryn corrected. "Like the—"

Her gaze darted to him. "Like Berolla, the fae queen's legendary dragon."

Teryn was surprised she knew. Faerytales were common enough, but he'd only heard about this one from Larylis. When he'd first found the falcon as a hatchling, he knew she needed a fierce name. Part of him thought it would improve her chances of survival. So when Larylis shared the tale of Berolla—the dragon who once ruled the skies in the days of the Elvyn and Faeryn—he knew it was the perfect namesake.

Cora averted her gaze and steeled her expression, as if she regretted showing interest in their conversation. She finished unwrapping the bandages and reached for a flask.

"What's in that—" Before Lex could finish, Cora poured it over the wound. The smell of strong spirits wafted into the air. Rum. Teryn could only hope it bore no poison.

He watched as she cleaned Lex's wound and began to stitch it closed with a needle and thread she'd taken from one of the pouches on her belt. When Lex began whimpering, she wordlessly handed him the mug of tea. This time, he accepted it. Her every move was steady and methodical as she continued her work. She'd clearly done this before. After the final stitch was made, she spread a mushy paste over Lex's arm, its odor pungent.

Lex wrinkled his nose. "This is disgusting. What is it?"

"Herbs," Cora said, then held out her palm to Teryn.

He stood at her side and handed her the cloth. By the time she was done wrapping his arm, Lex looked as pale as a ghost. His throat bobbed as he cradled his arm against his chest. "Do you have more tea?"

Cora didn't hide her smirk as she poured him another mug.

Teryn expected Lex to thank her as he accepted the offering, but instead he said, "You must be a witch."

Cora simply stared back at him.

Teryn stiffened. "Oh," he said, looking at her in a new light. "You are a witch." It made sense now. Her knowledge of healing and poison. The fact that she lived in the woods. Except... "I didn't know witches were real."

She faced him with a quirked brow. "I didn't know idiot princes were real, and yet here you both are."

Teryn bristled. "What did we ever do to you?"

"Do you honestly have to ask?" She stood and planted her hands on her hips. "You tried to kill Valorre—"

"Yes, remind me why the two of you seem to know each other," Lex interjected.

"—then you lied to me about who you work for—"

"I told you," Teryn said, "I didn't lie."

"—then you lied to me when you promised never to come near a unicorn again."

She had a point about that last part. "I'm...I'm sorry about that. About all of it. It was important that I try..." He ran a hand over his face, his fatigue bone deep. "I'd *thought* it was important to complete our mission. I'd thought..." He shook his head and returned to his seat on the other side of the fire.

Her brow furrowed as she studied him, her head cocked slightly to the side. After a few moments of silence, her shoulders fell, as if she too were overcome by the same exhaustion Teryn felt. She returned to sitting. "Tell me the truth then. Tell me why you came to hunt unicorns."

"Or else..." He expected a threat. Why else should he tell her anything? Why else should they do anything but part ways now, knowing not a single thing more about one another? She hated hunters. He was one. Perhaps his intentions weren't as dark as that of the men she'd poisoned, but she was right. He'd almost tried to kill her unicorn companion. He'd broken his promise—a promise he'd made without any intention of fulfilling it—and targeted another unicorn right after. Had James not planted suspicion in his mind, Teryn might not have been prepared to stop Helios in time. If Helios had taken the unicorn's horn, Teryn would have shared the responsibility.

His stomach turned at that. *All this time, Helios knew. He knew I'd be too soft for the truth.* Teryn wasn't sure if he should feel ashamed about that. It wasn't like he'd thought they could remove a unicorn's pelt without killing it. While it had never occurred to him that the horn would need to be taken while the unicorn was alive, he'd always known the creature would have to die. Was that where Teryn drew the line? He could kill, but not make an animal needlessly suffer?

He remembered his hesitation at the stream, how his body had seized up when he'd prepared to throw his spear at Valorre. He'd felt revulsion at the thought of killing the unicorn, a thousand times stronger than any distaste he'd felt during a normal hunt. Something inside him, whether he'd recognized it or not, had known a unicorn was not just another animal. That killing them to appease a spoiled princess' vanity was wrong.

Which meant Helios had been right. Teryn had always been too soft, right from the start.

Teryn realized Cora was still watching him. There was something discomfiting about her gaze. It was too probing. Too penetrating. He felt as if his heart were made bare, laid across his face in stunning detail like one of the illustrations in Larylis' books.

"I just...I want to know." Cora's voice was softer now. "I came here to rescue the unicorns from the hunters. To keep them from being captured. Now that I know the Beast is involved..." She shook her head. "I need to know more. Do more. And I have a feeling you know more about it than I do."

Teryn huffed a dark laugh. "You'd be surprised, then. Helios kept us in the dark about almost everything."

Cora leaned forward. Her expression took on a hint of pleading. It was the first time he'd seen anything close to vulnerability in her eyes. "Please."

Rubbing his brow, he released a heavy sigh. "It's called the Heart's Hunt."

TERYN TOLD HER EVERYTHING HE FOUND PERTINENT. HE KEPT ANY INFORMATION regarding his kingdom's debt to himself, telling her only that he was engaged to Princess Mareleau Harvallis, but had been slighted at Beltane when she invited other suitors to compete for her hand. She listened with rapt attention as he went on to explain his alliance with Helios and Lex. He told her what little information Helios had shared—how Helios had first come to learn of unicorns, how he'd made a treaty with Vinias to hunt their lands until unicorns could no longer be found north of Khero, how Duke Morkai had taken control over the hunt. He told her of their plan to steal a unicorn from the hunters, how they'd tracked them to the camp.

By the time Teryn was done with his tale, Lex had already retired to his bedroll and was fast asleep.

Cora, however, seemed more energized than ever. She paced before the fire. "Prince Helios said there are more hunting parties."

Teryn nodded. "I got the impression there were several more. When we arrived at the hunters' camp tonight, Helios knew exactly which name and location to say."

She stopped her pacing and faced him. "He showed them a writ as well. I want to see it."

Teryn's gaze went to Helios' horse. It was tethered next to his own, eyes closed. He hadn't had the heart to leave it at the site of a bloodbath, so he'd brought the mare with them when they'd followed Cora here. Besides, the horse was laden with Helios' bags, which could be full of any number of useful items for the ride home. But...did his saddlebag contain the writ? Or had he had it on him when the Beast attacked?

"I don't know if we have it. He could have kept it on him when we joined the hunters."

Cora started off toward the horses. "He put it back. I saw him."

Teryn blinked a few times, only realizing now just how unsettling it was that she'd been watching them the entire time. He followed after her and approached the horses. Berol launched from her branch and landed on Quinne's saddle. She nestled down as if to sleep but peeped an eye open to watch Cora step up beside Helios' horse. The mare was named Hara, if he remembered correctly. She was sleek and black, larger than Quinne. Cora opened a saddlebag while Teryn went to the one on the opposite side. Hara paid them no heed, for she clearly had a much better temperament than her former master. Teryn glanced over the saddle and realized Cora had to stand on her toes to get a look inside the bags. Meanwhile, his height provided him a clear view of the bag's contents—several knives, flasks, waterskins, leather pouches of dried meat, articles of clothing. He moved the items around until he found a stack of folded papers.

He took them out and smoothed out the top sheet, angling it so that the fire illuminated it. It was a map of the lower half of Risa, its main focus on the three kingdoms that comprised the land once known as Lela—Khero, Menah, and Selay. The forested areas were marked with either an *X* or a circle. Most of the *X*s were written over the southernmost parts of Selay and Menah, with only a circle or two drawn over their northern forests. Within each circle was a number. The ones in Selay and Menah bore ones or twos. Meanwhile, the circles drawn over the forests in Khero were marked with numbers in double digits. Could it possibly be the number of unicorns found in each region?

His eyes moved to northeastern Khero, which was the part of the map that hosted the most notations. There he found marks dividing the forests into regions, with a name next to each. These regions were contained to a radius around Ridine Castle. This must have been the *specific area* Helios had spoken of. Teryn sought out his current location. They were in northeastern Khero near the southernmost region noted on the map. There he found the word *Hammond*. Just northwest of there was the word *Drass*. Teryn remembered that name. That was whose hunting party Helios had pretended they'd come from when Gringe had questioned them.

Teryn gritted his teeth, his anger over Helios' refusal to share intel still sharp, even after the man's demise. What else had he been hiding? He moved the map to the back of the stack and studied the next paper.

His breath caught in his throat.

Two dark eyes stared back at him, keen, fierce, and intelligent.

He knew those eyes. They'd watched him from the other side of the fire mere moments ago.

Now they watched him from under the word *Wanted*.

No wonder Cora had looked familiar when he'd met her on the other side of her blade. It was because he'd seen her before, studied her likeness on the poster he'd found on his father's desk.

It made sense now why Cora was so well versed in poison. How she'd killed six men without batting an eye.

His gaze dipped to the bottom of the poster, even though he already knew what it would say. *For the murders of Queen Linette and Princess Aveline.*

He swallowed hard, his throat suddenly dry. When he'd first seen the poster, he hadn't given the murders much thought, but he remembered the deaths. Remembered how the people mourned, even in his own kingdom. The killer had left no sign of a wound on either body. Poison, it was deemed, but other theories circulated, spoken only in whispers.

A witch, they'd said. A young serving girl who'd dabbled in the dark arts and held a grudge against her royal masters. The queen was known to have been with child when she died, while the princess...

Teryn's chest felt tight. Princess Aveline had only been a young girl. He'd met her once when they'd both been children. Back when their kingdoms were friendly. Before her parents died in the plague that swept the continent for the better part of a year. At six years old, she'd been brave. Charming. Full of life and wit and beauty. She'd been his very first crush for all of the two weeks she'd spent as a guest at Dermaine Palace with her parents. She'd hardly looked his way the entire time, and yet he'd blushed and hid behind his mother's skirts whenever she was in the room. Teryn had almost forgotten. Now that he remembered, his heart plummeted with grief.

He stole a glance at Cora, her brows knitted as she read the parchment in her hands, oblivious of the truth he'd discovered.

He may not have learned much about her, but he now knew one thing. She'd killed Princess Aveline Caelan.

His eyes slid back to the poster and settled on the next words.

Reward: 500,000 gold sovas.

26

Teryn didn't seem to notice Cora's approach, even as she paused before him. He was too entranced by whatever he was reading. "You were right, it's a forgery," she said of the writ she'd found. The seal was almost an exact replica of Duke Morkai's crescent moon, but the word *Calloway*—the name of Morkai's duchy—was in the wrong script.

Teryn startled at the sound of her voice. He met her eyes over his stack of papers, his face a shade too pale. She opened her senses and felt his spike of alarm seep into her. But it wasn't her sudden appearance that had him so rattled. It had more to do with whatever he was looking at. She furrowed her brow. "What did you find?"

He went to hand her the top paper but ended up dropping the bottom of the stack. She bent to gather the loose papers before they could get soaked by the dewy grass. When she stood, he handed her one of the sheets. "You'll want to see this."

She took it from him and saw it was a map. Her heart sank deeper and deeper the longer she studied it. If the markings represented what she thought they did, there were several more hunting parties. It shouldn't have come as a surprise. She'd begun to suspect as much when she'd witnessed Gringe interrogating Teryn and his companions. He'd too readily accepted that they'd come from another company of unicorn hunters. Sure enough, *Drass* was labeled over the Cambron Pass, just as she'd heard Helios say.

Her lungs felt tight as she took a few steps back, slumping against the tree that met her back. "This is so much worse," she whispered.

"Do you intend to hunt all of them down? To...poison them?" She felt his judgment then, his condemnation of her actions.

She met his eyes. "If you have something to say, say it. You insisted they were no friends of yours."

He watched her for a few moments before averting his gaze, eyes unfocused. "No, they weren't. Nor were they good men. Still...it was a bit reckless, don't you think?"

"It worked."

"Barely. Three men didn't drink. What would you have done if Helios, Lex, and I hadn't been there to take the fall? To fight them for you?"

She clenched her teeth. "I didn't need you. Had you not been there, I would have taken them down with my bow one by one."

"What if you'd been caught?"

"I wasn't."

"What. If. Just think about it."

She did. Her heart raced as she imagined numerous ways her plan could have gone wrong. She could have been spotted. Even more of the men could have abstained from the rum. She could have tried to pick off the survivors and gotten a crossbow bolt to the heart. But that was the risk she'd taken from the start. She knew she was only one person. She knew the odds were against her. That didn't stop her from trying. It was a risk worth taking if it meant saving the unicorns. Denying the Beast its meal. Destroying whatever dark plans Duke Morkai was brewing. Now that she was no longer with the Forest People, this mission was all she had.

Crossing her arms, she pushed off from the tree, feigning more confidence than she felt. "You won't stop me. I'm going to find every last one of these hunting parties and wipe them out."

"When the duke sends men to replace them, what then?"

She startled every time he mentioned the duke. It was strange that he knew Morkai was involved but didn't show even an ounce of the terror that was due. That was probably because he didn't know the man was a mage. To him, the duke was just a businessman trying to turn a pretty profit.

Then his words sank in, flooding her with an overwhelming wave of exhaustion. He was right. The duke would send more men to replace the ones she killed. Did that mean there was no end to her efforts? No way to keep the unicorns safe for good?

Her next words came out with far less conviction. "I'll do whatever I can for as long as I can."

Teryn's posture stiffened. She sensed his tangled energy, felt him fighting against the words that were poised on his lips.

She gave him a pointed look. "What?"

He rubbed his jaw, then locked his eyes on hers. "Let me come with you."

Her face went slack. Surely she hadn't heard him right. Why would he want to come with her? She'd tried to kill him. She'd threatened his life. It had to be a ploy. Indeed she felt...*something* emanating from him. Some mixture of guilt, trepidation, and fear. It was heavy and cloying. She suddenly felt like they were standing too close, the three feet of space separating them not nearly vast enough.

He must have seen her reaction in her eyes, for he took a step back as if to appease her. "Hear me out," he slowly said. "Let me travel with you to the next camp. I assume that will be the Cambron Pass, correct? It's the closest."

She considered remaining mute on her plans, but she gave him a curt nod.

"Then let me aid your efforts in rescuing the captured unicorns there. That's all I ask. With my help—Lex's too, if he's willing—we could free the creatures, maybe without nearly as much bloodshed. If you find our aid useful, perhaps we can help you further, should you choose."

"Why? Why would you help me?"

"I owe you a debt. You treated Lex's arm. You must allow me to repay you."

"I don't want you to repay me."

"It doesn't matter. I'm a prince. Chivalry is my guiding compass."

She snorted a dark laugh. "It didn't seem like it when you aimed a spear at me."

"You tried to stab me first—" He shook his head. "That's beside the point."

"No, Your Highness," she said, tone mocking. "I don't care about your chivalry or your moral compass."

"Then care about what I could help you accomplish. Faster. Easier."

She eyed him through slitted lids. Suspicion prickled the back of her neck. "You're hiding something. What aren't you telling me?"

His eyes widened for a fraction of a second before he steeled his expression. When he spoke, his words were slow. Careful. "Now that I know what I know, I can't finish the Heart's Hunt. But perhaps I can do something worthwhile while I'm here."

She shook her head, not buying any of that. "What's in it for you? You may not have won your silly Hunt, but neither did anyone else. You could simply go home and claim your bride's hand—"

"I have a duty to my kingdom," he said, tone firm, "to do the right thing." He punctuated the last two words. With a deep inhale, she let herself feel his emotions. She sensed only truth.

"And you think helping me free some unicorns is the *right thing*?"

He hesitated before answering, but when he did, he was resolute. "Yes."

She heard soft steps coming up alongside the horses. Valorre. Berol ruffled her feathers at his appearance, edging farther down Teryn's saddle.

You could let him help you, he said.

She cast him a dark glare. *You can't be serious.*

It's dangerous doing this on your own.

I never heard you complain before, she silently conveyed. *You're the one who dragged me into this, you know.*

If you recall, I asked both you and your friend.

Her heart clenched at his reference to Maiya. But Valorre was right. He had implored them both to help, and Cora had sought the aid of the entire commune, only to be denied by Roije. She'd already fantasized about how much easier her mission would be if she'd had the Forest People to help. But the commune had skilled magic users, trackers, and hunters. Teryn and Lex were just...princes.

She returned her attention to Teryn. "How do I even know you'd be a help and not a hindrance? I saved your life from the Beast tonight."

He quirked a brow. "Technically, you saved the caged unicorn's life. The Beast only went for Helios, and I don't recall you intervening on his behalf."

"The creature wounded your friend and I bandaged him up."

He shrugged. "Still, wouldn't it help to have more than just you protecting Valorre? Your arrows wounded the Beast, but the monster didn't fall. I'm skilled with a spear, while Lex..." He trailed off, some of his confidence faltering. "Lex can wield a sword. You saw how he killed one of those hunters."

She rolled her eyes. "And nearly curled up in the fetal position after."

He sighed. "Give us a chance. Let us redeem ourselves. Let us do some good after everything we nearly destroyed."

Her gaze slid to Valorre. *I still think it's a good idea,* he said. *I like him. He's very tall.*

I take offense to that.

Why? He's very handsome and so concerned over my well-being. Did you hear him? He wants to fight off the Beast for me.

Oh, is that all it takes to win you over?

Valorre had nothing else to say.

She met Teryn's eyes, reached for his emotions. Her palms tingled as she sifted through his energy. She felt strength and fear. Hesitation and conviction. Something murky lurked at the edges, which told her he was still hiding things from her. But so was she. Could his secrets be any bigger than hers?

Finally, she released a grumbling breath. "I'll think on it."

He blinked a few times. "You will?"

"I'll tell you what I decide in the morning." She went to brush past him, but his hand landed on her shoulder. Her body went stiff, her pulse thrumming. She glanced down at his hand, felt the heat of his palm on her bare skin where her shift had slipped down her shoulder.

In an instant, he snatched his hand back. Even in the dark, she could see color rising to his cheeks. He cleared his throat before he spoke, fingers curling tight. "I just wanted to implore you...please give it serious consideration."

It took a few seconds to steady her breathing. "I will," she said, her voice a whisper.

〜

Teryn waited until Cora was fast asleep by the dying embers of the fire before he approached the horses again. He used the same technique he did while stalking prey—prodding the earth, taking one slow step after the other—to ensure he didn't wake her. Quinne softly nickered at his approach. He paused, waiting to see if Cora would stir. She didn't. Valorre, thankfully, was nowhere to be seen. He'd caught the unicorn wandering in and out of camp during the last couple hours that he'd feigned sleep.

He rifled through his saddlebags to retrieve parchment and quill. Berol landed quietly on his shoulder and nibbled his temple in greeting. After giving her a few affectionate scritches, he quickly scrawled his message. Then he took the Wanted poster he'd stashed inside his vest when Cora hadn't been looking and rolled it together with his letter. Finally, he sealed it and lifted it toward Berol. She clasped it in one of her talons.

"To Father," he whispered. "Home."

He then offered her a strip of pheasant he'd pocketed during dinner. She accepted it as well as more pets, then launched off his shoulder. He watched her silhouette against the dark sky until she merged with the night. A pinch of worry settled in his gut. He'd never sent her away this far from home, but she'd always returned with ease before, no matter where they were. Besides, this was the only way.

He needed to get a message delivered to King Dimetreus as soon as possible. Berol couldn't simply fly to Ridine Castle—a place she'd never been—and take up perch outside the king's study. The only way to let him know that Teryn had found the fugitive was to get a note to his father first.

Teryn stepped back from Quinne.

And froze.

The moon illuminated something white between a pair of trees. It was Valorre. He watched Teryn with his large russet eyes. How long had he been standing there? Teryn smiled at the unicorn, trying to exude innocence as he returned to his bedroll. The truth was, Teryn was anything but innocent. His string of broken promises was only just beginning.

At least he had one consolation.

The girl he was going to betray wasn't innocent either.

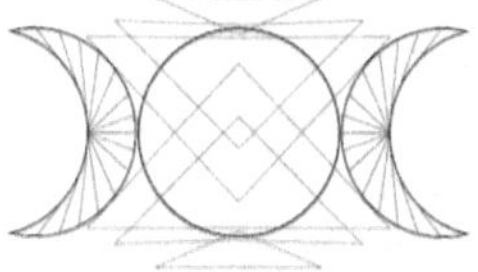

27

Lex, Teryn knew, would take some convincing.

"You can't be serious," Lex said, eyes bulging.

Teryn kept his voice far lower. "I am." They stood near the stream, watering their horses. He glanced toward their secluded camp and the tendrils of smoke that wafted above it. Cora had already been awake by the time Teryn had opened his eyes. He was almost surprised to see her there, tending the fire and boiling something fragrant in a cook pot. As much as he'd itched to ask if she'd made her decision, he dared not say anything more than a cordial greeting. The fact that she hadn't snuck away when she had the chance told him she was at least considering his offer. For now, that was enough.

He'd woken Lex after that, inquired about his arm. Trying not to be too obvious, he'd then pulled Lex away and had him bring his horse. Once they'd reached the stream, Teryn let him in on his idea. He hadn't told Lex everything. Only what he'd told Cora. Not because he didn't trust Lex to keep a secret. They'd successfully hidden their original alliance from Helios, after all. It was more that this situation felt particularly tenuous. The way Cora's dark eyes always held far too much intensity, how she always seemed to be watching, studying, reading between his words... he knew he needed to tread carefully. Letting Lex in on his secret would be a last resort.

"We only have to accompany her to the next group of hunters," Teryn said. "That's all."

Lex gave him a pointed look. "Oh, that's *all*? We nearly got ourselves killed by the last company."

"Yes, but that was when we knew nothing. Helios kept us in the dark. Cora was working against us. Now, we'll be working together."

"I don't see how this helps you get your princess."

"It doesn't," Teryn said. "If you want to return home now, I won't stop you, but I'd rather have your help. Should you come with me, I promise as soon as we return to Dermaine Palace, you can have anything you want. You want in on our trade agreement with Brushwold? You got it."

Lex made a bewildered face, but it was quickly replaced with a look of surprise. "Oh." A pause. Then another, more drawn out, "*Oooh.* I see what this is."

Teryn lifted a brow. Could he have guessed Teryn's true motive? "What?"

"You like her. Cora."

Teryn's heart did a strange thing in his chest. He opened his mouth to deny it but thought better of it. Perhaps he could use Lex's assumption—as incorrect as it was—against him. He decided to let Lex interpret his silence however he wanted.

Lex nodded, a crooked grin lifting his cheeks. "You no longer care about the Heart's Hunt because you've got a new hunt in mind." He waggled his brows. "A hunt up a certain pair of petticoats."

A flush of heat climbed up his neck, and his pulse quickened at the sudden visuals Lex's crass comment provided. It was far from the worst thing he could imagine. Cora was stunning. Terrifying, yes, but...

He recalled the feel of her skin beneath his palm when he'd unwittingly touched her bare shoulder last night, remembered the sharp heat that ignited his hand, warmed his chest—

No. He shook the outrageous musings from his mind. *She's a murderer. There's nothing enticing about that.* His blood quickly cooled, but he forced his momentary lack of composure to creep into his voice, letting his words tremble a little as he said, "Maybe it's more than that." It was almost too much for him to keep a straight face. Thankfully, Lex didn't know him well or else he would have called his bluff. Teryn was not the kind of man to do ridiculous things for love. To him, love was fiction. Folly. The breaker of peace and the bringer of wars. But Lex didn't have to know that.

Lex grimaced. "You can't want to...marry her. You're a prince, Teryn. Princes don't marry wood witches. Besides, isn't your kingdom—dare I say—broke?"

Teryn stiffened at that. They hadn't discussed Menah's financial state, which meant rumors must have spread as far as Tomas. It shouldn't have been a surprise. "Lex, I need you to trust me," he said, stripping all pretense from his tone. "Come with me or go home, the choice is yours. But there's only one option that's going to get you a contract for Aromir wool. What's it going to be?"

Lex puffed his cheeks as he considered. After a grumbling exhale, he said, "Fine. I'll do it for the damn goats."

Teryn's lips spread into a grin as he slapped his friend on the arm—the uninjured one, of course. "Thanks, Lex. One more thing. Please don't tell Cora about... you know. My feelings."

"All right," he said, "but if I see the two of you kissing or canoodling, the deal's off."

Teryn snorted a laugh. He took Quinne's reins as well as Hara's and began to walk them back toward camp. "Trust me, that's not going to happen."

"Clearly, you've never been in love," Lex muttered.

~

TERYN HAD BEEN SUSPICIOUSLY QUIET ALL MORNING. CORA HAD EXPECTED HIM TO bring up his proposition a hundred times already. Instead, he'd said nothing about it. Had he changed his mind? An unexpected disappointment sank her gut but she ignored it. Swallowed it down. Finished making breakfast.

Teryn and Lex returned from the stream and accepted bowls of root vegetable stew. They didn't even ask if the meal was poisoned. It wasn't, of course, and perhaps the fact that Cora was eating too eased any suspicions they might have. She watched them throughout the meal and found that Lex kept shooting strange looks at Teryn—ones she couldn't quite read. Whatever it was about, it had Teryn blushing furiously and wolfing down his stew as fast as he could.

After they'd all finished eating, a heavy silence fell. Cora could feel the weight of her decision resting on her shoulders, but she still didn't know what to say. Did she want them coming with her? She could admit she'd felt slightly safer last night knowing it hadn't just been her and Valorre at camp. Not to mention they had supplies, horses, cookware, weapons. Blankets and bedrolls. Meanwhile, Cora had only what she'd been able to steal and carry on foot.

She'd never been one to allow strangers to get close to her, and these two already knew far too much. They knew she was a witch and the one who'd poisoned the hunters. Facts that hadn't seemed quite so grim last night when their lives were at stake, but now the realization sent waves of anxiety through her. They could turn her in for what she'd done. And what if they found out who she really was? Teryn and Lex may have had no allegiance to the Kingdom of Khero, but after everything Teryn had said about duty and doing the right thing...

Cora picked up their bowls and wordlessly went to the stream to wash them. After a while, Valorre came up beside her. It was the first time she'd seen him all morning. She'd felt his presence close by, but she knew he wasn't content to stay in one place. He was a restless, wild spirit. Undoubtedly fae.

I'm certain those are clean by now, Valorre said.

She glanced down at her hands, realizing she must have been lost in thought. With a sigh, she stood and began walking down the bank, her steps slow. She knew it was time to make a choice. It was already well past dawn and if she wanted to reach the Cambron Pass quickly, she'd need all the time she could get. A sudden thought occurred to her. Teryn and Lex had an extra horse. If she accepted their company, she was sure she could use the mare for herself. She could travel faster than she ever could on foot.

Valorre rippled with indignation. *I am much faster than a horse. I could carry you.*

"Yes," she said with a grin, "but riding bareback isn't the most comfortable thing, and I'd never dare saddle you."

That seemed to satisfy him. *I would never stoop so low as to wear a saddle. What a silly contraption. I'd look very foolish indeed. Very well. Does that mean they're coming with us to help save my brethren?*

She nibbled her lip. Then the sound of clashing steel drew her attention. She paused, glancing back toward camp. Teryn and Lex were sparring just ahead. It seemed Lex's injured arm was his non-dominant hand, for he parried Teryn's attacks with ease. Teryn, she was irked to note, was once again without a shirt. She rolled her eyes as she approached them.

Teryn nodded at her with a grin, one that made her stomach tighten. Or perhaps it was the indecency of him being shirtless. She kept her eyes anywhere but his broad chest, his arms roped with muscle, his pants that seemed ridiculously low on his hips—

Crossing her arms, she returned his grin with a glare. "Do you ever wear a shirt?"

He shrugged and parried a halfhearted thrust from Lex. "Thanks to Lex and his refusal to let me turn his shirts into bandages, I only have one left. I'm not going to sweat in it."

"It's hardly safe to spar without one."

"Oh really?" he said as his shortsword clashed with Lex's. "I hadn't noticed because Lex isn't trying hard enough."

"My arm hurts," Lex said, then muttered something about Teryn showing off. That was when Cora realized what this little performance was all about. Teryn was trying to prove that they were useful. Skilled. That their aid would serve her.

Oh, the tall one is very strong, isn't he?

Cora cut a glare at Valorre. *Do you have a crush on Teryn?*

What is crush?

Never mind. She returned her gaze to the boys, watching as they set down their swords and drank from skins of water. Teryn shrugged on his hunting vest just as a familiar shape veered down from the sky. Berol landed on his padded shoulder, a scroll tucked in her talon.

He sent her away in the middle of the night, Valorre said. He didn't seem concerned, but she narrowed her eyes with suspicion.

"What's that?" she asked.

He met her eyes over the paper he was reading. "A letter from my father. I sent Berol with a note telling him I wouldn't be coming home for a while."

She clenched her jaw. That meant he'd already assumed she'd say yes to his proposition. It made her want to deny him outright.

He walked toward her, a questioning look in his eyes. "Have you decided?"

She found her words trapped in her throat as he held her gaze. He held it too long. Too unflinchingly. Blinking, she averted her eyes and pondered his question. Her time was up. She needed to choose.

Her gaze returned to his and she found that his eyes were in the process of sweeping over her form. His assessment made her breath catch. She dared not open her senses to him. Dared not read too much into his gaze. For surely he couldn't find much to be desired when he looked at her. She was a mess of tangles. Of soil and stone. Of petticoats tucked around her legs like pants. He was a prince, a man used to soft women with even softer demeanors.

She lifted her chin, reminding herself she didn't care what he thought of her. Not her appearance, not her personality, and certainly not her romantic appeal. He was a prince determined to make amends where his honor had failed. She was a witch with vengeance in her heart and violence in her soul.

"Put a shirt on," she said, sneering at his bare chest as if it were repulsive to her.

It wasn't, but that was one of many secrets she was determined to keep. "It's time for us to go."

"Us," he echoed. "As in...the three of us."

Valorre sidled closer to her, making his approval clear.

"Yes," she finally said through her teeth. "Now, hurry up or I'm leaving without you."

28

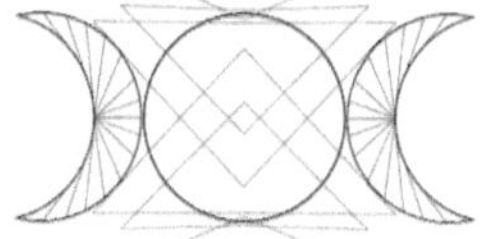

For two days, they traveled northwest for the Cambron Pass. They kept a decent pace with Cora riding Hara. After throwing most of Helios' personal items into the campfire, she'd kept all his useful belongings and took his mare for herself. She was surprised the animal was so amenable to new ownership. Based on the many snide remarks Teryn and Lex had made about Helios, she'd assumed his horse perhaps wouldn't respect her. Hara, however, was as even tempered as Cora could hope. Valorre took it upon himself to remind her who was the better of the two of them, and Cora always made certain to reassure him that, yes, he was the most magnificent and fearsome creature of hoof and mane.

Berol flew overhead, sometimes going so far as to become a pinprick in the distance, other times diving for prey or riding on Teryn's shoulder. She was curious about the prince's relationship with the bird. Not enough to ask him about it, of course. She made it her mission to speak as little as possible to the boys. The less they knew about her, the better, and she had no interest in getting to know them. They were temporary allies, not friends.

By the end of the second day of travel, the Cambron Mountains loomed large ahead. On the third, Cora found the first notable tracks.

She felt her nerves begin to fray the closer they came. Taking down the first group of hunters had been a harrowing enough experience. Now she was going to do it all over again. This time she had help, although it was still up for debate whether they would prove useful.

Each night, Cora's exhaustion was so deep that she'd fall asleep within minutes of bedding down on her newly acquired bedroll. Her slumber was—thankfully— deep and dreamless. But on the third night, after a day of tracking, stalking, and inching closer to her prey, she dreamed.

THE NIGHTMARE STARTED MUCH LIKE ANY OTHER. SHE WALKED DOWN A DARK CASTLE hall, following the pull of some terrible wrongness. Every step sounded hollow in her ears. The smell of dust and rot filled her nostrils, tickling the back of her throat. She walked forward, for that was the only direction that existed in this strange dream. A few steps more and a serving tray appeared in her hands. Then the door. That horrible, dreaded door.

She knew what she would find inside. This time, she didn't fight it. This time, she ran for it, knowing the sooner she saw the room the sooner this dream would end. Her feet flew beneath her as she reached the threshold. Even though she'd known what she'd find, the sight of the dead queen still took her breath away. She froze in the doorway, the tray slipping from her hands. Morkai stood at Queen Linette's side, his hands drawing the blood from the sheets, from her lips, from under her nose. Blood that seeped from no visible wound. He stopped and whipped his head toward her, and the scene shifted in an instant. Morkai wasn't manipulating the blood, he was gesturing out of shock or panic. Part of Cora knew that wasn't right, knew what she'd seen was real. But another part of her doubted. Doubted enough that when he called her over to help the queen, she obeyed. She gathered Linette's cold hand in hers, uncaring that the woman's blood was now smeared over her own palms.

The voice came next. One she expected but was startled by just the same.

King Dimetreus let out a soft wail as his eyes landed on his wife. His hand flew to his chest as he halted in the doorway. "What have you done?"

Morkai whispered to the king, "You recall what she said to the queen earlier."

"No," Cora said, rounding on them. She shuddered as the word left her mouth. There was something wrong about the way it failed to echo through the room. As if her voice didn't belong there. "I didn't mean it."

King Dimetreus gave no indication that he'd heard her. Instead, he rushed to her, anger replacing his anguish. "You did this. *You.* What have you done?"

Cora trembled before the king's rage. She knew what would happen next. Knew a dark cell awaited her. A demand for her death.

"No." The word was louder this time. She pinned the king with a glare. "No. This time, you will listen to me. I didn't do this. It was him." She pointed a finger at Duke Morkai. Her gaze shot to him, meeting his eyes. They shifted from an all-encompassing black to a blue so pale it was almost silver. His lips slid into a lazy smirk.

Returning her gaze back to the king, she was startled to find him frozen. Not just unmoving, but unbreathing, unblinking.

Morkai stepped up beside King Dimetreus. "You can't change the past by altering your dreams."

She clenched her jaw. A strange sense of duality washed over her as her hands balled into fists—fists that felt too small and too large at once, as if she were both the twelve-year-old version of herself that existed in her nightmares and her current self. The one who slept. Who dreamed. Who raged against this scene from the confines of her mind.

"You never fought against your sentence in the past," Morkai said.

"I was too shocked," she replied, her older voice mingling with her younger.

"It's useless. Besides, regardless of what you think, this *was* your fault."

"It wasn't. You did this."

Morkai waved his hand and the bedroom disappeared. Like an inkblot spreading over parchment, a new scene began to appear. Little by little, the colors grew brighter, her surroundings sharper. Her blood went cold when she realized where she was.

The dining hall at Ridine Castle formed around her. Its stone walls were decorated in intricate tapestries. The light from half a dozen candle-studded chandeliers cast everything in a warm, cheery glow. The tables were overflowing with courtiers dining, chatting, and drinking. Cora strode straight to the head table at the far wall. She knew she was late. It had been intentional. Her headaches had been coming on harder recently, and whenever she was forced to be around so many people, they became nearly crippling. No physician seemed to know what was wrong with her. There was no visible ailment. No disease of the body to treat. When she'd speak of feeling like she was being invaded by the hearts and minds of everyone around, she'd receive only unsettled stares. She'd hoped she could wait out the course of tonight's dinner, but Master Benedict had found her curled up beneath a staircase. Now she had no choice.

Master Benedict kept his hand on Cora's shoulder as she approached the table, his grip a reminder that there was no running away. She owed the king and queen an explanation, he'd said. Wincing at the pounding in her head, she lowered into a curtsy. She returned her eyes to the king and queen, bracing herself for the scolding. There wasn't one. Dimetreus was deep in conversation with Duke Morkai while Linette stared pointedly at her husband, her distaste in being ignored made clear by her pursed lips. Finally, Dimetreus turned from Morkai and gestured Cora closer to the table. Before he could say a word to her, Linette interrupted. "When shall we have a ball, my love? You promised me a ball this month."

The king claimed his wife's lips with a kiss. "You shall have a ball, darling, but not until our son is born. You are in no condition to dance. After he's made his appearance in the world, we'll celebrate. We'll have balls night after night until he's a year old. Then we'll host the finest party anyone this side of the Balma Sea has ever witnessed."

Linette's expression faltered as she shifted awkwardly in her seat.

"What is it?" the king asked.

"It's...oh, it's nothing." She batted her lashes and infused her tone with nonchalance. "It's just...I'm not very far along. Surely I can dance. I'd hate to let my newest gown go to waste before I grow too large to wear it."

The pounding in Cora's head increased, but the invasive energies shifted. They were no longer coming from the rows and rows of tables behind her but the one she stood before. Against her will, her attention focused on one person alone. Queen Linette. Cora felt a rippling anxiety turn in her stomach, a feeling that was not her own. With it came a sinking weight of guilt. Then something darker. Heavier.

"You aren't with child." The words left Cora's mouth before she could swallow them back. She hadn't yet learned which of her observations were better left unsaid. Had yet to understand why everyone else seemed blind to the things she gleaned so easily. So unwillingly.

Queen Linette's head whipped toward Cora. "How dare you say such a thing."

"It's true." Her voice came out tremulous. "You...you're lying. You were never with child."

"You wretched, awful creature—"

King Dimetreus held up a hand, silencing his wife. Master Benedict began to tug Cora away, but Dimetreus shook his head. His attention narrowed on Cora, voice soft. "Why would you say such a thing?"

Linette spoke before Cora could. "How many times have I told you, Dimetreus? She needs to be sent to a Godspriest. There's something wrong with her. She's infected by the seven devils and must have them cleansed from her soul."

Cora felt heat rise to her cheeks. "I do not need a Godspriest," she said, a frantic note to her voice. "I am not infected by the seven devils."

Linette looked around the dining hall. Cora was suddenly aware that silence had fallen over the room. She could feel the attention of innumerable pairs of eyes boring into her back. Linette spoke softly through her teeth. "Don't make a scene."

Cora's attention darted to Dimetreus. Why wasn't he speaking up for her? Tears sprang to her eyes as her blood began to boil like never before. It felt as if the energies she'd absorbed were compounding, the tightness in her skull growing sharper. She could still feel the queen's emotions the most, could feel her fear mixed with disgust, her guilt and her shame and so many things that Cora was too young to understand. "Tell him the truth," she yelled. "Tell him that you lied."

Linette rounded the table and grabbed Cora by the arm. "You rotten little witch."

Cora shrugged free, her breaths coming out in sobbing gasps. "I'm not a witch." That word had been a filthy thing then, something spoken with disdain. Cora hadn't yet learned that witches were real, that they were nothing like the storybook monsters she'd heard about.

Linette dragged her away from the table. "You are a witch," she muttered under her breath, all the while keeping a smile on her lips.

Cora glared up at her. She made no move to lower her voice as she said, "If I'm a witch, then I curse you."

Linette dropped her arm like she'd been burned. Her chest heaved, eyes roving the room and the eyes that continued to watch them. "Stop," she said, tears springing to her eyes. The queen shuddered. She was truly afraid of her. It was written in the emotions Cora sensed, writhing, contracting, spilling deeper into her until she felt like her head would explode.

She erupted with a shout. "I curse you to die."

Without another word, she kicked up her heels and ran from the dining room.

She crossed the threshold, desperate for the relief of the quiet halls.

But the doorway only led her to a room with a bloodstained bed.

"No," she breathed. The room was as frozen as it had been when she'd left it. The king remained locked in place, the queen staring sightlessly ahead. Only she and Morkai moved.

"You did that," he said.

"I didn't mean it," Cora said. This time, her voice was her own, without a hint of her younger self. "Even if I had, it wasn't a true curse. Witches don't curse people."

"How do you know? You spoke the words, sent them out into the ether. She died that very night."

"You killed her," Cora said through her teeth.

"Yes, but what if it was your fault? What if your words sparked a series of events that resulted in her death? Is it really so improbable? You killed the queen. You let Princess Aveline die. Deny it."

She opened her mouth to say she wasn't a murderer, but the words turned to ash on her tongue. The version of her that existed outside the dream had ended seven lives mere days ago. Erwin with an arrow to his throat. The hunters who drank her rum.

Morkai took a step closer. The lantern light glinted off the sharp planes of his face, making him look both beautiful and terrifying at once. "Maybe Linette was right all along. Maybe you're an evil thing. You kill without remorse. You choose death, violence, and solitude over the safety of a new home. You lied to people who loved you. Turned your back on your dearest friend without even a goodbye."

Her legs began to tremble as she tried to put more distance between herself and Morkai.

"Maybe you're even worse than me." With a flutter of his fingers, the room began to dissolve again, this time under swirling shadows. They crawled down her throat, filled her lungs, raked talons over her heart. Black filled her vision as she struggled to free herself from the strangling dark mist. No matter how she fought, where she turned, she was pinned in place. The shadows refused to abate. They simply pressed harder. Harder. Squeezing her lips like a kiss of death.

~

Cora.

Cora.

"Cora!" The sound of her name made her body go still.

Her muscles ached as if she'd run for miles, as if she'd thrashed and raged in her sleep the same way she'd done in her dream. She blinked into the night, but her eyes were glazed with tears, casting everything under a blur. Something heavy was still pressed to her mouth, the smell of sweat and soil filling her senses. It was wrong. Foreign. Her mind struggled to remember.

Where am I? Where am I?

Then she remembered. Somewhat.

Her body went limp, and the heavy thing left her mouth. A hand. She waited only a beat before reaching for her belt and unsheathing her knife. With her free hand, she thrust outward, striking blindly with her palm. A gasp followed, then a thud, and she shoved all of her weight into the other body until she felt it collapse beneath her. She blinked again and again to rid the glaze of tears from her eyes. When her vision finally cleared, she found Teryn looking back at her, eyes wide with surprise. He was flat on his back while she straddled his stomach, her knife at the base of his throat. She felt a slice of wind beat her cheek. As she turned her head to the side, she caught sight of a dark shape darting for her.

"Berol, no," Teryn said.

The falcon pulled out of her dive and lifted into the sky. Cora saw Berol's shadow cross the moon as she circled overhead.

She returned her gaze to Teryn, her chest heaving as she struggled to catch her breath. Their eyes locked.

"What are you doing?" Teryn asked, voice low, calm, steady. His eyes, however, revealed a tinge of fear.

"What were *you* doing?" she said, her words uneven, frantic. "You had your hand over my mouth."

"You were screaming."

She shuddered, reminded of her dream, the shadows that had tried to strangle her. "You had no right to touch me."

The fear left his eyes, replaced with indignation. "You wouldn't wake. Your screams nearly gave me a heart attack. I thought you were being murdered."

"So you decided to smother me in my sleep."

"I called your name a hundred times. The last thing I could think to do was muffle your shouts while I tried harder to wake you. Would you rather I let you carry on? I'm sure the hunters we're supposed to be sneaking up on would only be too happy to follow the source of a distressed woman's cries. And not to aid her, either."

That sent a spike of alarm through her. She lifted her chin, staring down at him with a glare. "Don't you dare touch me like that again."

He scoffed. "Do you think I wanted to? Do you think I took pleasure from it?"

The word pleasure sparked the memory of how his palm had felt on her shoulder. Her heart thumped heavily in her chest and sent a wave of heat to her cheeks.

His eyes landed on the very shoulder in question. When his eyes returned to hers, his lips quirked with a suggestive smirk. "Trust me, if I wanted to touch you, you'd know. And if I took pleasure from it, so would you."

Her breath caught, and something trilled low in her belly. She was stunned silent, her knife trembling in her hand. Without her permission, her eyes dipped to his lips, taking in their sensuous curve, the dimple at one corner. His smile slipped, an uncertain expression crossing his face. She was entranced as his lips parted, some word poised on them—

"Oh, for the love of the seven gods, get a room." Lex turned over on his bedroll.

Cora's eyes flew to the other man. Valorre stood off to the side, rippling with something that struck Cora like a snicker.

"No canoodling," Lex muttered, back facing them. "If I hear gasps or moans or even kisses, I'm going to throw rocks at your heads."

Cora returned her gaze to Teryn. She stiffened, realizing the impropriety of their position. He was on his back. She was on top of him. Sure, a knife's blade was between them, but...

She had to stifle her gasp of surprise when she realized where his hands were —at the base of her waist. Had they been there the whole time? He could have shoved her off him, and perhaps that was what he'd been prepared to do. But also...

Also...

It looked like so much more. For the tiniest splinter of a moment, it had—*maybe*—felt like more too.

She pushed off of him as fast as she could, nearly stumbling in the process. He rose much slower, his eyes never leaving hers. Then, trembling with rage, she stomped off, feeling his gaze follow her every step.

29

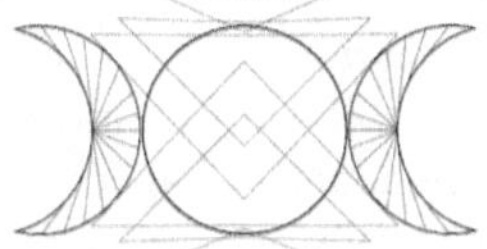

Teryn wasn't entirely sure why he followed after Cora. He told himself it was to spy, to see where she went and ensure she wasn't plucking poisonous berries to shove down his throat in retribution. But that wasn't the full truth. He was concerned. He'd heard the pitiful pitch of her cries that had roused him from sleep, had seen beads of tears clinging to her dark lashes as she'd held her knife to his throat. For a moment, it had been like she was somewhere else, trapped in her mind. He'd had every intention of pushing her off of him at the first chance, but instead...

He blushed as he recalled the look in her eyes when he'd brought up pleasure and touch. Seven gods, he'd *flirted* with her. With a woman who would sooner butcher him than bed him.

I only said what I did to shock her into calming down, he told himself. That too was a lie. He'd said it because he'd wanted to get a rise out of her. Wanted to taste her rage and test the bounds of her anger. Did he have a damn death wish? Who flirts with a woman he's planning to betray?

He shook the thought from his head as he trailed her. Valorre trotted past him, following after her too. They both disappeared into the dark. Still, he followed.

He spotted Valorre first. The unicorn stood at what Teryn realized was the edge of a rounded cliff. His white coat shone beneath the light of the moon, the ridges of his spiral horn glittering with reflected starlight. Teryn's heart leapt into his throat as he considered that Cora might be on the other side of the cliff's edge. She could have run blindly and taken a fall.

Then he saw her. Not far from Valorre, her small form was curled at the base of a tree, knees to her chest, shoulders heaving with quiet sobs. Teryn suddenly regretted coming after her. Her grief was not his to witness.

He took a slow step back, but Cora's face whipped up, stopping him in his tracks.

She rose to her feet and crossed her arms. "What are you doing here?"

"I..." He searched for words, his throat dry. "I just wanted to see if you were all right."

"Why wouldn't I be?"

Teryn knew he should leave. He was only making her more upset. If he wasn't careful, she might throw a knife at him. But despite telling his feet to walk the other way, he found himself stepping forward instead. Not toward her, but to the edge of the cliff. The Cambron Pass sprawled out before him, cloaked in darkness. Somewhere out there, the next group of hunters awaited. The thought chilled him, made him wonder if everything he was doing was reckless. He could lose his life doing what he was about to do. All so he could save his kingdom. Would the sacrifice be worth it? He glanced over his shoulder and found Cora watching him. His stomach sank with guilt. Would sacrificing *her* be worth it?

She's a killer, he reminded himself for the hundredth time. But right now, she didn't look like a killer at all. She looked...fragile. Not like a glass trinket. She was nothing like the soft women who fluttered about court. She was more like a blade, one that was forged to be mighty but still bore chips and scratches.

"I used to have nightmares." The sound of his own voice caught him off guard.

She stared at him, jaw set. At first, it didn't seem like she'd reply. Then, uncrossing her arms, she returned to the tree and leaned her back against it. Valorre nuzzled her shoulder, and Cora reached up to stroke the space between his eyes. "Let me guess," she said dryly. "You had them when you were young. Like every other child."

He gave her a weak grin. "If you'd consider me a child three years ago, then yes."

She met his eyes briefly, then returned her gaze to Valorre. "What were they about?"

He gulped before answering. "War."

"Why war?"

It really wasn't something he should talk about. Not only did he not enjoy talking about it but she had no right to know. Yet he found himself speaking regardless. "I...I don't know how much you know of my kingdom..."

She gave a noncommittal shrug.

"Well, a few years ago, my father attempted to replace my mother with his mistress." His lungs tightened. He remembered the yelling, the shouts. The way his sisters had cried. How he'd dragged them away to play games and pretend their family wasn't falling apart. "Dermaine Palace erupted with scandal. My mother fought to keep her crown while I...I was caught in the middle. Between Mother, Father, and my half brother. I loved all of them and realized I was about to lose at least one of them to some degree. My mother's home kingdom threatened war, and that's when I started having nightmares. Not all of them were truly about battles waged on Menah's shores but the familial war already wreaking havoc on my life."

Teryn glanced at Cora and found her staring, brow furrowed, hand frozen on Valorre's face. The unicorn nudged her to resume petting him. She tore her gaze from Teryn. "That sounds rough."

He released a heavy sigh and tried to make his voice sound casual. "I led a charmed life up until then, so who am I to complain?"

Her eyes flickered to his, and he saw her expression soften.

"What about you?" he asked. "What was your childhood like? Have you always been on your own?"

Her lips pulled into a frown. "In one way or another, yes. My parents died when I was young. I was devastated when Father died, but when Mother followed...a part of me broke. I felt like there was no one left alive who understood me." Her throat bobbed, and her expression grew hard again. "It's also when my...my *gifts* started developing and I realized I wasn't like other people."

A witch, she meant. His pulse quickened at that. Even though he knew it to be true, he was still bewildered by it. People didn't believe in magic or witches. They weren't supposed to be real. And yet, he'd met both a witch and a unicorn in a single week. He hesitated before asking his next question, unsure if she'd deign to answer. "What exactly does it mean to be a witch? I've never met one before you." He rushed to say the last part.

She snorted a dark laugh. "We're certainly not about blood-filled cauldrons and human sacrifice, I'll tell you that much."

"Well, what *are* you about, then? You know, aside from rescuing unicorns, threatening princes with sharp objects, and poisoning evil men. Is poison your only magic?"

"Poison is the least of my magic," she said with an indignant scoff. For a moment, he worried he'd offended her, but she spoke again. "I'm clairsentient," she explained, "which means I experience clear feeling. Every witch has an affinity for one of the senses. There are five others in addition to clairsentience. Clairvoyance is clear seeing. Clairaudience relates to hearing. Clairalience is smelling. Clairgustance is taste. And claircognizance revolves around knowing."

Teryn tried to keep the awe off his face. He'd only heard of such abilities in myths and faerytales. "So, what does it mean to experience magical feeling the way you do?"

"It...it's kind of hard to explain. Generally, a clairsentient witch uses her own emotions, internal physical responses, and touch to connect with her magic. A certain physical sensation could mean danger while a specific emotion could mean luck. Every witch is different and it takes some time to understand how to utilize one's magic. I, however, am a little different. I tap into my magic with feeling as well, but I am also able to feel the feelings of others. One of our elders told me I might be an empath."

"An empath?" Teryn echoed.

"A witch with very strong clairsentience. An empath's senses aren't limited to her own, and she can use them to perceive outside thoughts, feelings, and energies. It's something I've been able to do since I was a child. It was nothing but a curse when I was younger. It led to some...very bad experiences. It wasn't until I met other people like me that I learned to control it and shield myself from others' emotions."

"When you say people like you, do you mean...other witches? Are you part of a coven?"

She chuckled. "Something like that."

Teryn was once again struck with awe. Could it really be that magic was real and there were others like Cora? If so, was it a good thing? Or a bad thing? A startling realization dawned on him. She could read emotions. No wonder he'd always felt so unsettled by her gaze. She was probably absorbing his feelings all the while. Did that mean...did she know...

He shook the thought from his mind. His muscles tensed. Suddenly every single thought felt dangerous. "So, your powers," he said slowly. "Can you read my mind?"

She rolled her eyes. "No, it's not like that. I still have to process what I receive through my own feelings. While I can tune in at will, the level of information I glean varies. Some things jump out at me at random, overwhelming my own senses. It can happen even when I'm shielding. Other times it's just...just an emotion I have to put a name to. It's like reading a book in another language that you've only just begun to learn."

The visual worked surprisingly well for him. He'd been tutored in several languages, but he was only fluent in three. The rest he understood in fits and starts. His eyes fell to her hands. She'd begun brushing them through Valorre's mane, revealing the dark ink decorating her palms and forearms. The designs formed esoteric symbols like moon phases and geometric configurations unlike anything he'd seen before. In fact, he'd seen very few women with tattoos at all. He had to admit they were stunning. "Do your tattoos have anything to do with magic?"

"They are a tradition amongst the—" She paused and shook her head as if she were about to say something she didn't want to. Slower, she said, "Amongst my coven. They are symbolic of a witch's experience with magic. Some think they also help us channel our magic's flow."

"*Some* think?" He quirked a brow. "Do you not believe? Are you a skeptic when it comes to your own magic?"

"No, I believe," she said but there was certainly doubt in her tone. "It's just... sometimes I wish magic were more obvious. The most common feats of magic can be explained away by coincidence, imagination, or science. I've only ever seen one kind that couldn't." Her eyes took on a distant quality that reminded him of how she'd looked after her nightmare.

"Why are you on your own now?" he asked, mostly to guide her away from what was clearly a distressing subject. "Where is your coven?"

"I lived with them until recently. I left them after I met Valorre. I knew I needed to save his brethren, and my people...well, they couldn't help me."

"Why not?"

She stiffened, and Teryn could tell he was approaching yet another prickly topic. "I don't know how witches are treated where you're from, but here they aren't exactly considered upstanding members of society. They can't go gallivanting around the woods on crusades against fae creature injustice. Remember how you told me you've never met a witch before? That's because society doesn't treat us kindly. We stay hidden because it isn't safe for us to be found."

Teryn felt a weight in his chest, one that made him second-guess if he was doing the right thing. What if he was wrong about her? She couldn't have been very old when she killed Queen Linette and Princess Aveline. What if the crimes had been accidental? An unfortunate side effect of her growing clairsentience?

Both murders were deemed the work of poison, he reminded himself. *It doesn't get more intentional than that.*

He'd been tempted a few times now to simply ask her. But even if he did, what did he expect her to say? If she was guilty, she'd lie, which meant he couldn't trust her even if she denied the allegations. And if she *was* guilty, she'd be onto him. She'd know that *he* knew and would flee. Or try to kill him outright.

Besides, it was too late. The evidence was in the letter that was now tucked into his vest pocket. *It is done*, the note said. That was his father's response to the letter he'd sent Berol with. There was a chance this plan wouldn't work, of course. That the King of Khero wouldn't take Arlous' correspondence seriously. That the timing was terrible and nothing would come of Teryn's efforts.

The thought almost gave him relief.

Cora's voice drew him from his internal musings. "I can't imagine you think any better after what you saw me do to those hunters," she said, eying him warily.

He met her gaze, once again painfully aware of his own emotions and the fact that she might be reading them right now. With a sigh, he steeled his composure. "They were bad men and you were alone. You did what you had to do."

She seemed to relax a little at that, but her expression was cold. "I still can't fathom why you're helping me."

"I told you why."

She stopped brushing Valorre's mane. There was no jest in her tone when she said, "I don't entirely trust you."

He straightened, held her stare. "The feeling is mutual." He meant it. But for some unfathomable reason, his lips began to quirk up with a smile.

She lifted her chin and smiled back. "Good. Then we at least understand one another." She strode away from the tree and began heading in the direction of camp, Valorre following in her wake. Her back was turned to him as she paused. "Goodnight, Teryn."

His lungs felt tight at the sound of his name on her lips. *Fear*, he tried to label the sensation. *Revulsion. Hatred. Guilt.* The only one that held even the slightest truth was the last. In reality, the constricting sensation in his chest was something else entirely. It was...pleasant. Not to mention new and terrifying and highly inconvenient. "Goodnight, Cora," he replied and watched her swaying form disappear between the trees.

30

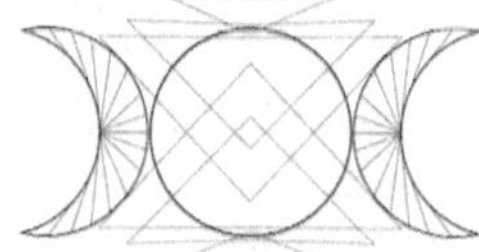

The next day, they followed the hunters' tracks until it was clear they'd entered their hunting radius. Which meant today was the day they'd spy on the camp itself. The prospect tied Cora's stomach in knots, but she tried to focus more on the fact that they were going to get another chance to free the unicorns. So far, she'd only saved two. Unless Valorre counted, which in that case it was three. But the three the Beast had slaughtered...

Cora steeled her resolve as she, Teryn, and Lex tethered their horses in a secluded grove at the far west of the Cambron Pass. Based on the sounds of hunting horns, the group was scouting west today. And if these hunters had similar habits to the previous group, the main party wouldn't be back until just after sundown. They only had about six hours to find the camp before it would be fully occupied.

They finished securing their horses. Cora could feel the tension radiating from Teryn and Lex, even with her shields in place. Valorre too had grown skittish since gaining so close in proximity to the new camp. He stood stiffly behind the horses, ears twitching back and forth. Even Berol seemed wary. She hadn't left Teryn's shoulder for the last hour.

"All right," she said, her own nerves creeping into her voice to give it a slight tremble, "I'll leave now and seek out the camp. Valorre will come with me, but he'll remain out of range once I think I'm close. If I find a decent vantage point to spy on the hunters, I'll stay. If I don't, I'll simply take in the lay of everything—"

"In what world did you think you were going to spy on their camp alone?" Teryn said.

His tone had her bristling. "In what world did you think I'd seek your permission?"

He shook his head. "We're coming with you."

Lex raised his hands, palms forward. "I'd rather stay and watch the horses, thanks."

Teryn rolled his eyes. "Fine. *I'm* coming with you."

Oh, yes, he can come, said Valorre.

"I don't need you," Cora said, ignoring Valorre and folding her arms. "I've done this before, you know."

"That's all well and good, but there's no way I'm waiting behind while you... endanger yourself alone."

Ah, he does have a point to be concerned, Valorre said. *I don't like when you endanger yourself either.*

Whose side are you on? she shot back.

His, obviously, he said without shame.

Cora furrowed her brow. Was that true concern in Teryn's eyes? Or something else? Suspicion, perhaps. She let down her shields just enough to sample his emotions. All she felt were conflicting elements. Fear. Trepidation. Something that made her stomach feel warm. With an exhale, she lifted her shields again. "This is the safest part of our plan."

Lex lifted a finger. "Remind me what this plan is again? Sorry, working together as equals is a foreign concept to me, considering Helios was a royal ass."

She felt a flash of guilt. They'd told her about what it was like working with Prince Helios. How he'd kept more secrets than he'd shared. Her instincts begged her to keep the boys from getting close to her, begged her to do exactly what Helios had done. She'd only let them come along because Teryn had practically begged her. Still...she'd agreed, for better or worse, which meant she now had to suffer the consequences. Even if that meant collaborating with people she'd sooner leave behind.

Valorre came up beside her and nudged her in the shoulder. *Are they not our friends?*

No, she conveyed back.

To the boys, she said, "Today, I will scout. Gather information. Study the camp. Valorre will warn me if he senses danger. I'll try to glean as much as I can about this party's habits. I'll report back everything I find, then we'll form a plan of attack."

"By attack do you mean..." Lex mimed throwing back a drink and tipping his head to the side, eyes closed, tongue lolling from his mouth. When Cora refused to acknowledge him other than thinning her lips, he whispered, "Poison."

Her mind filled with a vision of Paul's prone form at the base of a tree, of James lying by the campfire with blue-tinged lips. The sound of bodies falling, cries of alarm—

She blinked the memories away, but her pulse had kicked up to a rapid tempo. "I don't know."

"Ideally, we'll avoid bloodshed," Teryn said. "Which is why I'm coming with you. Two pairs of eyes are better than one. With both of our perspectives, we'll have a better chance at coming up with a viable plan that puts all of us in the least amount of danger."

She wanted to roll her eyes. Of course the goodly, dutiful prince wanted to avoid bloodshed. He was a fool if he thought it was possible. Perhaps it was a lesson he'd have to learn on his own. "You can help me form a plan but I'm going to scout alone. That's final."

Teryn released a mirthless laugh. He closed the distance between them, his posture mirroring hers until only a foot separated them. Berol ruffled her feathers but remained on his shoulder. Teryn was so much taller than Cora, she had to crane her neck to meet his gaze. "Then I suppose I will too," he said. Before Cora could argue, he brushed past her, took his sword from his saddle, and left the grove. "We'll see who gets there first," he called over his shoulder.

Cora stared after him, jaw hanging on its hinge.

Lex chuckled as he walked over to his horse and took a book and apple from one of his saddlebags. "The two of you are disgusting."

She whirled to face him. "Excuse me?"

"As if you don't know." Lex settled down at the base of a tree, opening his book with one hand and bringing the apple to his mouth with the other. "You must get a kick out of riling him up, making him act all protective like that. It's cute, I guess. But...ugh, so gross."

You know what's gross? Valorre said. *Taking an apple from one's bag without offering me one. I like apples.*

Cora stroked Valorre's neck and glared at Lex. "I promise you, I haven't a clue what you're talking about."

He opened his book and began to read. "We both know he fancies you."

Cora's hand froze on Valorre's soft hide while her heart thudded against her ribcage. No, Lex couldn't be right. It wasn't possible. The concept was utterly preposterous.

The only word that left her lips was, "What?"

He took another bite of apple, muffling his next words. "I saw the two of you sneak off last night after your sexy knife play. If that's what does it for you, I'm happy for you both. Still, I'd rather keep our mission professional."

Cora's cheeks burned hotter than ever before. "This arrangement is strictly professional, trust me."

Lex shrugged and flipped a page. "If you say so. But I must warn you, I've come to like Teryn. He's a good man and a good friend." His eyes shot from his book to her, simmering with threat. "So if you do anything to hurt him, either body or heart, you'll have me to contend with."

She wasn't sure if she should be amused or impressed. Lex was hardly an intimidating specimen, but it was heartwarming that he'd defend his friend like that. More than anything, she was annoyed. Flustered. Irritated beyond belief. With a huff, she shouldered her bow and quiver and left the grove.

～

She and Valorre caught up with Teryn not long after. His smug grin was more than enough to make her second-guess not having taken an alternate route, but it seemed he'd already claimed the best path to their destination. She wouldn't inconvenience herself just because Teryn had a superiority complex.

Or was it more about what Lex had said? Was Teryn's concern over letting her go alone fueled by...

She couldn't even think it.

They followed the hunters' tracks down several different game trails until the wear in the path grew denser, fresher.

I sense them, Valorre said. *My brethren. They're close.*

Then this is as far as you can go. Stay out of sight.

Valorre rippled with worry, but he quickly flitted between the trees.

Teryn startled at the sudden movement, then met Cora's eyes. Up until now, they'd spoken only when necessary and both made a clear effort to keep their distance. "Where did he go?"

"We're too close now. It isn't safe for him to come any nearer. He'll find somewhere to hide where his tracks won't be easy to follow."

Teryn gave only a curt nod and they were on their way again.

WITH ONLY TWO HOURS LEFT UNTIL SUNDOWN, THEY FINALLY FOUND THE CAMP.

Cora's palms were slick with sweat as they crept quietly toward the sound of a crackling fire. Once they caught their first glimpse of the clearing, Teryn fed Berol a strip of dried meat and gestured a finger upward. She immediately took off into the sky. Then he pointed at Cora and himself, silently conveying that they should circle the perimeter in opposite directions. She replied with a nod.

Teryn moved first, one slow step at a time. She wanted to mouth at him to be careful, but she kept the warning to herself. She was still a little peeved at how he'd insisted on accompanying her. However, she had to admit she'd come to feel comforted by his company today. Even now, having another person scouting made her feel safer than she had when she was alone. At first, she'd been worried Teryn would have no talent for stealth, but when she watched him take careful steps, prodding the earth with each foot before fully stepping down, she realized he knew what he was doing. She supposed that was one benefit to being a prince. Royal hunts were both a rite of passage and an expected pastime.

Cora circled the camp, pausing now and then to edge a little closer, stealing glances at what was beyond the veil of underbrush she kept to. No matter how many times she looked, she saw the same thing. A quiet camp. Four cages filled with unicorns. A single guard sitting by the fire. When she and Teryn met at the other side of camp—after they'd both startled at the sudden appearance of the other—she gestured for him to follow her away from the clearing.

Once they were well out of earshot, she whispered, "They have a baby unicorn." Her heart clenched just to say it out loud. She'd nearly stumbled when she'd first caught sight of it. Like the three adult unicorns, the baby was thin and frail. If she had to guess, based on everything she'd seen and overheard and all that Teryn had shared about what he'd learned, the creatures were close to harvest. Either the Beast would come to take them soon or the hunters would carve the horns from the unicorns' heads while the creatures were still alive.

Torture.

Slaughter.

One of the most inhumane acts of violence Cora could imagine.

They might not have days to continue spying. To brew another decoction of belladonna and establish the best way to infiltrate the camp.

"I saw," Teryn said. His lips were pulled into a frown, a disgusted look on his face that told her his feelings were much like her own.

She brought her thumbnail between her teeth to keep her hands from shaking. "And there was only one guard."

"I saw that as well." His voice held a note of concern. It probably wasn't hard to guess what she was thinking. "But he was only a boy."

That too made Cora's chest feel tight. She'd expected to find someone her own age, like James, if not a more grizzled guard like Paul. Instead, they'd found a boy who looked no older than thirteen. He bore no brand that marked him as a criminal. Had no hard look in his eye that made him seem like he was a mercenary in training. Cora would have thought they'd stumbled upon the wrong camp if it weren't for the occupied cages. Not to mention the deep reddish-brown stains that marred the earth before them.

"We have to free those unicorns," she said. "They won't make it much longer. And this," she gestured back in the direction of camp, "is too good of an opportunity to pass up."

Teryn's brow knitted. "Does it not seem *too* easy, though?"

She had to admit it did seem too good to be true. Still, she'd looked for signs that someone else was waiting out of sight, but there was nothing. No one. Every part of her itched to act. To finally do more than watch and wait. To save the unicorns for the ones she'd failed. Perhaps she was being a bit reckless, and had she been alone, she'd probably have chosen caution. But she wasn't alone. She had Teryn.

"We have to at least try, don't we? It's not yet sundown. The hunters are still far away." The last hunting horn they'd heard had been distant.

"We can try," Teryn finally said, "but we aren't killing the boy. Instead, we do this my way."

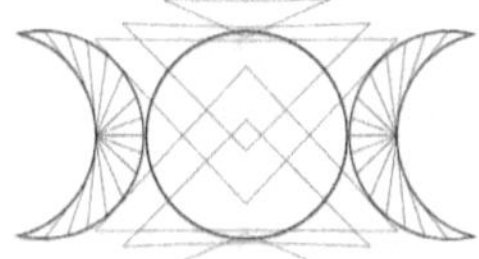

31

Teryn's way, it turned out, was humiliating. And yet, Cora agreed, having no better idea of her own. After stashing her bow and arrows, she circled the camp and paused just outside the clearing. The young guard was still by the fire in nearly the same position she'd last seen him—his posture slumped with an air of boredom, the side of his face resting on his hand as he poked the burning logs with a stick. Cora took a deep breath, untucked her skirts from her belt so they no were no longer wrapped around her legs, and twisted her expression into one of distress. She stumbled into the camp, feigning sobs.

The boy immediately rose to his feet. His hand flew to the hilt of a dagger at his belt, but when his eyes swept over Cora, he withdrew the hand. "Ma'am," he said, eyes wide.

She fell to her knees, her hair streaming around her. "You must help me," she cried.

He came closer. "What's wrong? What are you doing out here?"

She lifted her face, lips pulled into a pout. "I was kidnapped," she said, her voice high and feminine and breathy, "by...by...by bandits." Her words dissolved into a wail.

The boy stared at her, face pale and bewildered as if he couldn't comprehend what to do with her. Just then, a figure came up behind him. Before the boy even had a clue, Teryn hooked an arm around his throat and squeezed the sides between his bicep and forearm. The boy flailed but was out in a matter of seconds. Teryn aided his fall and settled him on the ground. With a nod to Cora, she rose, and they jogged over to the cages. Wordlessly, they got to work, severing the ropes that bound the frames. Cora opened the baby unicorn's cage first, then the one next to it. Soon all the cages were open, and all the unicorns were darting away.

We did it, she conveyed to Valorre, hoping he was still close enough to hear her.

If you can communicate with them, direct them to go east so they don't run into the hunters.

She felt Valorre's reply as a trill of joy, one that had Cora's lips stretching into a grin.

Teryn tugged her arm, nodding his head toward the edge of camp. She followed him out of the clearing to where she'd stashed her weapons. Her pulse was a roar in her ears as she shouldered her bow and quiver. They kept their pace as mindful as they could, but Cora felt like they were running for the way her body buzzed with elation and terror in the wake of their rescue. They'd done it. They'd truly done it. She had to stifle her desire to laugh.

Teryn stopped suddenly before her.

"What—" Then she saw it.

The baby unicorn was just ahead, its body quivering. Its thin legs quaked as it tried to take a step, but it seemed too overcome with fear or confusion.

"Seven gods," Teryn cursed. "The poor thing."

Valorre, there's a baby. She's so frail. She seems confused.

There came no reply. He was likely too busy guiding the others. Which left only her.

She took a slow step toward the tiny unicorn, her tawny fur thin and clinging to her bones. The creature startled, freezing in place as her eyes locked on Cora's. Cora halted as well. Lowering her shields, she opened her senses to the unicorn. She was immediately struck by panic, a desperation to find someone very important to her. Cora's throat constricted, and she was tempted to close the link if only to free herself from the emotions. Instead, she kept her senses open and tried to move them in the opposite direction. It had been effortless to converse with Valorre, but she'd never experienced the phenomenon with any other unicorn since. This time, though, she had to try.

Easy, she tried to convey, forcing her own emotions to calm, to exude safety and protection. The unicorn's energy softened a little. Cora took another small step. *I'm not going to hurt you. I'm here to help you. If you follow me, I'll take you to my friend. He's just like you.*

She filled her mind with thoughts of Valorre, letting warmth and kindness radiate from her heart, down her palms, into the space between them.

The creature calmed further and took a step forward. Cora mirrored her every move until they were almost close enough to touch. Then, crouching down, Cora extended her hands. The unicorn tottered the rest of the way on her tiny, shaky legs until Cora's hands met her hide. Cora nearly choked on a sob when she felt how prominent the unicorn's ribs were beneath her palms. "It's all right," she whispered to her, voice thick with emotion. "We're going to help you."

Remembering Teryn's presence, she cast a glance over her shoulder. Teryn's expression was nearly painful to witness. His eyes were glazed as he stared at the unicorn. He met Cora's eyes then, and she smiled at him. She wasn't sure why, only that she wanted to erase his pained countenance and remind him that they'd done something good, something worth celebrating. He smiled back, which was perhaps an even sadder look.

Berol dove down from overhead and landed on Teryn's shoulder. There was something uneasy about the way she perched, in the splay of her wings as she nipped Teryn's cheek. Cora didn't need to be bonded to the falcon to know the bird was delivering a warning.

A hunting horn sounded, shattering the air. It was too close. Far closer than the last one had been. The baby unicorn startled and made to dart away, but Cora lifted her in her arms. She wasn't exactly a creature made for carrying, but she was so thin, her weight was hardly a burden to bear. "Shhh," Cora whispered. "Easy."

Teryn ran to her, and Berol launched back into the sky to circle overhead. He angled his head in the opposite direction of the horn, and Cora followed him. They crept away, their pace hurried. "I can carry her," Teryn offered.

"It's all right," she said. "She feels comfortable with me."

Another horn blast, this one from straight ahead.

Then another off to the side.

Cora's heart leapt into her throat. They were surrounded.

"We need to get out of here fast," Teryn said.

He was right, but no matter where they turned, another echoing horn would sound. She glanced between the boughs. It wasn't yet sundown. The hunters shouldn't be back yet. But, of course, she'd chosen risk over caution today instead of ensuring she knew exactly when to expect them back. Now Cora and Teryn could be caught. The hunters would be upon them. They'd seize the unicorn and Cora would have failed again.

Her legs begged to run while another part of her burned for a fight. Teryn was the one who'd insisted on avoiding bloodshed, while she'd only grown more furious at seeing what these hunters had done to the creature in her arms. Her heart screamed for vengeance. Her head, on the other hand, reminded her they had no idea how many men they could be facing. It was only her and Teryn—her quiver of arrows and his sword—against what would undoubtedly be insurmountable odds.

Then I fight to the death, part of her said.

No, I flee and hope I make it out alive, said another.

She felt torn in two, unsure which instinct to heed. She'd followed her impulse to stay and fight when they'd thrown caution to the wind and rescued the unicorns right away. Had that been the right choice? Or the wrong one? Regardless of what was right or wrong then, which choice would serve her best now?

A wave of vertigo seized her, forcing her to stagger her feet. But it helped her remember the soil that stood beneath her, acting as a source of stability. It reminded her of other things too. Of the air surrounding her, filling her lungs. Of the fire that was her fury. The water that was blood. The elements. Her magic.

The last thing she wanted at a time like this was to slow down and turn inward. Not when she was feeling so frantic.

But, as Salinda always said, magic was strengthened by challenge, and the simplest challenge of all was doing what felt the hardest in any given moment. If there was ever a time for magic to prove stronger than weapons, it would be now.

Fighting through her more predominant instincts, she closed her eyes and focused on her breath. She detached her emotional bond from the unicorn to focus instead on the feel of a soft wind dancing over her skin, the sensation of her hair prickling at the back of her neck. She noted the way the ground felt beneath her feet, firm and strong but with subtle give. A sense of calm went over her, telling her she'd tapped into her deepest Art. Extending her senses around her, she sought nearby feeling. At first, she felt only the unicorn and Teryn, but she brushed past them to clusters of energies beyond. She was struck by a cacophony of emotions belonging to several others—excitement, trepidation, desire, hunger. There was a darkness to these energies, a density that made her stomach turn. At least half a dozen hunters were closing in on Cora and Teryn. A spike of alarm threatened to break her composure, but she breathed it away.

Another horn sounded, and Teryn placed his palm on her back, angling her away from it. "Cora, we need to go."

She put a hand on his forearm to still him. To tell him to stay. To do what, she still wasn't sure.

Hide.

The feeling originated deep in her gut, firm and calm and certain. Opening her eyes, she saw a wide tree straight ahead, its boughs low and dense. It wouldn't hide them, not if the hunters drew close enough, but she was going to try.

She met Teryn's puzzled expression. "You're going to have to trust me," she said.

"How so?"

She tugged him toward the tree, following the internal pull she felt with every fiber of her being. The baby unicorn struggled in her grasp, but she made a soothing noise at her. "You're going to have to trust me too."

The question was...could she trust herself?

She shook the doubt from her mind and hefted the unicorn closer to Teryn. "Help me hold her."

"What are we doing?" Teryn's whisper was laced with terror, but he helped her hold the unicorn between them.

With a deep breath, she said. "Close your eyes. Whatever you do, don't say a word. Don't move, no matter what you hear. Put..." She swallowed hard. "Put your free arm around me and don't let go until I tell you to."

His eyes searched hers, his face pale. "I don't understand."

Another horn blast.

The hunters would find them in a matter of seconds.

She held his gaze, trying to convey everything she was feeling. The urgency. The hope. The gut sensation that told her *this*—no matter how absurd it seemed— was what they had to do.

Finally, he stepped closer, the baby unicorn the only thing that separated their chests. He closed his eyes and hooked his free arm around her waist.

Her eyelids closed next, and she reached out for the trunk of the tree. Her palm met rough bark, thrummed with the pulse of its life force, of the elements surging through its roots, its branches, its leaves. She drew her attention to her feet, to the firmness of the ground below, and felt another thrum. The tree's roots extended deep underground, merging with the soil, the water that fed them, the air and sunlight that helped them grow strong. Cora pressed harder against the tree, imagined she was no different. She too was nourished by the same elements. They fed her body the same way they fed her Art. She was no different from the tree, her skin so like bark she might as well be a sapling. A steady energy began to pulse through her, stilling her mind. She was aware of two distinct energies pressed close to her and extended this same feeling outward.

They were one and the same.

She, the tree, the boy, the fae.

The heartbeat of the tree was her own. Hers was the unicorn's. The unicorn's was the boy's. The boy's was hers. She could almost hear it pounding through her, vibrating up the hand that held her waist, echoing the beat in her chest. When she breathed, he did too. When they breathed, so too did the unicorn, the tree, the soil, the sky. Everything breathed.

There was nothing here but a tree.

One with vast root systems that shuddered beneath the soil, stirring the top layer of dirt until not a footprint could be seen where once there'd been many. No longer was there a sign of the boy, the girl, and the small fae creature.

They'd never been there at all.

Just a tree.

A tree.

Only a tree.

The tree hardly acknowledged the men that stalked by. They prowled like wolves, eyes keen, but they found not what they sought. Nothing but a wood empty of everything but what should be there. The tree didn't count in minutes or seconds, but time did pass. Soon—or maybe not so soon—the men passed too, shoulders slumped with disappointment of a catch not had.

Only then did the tree unravel.

Only then did one become two, and two separated into three.

32

Teryn didn't know how many minutes had passed. All he knew was that he couldn't look away from Cora. He'd only obeyed her order to close his eyes for a few moments before his eyelids flew open. At first, it had been out of panic, but as her face filled his vision, calm settled over him. They were so close he could count every one of Cora's dark eyelashes, every freckle dancing over her nose. His hand felt warm on her back, and where they both held the unicorn, their arms touched. An *otherness* had surrounded them then, something Teryn wasn't sure he'd ever be able to explain. He didn't see it with his eyes or feel it with his senses. It was just there. The indescribable buzz of magic.

He hadn't known what Cora was doing, had seen nothing to explain what made the hunters walk by without giving them a second glance. He'd only seen *her*. For one strange moment, he'd felt connected to her in a way that defied reason. He'd felt her heart thrum as his own. Felt her breath move through his lungs. It was unsettling and yet completely noninvasive. He'd welcomed it. Yearned for it.

But now the *otherness* was beginning to fade with every breath. His pulse became his own, no longer entangled with Cora's and the unicorn's. He realized Cora's eyes were open now too and were locked on his. Slowly, she pulled her hand away from the tree trunk, but still, they didn't separate. She said something to him then, but his mind was too befuddled to comprehend it.

"What?"

"You're still holding on to me," she whispered, her voice unsteady.

He gulped, finding his tongue heavy as he searched for words. "You said not to let you go until you said so."

"Oh." A soft smile crossed her lips, a hint of a blush coloring her cheeks. "You can let me go now."

He held on a beat longer, then slowly slid his hand from around her waist. The baby unicorn, who'd grown surprisingly calm in the wake of such strange events, was all that connected them.

"I can carry her," Teryn said. "I think it's safe to say she feels comfortable enough with me now."

"All right." Teryn was surprised she didn't argue. She slipped her arm from the unicorn and stepped away. Teryn felt oddly cold. Empty. Whatever had happened at the tree...it had severely messed with his mind.

He wasn't even sure why he'd done what she'd told him to. He could have waited until the perfect moment and shoved her before the hunters—if that was even who those men had been. He'd been too focused on Cora when the figures had walked by, but when he'd first heard the hunting horns, he'd known his plan had worked. His father had sent word to King Dimetreus. The king knew they were heading to this camp next, knew Cora would try to rescue the unicorns. Because that was what Teryn's letter to his father had said.

I'll bring her to the Cambron Pass camp in exchange for her bounty.

He'd suspected his plan had worked as soon as he and Cora had stalked the camp and found only a young boy guarding it. Terror had surged through him then, even though he should have been pleased. He should have wanted his plan to come to fruition, right?

After that, he'd expected an ambush at any moment. It hadn't come. Part of him had hoped—as nonsensical as the hope was—that maybe his letter hadn't reached the king. Or perhaps it hadn't been taken seriously, or the king hadn't been prepared to react on such short notice. Relief had washed over him as they'd freed the unicorns, but it all fled the moment he'd heard the horns.

And now...

Now he didn't know what to think. He'd allowed Cora to hide them. Had *wanted* her to hide them. Even with his mind growing sharper, clearer, he had no desire to shout, to call back the hunters, to turn her in.

"We must go," Cora said and started off with caution.

If he took one step away from the camp, he knew what he was leaving behind.

500,000 *sovas*. Enough to save his kingdom.

All he had to do was turn in a wanted murderer.

Cora glanced over her shoulder, brow furrowed as she noticed his hesitation. She held out her hand, her tattooed palm extended his way. "Come on," she whispered. Her eyes were bright, her lips curled into a soft smile. She'd changed after what had happened at the tree. Whatever magic she'd used, she glowed with it now, radiated with it in unseen ways.

Teryn took a deep breath, knowing he was about to seal his fate. Hefting the unicorn in both arms, he returned her grin and followed after her.

～

CORA FELT ALIVE IN A WAY SHE'D NEVER BEEN BEFORE. HER USE OF MAGIC HAD DEFIED reason, obliterated coincidence, and negated any chance that she, Teryn, and the baby unicorn had evaded notice by happenstance alone. She'd made them *invisible*. Just like witch lore claimed was possible.

She understood now why it was referred to as quiet magic. Sure, her feat of invisibility was incredible to her, but to the hunters or anyone else that could have walked by that tree...to them it was like it never happened.

The aftereffects surged through her veins, pulsed in every line of ink on her skin. Resisting her instincts to run had been hard. Choosing magic over her bow had been harder. In overcoming her personal challenge, her magic had grown stronger. It still felt quiet and there was much more for her to learn, but now she believed the possibilities she'd once turned her nose up at.

Teryn too seemed changed. She'd sensed a shift in his emotions, from something dark and heavy to a lightness akin to relief. He still clung to a hint of the sorrow she'd glimpsed right after they'd rescued the unicorn, but his steps were lighter now, his smile freer. Perhaps it was just the comfort that came with knowing they'd escaped the hunters.

Valorre found them not long after. He was frantic with worry over not having warned them about the approaching hunters. Just as Cora had thought, he'd been out of range while he'd tried to direct his freed brethren to safer grounds. Thankfully, Berol had been there, even though her warning hadn't given them much of an advantage. She flew overhead now, keeping her distance from Teryn while he carried the unicorn.

What should we do with the baby? Cora asked Valorre.

The unicorn went still, ears twitching. Finally, he said, *I think her mother is near. Or...near enough. I can feel one of my kind lingering somewhere in the pass. She knows it isn't safe but she's...seeking something.*

Can you take us to her?

Valorre considered that. *No, the mother will fear you. I will take her myself.*

Cora was worried the baby unicorn might still be too shaken to walk. She turned to Teryn. "You can try putting her down."

He did as told, gently setting the unicorn on her hooves. She stumbled a little, legs splayed, but managed to keep her balance. She was no longer trembling like she'd been outside the camp.

Valorre took a few steps closer.

The baby lowered her head, posture startled. After a few moments of warily examining the much larger unicorn, she took a step toward him. Then another. Her gait was steady as she closed the remaining distance. Valorre gave her an affectionate nuzzle, then lifted his head toward Cora. *She will be fine. I will take her now.*

Cora's heart clenched as she watched Valorre guide the tiny creature away.

Teryn came up beside her. Berol was settled on his shoulder, preening. "We really did it," he said. "We actually freed four unicorns."

She turned to face him. "Thank you for helping me," she said, finding the words easier to say than she expected. She didn't want to admit that she'd been wrong in her hesitation to let him accompany her, but...perhaps she had been.

"You're welcome," he said, and again a hint of sorrow crept into the edges of her awareness. She strengthened her shields, blocking it completely. After what she'd accomplished at the tree, she needed a reprieve.

They made their way back toward camp, the sun barely a hint of light on the horizon. A comfortable silence fell between them, which was such a stark contrast to the tense quiet they'd kept earlier that day. They were nearing camp when Teryn whirled to face her.

Cora pulled up short. His expression told her that perhaps the silence had only been comfortable on her end. She frowned. "What is it?"

"We should leave this area tonight."

"What? Why would we do that?"

He folded his arms, shoulders tense. "The hunters will know someone knocked out their guard and freed the unicorns. They might try to track us. If not tonight, then tomorrow."

Cora's eyes widened, all of her pleasant feelings evaporating. "You're the one who wanted to avoid bloodshed. You only just now realize your plan has put us at a greater risk?"

"I'm sorry," he rushed to say. "Let's leave at once. Go...far from here."

She backed up a step, eyes narrowing. "My mission isn't done. You saw the map. There are still numerous other hunting parties. I can't let them continue to hunt unicorns."

"What are you planning to do? Poison all of them? What about when they're replaced with new recruits? These men are mercenaries and convicted criminals. There's no shortage of more like them."

Cora felt a crushing weight fall over her. He was right. It was too much. Still, she shook the overwhelming feeling from her heart and lifted her chin. "I will do whatever I can."

"To what end? You can't poison them all. Sooner or later, they'll catch on. They'll be waiting for you. This...this isn't sustainable. You can't do this on your own."

She threw her hands in the air. "You knew that when you asked to come with me. Is that not the very reason you begged to aid my efforts?"

He clenched his jaw, giving no answer.

She rolled her eyes with a scoff. "We ran into one close call and now you realize this isn't all fun and games. You should have known from the start that this wouldn't be some glamorous quest where you save the damsel in distress and come home the shining hero, bearing not a single scratch. I meant it when I said that I don't need you, but..." Her throat went dry. She tried to swallow her next words down, but they burst from her lips before she could stop them. "I liked having you around today."

His expression softened, eyes turning down at the corners, but he wouldn't meet her gaze. "Cora..." His voice was soft, strained.

She took a step closer, her heart pounding in her chest. With a slow exhale, she lowered her shields just long enough to feel his turmoil. His emotions were too jumbled to untangle completely, but she identified guilt. Shame. Fear. It left a bitter taste in her mouth. "What is it, Teryn? What aren't you telling me?"

Slowly, he lifted his eyes and met hers, his expression pure agony. "Did you kill Queen Linette and Princess Aveline?"

Her breath left her lungs. She was more stunned than if he'd slapped her. For several moments, all she could do was stare. Suspicion crawled up her spine, raking claws through her heart. "How long have you known?"

He paled. "You did it then."

She took a step back, a spike of fury sending heat to her cheeks. "No, of course I didn't."

His eyes narrowed as he watched her, his arms stiff at his side. Berol too stared from her perch on his shoulder, wings slightly lifted. Teryn's fingers flinched, a subtle movement toward his sheathed sword. She went to reach for her bow only to realize she'd already wrapped her hand around it. When had she done that? Suddenly she understood *that* was why his posture was suddenly defensive—because *she'd* reached for a weapon first. And yet he kept his hand open at his side, ready to fight should it come to that, but not willing to make the first move.

It was almost painful to force her hand away from her bow, to ball her fingers into fists. As soon as she did, Teryn visibly relaxed. Berol ruffled her feathers and nestled back down.

"I was framed," she said, voice quavering with restraint, "by Duke Morkai."

His eyes went wide. "The man orchestrating the hunt for unicorns? He framed you for murder?"

She nodded.

"So, what you're doing with the unicorns, with the hunters. It's...personal."

Another nod.

He studied her again, and she could feel the doubt pouring off of him. Of course he wouldn't believe her. How could anyone take the word of a poison-wielding witch over one of the most powerful men in Khero?

She waited for him to react. To ask her to prove her innocence. To sneer, argue, or condemn.

But he didn't.

"All right," he said, his voice barely above a whisper. Then once more, clearer, louder. "All right. Then it's even more important that we leave at once." Without another word, he stormed off.

She blinked in his wake, confused by his reaction. He was nearly swallowed by shadows far ahead by the time she started following after him. She had to jog to keep up with him when she reached his side. "What's going on, Teryn?"

He said nothing, only quickened his pace. It was enough to send Berol launching off his shoulder to follow them from above instead.

Her heart was a thundering, rioting mess as they marched into camp.

They pulled up short.

Lex stood as soon as he saw them. His eyes were wide as he searched their faces. Then his gaze swept over the five figures who stood silently around them. "I have no idea who these people are," he said, voice pitched with fright.

Cora, however, knew exactly who they were. Four of them wore black armor etched with a crescent moon. Guards. The fifth wore an elegant black coat embroidered with gold geometric designs that ran down the front and hems. Black leather gloves adorned his hands, and in one he gripped a gentleman's cane topped with an enormous amber crystal.

Cora's eyes locked on his face.

She recognized his black hair, his arched brows, and the pale shade of his blue irises. His cheekbones were sharp, his jaw sharper.

"Morkai," she said through her teeth.

The duke ignored Cora but nodded graciously at Teryn. "King Dimetreus was both surprised and pleased by your correspondence. Thank you ever so much for finding her. Your reward will be generous indeed."

Cora's gaze shot to Teryn. She saw the guilt written in his eyes and finally understood what she'd sensed all along. Her shoulders sagged as her heart crumbled inside her chest, pierced with icy talons of betrayal.

Morkai faced her, the smug tilt to his lips revealing how greatly he relished her pain. "Hello, Princess Aveline. It's been a while."

33

Cora hadn't been called by her first name in six years. Perhaps that was why —when next she dreamed—she saw not the shadowed halls of her nightmare but her childhood bedroom. She was face-down upon her bed, torn between shame and rage, when she heard her door open.

"Aveline Corasande Caelan," a deep voice said from behind her, tone pitched with warning.

Cora froze. Her brother only ever used her full name when she was in trouble. Steeling her nerves, she pushed herself to sitting and faced King Dimetreus. "I did nothing wrong."

With slow steps, he crossed the distance between them and took a seat next to her. His voice softened. "You acted brash at dinner tonight."

Her heart sank as she met his gaze. His dark eyes were gentle, a warm smile on his lips. With his shoulder-length brown hair and olive complexion, he reminded her so much of Mother. Only his nose and the stubble on his jaw resembled their father. Being reminded of her dearly departed parents made her wish he was angry instead. His sympathy only increased her guilt.

Still, she refused to back down. "Linette acted brash first and you did nothing to defend me."

"Linette is my wife and I love her dearly. I love you as well, Aveline, but you must learn to respect your sister-in-law. She is your queen. I need you to apologize to her."

She bristled. "But she's the one who lied. She's not with child, Dimi."

He chuckled. "Dearest sister, you're too young to speak on such matters. You know nothing about children or their conception. Just because her belly has yet to—"

"I know how babies are made and I know how they're born."

He gave her a patronizing look. "I assure you, sister, it isn't a stork."

"No, of course it isn't." She lifted her chin and put her hands on her hips. "When a man and woman feel desirous, a woman lifts her skirts and a man becomes engorged—"

He launched to his feet, nearly tripping in the process. "Seven devils, where did you hear that?"

She blushed, realizing she must have said something improper. She was always getting in trouble for things like that. "I overheard Lady Paulette discussing a novel with Lady Madeline."

"Banish such thoughts from your mind," he said, wagging a finger. His cheeks were as red as beets. "Regardless of what you think you know, you mustn't have acted as you did at dinner."

She stood and stomped a foot. "I didn't even want to be there. Master Benedict dragged me."

"Aveline," he said, his tone turning sharper, "you promised to attend dinner and you showed up late. To add insult to injury, you made a scene and upset Linette. She left the dining hall in tears. She's been inconsolable, sobbing in bed ever since. What you said to her was cruel."

She rolled her eyes. "I didn't actually curse her. I'm not a witch. I don't know how to curse people."

"It doesn't matter. What you said scared her. It's important that she is kept comfortable to keep the baby safe."

She had to bite the inside of her cheek to keep from arguing the fact that the queen was a liar, that she wasn't with child and had never been. She'd learned her lesson, though. Her brother was obviously never going to listen. She'd have to wait until later to say *I told you so*. Perhaps in the meantime she could try to sort out why a queen would feel the need to lie about such a silly thing in the first place. She knew queens were expected to bear sons, but she couldn't quite grasp the significance or the pressure involved. Maybe her brother was right. Maybe she was too young to speak on such complicated matters.

But still...

"I don't want to apologize."

Her brother's expression softened again as he took her hand in his. "I know, but you're a princess. The older you get the more you'll come to understand that being royal often means doing a whole host of things you'd rather not do. Please, Cora."

The name made her breath hitch. Only their mother had ever called her Cora, and usually only when they were alone. It was a nickname taken from her middle name—Corasande—a name that represented her mother's homeland in the Southern Isles. If she was being honest, she preferred Cora to Aveline. Aveline sounded like a stuffy old queen like Linette while Cora was fit for someone wild and free. Like whom she'd prefer to be.

She knew Dimetreus was manipulating her by using that name, but she found it effective nonetheless. "Fine," she ground out, "I'll apologize. But only for pretending to curse her. Everything else I said was true."

Her brother's expression hardened, but he released a resigned sigh. "It's a start. Now, get going."

"I have to do it now?"

His only answer was a pointed look.

Shoulders slumped, she dragged her feet down the hall in the direction of the queen's chambers. Linette had separate quarters from the king. Cora was rehearsing a stiff apology when her feet stopped moving of their own accord. A dark and hollow feeling formed in the pit of her stomach. She took another few steps but the sense of wrongness increased, prickling the hair on her arms—

"Your Highness."

She startled at the voice and found the queen's youngest maid brushing by, arms laden with a serving tray bearing tea and cookies. The girl was about Cora's age. "Where are you taking that?" she asked, even though she already knew the answer.

The maid paused and blushed, shifting anxiously from foot to foot. "Queen Linette, Your Highness."

Cora walked up to her and extended her hands toward the tray. "I'll take it."

"But...but it's what I'm supposed to do." The maid stepped back, expression struck with something between terror and indignation. "A princess cannot carry a tray."

Cora cut the girl a glare, but she only blinked back at her. With a grumbling sigh, Cora unclasped a bracelet—one of many cumbersome, shiny baubles she was forced to wear—from around her wrist and held it out to the girl. "Payment."

"I...I can't take that."

"You can and you will. That's an order. Now take it and go. I need to *apologize to the queen.*" She said the last part with a hefty dose of mockery.

The maid seemed too stunned to do anything but obey, her hands trembling as she passed the tray to Cora and accepted the bracelet in return. A flash of greed lit the girl's eyes once her fingers curled fully around the item. Then, with a vibrant smile, she curtsied and darted down the opposite end of the hall.

With a proper offer of apology in hand, Cora continued to the queen's rooms. Only then did she recall the eerie feeling that had first halted her progress. It crept into her bones once more, echoed through her blood. Shadows darkened the glow of lamplight lining the corridor. Sound became hollow as the halls emptied, dimmed, and closed in tight around her.

Cora remembered she was dreaming. With that realization came a reminder of everything she knew was coming. She struggled against her dream-self, tried to force her feet to stop. But the small version of her continued on, step after step, even as her terror grew.

Her next step brought her to the door.

The bedroom.

The blood.

Duke Morkai whirled to face her. With a devious grin, he lifted the queen's blood from the sheets. It rose to meet his palm in thin red ribbons that he played like the strings of a lute.

Cora dropped the tray.

Her scream jolted her awake.

～

SHE BLINKED INTO DIM LIGHT, FOUND SOMETHING SOFT AGAINST HER CHEEK. THE next thing she noticed was a rocking motion. She lifted her head, saw a shaft of pale sunlight peeking between a velvet curtain and a small window. Was it already sunrise? Another turn of her head revealed a door, leather-covered walls, and a seat beneath her draped with furs. She was in a coach. That explained the constant rocking. Perhaps that had been what had woken her. Not her scream but the jostling of the carriage.

She pushed herself to sit upright, surprised to find her hands unbound. Someone sat across from her, their upper body cast in shadow, but Cora didn't bother waiting for her eyes to adjust. Instead, she lunged for the door—

The bottom of a black cane smacked into the door, an inch from where her hand had been. She reeled back as the figure leaned forward. She wasn't surprised when Morkai's face was illuminated beneath the shaft of sunlight. He watched her with his silver-blue eyes, his lips lifted in an arrogant smile. "You'll find every exit locked, Aveline. Or should I call you Cora? It seems that's the name you gave the prince."

Cora's blood boiled at his mention of Teryn. It didn't matter that he'd seemed shocked when Morkai had mentioned her true name, nor did she care about the regret that had clouded his energy when their eyes met. What mattered was that he'd betrayed her. That he did nothing when Morkai's guards surrounded her. One of them had pressed a cloth to her mouth, filling her nose with an acrid scent. It was the last thing she recalled.

Her head spun. She resisted the urge to press a palm to her forehead and instead burned Morkai with a glare. "You made a mistake in locking yourself in here with me unbound."

He scoffed, eyes falling to the ink marking her forearms. "You're no threat to me. That's why you're unbound."

She assessed his relaxed posture, the way he sat with one leg crossed over the other, his crystal-topped cane resting in his lap. One hand stroked one of the crystal's facets while his other arm was draped over the back of his seat. He was the epitome of overconfidence. Everything about him was exactly as she remembered. His voice, his smug grin, the color of his eyes, his...face.

That was when she realized he hadn't aged a day. She remembered him looking ancient in her eyes six years ago, the same way all adults looked old to a child, but that didn't explain why he looked barely five years her senior now.

"How have you not aged?"

"Blood," he said, giving no further explanation. Then he added, "It's all right if you like what you see."

"I don't," she said through her teeth. It wasn't a lie. He might look young and beautiful, but it only fueled her disgust. Her arms begged her to reach across the coach and tear Morkai limb from limb. Then she'd climb from the carriage, find Teryn, and do the same to him. Unfortunately, she'd been disarmed while she was unconscious. Her bow and quiver were gone as was her belt, taking with it her knife and dagger. That left only magic.

She breathed in deep, letting her rage pour through her, directing it down her palms, to...to...

The blood left her face. She felt nothing.

Shaking her head, she tried again, breathing in deep. Her lungs, however, felt too shallow and her mind refused to stay in one place, refused to let her focus on her breath. She breathed in again, seeking any sign that her magic was there. A light tingle ran over her palms but that was it. Her magic lingered, just below the surface, but it felt tangled. Smothered.

By what? Was this Morkai's doing?

Morkai's grin widened. "I told you, Aveline. You're no threat to me."

She bit back her retort and forced herself to mirror his composure. Leaning back in her seat, she asked with feigned calm, "What do you intend to do with me?"

His answer came easily. "I'm taking you home to Ridine Castle, of course."

She huffed a dark laugh. "To be sent back to the dungeon? To be executed at last? Why did you even bother freeing me from the dungeon six years ago if you were only going to hunt me down later?"

"Whether you return to the dungeon upon our arrival at the castle is up to you. Should I will it, I can have you reclaim your rightful place as princess."

Her stomach flipped. She'd never dreamed of regaining her title. Had never wanted it back. Not after everything that had happened. Not after her brother had turned his back on her and condemned her. She'd let her old identity die the night she fled the castle and never said a word of the truth to anyone. Never enlightened any of the Forest People who'd brought up the poor princess' death.

"I can tell you don't believe me," Morkai said, "but I promise you it's true."

He was right. She didn't believe a word he said. "The world thinks I'm dead. How do you plan on resurrecting me?"

"That's a simple matter, for here you are breathing. Try bringing someone who's truly dead back to the realm of the living. That, my dear, is a far greater challenge but one I daresay will not be out of my reach for long."

Her mouth went dry at his words. She hadn't a clue what he was talking about, but it left a queasy feeling in her stomach. It did bring to mind a question that had haunted her these last six years.

"Who did you kill in my stead?"

"Just a maid wearing Princess Aveline's bracelet. So, in a way, you killed her. I couldn't have chosen better myself."

Fury surged through her. She balled her hands tight and considered launching herself at him. She may not have weapons, but she had fingernails. Teeth. Arms for punching and legs for kicking—

"Easy," he said. His knuckles went white on his cane. "One move from you and I'll rescind my offer to restore your title."

She deepened her glare but forced herself to ease back against her seat. Not because she was interested in hearing his offer but because she still had many questions. "I don't understand how you did it. My brother thinks a maid killed his sister, but I'm the one he convicted, knowing full well who I was when he found me with the queen."

"He was so deep in grief, he knew not what he saw. I reminded him of that when we found dear little Aveline's body. She was so swollen from whatever poison the maid had given her that she was barely recognizable. It wasn't hard to get him to accept a new truth."

A cold shiver ran down her spine. "You brainwashed him."

"Your brother has always been a weak-minded man."

"And yet you serve him most loyally."

His eyes took on a vicious gleam. "Do I, Aveline? Or does he serve me in every way?"

She swallowed hard. In all these years, she'd let herself despise her brother. Morkai had always held the greatest fault in her mind, but Dimetreus had stood by and accepted lie after lie while ignoring every truth she'd told him. When her brother found her with his dead wife's body, he didn't hesitate for more than a second before he condemned her. He heard not a word as she argued her case. He shed not a tear as he had his guards drag her into a cell beneath the castle.

What if Dimetreus' reaction hadn't been entirely his fault? If Morkai could manipulate the king into changing his own memories...what else could he do?

"What do you want from me?" she asked, a slight tremble building in her voice. Whether it was from fear or anger she knew not.

"To talk."

"You must want to do more than talk to offer 500,000 *sovas* for my capture. How did you do it anyway? The poster. My likeness couldn't have been sketched on a guess."

He rubbed his amber crystal again. "I kept a drop of your blood."

Her eyes went wide. It took all her restraint to keep from flexing the palm he'd once cut. "Why did you take it in the first place?"

"That's not for you to know right now. Besides, I'm not finished answering your previous question. I kept a drop of your blood which was just enough to catch glimpses of you over the years."

"Why did you..."

"Why did I want to check in on you?" He barked an indignant laugh. "How can you ask that, Aveline? Do you think I released you from the dungeon to be cruel? You were a child. I was curious to know if you survived."

She noted that he said he was *curious* if she survived, not that he *cared* if she had.

"By the way, where have you been these last six years?" His gaze swept over her briefly, landing again on her tattoos. "Those are interesting markings. Faeryn *insigmora*."

Her heart leapt into her throat. She hadn't expected him to recognize her tattoos. He was a dark witch, a mage, not a...

Her eyes wandered over his face, taking in his uncommon beauty. His sharp cheekbones. The slightest blue tinge to his black hair. And his ears...how had she never noticed the angled edge before? They weren't exactly pointed, but neither were they totally round. Could he be of Faeryn descent?

She shook the thoughts from her mind. What mattered most was that he'd asked where she'd been. That meant there was a chance the Forest People were safe from his knowledge. "Don't you already know where I've been? You confessed to spying on me through a drop of my blood."

He glanced at his nails with disinterest. "I saw your face, not your surroundings."

Relief swept over her, but she hid it behind a shrug. "I've been right where you left me. In the woods."

"In the woods," he echoed, his eyes narrowing, "where you just so happened to become marked with *insigmora*."

She held his gaze, her lips pursed tight.

The coach came to a stop.

"Ah, we're here." He leaned forward with a quirked brow. "What's it going to be, Aveline? Do I escort you from this coach as my prisoner or a princess?"

She bit her lip as a spike of panic laced through her. She still had so many unanswered questions. The hunters. The Beast. The unicorns.

"Only one of those choices will let you see your brother again," he said, a hint of taunting in his voice.

Her pulse quickened at his mention of Dimetreus. Her brother. The king. A man she'd come to hate almost as much as the duke. A man who may or may not have been controlled by a powerful mage.

There was only one way to find out. She took a deep breath and hoped Morkai couldn't hear her lie.

"I want to be a princess again."

"Well then," Morkai said, opening the coach door. "Welcome home."

34

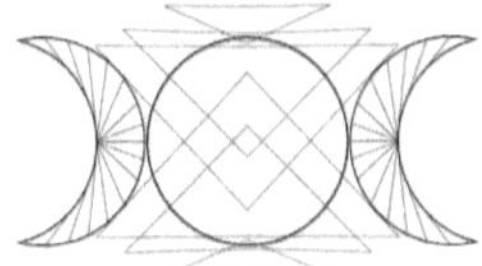

Teryn Alante felt like a dead man in his saddle after riding all night, but he hadn't been willing to let the duke's coach out of his sight. Not only was Cora inside it, but Teryn had yet to receive her bounty. To claim it, he'd have to meet with King Dimetreus at Ridine Castle. His reward for betraying Cora, however, was the least of Teryn's worries. He couldn't care less about it now. But that was a fact he'd kept to himself as soon as he'd realized how outnumbered he and his companions were against Duke Morkai's well-armed guards. It would have served him little to confront the duke, the very man Cora had been working against. No, Teryn would save his questions for the king himself. Perhaps he would explain why the woman he'd known as Cora was actually Princess Aveline.

He still didn't understand how it was possible. The princess was supposed to be dead, murdered by Cora's own hand. After the duke had ordered his guards to seize her and haul her into the coach, Teryn hounded him with questions. He'd been met with nothing more than an annoyingly condescending grin and the duke's assurance that Teryn could ask anything he wished once he arrived at the castle.

Which was where they were now.

It was an hour past sunrise when Ridine Castle came into view. Teryn and Lex rode through the gatehouse, following just behind the coach with two guards at the rear and two more at the fore. They entered a courtyard, which Teryn was surprised to find so empty. Perhaps he was used to the rhythm and regality of a palace, not the more practical nature of a castle. Ridine itself was a plain structure forged of stone with high walls, tall turrets, and an overall formidable appearance. Adding to that impression were the looming Cambron Mountains and the dark forests that skirted around the castle walls.

"I still wish I had any idea what the bloody hell was going on," Lex said, eying Teryn as they continued to follow the coach into the courtyard.

Teryn sighed. "I'll explain later." He'd said as much several times already, but Lex would only narrow his eyes. He had every intention of telling Lex the truth, but he wanted to wait until the duke's guards were no longer in such close proximity. Or maybe it was more that Teryn wasn't ready to admit what he'd done.

The coach rolled to a stop before the stone steps that led to an enormous pair of doors. Teryn dismounted at once and jogged toward the coach. He was stopped by one of the duke's guards. The guard said nothing, just held up a gauntleted hand and scowled through his helm. Teryn's shoulders tensed. Every part of him yearned to reach for his sword. His rational side stilled his hand. He may not have known much about Duke Morkai, but if the king had sent him to fetch Cora...

That is, if the king had sent him at all.

Teryn's chest tightened as the coach door opened. The duke stepped out first and extended his palm. No hand reached out to take it, but Cora slid out next, refusing to meet Morkai's eyes. Two more guards came down the stairs, each taking one of Cora's arms. She put up no fight as they escorted her up the stone steps.

"Cora." The word left his lips without him meaning to.

Cora froze in place, her eyes locking on his. Her expression shifted to one of murderous rage. She didn't need to say anything for him to know how she felt about him. It was there in her eyes. *Hate.* One of the guards tugged her forward and she continued up the steps, her head held high.

Like a princess.

How had Teryn not seen it before? She may not have been prim and proper like a royal, but there was a confidence to her he should have recognized. He'd seen it in the tilt of her chin, in her boldness, her refusal to apologize or follow anyone's orders but her own.

And he'd been a fool. He'd let a piece of paper and a tempting purse form his opinion of her before he'd tried to understand her on his own. He'd known she'd poisoned those hunters, murdered them without remorse, but as for what the poster claimed...

I was framed by Duke Morkai.

There was so much more going on than he understood, but nothing was going to stop him from finding out what that was.

❧

AN HOUR LATER HE SAT IN KING DIMETREUS' STUDY. ONE HAND WAS CLENCHED TIGHT around the arm of his chair while the other rubbed his brow. It was all he could do to keep from pacing around the room. He was alone aside from the guard standing sentinel before the closed door. Even so, he wanted to appear as composed as he could despite having been waiting for the better part of an hour. The duke had warned him it would be a while before he'd be granted an audience, but Teryn had refused to do anything else after he entered the castle. Lex, on the other hand, had nearly swooned at the offer of a soft bed and a bath.

Finally, the door opened. Teryn rose to stand out of respect for the king, but it was not Dimetreus who entered the study. It was Duke Morkai.

"Where is the king, Your Grace?" Teryn said through his teeth, not bothering to hide his irritation.

"The king is indisposed," Morkai said, striding over to the wide desk and sitting behind it. With slow, deliberate moves, he rested his crystal-topped cane upon the desk. He might as well have pointed a sword at Teryn for the unspoken threat the gesture carried.

Teryn held the man's gaze, studying him for further threat while he debated how to reply. He was surprised how young Morkai appeared. When Helios had spoken of the duke who'd taken over the unicorn hunt, he'd imagined a sinister old man. Not the dashing gent who sat across from him now, one who looked barely older than him. His pale eyes were uncreased, his jaw bearing not even a hint of stubble. How had this man become a duke? He certainly hadn't inherited the title, for Morkai was neither the name of a duchy nor a family surname of any prestige. Otherwise, he'd have learned the name during his many years of tutelage.

The duke leaned casually in the king's chair and gave Teryn a smile that didn't reach his eyes. "Worry not, Your Highness. The king has bidden me to settle your arrangement with him on his behalf."

Teryn clenched his jaw. "I demand to speak with the king."

Morkai cocked his head slightly to the side. "You forget yourself, Prince Teryn. This is Khero. You may have retrieved my kingdom's beloved lost princess, but you were found in the king's forest with only a forged writ of permission. A writ forged with my own sigil, might I add. I suggest you take what graciousness the king has offered you. At the moment, he's offered you me."

Teryn resisted the urge to glower and instead returned to his seat. It wasn't an ideal situation, but perhaps the duke could still shine light on some of Teryn's questions. "Your Grace, explain to me how the woman I turned in to the crown for the murder of Princess Aveline *is* the princess."

Morkai brushed a piece of lint off his black coat. "I did not grant you an audience to speak about the princess. That is a private matter belonging to this kingdom alone. Regardless, you will receive your reward. In fact, I took the liberty of paying off your debt to the Bank of Cartha."

Teryn blinked a few times. How did the duke know anything about his kingdom's debt to Cartha? Better yet, why the hell would he pay it back?

"Oh, don't fret," Morkai said with a chuckle. "You will get your 500,000 *sovas*. Think of my settlement of your debt as a bonus. You aren't just any bounty hunter. You're a prince."

Teryn narrowed his eyes. Sure, he could feel honored by such generosity, but he had a feeling this was no favor. Instead of clearing Menah's debt, the duke had only shifted the hands of who held it. He'd purchased his kingdom's allegiance.

Isn't that what Father wanted? Teryn thought to himself. *An alliance with King Dimetreus?*

No matter how hard he tried, he couldn't see this as a blessing. "I didn't ask you to do that."

"You didn't have to," Morkai said. "Let's just say it was in my kingdom's best interest."

Teryn didn't like the sound of that. Before he could argue, Morkai spoke again.

"I understand Menah has seen its share of hardship. Scandal. Threat of war. Pirates." He paused and gave Teryn a probing look. "Not to mention an unfulfilled marriage contract with the Princess of Selay."

Teryn tried not to appear flustered by Morkai's demonstration of knowledge about his kingdom. The duke reminded him of Helios in a way, but far more subtle.

Morkai waved a hand. "Lucky for you, your strife can end with the collection of a simple bounty."

"Lucky indeed," Teryn said stiffly.

"Now that your debt to Cartha has been repaid, I daresay your kingdom will look quite well to anyone who has scorned you thus far."

Teryn gave a grunt of agreement. He wished Morkai would get to the point already. Teryn had only known him for a handful of minutes, but he already knew exactly what kind of a man the duke was—one of smooth words to cover layers of pretense.

"Rumors run faster than horses," Morkai said. "Soon everyone will know of your kingdom's shift in status. I'm willing to bet that by the time you return home, your beloved princess will fall at your feet begging you to marry her. You'll never have to face the indignity of another ridiculous poetry contest again."

Seven gods, how much did this man know about him? Every kingdom had spies in every court, even his own. Still, it was unsettling to realize just how much more effective Khero's informants were compared to Menah's. Teryn forced a smile. "I'm sure you're right."

Morkai watched him through slitted lids. He leaned forward in his chair. "That is...unless you've changed your mind about her."

Teryn swallowed hard. His mind—for whatever strange reason—went to Cora. "Changed my mind?"

"Perhaps you're tired of being slighted by Selay. Had they wanted to sever your engagement to the princess, they could have done it with far more tact."

"They could have."

"And yet they pitted you against two other princes in a frivolous quest for unicorns. Is that why you came to Khero, Prince Teryn?"

There was no use denying it. "Yes."

"You didn't happen to have anything to do with the slaughter of an entire company of unicorn hunters, did you? They may have worked directly under me, but I serve the king." His tone was cordial, but Teryn could hear the threat laced between each word. It told him he knew Teryn had interfered with the duke's hunt. A hunt approved by the king himself. Teryn and his kingdom could be condemned for such a crime. Morkai clearly knew Menah couldn't afford war. Meanwhile, the elegant armor worn by the duke's guards was proof enough that Khero could.

Teryn's mind spun as he took it all in. Layers upon layers of the duke's words, actions, threats. He still felt like he'd barely begun to unearth the half of it.

Morkai's lips stretched into a wide smile. "It's fantastic that we are allies now, is it not?"

"Indeed."

"An alliance is reciprocal. You finding the princess is worth even more than what the king has done for you already. Should you wish it, we could do more."

Teryn shifted uncomfortably in his seat. "More?"

Morkai steepled his fingertips against his chin, brow furrowed as if deep in thought. "I think I might know what prevented your father from demanding that King Verdian honor the contract between you and the princess."

And we're back to the expense of war, Teryn noted. "Is that so?"

Morkai nodded. "That is no longer an issue, let me assure you. King Dimetreus has a prodigious army. One that would have Selay quaking with fear. Should you seek justice rather than matrimony, say the word and Khero will come to your aid."

Teryn's mouth went dry. Once again, the duke's words were generous at face value. But under the surface...

King Dimetreus has a prodigious army.

Teryn had already assumed as much, but Duke Morkai had wanted it reinforced in Teryn's mind. Not only that but the idea that Selay would easily fall beneath said army. And if Selay—a wealthy kingdom with a more-than-adequate military force—would so easily fall...

So would Menah.

Teryn kept his expression nonchalant. "Your Grace, Menah has no desire to go to war with Selay."

Morkai tore his gaze away from Teryn and pushed back from the desk. "No, I wouldn't think so," he said with a sigh.

He and Teryn stood at the same time. It was clear the conversation had come to a close. The guard opened the door and Morkai strode toward it. As he reached Teryn, he said, "Your reward is being counted and packed at this very moment. In the meantime, the king invites you to a celebratory dinner tonight. You will attend, yes?"

"Actually, I'd rather be on my way at once." The words were untrue. Teryn had no intention of leaving until he saw Cora again, but he was curious how far the king's—and the duke's—hospitality extended. Was he truly free to leave as he wished, or...

Morkai gave him a cold smile. "Better not, Your Highness. The king does insist."

"Then I'll simply visit the stables and see to my horse after such arduous travels."

"See to it then," Morkai said. "But you should know this. Should you try and take your horse beyond the castle walls, you will find Ridine's gates closed to those who deny the king's kindness."

"His kindness."

"Like I said. He insists you stay for dinner tonight."

As the duke swept away, Teryn was certain of two things. One, that he was a prisoner, not a guest. And two, that he'd get himself, Lex, and Cora out of there if it was the last thing he did.

<h1 style="text-align:center">35</h1>

For the first time in six years, Cora was dressed in a gown. She assessed herself in the mirror, startled by her own reflection. The last time she'd seen her full reflection was in this very mirror in this very room—her childhood bedroom. She'd been shorter then. Thinner. Paler. Softer. Now her skin had been browned by the sun, her arms chiseled with firm muscle built by her archery practice.

Her eyes swept over the gown. The skirts were layers of emerald-green silk trimmed with black lace while the bodice was sage brocade. The sleeves ended at her elbows and trailed more lace down her forearms. Cora felt a sharp pang of longing in her heart. This had been her mother's dress. As soon as the gown had been delivered to her bedroom an hour before, she'd recognized it. It had come with a letter written in her brother's familiar script, insisting she wear it and join him for dinner. It was so much like something that would have happened in her youth—her brother delivering a dress and extracting a promise that she'd attend some public function on her best behavior—that she could almost pretend she'd never left Ridine.

For a splinter of a moment, she let herself imagine the last six years had been full of nothing more than mundane activity. Dances. Dinners. Greeting dignitaries, courtiers, and guests. She pretended her brother hadn't accused her of murder. That Morkai had never come into their lives after their parents died, hadn't gained Dimetreus' favor and friendship, which would eventually drive a wedge between the king and everyone close to him.

In that split-second fantasy, Cora felt peace. Joy, even. Then her gaze drifted to her eyes, and the illusion shattered. Her eyes were too haunted to belong to a princess. Not to mention her tangled hair that made a mockery of her lovely gown. She'd been delivered an ewer of hot water for a bath, but she'd need a long soak in a tub to untangle her hair. In the end, she'd settled for a messy plait down her back. Loose strands were already slipping free around her face.

A knock sounded at her door, making her jump. A guard's deep voice rumbled from the other side. It was time for dinner.

Time to see her brother.

~

CORA STOPPED OUTSIDE THE CLOSED DOORS TO THE DINING HALL. THE TWO GUARDS who had shadowed her as she'd made her way down the familiar path stepped before her now, each reaching for a handle. She held her breath as they pulled the doors open. A shudder of fear ran through her.

The last time she'd been inside this room had been...

Had been...

I curse you to die.

She closed her eyes and forced the memory away. When she opened them again, the dining hall spread out before her. Her stomach sank at seeing it so empty. She'd been somewhat surprised to find the halls so vacant as she'd made her way here, but she'd assumed the servants had been busy with dinner. But that couldn't be true, for inside the dining hall, every table was empty save the head table. Only the back half of the room was lit by the lamps that lined the walls. The chandeliers overhead bore only cobwebs as if they hadn't been dressed with candles in years.

"Darling Aveline," a familiar voice said from the far end of the room.

Her eyes shot to the head table where three figures sat—Morkai, Lex, and... Dimetreus. Her heart skittered, then froze, skittered, then froze, as if it didn't know what to do as she looked at her brother. The last time they'd been face-to-face, he'd grabbed her by the arm and ordered his guards to haul her into a dungeon cell. But his voice was so warm and kind now. So much like the brother she used to love. Her throat constricted as she forced her trembling legs to move. Her eyes never left her brother's as she drew near, but with every step, concern began to darken her heart.

Dimetreus Caelan looked at least twenty years older than the version that existed in her memories and nightmares. His eyes were rimmed with shadows, lined with creases, his lips pale. Uneven blotches of color marred what used to be his golden-tan skin. His hair, once thick and black, was now sparse, shot with white beneath his crown. He was dressed in his violet royal coat, but she noticed how it hung loose on his frame as he rose to his feet. Morkai, outfitted in the same black and gold coat he'd worn earlier that day, stood as she approached the dais. Lex belatedly followed. Dimetreus spread his arms wide and gestured for her to take a seat next to him. Her breaths were sharp and shallow as she claimed the chair, and the men returned to their seats. Morkai sat at the king's right while Lex was at Cora's left.

Lex leaned in close and frantically whispered, "If someone doesn't explain what the hell is going on, I'm going to go mad."

She looked over at him, surprised to find he must have had a full bath. His blond hair was clean and brushed away from his face. His clothes were clean too but showed obvious signs of wear from his travels. The ruffled front of his shirt was tinged yellow while his waistcoat and jacket bore several frayed seams.

"Music," Dimetreus said, snapping his fingers.

Cora startled as strains of harp emanated from the back corner of the room. She hadn't noticed the woman sitting there until now, but the harpist began to play, a serene smile on her lips.

"That's better," the king said. "Ah, and here's our final guest. Just in time, for I'm certain dinner is soon to arrive."

Cora's eyes shot to the figure entering the room. Her heart hammered, fluttered, hammered, fluttered. Again, the fickle organ seemed confused. She supposed it wasn't the only thing confused, for even her feelings shifted from fiery rage to an absurd sense of relief as Teryn walked toward the dais. She blamed her confusion on the unexpected change in his appearance. He was no longer dressed in leather britches and his hunting vest. Instead, he wore evening attire—black pants, white waistcoat, a ruffled shirt with a white neckcloth, and a black frock coat. She assumed the outfit had been borrowed from her brother, based on how the coat strained across his broad shoulders. His hair, like Lex's, was freshly washed and neatly styled, a slight curl to his dark tresses. She couldn't suppress her shock. It had been easy to ignore that he was a prince when they were in the woods, but now...there was no denying what he was.

Cora resisted the urge to smooth out her hair.

"Prince Teryn," Dimetreus said in greeting. "You are a true hero."

Teryn's face flashed with confusion before he bowed. "King Dimetreus." His eyes slid to Cora, and she realized she was still staring at him. He bit a corner of his lip as if he was desperate to say something. She only narrowed her eyes to a glare.

"Come," the king said, "join us."

He kept his gaze locked on Cora's a breath longer, then strode up to the table and claimed the only remaining seat—to the right of Morkai.

Soon after, a pair of servants entered, far fewer than she'd ever seen attend one of the king's meals before. Where was everyone? Where were the maids? Where was Master Benedict, the castle's steward? The servants' faces were slack, eyes dull and glossy as they filled the plates with food and the glasses with wine. Lex dove in at once, but Cora could hardly bring a bite to her lips. Her stomach was tied too tightly in knots. There was so much she wanted to say, so much she needed to ask her brother, but she could do none of it with Morkai sitting so close. She'd have to find a way to get him alone.

She glanced at Dimetreus and found him looking right back. "Eat, sister. You must be starving after everything you've been through."

His expression was so kind, so full of concern, that she couldn't help but bring a spoonful of soup to her mouth just to appease his worry. She hardly tasted it, for her mind was wrapped around what he'd said. It was the first indication he'd given to suggest her appearance at dinner was anything but a pleasant-yet-not-unusual surprise. He'd expressed no shock over seeing her alive, shed no tears over how she'd aged, harbored no residual scorn over having once thought she'd murdered his wife.

She finished another sip of soup before facing Dimetreus. "After everything I've been through?" she asked, infusing her tone with only mild curiosity. She chose her next words carefully. "How much do you know?"

She could almost feel Morkai's stare burning straight through her brother, but she kept her gaze on the king. Dimetreus' expression fell. "A grave injustice was done to you, Aveline. I hope you believe that, had I known you were still alive, I would have come for you. Even when I thought you were lost along with my dearest Linette, I worked to avenge you. I *still* work to avenge you."

Her blood went cold with dread. "How are you working to avenge me?"

"Don't you worry, sister, Selay will pay for what they've done."

"Selay." Cora and Teryn uttered the word in unison.

"Yes," Dimetreus said. He took a deep drink of wine and turned toward Teryn. "If not for you rescuing my sister, I would have still thought Menah was involved."

"Involved with what?" Cora asked, drawing her brother's attention back to her.

"Involved with..." His throat bobbed. When he spoke next, his voice was strained. "I hate to even think about it. How Selay sent a spy into our midst, someone I unwittingly let get so close to my wife while I..." He slammed his fist on the table, making Cora jump. "That wretched maid. She took them from me. Linette and our unborn baby. I hadn't known. I hadn't...hadn't..."

Morkai put a placating hand on the king's shoulder. "At least your sister is alive."

"Yes," Dimetreus said, collecting his composure. "It's a miracle you managed to escape them. Thanks to Prince Teryn, our new ally." He raised his cup to Teryn.

Cora caught Teryn's eye. His expression was bewildered but she could sense that he simmered with a suppressed rage that almost matched her own. Who could he be so angry with? This whole ordeal was his fault. Wasn't he exactly where he wanted to be?

Teryn raised his glass in return, his gaze sliding to Morkai. "I helped her escape." It was a question without a question mark.

"Yes," Morkai said. "You rescued her from Selay, where she'd been held captive for six years."

Dimetreus nodded along. Cora's stomach turned.

"Am I the only one who feels like they woke up on the wrong side of reality?" Lex said, setting down his fork with a clatter. "Nothing that any of you have said tonight makes a damn lick of sense."

Dimetreus furrowed his brow and studied Lex as if seeing him for the first time.

Cora took a deep breath. "He's right, Dimi, I wasn't—"

"I wouldn't try and confuse him," Morkai said, pinning her with a warning glare. "He gets very upset when he's confused."

Dimetreus blinked a few times, then shook his head as if to clear it. He downed another drink of wine and released a dark chuckle. "He's right. I've been having... struggles with my memory as of late. I can't handle too much information or excitement at once. Which is why His Grace has been such a boon to me these last several years. He might as well be my whipping boy, but you won't hear him complain."

Cora's eyes slid to the duke's, taking in his smug grin. She remembered what he'd said in the coach after she'd mentioned how loyal he was to her brother.

Or does he serve me in every way?

"I don't like how grim the mood has become," Dimetreus said. "This is supposed to be a celebration. A joyous reunion. I've missed you dearly, Aveline." He faced her with a wide grin. There was a sweet quality to his expression that almost made him look like the version of him she remembered. But the closer she examined, the more she saw his facade fraying at the edges. His eyes were glazed over with a shimmer that nearly obscured the brown of his irises. She opened herself to his emotions, sensed a low hum of something...muffled. Suppressed. Confused. She could hardly make out a clear emotion, just a clash of vague impressions.

"I've missed you too," she said over the lump in her throat.

He clapped his hands, the sound far too loud for the quiet room. "I want to see my sister dance." Cora opened her mouth to protest, but Dimetreus shouted to the harpist, "A waltz."

"Dimi, please," she said, heat rising to her cheeks. "I can't. It's been too long."

"I insist," he said, oblivious to her discomfort.

"But—"

"Do not deny His Majesty," Morkai said. "You wouldn't want to upset him. Who knows what it could do. He might wake up and forget you were ever here."

Dimetreus chuckled. "I would do something like that, wouldn't I?"

Cora knew full well Morkai's words had been said in threat. If the duke wanted, he could make Dimetreus forget she'd come back. He could turn her back from princess to prisoner.

"Go, sister," the king said, gesturing at the floor before the dais. "Who will dance with her?"

Morkai stood easily from his chair.

But another voice spoke first. "Might I have this dance?" Teryn rose to his feet in a rush, sending his chair legs scraping against the stone floor.

Cora looked from one man to the other. Either way, she'd have to dance with an enemy. The decision, however, wasn't hard to make. She hated the thought of dancing with Teryn, but letting Morkai put his hands anywhere near her was far more repulsive. It didn't matter that he looked hardly older than Teryn. She'd rather die than dance with him.

Lifting her chin, she met Teryn's gaze with a glare. She spoke through her teeth. "Yes, Prince Teryn. I'd be honored to dance."

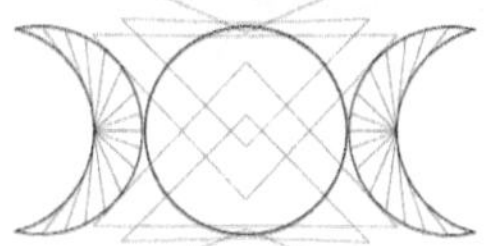

36

Cora's eyes locked with Teryn's as they left the dais on opposite sides of the table. His expression was neutral, unreadable, while hers was burning with malice. She felt as if she were meeting him for a duel rather than a dance. They met at the center of the floor, and Teryn gave a stiff bow. She offered an even stiffer curtsy. Her heart thudded wildly in her chest as the harpist began to play. Teryn stepped in close. He held one hand out to the side while the other came to her back. She stifled a gasp. Then, deepening her glare, she alighted one palm on his shoulder and draped the other over his waiting hand. She was grateful for the dinner gloves they both wore, creating barriers between their flesh. Even so, she could still feel the heat of his skin beneath them.

Teryn began to move. She stumbled, and her animosity was replaced with a flash of panic. While she'd been trained as a child in every sort of formal dance, she'd never been old enough to dance with a partner a public manner. Besides, her lessons had been years ago.

Her breaths came short and sharp as she tried to keep up with Teryn. Thankfully, it wasn't long before her feet seemed to remember what to do. Teryn must have foreseen that her dance skills would leave much to be desired, for she soon noted that they were moving far slower than the harpist's tempo. Teryn had probably enjoyed plenty of balls with plenty of capable partners, and yet he was keeping their waltz slow. Simple. For her sake.

It only enraged her more.

She lifted her eyes, realizing they'd fallen to her feet. It nearly made her lose her newly found rhythm when she took in just how close he was. They'd been this near before, primarily at knifepoint or perhaps when she'd hid them under the tree. But this, somehow, was different. She tried to keep her attention on the lower half of his face, noting how the bruising had faded from his nose, leaving only a slight yellow tinge where she'd once broken it. Then, against her will, her gaze inched up higher and higher until she met his eyes. For the first time, she noticed the emerald hue of his irises, a stunning shade even in the dim lamplight. They were turned down at the corners, brimming with unspoken apology that echoed the heavy waves of regret she sensed from him. She averted her gaze over his shoulder and raised her shields.

"Aveline," he whispered, his voice a deep rumble between them. It made her pulse quicken to hear him use her true name.

"Don't call me that," she muttered back.

He sighed. "Cora. Please believe me when I say I'm so sorry."

He led them into a turn, and she caught sight of the table. Her brother watched with a sappy expression while Morkai's stare was dark. Assessing. Lex, at the other end of the table, simply downed his wine and poured another glass. Teryn turned them again, leading her away from the table toward the unlit end of the dining hall.

"If I were armed, I'd kill you right now," she said through her teeth.

"I know."

She returned her gaze to his. "You think an apology is enough? What are you sorry for, anyway? That you've seen me in a dress, heard me called *princess*, and now realize you should respect me?"

His expression hardened. "I respected you the moment you held a knife to my throat. This was never about a lack of respect."

"Then what was it about?"

He shifted his jaw. "Desperation."

His emotions struck her again, and she felt their crushing weight. Desperation was indeed one of them, as was duty. Responsibility. Regret. Shame. It was a tangled burden of feeling, and an effort to breathe away. Her shields felt like they'd grown weaker ever since she'd been captured by Morkai. She shook her head. "Your desperation cost me my freedom."

He sighed. "You're not safe here, are you?"

She gave him a pointed look. "What do you think?"

His gaze slid over to the table. "I think there's something very odd going on here."

"Odd is one word for it." They turned, and now she had a view of the dais. Her brother still stared with a giddy grin, his eyes glazed and vacant. There was so much she didn't understand about what was happening. It was safe to assume her brother was indeed being manipulated by Morkai through means of dark magic. She could feel the duke's influence writhing through the castle, creeping into every corner and cobweb, dampening the air she breathed. But what exactly was he trying to accomplish? What reason did Morkai have to convince the king that Selay had been responsible for Queen Linette's death, not to mention Cora's supposed captivity? And where did the Beast and the hunt for unicorns fit in?

Her thoughts shifted to Valorre. He'd been helping the baby unicorn find its mother when Morkai had come. She hadn't felt his presence once since then. Hadn't heard his thoughts. His absence made her chest feel tight but she knew it was for the best. If she couldn't feel him, then he was far enough away to avoid whatever danger she was in now.

"We can escape," Teryn whispered, bringing her attention back to him.

She quirked a brow. "Escape? Why would you need to escape? You're the honored guest. My brave rescuer, remember?"

"No, I'm not."

"Have you received your precious bounty?"

His whisper turned sharp. "I don't want it. All I want is to get you and Lex out of here. Tonight. I've seen to our horses. All three are saddled and ready, but we can't use the main gates. If you know any other way out of the castle, any weaknesses in its walls, tell me."

A memory rose to the forefront of her mind from the night Morkai had set her free from the dungeon. He'd taken her not through the gatehouse, not out one of the patrolled exits, but a portion of the wall that stood closest to the woods. Ivy had covered most of that part of the wall, and somewhere hidden behind tangled green vines had been an opening. A passage.

"You know of a way," Teryn whispered. "Please, Cora. Tell me and I'll get you free."

There was so much conviction in his tone, she almost believed him. Almost. She scoffed. "You expect me to trust you?"

"I'm trying to help."

"I don't need your help." She stepped away from him. That was when she realized they'd stopped dancing. The music had come to an end. It must have been the song's natural conclusion, for she heard her brother break into applause. Only she was aware of her and Teryn's abrupt parting.

"Cora." He reached for her hand and grasped her fingertips.

She stared down at their gloved touch before wrenching her hand away. Then, without bothering to curtsy, she marched back toward the table.

Dimetreus waved his hands at her, shooing her away from the dais. "No, let's see another dance." He snapped his fingers at the harpist, who began another song.

Morkai's gaze burned into Cora while he spoke to her brother. "I think we've had enough dancing tonight, Your Majesty."

"Nonsense. Let the young people have fun."

"My feet are tired, brother," she said, painfully aware that Teryn had caught up to her and now stood by her side. "I can't possibly dance again."

Dimetreus gave her an indulgent grin. "You must forgive me, then, Aveline. I have just missed you so. Seeing you dance brought back the best memories. Besides," his grin took on a sly quality, "the two of you make quite the pair. Perhaps our kingdoms can take on a more formal alliance before long."

Cora's breath caught, her cheeks burning. She opened her mouth to speak but not a word came out.

Teryn, on the other hand, didn't share in her struggle. "I am honored at what you suggest, Your Majesty," he said with ease. "I am fond of your sister."

She whipped her head toward him, lips pursed to keep from emitting a string of curses. *The nerve. What a joke!*

"You forget, Majesty," Morkai said, his voice cold, "that the prince has yet to prove himself our ally."

Dimetreus gestured at Teryn. "He...he rescued her. It's quite romantic, Your Grace."

The duke's attention shifted to Teryn. "Romantic indeed. Still, he must demonstrate the extent of his heroics."

"He'll march on Selay with us," Dimetreus said. "Won't you, Prince Teryn?"

"March on Selay." Cora wasn't sure whether it was just her who'd said it because she, Teryn, and Lex were all staring bewilderedly at the king.

"Yes," Dimetreus said. His expression hardened, an edge creeping into his tone. "We must avenge what was done to my wife. We must make them pay for keeping my sister captive. For six years, I've been planning for this moment, building toward it. We will lay waste to the capital city, seize Verlot Palace, and make King Verdian regret that he ever lifted a hand against us."

A shudder ran down Cora's spine as she recalled the rumors of her brother's growing army. How Roije had to fight his way out of being recruited. All this time... the king's motive had been to build an army big enough to take down Selay? She narrowed her eyes at Morkai, but he only smiled back. This wasn't her brother's plan. It was *his*. But why?

She balled her hands at her sides and strode up the dais until she stood opposite her brother. "Selay didn't send a spy to kill your wife," she said, her words coming out with a tremor.

"Aveline," Morkai said, tone pitched low.

"I wasn't kept captive there for the last six years."

Dimetreus blinked a few times, his face going a shade paler. "What is she talking about, Your Grace?"

She expected Morkai to answer, but he didn't. Amusement danced in his eyes, which should have been warning enough to keep her from saying another word. Still, she had to try. Had to test the bounds of Morkai's control. "I've been hiding for six years because *you* sentenced me to death for the murder of Queen Linette. A crime I didn't commit. A crime *he* did." She pointed at the duke. "He framed me for it, let me take the fall, and you believed him. You believed him when he told you I'd died, but now you see me standing before you. You believed him when he said it had all been a mistake and I'd been captured by Selay, but I promise you that is untrue. Brother, do not believe another word he says."

Dimetreus trembled and closed his eyes. At first, Cora thought he was crying. Then he stood from his seat and pounded his fists onto the table, sending the dinnerware rattling. Lex scrambled back from the table while Morkai took a sip of wine, watching the spectacle with a grin.

"Lies!" the king shouted. "You lie! You are not my sister." He reached across the table for her, but she launched back—only to recall she was upon the dais. Her foot slipped on the top step, and she began to fall.

A steady arm encircled her waist, catching her. She didn't care that it was Teryn. Didn't care that he kept his hand on her lower back once her feet were planted firmly on the ground. She only cared about the rage distorting her brother's face. He looked so much like he had the day he condemned her to die.

"She speaks the truth," Teryn said. "Every word she says is true."

Dimetreus began to round the table toward them. "You're both spies. You aren't my sister, and you aren't the prince." He whirled toward where Lex stood plastered against the wall. "Who even are you? Who are any of you? Guards!"

The door opened at the end of the dining hall, and in strode several guards. Cora noted that not one bore the king's sigil, only the duke's crescent moon.

"Get them out of my sight," Dimetreus said as he stormed away from the dais.

"Dimi," Cora called after him, but he didn't give her a second glance before he left the dining hall entirely. She pressed in close to Teryn as the guards surrounded them in a half circle. There was no getting to the door without going through the guards first. Cora waited for them to start forward, draw their weapons, and attack. They didn't.

Slow footsteps drew her attention to Morkai. He sauntered down the dais, cane in hand, and addressed his guards. "The king is having one of his fits again. He'll be right by morning. For now, ignore him."

The guards obeyed, making no move to close in.

It didn't ease the feeling of dread that had crawled into her heart.

Morkai approached Teryn and Cora, eyes narrowed to slits.

Cora felt something squeeze her hand and realized Teryn had been holding it. Gritting her teeth, she wrenched it away and took a step back. Teryn remained rooted in place. He met Morkai with his chin held high. They were nearly the same height, although Teryn was of a much broader build. In contrast, Morkai was lithe and lean, which only somehow added to his terrifying beauty.

"Prince Teryn," Morkai said, a hint of mocking in his tone, "I do believe it's time I showed you the garden."

37

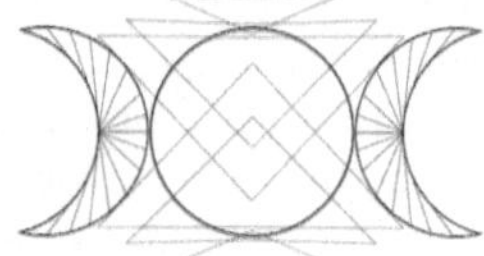

Teryn knew Duke Morkai's words were not to be taken as a request. It was a demand, and not just for him. The duke motioned Lex forward. Teryn found his friend against the wall, shoulders nearly as high as his ears. Lex's eyes darted from Teryn to Morkai, then to the guards. Teryn still hadn't had a chance to speak with Lex alone. He'd tried to call upon Lex earlier but had been turned away by a guard. The duke clearly had every intention of keeping them from communicating outside his presence.

Lex slowly pushed off from the wall and joined Teryn and Cora.

"Come," Morkai said. "We shall all visit the garden together." He started off toward the door and the guards gestured for Teryn and his companions to follow.

Cora didn't hesitate before she marched after the duke, which was all it took to get Teryn and Lex moving too. Teryn saw no point in arguing. No point in facing off with the guards—heavily armed ones, he was quick to note. He'd been disarmed upon arriving at the castle, which meant he had absolutely no defense but his fists. His consolation was that visiting the garden meant going outside, which would offer Teryn a chance to scope out the castle grounds. All he needed was to find an empty part of the wall. A gate left unattended. He'd done more than simply tend his palfrey when he visited the stables earlier. He'd tended all three of their horses, gathered their belongings, hid them inside each pen in anticipation of a hasty escape. He'd meant to convince Cora to agree to work with him, but it seemed their dance had only widened the chasm he'd regrettably created. Regardless, Teryn was determined to get her out of the castle. Princess or no, she was in danger here. Her brother was a madman, and the duke...Teryn wasn't entirely sure what the duke was just yet, but he had a feeling he was going to find out.

Lex leaned in close as they wove through the halls. "Care to share what in the name of the seven devils is going on?"

"We need to speak alone," Teryn whispered back. "For now, know we aren't safe here. None of us are. Don't trust a word the duke says. I'm getting us out of the castle tonight."

Lex opened his mouth to reply, but one of the guards gave him a shove between the shoulders, forcing them apart. Teryn bristled, his hands curling around air while yearning for a weapon. He'd never known a guard of any rank who'd consider laying a hand on a prince like that. In any other situation, the guard would lose his position, his hand, perhaps even his life.

Lex cut the guard an affronted glare but kept silent. He'd probably come to the same conclusion Teryn had—that these weren't regular guards. They didn't respect royal hierarchy. They followed Morkai, a duke, a man who stood below their king.

No duke should have the authority Morkai did.

The party came to an empty courtyard. It stood beneath a black sky, the sun having already set before dinner. Cool night air brushed Teryn's skin as they crossed the stone floor and funneled through a door in a low stone wall at the other side. Morkai stopped just beyond it and beckoned the rest of them to come forth.

Cora halted as soon as she took a step beyond the wall. She released a gasp, her body going rigid. Teryn and Lex quickened their pace and came up beside her.

"The garden," Cora whispered, but Teryn could see nothing resembling anything close to a garden. Instead, he found a charred field riddled with black stumps of gnarled trees. Nothing stood beyond the field save for the castle wall. He studied the towering perimeter, noting the many silhouettes of sentries atop it. It didn't bode well for his escape plan.

He scanned the sky out of reflex, but he knew he wouldn't find Berol. The last thing he'd done after preparing their horses was to scrawl a note that simply said, *Ridine Castle. Not safe. Trying to flee.* He'd left the rolled-up parchment on a bale of hay outside the stables, careful not to let any of the duke's guards see. Before he'd returned indoors, he'd caught a glimpse of Berol diving from the sky, then flying away with the scroll clutched in her talons. She'd known better than to fly inside the stables or the castle before then, just like she'd understood to keep her distance while he'd traveled with the duke's entourage to Ridine. The less Morkai knew about Teryn's assets, the better. Now he just had to hope Berol brought it to his father at once. He hadn't been close enough to convey where he wanted the letter delivered, but he trusted her to understand he was in trouble.

"This is not at all what I'd call a garden," Lex whispered.

Cora faced Morkai. "Why did you bring us here to show us *this*?"

Morkai chuckled. "This isn't what I brought you to see, but I'm glad you're impressed."

"This was my mother's garden."

"Everything comes at a price, Aveline."

"Do you have a point or do you simply like hearing yourself make vaguely ominous statements?"

Teryn nearly barked a laugh. If Cora was afraid of the duke, she was doing a damn good job of hiding it.

Morkai planted his cane in the earth and rubbed his thumb over the amber crystal. "You might have gleaned that King Dimetreus will soon be declaring war."

"I gathered," Cora said, "although I've yet to understand why. Selay is no enemy to Khero. Everything you've told my brother is a lie."

"Everything the king believes is true to him," Morkai said with a wry grin. "When he said we've been planning this for six years, that was true. And I've been planning even longer in ways you couldn't comprehend. We have the means to wage a very fast, very bloody, and very successful war. Harbor no doubts that our enemies will fall."

Teryn's blood roared in his ears. He may not have had the greatest respect for Selay and its rulers, especially after King Verdian had allowed his daughter to publicly snub their engagement. But that didn't mean he relished the thought of the kingdom falling to war. "Aside from the story you've fabricated over Princess Aveline's captivity, what reason does the king have for marching on Selay?"

"I too would like to know," Lex added, although his tone held far less fire. "I visited Verlot Palace recently, and the king and queen seemed rather...nice..." His words dissolved into nothing as Morkai pinned him with a glare.

"My reasons are not for you to concern yourself with," the duke said.

Teryn noted that he'd said *my reasons*, not the king's.

Morkai's lips lifted in a taunting grin. "But it may serve you to know that Selay is not our only enemy."

Teryn's blood went cold. "Are you suggesting the threat holds true for Menah as well?"

"I'm suggesting you choose your alliances well, Your Highness. Whether the king's army marches on one kingdom or two is in your hands."

Teryn knew the duke was baiting him but he had to know the truth. "What does that mean?"

"It means you can either act as a voice of reason or serve me as a mute pawn. Your presence here is a gift."

"Is that so?"

"Quite. I'm sure you are well acquainted with the costs of war. Not only in coin but in lives. Time. Resources. Like I said, Khero is fully prepared for battle but that doesn't mean Dimetreus wouldn't settle for a peaceful resolution instead."

"What are you getting at?" Cora said. "Stop talking in circles and tell us what you brought us here to say."

Morkai ignored her, keeping his eyes fixed on Teryn. "You, Prince Teryn, create the possibility for negotiation. Instead of marching for war, the king will demand surrender. Tomorrow morning I will send messengers to both Selay and Menah. I will call for a meeting at Centerpointe Rock in two weeks' time where we will discuss the terms for both kingdoms' surrender."

"Two weeks' time," Teryn echoed. "You're only giving them *two weeks* to prepare for a war meeting?"

"Two weeks will be more than enough time for all three parties to reach Centerpointe Rock. There will be no need for any of us to come with heavy forces in tow. For this is not a war meeting but a meeting of peace."

Teryn scoffed. "*Peace*? Not once have you demonstrated anything resembling peace. Instead, I've watched you present lies as truths, wield threats like knives, and cast a princess as a common criminal. Not to mention treating me and Prince Lex like prisoners."

Lex's eyes widened. "Wait, we're...prisoners?"

"Of course not," Morkai said. "Until you expressly refuse the king, I'll consider you allies. Anyone who'd rather not stand opposite Khero's army in the future will choose to *remain* allies."

Teryn's neck prickled beneath the threat, but he kept his expression stony.

"You know what?" Morkai turned and marched closer to the charred field. "Enough chit-chat. I think what you need is visual proof."

Teryn's eyes sought Cora's. She met his gaze and he saw all of his own fears and confusion reflected back at him.

Morkai crouched at the edge of the field and pressed his hand to the charred earth. At first, nothing happened. Then movement at the far end of the field. One of the charred stumps...was growing. A shape formed from the shadows, creating a silhouette of an enormous head on a hulking body. That was when Teryn realized it hadn't been a stump at all. It was the Beast.

Lex edged closer to Teryn, as did Cora, her hands fumbling at her back, her waist, searching frantically for the weapons that weren't there. She froze when Teryn's hand alighted on her shoulder. This time, she didn't glare or pull away.

The Beast paid them no heed as it plodded forward, showing no sign that it had ever been injured by Cora. Both of its beady eyes were intact and its raw-looking red skin hid any sign of puncture. It stopped next to Morkai and sat back on its haunches. The creature towered over the duke, but Morkai patted its hide as if it were only a dog. Then, keeping one hand on the Beast, he lifted his other palm to the sky.

Teryn didn't dare blink as he watched a fog slowly creep over the field. Little by little, the misty patches began to grow brighter, reflecting the light of the moon. Soon shapes began to solidify and disperse, forming something akin to bodies. Teryn saw a hand here, a leg there, heads with dark holes where eyes should be.

Cora stepped back, flinging out a hand. Her gloved fingers came around his wrist and she made no move to let go. "Wraiths," she whispered.

Teryn's heart slammed against his ribs at the word. The longer Teryn stared at the humanlike shapes forming on the field, the more he realized there was no other word to describe them. There were hundreds of the semi-translucent figures all clustered together over the charred soil, and in each of their hands was an equally translucent weapon—swords, spears, axes, bows. They wore armor the same color as their ghostly bodies but the style was outdated. Ancient.

"What...who are they?" Cora asked.

"Spirits from a nearly forgotten war," Morkai said. "They died trapped between two realms and have wandered the planes between the living and the dead ever since. Now they serve me. I sacrificed the garden for them, traded death for life. Or something like it at least."

Lex's voice rose a few octaves as he muttered, "What the bloody hell."

Morkai stepped away from the Beast, and the creature plodded off to lie down a few paces away. The duke turned to face Teryn and his companions, his eyes lighting up with satisfaction at seeing the three of them huddled together. "Come, Aveline," he said, waving Cora forward.

She remained in place, her fingers still clasped around Teryn's wrist.

Morkai's gaze slid down to their hands, and his expression turned hard. Cora seemed to realize the source of his attention and stepped away from Teryn, releasing her grip and fisting her hands in the folds of her silk skirts. "I have no desire for a closer view." Her eyes darted from Morkai to the wavering forms of the wraiths.

"Oh, I'm not inviting you over just to look." He gestured to someone behind them, and one of his guards stepped forward carrying Cora's bow and quiver. "You're to participate in the demonstration." To the guard, he added, "Bring them."

Teryn tensed, assuming Morkai meant him and Lex. Instead, two more guards entered the garden from the courtyard. They hauled two bedraggled men whose hands were cuffed in iron, and shoved them before Morkai. The older of the two stumbled to his knees. His face was bruised, and an open cut seeped above his eyebrow. The younger man tried to help him up, but the duke held his cane between them.

"Monster," the younger man bit out. "Usurper. Filth—"

In a flash, Morkai snapped his cane against the side of the older man's face, opening his wound further.

Teryn started forward, his fists curled so tight he felt his nails dig straight through his dinner gloves to his palms. He halted in place at a sharp look from the duke. Another guard stepped forward, hand on the hilt of his sword. *Damn it.* He hated being unarmed. He hated himself for getting into this mess.

"Enough," the duke said to the younger man. "One more word and I'll break your father's legs."

The younger man's throat bobbed. His eyes burned with rage but he pursed his lips against further argument.

"Now," Morkai said, "walk eight paces onto the field. Refuse and your father dies. Take one step after your eight paces are complete and he dies. Go."

"Don't do it, Bradley," the older man begged. "Obey not a word the usurper says."

Bradley only hesitated a moment, just long enough for Morkai to slightly lift his cane. On trembling legs, he strode eight paces forward.

Toward the waiting wraiths.

Only a dozen or so feet stood between Bradley and the apparitions.

The guard bearing Cora's weapons handed her the bow and quiver. She took them with a wary expression that echoed the dread Teryn felt inside. Arming Cora felt too good to be true. She kept her eyes trained on the duke as she slung her bow over her shoulder, creating an odd contrast with her elegant gown. "What is this about?"

Morkai gestured at Bradley. "He will face my wraiths while you, Aveline, defend him. If he still lives after one minute, both he and his father go free."

Teryn glanced from Cora to the wraiths, then the two prisoners.

Before anyone could argue, Morkai's voice bellowed across the field. "Attack!"

The wraiths surged forward at a run. Their moves were neither silent nor loud but something in between. Something hollow and wrong and unsettling. Cora bit back a cry of alarm and nocked an arrow. She sent it flying into the heart of one of the first wraiths. The wraith disappeared in a puff of mist. Teryn watched as her arrow shot through the ones behind it as well, carving a line through the oncoming hoard. For a moment, Teryn thought the duke's plan had backfired, but just as Cora shot another arrow, clearing yet another line through the translucent bodies, wisps of mist filled the previous gap, and the bodies reformed. They stumbled, paused, but soon the reanimated specters were running again. Cora shot another. Another. But there were too many. No sooner did she obliterate one did another take its place. They couldn't be killed. They could hardly be slowed.

Too soon, they surrounded the handcuffed man, their ghostly weapons slicing through his flesh as if they were made of steel. Cora continued to shoot, tears streaming down her cheeks as her efforts proved more fruitless with every arrow.

Until there was nothing left to defend.

"Stop." Morkai's voice no longer bellowed but caressed the night, a whisper against the not-quite-soundless slaughter on the field. The wraiths stopped at once and retreated to their previous positions, leaving the body crumpled and alone.

The older man cried out, wailing for his son.

Cora angled herself toward Morkai, but a guard was already at her side, wrenching the bow from her hands. He made no move to take her quiver, however. The prisoner continued to weep for his son as Morkai strode over to the body. Stopping just before the corpse, the duke lifted his hands, palms level with his waist. Teryn could hardly breathe, hardly blink, as he watched Morkai's strange posture. Then something began to move over Bradley's body. It started as a strange undulating motion, like snakes sliding over the dead man's skin.

It was blood.

Teryn's throat went dry as he watched a ruby pool gather in the hollow of the man's collarbone, then—against all impossibility—began to rise into the air. Crimson tendrils lifted from the body to the duke's hand, forming an orb. The ball of blood remained suspended midair, following Morkai's palm as he rotated it upward.

The duke turned away from the corpse and approached the weeping prisoner. "I'm sorry Princess Aveline failed you and your son."

Cora made a strangled sound.

The duke kept his attention on the man, still sprawled on his knees, cuffed hands clasped together as if in prayer. He muttered something too quiet to be heard. "What did you say?" Morkai said gently.

The man lifted his head, his wounded temple still seeping. There was not grief but defiance in his eyes. "I said, I pray the seven devils drag you to hell."

Morkai looked down his nose at him. "They can try." Then, with the orb of blood still hovering over one palm, he raised the other toward the man. A thin tendril of blood lifted from the man's open wound, then snaked through the air and wove between the duke's fingers. The first orb of blood stretched out until it too resembled thread. The two sources of blood began to connect, swirling around one another, bending, twisting, weaving, until they merged as one.

The prisoner made a choking sound.

Morkai fluttered his fingertips, and the tapestry became solid. Then, with a snap of his fingers, the blood-weaving disappeared.

The man dropped at the same moment, sprawled limp on his side.

Lifeless.

Sightless.

Dead.

Teryn's gaze shot to Morkai. "You're a..." His words were trapped in his throat. It seemed an insult to call him a witch. Cora was a witch. Witches used magic. The duke, on the other hand...

This was something else. Darkness. Sorcery.

"I prefer the term blood mage," he said, "but someday you will call me your king."

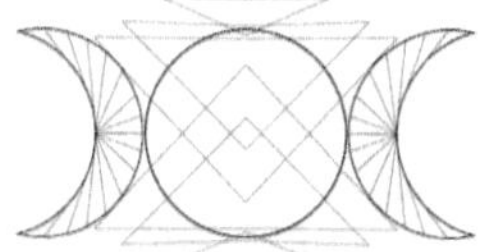

38

Cora stared at the two bodies, her mind reeling over what she'd seen. He'd taken their blood. The same way he'd taken Linette's. And her own. He'd woven the prisoners' blood between his palms, just like he'd done with hers the night he freed her from the dungeon.

What did it mean?

Teryn's voice stole through her thoughts. "You seek to be king?"

"Let us not get ahead of ourselves," Morkai said. "You must first bow to King Dimetreus."

Cora swallowed hard, seeking her voice through the tangle of emotions that threatened to crush her. "What are you implying?"

"Dimetreus shall become King of Lela," he said.

She furrowed her brow. The three kingdoms of southern Risa hadn't been called Lela in hundreds of years. If Morkai sought to reform Lela...

"That's the reason for the war," she said. "You want to conquer Menah and Selay to rule over all three kingdoms."

"Dimetreus wants to conquer Menah and Selay. I am simply helping him execute his plan."

She shook her head. Regardless of what Morkai tried to insist, she knew better than to attribute any of this to her brother. He may have been signing the documents and approving the plans, but every seed was being planted by Morkai. "You just said you'd one day be king. How in the name of the Mother Goddess is that possible?"

Morkai lifted his chin and pinned her with a sly grin. "I am Dimetreus' heir."

"No. No, you're...you're a duke. My brother gave you that title. You didn't inherit it. You hardly earned it. You've no royal blood. I..."

"Oh, did you think *you'd* be his heir? Think twice, Aveline. To the rest of your kingdom, you're still dead. There is only one way you will ever be considered his heir again, but that's a conversation better left for when we're alone."

Cora shuddered at the thought of being alone with him. The coach ride had been enough.

Morkai turned to Teryn and Lex. "Let's get things moving, shall we? Prince Lexington, my offer to you is simple. You've seen my power. You've met my wraiths. I assure you the king's living army is equally as impressive. Dimetreus' reign over Lela will come swift. Unless you leave Ridine Castle as an ally, we will come for Tomas next. We will wipe out your pitiful kingdom in a single day and put an end to every life you cherish."

Lex's face was pale as he fumbled with the hem of his waistcoat. When he spoke, his voice was a trembling whisper. "What must I do to be an ally?"

Teryn stiffened.

"Go home, gather your father's army, and send them to me," Morkai said.

Lex's eyes went wide. "His...army."

"I'll even take half," Morkai said with a smile that didn't meet his eyes. "Believe me, you will get far more out of an alliance with King Dimetreus than you will with Prince Teryn. Whatever belongs to Menah will soon belong to Lela instead. It's a simple choice, really. Life or death to put it plainly."

Lex took a step away from Teryn, his eyes on his feet. "When...when can I leave?"

"You can leave tonight if you wish. It seems someone has taken the liberty of readying your horse." Morkai shot a glare at Teryn at that last part. "However, I will send you home in the king's own coach. You can stay at the finest inns along the way."

Lex lifted his head at that. "Will the king pay for my meals too?"

"Anything you like," Morkai said, an edge creeping into his voice.

"All right," Lex said.

Teryn turned slowly toward him. "Lex."

"I'm sorry," Lex muttered. At first, he couldn't seem to meet Teryn's eyes. Then his expression shifted, turning to steel. "You know what? I'm not sorry. You dragged me into this and I've still yet to understand how or why."

"Lex, I wanted to tell you—"

"No, it's too late for that. I've been asking you to explain what the hell is going on ever since we met Mister Scary over here. All I've come to glean—on my own, mind you—is that you're a liar." He jabbed a finger toward Teryn, then pointed at Cora. "You're a lost princess, and you..." He shrank back as his eyes landed on Morkai. "Well, you have ghosts, an army, and a monster and I'm terrified of all three."

"The only sensible one of you all," Morkai said under his breath.

Lex returned his attention to Teryn. "From what I understand, you already made a deal with the king in exchange for some bounty. I'm only following your lead."

"It's not like that."

"It doesn't matter," Lex said with an exasperated shrug. "I understand duty as well as you do. I also know how to identify the losing side in a battle. You forget,

Tomas has watched two kingdoms fall to Norun. We've already done too much to keep from falling next."

"So you'll help him destroy my kingdom instead?"

"I'll do whatever it takes to save those who are important to me. Trust that."

Teryn's throat bobbed, his expression pained.

Cora tried to take pleasure in that look, knowing he was feeling a fraction of what Cora had felt when she'd learned what he'd done. Instead, she felt empty. She was still struggling to process everything Morkai had said. Everything he'd still left unexplained.

"Escort Prince Lexington to the royal coach," Morkai said to a pair of guards. Lex went with them willingly, offering not a single parting glance before he was out of sight.

Morkai angled away from Cora to face Teryn. With his back to her, she studied her surroundings, her assets. The guard with her bow watched her through the slit in his helm, while another stood a few feet away. She noted more guards standing in the shadows along the wall between the garden and the courtyard. They were all heavily armed while all she had was a half-empty quiver. The rest of her arrows littered the charred field. Her fingers flinched, begging her to reach for one of the arrows anyway, if only to have something solid and potentially lethal in her hand.

"What about you, Prince Teryn?" Morkai said. "Will you play the hero or the fool?"

"If I agree to be your ally, will you let me leave tonight too?"

Morkai let out a dark laugh. "No. I've already told you. You are a gift, one too valuable to part with. So long as you are in my custody, I have the upper hand, and I will play that hand in the name of peace. As heir to Menah and the fiancé of Selay's princess, you make a most effective bargaining piece. Your survival will be contingent upon both kingdoms' surrender. Should you value your life, you will convince your father to accept my terms for a peaceful resolution. When I send word tomorrow about our forthcoming meeting, I will include a letter from you written in your own hand. In it you will sincerely implore Arlous and Verdian to meet King Dimetreus with surrender in mind."

Teryn held Morkai's gaze without falter. "If I refuse?"

"If you refuse, then you will be a silent hostage. The result will be the same. Either you speak and urge your father to see reason, or you remain silent, captive, and hope your father has the foresight to know—should he refuse to surrender and enter war with Khero—he will not win."

Cora's heart raced as she watched Teryn's face. She tried to open herself to sense his emotions, but she found her shields had already crumbled. Her nerves were raw, her senses frayed. She was already feeling everything at once and hadn't even realized it. With a deep inhale, she focused on her breath, on the solid ground beneath her feet. Little by little her mind began to clear.

"What will it be, Prince Teryn?" Morkai said.

Teryn narrowed his eyes. "I will not encourage my father to yield to you, regardless of your threat to my life. You made a mistake in telling me you sought to inherit Dimetreus' crown. You made a mistake in showing me your dark magic. I would never let Menah bow before a blood mage."

Morkai took a step closer, his tone icy. "No, Prince Teryn, the mistake is yours." He lifted a hand. "Take him."

Four guards surged forward but Teryn immediately put up a fight. Cora watched his hand come around the hilt of one of the guard's sheathed swords. That was the last thing she saw before she plucked an arrow from her quiver and charged the guard who held her bow. The guard was surprised by Cora's sudden attack and stumbled a step back, arms spread for balance. Cora closed in and plunged her arrow into a gap in the guard's armor, burying it into his armpit. The guard dropped Cora's bow to remove the arrow, taking several more steps back. He tripped again, this time over the body of the old man. The guard went down on his back, his helm tumbling off in the process. Cora gathered up her discarded bow in one hand and took another arrow from her quiver with the other. Without hesitation, she straddled the guard and thrust her arrow through his throat. Only then did she see the guard's face. It was...a girl, not much older than Cora. Her pupils were unnaturally wide with an odd sheen over her eyes. As she choked on her own blood, the sheen began to fade, her pupils constricting to a more regular size. The girl died with tears streaming from the corners of her eyes.

Cora leapt off the guard, bile rising in her throat. She didn't know why it should matter that the guard had been a girl. And perhaps that wasn't what had Cora feeling so rattled. It was more that the guard wasn't what Cora had been expecting. She'd assumed Morkai's guards were of the same ilk his hunters had been. Rugged criminals. Mindless killers. But this guard, her eyes...they held the same sheen she'd found in Dimetreus'. These guards weren't vile monsters cloaked in armor but *people*. People he was likely controlling in the same way he was Dimetreus. And she'd just killed one of them.

"Well done, Aveline," Morkai said.

She whirled around, an arrow nocked in her bow. The only guards around were the ones who stood by the wall. Her eyes shot to where she'd last seen Teryn but he was nowhere to be found. She'd been so distracted with the guard, she hadn't noticed when his fight had ended. Or *how* it ended. Was he...

She shook the question from her mind and drew her arrow. Morkai lifted a palm, and she felt a sharp pain strike her chest. Her shot went wild as she heaved over, grasping her heart. The pain disappeared, but her lungs felt tight in its absence. Her gaze flew to his upturned palm. A tiny ball of crimson floated above it.

"I still have a drop of your blood." Morkai strode closer, the red bead suspended over his palm. She held her breath, eyes locked on his hands. His grin widened. "Let's have a private chat, Princess Aveline."

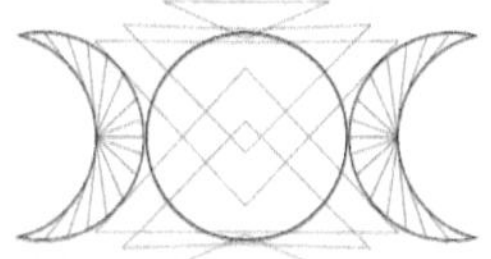

Every muscle in Cora's body was coiled tight, every limb poised for attack. Yet Morkai simply sat in a wingback chair opposite her and sipped his tea. They were in what used to be the North Tower Library, which seemed to have become Morkai's personal study. It was a wide circular room lined with bookcases, save for one wall that bore an enormous hearth. She and the duke sat before it, a fire blazing in its core.

Cora tried not to let her eyes leave Morkai's, but she couldn't help noting all the changes he'd made to the room since she'd last seen it. Every window had been sealed with a tapestry. Every shelf bore far more books than there was space for, every spare inch brimming with unfamiliar volumes, some boasting unsettling titles on their spines. *The Art of Blood. Grimoire Sanguina. Mastering the Ethera.* A desk was pushed up against one of the bookcases, its top strewn with parchment and several enormous leather-bound tomes. A table sat at the center of the room, littered with more parchment, more books, stoppered indigo bottles, and a crystal bowl filled with some dark liquid. The most terrifying thing of all was the enormous shape of the Beast dozing next to Morkai's chair. The creature took up a good portion of the room, its rumbling snores filling the air with a grating sound. This was the closest she'd been to the Beast. Her eyes fell on the ridge of spines running down its back. Spines she now realized weren't spines at all but unicorn horns. Valorre came to mind again, sending an ache to her heart.

If the Beast is here, Valorre is safe, she told herself.

But what of the hunters? If they find him...

With a shudder, Cora returned her study to the duke. He sipped his tea again, then tipped his chin at the cup and saucer she held in her shaking hands. "I promise it isn't poisoned," he said. "Besides, that's more of your realm of expertise, isn't it?"

She set her tea on a small table next to her chair and gripped her armrests instead. He'd let her keep her bow and quiver. Another gesture to show how little he feared her. Her weapons lay next to her chair, tempting her to reach for them. Each time she considered the action, she remembered that ball of blood Morkai had. He'd summoned it so quickly. So easily. Where was he even keeping it?

"You said you wanted to talk," she said, her voice coming out far shakier than she liked. "So let's talk."

"You have questions. Ask them."

"You're truly going to answer?"

"I have nothing to hide from you. It is my deepest wish to make you my strongest ally. I already know it is folly to lie to you, what with your Art. I can only imagine you've honed your talents these last six years." His eyes dropped briefly to the ink on her forearms, once again eying them without even a hint of reverence. "So ask. I'll answer."

Cora pored over everything she'd yet to make sense of. A vision of the dead guard's glassy eyes flashed through her mind. She closed her eyes against the guilt, banishing the sight of her hands on the arrow that killed the girl—

"How are you controlling people?" she managed to say. Forcing her eyes open, she focused on her breath to steady her. "How are you able to get people to follow you and blindly obey?"

"Not everyone who works for me follows me blindly, Aveline."

Cora thought of his hunters. No, she supposed some wouldn't take much convincing to do his bidding. "But I know you utilize magical influence for control. You've changed my brother's memories. You've convinced him Selay and Menah are his enemies." She didn't mention the guard. Couldn't mention her.

"It's called a glamour. Do you know what that is?"

She nodded. She'd learned about glamours from the Forest People. Similar to her feat with Teryn and the baby unicorn, a glamour was a way to shift another's perception to make them see what one wished for them to see. Cora had never witnessed it in action. Or, if she had, she hadn't known. Still, it seemed to have very little in common with what Morkai was doing.

He seemed to pick up on her train of thought. "What I do goes beyond the realm of a common glamour. My specialties lie less in changing what people see and more in changing what they believe. I weave thoughts into one's mind, give them images, impressions, and beliefs. It only works on the minds of the weak or willing."

"Are you saying my brother is weak?"

"I'm saying your brother has always been quick to accept exactly what I've offered him. He's always wanted an explanation for his wife's death. An enemy to blame other than himself. My explanations suit his sphere of plausibility. He's never wanted the enemy to be me, which is why your efforts to convince him otherwise fall on deaf ears."

"And what of others who work for you? Others you control?"

His lips curled into a smirk. "Like the guard I watched you kill? She had ambitions. People she wanted to prove her worth to. I merely helped her along. Impressed upon her a vision of what could be accomplished in my service."

"How do you do it? How do you keep your illusions constantly in place?" As far as Cora knew, a glamour lasted only so long as one was focused on it. Expending that kind of magic on multiple people at once for any extended length of time…it shouldn't be possible.

Morkai glanced at his sleeping Beast. "That's where my Roizan comes in."

"Roizan." Cora echoed the unfamiliar word. "What is a Roizan?"

"A creature made with the forbidden Arts—the magic of the sanguina and ethera. A Roizan is forged from death and given new life. It is no longer a natural being. No longer susceptible to mortality. Its life is bound to mine and my powers to it. A Roizan is a living vessel. It can hold unimaginable power that I am able to channel from without expending any of my own vitale."

She was unfamiliar with some of the terms. *Sanguina. Ethera. Vitale.*

Morkai continued. "Because of my relationship with my Roizan, I can maintain hundreds of glamours at once. All I have to do is weave them."

"What does the Beast—the *Roizan*—have to do with the unicorns you're hunting?"

He set down his teacup and placed his cane in his lap, caressing the crystal like she'd seen him do many times now. Was it simply an idle habit or did the crystal hold some significance? "The unicorns are a complicated subject," he said slowly.

"You said you'd answer my questions."

"I mean to. But where to start?" He gazed at the fire, but his expression was not one of deep thought. His face was smug. "There's an ancient prophecy I've spent most of my life fighting against. One that mentions unicorns, a mother, and a child. Three things I should have no reason to fear. And I don't, for there is but one element of the three that all the others hinge upon, and I've already taken an action against it that has nullified the prophecy in its entirety."

She felt cold despite the warmth of the fire. "What action have you taken?"

"You asked about the unicorns, so let us remain on topic. The unicorns are part of the prophecy, which as I've said, is null. And yet, the prophecy itself doesn't seem to know that. The appearance of the unicorns is a personal affront to my efforts, so I've made it my mission to be rid of them."

"That sounds rather petty."

Morkai shrugged. "Petty, perhaps, but quite beneficial to me. Unicorns hold some of the strongest fae magic that exists. Harnessing that magic creates a well of power. I need sources of power to work my magic, for every feat expends it."

Cora's stomach churned. "That's why you feed the unicorns to your Roizan. It… holds their magic."

"Which I, in turn, draw from at will."

"Why do you starve them? Torture them?"

"Unicorn magic is pure light, Aveline," he said, a condescending lilt to his tone. "It has been known to heal, to burn away darkness."

Cora huffed. "That's supposed to be a bad thing?"

"It is neither a good thing nor a bad thing because darkness isn't evil. Darkness is simply an aspect of light the same way death is an aspect of life. My Art deals in darkness, which makes light magic detrimental. But light can turn to dark the same way day turns to night. Unlike the natural passing of dawn to dusk, light magic needs help to transmute itself into darkness. Starving the unicorns, trapping them in iron, and letting the deadly metal drain their vitale...it corrupts their magic. Changes it. No unicorn would ever wield corrupted magic themselves, but I would. And I do. You saw my demonstration. Saw how easily I drew living wraiths from dead, scorched earth. You've seen how I can change the minds of the weak. Saw how easily Prince Lexington accepted my offer. Menah and Selay will fall, as will anyone who stands against us. Dimetreus will become King of Lela. Your only choice is to stand at his side."

Cora squeezed the arms of her chair until her knuckles turned white. "To what end? You've implied that you intend to usurp my brother once he's claimed rule over the three kingdoms. Why? My brother has already given you more than you deserve. He made you a duke. Set you at the head of his council. How is that not enough for you?"

He scoffed. "The title of a duke. I'm already a prince of two kingdoms—a kingdom of men and a kingdom of fae. If neither of those titles are enough, what makes you think I'll settle for being a duke?" He shook his head. "I'll settle only for King of Lela."

Cora frowned. Since when was Morkai a prince? Not only that but a prince of fae? She'd already suspected his fae heritage when she'd studied his features in the coach. But...there were no living fae aside from the Faeryn descendants. No fae kingdom left to rule. As for the human kingdoms he sought to overthrow...

She gritted her teeth. "You have no right to rule all three kingdoms of Lela. Not even Dimetreus has that right."

Morkai's silver-blue eyes flashed with indignation. "I do have that right. My blood is the blood of an Elvyn king. My claim is to Lela's magic, and I will inherit it."

"What are you talking about?"

"Lela is more than it seems, Aveline. It is not a human land, but the heart of the fae realm. Fae magic seeps through every blade of grass, every root, every tree, but it does nothing but dissipate into thin air. The magic must be harnessed, and the person to harness it will be me." He shifted in his seat, some of the fire leaving his words. "First, though, I must *inherit* the land itself. Not just a portion of it. Not just Khero. All of what was once considered Lela."

"That's why you're having my brother conquer the other two kingdoms."

He nodded. "I cannot conquer Lela myself, I can only rightfully inherit it. That is a condition of the prophecy I cannot fight. Your brother, on the other hand, can claim rule over the three kingdoms through battle, brutality, lethal force—whatever means necessary. Then he will pass his crown to me after his death."

Cora bristled. "You're going to murder him."

"He's going to die," the duke corrected, lips quirked into a sly smile.

She shook her head. "You can't be his heir. Your rule will be contested—"

"Who will dare stand against me?"

Cora wanted to say her brother's other councilmen, but she realized they were likely already under Morkai's thumb. If they were even still alive. Based on the two prisoners she'd met today, it seemed Morkai didn't let those who stood against him live.

"It won't matter," Morkai said. "By the time anyone thinks to contest my rule, I will have control over fae magic. Not just the Elvyn magic that lives in my blood but the magic of the Faeryn too. Whatever magic you've seen and studied, whatever magic you think you know, it pales in comparison to what I'll have once I'm king. I will direct the flow of magic in this land, whether it's the Art of witches or the Magic of the Soil. I will give power where it is due and take it from where it is not."

Cora's mind reeled at the hidden implications. He hadn't admitted to knowing about the Forest People, but he knew about the Faeryn, the Magic of the Soil. He claimed to be an Elvyn prince. If he attained the power he sought…what would happen to the Forest People? Their magic? To witches like her and anyone who refused to bow to his control?

Keeping her voice level, she asked, "Why do you want this power so badly?"

He lifted his chin and studied her for a few silent moments. "I will do great and wonderful things, Aveline. My allies will be blessed. My enemies will be vanquished. I will shape the future of the world as I see fit. My magic will allow me to accomplish feats you can't imagine. I will put an end to death for those I protect." His expression took on a fierce quality as something dark flashed in his eyes. Slowly, he stood from his chair, planting his cane firmly before him. "You could be one of those people."

An end to death. What was he talking about? She recalled what he'd done with the prisoners' blood. What he'd done with *her* minuscule drop. She recalled the wraiths, heard their ghostly blades carving apart living flesh. If Morkai could do all that, what else could he do? What could he do to an army? What could he do during a bloody battle? Even more frightening was the thought of what he could do if his powers were increased by the magic he sought.

Cora knew in the depths of her heart, blood, and soul that—should Morkai succeed—he would destroy the world.

"You're right about one thing," he said, voice gentle. "Some will contest my right to the throne after your brother dies, and I will deal with them swiftly. I will spill their blood without remorse. You, however, can stop that from ever happening. You can save others from bloodshed by helping me strengthen my right to the throne."

"How?" she asked, although she dreaded the answer.

His pale eyes locked on hers, devoid of warmth. "Marry me."

She rose from her chair and took a step away, knocking the tea table over in the process. Her teacup and saucer clattered to the floor, but she refused to take her eyes from Morkai's. "You're out of your mind."

He took a step closer. "I can give you half my heart."

She barked a laugh as she stepped back again, feeling porcelain crunch beneath her shoes. "*Half* your heart? Is that what you consider a proper proposal?"

"The other half doesn't belong to me," he said without inflection. "But you could. I think my heart would like you. It's a jealous heart, but it could come to understand."

Another piece of porcelain crunched under her foot. This time she slipped. She caught herself on her hands and knees, making an effort to heave a few breaths as her fingers stretched toward her quiver. Her hand came around the fletching of an arrow. She rose to her feet and rushed Morkai, colliding with his torso. Her arrow slid through flesh as she angled it up beneath his ribs—

She gasped as a surge of pain struck her chest. Her vision blurred, but she refused to collapse. Clutching at her heart, she took a wavering step back, her lips curled into a wicked grin. Morkai held her drop of blood over his palm, but Cora didn't care. So what if he killed her, as long as she took him with her. His black coat was already darkening around the shaft protruding from his torso. He stared down at it for a moment. Then, to Cora's horror, he smiled. Tucking his cane beneath his arm, he brought his free hand an inch from his wound and began to gather tendrils of his own blood.

He met her eyes as her tiny drop stretched thin and began snaking toward his. "I could bind us by blood, Aveline. I could wind our fates together, force you to be my bride."

She stumbled back, her chest still throbbing with pain as she doubled over. Her vision was nearly black now.

Then the pain abated. She lifted her eyes and found Morkai frowning down at her. His blood no longer hovered over his palm and hers had returned to a tiny drop. He lowered his palm and the ball of blood disappeared.

"I won't bind you to me," he said, voice barely a whisper. "Weavings of fate take more power than I'm willing to expend. Instead, I will give you time to choose me. And you will. You will choose one half of my heart willingly, or you will take the other half unwillingly." He said the last part through his teeth as he wrenched her arrow from his flesh and threw it into the fire. Then he took his cane from under his arm and pointed it at the sleeping Roizan. He pressed his other hand to his seeping wound. In a matter of seconds, he stood straighter.

He'd healed himself.

"I will give you time to think."

"I don't need time to think," she spat out. "I will never choose you."

A tic formed at the corner of his jaw. "Is it the boy then? The prince?"

Her pulse kicked up. "Teryn? He's...he's nothing to me. He betrayed me."

Morkai scoffed. "I see the way you look at him. I've been on the receiving end of looks like that. I know what it means."

"You mean hatred? Yes, I imagine you've received many looks like that."

"You could never be Teryn's queen. Do you know what the prince's father did to *his* queen? He tried to have her replaced with his mistress. Teryn would only do the same to you."

She clenched her teeth. "I never said—"

"Haven't you figured out why I took your blood all those years ago? Why I wove it with Queen Linette's?"

Cora's breath caught. All she could manage was a shake of her head.

"I bound your fate to the queen's. It took all the power I'd stored in my Roizan up until that point, but I succeeded."

"Then why am I still alive? What are you waiting for?"

"Death was not the bond I wove. A death weaving doesn't take nearly as much power, for it is an immediate sentence, not a long-term curse. It was your fate I wove, one that guaranteed—like the queen—you would die childless. It was an idea you inspired. I don't have your ability to sense others' emotions. I can only give thoughts and feelings to weak-minded beings, not receive them. But you knew the queen had lied about providing an heir. I'd already known I'd have to do away with her one way or another. She'd already begun trying to turn Dimetreus against me. And letting her further Dimetreus' line would only hamper my plans. But your little scene at dinner that night made me realize I could take care of two problems at once."

Cora's stomach turned over with a wave of nausea. She resisted the urge to bring her hand to her stomach. "Why would you do that? Why would you try to keep me from having..." She couldn't even say the next word. The prospect of having children had rarely crossed her mind. She was nowhere close to ready when it came to becoming a mother. But the realization that he'd tampered with something so personal, so intimate....

Her legs gave out and she sank into her chair. Sweat beaded behind her neck, down her back. The laces of her corset felt too tight, too smothering. "Why?"

"The unicorns. The mother. The child. Who do you think you are in that prophecy?" When she didn't answer, he said, "The mother, Aveline. You are the mother and your child would have been my enemy. I knew of the prophecy long before I came to Khero, and I knew who you were the moment I met you. I sensed your magic, respected it. That's why I never wanted to kill you, regardless of the threat you posed. Weaving your fate was the only thing I could do to let you keep your life."

He said it with so much false kindness, it made her want to retch. Fury roared through her blood, and it demanded his life. She extended a hand toward her quiver, even as Morkai's eyes trailed her every move. She didn't care if he stopped her. She didn't care if she died trying—

The door flew open and a guard stormed in. "There's a unicorn circling the castle wall."

Morkai's expression shuttered. "A unicorn?"

"It's been trying to get in."

Cora was frozen halfway toward reaching for her quiver. Her mind went to Valorre. It couldn't be...

The Roizan stood and growled at the open door.

Morkai turned narrowed eyes upon her. "Do you have a friend, Aveline?" Her guilt must have shown on her face for he broke into a dark laugh. Turning to the Roizan, he shouted, "Find it." The Roizan darted across the room, sending the guard diving out of the way as the creature squeezed through the door.

Cora's hand closed around the strap of her quiver—

"Seize her," Morkai said. Cora dove for her bow, but the guard was faster. He tore the weapons from her grip and twisted her arms behind her back. Morkai gathered up her bow and quiver as the guard hauled her out the door. She struggled the entire way down the stairs, through the dark halls, but it was no use. The guard evaded her every attempt to free herself. Soon the stench of rot filled her nostrils. Panic set in as they entered an eerily familiar part of the castle. Not eerie in the same way she'd feel if they'd been heading for the former queen's chambers. This sense of terrifying recognition came from returning to a place Cora had only been once before.

The dungeon.

40

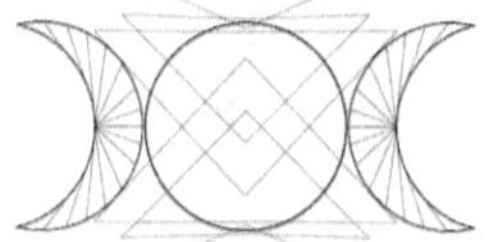

The fight left Cora's body. Dread filled her core as the guard hauled her over one armored shoulder. They marched past cell after cell, some doors closed while others gaped open. The dungeon hall was lit only by the occasional lamp. It was exactly how she remembered it. Dim. Terrifying. Cold. The unsettling familiarity swept Cora into memory. She was small again. A girl who'd just been on the receiving end of her brother's misplaced wrath. Tears had streamed down her cheeks as her pleas went unheard. Her brother had refused to step foot in the dungeon hall and instead stood at the doorway, watching as she was dragged away from him without an ounce of pity in his glazed eyes.

She looked at the same doorway now. It was empty this time, shrinking behind her with every step the guard took. But she remembered the sheen in Dimetreus' hollow gaze. Her brother had been under Morkai's glamour even then. It made sense now. She'd met the Roizan that night six years ago, which meant the duke had already created a vessel for dark magic, already had the ability to weave a long-standing glamour.

Her captor stopped outside a closed cell. She renewed her struggle, but the guard only squeezed her tighter. From ahead, she heard the clang of metal on metal. A door being unlocked. The guard set her roughly down and shoved her inside the now-open cell. She stumbled back into darkness and landed on the damp stone floor. Pushing herself off the ground, she whirled toward the door. Two figures were backlit by the dim light outside the cell. One was unmistakably Morkai. She hadn't noticed he'd come too.

He threw something at her feet and slammed the cell door. His voice came through a thin barred window. "If only one of you remains alive by sunrise, that person can leave."

Two sets of footsteps retreated.

She blinked into the room, willing her eyes to adjust to darkness. The tiny window provided barely enough light to see her own hands at first. But soon she began to make out shapes from the shadows. A pile of straw. A chamber pot. And a humanlike form in the corner.

She'd already known she wasn't alone.

If only one of you remains alive by sunrise, that person can leave.

Her gaze darted to her feet where she found her quiver with not even a dozen arrows left inside. That must have been what Morkai had thrown inside the cell with her. He wanted Cora to kill whoever was in here with her.

Or...he wanted the other person to kill her.

The form stirred, shifted. She bent down, grabbed an arrow in each hand. The figure rose to standing at the same moment she did. It stepped closer while Cora stood her ground, prepared to fight. She assessed every edge of her adversary's silhouette, seeking any sign that they held a weapon too, until...

Until they stepped into the sliver of light streaming in from the barred window.

It was Teryn.

~

She wasn't sure whether to feel relief or anger, but she didn't have time to consider either emotion. He moved toward her, and she drew her arm back, ready to plunge her arrow—

He didn't close in.

Instead, he leaned against the opposite wall with a sigh. She shifted her stance so she could see him more clearly. He was still dressed down to his shirt and trousers, his neckcloth hanging untied around his open collar. His face was bruised, his lower lip split. He closed his eyes and rested his head against the wall. "He doesn't expect us to kill each other, nor does he want us to," he said, voice heavy with fatigue. "He needs me alive, remember?"

She looked down at the arrows in her hands. "Then why did he leave me with these?"

"Because he wants us to distrust each other. Either that or...or he wants to test our friendship so he can use us against one another."

She pointedly ignored the second part of his statement. "Distrust has already been well established between us, thanks to you."

"I can't keep saying I'm sorry if you won't believe it."

"You haven't said it nearly enough for me to even start to believe it. We're here because of you."

She expected him to argue, to say they were there because of *her*, because she'd lied about her identity, because she was a wanted fugitive.

But he said none of that.

"I know, Cora. I'd take it back if I could."

She felt the truth of his statement. As much as she wanted to hold on to the comforting weight of her rage, she felt some of it begin to fray. He hadn't taken Morkai's deal. Hadn't agreed to convince his father to surrender. Unlike Lex. She felt a flicker of resentment at how easily Lex had given in. Not that she could blame him. What was happening here had nothing to do with the Kingdom of

Tomas and everything to do with the three kingdoms of Lela. For now, at least. What Lex had failed to understand was that if Morkai became King of Lela, he'd be a force the rest of the continent should fear. A force the rest of the *world* should fear.

She could forgive Lex for being a coward, but she wouldn't be so easy on herself.

With a deep breath, she tossed her arrows back inside her quiver and began unhooking the closures of her gown. When that didn't work, she tore her bodice and pushed her skirts down her hips until only her shift and corset remained.

Teryn straightened with alarm. "What are you doing?"

"I'm not lounging around in a dungeon cell wearing an evening gown." She turned away from him and began loosening the laces of her corset until she felt her ribcage expand. Her cheeks grew hot despite the fact that modesty was pointless in their situation. Still, she refused to meet his eyes as she marched to the cell door. There was no keyhole on this side, only solid metal. She hadn't heard the scrape of a key after Morkai had shut the door, which meant the locking mechanism must be automatic. The barred window was far too high for her to reach through and try to pick the lock. And yet, it was a lock like any other. And the door...it was just that. A door. A medley of elements.

Closing her eyes, she pressed her palms to the metal.

And pushed.

～

NOTHING HAPPENED. FOR HOURS, CORA SOUGHT THE ELEMENTS WITHIN THE DOOR. She should have been able to connect with them. In theory, at least. She'd heard tales of witches who could walk through walls, of Faeryn who could carve paths through stone with a touch. After what she'd done under the tree, she believed those stories now. Believed it was possible. The door was iron. Earth that had been heated with fire, transmuted into liquid, solidified with air. The same elements that comprised her body, animated her life force. She should be able to melt it. Move it. Seek the locking mechanism and lift it from its latch. She went through the same thought process she'd gone through at the tree, but not once did she feel a connection to her magic.

It was Morkai. It had to be him. She hadn't felt her magic as strongly ever since he'd captured her. Not even her shields had felt as firmly under her control. The duke was blocking her magic somehow.

With a frustrated groan, she slammed her fist against the door.

"Are you going to do that all night?" Teryn asked. They hadn't spoken more than a handful of terse words.

"I'm trying to get out of here," she said through her teeth. She pressed her palms to the door, but her magic felt more muted than ever. Why had it been so much easier at the tree? She'd felt so strong afterward. Exhilarated.

Then she remembered why she'd done it in the first place.

She'd felt an internal nudge, a clairsentient *feeling* that told her to do what felt hardest in that moment. Her instincts had begged her to fight or flee but her magic had urged her to stay and hide. She'd faced a challenge and her magic had grown from it.

If that was the case, where was her magic now? Where were the great feats she'd allowed herself to believe in?

She closed her eyes and focused on her breath, stilling her thoughts until they narrowed on the feeling of air filling her lungs. The stench of rot threatened to shake her concentration, but she told herself the aroma was nothing more than air and earth and water and fire. She shifted her feet against the stone floor, letting it anchor her. She felt the damp air on her skin, could hear the trickle of water dripping in a nearby cell. She opened her eyes and studied the shaft of lamplight streaming through the barred window. With her connection to the elements made, calm settled over her. But there remained a heaviness that darkened the edges of her awareness, snagging her senses. She followed it, pursued the source, expecting it to lead her to Morkai.

It didn't.

It led her to Teryn.

From her periphery, she saw him leaning against the wall, head lowered, arms folded. The darkness she'd sensed collected all around him, but it wasn't coming *from* him. It was coming from her. She could feel it spilling from her chest in angry waves.

Morkai wasn't blocking her magic. She was.

The realization was so enraging, she felt the darkness gather even thicker. She knew then what her current greatest challenge was.

Hands on her hips, she whirled to face the prince. "Why should I forgive you?"

He looked up and met her eyes. "I never said you should, only that I'm sorry."

"Why did you do it? What great need did you—a prince—have for my bounty? Why was it so important that it compelled you to trick me into accepting your company, trick me into thinking you wanted to help the unicorns—"

"I did want to help them," Teryn said. "Perhaps that hadn't been my motive at first, but I was repulsed by what the hunters were doing. By what Helios had wanted to do. It's just that..." He stepped away from the wall and rubbed his brow. "I thought you were a murderer, Cora. I thought you'd murdered the queen and princess."

"You could have asked. You know, *before* you betrayed my trust."

"What would you have done?"

She opened her mouth but her answer died on her lips. Had he revealed that he knew who she was—knew she was wanted by the crown—she'd have fled at her first chance. And that was only if she hadn't felt threatened. If she had, well...it would have ended in a fight. Her heart sank when she imagined how such a confrontation could have ended. "You still haven't answered my question. What did you want with my bounty?"

"I told you about the scandal," he said, voice hollow with exhaustion. "About the threat of war my kingdom faced a few years back."

She nodded, trying not to think about what Morkai had said on that topic.

You could never be Teryn's queen.

The unicorns. The mother. The child...

Do you know what the prince's father did to his queen? He tried to have her replaced with his mistress. Teryn would only do the same to you.

The curse he wove with her blood...

"My father took a loan from the Bank of Cartha to compensate my mother and keep her father from declaring war on us. We hadn't been able to pay the bank back so Cartha resorted to sending pirates. They've been raiding our ships, halting trade between us and Brushwold. My kingdom...we were on the brink of ruin. It was my duty as heir to fix what my father had nearly destroyed. That was why I went after the unicorns in the first place."

"The Heart's Hunt," she said, remembering what he'd told her when they'd first met. He'd come to Khero to win Princess Mareleau's hand in marriage. The thought sent an odd prickle to her heart.

"I found the poster with your face on it shortly after I realized I couldn't complete the Hunt." He ran a hand through his hair before he met her eyes again. "I regret it. I regret lying to you. I regret putting you in danger."

Again, she felt the truth of his emotions. "What about for yourself? Don't you regret getting captured?"

He let out a dark laugh. "Maybe I've gotten what I deserve."

They fell into silence. Cora nibbled her bottom lip. She could feel the darkness dissipating between them, felt something like relief lighten her chest. But she still felt a block. A challenge. One that aggravated her to no end.

"I won't let my father yield to him," he said. "I promise you, in whatever way I can, I will stop Duke Morkai."

She wanted to bark a laugh and remind him there was nothing he could do. He was a prisoner. A hostage. Morkai would send his summons to Menah and Selay in the morning. When they met at Centerpointe Rock in two weeks' time, there would be very little chance the duke would give Teryn the opportunity to speak. If the prince hadn't been such a stubborn fool, he could have lied to the duke the same way he'd lied to her. He could have let Morkai think he'd won him over only to bide his time until he could act against the duke in a way that mattered. Instead, Teryn had gotten himself thrown in a cell.

As did I, she reminded herself. Perhaps they weren't so different.

She had to admit, there was something admirable about him refusing to play the duke's game. Her admiration bloomed, softening the edges of the thorns that had embedded themselves around her heart. His betrayal still ached. She breathed it in, feeling the sensations sink her stomach, letting them thrum through her, weaken her bit by bit, crumble her, and then...*strengthen* her. Her mind grew clearer, her breaths fuller.

"All right," she whispered.

"All right, what?"

"All right, I..." She tried to form the word *forgive*, but her mouth wouldn't obey. It was too soon to feel genuine forgiveness, but she felt *something*. "I understand. I...I know why you did what you did, so...all right."

His posture relaxed. "Cora—"

She turned away from him and went back to the door. This time, when she placed her hands against the metal, a thrum of magic ran through her palm. She felt equal parts elation and annoyance. Why had her magic insisted on her making peace with Teryn? Then again, maybe it hadn't been about him at all. Maybe it had more to do with the rage and hate she'd let consume her senses. Her powers had grown when she'd hid herself and Teryn under the tree, but she'd so quickly reverted to her base instincts afterward. It was a lesson she was constantly having to revisit—the cost of ignoring the whispers of quiet magic in the face of far more tempting noise.

She could hear her magic now, though, the same way she had at the tree. It wasn't a voice that spoke but a feeling. One that guided her hand to where the door met the frame. She felt the cool metal pulse beneath her hand, echoing the rush of her blood. Once, this door was molten. Once, this door was as soft and pliable as her flesh. Once, it was but a collection of metals. Small. Separate. Movable. Even now, she could sense space in the steel, the same space that existed between her fingers, between the strands of her hair, in the pores of her skin. It moved, it buzzed, it hummed like anything else. She slid her hand slightly up, sensed movement mirrored within the door. Then she brushed a finger to the left.

A soft click sounded on the other side. She gave the metal a gentle push.

Beneath Cora's palm, the door opened.

41

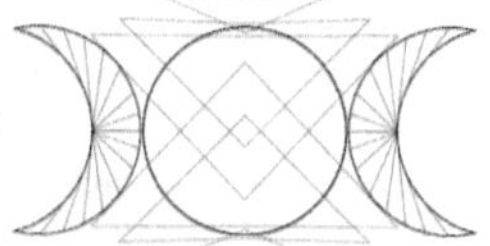

Cora stared at the gap in the cell door. Her body tingled with residual magic from her feet to the center of her scalp. She was so lost in her moment of surprise that she didn't realize Teryn had come up beside her until she heard the soft rumble of his voice.

"You...you opened the door."

All Cora could manage was a nod.

"You did that with your magic?" He was looking at her as if seeing something he'd never noticed before. Even to her, this was more impressive than what she'd done beneath the tree. She'd unlocked the door with clairsentient magic. Moved physical matter using sensation, feeling, connection.

If I can do this, what else can I do?

She couldn't help the smile that formed on her lips, but she reminded herself that her pride could wait. There was still a need for haste. She opened the door a little wider and glanced down both ends of the hall. One side ended in shadow where the dungeon hall led to deeper areas, more cells, places Cora had never seen. The other side revealed the closed door she'd been led through earlier—a door that would take her to the upper levels of the castle. With her magic still thrumming strong in her veins, she extended her senses and searched for nearby minds, emotions. Most of the energies she could sense were condensed in the deeper areas of the dungeon. Closer to her cell, she sensed only a few minds, their emotions dulled in slumber. She was struck with the sudden impulse to free the other prisoners but halted that thought before it could bloom. There most certainly were more prisoners like Bradley and his father, but there also could be dangerous people like the hunters. Besides, who knew how long she had before another guard would be back. Before Morkai returned.

If only one of you remains alive by sunrise, that person can leave.

Cora had no idea what time it was. For all she knew, it could be nearing sunrise already.

With a steadying breath, she took a step outside the door. She paused, waiting, feeling. When the path seemed clear, she returned to the cell, shouldered her quiver, and gestured at Teryn. "Come on. We must hurry." She took another step. When she didn't hear Teryn follow, she cast a glance back at him.

She watched his shoulders fall. Watched a flicker of hope crumble until his face was left slack. His response was strained. "I can't leave."

"What? Why?"

"You heard what he said. He needs me alive."

Cora took a step back inside the cell. "He only needs you alive to use as a bargaining piece."

"Yes, and if he finds me gone come morning, he won't send his summons for my father and King Verdian. He won't meet with them for talks of peace."

"I thought you didn't want your father to surrender."

"I don't."

Cora took another step closer. "Then why would you let yourself be used by Morkai?"

"So long as he has me as a hostage, we know his next move. We know he'll proceed with the meeting."

"How does it help for us to know his next move if Menah and Selay don't? They don't know he's a mage. They will only know what the duke's missive tells them. I guarantee he will make terms for surrender sound favorable. Not only that, but his magic...he can influence people's minds. Change how they think."

"I've gathered that," Teryn said. "But, Cora, we're both prizes to him. He needs me for negotiations. As for you..." His fingers curled into tight fists. "I don't like the way he looks at you. The way he talks to you. The way he framed you for murder only to hunt you down now. I have a feeling he wants to do so much more."

Cora pursed her lips to keep from telling Teryn he was right. Morkai had plans for her indeed, and she wasn't sure she even knew the half of them.

Teryn spoke again. "If he finds this cell empty in the morning, discovers both his prizes are gone, who knows what he'll do, when he'll strike. I can't leave, but you can. You can warn my father not to listen to a word Morkai says. Warn him of the duke's true nature. Perhaps then we can beat him at his own game."

She felt the wisdom of his words, and yet it did nothing to stop the ache in her chest. Now that she'd rid her heart of its icy thorns of hatred, it was left open to other emotions. His. Hers. Pain, regret, fear.

"I can't leave you here," she said, her voice breaking.

"Tell my father—"

"Come with me and tell him yourself."

"—everything you know. Everything we've seen. Tell him—"

"No." She reached for his wrist, closed her fingers around it. Her palm pulsed at their touch, no longer separated by gloves, and her heart thudded in a wild echo.

Teryn stepped in close, and for a moment, Cora thought he was going to agree.

But his expression was not one of resignation. It was one of pain. "Tell him to let me go."

She felt the weight of what he meant. He wanted his father to let him die. It shouldn't have come as a surprise. She knew Morkai intended to kill Teryn if the royals refused to surrender. Only now did that strike her as something she couldn't bear. She almost wished she'd held on to her hate, for maybe then it would be easier to leave him. Easier to do what needed to be done.

She gripped his wrist tighter, took another step closer. "You stubborn son-of-a—"

Her words dissolved as he gave her a sad smirk and lowered his face to hers. In the next breath his lips were against her own, the kiss so sudden and startling she froze. Then a rush of fire swept over her, and she wasn't sure whether it was renewed rage or some absurd flood of desire. Whatever the case, she felt her lips yield beneath his, felt her hand leave his wrist to cradle the back of his neck. She buried one hand in his hair while the other ran up his chest, resting on the curve of his shoulder. His arms came around her back, pulling her tight against him, as if even the slightest inch between their bodies was unbearable. She bit back a gasp, but it only made her lips part. His tongue swept against hers and she met it with a fervor she'd never felt before. Something small inside her shouted that this was hardly the time for a kiss, but a greater part of her banished the thought, consumed by a sudden need to taste him, feel him—

He pushed away from her before she realized what was happening. She opened her eyes, found a door slamming shut before her, heard the click of the lock snapping automatically in place. Catching her breath, she stared at the closed door and realized she and Teryn now stood on opposite sides of it—she in the hall and Teryn in the cell. All previous desire drained from her body as her mind reeled over what had just happened.

"You tricked me."

"I did what I had to do," came his muffled voice from the other side.

Her hands trembled, her skin still warm from where it had been pressed against him. "I...I despise you."

"Good." His shadow shifted behind the barred window. "Then it will be easier for you to leave me here. Go. And know that if we never meet again, I think you're—"

She gritted her teeth, expecting him to say something patronizing like *pretty*, *beautiful*, or *great*.

"—formidable." The way the word rolled off his tongue with the deepest respect and admiration made Cora feel as if he'd just called her the most desirable woman in the world.

Her anger dissipated. Not fully, but enough to clear her mind. The warmth from their kiss was gone, leaving her shivering in the cold hall.

"Go," he whispered, then she heard him shuffle away from the door and shift against the far wall.

Without another word, she turned from the cell and left him behind, ignoring the tears that managed to squeeze from the corners of her eyes.

~

CORA BANISHED ALL THOUGHTS OF TERYN AS SHE CREPT THROUGH THE DARK HALLS IN the lower level of the sleeping castle. Her steps were slow, quiet, careful, as she followed a familiar route to the servants' passage. It was the same path Morkai had taken her down six years ago. She kept her shields lowered, her senses open, stopping every time she felt guards drawing near. When they did, she pressed herself close to the walls, merging with stone and shadows until they passed her by. The servants' passage was thankfully empty. It wasn't too surprising considering the lack of staff she'd seen at dinner. She was starting to understand more and more why Ridine was so empty. Anyone who couldn't be swayed by Morkai was probably dismissed, imprisoned, or killed. Perhaps it was a good sign that the castle wasn't teeming with mindless, brainless sycophants. It could mean Morkai's influence was weaker than he'd made it seem.

Cora reached the back end of the castle. After testing a few doors, she found the one that led from the passage to the yard outside the kitchens. Enormous outdoor ovens, washbasins, and lines for drying linens stood empty as Cora crept past. She focused on her breath, on the firmness of the earth, silent beneath her soft steps. The air was cool, the sky just beginning to pale toward dawn. She fixed her gaze on the dark forests looming beyond the wall, her hope tenuous as she paused behind an overgrown shrub. With a deep breath, she turned her attention to the wall itself, seeking signs of sentries. She saw some silhouettes farther down, closer to the nearest gate, but none straight ahead. That was where the vines of ivy crawled up the wall, blanketing it like a tapestry.

That was where she hoped to find the hidden break in the stone.

With another deep breath, she drew air against her skin, earth against her feet, calling upon the elements to shield her, hide her, obscure her. Then she stepped out from behind the shrub and crept toward the wall. She kept her senses reaching outward, seeking any nearby emotions that rippled with shock or alarm.

Finally, she reached the wall and pressed herself against it. There she paused, once again assessing her surroundings for threats. The sentries remained near the gates. She tiptoed along the wall, feeling beneath the ivy for any sign of crumbling stone. Her heart slammed against her ribs, her muscles clenched in panic. Every touch revealed only solid wall. Terror nearly threatened to overtake her, but she forced herself to be calm. Breathe. Turn inward.

She closed her eyes and pressed both palms to the stone beneath the ivy, extending her senses out along the wall. To the right, she felt only dense, solid energy, but to the left...

There was a hollow, a lightness in the wall's density. She followed it, ran her hand to where she was guided, freezing when her fingers sank beneath the ivy. She bent down, spread the ivy aside, and found an opening only chest high. In her memories, the opening had been almost as tall as her, but she'd been twelve then. Smaller. It stood to reason that the hole would seem much lower now. She peered inside, seeing nothing but darkness beyond. A ripple of revulsion passed through her when she considered what kinds of creatures or creeping things could be hiding inside such a hole, but now was not the time to be afraid.

Biting the inside of her cheek, she slipped beyond the ivy.

Hurry. Danger.

Her heart nearly leapt out of her throat at the voice. Relief and joy and surprise flooded through her, so potent it made her quicken her pace as she squeezed through the gap in the wall. *Valorre?*

She could feel him somewhere nearby, his presence growing closer with every breath. But he didn't seem to share in her relief. Instead, his energy was panicked. *Hurry. Hurry. Hurry.*

A subtle light broke through the dark space she traversed, giving her a glimpse at where the hidden gap let out. The sound of Valorre's hoofbeats hit her ears next. He was right on the other side of the wall now.

His hoofbeats were drowned out by a sudden rumbling coming from behind her. It sent the wall shaking, sending crumbling bits of rock raining down on her head. She moved faster in the narrow space. The exit was almost in reach, just as hot, moist breath blew against the back of her head. She didn't need to look behind her to know the Roizan was there. Only a few feet remained, then she'd be free—

Shouts of alarm erupted from above. The Roizan growled into the gap, setting her teeth on edge, but then it was gone. She broke through the ivy on the other side of the wall and nearly stumbled into Valorre.

Danger. It's coming. He sidled closer and lowered his head, inviting her to mount.

One of the sentries called for someone to open one of the gates. Cora gripped Valorre's mane and hauled herself onto his back. She barely had her seat before he took off. They darted through the trees behind the castle. Cora kept her head lowered as a defense against the branches that reached out to graze her flesh while they tore across the forest floor. A rumbling followed behind. Valorre wove, dodged, shifted direction, but the Roizan was persistent.

She reached for her bow but all she had was her quiver. "Damn," she muttered and retrieved an arrow anyway. Should the Roizan gain on them, she wouldn't go down without a fight. A wary glance over her shoulder revealed trees trembling, a flash of red skin in the distance.

Worry only a little, Valorre said. *I spent most of last night learning to evade the abomination. I run faster. Longer.*

"You...you found me. You've been waiting for me."

You're my friend, he said, as if that explained everything. Explained why he'd been battling a unicorn-eating demon creature when he could have kept himself safe instead. *But where is the handsome one?*

Her chest constricted with thoughts of Teryn. Heat rose to her cheeks as she replayed the kiss he'd tricked her with. "I had to leave him behind."

Valorre rippled with disappointment. Or was it Cora's own that she felt?

Where do we go next? he asked. His words were calm despite the breakneck pace he kept. Their pursuer still followed.

Cora considered the question. Her first instinct was to flee far from Khero, away from Lela, away from Morkai and his war to rule fae magic. They could keep to the forests and hide at the far north of the continent, leaving all of this behind them. But the thought was only a fleeting fantasy. No matter how much she wished to escape what was coming, she felt in her blood that she was already entangled.

The unicorns. The mother. The child.

She knew Teryn wanted her to warn his father, but how could she hope to convince a king of anything? Now that she'd run away, Morkai would not be spreading tales of the princess who'd returned from the dead. That meant she was once again a fugitive. Still, that didn't mean she could do nothing. Her meager existence had been such a threat to Morkai's plans that he'd intervened with her fate. She didn't know much about prophecies, but the faerytales had always insisted upon their persistence. Maybe her role wasn't over yet. Maybe it had only changed.

It was a daunting thought. A terror. A burden.

But she'd faced terrors and she'd carried burdens. She could carry this one too.

She gripped Valorre's mane tighter, her blood burning with resolve. "It's time for me to go home."

42

Teryn had no concept of day or night in his cell, but he knew the sun had risen when he heard footsteps marching down the hall. They were too swift to be a guard's. Too confident to belong to anyone but Duke Morkai.

He rose to his feet as his cell door opened. Morkai strode in, a smug smile stretched across his face. It fell when he found only Teryn inside. Morkai's gaze rested on Cora's discarded gown. In a flash, the duke surged toward Teryn, bringing his cane against Teryn's throat. "Where is she?"

Teryn fought to keep his composure despite his constricted airways. Even if he'd wanted to answer, the duke's cane made it impossible.

Morkai seemed to come to the same conclusion and shoved away from him. His pale eyes flashed with rage. "Tell me."

Teryn rubbed his throat, taking in heavy gulps of air. He shot the duke a smirk. "You said only one of us could remain alive by sunrise."

Morkai took another step back, a vein pulsing in his temple. "She isn't dead."

"She could be," Teryn said with a halfhearted shrug. It took all his effort to hide the truth of his feelings—the emptiness he felt at not knowing how Cora fared after her escape. His only consolation was that Morkai had no clue where she was. Which meant she *had* escaped.

"What. Happened." The duke said each word through his teeth.

"She walked straight through the wall and left me behind."

Morkai froze.

"Oh, did you not know she's a witch?"

"She's more than a witch," the duke ground out.

"Then did you underestimate her powers?"

Morkai lifted his chin, jaw clenched tight, but Teryn could see the hint of fear in his eyes. He *had* underestimated her. The duke had expected to enter the cell and find them sitting at opposite ends, not daring to trust one another in light of

Morkai's bargain. Or perhaps he'd thought to find them huddled together, cowering with fear over what the duke would do to them come morning. Not once had Morkai considered Cora would use her magic to break herself out. The fact was written plainly across his face.

The realization filled Teryn with such satisfaction, he couldn't stop the grin that spread over his lips. Teryn had never underestimated her. Had never seen her as anything but what he'd called her before she'd left.

Formidable.

She was a force to be reckoned with, a storm wind, an inferno. She was a wind-tossed sea and a snow-capped mountain. Beautiful like the edge of a blade.

Morkai didn't see that, but Teryn did.

"Don't look so smug, prince," Morkai said. "Like you said, she left you behind."

Teryn shrugged.

Returning to his carefully curated composure, Morkai planted his cane before him and folded his hands over the crystal. "Never mind the princess. I will find her again, have no doubts. My business is with you. Have you reconsidered my offer?"

"A night in the dungeon has done nothing to convince me to ally with you."

"Are you certain? This is your final chance. I will send out my summons this morning. Ally with me, send a letter for your father, and I'll award you with a personal guarantee that I'll let you live even if your father refuses to surrender."

"Can my letter say anything I choose?" Teryn already knew the answer but he couldn't help baiting the duke with his own words.

"Of course not. Your letter must be penned in favor of surrender."

Teryn leaned against the wall. "Then I refuse."

Morkai's jaw tightened. "I will make you pay, then. Should Menah and Selay surrender as they should, I will make you grovel at my feet. Should they choose war instead, then I will flay you alive before your father's eyes and make him watch as I cut you apart piece by piece."

Teryn swallowed hard. He knew standing against the duke meant his death, especially if his father made the choice Teryn wanted him to make. That didn't mean he didn't dread his fate. It also didn't mean he was resigned to it just yet. There were two weeks until the meeting at Centerpointe Rock. Two more weeks in the duke's company. Two more weeks to find a way to undermine him. Two more weeks to hope his father would make a plan. One that didn't involve bowing before a blood mage.

Morkai narrowed his eyes. "Perhaps I could start carving you apart right now. A finger would work nicely in my summons. Perhaps fill your father with a sense of urgency."

Teryn felt the blood leave his face. Despite the revulsion that turned his stomach, he forced himself to extend his hand. "Take your pick. It's a sure way to turn my father firmly against you."

The duke assessed him, eyes flicking briefly to Teryn's outstretched hand. Then, with a dark huff of laughter, he took a step back. "No, let us save the theatrics for the meeting."

"If we must."

Morkai's lips pulled into a sneer before he swept out the door. A guard closed it behind him. The duke's voice rumbled from the other side. "I'll see you at the meeting, Your Highness."

Teryn listened to the sound of footsteps receding until he could hear them no more. Only then did he let his guard down. He slumped against the wall and slid down it, his arms trembling as he draped them across his knees.

The meeting at Centerpointe Rock loomed in his mind like a dark cloud. It felt both too soon and too far away. His skin crawled with the thought that he'd be trapped in this dark cell until then. He was desperate to move, to act, to fight.

Instead, all he could do was wait.

~

King Dimetreus' demand for surrender arrived at Dermaine Palace two days later. Another day had passed since then, and yet Larylis Seralla held firmly on to his disbelief in what the letter had said. Refused to accept his brother was being held hostage. All evidence pointed to it being true, however, starting with the hastily scrawled note Berol had delivered a few days ago.

Ridine Castle. Not safe. Trying to flee.

Now his father had been summoned to meet at Centerpointe Rock in less than two weeks' time to discuss terms for a peaceful surrender. Peace—while Teryn was being kept as a bait.

Larylis was sick with worry over his brother's fate. He paced across his balcony, which he'd been doing for the better part of the morning, stopping only when he heard wings beating the air. He turned to see Berol diving toward the balustrade. Larylis rushed to her as she landed, his pulse leaping as he saw something clutched in her talon. He hoped against all hope that it was a letter from Teryn, proof that he was all right. Proof that their world hadn't been turned upside down.

His heart sank as he saw Berol carried not a piece of parchment but a charred tree branch. Larylis took it gingerly from the falcon and fed her a strip of meat he'd set aside in anticipation of her return. This was the third time she'd come back without any communication from Teryn. When Larylis had gotten Teryn's letter about being unsafe at Ridine Castle, he'd sent a note back asking for more details. Berol had returned with it still clutched in one of her talons, no sign that it had been read.

Larylis ran his thumb over the charred branch, watching it blacken the tip of his finger. Wherever Teryn was, Berol couldn't reach him. He fled the balcony and went to the bureau inside his room, surprised when Berol followed him. She rarely came inside, spending most of her time on Teryn's balcony or in her mews. The falcon landed on the top of Larylis' bureau, wings splayed as she screeched her distress.

"I know," Larylis said as he placed a fresh piece of parchment over his desk. He knew it was fruitless to send another letter, but he...he had to try.

He reached for his inkwell, but in his haste, he spilled it over the parchment. Cursing under his breath, he righted his well and sopped the ink with the paper, then began rummaging through the drawers of his bureau. Empty. Damn. He had to have more ink somewhere.

With quick strides, he went to his bookshelf, shoving aside books and stacks of paper. Finally, he found a stoppered bottle of fresh ink beside a stack of old letters and a pile of his favorite novels. He moved the books aside and reached for the ink. When he pulled it from the shelf, the letters came with it, spilling all over the floor. Larylis bent down to gather them up. He was halfway through retrieving them when one caught his eye. The letter was open, its familiar script flowing over the parchment. Gingerly, he picked it up, scanning words that had already been branded on his heart.

> *Larylis,*
>
> *We cannot see each other anymore. I can't explain. All you need to know is that I can't love you. I could never love a bastard.*
>
> *Mareleau*

Whatever had possessed him to keep the letter was beyond him, for even now, three years later, the words still stung. Perhaps more so with his brother being held captive after running off to fulfill *her* Heart's Hunt. Resentment boiled in his blood, a much more welcome feeling than fear. He crumpled the letter in his fist, strode to his desk, and tossed the princess' letter in the hearth on the way. His chest felt tight as he caught sight of it igniting beneath the flames.

"Good riddance," he muttered and poured the fresh ink into his inkwell. Berol screeched at him, her wings still splayed with agitation. He grabbed fresh parchment and his quill and began to write. "I know, Berol. I'm trying again."

The falcon hopped down from the top of his bureau to the desktop, nipping at his fingers to stop him.

"Berol, I need to write to him—"

She nipped again, forcing him to drop the quill.

He glared at the bird, prepared to shoo her off his desk, but there was something in her eyes that made his shoulders sink—a deep sadness that echoed the emotions he was trying to shove aside. A heart-wrenching possibility dawned on him, one too unbearable to consider. He ran a hand over his lower face and took a step back. "Seven gods. Berol, is Teryn...is he..."

She seemed to calm down a bit and flew back to the top of the bureau. Her shift in countenance sent him some small relief. He didn't know how to communicate with the bird like Teryn seemed able to, but he wanted to believe she was trying to tell him his brother was alive. It was clear she was also trying to convey that writing another letter would do nothing. But what else could he do? His father had shut himself in his study ever since the missive arrived from King Dimetreus. Arlous had immediately blamed himself for what was happening to Teryn, saying it was all his fault because he'd told Teryn about some outlaw's bounty. A bounty Teryn had attempted to collect, thanks to their father sending a communication to the king a while back. Never mind the fact that their father had only acted because of the letter Teryn had sent Berol with in the first place.

Larylis didn't understand the full story, and the fact that he couldn't talk to his father about it was driving him half out of his mind. He slammed a fist onto the desk. "We have to do something."

A heavy knock sounded at his door. He whirled to face it, finding it swinging open before he could grant the caller permission to enter. He may have been a bastard but the palace staff knew better than to treat him as such.

But it wasn't a servant on the other side of the door. Instead, Prince Lexington of Tomas charged into Larylis' room, a mortified guard following in his wake.

"He wouldn't take no for an answer," the guard said, her eyes brimming with apology. "Your father wouldn't see him, but I can't turn him away. He's a..."

"A prince, yes," Lexington said, although his appearance was the opposite of regal. His cheeks were smudged with dirt, his hair a blond windswept mess, his clothing torn and stained. "And yet no one seems to respect that fact nor how long or how fast I've been bloody riding."

Larylis blinked back at the man, uncertain what to make of his presence. The guard gave Larylis a questioning glance, one hand on the hilt of her sword. "It's all right," he said to her, then turned his gaze to the prince. "To what reason do I owe this pleasure, Prince Lexington?"

"Call me Lex, and—" He held up a finger, then doubled over, hands braced on his knees. "Seven devils I'm out of breath."

Larylis watched as Lex took several deep breaths before straightening.

"Teryn is being held hostage by Duke Morkai," the man said in a rush.

"I know," Larylis said, then paused. "Wait...Duke Morkai? Not King Dimetreus?"

Lex gave a flippant wave of his hand. "They're basically one and the same, but the worst part is the duke is a bloody blood mage and he's the one who really wants to become king. You cannot surrender to him."

"If we don't, he'll kill Teryn—" He shook his head. "How do you even know this?"

"It's a long story, but I was captured with Teryn. Duke Morkai offered me a deal in exchange for my father's allegiance. Little does he know, my father would rather build a wall to hide behind than join forces with a conqueror. Which left me one choice—to warn you about the duke's monsters and wraiths and try to find a way to save my friend."

Blood mage. Monsters. Wraiths. His words made no sense, but Larylis only questioned the one that seemed at least partially grounded in reality. "Your... friend."

"Teryn," Lex said as if that was supposed to be obvious from the start.

"Since when are you friends with Teryn?"

"Another long story, and if you don't mind, I'd rather only tell it once. Which means we should speak to your father." Lex turned on his heel and marched down the hall like he owned it. "In fact, we should probably head for Selay straight away. They'll want to hear this too. Besides, I've got a Heart's Hunt to forfeit."

Larylis followed after Lex, unsure whether the prince was a hero or a madman.

43

Cora could feel her destination drawing near. Her heart grew warmer with every racing step Valorre took across the forest floor. He'd hardly slowed his pace after escaping the pursuit of the Roizan three days prior. They'd stopped only to rest and eat, although without Cora's bow or belt of necessities, she'd been limited to whatever she could harvest with her hands or an arrow. She was weak. Hungry. But at least she had Valorre. He carried her to the Ishvonn Woods where they first met. Where she hoped beyond hope that the Forest People had remained since she'd parted from them. Thankfully, it was not yet summer, so the commune had little reason to have departed.

As Valorre galloped past the hot spring caves, weaving along the familiar path she'd trod mere weeks ago, she felt the call of home. Of family.

Of people who might turn her away the minute they saw her face.

We're here, Cora thought to Valorre when she sensed the commune's proximity. He slowed his pace and paused near a thicket of trees. Cora dismounted, wincing at the soreness in her thighs, the ache in her legs, the hollow in her stomach. She felt a sudden stab of self-consciousness when she realized what she must look like. Dressed only in her corset and shift, no petticoats, no overskirt, filthy, her hair a mass of tangles...she imagined she appeared half mad.

I'll stay close, Valorre said and trotted away.

She felt cold without her friend, but she knew it would be best to enter the camp alone. Her mission would be much easier if the others weren't gawking at a unicorn. Then again, perhaps if they had him to gawk at, they wouldn't do so at her.

With a deep breath, she made her way toward the camp.

Familiar smells of herbs, food, and campfire invaded her nostrils, sending her stomach growling. What she wouldn't give for one of Chandra's stews. The yearning almost sent tears to her eyes, along with a hefty dose of regret. What would it have been like if she hadn't left? If she hadn't even gone to the hot spring caves at all that night? Remorse sank her heart, but she was surprised that it didn't linger. If she hadn't gone to the caves, she wouldn't have met Valorre or Teryn or been captured by Morkai.

But that would only have changed things for her.

Morkai's mission would have stayed the same. Without Teryn to hold as a hostage, without her to have brought the entire mess together...no one would have a clue the duke's war was coming.

Which is why I'm here, she reminded herself. Not for comfort. For war.

The clearing became visible between the trees just ahead. She slowed her steps and halted as she heard a soft step behind her. Just as she'd expected, her intrusion was detected.

"Cora?" She knew the voice before she saw him. Slowly, she turned to face Roije. He lowered his bow, brow furrowed, but there was something knowing in his expression. "Maiya said you were coming."

Her chest constricted at her friend's name. "Maiya...knew?"

He nodded, then shifted his feet as if he wasn't sure whether to block her path or welcome her back. She opened herself to his energy and found it cloudy. Hesitant.

"What is it?" she asked.

He lowered his voice. "The last group that went out to trade with the village... they brought back your poster."

Her stomach took a dive. Perhaps she'd left the commune at the right time after all.

His expression turned apologetic. "I don't think it's the best idea that you're here."

"Nonsense." Salinda stepped from between the trees. Her face was so warm, so kind, so motherly and familiar that Cora's throat felt tight. She wasn't sure who reached for who first, but the next thing she knew, they were wrapped in a tight embrace. Cora found herself sobbing on the woman's shoulder despite her every effort to compose herself. "It's all right," Salinda soothed, rubbing her back like she'd done every night during the first inconsolable weeks after the Forest People had found her. "You're home. You're home."

Cora wished they could stay like that forever. That she could forget what Roije had said about the Forest People's knowledge of her Wanted poster, about the dark tidings she carried on her shoulders. She wished she could pull away from Salinda and promise her she'd never leave again. But that was folly.

Once she managed to rein in her tears, she gently unraveled from Salinda's comforting arms and delivered the words she needed to say. "I need to speak with the elders."

Salinda frowned, her mouth falling open. No words came out, but Cora knew what the woman was poised to say—that Cora had no right to call such a meeting. Only another elder could, and Cora had lost that right when she refused to take the path Salinda had offered. Furthermore, she'd lost her right to even sit amongst the elders when she departed from the commune without a word. Even more so now that they knew she was a wanted fugitive.

A flash of panic struck her. If Salinda turned her away now, her visit would be all for naught. Her plans would be foiled.

Salinda's lips curled into a sad smile. "You do have much to tell us, don't you?" Then, with a heavy sigh that seemed to share the weight of Cora's burden, she said, "I'll gather the elders."

TEN MINUTES LATER, CORA SAT IN THE TENT OF THE ELDERS. IT HAD TAKEN SOME work sneaking Cora into camp without being seen, but Roije had brought her a cloak and used his connection to the Magic of the Soil to navigate the clearest path there. It was past midday, which meant most within the commune were busy with their daily tasks, leaving very few idle enough to stare. Now she just had to wait for Salinda to return with the elders.

She wandered the tent, focusing on her breath, on the aromas of herbs and oils filling the air, on anything that could distract her from the anxiety that plagued the back of her mind. The tent of elders was the largest in the camp, used for celebrations, elder meetings, and *insigmora* ceremonies. Cora stared down at her forearm, remembering the last time she'd received a new design several months ago. She frowned as she stared down at her inner elbow crease. A dark spiral was there, an inch above her most recent tattoo. Surely that hadn't been there before—

Cora froze as the tent flap opened to reveal Salinda. She held the flap for the twelve other figures who followed. Nalia, the Forest People's High Elder, brought up the rear. She was thin, hunched, and wrinkled, as ancient-looking as the oldest tree in the forest, and—surprisingly—without a single *insigmora*.

The silence was stifling as the thirteen elders took their places in a circle around the tent. Cora didn't need to use her Art to know the elders weren't pleased about being called into a meeting with her. It would have been one thing if she were simply *Cora, Salinda's foster daughter*. It was another now that she was known as a murderer. She doubted they'd be any happier to learn the truth.

Once they were seated—six elder witches to Nalia's left, the six elder Faeryn to her right—the High Elder motioned Cora to stand at the center of the circle. Trembling despite the warmth of her borrowed cloak, she did as told and took her place.

Nalia gave a bow of her head. "You may speak, child."

She drew a long, shaking breath. "You know me as Cora, but my true name is Aveline Corasande Caelan. I'm the Princess of Khero. Fae magic is in danger."

WHISPERS SURROUNDED HER. SHE'D DELIVERED HER STORY AND NOW STOOD trembling in the wake of her truth. She kept her gaze above Nalia's head, not daring to meet anyone's eyes as they deliberated her tale. They'd remained respectfully silent as she'd explained who she truly was, where she'd come from all those years ago when they'd found her, and why she'd kept her identity to herself. She'd felt their trepidation turn to terror as she'd described the gruesome hunt for unicorns and how it was tied to Morkai's magic and his Roizan. They'd stared unblinking as she'd revealed his plans for war in the name of harnessing fae magic.

Now she breathed deep, focusing on the canvas walls of the tent to keep from being overwhelmed by the emotions growing and clashing all around her. Soon the whispers turned to much louder questions and the voices of the elders rose to match the roar of feeling. Cora closed her eyes and tried to raise her shields against the cacophony, but her fatigue was too great.

"Enough," Nalia said, her soft voice somehow cutting through the noise. "We will now peacefully discuss."

"What is there to discuss?" asked one of the witches, a man named Druchan. "We live by simple rules, one of which is to never involve ourselves in royal matters."

Salinda pinned him with a glare. "Did you not hear a word she said? This may be a royal matter, but it ultimately concerns magic."

Another Faeryn elder nodded beside her. "He calls himself Morkai. *King of Magic.* He's trying to become the Morkaius. You know what that means."

Nalia's face went slack. "High King of Magic."

Cora straightened at that. She'd never heard the term *Morkaius* before, nor had she considered Morkai wasn't the duke's true name. She'd always known him as such. Only now did it seem strange to her that he hadn't taken on the title of his duchy—Calloway—when Dimetreus named him duke.

"If the prophecy is true," one of the elder witches said, "the Morkaius cannot claim the magic without being destroyed by it."

"He has created this...this Roizan thing!" argued another witch. "A channel between his body and the magic."

Cora's eyes darted between the arguing elders. "You know about the prophecy?" That was one part of her tale she'd kept vague. She hadn't mentioned what he'd said about her role in the prophecy or the curse he'd laid upon her with his blood weaving. Her question, however, was drowned out beneath the sounds of further arguments.

"War is not our way. Let the armies do the fighting."

"There will be no fighting if the royals surrender."

"And if they surrender, the duke wins."

"It doesn't matter. We protect our own, that's all."

"What do you mean it doesn't matter? We protect the land and the Arts. If the duke becomes Morkaius, he will have control over magic. He could take our Art from us. We must act."

"What can we even do? He's an Elvyn prince. A weaver—"

"He is not a true weaver," Nalia interrupted, voice fiercer than Cora had ever heard. "He may have Elvyn blood as he claims, but Elvyn weavers need only magic. This Morkai wields blood and animates spirits because he is no true weaver at all. He is weak. He relies on curses and tricks and the forbidden Arts."

Cora wanted to argue that Morkai's powers were hardly what she'd call weak. As far as she could tell, his blood sorcery was far stronger and more terrifying than the Forest People's quiet magic.

"High Elder," one of the Faeryn said, giving Nalia a respectful bow of her head, "that still doesn't explain what we can do."

"Nor do we know if we can trust a girl who's been hiding a secret identity from us the entire time," Druchan added.

"We can trust her," Salinda shot back. "I've raised her since she was a child. She told us why she hid who she was. Can you blame her?"

"She should have left the minute she learned we don't involve ourselves with royals."

"She was twelve!"

"She could have brought danger to our camp at any time."

"But she didn't. When she realized her presence was a threat, she left."

Druchan narrowed his eyes at Cora. "She should have stayed gone."

"This isn't about Cora," Nalia said, silencing the tent once again. "This is about magic. This is about the fate of this land that we work to nurture and protect. I assure you, nothing good can come from the Blood of Darius. He will destroy not one realm but two. He will corrupt fae magic until there is nothing left of the lives we know."

Cora felt the hairs on her arms rise. Who was the Blood of Darius? Was that... Morkai?

Druchan shrank down. "It's just...stories, though. Isn't it?"

Nalia slowly turned to look at him, her expression both hard and sad at once. "No. What you call stories are merely a fraction of the truth."

Salinda nodded. "What can we do, High Elder?"

Nalia's tone was resolute. "We must kill the duke."

"How?" Druchan asked.

Nalia turned her gaze on Cora, expression penetrating. "What do you suggest, Your Highness?"

Cora's throat constricted at the honorific. She nearly told her not to call her that but swallowed the words down. Perhaps it was time to be a princess after all. She had no desire to reclaim her title, but in coming to the Forest People with the truth, she'd already taken on that responsibility. If her brother couldn't protect Khero, that left only her.

Lifting her chin, she said, "I know where Morkai is going to be next."

44

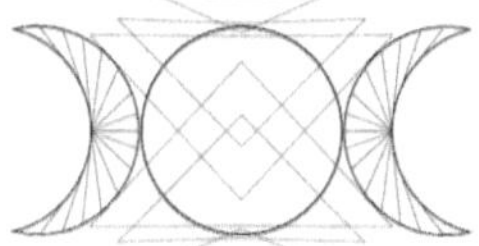

Two hours later, after Cora had visited the bathing wagon and thoroughly washed her hair, she went to her old tent. Her chest felt tight when she noticed her side still held all of her things—her cot, her blankets, her clothes—as if Maiya had never given up on her returning. She changed into a fresh shift, bodice, and skirt, relishing the fragrant lavender that wafted off the clean textiles. Her heart yearned to bask in the comfort of being home again, but the sinking in her gut reminded her that she wouldn't be staying for long. Druchan had been evidence enough that even though many amongst the Forest People would accept her return, there would be many others who would not. At least Salinda had promised to spread word that Cora wasn't the outlaw her poster claimed she was. It wouldn't be long before the entire camp learned what had occurred inside the elders' tent too—that some of them were going to fight an Elvyn blood mage.

She rifled through more of her belongings, finding a spare belt, a knife, her extra bow, and more arrows for her quiver. As she began to stuff the arrows inside, something caught her eye. She peered into her quiver and saw the white unicorn-horn blade that had belonged to the deceased Prince Helios. She'd nearly forgotten about it, having not seen it since she took it from beside the dead body and tossed it in her quiver. A subtle pulse of dark energy entered her awareness, heavy and sorrowful.

"You aren't leaving already, are you?"

Cora dropped the arrows the rest of the way inside, hiding the dagger and muting its dark resonance once again, and whirled to face Maiya. They collided in a hug that included much crying on Maiya's part.

"I woke up this morning and *knew* you'd come," said her friend. "Just like I knew that poster was wrong about you when the traders brought it back last week."

They separated, and Cora studied Maiya's face, curious what else she knew.

Maiya blushed and averted her gaze with a shy smile. "Should I call you Your Highness?"

Cora gave her shoulder a playful shove. "Don't you dare." If there was one person she wanted to continue to be *Cora* with, it was Maiya.

Maiya grinned but her expression quickly turned somber. "Mother told me about the meeting with the elders, but I still can hardly believe it. Mages, dark magic, war. It's...terrifying."

Cora could only manage a nod.

Maiya nibbled a corner of her lip and said, "I understand why you did it. Why you never told me who you truly were. Still, I wish you had. I could have been there for you."

"You were there for me," Cora said, gathering one of her friend's hands and giving it a squeeze.

"Not as much as I could have been."

"What else could you have done?"

Maiya sighed. "I just...I just wish I'd known. You must have been through a lot before you came to us."

Cora wasn't sure what to say about that. She had been through a lot, but her past wasn't a topic she felt like talking about at the moment. Her mind was too wrapped up in the pasts of those she *didn't* know. She was desperate to learn more about what the Forest People knew—about Morkai, about whoever the Blood of Darius was, about the prophecy. Thankfully, she was saved from having to shift the subject when the tent flap opened again.

Roije took one step inside and froze, his eyes darting between Cora and Maiya. He seemed flustered at finding them both there. Perhaps he'd been looking for Cora to ask more details about the dark tidings she'd brought. "I'll come back," he said as he began to back out of the tent.

Cora was about to tell him they could talk about anything in front of Maiya, but her friend spoke first.

"No, Roije, it's all right." With a flutter of her lashes, Maiya took his hand.

His eyes locked on hers. The soft grin that stretched across his lips made him look more boyish than Cora had ever seen. He lowered his voice to a whisper. "I came to ask if you still wanted to go to the hot spring caves together."

Cora's cheeks burned as she suddenly realized what she was witnessing. Her eyes landed on the pair's clasped hands, the nervous, desire-fueled emotions radiating off of them in droves, the implications of Roije's invitation to the hot springs. Maiya and Roije were...courting.

Maiya glanced at Cora, brows knitted. Her energy clouded with regret. "I wanted to, Roije, but now that Cora's back—"

"It's fine," Cora said, her words coming out in a rush and with far too much enthusiasm. A strange blend of surprise and jealousy flooded through her. Her envy wasn't of Maiya. She'd never fancied Roije and had always wished the two of them would confess their feelings for each other. It was more that she was struck with a sudden longing for what her friend was experiencing. Or perhaps it was only regret over not having been there for such an exciting development in

Maiya's life. Whatever the case, it brought a sudden memory of Teryn's lips against hers—

She shook her head, banishing the thought.

"Don't worry about me," Cora said, her voice back to normal. "I need to speak with your mother, anyway. Go have fun."

Maiya grinned, her cheeks flushing a deeper shade. "You won't leave tonight, will you?"

Cora had originally considered making camp with Valorre not too far away, but the pleading look in Maiya's eyes made her reconsider. She almost asked if Maiya was planning to return to their tent tonight or stay with Roije, but she quickly swallowed the question. Her friend was shy enough. She'd probably be mortified by such an indelicate suggestion. Instead, Cora gave her a reassuring grin. "I'll be here when you get back."

After Maiya and Roije left for the hot springs, Cora made her way to Salinda's tent. She found the woman sitting outside it, a quill and stack of parchment in hand. Salinda's brow was furrowed as she wrote, her energy heavy and murky. Cora realized Salinda must be recording what had transpired today. As Keeper of Histories, it was Salinda's duty to keep records of not only the past but any new events that dealt with the Arts. Salinda always put her stories to paper first before committing them to memory where she carried them thereafter. With the Forest People being nomadic, they didn't have space or the means to carry physical tomes.

Salinda didn't look up from her writing until Cora cast a shadow over her work. "Forgive me," Salinda said with a smile as she looked up at her. "I was wrapped up in words."

"You can keep writing," Cora said, stepping out of the sunlight so it could illuminate the parchment again. "I'll wait until you are finished."

Salinda shook her head and set her quill and stack of papers inside a leather sheath, then motioned for Cora to follow her inside the tent. It was the same size as the one she shared with Maiya but far messier. Furs, papers, and clothing were draped all over. Salinda's husband—and Maiya's father—had passed away some years ago. Whenever Cora had glimpsed Salinda's living space, she'd wonder if the mess helped distract her from the absence of her missing half.

Salinda took a seat on a pile of furs and poured two mugs of herb-infused water. Cora sat down across from her and took one of the clay mugs. The water tasted of mint and rosemary, two aromas she'd always associate with her foster mother.

As she lowered the cup, she noticed Salinda's gaze had fallen to the crook of her arm. "Your *insigmora* has grown since you've been gone."

Cora's eyes went wide. She'd almost forgotten the strange spiral she'd noticed in the elders' tent. "How is that possible?"

Salinda gave her a sly smile. "You didn't think all of our tattoos were inked by hand, did you?"

She blinked back at her. "Yes, that's exactly what I thought."

"For many of us, it's true. For others...well, some of us have deep enough connections to our magic that our *insigmora* grow of their own volition."

"But it's a Faeryn tradition," Cora said. "I'm not Faeryn. I'm just a witch."

"*Just* a witch," Salinda said with a scoff. "When are you going to appreciate your magic for what it is?"

Cora opened her mouth but snapped it shut. In truth, she'd been learning to appreciate her quiet magic more and more.

"You overcame a challenge that was directly related to your magic, didn't you?"

"I did. A couple of them."

"And your magic grew stronger?"

Cora nodded. "It was...frustrating," she said, remembering how difficult it had been to work against her own resistance.

"Your journey with the Arts has taken a new path, and your *insigmora* has reflected that." Her eyes crinkled at the corners. "And here I thought I'd be the one to guide you on the path of the empath."

"Empath." Cora pulled her head back. "I don't feel like my magic has grown *that* strong."

"Are you sure about that? Since you've been away, has there not been one new thing you've learned to do that no one else can?" Cora opened her mouth to deny it, but Salinda said, "Think. Is there anything you couldn't do before? Anything that has to do with emotions or sensations?"

Her ability to speak with Valorre came to mind, but she'd never considered whether that had anything to do with advanced clairsentience. If anything, she'd credited the phenomenon to Valorre being a fae creature. It wasn't like she was suddenly able to speak with every chipmunk, rabbit, and squirrel she came across. But it also didn't explain why Valorre couldn't seem to speak with anyone else but her.

Salinda nodded knowingly. "You've experienced something."

"Perhaps," Cora said slowly.

"As you step more and more into your role of empath, you will face even more challenges."

Cora grimaced at that. Not that it was a surprise. She only hoped it would get easier to accept such challenges instead of fighting against them. Then again, wasn't that the point of a challenge in the first place? For it to be hard? "Does every witch face a challenge to grow their power?"

"Every strong witch, whether they're following the path of the empath, oracle, seer, muse, alchemist, or narcuss."

Cora frowned at the last word. It was the only one she wasn't familiar with. "What's a narcuss?"

"It's a rare witch's power," Salinda said, tone grave. "One I believe this so-called Duke Morkai possesses. A narcuss is the shadow of an empath. Instead of feeling the emotions of others, taking them on, or absorbing them, a narcuss projects emotions outward. He can control and manipulate the people and objects around him. He can project what he wants others to see and feel. He is entirely focused on self-protection, self-advancement, and personal power."

That certainly sounded like Morkai. "But he said he's an Elvyn prince. You think he's part witch too?"

"I believe so. But I doubt he's faced the kind of challenge that would require him to become the strongest kind of narcuss. And Nalia was right about his Elvyn powers. If he were a true weaver, he wouldn't need to rely so heavily on the forbidden Arts."

Cora pondered that. She didn't know much about Elvyn magic, only that they wove the Magic of the Sky—whatever that meant—while the Faeryn worked with the Magic of the Soil.

Salinda continued. "What Morkai is doing is a corruption of true weaving. Elvyn magic was never used for harm, just like Faeryn magic. The power Morkai seeks is the same power that started the war that destroyed the fae several hundreds of years ago."

"Does that have to do with what the elders said about a Morkaius?"

"Yes. This duke is not the first to have attempted becoming High King of Magic. If he truly is the Blood of Darius, then he will believe he has a right to Lela's magic."

"He doesn't have a right to it," Cora said, "does he?"

Salinda looked thoughtful for a moment. "That very question is the reason the ancient war began. It's the reason the fae were destroyed."

"But where did they go? Why are the unicorns returning? And if unicorns are back then where are all the other fae creatures?"

Salinda released a heavy sigh. "We don't know, my dear. All we have are our stories."

"What do the stories say about the Morkaius?"

"The first Morkaius was the illegitimate son of the Elvyn queen and her human witch lover. His full-Elvyn sister was chosen as heir over him, and he sought to overthrow her."

A chill ran down Cora's spine. Half Elvyn. Half witch. "You think the duke is this same man?" It should have been impossible. But was it? She already knew Morkai was ageless. When she'd asked him how he hadn't aged, he'd answered *blood*. Had he meant his Elvyn blood kept him from aging? That he'd been alive for hundreds of years? Or had he simply been referring to blood magic?

Salinda shook her head. "No one knows for sure. Our stories claim the Morkaius was destroyed in the final battle. The fight ended at the Elvyn palace in a massive explosion that turned the structure into a ruin. A ruin that stands today. A ruin that our stories claim holds the source of what little fae magic flows out into the land."

Cora furrowed her brow, wondering what ruin she was talking about. Then it hit her. "Centerpointe Rock."

She'd never seen the rock before, only knew it was a landmark that stood at the very center of the three kingdoms, a neutral place where all three borders met. Cora had assumed that was the only reason the duke had chosen it for his meeting, but now she was starting to suspect more sinister motives.

"If Centerpointe Rock is the source of fae magic," Cora said, "and he's determined to harness the source..."

"You were right to come to us, Cora," Salinda said. "Not everyone in the commune will agree, but I do. This is a matter of magic. Of a fate greater than any of us can comprehend. Even if the meeting of the royals culminates in peaceful surrender, it will not be peace that follows. It will be the beginning of the return of the Morkaius. The beginning of a reign of darkness."

Cora's fingers curled into fists. "We must kill him."

Salinda nodded. "Thanks to the information you've given us, we stand a chance."

Cora left Salinda's tent filled with a new sense of burden and hope. This was so much bigger than she'd thought. She returned to her own tent with rest in mind, only to realize she still hadn't brought up her place in the prophecy or asked what Salinda knew about it. But as she laid down on her cot, their plans for attack buzzing through her mind, she wondered if it might be better that she hadn't confessed her role as some prophesied girl. A mother who'd been cursed to die childless. She ignored the ache in her chest when she considered what his blood weaving had taken from her and instead focused on hope.

For if all went to plan, Morkai would soon be dead.

And her place in the prophecy would die alongside him.

45

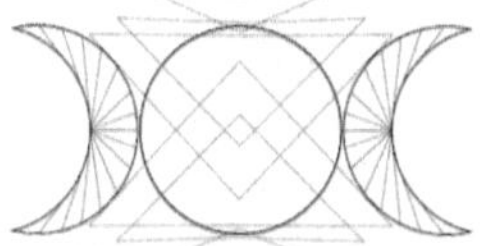

Larylis had figured the third time hearing Lex's description of the events at Ridine Castle would be easier to bear. He was wrong. It seemed with every new repetition, Larylis heard some new detail that flooded him with an eerie chill. The first time he'd listened to Lex's story had been in his father's study. The second time had been later that evening when Larylis had asked Lex to go over all the details yet again. Now, three days later, they sat around the elegant mahogany table in King Verdian's council room, with Lex relaying everything all over again. The day was early but the tall windows lining the far wall had been drawn shut against the sunlight, giving the meeting an even more daunting feel.

At least Larylis had finally come to accept that his brother was indeed captive, and war was looming on the horizon.

When Lex finished speaking, he was peppered with questions by King Verdian's council. King Arlous' councilmen were present too, but they'd already heard most of the tale before they'd departed Dermaine Palace.

"What joke is this?" Lord Ulrich said. He was one of Mareleau's uncles, and the man Larylis had once served as ward to. He was stout and clean-shaven with a double chin, gray eyes, and a head of brown hair cropped just below his ears. "You expect us to believe King Dimetreus is being puppeteered by a mage who uses blood magic and has a monstrous wolf-boar as a pet?" With a disbelieving scoff, he leaned back in his chair.

Larylis couldn't blame him for his doubts. He'd shared them at first. It was hard to believe in dark sorcery when no one believed in magic anymore. Magic had died with the fae. It only survived in Larylis' favorite novels. Then again, the same could have been said for unicorns, months ago.

Lord Kevan, Mareleau's eldest uncle and the head of King Verdian's council, rubbed his jaw. Unlike his younger brother, Kevan had a bushy brown beard and gray-brown hair that reached his shoulders. "No, some of the story rings true.

When I spotted the unicorn last year, I sent dozens of men after it. One man came back reporting that some monstrous creature had intervened and chased the unicorn beyond the border into Khero. I took the tale as folly, but perhaps it wasn't."

"What does that have to do with anything?" Lord Ulrich said. "The rest of Prince Lexington's story could be fabricated. He could be working with King Dimetreus, weaving tales of sorcery so that we'll be more inclined to surrender."

Lex's mouth fell open. "I am not working with King Dimetreus. I risked my life in coming here. My own kingdom stands in peril because of my deception. If you surrender, Tomas is done for."

One of Verdian's other councilmen snorted a laugh. "Remind me how you supposedly got away."

"Oh, sure," Lex said. "Right after you remind me why I was in Khero hunting unicorns in the first place."

King Verdian's cheeks flushed. This was one of the rare times Larylis had seen the man without his powdered wig. His gray hair was kept close to his scalp, his blue eyes the same shade as his daughter's. "No one told you to go to Khero, Prince Lexington. If you'd had any sense, you would have kept to Selay's borders."

Lex held the king's gaze without falter. "If you'd had any sense, you would have kept your daughter from sending me on some idiotic quest without aid."

Larylis was impressed with Lex's ability to bluff so easily. He supposed it had come in handy when he'd pretended to take the duke's offer only to escape his guards when they set him up at an inn the first night of their journey. According to Lex, he'd slipped away before dawn and bought a messenger horse to take him to Dermaine.

Only Larylis and his father knew the truth—that Teryn hadn't been captured by the duke solely because of the Heart's Hunt but because of his efforts to claim the fugitive princess' bounty. The three of them had agreed to keep that part of the tale to themselves for the time being. Perhaps it was a bit underhanded to make Verdian think his kingdom was responsible for Teryn's captivity, but if it gave Menah a respectable place at the council table, Larylis was happy to carry the lie.

King Verdian glared at Lex but seemed to think he wasn't worth arguing with. Waving a hand, he said, "Selay will not surrender regardless."

King Arlous rubbed his brow. "If we don't surrender, Teryn dies. I will not let that happen."

"Prince Teryn's fate is contingent upon both kingdoms' surrender," added one of Arlous' councilmen.

Verdian shook his head. "It is not up for debate. We weren't going to surrender to a mortal king. I'll be damned before I surrender to a sorcerer."

"So you'll have me risk my son? Your daughter's *fiancé*?" Arlous pinned Verdian with a hard stare, daring him to contradict the engagement.

Larylis shifted uncomfortably in his seat. With Prince Helios dead and Lex having forfeited, Teryn was the clear winner of the Heart's Hunt. King Verdian's guilt over Teryn's capture had been enough to solidify the betrothal between Teryn and Mareleau. Adding to that was Menah's shift in fortune. Larylis had learned of their kingdom's cleared debt in the same letter that had threatened Teryn's life and summoned his father to Centerpointe Rock. Arlous had been sure to flaunt their financial state as soon as they arrived at Verlot Palace.

Verdian spoke through his teeth. "We would be devastated by Prince Teryn's loss, should it come to that, but surrender is not on the table. I say we ignore the summons and prepare for war at once."

Larylis gripped his armrests, forcing his eyes to remain on the table instead of cutting a glare at Verdian. How could he refuse to even consider an option that saved Teryn's life?

Arlous slammed a fist on the table. "What of my son?"

"What of him?" Lord Kevan spat. "We will not surrender, therefore it is time to speak of our plans for war."

The table dissolved into a fray of arguments as the kings and councilmen began to talk over each other. Larylis' head spun, the chatter becoming a tidal wave of sound. He could hardly separate one voice from the other as they clashed with the weight of his own thoughts. Surrender. War. Surrender. War. Larylis wanted neither. All he cared about was getting his brother back. Why wasn't anyone discussing a solution that involved neither surrender nor Teryn's death?

Words burned on his tongue. He'd done his best to stay silent during the meeting thus far. His presence here today had already been met with enough scorn from King Verdian's council. No one wanted to see a bastard born of scandal at their table. But something had cracked in his father's heart after learning about Teryn's captivity. Once they'd left for Verlot, he'd refused to let Larylis out of his sight for long.

The arguments rose and crashed against each other, and still, their words remained a jumbled mess in Larylis' mind. His stomach churned, his blood turning to fire as he fought to stay quiet, stay seated—

"We must get my brother back."

Silence echoed. It took Larylis several breaths to realize the words had come from him. He stood at the table, his chair flung back behind him. He'd said nothing profound, nothing shocking, and yet the eyes of everyone at the table locked on him. It was only the element of surprise that had drawn their attention. *The bastard speaks.*

It was better than nothing, he supposed. He might as well make use of the quiet. "We cannot surrender to a blood mage, nor can we let the Crown Prince of Menah die."

Lord Ulrich scoffed. Larylis may have been his ward once, but the man hadn't liked him then. It stood to reason he didn't like him now either. "Do you have some brilliant plan, Lord *Seralla*?" Ulrich enunciated Larylis' surname as if to remind him of his place.

Lord Kevan turned an amused gaze to Larylis. "I too would like to hear what Lord Seralla's plan is. Amongst war generals, nobles, and kings, surely a whore's son knows best."

King Arlous rose from his seat, a vein pulsing at his temple. "How dare you speak to my son that way!"

Kevan opened his mouth but Verdian held up a hand. "We'll give the boy one minute to speak," the king said grudgingly. He seemed more concerned about offending Arlous than defending Larylis. At least Menah's change of fortune had that benefit.

The eyes of the councilmen burned into Larylis. Now that they'd granted him permission to speak, he didn't know what to say. He didn't actually have a plan. Fantasies of vengeance, certainly. He couldn't count the number of times he'd imagined himself as the heroes in his favorite war novels, or perhaps General Bralish, the famed savior of the Medlon army at the Battle of Delton in 94 Year of the Wolf.

His gaze swept the mocking faces of the men at Verdian's end of the table. Then his eyes found Lex's. And his father's. Arlous gave him a subtle nod.

He released a shaky breath. "We...cannot surrender to a mage."

Lord Kevan snorted a laugh. "That has been established."

Larylis opened and closed his fists, a cold sweat breaking out behind his neck. Kevan was right. Larylis was only repeating himself. If he didn't have anything to add to the conversation, he might as well sit down.

He took a step back toward his chair but his feet refused to take another. This was his chance to be heard. There had to be something he could add to the debate. Clearing his throat, he forced himself to stand a little taller, summoning the side of him that knew how to play it cool under supercilious scrutiny. "We must get Prince Teryn back *and* refuse surrender."

"You still aren't saying anything new," Ulrich said.

Larylis ignored him, running histories, fictions, and fantasies through his mind. How had General Bralish stolen the hostages back from the Allerton Horde? His words came out slow. Careful. "We'll go to the meeting and figure out where they're keeping Teryn. He'll be somewhere in King Dimetreus' camp."

Verdian narrowed his eyes. "How are you so certain? They could keep him at Ridine Castle."

"They'll expect us to demand to see Teryn alive and unharmed before we consider surrender."

"What then?" Arlous asked, his skeptical tone in contrast with the hope in his eyes.

"Once we know where Teryn is being kept, we'll send in a covert force to break him free. Until then, we will draw out negotiations."

"Stealing a hostage is akin to a declaration of war," Kevan said.

Larylis gave him a pointed look. "Which we've already resigned ourselves to in refusing to surrender. We will plan for war, but first we rescue Teryn."

"How do you expect to free our prince without the sorcerer taking notice?" asked one of Arlous' councilmen. From the look on his face, he was taking Larylis seriously. "We can't simply march in and search from tent to tent."

"I have an idea of how to locate him before we send in any of our men." He didn't elaborate, knowing it would take some work to convince them to put their faith in a falcon. But Larylis knew if anyone could find Teryn in an enemy camp it was Berol.

"It's reckless," Verdian said, running his hands over the ruffled collar beneath his royal white and gold coat. "But if we're already set on war, we might as well attempt to free the crown prince."

"You can't seriously consider this," Kevan said. "Larylis Seralla has no place on this council. He's a bastard—"

"Enough with that word." Arlous' voice came out hard. "Larylis *Alante* is my son and heir."

Verdian's eyes went wide. "That's taking things a little far, Arlous. Naming your illegitimate son your heir?"

Larylis couldn't argue with that. He wasn't even sure his father had meant what he'd said. He'd called Larylis...an Alante. The king's royal name. A name Larylis had been forbidden to take due to his illegitimate birth. Arlous' last attempt to legitimize him had nearly ended in war. If the queen found out, it very well could come again—

No. The threat of war was already here. It just wasn't coming from the same place it had before.

Lord Kevan scoffed. "Have you given up on getting Prince Teryn back so soon?"

Arlous held back a smug grin. "If we are to hide our plans at rescuing Teryn, we need the mage to think we've fully given up on getting the prince back when we refuse to surrender. Larylis will stand at my side during negotiations as my new heir. We won't officially refuse the king until we've received a sign that Teryn is safe."

"Dimetreus will never believe you've made your bastard your heir," Kevan said.

"Why?" Arlous met the man's gaze without any hint of shame. "I almost succeeded before."

Larylis felt sick. He'd hated how it had felt to be pitted against his brother when the scandal erupted. He didn't like it any better now, even if it was only an act. But if it got Teryn back...

"Well, Prince Larylis," Kevan said, voice mocking, "since you seem to have everything all figured out, will you be the one to organize the prince's rescue force?"

Larylis took a deep breath, forcing far more confidence than he felt. There was no use backing down now. No use revealing just how terrified and intimidated he felt. Instead, he imagined he was General Bralish, undaunted in the face of an enemy horde. Lifting his chin, he met Lord Kevan's taunting stare. "Yes, I will."

46

Mareleau Harvallis ignored the soft flutter inside her chest. It was a traitorous thing, the way her heart refused to recall that Larylis Seralla was no longer her beloved. Still, she had to admit he looked...brilliant. Brave. Standing up to her father and her uncles, coming up with a plan to save his brother.

She pushed the door open a crack wider, then resumed winding her fingers through the braid she'd been nervously plaiting for the last several minutes.

"We shouldn't be spying," Lurel whispered from behind her. They were in the drawing room that stood between the library and council room. It was mostly used by servants to stage food and libations during formal events or much larger meetings. This meeting, however, was private. Not even servants were allowed to be present. Neither was Mareleau but she didn't need her cousin to remind her that. Seven gods, the girl was annoying. Always so prim and proper.

Lurel tugged the sleeve of Mareleau's gown. "Our fathers wouldn't want us listening in. It's men's business."

Mareleau clenched her teeth. *Men's business.* So far, nothing that she'd heard had seemed particularly masculine. Why were women thought to be too soft for matters of war? Did breasts somehow make her unable to consider death and bloodshed? She had to deal with blood every month, which was more than any of the men in that room could say.

Lurel tried to pull her away again, but Mareleau elbowed the girl before she could. Doing so jostled the door, drawing the peering eyes of Uncle Ulrich. Mareleau darted away from the gap in the door. She held her breath as footsteps slapped across the floor. A second later, the door was shut the rest of the way with an exaggerated slam.

Damn her uncle.

With her view sabotaged, she spied on the remainder of the meeting by pressing her ear to the closed door, but all she could glean were snippets here and there. From what she could understand, it seemed both Selay and Menah were set on war. It was a terrifying prospect, and that was without considering the part about wraiths and mages. Her only experiences with war were secondhand accounts of battles that happened in other kingdoms. She never thought it was something she'd witness in Selay during her lifetime. Up until now, her life had been one of luxury and peace. Politically speaking, that is. Her love life was another issue all in its own.

A vision of Larylis filled her mind, for reasons she'd rather not dwell on.

Once she heard the meeting come to a close, she strode away from the door and sank into one of the chairs in the drawing room. Lurel wrung her hands before her. "Shall I call for tea, Highness?"

"I don't want tea," Mareleau said, eyes unfocused. As much as she didn't want to admit it, she felt a slight pang of guilt over Teryn's fate. He'd gone to Khero for her Heart's Hunt, after all. She'd wanted to rid herself of her suitors, but she hadn't expected it to end like *this*. Adding to that guilt was the fact that part of her *wasn't* sorry. She'd gotten what she wanted. For now, at least. If Larylis' rescue mission failed, she'd never have to worry about her unwanted engagement again.

Was it so terrible that she was considering such a benefit?

The door from the council room opened, sending her sitting upright. She expected Uncle Ulrich to come storming in to see who'd been spying on the meeting, but it wasn't him.

It was Larylis.

They both froze at the same instant, their eyes locked on one another.

His mouth hung open for several seconds before he found his words. "I...I was just heading for the library." He gestured toward the door at the other end of the drawing room. Then, backing up a step, he said, "I can use the main door."

"No," Mareleau said, keeping her expression neutral as she rose from her chair. "Lurel and I were just leaving anyway."

He offered her a bow and began to brush past, not giving her a second glance. She glared at him, her chest bubbling with words she'd smothered in the depths of her heart for the last three years. Pursing her lips, she willed herself to say nothing, to follow Lurel out the door and back to her chambers. Larylis was almost at the opposite door when the words flew out of her mouth.

"Why didn't you ever reply to my letter?"

Larylis froze with his fingers on the door handle. He turned to face her, expression hard. "Why would I have?"

Heat burned her cheeks, her body flooding with every ounce of rage she'd held on to since he'd broken her heart.

Lurel turned a pleading look on her. "Your parents wouldn't want you talking to him," she whispered.

"Leave us," she said through her teeth.

Her cousin's eyes bulged from their sockets. "I can't leave you unchaperoned with a man. Your reputation—"

"My reputation can go to the seven hells."

"If anyone found out I left you with him, we'd both get in trouble."

She burned the other girl with a glare. "Then don't tell anyone." Lurel was right, of course. Mareleau would never hear the end of it if either of their parents found out. Still, Mareleau hated being told what to do. And her confrontation with Larylis was long overdue. "Shut the door on your way out."

"But—"

Mareleau raised her voice to a shout. "Out, you simpering fool. And if you tell anyone about this, I'll...I'll tell your friends about the time you wet your skirts last year."

She gasped, her cheeks flushing crimson. "It was two years ago and I was sick."

Mareleau only shrugged.

"You're...you're so cruel. I'm only trying to help you." Without another word of argument, she turned on her heel and fled into the council room, closing the door behind her.

Mareleau shot a withering look at Larylis, but her stomach flipped as she met his stare. He leaned against the other door, arms crossed. His gaze locked on hers, his eyes narrowed to remind her that he didn't love her anymore. Maybe he never did. She bit her lip, wondering if it had been a grave mistake to speak to him. Did she really want to know why he'd chosen to abandon her?

She wound her fingers through her makeshift braid, desperate to do something with her hands. "Then you admit you at least received my last letter."

He shrugged. "If you can call it that."

A stab of pain struck her chest. She'd poured her very soul into that letter. "Then why didn't you respond? You could have said *something*."

"You made it clear you never wanted to hear from me again."

She blinked at him. "What are you talking about?"

He pushed off from the door and began walking toward her, his words dry and rehearsed. "*We cannot see each other anymore. I can't explain. All you need to know is that I can't love you. I could never love a bastard.*" He paused several feet away from her. "Do you deny you wrote those things?"

She opened her mouth to do exactly that, but she stopped herself. His words echoed through her mind, slamming against ones her heart had never let herself forget. "Why are you taking my words out of context like that?"

He gave her a bewildered look. "What other context was there? You wrote me three lines."

"I wrote you far more than that," she said, voice catching on the lump in her throat. She mirrored what he'd done moments ago, walking toward him while she recited her letter, every word punctuated with rage. "*Larylis, Father has said we cannot see each other anymore. I've told him how much I love you. I've told him that I will have only you. He will not listen. He thinks you're simply a fancy I'll grow out of. No matter what I say to try and explain the depths of my feelings, he tells me I could never love a bastard.*"

She paused when only a foot of space remained between them. Larylis' complexion had gone pale, his face slack. She wasn't sure what his countenance meant but it gave her no small amount of satisfaction.

She continued reciting her letter, her voice quavering with emotion. "*But he's wrong. I love you. You need to know that. No matter how they try to keep us apart I will always love you. I can't live without you, and I know you feel the same about me. Let us proceed with our plans without their blessing. Meet me at the Godskeep in Salissera at dawn on the twenty-first. I don't care if I lose my place as heir. All I need is you. Please come. Please. I'll be there."*

Mareleau felt cold in the wake of her words. She felt empty, stripped of pride and anger alike. All that was left was truth. Vulnerability. She searched Larylis' face, aware of the way he trembled, the way his hands curled into tight fists. When it was clear he had nothing to say, she spoke again, doing her best to keep her voice level. "You never came. I waited for you for two days. I was...humiliated. Heartbroken. Mother found me."

Larylis let out a shaky sigh. They stood so close, Mareleau felt his breath warm her face. She knew she should put space between them, but she couldn't move. Finally, he spoke, voice barely above a whisper. "I don't understand. I never received that letter. I received only those three lines."

She frowned. How was that possible?

"The letter you wrote to Teryn—"

"I never wrote him a letter."

Larylis dropped his eyes from hers and ran a hand over his face. "Seven devils," he said under his breath. "Your letters were forged. Two taken from one, each word copied from truth."

A chill ran down her spine. She wanted to deny the plausibility, but the facts made it painfully clear. No letter left the palace without someone knowing about it. After she was caught kissing Larylis in the stables three years ago, which resulted in her being forbidden from seeing or even speaking to him, it made sense that her parents would do anything to keep her from *embarrassing herself further*, as they'd liked to say. She'd thought she'd been discreet when she'd sent the letter, but was it possible she'd overestimated her own cunning?

Larylis slowly met her gaze again. "Everything about that letter, from the slant of your script to the length of your loops looked exactly as if it had been penned by your hand. Teryn showed me the letter he'd received. It looked the same."

She threw her hands in the air. "Neither letter's content clued you in to the truth? You couldn't possibly have believed I'd be so cold to you while being even remotely warm toward your brother."

"I found out about your engagement to him as soon as I returned home. I figured you'd changed your mind, that you realized he was a better match—"

"How could you believe such a thing?"

"What else was I to believe? Every word in that letter was true." His face twisted with agony.

"No—"

"It was. I am a bastard. You...you can't love me."

"But I..." She paused, debating what to say. Everything inside her yearned to reach for him, to wipe that look off his face. She didn't know what would happen if she did. If she let go of three years of hatred, resentment, and indignation...what would be left? He'd broken her heart, unwittingly or not. Then again, if she was honest with herself, she'd have to admit she'd never fully given up on him. No matter how shattered she'd become, no matter how many thorns had pierced her aching heart and split it into shards, threads had remained, connecting every fragment. She'd ignored them, burned them into rage, but despite her best efforts over the last three years, they'd come back. Every time she'd thought of him, remembered their time together, a thread would return, weaving through the hurt and the betrayal to repair the broken pieces. Now more than ever, those threads were there, growing. Piece by piece by piece, what she'd thought was broken collided back together. Her chest felt warmer than it ever had before. It bloomed into words that she rolled around on her tongue, warm and sweet with only a hint of bitter. She tasted them, tested them, before they breached her lips. "I still do," she whispered.

Larylis' throat bobbed. His brow was furrowed, eyes glazed.

She took a trembling step closer and reached a tentative hand for his chest. He inhaled a sharp breath as her fingers landed on his silk jacket. Her own breaths came hard and fast, her breasts heaving above her lace bodice. Part of her dreaded his answer to her next question, but she had to know the truth. Locking her eyes on his, she asked, "Do you? Do you still love me?"

His answer came out low and deep. "I've never stopped."

Her hands came to his collar at the same moment his wound behind her back. She claimed his lips with a greedy kiss, one of fire, desperation, and regret. They'd never kissed like this, like the other's lips were their only source of air. She arched into him, pulling him closer, parting her lips to deepen the kiss. His tongue moved against hers and hers against his. They were in perfect tandem, perfect agreement. One of his hands wove into her hair, sending pins clattering to the ground, while the other cupped the front of her bodice. She gasped against his mouth and reached for his neckcloth, untying it with frantic fingers. Once it was free, she slid her hands down his chest, beneath his jacket. He aided her efforts to free himself from it. Then she began working the buttons of his waistcoat, all the while never taking her lips from his. His palms moved to her shoulders and down the length of each arm, pausing when his hands landed on top of hers. She was still struggling with his buttons when he gave her fingers a soft squeeze. Only then did she realize he was pulling away from her. Her heart sank as her lips left his. She searched his face, saw desire still burning in his eyes. But the longer she watched him, the more his expression began to fall.

With her hands still gathered in his, he removed them from his waistcoat and took a step away. "I can't do this," he said, letting her hands slide from his palms. "You're engaged to my brother."

She gaped at him for several moments before she could find her voice. It came out breathy, still shallow in the wake of their passion. "I will never marry him."

"Your engagement is more final now than it was before."

She shook her head. "No, I will never allow it to be. I was set against it when I thought you despised me. Now that I have your love again, I won't give it up. I promise you, Lare, I will do everything in my power to end it. To be with you instead. And that's only if he returns—"

She knew at once she'd said the wrong thing. All remaining desire drained from Larylis' face as he took another step away from her.

"That's not what I meant," she said.

"It is, though, isn't it?" His voice was cold now. Empty. "That's why you sent him on some ridiculous quest for the Heart's Hunt, right?"

A spike of anger surged through her. "You can't blame me for not wanting to marry him."

He studied her for a few moments. "You've said that before. The evening of the poetry contest. I thought then...I thought it had been because of the scandal. Because of Menah's debt. All this time...you've been cruel to *him* because of *me*."

"I never chose to marry him. Our parents arranged it. But it's you I want to be with. I'm tired of letting them keep us apart. I was able to bear it these last three years only because I thought you didn't love me." She closed the distance between them, reaching for him. "Now that I know the truth, I can't—"

"No," he said, stepping out of her reach. "I...I'm not like my mother. I will not do what she tried to do."

Mareleau balled her hands into fists. "You stubborn fool! This is nothing like what happened with your mother and father, because Teryn and I aren't married yet. I'll be damned before we ever are. Besides, doesn't it matter what I want? Why has no one asked what *I* want?"

He looked at her as if seeing her with new eyes. "What do you want?"

The answer was easy. "I want the crown in my own right. I want out of an arranged marriage. And I want you. Larylis, with everything I am, I want you." She placed her hands on his chest again. "Tell me you don't want me too." His heart hammered beneath her palm. She could see his answer written in the depths of his eyes as they flickered to her mouth.

"I can't," he whispered, his words gravelly. "I can't say I don't want you. So badly I do."

Mareleau unraveled with relief. Heat spread low in her belly at the timbre of his voice. She tilted her head back, desperate to taste his lips once more.

"But I can't be with you. I...won't do that to him."

Her heart plummeted to her feet as he moved away from her once more. Without another word, he grabbed his discarded jacket and neckcloth off the floor and left.

She wasn't sure which door he'd used.

Wasn't sure she'd even watched him depart.

All she knew was she'd give anything to erase the last several minutes they'd shared—that instead of opening her heart, she'd stayed quiet. Angry. Resentful. Any of that would be better than the pain of his rejection renewed.

47

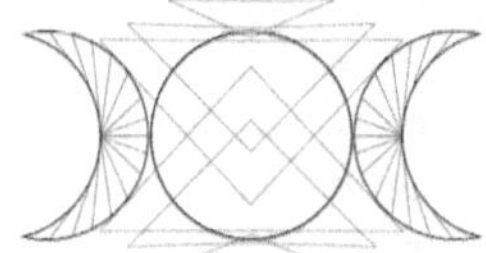

Cora eyed Centerpointe Rock from her vantage point on the hillside. Dawn had just broken over the horizon, illuminating the valley that surrounded the rock and casting a crown of gold upon the hills that stood sentinel around it. The rock itself was an enormous piece of weathered stone with a flat surface. It looked nothing like an ancient ruin from a forgotten war, nothing like a remnant of a fae palace. Now that she knew what it was, she couldn't help wondering what part of the palace the ruin stood in memory of. Was it once the floor of a throne room? A library? Some ancient fae queen's bedroom?

Her gaze wandered to the surrounding valley. The ground was green and plush, covered in a light morning frost. On one side sat her brother's camp, a sea of tents beneath standards of indigo and violet—indigo for the duke and violet for the king. The king's entourage had been camped there for three days—as long as Cora and her company of Forest People had been stalking the hillside—while the delegation from Selay and Menah had been camped at the opposite end of the valley since two days prior. Today was the day the meeting would commence.

She wrapped her wool cloak tight around her, chilled at the thought of what was to come. The Forest People had a plan that would end in the duke's death, but it didn't stop her from agonizing over every way it could go wrong. Cora had come to Centerpointe Rock with a small group of some of the strongest magic users among the Forest People. Roije for his tracking. Druchan for his proficiency at wards and concealing. Their elder seer. Two witches with incredible clairaudience who could listen for threats at a distance. A host of their best archers and spearmen. Several other highly accomplished Faeryn. The latter included Salinda and Nalia, despite neither having an Art honed for fighting or hiding. Cora felt a bit overshadowed by her companions' statuses, but there had never been any doubt as to whether she'd come along. This was her plan, after all. Mostly.

Cora may not have had firsthand experience with war, but her childhood education in history and warfare had been thorough. She understood what to expect from the proceedings. The meeting would begin with Khero delivering their demands and terms for the two kingdoms' surrender. If Menah and Selay didn't surrender right away, they'd be given a short time to deliberate. A second meeting could be set, at which the royals would need to deliver their final answer. If they surrendered, they'd get Teryn back. If they refused, they'd settle on terms for war.

A dark cloud of dread filled her gut. She knew Morkai had every intention of harnessing the magic and becoming Morkaius before leaving the meeting, regardless of what the royals decided. The fact that the negotiations were taking place at Centerpointe Rock—the very source of fae magic—was proof of that. If the two kingdoms surrendered, Dimetreus would be named King of Lela. Until Morkai killed him and took his place, of course. As terrifying as that thought was, it was the outcome she both expected and hoped for. Not the part where her brother was killed but where the royals surrendered. Because—as soon as Teryn was safely returned to his people—the Forest People would act. Morkai wouldn't get the chance to kill Dimetreus or harness the magic he sought.

But if the royals refused to surrender, it would mean—

Cora shook her head against the thoughts that filled it. Thoughts of Teryn. His fate. What Morkai would do if Menah and Selay rejected his terms. What Teryn had asked of her before she'd fled the dungeon.

Tell my father everything you know. Everything we've seen. Tell him to let me go.

A pinch of guilt prodded at her heart. She knew she was working against his wishes, but her plan was better. Her plan would save Teryn's life and the fate of Lela. It didn't assuage her guilt, but she supposed it was better than what lingered beneath it—the memory of their shared kiss, of his trickery, of the way her body had so eagerly responded to his.

She bit the inside of her cheek to distract herself from the tingling warmth in her stomach and brought her mind back to thoughts of war.

Her gaze swept toward her brother's end of the valley. His party was moderate in size—about the same as the combined entourages from Menah and Selay—which boded well, for it meant Morkai might not be planning to strike immediately should negotiations turn to war. Roije and the other scouts had confirmed that no hidden armies were waiting beyond the hills, no secret reinforcements were poised to invade. Then again, the duke could summon wraiths to bolster his numbers. While she'd seen the specters contained only to the charred field, she had a feeling Morkai could conjure them elsewhere.

The plan remains the same no matter what, she reminded herself. *Get the Roizan away from Morkai. Keep him from amplifying his powers through his well of dark magic. Then kill him.*

Still, thoughts of Teryn lingered in the back of her mind. If they didn't surrender...

They must surrender. They must. It's the only way he lives.

Something soft bumped into her shoulder. She turned to find Valorre at her side, his presence immediately settling her nerves. With a weak smile, she stroked the side of his face, then rested her hand at the base of his horn. She frowned at the layer of cotton surrounding it. Even though the Forest People kept their hiding place safe behind wards and illusions, Cora figured extra precautions couldn't hurt. She'd glimpsed the Roizan at a distance a few times, stalking her brother's camp with its loping gait. She wasn't sure how far it could sense a unicorn's horn, but she wasn't willing to find out. Not when Valorre was so integral to their plans. If there was one thing that could separate the Roizan from its master, it was a unicorn. "That isn't uncomfortable, is it?"

I am not so easily bothered, he said, in contrast with the flutter of embarrassment that rippled through him. *I must look foolish though.*

"No, you look rather imposing in that pink floral pattern."

Do I? All right.

"You don't grasp sarcasm, do you?"

I...don't think so.

Cora's laugh was cut short by her sudden awareness of an approaching presence. Her walls had been kept down to allow her to perceive nearby threats. But this presence was no threat.

Salinda appeared a few moments later. She was dressed the same as Cora, in britches, a wool tunic, and a boiled leather breastplate and gauntlets. With a warm smile, she came up beside Cora and put a comforting hand on her shoulder. "Rianne has seen it. The meeting will happen very soon."

Her mouth went dry. "Did she see how it would end?"

"She saw possibilities," Salinda said. Rianne was a seer but that didn't mean she could see the future. Her magic was more about catching glimpses of possibilities. Quiet magic, not certainty. Salinda gave Valorre a reverent nod. "Speaking of seeing, I still can hardly believe what stands before my eyes. He's a faerytale come to life."

I am majestic, yes, Valorre said. *She may pet me if she wishes. One could hardly blame her. I am so very strong.*

Cora rolled her eyes. She hadn't introduced Valorre to the entire camp, only the small party she'd come here with. Not wanting to overwhelm him with a flurry of starry-eyed admirers, she'd waited until their task force had begun their journey to Centerpointe Rock before revealing him. He'd received a warm welcome and had relished their adoration. It made her think he wouldn't have minded being the center of the entire commune's attention after all.

Salinda gave him a gentle pat on the side of his neck, then turned to Cora with a more serious expression. "Are you ready?"

Cora nodded, one hand wrapping around her bow. It may not have been the bow she favored, for she'd lost that one at Ridine Castle, but it was still a bow. Her preferred weapon. A source of comfort and strength. She brought her other hand to her belt and the three knives slung there. She froze when her fingers brushed the hilt of the dagger she'd finally removed from the bottom of her quiver that morning. Repulsion shot through her, but she breathed it down. She hated carrying a weapon that had been wrought from death and suffering, but if Valorre's role in her plans became compromised, it might help to have alternate means to draw the Roizan away from Morkai. She wasn't sure if the blade was as potent as a living unicorn, but it had brought Prince Helios to his unfortunate doom.

She lifted her hand from the dagger and balled it into a fist at her side. "I'm ready."

Silence fell between them, the burden of what was to come hanging heavy like a shroud. Together they stood watching the valley.

Waiting.

Waiting.

Waiting.

Until someone strolled onto the field.

Cora's blood went cold as the figure left Dimetreus' camp. With slow, confident moves, Morkai walked toward Centerpointe Rock.

Cora met Salinda's eyes. The woman gave her a knowing nod.

It was time.

48

Teryn didn't put up a fight as he was hauled from the prison tent. He knew where the guards were taking him as they dragged him through camp, their pace too fast for him to keep his feet beneath him. His legs felt like water even when he did manage a few steps, as he hadn't been allowed to walk much since arriving at Centerpointe Rock. He'd been chained, guarded, and given only the bare essentials to keep him alive. Now he was about to see his father for the last time. His only regret was that he wouldn't get to speak with him. The gag tied over his mouth wouldn't allow him to tell his father it was all right. That he could let him go.

Hopefully Cora had. Otherwise, his father might not know enough about Morkai to reject his terms for surrender. And that...that just wasn't a possibility. His kingdom *had* to fight, war or no. They could not yield to the mage. They had to destroy him.

The guards halted just outside the camp at the edge of the wide-open field. Teryn gathered the crisp morning air into his lungs, savoring what might be one of his last easy breaths. Several more guards and soldiers were already waiting, along with King Dimetreus. Teryn looked out at the field, seeking any sign of the opposing camp, but the valley was enormous. He could see nothing beyond the shape of the rock. Before it, however, was the silhouette of Morkai. Once the duke reached the Rock, he climbed upon it. It was brazen the way he stood unguarded, as if he were taunting the other side to act against him. Teryn almost wished they would. Any act of violence would result in retaliation. Should anyone attack Morkai now, Teryn—as hostage—would be put to death.

A price he was willing to pay.

He turned his eyes to the sky, basking in the sunlight on his skin. There was hardly a cloud to be seen, only the blue, pink, and orange hue of sunrise. It was beautiful. Perhaps the last beautiful thing he'd see.

A shadow darted over his vision—a bird. With a start, he noted the familiar flight pattern, the wingspan. His heart ached to see Berol. Of course she'd come. She'd always been able to find him. He could only hope that she wouldn't act when the time came for him to die, for if she got herself killed in the process, he wouldn't be able to leave this world free of regret.

"You played the hero well," said a mocking voice. Teryn shifted his gaze from the sky to find Dimetreus watching him with disdain. "But you ended up being a traitor. You and that...that vile girl."

Teryn bristled at hearing Cora called vile by her own brother. He started to speak but found his words muffled by the gag. Instead, he bit down on it and burned the king with a glare.

Dimetreus sneered back. "To think I let you into my castle. Fed you. Clothed you. To think I showed that wretched girl kindness when I should have sent a knife through her heart—"

Teryn lurched forward, but the guards kept him in place. He gave up his struggle and shouted at the king through his gag.

Dimetreus fully faced him and closed the distance between them.

"Your Majesty," one of the guards warned.

"I want to hear his last words," Dimetreus barked. With rough hands, he pulled the gag from Teryn's mouth. "Speak, filth. Let me hear your excuses for the last time. Fuel my vengeance and make it that much sweeter when justice comes."

Teryn held the king's gaze. "That girl is your sister." His voice felt rough in his throat. He'd been gagged since his arrival at Centerpointe Rock. "The one you call wretched. Vile. She really is Princess Aveline."

Dimetreus gave a disbelieving shake of his head. "My sister is dead. That girl was an impostor. I should have known better than to believe such a fantasy."

"If your sister is dead, then that means Selay never held her hostage. If that's the case, why are you trying to conquer them and Menah?"

"Selay sent the spy who killed my wife and sister. Menah was in on it. They sent you—"

"To do what? To claim a bounty on a woman I thought was a killer only to find out she was a lost princess?"

"No, you infiltrated my castle with a girl parading around as Aveline."

"Again I ask you, to do what? What reason did I have? What reason has anyone —Selay, Menah—had for their supposed crimes? What threats have you received? Seen with your own eyes?"

Dimetreus blinked hard several times. His glazed eyes held the same confused quality they'd had when Cora tried to tell him the truth. "You...you have no right to question me—"

"She told me her name was Cora."

Dimetreus' face went slack. He took a step back, blinking hard again.

Teryn was emboldened with the hope that he was—at least somewhat— getting through to the king. The one that existed beyond the duke's control. "It makes sense now," Teryn said, speaking carefully to keep Dimetreus' full attention. "Aveline Corasande Caelan, Princess of Khero. You watched her dance. You sat next to her at dinner. Do you honestly believe in your heart of hearts that she wasn't your sister?"

The king's throat bobbed, face pale.

"She's still alive. And...and she loves you." Teryn wasn't sure that last part was true. After everything Cora had been through, he'd understand if she hated her brother.

"The signal, Your Majesty," said a guard.

Dimetreus' lips curled away from his teeth. "Lies. Every word a lie." Just as roughly as he'd taken the gag down, he shoved it back over Teryn's mouth. This time it didn't make it between his teeth. Instead, it was pushed only over his lower lip, something that neither the king nor any of the guards seemed to notice.

Teryn was once again forced to move forward. As he followed after the king's entourage toward Centerpointe Rock, a spark of hope filled his chest. Not over his exchange with the king, for that had served no purpose in the end. His hope was that, if he could work his gag just a little lower, he might be able to speak to his father one more time after all.

~

LARYLIS THOUGHT HIS HEART WOULD SHATTER IN TWO AS HE LOOKED AT HIS BROTHER standing on the opposite side of Centerpointe Rock, flanked by guards and the traitor king. Duke Morkai stood with Arlous and Verdian upon the rock, but Larylis only had eyes for his brother and his shockingly awful state. Teryn's hair stood in disarray, the already dark strands heavy with grease. His skin was smudged with dirt, his tired eyes shadowed with dark circles, his cheeks far hollower than they normally were. His clothing—a pair of black trousers and what appeared to be a once-fine shirt—was torn and stained.

Teryn met his eyes, but all Larylis could see was Mareleau's face. Her lips. Her eyes heavy with desire. His brother had been imprisoned, starved, and perhaps even tortured, while Larylis had been kissing his fiancée. They would have done more had he not regained his senses. It had taken all his restraint to leave Mareleau, the woman he loved, the woman who loved him back, but it had been the right thing to do. They could love each other all they wanted, but they could never be together. Her father would never allow it, and Teryn...

His heart ached to look at him. It only deepened his guilt knowing that Larylis now stood in their father's entourage as a false prince. Arlous' newly legitimized heir. A necessary ruse for when they'd attempt to make their refusal to surrender convincing. Morkai had to think they'd given up on getting Teryn back, all to provide enough time to spirit Teryn away and flee Centerpointe Rock before the duke learned of their duplicity.

Larylis had a plan. One that was not allowed to fail.

Larylis pulled his gaze away from Teryn to assess the proceedings on the rock. Arlous, Verdian, and Morkai stood several feet apart from each other on the rock's surface. Their respective entourages stood on the ground behind them. Arlous and Verdian had each brought their war generals and a small group of soldiers to form their retinues, while Dimetreus stood only with soldiers bearing Duke Morkai's sigil. It was no surprise that the duke was speaking for the king, both as his proxy and war general. If everything Lex had said was true, the king was merely a puppet.

The three men upon the rock kept their voices low and calm, but Larylis could still hear most of what was being said. Morkai had already reminded the two kings what was at stake—Teryn's life if both parties didn't surrender. They would not get another chance to see Teryn alive if they didn't acquiesce. Now the duke was delivering each kingdom's terms for surrender.

"Verdian, along with your surrender to your new king, you must claim responsibility for sending the spy that killed Queen Linette."

Verdian opened his mouth, his face crimson, but he managed to hold his tongue. His shoulders tensed, hands curled so tightly his knuckles went white.

Duke Morkai gave him a taunting smile. "You may be offered a dukedom should you easily comply. Your crown, palace, fortune, and all trade agreements will be transferred into King Dimetreus' possession."

Verdian's lip curled as if he were cursing the duke under his breath. Larylis was impressed the king was able to remain silent. It had been part of their plan—hear the duke's terms, make no argument, request time to deliberate—but Verdian wasn't known for restraint.

Morkai turned his gaze to Arlous. "Along with Menah's surrender to King Dimetreus, you will confess to colluding with Selay in orchestrating Queen Linette's murder as well as sending Prince Teryn as a spy to Ridine Castle. You'll be made a viscount should you readily comply. Your crown, palace, fortune, and all trade agreements will be transferred into King Dimetreus' possession."

Arlous pursed his lips against the arguments that were sure to be brimming behind his clenched teeth. Larylis, on the other hand, felt as if his blood had been doused in ice. These ridiculous terms, confessing to crimes they didn't commit... would they not result in severe punishments for Arlous and Verdian both, regardless of any titles bestowed? He had the prickling feeling they were all being toyed with. As if the duke didn't care whether they surrendered or not.

Only that they were here.

The armor he wore suddenly felt too light. Too insubstantial. Aside from the soldiers, who wore full plates, and Teryn who had no protection, everyone present wore only breastplates and gauntlets. Anything heavier would have signaled an expectation for battle. Anything less would be foolish.

Larylis was starting to think that coming here without a full army behind them had been the foolish choice.

"Is that all?" Verdian said through his teeth.

The duke nodded. "Simple terms. A simple choice."

Larylis held his breath, waiting for his father or Verdian to deliver the next piece of their plan.

Arlous shifted his jaw and spoke, words clipped. "We will inform you of our decision at midnight tonight."

Larylis released a relieved sigh. That was what the rest of his plan hinged on. They needed the cover of darkness to act. Needed to get Morkai out of the camp while there was limited visibility. Larylis already knew how to find Teryn. Berol had located his tent before the delegation had even arrived. They'd spied on it the night before, hiding on the hillside. The only thing that had kept them from acting right away was the presence of the damn duke. He and his monster stalked the camp every hour of the night, and Larylis dared not face him head on. But tonight...

Tonight, they'd act. Larylis would stand at his father's side, drawing out negotiations and arguing over everything they resisted bringing up now. It would give Larylis' force of covert operatives the chance they needed to sneak into camp while the duke was distracted.

Arlous stood taller. "We'll meet you back here—"

"No," Morkai said.

The word sent a shard of glass through Larylis' heart, puncturing his hope, his well-laid plans.

"Excuse me?" Verdian said. "You cannot deny us time to deliberate."

"I can," the duke said, his expression devoid of shame. "You will surrender now. It is a matter of Prince Teryn's life. The choice should be easy." He slowly angled his head toward Verdian. "Or perhaps it isn't easy for you. Perhaps you don't care enough about the prince's fate to be moved. Perhaps my terms weren't gracious enough for you."

Arlous leveled a dark stare at Verdian, but he refused to meet it.

"How about I provide a royal marriage for your daughter?" Morkai said.

Larylis' veins burned with anger. How dare he bring Mareleau into this!

Verdian narrowed his eyes. "Selay will surrender if my daughter is married to King Dimetreus. Our surrender will only be made after she has borne the king an heir and you have left the continent."

Morkai let out a dark chuckle. "Your daughter will be given a marriage of my choosing, your surrender will happen now, and I will not be going anywhere."

"No!" The word erupted from Verdian's lips. "I've had enough of this farce, sorcerer. Selay will not surrender. You now have my answer." With that, Verdian stepped off the rock and stormed away, his retinue following behind. Larylis blinked after him, his body seized with terror.

To save Teryn's life, both kingdoms had to surrender.

"My...my son..." His father's anguished voice drew Larylis' gaze back to the rock. He expected to see a knife at his brother's throat, a sword over his bowed head. Instead, Morkai had stepped closer to Arlous, a mocking frown turning the corners of his lips.

"I'm a sympathetic man, Arlous. I'll give you one last chance. I will spare Teryn's life if you surrender. I will make you an ally and we will stand up against Selay together. You can get revenge for the final insult Verdian has made to your son. What will it be?"

Arlous' expression was vacant. Hopeless.

Muffled shouts came from Dimetreus' entourage. Larylis' gaze shot to Teryn as he struggled against the guards that held him back. He rubbed his chin against his shoulder again and again. Finally, he managed to get the gag beneath his mouth and his voice came out clear. "Do not surrender. Whatever you do, do not surrender. I've made peace with my fate, Father. I promise you I have. Fight him."

One of the guards backhanded Teryn with an armored glove, splitting Teryn's cheek. Another shoved Teryn's gag back into his mouth.

Morkai sighed as if the outburst had been merely a minor irritation. "What is your decision?"

Arlous stared at Teryn, his brows furrowed. Agony was etched into every crease on his face. Their father had always been strong. Stubborn. Willing to stand for what he wanted regardless of the cost or conflict. He was a steadfast ruler and a kind father. He was unflappable in all things.

Except when it came to love.

That was where his father was weak.

A strange mixture of terror, defeat, and relief swarmed through Larylis as he realized his father had only one choice. He was going to surrender. Lela would fall to the rule of a blood mage to save Teryn's life. Larylis didn't blame him. Not at all. He only dreaded what would happen to this land in the days, months, and years to come.

Arlous spoke, his voice far stronger than Larylis expected. "Very well. We will give you our final decision. First, I request an exchange of hostage."

A chill ran down Larylis' spine. Not once had they discussed a change of hostage.

Morkai scoffed. "A change of hostage? Who do you suggest to take his place?" His gaze slid slowly to Larylis.

He blanched, his legs nearly giving way beneath him. His father was going to... to sacrifice *him*. A surge of betrayal twisted his heart, but he pushed it away along with the tears that pricked his eyes. This was a sacrifice that needed to be made. If Menah didn't surrender, death would be the toll. Better to kill the bastard than the heir.

Another spike of betrayal tightened his chest.

"No," Arlous said. "I want you to take me."

Larylis froze, his mind reeling to comprehend his father's words.

Morkai grinned as if the proceedings were an entertaining spectacle. "I cannot allow you to decide your kingdom's fate and play hostage at the same time."

Arlous shook his head. "My son will take my place. His decision will be final."

"I can hardly trust the crown prince to make such an important decision on Menah's behalf," Morkai said. "He's already made his stance clear. Not that I blame him. I believe he's feeling rather sore about being a hostage."

"Not Teryn," Arlous said. "But my other heir, Larylis Alante."

Larylis looked from his father to Teryn. None of this made sense. He wasn't truly an Alante. It was only supposed to be an act in the service of a plan that had already failed.

Morkai turned his gaze on Larylis, studying him as if seeing him for the first time. "Larylis Alante?"

Larylis shook his head to deny it, but his father's voice rang out. "You are an Alante, Larylis. It is my final wish."

"I accept," Morkai said. He snapped his fingers and two guards dragged Teryn onto the rock. Everything seemed to happen in a blur as Teryn—still bound and gagged—was turned over to Arlous' war commander, General Nellman. Meanwhile, Larylis was beckoned onto the rock. Arlous now stood where Teryn had been, his wrists tied behind his back. It took Larylis a moment to realize his father had been stripped of all weapons and armor, and they now lay on the ground at Teryn's feet.

He met his father's gaze, who held his eyes with a knowing look. "I trust you. You will make the decision we've already settled on. Do you understand me? I believe in you. I love—" His voice was cut off as a guard tied a gag around his mouth. With nothing left to say, Arlous only gave him a resigned nod.

Larylis' heart hammered so hard he could hear it. It pounded in his ears, mingling with the echo of his father's words.

You will make the decision we've already settled on.

His stomach churned, sending bile rising to his throat.

Do you understand me?

Larylis understood completely.

Morkai gave him a wry grin. "What's your choice, Larylis Alante?"

I believe in you.

He swallowed hard. His voice sounded far away when he finally spoke. "We refuse to surrender."

"Very well." Morkai lifted his cane and tugged on the amber crystal that adorned the top. In a flash, the cane separated in two, revealing a long, slim dagger attached to the crystal, its hilt the same black color of his cane. Then, with a swipe, he slashed it over Arlous' throat.

49

Teryn roared against his gag as he watched blood seep from his father's throat. The guards stepped away, leaving Arlous staggering, writhing, his bound hands preventing him from covering the wound. Teryn struggled against the arms that restrained him. This time it wasn't Morkai's guards but his father's own men. He was desperate to run to him, to save his father before he could bleed out. But all hope of that was lost when a flash of silver swept between Arlous' head and shoulders. Teryn hadn't seen the soldier come up behind his father, hadn't seen him unsheathe his sword. He only saw as Arlous' head was separated from his body before falling to the ground. Hot tears streamed down Teryn's cheeks as he renewed his struggle to get free. "No, Your Majesty. No," General Nellman kept saying over and over. At first, Teryn thought he was quietly lamenting Arlous' death.

Then he realized Nellman was talking to *him*.

He was king now.

Morkai stepped toward Larylis, who stood trembling, eyes fixed on their father's corpse. "Do you feel satisfied with your choice, Larylis Alante?"

Larylis' gaze shot toward the duke. His throat bobbed. Once. Twice. When he spoke, his words came out trembling. "We...we will now discuss terms for war."

Morkai released a sigh and extended his free hand to the side. His cane was clenched in the other, his hidden blade back in its sheath. "No, we will not."

The ground rumbled all around. A dark shape bounded over and leapt onto the rock. It was the Beast. Just then, one of the duke's soldiers blew a deep and baleful horn.

THE HORN BLAST ECHOED THROUGH THE VALLEY, ITS TONE REVERBERATING THROUGH Cora's bones. She couldn't take her eyes off the dead king. They didn't surrender. They were *supposed* to surrender. She'd thought that was what had happened when Teryn had been transported to the other side of the rock. But now King Arlous was dead, and the horn...

It signaled battle.

She could spend no more time waiting for Teryn to get to safety. If the Forest People were going to take down the duke, they'd have to act now.

She assessed the figures who'd come to stand beside her, all dressed in the same leather armor she wore. The archers and spearmen had their weapons drawn. The Faeryn had their hands raised, ready to summon the Magic of the Soil.

A glance back at the valley showed the Roizan leaping onto the rock. It must have charged from her brother's camp when she hadn't been looking. With a spike of terror, she whirled toward Valorre and tore the cotton sheath from his horn. "Go," she whispered.

The unicorn took off running.

Cora and the Forest People followed.

~

TERYN SHOUTED LARYLIS' NAME, BUT HIS MOUTH WAS STILL GAGGED. HIS MUFFLED cries were drowned out by the war horn, by General Nellman's call for retreat. Larylis obeyed the call and dove off the rock. One of Menah's soldiers got hold of Larylis and began ushering him away from the rock. Teryn stumbled, his movements made far more difficult with his hands still bound, but he was quickly hauled to his feet. He found Lieutenant Griff at his side, a knife in hand. He cut Teryn's bindings and gag, then hastily dressed him in a belted sword and breastplate. All of his father's soldiers—no, *his* soldiers now—formed a wall around him and Larylis against the duke's men.

Larylis sidled closer, sword raised. His hand trembled, his face as pale as a ghost as they continued their retreat. The duke's men were gaining on them. Teryn exchanged a terrified glance with his brother. Neither needed words to express how they were feeling. They were both terrified. Reeling in the wake of their father's death. "Your sword," Larylis said, voice wavering.

Teryn glanced at the sword that had been belted at his waist. Only then did he recognize it. His father's sword. His father's breastplate. Both had been stripped from his father when Arlous had taken Teryn's place. The armor was light. Not what a royal would wear into battle, but his father hadn't anticipated how the meeting would end. It wasn't how so-called *peace talks* were supposed to work .

This isn't how anything *is supposed to work.*

Arlous' death replayed before Teryn's eyes, but he forced himself back to the present. Grief lanced his heart as he unsheathed his father's sword. Morkai's men were gaining on them, and the horn had likely summoned the rest of his forces back at camp. Hopefully it had summoned reinforcements from Menah and Selay as well.

Teryn caught a glimpse of the rock where Morkai stood next to his Beast, lips pulled into a smug grin. The view was quickly obscured by a misty fog. It sprouted from the earth in patches that were growing denser by the second.

His blood went cold.

This wasn't fog.

A patch of mist turned corporeal before his eyes, forming a towering figure with a semi-translucent battle axe. The wraith swung the weapon, but not at Teryn. He was facing away from him…toward Lieutenant Griff.

Teryn's warning came too late, and the man took the axe in his shoulder. With a grunt, Griff staggered forward and whirled to face his opponent. Through the wraith's body, Teryn saw the lieutenant's eyes go wide, saw where his armor was rent open to reveal a seeping wound. The man's arm hung useless at his side, but he kept the other hand wrapped tight around his sword. The wraith swung his axe again, but Teryn dove into action. His father's sword cleaved through the specter, making it disappear into a puff of mist.

Lieutenant Griff met Teryn's gaze with a haunted look, his face already pale from blood loss.

"It's going to reanimate in a matter of seconds," Teryn said. "Be ready—"

Griff charged to Teryn's right and met the shaft of a spear that had been aiming for the flesh above Teryn's breastplate. Teryn launched back. Griff's sword knocked the spear away. Another swipe and the wraith was gone. At least the apparitions' weapons could be parried like any other, and their bodies could be vanquished by the lightest interference. Teryn had witnessed that when Cora had shot them with her bow. Her arrow had soared straight through every wraith in its path and took them out with ease.

The problem was that they kept coming back.

The axe wraith reformed before Teryn's eyes, staring down at him with two black hollows. Teryn cut through his middle before he could swing his axe, but the spear wraith was back now too. Teryn blocked his spear then swiped through his body. Turned, cut down another. Turned. Another.

They were everywhere.

Everywhere.

He turned again, watched Lieutenant Griff fall to the earth, his gut gaping open where the axe wraith had split his armor yet again. The next swing of the axe severed Griff's head. Teryn's stomach lurched. He stepped back, forcing himself to keep his nerve. Mist formed at his left but he cut it down before it could take a human shape. Another appeared on his right. Another straight ahead.

A flurry of wings stole past his vision, cutting through the bodies of the wraiths and sending them scattering into mist. *Berol.* She flew back up, her wings beating the air.

A specter holding a mace charged him. Again, Berol dove down. The wraith swung his mace. It nearly collided with her. She veered left at the last minute, missing the weapon's spiked head by an inch.

She landed on Teryn's shoulder and frantically nipped at his cheek. "Go!" Teryn shouted, waving her away. The mace wraith renewed his charge on Teryn. Berol launched off Teryn's shoulder and flew at the apparition. This time, its mace connected with one of her wings. "Berol!" Teryn saw her fall to the ground just as he cut through the wraith. As soon as it disappeared, he turned toward the falcon. She rolled on the grass and righted herself, then flew back toward Teryn. Her feathers were bent at odd angles where the wraith had struck her, making her flight uneven. She flapped her wings in his face, ushering him back. His heart squeezed tight at the sight of those twisted feathers. "Get out of here, Berol. Home! *Go home.*" She beat her wings at him a few more times, but he gently shoved her away. "Go!" he shouted as fiercely as he could. "Go away!"

She launched back into the sky and circled overhead.

"Please." The word was barely a whisper. With all his heart, he willed her away. Whether it was home, the woods, or some far off place, he didn't care. He'd rather never see her again than watch her die protecting him.

Finally, she flew out of sight.

With a bone-deep weariness, Teryn returned to the fight.

He barely noticed when a small cavalry charge came from behind. Reinforcements had arrived but it still wasn't enough. There were too many wraiths.

He swung his sword again and again, his arms aching with every slash. His father's longsword was far heavier than the shortsword he'd brought on the Heart's Hunt. Still, he fought on. The wraiths were relentless. A particularly skilled apparition pursued him, blocking every swipe and slash with his translucent sword. The sounds their two weapons made when they made contact was wrong. There was no clang of steel on steel, only a muffled crash. Sweat dripped into Teryn's eyes. His muscles screamed with every move. He parried. Stepped back. Parried. Stepped back.

His next step landed on something hard. The body of another one of his soldiers, he realized with terror. He lurched back as the wraith swung his sword, sending him tripping over the man. The wraith took his chance to close in on Teryn. Teryn lifted his sword, but the wraith was faster, his weapon darting straight toward his throat.

The wraith froze and puffed into mist. Teryn scrambled to his feet and found a thin, twisted root where the specter had been. Not too far away he saw a woman with tan skin, dark hair, and inked forearms. His heart stuttered as his first thought was that the figure was Cora. But another look revealed this woman was much older. He glanced around the battlefield and noticed a few other similar figures, their tattooed palms raised as more roots rose from the earth, tearing wraiths in two, snuffing them out before they had the chance to fully form. He saw others with spears and bows, some in direct combat with Morkai's soldiers.

Teryn wasn't sure how it was possible, but Cora must have brought her people. Her coven. She might even be there herself. The prospect wasn't entirely comforting, as he hated the thought of her being in harm's way. Still, the odds were no longer so firmly against him, especially as an infantry charge stormed into the fray.

A wraith formed in front of him, and he cut it down, ignoring the scream of his muscles. Gritting his teeth, he turned his mind away from retreat. There was one person he needed to find.

One person to kill.

50

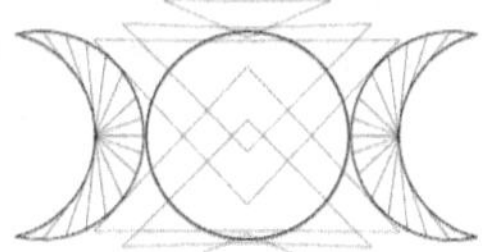

The air grew heavy with plumes of dirt, left in the wake of the Forest People's manipulation of roots and vines. It was some of the most impressive feats of visible magic Cora had ever seen. She couldn't gape for long, though. Not only was her vision growing increasingly obscured as she wove through the battlefield, but she had a job to do.

Salinda stayed at her side, fending off threats with her Magic of the Soil while Cora used her bow. They kept to the east side of the valley, where the field was devoid of wraiths. The specters remained to the west, the side closest to Menah's and Selay's camps, where very few of Morkai's men kept up pursuit. It didn't take long for Cora to learn why. The wraiths cut down anyone they came across, regardless of what side they served or what sigil was etched into their armor. She supposed that was the cost of employing the dead—beings whose bodies had been stripped from mind and spirit. Morkai had said they were the souls of warriors who'd served in a war long passed. They were living memories gifted with the power to kill, nothing more.

The ground rumbled beneath her feet. Cora and Salinda pulled up short as Valorre streamed past, the Roizan charging after. Cora had been too late to prevent Morkai from using his creature to summon the wraiths, but Valorre's appearance on the field had been enough to get the Roizan away from Morkai shortly after. Valorre had then begun circling the perimeter of the field, drawing the Roizan up the hillside, between the trees, anywhere to keep him out of range from the duke. But whenever Valorre had tried to lead the creature too far, the Roizan would come barreling back, forcing Valorre onto the field to tempt the beast away again.

Cora coughed into her cloak as she and Salinda moved through a particularly dense cloud of dirt. She blinked the grit from her eyes once they were past it. They were nearing Centerpointe Rock. Through the haze, she saw half of it was framed by roots, as if one of the Forest People had tried to create a cage around it. Finally,

Cora caught sight of Morkai. He was battling Roije. The tracker had a spear in one hand while his other palm was raised toward the earth. He sent root after root to harry the duke, but Morkai sliced through every vine that tried to wrap around his ankle, hacked through every root that shot toward his chest. Not only did Morkai have his long dagger—the one he'd had hidden in his cane—but he now held a broadsword as well. Salinda and Cora took off toward the fighting pair. Cora's heart leapt into her throat when she passed a familiar body lying in the muddy grass.

Druchan.

He was dead.

She didn't have time to grieve or feel guilt. Only to nock an arrow and aim for Morkai. Something heavy slammed into her, and she lost her footing. Her bow skittered out of her hands as she landed on her back. A dark silhouette stood over her, backlit by the rising sun. The light glinted off a broadsword pointed over her heart.

"You," growled a familiar voice.

Her lungs tightened. "Dimi."

"Impostor," he said. As her eyes adjusted, she saw his furious glare. "How dare you come into my home and try to manipulate me. To pour salt in a wound already gaping."

"Brother," Cora said, trying to keep her voice level. "It's me. It's...it's Aveline. It's...Cora."

He froze on an intake of breath. "How do you know about that name?"

"Because it's *my* name. It's what our mother used to call me in private. You know that."

"All you speak are lies," he said, shaking his head. He continued to glare, but for the briefest moment, she thought she saw the glossy sheen over his eyes retreat.

Hope sparked inside her, and she held on to it like an anchor. "Do...do you remember when I told you how I'd learned where babies came from? How I'd overheard what Lady Paulette had been discussing with Lady Madeline? Do you remember what you said to me after? You said—"

He took a forbidding step closer, the tip of his sword pressing against Cora's thick leather breastplate, the haze once again clouding his eyes. "It doesn't matter what I said. There was a spy in my house that night. I trust nothing that was uttered where that wretched poisoner could have overheard."

He lifted his sword slightly, as if preparing to thrust.

"What about the wildflower meadow?" she rushed to say.

He paused. "What about it?"

"Do you remember when we used to have picnics on our secret cliff?" The memory played out in her mind as she said it. She hadn't even remembered it until now. "Remember how we used to watch the meadow beneath the cliff and pretend it was home to faeries? We used to imagine we could leap from the ledge and land in another world. Another realm. You took me there after our parents died." Mentioning her parents brought a lump rising in her throat. She searched his eyes, hoping to see the haze lift. It didn't. Grief snagged her heart, and rage began to bloom there. Her voice quavered, growing louder, firmer, with every word she spoke next. "You told me it would be all right. That you'd always protect me. You said you'd never let anyone hurt me. You said that, Dimi. You promised."

She no longer cared about the sword pressed over her chest, only the relief that came from uttering truths she'd let lie buried too long. "You asked me a question the night you found me next to Linette's bedside. You said, *What have you done?* I ask you the same, Dimetreus. What have you done? What have you done to *us*, to all that was left of our family? What have you done to our kingdom?"

"Enough!" he shouted. His torso heaved as he stared down at her, blinking furiously. "Enough," he said again. His voice, his posture, his expression...everything began to deflate. His sword still stood between them, but his sword arm trembled. The haze...began to lift.

She extended her senses toward him, felt his conflict, his confusion. His dulled emotions seemed to slam up against invisible walls. She swallowed hard, willing her anger to abate as she brought her palms out in a placating gesture. "It's all right —" Her words cut off as two shapes came barreling toward them. A pair of fighters on horseback locked in battle. The horse and soldier closest to them were wounded, the mount rearing back. Back. Edging dangerously near. "Dimi."

"No," he said, the word like a plea. "It can't be..."

"Dimi!" She shouted his name and began scrambling back on her forearms, her brother's sword no longer her greatest concern. She rolled onto her stomach, clawing at the earth to gain enough purchase to rise to her feet. The sound of hooves closed in, followed by a guttural neigh. A glance over her shoulder showed the wounded stallion bucking as his rider received a fatal blow. His rear hooves caught Dimetreus in the gut, sending him tumbling back. His head struck the earth. Cora was halfway to rising when the stallion bucked again. She ducked, covering her head, and caught a hoof in the shoulder instead. It sent her to the ground, several feet from where her brother lay unconscious. Perhaps even dead.

Another guttural sound came from the horse. The other soldier had opened the stallion's throat. It fell back, its body plummeting straight toward Cora. She half ran, half crawled. But when the horse landed, her legs were pinned beneath it.

⁓

THE GROUND WAS RIDDLED WITH ROOTS AND VINES, IMPEDING TERYN'S PROGRESS along with the relentless reappearance of the wraiths. His one consolation was that the longer the battle went on, the slower the wraiths began to reanimate. It seemed there were limits to the duke's magic. Or perhaps the wraiths' patience in following his will was wearing thin.

Teryn was nearly out of breath, his brow slick with sweat, by the time he finally found Morkai. The mage stood upon Centerpointe Rock, locked in combat with two witches, a male and female. Both had tattoos like Cora's and worked with roots the same way he'd seen others doing on the battlefield. Morkai parried every attack they threw his way, his moves swift and sure. The female sent roots crawling from the earth around the rock, snaking over the surface and weaving around his ankles while the male charged with a spear. Morkai broke free and parried the spear with his broadsword. With his dagger, he cut through the vines and kicked the tangled limbs free.

Another root erupted from the earth, this one large enough to make the ground tremble as it shot toward the rock. It wrapped around the mage's middle and squeezed. Teryn saw the duke's breastplate begin to warp. The male witch came in for another attack with his spear. With a mighty swing, Morkai hacked through the root with his sword. With his dagger, he severed the leather straps securing one side of his breastplate. He shrugged off the armor just as the witch swung out with his spear. The spearhead sliced open Morkai's side, but the duke didn't falter. He stepped forth and swung his sword in an arc.

And severed the man's arm at the elbow.

"Roije!" the female witch called out. She ran to the injured man.

Morkai pursued them both, turning his back fully to Teryn.

Teryn raced the rest of the way to the rock, determined to plunge his sword into the duke's back, straight through his ribs, his heart—

Morkai turned around and parried Teryn's attack.

"The new King of Menah," Morkai said with a smirk. Now that they were face to face, Teryn could see the blood splattered over the mage's face and neck. How many others had the duke killed? Teryn was vaguely aware of the unmoving shapes of other bodies strewn about the rock. He had a feeling most were soldiers from Menah or Selay.

"I appreciate you making things easy for me," Morkai taunted. "After I kill you, I'll kill your brother. Menah is as good as mine."

Teryn's blood boiled with rage, fueling his every move as he struggled to get under Morkai's defenses. The mage fought with surprising skill and unnatural speed. Teryn knew the mage worked terrifying feats of blood sorcery, but he hadn't expected him to fight like a trained soldier.

Teryn's eyes stung as sweat dripped into them. He blinked the moisture away, swung his father's sword. It clashed with Morkai's dagger, but the force of Teryn's swing was so hard it sent the mage's weapon flying from his hand—

A sharp pain struck Teryn's ribs. He staggered back. Glancing down, he found a gash in the right side of his breastplate. Morkai may have been partially disarmed but he still held his broadsword. Thankfully, the wound didn't appear terribly deep. Or was he simply in shock? Whatever the case, he gritted his teeth against the pain, set his feet, and strengthened his grip on his sword.

Morkai raised his empty palm.

To Teryn's horror, streams of his blood began to float from his wound to dance through the air between him and the mage.

In a matter of seconds, the duke held a ball of Teryn's blood in the palm of his hand.

51

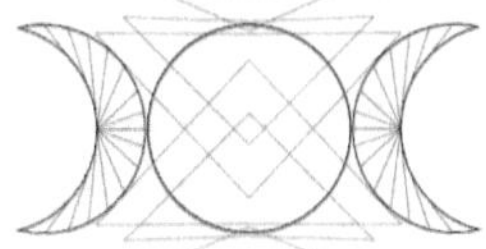

Cora was forced to watch the horrible scene unfolding before her. Roije and Salinda's attack. Roije's severed arm. Teryn charging Morkai. Salinda wrapping Roije's wound and helping him limp away. Cora lost sight of them in the haze, but she was close enough to see Teryn and Morkai's fight. Close enough to watch as his plate was rent open.

She could hardly peel her eyes away, even as she struggled to free herself from beneath the dead horse. At least none of the enemy soldiers had seen her, nor had anyone found her brother. With the plumes of dirt clouding the air and mingling with the bloody chaos of battle, Dimetreus looked like any other dead body.

But he wasn't.

She could feel his life force even as he lay prone a few feet away.

Her pulse thudded wildly as she watched Morkai step toward Teryn. The prince was frozen, his hand over his heart, his eyes on the ball of blood. She clawed her hands into the dirt, tried to pull her bottom half free. There was a sharp pain in one of her legs. Likely fractured from the horse's fall. Her shoulder screamed where the stallion had kicked her.

Morkai lifted the ball of blood higher and let it rotate in his hand. Teryn gasped, raking his breastplate with his fingertips as if desperate to reach his heart. She remembered that sharp pain when Morkai had used her own blood against her. But could he kill with it? She knew he could weave death by merging it with a deceased person's blood, but what could he do with just a single source?

Teryn winced. His sword clattered to the surface of the rock.

Morkai dropped his broadsword.

Cora's heart slammed against her ribs as she realized what he was going to do.

There were several bodies littered around the rock.

Gaping wounds.

Sources of blood.

Morkai lifted his free hand toward the nearest body. Tendrils of crimson rose like ribbons toward his palm.

Cora renewed her struggle, straining against the horse's weight.

Stop fighting.

The demand came from within her. Not a voice but a feeling. She ignored it.

Stop struggling.

She only struggled harder.

Slow down.

Feel.

She gritted her teeth against the urgings, raging at them, hating them. How could she be expected to slow down and *feel* at a time like this?

A spike of resentment shot through her. Resentment at her own futility, her weakness, her stupid worthless magic—

Subtle awareness cleared a path through her anger, something soft and yielding. She continued to rage against it, but it was stronger than her resistance.

It was her magic.

She suddenly knew what this was. Another challenge.

Hot angry tears streamed down her cheeks. She didn't have time for a challenge. She didn't have time to slow down and turn inward. Not when Morkai was transforming both sources of blood into threads—threads that were now beginning to twine together.

Again, that soft, quiet urging cut through her resistance.

She hated it. Oh, how she hated it.

But she gave in. Gave in to the hate, the anguish, the panic. Let herself feel it, let it twist her heart and weaken her body. Let herself slump beneath the horse and close her eyes. Her weakness turned to calm, and calm turned to strength. Magic flooded her chest and trailed down her arms, humming through the ink that marked her skin.

She breathed.

In. Out. In. Out.

And felt.

Pain. Grief. Urgency. Fortitude.

Then something softer.

Protection. Devotion. Friendship. Love.

Open your eyes.

She followed the internal urging, saw Morkai's blood weaving growing tighter, the strands of blood nearly fully merged. Teryn was now on his knees, still clutching his breastplate.

Allowing her quiet magic to still her mind, she followed its pull, its guidance. Followed it as it narrowed in on the space behind Morkai. She felt an overwhelming *need* to be there, to free Teryn. It was so strong she could feel it down to her bones. It tugged her palms, her body, her soul, tugged every part of her until she felt as if it would carry her there on an invisible wind.

Teryn's face warped with pain as the mage threaded another strand through his tapestry.

Her heart swelled with determination. Resolve. Conviction.

With a slow exhale, she focused on her legs, on the foot that wasn't radiating with piercing agony. She moved it against the dirt, the horse, and pictured it pressing against the very place she needed to be. Not against soil, not buried beneath a dead animal, but upon the rock—

She hobbled on one leg, suddenly upright.

Blinking at the startling shift in light, she realized she now stood directly behind Morkai on Centerpointe Rock.

His back was facing her as he continued to weave his crimson tapestry. He hadn't a clue she was there. It shouldn't be possible that she was. She couldn't have been able to move from under the horse to the rock in the blink of an eye.

But it had happened. And this was no time to second-guess what could be her last shot.

A ripple of pain shot through her injured leg as she shifted her stance. She reached for one of her daggers, stepped forward, and plunged it into Morkai's back. She twisted it as far as she could before he whirled to face her.

His eyes went wide as they met hers. His blood weaving fell to the surface of the rock. It didn't disappear like it had before he'd killed the prisoner or after he'd woven her blood with Linette's. It simply spilled as ordinary blood should. His magic ruined. His tapestry incomplete.

Cora held his gaze and unsheathed her next dagger. With a thrust, she drove it into Morkai's abdomen. She grabbed her final knife, thrust toward him, but he knocked her hand away. Unfazed, she swiped and slashed and stabbed. He backed up a few steps and held out his hand. She expected him to reveal her tiny ball of blood again. Expected to feel the searing pain strike her chest at any moment.

It didn't.

She plunged her final knife into Morkai's side and grabbed an arrow from her quiver—

Teryn gasped.

Her eyes flew toward him. He'd been halfway to standing but now doubled over. Fresh tendrils of blood seeped from his wound as Morkai drew it toward his palm.

She glanced back at Morkai, saw blood spreading over his padded tunic everywhere she'd struck. He held her gaze with a sneer and wrapped his free hand around the hilt of the knife in his side. As he pulled it free, more blood darkened his tunic.

Her lips curled into a wicked smirk. If he pulled all of her blades free at once, he'd bleed to death before long.

He narrowed his eyes as if he had come to the same conclusion. Gritting his teeth, he pressed his open palm over the wound while the other continued to summon Teryn's blood. "I need my Roizan," he said.

"He's busy right now." She clenched her hand around the shaft of her arrow, assessing where she could strike next.

"Drop your arrow and call off your unicorn friend—"

"No."

"—or Teryn dies."

Teryn bit back a cry as Morkai drew more blood from his wound. He sank back to his knees, his face white. He was losing blood far faster than Morkai. He'd die, even without a blood weaving.

"All right." The words left her mouth in a rush. She let the arrow fall to her feet. "All right. I'll call off Valorre. Drop Teryn's blood."

"Call off the unicorn first."

She released a slow breath and sought her connection to Valorre. She sensed him on the hillside, his energy frantic, fatigued. *Run out of range.*

He rippled with defiance. *The abomination will come back to the field.*

It's all right, she said, trying to convey her certainty. Her sense of calm amongst a storm of fear. *Just do it.*

She felt the unicorn's grudging acceptance.

"It is done. The Roizan will return."

Morkai turned his palm down. She noted that the blood didn't fall. It only disappeared. That meant he still had it, the same way he still held her tiny drop somewhere. He took a step toward her, his face distorted with rage. "Stop fighting against me, Aveline. I have already won. Lela will be mine by the end of this battle. There will be no war. No surrender. It ends here. This is your last chance to choose me."

She hobbled a step back, her injured leg screaming in protest. Catching her balance, she lifted her chin and tried to exude far more confidence than she felt. "You already know my decision. I will never choose you. And you haven't already won. You've lost. You may have killed King Arlous and may think you can kill Teryn too, but King Verdian has fled to safety." She didn't know if that last part was true, only that she hadn't seen the King of Selay on the battlefield yet. No one could see far in this haze. Her chest squeezed as she pondered her next lie, uncertain if there was a chance it could be true by now. The thought tinged her voice with sorrow, giving weight to her possible deception. "My brother is dead. You have no one to inherit Khero from."

His lips tightened into a line.

"You made a mistake in keeping him on the battlefield," she said.

Morkai spoke through his teeth. "He wasn't supposed to be on the battlefield. I ordered him back to camp."

Cora frowned. If her brother had been ordered to safety...why had he been out there? Had he purposefully sought her out? If so, why? Based on the anger he'd shown during their initial confrontation, it could have been for revenge.

She remembered how his eyes had briefly cleared of their sheen. It hadn't lasted long, but for a moment she'd felt like she'd connected to a piece of his true self.

Perhaps it had been hope that had driven him after her.

Over Morkai's shoulder, Cora saw the lumbering shape of the Roizan breaking through the dusty haze. It set the rock rumbling as it clambered toward its master.

The duke shook his head with a dark laugh. "You're wrong about one thing, Aveline," he said as he removed another one of her daggers. "I do have someone left to inherit Khero from. You."

The Roizan ambled closer and closer, panting with fatigue, lips coated in froth. Morkai pressed his hand over the freshest wound and reached for the final embedded dagger. The one she'd plunged into his lower back when she'd first found herself transported onto the rock. His face contorted as he reached behind him and wrenched the blade free.

Cora stepped back, stifling a cry as her injured leg made contact with the rock. She angled herself slightly toward Teryn. He'd managed to remove his breastplate and now pressed his palm over his wound.

With the final dagger free, Morkai locked his eyes with hers. "If your brother is truly dead, then I need you more than ever to claim the throne."

The Roizan reached the edge of the rock.

"But I don't need you alive. All I need is your body." A wild grin stretched over his lips, his pale eyes flashing with menace. He held his hand—the one still clutching her dagger—toward the Roizan. He hadn't looked at the weapon after he'd removed it. His attention had been too fixated on Cora. Too engrossed in his own wicked plans to question whether Cora had any of her own. Didn't think to wonder why Cora had stopped fighting him. Why she didn't flinch or cower as the Roizan leapt upon the rock.

Morkai's expression shuttered with relief, his free hand still pressed to one of his wounds. A wound that was surely knitting back together at that very moment.

It didn't matter.

The Roizan's eyes narrowed on the blade in its master's hand, a blade forged from a white horn. It opened its salivating maw over Morkai's arm and snapped its teeth shut. With a cry, Morkai faced his creature, eyes wide with surprise. The Roizan didn't seem to see Morkai at all, not even as the duke swung out with his free hand, shoving at the beast's snout, desperate to free himself.

Cora edged the rest of the way toward Teryn and linked her arm through his. Together they scrambled off the rock, tumbling to the root-strewn grass. She looked back at the rock just as the Roizan opened its mouth again, this time snapping its teeth over Morkai's head. Then his body. Blood poured between the Roizan's teeth as he continued to crunch through flesh and bone. The monster devoured his master, his maker, until there was nothing left that could be called a being at all.

<h1 style="text-align:center">52</h1>

Larylis fought, certain that his next breath would be his last. Part of him wasn't sure he deserved another breath. Not after what he'd done. Not after the choice he was forced to make. One that ended in his father's death. Still, he swung his blade. Whether he fought a man of flesh or a wraith of mist, every cut conjured visions of father's ruined neck, his severed head, his lifeless eyes. He saw the pride, the trust, right before Larylis condemned him to die. It didn't matter that it was what his father had wanted. All that mattered was that his voice had delivered the sentence. His words had driven the blade.

Part of him yearned to quit fighting, but somehow a fire remained kindled deep in his heart. It drove his arms to move when they were too fatigued to feel, planted his feet on the slick mud when all he wanted to do was sink to his knees and weep.

He fought that urge now as he battled a wraith. Their swords clashed again and again. Larylis' reaction time was getting slower. His weapon heavier in his hand. But that ember still glowed. Still begged him to fight.

The wraith seemed to slow as well. It had already reanimated several times. Each time it reformed, its misty body took longer to condense into a humanoid form. He'd noticed it with other wraiths as well. The longer a wraith fought, and the more times it was felled, the more hampered it would become, as if the act of reanimating was too much work. The will to fight and die over and over too burdensome to bear. Larylis had already seen numerous wraiths wander off the field and disappear. Others simply refused to reanimate.

Larylis parried a particularly lethargic swing and swept his blade through the wraith's middle. As it disappeared, he took the chance to assess his surroundings. The haze was still heavy where he fought, as a few of the tattooed vine-wielders battled wraiths nearby, sending new plumes of dirt into the air with every root they drew from the ground. He'd been terrified when he'd first seen them, certain they served the mage. But his fears were quickly assuaged. They were fighting *against* the duke and his men.

Nearby, he spotted Lex facing off against a mace-wielding wraith. The prince had joined the fray with the infantry charge and had fought with alarming tenacity ever since. He heaved and stumbled, but not once did he give up. Larylis wondered if the same persistent fire that kept him on his feet burned within Lex too.

A misty shape drew his attention. The wraith Larylis had been fighting began to reform in front of him, but he slashed through it before it could fully solidify. A strangled cry rang out, pulling his attention to his surroundings once more. It didn't ring with the same tenor as a yelp of injury or a grunt of strength. It was neither a battle cry nor a shout of vengeance or rage. Instead, it was a long wail of anguish. Terror. He squinted into the haze and saw a soldier fall to his knees and tear off his helm, his posture slumped. He wore the black armor of the duke's men. His opponent, a soldier from Selay, went in for the kill. The other man held up his hands in surrender, falling on his back.

Another similar wail echoed elsewhere on the field. A man stumbled by, peeling off his plates of armor, eyes bulging as he stared at his surroundings as if seeing them for the first time.

A shiver ran down Larylis' spine.

He forced his gaze back to the place where his wraith opponent would surely rise.

It didn't. No matter how long he looked, the wraith didn't return. He scanned the field around him. More bewildered soldiers stumbled past. Some fell to their opponent's swords while others cried out to surrender. Still, others continued to fight, unplagued by whatever drove their comrades to confusion.

Larylis had no idea what was going on.

One thing was certain, though.

The wraiths were gone.

~

A screeching bellow echoed throughout the valley. Cora watched as the Roizan pressed its snout to the surface of the rock, sniffing, tasting. Then, with another piercing howl, it began to buck and thrash. Cora and Teryn backed farther away from the rock, their moves hampered by their respective injuries. Cora didn't dare look away from the Roizan as crimson saliva frothed at its lips. It tossed its enormous head and scraped its front hooves over the rock. Howls turned to grunts. Grunts turned to whimpers.

Then it stilled.

The Roizan's head drooped as if suddenly too heavy for its shoulders. Its eyes closed, its hindquarters quavered. With a final tremor, it fell upon the rock with a rumbling thud. Its red skin began to blacken and char, burning everything from its snout to its tail to the ridge of white horns running along its spine. Fiery veins of red began to spiderweb through its charred flesh. The Roizan slowly opened its maw and released a deep moan. With a final breath, the body of the Roizan collapsed into a pile of ash.

Cora watched as a gust of wind stole some of the ash and sent it scattering over the field. Part of her expected the beast to reform, for Morkai to rise from his bloody remains. The longer she watched the more certain she became.

Morkai was gone.

Just as the duke had said, his magic was connected to the Roizan, and the Roizan's life was bound to his. The duke's death meant the end of the Roizan. An end to his well of magic. And—hopefully—a severing of Morkai's control. Without the duke's numerous glamours being fueled by the Roizan's magic, those he'd been controlling should now be free.

That was her theory, at least.

Teryn let out a pained gasp. She whirled toward him, his name lurching from her lips. A spike of terror surged through her. He was badly injured and his wound was still bleeding. Thanks to Morkai, he'd already lost far too much blood. He swayed on his feet. She reached out to steady him, wincing at the pain in her leg. Her own injuries could wait. Without a second thought, she retrieved an arrow and slashed the head through the bottom of her cloak. It wasn't as effective as a knife, but all her blades were still on the rock. The two the Roizan hadn't eaten, that is.

With frantic fingers, she wrapped the strip of wool around his torso, relieved that the lesion over his ribs wasn't worse. It was a jagged cut, both from the sword Morkai had struck him with and the armor that had bitten into his skin as a result. It certainly wouldn't help that the strip of wool she'd bandaged him in was dirty. At least it would slow the bleeding before he could get to a field surgeon.

Once the wound was wrapped, she stilled her fingers and lifted her eyes to his. He stared down at her with a thoughtful expression. One that made her breath hitch. She realized now that they hadn't been this close since he'd tricked her with a kiss. Nor had they exchanged a word since then either. When she'd seen him fighting Morkai, her only thoughts had been to save him, protect him, defend him. Their last meeting hadn't mattered, nor had his betrayal or their kiss or any of the other conflicting emotions she felt around him. But now...

Her cheeks warmed as she noticed her hand was still pressed to his chest. Over the other side of his ribs. Beneath his heart. She was about to lift her palm when his hand closed over hers.

"Thank you," he said, his voice a quavering whisper. He ran his thumb over the back of her hand, his touch so soft it almost made her shudder.

"Teryn," a male voice called out from nearby.

Cora slid her hand from under his and took a step back.

Teryn slowly angled his body to face the figure that ran toward them. Cora recognized the man from his presence at the negotiation. His resemblance to Teryn made it easy to guess who he was.

"Larylis," Teryn said, voice heavy with relief. The two embraced with the affection of brothers. Cora, feeling like an interloper, took another step back. She stifled a cry as her heel caught on something in the grass. Shifting her weight more evenly over her uninjured leg, she glanced down at what had nearly caused her fall. There, almost hidden amongst the overturned earth and muddy grass, was a long, slender blade. An amber crystal lay beside it, broken off from the hilt. She bent down and gingerly lifted the crystal. Her palm thrummmed against its cold facets. A murky energy pounded against her hand, turning her stomach. She nearly dropped it when she noticed red dripping from the bottom of it.

Blood.

Was the crystal where Morkai had stored the blood he'd stolen?

Swallowing down the bile that rose in her throat, she prepared to throw the crystal into the pile of ash. Then something caught her attention. Some swirling movement behind the amber facets. Her palm thrummed again, this time sensing a new energy. It wasn't dark or murky but...different.

A hand fell softly on her shoulder. She bit back a gasp and shoved the crystal into an inner pocket of her cloak. Teryn gave her a sad smile. "Larylis, this is Cora."

Larylis gave her a solemn nod. "Lex told me about you."

Teryn furrowed his brow. "What do you mean, Lex told you?"

"He came to Dermaine to warn us about the duke's true intentions, then joined our entourage when we left for Centerpointe Rock. He fought with our forces."

Cora and Teryn exchanged a befuddled glance. The last time they'd seen Lex, he'd taken Morkai's deal.

"He's apparently a master of deception," Larylis said. He gave a humorless laugh, one in contrast with the sorrow in his eyes.

It reflected her own sorrow as she looked past the two men to the field beyond, where bodies lay strewn about. Horns bellowed from the east, signaling Khero's retreat. Morkai's death couldn't be widespread yet, but it was clear the tide had turned. The duke's magic had been severed.

It's over. She felt Valorre's words. Glancing around, she sought sight of him to no avail.

It is, she conveyed. *Where are you?*

Close. Your people flee back to the hillside. Will you go with them?

She turned toward the hill where the Forest People had hidden the last few days, but the haze was still too thick to make out any retreating forms. Extending her senses, she felt them near. The survivors at least. Salinda had made it. Roije too, although she sensed him only faintly. Her chest tightened at the knowledge that some of the Forest People had died today and more still could from injuries. Because of her.

Because we had to do what was right, she reminded herself.

She imagined how the battle would have gone without the Forest People's aid. The wraiths would have overpowered Selay's and Menah's forces if not for the roots and vines that tore through the specters with ease.

"What is it?" Teryn asked, his fingertips lightly brushing against hers.

She met his eyes and felt as if her heart were suddenly torn in two. Valorre's question echoed through her mind.

Your people...will you go with them?

The Forest People had fought at her side. They'd intervened with royal affairs in the name of protecting fae magic. But were they truly *her* people? Or were the citizens of Khero—

A dreadful realization sent her heart skittering.

"Dimetreus!" She whirled toward where she'd seen him last. There were too many bodies. Too many figures still darting across the field, some in retreat, some in combat. Finally, she spotted the dead stallion. Not far from it, a cluster of soldiers stood. She began limping in that direction. An arm caught hers and helped her forward. She flushed as she glanced to the side, expecting to find Teryn.

Instead, it was Larylis. "Let me help you."

Disappointment struck her. Of course it wasn't Teryn. Teryn was injured. He walked slightly ahead of them, his gait uneven, his hand pressed against his bandaged ribs. "King Verdian," Teryn called.

A man turned around, and Cora recognized the King of Selay. His eyes widened. "Prince—" He cleared his throat. "*King* Teryn. You're alive."

"I am."

The king shifted his stance, his posture stiff. Cora sensed guilt wafting off of him. "I'm sorry for your loss."

Teryn accepted the king's condolences with a nod.

Verdian's jaw shifted side to side. Lifting his chin, he said in a somewhat begrudging tone, "It will be an honor if you'd take my daughter as your bride when we return home."

A jolt of something fiery sparked in Cora's chest. She breathed it away, forcing her attention from Teryn to the group of soldiers who still stood in a cluster near the felled horse. One turned around. "Your Majesty, the traitor king is awake."

Cora's heart leapt into her throat as she watched the men part to reveal her brother. His eyes darted wildly about as he tried to rise from his knees. A soldier had Dimetreus' arms behind his back and kicked him in the shoulder to keep him down.

A strangled sound left her brother's lips. "What's happening? Where...where..." He blinked several times and shook his head. "A nightmare. No, a nightmare."

Cora surged forward. "Dimetreus!" Another soldier stepped before her, shoving a gauntleted hand out to halt her progress. She hobbled back, eyes darting from the soldier to her distressed brother.

"Who the hell is this?" came King Verdian's sharp tone. Cora met his gaze and found cold eyes looking back at her.

"This is Princess Aveline," Teryn said, coming up beside her.

Verdian let out a bark of humorless laughter. "The dead princess brought back to life?" He scanned her until his eyes landed on her tattooed palms. His lips curled in disgust. "She's a witch. Like the others. The ones with the...vine sorcery."

"The witches fought *with* us," Teryn said, voice surprisingly calm.

Verdian spread out his arms, glancing exaggeratedly from side to side. "Then where are they now?"

Teryn's tone darkened. "Princess Aveline killed the duke."

The king gave him a patronizing look. "Princess Aveline is dead, Majesty."

"Aveline?" The voice was weak, trembling.

Cora met Dimetreus' eyes. They were no longer cast beneath a glossy sheen. They were still shadowed with dark circles and lined with creases that belied his age. Proof that Morkai's death didn't immediately return his well-being.

"Dimi, it's me," Cora said.

"She's working with the traitor," Verdian said. "Take her too."

The soldier with the upraised palm darted forward but Teryn stepped in front of her.

"Out of the way, Majesty," Verdian said through his teeth.

"She's no criminal," Teryn argued. "And she's injured."

The king raised his brows and glanced briefly at Teryn's torso. "So are you. We need to get you to a surgeon."

"Just let Cora go."

"Cora," Verdian echoed. "I thought she was *Princess Aveline*." He said the last part with clear mocking.

"She is," Teryn said, his voice tinged with desperation. "Did Lex not tell you?"

The king denied it at the same moment Larylis said, "He told *me*."

"Just let her explain," Teryn said.

Verdian shook his head. "If she really is who she says she is, she can come with us willingly and explain during questioning." He leaned to the side and met Cora's gaze.

Fiery rage flooded her core. She spotted her discarded bow, left beside the stallion when she'd been knocked down. Her quiver was still strapped to her back. She could dive for her bow, fight her way out. Or...

She glanced at the hillside where the Forest People were waiting. Where Valorre was waiting.

Your people...will you go with them?

She could close her eyes and try to do what she'd accomplished earlier. She hadn't had the opportunity to revel in what she'd done. Somehow, she'd managed to step across time and space. One moment, she was trapped under the horse. In the next, she was on the rock.

Her body flooded with calm. Perhaps she could do it again. Morkai was dead. Her mission was complete. She could leave this all behind. If the Forest People wouldn't have her back, then she and Valorre could go out on their own—

"Aveline," Dimetreus cried out again. "What...what has happened?"

Her gaze slid back to her brother.

Questions invaded her mind. What would happen to Khero now? The other kingdoms saw Dimetreus as a traitor. An invader. Cora couldn't call him fully innocent, for she still felt the ghost of resentment clawing her heart. But he didn't know what was happening. He might not remember anything between now and when Morkai had first begun manipulating his mind. How could he defend himself and explain what Morkai had done if he didn't understand any of it?

She was reminded of something she'd said to herself only days ago.

If my brother can't protect Khero, that leaves only me.

Her shoulders slumped, her fingers unclenched to hang open at her sides. She thought not of the hillside and the freedom that beckoned her nor the bow that demanded blood. Instead, she met Verdian's hard stare with defiance. She stepped out from behind Teryn, doing her best not to limp or wince. "I am Princess Aveline," she said. "I will go with you and provide whatever proof you require. You will hear me out and you will give my brother a chance to defend himself."

Verdian's face slackened with surprise but he quickly steeled it. "Very well," he said. "Take the traitor and the supposed princess."

"Treat them as befits royalty," Teryn added, his voice firm. The voice of a king. He stared at the soldiers, gaze unflinching, daring any of them to contradict him.

Verdian released a grumbling sigh. "Get King Teryn to a surgeon." The king strode away, his final order sending the soldiers into a frenzy of movement. Two men took Cora by each of her arms.

"Treat her well," Teryn called. She could no longer see him through the commotion, and his voice sounded farther away now. As the soldiers hauled Dimetreus to his feet, she finally caught sight of Teryn. He was being escorted away by far gentler hands. Glancing over his shoulder, he met her eyes and gave her a small nod. She felt his reassurance. His worry. His unspoken apology tinged with a promise—he wouldn't let anything bad happen to her.

A voice crept into her awareness. *Shall I fight them?* Valorre's unseen nearness filled her with a steadying warmth.

No. I'm going with them willingly.

Then I'll go too.

You can't, she said. *We don't know what they'll do to a unicorn.*

His energy rippled with something like a scoff. *They will not see me. But I will follow. I'll be near. I go where you go now.*

Her lips curled into a small smile, fueling her strength as she let the soldiers lead her to the western side of the field. Despite her aching leg, her fatigue, and the storm of questions that tangled in her mind, she kept her head held high. Kept her shoulders back.

Whatever came next, she'd be the princess she needed to be.

A CAGE OF CRYSTAL

BOOK TWO

1

———————

Aveline Corasande Caelan had been a prisoner before, but never in so lovely a cage. By appearances, she was in a luxurious bedchamber. It was twice as large as her childhood bedroom with white marble floors bedecked with opulent carpets and walls papered in a white and gold rose motif. Despite the room's comforting display, Cora knew the truth. She was stuck here. The room was certainly an improvement upon the wagon she'd been kept in after she was captured at Centerpointe Rock, but it didn't change the fact that she was on trial. It was a quiet trial, one of secret conversations and endless questions held behind the closed doors of this gilded prison, but it was a trial nonetheless.

And Cora was getting godsdamned tired of it.

She strolled from the mahogany bureau to the plush bed, ignoring the quiet company of the ever-present guard who stood before her closed door. With an aggravated sigh, she sat at the edge of the mattress. The comfort of her seat helped take the edge off her restlessness, not to mention the slight throb she felt in her still-recovering ankle. Thankfully, getting trapped under a dead horse had resulted in only a few sprains and not fractures.

Almost a month had passed since the battle at Centerpointe Rock. After her injuries had been tended to, nearly every waking moment had been spent trying to prove her identity and the—at least partial—innocence of her brother, King Dimetreus. They'd both been hauled off the battlefield and taken into custody. King Verdian of Selay had become their captor. Nameless men and women had become her inquisitors, asking her to recount everything about Duke Morkai, his magic, her childhood, and her brother while they listened with intimidating silence. She was certain the only reason she and Dimetreus hadn't been sent to the dungeon upon arriving at Verlot Palace was because Teryn Alante, Prince of Menah, had intervened on her behalf.

Thoughts of Teryn did strange things to her heart. She wasn't sure if he made it sink or flutter. Both perhaps. She was sure of one thing though; she needed to stop thinking of him as a prince. With his father dead, he was king now. Or would be soon. She hadn't a clue how he'd fared since the battle. When last she'd seen him, he'd been wounded. It hadn't been the deadliest of wounds, but it didn't stop her from worrying about him. No matter how many times she'd hounded her captors with inquiries, no one would say a damn word about Teryn's well-being.

Today no one had said a word to her at all. This was the first day she hadn't been visited by inquisitors at the crack of dawn. She couldn't help but assume the worst. That King Verdian had made his decision regarding Cora and her brother's fate.

Panic rippled through her, mingling with a flash of anger. Curling her fingers into fists, she pushed off the bed and marched to the nearest window. At least, she intended to march. As her first hard step on her right leg sent a sharp pain through her ankle, she forced herself to slow. Keep her steps even. Careful. She'd only been given the go-ahead to walk on it this week. She supposed she should feel grateful that her wounds had been tended to at all.

She reached the velvet-draped window and tugged the curtain aside. Morning sunlight winked back at her, rising over the sprawling mountains in the distance. Her nerves stilled at the sight of those mountains, at the thought of those forests. What she wouldn't give to be transported straight there, to escape these stifling walls and fill her lungs with early summer air.

Can't I? a small voice inside her asked. *Can't I just...leave?*

She remembered what she'd done at the battle, how she'd somehow managed to cross time and space, bringing her from beneath the dead horse that had pinned her legs, to the rock where the duke had stood. It had happened in the blink of an eye.

And yet, the more time that passed between then and now, the more she began to doubt it had truly happened that way. Surely there was another explanation for it. She'd heard of witches who could astral project and astral travel, but those powers were rare. What were the chances Cora had accomplished such a feat?

Besides, even if she could disappear, she knew she couldn't. She'd made her choice. Now she had to see it through. At least there was one way she could experience what stood outside her prison. Sort of.

Pressing her forehead to the cool glass, she closed her eyes and extended her senses outward. It didn't take long to connect to a sense of warmth. Hoofbeats echoed the pound of her heart. She could almost feel the soil beneath her feet, smell the dew-speckled leaves glistening beneath the morning sun. Then a voice came to her, formed from feeling, shaped into words.

I'm still close by.

Her lips curled into a sad smile. Even though she was a prisoner, it gave her comfort to know that Valorre, her unicorn companion, was free.

The door opened behind her, and her connection to the unicorn vanished. Forest trees and dewy leaves dissipated as her senses returned fully to the room. She turned away from the window just as a young woman entered.

"Is this her?" the girl asked the guard. She appeared to be perhaps fourteen or fifteen years of age with dark blonde hair and blue eyes. She was dressed in maroon velvet; a simple gown but far too fine to mark her as a lower servant.

The guard nodded. Without a word, he exited the room and left the two women alone.

Well, that was a first. Save for her use of the toilet, there was always a guard around, even while she slept. Or tried to. For someone who once had to rely on a sleeping tonic to achieve some semblance of peaceful slumber, trying to rest while being watched was no easy feat.

The girl dipped into a deep curtsy. Her face was alight with a bright smile as she rose. "It's wonderful to meet you, Princess Aveline."

"Cora." The word slipped from her mouth before she could take it back. She'd gone by *Cora* for the last six years. *Princess Aveline* still felt foreign to her. Forgotten. Forbidden. She hadn't even liked the name before she'd fled her childhood home and had preferred the nickname her mother had given her. After she'd started her new life with the Forest People—a commune of witches and Faeryn descendants who scorned royals—she'd discarded her former title. Buried it deep alongside her past.

But she wasn't with the Forest People anymore. She'd relinquished her chance to return with them after the battle when she'd chosen to defend her brother instead. In doing so, she'd turned her back on magic. On her true self. On *Cora*. But Cora had never belonged with the Forest People. Not truly. Had they known she was a princess when they'd found her wandering the woods alone as a child, they never would have accepted her into their midst. The question now was: did she belong with the royals either?

"Cora," the girl echoed. "Ah, that's what the prince calls you, isn't it?"

Cora's pulse kicked up at her mention of the prince. Of Teryn. Her mouth fell open, her tongue prickling with the questions she was desperate to ask. How was he? Had he recovered from his wounds? But the girl was already speaking again.

"I'm honored you would allow me to call you Cora in private," she said, smile widening. "I assume it's a name reserved for your dearest friends, and I do hope you will consider me a friend, for we will be spending much time together. As for me, my name is Lurel."

Cora frowned. "Why will we be spending so much time together?"

A blush rose to her cheeks. "Silly me. I should have explained myself better. I'm your new lady's maid."

Cora's pulse hammered. If she'd been given a lady's maid, did that mean...

She swallowed her hope before it could fully rise. Until she met with King Verdian himself and heard from his lips that she and her brother were pardoned, she would assume nothing.

A knock sounded at the door, and Lurel bounded over to open it. Three older women entered the room, bearing several boxes each. They paused to curtsy, then proceeded straight for Cora. She stiffened as they set their boxes down at her feet and began to assess her with furrowed brows. Emotions flooded her at once, an odd mixture of aversion, curiosity, and dread. She realized then that her mental shields were down; she'd lowered them to connect with Valorre. The emotions she was experiencing now were coming from the three women who were circling her with furrowed brows, *hmm*-ing, huffing, and whispering amongst themselves.

With a deep breath, Cora focused on the marble floor, firm beneath her feet. She imagined the air around her thickening, growing denser and stronger until it felt like a protective shroud. With her mental shields back in place, the unwanted emotions faded away.

Being a clairsentient witch had its benefits, but there were times when it was highly inconvenient. Her empathic ability to feel the emotions of others had served her numerous times, but in everyday situations, it was a hassle that required constant vigilance to block out unwanted outside stimuli.

And now that she was trying to reclaim her place as a princess amongst royals who feared magic, it was a secret she kept to herself.

The women continued to circle and assess her like a horse up for auction, making her discomfort grow. Were they determining her coffin size? Deciding on which length of rope to use at her hanging? Perhaps she was jumping to ridiculous conclusions, but if someone didn't explain why she was the sudden object of these women's scrutiny, she would lose every last shred of good sense.

"Pardon, but what is your purpose in being here?" Her voice came out sharper than she intended, but the three women didn't balk.

"I'm so sorry," Lurel said, wringing her hands as she approached. "I'm off to a terrible start at being your lady's maid, aren't I? I'm so used to serving Princess Mareleau, and she—well, I forgot that you haven't lived as a princess for quite some time."

Cora clenched her jaw to keep from snapping at the girl, who still hadn't answered her question. One of the women lifted Cora's arm and ran a measuring tape from her armpit to her wrist. That was when Cora understood. She hadn't been fitted for clothing since she was a young girl. "You're seamstresses."

Lurel nodded. "You're being fitted for a new wardrobe by Princess Mareleau's personal dressmakers. Ordered by King Verdian himself."

She raised a brow. "Why would he do that?"

"Rumor has it that Selay and Khero are allies now. He's helping you reclaim your title as princess. Of course he would want to help you look the part. You can't return home looking like that."

Home. She was...going home?

"I'm surprised you weren't offered finer clothing sooner. Or a bath." Lurel's tone was devoid of disgust or condemnation, but it made Cora bristle just the same.

She glanced down at the plain gray dress she wore, one she'd received upon arriving at the palace, along with a nightgown and undergarments. She'd been given a daily ewer for washing, but her hearth was never lit unless she requested it. Since she was too proud to beg anyone here for help, she'd donned her cloak on cold mornings instead, and today was no exception. It was the same cloak she'd worn during the battle, and the wool was stained with soil and blood. She splayed her hand, noting dirt caked under her nails as well as the loose strands of frizzy hair that floated about her face.

Now she understood the emotions she'd sensed from the seamstresses. If they were used to fitting the Princess of Selay, they had their work cut out for them with Cora. They didn't bother having her undress and they seemed loath to touch her or her filthy clothes more than necessary.

After a few more basic measurements were taken, the women stepped back and began holding bolts of fabric and even some finished dresses next to her as if testing the colors against her skin tone.

"These are Princess Mareleau's old dresses, Highness," one of the seamstresses said, addressing Cora for the first time. She held up a gown of gold taffeta and squinted at it before giving the dress a nod and taking it to the bed.

"More like rejected designs," the eldest woman muttered, a wry smirk on her face. That earned a titter from the other two.

"I can't imagine why Mareleau would reject any of these," Lurel said, tone wistful as she watched the women lift dress after dress and hold it next to Cora. The seamstresses were careful not to let any of the gowns come within an inch of her current ensemble.

Once they seemed satisfied, they packed all their things back in their boxes. "We'll have these gowns hemmed and adjusted by evening, Highness," one said. "They won't be perfect but they'll do until you get home to your own dressmaker."

There was that word again: *home*. She tried to associate it with Ridine Castle but forest trees and archery seemed more suited to it.

She shook her head. Maybe someday she could return to just being Cora, forest witch, friend to unicorns, and poisoner of enemies. Not yet. She'd chosen her brother. The safety of Khero. Until she knew both could flourish without her, she had to stay. Had to be Princess Aveline.

"You must be exhausted after everything you've been through," Lurel said, rousing Cora from her thoughts. Only now did she notice that the seamstresses had left and had been replaced with servants hauling in a large washbasin and pitchers of steaming water. "Now, come. Let's get you washed and styled. We'll have you feeling like a princess again in no time."

2

The bath was heavenly. Aromas of jasmine filled her senses while the enormous tub accommodated enough water to let her submerge up to her neck. The only part of her bath that was less than ideal was Lurel's presence. She hadn't bathed in front of an attendant since she was a child, but the girl had only scoffed when Cora suggested she wait outside her room.

"Nonsense," she'd said. "You won't get those tangles out of your hair without aid."

Lurel had been right, and Cora was now suffering from it as the knots were combed from her dark strands. Cora could feel the other girl's frustration, even with her mental shields in place.

"I've never met a more stubborn knot," Lurel said through her teeth.

"You can cut more of my hair," Cora offered, ready for her torture to end.

"I already cut six inches, Highness. I'll take no more."

Cora made no further argument. By the time her hair was combed, her scalp felt like it had been grated off. But when she ran her hands through her silken tresses, she thought perhaps the torment had been worth it.

"We must hurry," Lurel said as she ushered Cora out of the tub and behind a dressing screen. "Your bath took far longer than I expected and you have a meeting to attend."

Lurel left Cora to dry herself with a plush towel, then returned with her arms full of cream-colored silk and linen, which turned out to be a shift, corset, petticoats, and stockings. Cora's cheeks heated as the girl took Cora's towel and began dressing her in undergarments as if it were the most normal thing in the world. She supposed it was for a lady's maid.

"A meeting with whom?" Cora asked as Lurel flounced off again, this time returning with the gold taffeta gown the seamstresses had left behind.

"With King Verdian, of course," Lurel said.

"I'm meeting with King Verdian?" Her voice was muffled as Lurel pulled the dress over Cora's head.

"Of course. Hasn't anyone told you?"

When Cora's head popped above the bodice, she gave the girl a pointed look. "You're the first person I've had any lengthy conversation with who isn't an inquisitor."

Lurel paused, her face going a shade paler. "Oh. I hadn't realized—well, there I go being a rotten lady's maid again. No wonder Mareleau offered me up to you. I may be her cousin, but she doesn't like me much."

I wonder why, she thought with sarcasm, but chastised herself. Lurel may be a bit vague but she was kind. That's more than she could say for the inquisitors. They had been some of the most abrupt, skeptical people she'd ever had to converse with.

Once Lurel secured the laces at the back of the dress, she rounded the front and assessed Cora through slitted lids. "It will have to do. The dress is a bit too modest for your age, but it was the only one that would fit without being hemmed first. It belonged to Mareleau when she was eleven."

Cora glanced down at the gold and cream taffeta, the ivory lace at the hem and sleeves. The bodice was high enough to leave no sign of cleavage, but it wasn't terribly modest. Then again, her ideas of fashion were likely out of date.

Lurel's words suddenly dawned. "You're saying I have the body of an eleven-year-old?"

"An eleven-year-old *Mareleau*," Lurel corrected. "She's much taller and curvier than you are. You really ought to wear a crinoline or a bustle—but we don't have time for that. Your hair! Oh, it looks terrible."

She wasn't sure if she should feel offended by Lurel's comments, but she pursed her lips and let the girl finish her flustered ministrations.

❧

CORA FELT MORE LIKE A PEACOCK THAN A PRINCESS AS SHE LEFT THE ROOM. HER HAIR had been woven into four braids that had been pinned around the crown of her head and dressed in feathered ornaments to hide that her tresses were still damp from her bath. Rouge colored her lips and cheeks, but she'd managed to convince Lurel to forgo the face powder and kohl. She hadn't been this overdressed since she was a child and never had she been expected to wear cosmetics.

A pair of guards flanked her as they escorted her down the elegant halls of Verlot Palace. She tried her best not to gawk at the splendor around her, but this was the first time she'd been allowed out of her room all week. Equally as distracting were the many curious eyes that looked her way, the courtiers who stared shamelessly as she passed.

The guards stopped outside a pair of double doors. Her heart raced as they opened them, and she fisted her hands in the folds of her skirt. She found the room beyond to be a study, with the familiar face of King Verdian standing behind a large desk. He looked different from how he had on the battlefield. Instead of short gray hair, he now wore a powdered wig, and instead of armor, he bore a regal gold and white coat emblazoned with Selay's rose sigil over his breast. An imposing-looking woman sat to his left, her golden hair arranged in a tight coronet, lips tightly pursed, eyes hard and assessing.

The guards closed the doors behind Cora, and she dipped into a curtsy several seconds too late.

"Princess Aveline," King Verdian said, tone flat, "this is Dowager Queen Bethaeny."

Cora blinked a few times. She'd assumed the woman was Verdian's wife, Queen Helena. Instead, it was...Teryn's mother. Now that she reassessed the woman, she saw some similarities between her and the boy she knew. While Teryn favored his late father's looks with his green eyes and dark hair, his tresses glinted gold in the sun, a similar shade to the queen's.

More surprising than the unexpected presence of Queen Bethaeny, though, was the figure that rose from his seat. She hadn't noticed him behind the high leather back of his chair, but as her brother faced her with a worn, tired smile, she couldn't look anywhere else. Her heart skipped and lurched, just how it had when she'd first seen him at Ridine Castle over a month ago. It seemed her emotions still didn't know what to make of Dimetreus. For too many years, she'd hated him for believing she'd killed his wife. She'd despised him for ordering her to a dungeon cell without remorse. Only after she'd been captured by Duke Morkai had she realized her brother was being controlled by the mage.

At the end of the battle, her brother had been surrounded by soldiers, called a traitor for having attempted to conquer Selay and Menah. Dimetreus, however, hadn't had a clue as to what the accusations were about. Morkai's death had severed his magic and the multiple glamours he'd woven. Once the glamours had been lifted, Dimetreus—and all the others who'd been freed from the mage's hold —had been confused. Lost. His memories a tangle of truth and lies.

Cora still blamed her brother for many things, primarily for letting Morkai into their lives in the first place and not being strong enough to withstand the mage's glamour. But she knew he wouldn't have waged war on Selay and Menah if he hadn't been under Morkai's spell.

At least, she hoped that was the case. It was the gamble she'd taken, the sole reason she was here and not far, far away, basking in the solitude of the woods. If Dimetreus was innocent, he deserved to keep his crown, and she owed it to their kingdom to ensure that happened.

She assessed him, noting the dark circles that still hung beneath his eyes, the wrinkles he was too young to have, and the thin gray hair that should have been lustrous and black. These telltale signs of Morkai's abuse fueled her conviction. There was no way he'd have endured Morkai's sorcery willingly. He *was* innocent.

"Aveline," he said as he walked toward her, voice strangled. His dark eyes glistened with tears, reminding her too much of how they'd looked when under the sheen of the glamour. He extended his arms, inviting her into an embrace, but she couldn't bring herself to move.

A flash of memory shot through her, of him storming into Queen Linette's room, of the rage on his face when he'd turned to Cora and blamed her for his wife's death...

Slowly, he lowered his arms and gave her a knowing nod. "I'm so sorry, my dear sister."

Cora shook her head to clear it and tried to summon a smile. All she conjured was a subtle flicker of her lips. "It's all right," she whispered. Then, with a deep inhale, she took her brother's arm and allowed him to escort her to the desk. Her breath caught when she felt how slim his arm was. Her momentary resistance drained, leaving only sympathy in its wake. She looked up at him, this time managing an almost-full smile. "I'm glad you're well. You seem to have recovered from the wounds you sustained at Centerpointe Rock."

"I have. As have you, I presume?"

"Yes," she said, and they separated to take their seats.

Verdian's expression remained hard, unmoved by their reunion.

Queen Bethaeny spoke first. "My son has done much on your behalf, Princess Aveline. He's been tireless in proving your identity and corroborating your story. I was curious to meet the woman who had my son so transfixed that he'd delay both his coronation and the burial of his father."

Heat flooded Cora's cheeks, her heart flipping in her chest. It took no small effort to keep her voice level. "I am grateful for everything Prince Teryn has done, and for Your Majesties' willingness to listen."

She meant every word. Trusting Teryn had been another gamble. He knew her secrets, knew she was a witch. Knew that she'd poisoned an entire camp of hunters and that she had a dark history with Morkai. The things he knew could have condemned her. She'd put blind faith in him the last few weeks, trusting he'd say only what the royals needed to hear and nothing more. She knew from firsthand experience how convincing he could be, even to someone who could sense emotions. She'd been on the receiving end of his lies when he betrayed her to Morkai. If anyone could keep a secret, it was him.

"Have you been treated well?" Bethaeny asked. "I was told my son demanded that you were."

Cora paused, debating her answer. "My accommodations have been fine, but I much prefer the freedom to leave my room."

The queen gave a smile that didn't reach her eyes. "You must forgive us for the lengthy questioning period you endured. Even with my son so invested in your plight, precautions were necessary."

"After what we've been through, we weren't willing to take any chances," Verdian said, his tone far brusquer than Bethaeny's. "Lives have been lost. We couldn't risk the possibility that either of you posed the same threat the duke had."

"I assure you," Dimetreus said, speaking slowly, carefully, "I hold none of the ambitions the former Duke Morkai held, nor do I believe any of the lies he once fed me. I only wish to return to Khero and set everything to rights. As I've promised, I will do whatever it takes to secure the trust of Selay and Menah."

"Yes, we've heard your promise," Verdian said, "but now we need the princess' word as well."

"I feel the same as my brother," Cora said. "I will support him in any way I can."

Verdian leaned back in his chair, pinning Cora with an icy look. "First, I must remind you what is at stake. Even though we're willing to believe Dimetreus was not acting of his own free will, those who fought at Centerpointe Rock saw him as a traitor. Rumors have spread, and even citizens of his own kingdom have reasons to doubt him. It would be no difficult task for me to seize control over Khero during this time of unrest for the kingdom's own good. If you and your brother fail to agree to our terms, I will enact this plan, and you will remain hostages here. Any resistance from you as hostages, and you will be executed."

Cora clenched her jaw. This was the first time she'd been referred to as a hostage. She'd known that was what she'd been all along, but it was one thing to know it and another to hear it stated outright. Not to mention his threat to seize her kingdom as his own. A fiery rage sparked in her chest but she breathed it away. "What are your terms?"

"Your brother will be allowed to resume his place as King of Khero, but his council, staff, and military will be selected by me. All positions will be filled by men from Selay. Dimetreus has already agreed to this."

Cora met her brother's eyes. He gave her a resigned nod, and her muscles began to uncoil. Those terms weren't terrible.

Verdian continued. "But we need something from you too. Based on the widespread belief of your death, as well as your questionable...*history*...we've struggled with how best to secure trust with you."

He glanced briefly at Cora's forearms where a hint of black ink trailed over the tan skin above her silk gloves. Lurel had wrinkled her nose when she'd first caught sight of the tattoos during Cora's bath, her feelings made clear despite how she'd insisted she thought they were *pretty*. Cora hadn't argued when Lurel dressed her in gloves before leaving her room. She tugged the silk a little higher now, pursing her lips against the indignation that colored her cheeks.

Verdian didn't know that the tattoos were *insigmora*, a Faeryn tradition meant to convey what level of the magical Arts one was practiced in. Hiding her tattoos—and her magic—felt like a betrayal, but these were secrets she needed to keep. She'd already drawn enough suspicion when she'd admitted to having lived with the Forest People. Even though they'd fought against Morkai at Centerpointe Rock, there was no denying their use of magic. Everyone on the battlefield had witnessed them wielding roots and vines like weapons. During Cora's questioning, she'd sensed the inquisitors' fear and disgust for all things magic. That was when she'd decided to bury that side of her. Hide it. Ignore it. Pretend she was just a princess. Just a girl eager to restore her title and save her brother's crown. It was the only way to convince them she was who she claimed to be.

Verdian spoke again. "While our current terms have established trust between Selay and Khero, you and Dimetreus owe Menah a debt as well. It is imperative that we forge an alliance between all three of our kingdoms, so that true peace can be secured between us."

"My son has come up with a proposal," Bethaeny said. "A solution that will bind you to Menah and forge that trust we seek."

Sweat slicked Cora's palms. "What proposal would that be?"

"Marriage," Verdian said.

Cora froze. She repeated their words in her mind to make sure she understood them correctly. *Teryn has proposed...*

"Marriage?" she echoed.

Verdian and Bethaeny nodded in unison.

"To me."

Another nod.

Emotions clashed in her heart, anger warring with something softer. How dare Teryn propose marriage without asking her directly! She...she...she would stab him for this. Surely she deserved a far better proposal than one of contractual obligation. But of course he didn't *want* to marry her. This was a matter of politics and alliances, as all royal marriages were. It was all for the better this way. She wasn't certain she wanted to keep her title longer than it took to reestablish her brother's rule. A marriage of the heart would only complicate things.

Still...he'd come up with this plan for *her*. That had to amount to something. Perhaps he did want the union, for reasons other than necessity.

Warmth crept into her chest, barreling through her anger, her shock. Memories of the kiss they'd shared in Ridine's dungeon came to mind, of that moment of pleasure and desire that had ended in trickery. He'd kissed her to trick her. He'd tricked her to force her to leave him behind. She'd resented him for using her own hidden desire against her, but...

Could he have wanted the kiss as much as she secretly had?

Verdian's voice was an unwelcome distraction from her thoughts, especially with the taunting lilt to his voice. "Your betrothal contract will be drafted at once. You will marry the Prince of Menah in one year."

Cora frowned, puzzling over the mocking way he'd said *Prince of Menah* and that he'd referred to Teryn as *prince*. Bethaeny had said Teryn postponed his coronation, but Verdian had begun calling Teryn *king* as soon as the battle was over. A cloud of dread began to sink her stomach.

"Once you agree, we will speak with Prince Larylis," Verdian said. Then, with a smirk, he added, "I doubt he'll have any qualms over it. He's lucky to be a prince, much less marry a princess."

Cora felt as if the floor had opened a gaping hole beneath her. Her disappointment was so heavy, it made her head spin. "Just so we're clear," Cora said, her voice trembling, "I am to marry Teryn's brother...Larylis."

"*Prince* Larylis," Bethaeny said, tone brimming with disdain. "Thanks to my late husband's last wish."

Cora curled her fingers around her chair's armrests.

Teryn hadn't made a proposal of marriage between himself and her. He'd made it between her and his *brother*.

Every soft feeling that had awakened inside her dissipated beneath the new wave of fury that roared through her. She wasn't mad at Teryn. No, what he'd done made sense. He was already engaged to Princess Mareleau. He had no romantic inclinations toward Cora. Her anger was with herself. For that pathetic spark of hope she'd allowed herself to entertain.

"Oh, Highness," Bethaeny said, voice soft, "you didn't think..."

Cora met her eyes and found the queen's expression held equal parts sympathy and amusement. It was the latter emotion that had Cora's chest heaving. She tore her gaze from Bethaeny's and turned her attention to Verdian. "Is that all?"

"There are finer points to this arrangement," he said, sharing neither Bethaeny's sympathy nor her amusement. "Should Dimetreus fail to secure a proper bride and provide a suitable heir, rule will pass to you upon his death or abdication. If Dimetreus' council deems him incapable of the crown at any point, he will be forced to abdicate at once. If this occurs before you and Larylis have officially wed, you'll need to formalize your marriage immediately. Your council will not recognize you as Dimetreus' heir until this marriage alliance is secure."

Cora glanced at her brother again only to find resignation in his eyes. This was another term he'd already agreed to. What else was there for her to do but resign herself to it as well? She was too angry to think things through, too irritated by her own fickle heart to do anything but say, "I accept. All of it. Whatever it takes. When can we return home?"

Verdian tilted his head back as if he hadn't expected her to agree so readily. "We've arranged transportation and lodgings. My brother, Lord Kevan, will host you at his estate for a few days while we finish preparations. He will serve as Dimetreus' Head of Council and will escort you and some of your new household staff to Ridine—"

"Great," Cora said. She was disturbed by how much had already been arranged before she'd agreed. More than that, she was desperate to end the meeting. "We will leave for Lord Kevan's estate at once."

"Very well," Verdian said. "The sooner we can bring stability to Khero, the better."

With her cooperation secured, she took the opportunity to excuse herself. She felt a flash of guilt for abandoning her brother, but she needed to get out of there. To breathe. To be alone—

"I hope you didn't think it was going to be that easy."

Cora had just left the closed doors of the king's study behind her when a tall female figure blocked her path. She expected it to be one of the guards who had brought her here, but she spotted both of them waiting farther down the hall. Instead, she was confronted by a woman dressed in a turquoise silk gown with a plunging neckline that revealed an ample bosom. Her skirts flared out at her waist in every direction. Her silver-blonde hair fell in perfect curls over one shoulder. Cora blinked at her a few times. "Excuse me?"

"Don't get comfortable," the girl said, blue eyes flashing with menace. "You aren't marrying Larylis."

She wanted to say that she didn't give two licks about Larylis, or her, or anyone here. Instead, she lifted her chin to meet the other woman's eyes. Batting her lashes, she said, "Should I know you?"

The blonde's cheeks heated with indignation. The truth was, Cora knew exactly who she was. It didn't take a genius to guess this was Princess Mareleau Harvallis, the woman who'd spurned her engagement to Teryn and sent him on a hunt for unicorns. Until this moment, Cora hadn't realized just how much she already despised her.

Mareleau took a step closer, hands on her hips. With a cruel grin, she looked Cora up and down. "Nice dress. Do you always wear children's clothes?"

Cora gave her an innocent smile. "When my only options are the leftovers from some spoiled harpy with poor taste in fashion, yes." With that, she skirted around Mareleau and stormed down the hall, her fury burning hotter with every step she took.

3

There were few things in life Teryn Alante truly despised. Sitting still for any extended period was one of them. His disdain for inertia had sprouted when he'd been kept prisoner by Duke Morkai before the battle at Centerpointe Rock. He'd been helpless. Powerless. Unable to prevent what came next. Those feelings had only worsened after the battle. After his father's gruesome demise.

Now if he stayed still too long, his mind would fill with blood.

With screams, cries, and the clash of steel.

With his father's lifeless eyes.

He'd found a way to channel his angst, and it was in fighting for Cora's freedom. After his injuries had been tended at Centerpointe Rock, he'd requisitioned a coach and followed King Verdian's retinue to Verlot Palace.

For that was where Cora had been taken.

His half brother Larylis had remained by his side. When Teryn's fractured rib kept him from writing, Larylis wrote for him. Together, they'd recorded everything Teryn knew about Cora, Morkai, and Dimetreus—anything that could prove Cora's identity and innocence.

Once he'd arrived at Verlot Palace, he'd redoubled his efforts, dogged in his determination and refusing to return home to Dermaine Palace until the matter was settled. Not even his own coronation nor his father's burial could tempt him away.

Not yet.

Not until she was safe.

Not until he'd fixed everything he'd nearly destroyed.

Teryn stood in the Great Hall of Verlot Palace, anxiety tickling the back of his mind. The emotion was a constant passenger and would be until Cora's fate was sorted. He tried his best to ignore it, however, as a friendly face came bounding toward him.

"Prince Lex." Teryn greeted his friend with a grin.

"Come to see me off?" Lex asked as they grasped each other's forearms in a gesture of camaraderie. After the battle, Lex had come back to Verlot Palace. He'd done more than his share to confirm everything Teryn had said about Cora. And to keep quiet about all the things Teryn had left unsaid.

Teryn nodded. "Thank you for everything you've done."

Lex gave a halfhearted shrug. "I had to make up for tricking you into thinking I'd abandoned you at Ridine Castle."

"I would think fighting with our armies was already more than enough." He glanced around the Great Hall. The gilded walls and marble floors echoed with sound, as the palace was already bustling with activity this morning. He caught several courtiers looking at him and Lex as they passed. Lowering his voice, he added, "But I do appreciate everything you've done for Cora."

"Yes, well, I figured going the extra distance might remind you of a certain discussion we once had. One regarding Aromir wool."

Teryn's expression fell. He'd almost forgotten their bargain. It had begun as an offer from Lex to help Teryn win the Heart's Hunt in exchange for inclusion into Menah's most exclusive trade contract. After they'd met Cora, Teryn had renewed the promise to Lex, as long as he'd agree to come with them and rescue unicorns. Now that Menah was no longer in debt to Cartha, Teryn could afford to reward Lex's loyalty. Still, he wasn't officially king yet. He wasn't sure what promises he could make.

Lex chuckled and slapped Teryn on the shoulder. "I'm kidding. I didn't come to Verlot because of our alliance but because you're my friend."

Hearing Lex call him a friend warmed his heart. It was almost enough to quiet the incessant buzz of anxiety that fluttered in the back of his mind. "What about your father? Won't he be cross that you've returned home empty-handed?"

Lex's mirth faded. "Hopefully he'll be proud enough that I helped save the damn world. Though, I bet he'd sooner chastise me for not hiding from the conflict. Either way, I hope you think of Tomas as an ally."

"I do. Menah is yours as well."

"What about Selay?" Lex asked with a grimace. "How much does King Verdian hate me?"

Teryn released a sigh. "No more than he dislikes me." Proving Cora's royal identity had required them to confess that Lex had withheld information from Verdian when he'd brought news of Morkai's plans. It meant Selay could no longer carry the full blame for Teryn's imprisonment at Ridine Castle. Teryn had learned that his father had decided to let Verdian think the Heart's Hunt had been the sole reason Teryn had crossed paths with Morkai. It would be an understatement to say Verdian had been furious to learn the fault lay more with Teryn's attempt to collect Cora's bounty.

Lex squinted at Teryn. "Have you told her yet?"

"Told who what?"

"Cora," Lex said, in a too-loud whisper. "Or Aveline, or whatever I am to call her now. Have you told her how you feel?"

Teryn didn't know what to say. He hadn't realized Lex still believed Teryn had feelings for Cora. He'd allowed his friend to believe as much when they'd first met her. It had been a ruse to convince Lex to join her unicorn rescue mission without Teryn having to admit the real reason he wanted to travel with her—to turn her over to the crown as an outlaw. He wasn't sure why he kept quiet now. Perhaps because the lie no longer felt so false.

"You should tell her," Lex said.

"I will." It came out too fast, his cheeks suddenly too warm.

With that, they said their final farewells. Teryn watched his friend leave the Great Hall. As soon as he was out of sight, his fluttering sense of urgency crept back up. Dread filled his bones as it did during every quiet moment, every time he stood still without any direct destination toward which to move his feet. He bit the inside of his cheek just to feel something else. Something—

"Your Highness."

Teryn found Captain Braze of his personal guard beside him. He'd sent the man to check on Cora. His heart climbed into his throat. "Do you have news of her?"

The man nodded. "She's been released. She's meeting with King Verdian now."

~

Teryn moved so fast, his side ached where his stitches strained against the full breaths he took. He turned down the hall that led to Verdian's study—and halted. His entire body froze save for the mad thumping of his heart.

It was the first time he'd seen Cora in nearly a month, and he was overjoyed to find her hale and whole, uncowed by her imprisonment. He'd been worried she might have been mistreated despite his orders, but the way she walked with her head held high, carving a line through gaping courtiers like a wildfire surging through a forest, he knew she held the same spark she had before. Perhaps more of it. Her dark eyes were fierce, her rouged lips and cheeks doing nothing to soften the intensity of her gaze. She walked on swift feet, leaving no sign of the injuries he knew she'd sustained, and with the confidence of someone who'd never stopped being a princess. Two guards trailed in her wake, but she paid them no heed.

Her eyes landed on him, noticing him for the first time, and she pulled to an abrupt halt.

His lips spread into a grin while her face flashed with surprise. He nearly bounded over to her but stopped himself as her expression turned hard. Cold. Not a look he was unaccustomed to, but one he hadn't expected to find upon their reunion. She closed the lingering distance between them, stopping a few feet away. Everything inside him begged to reach for her, to turn her head this way and that to assure she remained unharmed. If he discovered anyone had laid a finger on her...his blood boiled at the thought. He fisted his hands at his sides to keep them still.

She tilted her head back to lock her eyes with his. "Am I just a pawn to you?"

Teryn inhaled sharply, her tone so barbed she might as well have slapped him. "What?" It was the only word he could utter.

"You proposed marriage," she said, voice quavering, "which you had no right to do."

Heat crawled up his neck. "What—how do you know—"

He couldn't find the words to finish. He'd brought up the idea of a marriage alliance between Khero and Menah to his mother just two days ago, but he hadn't spoken to Verdian yet. There were still details to work out. Bonds to break. New ones to forge. Most of all, he'd wanted to talk to Cora first.

"Your mother told me," she said. "I had to hear it from her. Meanwhile, you didn't even ask me if that was something I wanted." The tears glazing her eyes struck him like a blow to the chest. He was torn between the pain that came from knowing he'd once again hurt her and the weight of her rejection. He hadn't had the chance to ask her himself. Perhaps it was best that he hadn't.

"I wanted to talk to you about it," he said, unable to meet her eyes. "I didn't think..." Confusion tangled his thoughts, stalling his tongue. Why the hell had his mother intervened? What he'd conveyed to her had only been the barest idea. A hint to test her response. A seed that would first require Cora's acceptance before it could grow.

Cora shook her head. "You didn't think what? That this would hurt me?"

Teryn opened and closed his hands, his fingers desperate to reach for hers, to comfort her, to seek forgiveness. When he'd come up with his idea, he'd known there was a chance it could strain things between them, especially if she said no. However, he'd hoped they could at least remain friends if that ended up being the case.

Then again...were they *ever* friends before?

They'd exchanged as many smiles as they had blows, verbal and physical alike. They'd been enemies. They'd been allies. He'd betrayed her. He'd kissed her.

Where did that leave them now?

Not for the first time, the memory of their only kiss played through his mind. In the moment, he'd been driven by desperation. On one hand, he'd wanted her to leave him behind at Ridine Castle and flee while she had the chance. He'd known shocking her with a sudden kiss would work in his favor. On the other hand—and more importantly—he'd wanted to feel her lips against his. Wanted to give in to the spark of desire he'd felt. It was the desperate last wish of a man who thought he'd never see her again.

Whispers drew his attention back to the present. To Cora's tear-filled eyes. To the courtiers who surrounded them, muttering behind their hands. He took a step closer and lowered his voice. "Can we speak in private?"

She shook her head. Her voice calmed as if she too had noticed their audience. "What more is there to say? The only way for me to get my kingdom back is to resign myself to a loveless marriage."

The last part stung worse than he could have imagined. He swallowed hard. "You really think it would be loveless?"

She let out a humorless laugh. "I'm such a fool. I'm always such a fool when it comes to you." With that, she brushed past him.

His throat constricted. He knew he should let her go. End this scene before they stirred more gossip than they already had. Against his better judgment, he turned and took a step after her. His fingers closed softly around her wrist.

She stopped at once, frozen midstep. Then, after a glance at his hand, she slowly lifted her eyes to his. A sad smile curled her lips. Her voice was small, frag-ile. "For one moment, I thought she meant you."

His breath caught in his throat. He was so stunned that when she tugged her wrist from his grip and stormed off, he could do nothing but stare after her. Dread crept into his heart. What had she been implying by her last statement?

I thought she meant you.

Teryn fought the urge to chase after Cora and turned his attention to the other end of the hall. Toward King Verdian's study.

4

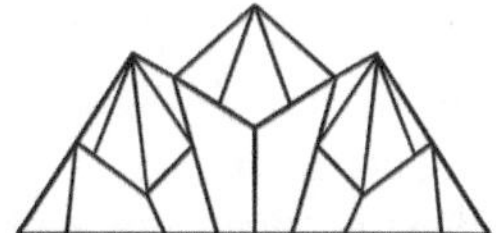

Mareleau Harvallis stood before the closed doors to her father's study several moments before gathering the courage to enter. King Dimetreus had already taken his leave, which meant now was her chance. Yet she lingered, still stewing after her interaction with Princess Aveline. She required a clear head to do what she had to do next, so she needed to rein in her emotions. She'd been planning this for weeks. She wouldn't let her plan fail now.

It was time to utilize her *magic trick*. She planted a false smile on her lips and envisioned the persona she wanted to project. Confidence. Dignity. Authority. Not that manipulating her outer composure ever really worked with her father. King Verdian and Queen Helena were amongst the few who often seemed immune to her charms. Still, it was worth a shot. She needed all the pretend magic she could muster for the reckless actions she was about to take. With a deep breath, she pushed open one of the doors.

"Princess Mareleau." Dowager Queen Bethaeny greeted her with a warm smile. It took no small effort not to sneer at the woman as Mareleau lowered into a polite curtsy. Mareleau had never had a reason to dislike Bethaeny before, but after the meeting she'd overheard, she found it hard not to despise her. She knew the queen wasn't to blame for the proposed marriage between Larylis and the lost princess. According to Bethaeny, it had been Teryn's idea. His mother had only played messenger. Either way, it gave Mareleau yet another reason to hate Teryn Alante— her fiancé—from the depths of her soul.

Once she rose from her curtsy, she faced her father's desk.

King Verdian gave her an impatient look. "I did not summon you, daughter."

"Yet I came anyway."

"I am expecting someone else."

She cocked her head innocently to the side. "Who might that be?"

He released a sigh and pinned her with a pointed glare. "Prince Larylis."

"Oh, how convenient. He's exactly who I came to speak to you about." She opened her mouth to say more when the study doors opened again. Her pulse kicked up as she expected Larylis to enter the room. Instead, she gritted her teeth at the sight of Teryn. Her sneer was lost on him, for he didn't so much as look at her. His eyes were locked on his mother.

His rigid posture—broad shoulders tense, chest heaving—stripped Mareleau's mind of all previous thought. She'd never seen him looking anything other than the arrogant, composed prince he was. What in the name of the seven gods did he have to be so enraged about? More than that, did he not realize he was interrupting a very important meeting? One she'd plotted with stringent care?

Teryn's voice came out strained as he spoke to Bethaeny. "Mother, did you offer a marriage alliance to Princess Aveline?"

She gave a gracious nod. "I did."

"Between Aveline and whom?"

"Between Aveline and Larylis, of course."

Mareleau internally roared with anger, but before she could let it out, her father cut in.

"Was it not your idea?" he barked.

Teryn's jaw tightened as he looked from Verdian to Bethaeny. "It was my idea to form a marriage alliance between Menah and Khero. I had suggested nothing beyond that."

Bethaeny skirted around to the front of Verdian's desk and laid a placating hand on Teryn's arm. "Darling, I simply executed your idea in the best possible way."

"I didn't ask you to do that, nor did I express the intricacies of my plan."

The queen gave Teryn a knowing look, one Mareleau couldn't quite decipher. "I had some inkling as to your *intricacies*," Bethaeny said, tone terse.

Teryn returned the look, green eyes flashing with anger. His words were clipped as he spoke through his teeth. "Clearly you didn't."

"I have something very important to discuss with my father," Mareleau said, giving Teryn and Bethaeny an exaggerated smile that probably looked more like a snarl. "You'll excuse us, won't you?"

They both ignored her.

"Princess Aveline is not marrying Larylis," Teryn said.

Mareleau blinked at him in surprise. When she managed to find her voice, she rushed to say, "I agree. She most certainly is not."

Teryn frowned at her as if he hadn't realized she was there until now.

"The princess has already agreed," Verdian said.

"She agreed under false pretenses," Teryn argued. "It was never my intention for her to marry Larylis."

Verdian released a grumbling breath. "Then who did you intend for her to marry?" When Teryn didn't answer, the king continued. "If Queen Bethaeny hadn't brought your idea to my attention, I would have come up with a similar solution myself. We need more than spies and allies at Ridine Castle. To ensure Khero is never again a threat—"

"Cora isn't—" Teryn shook his head and started again. "Princess Aveline isn't a threat."

"To ensure that is the case," Verdian said, enunciating each word, "we need a stronger alliance. Your marriage to my daughter will seal peace between Selay and Menah. Aveline's marriage to Larylis will do the same between Menah and Khero."

"Aveline cannot marry Larylis," Teryn said. "And I...I cannot marry Mareleau."

Mareleau's eyes shot to him. Never had she heard sweeter words. She shuttered her eyes, certain she was hallucinating. "You...can't?"

He met her gaze with a sympathy that almost made her bark a laugh. "I'm sorry."

She huffed. "Don't waste an apology on me. If you weren't going to end it, I was."

Verdian rose from his seat. "Have the two of you lost your minds? What is this?"

Bethaeny's cheeks flushed pink as she took her son's hand in hers. "What are you thinking, my dear? This marriage alliance has been secured for three years."

He quirked a brow. "I think we can all agree that this marriage alliance has been anything but secure. I will sign a treaty for peace. I will promise my kingdom's loyalty. But I will not go forward with this marriage."

Mareleau lifted her chin, mildly disturbed that she was agreeing with the man she'd been fighting against for three years. "Nor will I."

Verdian scoffed and planted his hands on his desk. "You have no say in this."

"I do," she bit out, despite her father's warning glare. She knew she should stay silent. With Teryn's refusal to go through with their betrothal, her most pressing battle was won. But there was something left to fight for. Something she'd given up on once before, only because she'd been tricked. This was her chance to try. "*I'm marrying Larylis.*"

A vein pulsed at her father's temple. "You've gone mad."

"You knew I wanted to wed him three years ago. Did you think my heart would change because you and Mother stole my letters and forged a mockery of my words?"

His face paled. It was the only confirmation she needed; both he and her mother had been involved with intercepting her letters. He revealed no shame as he spoke. "We've been over this. You are not marrying a bastard."

Her blood boiled at the word. That despicable, hateful word. It had driven her and Larylis apart three years ago when Uncle Ulrich caught them kissing in the stables. Moments before, they'd confessed their love for each other, their wishes to marry. Then, just like that, their dreams had been murdered, buried beneath the headstone of *Bastard*.

Larylis' parentage hadn't mattered to her then, and she wanted to argue that it didn't matter now. But she knew it wouldn't move Verdian. Her father didn't care what she wanted or how she felt. He only cared about his throne and his legacy. Well, if it was a legacy he cared so much about, she'd play that card.

"Larylis Alante is not a bastard, Father. He's been legitimized. He's a true prince now."

Verdian shook his head. "It may have been Arlous' last wish to give Larylis the

Alante name, but it doesn't change the boy's origins. You are my heir, Mareleau. As a woman, your claim to the throne is tenuous."

"*As a woman,*" she echoed, every word laced with venom. She curled her hands into fists to keep herself from shaking. "You do realize that if you were dead, Mother could run this kingdom just fine. Perhaps even better."

He snorted a humorless laugh. "That might be true, daughter, but Helena will not rule after I'm gone. My heir will. However, both of your uncles would rather see themselves on my throne than you. Should you marry someone of questionable blood, you won't stand a chance. The crown will never make its way into your hands. Not unless you make a proper match. Teryn is that match. He is a king. You will be his queen."

She threw her hands in the air. "How can I be queen of one kingdom and heir to another? Are you simply trying to get me out of the way so you can give your crown to one of my uncles? Are you so desperate to be rid of me as your heir?"

"You are my heir and I plan on keeping it that way," he said, with so much conviction she was partial to believe him. "Whether you keep my crown after I die is dependent upon your standing in the eyes of your competition. Should you marry a crown prince, or even a second or third son of distinguished royal lineage, that would be enough. Anything less..."

"Anything less...what?"

He ran a hand over his face. "Do you know what happens to monarchs with a weak claim?" He walked around to the side of his desk, stopping when he was a few feet away. "Queen Marion, 29 Year of the Fox, ruled for fifteen days before she was beheaded by her younger brother. Queen Jesebel, crowned 76 Year of the Sheep, overthrown in her second year of rule and imprisoned until her death. Princess Vilas, 102 Year of the Tiger, disappeared three days before her coronation as queen and was never seen again. Her cousin took the throne. Do you understand?"

Mareleau suppressed a shudder at what her father was insinuating. She'd never been overly fond of her uncles, and they bore very little love for her. But... did he really think they'd do something so sinister? The names he'd listed filled her mind, followed by other famed monarchs in history who'd been overthrown by powerful relatives. She kept her voice level as she said, "You underestimate my own cunning."

"You may be cunning, daughter," her father said, tone softening, "but I cannot risk your safety. You think I've been hard on you, but I will not set you up to fail. It is better that you are strong and safe. As Teryn's queen, you will be. Upon my death, you and Teryn will merge two kingdoms into one. Forge a power so great your uncles won't stand a chance. Even if they did manage to wrest Selay from your control, you would still have Menah. My legacy would die in this kingdom, but it would live on through you elsewhere. That would be enough for me."

Her heart shattered at the care she saw in his eyes. It was the first time she considered that his unwavering austerity toward her could have been fueled by something other than cruelty. And yet, she couldn't give him what he wanted. "I can't marry Teryn."

Verdian's composure hardened once again. "You will marry King Teryn. The two of you will rid your minds of this nonsense."

"I don't love him, Father. You know this. I love Larylis."

"We're not talking about love. We're talking about politics. About your own safety."

Her stomach churned. It was time to play the card she'd been keeping close to her heart. One she knew would damn her soul as soon as she uttered it aloud. Folding her hands at her waist, she met her father's eyes with contrived calm. "I will marry Larylis, Father, for it is the only reasonable course of action now that I'm with child. *His* child."

Silence echoed in the wake of her words, the tension so thick she thought it might smother her. Then a sound cut through. The only sound that could shatter her composure, her resolve, and her heart all at once.

Larylis' voice trembled from behind her. "What did you say?"

Slowly, she turned to face him. He stood in the doorway, his expression brimming with a flurry of feeling. Confusion. Anger. Guilt. Hurt.

His emerald gaze turned to steel, hardening on one final emotion.

Betrayal.

5

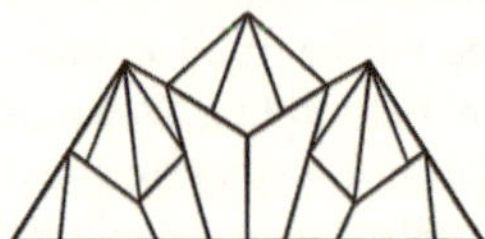

Teryn didn't know what to feel. His first reaction upon hearing Mareleau agree not to marry him had been relief. It hadn't been the biggest surprise, considering her previous attempts to court other suitors. But when she'd spoken of her love for Larylis, he'd been...shocked. Ashamed. Embarrassed.

He realized now that she hadn't spurned their engagement all this time because his kingdom was poor, nor because of his father's scandal. She'd done it because she was in love with someone else, and Teryn had stood directly between them. For the first time, he saw himself the way she must have seen him all along. An unwelcome interloper.

Did his brother see him the same way? The thought made his chest feel tight.

"You aren't serious, Mareleau." Queen Helena's voice teetered between disbelief and hysteria. Teryn hadn't noticed her enter behind his brother, but now she swiftly closed the study doors, eyes darting quickly around the room as if to assess who'd heard Mareleau's scathing admission.

"She isn't." Verdian's voice was almost a growl. His face was so flushed it was almost purple. "This is just another one of her games. Another childish attempt to flee an engagement."

"I think we've heard enough," Bethaeny said, taking Teryn's arm to pull him away. His feet were rooted to the spot.

"It's not a game," Mareleau said. Her words were for her father, but her eyes remained pinned on Larylis. She'd gone pale since his arrival, and her composure seemed shaken. "I'm pregnant with Larylis' child. It's a truth we no longer have to hide."

"No." Larylis' voice broke on the word. "We never..." He turned toward Teryn. "We didn't..."

Teryn studied him, searching for layers of truth behind his pleading eyes, between the words he wouldn't say.

Larylis had once admitted to having kissed Mareleau, but according to him, it hadn't meant anything. The disdain Larylis had demonstrated for the princess over the last three years had only served as evidence to support the claim.

But Teryn could still recall the pained look on Larylis' face during the poetry competition. During every conversation where Mareleau had come up. It was the same expression Larylis wore now.

The look of a man whose love was equal only to his agony. Both of which he tried to hide.

How had Teryn not recognized this before?

Was it because he'd never been in love?

If so…why did he recognize it now?

His mind went to Cora, but he couldn't think of her without recalling how he'd failed her. Betrayed her. He'd chosen duty over friendship. Lies over truth. He'd tried to fix his mistake but only when it was too late.

He would never be too late again.

Not for anyone.

Larylis took a deep breath and gathered his composure. "It isn't what you think, Teryn. I promise you, we never—"

"You don't get to speak, bastard," Verdian roared.

Mareleau rounded on her father. "Don't you dare talk to him like that!"

"You shouldn't talk at all."

"No, she *should* talk," Helena said, forcing calm into her voice. "Let her take it back. She knows better than this. Such a false statement would ruin her."

Mareleau lifted her chin with defiance. "I won't take it back."

Verdian opened his mouth, but Helena rushed to him and put a hand on his arm. "Let us not say a word more. Our daughter needs some time to contemplate—"

"There's nothing to contemplate. I am with child. Larylis is the father."

"Nonsense," Helena barked, her composure shattering into fury. "Your moon cycle—"

"My moon cycle is late. Ask my maids about my laundry. They will confirm it. Larylis and I conceived the night of the Heart's Hunt."

Larylis stepped forward. "Mareleau, stop. Please."

Helena shook her head, setting loose a graying brown curl from her towering updo. "That's not possible. I made sure to keep the two of you separate."

Mareleau shrugged. "You think I don't know how to navigate the servants' passages?"

Verdian's lips peeled back from his teeth. "You've ruined yourself!"

Mareleau didn't respond to her father's statement. "If you'd like proof of further indiscretions, just ask Lurel. She left me and Larylis alone in the drawing room adjacent to the library after the war meeting. I threatened her to keep it a secret."

"Seven gods, Mareleau," Larylis said as he ran a hand over his face. His shoulders drooped with fatigue. Or was it remorse?

Teryn realized he still hadn't moved. Still hadn't spoken. His blood stirred with a sensation he'd grown accustomed to over the past weeks. A desperation to not be idle. To fill every possible silence with a flutter of activity. To work, to strive, to fix.

This...he could fix this too. Before it was too late.

Teryn cleared his throat. It took a few attempts to find his voice. "Do you love her, Larylis?"

His brother opened and closed his mouth, eyes darting between Mareleau and Teryn. "We didn't..."

He repeated his question, tone firm. "Do you love her? The truth."

Larylis' throat bobbed. "Yes."

Teryn nodded. "Then you should marry her."

"You don't get to make that choice," Verdian said. "She's my daughter and she will not marry that—"

Teryn cut him off before he could say the word *bastard* again. "Why? My brother has been named an Alante. He's a prince. You were willing to see him wed the Princess of Khero. Why should he not marry the Princess of Selay?"

"The Princess of Khero isn't my daughter. Aveline's kingdom has no other contenders for the throne. Prince Larylis will suit fine for our purposes there. Here..." Verdian shook his head. "He does not have the respect required to allow my daughter to keep my throne after my death. Unlike you, he can offer her nothing else. He cannot merge our two kingdoms, nor can he make her a queen."

Teryn's stomach sank. As much as he hated to admit it, Verdian was right. Mareleau was Verdian's heir. His only child. He wanted his daughter made queen at any cost. Kept safe at any cost. And Larylis...well, he may have been given the Alante name, but he was still only a prince.

"It humbles me greatly to say this," Verdian uttered through his teeth, "but you're her only hope now. Should you find it in your heart to take my daughter as your bride and bury this scandal—"

"How dare you suggest such a thing." Mareleau's voice quaked as tears gathered in her eyes. "I love Larylis. I'm pregnant with *his* child."

Verdian's voice took on an empty quality. "If Teryn agrees to marry you, no one need know of your shame. Otherwise, you are ruined. You will neither be queen nor my heir."

"If I'm so ruined, why not just let me marry the man I love? Disinherit me. Make one of my uncles your heir. Do whatever you must, just—"

"I will not reward you for what you've done!" Verdian's voice boomed from wall to wall.

Another silence fell, and in its wake Teryn felt that familiar itch return. To move. To act. To fix. He opened and closed his fists as he worked up the courage to do what must be done.

Finally, with a trembling sigh, he said, "I abdicate my claim to the throne."

~

LARYLIS ALANTE NEVER IMAGINED HOW AWFUL IT WOULD FEEL TO HAVE HIS DEEPEST desires come true. When he'd dreamed of earning the Alante name, he'd always imagined it would come about through perseverance, through gaining the respect of Queen Bethaeny, through his own merit. Not seconds before his father's death—a fate that was delivered by his own words.

When he'd dreamed of being with Mareleau, he'd never imagined it would come through deception and lies. Never imagined the woman he loved would twist their forbidden ardor into a tale of some treacherous liaison. Never imagined he'd be offered a crown in exchange for their perceived indiscretions.

He'd never—*ever*—dreamed of being king.

The thought of being given a throne he didn't deserve made his shoulders feel as if they bore leaden weights. There was only one reply he could give to Teryn's outrageous statement.

"No."

The word was shared with everyone else in the room, save Teryn and Mareleau. Verdian, Helena, and Bethaeny all looked at Teryn as if he'd gone mad. Teryn, meanwhile, stood taller, prouder, as if he'd already shrugged off the burden of their father's crown. Was that why Larylis suddenly felt so heavy?

"I won't take it," Larylis said, as if his refusal could shift the weight back where it belonged. He caught Mareleau's injured expression from the corner of his eye, but he couldn't bear to look at her. Not because he was angry. He certainly *was* angry, but he was more concerned that—should he meet her eyes, should he remember the desire in them when they'd shared their last kiss, should he recall the sweetness of her lips—he might be tempted to play along with her lie.

"It seems the boy has some modicum of sense after all," Verdian muttered.

"What I said stands." Teryn's voice was stern. "I abdicate, and that is final. I will gather Menah's council to make it official, but I have made my choice." In that moment, he reminded Larylis so much of their father, he thought his heart might shatter in two. Teryn held Verdian's stare with the same conviction Arlous had demonstrated when he'd first referred to Larylis as an Alante.

It was too much.

His throat closed up, seared by blood, by battle, by the words that had condemned their father to die.

We refuse to surrender.

"This will not stand," Verdian said. "You are King of Menah—"

"I've yet to be crowned," Teryn said. "Larylis will be in my stead."

"No." Larylis ground the word through his teeth.

Mareleau took a step toward him, her expression begging him to be silent.

"No," he said to her as well.

Teryn rounded on him. "I'm trying to fix this."

"There's nothing to fix." His lungs felt too tight. He could almost smell the blood on the battlefield, could almost hear the clang of steel. Red filled his vision. His next words came out in a rush. "I will not be rewarded for killing him."

He felt empty in the wake of his confession. It was the first time he'd spoken the truth out loud. That he'd killed King Arlous.

Teryn's expression flashed with pain, but it quickly hardened. When he spoke, his voice was cold. "You don't get to carry that burden on your own, brother. Father traded his life for mine."

"But I'm the one who refused to surrender." He hated the way his voice trembled. Hated how small he felt in that room, despite being one of the tallest there.

Teryn's tone softened the merest fraction. "You did what I wouldn't have had the strength to do. You made the choice only a king would make. That's why Father put you in charge of that decision. That is why you will take my place."

Larylis shook his head. "You don't understand what you're giving up. What you think Mareleau and I have done—"

"It doesn't matter. Take the crown. I will not be swayed otherwise. If you won't take it as your right, then take it as your punishment."

His punishment.

There was something about that concept that silenced any further argument. There was a rightness about it. A cruel justice.

Perhaps it was what he deserved. To bear the crown of the man he killed. To win the hand of his beloved not through love but lies.

It would hurt so much more to accept than to refuse. It would hurt more to be king than to watch Teryn make all the impossible decisions from now on. It would hurt more to start a marriage based on deception than simply loving Mareleau from afar.

It was that pain, that aching punishment that drove him to finally say, "I accept."

6

Teryn felt every muscle in his body uncoil. He hadn't realized how badly he hadn't wanted his father's throne until he felt the responsibility slip from his hands. His lungs felt stronger. His heart lighter.

As he assessed his brother, he knew why. Larylis now bore all that Teryn had shrugged off. Guilt sank Teryn's gut. He knew his brother didn't want it. Knew Larylis held much of the same anguish over their father's death. Perhaps it was cruel of Teryn to do what he'd done—to give him a crown he didn't want—but it was the only way he could think to fix the mess they found themselves in. This way, Larylis could marry the woman he loved. And Teryn...

He shuddered at the void that stood in the space his father's crown once filled. Without the mantle he'd been raised to bear...who was he?

The itch returned. He fluttered his fingers and shifted his stance just to feel his body move. He faced Verdian. "We've made our choices, Your Majesty. What's yours?"

"Choice," Verdian said with a scoff. "You've hardly given much thought to your so-called *choice*. How will your brother keep his rule strong?"

He felt Mareleau's eyes burning into him, a silent plea for him to answer well. She'd gone silent since Teryn's announcement, as if she feared any word from her would shatter what Teryn was attempting to fix.

Teryn glanced at Larylis. He stood as still as a statue, jaw set. His eyes were unfocused as if he were only half there.

Turning his gaze back to the king, he said, "Larylis' rule will be strong, for he will have all our support. Selay's. Khero's. We're already in the process of forging a peace pact between our three kingdoms. Let us write these new terms into it. If you're determined that Selay and Menah will merge as one kingdom upon your death, then we'll write it into the pact. That way anyone who defies Mareleau or Larylis will draw the wrath of all three kingdoms. As for other allies, I'm sure even the Kingdom of Tomas will support him, thanks to Prince Lexington. I too will support Larylis as my king with all my heart, and..." He swallowed hard as he glanced at his mother. "He'll have Dowager Queen Bethaeny's support as well."

She paled, stunned silent. Then color pinked her cheeks. "You reckless, insensitive boy," she said, voice trembling with restraint. "You ask too much of me. Too much of my heart."

A lump rose in Teryn's throat as he watched her turn on her heel and flee the study. He wanted to run after her, to explain, to apologize, but he needed to see this through.

He returned his attention to Verdian and continued. "King Larylis will be crowned on the fifth of July. If you would like your daughter to be made queen the same day, I suggest you accept these new terms."

Queen Helena brightened at that. Gone was her previous disdain as she smiled up at Verdian. "The fifth! That's only a few days from now. Our Mareleau could be queen so soon."

Verdian ignored his wife and huffed a laugh, his eyes still trained on Teryn. "Is that when you were supposed to be crowned? You're cutting it a little close to still be here."

He was right, but he'd had his reasons. "I didn't want to return home until I was assured of Princess Aveline's safety."

With a grumble, Verdian returned to the other side of his desk and sank into his chair. "And what shall we do with Princess Aveline?"

Teryn bit the inside of his cheek before answering. "I will marry her, pending her acceptance. The marriage alliance will be just as we'd planned before. Only a change of groom will be required. But I implore you, do not speak of this to her until I have spoken to her first." His heart ached to recall her anger at him when they'd met in the hall. He couldn't bear it if she learned of yet another development made without her prior knowledge.

Verdian rubbed his brow, sending his powdered wig slightly askew. Teryn held his breath as he awaited the king's answer. Finally, he spoke, his voice brimming with grudging resignation. "Very well. But I have conditions."

Mareleau stepped forward and took one of the chairs on the opposite side of his desk. She perched at the edge of her seat, fingers clawing into the armrests. "What might they be?" she said, her voice barely above a whisper.

Verdian spoke only to Teryn. "Following Mareleau's coronation, my daughter will leave for Ridine Castle. She will travel with Lord Ulrich. He's already planning to lead the rest of King Dimetreus' new staff and council to Ridine anyway."

Mareleau lifted her hands from the armrests to anxiously weave her fingers through a lock of her silver-blonde hair. "Why would I go to Ridine?"

Verdian met his daughter's eyes. "I want someone there who can get close to Aveline. Someone she will feel comfortable enough to confide in. I'd previously had it in mind that Larylis would stay at Ridine during their period of courtship and act as a spy."

Teryn took a step forward. "Then I will take Larylis' place."

"No," Verdian said, his lips lifting into a smug grin. "You must stay with your brother. Now that you've decided to turn over your crown to someone who is wholly unprepared, you'll need to guide him."

"But I'm pregnant," Mareleau said, lifting her chin. "I can't travel."

Helena stood by her daughter and rested a hand on her shoulder. "She's right. She's in no condition to travel all the way to Ridine. It's bad enough that she'll have to journey to Dermaine Palace."

"Have some sense, Helena," Verdian barked. "She isn't far along. Besides, no one knows she's with child yet. She'll need to keep up the ruse that she conceived on her wedding night. Until it is proper for her to announce her condition, she will act as normal."

Mareleau rose from her chair. "That's unfair."

Verdian pinned her with a hard look. "Those are my terms."

Mareleau's eyes darted from Verdian to Helena, then to Teryn, as if hoping one of the latter two might intervene. Teryn knew better than to argue now. Finally, her gaze locked on Larylis. He still stood frozen, hands behind his back like an obedient soldier. Her expression flickered with hurt.

Verdian followed her gaze. "What do you think about my terms, King Larylis?"

Teryn bristled at his mocking tone, but Larylis was unflustered. "I will agree to whatever terms you deem necessary."

Mareleau pursed her lips as she burned Larylis with a glare he refused to meet. Turning back to her father, she said, "How long do you intend for me to stay there?"

Verdian rubbed his jaw, eyes unfocused, before he answered. "Until the end of July. On the final day of the month, we will convene at Ridine Castle to sign the official peace pact, solidifying these terms we've discussed. That will give us a chance to ensure once and for all that Aveline and Dimetreus can be trusted. Until then, keep close to Aveline. Report on her actions. Once the peace pact is signed, you may return home with your husband. Do you agree?"

She resumed weaving her lock of hair until her mother laid a hand on her fingers to still them. Mareleau dropped the tangled braid and folded her palms at her waist. "Yes."

"Then I suppose it's time to draw up a marriage contract."

Teryn released a sigh. He'd done it. He'd managed to fix something before it was too late.

But there was still more to do. More amends to make. And a very important question to ask.

～

THE DOORS TO CORA'S ROOM SPRANG OPEN. CORA HALTED HER PACING BEFORE HER window and turned toward the door, grateful to have some distraction from her thoughts. She was desperate to rid herself of the memory of Teryn's stricken face when they had spoken in the hall, of the courtiers who'd watched them with amused grins, of the betrothal she'd agreed to.

Lurel skipped into her room, a large box in her hands. The girl's smile grew with every step she took toward Cora. "I have so much news to share with you, Your Highness!"

"What news is that?"

"First of all," she said as she set the box on Cora's bed, "everything is settled for your journey to my father's estate."

Cora furrowed her brow. "Your...father?"

"Lord Kevan," she said.

Cora recalled the girl mentioning she was Mareleau's cousin, but Cora hadn't realized Lurel was the daughter of the man who'd be accompanying her to Ridine.

Lurel spoke again. "My next piece of news is even better! I'm coming to Ridine with you. I get to remain as your lady's maid even after you leave here! I wasn't sure Father would let me come, but since he'll be going to Ridine too, he gave me permission. Isn't that great?" The girl bounced on the balls of her feet. Her excitement was somewhere between endearing and annoying.

Cora gave her a weak smile. "How wonderful."

Lurel beamed and lifted the cover off the box she'd brought. "This is my next piece of news." From inside the box, she extracted a cloak of teal wool with brown leather running along the front seams and bottom hem. "It's your new riding cloak, made from the finest Aromir wool. Do you love it?"

Cora stepped closer to examine it. She ran her fingers over the wool, finding it impossibly soft yet dense. Aromir wool wasn't something she'd had access to when she'd lived with the Forest People, for it was more of a luxury than a necessity. When it came to practical use, regular wool sufficed.

But when it came to a garment fit for a royal...

"It's perfect."

"Try it on," Lurel said, already draping it around Cora's shoulders. "The seamstresses will have a riding habit hemmed for you within the hour. If you're still set on leaving tonight, we can depart by early evening. My father's estate is only an hour away, so we'll make it there by nightfall."

"My brother is prepared to leave tonight as well?" A pinch of guilt squeezed her chest. After her confrontation with Teryn, she hadn't had the courage to leave her room, which meant she hadn't seen her brother since she'd abandoned him at the meeting.

"He has left it up to you, Your Highness." Lurel straightened the length of the cloak while Cora secured the clasp. She noted its shape—a purple oval with a black mountain. Khero's sigil. She hadn't worn something bearing her kingdom's sigil since she was a child. It made her throat feel tight. Lurel's voice called out from behind the dressing screen. Cora hadn't noticed when she'd flitted over there. "Can we throw this one out then?"

Cora frowned at the stained garment Lurel held by the tips of her fingers. She took the battered cloak from Lurel, her eyes falling on the torn hem where she'd cut a bandage for Teryn's wound after the battle at Centerpointe Rock. She remembered how he'd looked at her then, how he'd placed his hand on hers after she'd finished wrapping the wool around him. The thought was quickly replaced with the pain she'd felt at discovering he'd bargained off her hand to his brother.

"Might as well burn it." Gritting her teeth, she folded up the cloak with far more force than necessary and strolled over to the hearth and the warm blaze within. Now that she'd officially reclaimed her title as princess, she didn't have to beg for her hearth to be lit; it was simply done. She folded the cloak tighter and prepared to toss the bundle on the flames when she felt something hard beneath her palm. Frowning, she paused and searched for the source. From within one of the inner pockets, she extracted a large amber crystal.

Her heart leaped into her throat. Murky energy thrummed against her palm—

"What is that?" Lurel appeared at Cora's side, eyes wide.

"It's nothing." She threw the cloak into the fire. As Lurel's eyes followed the garment, Cora stashed the crystal into the pocket of her new cloak. Her mind reeled. How had she forgotten that she'd taken Morkai's crystal from the battlefield?

Lurel looked back at Cora, eyes searching her now empty hands. She opened her mouth, but a sudden chime of bells drowned out whatever she was about to say.

"What is that?" Cora asked. The bells resounded far too many times to mark the hour.

Lurel clasped her hands to her chest. "That must have to do with my next piece of news! I heard the gossip on my way here. Princess Mareleau is getting married. Well, those chimes must be announcing that it has already happened. It seems there will be no fuss or ceremony. It's rather last minute, don't you think? But her engagement has already lasted three years. It makes sense they would wed so fast, I suppose. There is to be a feast tonight. We cannot go, for we will be on the road by then. Unless you want me to ask my father to postpone?"

Cora tuned out the girl's voice as she spun on her heel. Her steps were slow and heavy as she made her way to one of the windows. She watched as courtiers chatted animatedly in the garden below, probably gossiping about the princess' surprise nuptials. Something dark heaved in her chest, but she refused to let it out. She was too afraid it might be a sob.

No, she wouldn't cry.

She wouldn't.

Why should she, anyway? Had she not admitted that a loveless political marriage would be better for her? If Teryn had wanted her hand, it would only complicate things. Her feelings for him represented something she wasn't ready to accept—surrender. Should she marry for love, she'd have to give a piece of herself away. Her magical self. She knew she'd never be accepted as both a royal and a witch. Should she forge any heartfelt ties beyond what was necessary for the safety of her kingdom, she'd never have the option to return to the woods. She'd be nothing but Princess Aveline forevermore.

No, that was not something she could give in to just yet. While she knew she no longer belonged with the Forest People, she didn't fit with the royals either. Her place was yet to be discovered. In the meantime, she'd play the royals' games. Agree to their terms. Serve her kingdom. So long as she kept one foot out the door, she'd have means for escape. For freedom. For a future where she could be herself again.

Lurel came up beside her and handed her a folded piece of parchment, sealed with a simple, unmarked blot of wax. "Here is my final piece of news, though I can hardly call it that. I don't know what it is. A servant brought it to me and asked that I deliver it to you."

Cora took the note from the girl and flicked the seal with her thumbnail. She unfolded the paper to find a short letter that read:

> Cora,
> Meet me in the garden after dinner.
> Please.
> —Teryn.

"What does it say?" Lurel asked.

Cora crumpled it into a ball and brought it to the hearth. "Nothing important. Come. Let us prepare to leave. We'll make no fuss about it either. Tell your father to keep our departure quiet. We wouldn't want to take away from the princess' happy day." She said the last part with no small amount of malice and tossed the letter into the flames.

7

Mareleau Harvallis had never felt so anxious as she did now. Her stomach was a swarm of butterflies. Her heart the rapid pulse of hummingbird wings. She walked down the dimly lit halls of Verlot Palace next to the man she loved. The man she was now married to. The man who hadn't so much as looked at her since they'd marked their names side by side on a binding contract.

That was all her wedding had been.

No ceremony. No Godspriest. No elaborate gown. Not even a kiss to seal their nuptials.

Just a quill, a contract, and a flurry of bells.

Her mother had convinced Verdian to agree to host a dinner at least, but Mareleau could have done without that. The last-minute formality meant Mareleau had been pulled away from Larylis immediately following the signing of their marriage contract to be fussed over by her lady's maids. They'd cooed congratulations while whispering behind their hands when they didn't think she was listening. They'd worn smiles while they'd styled her hair, dressed her in the prettiest gown she owned, then smirked and gossiped over the suddenness of her wedding and her unsettling choice of groom.

Dinner had been more of the same. She'd endured cold congratulations, perplexed stares, and too-loud whispers as her dinner guests speculated upon why she'd married the bastard and whether it was true he was now King of Menah in lieu of Teryn. She'd suffered it all with a tight-lipped grin, her composure curated to hide the mess of emotions tangled within. All the while, Larylis—her husband, her beloved—had sat mute by her side. Not once had they gotten the chance to speak. Not once had he turned to her with a smile or a kiss. Her dread had only grown from there.

Now that dinner was over, she and Larylis were forced to engage in one of the most barbaric and outdated traditions Mareleau's kingdom observed during royal marriages. The procession to the wedding chamber.

The corridor echoed with strains of violin, shuffling feet, and muffled whispers. Thankfully, their retinue wasn't overlarge, but even the dozen or so spectators were more than enough to tie Mareleau's stomach in knots. She and Larylis were near enough to touch as they walked with slow steps. That they didn't so much as brush fingertips showed her what efforts Larylis was taking to prevent it. She no longer tried to catch his eye, for she was too preoccupied with her own dread and humiliation. Surely, if she'd been denied a formal wedding ceremony, she could have been denied this ridiculous tradition as well. But no matter how hard she'd argued against it, her mother had refused to hear a word of it. *This is more important than the wedding*, Helena had said. *Especially where you're concerned.*

Mareleau had guessed what her mother had been referring to. The procession to the wedding chamber was meant to prove a royal marriage was consummated. She could only thank the seven gods that her kingdom had long ago done away with the requirement that the consummation be witnessed by a Godspriest. To think that was ever considered civilized!

They reached the end of a short hall where a pair of red and gold doors stood. Mareleau had never entered them before. She'd never had need to, for the room was reserved specifically for newlyweds. Mareleau had to resist the urge to fiddle with her hair as they paused before the doors. She hazarded a glance at Larylis just as he did the same to her. Her heart climbed into her throat, sending it thudding even faster. Too soon, he looked away and faced the crowd behind them.

Mareleau did the same. She kept her eyes fixed firmly above everyone's heads, grateful for how dark the hall was. Breah, one of her lady's maids, stepped forward with a curtsy, then loosened the laces of Mareleau's gown and removed pins, jewels, and sashes from her ensemble. Breah helped her out of her dress next, leaving her in her petticoats, corset, and shift. As she let down Mareleau's hair, a young man went to assist Larylis out of his jacket and waistcoat.

Mareleau swallowed hard and briefly scanned the crowd. She found her other two lady's maids—Ann and Sera—as well as her mother. It was no surprise her father was missing, for he'd hardly deigned to join her wedding feast. His actions spoke clearly of his disdain for her marriage, regardless of his grudging acceptance.

Once Larylis was left in only his shirt and trousers, the audience rumbled with polite applause. Everything inside her wanted to curl forward, to fold her arms over her chest, but she forced herself to stand tall, to lift her chin, to exude the confidence she didn't feel.

Queen Helena clasped her hands to her heart and faced the crowd. "It is now time for the bride and groom to become true husband and wife. Wish them many blessings, so they may bring forth an heir." Another wave of applause. A few disbelieving snickers.

Breah curtsied once again, bowing her blonde head. "Is there anything you desire to be brought to you before we bid you goodnight, Your Highness?"

"Wine." The word came out in a rush.

Helena cut a glare at her daughter, then glanced suggestively at Mareleau's abdomen.

It took no small amount of restraint to keep from rolling her eyes. "For my husband," she amended, lifting a hand toward him. She nearly alighted it upon his arm when she remembered they hadn't touched since their stolen kiss over a month ago. She folded her hands at her waist and gave her mother a demure smile. "My husband would like wine. I do not."

Breah nodded and scurried into the crowd, returning with a bottle and glass. Breah handed both to Larylis.

Helena gave a satisfied nod, and two servants opened the pair of doors. As Mareleau and Larylis turned toward them, her pulse kicked up. She was relieved to escape the eyes of the spectators, but she dreaded what would come next. Not the consummation they were expected to perform but something far more mundane.

A conversation.

She'd been desperate to speak to him all night, to explain, to apologize, but as she entered the wedding chamber and heard the doors close behind them, she wished she were anywhere else. The longer Larylis had avoided speaking to her, the more certain she'd become of his displeasure. He had every right to be upset, of course. Hopefully his love for her was stronger than his anger.

Silence hung heavy as they stood just beyond the closed doors. They studied the walls, the bed, looking everywhere but at each other. The candlelit room was relatively small while the bed was enormous, piled high with plush pillows, silk sheets, and velvet blankets in the deepest shades of red and gold. Old-fashioned tapestries adorned the marble walls, displaying romantic scenes of courtship and lovemaking.

Mareleau couldn't help but wrinkle her nose. "This is the most hideous room I've ever seen."

Larylis snorted a laugh. The sound was so familiar, so cherished, it had Mareleau's chest warming. She glanced his way to see if he held a smile on his lips, but he was already turning away from her. He strolled over to the bedside table and set down his armload. With slow moves, he poured the deep ruby wine into the glass. She expected him to drink from it, but he didn't. Instead, he set it back down and moved to the sole window in the room. He drew back the crimson curtain and stood silent, hardly moving but for the rise and fall of his chest. The blush of the setting sun streamed through the window, amplifying the red and gold glow of the room, glinting off the copper tones in his dark hair.

Mareleau watched him for a few moments, studying the broad expanse of his shoulders, the slim taper of his waist visible beneath his untucked shirt, the way his overlong hair curled at the nape of his neck. She was desperate to break the silence, but no words would come. So she swept over to the glass of wine, drained it in two gulps, then filled another. The burn of the fiery liquid warmed her stomach and muted her swarm of thoughts. She closed her eyes as she took another sip, relishing the way her muscles unwound.

"What about the baby?" Larylis' voice had her eyes flying open, his tone equal parts taunting and condemning. He watched her from the window, lips pressed into a tight line.

Her heart hammered so hard, she was surprised her entire ribcage didn't shatter in her chest. With trembling hands, she set down the cup and took a few steps toward him. She immediately set to braiding three strands of hair, hating how her stomach turned beneath his unyielding scrutiny. She paused and considered wielding her *magic trick* to summon one of her false personas. It would make it easier to have the conversation they needed to have, but...it wasn't right. Larylis deserved her true self now.

"I'm so sorry I lied, Larylis," she said.

"Why did you do it?"

She frowned. "Why do you think I did it? I had to get out of marrying Teryn."

He shook his head. "You could have gotten out of your engagement a hundred different ways. Why did you bring me into it? With a lie, no less. One that made me look like a traitor to my brother."

She bristled at his rising tone. Her own voice grew sharper. "It was the only way I could think that would finally allow us to be together."

"You should have asked me first."

"You would have said no."

He took a step closer. "And you'd have had my answer. What are you going to do in a few months when it's clear you aren't with child?"

"I have plans for that," she said slowly. "In a few weeks, I will announce that my condition came to...to an end. My parents won't expect me to mourn, for I am supposed to be hiding my supposed pregnancy."

She expected some relief to show on his face after hearing she had it all under control. If anything, he looked angrier. "You shouldn't have done this."

She narrowed her eyes. "You'd have let me go so easily? Even after everything we confessed in the drawing room, after learning what had happened to our letters...you'd have let me go? Answer me honestly."

He opened his mouth only to snap it shut. With a slow sigh, he dragged a hand over his face, and his expression finally eased. His tone turned soft. Resigned. "Only on the outside. Inside...inside, I would have held you tight and never let you go."

"Well, I'm not quite so noble as you. I wasn't willing to let you go inside or out. I had to fight for you, whether it damned my reputation, ruined my chances at inheriting my father's crown, or had me cast out as a traitor. I had to try. I had to risk everything."

Again, he opened his mouth only to say nothing for several breaths. Finally, he whispered, "It was wrong. We shouldn't...we shouldn't have been rewarded for your lie. I shouldn't have been rewarded for what I did to my father."

Her heart clenched at that. She remembered what he'd said in her father's study, how he'd taken the blame for his father's death. She'd heard the details of what had happened during the battle. Had she been less wrapped up in her own schemes, she might have reassessed the timing of her plan. She bit her lip and took a few steps closer. Her hands begged to reach for him, but she was too afraid he'd evade her touch. "It wasn't your fault."

He averted his gaze. "You weren't there."

"I didn't have to be." She stepped closer again, and this time she did reach for him. Her hands shook as she pressed them to his chest. His heart thumped against her palms. Despite their years of animosity that had resulted from her parents' trickery, touching him now felt like coming home. Like she hadn't spent three years thinking he'd abandoned her. "I know you, Larylis. You are the most intelligent man I've met. You do nothing without analyzing the alternatives first. You make no choice without weighing it against histories, facts, and probabilities. You are selfless and are constantly trying to make those around you happy and comfortable. You think too little of yourself, but I see you. I know about the difficult choice you made, and I know you made the only one you could."

He looked down at her, a flash of surprise in his eyes. Then his expression fell, and he looked away from her again. "I can't help but wonder if it was the wrong decision."

"You can't go back." She lifted a hand from his chest and placed it on his cheek. "*We* can't go back. I'm sorry for what I did and for all the pain I've caused. I'm sorry for the rift I may have driven between you and your brother, but..."

She gently turned his cheek until his eyes met hers. Lifting her chin, she spoke with fierce truth. "I don't regret it. I'd do it again a hundred times if it meant no one would keep us apart again."

His eyes widened. Mareleau wasn't sure if they held awe or terror. She didn't care. This was the real her. If he was to be her husband, he should know she wasn't a pretty flower. She was a dragon. She would consume the world and burn it to ash to get what she wanted.

Right now, what she wanted was him.

She stepped closer until her chest brushed his. He stiffened but kept his eyes trained on hers. "Tell me this is wrong," she dared him, angling her head back. "Tell me you don't want this. Say the word and I'll step away from you. We can be husband and wife in name only. You can punish me for my lies and punish yourself for your own perceived crimes."

He said nothing.

She ran her thumb along his jaw, feeling the slightest hint of stubble beneath the pad of her finger. "Tell me, Larylis."

His breaths turned sharp and shallow, his wide chest pulsing against her breasts. She refused to widen the space between them, refused to give an inch unless he told her to. His moss-green eyes swam with a hunger that sang through her blood, echoing the desire thrumming in her core.

Finally, he slid an arm around her, his palm skating over the laces of her corset. His other hand covered hers—the one still pressed against his cheek. It sparked a memory from the last time they'd stood this close, the last time he'd placed his hand over hers. They'd been in the drawing room, and she'd been working to frantically undress him when he'd stilled her hands and pulled away.

Her heart lurched as she expected him to do the same now. She held her breath, bracing herself for his rejection—

His lips came down to hers, soft and slow and hungry. She gasped with surprise, with relief, and wound her arms around his neck. They were a tangle of limbs as they moved away from the window. She opened her mouth to deepen the kiss, felt his tongue caress hers. Her legs trembled from the desire that coursed through her, gathering in a burning warmth low in her belly. She gave more and more of her weight over to him, let him lift her beneath her thighs and carry her the rest of the way to the bed. Her back met the plush mattress, the velvet blankets soft against her bare shoulders.

She tugged Larylis closer, searching for buttons to pry loose. He pulled away from her long enough to shrug free from his shirt. She lifted herself on her forearms, desperate not to let the distance between them grow too vast. When he returned to her, his hands moved to her back. With one hand, he untied the laces of her corset. With the other, he unhooked the front closures. Once she was free, he threw the garment on the floor. Her petticoats went next, leaving only her cotton shift to cover her naked flesh.

He paused and pulled back, eyes roving the length of her. The desire filling his gaze was so heady, it emboldened her. With slow motions, she reached for the top of her shift and slowly slid it down her shoulders. Inch by slow inch, she let the cotton skate down her skin, baring her breasts, her torso, her stomach. Finally, she slid it over her hips until she was fully naked before him.

He assessed her again, then leaned in to claim her lips. She pulled back and shook her head. "It's your turn."

His lips quirked into a crooked grin—the first smile she'd seen from him all day—and it was the most beautiful sight she'd ever witnessed. Her hands moved to the buttons of his trousers. He trailed kisses down her neck, over her collarbone, over the crest of each breast, as she freed him from his pants. Then, slowly, he lay beside her on the bed, his hands roving her side, her hip, her upper thighs. His gaze turned suddenly timid, but his touch was fire, igniting everywhere their skin met. She bit her lip as his hand curved around her bottom.

"Larylis." His name came out with a tremor. "I need you. So badly, I need you closer." She meant it in more ways than one. She wanted his body in this moment more than she'd ever wanted anything. But she wanted his heart too. His mind. His love. The coldness that had stood between them today was too sharp to endure again. They'd already been pulled apart for three years. Now they would be separated again in a matter of days. She'd be stuck at Ridine Castle for at least two weeks, and that didn't include the travel time to get there. She needed to know a chasm wouldn't grow between them in her absence. "I need you to love me."

He drew his hand back up the length of her body, over her thighs, her stomach, her breast, her neck, until he cradled her cheek. Locking his eyes with hers, he said, "With everything that I am, I love you."

She pulled him down to her and lost herself in his lips, his limbs, his touch. Their hearts met. Their bodies tangled. Amidst the web of lies she'd spun, through the cracks rent by the ferocity of her affection, love dug roots and bloomed.

8

Dinner had been over for two hours, and still Teryn waited. He stood in the courtyard just beyond the doors that led from the palace to the garden, ensuring he wouldn't miss anyone who entered. No matter how many times footsteps resounded on the stone steps, not a single pair belonged to *her*.

His heart had sunk with the sun, and now that night had fully fallen, he wasn't sure he dared hope any longer. He glanced away from the palace doors to the windows of the upper levels. Music streamed from the open balcony of the ballroom, where a celebratory dance was being held. The newlyweds had already been escorted to their wedding chamber, but it seemed the festivities being held in their honor were ongoing. Teryn scanned other balconies, most of them dark, seeking Cora's room. He knew he could go to her, but there was a reason he'd asked her to see him in the garden tonight. Yet the longer he stayed out here, the more pathetic he found his reason to be.

He released a heavy breath. "Was it really so foolish of an idea to think I could romance her?"

The only answer he received was a sharp peck on his cheek. With a grin, he glanced at Berol, his peregrine falcon. She was perched upon the leather pad he wore over one shoulder, strapped across his dinner jacket. He dared not go outside without it, for Berol refused to let him out of her sight when he was outdoors lately. The falcon had found him the day he'd arrived at Verlot Palace after leaving Centerpointe Rock. Teryn's relief at seeing her both alive and having forgiven him for yelling at her to go away during the battle had nearly been enough to bring tears to his eyes. He'd been willing to upset her at Centerpointe Rock if it meant keeping her safe, but her short absence had been almost as painful to endure as his physical wounds.

He gave her neck some scritches, which she returned in the form of more nibbles to his cheek.

The sound of a door opening caught his attention, followed by the swoosh of skirts and the patter of feet. Hope bloomed in Teryn's chest as he angled himself toward whoever had come—

His shoulders slumped as he found his mother strolling into the garden. He should have recognized the cadence of her steps. Dread replaced his hope, for it was clear she'd come to talk. He owed her an explanation for what had happened today, for how he'd claimed she'd support Larylis' rule. However, he'd hoped he'd have more time to prepare for it.

Her lips were pursed as she walked up to him. Berol launched off his shoulder as if she dreaded the scolding as much as Teryn did. What Teryn wouldn't give to sprout wings and fly away too.

"Mother," he said with a nod.

Her eyes blazed with fury as she spoke. "Everything I've done, I've done for you. In a single sentence, you've done away with all of it."

"I'm sorry," he said, filling his voice with the full weight of his apology. He didn't regret abdicating, but he was agonized over how much it must have hurt his mother.

"What is your apology worth now? They've won. They got what they wanted all along."

Teryn frowned. "Who won?"

"Lady Annabel and your father," she said through her teeth. "Why do you think I sent Larylis away all those years ago? My ladies heard Annabel bragging that her son would one day be king. Her ambition had become dangerous, so I fought hard against it. I fought with everything I had to protect you. To protect your crown."

"I never asked you to protect my crown," he said as gently as he could.

"I'm your mother. My protection comes with or without your request or permission. Now that you've turned your crown over to Larylis, everything I fought for has been for naught." She let out a humorless chuckle. "With Arlous' death, *we'd* won. You and me. Even with Larylis named prince, we'd still won."

Teryn shook his head. "I'm tired of war, Mother. The battle of crowns was never one I wanted to fight. I never wanted to be pitted against my brother. I never wanted to be torn between you and Father."

She huffed. "Are you saying I was wrong to fight for my crown? I was defending my right and yours."

"I could never deny you that right, nor could I have condoned what Father did when he tried to replace you. You're my mother. I love you. But...I loved Father too. And Larylis."

"Your love won't make him a good king."

"I believe in him."

"What about me? Have you no sympathy for what this means for me? With Larylis as king, Lady Annabel will have the run of Dermaine Palace. She'll be Queen Mother Annabel. I'll be relegated once more to my little palace, never again welcome in the place that once was my home." Her voice broke on the last part.

Teryn's heart sank. He gathered his mother's hand in his. "You will be welcome."

She turned up her nose. "Larylis could ensure I'm not."

"He's better than that. He's better than Annabel, and you know it."

She turned her head but made no argument.

"He and I will both take care of you." He hesitated before saying the next part. "There was once a time when you took care of him. Until you banished him from Dermaine, you were far more of a mother to him than Annabel was. He hasn't forgotten the kindness you once showed him."

Her shoulders drooped. She met Teryn's eyes briefly before shaking her head. "I couldn't let myself love him. It was too dangerous. He won't forgive me for banishing him."

"He will. It's himself he'll struggle to forgive. Besides, Larylis and I have seen true danger. We met it on a battlefield. We fought wraiths, a monster, and a blood mage. This...this is just politics."

"You're really willing to let go of your birthright so easily?"

"I won't say it's easy, but I believe it's the right thing to do. If you trusted me to be king, then I ask you to trust me with this too."

Silence fell between them. Finally, she squeezed his hand. "I can't say my heart isn't broken, but I...I'll support your brother's claim to the throne in name only. Do not ask me to do anything more on his behalf."

"That's fair," he said, trying not to sound too shocked that he'd won her agreement.

She released his hand and made to leave. Just as she turned away, she whirled right back around. "Who are you waiting for?"

"How do you know I'm waiting for anyone?"

"You've been out here for two hours, my son. It's the longest I've seen you stay in one place in weeks. So tell me. Who is it?"

He couldn't help the flush that heated his cheeks as he spoke her name. "Princess Aveline."

His mother's eyes flickered with a sympathy that seemed suspiciously feigned. "Did no one tell you? She already left."

Teryn's muscles went rigid. "When? Why didn't I hear about it?"

She gave a flippant shrug. "One of my ladies told me the princess left while everyone was at dinner. Rumor has it, she didn't want to take away from such a special occasion with her hasty exit."

He rubbed his temples as if it could grind away his disappointment too.

"My suspicions were correct," Bethaeny said, an edge to her tone. "You have feelings for the princess. You intended to wed her when you proposed the marriage alliance."

He gave her a pointed look. "Yes, and you shouldn't have intervened."

"Like I said, Teryn. I am your mother. My protection does not need permission. I was worried you were about to make a hasty decision and destroy your engagement to Mareleau. That was before I knew the girl was a scheming harlot, of course."

"I fear your protection has made things far more difficult," he said, trying his best to keep his voice level.

"Tell me this, son. Is *Cora*, as I've heard you call her, worth giving up your crown for?"

"I didn't do it for her." His words were true. He'd done it for Larylis too. He nearly left it at that but there was a deeper truth yet to be said. "But yes. She's worth it."

"Do you love her?"

His heart hammered at the question. Heat crawled up his neck, his cheeks. He was grateful that night had fallen to hide the blush that had certainly taken over every inch of his skin. "One step at a time," he said, trying to sound nonchalant. "First, I need to make sure she doesn't try to shoot me in the heart with an arrow when she sees me next. Which...I don't know when that will be."

"Promise me you will not go after her," she said with a stern raise of her brow. "Promise me you will be there for your brother. You owe it to him and your kingdom."

He hated that she was right; Larylis needed him. His brother had a heavy responsibility he'd never expected to take on. And yet, Teryn couldn't find it in his heart to make the promise his mother asked for. He'd long since learned not to utter promises he knew he wouldn't keep. "I'll do what is needed of me."

She narrowed her eyes but made no argument. Seeming satisfied with his answer, she left him alone. Berol flew back to his shoulder. He fed her a strip of duck he'd taken from dinner, but in his mother's absence, the uncomfortable itch to move returned. He'd managed to keep it at bay while he'd been waiting for Cora, but now that he knew he wouldn't get to see her tonight, he was back to feeling unsettled. Stuck.

With a heavy sigh, he turned from the palace doors and headed deeper into the garden, past the candlelit alcove where a single table stood, upon which sat a bottle of wine and a pair of glasses. He couldn't bring himself to look at it. Cora probably would have hated it anyway. He walked past the harpist and shook his head. With a nod, the musician rose from her seat at the edge of the fountain and departed. Cora would have hated that too. They'd danced to a harpist once, but... what had he been thinking? She'd hated him then. She probably hated him still.

And yet...

For one moment, I thought she meant you.

Damn it all, it *was* him. It had always been him. He couldn't tell her now, and maybe he couldn't tell her any time soon. But he would. Eventually...he would.

Deeper and deeper, he walked into the garden, Berol his lone companion, determined to walk until he was tired enough to sleep and forget the hollow ache in his heart.

9

The smell of the forest was so soothing, Cora almost wept. Aromas of earth and pine surrounded her, carried by the mild breeze. Closing her eyes, she tilted her face to the sky, basking in the morning sun that warmed her skin. If it wasn't for the dozens of hoofbeats that echoed on the road around her, she could almost pretend she was deep in the woods, riding one of the Forest People's horses alongside Maiya. Instead, she rode a borrowed palfrey alongside her brother on their way home.

She still didn't know how to feel about the word *home*, nor the pain that lanced her heart at the thought of Maiya. She hadn't communicated with any of the Forest People since the battle, and she was desperate to know how they fared. They'd come to her aid, fought Morkai's wraiths, defended royal soldiers. All in the name of protecting fae magic. They'd come out victorious, but she knew not all the Forest People had survived. She'd seen Druchan's dead body. Witnessed Roije get his arm severed by Morkai. Had he survived such a grave wound? And if not... would Maiya ever forgive her?

She shook the question from her mind, for it would only plague her to no end. Perhaps someday soon she could seek out the commune, at least for a visit, but this was not the time. Right now she needed to be Princess Aveline.

She turned her face away from the sun and opened her eyes. Her gaze landed on a less pleasant view—Lord Kevan's backside. He rode ahead of her while Dimetreus kept to her side. Guards took the lead and rear, while dozens of other horses, wagons, and coaches filled the middle of their entourage. Lurel rode in one of the coaches, alongside other handpicked servants and staff, all selected by Lord Kevan.

Cora and Dimetreus had stayed at Kevan's estate for three days while their preparations had been finalized. That had given Cora more than enough time to set her opinion of her kingdom's new Head of Council. He was gruff, short tempered, and the complete opposite of his bright and bubbly daughter. The more she got to know him the harder it was to believe they were related. Even their looks were at odds. Where Lurel was willowy and fair, Kevan was a brutish bear. He was barrel-chested with piercing blue eyes, gray-brown hair that framed his face like a wild mane, and a thick beard. He was never short on cutting remarks and made no effort to venerate Cora and Dimetreus more than necessity required.

Cora had been eager to get out of his home and on the road to more neutral territory. Yesterday, she'd gotten her wish, and today had brought them to the forest road. To pine and birdsong and a mountainous view beyond a sea of endless green. It was the closest she could get to the forests she craved.

Closing her eyes again, she focused on her breath, on the air caressing her nostrils, brushing her cheeks, dancing over her gloved hands as she held her reins. She let the horse beneath her root her to the earth, every hoofbeat serving as an anchor. The warmth of the sun connected her to the element of fire while her emotions, her blood, and the aroma of dew-speckled leaves connected her to water. The elements thickened around her, feeding her mental shields.

Her shields had been especially necessary lately. Without them, she'd likely have a migraine by now from all the emotions she'd have picked up from the strangers around her. But that didn't mean she couldn't let them down for at least a moment...

With a slow exhale, she pried the smallest hole through her mental shroud and extended her senses outward, beyond the road and her retinue, reaching deeper into the woods that flanked their path. Finally, she located what she'd been searching for.

Warmth greeted her like a friendly wave.

I am nearby, Valorre said. She smiled at the feeling-thought that was his voice, although she could sense a tinge of impatience with it. The unicorn was not overly fond of how slowly her entourage traveled. He'd already galloped ahead and doubled back several times. *You will be pleased to know I have found no hunters.*

That's good, she thought back to him. However, she wouldn't be fully comforted until they left northern Selay and confirmed the forests in Khero were empty of Morkai's hunters as well. She figured word of their master's death had likely driven them to abandon their efforts, but she couldn't be certain. Unicorn horns were still a rare commodity. And unlike many of the soldiers who'd awoken confused on the battlefield after the duke's glamour had been severed, the unicorn hunters Cora had once pitted herself against weren't being controlled by dark magic. Instead, they were mercenaries and convicted criminals. Cora wasn't sure what Verdian and her other new allies were doing to sway public opinion about her brother and present him as an innocent victim, but if Morkai's men thought Dimetreus was still in league with the duke's former plans, they might continue their work.

That was yet another thing Cora was determined to see finished before she considered leaving Ridine Castle to find the Forest People—unicorn hunting had to be abolished. Not just in Khero, but across the continent.

"You used to love to ride." Her brother's voice roused her from her thoughts. Closing her mental shields, she turned and met his grin. It was the same tired smile he'd greeted her with in Verdian's study, but the fresh outdoor air seemed to be doing him some good. His complexion had regained some of its golden-tan hue, the blotches that had once marred it now fading. Her heart tumbled with the same confused reaction it always gave when she looked at him—love and hate. Fear and sympathy. She stiffened as he reached across the space between their horses to squeeze her hand. "Do you still love to ride?"

His tone was so much like how it had been when she was younger—soft and slow, like he was speaking to a child. She didn't have it in her to be offended. His last clear memories of her were as a young girl. It was the only way he knew how to talk to her. They'd have to get to know each other all over again.

She gave him a nod. "I do."

"I remember that," he said, a note of pride in his voice. He returned his hand to his reins. "More of my memories are coming back. I recall almost everything clearly from...from *before*."

He didn't have to elaborate. She knew he meant before Morkai had come into their lives. The duke—though not a duke yet at that time—had arrived at court two years after she and Dimetreus had lost their parents to a plague. She wondered how soon Morkai had begun using his magic to influence her brother...

A chill ran over her, so she tucked her hand into one of her pockets. A deep pulsating beat thrummed against her gloved palm—the energy of an object she'd forgotten was inside. She extracted the hand faster than if she'd been burned. Repulsion swept through her, as well as annoyance that she kept forgetting the crystal's presence. Even more frightening was the thought that it might be enchanted. Though it would explain why she found herself surprised by its existence, it was too unsettling to think Morkai's magic might linger beyond his death. Still, it wasn't an impossibility. His glamours had been severed, but those had been woven using his Roizan, which had died along with its master. That didn't mean all Morkai's spells had dissolved. It stood to reason that any magic he'd made without the Roizan could remain.

She hated keeping the crystal on her person. She'd chuck it into the woods if she didn't suspect it was too dangerous to discard so carelessly. It undoubtedly held vast darkness, but when she'd first touched it on the battlefield, she'd felt something else. Some unfamiliar energy. Whatever it was, the crystal needed to be cleared by magical means. The Forest People had taught her several ways to clear objects of unwanted energy, but she didn't dare do it until she had ample privacy.

"What else do you like, Aveline?" her brother asked. "Do you like when I call you Aveline? I've been told Prince Teryn calls you Cora, like...like our mother used to." His eyes turned down at the corners.

She could be honest and tell him she strongly preferred being called Cora, but she was supposed to embrace being Princess Aveline from now on. "You can call me whatever you prefer."

He opened his mouth but his words were halted when a rider came up alongside them, edging in beside Lord Kevan. The messenger was not from their entourage, for he bore the white and gold rose sigil of Selay. Cora's retinue rode beneath Khero's standard—the black mountain on a purple background. "Message from King Verdian," the rider said.

Cora watched as Lord Kevan took a letter from the messenger. He scoffed as he read it, then looked over his shoulder at Cora and Dimetreus. He offered a grin that looked more like a sneer. "It appears a guest will be joining us after we arrive at Ridine."

"Who?" Cora asked.

"Queen Mareleau," he said with a mocking laugh. "She is to serve as your companion while you get settled back into your role as princess."

The news couldn't have been more unfavorable. Her sole encounter with Mareleau had been enough to turn her heart against the girl until the end of time. Now that the brazen harpy was married to Teryn, Cora despised her even more. Before she could dwell on her sudden spike of jealousy, she bit out, "Why?"

Kevan nodded at the messenger, dismissing him, before returning his attention to Cora. His lips curled into a cruel smirk. "Probably to punish her for marrying a bastard." He chuckled and faced forward again. "Pardon, I meant *King Larylis*."

Cora nearly dropped her reins in her shock. She blinked a few times, her mind reeling over what he'd said. "Lord Kevan, are you saying Mareleau has wed... Larylis Alante? Not Teryn?"

"So it would seem."

Her mind flashed to the letter Lurel had delivered. The one she'd ignored, crumpled, and tossed into the hearth. She'd thought he'd wanted to meet with her as a married man, a friend seeking a fond farewell. She'd been too angry to respond, too hurt by the unwanted engagement he'd orchestrated, too desperate to leave Verlot to consider...

Regret pierced her heart, but she hardened it against the sting. It didn't matter now. Whatever marriage politics had befallen Teryn, Larylis, and Mareleau, it was none of her concern. At least it meant she no longer had to marry Larylis.

And yet, a marriage alliance might still be required between Menah and Khero. It was one of Verdian's terms.

Teryn might...*no.*

She shoved him from her mind. Never again would she give in to hope without due cause. Never again would she let her heart distract her from the reality at hand. She'd already established that love was the last thing she needed. Love equated to permanent attachments. To vulnerability. To giving up on who she really was.

She tried to focus on her current reality. That gave her far more pressing matters to concern herself with—getting home, ensuring her brother could make peace with his lost memories, helping him reestablish his role as king, and...

She gulped.

Tolerating the company of Mareleau.

Despite her best efforts to distract herself, her mind and heart conspired against her, forming a solitary wish: that she could go back in time and stay long enough at Verlot to hear what Teryn had wanted to say.

10

Mareleau had enjoyed one night of bliss, one night of passion, one night to experience the pleasure of being fully and completely loved. It had been beyond anything she'd imagined, anything she'd ever had a right to hope for. Now she stood to lose everything.

Well, perhaps not everything. Larylis was her husband and nothing could change that. But if he didn't show up for his own coronation, she wouldn't be crowned either.

She paced the length of the hall outside the Godskeep at Dermaine Palace, grateful that the only witnesses to her panic were a handful of guards and her three lady's maids. Breah trailed after her, keeping the long train of Mareleau's white silk dress from touching the ground. Whenever Mareleau would pause, Ann and Sera would rush to her, dabbing her face with powder, patting her hair, or straightening her red velvet cape.

Seven devils, where was he?

Sounds of chatter slipped beneath the Godskeep door. The room was full and the audience had already been waiting for fifteen minutes. If Larylis didn't show up soon, the courtiers, nobles, and guests would have more to gossip about than Teryn's unexpected abdication and Larylis' equally unexpected marriage to his brother's former fiancée.

She reached for her hair, seeking a lock to braid, but found her tresses out of reach. Her maids had done her hair in an elaborate updo specifically suited for the crown she'd be given. *If* Larylis showed up.

She'd seen less of him than she'd wished over the last few days. The morning after their union, they'd hastened to leave for Dermaine. Everything that followed had been rushed activity and travel. They'd slept separately at night, traveled separately by day. They'd exchanged only a few stolen glances and too-short embraces. Even the one night they'd spent together after arriving at the palace had been brief, with Larylis being called into a meeting with his council until well after Mareleau had fallen asleep. Still, their sparse interactions had been enough to show her the melancholy he'd returned to.

What if he'd changed his mind about becoming king? She imagined what that would mean for them. If they weren't king and queen, if her marriage to Larylis lost what little credibility her father was willing to see in it, if she was disinherited...

For one moment, she felt the strangest twinge of relief. If they were no longer beholden to their parents' thrones, they'd be...free. They could run away together, live a simple life—

She shook the thought from her head. Wherever Larylis was, he hadn't chosen to bring her along. Besides, she may have enjoyed the occasional fantasy about living the simple life, but she knew as well as anyone that she was not a simple woman. She enjoyed her luxuries. Already, the walls of Dermaine Palace felt too close compared to the wide halls of Verlot. The lights too sparse, too dim. The floors too plain. Her footsteps too loud. Her pulse too fast.

She paused her pacing and steadied her breaths. Sera came to powder her forehead, but Mareleau slapped her hand away. "I'm fine." The girl took a step back and exchanged a glance with Ann.

"He'll be here," Breah said, tone calm. Mareleau wanted to believe her, but Breah didn't know a damn thing.

The Godskeep door opened, sending Mareleau's heart leaping into her throat. Hope bloomed in her chest but she crushed it even before the figure emerged from the other side. It couldn't be Larylis, for he was supposed to be entering the Godskeep, not emerging from within it. If he were already inside, she wouldn't be an anxious mess.

Teryn stepped into the hall and closed the door quickly behind him. "He still hasn't shown?"

"No." Mareleau put her hands on her hips. "Do you know where he might be?"

Teryn's eyes unfocused. "I think I have an idea."

~

LARYLIS NEVER IMAGINED HE'D FIND SOLACE AMONGST THE DEAD, BUT THE CRYPTS beneath the Godskeep were oddly soothing. It was the quiet that comforted him, something he used to only find in libraries. But with Dermaine Palace so busy in the wake of his and Teryn's return, his favored haunts were devoid of their usual silence.

He placed his hands on the cool stone of his father's sarcophagus. The sides bore an intricately carved relief of seven faces to represent the seven gods. The top was carved with Menah's eagle sigil. Arlous' effigy was still being carved, but soon it would grace the sarcophagus as well. Footsteps echoed from the entrance to the crypts, telling Larylis his respite was at an end. Teryn came up beside him.

"I figured you were down here," his brother said without a hint of reproach. Instead, Teryn's voice sounded as tired as Larylis felt. It was an exhaustion that no amount of sleep seemed to dissolve.

They stood in silence for several moments before Larylis found his voice. "We laid his body to rest this morning, and by afternoon I'm expected to take his crown."

"I know."

Larylis realized this was the first time they'd been alone since the meeting in Verdian's study. Before Teryn gave up everything and laid it at Larylis' feet. Slowly, he turned to face his brother. "I'm sorry, Teryn."

Teryn released an exasperated sigh. "What are you apologizing for?"

"You know what I'm apologizing for. I've taken everything from you."

"You've taken nothing that I did not freely give. And it's nothing you don't deserve." His voice held an edge that wasn't lost on Larylis.

He certainly *did* deserve it. Deserved whatever scorn his brother held.

Teryn's expression softened. "I'm not mad at you."

"I can't imagine how you could feel anything but hate for me."

"I could never hate you. You're my brother." He turned to face their father's sarcophagus. "It's myself I'm angry with. I should have known how you felt about Mareleau. I should have seen it, even when you told me you didn't love her."

Larylis' stomach turned. "No, I should have been honest. It's just...it was complicated. I didn't think I loved her anymore, nor she me. I didn't think we could ever be together, didn't think I'd ever be worthy of her. And it was your duty—"

"My duty can go to the seven devils," Teryn said with a dark chuckle. "I've made more mistakes in the name of duty than I care to admit." He turned to face Larylis with a pointed look. "It's your duty now. One you're rather tardy for."

Larylis' fingers curled into fists. "How can I wear his crown after what I've done?"

"I meant what I said before. You made an impossible choice."

"What if I'd surrendered? He could still be alive—"

"We don't know that," Teryn said, tone sharp. "We will never know what might have been. If you're worried about being worthy of Father's crown, then *be* worthy. Stop asking if you are. Just be the king he'd want you to be."

Guilt and shame twisted in his heart. Teryn was right. "I've done a terrible job of accepting my punishment, haven't I?"

Teryn's eyes turned down at the corners. "I didn't mean it when I said you should take the crown as your punishment. I only said that because I needed you to accept. Because I knew your capacity for self-hatred was greater than your willingness to be happy. But that's not what Father would have wanted."

Larylis opened his mouth to argue but couldn't find the words.

"I've seen what you're doing, Larylis. You've been distant with your wife. You're refusing to let yourself enjoy one of the best things life has to offer. Carry Father's crown like a burden if that is your wish, but...don't shun love."

"Weren't you the one who always said love is for the weak? That duty is greater when you're a royal?"

"I told you how I feel about duty. Besides, you're lucky. Your wife is both your love and your duty. Don't push her away. And don't you dare say you don't deserve her. She deserves *you*. A woman who's willing to fight for your sorry ass deserves better than a cold bedfellow."

Larylis' cheeks flushed. His and Mareleau's one night together in bed had been anything but cold. Yet Teryn was right. He'd gone to great lengths to distance himself from his wife ever since. The warmth of his love, the depth of his joy at being near her...it terrified him. He was so afraid to give in, to revel in the love he'd been given, to take pleasure in anything that had come from either his treachery or hers. What exactly he was afraid of, he wasn't sure.

He met Teryn's eyes. "You've changed...since before..."

"Since before I betrayed someone I cared for and got myself captured by a blood mage? I know."

"The person you care for...that's Cora, isn't it?"

Teryn's throat bobbed. He gave a curt nod.

"She's the reason you've been acting like a maniac, isn't she?"

"What do you mean?"

"Don't think you're the only one who's noticed odd behaviors, brother. I've seen what you're doing too. You're constantly in motion, constantly fixing things you don't need to fix."

"I just want to be useful."

Larylis leveled a look at his brother. "You helped fix a wagon wheel on the road. We pay people to do that, yet you aided repairs with your own hands. When we arrived home, you organized the study. You cleaned Father's desk. You alphabetized correspondences by sender, then rearranged them by date received instead."

Teryn shifted from foot to foot. "I'm supposed to be helping you."

"But you'd rather be somewhere else."

A flush crept up Teryn's cheeks. His voice was low when he spoke. "I need to talk with Cora about our...potential engagement. I don't want her to find out in a letter, nor do I want it arranged before she's had a chance to say yes. And if she says no, then we need to find another way to formalize an alliance with Khero." He said the last part in a rush.

Larylis recognized something in his brother. Something he'd never seen in Teryn, only in himself. He wasn't sure if Teryn knew just yet, but his concern over Cora was more than politics. More than alliance. More than friendship. A flash of treacherous joy crept into his heart, but for once he didn't try to tamp it down. Surely he could stand to be happy for someone else, couldn't he?

"You should go to her," Larylis said.

"I will. Perhaps in a few months after you're settled—"

"No, you should go to her now. Leave in the morning with Lord Ulrich."

Teryn blinked a few times, shifting from foot to foot again. "I can't go now. You need me. There's so much I haven't told you about running our kingdom, so much I've yet to pass on. Moreover, Lord Ulrich would never allow me to come. Verdian is determined to punish us, and I doubt Ulrich would act against his brother's wishes."

Larylis' heart sank. Teryn was right. Verdian wanted his daughter punished by sending her to Ridine. He wanted Larylis punished by keeping him from his wife. And Teryn...did Verdian realize keeping him from Cora was punishment too? Larylis wasn't even sure Teryn realized as much. Whatever the case, he didn't think he was ready to face Verdian's wrath. Larylis may soon be king, but Verdian was his father-in-law. He'd witnessed both the power and rage such a familial tie could bring when Queen Bethaeny's father threatened war when Arlous tried to divorce her. But still...Larylis' crown had to be good for something.

"Then wait a few days and leave on your own. You are the least beholden to Verdian. And is it not essential we secure an alliance with Khero? If you're deter-mined to do it in person, then I say it's a pressing matter."

Teryn's expression brightened, his lips quirking into the ghost of a grin. "You really think so?"

Larylis straightened, shoulders squared. "As your king, I command it." It felt like a mockery to refer to himself as king, but he supposed he should start getting used to it.

"Very well," Teryn said, "but if I am to listen to a damn word you say, you better get to the Godskeep before Mareleau wears a hole straight through the floor with her pacing."

Larylis forced a smile. "Deal."

Together, they left the crypts and ascended the stairs to the hall outside the Godskeep. There he found his wife, a vision in white silk, her shoulders adorned in a velvet cape. A queen's cape. Just as Teryn had said, she was pacing frantically across the floor. She paused when she caught sight of him. His heart lurched in his chest as their eyes met. Her gaze held a question steeped in worry, laced with trep-idation.

He knew then how much his distance these last few days had hurt her. Knew how selfish he'd been in clinging to his pain. He wasn't ready to let go of it completely, but he could push it aside, just enough so she could fit beside it.

His valet approached him with the royal cape—red with sable trim to match Mareleau's—while a servant darted forth with a brush for his coat, frowning at the thin layer of dust Larylis had accumulated from the crypts. Larylis stepped past both of them, heading straight for Mareleau instead. He didn't stop until she was against him, until both his hands had framed her face, and her soft lips were pressed to his. She met his kiss first with tense surprise, then with yielding. He felt her smile against his mouth, felt her grip tighten around his waist. With every tender brush of his lips, he conveyed his apology, his love, his promise.

I'll never push you away, he thought. *I'll make today count. And when it's time to go to Ridine for the signing of the peace pact, I'll be ready to bring you home.*

His valet cleared his throat while Mareleau's ladies giggled. He reluctantly pulled away from the woman he loved. She smiled at him and he let himself grin right back.

This. He'd let himself enjoy this. He may not deserve it, but damn it, Teryn was right. *She* did. His fierce, beautiful, devious wife deserved his love.

They faced the closed doors and let their servants clean them up once more. Then they entered the Godskeep hand in hand and claimed their burdensome crowns together.

11

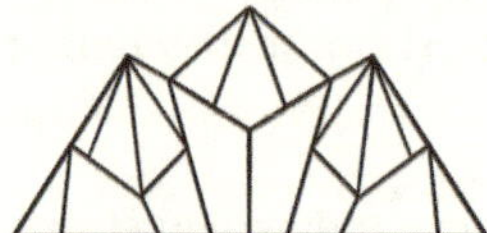

Cora's arrival at Ridine Castle felt less like coming home and more like stumbling upon a traveling circus. The location was familiar but had been transformed by the uncanny. As she entered the great hall with her brother, she found it looked nothing like the understaffed castle Morkai had brought her to, nor the dark, chilling place of her once-constant nightmares. It bustled with activity, much like it had during her childhood, but with unfamiliar faces.

Servants and staff bowed low as Lord Kevan barked orders and made introductions. Chests and furnishings were brought in from the wagons that were being unloaded in the courtyard. The chaos was so unsettling, Cora found her shields weakening. She took a deep breath to steady her nerves and forced herself to focus on the latest introduction.

An older man with a slim build and kind face greeted her and her brother with a bow. "Your Majesty. Your Highness. I am Master Arther, your new steward."

Cora nodded in greeting, then faced Lord Kevan. "Has Lord Ulrich already come?"

"No," Kevan said, "we are not expecting him for another three days at least."

Cora furrowed her brow. If Ulrich hadn't arrived with the rest of their newly appointed staff and councilmen, then who were all these people? Neither Master Arther nor half of those scuttling about the halls had come with her retinue. None showed any familiarity with Dimetreus but seemed well enough acquainted with Kevan. That meant they hadn't served under her brother when Morkai had had the run of the castle. Considering how empty Ridine had been the last time she'd been here, it was no surprise it required an overhaul of staff. Still, she hadn't expected it to have been done in her and Dimetreus' absence.

When Kevan didn't elaborate, she turned a questioning look to her brother.

Dimetreus released a grumbling sigh. "King Verdian seized control of Ridine immediately after the battle," he said, speaking low. "He'd already had it restaffed before we'd come to our agreement."

A spike of indignation surged through her blood. While she understood Verdian's suspicion over her brother's involvement with Morkai, it felt wrong that he'd taken over Ridine Castle so prematurely. It served to remind her that until the peace pact was officially signed, she and Dimetreus were essentially on probation. Should they give Verdian—or his brothers—any reason to doubt their innocence, he could pull Khero right out from under their grasp.

Kevan narrowed his eyes at Dimetreus. "Yes, and you should be quite thankful for my brother's generosity. Had he not acted when he did, you'd be coming home to cobwebs."

"I am ever so grateful," Dimetreus said through his teeth. This was the first sign Cora had seen to suggest he might share in Cora's annoyance. For the most part, he'd demonstrated nothing but eager submission and a willingness to comply with whatever was demanded of him. She studied him closer and saw a tic forming at the corner of his jaw.

Lurel bounded up to Cora, her face alight with a wide smile. "You're home, Your Highness! How does it feel? I bet you missed it greatly. You haven't been back to Ridine in so long, have you?"

Cora nearly admitted that it hadn't been long at all but decided against it. She hadn't shared many personal details with her lady's maid, so all the girl knew about Cora's past was whatever was being said through gossip. Kevan had urged Cora and Dimetreus to speak little of recent events until they could hold a council meeting and agree upon the official story that would be publicly shared. That meeting, however, couldn't commence until the rest of the council arrived with Lord Ulrich.

Lurel glanced around the great hall, her smile shifting into something like a grimace. "It's rather...different from Verlot, isn't it?"

"Different is a word for it," Cora said. She'd been too consumed with her and Dimetreus' fates to appreciate the luxury of Verlot Palace, but as she stared at the plain stone walls, bare wooden beams, and flagstone floor, she couldn't help but admit Ridine left much to be desired.

Lurel bounced on the balls of her feet. "We can spruce things up, Highness. You're the lady of the castle. It will be up to you to bring a..." She trailed off, frowning at a faded tapestry bearing a gruesome hunting scene that hung on the wall beside them. Her expression brightened as she met Cora's eyes with a hopeful smile. "A feminine touch. That is what you'll bring."

"Your composure, Lurel," Kevan said, tone gruff.

Lurel pursed her lips, steeling her features. In a softer voice, she said to Cora, "Might I take your cloak and riding gloves, Highness?"

"Oh...yes." Even after spending over two weeks with a lady's maid, she was still unused to being waited upon. Lurel unclasped Cora's cloak and slid it from her shoulders while Cora peeled off her riding gloves. As she handed them to Lurel, she caught sight of Kevan staring at her bare hands, her tattooed palms now visible.

His lip curled behind his bushy beard as he addressed his daughter. "From now on, Lurel, be sure to keep an extra pair of gloves on hand so the princess always has something to change into."

Cora bristled at the disdain in his voice. Was the sight of her tattoos so repulsive to him? Her palms tingled as if the magic thrumming through her veins wanted to show him exactly what he should fear. But the fiery urge quickly cooled to a simmer. She'd already chosen to bury her magic when she'd asserted her innocence before the inquisitors, convincing them her *insigmora* were simply traditional markings borne by the peaceful commune that had provided her sanctuary for six years. When she'd been pressed for more information regarding their magic, she'd feigned ignorance, claiming she knew nothing of magic herself. She'd sensed her questioners' approval then, which had made Cora wonder if they cared less about the truth and more about her delivery of acceptable answers.

A rebellious fire burned in her belly. Holding his gaze, she rolled up the sleeves of her riding habit, showing off more of the black ink.

With a derisive snort, Kevan gave a shallow bow and departed.

"Your Majesty, Your Highness, shall I show you to your rooms?" Master Arther said. "I imagine you must be tired from your journey."

"I may have what many consider a befuddled mind, but I know how to find my own living quarters," Dimetreus said, tone sharp enough to stiffen Cora's spine.

Arther paled. "Yes, Majesty, I understand. It's just...very few of the rooms had been kept with much care. We've focused our efforts on preparing living spaces for our most prominent residents, but not all rooms are ready for occupation. We are awaiting delivery of fresh linens before we can finish the rest of the rooms. In the meantime, we have assigned sleeping quarters that may not be what you were used to."

Dimetreus rubbed his brow and forced a smile. "Of course. Lead the way."

Cora eyed her brother as Arther led her, Dimetreus, and Lurel upstairs. Dimetreus seemed to have grown fatigued since stepping foot inside the castle. The tic still pulsed at the corner of his jaw, and his shoulders were nearly to his ears. "Are you all right?" she whispered.

He grunted his assurance, but Cora wasn't so convinced.

She continued to watch him carefully as they proceeded past a dimly lit portion of the keep which was clearly uninhabited. The only light came from the pink blush of the setting sun that peeked through the occasional window.

Lurel wrinkled her nose and muttered something about a draft. She edged closer to Cora, hugging Cora's cloak close to her chest. "I certainly hope the whole castle isn't always this cold. It is summer, after all."

They approached a well-lit hall that Cora was quite familiar with. One end led to her childhood bedroom, the largest guest bedrooms, and the king's suite. As for the other end...

Cora's pulse quickened as Arther turned to the left and entered another corridor.

Her feet rooted in place. Shadows gathered at the corners of her vision, her heart thumping with a dread she hadn't felt since her last nightmare. Her sleep had been mostly dreamless since Morkai's death, but now her mind rang with echoes of the past.

She knew where this hall led. Knew it ended in a single door. A bed.

And blood. So much blood—

Dimetreus stumbled, his hand clutching his chest. In an instant, Cora's mind returned to the present. As her vision regained its focus, she found her brother's face, twisted with anguish.

Arther doubled back, seeing that they were no longer following him. "Is everything all right, Your Majesty?"

Dimetreus' voice came out strained. "Why isn't there a wall here?" He blinked hard several times. "I...I thought there was a wall. This hall isn't supposed to exist."

Arther frowned. "There was no wall, Majesty. This hall was crowded with dusty furniture, but—"

Before Cora could think to stop him, Dimetreus charged past Arther into the corridor. Belatedly, she started after him, ignoring how the walls felt as if they were closing in on her. On trembling legs, she reached the dreaded door.

And found her brother slumped in the doorway.

Cora's first reaction was relief. The room inside looked nothing like the one from her nightmare. The bed had been moved from its previous location, the linens elegant and new. Violet brocade curtains were drawn open to welcome the last glow of sunlight as it dipped behind the Cambron Mountains.

Cora's muscles uncoiled as every remnant of fear faded away. In its place, calm settled over her, and her attention narrowed on her brother. She approached him with slow steps.

He held his face in his hands while his shoulders heaved with sobs. "Linette!" he wailed.

Cora reached out a timid hand and let it hover just above his shoulder. She wasn't used to comforting others. Over the last six years, she hadn't allowed herself to become close to anyone but Maiya and Salinda. Sympathy had become something she'd refused to accept. In turn, she wasn't sure if she knew how to give it.

Then she recalled the way she'd opened up to Valorre as her friend. The softness that had melted her heart when she and Teryn rescued the baby unicorn. The fierce protectiveness she'd felt when Teryn was wounded at the battle.

She had been capable of sympathy, kindness, and care, even when she hadn't meant to be.

Right now, her brother needed that from her.

She let her hand fall the rest of the way onto his shoulder. "Dimi."

He cried harder as he angled his head toward her. "I remember. I remember it, Aveline." He pointed to the room. "You were there. And I thought...oh, seven gods, I let him convince me..."

"It's all right," she whispered over the lump in her throat.

"You tried to tell me. You tried, and I...I ordered you to the dungeon. I condemned you to die."

"It's over now."

He leaned against the doorframe, shoulders slumped. "But then...then I saw your body. You'd died too." His eyes met hers, and there was a wild quality in them. "You'd died, Aveline. I saw that too. I saw—" He blinked hard several times, his body trembling with convulsions.

Lurel came up beside them while Arther wrung his hands farther down the hall. Lurel's face was pale as she watched the king. She pointed a thumb over her shoulder. "I should go. I must tell my father the king is unwell."

An urgent feeling, a clairsentient warning, had Cora rounding on the girl. She wasn't sure why she was suddenly so panicked, until something dawned on her.

Verdian's threat echoed in her mind.

If Dimetreus' council deems him incapable of the crown at any point, he will be forced to abdicate at once.

"You will not," Cora said, pinning the girl with a hard look. "This is a private matter. The king is grieving."

"But...but my father asked me to report to him if—"

"I don't care what he asked of you. You will not embarrass the king in his time of need. You will stay here until he has recovered and speak not a word of this incident."

Lurel worried her lip. Even through her shields, Cora could feel the girl's conflict. Lurel desperately wanted Cora to like her but knew better than to disobey her father.

Cora softened her tone. "I'm sure your father only had the king's best interests in mind when he asked you to report on his actions, but this isn't the kind of situation he meant. This is simply grief. You don't understand my brother's complex past nor the dark history this castle bears, and to spread word of this would be a great dishonor to the king you now serve."

Lurel sank to her knees, head bowed. "Forgive me, Highness. I didn't mean to offend you or the king. I'm sure you're right."

Cora stalked past Lurel toward the steward. "Master Arther, how about we show *you* where our rooms are, and if they are not ready for us, then do whatever it takes to have them prepared by the end of the day." She was surprised at the demand in her voice. It was a tone she hadn't spoken with since she was a child. Or perhaps the few times she'd argued with Teryn.

Master Arther straightened and gave her a nod. "It will be done, Your Highness."

Satisfied that she had the situation under control, she returned to her brother. Doing nothing more than resting her hand on his shoulder, she let him cry. Let him grieve the memories that pained him and rail against the ones he'd lost. She kept her eyes dry, her composure strong.

Later, she told herself. Later she'd let herself cry too.

Now there was work to be done.

12

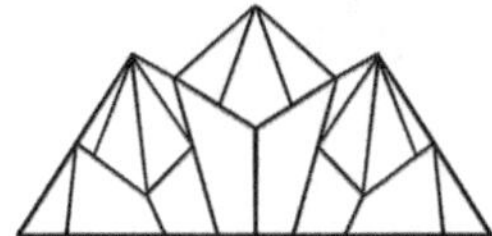

Mareleau never imagined she could be so physically close to a person yet feel so lonely. But as she rolled from side to side on the old mattress, sandwiched between her lady's maids, lonely was all she felt. She wanted her husband. The bed they'd shared at Dermaine Palace. Not these three snoring harpies and a stale bedroom.

She rolled onto her opposite side, wincing as the wooden bedframe creaked in response to her movement. Ann mumbled in her sleep, Sera erupted with a gasping snore, and Breah's arm flew across Mareleau's face. Mareleau sat up with a scoff and cut a glare at the three sleeping girls. How could they sleep in accommodations as shoddy as this? Their rooms back at Verlot were almost as nice as her own. Yet there they were dozing like three baby pigs in a stall.

A stall. Yes, that was all she could say of this room. It certainly wasn't appropriate for a supposedly pregnant woman, much less a queen. This wasn't the first time she'd been relegated to such accommodations during her recent travels either. Instead of staying at grand estates and being hosted by lords, viscounts, and barons, she's been shuttled from one inn to the next. They were fine inns, she supposed, but they were nothing like what she was used to. She wasn't sure whether she had her father's malice or her new kingdom's lesser financial wealth to blame for her environment, but she suspected it was the former.

She gritted her teeth as her eyes shot to the closed door of the tiny bedroom. She was tempted to stomp across the hall to Lord Ulrich's room, pound on his door, and demand he find private lodgings for her at once. But she knew it would do no good. Her uncle never had much patience for her before, and his opinion of her seemed little improved now that she was queen. If anything, it had the opposite effect. At least they were finally nearing the end of their journey.

An unsettling question came to mind. Would Ridine be any better? It was a castle, not a palace, after all. A structure built for defense. With a sigh, she laid back down only to find Breah had taken up more space in Mareleau's absence. Cursing under her breath, she stood and grabbed her cloak, wrapping it tightly around her as she crept from the room.

The hall outside was chilly, lit with a single lamp. She made her way down the stairs and into the empty dining room. The clang of pots and pans and the giggling voices of maids echoed from the kitchen. Dinner had been hours ago, and since Ulrich had had the decency to buy out the inn for the night, there were no other guests lingering about. She went to the hearth and pulled up a chair next to the dying embers. A shiver ran through her, and she pulled her cloak even tighter around her nightdress.

Now that she was fully alone, her annoyance began to fade, replaced with the full weight of what lurked just beneath it: loneliness.

Mareleau had never considered herself a friendly person. The last friend she'd had—a former lady's maid named Katra—had dallied with one of her suitors. She wouldn't have cared much, had the man not been the only person she'd been even remotely attracted to after Larylis. The memory filled her with guilt now that she and Larylis were together at last, but at the time, that mild attraction had felt like hope. What Katra had done had broken something inside her. She hadn't realized it before. She'd been too preoccupied with the Heart's Hunt. Then the threat of war. Then her plot to marry Larylis.

In the wake of everything she'd won and everything she'd risked, now that she was away from the man she loved and the two parents who despised her, she felt that gaping void like never before. It was a hollow ache, one that made her shrink into herself as if that could close it.

She hugged her arms around her torso, then startled as the kitchen doors swung open. In an instant, she sat up straight, evoking her *magic trick* to help her appear calm. Collected. Regal. A maid left the kitchen, arms full of clean plates, and tossed a snide remark over her shoulder. It was met with much laughter from the other maids. As the girl fully entered the dining room, she caught sight of Mareleau. The smile disappeared from her face. In a rush, she set the plates on the counter and hurried to Mareleau. With a low curtsy, she said, "Forgive me, Your Majesty. We weren't expecting anyone to be awake. What can I get for you?"

"It's all right," Mareleau said curtly. "I need nothing but what you cannot provide."

The girl took that as her dismissal and scurried back into the kitchen. Mareleau heard no more giggles or gossip from behind the door after that. She settled back into her chair, sulking into the backrest, and reached into her cloak. From within, she withdrew a folded piece of parchment. The sight of her name written in a familiar script was enough to fill her heart with warmth and longing in equal measure. Larylis had pressed the letter into her hand before she'd left Dermaine for her journey north. She'd waited until she'd been alone the first night before reading it. Gods, was she glad that she did. For no sooner than she'd read the first sentence had her chest heaved with a sob.

With a deep breath, she opened it now. Tears welled in her eyes as she read the words her heart had already committed to memory.

Mareleau,

For all the letters we didn't write over the last three years, I will write you a thousand more. For every kiss we didn't share while we were apart, I will give you a million kisses more. And every moment you doubt my love, remember my heart is yours. These seconds may be torture while you're away, but my love will only grow.

It will grow, Mareleau.

I will be waiting.

Writing.

Loving you.

Forever and always yours,

Larylis

She reread the words over and over until her eyes were raw and her lungs were sore from silent sobbing. When she could no longer handle being so ridiculously pathetic, she refolded the paper with care and tucked it back into her pocket. Wiping at the moisture on her cheeks, she stood to return to her room—only to sink back into her seat as the dining room door opened.

The old innkeeper entered, followed by a hooded traveler. Mareleau kept still in her chair, hoping they wouldn't notice her in the dark room. After crying like a wailing babe, she had no desire to speak to anyone, nor did she have the energy to control her composure. "We weren't expecting you, Your Highness," the innkeeper said, his tone laced with anxiety. "You didn't arrive with the others."

"Others?"

Mareleau's spine went rigid. The voice was gratingly familiar. She turned in her seat, getting a clearer look at the newcomer as the innkeeper led him through the dining room. Sure enough, just as they turned toward the stairs, she caught sight of his profile.

She rose to her feet and planted her hands on her hips. "What the hell are you doing here?"

Teryn startled. With a frown, he faced her.

The innkeeper shrank down, eyes darting between the two of them. "Is the prince not of your party, Your Majesty?"

"That depends," she said through her teeth. "Did he come alone?" Hope threatened to swell in her chest as she awaited his answer. *Please say Larylis is here. Please.*

"Yes, I came alone."

Her heart plummeted to her feet, and rage funneled in its place. "No, he does not belong to my party, and my uncle gave you orders not to allow anyone else to stay here tonight."

The innkeeper opened his mouth but Teryn spoke first. "Might I have a word with the queen?"

She lifted her chin, tempted to deny him. She wasn't even sure what drove her sudden rage. Teryn was only guilty of the same crime she'd always accused him of. Not being Larylis. But he wasn't a threat to her happiness anymore, was he?

"Very well," she said.

The innkeeper bowed low and rushed from the room as if he were eager to be anywhere else.

Mareleau repeated her question. "What are you doing here?"

Teryn gave her a bewildered look. "What are *you* doing here? Ulrich has you staying at an inn? I thought you'd be hosted by nobles."

She crossed her arms. "You don't need to rub it in. Besides, I asked you first. I am your queen, remember?"

He glanced around the empty room, then released a heavy breath. "I'm heading for Ridine to speak with Princess Aveline. I'd meant to follow behind your retinue and arrive afterward, but it appears I've caught up too quickly. Promise me you won't tell your uncle I'm here."

"Why shouldn't I? I was ordered to go on this journey against my will, and you were told to remain at Dermaine. Why should I, the queen, follow orders while you get to break them? Why should I be separated from my husband—" She cut off as her voice broke on the last word.

His face softened. "Larylis wishes he were with you, trust me. I haven't seen him so morose, since...ever. He doesn't want to risk going against your father. I, on the other hand, have less to lose. For now."

She averted her gaze. "It isn't fair, you know."

"I know it isn't." He took a few steps closer. "I also understand why you resent me. If I'd known about you and Larylis..." His lips quirked into a wry grin, one that reminded her too much of his brother. "Please don't take this the wrong way, but I never wanted to marry you either. I found the prospect just as awful as you did."

She was overcome with a sudden urge to bark a laugh. Her animosity softened at the edges, making her wonder if Teryn hadn't been her enemy all along.

"Can we be allies? We are brother and sister now. Plus, you owe me." His smile turned devious.

She could tell he was teasing, but she didn't feel generous enough to play along. Instead, she pursed her lips and burned him with a scowl.

He wasn't the least bit cowed. "Don't you agree? I helped you marry the love of your life."

That managed to weaken her resolve.

"Can I count on you to keep my presence here a secret from your uncle? I promise not to show up at your next stop. I'll simply stick to far finer establishments."

She snorted a begrudging laugh at that. "That will certainly keep you from wherever Ulrich has me sleeping."

He raised a brow, reminding her she had yet to answer his question.

She rolled her eyes. "Fine, I won't tell Ulrich." It was almost painful to say. Everything inside her wanted to see him punished as badly as her. But she reminded herself of what he'd given up. He'd abdicated, set aside his crown, his birthright, for Larylis. To clear the final obstacle that had kept them from being together. Uncrossing her arms, she let her shoulders relax and tried to smile. All she managed was a grimace. "So...I have a brother now?"

"Unfortunately for us both, you do."

"Ugh. I never wanted one." She brushed past him and ascended the stairs. Despite her abrupt last words to him, she was surprised to find the aching void in her heart had lessened. Whether it was due to reading Larylis' letter or entertaining the prospect of having a new—albeit unwanted—brother, she knew not. All she knew was that, as she climbed back into bed between her annoyingly peaceful lady's maids, she felt a little less alone.

13

Cora wasn't sure why she chose to return to her childhood bedroom. She could have had her pick of rooms, ones that didn't bear memories of the last time she was here, dressing in a gown in preparation to meet her brother for the first time in six years, only to find him controlled by dark magic. Nor the time before that, when she'd pouted on her bed after pretending to curse the queen. The queen who'd later died...

She shook the morbid memories from her mind and returned her attention to the present. She sat at her vanity while Lurel brushed her hair. Even after two days back at the castle, she still wasn't used to being waited on like this. Dressed. Brushed. Bathed. Forced to sit idly while others served her. It aggravated her, reminded her that this princess persona was all an act, made her want to flee the confines of the castle walls and leave this curated world of cruel politics and false politeness behind.

This is all for Dimetreus, she told herself. *It's for the sake of Khero.*

Lurel continued to comb Cora's hair, a task that seemed endless despite the girl tending to it twice a day. Cora's eyes darted toward the window and the glow of the setting sun. It was a most welcome sight, for as soon as night fell, Cora had plans to escape the castle and throw off the guise of princess. Temporarily, of course, but the thought had her antsy with anticipation.

She was desperate to be surrounded by trees, close to the elements the Forest People had taught her to revere. To feel her magic buzz around her so she could embody the witch she was. It was a part of herself she couldn't fully let go of, only hide, betray, and publicly refute. All for the sake of being a princess and proving to those who distrusted her that she was nothing like Morkai. If only she could trust *them* to understand that there was a stark difference between witch magic—*quiet magic*—and the sinister sorceries the duke had dabbled in.

But no, they did not understand. Which meant if she wanted to utilize the Arts in any obvious way, she needed to do it where no one would see her. That was exactly what she intended to do tonight. Once she was in the woods, she could perform a clearing ritual on Morkai's crystal.

There was an additional reason she was eager to sneak out tonight: to see her unicorn friend again.

Her knee began to jiggle, and she sat on her hands to keep from fidgeting. What she really wanted to do was shake off Lurel. The sooner the girl bid her goodnight, the sooner Cora could proceed with her plan. Still, she knew her maid was ordered by her father to keep a close eye on her. The last thing she needed was to cast herself under a suspicious light.

Lurel, though, seemed perfectly oblivious to Cora's anxious state. "How can your hair get so tangled after just a day?" she said with a grunt as she worked at a large knot at the end of Cora's dark tresses.

"Is that abnormal?" Cora asked.

"Perhaps I'm only used to Mareleau's hair. Her hair is always tangled in random braids by the end of the night, but her hair is smoother than yours and easier to brush."

Cora tried not to take offense at that, but any mention of Princess Mareleau— no, Queen Mareleau now—set her teeth on edge. She still couldn't shake their first meeting and the woman's icy demeanor. Worse was the fact that she was expected to arrive at the castle in the next few days.

"Why was the king so distraught yesterday, Your Highness?"

Cora tensed at the unexpected question.

When Lurel received no answer, she elaborated. "When we went to...to that room. You said he was grieving and that I didn't understand his complex past or the castle's dark history. What did you mean by that?"

Cora considered not answering. It wasn't Lurel's business, after all. But if it helped the girl understand the king, then perhaps she'd take her duties to spy on Cora and Dimetreus less seriously. "His wife died in that room."

"Oh my. Queen Linette, right? That was a tragedy. But you were said to have died that night too. If you're still alive...what really happened?"

Cora narrowed her eyes at the girl's reflection in the mirror, wondering if she was testing Cora's response at the command of her father. Lord Kevan had insisted she not speak about her false death, disappearance, or resurrection until after their council meeting could commence. Cora opened her senses to her maid but found only naive curiosity in her emotions. Regardless, she'd follow Lord Kevan's rules. Until the peace pact was signed, she had to toe a fine line. "I'm not at liberty to say."

Her lips curled into a frown. "Father won't tell me either. All I hear is rumors from the staff. Is there anything you *can* tell me? Is it true what they're saying about your brother?"

Again, Cora's muscles tensed. "Who's *they* and what are they saying about him?"

"Well, I've heard some of the servants whispering that a sorcerer had chained the king in the dungeon for several years and was acting as the king in his stead, and that the mage is the one who instigated the battle at Centerpointe Rock, not the king. Others say the king was working alongside the sorcerer and truly wanted to conquer Menah and Selay. The oddest rumor is that the king was being puppeteered by dark magic and hasn't had control of his mind or body for countless years. Almost all accounts claim Duke Morkai was the evil mage. That paired with the tales I've managed to overhear about the battle makes me wonder if it's true. Were there truly...ghosts on the battlefield?"

Lurel paused her brushing and met Cora's eyes in the mirror. Her face was pale but there was a note of excitement playing around her mouth.

"Again, I am not at liberty to speak on such matters until I've had further counsel with your father."

Lurel resumed brushing, shoulders slumped. "I thought you might say that. Well, what about the rumors regarding the North Tower Library?"

Cora's blood went cold. "What about it?"

"Is it truly haunted? I heard we aren't allowed to go in there. Naturally, some of the servants are speculating that there's a ghost in the tower, and that if we open the door, it will come out and terrorize the castle. Sometimes I think I'd give anything to see a ghost. It would be a fright, but...oh, there's just something so romantic about a haunted castle, isn't there?"

Cora couldn't agree. She'd seen wraiths, souls of the dead reanimated to fight living men. There was nothing romantic about watching men get cut down by spectral blades.

"You must have been to the tower yourself. This was your childhood home! Tell me, is there really a ghost? Perhaps the spirit of the dead queen—"

"Lurel." Cora whirled in her chair to face the girl, pinning her with a stern look.

Lurel took a step back, cradling the brush against her chest. "I'm being insensitive, aren't I? I'm so sorry, Your Highness. Mareleau was always saying as much, so I suspect it must be true. I was always either annoying, insensitive, or too weak-minded, according to her. I beg your forgiveness, Highness. I seem to forget myself around you."

Cora clenched her jaw at being compared to Mareleau. She gentled her tone. "You're just getting a little carried away. The North Tower Library is not haunted."

"Then why are we forbidden from entering it?"

Cora imagined it was because Morkai's belongings were still there. She remembered what the room had looked like when the duke had brought her there for a tense chat. He'd turned the library into his personal study and filled it with an array of ominous-looking books and vials of strange liquids. With Master Arther so focused on preparing the living quarters in the castle, it stood to reason that other parts of the castle had yet to be touched. She couldn't blame anyone for wanting to avoid the library for as long as possible.

"The library is dirty, that's all," Cora said. "Until the room has been cleaned, it poses a hazard."

Lurel's expression fell as if the answer disappointed her. Cora turned back around to face the mirror and let Lurel resume brushing. The girl's moves were slower this time, distracted.

Finally, Lurel spoke, her voice small. "Can I stay in your room again tonight? I know I only stayed last night because I didn't have a room of my own yet, but all this talk about ghosts has me frightened."

Cora assessed the girl in the mirror with a quirked brow. "Your room has been furnished now. Besides, I thought haunted castles were romantic."

"Yes, but in a morbid sort of way, and...well, if I'm being honest, Father told me to stay with you again."

"To spy on me."

"Highness, please don't hate me for what he's asked of me. I have no intention of betraying you, but—just like my cousin has always said—I am weak of mind, and I find it rather difficult to say no."

Cora's lips flattened into a line. She just had to bring up Mareleau again. Every mention of the woman had Cora itching to prove she was the opposite. She sat up straighter. "You aren't weak-minded, Lurel. Your father is a powerful man and he has his reasons for distrusting me and my brother."

"But I don't distrust you in the least. Either way, you're a princess. Should you demand it, I'll go to my own room. Although...I really have put myself ill at ease about the ghosts, especially now that I know about...about the queen's room." Lurel's voice climbed higher until it ended in a squeak. "My quarters are in that hall."

Cora nibbled her bottom lip and cast a glance at the setting sun once more. Lurel's presence would put a hitch in her plans. It was why she hadn't snuck out to clear the crystal the night before. But at least she'd determined that Lurel was a deep sleeper. The girl had spent most of the night snoring from the other side of the large bed. Cora had tested her ease of waking when she'd left the room to visit the toilet, but Lurel had remained in the depths of slumber.

Cora released a resigned sigh. "You can stay."

～

It was nearing midnight when Cora finally left her room. Dressed in her shift and teal riding cloak, the amber crystal weighing down one of her pockets, she entered the hall outside her room, finding it empty. Her shields were down, allowing her to sense nearby emotion, but every strain of feeling that reached her was calm. Muted by sleep. On silent feet, she crept down the stairs. Unlike when Morkai had the run of the castle, there weren't guards pacing every corridor, so she didn't have to worry about evading them. In contrast, the castle was far more heavily staffed than it had been under the duke, which made the servants' passage a risk. So instead, she kept close to the walls, kept her shields down, and made her way straight from the keep to the kitchen.

Her heart climbed into her throat as she tiptoed out the same door she'd fled through when she'd escaped the dungeon, following the same path that led to the ivy-covered gap in the castle wall. She wrapped the elements around her, concealing her, masking the sounds of her steps. It might have been an unnecessary precaution, considering she'd yet to come across anyone, but the memory of what she was doing now echoed the escape she'd made almost two months ago, reminding her of when sentries stalked the wall, when a beastly creature shadowed her steps, pursuing her into the crevice—

She took a deep breath, forcing herself to pause and look around. This was not the Ridine Castle she'd escaped from. Morkai's men weren't patrolling the wall this time, only a few bored sentries near the gate. And the Roizan wasn't nipping at her heels. It was gone. Dead. Like Morkai.

With her nerves settled, she proceeded the rest of the way to the wall and located the opening. The narrow crevice wasn't the most welcoming of places, but it was her ticket to momentary freedom. Shoving the ivy aside, she plunged into the dark fissure.

14

Anxiety tickled Cora's chest the deeper she went into the pitch-black crevasse, but soon a calming presence cut through every dark emotion.

I'm here, Valorre said from the other side of the wall.

Emboldened, Cora rushed the rest of the way out of the opening and found her friend standing on the other side. The moonlight glinted upon the slender horn at the center of his head and sent his white coat gleaming. Her heart swelled in her chest as a sudden wave of emotion constricted her throat. This was the first time she'd laid eyes on Valorre since the battle.

She was so relieved, so overjoyed at seeing him that she ran to him at once. He startled only a little as she threw her arms around his thick neck and buried her face into his hide. It wasn't something she'd done before. Valorre wasn't a pet, after all, but a fae creature. A person. And his temperament wasn't always cuddly. But Cora couldn't find it in her to care. Not with his soft coat pressed against her cheek, the aromas of dirt, leaves, and soil surrounding her, wrapping her in a blanket that felt so much more like home than a dusty castle did.

Yes, I am quite soft, aren't I? Valorre said, bumping her shoulder with his muzzle. *You will find the base of my ears are soft too. Perhaps you can scratch them?*

With a chuckle, she stepped back and gave in to his request. "I missed you, Valorre. I...I think you're my best friend."

Ah. That's nice. Teryn is my best friend.

She halted her scratching, mouth falling open as her euphoric joy turned to indignation. "Teryn? Why the Mother Goddess is he your best friend? You hardly know him."

He rippled with something like laughter. *I think it's called humor.*

She blinked at him a few times, at the twinkle in his russet eyes, and arched a brow. "You were teasing me."

It was fun.

"Then I am your best friend, right?"

Yes, I suppose you are.

She rolled her eyes at his begrudging tone. "So, you've been so bored without me that you learned humor in my absence. How does that work? Aren't fae creatures unable to lie?"

That sounds false to me.

"Well, it was a very rude joke. Teryn, of all people." Her heart stuttered. Even saying the prince's name brought to mind their last encounter. The anger she'd expressed to him. Her humiliation over having been promised to his brother at his behest. The note he'd sent that she'd thrown in the fire. The meeting he'd requested that she never attended. What was it he'd wanted to tell her?

You miss him too. Like you missed me.

She forced her thoughts away and scoffed. "Why would I miss him?"

Well, your heart gets quite loud and thuddy whenever you or I mention him. And I know you often think about that time when he put his mouth on your mouth—

"How do you know about that?"

Ah, yes, and then you get angry and admiring the same way you did whenever you saw him without a shirt—

"Let's stop talking about Teryn."

Valorre obeyed her request for all of five seconds. *But you do miss him, don't you?*

"No. I...why does it matter?"

You're my friend. He's my friend.

Cora waited for him to continue, but it seemed his explanation ended at that.

I'll make a bargain. Admit you miss him, and I'll let you ride on my back. He lifted his head, radiating pride if not a little arrogance.

Cora hadn't intended for a midnight ride when she'd planned on sneaking out of the castle. All she'd wanted was to greet her friend, surround herself with trees, and drink in moonlight. That and find a quiet place to perform an energy clearing ritual on the crystal, of course. She'd made a habit of shoving her hand in her pocket to remind herself of its existence. It continued to unsettle her how easy it was to forget.

Still, it wasn't absolutely dire that she perform the ritual right away. She could ride first. In fact, it might help her find the perfect place to proceed with her chore. The thought of speeding through the trees on Valorre's back, neither racing for their lives nor traveling with any destination in mind, was too good to resist.

However, something told Cora the unicorn wasn't going to compromise on his terms.

"Fine, Valorre," she muttered through her teeth, "I miss Teryn." She'd meant for her words to be meaningless, a way to get Valorre off the subject, but as soon as she said it, a thrum of truth warmed her chest, steadying her. Memories melted over her, of her and Teryn rescuing the baby unicorn. Of the two of them standing close while she used her magic to hide them under the tree. Of his lips on hers before she escaped the dungeon. Of the split second when she thought Queen Bethaeny was proposing a marriage alliance between Cora and Teryn.

I thought she meant you...

"I miss him, all right?" she said, voice firm and devoid of the emotions still playing inside her. "Are you satisfied now?"

Quite. Now climb up and I will remind you why I am so much stronger and better than the brainless creature you traveled here upon.

A wry grin curled a corner of her mouth. He really was a prideful creature. But if it garnered her a stolen moment of unbridled freedom, she'd play into that arrogance.

Valorre ducked his head, allowing her to gather his mane in her hands. No sooner than she was properly seated did he take off into the night. Shadows streamed past as the thud of the unicorn's hooves filled her ears, resounding against the beat of her heart, the exhilarating rush of her blood. Moonlight speckled the forest floor, and Cora let herself pretend—for a short time at least—that this was all that mattered.

∿

CORA WAS FULLY READY FOR SLEEP BY THE TIME VALORRE RETURNED HER TO THE castle wall. The ride had been exactly what she'd needed, and now she felt rejuvenated in a way that left her equally exhausted. Only when she was halfway back to the castle, hand tucked in her pocket, did she realize she'd never performed the clearing ritual. She'd forgotten about the crystal again.

She halted, glancing back at the wall. Her bones begged for sleep, and she had to admit her weary state would likely hinder any ritual she'd perform. Starting back toward the castle, she told herself she'd have to try again the next day. A day that was soon approaching dawn, now that she considered how long she'd been out. If she didn't get some sleep soon, she'd be miserable come morning.

And yet...

A strange feeling settled over her. Not for the first time she wondered whether the crystal was enchanted, making it slip from her mind far too easily. Just the thought of being touched by leftover strains of Morkai's magic made a shudder run through her. Her eyes flicked up to the North Tower Library, barely visible behind the other turrets and crenellations—

She froze, her heart leaping into her throat. Subtle illumination flickered beyond the library window, soft like candlelight. It was so faint, she tried to convince herself she was imagining it. But the longer she looked, the more certain she was. Someone was inside Morkai's tower.

∿

IT'S PROBABLY NOTHING, CORA TRIED TO TELL HERSELF AS SHE MADE HER WAY THROUGH the lower levels of the castle, past the kitchen and the staircase that led to the keep. But the hair bristling at the back of her neck, the hollow pit in her stomach, told her it wasn't nothing. This feeling wasn't just a tinge of unfounded fear. It was a clairsentient warning.

She hoped she was wrong. She hoped there was a reasonable explanation for why someone would be in the library—the very room Lurel had claimed was forbidden to castle staff—well after midnight. And someone *had* to be in there. Why else would there be a candle burning in a forbidden room at this hour?

Nausea turned her stomach as she reached the dark stairwell that led to the tower. She placed one foot on the bottom step but found her body unwilling to move. Breathing deep, she called upon the elements to steady her—air to fill her lungs, earth to anchor her feet, water to calm her emotions, and fire to fuel her resolve. It smoothed the edges of her growing fear, but pain pulsed at her temples, pounding with the effort it took to ward off darker memories...

Of her and Morkai, sitting in the room at the top of these very stairs...

The hulking shape of the Roizan curled on the floor...

The duke confessing secrets she still didn't understand...

His claim as an Elvyn prince.

The reasons behind his war.

A prophecy.

The unicorns. The mother. The child. Who do you think you are in that prophecy?

His offer to give her half his heart.

His threat to bind her fate to his in a blood weaving—

Cora closed her eyes and flung out a hand, pressing it to the cool stone of the stairwell. Her palm thrummed with the steadying energy of the stone. She felt it move through her hand, her arm, warming the inked designs of her tattoos until she managed to catch her breath.

He's gone, she told herself. *It's over. There's nothing to fear from him any longer.*

Swallowing hard, she forced herself to take the next step. Then the next. Soon the library door came into view. It was left partially open, and the same flickering light she'd glimpsed outside shone from beyond the door. Daring to open a hole in her mental shields, she extended her senses, seeking whoever might be inside. She connected with a familiar energy, someone she knew—

The door flung all the way open, and Lurel's silhouette shone against the candlelight behind her.

Cora sagged with relief. She wasn't sure what—or whom—she'd expected to find, but now that she saw her lady's maid, all her fears seemed embarrassingly irrational. *I'm a witch, damn it. I'm supposed to be stronger than fear.* Perhaps suppressing her magic, betraying her true nature, had made her soft.

Her internal chiding turned to concern as Lurel came rushing down the stairs, her shoulders trembling with silent sobs. Her moves were so erratic, so panicked, Cora feared the girl would tumble down the stairs.

"Lurel," Cora said softly, so as not to frighten her.

The girl let out a startled squeak, but as soon as she saw Cora—or whatever she could see of her in the dark stairwell—she heaved an audible whimper and rushed the rest of the way to her.

Lurel threw her arms around Cora in a relieved embrace.

Cora was stunned at the sudden hug, and for a few moments, she didn't know what to do. Then her softer instincts took over, ones she admittedly wasn't too well-practiced at, and she returned the embrace with a few consoling pats on the other girl's back. She kept her tone gentle as she asked, "Lurel, what are you doing here?"

"You were gone when I awoke," she said, heaving a sob. "You didn't come back and I...I couldn't sleep. I was worried about you so I went looking to see where you might have gone. Then...then I kept thinking about the tower. I was scared."

Cora placed her hands on Lurel's shoulders and gently put space between them. Lurel reluctantly released Cora. The faint candlelight still streaming from inside the room at the top of the stairs cast half of her maid's face in shadow, but it was enough to show the streams of tears running down her cheeks. "So you came to the very place you thought was haunted?"

"You said it wasn't, so I wanted to prove to myself it was nothing! Besides, what if it *was* haunted? What if you'd been taken in your sleep by the ghost? But then...I saw...I saw all those things..." She gestured toward the open door, eyes wide, and shuddered.

Cora nearly did the same at the haunted look in Lurel's eyes, but she forced herself to keep her composure.

Lurel wrenched her gaze from the room and returned her attention to Cora. Her face twisted as her sobs renewed. "I'm so sorry. I shouldn't have gone in there. Please forgive me."

A pinch of sorrow struck Cora's chest. She wasn't sure if it was her own emotion or Lurel's, but it softened her feelings for the girl. Lurel may be irritating at times, but she was sweet. Kind. Determined to be liked. And the poor thing was trembling with fear. Cora forced her lips into a reassuring smile. "It's all right, Lurel, you're not in trouble."

Lurel shook her head. "Something happened. I pricked my finger on a book when I tried to open it...and..." The girl wobbled on her feet, and one slipped off the edge of the stair. Cora caught her, but Lurel grew heavy in her arms, sinking down until she planted her bottom on the step.

Even sitting seemed too hard for Lurel. Her head hung low and she slumped against Cora. "I don't feel well, Highness," she said, voice weaker now.

Dread filled every inch of Cora's body. She shifted to the side and propped Lurel's shoulder against the wall of the stairwell. "Stay here. I'll get help—"

Lurel's eyes shot to Cora's. "Don't leave me."

Terror froze Cora in place. The candlelight from above still cast most of Lurel's face in shadow, but the portion it illuminated revealed her tears had grown tenfold.

No. Not tears.

Blood.

Rivulets of dark crimson turned black by the shadows of the stairwell trickled from the girl's eyes, her nose, the corners of her lips.

Lurel whimpered, then hung her head once more.

Cora couldn't cry, couldn't scream, couldn't move, could do nothing as she felt the emotion, the energy, and the life leave Lurel's body.

15

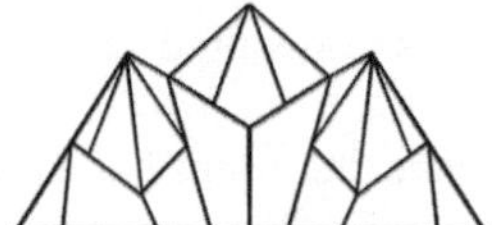

Cora was no stranger to death. It had first entered her life when her parents died. Next, it had arrived courtesy of Morkai when he'd murdered Queen Linette. More recently, she'd delivered several souls to death's door; first with Erwin, the hunter who'd tormented Valorre with an iron-barbed whip, then a camp of hunters, their rum poisoned by belladonna placed by Cora's own hand.

But this...

Lurel was different. Her death was senseless. Unfair. Untimely. Just like Cora's parents' deaths had been. Linette's too. And yet, Lurel's carried the same weight Erwin's and the hunters' did.

Because this too was Cora's fault.

Words of blame echoed around her, shouted by Lord Kevan. They resounded up the stairwell—now lit by several lanterns and the first blush of dawn peeking through the windows. All she could do was accept his condemnation. She couldn't refute what Lord Kevan was saying.

"She was supposed to stay with you. She was not to leave your side. Why was she in the tower? Why? *Why?*"

Because I told her it wasn't haunted, she said to no one as she let Kevan continue to shout at her. *Because I left the castle. Because Lurel woke up alone and came to find me.*

Her eyes stared sightlessly at the space where Lurel had lost her life. A stair now empty after the girl's body had been hauled away. By the time Cora had shouted for help, it had already been too late. Lurel had taken her last breath in Cora's arms.

"Look at me and give me a reason why my daughter is dead."

Cora managed to tear her gaze away from the empty stair to take in Kevan's stricken face. He stood several steps down from her, still dressed in his nightgown and robe. A robe that bore a crimson stain from where he'd cradled his daughter's face to his chest with a wail Cora could still hear piercing the air. His face was pale, his eyes rimmed with red. Sorrow poured out of him, slamming into Cora's threadbare mental shields and pummeling her with emotions that were not her own. Or perhaps they were. She was in a state of shock. Of numbness. Of feeling everything and nothing at once.

"Tell me why you're dressed in a riding cloak in the middle of the night."

The lie would be a simple one. *Lurel left my room in the middle of the night. I donned my cloak to go look for her.* But she couldn't utter the words.

Lord Kevan took a forbidding step up the stairs, his face contorted with rage. "Tell me why my daughter had blood streaming from her eyes! Give me an explanation, or for the love of the seven gods—"

"Lord Kevan."

Cora stiffened at her brother's voice. He hadn't been awoken when the chaos erupted, which meant he might not yet know what had happened. Kevan whirled to the side, revealing Dimetreus at the base of the stairs, shadowed by two guards.

"Watch your tone with my sister," Dimetreus said.

Kevan's chest heaved as he stared down at Dimetreus, but he managed to cut off his tirade.

"I've been informed a great tragedy has befallen us," Dimetreus said with gentle calm as he ascended the staircase, stopping when he was next to Cora. Placing himself at her side was a silent statement, demonstrating his support of Cora while reminding Lord Kevan of his place. Or what should be his place. Dimetreus' demeanor reminded her so much of the confident monarch he used to be that it cleared some of the grief clouding her mind. "You have my condolences, but please do not take your sorrows out on my sister. We are lucky she found Lady Lurel."

Kevan huffed. "Lucky. Perhaps you, Majesty, can shed some light on why my daughter was in the tower in the middle of the night."

"It is a fool's errand to seek such explanations, trust me." A note of sympathy deepened his voice. "My only guess is that she couldn't sleep. The library is stocked with ample reading material—"

"Reading material," Kevan echoed. "What in the name of the seven devils would she possibly have wanted to read in there? She was forbidden from stepping foot inside the cursed room. And...trust you? *Trust* you? You were in league with a sorcerer. Perhaps you still are. Perhaps you're the reason my daughter wept blood when she died."

"Wept blood," Dimetreus whispered, his face going a shade paler. "Cursed room."

Cora's stomach bottomed out. Whatever Dimetreus had been told about Lurel's death, he hadn't been given the whole story. A dark dread crept over her, clearing the remainder of her somber fog. This was not the time to get lost in her grief. In her guilt. She took a step closer to her brother and laid a gentle hand on his forearm. "Dimi."

He flinched at her touch and whirled to the side, casting a glance at the closed door at the top of the stairwell. His eyes grew wide. Haunted. "What significance does this room hold? Why was Lady Lurel forbidden from entering the North Tower Library?"

Kevan gave a disbelieving shake of his head. "You're going to claim ignorance about that too, then? That you had no idea your own library had been turned into a sorcerer's lair?"

Dimetreus flinched at his words, and he began to shrink in on himself. His regal demeanor drained to match the sudden pallor of his skin. "Sorcerer's lair?"

Cora put a hand on his shoulder and tried to turn him away from the door. "Dimi, let's leave the man to grieve alone," she whispered.

He ignored her, rounding on Kevan. "You said your daughter died with...with tears of blood. And that...that..." He gestured at the closed door, his throat bobbing. "Beyond that door is...*his* lair."

Kevan said nothing, only narrowed his eyes.

A tangled web of emotions—terror, confusion, panic—flooded Cora with a force that nearly made her knees buckle. She was still too raw, too drained, to strengthen her shields, but she breathed as much of the unwanted energy away and gripped her brother's arm tighter. "Dimetreus, we should go—"

He wrenched himself from her grip and cast another glance at the closed door. He trembled so hard he slipped down a step but caught himself against the wall before he could stumble down another. "He's here," the king muttered. "He's still here. We'll never be rid of him."

A low chuckle slipped from Kevan's lips, expression smug. "Ah, and now the king unravels. I've been waiting for this moment."

A spark of rage lit Cora's blood, burning away all her sympathy for the man. Her voice came out with a sharpened edge. "You are dismissed, Lord Kevan."

"I think not, Highness. It is my duty to make a sound judgment on the king's stability. You agreed to the terms. You know what will happen if your brother proves ill-suited to the crown."

She did know; Dimetreus could be forced to abdicate at any time.

Oblivious to her and Kevan's conversation, Dimetreus leaned against the wall and lowered himself onto one of the stairs. Cora tried not to think about how Lurel had done exactly that before she'd—

Cora shook her head, patting her brother's shoulder as he began to weep, his sobs punctured by a single name. "Linette. Linette. Oh, gods, I remember the blood."

Kevan lifted his chin and opened his mouth, but before he could utter a word, Cora said, "If anyone is incapable of sound judgment right now, it's you. You're grieving, Lord Kevan. Go tend to your daughter's death rites and keep your nose out of business you don't understand."

"Oh, I understand—"

"You understand nothing." Her voice rose nearly to a shout. Movement shifted at the bottom of the staircase, reminding her of the presence of the two guards who'd followed her brother. She clenched her jaw, hating that there were witnesses to the king's current state. The guards may have been assigned to Dimetreus, but they were appointed by Verdian and Kevan, and likely held a stronger allegiance to them than to the king they now served.

She descended a few steps closer to Kevan until they were nearly at eye level. "Had you a sympathetic bone in your body, you'd recognize the king's sorrow and understand where it was coming from. But seeing as you choose to berate a grieving man rather than confront your own pain tells me you are in no position to judge us. Go, Lord Kevan. I've no need for your council at this time."

His face burned crimson, and a vein pulsed at his temple, but he made no argument. Whirling on his heel, he stomped down the stairs. "To the seven devils with you."

Cora's muscles uncoiled with every step the man took. Once he was out of sight, she released a heavy sigh and turned toward her brother, taking a seat next to him. For a while, that was all she did, sitting in silence while she let him cry, not forcing him to move or talk or leave. She caught the two guards exchanging a wary glance or two, but at least they left them alone.

"Aveline," Dimetreus said, acknowledging her presence for the first time since his breakdown had begun. He lifted his head and turned his tear-stained face to her.

Her breath caught in her throat as she recalled Lurel's face, eyes leaking crimson tears. She almost expected her brother's to look the same.

But the moisture on the king's cheeks was the benign sort, sending her panicked memories to the back of her mind. Shifting her focus to the cold stone beneath her, she anchored her energy and rose to her feet. "Come," she whispered softly to her brother, extending a hand. "Let's get you back to your room."

And away from the godsforsaken tower.

~

The sun had fully risen by the time Cora returned to the stairwell. As much as she never wanted to step foot there again, she knew she needed to. She couldn't rest until she saw what Lurel had seen. Until she had some inkling as to what had led to her death.

Rumors had already circulated the castle regarding Lurel's demise. The official story was that she'd taken a tumble down the stairs, but whispered gossip told of the cursed tower, tears of blood, and a vengeful ghost. Cora wanted to flay whoever was spreading the latter rumors, no matter how close to the truth they were. Only the guards who'd been summoned to help would have seen Lurel's body. Known where she'd lost her life. Which wouldn't make it difficult to pinpoint exactly who had broken Lord Kevan's order to keep quiet.

But that wasn't the task that took precedence in Cora's mind. She crept up the North Tower stairwell, thankful it was devoid of guards. Her throat tightened as she reached the closed door at the top of the staircase. At least the daylight made it harder to conjure images of what had happened earlier that morning. Made it less daunting to turn the handle and step inside the room...

Cora shuddered as she took in the circular library. It was dimmer than the stairwell, each window covered by a tapestry—the same as it had been when Morkai had brought her there to talk. In fact, everything was exactly as she remembered it. There was a tea table and a pair of wingback chairs by the empty fireplace, a cluttered desk shoved haphazardly against one of the many bookcases that lined the walls, books upon books upon books bearing spines with titles she hadn't been able to forget: *The Art of Blood, Grimoire Sanguina, Mastering the Ethera.* Then there was the table that stood at the center of the room.

Her gaze lingered there, and she crept toward it. Upon the table she spotted the one item that had not been in the room before—Lurel's candlestick holder, the candle's wick extinguished after having burned down to the base. Beside it sat an open book.

Lurel's words echoed through Cora's mind: *I pricked my finger on a book when I tried to open it...*

Cora's heart hammered as she stepped closer to the table, to the book. She dropped her mental shields, assessing the energy in the room, and immediately felt the air darken, its weight prickling the hair on her arms. It was condensed around the book, saturating the metal clasp that hung from the cover, crawling over the page it had been opened to.

Cora breathed away the darkness and maintained focus on the stone floor beneath her slippered feet, rooting herself to the earth, to safety, to protection. Careful not to touch anything, she lifted a hand above the book. Her inked palms tingled against the darkness, buzzing against her flesh in an almost painful way. Her stomach churned the closer she let her hand drift to the book. The energy thrummed near the clasp, and as Cora leaned closer to investigate, she caught a glint of sharp metal protruding from the top edge. That must have been where Lurel had pricked her finger. The clasp must have been fitted with a mechanism that pricked anyone who tried to open it. Anyone aside from Morkai, perhaps, for how else would he have accessed the book? And it was certainly his; it writhed with the sorcerer's essence, as potent as his living presence had been. But how did Lurel die?

A hollow feeling drew her attention to the open page of the book. It was one of the first pages. On the left was blank paper, but on the right...

Cora launched a step back as bile rose in her throat.

Rust-colored ink crisscrossed the sheet, almost too faint to see beneath the dim lighting. It was a pattern of intersecting lines like a tapestry.

A blood weaving.

She understood then that the book had been enchanted to kill anyone who dared open it. The clasp had pricked Lurel's finger, drawn her blood, and woven it with whoever's this page contained. Perhaps even Queen Linette's, considering the similarity of their deaths—blood that seeped not from any ordinary wound but the eyes, nose, and mouth.

Cora's breaths grew sharper as panic threatened to seize her. But she couldn't give in. Neither to panic nor to sorrow. She needed to be strong. For her brother. For Khero. For the safety of Ridine Castle.

She swallowed her fear and let anger take its place, let it crawl down her arms, spiraling through the inked sigils she bore, driving the dark energy away from her, shoving it back, back, until it retreated into the pages of the book. Then she slammed the cover down, containing the energy. She sneered down at the closed book, the dark leather cover hiding the blood weaving that marred the inner page.

She turned her scowl to the vials littering the table, then to the volumes of books cluttered upon the bookshelves around her. The objects leered, taunting her, but unlike their master, they were easily destroyed. One simply had to know how. And Cora did. She was the only person in the castle who could make this room safe again.

She'd been wrong when she'd told Lurel the tower wasn't haunted. It was. Now she was determined to rid every last scrap of Morkai's memory, his essence, his energy, if it was the last thing she did.

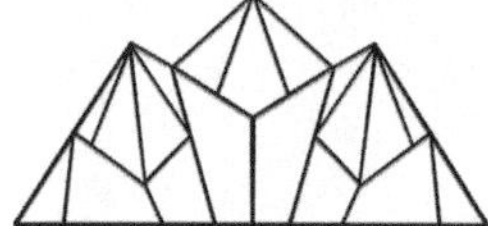

16

Mareleau blinked several times as if that could help her make sense of the words that just left Uncle Ulrich's mouth.

"My cousin," Mareleau said.

Ulrich nodded, not bothering to look at her from his seat opposite her in the coach they rode in.

"Lurel."

Another nod.

"She's...dead."

"A tumble down the stairs, the letter says. Just a few days ago," he said, tone distracted. His attention was consumed by the letter in question, although not by the subject matter Mareleau expected. While she continued to reel over the upsetting news, her uncle was already mumbling his approval that the council meeting would commence upon their arrival at the castle that afternoon as planned.

Mareleau blinked at him again, willing his countenance to reflect her internal unrest. But no, he remained unflustered, his grin stretching above his clean-shaven double chin, his gray eyes free of sorrow. Surely he should do more than say *a tumble down the stairs* before moving on. The girl was his niece, after all.

"My condolences," Breah said. She was the only other person in the coach with them, as Mareleau's other two lady's maids were riding separately. Mareleau turned a furrowed brow to the girl beside her, trying to determine if she too was reeling despite her simple words. Breah had served alongside Lurel. Even though she'd shown a stronger preference for Ann and Sera, she must feel the way Mareleau did. She must feel...

Well, how did Mareleau feel? Shocked, she supposed. Lurel was younger than she was. She'd been perfectly fine and healthy when last they'd spoken. Which was, of course, when Mareleau had informed her that she'd selected the girl to serve Princess Aveline. Mareleau's decision had been an easy one. Of all her maids, it pained her the least to part with Lurel.

But now it struck her that she'd had an indirect hand in Lurel's fate. Much as had been the case with Prince Helios' death. She hadn't felt as sorry as she should have that her Heart's Hunt had gotten one of her champions killed. There was little that could fluster her. Little that could shake her composure. She'd experienced her share of grief, of life's unfairness. But this was the closest Mareleau had ever come to feeling death's touch.

Lurel, her irritating, naive, endlessly prattling cousin...was dead. And Mareleau, the ever-unshakable, ever-scheming, ever-resilient newly crowned queen, felt smaller and weaker than she ever had before. What was this horrible feeling? Guilt? Grief? It felt almost as bad as when she'd broken Larylis' heart with her lie.

Her hand went to the nape of her neck, seeking loose strands of hair. She was desperate to move her fingers, to wind them through a braid like she often found herself mindlessly doing, but her silver tresses were pinned in a coronet.

"Stop touching your hair," Ulrich snapped, glancing up from the letter and tucking it into his waistcoat pocket.

She dropped her hands to her lap. Heat rose to her cheeks at having been chastised by her uncle. *At least I have hair to touch*, she wanted to say. His dark tresses, cropped just below his ears, looked more like an upside-down bowl that did his dour face no favors.

"Lurel was Princess Aveline's lady's maid," he said. "Now that she is once again without a proper attendant, you might loan her another one of yours."

Panic constricted Mareleau's chest. She had to choose another girl to serve Aveline? Make another choice that would lead to consequence, for better or worse?

"Certainly not me," Breah said in a rush, sitting up straighter. Ulrich arched a brow at her, so she swiveled toward Mareleau. In a much more composed tone, she said, "Sera would do a wonderful job, Majesty. She's much more skilled at serving a princess than a queen. Wouldn't you say? I can't imagine you'd be able to part with *me*."

Mareleau had to admit Breah was right. If she had to keep only one of her maids, it would be Breah. She was the only sensible one of the bunch. That didn't mean she considered the girl a friend. Katra was the last lady's maid she'd called *friend*. And that girl had betrayed her by trysting with her suitor.

The memory made her stiffen and reminded her why she kept her maids at a distance. Why she refused to coddle them. Katra's betrayal had broken Mareleau. It had taught her the futility of friendship and the necessity of being sharp. Suspicious. Relentless. In a way, she was grateful. The experience had made her cold enough to fight for what she deserved. To care less about those who only pretended to care about her. To extend her heart only so far as she was willing to let it be broken.

She'd done enough of that lately with Larylis. Now it was time to be a queen. A leader. Someone who could sit tall in the face of tragedy instead of wanting to curl up and plait her hair like a child. She couldn't fall apart just because a family member took a tumble down the stairs.

Her heart pulsed in rebellion at such an unfeeling statement, but Mareleau swallowed the treacherous feeling down. Donning the graceful mask that was Queen Mareleau, she said, "I suppose I can live without Sera. Temporarily, of course. I assume Princess Aveline will soon have her own ladies appointed to her?"

"By the time you're done serving as her companion," Ulrich said, "she'll have new ladies. For now, it is in our best interest to keep her circle of influence small and controlled."

Mareleau bristled at how her uncle referred to her task as *serving* the princess. She was queen now. She should have to serve no one. Up until this morning, she'd hoped her father would see that and take back his insistence that she complete this ridiculous errand. But today was the last day of their journey, crushing all hope that Verdian would have a change of heart. Her entourage would arrive at the castle in the next couple of hours. Once she was there, her sentence would begin.

It's really going to happen, she thought, watching the dense forest flanking the road fly by in a blur of brown and green. *I'm going to be stuck at Ridine Castle for at least two weeks.* The trees seemed to extend claws toward the coach in answer. They were so tall, so dark for such an early hour, that she couldn't help but see them as sinister. Not to mention the Cambron Mountains leering behind them like a sleeping giant. Such a dreary backdrop lacked both the elegance of the snow-dappled mountains in Selay and the charming green hills she'd glimpsed in Menah. What she'd seen of Khero so far was rugged, rough, and far from enchanting.

"Aveline needs your help, Majesty," Ulrich said, drawing her attention back to him. "She hasn't lived as a princess for six years. She's likely forgotten the rules of royal propriety and tradition. You must teach her your wisdom."

She couldn't tell if he was being earnest or not, especially with that flippant tone of his. Ulrich had never treated her like she held even an ounce of wisdom. There were times when he was downright disrespectful. After everything her father had said regarding her lack of safety as his heir, she had even less reasons to trust her uncle's sincerity.

"Princess Aveline is so lucky to have you, Your Majesty," Breah said.

Mareleau wasn't certain the princess would feel the same. Their first and only encounter had been rife with tension. Now that everything with Larylis was settled, she could admit she'd been perhaps a little brusque with Aveline. She'd all but accused her of trying to steal the man she loved. When she looked at the situation objectively, it was clear Aveline had no ulterior motive and was simply agreeing to terms that had been delivered to her. It had been desperation, not desire, that had driven the princess to agree to a marriage with Larylis.

Mareleau was a jealous creature, but she could try to forgive the princess for having posed a short-lived threat to her happiness. Couldn't she? She'd at least have to pretend.

Breah's words took on a conspiratorial tone. "I heard she's been living in the forest this entire time. Raised by wolves if you can believe it."

Ulrich released a disapproving grunt and opened his broadsheets. The messenger had delivered the paper alongside the letter bearing word of Lurel's demise. His voice came from behind the front page. "She was raised by a group of covert operatives tasked with keeping the princess safely hidden from the traitorous duke."

Mareleau couldn't help but note his rehearsed-sounding tone. She wasn't privy to all the details of the battle with Duke Morkai, the truth of King Dimetreus' captivity, or the secrets of Princess Aveline's faked death, but every rumor she'd heard involved dark magic shrouded in secrecy, all of which her uncle constantly refuted. It would have been a comfort to hear such claims dismissed had Mareleau not known Ulrich's very duty was to create official statements for public consumption. In other words, everything he'd just said to her could have been a lie.

"Act kindly to Her Highness," Ulrich said, "but do not let your guard down. Remember that your job is not to be her friend but her confidante."

She sniffed, not bothering to respond. If anyone understood her duty, it was she. Mareleau knew she was a spy and nothing more, entrusted with a task that would earn her father's trust. Or whatever was left of it.

Under no circumstances did she intend to make friends.

17

For the third time that day, Cora strolled past the stairwell to the North Tower Library. Just like the first two times—and every time she'd come here the last two days—a sentry patrolled the entrance. The guard noticed her approach and offered a stiff bow. She nodded in reply before gritting her jaw and scurrying past. Once she was around the next corner, she paused and slumped against the wall. Damn. She'd hoped she could sneak back into the tower library, but she'd had no such luck.

She supposed she should feel grateful for the guards, if only for the fact that it meant Lord Kevan understood the threat the tower posed. But stationing sentries in the stairwell day and night was not a sustainable solution. Sooner or later, one of the guards would get lax. Leave their post. Someone would get too curious. Too brave. Or perhaps too skeptical. Whatever the case, so long as the tower remained as it was, someone could get hurt. Or worse.

Cora hadn't let herself look around much when she'd come the morning after Lurel's death. It wouldn't have been safe. Not until she had the items she needed for a clearing ritual. Earth for grounding. Water for cleansing. Fire for transmutation. Air for dissipation. By the time she'd pilfered a few items from the kitchen, the guards had taken their posts. Cora had lost her chance to do her work unseen.

She glanced around the corner toward the stairwell and spotted the sentry's armored shoulder peeking from the archway. Opening her senses, she caught strains of boredom mingling with discomfort. She wondered if there was anything she could do to inflate the latter emotion and trick him into leaving his post. But what good would that do? Cora needed ample time to do what she needed in the tower. It would take days. Weeks. Months perhaps.

It left her only one option; she'd have to propose her plan to Lord Kevan.

She grimaced at the thought. After their argument in the stairwell two mornings ago, she'd done her best to avoid him. Maybe he was avoiding her too. Still, until she and Dimetreus established firm trust with their new allies, the castle was essentially under Lord Kevan's command. The guards listened to his orders. Followed his rules.

"Mother Goddess," she cursed under her breath, leaning her head against the wall behind her. If only she could repeat the strange feat she'd accomplished at Centerpointe Rock. Then she could cross the distance from here to the tower room with no one else being the wiser. That is, if she'd truly done what it had felt like she'd done. Despite her growing doubt over the singular incident, she'd attempted to replicate her feat of spontaneous transportation a few times. She'd tried to will herself to the other side of her bedroom. To the forest. To...anywhere. But it hadn't worked. She couldn't determine what was missing.

In the past, her magic had grown each time she'd overcome a personal challenge regarding the Arts. It was a concept the Forest People were well acquainted with. When a witch would overcome a point of resistance along their path with the Arts, their magic and abilities would grow. Cora had experienced this a few times now, and it had always come from doing what had felt the most difficult in any given moment. So far, her challenge had always been to tune in to her Art. To get out of her head and trust her magic. To release her skepticism and believe she was capable of doing more than she dared dream of. Lately, though, the most difficult thing she'd had to do was publicly reject her relationship with magic. It would have been so much easier to run away. To flee to the woods and let her brother sort out his own problems. Didn't that mean she was doing the right thing?

If so, her magic should be growing now. Instead, she felt like it was being smothered by a heavy weight in her chest. Sure, the base functioning of her clairsentient magic remained. She could open her senses, feel others' emotions, and raise or drop her mental shields, but those were all things that had become inherent to her. She tried to remember what it was like to be the witch who had rendered her and Teryn invisible. Who had manipulated matter and opened a locked door. The witch who had crossed a distance in the blink of an eye and killed a sorcerer. She simply...couldn't.

It reminded her of when her magic had become muted after getting captured by Morkai. Her anger over Teryn's betrayal had smothered her connection to her Art. If that was happening again, why? Was it guilt over leaving the Forest People? Anger over having to pretend to be someone she wasn't?

All she knew was that she'd felt somewhat like herself again when she'd faced Morkai's deadly book and vowed to destroy all that was left of him. If she could perform a clearing ritual in the tower, she could connect to her magical side. To the witch she couldn't be until her duty as a princess had been served.

"Your Highness, there you are."

Cora startled at Master Arther's voice. The steward came marching toward her, shoulders tense. She pushed away from the wall and took on a more regal bearing. "Greetings, Master Arther. I was just—"

"They're here, Highness," he said, wringing his gloved hands. "The queen's entourage. You must greet her and Lord Ulrich at once. His Majesty and Lord Kevan are already in the courtyard."

Cora paled, her throat going dry. She'd been so focused on trying to get back into the tower that she'd forgotten the upcoming arrival of Queen Mareleau. The last thing she wanted to do was greet the prickly woman. "You'll have to send her my sincere apologies. I'm not feeling well—"

"The council meeting will commence as soon as Lord Ulrich exits his coach. You cannot leave the queen to such a cold welcome."

Cora bit off all further argument. Queen Mareleau could have the iciest welcome for all she cared, but her brother's first council meeting wasn't something she intended to miss.

"Very well," she said, "I shall greet Her Majesty."

Relief smoothed the furrows in Master Arther's brow, but it was short-lived. His eyes swept over her ensemble. "Are you going to greet her in that, Highness?"

Cora glanced down at the green wool riding habit she wore. It was one of her simplest outfits, and the easiest to don without assistance. Master Arther seemed to realize exactly that and took a sharp inhale. "Highness! Oh, dear. You must forgive me for neglecting my duties. I...I never..."

She knew what he was struggling to say. In the aftermath of Lurel's demise, she hadn't been appointed a new maid. Servants had come to call on her, but she preferred tending to herself. She wasn't about to bring any attention to the quiet solitude she'd been granted the last couple of days.

"It's all right, Master Arther," she said, lifting her chin. "I'm perfectly content to greet the queen in my riding habit."

"I suppose there's nothing to be done about it now," he muttered and led the way toward the front of the castle, past the dining hall, and out to the courtyard. As soon as they exited the front doors, a flurry of activity erupted around them. Several coaches pulled before the stone steps of the entryway, followed by dozens of wagons and countless figures on horseback. Cora's mental shields faltered beneath the weight of so many new faces, new energies, new emotions. She breathed deeply, strengthening the elements around her, and shifted her stance to root her energy into the stone under her feet.

Only then did she make her way to the bottom of the stairs to take her place next to her brother. He greeted her with a smile while Lord Kevan, who stood on the king's opposite side, didn't bother glancing her way at all. She wondered how he'd look at her once she brought up her plan...

"It will be nice for you to have a companion, don't you think?" Dimetreus asked in that doting tone that echoed how he'd spoken to her as a child. "Queen Mareleau is your same age, I believe."

Cora internally groaned. She'd almost forgotten the purpose for Mareleau's visit. While most of the people were here to serve as the remainder of the king's staff and council, the queen was to act as her companion and help Cora get acquainted with her role as princess. When Lord Kevan had relayed this information to her, she hadn't dared argue, but that had mostly been due to shock over having learned that Teryn hadn't married Mareleau. She could try to convince herself the queen might not be as bad as their first impression had suggested, but after everything Lurel had said about her...

Sympathy tugged Cora's chest at the thought of her lady's maid. While Cora had only known the girl for a short time, she was Mareleau's cousin. Despite whatever tense relationship Lurel had suggested they'd had, they'd been family. Mareleau might be grieving.

"Ah, here comes Lord Ulrich," Dimetreus whispered.

Cora's eyes fell on the nearest coach from which a stout, middle-aged man exited. He bore some resemblance to Verdian and Kevan but was the shortest of the three and had the most unfortunate bowl cut. With a bored expression, he extended a hand to help the next passenger exit the coach. White silk gloves grasped his leather ones, which reminded Cora that she wasn't wearing any. She hid her hands in the folds of her skirt, certain Mareleau would likely faint if she saw Cora's tattooed palms.

The queen in question exited the rest of the way from the coach in a waterfall of pale blue silk patterned with chrysanthemums, followed by a blonde who appeared to be one of her maids. Mareleau's wide skirts made Cora wonder how she'd even managed to fit inside the coach without smothering her traveling companions. It also negated the chance that the queen was deeply mourning her cousin's death, for blue certainly wasn't an appropriate color. Even Cora knew that, and she'd spent the last six years with the Forest People, who did not observe such traditions.

Then again...had the queen heard the news yet?

Ulrich escorted Mareleau up the stone steps to greet them. "King Dimetreus, Princess Aveline, may I present to you Queen Mareleau Alante." His words lacked sincerity, much like Lord Kevan's did whenever he spoke of Mareleau. Cora, her brother, and Kevan sank into obeisance.

"Gather the councilmen that have just arrived," Kevan said to Master Arther before Cora had even risen from her curtsy, "and direct them to the council room. The rest of us will wait there for them."

Arther rushed down the stairs while Kevan, Ulrich, and Dimetreus turned and marched inside. Cora felt a flicker of betrayal strike her heart at the sight of her brother's retreating back. Hadn't he thought of including her in the meeting?

Well, it didn't matter. She was going to go regardless—

An unwelcome figure blocked her view, mostly due to her ridiculously wide skirts and much taller height. Mareleau looked down at Cora with what was clearly a false smile. "Charming castle."

"Thank you, Majesty. Now if you'll excuse me—"

"We met under less-than-ideal circumstances at Verlot Palace," she said, tone placating, "but we can put that behind us, can't we? I am determined for us to be cordial. Besides, you heard what my uncle said. I'm Mareleau Alante now, Queen of Menah, and Larylis is my husband."

Cora bristled. She could hear the smug taunting in Mareleau's voice, as if...as if Cora should envy her. Over Larylis! Her preoccupation with following her brother fled as her mind became consumed with how best to convey just how little she cared about the queen's husband. Before she could sort out the most cutting retort, Mareleau spoke again.

"Congratulations are in order."

Cora blinked back at her.

"To me," Mareleau clarified. "You should have congratulated me on my coronation and my marriage. It would have been the appropriate response. We only have two weeks to school you in the proper behavior of a princess, so we'd best start now. Your curtsy must be improved upon. What you greeted me with was more like a half curtsy, not at all appropriate for meeting a queen. You should have dipped another six inches lower."

Cora bit back a humorless laugh. This was what Mareleau had meant when she'd said she was *determined for them to be cordial*? Fire heated her blood, and she let it rise, let it lift her chin and pull her to her full height despite being several inches shorter than the other woman. "That would be true, Majesty, if you were *my* queen. In that case, I'd have been required to lower in the appropriate twelve-inch curtsy, but since you are merely a visiting monarch from a neighboring kingdom, I need only demonstrate respect."

Heat flushed Mareleau's cheeks, and she pressed her lips into a tight line. She reached for the nape of her neck and twirled a wisp of hair around her finger before she abruptly folded her hands at her waist.

Cora extended her senses far enough to feel the queen's flustered state.

"You are correct, Princess," Mareleau said through her teeth. "I was merely doing my duty in helping you—"

"I honestly don't have time," Cora said, finally managing to skirt around her. "There's a council meeting about to begin."

She marched inside but found Mareleau keeping pace with her. "You aren't serious. They aren't going to let us sit on the council."

Cora halted and whirled toward the queen. "No, of course they aren't going to let *us* sit on the council, for you do not belong to this kingdom. But *I* do, and I have every right to attend."

Mareleau gave her a pandering grin. "If it were that simple, I'd have attended every meeting at Verlot Palace. You do realize those are *my* uncles leading your brother's council, don't you? Do you know how many times they've refused me?"

"Many times, I'm sure, but this isn't Selay, nor is this Verlot Palace, and this isn't your father's council. I'm going to that meeting."

She turned away from the queen, nearly colliding with Master Arther. He was leading half a dozen men down the hall, but upon seeing Cora and Mareleau, he paused and directed the men to continue toward the council room.

Cora made to follow in their wake, but Master Arther shadowed her steps. "Your Highness, perhaps now we can settle on new linens for the remainder of the bedchambers."

She suppressed the urge to roll her eyes. Approving linens. Of course that was all a princess was good for. With an exaggerated smile, she gestured toward Mareleau. "You know who would do a wonderful job at selecting linens? Her Majesty."

Determined to let nothing more distract her, she marched away.

Master Arther called after her while Mareleau let out an affronted gasp. The last thing she heard before she reached the council room door was Mareleau's purposefully too-loud voice. "Linens. What nerve. Very well. Show me the most hideous linens I can choose from."

<h1 style="text-align:center">18</h1>

By the time Cora entered the council room, all the other members had taken their seats. She was momentarily stunned by the look of the room, for it appeared almost exactly as it had the last time she'd been inside. Not that she'd had much reason to enter it as a child. Still, she'd always been impressed with its imposing grandeur. She felt the same now as she studied the walls of dark wood, carved with reliefs of battle scenes. These were interspersed with portraits of previous kings from the Caelan bloodline, including her father, whose portrait stood at the far end of the room. Beside it hung a purple standard bearing Khero's black mountain sigil. The head of a large rectangular table was placed directly beneath it, where her brother sat now. Several smaller tables covered in maps and books lined the room.

Cora strolled straight for the table. A trio of servants fluttered about it, filling glasses with wine and water while the councilmen got situated. Conversation filled the room, masking the sound of Cora's steps. After the servants finished filling the last glass, they hastily made their exits, closing the door behind them. No one noticed Cora's approach until she placed her hand on the back of the empty chair at the far end of the table and slid it out.

Dimetreus was the first to rise to his feet. Others belatedly followed, some offering hasty bows, while Lord Kevan stood less out of respect and more out of annoyed surprise.

The king rushed over to her. "Oh, darling Aveline," he said, voice low. "You don't need to worry yourself with this meeting. I daresay it will be tedious and rather bleak of topic."

She tried not to feel offended by his tone or his words. When would he stop treating her like the twelve-year-old girl he last knew? Had she not been the one to comfort him all week? To play parent to him and soothe his emotions, all while controlling the narrative surrounding his sudden breakdowns?

Cora did her best to keep her voice level, but she didn't bother meeting his low volume. "Yes, dear brother, but you should recall that many of these bleak topics have to do with me. Lord Kevan has reminded us of this meeting's importance time and again, and that we are to say little about anything regarding our pasts and recent events until our stories have been agreed upon by your new council. That is precisely why I'm here."

Kevan's voice shot across the table with unmasked ire. "You're supposed to be showing hospitality to the queen, Highness."

"I showed her what hospitality was due. Right now my place is at this table."

Kevan's cheeks reddened, his mouth falling open.

Before he could speak, Dimetreus addressed the council. "Consider the oversight mine. I should have invited Princess Aveline to attend our meeting from the start. She is right. Today's agenda involves her."

That silenced further argument from Kevan, but Lord Ulrich's snicker still carried across the table. Whether he was amused at his brother's irritation or laughing to undermine Dimetreus' authority, Cora knew not. Her nerves were wound too tightly to allow her to extend her senses.

Dimetreus faced Cora with an apologetic smile. "Forgive me," he whispered, giving her shoulder a gentle squeeze.

Her heart softened. "Of course."

The king returned to the head of the table and Cora finally lowered herself into her chair. She glanced around the table, meeting a few stares from the men around her—some curious, others icy—and held their eyes without falter. All looked quickly away, turning their gazes to the king. The council was comprised of twelve men total, aside from the king, half of whom had arrived today with Ulrich. Kevan and his men sat on one side of the table while Ulrich and his sat on the other.

"Shall we get started, Your Majesty?" Lord Kevan said, tone curt. "Perhaps we shall begin with the topic of Princess Aveline. Then she need not stay for the duration—"

"We shall," Dimetreus said, cutting Kevan off. "Lord Ulrich, I've been told you bear the responsibility of forging the official statements we'll be making to the public. What shall we say to prove my sister's assumed death was false?"

Cora was impressed with how effortlessly her brother spoke on a topic she knew distressed him. It bolstered her conviction that she'd done the right thing in aiding his return to the throne. Regardless of the trauma that continued to afflict him, he *was* king. Without Morkai's influence, he could be a great king.

Lord Ulrich shuffled the stack of papers before him. Selecting one, he leaned back in his chair. His casual posture contrasted Kevan's tense demeanor. "The official statement," Ulrich drawled, "is that six years ago, King Dimetreus learned of a threat to the crown. While it had been too late to save the queen, he was able to spirit the princess away and fake her death to protect her."

Cora's gaze locked on her brother, seeking any sign that mention of his wife's demise was causing him anguish. The last thing she needed was for him to fall apart before the council. Thankfully, all she noted was a slight twitch beneath his eye.

Ulrich continued. "She was raised in a secret location in the Cambron Mountains by a group of operatives tasked with keeping her safe until the threat could be dealt with. That is why claims of her death are now being refuted."

"What is being said to clear our king's name?" asked a man with thinning auburn hair and a heavy mustache that hid his upper lip. Cora recognized him as Lord Danforth, one of the councilmen who'd journeyed with her retinue from Lord Kevan's estate.

Ulrich rifled through his papers again and selected a new one before returning to his slumped pose. "Although His Majesty first learned of the threat six years ago, it took almost as long to uncover its source. He nearly lost his life when he and his spies uncovered Duke Morkai's sinister motives, but he was able to flee to Selay. There the king and his allies from Selay and Menah rallied a force to confront the duke, which resulted in the battle at Centerpointe Rock."

Dimetreus furrowed his brow. "The people are accepting this story?"

"Yes, Your Majesty," Ulrich said. "It seems the duke kept very few witnesses at the castle, save for those who served him. We've questioned the survivors from the battle. Most had minds too addled to understand anything that had occurred, much like you'd claimed. Only a small handful knew of the lie Morkai had fed you about Selay's and Menah's involvement in your wife's death. The general public has no clue that Khero was ever pitted against Selay and Menah, and any rumors will quickly be smoothed over by our official statement. The worst crime your citizens see you as guilty of were your aggressive recruitment attempts, but those too will be forgiven when word spreads that you'd been countering a coup all along."

"What of the prisoners taken at the end of the battle?" one of the men from Ulrich's party asked. "Have all the soldiers who served under Morkai been put to death?"

Cora's blood went cold. While she knew Morkai had earned the loyalties of some of his soldiers, there had to have been countless more who'd simply fallen under his glamour.

"Many have," Kevan said, running a hand through his thick beard. "Any who revealed hostility or unwavering loyalty to the departed duke were executed at once. Their families have been informed that they died in battle serving the king. As for the rest, we're taking it one day at a time. We can't release a host of soldiers claiming to have lost their memories. And those who have retained their memories know of certain facts we can't let them share. Should too many similar tales begin to proliferate—"

"You can't kill them all." The words burst from Cora's lips. "Most have been afflicted in the same way my brother has. Duke Morkai's dark magic is to blame, not his victims."

Kevan pinned her with a glare. "If you'd waited until I'd finished, you'd have heard me state just that. Considering this is your first time sitting with a royal council, your childish behavior is excusable, Highness, but going forward do respect the speaker and wait your turn."

Heat rose to Cora's cheeks. She hated being scolded by him but arguing would only further his point. Pursing her lips, she funneled her rage by gripping the armrests of her chair.

"And going forward," Dimetreus said, steely gaze on Kevan, "you will speak to the princess as befits any other man on the council. Understood?"

Kevan's beard twitched as he shifted his jaw side to side. It seemed to pain him greatly to offer the king a tight-lipped, "Understood."

Ulrich sat a little straighter, amusement dancing in his eyes. "What my brother was going to say is that we are aware that we cannot execute all the soldiers who fought at Centerpointe Rock. Many have only good things to say about their king. We are going to use their confusion in our favor. We've begun feeding them a tale that the duke had utilized a chemical poison during the battle which resulted in hallucinations and memory loss. Those who accept this story are being sent home, honorably discharged from service, after a thorough interview."

Cora relaxed at that, and she regretted her earlier outburst.

"That will help explain away all mention of ghosts and monsters," one of the men said with an approving nod. "Even if rumors do spread, the official statement will counter it."

"A similar story has been fed to the soldiers who fought for Menah and Selay," Ulrich said. "Since they lack the memory loss of those who'd been controlled by the duke, their conviction over what they witnessed is stronger. But it's less important that they believe the story and more that they understand to keep quiet. No civilians were present at Centerpointe Rock, only military personnel. Anyone caught spreading rumors about dark magic and sorcery will be dishonorably discharged."

This time when Cora spoke, she kept her tone neutral. "So all word of magic is being stripped from the official story?"

"Yes," Kevan said. "There is no point in frightening the public. Now that the duke is dead, magic can return to being a thing of myth."

"But magic is real." Cora's heart hammered at the confession.

Some of the men paled while others shifted uncomfortably in their seats.

"No, it is not," Lord Danforth said with a sniff. "Whatever happened at Centerpointe Rock was a singular occurrence. Our story about chemical poisons and hallucinations very well might be true. It makes a hell of a lot more sense than sorcery."

Cora lowered her shields to sense the emotions coming from the men around her. She was struck with fear, discomfort, and dissociation. Conflict writhed through them, a war between the terrifying truth and the far more comforting lie.

Only now did it strike her that no one had referred to Morkai as a sorcerer or mage, only a duke. They were not only lying to the public...but to themselves.

With her shields back in place, she sank against the back of her chair, regarding the men before her. They knew the truth. They knew dark magic existed, yet they were content to pretend it had never happened.

She supposed she shouldn't have expected anything more. The average citizen didn't believe in magic, and anything deemed *too different* was often met with suspicion. Which included witches—people born with one of the six sensory magics. If their Art caused them to reveal strange tendencies, keen senses, or miraculous abilities, they were often cast out of society. That was the very reason the Forest People, who'd once only been comprised of Faeryn descendants, began to welcome witches into the commune. Just like they'd welcomed Cora. Nurtured her Art.

A heavy sorrow filled her chest as she realized she was right back where she'd been as a child—hiding her magic lest she be judged for it.

It doesn't have to be forever, she reminded herself. *In the meantime, there are still things I can do. Issues only a princess can solve.*

She sat up straighter. "What of the unicorns?"

"What about them?" Kevan asked. "They are no more evidence of magic than a horse is. They are simply an ancient species that has recovered from extinction."

He was wrong about that. Unicorns were fae creatures, and where they'd suddenly returned from remained a mystery. However, that was not the topic she wanted to discuss. "What is being done about those who hunted them? I'm sure you've been told in the final report compiled by King Verdian's inquisitors that I came across multiple parties of unicorn hunters who served Morkai."

It had been a necessary truth to confess since it explained how she and Teryn had crossed paths. Of course, she'd neglected to admit anything about having poisoned a group of them. Teryn, it seemed, had stayed quiet on the subject as well.

Ulrich answered. "A proclamation has been publicly made against any hunters continuing work in the duke's name, and bounties have been offered in exchange for the recapture of the criminals the duke had freed."

Cora narrowed her eyes. "Has unicorn hunting been abolished? It is a cruel practice and should not be allowed, especially when a species is endangered, as Lord Kevan has pointed out."

"You can rest assured," Lord Danforth said, "that unicorn hunting has been strictly regulated."

A sinking sensation struck her gut—a clairsentient nudge. She pried a hole in her shields, just enough to sense Danforth's emotions, and found him lacking sincerity. He was...hiding something. She glanced from Danforth to Ulrich, then to Kevan. They wore smug expressions and writhed with greedy energy.

She could feel the truth then. *They* were continuing the hunt. They'd probably only issued warrants to lessen competition. Her mouth fell open, her tongue tingling with accusations...

But what could she possibly say? What could she accuse them of without confessing to her Art?

She'd have to wait and bring the subject to her brother alone. Not that he'd ever listened to her clairsentient warnings before. He may not have condemned her strange abilities the way Linette had, but he hadn't understood them either.

Damn it. I'll have to warn Valorre.

"Now, Highness," Kevan said, tone mocking, "do you have any other pressing matters to bring to the table? Perhaps the welfare of dragons and pixies?"

A rumble of laughter echoed over the table. He could laugh at her expense all he wanted. She was about to see that jovial expression stripped clean off his face.

Sitting straighter, she locked her eyes with his. "I do, actually. I'd like to discuss the North Tower Library."

19

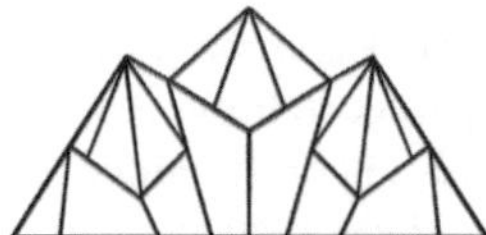

Silence fell over the council table. Not all eyes turned to Cora, for only the men who'd already been at Ridine knew the significance of the North Tower Library. But the faces that had locked on hers were ashen.

Lord Kevan, on the other hand, grew flushed. He spoke through his teeth, each word clipped. "What about the library?"

She kept her tone neutral, her composure steady. "I'd like to oversee its..." She paused to consider the best word to complete her sentence, knowing she needed to tread carefully with this topic. "Renovations."

Kevan scoffed. "There will be no renovations of the North Tower Library. The door has been locked and the stairwell leading to it will be guarded night and day."

"How long?" Cora countered.

"I just stated night and day—"

"Yes, but for how long? Forever? Shall guarding the stairwell become some grand tradition passed down through every ruler to come?"

With the hole still open in Cora's shields, she could feel his growing discomfort. Not because the topic was related to his daughter's death, but because he had no answer to give.

She arched a brow. "You haven't thought it through, have you?"

Ulrich lifted a hand from his slouched position. "Is this stairwell the same that Lady Lurel took a tumble down?"

Cora flinched at his careless tone. Even she would have had more tact out of respect for Kevan's emotions. She wondered how much love the brothers shared. Perhaps very little.

Kevan glanced across the table at Ulrich. "Yes, and I am determined to see that her fate goes unrepeated. Meanwhile, Her Highness wants to gallivant around hanging tapestries."

"You mistake me, Lord Kevan," Cora said. "When I said renovate, I did not mean redecorate. I meant that I want to dispose of every item in that room."

Kevan had nothing to say to that. She slid her gaze to Dimetreus. He'd been quiet since she'd brought up unicorns and now the library. But when she met his eyes, he gave her a solemn nod.

Emboldened by his approval, she addressed the council. "What most of you don't know is that the North Tower Library was once the duke's private study. It is full of deadly items."

"What kinds of items?" one of Ulrich's men asked, tone skeptical. "Knives? Swords? A guillotine?" He grinned at the councilmen across the table but none shared his amusement.

"Grimoires," Cora said. "Poisons. Traps. You may have decided to dissociate the duke from magic, but that won't change the things he left in that room. We must get rid of them."

Ulrich waved a flippant hand. "So we'll haul everything out and burn it."

"Not everything can be burned. Besides, some things are too dangerous to be touched by those unaware of the threats the objects pose." She was tempted to tell the truth about Lurel's death, but it wasn't her place. Kevan was the girl's father, and regardless of how much Cora despised him, he was grieving. She couldn't bring herself to illustrate the gory truth if Kevan didn't want it known. She'd let him stick to his tale about a tumble down the stairs if that's what he needed. So long as it didn't prevent her from doing what needed to be done, that is.

Kevan spoke, and this time his tone was tired. Empty. "Which is why I've decided to keep the room locked instead."

"Which is admirable," Cora confessed, "but not sustainable. The only way to make that room safe is to destroy everything inside it."

"But you just stated that the room is too dangerous," Ulrich said.

Cora nodded. "For those unaware, yes."

He quirked a brow. "But you are...aware?"

"Yes."

"How?"

Cora's pulse quickened, her heart rocketing in her chest. It was time to take the conversation into more dangerous territory. Should she make one wrong move, she could undo all the work she'd done to get Dimetreus back on the throne. She could contradict all the necessary lies she'd told the inquisitors to convince them she wasn't a witch. Maybe she should wait to ruffle feathers until after the peace pact was signed, when Verdian's threats to seize her kingdom could no longer bear fruit.

But this couldn't wait.

A little bit of truth. A little bit of lie. That will keep me safe.

Her words came out slow. Careful. "I've been trained to detect and dispose of the threats that are in that library."

Silence fell over the table once more. She couldn't bear to look at anyone but her brother, and when she met his eyes, she found a flash of confusion in them.

One of Ulrich's men broke the silence. "Clarify for me, Highness, but are you talking about magic?"

Her throat felt dry as she worked out her answer, but before she could speak, Kevan's icy tone struck her. "You told the inquisitors you harbored no magic. That you were not like those...those *people* we saw during battle."

She stiffened, knowing he was referring to the Forest People. She'd wanted so badly to keep them out of the inquisitors' report, but the soldiers from Menah and Selay had seen them. They'd witnessed them wielding roots and vines—a stunning feat only the descendants of the Faeryn could do with their Magic of Soil, and something Cora hadn't even known was possible until she'd seen it with her own eyes.

Every other Art Cora had witnessed before that had been quiet magic: a clairvoyant witch's vision of a future event that came to pass, a Faeryn's miraculous ability to track prey long since gone, a claircognizant witch's keen knowing that something was true, a Faeryn's gift to nourish poisoned soil and bring dead plants back to life. All things that could be easily explained away. Cora often felt that way about her own magic.

But what the Faeryn had done at Centerpointe Rock...that kind of Art was the opposite of quiet. It had been loud. Obvious. Irrefutable. And the only way to protect the Forest People had been to admit that they'd been on their side. That they'd seen Morkai as an enemy and used their magic to aid Menah and Selay.

Lord Danforth shifted uncomfortably in his seat. "Are we referring to the...the vine witches?"

Sweat prickled the back of Cora's neck. She knew it was a losing battle to try and explain what a witch truly was, that they didn't deserve the fear and scorn they received. Instead, she confessed what might be a little easier to swallow. "The people who aided us at Centerpointe Rock—the people who kept me safe from Morkai for six years—are descendants of the Faeryn people."

"Faeryn people," Ulrich echoed with a laugh. "We're talking about faeries now?"

"The Faeryn are the same as the unicorns are," Cora said. "An ancient race that has survived extinction."

"And can wield deadly magic," Kevan said. He threw his hands in the air. "Why the seven devils are we talking about the library when we should be discussing how to round up these dangerous earth mages?"

Cora shot forward in her seat. "They aren't dangerous."

"Those who were at Centerpointe Rock will disagree."

"They fought on *our* side."

"This time," one of Ulrich's men muttered. "Who's to say they won't fight against us next time?"

"They are living on the king's land," another man said, "paying no taxes, no dues. They must be hunted down."

"No!" Cora shouted, but her voice was drowned out by sounds of agreement.

"Especially if they taught the princess magic," Danforth said.

One of Kevan's men looked at Cora sidelong. "They may have planted her here to claim the dead princess' identity."

She rose to her feet, her palms slamming against the edge of the table. "My identity has already been determined."

Kevan narrowed his eyes. "Perhaps my brother made a mistake. A mistake he still has time to remedy."

Rage coursed through her, burning through her mental shields. Strains of emotion slammed against her—suspicion, repulsion, amusement, fear. The energies threatened to overwhelm her, to pull her down and override her self-control, but her anger somehow steadied her. That and the feel of the table's hard edge beneath her curling palms.

She honed her attention on Kevan, the instigator of this sudden chaos, and felt a violent pull toward him. Every inch of her body felt the ease with which she could take a single step—not the twenty or so paces she'd have to travel by foot, but a singular move through time and space—to reach the man and strangle the stubbornness from his bearded neck. Her palms tingled, as if she could already feel his flesh—

"Enough!"

Dimetreus' voice bellowed through the room, leaving tense silence in its wake. He stood at the opposite end of the table, hands planted on the table much like her own. His chest heaved as he glared from one man to the next. When he spoke, his voice came out with a deadly chill. "What kind of circus has King Verdian appointed to my council table?"

The men had the good sense to keep quiet.

"My sister's identity is not up for debate. Fail to respect that and I'll dismiss you from this council at once. Should King Verdian have a godsdamned thing to say about that, he can take it up with me, as *I* am his equal. I am King of Khero. This is my kingdom, my home, and my council. Don't you dare forget it."

Cora's rage began to melt away, leaving her trembling as she attempted to steady her breathing. Slowly, she lowered herself back into her chair. Thoughts of Kevan's neck beneath her hands filled her memory. For a moment there...she'd felt like she was about to use her mysterious ability again. Or had that simply been a violent fantasy? Whatever the case, it left her head spinning. Closing her eyes, she touched upon the elements and let her shields wrap around her.

When she opened her eyes, her brother spoke again. "We can try to pretend magic doesn't exist, and I agree that for the public, it is safer if we do. But not here. Not behind these closed doors where such matters are tantamount to this kingdom's safety. Six years ago, I ignored the possibility of magic, and I ended up ensnared in its web. Duke Morkai was a sorcerer, and my ignorance allowed me to be controlled by him, my mind invaded, my memories altered. I will not let that happen again. Not to me. Not to anyone else."

Dimetreus returned to his seat. "Now, we are not here to talk about the people who gave sanctuary to my sister. Yes, they used magic. Yes, they fought on our side. We will do our due diligence to ensure they pose no threat to this kingdom, but we want them as allies, not enemies. So we will not be hunting them down or rounding them up. Once this council has proven itself capable of good sense, then perhaps we'll send an envoy to open peaceful talks between us and them."

Cora's chest warmed. Despite his shortcomings, both recently and in the past, she was growing more and more impressed by him.

Kevan opened his mouth, but Dimetreus continued before he could utter a word. "We will return to the topic Her Highness has brought forth. While she has been considerate of your sensitivities to the subject of magic, I will not be. The North Tower Library is filled with dark magic, poison, and enchanted objects. If Princess Aveline has a way to neutralize the threat, we must hear her out. Sister, please continue."

Twelve sets of eyes turned toward Cora. She didn't need to lower her shields to feel the tension in the room or know that the councilmen gave her their attention begrudgingly. It didn't matter, so long as it allowed her to do what needed to be done.

"My brother is correct," she said, doing her best to keep her voice calm. Even. "The library is filled with dark magic. It doesn't matter if you believe that to be true or not. Should you care only for science, then let me tell you that there are violent compounds in that room, ones too dangerous to discard in a lake or pour onto the earth. Additionally, there are secret traps laced with poisons. Ones too small to see with the naked eye but deadly enough to kill. For example, following Lady Lurel's unfortunate accident, I investigated the room and found a book affixed with a needle hidden in its clasp. The needle had been laced with poison, pricking anyone who opened it and resulting in a quick death."

She met Kevan's gaze to see if he understood that she was describing how Lurel had died. The only sign he gave was a slight widening of his eyes. Of course, she still hadn't told the full truth. She'd left out the part about the blood weaving and replaced it with poison, as that was something Kevan and the other councilmen could accept.

Lord Danforth's throat bobbed. "How are you able to detect traps and poisons?"

She took a deep breath. *A little bit of truth. A little bit of lie. Focus on the things they can easily understand.*

"The Faeryn descendants I lived with for the last six years taught me many things. Healing practices. Herbal remedies. Living so deep in the woods required many precautions. I was taught to smell for poisonous herbs and flowers. How to detect hidden traps laid by hunters. I know the signs. I know the scents. Most importantly, I know how to safely discard these things. I know how to navigate a trap without setting it off. I know which compounds can be burned, which can be diluted in water, and which must never be opened under any circumstances. The duke's poisons bear labels only I can decipher with my knowledge of plant species."

"It's too dangerous," Kevan said, speaking slowly as if any inflection might spark Dimetreus' wrath again. "You're the king's heir. Or you will be once we've formalized the peace treaty." He rushed to say the last part.

Cora blanched. His words reminded her of the marriage alliance she'd agreed to, one that would secure her position as Dimetreus' heir in the eyes of his council. Now that Larylis had married Mareleau, would she be paired with...no, she couldn't let herself think of that. Matrimony was the least of her worries.

"I appreciate your concern over my safety," she said, trying not to sound too mocking, "but this is something I *must* do. Even if we keep the stairwell guarded, the day will come when one of the sentries makes a mistake. Someone will grow too daring. Or a guard will leave his post and let a curious servant slip past.

Keeping the room locked and shrouded in mystery will only draw more attention to it. We cannot risk another *accident* happening again. The sooner you agree to support my work, the sooner we'll truly be free of the last vestiges of Morkai's influence."

The councilmen exchanged glances while Cora looked to her brother again. His face had grown wan, which told her his composure was beginning to dissolve.

"If we support this plan," Ulrich said, "I must insist that the room remains guarded at all times for your safety."

She pursed her lips to keep from smirking; she knew he cared less about her safety and more about having her under surveillance. It didn't matter. They could watch all they liked. She'd be using quiet magic. No one would be able to claim she was up to anything sinister.

"As long as no guard steps foot beyond the threshold of the room," she said, "I am grateful for the protection you offer."

"I approve of your proposal, Aveline," Dimetreus said. His lips flickered with a sad smile. "Please be careful."

She dipped her chin in a gracious nod.

Kevan released an irritated grunt. "Shall we conclude and reconvene tomorrow? I think we'd all benefit from a fresh start in the morning."

Without you, his glare told Cora.

It didn't matter. She'd leave the councilmen to their own devices on the morrow. While she was far from finished regarding the hunting of unicorns, she'd at least succeeded in regard to Morkai's tower.

The meeting ended, and she scurried out of the council room, unable to stop the victorious smile that curled her lips.

Maybe a witch can *be a princess.*

20

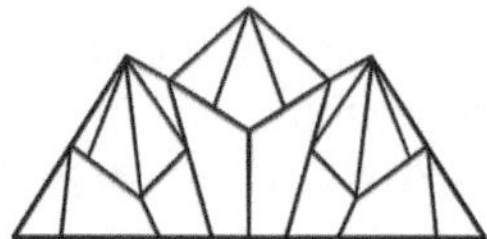

Mareleau had known from the start that her time at Ridine Castle would be time poorly spent, but she'd underestimated just how pointless it would be. She sat on an old-fashioned divan—furbished in a mauve brocade that had already been out of date last year—in her appointed room, doing the needlework she was supposed to be teaching Princess Aveline. Mareleau had been at the castle since yesterday, yet not once had the princess paid a visit. And Mareleau certainly wasn't going to call upon *her*. Aveline had proven herself quite capable of reciting proper protocol for royal behavior, which meant she damn well knew she owed Mareleau the first visit. Perhaps an apology too. Come to think of it, she never did receive the congratulations she'd been due, and she'd fully spelled it out for Aveline.

Gritting her teeth, she pushed her embroidery needle through the linen with more force than necessary, pricking her finger on the other side. Dropping her embroidery hoop to her lap, she brought the stinging finger to her mouth. She glanced at her two ladies, Breah and Ann, to see if they noted her distress, but they were too embroiled in gossip at the other side of the tea table, their own embroidery hoops barely touched in their laps. Not that she wanted their attention. She hated when they doted on her too much. Thankfully, Breah was too practical to get flustered by small things and Ann was too vapid to care more than she should. If anyone would fret over the queen's pricked finger it would be the simpering Sera, and she was officially serving the princess now. She supposed Lurel would have made quite the fuss too, but she...

Mareleau's heart sank. She still couldn't reconcile that her cousin was no longer living. Time and again, she found herself forgetting, found herself expecting her cousin to pop around the corner and chide Mareleau over some perceived wrongdoing. As annoyed as Mareleau had been with the girl most of the time, she now realized that much of that annoyance had been tangled with a thread of affection. It struck Mareleau as cruel that she'd never get to say goodbye. And since she hadn't had the foresight to have her ladies pack mourning attire, the closest she could get to showing outward respect for her loss was the navy gown she wore today.

She removed the injured finger from between her lips and found that it had already stopped bleeding. Setting aside her hoop, she left the divan and wandered to the window, winding three strands of hair between her fingers as she went. The view outside revealed the dense forest beyond the castle wall, crowned in a misty morning fog. It wasn't the most spectacular view, but it was tolerable enough to make her wish she could curl up on the ledge and press her forehead to the window glass, much like she often did in her favorite alcove at Verlot. Even if the sill was large enough to sit on—which it wasn't—she couldn't show such unqueenly behavior in front of her ladies.

She glanced back at them, still chattering away. Breah's blonde head bobbed as she laughed at something the crimson-haired Ann had said. Mareleau envied Ann's red hair and Breah's slender, willowy form. More than that, she envied the ease with which they laughed. Mareleau hadn't laughed with such unbridled restraint since she was much younger. Perhaps not since before she and Larylis had first been forced apart three years ago.

Her heart pulsed with longing for her husband, sending a wave of sorrow so strong, it nearly tore a sob from her throat. She gripped the edge of the windowsill hard enough to distract her, to steady her while she breathed away the urge to cry.

She would not let a tear fall.

Not a single one.

When her sudden grief had passed, she found anger in its wake. Whirling from the window, she faced her ladies. "This is incredibly unfair."

Breah and Ann halted their chatter and turned wide eyes toward the queen. Ann shifted anxiously in her seat, then began winding her embroidery floss around her finger. Meanwhile, Breah set aside her needlework and rose from her chair. "What can we do for you, Majesty?" she asked.

"You can tell me why the seven devils we're here," Mareleau said, marching past Breah to Ann and lifting the girl's embroidery hoop from her lap, "doing *hideous* needlework while the princess does gods know what."

Ann frowned at Mareleau's insult. "It's a bird."

Mareleau frowned just as deeply at what she'd been certain was a misshapen mountain. She dropped the hoop back onto her lady's lap and sank down onto the edge of the bed. It was bedecked in the same outdated mauve brocade as the divan. "Why am I in a room rumored to have belonged to a dead queen? One who died in this *very* room, no less?"

Breah nodded. "It's in rather poor taste, Majesty. But it might just be a rumor."

Ann swiveled in her seat to face them. "I heard it repeated by at least four—"

Breah silenced the girl with a glare.

"You're right," Ann rushed to say, "it's probably just a rumor."

"I had a plan," Mareleau mumbled. "I was supposed to at least *pretend* to be useful here."

Despite Mareleau's dread over having to spend two weeks at Ridine, she'd managed to give herself some sense of purpose. During her travels, she'd organized lists of all the wisdom she'd share with Aveline, all the etiquette, manners, and feminine arts she could pass on. She wasn't normally a fan of anything considered *feminine arts*, nor was she one to go to such great lengths to help others, but her mission at Ridine was a scheme of sorts, and scheming was something Mareleau excelled at. If she was forced to be a spy, she'd be a damned good one.

"It's only been a day, Majesty," Breah said. "Aveline will come to call soon enough, and you'll be able to chastise her for her poor behavior."

Ann rushed to stand beside Breah. "Have you asked your uncles where she is?"

Mareleau scoffed. She *had* asked her uncles, and when she'd inquired how the seven devils she was supposed to get close to the princess when the girl wouldn't even observe respectful protocol, they'd told her there had been a development. According to Kevan and Ulrich, the princess was in charge of refurbishing some library that Mareleau was forbidden to step foot in. When she'd asked for more of an explanation, they'd refused.

Never before had it been clearer; her purpose at Ridine was less about being her father's spy and more about being punished.

A knock sounded at the door, and Mareleau's heart leaped, half with hope, half with dread. While she was eager to busy herself with something—even if that *something* was a princess whom she didn't exactly get along swimmingly with—the thought of conversing with Aveline set her teeth on edge. She'd humiliated her yesterday, going on about how Mareleau wasn't *her* queen, and she didn't belong to *this* kingdom. Mareleau was almost of a mind to take everything back and feel gratitude for her state of boredom, but when Breah opened the door to reveal an unfamiliar face that did not belong to Aveline, Mareleau felt her anger return.

How dare the princess still not visit! *She* was a queen.

Breah closed the door without inviting the caller in and brought an envelope to her. "You have a letter, Majesty."

Mareleau tore it from the girl's grasp and rushed to the window. All prior thoughts fled her mind as she flicked open the seal without even looking at it, hoping to see a familiar script—

She pursed her lips. Why she wasn't used to disappointment by now was a mystery. She should have known better than to expect a letter from Larylis. Not because he hadn't been writing, but because she'd already received one from him that morning. She rarely went a day without one, and they'd become the singular bright spot in her current state of existence. If she could reread them all day, she'd never suffer from boredom. However, along with joy, her husband's letters brought sorrow too, simply because they were apart. Her emotions had already grown volatile as of late; everything seemed to bring her to the edge of either tears or rage. Should she spend all day reading her beloved's words, she might forget how to keep her composure at all.

She scanned the brief letter with a scowl, then tossed it on the windowsill. "Teryn," she said between her teeth. "Have I not done enough for you as it is?"

The answer rang through her, a clear *no*.

While she'd kept her word and made no mention of Teryn's secret travels nor his appearance at the inn to Uncle Ulrich, she knew in her heart that she'd always be in his debt. Nothing could repay him for what he'd done. She didn't know whether he'd acted out of love for his brother or dislike for Mareleau, but it didn't matter. He'd been on her side when no one else had been. He'd abdicated his right to the crown so Larylis could be king, erasing every last obstacle that stood between her and the man she loved.

Her heart softened, smoothing the edges of her ire. She glanced back at the discarded letter. Its contents relayed a request for another favor. Since it was a scheme of sorts, Mareleau supposed she could oblige. He was her brother now, and if she couldn't do her duty as a spy, she could assist her unwanted sibling's request to get him into the castle without being intercepted by her uncles.

With a soft smile curling her lips, she turned away from the window. She was about to exit the room for the sake of reconnaissance, but the look on her ladies' faces pulled her up short. Breah's eyes turned down at the corners while Ann wrung folds of her silk skirt in her hands.

"What?" Mareleau bit out.

Breah and Ann exchanged a look but said nothing.

"Out with it."

Breah worried her lip before taking a step closer to the queen. "It's just...I was wondering...is it strange?"

Mareleau's irritation returned in a flash. "Is *what* strange?"

"Being married to...to King Larylis instead of Teryn?"

"Why the seven devils would that be strange? Strange would be being wed to Teryn."

"Because Teryn isn't king?" Ann said.

"Because Teryn isn't my husband."

"But you wanted him to be, didn't you?" Breah asked. "The two of you were engaged for three years."

Mareleau barked a laugh. "What gave you the impression I'd *wanted* to be engaged to him? Banish it from your minds."

Ann shifted from foot to foot and let out an awkward laugh. "I did find it strange that you were always courting another suitor."

"Courting other suitors went against my will, just as much as being engaged to Teryn did. The only man I've ever loved was Larylis."

Breah's eyes bulged from their sockets. "Truly?"

Mareleau was perplexed by her ladies' shock. Hadn't they known about her friendship with Larylis when he'd lived as a ward to Uncle Ulrich? The budding feelings she'd begun to develop? Then she recalled that she'd only confided in Katra, the lady's maid she'd trusted most. The one person aside from Larylis that she'd considered a friend. Before Katra had betrayed her, of course.

No wonder her maids knew nothing of her true feelings. She'd kept them well hidden. Now she felt a little self-conscious that she was sharing so much. Being at Ridine truly was messing with her emotions. Either that or—

That's right!

Her moon cycle was due any day now. Her pregnancy ruse was coming to an end. That explained her irritation, her fraying nerves.

She studied her ladies through slitted lids. She supposed it wouldn't hurt to tell them the truth about her feelings. The last thing she wanted were rumors spreading that the queen had only married Larylis because he'd been named king. She needed the world to know of her love. Of her victory.

"Yes," Mareleau said, lifting her chin, "I've only ever loved Larylis. I've never had an ounce of feelings for anyone but him. I would have given up my royal right for him, would have burned down the world for him. And now he's mine and I'm happier than I've ever been. Or I will be, once I leave here and go back home to Dermaine Palace."

Ann brought a hand to her lips while Breah blinked a sheen of tears from her eyes.

Mareleau threw her hands in the air. "Now what?"

Ann lowered her hand to reveal that she was grinning like an idiot while Breah bounced on the balls of her feet. "It's just," Breah said, "we've never heard you speak like that before. You've never talked about love or romance, or feelings at all. It's so good to know you're happy."

"I am," Mareleau said, but the words formed a sudden lump in her throat. Tears welled in her eyes, and a sob was building in her chest, too heavy to suppress.

Breah's lips curled into a sappy smile, and she took a step forward to reach for her hand.

Mareleau whirled back toward the window before the girl's fingers could make contact with hers. Blinking furiously to clear her eyes, she managed to say, "Find me chocolate. Both of you."

"I already have, Majesty," came Ann's voice. "The cook said she didn't have any."

"Ask again," Mareleau ground out between her teeth. "And if she still doesn't have any, tell her to order some. While you're at it, bring me a slice of cake."

"Yes, Your Majesty," both girls said in unison. A swish of skirts followed, then the close of her chamber door. Only then did Mareleau release a heavy sigh. Only then did she let a tear slip over her cheek.

21

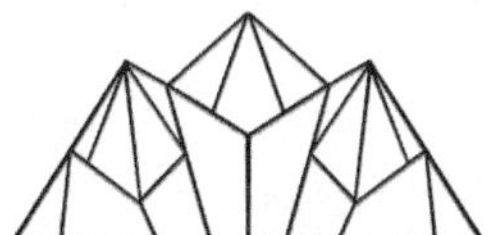

Cora could only guess how long it had been since the North Tower Library last felt the touch of sunlight. Now that the windows had been freed from the heavy tapestries that had covered them, the room looked half as sinister as before. She wiped her hands on the apron covering her simple wool day dress and gave the room an approving nod. She could work with half as sinister.

Warm afternoon air wafted through each open window, bringing with it the smell of the not-too-distant mountains mingling with the hawthorn, laurel, and rosemary burning in the hearth. The herb smoke and sunlight, along with the droplets of spring water and rows of salt lining each sill, would ensure any dark energies that managed to escape the room through the open windows would be purified.

Earth, fire, water, air.

That was all a witch needed to cleanse an item of energetic impurities. Her efforts were working. Already she could feel the room growing lighter, brighter, clearer. A safer space to navigate. But that was just the room itself. As for the objects in the library...well, that would take far longer. She predicted weeks of emotionally draining work lay ahead of her. Luckily, it was work she was well suited to.

She'd spent the last day and a half gathering supplies—herbs, plants, spring water, and stones—to accompany the items she'd already taken from the kitchen. This morning, she'd spent a few hours taking energetic inventory of the room, wandering from wall to wall with her palms extended, sensing beats of pressure, darkness, enchantments. The strongest pulse had come from the book that had killed Lurel. It remained closed as Cora had left it, but one of the first things she'd done this morning was carefully slice the leather strap that attached the metal clasp to the cover and toss it in the fire. The hidden needle was the only trap she could sense on the book, and she wasn't willing to risk anyone else being pricked.

She couldn't guarantee that the blood weaving Morkai had armed the book with could only be forged once.

She glanced at the book now, sensed it thrumming with the murky darkness contained between its covers. With her shields only partially up—for protection only—she could sense fluctuations in the energies around her. She had every intention of purifying and destroying the book, but she knew it would be a challenge. Something with that much dark energy would fight her. While the Forest People had taught her and all the other witches and Faeryn descendants how to clear energies, she'd only had experience with small items. A patch of earth here and there. Her tools and weapons. Never had she been responsible for an undertaking like this, and it would doubtless be a draining endeavor. Until she'd warmed up to the process and assessed her energetic stamina, the book would remain as it was.

Her gaze slid to the amber crystal resting beside the book. She couldn't count the number of times she'd forgotten it by now, but today, when she'd found it in her apron pocket, she'd refused to remove her hand from it until she'd entered the room. Then she'd set it on the table, out in the open where she wouldn't be able to forget its existence, regardless of the enchantment Morkai had placed on it. She squinted at it, then at the two copper basins on the floor before the fireplace. One held salt while the other would soon be filled with water. She could try the crystal first...

A rushing sound reached her ears, of wings beating wind. She caught sight of a dark silhouette from the corner of her eye and nearly jumped out of her skin as a large bird landed in one of the open windows, opposite the row of salt lining the ledge. There it stood, head cocked to the side. Backlit as it was by the bright sun, she couldn't clearly make out its distinguishing features. She blinked a few times and took a few steps closer, trying to get a better glimpse.

Its size, its form, the emotional energy she was just beginning to connect with, slowly took shape as something familiar...

Could it be?

"Berol—"

"I've brought another jug of spring water, Highness." The disgruntled voice of Cora's new lady's maid sent the bird flying from the sill and out of sight.

Cora whirled toward the doorway just as Sera began to duck beneath the dangling bundles of rosemary hanging from the doorframe. All thoughts of the bird fled her mind. "Do not take a step inside this room," Cora barked, her voice harsher than she'd intended.

Sera pulled up short, muttering under her breath. "Like I even want to be here at all."

Ignoring the girl's retort, Cora met her at the doorway. With a poorly hidden scowl, Sera handed her the jug of spring water beneath the hanging rosemary.

"What is this anyway?" Sera asked, casting a wary glance first at the rosemary, then at the row of salt sprinkled in a distinct line over the threshold. The girl seemed more annoyed than curious, wrinkling her nose in distaste. Then again, Cora had never seen Sera looking anything other than displeased. She was starting to wonder if that was simply due to her face. She had a small mouth, an upturned button nose, and a pointed chin a little too sharp for her rounded cheeks. There'd be something cherubic about her looks, were she not always looking at Cora like she'd rather be anywhere else.

Cora noticed movement farther down the stairwell where one of her guards—or Kevan's spies, more like—awaited. He was around her brother's age, perhaps nine-and-twenty, but his shrewd expression made him seem much older. Another sentry stood at the base of the stairwell, but the man upstairs was tasked with keeping an eye on her at all times. His gaze narrowed on the bundled herbs as if he too sought an answer to Sera's question.

Cora relayed her lie with practiced ease. "Since I've been ordered to keep the door to this room open while I work, I've had to take precautions to ensure no one but me enters. It is for everyone's safety that I be the only one allowed in here. Should I see smeared granules of salt across the floor or hair tangled in the rosemary, I'll know someone has been inside."

Sera nodded absently, accepting Cora's fabricated tale while she twirled a strand of straight brown hair around her finger. The guard seemed to accept her story too and averted his gaze from the doorway.

Cora turned away, smiling to herself with satisfaction that quiet magic could so easily be masked with logic. The true purpose of the salt and rosemary was to keep the energies contained to the room, utilizing the magical properties of the herbs. They acted as a ward of sorts, preventing the dark energies from fleeing down the stairwell and into the rest of the castle. If the energies wanted free, they'd have to depart through the windows where they could be purified upon crossing the sill.

She crouched on the floor before the water basin and reverently poured the spring water from the jug. A tingle of euphoria moved through her. Mother Goddess, this felt good. Not so much being surrounded by Morkai's dark items, but embodying her magical side, even if only in secret. To think she used to scoff at quiet magic, used to undermine its soft and unassuming effects in favor of weapons. Now she was grateful to be surrounded by the invisible Arts. It made her feel powerful. Useful. A witch hiding in plain sight. A princess with a purpose.

"You don't need me anymore, do you?" Sera asked from the other side of the threshold. Then, as an afterthought, tacked on, "Your Highness."

Cora rolled her eyes. Ever since Lord Kevan had hauled Sera into her room and deemed her Cora's new lady's maid, the girl had made no secret that she'd rather be with her beloved queen. It served Cora well, though, for it made Sera easy to get rid of. And she'd certainly need her gone before she could get started. It was already bad enough having a guard hovering at the top of the stairs.

"You may go," she said over her shoulder. As soon as the words left her mouth, she felt Sera's emotions lift into bubbly excitement.

"Do you need me to return at all today? Perhaps not until this evening when I ready you for bed? In the meantime, I really should check on Her Majesty. It must be dreadful managing with only two of her ladies. She really needs me, you know. Especially because of the baby." The last part came out as a loud whisper.

Cora shifted slightly toward the door. "The queen is with child?" This was certainly the first time Cora had heard of the news.

Sera continued to wind a strand of hair around her finger. Taking on the telltale tone of someone relaying a juicy bit of gossip, she said, "According to Queen Helena, yes. The morning we left Verlot, she told us she was absolutely certain her daughter had conceived on her wedding night and ordered us to forbid the queen even a single glass of wine while she was away. I daresay she must be right, for of course Her Majesty would conceive easily. She is queen, after all, and knows her duty is to bring Menah's next heir into the world. Her son will be heir to two kingdoms because when her father dies, she'll inherit Selay too. Can you imagine how great a kingdom she'll have when Selay and Menah merge as one?" She lowered her voice to a whisper again. "Much larger than your own kingdom, Highness."

Cora stared blankly at the girl. That was the most Sera had ever spoken to her. Apparently, if the topic was Mareleau, she'd be impossible to stop. Well, that was a subject Cora could do without.

Before Cora could dismiss her once more, Sera spoke again, eyes going suddenly wide.

"Is it really possible to know if one's pregnant immediately after one's wedding night?" Trepidation and a hint of panic wafted from the girl. "Or one's...*you know*... night?"

The guard let out a cough to mask what had started as a bark of laughter.

Sera stiffened, cheeks turning pink as if she'd forgotten the man's presence.

Cora debated the best answer she could give—one that wouldn't undermine whatever Queen Helena had said while also convincing Sera to leave her alone already—when a clairsentient feeling struck her, telling her she was on the verge of a truth she wasn't supposed to know. She shouldn't care; this situation had nothing to do with her. But the niggling feeling had her stringing facts together in her mind: Queen Helena's certainty that her daughter had conceived, Mareleau's sudden marriage and surprising change of groom, her aggressive protectiveness over Larylis...

Mother Goddess, Mareleau and Larylis had had an *affair*.

It was the only explanation that made sense. Why else would Teryn not have married her? Why else would Larylis be King of Menah in Teryn's stead? There was no way Teryn would have *chosen* such a thing were it not a last resort.

The thought tied her heart and stomach in knots.

"Never mind," Sera said with a huff, clearly frustrated by Cora's lack of answer. "I was only asking for a friend. *I* trust Queen Helena's judgment." Then, without offering any kind of formal farewell, she turned on her heel and rushed down the stairs.

Cora roused herself from thoughts of Mareleau, Larylis, and Teryn.

And Teryn.

Teryn.

She shook her head, forcing him from her mind at last. She had a vital task to perform, one that required a clear head and emotional fortitude. Rising from the floor, she strode to the table, retrieved the amber crystal, and brought it back to the water basin. With a deep breath, she dropped it beneath the surface and gave herself over to the miracles of quiet magic.

Until quiet magic turned to blood.

22

Cora watched with terror as the water in the basin turned crimson. She wanted to believe it was a trick of the light, the orange glow of the crystal reflecting off the copper bowl, deepening into scarlet. But she knew the truth. It filled her with a sickening certainty.

The crystal was leaking blood.

It shouldn't have surprised her. She knew this was Morkai's crystal, remembered how it had dripped blood when she'd found it on the battlefield, broken off from his cane dagger. She'd suspected that he'd somehow used the crystal to store the blood he'd stolen for his weavings.

And now it was filling the basin, flooding it with the essence of countless victims, most of whom were probably dead.

Her own ball of blood was likely in the pool, swirling, mingling...

Bile rose into her throat, but she couldn't look away. Couldn't move. Her shoulders began to tremble, her mind reeling between shock and panic. The water was so dark, the crystal was almost invisible now.

Cora.

Valorre's familiar energy reached through her frazzled emotions, cleaving through her panic, and separating her from her fear. She hadn't been out to see her unicorn friend since the night of Lurel's death, but he'd come close enough to the castle walls to check in with her now and then.

Are you all right?

She forced herself to her feet, averting her gaze from the basin. Then, focusing on the elements—on the heat from the hearth, the smell of herbs wafting from the fire, the feel of solid stone beneath her leather slippers, the glittering dewdrops lining the windowsill—she drew her shields tight around her. She'd need to lower them again before she got back to work, lest she fail to sense hidden dangers, but for now they served as a sense of safety.

I'm all right, she conveyed to Valorre.

I worry, he said from somewhere in the forest.

So do I. But I'm fine now.

With a slow exhale, she glanced back at the blood-filled basin. The sight still repulsed her, but she could think objectively now. Of course the crystal leaked blood. And it was a good thing. It meant the cleansing was working. All that was left for her to do was empty the dirty basin, bring it back inside, refill it, and start again. She'd do it over and over until the water ran clear.

She'd made a mistake in starting with the crystal, assuming it would act like an ordinary stone. Had she wanted to start off easy, she'd have chosen something far less personal to Morkai. But she'd already begun and now she would see it through.

Setting her jaw, she bent down and hefted the basin in her hands. Thankfully, it wasn't overfull, even with the blood. She'd purposefully poured only one jug of spring water inside it, knowing she'd have to change the water frequently over the course of her work. Even so, she kept her steps even, determined not to let even a drop of the basin's repulsive contents get within inches of the bowl's rim. Then, keeping her composure nonchalant, she ducked beneath the hanging rosemary and strolled past the guard. He stiffened at the sight of what she carried, but she commented, "Rust," and left it at that.

Every step felt tenuous as she descended the stairs. Her heart slammed against her ribs, making her arms shake. She dreaded even the slightest stumble. If she got even a drop of that vile blood on her, she'd retch. She managed to reach the bottom of the stairwell without any incident and proceeded through the castle. The guard's footsteps sounded behind her, echoing the pound of her racing heart, but she paid him no heed. She had no choice but to let him follow her.

She moved more on instinct than design, making her way outside past a familiar courtyard, then through a door in a low wall, stopping only when she reached the charred field that once was Ridine's garden. Her composure began to crack at the sight of it; it was somehow even more sorrowful under daylight. Morkai had sacrificed the life that had once grown there to animate his wraiths. It remained as she'd seen it last, an expanse of black earth dotted with gnarled stumps.

A shudder ran through her as she recalled the duke's demonstration. How he'd killed two prisoners, one slaughtered by his wraiths, the other murdered by a blood weaving. She understood now why her instincts—no, her Art—had drawn her here. While she couldn't change what had happened, couldn't bring Morkai's victims back from the dead, she could return the blood he'd stolen. Give it back to the earth where the dead belonged. Feed the land where Morkai had taken. Killed. Destroyed.

Crouching at the edge of the field, she emptied the basin until every last drop of blood seeped into the charred soil.

IT TOOK TWO MORE JUGS OF SPRING WATER BEFORE THE CRYSTAL STOPPED BLEEDING. Her chest unraveled with relief. Even more so when she dried off the stone and buried it in the bowl of salt. She half expected the salt to turn red, but it remained untainted. Blowing out a breath, she shifted her weight and sat back on her heels.

You can stop being such a mother hen now, Valorre, she relayed to her friend. With her shields lowered again, she could practically feel the frantic pacing of his hooves along the outer length of the castle wall.

Hen? I am no hen, came his affronted response. *Nor am I a mother.*

Her lips quirked into a weak smile. *No, you are a valiant unicorn. But I'm all right. Truly.* Her heart sank with regret. As much as she liked knowing he was always nearby, she felt guilty too. The only reason he kept close was because of the choice she'd made. He could go wherever he wanted. Roam the woods. Find more of his kind. Instead, he chose to stay near Ridine, for a person who hadn't had the decency to visit him more than once—

Valorre's voice cut in on her thoughts. *I am not to be coddled. I stay because we are friends. You think I need to see your face to be your friend?* He scoffed into her mind. *You confuse me with a pet.*

She blinked a few times, surprised at his sudden ire. His presence waned, and she sensed him trotting off. A flash of concern pinched her heart, but it quickly abated. Her too-proud companion would be back. In the meantime, he was giving her the space she'd inadvertently requested.

And she needed that space. That silence. That focus.

Returning to her kneeling position before the salt basin, she smoothed her hands over her apron, then reached inside the bowl and retrieved the crystal. She rinsed it briefly once more and brought it before the hearth. A fresh bundle of herbs burned alongside the cedar logs, filling the space with the heady aroma of woodsmoke, hawthorn, laurel, and rosemary. She ran the crystal through the smoke, turning it in her hand so every facet could feel the heat of the flames and the gentle touch of the smoke. Now that every element had done its work—earth for grounding, water for cleansing, fire for transmutation, and air for dissipation— she took it to the empty tea table and placed it at the center. There she'd formed a protective sigil using twigs and stones, shaped in overlapping triangles and circles, much like her *insigmora.*

The tea table was far enough from the doorway that the guard, or anyone watching from the other side of the threshold, wouldn't see the strange symbols. With her back facing the door, she could hide what she did next. Not that she was about to do anything impressive. It was only that some aspects of quiet magic looked odd to those ignorant or fearful of magic.

Her inked palms tingled as she closed her eyes and lowered her hands around the crystal, not touching it but sensing. *Feeling* with her Art alone. She extended her senses, connecting with the energy of the crystal. An energy she hoped to find vibrating with pure light—

Disappointment sank her stomach.

She opened her eyes and frowned down at the crystal. While the stone's energy certainly felt lighter, there was still a weight to it. A murky energy mingling with something she couldn't identify. Something that felt alive. Trapped. And not necessarily dark.

Cora released a frustrated sigh, sending loose tendrils of tangled dark hair off her forehead. What could she do next? A normal stone would be cleared by now, but this wasn't a normal stone. Perhaps heat from the fire hadn't been enough to fully transmute the energy. She could throw it in the flames. But would it melt? If so, would that be a good thing? She supposed that all depended upon what exactly that trapped energy was. Not to mention the murky energy beside it that felt far more malevolent.

Curiosity had her furrowing her brow. She reached into her apron pocket and retrieved the paring knife she'd taken from the kitchen. Bending over the table, she held the crystal in place with one hand and carefully pressed the blade's edge into the stone with the other. No matter how much pressure she applied, the crystal didn't so much as splinter. That meant it was only amber in color, not composition. That didn't mean it couldn't be broken. Still, breaking it should be a last resort. It would be best if she could purify more of the murky energy before doing anything that could either destroy the neutral energy or release the darker.

But what else was there to try? She was running out of tools in her arsenal. The Forest People hadn't taught her much beyond this, for whenever they'd come across something that required extra care in regard to clearing, it had been handled by an elder. If only she'd taken magic more seriously when she'd been with them. If only she'd accepted Salinda's invitation—

No. She could not allow her thoughts to get tangled up in *if only*. The truth was, had she taken her magic more seriously and accepted Salinda's offer to take the path of elders, she wouldn't be where she was now. She'd have gone to the Beltane ceremony instead of the hot springs the night she met Valorre. It was impossible to say if fate would still have led her to leaving the commune, meeting Valorre, or crossing paths with Teryn. All she could do was accept that *this* was the path she'd taken. She'd have to solve the puzzle of the crystal with the skills she had at her disposal.

With a groan, she swiped the crystal off the table and stormed back toward the basins. As she passed one of the open windows, a beam of sunlight caught the object in her palm, sending glittering light across her vision. She halted in place and faced the window.

"Sunlight," she said under her breath, realization dawning. While heat from the fire might have been too mild and flames too strong, sunlight could be just what she needed. Taking a step closer to the open window, she lifted her hand and let the warm glow of the afternoon sun fully encompass the crystal. It glittered with light, casting the walls and floor in shards of rainbow luminescence.

Why did Morkai have to use something so beautiful for such sinister purposes?

She rotated the crystal, allowing another portion to face the sun, but when she held it still, she caught movement swirling at the stone's center. With a frown, she watched closer as the crystal's amber depths undulated, its movements like slow honey.

"What are you?" she whispered, tilting the crystal higher, creating more contrast between the sunlight and the stone's core.

Her palms thrummed in warning.

Her heart echoed with a heavy beat.

She lowered the crystal, forcing her eyes away. But when she blinked into the light of the room, her vision was blanketed in white.

23

The white that surrounded her was blinding, like the forest after a heavy snow, masking every tree, every blade of glass, turning the world shapeless. Formless. Panic crawled up her throat, seared every nerve. She tried to focus on the ground beneath her, to root her energy through the soles of her feet, but...there was no ground. No sense of purchase beneath her. It felt more like she was floating.

In nothingness.

Trapped.

Without shape.

She glanced down at her body, her hands, her feet and saw...

Nothing.

Nothing.

Nothing.

"It's all right, it's all right," came a soft feminine voice. The white light dimmed, muted hues bleeding into it like watercolors on a canvas, painting the scene in earth tones. Of stone and wood and sunlight. The tower library took shape around her, but there was something hazy about it. Tenuous.

"This is where you are, isn't it?" the voice asked. Cora looked around for the source, feeling another spike of anxiety when she saw no one.

"I'm here."

Cora faced forward again, and this time she saw a figure standing before her. She was unfamiliar to her, a woman perhaps a year or two her senior. Her skin was deep brown, her hair falling in black curls that just reached her shoulders. Shoulders Cora now realized were bare, as the woman wore a silky gown that hung from her neck and fell in sweeping folds to her ankles. The dress was unlike anything she'd seen before and certainly wasn't suited to this climate.

This climate, her mind echoed.

But what was *this climate*? Her eyes slid from the woman to the room, and a feeling of wrongness struck her. The warmth of summer no longer touched her skin. *Nothing* touched her skin. Panic threatened to seize hold of her again, but the girl's calming voice stole her attention.

"Don't focus on anything but where you are."

"But why am I in this room at all?" Cora startled at the sound of her own voice. It was hollow. Flat. "I...I can't remember why I'm in the tower library." She took a step toward the woman, but the stranger leaped back at the same time, palms facing Cora in warning.

"Be very careful not to touch me," she said.

Cora froze. Despite her sudden inertia, a tingling sensation hummed all around her. Through her. Like she was no longer a solid being.

"Remember what you were doing just a moment ago. Start with what you were wearing."

She glanced down at her body and saw that she wore a gray wool dress covered in a linen apron. In one hand, she held a paring knife. Her mind flickered between sharp memories and hazy confusion. She chased the former, trying to recall why she was in the tower library. What had she been doing with the knife? She glanced at her other hand but found it empty. Hadn't she been holding something?

"The knife," the woman said. "Focus on the knife."

She did as told, but as she studied it, the color of the hilt flickered from black to brown and back again.

"Don't focus on what it looks like. Focus on how it feels in your hand. Close your eyes and *feel*."

Cora didn't want to close her eyes. She wanted to understand what the hell was happening. "Who are you? Where did you come from?" Again, the hollow sound of her voice struck her as wrong. Why didn't it echo even the slightest?

"You cannot focus on me," she said, a note of panic in her tone. "Focus on you. Focus on your body, your surroundings, your breath. Focus on—"

The woman's eyes darted to the side, and a flash of fear crossed her face. Cora shifted to follow the stranger's line of sight, but she barked, "Don't look."

Cora halted, but this time she couldn't stop the panic from tightening her chest, her lungs. Her eyes remained on the woman, but she could sense something behind her. Something dark, murky...

"Focus on yourself, Highness," the woman said, but the terror in her voice was palpable. "Please. You must remember where you are. Focus on the knife. Focus on your breath."

Cora tried to do as the woman suggested, but the dark energy building behind her grew too strong to ignore. Against her better judgment, she cast a glance over her shoulder. At the center of the room, the air vibrated, shuddered, like an enormous fist was slamming against an invisible door.

The woman rounded Cora until she stood between her and the strange phenomenon warping the center of the room. She angled her head until Cora was forced to look at her. "I can't keep us locked here for much longer. You must focus on yourself. Close your eyes."

Just then, a sound like breaking glass pierced the hollow silence around them.

Where the air had shuddered, there now was a crack. A crack in what, Cora didn't know. It splintered the center of the tower room as if her surroundings weren't real but something reflected behind a mirror.

Another thud. Another crack. Then wisps of black smoke oozed through the cracks.

On instinct, Cora lifted her blade...

But her hand was empty.

"No," the woman said, reaching for Cora without touching her. "The knife. Remember the knife! Feel it!"

Cora opened her palm. Closed it. Felt nothing. Nothing.

The tower room began to drip and bleed, returning to the blinding white. The woman was nowhere to be seen, only the darkness that continued to spill through cracks that were now invisible. It took shape before her, swirling from the ground up to form legs, hips, a torso, a pair of shoulders—

Cora opened her mouth to scream.

~

WITH AN INTAKE OF BREATH, SOUND AND COLOR RUPTURED AROUND HER, BRINGING with it the heavy awareness of her body, her limbs, her hands, things she'd been disconnected from a moment ago. Another body pressed close to hers, touching her, shaking her. She curled her palm around her paring knife, and this time she felt its hilt, a comforting weight in her hand. In a flash of movement, she flicked the blade up and pressed it to her assailant's throat.

She blinked several times, clearing them of the haze lingering in the wake of the change of light, until a familiar face took shape before her.

Dark hair flecked with gold. Chiseled cheekbones. Green eyes the color of moss.

She had the strangest sensation that this wasn't whom she'd been expecting.

But whom had she been expecting?

What had she been doing?

Why was she holding a paring knife...to Teryn's throat?

His hands went still on her shoulders, throat bobbing as his lips curled into a hesitant smirk.

"This brings back memories," he muttered.

Cora's chest heaved with sharp breaths, her knife hand trembling. Her emotions shifted between terror and relief. Confusion and shock. Part of her wanted to scream while the other wanted to collapse into Teryn's arms and sob with relief. Then she recalled he had no reason to be there. He *couldn't* be there. He was supposed to be at Dermaine Palace. No matter how hard she tried, she couldn't reconcile this moment with the one that came before it. Both were equally impossible, but one was slipping from her mind with every beat of her heart until...it was gone. *Now* was all she had left.

Teryn looked down at her with the most tender concern. "Are you all right?"

Cora gave a shaky nod.

"Then will you lower the knife?"

She'd forgotten about the blade. Forgotten why she'd been driven to defend herself with it. Why was she so shaken up? Had Teryn simply startled her while she'd been concentrating on her work? But what had she been working on? Hadn't she been holding something other than the knife...

"Highness," came a voice from behind them. It belonged to Cora's guard, and his tone was laced with the frantic impatience of someone who'd been repeating himself to no avail. "Is everything all right?"

"Yes," Teryn called over his shoulder.

Cora drew back her knife and took a step away from Teryn, just in time to see the guard's head ducked beneath the rosemary, his foot planted over her line of salt.

Solid sense eradicated the remainder of her disorientation. "You can't be in here," she shouted at the guard. Then her eyes slid to Teryn, going wide when the implications of where she was—where *he* was—began to dawn. "Damn it, Teryn, you can't be in here either."

Her pulse kicked up, propelling her to return her knife to her apron pocket and press both hands against Teryn's chest. She blushed at the feel of his solid torso beneath her palms, but she blamed it on her fury. Forcing him around, she pushed him toward the doorway.

"Have you any idea how dangerous it is in here?" she said to his back as she shoved him by the shoulder blades. "How did the guard let you in?"

"I didn't exactly give him a choice," he said, voice low. "And...you weren't moving. You were just standing frozen. Unresponsive. I was worried about you."

She paused. *I was frozen?* For the life of her, she couldn't recall what might have had her so transfixed. Never mind that. The thought of Teryn meeting Lurel's same fate just to save her had her redoubling her efforts. Hands on his lower back, she pushed him the rest of the way out the door. Had he wanted to, he could have set his feet and laughed while she tried to move him without gain. They may have been well matched with weapons, but when it came to size and strength, Teryn was the indisputable winner. So it wasn't lost on her that he let her push him, let her guide him out the door and into the stairwell.

Cheeks flushed, she stepped over the threshold and faced Teryn with her hands on her hips. With him standing on the top stair and she on the landing before the doorway, their bodies were noticeably close. She lifted her chin to meet his eyes and found that she didn't have to lift them far. With him a step down from her, they were nearly eye to eye. Lips level. Chests close enough to collide—

"What are you doing here?" she bit out, her voice laced with fury. Whether her ire was driven by lingering worry over him having crossed such a dangerous threshold or resentment over their last meeting, she knew not.

Teryn opened his mouth then snapped it shut, steely gaze moving to the guard that hovered on the stair beside him. He arched a brow. "Do you mind?"

The guard glanced from Teryn to Cora, then moved down a few steps.

Teryn returned his gaze to hers. His emotions slammed into her, buzzing with trepidation, timidity, and...something warmer. Softer.

Cora took a deep breath and fully raised her shields.

"I...I came to speak with you," he finally said.

"About what?"

A flush crept into his cheeks.

Even with her shields now fully in place, she knew the answer. She'd been half expecting this, though she hadn't let herself dwell on it. A marriage alliance still needed to be made to secure trust between her and her new allies. Teryn was here to forge that alliance. Between himself and her.

She startled at the happy trill that sang through her chest, but she smothered it down. *I'm his only option*, she told it. He was not here for a love match, just politics.

A heavy disappointment clawed at her heart.

Another thing she smothered down.

He lowered his voice. "Can we go somewhere private?"

Her stomach tightened. He wanted to go somewhere private to...to ask her to marry him. It was a fact. Logical. She *felt* in her deepest core that this was happening. Knew it *needed* to happen.

This is just a cold, calculated alliance.

Then why the Mother Goddess did it send her heart hammering?

Her throat constricted, forcing her voice higher than she intended. "Right now?"

"Yes, right now."

She angled a thumb over her shoulder. "I...I have work to do—"

"Then we'll speak here if we must. I'm not willing to let this matter stretch on a second longer. I've gone to great lengths to ensure no one and nothing will come between us—between this matter at hand—until I've said what I've come to say. I'd prefer we speak before Verdian's brothers return."

Cora focused on the last part of his statement, not the parts that made her heart feel like it might take flight from her ribcage. "Where are Lord Kevan and Lord Ulrich?"

"Hunting with your brother and his council."

She pulled her head back. "Hunting?"

"Yes, in the royal forest."

That cured some of the fluttery madness writhing through her. Dimetreus had gone out hunting with the council...and he didn't even tell her! What was he thinking? Should he even be going on such an excursion? What if something happened? What if he had another breakdown in front of those men—

She closed her eyes and forced the thoughts from her mind. Her brother may not be in the most stable of states, but he was king. He'd proven that he could hold his own at the council meeting. Royal hunts were expected of a monarch. What was the worst that could happen?

Her stomach sank. Perhaps she shouldn't let her mind go there. Plenty of things could go wrong, but—

The blood drained from her face.

Valorre!

She cursed under her breath. Valorre was out there somewhere, well beyond the castle wall. She extended her senses to try and connect with him, but it seemed he'd yet to return to close range. If Kevan or Ulrich caught sight of him...

She remembered the clairsentient warning she'd felt at the council meeting; she knew some of the councilmen were eager to continue hunting unicorns.

"Are you all right?" Teryn whispered.

Her eyes snapped to his, and she was forced to recall just how close he stood to her.

"Yes," she said in a rush, caught between worry for Valorre and anxiety over what Teryn had come to talk to her about. Perhaps she could handle both issues at once. She swallowed hard and gestured down the stairwell. "Very well, Teryn. Let's go speak in private."

24

The air between Cora and Teryn crackled with tension, thick enough for Cora to feel even through her shields. They walked side by side down a narrow path through the woods just outside the castle walls. The three feet of space between them meant their shoulders were in no danger of touching, yet she felt Teryn's presence with every fiber of her being as if he were pressed to her side.

She'd brought Teryn outside so she could check on Valorre and ensure he hadn't crossed paths with her brother's hunting party. But with Teryn so close it was hard to focus on anything else. Not even the presence of the two guards who tailed them lessened her awareness of him.

Shaking thoughts of her distracting companion from her mind, she extended her senses and sought Valorre's familiar energy. She'd tried it several times since exiting the castle to no avail, but this time she felt their connection snap into place. He was just barely within their communication range.

Valorre! Where the hell are you?

She felt a tinge of annoyance coming from him, but it melted away. Softened. His voice reached her without an edge. *I'm not too far.*

My brother is in the royal forest with a hunting party. I don't trust his councilmen when it comes to your kind. You haven't crossed their path, have you?

He scoffed, and she could almost see him puffing his large white chest with pride. *They are a pathetic hunting party. They could never find me or my kind. I could trot beside them and they'd pay me no notice. They rely on hounds to alert them of prey, not their brains.*

They have hounds? How is that supposed to comfort me?

Hounds like me.

She waited for him to elaborate, but that was the only explanation he gave. *Fine. Just be careful.*

Who's being the female chicken now? he said with a smug chuckle.

The phrase is mother hen—never mind. I guess we're even.

Her lips curled into a small smile.

Cora startled as something brushed her hand. A glance to the side revealed Teryn had stepped in close, and his knuckles lightly skated over hers.

He threw a look over his shoulder at the guards, then lowered his voice. "Is Valorre nearby?"

She suppressed a shudder at the way his deep, whispered tone rumbled through her. "He is."

"I thought so." He took a small step away, but not far enough to regain all the distance he'd closed. "You had that look on your face just now. The one you often got during our travels. I always felt like you and Valorre were sharing some secret language."

She pursed her lips. She never did confess just how well they could communicate. "What about Berol?"

He tipped his chin toward the sky.

Cora glanced up and saw a dark silhouette circling high above them. Realization dawned as she recalled the bird that had landed in the tower window. *That had been Berol after all!*

"So..." Teryn sidled slightly closer. "Should we talk about—"

"Not yet," she said, heart leaping into her throat. "Not until we get to where we're going."

"Ah, so you do have a destination in mind. We aren't simply wandering the woods until you find an ample cliff to shove me from?"

"Oh, we are heading for a cliff. I'm undecided whether I'll be shoving you off it." She met his gaze with an easy smile and found him grinning right back. The sight made her pulse quicken. When had she last seen him smile like that? For a moment, it felt as if they'd slipped back in time to just under two months ago, when their banter and arguments had begun shifting into friendship. The echo of the past unsettled her. It felt...wrong. But why? Because they were less than friends now?

Or because they were more?

She couldn't help but think of their kiss. Or before that, of the moment they'd shared beneath the tree when she'd rendered them invisible. Or at Centerpointe Rock when her hand had stilled on his torso after she'd bandaged his wound. Her mind lingered over that moment now, remembering how his eyes had flickered as he'd looked down at her, stirring the energies between them into something new. Even more so when he'd placed his hand over hers and caressed the back of her hand with his thumb.

That moment had felt so heavy. So meaningful.

But then everything changed. Cora had gotten herself captured by Verdian.

And Teryn...

Teryn had proposed an engagement between her and his brother. Regardless of the reason that had brought him here now, she couldn't let herself forget that she hadn't been his first choice. He was here because he had to be.

The forest path split into a fork, and Cora paused to recall which way led to her destination. After a moment of hesitation, an internal tug pulled her to the left. "This way," she said, starting off down the left-hand path and taking the opportunity to place another foot of space between them.

Keeping her voice nonchalant, she changed the subject to neutral territory. "How did you know my brother and his council had gone hunting?"

Teryn's smile no longer brightened his face. "Mareleau told me."

"Mareleau?" A spike of annoyance shot through her. So his former fiancée was simply...Mareleau. Not Her Majesty. Not Queen Mareleau. Cora wasn't sure how to feel about that, but the jealousy that clouded her chest was most certainly uncalled for. But that didn't stop it from growing.

Teryn nodded. "She'd discovered my plan to come here and speak with you. I begged for her silence and requested her help in getting me inside the palace while her uncles were away."

Cora arched a brow and cast him a disbelieving look. "She helped you? As in... she did something for another person?"

"More like she sent me a curt letter informing me of her uncles' hunting excursion, and I took advantage of their fortuitous absence."

"Why did you ask for her help and not mine?" Cora wished she could swallow her accusing tone, but it was too late. *I shouldn't care. It shouldn't matter.* She cleared her throat. "If your business at Ridine involves me, you could have sent me a letter informing me of your visit. Why the secrecy?"

Teryn cast her a sideways grin. "I wasn't sure you'd reply. Worse, I thought perhaps you'd tell me not to come at all."

He had a point.

But still...

"So instead, you schemed to infiltrate my home and sneak up on me unannounced?"

"Technically, I didn't infiltrate the castle. Master Arther greeted me and—" His voice cut off and his expression turned serious. "I was willing to do whatever it took. I told you, Cora. I wasn't going to let anything come between us again."

Us.

The word sent her pulse thundering.

She shifted her gaze ahead and saw the trees thinning, opening to a familiar sight. One she hadn't seen since she was a child. She picked up her pace, pouring all her focus into her destination to distract herself from Teryn.

From the way he'd said *us.*

Teryn kept pace at her side while the sound of the guards' footsteps lagged farther behind. Finally, they reached a small clearing at the edge of a low, grassy cliff. Beneath it spread a wide meadow dotted with wildflowers in every shade imaginable. A smile stretched Cora's lips. It was even more beautiful than she'd remembered.

She halted a few feet before the cliff's edge and breathed in the fresh summer air. A shadow crossed the sun as Berol descended and landed in a nearby tree.

Teryn came up beside Cora. His knuckles caressed hers again, making her breath catch. He made no move to pull his hand away, only let their fingers brush once more before he said, "It's beautiful."

She angled her body to the side, sliding her hand out of reach. "I used to come here with my brother when I was a child. It was our secret place."

He met her eyes, sunlight catching his emerald irises. His mouth lifted at both corners. "Thank you for bringing me here."

Her shoulders tensed as a sudden wave of self-consciousness swept over her. She hadn't considered the implications of bringing him to a special place to have their private chat. To be honest, she hadn't thought of where to take them until they were several minutes into their forest stroll. It was the only place she could think of that was close enough for the guards not to make a fuss but far enough away to give her the time she needed to mentally prepare for the matter at hand.

Teryn faced her fully. His throat bobbed once. Twice.

She held her breath, knowing what he was preparing to say...

"Why didn't you meet me in the garden at Verlot Palace that night?"

She blinked a few times. Those weren't quite the words she'd expected, but they filled her with no small amount of anxiety. She opened her mouth to answer, but her eyes darted to the side, taking in the bored postures of the two guards who stood several feet away.

Teryn released an aggravated grumble and addressed them. "Can you *please* give us some damn privacy?"

The guards exchanged a glance but begrudgingly obeyed, taking a dozen or so paces out of the clearing to flank the forest path instead.

Teryn returned to face Cora, brow raised in question.

It seemed he wasn't going to let her off that easy.

She resisted the urge to fidget and hid her hands in the folds of her skirt. Only then did she realize she still wore her apron and her dress was embarrassingly plain. She'd had to borrow it from a servant just to have something comfortable enough to work in. She was likely covered in salt, herbs, and soot as well. Not to mention what her hair must look like. Meanwhile, he was dressed like a true prince. A man who'd almost been king. His dark trousers were clearly made for riding, but the way they hugged his thighs told her they were custom tailored to the finest precision. His waistcoat was leather, but not in the style worn by a hunter. His was of a supple blue suede, embossed with Menah's eagle sigil. Not even the rolled-up sleeves of his shirt or the cravat hanging loose around his neck belied his title.

He was a distinguished royal. *She* was a witch playing pretend until she'd served her purpose as a princess.

Besides, it didn't matter what either of them looked like. He was only here for politics. It was better that way. She'd already determined that a political alliance was all she could commit to. A love match represented danger. The potential for heartache. She wasn't yet ready to let go of the life she'd had with the Forest People. Of freedom. The Arts. If she married for love, she'd have to give that all up. Be Princess Aveline forevermore.

But isn't Teryn the one person I can be both a witch and a princess with?

She banished the thought and reminded herself he was still waiting for an answer. She supposed he deserved one.

Forcing herself to meet his eyes with a neutral expression, she said, "I didn't think it was proper to meet with what I assumed was a married man alone in a garden at night."

"You thought I'd married Mareleau."

Cora shrugged. "She was your fiancée."

"No, Cora, everything changed—"

"I know what changed. I know about Larylis and Mareleau. Or...her pregnancy at least."

Teryn frowned. "You do?"

She let out a halfhearted chuckle. "One of the queen's maids—well, I suppose she's my maid now—isn't the keenest when it comes to discretion. Or even logic."

Teryn looked relieved that she'd freed him from the burden of having to explain. Perhaps she should free him from the rest of his burdens too. They might as well get this over with.

Turning back toward the edge of the cliff and the bright meadow beyond, she said, "I know why you're here, and I know what you came to say. What you came to ask me. I agreed to an alliance with Menah, one that will be solidified in a peace pact at the end of the month. Its terms include a betrothal to Menah's prince and will result in an official marriage one year from now. But there's been a change of groom. Now I must be engaged to you to secure trust with my allies. Marrying you is the only way my brother's council will recognize me as his heir. Until Dimetreus remarries and has children of his own, I'm the only heir he has. Which makes our engagement necessary on all fronts."

Teryn was silent for a moment. Then he came up beside her. She could feel his gaze burning into her profile, but she refused to meet his eyes.

"You don't have to marry me, Cora," he said, voice low, somber. "You have a choice. Should you wish to refuse me, I'll convince Verdian of some other way to secure trust. I promise."

She let out a humorless laugh. "Have you learned nothing about the folly of making empty promises? King Verdian is your queen's father. He's threatened to take my brother's birthright away if I so much as step out of line. You can't go up against him."

"Try me."

Cora couldn't help but look at him then. His expression held no jest. She didn't dare open her senses to him, to feel the intensity hidden behind his words.

"It doesn't matter," she said, forcing her composure to remain cool. Calm. Disconnected from emotion. "My answer is yes."

"It is?" When she gave him nothing but a curt nod in reply, he lowered his head and pinched the bridge of his nose between his fingers. "This isn't going how I'd imagined."

"Were you expecting me to say no?" She clenched her jaw, a flash of fury sparking in her veins. "Do you...want me to say no?"

"It's not that. I just thought...I thought this would be a bigger deal to you."

"Well, it's not. You're giving too much weight to a small matter. You didn't need to come here, Teryn. You could have written this all in a letter—"

"I didn't want to write it in a letter," he said, voice rising. "I came so there'd be no mistaking my intentions...and yet of course you're mistaking them anyway because I'm a blundering fool..."

His words dissolved into a string of muttered curses. With a sigh, he ran a hand over his face and looked out at the meadow. Cora's brow furrowed as she took in his tense shoulders, the fist planted on one hip, the sharp rise and fall of his chest. She wasn't sure she'd ever seen him so flustered.

"You may be content to agree to a cold, loveless betrothal," he said, opening and closing one hand as if he didn't know what to do with it. "If that's what you prefer, I'll respect that, but I don't want you agreeing to a thing until you understand my side of things."

"What's your side?" she asked, almost terrified of the answer.

Slowly, his eyes returned to hers and he held her gaze without falter. His voice came out slow, broken only by the slightest tremor. "When last we spoke, you said you'd thought my mother had meant for you to marry me when she conveyed my proposal."

Cora shrank back, wishing she could disappear entirely. Her cheeks flooded with heat. "I...that's not—"

"It *was* supposed to be me. It had always been me."

Cora's breaths grew sharp, her pulse rioting. "I don't understand."

He took a step closer. "I told my mother of my idea to forge a marriage alliance between Khero and Menah, but that was all I'd said. She had no right to take my proposal and offer it to you before she fully understood—no, that's giving her too much credit. She did understand my heart and interfered on purpose. She never should have done that. It was supposed to be you and me from the start."

Teryn's words did strange things to her chest, her stomach, threatening to upend the balance of the entire world. She felt a flicker of hope—one that had proven traitorous before.

Shoving aside all warm feelings, she latched onto steely logic instead. "That's impossible," she said, voice calm. "You couldn't have meant to marry me from the start. Not until you found out about whatever scandal befell Mareleau and your brother. You were engaged to her. Had you rejected her without due cause—"

He stepped even closer. "I wasn't thinking about her. Not for a moment. I was only thinking about you. About us."

Us. There was that word again.

A corner of his mouth quirked up. "Thankfully, my unwanted fiancée had secrets that aided my own."

Her gaze lingered on his lips, on that crooked smile. On the mouth that just confessed he'd wanted her from the start. That he'd intended to choose her over the woman he'd been promised to.

Again, that flicker of hope tried to spark into a blaze, but she breathed it away. She crossed her arms over her chest and lifted her chin in defiance. "You've tricked me before. Used my own emotions against me."

His smirk stretched wider, revealing the depths of his amusement. "Are you talking about our kiss?"

She pursed her lips. "I don't see anything funny about it."

"The only thing funny about it is that you think I did it to be cruel." He stepped in closer, forcing her to take two steps back. He shadowed her retreat, but she refused to let him close—

Her breath caught as she felt her back come up against the trunk of a tree.

He stared down at her with unbridled intensity. "Do you honestly believe my only motive for kissing you was to trick you? Had I wanted to be cruel, I could have said or done a thousand other things to hurt you. And if I'd simply wanted you to leave me behind in that dungeon cell, I could have hefted you over my shoulder and set you on the other side of the door before you knew what was happening."

The thought of Teryn picking her up with such ease sent heat building low in her belly. But the image fled her mind as he leaned down, planted his forearm against the trunk over her head, and brought his face mere inches from hers. His voice left his lips in a whisper. "I kissed you because I wanted to. Because I wanted to feel your lips against mine before I died. Because it was my desire."

"Desire," she echoed. The word sent her knees quaking.

"Yes, desire."

Mother Goddess, she was losing hold of everything. Of her anger, her logic. That spark of hope was growing, searing through her carefully constructed walls.

She forced herself to straighten, to hold his gaze and pretend every inch of her wasn't burning from the inside. She waved her hand in a flippant gesture. "So now you want to go straight from desire to an engagement? Is there nothing missing between those two steps?"

"Oh, there's plenty missing. Could I disentangle our necessary betrothal from my feelings, I would, for that would allow me to court you the way you deserve to be courted. And I'll do it no matter what. Our engagement need only satisfy King Verdian, and we have a year before we're expected to wed. A year for you to change your mind. A year for me to win you over. Regardless of your answer, of whatever is expected of us, I'll woo you, Cora. I'll court you as befits strangers. Lovers. I'll deny myself the pleasure of kissing you until I've fully won your heart."

Cora's cold façade crumpled. His words cleaved through all remaining resistance, obliterated every argument she had in her arsenal. She could no longer deny the truth she'd tried so hard to suppress—that when Queen Bethaeny had offered the proposal, she'd *wanted* it to be with Teryn. And when he'd kissed her in the dungeon, she'd *wanted* that kiss. Wanted him. She slackened against the tree trunk and surrendered to Teryn's relentless barrage. "All right," she whispered, and her chest pulsed its satisfaction.

"All right," she said again, louder this time. The spark of hope ignited, melting the remainder of her walls, heating her blood, and filling her head with the most tantalizing euphoria. "But under one condition. I want you to kiss me now."

25

ora's request sent heat radiating through Teryn's chest. His eyes dropped down to her full, slightly parted lips, wondering if he hadn't imagined the words that had left them. As if in silent confirmation, she tilted her chin, lashes fluttering closed.

That was all Teryn needed. All the agonizing seconds he could resist before he lowered his mouth to hers. She met him halfway, her lips impossibly soft as they crushed against his. Her arms wound around his neck, fingertips sliding into his hair and sending a shiver down his spine. He pressed her closer to the tree, one hand snaking behind her back while the other trailed down her hair, the side of her face. Then, cradling her jaw, he gently tilted her chin, allowing their kiss to deepen. Her lips parted, and their tongues met in a languorous sweep. His hand stiffened on her back, pulling her ever closer. She yielded to him, her soft, small body somehow fitting perfectly against him. Their breaths grew heavy, sharp, and with the next sweep of his tongue, she released the most delicious of moans.

It nearly unraveled him, nearly made him slide his hands to places better left explored in private. He ached to palm her backside, to untie her apron and feel at least one less layer between them. Yet, despite his near-feverish desire, he remained vaguely aware of the two guards nearby. Guards that were surely getting an eyeful regardless of where Teryn kept his hands.

Cora arched into him, releasing another soft moan, her fingers clawing into the hair at the nape of his neck. Teryn was about to throw caution to the wind and heft her into his arms to close more of the sparse distance between them—when Cora suddenly pulled back with a gasp. And not one of pleasure. Of...something he couldn't comprehend.

Teryn froze. Had he done something wrong? Had he let his passion get out of control after all? The tightening in his trousers suggested as much, and she certainly would have noticed *that*, but—

She gasped again. Only this time he realized it wasn't a gasp at all but a snort. Of laughter.

Which might have been worse than whatever he'd been imagining.

Still, her smile sent a fluttery feeling to his chest, and he found his lips lifting too. Her arms were still around his neck, her body still close to his. "What is it?"

She pursed her lips, gaze lowered. Then she lifted her dark eyes to his and her smile grew. "It's Valorre," she said, her voice quavering with restrained laughter. "That smug little bastard is smirking."

Teryn cast a glance over his shoulder but saw only the edge of the cliff and the wildflower meadow. The other direction revealed nothing but trees and the forest path. Well, that and the pair of guards who were absolutely looking at them. Perverts.

"I don't see him," he said.

"He's not here," she whispered, "but he is close by. I can *feel* him smirking."

Awe washed over him. "You really can communicate with him, can't you?"

Her expression turned timid, but she gave him a small smile. "Yes."

Seven gods, she was incredible. Their moment of passion may have been broken by Cora's sudden amusement, but it hadn't changed his feelings. With his hand still pressed against her back, he gently stroked his thumb over the wool fabric of her dress. "I wish you didn't have to hide who you really are. You are too godsdamned amazing for that."

Her expression took on a teasing quality. "I think I liked it best when you called me formidable."

"You're always formidable."

She leaned against the tree, placing space between them. Her hands slid from around his neck but lingered over his chest. "I never did thank you," she said, eyes flashing toward the guards. "For keeping my secret. About my magic, about...well, a lot of things."

He gave her a wry grin. "Yes, I seem to recall you being too busy yelling at me when last we spoke to properly thank me."

She playfully swatted his chest, but he caught her fingers and brought them to his lips. Holding her gaze, he planted a kiss over the back of her bare, gloveless hand, right over the rounded curves of her knuckles. She bit her lower lip as if that could hide the grin splitting her face. And if it wasn't the most beautiful godsdamned smile he'd ever seen. He didn't think she'd ever looked at him like that, and now that he'd seen the expression, he was determined to inspire it a thousand times more.

Her face fell slightly, eyes darting toward the guards again. "We should probably get back before we lose our senses and give them another show."

Losing his senses was exactly what Teryn wanted to do with her. Just the thought of how good she'd felt against him, against that tree, nearly had him pulling her into his arms all over again. But she was probably right. So instead of kissing her swollen lips and eliciting another one of those glorious moans of hers, he took her hand and placed it at the crook of his elbow. Angling his head toward the path, he said, "Shall we?"

THEY FELL INTO SILENCE AS THEY MADE THEIR WAY BACK TOWARD THE CASTLE. BEROL soared overhead, sometimes swooping low enough that he could hear the beat of her wings. As much as Teryn wanted to fill the void with conversation, he was grateful for the quiet, for it allowed him to simply enjoy the feel of Cora's company, of her slender hand warm against his forearm, of the pound of his heart dancing in rhythm with their steps. A pinch of fear crept up now and then, and he'd worry their silence was shifting into the awkward sort. But then he'd glance her way and she'd grin back.

Perhaps there was some awkwardness to their silence, but it was a good kind. One that marked new beginnings. Two people getting to know one another in an entirely new way.

In fact, all of this was new to Teryn. While he'd had his share of lovers, he'd never entertained anything serious. His marriage prospects had always been filtered through political advantage. Which, of course, had resulted in his engagement to Mareleau. Regardless, he'd always been resigned to his fate. After seeing what love had done to his parents and his kingdom, he'd been determined to accept his duty with a cold heart.

But meeting Cora...

She'd changed him in such a short time. He'd made mistakes with her, ones that taught him the dangers of blindly following what he thought was his duty and going against his heart.

Now his duty and his heart were aligned. Because Cora was both.

"What will you do now?" Cora asked, finally breaking their silence. Ridine's towers peeked over the trees in the distance.

"Well, I..." Teryn frowned. "I don't actually know. My mind has been so consumed with simply getting here and speaking with you about our engagement, I haven't thought about what comes next now that the alliance is secure."

She arched a teasing brow. "Oh, so the alliance is all you came here for?"

"You know I came for more than that," he said. It was true, although he'd never expected their conversation would end in a kiss. He'd intended to tell Cora the truth. That regardless of her feelings, or lack thereof, his own ran deeper than politics. He hadn't realized just how deep they ran until she'd refused to entertain such a notion at all. Until he was forced to spell it out—both to himself and her—that he *wanted* their union to be a romantic one. A passionate one.

Had she told him she wanted to keep things platonic between them, he'd have agreed. Grudgingly, yes, but respectfully. But gods, was he thrilled she'd accepted his affection. He wasn't ready to call it love. Not yet—

"Will you stay?"

Teryn glanced at Cora and found her worrying a corner of her lip.

"Now that you've secured the...the alliance, will you return to Dermaine Palace, or will you...stay? For a while at least? Maybe until the peace pact is signed?"

He paused and turned toward her. "I'll stay. For as long as I can."

He hoped it would be long indeed and that Verdian and his brothers wouldn't interfere. He hated that they had a stranglehold on Ridine Castle and the kingdom at large. On *Cora's* kingdom. He hated that they treated her and her brother like they were still prisoners. Perhaps now that the engagement was secure, they'd respect her title more.

"I'd like that," she said.

A tendril of dark hair unraveled from her messy updo and fell onto her cheek, but before she could sweep it away, he gently took hold of it. He ran the silken lock between his fingers before tucking it behind her ear.

"My hair is probably a mess right now," she said, cheeks flushing.

"I like when it's a mess." And for the love of all things, he liked it when she blushed. The fact that he could make this fierce, gorgeous little creature blush made his stomach tighten.

She averted her gaze with a poorly hidden smile, and they proceeded toward the castle once more.

By the time Teryn returned Cora to the stairwell leading up to the tower room, she'd told him about the task she'd taken on. It gave him no small amount of terror to imagine her in that room surrounded by a dead mage's possibly enchanted belongings. He knew better than to ask her to stop her work. All he could do was offer his help, which she'd predictably refused.

At least she said yes to dinner tonight.

Teryn let that warm his heart as he left the stairwell, left Cora to proceed with her work alone, but it did little to calm his nerves. He trusted Cora's powers, knew she was so much stronger than anyone gave her credit for. And yet, he couldn't shake how she'd looked when he'd first climbed the staircase and saw her standing frozen, staring at...

At...

Teryn's mind went blank.

Hadn't she been staring at something? Something she'd held in her hand? The more he tried to remember, the hazier his thoughts became. That in itself was worrisome, not to mention the fate of Cora's lady's maid, Lurel. His muscles tightened, begging him to turn around. Begging him to take up post next to her useless guards and ensure she was safe every moment she spent in there.

But he couldn't.

He wouldn't.

He'd trust her. Believe in her.

Because he knew there were few others who did right now.

He released his worries in a heavy sigh and made his way through the castle halls...only to realize he hadn't a clue where he was going. This was only his second time at Ridine, and the first had been so fraught with tension that he'd hardly paid heed to the castle's layout. This time, his arrival had been overshadowed by his single-minded focus to find Cora. Master Arther had greeted him, given him a room, and set an appointment for him to be received by King Dimetreus that evening, but he'd evaded every question Teryn had asked about Cora's whereabouts. Which had left Teryn to investigate on his own. Thankfully, other members of the castle staff had been far more amenable to his inquiries, especially when they realized who he was. It seemed *some* respected royal title over the influence of two self-righteous lords who'd been given more power than they deserved.

Was Teryn bitter at seeing Cora's castle swarming with Ulrich's and Kevan's guards and staff? Yes. Yes, he was. And was he perhaps growing just a little too protective over her? Also yes, but that simply couldn't be helped, not after they'd shared that heated, incredible, mind-blowing kiss—

He rounded the next corner and almost collided with a figure coming his way. A feminine yelp had him leaping back a step, but it was followed by a familiar aggrieved tone.

"Ugh. You." Mareleau's lip curled at the sight of him.

Teryn returned her sentiment with a flat look. "Ugh. Likewise." He offered a shallow bow and stepped aside for her to pass. She started to sweep by but faced him with a roll of her eyes.

"I suppose you found her then, with no trouble from my uncles?" Her tone suggested she couldn't care less, but if that were the case, she could have said nothing at all.

"I did." He'd meant to keep his expression stony, but admitting he'd found Cora filled his mind with the memory of her lips.

Mareleau's eyes went wide. "Seven devils, I know that look."

His cheeks flushed. "What look?"

Her expression softened the slightest bit. "Larylis gets the same one sometimes."

"And?"

She popped a hip to the side with a huff, as if their continued conversation were becoming more and more offensive to her by the second. Finally, she deigned to answer him, her face impassive while her voice held a note of genuine curiosity. "You like her, don't you? The princess."

He gave her a pointed look. "Did you think I was going through all this trouble to see her because I barely tolerated her?"

She shrugged. "I assumed you were tasked with formalizing a betrothal to her now that Larylis was no longer an option. But just because you were assigned as her groom didn't mean you had to like it."

He gave her a humorless grin. "We'd both know a thing or two about that situation, wouldn't we? Regardless of politics, I do like her. She's part of the reason I was so set against marrying you. That and your revolting personality, of course."

She scoffed, but she seemed to take his insult in stride. "I'd be offended were I not so completely and utterly grateful for your dislike of me. I suppose we're even then? You have your beloved and I have mine."

He gave an exaggerated wince. "Not quite. You see, you and Larylis are already married, while Cora and I must wait a year. So how about we call it even on my wedding night? In the meantime, you can work off your debt to me by directing me toward the keep."

She crossed her arms. "I'm your queen, not your servant. Besides, I'm going to the kitchen."

The kitchen. That was on his list of places to visit too. He'd asked Cora to dine with him, but he hoped he could arrange something a little better than a public meal in the dining hall. Something to make up for everything Cora had missed when she'd refused to meet him in the garden at Verlot. He may not have access to a harpist or an elegant candlelit alcove, but he could do something to show her the efforts she hadn't gotten to see.

"You know where the kitchen is?" he asked.

"No, of course I don't. But I'm determined to find it, if only to prove to my maids just how incompetent they are. They've assured me there's no chocolate in this castle. Can you imagine? There has to be chocolate. At least chocolate cake."

Teryn resisted the urge to bark a laugh. Of course the pampered Mareleau wouldn't realize just what a luxury chocolate was in some places. However, he recalled seeing a chocolatier's shop in one of the cities he'd traveled through on his way here. He'd stopped before the window and considered going inside to buy a peace offering for Cora. Before he could act on it, he'd talked himself out of the idea, reminding himself that Cora might send him packing before he even got the chance to offer gifts.

Oh, how wrong he'd been...

He shook his head before memories of a kiss beneath a tree—of Cora's body against that tree—could render him brainless.

"How about this," he said. "I'll place an order for chocolate if you do me a favor tonight."

She threw back her head with a groan. "For the love of the seven gods, not again."

"It's a small favor," Teryn rushed to say. "I need to talk to the royal chef. If all goes well, I'll simply need your help procuring a spare table and maybe some candles. Perhaps a nice cloth. And, if you're feeling generous, you can locate somewhere Cora and I might dine undisturbed tonight too."

"Oh, that's all," she muttered with sarcasm. "Why do you call her Cora, anyway? And why can't you do any of this yourself?"

He ignored the first question, but it served as a reminder to call Cora by her royal name in front of others. To address her second question, he said, "I still have an audience with King Dimetreus to attend once he returns from his hunt, and I'm not entirely convinced your uncles won't thwart my efforts to enjoy myself while I'm here. They are your father's brothers, after all."

She nodded as if to admit *fair enough*.

"If you do it," he said, "you can tell your uncles it's for the sake of teaching the princess proper dinner etiquette. They'll believe that."

She narrowed her eyes and tapped her foot rapidly against the flagstones. Finally, she blew out a long breath and said, "You're lucky I'm bored."

"And you're lucky I know of a place that sells cream-filled truffles. Now, sister, if you don't mind, let us make haste to the kitchen where our mutual schemes might be realized."

She burned him with a scowl but it lacked venom. "Very well...brother."

26

———

Cora's lips continued to tingle even hours later, forcing her to recall the feel of Teryn's mouth against hers again and again. It was a pleasant reminder, yet a dangerous distraction considering where she was and what she was doing. She bit her bottom lip, letting the pressure override the far gentler memories, and focused on what was before her—a hearth filled with flame, consuming pages of a very dangerous book.

She hated burning books on principle alone. The thought of permanently destroying knowledge, eradicating words that had been carefully recorded on paper for a distinct purpose, weighed her stomach down with guilt. She knew to cherish knowledge. Stories. Traditions. For six years, Cora had been raised by Salinda, the Forest People's Keeper of Histories. Passing knowledge of the Arts down from one generation to the next had been Salinda's job as one of the commune's Faeryn elders.

But Cora knew even Salinda would approve of her burning this knowledge now. Knew she'd insist upon it.

Cora shuddered with revulsion, recalling the unsettling images she'd found within the book's pages.

A wolf and a stag, facing off in the forest. One with bared teeth and raised hackles, the other with a lowered head of deadly antlers.

On the next page, the two creatures colliding in a battle of teeth and claws, hooves and tines.

On the following page, the animals collapsing in a heap of blood and torn flesh, eyes devoid of life.

Then, concluding the chapter, a single creature with paws and hooves, a sweeping tail, and a head crowned with antlers emerging from the two bodies...

She hadn't seen the word Roizan anywhere on the page, but she knew that was what it was. That was how Morkai had created his creature, his vessel for dark magic.

Part of her had been tempted to keep the book for informational purposes, if only to learn more about Morkai, his magic, how he'd constructed his spells—

And that idea had made her slam the book entitled *Mastering the Ethera* shut.

Her desire to keep the book hadn't been sinister in any way. There was logic to learning more about an enemy, even a dead one, especially when his dark magic lingered beyond his death. But the fact that she'd almost felt justified in keeping a book on the forbidden Arts had terrified her.

So now it burned. Just like the dozen she'd burned before it and the hundreds still left to toss into the flames. It was a slow process. She couldn't simply pick up a volume from one of the many shelves lining the circular room and chuck it in the fire. Instead, she had to extend her senses, *feel* for any threat radiating from the spine or cover. Then, handling it with care, she'd have to flip open the cover with the edge of her paring knife, investigate the pages, seek any sign that they were laced with poison or woven with enchantments that needed to be broken with salt or water before succumbing to fire and air.

She glanced around the room at the leagues upon leagues of books, bottles of poisons, and stacks of paper cluttered everywhere. Her shoulders sank with how heavy this task was. How lengthy. How vital. She'd only been working in the tower for a few hours today, and already she was exhausted. Her stamina nearly spent.

But she was the only one who could do this.

It would take time, but she *would* do this.

She watched the book turn to cinders and added more of the purifying herbs to the fire. Then, returning to where she'd found *Mastering the Ethera*, she assessed the shelf. One more book to burn and it would be empty. One more and she'd have cleared an entire shelf.

A glance out the window showed the sun was close to setting. Not only was she determined never to work in the tower after dark, but she had something very important to do tonight. Dinner with Teryn. The thought tugged her lips and reawakened her awareness of how they tingled. If she wanted time to bathe and dress and look something like a princess meeting her betrothed for a romantic meal, she needed to leave the tower soon.

But the near-empty shelf taunted her.

I suppose I can do one more.

She lifted her palms. They tingled at once, but she resisted stepping closer to the shelf until she reconnected with the elements: the stone beneath her feet for grounding and safety, the air in her lungs for intellect, the heat of the hearth for her strength of will, and the water on her tongue that connected her to her emotions, to the very root of her clairsentient magic.

Only then did she step closer to the book.

Her palms immediately pulsed with warning, tingling along every line of her *insigmora*. She breathed out deeply and brought her palm closer to the book, careful not to touch it with her flesh, only the extension of her Art. The spine felt neutral, as did the cover. Lowering her hand inch by inch, she carefully grasped the spine and angled the book to the side. The edges of the paper nearly shouted at her magic, and as she turned it farther around, she saw they were discolored. It wasn't from age, either. It was poison.

She cursed under her breath, knowing she couldn't burn poison. Without knowing exactly what herbs or botanicals Morkai had used, she couldn't guarantee they wouldn't carry on the smoke and kill everyone who dared inhale it. Instead, she gathered up a piece of cloth and carefully wrapped the book. She brought it to the table at the center of the room, setting it next to another book. The one that had killed Lurel.

The table had become her place for collecting items that would require extra care before being rendered harmless. That included most of the vials of poisons and bottled herbs Cora had found around the room. She didn't dare pour them in any soil or stream, for the same reasons she couldn't burn the poison-laced book; they could pose too great a harm. Those items she could only lock in a chest filled with salt and bury deep underground.

She glanced at the book that had killed Lurel and had the strangest sensation there was something missing from beside it. Hadn't there been another item... something she'd tried to clear this morning...

Her mind went blank.

Perhaps it was the book itself that made her uneasy, gave her the niggling thought that she was forgetting something. She shifted her focus, narrowing her eyes on its leather cover. She'd already determined the book was too dangerous to destroy without knowing the extent of her stamina, but now she wondered if that hadn't been another justification. A temptation to keep it in the off chance that something within its pages could eventually serve Cora in some way.

The thought alone brought several *what ifs*...

What if it contains a spell to undo some other enchantment?

What if it holds information about the fae?

What if it mentions unicorns and where they came from?

What if...

Cora shook the notions from her head. While this book was clearly one of Morkai's most personal items, there was nothing that could justify keeping it for any extended period of time. Perhaps she should just throw it in the fire now.

Her stomach sank in warning.

No, she couldn't be reckless. Like everything else in this room, the book needed to be handled with care. Caution. Her Art.

With a deep breath, she assessed her connection to the elements and found it strong. Then, swallowing hard, she slid the book closer. From her apron pocket, she withdrew her knife and used it to carefully flip open the front cover.

It opened to the page she'd seen before, the one bearing the blood weaving that had sealed Lurel's fate. The rust-red color hadn't faded, nor had the design. Still, it was just paper and blood. It could be burned. As for the rest of the pages...

Her palms pulsed with heat, reminding her of why she'd chosen not to clear the book just yet. It wasn't like the other books she'd discarded already. While those contained instructions in the forbidden Arts, this one held more than that. It was laced with darkness. Personal intent. She should slam it shut. She knew she should.

But something inside it called to her. Not in a tempting way. Not like a siren's song. It was more like...a part of her. A missing piece of a puzzle she could recognize by size and shape alone. *This* was the feeling that called to her, coalescing somewhere in the middle of the book. It thrummed with an energy that matched the cadence of her pulse, vibrating alongside the darkness that compressed all around it.

Cora's throat tightened, fear strangling her chest.

But she had to know.

She had to.

Using the edge of her blade again, she tucked it between the pages, right at the center of the gathering energy. She lifted the pages and the worn spine complied, splaying open to reveal a spread of two inked pages. Unlike the page that had killed Lurel, the ink on these was not red like blood but black. Yet their design was of a similar nature, marking both pages in a complex pattern of crisscrossing lines. They may not have been actual blood weavings, but Cora felt with certainty that these were designs for ones. Blueprints. Curses invented to be forged with real blood later.

And at the top of each page was a name.

On the left, *Linette Rose Caelan*. Cora's dead sister-in-law and Dimetreus' dearly departed wife.

On the right, *Aveline Corasande Caelan*.

Cora's name.

Cora's fate.

Cora's death.

27

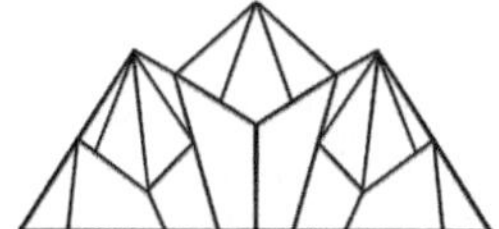

Cora hadn't forgotten about Morkai's blood weaving that had bound her fate with Linette's. But knowing about the curse was one thing. Seeing the origins of its inception was another. It made her stomach bottom out, made every hair on her arms stand on end.

When Morkai had confessed to her about the fate weaving—told her about it in this very room, no less—she'd felt violated. Shocked. Ashamed. He'd taken a twelve-year-old Cora's mistake and twisted it for his own sinister use. After Cora had publicly declared before the court that Queen Linette had been lying about being with child, he'd used that knowledge to forge a devious plan, killing the queen and gathering her blood. Then he took Cora's blood too, cutting her palm and weaving a horrible tapestry with it before her eyes. She'd fled the castle right after, unwitting as to why he'd cut her or what purpose that strange blood weaving had served.

But she knew now.

Morkai had bound her fate to Linette's so that she, like her sister-in-law, would die childless.

All because of a prophecy he'd been determined to thwart.

Morkai's voice echoed through her mind, recalling the words he'd said the night he'd confessed the truth.

The unicorns. The mother. The child. Who do you think you are in that prophecy?
Then after that...

You are the mother and your child would have been my enemy.

Weaving your fate was the only thing I could do to let you keep your life.

She hadn't forgotten. No, she'd carried the burden of the curse, hating what he'd done if only because it robbed her of choice. And yet, she had grown complacent, hadn't she? Upon Morkai's death, she'd seen proof that his glamours had been severed. She'd assumed every bit of magic he'd cast had died along with him.

But that wasn't true. She knew that now. The evidence was all around her, mocking her from the shadows of Lurel's demise. Only the glamours, spells, and enchantments that had relied upon a continuous stream of magic from the Roizan had been broken when the creature died. When Morkai died. But everything else remained. Every curse he'd placed—using just a single instance of dark magic—stayed unbroken.

Which meant her fate was sealed. She'd die childless.

Her stomach plummeted further, taking her heart with it, but not for the reasons she expected. Having children might be a blessing she'd someday desire, but it had never been at the front of her mind. She was nowhere near ready for maternal responsibilities.

But that curse—that fate—was tangled up in something else now. Something far more pressing. Present. Cherished.

More of Morkai's words rang through her mind.

You could never be Teryn's queen. Do you know what the prince's father did to his queen? He tried to have her replaced with his mistress. Teryn would only do the same to you.

She wanted to believe Morkai had been wrong. Her heart told her he had been. Teryn wouldn't cast her aside for being unable to bear him children.

No, he wouldn't, he'd...never...

He betrayed you before, came her own voice from deep inside her. It was stoic and steady, the part of her that remained within the walls she'd erected around her heart. *He said he desired you. He never said love.*

And even love could be broken. Even love could twist hearts. She'd seen it happen.

As much as Dimetreus had loved Linette, the queen had been so afraid of disappointing him that she'd lied. Pretended to be with child to keep his attentions from wandering. Back then, Cora had been perplexed over Linette's motive. Why would anyone—a powerful queen, no less—lie about being pregnant?

Cora understood, now that she was older. She knew full well the expectations placed on royal women, even more so after her recent experiences with Verdian and his brothers. Queens were expected to bear heirs. If they failed...

Teryn would only do the same to you.

She shook her head. Teryn was no longer beholden to the pressures of the crown; he didn't need an heir. He only needed to marry Cora to fulfill the alliance, and in turn, position Cora as Dimetreus' heir. His *temporary* heir. Once he remarried...

Cora stepped back from the table, as a complex layer of truth peeled back before her. In what world could she imagine Dimetreus—her hurt, traumatized brother who still agonized over his dead wife—getting remarried? If he didn't, Cora's place as heir would be permanent. She'd be expected to ascend to queen one day. A queen forced to carry all the same burdens and pressures Linette had caved under. That Teryn's mother nearly lost her crown over.

Cora had never wanted to reclaim her role as princess permanently. She'd only wanted to help her brother get his throne back and ensure Khero was taken care of. Agreeing to a loveless marriage alliance had been a necessary evil, and she'd still considered it something she could escape once her duties had been served.

Then came Teryn's confession. It had opened her heart, made her think that being stuck in her role wouldn't be so bad. Not with him by her side.

Half her heart told her she was in no danger of losing that now. This was Teryn, after all. He wouldn't reject her for being unable to bear children, even if he wanted them. But the other half of her heart shrank back, reminding her that all royal men—even those with lesser titles like dukes and lords—were forever fixated on heirs. On sons. On their legacies.

What if she couldn't provide that?

Regardless, if the worst came to pass and Cora ascended to the throne, the curse had potential to upend her life in the future. Wars sprung easily where bloodlines were broken. Where queens failed to produce sons.

Even if Teryn decided he didn't care about having children, could she truly subject him to the chaos that might one day ensue in her kingdom?

Mother Goddess, it was too much to think about.

Her lungs tightened. The room felt too small, the walls closing in around her, smothering her. She felt...trapped.

Trapped in a curse.

Trapped as her brother's heir.

Trapped in a game of royal politics.

Trapped under fragile, breakable hopes.

"Your Highness."

The voice sent her whirling away from the table and toward the door. Her guard stood on the other side of the rosemary bundles, his face cast in shadow from the stairwell. She glanced out the nearest window and saw the sun sinking over the horizon. How long had she been lost in her thoughts? Something small and wet landed on her collarbone. Belatedly she realized it was a tear, and more were pouring down her cheeks.

She cleared her voice and addressed the guard. "What is it?"

"His Highness Prince Teryn is here to see you."

Cora's heart leaped into her throat. He was early! No, she was late. They were supposed to meet for dinner, one she most certainly couldn't attend. Not in this state. Not with her mind so consumed with blood magic and curses.

"Tell him..." Her voice dissolved into a quaver. She found herself unable to continue.

"Cora." This time it was Teryn's voice coming from the other side of the threshold. She hadn't realized he was at the top of the stairwell too. Damn her guards. She'd have to tell the sentry at the bottom of the stairs to block all visitors from ascending from now on. Just because she was inside the room didn't mean it was safe. "Is everything all right?"

Before she could say a word, he brushed aside the hanging herbs. Their eyes met, and his grew wide. He surged forward, ready to cross the line of salt—

"Stop!" she shouted, charging toward the door. "Get out, Teryn!" Her voice came out harsher than she'd intended. A look of hurt crossed his face, but he halted in place—that was what mattered. It was too dangerous for him to step inside this room. He'd already done it once and she'd be damned if he made a habit out of it. Besides, she didn't want him to see her like this. It was too late, of course. Now that she was closer to the doorway, he could fully see her through the rosemary. His gaze slid to her cheeks, and his expression of hurt shifted into one of concern.

"Cora, what's wrong?"

She opened her mouth to try and shape her current state into words, but no sound would come. Instead, she breathed in the truth on an inhale, burying it in her heart, and donned a casual demeanor on an exhale. "It's nothing," she finally managed to say.

His voice deepened into a growl. "It's clearly not nothing. Who hurt you? *What* hurt you?"

"I'm fine." A lie. The deepest of lies. She had been hurt by someone and something, but how could she express that? The thought alone made her throat tighten all over again, summoning painful memories to the surface. She'd spent most of her life keeping secrets, and for good reason. Telling the truth had rarely served her well. Evidence flashed before her mind's eye.

Queen Linette condemning Cora's clairsentience, calling her a witch and begging Dimetreus to have her exorcized by a Godspriest.

Dimetreus ignoring Cora's strange powers and telling her that her insights were untrue.

The Forest People boasting of their distrust of royals.

Cora's meeting with the Forest People elders where some denounced her for her lies. Her secrets. Her identity.

Cora gaining the acceptance of Verdian's inquisitors only after pretending she knew nothing of magic.

Dimetreus' new council feigning that magic didn't exist. Fearing her relationship to the Arts. Mistrusting her motives in the tower.

She shook the memories away, reminding herself that this new situation wasn't like the rest. This was about her and Teryn. Even so, with these wounds still darkening her past—many of which were still fresh—she found herself shrinking deeper and deeper into herself. She wanted to talk to Teryn, but she was still learning how to open up to people, especially to him. This curse was no small matter, nor were the repercussions it could have on their relationship. On her responsibility as potential future queen. She needed time to prepare for that conversation.

"Please come out here and talk to me."

She shook her head. No. No, she wasn't ready.

Another look of hurt flashed across his face. "We can sit in silence then. Let me be there for you, whatever is wrong."

"No, Teryn." His name on her lips nearly shattered her heart in two. But it was nothing compared to the pain she'd feel if he rejected her upon learning about the curse. Teryn may desire her, but what if he desired furthering his bloodline more? She tried to tell herself such a fear was silly, but it didn't *feel* silly. It felt crippling. Smothering. Before she'd be ready to tell him the truth, she'd need to prepare herself for possible heartbreak. Fortify the walls she'd so recklessly abandoned, just in case she needed to retreat behind them once more.

She was nowhere near strong enough for that right now.

"I just need one night to be alone," she said, tone softening.

Teryn's throat bobbed, expression struck with agony. "I don't want to leave you."

"I need you to. Please. Just one night." She wasn't sure a single night would be enough to sort through her feelings, but she hoped it would be. She forced a reassuring smile to her lips. "Please."

Teryn held her gaze for several silent moments. Finally, he gave her a nod and turned away. She watched his back until he was out of sight. Fresh tears trailed down her cheeks.

It killed Teryn to do as Cora had bid and leave her behind. To think only hours ago she'd requested a kiss that he'd been all too eager to deliver. Now she was asking for space.

Every step that took him farther from the tower room made him question whether he was doing the right thing. He wanted to trust her. Believe in her strength. But seeing her like that, her cheeks glistening with tears, her shoulders hunched with grief...it nearly cleaved his heart in two. He knew she was capable of combating dark energies, of using her magic to accomplish incredible feats.

But what the bloody hell had made her cry?

Rage sparked in his blood, and his fists closed around air. He wished he held his hunting spear right now. If he did, he would chase down the source of Cora's distress and destroy it.

What if I'm the source?

The question sank his gut, but he had to consider if it was true. Had he pushed her too far? Had she changed her mind about him? About *them*? If so, he couldn't force his presence upon her. The best thing he could do was let her work through it. And if she had changed her mind...

He found himself outside the door to the guest bedroom he'd been given. With a sigh, he pressed his forehead to it.

If she's changed her mind, I have to respect that.

Telling her about his feelings had already been a risk. He'd known she could have rejected him, and he'd been prepared for that. But to lose her now, lose the small, beautiful thing that had begun to bloom between them, tore him up inside.

Feeling as if his feet were made of lead, he opened his bedroom door and dragged himself inside, stopping only when he reached one of the windows. There was no balcony, no balustrade to lean upon, so the windowsill would have to do. He opened the glass pane, relishing the fresh air pouring in, and gathered lungfuls to counteract the tightening in his chest.

His eyes were unfocused, but not enough to miss the feathered shape darting from the trees outside the castle wall. Berol landed beside Teryn on the windowsill, giving his forearm an affectionate nibble. He reached into his pocket in search of the dried meat he always kept on hand for his falcon, only to realize he wasn't wearing his traveling vest but an elegant frock coat.

He'd changed his clothing before his audience with King Dimetreus, during which the king had granted him permission to dine privately with Cora instead of attending the meal in the dining hall. After that, he'd changed again, outfitting himself in the finest ensemble he'd brought. He didn't have the heart to join the main feast now, to sit amongst the king and his council, trying to pretend there wasn't somewhere else he'd rather be.

He was about to fetch his leather vest from where it was draped at the foot of his bed, when his hand brushed over a lump in his waistcoat. Had he tucked some treats in there after all and simply forgotten? He reached inside the pocket to extract what he expected to be a strip of meat...but came away with an amber crystal.

He blinked at it a few times, confusion blanketing his mind. Why did he have this? Was this...no. It couldn't be.

Yet the color, shape, and size were hauntingly familiar. There was no denying what this was. The last time he'd seen it, it had been attached to the dagger that had opened his father's throat.

Wait, that wasn't true.

The last time he'd seen it had been...

A memory snapped into place, of him changing his clothing and finding the crystal in his trouser pocket. The same confusion had struck him then. He hadn't understood why he had it or where he'd gotten it until—like now—his memories returned.

Now he remembered it all.

He recalled Cora standing frozen in the tower room, her fingers clutched around the crystal. She hadn't moved, hadn't responded to the sound of her name or the feel of his touch. Not until he'd wrenched the crystal from her hand and shook her by the shoulders once more. He must have tucked it in his pocket to free his hands then. And when he'd found the crystal while he'd been getting changed, he'd moved it to his waistcoat pocket with the intention of returning it to the tower.

But...he'd forgotten. Twice now.

The thought chilled his bones.

With a screech, Berol nipped at his fingers, then raked a talon over the back of his hand. He winced and dropped the crystal to the ground. It rolled toward the bed, and he watched it settle at the corner of the rug. Berol screeched from the windowsill again, wings splayed.

"Hush, Berol," he said to her, tone soothing. His eyes remained locked on the crystal. He still couldn't fathom how he'd forgotten about it. Sure, he had his reasons for being distracted, but forgetting that he'd tucked a strange object into his pocket? It had to be enchanted. Possibly triggered by touch.

He frowned, stepping closer to it. Berol screeched once more, but he held out a hand to quiet her. "I know, Berol. It's dangerous. I won't touch it. I just need to tuck it somewhere safe until I can tell Cora about it."

Saying Cora's name wrenched his heart, but he was too preoccupied with the mysterious crystal to linger over his pain. Instead, he kept his attention on the stone, afraid to blink lest it somehow flee his memory like it did before. Inch by inch, he crept toward the crystal as if he were stalking prey on a hunt. He untied his white silk cravat from around his neck and stooped over the stone. Careful not to let his skin touch the object, he lifted it with the cloth.

He faced the window, ready to fold his cravat fully around the crystal, when shards of light exploded around him. The light from the setting sun had caught upon one of the facets. The glittering effect was...beautiful. He'd never seen that happen when the duke had carried it atop his cane.

His fear and trepidation fled his mind. What had he been so worried about a moment before? Entranced by the dance of amber light, he lifted the crystal higher, let the waning sunlight catch more of its facets...

Berol let out a sharp cry, startling him as she launched off the sill and into the room.

"Right," he said, closing his fist around the crystal and smothering it in the folds of his cravat. But when he looked back at his surroundings, all he saw was blinding white light.

28

Mareleau had never arranged a bouquet with her own hands, and as she assessed the sparse collection of greenery and wild poppies she'd picked from the castle lawn, she realized there was a very good reason for that. If she'd seen such a sad spectacle gracing the vases at Verlot Palace, she'd have insisted upon whoever had made it be fired at once. But this wasn't Verlot. Nor was it the slightly more modest Dermaine. This was Ridine Castle, and the tiny bundle of drooping flowers was the brightest thing about it.

The bouquet sat in a cracked porcelain vase upon a small table. The table itself was nestled in a narrow courtyard surrounded by overgrown shrubs outside the kitchen. An array of half-melted candles lit the table's surface, illuminating two sets of empty dishes. Soon the dishes would be ladled with food, and Mareleau's mission on behalf of her brother-in-law would be complete. With the last vestiges of the sunset painting the sky from pink to indigo, the end result was rather charming, if she did say so herself.

Mareleau jumped at the loud clatter that carried through the open kitchen windows. All right, so the noise was less than charming, but the location was the best she could find. Inside the kitchen, dozens of cooks and servants bustled about in preparation for the king's dinner. One she'd be expected to attend, same as she had every night she'd been here.

A pang of envy struck her as she glanced at the quaint dining area she'd arranged. While it wasn't the most elegant of spaces, she regretted that she wouldn't get to enjoy the fruits of her labor. Her gaze landed on the bottle of wine sitting beside two glasses. That was perhaps the most tempting part of the whole setup. Seven gods, she missed wine. She was so desperate for a sip, it made her sick to her stomach. Literally. Or...maybe the sudden nausea was more due to hunger. Regardless, she knew she couldn't imbibe, for her ladies were watching, and they'd report back to her mother and father. Until her ruse was up, she needed to act like the epitome of the careful, pregnant queen. That way, when she confessed to the surprising return of her moon cycle, she'd be blameless. Her father would have to carry that guilt, for she was fully prepared to lament over the castle's agonizingly chilly drafts and the musty air quality.

"It's lovely, Your Majesty," Breah said, coming up beside her.

Ann nodded in agreement. "You have a knack for creating elegance, Majesty."

The girls were pandering to her, but Mareleau didn't care. Despite her shoddy attempts at setting up a romantic meal, she couldn't ignore the pride flaring in her chest. She'd never done anything like this before. Perhaps she could do it for Larylis when she returned home to him.

The thought warmed her heart, and a soft smile curled her lips. Before her longing could dip into sorrow, she adopted a flippant tone and said, "It beats picking out hideous linens with Master Arther. Come. Let us prepare for dinner."

Sera released a groan. "I suppose I should fetch my lady from her horrible tower."

Mareleau cut a glare at the girl. She was so used to Sera's presence, she kept forgetting the girl was supposed to be serving the princess. "Sera, you should have readied her for dinner an hour ago."

Sera shifted from foot to foot. "I...I figured you were more in need of assistance than she, Majesty."

"Yes, well, *she* is supposed to attend a romantic meal with my brother. You can't have her looking like a pauper, for it will surely be the ruination of my efforts. Go get her cleaned up at once."

Sera's shoulders slumped, but she sank into an obedient curtsy before shuffling out of the courtyard and into the kitchen. Mareleau and her ladies followed just behind, turning toward the keep as they exited into the hall. She halted in place, glancing in the opposite direction to where Sera was heading for the North Tower Library stairwell. A strange feeling fluttered in her chest, and it wasn't entirely pleasant. She wasn't sure what to call it, but it might have been something akin to sympathy.

"The two of you go with her," she said to Ann and Breah before she could stop herself.

Her maids stared back at her as if she'd lost her mind. And maybe she had.

Breah's tone turned simpering. "Why, Majesty?"

"Sera will need your help to ready the princess with haste," Mareleau said.

"Don't *you* need our help?" Ann asked. "Surely you want to change into a new gown for dinner."

"Why? Is there something wrong with how I look now?" She knew it was only habit that drove her maids to expect a change of clothes, but she needed them to stop their whining. "I can manage looking appropriate for dinner just fine. The princess, on the other hand, needs all the help she can get. I won't have her making a mockery of all the hard work I did tonight. Now go. Follow after Sera and make certain the princess is presentable in the next half hour. Understand?"

The girls bobbed into curtsies before making their grudging departure. Meanwhile, Mareleau ascended the stairs to the keep. She had every intention of heading straight for her room, but when she passed the door she knew belonged to Teryn's guest quarters, she paused.

Again, that irritating feeling fluttered in her chest. It was less about sympathy this time and more about...was it care? Pride? All she knew was that she wanted to brag to Teryn that tonight's dinner was going to be fabulous, thanks to her. With her chin held high, she marched to his door and rapped on it with her gloved hand. The lamps illuminating the hall revealed several smudges of dirt on the white silk. She certainly wasn't used to seeing that.

The door opened in a rush, tearing her from her thoughts. Teryn's form stood on the other side of the doorway, but she could hardly separate him from the shadows. She frowned, wondering why he was in a dark room.

Some of her excitement waned, and she took a step back, folding her arms over her chest. "You better not tell me you've been napping while I've been doing all the hard work for you, brother."

"Brother," he echoed, a hint of taunting in his tone.

She frowned. That hadn't been the first time she'd used that word to his face, and he was the one who'd started it, calling her *sister*. Why did he sound so amused?

He stepped out of the doorway and into the light of the hall.

Mareleau's eyes went wide as she noted the gash on his cheek, then the way he cradled his hand. A white cloth—his missing cravat, perhaps—was wrapped around it like a bandage.

"Teryn, what the seven devils happened to you?"

He glanced down at his hand and huffed a chuckle. "Ah, that. I broke a glass."

It must have been quite the violent break for it to have sliced his cheek. And... was there a portion of his shirt missing? His ruffled collar appeared to have been torn. Maybe that was what he'd used to tie his hand. Whatever the case, he looked quite the mess.

She waved at him, motioning him back toward his room. "Clean yourself up at once. You can't meet Princess Aveline looking like this."

He narrowed his eyes, as if trying to decipher the meaning of her words. Then, with a shake of his head, he said, "For dinner tonight. The one I asked you to help me with."

There was something strange about the way he spoke, uttering each word slowly as if he wasn't quite sure what he was saying. "Are you still asleep? Go! Get changed. Princess Aveline will be coming by at any moment to do the same. I didn't offer my maids to her for nothing, and I'll be damned if the both of you embarrass me."

"Who are we embarrassing you before?"

Mareleau pulled her head back with a scoff. "Me, of course. For two people so madly in love, neither of you seem to know how to impress the other. Perhaps I'll have to play the mentor to you both."

He narrowed his eyes again. "Because you're at Ridine Castle to mentor Princess Aveline."

Once more with that careful way of talking. It almost seemed like he was asking a question rather than stating a fact. What was wrong with him?

"You know this," she said. "Now go before I lose my mind and promise never to help you again."

Teryn watched her with a probing look that was almost unsettling. Then he crossed his arms and leaned against the doorframe. "I regret that your aid will come to naught. The princess will not be joining me for dinner tonight."

"No, she's simply running behind. My ladies will return with her soon and have her dressed and ready in no time."

"You don't understand," Teryn said with a sigh. "I've already been to see her tonight and she refused to come to dinner with me."

"But...but my ladies—"

"She will refuse them. Trust me."

Disappointment sank her stomach. Then anger took its place. "Don't you dare tell me you're going to waste the wine I picked out for you. And the cake!" She clenched her jaw with a growl. It wasn't chocolate cake, but it was lemon chiffon. Mareleau had nearly burst into an inferno of rage when the baker told Teryn she'd make a small cake just for him and Aveline. Where was Mareleau's cake?

A corner of Teryn's mouth lifted into a smirk she'd never seen grace his face before. "Wine and cake, you say? Well, we certainly can't let that go to waste."

She huffed. "You seem awfully buoyant for a man whose dinner offer was rejected by his beloved. I would have expected you to be more upset." Or maybe she just didn't know Teryn well at all. She was finally beginning to warm up to him, but the way he was acting now...it didn't seem quite right.

"What is there to be upset about? She's simply busy. I respect her. There's no need to cling to someone you trust."

Mareleau felt abashed at that. She may not know her brother-in-law well, but she knew even less about separating love from obsession. She'd clung to her chance at love so hard, she'd lied for it. Betrayed the trust of the person she'd been fighting for. She waited for the guilt to come, but most of it had already faded when Larylis forgave her.

Larylis. Gods how she missed him.

She pushed the thought away. "You must really like her."

Teryn's expression shifted, his smile tightening with his jaw, eyes suddenly devoid of mirth. "An understatement."

"Then why don't you march over to that tower—"

"No." The word came out cold, edged with finality. It hung between them, chilling the air. Then his smile returned, and it was no longer angled into a smirk. "Why don't you join me for the meal you worked so hard to prepare, sister?"

"Me," Mareleau said with a grimace. "Dine with you?"

"You seemed quite passionate over the wine and cake. If anyone deserves to enjoy it, it's you, am I wrong?"

He had a point. She had worked hard, and if Aveline was going to force all that effort to go to waste, then the least she could do was enjoy it. "But...but my presence will be missed at dinner in the hall."

"Will it, though?"

Another good point. She doubted anyone would even note her absence. Besides, she was only going for cake. She could always join the feast after.

Her stomach churned, rippling with the same nausea she'd felt earlier when she'd lusted over the wine. Seven gods, she was ravenous. She supposed it made sense after all her hard work.

That left her only one answer she could give. "Fine."

~

BBY THE TIME THEY REACHED THE LITTLE COURTYARD, THE PLATES HAD ALREADY BEEN filled with food, and a small round cake rested upon a tray at the center of the table. Noise still carried from the kitchen, but with most of the staff busy in the dining hall, it was somewhat less chaotic. Still, Teryn didn't hesitate to close the shutters over the kitchen window and seal the door leading to the courtyard. It cut off even more of the noise, leaving them some semblance of peace.

Teryn lowered himself into one of the seats, his posture casual as he sank into the chair. He seemed...tired. Fatigued. As if he'd been the one slaving away over table decorations the last couple of hours.

Mareleau resisted the urge to sneer at his lax composure and dragged her chair far from his. When they were on opposite ends of the table, she took her seat. She leaned toward the glorious display of lemon chiffon, only to pause with her hand an inch away from the serving knife. Teryn had insisted that his dinner with the princess be unattended by servants, and while she'd found the notion crass then, it was even more so now. She'd never had to slice her own cake before...

Teryn released a soft chuckle and took the knife from under her hand. Then, with deft movements, he sliced the cake with two flicks of the blade and placed the piece on her plate.

"Thank you," she mumbled, taking up her fork. She was about to take a dainty bite as befitting a queen, when she decided—*to hell with it*—since no one of import was watching, she might as well shove the largest forkful she could fit. One with equal parts frosting and cake.

She closed her eyes as the sweet lemon flavor melted over her tongue. It made her want to dance in her seat. Were she a younger girl, she would have. She was far too reserved for that now.

The sound of pouring liquid made her open her eyes. Teryn filled his glass with wine, then did the same for hers. Her stomach rumbled at the sight of the ruby liquid before her. It took all her strength of will to force her eyes away so she could burn Teryn with a glare. "I can't have that."

He arched a brow. "Why not?"

"You damn well know why not."

He shrugged, taking a long pull from his glass. "Gods, it's been too long since I've tasted wine. Why can't you have any?"

She glanced around, but she already knew they weren't being watched. "The baby," she whispered.

"Ah. Right. You're pregnant with my brother's child."

"Why do you keep acting like that?"

"Like what?"

"Like...like you've forgotten things."

He leaned farther back in his chair and tipped his face toward the sky. "It's been a long day. A day that has felt more like months. So forgive me if I'm beyond caring whether you imbibe."

She studied him, studied his too-relaxed posture, his loose limbs. Maybe courting Aveline had done a number on his brain. Or was it more that...

Her pulse racketed as realization dawned.

"Did Larylis tell you? Is that why you're being so lax about this?"

"Tell me what?"

"About...my lie."

He swirled his glass and watched her over the rim of his cup. "He tells me many things. He's my brother."

She felt suddenly small. Abashed. While she couldn't blame Larylis for wanting to relieve some of the guilt he carried, she hated that he hadn't warned her in advance that he'd be telling Teryn the truth. "So you know I'm not truly with child."

An amused grin lifted his lips. "I do now. What an entertaining twist."

Heat seared her blood and crawled up her cheeks. "Did you just...trick me into confessing—"

"Seven devils, Majesty," he said with a roll of his eyes. "Drink. Enjoy yourself. Or don't. I care not about whatever lies you've had to tell to get what you want."

She was flustered beyond belief, unsure whether Teryn had been teasing her or if he still was. Either way, it didn't seem like he was at all concerned about reporting her actions to her parents.

"Fine," she said, snatching the glass from the table and bringing it to her lips. She swallowed half the glass in a single gulp, then drained the rest between bites of cake. While she knew she should savor the wine's taste—it was a lovely vintage, after all—she couldn't help but fear it would be taken away at any moment. If one servant exited the door, if one of her lady's maids came looking for her, she'd have to return to her ruse.

Just a few more days, she reminded herself. Her cycle was due soon. Or was it overdue? It didn't matter. As soon as she could release herself from her lie, she could have all the wine she wanted. Then maybe, just *maybe*, her remaining days at Ridine would be somewhat tolerable.

"Your Majesty," Teryn said, refilling both their empty glasses, "I think we should get to know each other better."

"I suppose," she muttered, mouth full of cake. She gathered another forkful, noting her movements were growing sloppy. Damn. She should have known better than to drink so fast. Especially with how long it had been since her last drink. Even so, she'd enjoy the wine while she could, no matter how drunk it got her. Rebelling against her own good sense, she drained the rest of her glass and poured more. She chased that with the rest of her cake. With her nerves so unwound, she leaned back in her chair and released a satisfied moan, luxuriating in the sugary fullness of her belly, the burn of the wine, the lightness in her head.

"Tell me, sister. What is your deepest secret? Aside from the one I already know about, of course." He said the last part with a wink.

"My deepest secret...is that I have no secrets." She snorted a rather unladylike laugh at her lie.

"Then what is your greatest desire?"

That she could confess. "That I was back home at Dermaine with my husband."

Teryn's expression fell with pity. "You've been treated unfairly, Majesty. You deserve better."

"You don't need to tell me that." She lifted her chin, and a wave of dizziness had her swaying in her seat. "I already know."

"It must be so hard for you to be here alone. Without friends. Without family. All the while watching Princess Aveline get everything she wants. Her home, her lover. And what do you get?"

His words rang true, yet they sounded wrong coming from his lips. Why was he saying these things about the woman he adored? A shudder ran down her spine, and the warmth from the wine, the tingling in her mind and stomach, no longer felt so pleasant.

She stood on unsteady feet but forced herself to seem composed. "I've had enough cake," she said, voice slurred. "I'm going to bed now."

"No, you should enjoy yourself more. Besides, do you really want people to see you swaying through the halls? Courtiers talk, you know."

She glared at him, but a swirl of nausea had her dropping back into her seat.

Teryn brushed past her, pausing at the door that led to the kitchen. "If ever there is something you want, do tell me. You'll find I make a formidable ally and a terrifying enemy."

She forced herself to turn around in her chair. "Is that some kind of a threat?"

"An offer, Majesty. We're on the same side."

"What side is that?"

"The one where we get everything we want." He winked at her and left, closing the door behind him. As soon as it was shut, she lurched to the side and heaved her precious cake onto the courtyard stones.

29

Teryn woke with a sudden start, though he didn't feel as if he'd been asleep. He felt more like he'd been...lost. Floating. Clinging to the fraying edges of his consciousness. Now wakefulness dawned on him in a violent rush. He sat up—at least he thought he did—but all he saw was blinding white light. Not even his body stood out against it. He glanced down at his hands, his legs, but there was nothing to see.

Panic raced through him, sending him teetering back toward the opposite edge of consciousness.

"Calm, Your Highness." A feminine voice reached his ears. It was a hollow sound, devoid of resonance, but the fact that there was someone near him, calming him, gave it a soothing quality.

"Where am I?" His voice held the same lack of resonance, but there was nothing soothing about it. The words left his lips, but instead of reverberating from his vocal cords, they simply took shape in the nothingness around him. That only renewed his sense of panic.

"It's all right, Prince Teryn."

"Who are you? Why can't I see anything?"

"My name is Emylia. I'm here to help you."

"Help me with what? Where the seven devils am I?"

As if in answer, the light grew muted, slowly fading into shadows. Those shadows spilled over the surface of white, like ink staining a blank page. But instead of pure darkness, the shadows took form, creating distinct edges, shapes, and textures, until it became a moonlit bedroom. *His* bedroom at Ridine Castle. He saw his four-poster bed, the flagstone floor, the tapestries decorating the walls.

He released a sigh of relief...but the breath leaving his lungs didn't feel normal. It tingled against his lips without warming them and it lacked the rushing sound he was used to. He glanced down at his body, and this time he could see hands. That was a small comfort.

"Just breathe, slow and steady," the woman named Emylia said. A woman he'd still yet to see.

He glanced up from his hands and nearly leaped out of his skin at the sight of the unfamiliar woman. If he had to guess, she was around his age, perhaps a year older. Her skin was a rich brown while her curly hair was the color of the midnight sky outside his room. A beautiful woman. And one who was only half dressed. The shift she wore was of a flowing, floor-length silk in a color he couldn't distinguish in the unlit room, but the way it bared her shoulders told him it had to be a night-gown at best.

Suspicion darkened in his mind. Averting his gaze, he set his jaw and said, "Miss...Emylia, who are you and what are you doing in my room?"

It was all he could do not to order her out at once. The last thing his relation-ship with Cora needed was a scandal. A nagging thought pulsed through him, telling him this was the least of his worries. But...why? Something had happened after his conversation with Cora...

Something that would explain the terror lurking in the back of his mind...

"I told you. I'm here to help you."

"With what?" He allowed his gaze to return to her and saw she now wore a capelet over her shoulders in the same flowing silk as her gown. It struck him as odd that her ensemble would change so suddenly, but he was more concerned with getting her out of his room. There was no way he was letting this stranger ruin what he had with Cora. "Never mind. You shouldn't be here. Please leave at once."

When she made no move to obey, he reached forward to assist her, determined to drag her out if he must.

"Don't touch me," she barked, leaping away from his touch.

Teryn froze.

The woman made a placating gesture, and her tone turned gentle again. "It's... it's probably fine, but we can't risk it."

"I don't want to touch you," Teryn said through his teeth, trying to ignore that his teeth felt...well, there was something wrong with them. Something wrong with *him*. Everything about his body felt...too light. Too fuzzy. Was he dreaming? It felt like a dream. But not even in his dreams did he fancy having a strange woman in his private quarters when he could have been dreaming about someone else. "I just want you out of my room before someone gets the wrong idea."

Her shoulders sank, eyes turning down at the corners. "Highness, we aren't in your room."

"What do you—"

"Do you remember anything about what you were doing before?"

"Before what?"

"What's the last thing you recall? Stay calm but try to remember. It's better if you remember on your own."

Teryn was torn between fear and irritation. A nagging notion—too hazy to decipher—continued to plague him, trying to remind him...

He closed his eyes, and a vision played through his mind. First he saw himself holding the crystal in his room, saw the light catch on its facets. Then there was nothing but white. He'd heard a woman's voice. Emylia's voice, he realized now. Then dark tendrils like black smoke took shape before him, forging legs, hands, a torso. Then a face. One he recognized. The shadowed figure was colorless, revealing neither Duke Morkai's dark hair nor his silver-blue eyes. But Teryn knew it was him. Emylia had shouted not to let Morkai touch him, but the voice had been too far away, too lost in the tumult of Teryn's fear and confusion. The figure reached out, grasped Teryn. Pain had surged through him, searing his skull as if it were being cleaved in two, and then...

Then nothing.

Teryn stumbled back, swiping a hand over his face. But when his palm made contact with his skin, it lacked the pressure he was used to. Instead, it simply... buzzed. Thickened the air. He drew his hand back and examined it. It was still his hand, but the closer he looked, the more he realized its edges were slightly blurred, its shape in a constant flux of swirling particles.

His breaths grew sharp and shallow. Breaths that didn't feel like true breaths.

"You need to stay calm," Emylia said, but her words only reminded him of the wrongness of their voices. They still lacked resonance. Still struck hollow in the space around them.

"You expect me to stay calm? What the seven devils is happening? Where am I —*really*?"

Her expression sank with pity. "You're inside the object you know as Morkai's crystal."

Teryn glanced around the room, no longer trusting his surroundings. They seemed as tenuous as his form, something real but not real. This was wrong. All of this was wrong. He could only hope this was a nightmare and that he'd wake from it at any moment. But if this wasn't a dream and Emylia was telling the truth...

He was inside Morkai's crystal.

Not his body, though. He knew enough to comprehend that whatever he was now, it wasn't a being of flesh and blood.

A question formed on his lips, one he wasn't sure he was ready to hear the answer to. "Am I dead?"

"No, Teryn," she said with a gentle smile. "You're alive."

He swallowed hard. "Then what am I?"

She clasped her hands at her waist. "The part of you that exists inside this crystal is your ethera. You might call it your spirit. What you see now is the outer layer of your ethera, the part that most resembles your physical form."

"And you? What are you?"

She gestured at her body. "This too is the outer layer of my ethera. But unlike you, I died many years ago. I don't have a body to return to."

"Does that mean I can go back? I can get out of the crystal and...return to my body?" Referring to himself as something separate from his body ignited a fresh wave of panic.

"Yes, but you need to keep your breathing steady, Highness. It's your best defense against him."

Him.

The shadowed form of Duke Morkai.

"Was that...*thing* I saw...was that the sorcerer's ethera?"

She nodded. "He tethered it to the crystal as a way to fully evade death."

"But you said you're considered dead because your body is gone. So is his. He has nothing to return to."

Emylia wrung her hands before forcing them to still. "Returning to his *former* body isn't his goal."

The way she emphasized *former* sent a chill through him. She must have been implying that Morkai intended to forge some new body. What did that have to do with Teryn? Why was his spirit stuck inside a crystal—

Truth dawned like a dagger to his heart. "He wants to use my body."

Her nod of confirmation sent his head spinning. Or whatever part of this so-called ethera that felt like his head.

"He...already has," she said. "Somewhat."

"What the seven devils is that supposed to mean? Is his spirit in my body right now?" What were these words leaving his mouth? These kinds of things weren't possible. They weren't real. Months ago, he hadn't believed in magic. Magic had been a thing that existed only in faerytales. Then he'd met Cora, caught his first glimpse of a unicorn. Magic then shifted into a beautiful truth, one that gave Cora the ability to sense emotion and even go so far as to hide them from sight. But when Morkai came along, his view of magic changed yet again, and he'd learned of its dark side. One of wraiths and blood sorcery. Somehow, Teryn was now entangled in that malevolent kind of magic.

No, this can't be happening.

His chest tightened, lungs contracting. Or were they his lungs at all? Emylia had told him to breathe, but if he was separate from his body, then...then that was impossible. His legs-that-weren't-legs gave out beneath him and he slid to the floor. But the floor wasn't solid; it was nothing but a buzzing resistance against his thighs and hips.

Emylia crouched before him. "I can't answer any more questions until you strengthen your connection to your vitale."

"My what?"

"Your vitale, your life force energy. Your ethera is connected to it. Now close your eyes and focus on your breath. Breathe slow and deep."

It was hard to focus on anything except his growing panic, but she'd said breathing was his greatest weapon against the sorcerer, right? He didn't know how or why or even half of what was happening to him, but if Emylia was telling the truth, he had to try.

Closing his eyes, he took a breath. It was shaky and shallow, but he poured all his focus into making the next one deeper, stronger. Then the next.

"Can you feel the air moving through your lungs?" came Emylia's voice.

"Yes," he said, though he didn't understand how it was possible.

"Can you feel the beating of your heart?"

He shifted his attention to the rhythmic pounding. The thud of his pulse. The melody drained some of his fear, smoothing the edges of his panic. His next breaths were even deeper.

"Good. Sink your attention into what makes you feel alive. The pulsing of your blood. The workings of your heart, lungs, and other organs. That is your vitale. It is your life force, the part of your body you still maintain control over. Do not open your eyes until you feel like you can maintain this connection without conscious thought."

Teryn sat in stillness for countless minutes until his breaths were steady, his pulse uninterrupted by spikes of anxiety. Finally, he opened his eyes and saw Emylia sitting across from him. She no longer wore her dress and capelet but billowy silk pants and a matching tunic. It was yet another strange outfit, following neither current female fashions nor ones from the recent past. If Emylia's ethera resembled who she'd been when she was living, she hadn't been from the continent of Risa. The Southern Islands perhaps?

While his calmer state of consciousness allowed some curiosity to bloom, he had far more pressing questions.

"You said my vitale is the part of my body I still maintain control over. Does that mean..." His words snagged on a thorn of fear, but he quickly refocused on his breath, on the steady rise and fall of his lungs, on the steady beat of his heart. He tried again, and this time he managed to speak past the terror that threatened to overwhelm him. "Does that mean Morkai has control over the other parts of me?"

Emylia kept her tone steady. Gentle. "Morkai has control over your cereba. That is the spiritual aspect of your mind that allows your soul to animate your physical body. It controls movement. Speech."

Ethera. Vitale. Cereba. These were all strange words he'd never heard before. Were these scientific terms? Or did they have more to do with magic?

"If we're both souls, how are we talking?"

"Our etheras are beyond the restraints of the human body. We can communicate, even without forming words with our lips. However, the instinct to move our lips when we speak is deeply ingrained with the outer layer of our etheras."

"Are you saying we could communicate with just our minds if we wanted to?"

She pursed her lips. *Yes, we can. See?* This time, he heard the words despite her lips remaining pressed tight.

A shudder tore through him. If he had a body, his hair would stand on end.

"I figured you'd prefer it if we continued speaking like this," she said, moving her lips this time.

She was right. Speaking mind-to-mind was not something he was ready for.

Changing the subject, he asked, "How did this happen? You said Morkai tethered his ethera to the crystal. The last thing I remember from inside my body was looking at the light on the stone's facets."

"Eye contact with light from the crystal gave him temporary access to your cereba. He held you in place and drew your ethera into the crystal through that link."

Teryn shuddered, wondering if that was what had happened to Cora when he'd found her in the tower room. She'd had the crystal in her hand, but...she'd probably been looking at it too. He'd only taken the precaution of not letting the stone touch his skin, but he'd let himself look. Let himself become entranced by its dazzling light. How foolish could he be?

"Don't blame yourself," Emylia said. "Morkai wove countless enchantments around the crystal over the years, ones that were meant to be triggered upon his death, should it come to pass. As a result, the crystal is easy to forget, evading one's memory when it's out of sight. It's alluring, which makes one forget danger and want to look at it. And it's unbreakable. These enchantments were too strong for even the princess to break with her efforts."

"You know about Cora, then? I think she was stuck in here too, she—" His pulse racketed, surging out of his control. "Has he gained some hold over her ethera too?"

"No, you freed her before he could touch her ethera, and he...he didn't intend to touch hers at all."

That gave him some relief. Enough to steady his breaths again. "Does that mean when his shadowed form touched mine, he took control?"

"Yes. Touching your ethera with his own strengthened the link to your cereba. That allowed him to manipulate your body. A difficult task with such a temporary connection, but it was enough to force your hand to lift the crystal and hold it over your body's sternum. That closed the circuit, creating a sustained link from Morkai's ethera, to your cereba, to his heart-center."

Teryn furrowed his brow. "Heart-center?"

"The spiritual aspect of the heart. His is stored inside the crystal. So long as the crystal is near your body, within at least sixteen inches of where your heart-center should be, the circuit remains closed, giving him primary control over your cereba."

Primary control. Over *his* body.

Nothing good could come of that.

"Where is my body now? What is he doing with it?"

Emylia held his gaze, nibbling her bottom lip as if debating whether to answer. Then, with a sigh, she waved a hand. A ripple of shadow crossed his vision. As it settled, the bedroom grew somewhat sharper, the walls and furnishings more distinct. She stood and gestured toward the bed. Teryn rose too, feeling that strange buzzing resistance between his feet and the floor. Slowly, he turned toward the bed, dreading what he was about to see. He was right to feel dread. For there, upon the bed, lay himself. Asleep. His own body separate from the soul he was now.

"Is this real?" Teryn asked. "Is this truly my bedroom? Truly my body?"

She nodded. "I can utilize some of the magic in the crystal. With it, I can forge a likeness of any place I've seen. That is what I first showed you when you awoke. I muted the light of the crystal and showed you something familiar to set you at ease. But what you see now is real. In addition to casting illusions, I can create a window of sorts that allows me to project my ethera—and yours—outside the crystal."

"So we're free from the crystal now?" Even as he asked, he knew the hope was too good to be true.

"No, our etheras are tethered. Mine even more than yours, as I have no link to a living body. We can experience the crystal's immediate surroundings, but that doesn't make us free of our captivity."

Teryn wondered if Morkai had been able to project his ethera in the same way. If so, Morkai could have been watching Cora the entire time she'd possessed the crystal. Rage burned through him at the thought.

"Where is the crystal now?" he asked, stepping closer to the bed.

She angled her head at the sleeping Teryn's chest. "It's beneath your shirt."

"And Morkai is…"

"Resting his ethera. Controlling your cereba is taxing, especially since he has no link to your vitale. He'll need to sleep, and that is when you have the highest chance of regaining control. It will be hard, though. He maintains the primary connection even during sleep. To loosen his grip, we must move the crystal more than sixteen inches from your sternum and open the circuit between your cereba and his heart-center."

Teryn studied his body, saw the lump beneath his shirt that must be the crystal. If Morkai's spirit was sleeping, now was Teryn's chance. He surged toward his sleeping form and reached for the collar of his shirt—

His ethera's hands went straight through the cloth, resulting in nothing but that buzzing resistance. That thickening of the air.

"Breathe," Emylia said, and Teryn realized his lungs had begun to contract again.

Teryn took a few steps back, deepening his breaths and watching his body's chest rise and fall in tandem. "Seven devils, this is madness."

"I know, and you had the right idea. But before you have any chance of manipulating physical matter, you need to strengthen what little connection you have to your cereba. You maintain a slim link between it and your vitale."

"What can I do?" He had to do something. Anything. Morkai was in his body. He would wake. He would…

Teryn didn't want to think about what he might do. *Whom* he might do things to.

"For now," Emylia said, "align your ethera with your body and simply breathe. Feel your heart. Your pulse."

"You want me to just…lie down and breathe."

"Do not underestimate your connection to your vitale. So long as your awareness of it remains strong, you hold the upper hand. If you let fear disconnect you from it, you leave it open for Morkai to take. He isn't strong enough to take it yet, but he has plans to do so. I know he does."

What were his plans? And how did Emylia know so much about Morkai, about utilizing the crystal's magic? Who was she aside from a trapped spirit? Could he even trust her?

Emylia opened her mouth, but before she could speak, he said, "If you tell me to breathe one more time, I'm going to lose my godsdamned mind."

She pursed her lips and gestured toward the bed with a pointed look.

With nothing else to do, he climbed upon the mattress, sank into his sleeping form, and tried to become one with a body that was no longer his own.

30

Morning dawned, but peace did not rise with the sun. Cora stayed in bed as sunlight streamed through her window, crawling up the walls and dancing over her ceiling. All the while she hoped she'd feel some of that light reflected in her heart. But she didn't. She remained burdened with the same dark revelations she'd stumbled upon last night. No matter how she wished otherwise, a curse placed by a dead man had invaded her life, throwing all her carefully laid plans into disarray.

And yet, when it came to said plans, she had to admit some of the folly lay with her. She'd been naive to think she could easily exit her role as princess. That all she had to do was ensure Dimetreus was secure on his throne. There was more to this political game than she'd anticipated. A game of heirs and royal bloodlines. Now, because of Morkai, she was unable to play the game at all. She'd lost the one piece that had made her a contender on the board.

The ability to further the Caelan bloodline.

She hated that something so small—something so intimate and personal—determined her worth as a royal woman. Hated it so much that it burned away the edges of her sorrow, replacing them with something sharper. Wilder. Fiercer.

Where last night she'd felt pain, only anger existed in her now.

It was enough to drive her out of bed, to make her throw back the bedsheets with awakening resolve. She stomped over to her vanity, splashed water on her face from the ewer, and set about getting herself dressed. Sera hadn't returned since Cora had sent her and Mareleau's other two ladies away when they'd tried to fetch her from the tower last night. Cora hadn't even deigned to deny them to their faces. Instead, she'd ordered the stairwell sentry to forbid anyone from coming upstairs. By the time she'd gathered her composure enough to leave the tower room, the three girls were long gone. Perhaps they'd been offended by her refusal to entertain their efforts, but Cora didn't have it in her to care.

She donned a linen summer dress that laced up the front, tightening each row with far more force than necessary. Each pull was infused with her rage. Her hatred.

How dare Morkai. How dare he make a lasting impact on her life in such an invasive, perverse way. How dare he have so much influence beyond the grave, great enough to shatter Cora's heart. To break what she and Teryn were beginning to forge.

Teryn.

Her hands went slack on her laces, and her shoulders dropped. The thought of him broke through her anger, blunting it with sorrow yet again.

Her eyes went unfocused as she tried to imagine what she should say to him today. How she should act. She couldn't avoid him after insisting she only needed one night alone. Yet she didn't know what to do. Didn't know how to tell him about Morkai's curse. Sure, she knew the words she needed to say, but it was one thing to *know* and another to actually confess something so deeply intimate, something that pertained to the inner workings of her body. Her heart. Her soul.

Her chest constricted, but she breathed the tightness away. Shifting her gaze to the morning light streaming through the window, she called upon the element of fire.

Light. Heat. Warmth.

Passion. Anger. Rage.

Life force. Strength. Transmutation.

The sunlight heated her insides, evoking her anger. It surged from her chest to her palms. With renewed vigor, she finished lacing her bodice and tied off the ends. Then, closing her eyes, she strengthened her connection to the other elements.

She rooted her feet to the stone floor.

Earth. Safety. Protection.

Took a fortifying breath, in then out.

Air. Thoughts. Intellect.

She acknowledged the element of water—*feeling, emotion*—but it was already too strong. She needed less water right now. Less emotion and more strength of will. Steady logic. Keen insight.

Calm settled over her. It wasn't the most peaceful calm, for she still didn't know how to express herself to Teryn. A night of agonizing over the situation hadn't given her any answers. Perhaps there weren't any. None that were easy, at least.

But she knew what she *could* do. What she *must* do.

She'd funnel her rage, her attention, and her energy into the only suitable recourse: clearing Morkai's tower. And maybe—just maybe—if she was willing to take a risk and do something just a little reckless, she might be able to find the information she needed to break this damn curse.

～

TERYN HATED SITTING STILL. HE'D FORGOTTEN THIS FEELING. FORGOTTEN THE anxiety that had plagued him in the wake of his father's death. The time between

Centerpointe Rock and Cora's official release from Verlot had been pure agony when he hadn't been moving. Doing. Fixing. He'd felt some relief after Cora had been given back her title, and every moment since had been filled with distraction —first helping his brother step into his role as king, then focusing all his efforts on reuniting with Cora.

Now sitting still was all he could do.

And it was torture.

He'd kept his ethera aligned with his body for hours on end. At least, he assumed hours had passed. His ethera didn't feel the passing of time the way his body had been able to. There were no hunger pangs, no bodily urges. His primary relationship to time now was his growing anxiety.

"Breathe, Teryn." Emylia's words made him want to clench his jaw, but the mild buzzing resistance his ethera generated lacked the satisfaction he was used to.

Which gave him no choice but to listen. To tune back in to the feel of his breath, the rush of his blood, the rhythmic pulse of his heart. Despite his irritation over Emylia's constant reminders, she was right. The strength of his connection to his vitale—the one bodily sensation he could consistently feel—always calmed his nerves. With his soul lying in perfect harmony with his body's shape, his spiritual heart-center aligned with his sternum, his ethera's eyes aligned with his body's eyes, his soul's feet nestled within his body's feet, he could almost pretend he was whole again.

"Good," Emylia said. "You're going to try some subtle muscular movements again."

A spike of panic flared inside him. He'd tried to control small muscular movements already and failed miserably. According to Emylia, if he had any chance at reclaiming his body, he needed to not only strengthen his connection to his vitale but also to the thin thread that linked him to his cereba. The only reason he even had that tiny link was due to his connection to his vitale. While Morkai reigned over Teryn's conscious movements, Teryn maintained a sliver that controlled his automatic functions like breathing, blinking, and swallowing. Emylia had surmised that if Teryn could intentionally create small movements related to these automatic functions, he could learn to control larger ones next.

He hadn't managed so much as a flinch the first time he'd tried, which had resulted in him flying into a panicked rage and losing his connection to his vitale entirely.

"You must start small and be patient," Emylia had said. "You will get there."

That same anxiety filled him now—of being inside his body, yet unable to move it. He tuned back in to his breath, his pulse, his blood, and felt the panic melt away.

Emylia kept her voice slow and gentle. "Now shift your attention to what's outside your body. Focus on the sensation of the blankets against your back. Feel the pillows cradling your head, brushing against your cheek."

He followed along, noting the various levels of resistance generated between each object and his ethera. It didn't feel quite the same as it should, but he tried not to dwell on that.

"Now focus on a single finger on your right hand," Emylia said. "Pour all your attention there. Feel the pressure of your fingertip against the blankets. The connection between the finger and your hand. Then your hand to your arm. Arm to shoulder. Shoulder to neck. Neck to spine. Spine to mind. Then follow it back down to your finger."

Teryn did as she said, following his awareness of each part of his body. Or was it just his ethera he was noting? He supposed it didn't matter. Emylia moved him through the exercise again and again until he felt a strange hum in his ethera, filling the space he was focusing on, rippling from his mind to his fingertip.

"Good," Emylia whispered. "Now send a single surge of awareness from your mind to your finger. Don't try to figure out how. Just trust. This is an automatic function. A flinch. You maintain that link. You can send energy through that circuit. That's all you're doing now. Are you ready?"

He breathed in deeply, felt his lungs expand. Felt the resistance between his back and the mattress shift with the movement. Felt the subtle sway in the energy from his mind to his hand, then back to his mind. He settled his attention at the top of his head. Then, with a rush of single-minded intent, he sent his awareness down his neck, his arm, his hand, and into his finger. The energy echoed back his intent with a flinch of movement.

"You did it," Emylia said, keeping her voice level despite the excitement it contained. "You moved your finger."

Teryn's pulse quickened in response to his shock. He...did it. He finally managed to move something—

A sudden wave of energy tore through his chest, and he felt as if he were torn in two. He shifted his attention to his surroundings, to the bed in the dark bedroom, the pale morning light creeping in through the closed curtains. His eyes fell on his own back, upright and no longer aligned with his ethera. His body moved of its own accord—no, Morkai's accord—glancing left and right, eyes blinking furiously.

This was the first time he'd witnessed his body being operated by Morkai, and it drained all the pride he'd felt in having made his finger flinch. What good was a damn flinch when Morkai could make his body sit? Stand. Walk. Talk.

Keeping his eyes on his now-awake form, he slowly shifted away from Morkai and slid from the bed. "You did great," Emylia said, standing at his side. "We will practice again next time he rests."

Teryn could only nod, eyes trained on Morkai.

The sorcerer ran a hand through his stolen body's hair, then threw back the covers.

Before Emylia could chastise him for his growing anxiety, Teryn focused on the sensations of his vitale, reminding himself that his heart was still his own. *His* breath kept his body alive. *His* blood pulsed through that body, even as Morkai made it walk across the room to the wardrobe.

"Does he know we're here?" Teryn asked. "Can he see us? Hear us?"

"No," Emylia said. "He's fully immersed in operating your body. He has no awareness of the spiritual plane we stand in now."

That gave him some relief.

"Now that he's awake," Emylia said, "you should rest your ethera. If you don't rest it on purpose, your ethera will eventually give you no choice. It's better you do so now so that you'll be at your best when Morkai sleeps. You aren't strong enough to wrest control of your body while he's awake yet."

Teryn debated the wisdom of her words, but he couldn't stand the thought of resting while Morkai did devils-know-what in his body. "I want to see where he goes. What he does. I need to know what his plan is."

Morkai stripped off his nightshirt, giving Teryn the first glimpse of the crystal. It was wrapped in a thin strip of leather and secured around his neck on a long cord, the crystal itself resting at his sternum.

"We know what his plan is," Emylia said. "It's the same as it's always been. He intends to become the Morkaius of Lela."

Teryn whipped his gaze to her. "Morkaius? What is a Morkaius?"

She frowned. "Princess Aveline hasn't told you everything."

Mention of Cora struck him with a hollow ache. He recalled her tears last night, how she'd begged him to leave her alone. Now he'd give anything to take it all back, to storm up those stairs and refuse to leave her. He'd tolerate her rage, her ire, if it meant preventing what was happening now. If only he'd remembered the crystal. Perhaps she'd have had some idea how to destroy it...

Or would that only have gotten her trapped in his place?

Emylia's voice roused him from his thoughts. "*Morkaius* comes from the ancient fae language. It means High King of Magic. Morkai is not the sorcerer's real name but a title he's given himself. It means King of Magic. He intends to become Morkaius by ruling all three kingdoms of the land once known as Lela."

"Why?" Teryn shifted his gaze back to Morkai, saw him securing the buttons of one of Teryn's shirts, then donning a waistcoat.

"Ruling over Lela will allow Morkai to tap into an immense well of fae magic. That magic isn't meant to be wielded by a single person, and if he does harness it, he'll be able to do terrible things."

Teryn shuddered. He remembered how Morkai had boasted that he'd one day be King of Lela—that Dimetreus would conquer the three kingdoms, and Morkai would inherit rule after the king's passing. "If ruling over Lela has always been his goal, why did he even bother going through King Dimetreus and using him as a puppet?"

"To claim the magic," Emylia explained, "he must first inherit the land. Not through conquest either. Specifically, the crown must be *given not taken*, which suggests his best bet is to insert himself into the line of succession."

Morkai finished dressing and assessed his reflection in the mirror beside the wardrobe. Outfitted in Teryn's trousers, shirt, waistcoat, and jacket, no sign of the crystal or the leather strap could be seen. Seemingly satisfied with what Morkai saw in the mirror, he lifted Teryn's lips in a smug grin that looked nothing like his own.

"Are you starting to understand why Morkai chose you?" Emylia asked.

"What do you mean he *chose* me?"

"You were his target all along, which is why the crystal's magic was so strong with you. Why you forgot its existence so easily. Why you were so drawn to look at it. While the crystal is enchanted to have some semblance of self-preservation, its magic works strongest around Morkai's targets."

Dread filled every inch of his ethera. "And he specifically wanted me so he could..." He couldn't bring himself to finish, to even think it.

Emylia filled in the blanks for him. "He wanted your body so he could use your identity, your title, and your position to become Morkaius. To inherit the three kingdoms of Lela and control the magic of the ancient fae."

He still didn't understand the magic of the fae or even the full extent of what it meant to be Morkaius. The implications of Morkai's intent were enough to occupy his thoughts. If the sorcerer intended to use Teryn's body to accomplish his means, then his first step...

"It's because of Cora, isn't it?" His voice came out with a tremor, even though his words were no longer shaped with vocal cords. "It's because I am betrothed to her, and she is Dimetreus' heir. Through her, he could position himself as future King Consort of Khero."

Emylia's face fell with sympathy. "That is undoubtedly his first of many steps."

Teryn felt that agonizing urge to move, to act, to fix. Morkai was going to try to marry Cora in Teryn's stead. Surely she'd see through him! She had her magic, her ability to sense others' emotions. She'd notice Teryn wasn't who he appeared to be.

Wouldn't she?

Or would she continue to sense Teryn's soul as his own, oblivious to the fact that he was trapped in a crystal?

His only solace was that Cora and Teryn's marriage wasn't set for another year. If Morkai had the patience to play such a long game, Teryn could too. He'd strengthen his vitale, reclaim his cereba, and then—

A strange pulling sensation sent Teryn's ethera surging forward. Morkai had left the mirror and was now exiting the room.

"You and I are bound to the crystal," Emylia said, following after Morkai. "We are only able to project our etheras within the stone's immediate surroundings. So when the crystal moves, so do we. If not willingly, then by force."

Teryn caught up with the sensation pulling his ethera and measured his steps behind Morkai's. Belatedly, he realized he probably didn't need to walk at all. Surely the act of setting one foot before the other was only for show. An instinct belonging to the outer layer of his ethera, like how Emylia had explained about their means of communication. Should he want, he could probably float in Morkai's wake.

The thought was as disturbing as speaking mind-to-mind had been. No matter what he was now—disembodied spirit or no—he would continue acting as alive as he could.

"Are you certain you wouldn't rather rest your ethera?" Emylia asked as they trailed Morkai through the halls of the keep. "Since I have no ties to a mortal body, I don't require rest the same way you and Morkai do now. I can keep watch and wake you if there's anything I think you should see."

He knew she was right, and he thought he could trust her. She was trapped, same as he. And yet, now that he knew what Morkai planned—that marrying Cora was his primary goal—he couldn't stand the thought of not witnessing his every move.

"Just a little longer," Teryn said. "I just want to see where he's—"

All thoughts fled his mind as Morkai rounded the next corner...and froze. It seemed Teryn and Morkai were of the same mind, equally as unprepared to see the person who halted before them.

Teryn's heart thundered in a chest that was no longer his own. He breathed her name in a voice she couldn't hear. "Cora."

31

A thousand different things happened to Cora's heart in the split second that she realized Teryn stood before her. First was a joyful flip, an automatic response to seeing his green eyes, the tousle of his gold-touched dark hair, the broad expanse of his chest beneath the fine silk jacket he wore. Then came the sinking, the guilt over seeing his frozen posture, the tense set of his shoulders, his look of mild shock. Next, she felt a wave of anxiety along with the reminder that she still didn't know what to say to him. With the next beat of her rioting heart, Teryn's composure relaxed and a casual smile crossed his face. That sent a flutter of hope, a fragile, dangerous promise that everything would be all right.

"Princess Aveline," Teryn said with a bow.

She wasn't sure if his formality was more of a show for the passing servants or a response to her treatment of him last night. His smile remained present, but it only made her heart shift into a new emotion. This time it was shame. Shame because she knew—regardless of those precious hopes that all would work out as she wished—she wasn't ready to tell him about the curse.

Still, she couldn't pretend last night didn't happen. Nor could she avoid him. Certainly not while he was standing before her. Not when her heart was so tangled with his.

She took a step closer to him. Her muscles tensed, half with dread, half with longing, as she expected him to touch her. So badly she wanted to feel his reassuring embrace. Just as badly she feared she'd fall apart if he so much as held her hand.

But he didn't. He made no move to reach for her at all. He remained where he was, posture tall and stiff, hands behind his back. Was he merely being respectful after last night? She extended her senses, desperate to read what he was feeling, but she got back...nothing. Perhaps her own frazzled emotions were too loud.

"Teryn, I..." The overwhelming urge to fidget sent her fingers fluttering at her sides, so she folded her hands at her waist instead. She studied his face, as if she could read the words she needed to say, written somewhere on his visage. Her eyes caught on his cheek. The light from the hall window had cast part of him in shadow, but now that she was closer, she noticed a thin slice over his cheekbone. Concern replaced her anxiety. "What happened to your cheek?"

She lifted a hand to his face, but he took a step back. With a timid smile, he covered the wound with his hand. "Ah, that. It's embarrassing to say, but I accidentally cut myself with the straight razor while shaving. I suppose that will teach me not to travel without my valet."

"Oh." She frowned, noting how he hadn't let her touch him. Releasing a slow exhale, she searched his energy again, seeking whether he was truly shying away out of embarrassment...or if it was something else. Again, she sensed nothing. Not a hint of his emotions.

At least the unexpected topic had managed to banish some of her trepidation. Before her anxiety could return, she blurted out what she needed to say. "I'm so sorry about last night, Teryn. I shouldn't have pushed you away. I was just...dealing with something and I needed time alone."

He dropped his hand from his cheek. "There's nothing to be sorry about," he said, but there was something hollow in his words. Was he hiding his hurt after all? He continued to grin but she realized it didn't meet his eyes. "You were right to ask for space."

"I...was?"

His expression shifted into one of resignation. Or was it apology? His smile turned sad. "I was wrong to push you into something you weren't ready for. You accepted my proposal, but I pressured you for more."

Cora's brow knit into a furrow. Did he really think she'd asked to be alone last night because she hadn't been ready for their relationship to progress romantically?

Her heart raced as she spoke the next words. "That's not it, Teryn. I didn't ask for space out of some need to pull away emotionally. I...I just didn't know how to talk to you about what I was going through. But..." She swallowed hard. "I'm ready to talk now."

"You don't have to tell me anything."

Her stomach sank, though she wasn't sure if it was due to disappointment or relief.

"I trust you," he said. "You know that, right? You're free to keep your secrets. I'll never pry them from you or begrudge you your time alone. Besides, you have important work to do in the tower. It would be selfish for me to keep you from it."

Her lips flickered between a smile and a frown. While she'd hoped he wouldn't be too concerned over what had happened last night, she hadn't expected him to be so accepting. So dismissive. Was he posturing to hide any hurt he may feel? Or was he simply being supportive?

As if he could read the conflict in her expression, his tone turned warm. "My feelings haven't changed. We have all the time in the world to fall in love. There's no need to rush."

Before she could say anything else, he took a step back and gave her another formal bow. When he rose, his eyes danced with mirth, lips quirked in a sideways grin. Then, with nothing more than the word "Highness," he left.

Cora stood frozen for a few beats more, unsure how to feel about their exchange. Her emotions were still too tangled, too loud. Most of all, her skin felt cold, chilled beneath the broken expectations that she'd at least receive a kiss on the hand, if not a parting embrace. The absence of his touch was as painful as a slap, as was his failure to request her company for some later date. Instead, he'd just...walked away.

He'd given her what she needed though, hadn't he? The space to finish her work in the tower. Permission to keep her secrets to herself. She'd let that be enough.

In the meantime, she could do what needed to be done.

Clean the tower.

Learn how to break her curse.

She marched from the keep to the tower stairwell and up the stairs. Both guards acknowledged her with a bow of their heads. The room was as she'd left it, the windows having been closed for the night, the hearth filled with nothing but soot.

Summoning the fiery resolve she'd felt earlier, she set everything back in place —donning her apron, opening windows, adding fresh salt to the threshold and sill, tossing her blend of herbs upon the cedar logs in the hearth. Once she was ready to begin her work for the day, she strode to the bookshelf, selected a book, and analyzed its energy. Deeming it safe enough to touch, she brought it to the hearth. But instead of tossing it in the growing flames, she set it on her lap, retrieved her knife from her apron pocket, and flipped open the cover.

This time, without guilt or shame or worry that she was doing the wrong thing, she read.

And read.

And read.

~

Teryn floated in nothingness, his surroundings shapeless and awash in pale light. He vaguely noted that *this* must be how it felt to rest his ethera. It was the same sensation he'd had before he'd awoken inside the crystal for the first time. His mind lingered somewhere between rest and consciousness. Thoughts began to sharpen at the edges, forming his last waking memory.

Cora.

Beautiful, fearless, formidable Cora standing in the hall.

Cora, frozen in place as her eyes fell on his body.

Cora, trying to confess a hurt she'd endured.

Cora, crestfallen as Morkai's retreating footsteps dragged Teryn away from her, forcing him to follow the crystal's path.

He woke with a jolt and found himself in an unfamiliar place. Instead of the muted gray stone of Ridine's walls and regal tapestries, he found himself surrounded by pale marble carved in intricate patterns. Rugs covered the floor of the small room, and an array of bright pillows stood in lieu of tables and chairs. To the left was a low bed draped in gauzy curtains that hung from the ceiling, sheets the color of ruby and saffron haphazardly tucked in place.

"This was my bedroom when I was alive." Emylia's voice startled him, and he found her suddenly at his side. She was dressed in a sleeveless linen gown the same shade of saffron as the bedsheets. Her curly black hair was pulled into a bun at the top of her head. "I spend most of my time here. Is that all right? Or would you prefer I shape the crystal to mimic your bedroom at Ridine again?"

"It's fine," Teryn said, his mind still sharpening from the haze of rest. "But where are we really? Where is Morkai right now? How much time has passed since…" Fear clenched his chest as he realized he couldn't remember anything after he saw Cora. His ethera must have forced him to rest, just as Emylia had said it would.

"Connect with your vitale first."

He bit back a curse, but she was right.

With a deep breath, he focused on the feel of air moving through his lungs, the pulse of his blood, the beat of his heart. Calm settled over him.

Only then did Emylia answer his question. "A few hours have passed. King Dimetreus is holding court and Morkai is in attendance."

"Doing what?"

"Just watching."

Teryn arched a brow. "That's all?"

"For now."

Teryn had expected something more sinister, but as long as he wasn't anywhere near Cora, he could let himself relax.

Emylia gave him a sympathetic smile. "You're worried about the princess, aren't you?"

"How can I not be worried? He's using my body to marry her and become king. He—" His voice cut off as he recalled Morkai and Cora's interaction. He'd nearly exploded in a futile rage, expecting Morkai to put his hands on her, to touch her or kiss her the way Teryn would have. Instead, he'd kept his hands behind his back, maintained a steady distance between their bodies. Then there were the things he'd said, telling her she was right to ask for space. The fact that he knew about what had happened between them in the tower last night told him Morkai had indeed been spying on them, the same way Teryn had begun watching Morkai.

But why had he acted so cold?

Teryn faced Emylia. "If Morkai is determined to marry Cora, why did he try to keep her at bay today? Wouldn't it serve his purposes to keep her close?"

Emylia shook her head. "He will have to ensure your engagement remains secure while avoiding her as much as possible until the marriage contract is signed. Cora is dangerous to him because of her magic. The crystal likely keeps her from reading Morkai's true emotions, and it might be muting yours as well, but she may grow suspicious if she realizes she can no longer read you."

"You know about Cora's magic?"

"I've been in this crystal a very long time, and I've spent most of my time projecting myself outside of it, watching. I've witnessed every moment between her and Morkai, starting with when he first arrived at Ridine Castle. I watched her struggle with her magic as a child, long before she'd learned what she was. But I've always known she was a clairsentient witch. A strong one. She's what my people call an empath."

"An empath," Teryn echoed. He remembered Cora saying that word when she'd confessed about her magic. She'd told him about witches and their six sensory magics, said that an empath was a witch with the strongest form of clairsentience.

"I'm from Zaras," Emylia said, "in the Southern Islands. There we respect magic. Almost everyone feels a connection to at least one of the six sensory magics. The strongest in the Arts train as priests and priestesses at the Zaras Temple. This bedroom was where I lived while training as an acolyte at the temple. I was a promising seer before I died."

That explained why Emylia knew so much about magic, and perhaps why she could utilize the crystal the way she did. Yet it reminded him just how much he *didn't* know about her.

"How did you die? Why did he trap your ethera?"

"He trapped me for the same reason he trapped you. He has plans for me."

He didn't fail to note that she hadn't answered the first part of his question. Was she hiding something? He narrowed his eyes. "Why are you helping me?"

"Our goals are the same," she said with a shrug. "I want out. I want my soul to be at rest. And there's only one way to solve both our problems."

"What's that?"

"We must destroy the crystal."

Teryn's eyes went wide. "How?"

"I don't know yet," she said, wringing her hands at her waist. "You need to strengthen your connection to your vitale and cereba first. You'll likely get only one chance to do what needs to be done. That flinch you created today? You'll need to do that with your whole body. If you can gain control over your movements, you'll have a chance at removing the crystal from your body. You must force it at least sixteen inches away, remember? That's the first step."

"What will that do?"

"Like I told you, removing the crystal from over your body's sternum will compromise the connection between Morkai's heart-center and your cereba. He will fight you for dominance, but without the crystal closing the circuit that gives him primary control, you'll have an equal chance at retaining motor function. You'll need to act at once to break the crystal."

He gave her a pointed look. "Didn't you tell me it's unbreakable?"

"Yes, but I'll work on figuring that part out. For now, you must get strong. You have time. I promise."

Teryn bristled despite her placating smile. He knew what empty promises sounded like, for he'd delivered his fair share, and hers rang as hollow as an unfilled vase. But that didn't mean he couldn't trust her. Right now, it was his only choice. And he did have time, didn't he? His marriage to Cora wouldn't commence for another year, and if Morkai was determined to avoid her until then, she'd be safe in the meantime. He'd be able to free himself before then.

Right?

Yes. He affirmed the word again and again.

Yes. Yes, I will do this.

No matter what it took, no matter how many sessions he had to spend laying in his empty body, trying to get his limbs to obey his mental commands, he'd get his body back.

And if he couldn't...

Well, he knew one thing that would prevent Morkai from attaining his goals. It would be a last resort. A dreadful one at that. But if it meant keeping Cora safe—keeping the three kingdoms he sought to control safe—then Teryn Alante was willing to die.

32

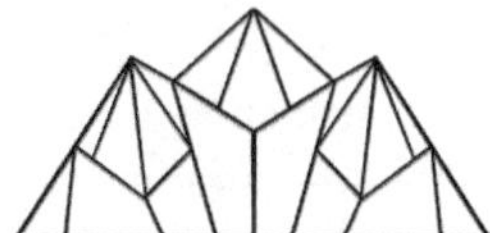

Witches didn't deal in curses. Cora knew this, knew every bit of information she pored through stood in contrast to her ethics. But if there was any hope in breaking Morkai's fate weaving, it had to be in one of these books. And yet by sunset, with over a dozen books read and burned, she'd found nothing to fuel that hope. Nothing of immediate value, at least.

Only three of the books had mentioned curses at all, and when it came to breaking them, all had said some measure of the same thing: *To break a curse, one must cast the same spell in reverse.*

That wasn't helpful. Cora may have had access to Morkai's blueprints for the fate weaving he'd cast, but she couldn't make heads or tails of the complex intersecting lines he'd drawn in his book. Would it be enough to draw the pattern in ink, or did she need blood? Would she have to suspend it in the air, make the pattern weave itself, like Morkai did? And if she was supposed to cast the spell in reverse, didn't that mean she needed to know which part of the pattern was the starting point and which was the end?

She'd found only one other option, a single sentence mentioned in the most recent book she'd read: *A curse may be rendered neutral if one casts a counter curse of equal or greater power to the opposite effect of the original curse.*

Yet another unhelpful piece of information. Because—as Cora had already surmised—witches didn't deal in curses. Even if she knew how to cast a counter curse, how could she make one strong enough to neutralize Morkai's dark magic? And what would the opposite effect be? A fertility spell?

She curled her fingers into fists as she watched the book burn, witnessed every page crumble to ash in the hearth. That single line of relevant, albeit unhelpful, text was all she let remain in her mind. Everything else, every unsettling spell, every instruction on using dark magic, she'd refused to take in. She may have decided to use Morkai's books as a means for education in a single subject, but she wasn't a fool. She wouldn't be seduced by the excerpts scrawled within these tomes, nor would she allow any excuse to save a single book from burning. Aside from those that couldn't be burned, of course, like the ones with pages laced with poison. But even those were fated to be discarded, not kept.

Even if she never found a way to unravel the weaving Morkai had placed upon her, she'd at least have the satisfaction of watching everything he'd owned be destroyed. That was where her true motive lay. This was less about gaining the ability to bear heirs and more about defeating a sorcerer who held too much power beyond the grave.

The sun began to set just as the last remnants of the book joined the ashes in the hearth. She debated returning to the bookshelf and selecting her next target, but she stopped herself, noting the heaviness of her bones, the fraying edges of her protective shields. As desperate as she was to do more, she knew better than to push herself. After expending so much energy sensing, reading, and clearing, she was at her limit. Her magic needed rest, as did her mind.

She set to the task of closing windows, putting out the hearth fire, and readying the room for the morrow. All the while, she couldn't shake her growing ire. She'd hoped she'd have gained something from reading Morkai's books today. Considering what little value she'd gained from the two excerpts she'd committed to memory, all she'd manage to accomplish was a slower pace than the day before.

Her frustration grew and grew as she left the tower and returned to the keep. Every step up the stairs carried the weight of her anger—an anger that hadn't diminished with her day's work.

All the better, she told herself. *It will carry me through tomorrow and keep me from thinking about...*

She cursed under her breath as Teryn entered her thoughts for the first time since she'd begun her day's work. Her mind had been too occupied to stray to him while she'd been reading and clearing, but now she remembered how his face had looked that morning. The smile that didn't reach his eyes when he'd told her she was right to ask for space. The distance he'd kept as they spoke. The rigidity of his spine as he'd stood with his hands behind his back, as if forcing himself not to touch her.

Or had he not wanted to touch her?

She shook her head, preferring her previous irritation to what she felt now, teetering on the edge of grief. She reached the main floor of the keep and saw the lamps had been lit in the hall.

Fire, she thought as she passed by the first, willing the element to grow within her, to spark the rage that served as a comforting barrier around her heart.

Fire, she thought again, striding past the next several sconces. She imagined the light dancing up her skin, settling over her core, and fueling her strength of will—

A startled squeak interrupted her focus, and she found Sera at the end of the hall, face pale as her eyes locked on Cora's. She lowered her eyes to the floor and dipped into a curtsy. Her voice came out with a mild tremor. "Highness."

A sense of guilt washed over Cora, but it wasn't her own. She'd left her mental shields as they'd been in the tower, strengthened only for protection, not sensing.

Breathing deeply, she fully sealed them, but not before gaining a full understanding of Sera's state of remorse.

"I'm sorry I haven't attended to you today, Your Highness," Sera muttered, eyes still locked on the floor. She began to fiddle with the ends of her brown hair.

"It's fine," Cora said curtly as she reached the girl. "I had no need of your aid."

A rush of air left Sera's lips as she finally lifted her face. "That's a relief, Your Highness, for I couldn't have been spared to aid you even if I'd wanted to come. Queen Mareleau has been dreadfully ill all day, you see. She can hardly keep anything down."

Cora began to brush past the girl. "Do what you must. I'm sure the royal physician will take care of her." She paused. Did they even have a royal physician on staff yet? Surely such an appointment would have been a priority...

Sera lowered her voice to a whisper. "She refuses to allow any of us to fetch him or tell anyone about her condition. I'm only telling you because you're my current mistress, and I didn't want you to think—"

Cora rounded on the girl. "Her Majesty is ill and she refuses to be seen by the physician?"

Sera gave a frantic nod. "She insists she can cry and throw up well enough on her own."

Finally, Cora found an appropriate target for her anger. What was Mareleau thinking refusing help while ill? Wasn't she with child?

A dreadful thought occurred to her. What if she was having complications with her...her pregnancy? And didn't want to tell anyone? Cora's heart softened the slightest bit.

"Take me to her."

Sera blinked at her a few times. "To...Her Majesty?"

"Yes." Cora wasn't even sure why she insisted. Whatever Mareleau was going through was none of her business. But with the dreadful pressures of queens and royal women so fresh in her mind, she couldn't stand idly by if the woman was suffering.

Sera led her down the halls toward a familiar wing of the keep. Cora shuddered as they neared the late Queen Linette's former chambers.

Master Arther put her here?

It made sense considering both Cora and Dimetreus had refused to claim the room, and it was one of the largest in the keep. Of course the steward would appoint it to the visiting queen.

Sera opened the door and ushered Cora inside before quickly closing them in. Cora nearly gagged as the scent of vomit reached her nostrils. The windows were open, allowing a gentle evening breeze inside the room, but nothing could hide the smell of sick.

Cora took in the state of the room, saw ewers of water, soiled rags, and clothing haphazardly strewn about. There was no sign of blood, but that didn't mean the worst hadn't happened. Mareleau lay upon her bed, the back of her forearm covering her eyes. Her hair was slightly damp around her forehead and her cheeks were pale. Her two other ladies, Breah and Ann, fluttered about next to her, trying to coax her into taking a bite of bread.

"I don't want any more bread," Mareleau said with a grumbling moan. "Just leave me alone and stop fussing."

Sera led Cora to Mareleau's side. Cora addressed the queen's ladies. "What are her symptoms?"

With an affronted gasp, Mareleau threw back her arm, revealing her blue irises, the whites of her eyes bloodshot. "You can ask me myself. I'm not dead, you know."

"Fine," Cora said through her teeth. "What's wrong with you?"

Mareleau's eyes widened as she took in Cora's presence. "What the seven devils are you doing here?"

"I'm here to check on you, Majesty." Cora's barbed tone relayed just how much she was already regretting doing so. "Tell me your symptoms."

Mareleau scoffed. "Do you fancy yourself a physician?"

"Do you fancy yourself a fool? Surely you know better than to neglect your health in your condition."

"My condition?"

"Your pregnancy, Majesty." Cora was done dancing around the subject. If Mareleau wanted to be difficult, then Cora would be blunt. "The child you bear. Whether you're suffering from the condition itself, the loss of it, or some other ailment, it's folly to refuse proper care."

The queen's mouth fell open and color rose to her cheeks. "It's...it's not—who told you? Never mind. Get out!"

Cora lifted her chin. "No."

"I am the queen—"

"Not mine, though you keep forgetting. Now tell me your symptoms or I'll plant myself in this room until you do."

Mareleau bared her teeth with a growl of frustration. Her gaze shifted to her ladies. "Out! The three of you."

The maids exchanged wary glances, but as Mareleau added a sharp, "Now," the three scurried from the room and closed the door behind them.

Mareleau groaned as she pulled herself to sitting, struggling to arrange the pillows behind her. The shoulders of her silk gown hung loose as if the back had been left undone. Cora almost felt bad for the queen as she winced with every move, but her pride was too strong to offer help. Mareleau likely wouldn't want it anyway.

Once she was able to comfortably recline while sitting, she spoke. "It's not about the baby, trust me." Her eyes flashed to Cora's, then quickly away. A flicker of emotion—something like guilt or shame—crept past Cora's shields.

"Then what's wrong?"

Mareleau released a huff. "I'm nauseous, all right? That's all. It started yesterday. My stomach was rumbling most of the day. I worked too hard and got too hungry. Today, I can't keep anything down. My head is pulsing like it's about to split in two. I smell terrible. *Everything* smells terrible...and I...well, I simply ate too much cake last night, that's all."

Cora's muscles relaxed. What Mareleau described didn't sound too dire. But what reason did she have for refusing the attention of a physician?

"It's all your fault, you know," Mareleau said.

"My fault?"

"Yes, your fault. I spent hours—*hours*—slaving away in the courtyard behind the kitchen setting up the perfect romantic dinner for you and your beloved prince. I should have said no, but he begged me. Can you imagine? A prince begging a queen! But I said yes, and—"

"Wait." Cora frowned. "Teryn had you set up a private dinner for me?"

"Obviously. You refused to attend, did you not?"

Cora's mouth fell open but she couldn't find her words. When Teryn had asked her to dine with him last night, she'd imagined them sitting side by side at the feast in the dining hall, not a private meal made especially for her. Her shoulders sank, as did her heart. Though she supposed it made no difference. Even if she'd known about Teryn's efforts on her behalf, she still wouldn't have been able to face him last night. She'd needed that time alone. But now she felt the weight of her rejection, regretted that she never saw what he'd planned for her.

"You shouldn't spurn him, Princess," Mareleau said, oblivious to Cora's inner turmoil. Cora was only half listening as the queen continued. "I was just getting used to having a brother, but I daresay I liked him far less last night than usual. Still, I couldn't let all my hard work go to waste. If you weren't going to enjoy the bounty, I might as well, though I regret it now." She lurched as if about to be sick, but quickly settled.

Cora's mind sharpened, and her gaze snapped back to Mareleau. "Are you saying you dined with him in my stead?"

"Don't act jealous with me," she said with a scoff. "If you'd wanted to sit in my place, you very well could have. And I didn't *dine* with him; I only stayed for cake. One that was clearly underbaked."

Cora tried to ignore the pinching sensation in her heart and gave Mareleau a pointed look. "I highly doubt your nausea is due to an underbaked cake."

Mareleau pursed her lips and reached for a lock of silver hair. She began winding three strands into a braid but halted. With a grimace, she glanced down at her tresses where they tangled in something slick. With a whine, she dropped her hair and clasped her hands at her waist. Returning her attention to Cora, she rolled her eyes. "Fine, I admit it. I might have had wine too. Just one glass! All right, two."

Cora crossed her arms. "That's not what I meant either. I'm referring to the baby. Morning sickness. Though it isn't uncommon to be more sensitive to liquor while pregnant."

"Oh, and how would you know anything about it?"

"Pregnancy and childbirth were common occurrences amongst the people I lived with for the last six years. It wasn't a taboo subject like it is amongst royal society. We were open about it. Most of us trained in general aid, and I attended my share of births. While I've never experienced the condition myself—"

And never will, thanks to Morkai. The thought invaded her mind so suddenly, her breath caught in her throat. Breathing deeply, she forced the unwanted thought away and focused on what she'd been trying to say. "I have knowledge that can help, should you want it."

Mareleau quirked a brow, unimpressed with Cora's credentials. "And what knowledge is that?"

"First, that you really should see a physician when you're feeling ill. It isn't safe to neglect such care. Why did you, anyway?"

The queen shifted awkwardly in the bed, a hint of embarrassment on her face. "I didn't want him to know I'd had wine. If word got back to my mother...ugh. Must I spell it out for you? She wouldn't approve because of this..." She waved a hand at her belly. "*Condition*. Don't you dare say a word to anyone."

"I won't, but I doubt the royal physician would have been able to read your perceived sins through your vomit."

She lifted a shoulder in a shrug. "How should I know what a physician can and can't do? Is it not their job to read the inner workings of one's body?"

Cora would be amused if she weren't so tired. Now that she knew Mareleau wasn't in any immediate danger, she was desperate for sleep. Brushing her hands on her skirts, she took a step back from the bed. "I'll request a cup of ginger tea be brought to you at once, which you should have daily from now on."

"Why is that?"

"Morning sickness can last weeks, and you're certainly far enough along for it to begin."

"Surely I'm not. My wedding night wasn't yet three weeks ago."

"Oh, right," Cora said, tone flat. She recalled what Sera had said about Queen Helena preemptively spreading word that her daughter had conceived on her wedding night. All to cover the fact that her daughter was already with child. "Even if that *were* the case, it still isn't too soon for these symptoms to begin."

Mareleau released a disbelieving snort. "What do you know? I already told you it was underbaked cake and wine..." Her words dissolved, taking with it the color in her face. "Wait, what do you mean it's not too soon to experience...symptoms? That...that even if I'd conceived on my wedding night, I could..."

"It's exactly what it sounds like."

"No," she said with a light chuckle. "That's not possible." She held Cora's gaze with a hopeful grin as if waiting for Cora to agree with her. When Cora remained mute, Mareleau's expression went blank, eyes wide as they locked on Cora's. "No!"

A spike of the queen's emotions slammed into Cora. Terror. Shock. Panic. They made Cora stagger back before she could strengthen her shields. Breathing deep, she closed her eyes and connected with the elements, weaving them tighter around her.

When she opened her eyes, Mareleau's face had crumpled.

"Seven devils, no," the queen said, chin quivering, before a sob tore from her throat. She hung her head and covered her face with her hands, shoulders heaving as she dissolved into a pool of tears.

Cora stared at the other woman, too startled to know whether she should comfort her or leave her in peace. She chose the latter and backed out of the room. The last thing she heard as she softly closed the door was Mareleau's distressed, high-pitched wail that ended in, "I'm godsdamned pregnant."

33

Larylis Alante never would have believed there was anything lonelier than being a bastard. Now that he was king, he knew it to be a far lonelier endeavor. He had guards. A bevy of attendants. His late father's councilmen. But being surrounded by all these people, most of whom were no better than strangers to him, made him feel even more alone than if he were in an empty room. Empty rooms, in fact, held a certain comfort no space filled with strangers could have.

He felt this now as he sat in King Arlous' place at *his* council table in *his* council room with *his* councilmen. As the king's bastard son, he'd never been allowed to attend such meetings before. Now, with his father gone and Teryn having abdicated, he had no choice but to attend them. He sat in his father's mahogany chair, wore his royal coat and crown of gold, yet he struggled to reconcile his change of station. The same doubt shone in the eyes of at least half of the councilmen who sat around the long oak table. They may address him as *Your Majesty* and pay him the outward respects required, but how many of them wished to see Teryn sitting in Larylis' place?

Larylis certainly did.

Or that Teryn was there, at least. Not that he had any intention of admitting as much to his brother. It wasn't pride that drove his silence but sympathy. He knew Teryn would come home at once if Larylis confessed just how much he could use Teryn's lifetime of knowledge as future-king-in-training. But Larylis was willing to suffer—willing to pretend he felt an ounce of confidence when he passed laws, made judgments on petitions, or sent correspondences marked with Menah's royal seal—if it meant Teryn had all the time he needed with Cora.

His own relationship may be temporarily stunted by distance, but that didn't mean Teryn's should be too.

Besides, Larylis had the means to adapt to his current struggles. He didn't have

Teryn's lifetime of royal tutelage, but he had one reliable resource that had never let him down—books. Every night, he read about the kings of history. Great kings to emulate. Terrible kings to learn from their mistakes. During the day in his father's study, he learned from another form of the written word—his father's. He read over Arlous' correspondences, studied his diary, memorized the names of his allies, spies, and other important contacts.

He hadn't learned much to instill confidence in his capabilities, but facts, stories, and histories had always made him feel at least somewhat secure. They helped him pretend. If he could step into a role from fiction or history, he could separate himself from all his worries.

Right now, he was pretending to be Marsov, Fifth King of Rezkos, crowned Year 87 of the Sheep. Like Larylis, Marsov had been born a bastard. He, however, had claimed the throne without being legitimized and kept his crown despite many other contenders. It would have been an inspiring tale, were it not for the sixty years of war King Marsov put the Kingdom of Rezkos through, but that wasn't the part Larylis was emulating. Instead, he was mimicking the confidence he'd read about, the way King Marsov always sat with his chin held high, refusing to acknowledge any slight against his lesser birth.

Larylis wasn't sure if it helped or just made him look like an ass, but either way, his council continued to defer to him in every decision as the meeting continued. He wondered if King Dimetreus was receiving the same respect from his council. What was it like being served by a council made up of men from another kingdom? Larylis had that to be grateful for. Had it not been for Verdian's wariness of Dimetreus, the king may have tried to position his brothers at Dermaine instead.

Larylis' Head of Council, Lord Tolbrook, brought up the next subject for their discussion. "Are you certain you want to grant the Kingdom of Tomas inclusion into our trade with Brushwold?"

Larylis met the man's shrewd eyes and saw disapproval in them. His councilmen may have deferred to Larylis, but that didn't mean they ceased questioning some of his stances. Still, this was something he wouldn't budge on.

Sitting tall, he addressed the table in his best King Marsov voice. Or what he imagined his voice might have sounded like. Confident. Steady. "Prince Lexington came to our aid when my brother was captured by Duke Morkai. He fought at our side at Centerpointe Rock. His kingdom deserves to be rewarded for their prince's valiant efforts."

He didn't add that Teryn had promised the prince as much when they'd made a secret alliance during the Heart's Hunt, though he would if it came down to it. He'd learned that declaring something as *supported by Teryn* had its merits, for it proved that a change of heir would have made no difference.

Silence echoed over the table, and he felt his confidence waver. Then his eyes met those of Lord Hardingham, the councilman who had supported Larylis the most since he'd taken the throne. Hardingham had been his father's most trusted advisor, and unlike most of the others, he respected Arlous' dying wish to see his bastard son legitimized. Hardingham gave a subtle nod of encouragement.

With his confidence bolstered, he met Tolbrook's gaze without falter. "I will not yield on this."

"Very well," Lord Tolbrook said, tone grudging. "For the first time in forty years, we relinquish our exclusive rights to Aromir wool."

~

EVENING HAD FULLY FALLEN BY THE TIME THE MEETING CAME TO ITS MUCH-WELCOME close. His feet felt as heavy as bricks as he climbed the stairs to his sleeping quarters—chambers that once belonged to his father. Four guards followed in his wake, but he dismissed them once he reached his bedroom, along with his valet and other attendants who were ready to prepare him for bath and bed. Despite his fatigue, he wasn't ready for bed. His mind was simply set on being alone for the first time all damn day.

Alone yet far less lonely.

Part of his motivation was tucked in his waistcoat pocket, inaccessible beneath the royal coat he'd worn to the council meeting. As soon as his guards and attendants exited the room and closed the doors behind them, he stripped off his jacket and extracted the piece of parchment that had been nestled against his heart all day. It was a letter from his wife. He'd gotten one almost daily since she'd left for Ridine, and they were the highlights of his days. This one, even before reading a single letter of her elegant, achingly familiar script, was no exception.

With a heavy sigh, he broke the seal and sank onto the bed. It was twice as large as the bed he'd had in his old chambers, which only made it feel emptier without Mareleau. But as he unfolded the letter and took in her words, a smile curled his lips. He could almost hear her voice, could almost pretend she was relaying her day's woes from beside him.

Ridine is a dark cruel place, my love. Is this a prison or a castle? I insist it's the former because they are highly lacking in sweet treats.

Larylis snorted a laugh at that. He'd have to send his reply first thing in the morning along with a jar of the finest cocoa. He knew how much she liked chocolate. With the speed a messenger horse could travel, she'd have her sweet treat in less than three days. His heart ached with envy. What he wouldn't give to travel by messenger horse himself. At least he didn't have to wait much longer to depart for Ridine; in two days, he'd start his journey north for the peace pact signing. But with the size of his retinue and the ridiculously slow agenda his council had planned for him, he wouldn't arrive until at least a week later.

He finished reading Mareleau's letter, then started over at the beginning, once again imagining every word in her sometimes playful, sometimes haughty voice.

My dearest Larylis—

A shuffling sound drew his attention from the letter. Sitting upright, he glanced around the room, seeking its source. The room still felt alien to him with its ample space, luxurious rugs, and elegant tapestries. Sound didn't travel the same way it had in his former bedroom. There could be a servants' passage behind one of the walls, for all he knew.

He heard the sound again, but this time he knew it was coming from his balcony. Frowning, he set down Mareleau's letter and approached the doors. The curtains were drawn shut, so he couldn't see the balcony beyond. He set his fingers on the handle, pausing to consider if he should call one of his guards inside instead...

Another sound, and this time it carried a note of familiarity. It was the telltale flap of...wings.

Larylis pushed the door open and found Berol staring up at him with what was undoubtedly an impatient look. Her wings were splayed, beak open, and before he could step out onto the balcony with her, she darted inside. She launched from the floor to one of his towering bedposts, then to his desk.

Larylis approached her, noting something tucked inside one of her talons. "Did Teryn send you?" From the agitated splay of her wings, he guessed she'd struggled to find him. It made sense considering she was used to the location of his former chambers. But why did Teryn send her? She could travel far faster than a messenger horse, and he was known to utilize her to send messages now and then. Regardless, her flustered state unsettled him.

He extended his hand and took the missive from Berol's talon.

Only it wasn't a missive at all.

Larylis stared at the piece of torn fabric, at the rust-colored splatter that looked an awful lot like blood.

His throat went dry as he was forced into a memory from not long ago.

It reminded him of...

Gods, he didn't want to think it.

But it was impossible not to see that scrap of fabric, the frantic splay of her wings, and *not* recall what had happened the last time she'd brought Larylis something while Teryn was at Ridine.

Why did she bring a scrap of cloth? Was this a piece of Teryn's shirt? Someone else's? Was he in trouble?

He sat at his desk and took out a quill and sheet of paper. He hadn't intended to write any letters until the morrow, but this one couldn't wait. Not with the dread sinking his heart.

It's nothing, it's nothing, he told himself again and again as he penned his inquiry to Teryn, asking if he was all right. If it truly was nothing, then he'd receive confirmation in less than three days' time. Sooner, actually, for he'd send a copy with Berol. There was a chance he'd get a reply as early as tomorrow evening.

It's nothing. Teryn's fine.

He rolled up the first letter and handed it to Berol. "To Teryn," he said aloud. She clutched it in her talons and set off at once. That was a good sign, right? She wouldn't have flown off if she didn't know where he was.

He tried to let that comfort him as he finished the second letter and handed it to one of his guards, insisting a messenger leave with it tonight. Then he returned to his desk and examined the torn strip of cloth Berol had brought him. He tried not to panic at the spatter of blood.

Yet try as he might, his mind kept wandering to the worst-case scenario. Teryn injured. Teryn hurt. Teryn...*no*. That was as dark as he'd let his thoughts get. Whatever was happening, he'd sort it out soon enough.

In the meantime, he could only wonder...what the seven devils was happening at Ridine?

34

Teryn spent another night lying within the intangible bounds of his body, trying to influence muscle movement. After two hours, he managed another flinch of his finger. After three, a flutter of his eyelids. At least he thought he did. Unless it was merely coincidence that Emylia had witnessed Teryn's lashes lift just as he'd been directing all his intent to those minuscule muscles, he'd succeeded.

Yet it still wasn't enough. It was nothing compared to what he needed to do. Trying to force these subtle movements took all the strength of will he had. He couldn't imagine how long it might take to control enough of his body to remove the crystal from around his neck. He might go mad before then.

No, he told himself. *I will not give in to my own futility. I will build the strength required to do this or I will die trying.*

He shifted on the bed, feeling the edges of his ethera buzz from the contact it made with his body and the mattress beneath it. After connecting to his breath, blood, and pulse, he tried to refocus on his current task: parting his lips. No matter how he tried, his mind kept shifting to Cora. To worry. To fear.

He hated that Cora had no clue what was going on. Hated that she perceived Morkai's coldness to her as his own. At the same time, he was grateful for Morkai's outward indifference. If it kept Cora from getting too close to Morkai, Teryn would let her think anything at all. He'd sever ties with her for good if it prevented the sorcerer from using their relationship the way he intended. Furthermore, Morkai's avoidance of Cora gave Teryn the time he needed to reclaim his body. There wasn't much Morkai could do to further his goals until he was married to Cora. Right? Surely he could defeat this challenge by the end of a year.

Just the thought that it could take even a fraction of that time sent a flicker of anxiety through him...

"Breathe, Teryn," Emylia reminded him.

He clenched his jaw, creating a buzz of resistance tingling over the bottom half of his face, but he did as she suggested. He refocused on the air filling his lungs, on the steady thrum of his pulse, until his mind cleared of panic. Then he shifted his attention to his mouth, feeling the energy hum where his body and ethera were perfectly aligned. On an inhale, he experienced the air moving through his nostrils, unsure whether this sensation belonged to his body or ethera. Perhaps some place between where the two were connected. Slowly, he exhaled and felt the air tingle his upper lip. He repeated this meditation several times until he could imagine he was simply resting like normal—whole and alive. Then, on his next exhale, he shifted the course of the air escaping his lungs, sending it out his mouth instead.

His lips parted. The air left his mouth in a soft, easy breath.

Surprise sparked the edges of Teryn's consciousness, but he reined it in, determined to stay focused. He controlled several more mouth breaths, then shifted his attention to the back of his throat. To his tongue. The roof of his mouth. His vocal cords.

Excitement rippled through him as the idea took shape. If he could simply control his voice—form words for just the right person—he wouldn't need to wait until he could move his entire body. He could shout a warning. Get help.

His throat was warm with the heat of his breath, with the harmonious vibration humming between his body and ethera. On his next exhale, he sent a surge of energy, will, and intention, through his throat and vocal cords, lifting his tongue to the roof of his mouth—

Energy tore through him, ripping, separating, and his body bolted upright, leaving his ethera reclined on the bed. Morkai heaved a cough and pushed back the covers, motions agitated.

"Seven devils," Teryn cursed, leaving the bed to stand beside Emylia.

"Don't be discouraged." Her smile was warm, dark eyes glittering. Today she was dressed in billowing ivory pants and a knitted cream tunic. It occurred to him that he never had any awareness of his own appearance, much less what he was wearing. A quick glance down revealed the same articles of clothing he wore the night he was trapped in the crystal. It didn't matter to him, for it wasn't like he had any sense of comfort or discomfort when it came to his ethera's state of dress. He assumed it was merely a construct of his mind, anyway. Or perhaps a mirage shaped by Emylia's magic.

Emylia's smile grew wider. "You did really well this time. You accomplished three muscular manipulations, and I could sense what you were trying to do at the end."

Teryn shook his head. "I failed. It woke him up."

"You didn't fail. You've already gotten stronger."

Teryn narrowed his eyes at the sorcerer who paraded about the room in Teryn's body, donning clothing with haste.

"You should rest your ethera," Emylia said. "It must be exhausted after what you accomplished."

"No, not yet," Teryn said. "Not until I see what he plans to do today."

~

Teryn and Emylia followed Morkai through the castle as he strolled, dined, and greeted courtiers and councilmen. He seemed to lack an agenda until he began making inquiries of servants and staff, asking whether the king was holding court today and if Teryn had received any new correspondences. Teryn saw no sign of Cora, and he wasn't sure whether to feel sorrow or relief.

Finally, Morkai left the great hall to enter a separate building Teryn had never seen before. Its outer walls were crumbling and marked with ivy-shaped shadows that suggested the trailing vines had recently been removed. The building rose into a tall arch, its apex carved with a circle bearing seven interlocking spheres, marking it as a Godskeep. Teryn's eyes trailed back down the building, landing on two guards who stood outside the door. As Morkai approached, the guards made no move to open it.

One guard stepped forward. "His Majesty is at prayer."

"I too came for prayer," Morkai said, far more brazenly than Teryn would have dared. "I am soon to be the king's brother-in-law. He will not mind my attendance, for we pray for the good of the same kingdom."

Teryn cringed at the sound of his voice. It was *his* voice, *his* tone, but the way Morkai spoke...it sounded nothing like him. Yet of course these guards wouldn't know that. They'd been planted at Ridine from Selay. The only person here who could possibly see through Morkai's ruse was the very woman the sorcerer was determined to avoid.

When neither guard showed any sign of allowing Morkai inside, he lowered his voice. "To be honest, Lord Kevan asked me to come here for reasons I'm sure you understand."

The guards exchanged a look that set Teryn's teeth on edge. Despite now serving the king, they clearly maintained allegiance to Kevan. Had Morkai already gleaned the tense power dynamic here at Ridine? Did he know Dimetreus was still under scrutiny by Verdian and his brothers—the men who were supposed to be the king's new allies? If Morkai had been able to project his ethera outside the crystal the way Teryn and Emylia could, then he must have been able to collect at least some intel before having taken over Teryn's body. Not to mention the fact that he'd been off on his own much of yesterday while Teryn had been resting his ethera.

"I'll inform the king of your request," one of the guards said and entered the Godskeep.

Teryn frowned. What did Morkai want with the king? Whatever it was, it filled Teryn with a sinking sensation.

"Are you certain you wouldn't rather rest?" Emylia asked, tone wary. He met her eyes and found trepidation in them. She wrung her hands but stilled them when the movement caught Teryn's gaze.

"Is there something you know that you aren't telling me?" he asked.

She released her arms to her sides, donning a casual posture. Too casual.

Teryn *could* trust her...right?

"I'm telling you what's for the best," she said. "If you overexert yourself, you'll be forced to rest anyway. Remember what happened yesterday?"

Teryn knew she was referring to the way he'd lost consciousness after witnessing Morkai's conversation with Cora. He shrugged. "So be it. I want to know what business Morkai has with Cora's brother. I will watch their interaction for as long as I can."

"Just...just know that there's nothing you can do right now." She spoke slowly. Carefully. "Whatever happens, whatever you overhear, we can only continue with our plan."

Teryn's sense of unease increased, but the guard returned, pulling Teryn's focus back to the Godskeep door.

"The king will see you," the guard said, opening the door for Morkai to pass.

Teryn and Emylia shadowed Morkai through the antechamber, then to the nave. It was much smaller and darker than Dermaine's, with no bright tapestries, no painted ceiling, and no stained-glass windows. Its only adornments were a red carpet that ran from the doorway to the dais, a long wooden table that served as an altar, and seven statues of the seven gods that rested upon it. At the foot of the dais, Dimetreus kneeled. He was dressed in ceremonial robes in Khero's violet, embroidered with threads of gold and the kingdom's black mountain sigil on the back. A simple gold circlet rested upon his brow, while a bejeweled dagger hung at his waist. Teryn's gaze slid to Morkai's hip, relieved to see he was unarmed. Even if the sorcerer had thought to bring a weapon, the guards would have disarmed him upon his entrance to the Godskeep. Only the king and his guards could enter a Godskeep armed.

Morkai strolled past the rows of benches until he reached the king. "Your Majesty," he said with a deep bow.

Dimetreus nodded in reply. "Prince Teryn, how good of you to join me for prayer."

"I appreciate you allowing this intrusion."

"It's no intrusion," the king said, "for I am merely posturing. I've never been a man of prayer. A man of faith, yes, but not as faithful as I should be."

"Is that so, my king?" Morkai strolled up the dais and lit seven sticks of incense on the small brazier burning at the center of the table. Then he placed one stick before each of the deities before returning to the king's side. Teryn watched his every move with keen awareness, a tense wave of energy tightening his ethera. He expected Morkai to do something sinister, but he simply kneeled beside Dimetreus, positioned slightly behind as was deferential to the king.

Dimetreus spoke again. "Lords Kevan and Ulrich insist I make a show of being a penitent king to improve my image. Though I can't see how it would help when there's hardly a soul to witness me in here."

"I wouldn't say you're without witnesses, Majesty." Morkai gave a subtle nod toward the dais. Teryn's gaze followed to where the king's personal guard stood, two men on each side, nearly hidden amongst the shadows of the dark nave.

The king snorted a laugh. Lowering his voice to a whisper, he said, "I suppose you know more than anyone what position I'm in, as you had a strong hand in negotiating for my and Aveline's pardon."

"Yes, though I would have prevented Verdian's stranglehold on your castle if I'd held more sway. Kevan and Ulrich are too ambitious for their own good." Teryn hated hearing Morkai utter words that held true for Teryn. Perhaps the sorcerer was adept at playing this role after all.

"I appreciate you saying that, Prince, but...but I am in a situation of my own making. Though I wasn't of the right mind when I attempted to declare war on Selay and Menah, I can't change that it happened. I am willing to do whatever it takes to demonstrate my peaceful intent to my allies." His tone was dry, rehearsed.

"Majesty, I hope you won't fault me for being blunt, but you need not speak with caution around me. I'm on your side."

Dimetreus gave him a warm smile. "Of course you are. You were quick to forgive me, for you saw how I was being controlled firsthand when the sorcerer brought you here. Still, I bear the burden of having neglected to see Morkai's vile intent long before I named him duke. Even after, I'd had a choice. I could have listened to Aveline..."

His voice trailed off, eyes vacant. Haunted. Then he shook his head and rose to his feet. One of his guards rushed forward to offer him a hand, but he waved him off. The guard hesitated, then returned to his post at the end of the dais.

Morkai stood as well and faced the king with a bow.

"I'm glad my sister has you, Prince Teryn," Dimetreus said. "I can tell your affection for her goes beyond a betrothal contract."

Teryn was torn between feeling elated and enraged at the king's words. Though he said them to Morkai, the sentiment was true. Teryn's affection for Cora went beyond what he'd confessed to Dimetreus during the audience he'd had with him the night Teryn arrived. He was glad the king understood that.

But Morkai didn't deserve to hear those words, to receive them with that smug grin of his, one that made Teryn's face look nearly unrecognizable.

"You honor me, Majesty," Morkai said. "I am most *eager* to wed the princess."

Teryn tensed at how Morkai had emphasized *eager*.

"Next year, Khero will have regained enough stability to allow us to host a grand wedding," Dimetreus said.

"I await that day with the most ardent anticipation. However, I'm surprised your council has allowed for such a lengthy engagement."

Dimetreus gave a lighthearted chuckle. "I thought you were the one who'd suggested a yearlong betrothal, Prince. The marriage alliance had been your idea."

Morkai's face flashed with the slightest hint of alarm before he donned an easy smile. "Yes, I did propose the alliance, but I didn't set the timeline."

False, Teryn wanted to shout. He had set the timeline. He'd proposed a yearlong betrothal out of respect for Cora, out of consideration for the time he knew she'd need to adjust. The time they'd both need to fully enjoy their courtship.

"Ah," the king said, wagging a finger. "Your heart has made you impatient. I remember that feeling well."

"Yes, you are very right about that," Morkai said, but his voice lacked the warmth necessary to suggest the words were true. He furrowed his brow as if deep in thought. "I am concerned with one thing. Aren't you essentially without an heir until Aveline and I marry? Doesn't the peace pact state that your council will only accept your sister as heir after she and I are wed?"

"That's technically true," Dimetreus said. "It seems you are the key, Prince Teryn, for your neutrality secures Verdian's trust as well as that of my council." The king's tone turned grudging as he spoke the last part.

Morkai narrowed his eyes. "You don't seem too happy about that."

Dimetreus forced a smile that crinkled the skin around his eyes, but there was no mirth in it. As he glanced over at his guards, it waned completely. He lowered his voice, eyes still on his guards. "It isn't a matter of being happy or unhappy. Aveline deserves to be heir in her own right. Yet the marriage alliance is a necessity. I'm only grateful it's a happy one."

Morkai's lips lifted at the corners in another smirk that had no right twisting Teryn's face. The expression disappeared as the king returned his gaze to Morkai.

"So, in a way," Morkai said, "I'm just as important of an heir as the princess is. When it comes to the council's point of view, that is. Wouldn't you agree?"

Teryn's pulse kicked up. He didn't like where this conversation was going.

Dimetreus frowned. "In a manner of speaking, I suppose you could say that."

"And you don't think you'll remarry?"

"No, my heart cannot part from my darling Linette. Due to my loss of memories, I feel like it's been far less than six years since her death. I have no intention of choosing a new queen. Aveline will further the Caelan bloodline, not me."

Morkai's face fell with false sympathy. "You must miss her dearly."

Dimetreus inhaled a sharp breath, and when he spoke, his voice held a quaver. "More than I can say."

"I bet you'd do anything to bring her back."

The king nodded.

"You'd sacrifice your own life, if need be, wouldn't you?"

"Without question."

Morkai stepped slightly closer. His voice dipped so low, Teryn had to move closer to hear.

"Teryn," Emylia said, a warning in her tone, but he couldn't be bothered to pay her heed. He *had* to know what Morkai was saying.

"What else would you trade, Majesty?" the sorcerer whispered. "Your kingdom? Your mind? Would you make a blood mage your heir in exchange for a promise that he could bring your wife back from the dead once he gained power over your kingdom? Or...or have you already done that?"

Teryn's heart slammed in his chest, his lungs constricting.

"Breathe, Teryn," Emylia said. "Keep your breaths slow and steady. Don't lose contact now."

Dimetreus took a trembling step back. "What...what are you saying?"

Morkai's voice shifted into a softer tone, one far more sinister than anything that left Teryn's lips before. It was so quiet, Teryn could barely make out the words. "Were you a willing participant after all, my king? Did you...*let* the duke take over your mind?"

"No, I..." Dimetreus' chest heaved, his eyes going unfocused. "No. No, it can't be. I wouldn't have..."

"I'm still here, my king. We can make the deal again. Give me your mind and I'll give you your wife. I'll bring her back—"

"No!" The roar leaped from the king's throat. His lips curled up in a snarl, eyes wild. "Monster! Demon! What are you? *What are you?*" In the blink of an eye, Dimetreus surged toward Morkai, the dagger at his belt suddenly unsheathed in his hand.

The guards darted from the dais, and Morkai threw up his hands and stumbled back. He fell to the ground, eyes wide with feigned terror.

Teryn watched, frozen in place, as Dimetreus tackled Morkai and held the dagger to his throat—to *Teryn's* throat. A line of crimson erupted from his flesh, but Teryn couldn't feel the cut. No, just the frantic beat of his heart. The race of his pulse. The tightness in his chest.

Spittle flew from the king's lips as he shouted, "Demon! Demon!"

"What are you doing, Majesty?" Morkai's voice had returned to normal, brimming with horrified innocence. "Seven gods, Majesty, look at me. Look at me! It's me, Prince Teryn!"

Dimetreus shuttered his eyes and pulled the blade back just as the king's guards reached them. They hauled Dimetreus up at once, eyes darting between their king and Morkai. "What happened?" one of the guards shouted.

Dimetreus continued to blink rapidly, then stared down at the knife in his restrained hand. With a cry of alarm, he dropped the blade. "Seven gods..."

Morkai slowly rose to his feet, shoulders almost as high as his ears, expression wary. "The king attacked me. We were talking and then...and then..."

Teryn's blood burned with rage as the guards showed no sign of seeing through Morkai's farce. Even Dimetreus seemed to take his performance as truth, a wail escaping his lips. With his crown askew and spittle speckling his chin, he looked every part the crazed king. "I'm...I'm so sorry. I don't know what came over me. It... it was a moment of hallucination. I've never had one so strong, so..."

"Keep him restrained," one guard said to the others. "This is a matter we must take to Lord Kevan."

The king went willingly as the guards led him through the nave. Morkai followed just behind. With the guards' backs turned, the sorcerer's lips curled into a satisfied smile.

Cold certainty washed over Teryn. This must have been his plan all along. He wasn't sure of the repercussions, but they couldn't be good. No, they could be terrible indeed.

Emylia tried to remind him to breathe, but his breaths were already too sharp, too shallow, his vision going hazy at the edges. The next thing he knew, the Godskeep faded from view and sent his mind drifting into nothingness.

35

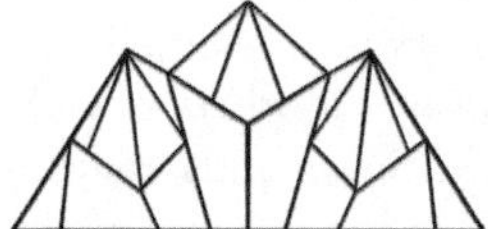

Cora had gotten used to the smell of burning paper, but she hadn't grown accustomed to the grim contents of Morkai's books. Nor the disappointment at finding nothing useful amongst all the references to blood magic, curses, and manipulations of mind and will. It was almost a relief to reach a portion of the bookcase filled with nothing but benign volumes—herbal encyclopedias, folk medicine, a regional guide to plants and animals. These made her feel far guiltier for burning them. Yet she followed her own rule: anything in this room that could be burned would be.

Her heart ached as she watched botanical illustrations blacken at the edges as fire lapped over a guide to flowers, but she reminded herself of the risk involved should she try to salvage anything. Should there be an unremarkable-seeming notation scrawled in the book, hidden amongst legitimate illustrations and documentations but bearing hidden treachery and dark magic, she'd be responsible should anyone find it in the future. She couldn't risk that. Everything in the tower room belonged to Morkai, bore his essence, carried his energy. It all had to go.

As the book dissolved into ash, she tossed more herbs onto the fire and returned to the bookcase. It was three-quarters empty now. She felt accomplished so long as her gaze didn't stray to the multitude of other bookcases awaiting their turn at being cleared.

One at a time, she reminded herself. *No matter how long it takes, I will do this one at a time.*

In preparation to sense the energies of the next book on the shelf, she reconnected to the elements. Shifting her feet, she grounded her energy, rooting her stance upon the stone floor. Then she breathed in the afternoon air carrying scents of herbs and smoke. To connect to the element of water, she glanced at the basin on the floor, filled with clear liquid. Fire was easy. Not only did it fill the hearth, but the open windows drew in sunlight, filling the room with a golden glow, warming her skin, her hands. She cast her gaze out the window and looked upon the vibrant greens of the forest beyond the castle wall, the emerald mountains dappled in chartreuse.

A note of longing cut through her meditation. It was such a gorgeous summer day. What she wouldn't give to be outside, enjoying the scents of warm soil, a breeze that didn't carry dark energies and the ghosts of murdered books. She imagined the freedom of the forest, could almost feel the soft earth beneath her feet, could almost hear the birdsong increase.

Mother Goddess, if I could just be anywhere right now...

Her thoughts drifted to the Forest People's camp, and her longing deepened. She missed Salinda and Maiya so much more than she'd realized. The past several weeks had given her plenty to occupy her mind and time, and the same was true now, but such distractions had only prolonged her grief over losing her adoptive family. Would she ever see them again? She'd promised herself she would find them as soon as her kingdom was secure...

Her heart sank to her feet at the realization that the Forest People were no longer at the camp she'd left. It was well after Litha now, which meant the commune had already relocated, as they did with every season. To find them again would take tracking skills she didn't have.

Would she ever find them again?

We will, came Valorre's voice, and her heart trilled at the comfort it brought. *If you can feel them, we can find them.*

She wasn't sure if she *could* feel them, but she knew it was folly to worry about that now. Not when she had so much work ahead of her. Her kingdom wouldn't be secure until after the peace pact was signed. As for the tower room...that could take weeks longer. Months.

Darker thoughts lingered at the edges of her consciousness, questions she still had no answers to. Would she ever get the chance to take leave of the castle? Could she ever return to being the witch she longed to be? Was her role as princess shifting into a commitment as future queen?

You've been sad, Valorre said.

I have, she admitted.

But furious too.

Yes. She moved to the window, giving herself a better view of the castle's sprawling property and the towering walls that surrounded it. She felt how near Valorre was, could sense him on the other side of the wall, just out of sight.

You could sneak out again.

Her lips curled into a small smile. The offer was tempting, but she knew she couldn't risk it during the day. Night was the safest option, but lately she'd been so tired after her work in the tower, she hadn't even considered it.

Soon, she said and was about to apologize for neglecting him. Then she recalled his speech about treating him like a pet, and she decided to hold her mental tongue. Not that he wasn't likely reading her thoughts right now. She could sense the strength of their mind link, could feel his care and concern. And perhaps a note of confusion. He'd checked in on her enough the last couple of days to understand what she was upset about, but as a unicorn, he couldn't grasp the complexities of royal politics.

Valorre's energy turned distracted. *Oh, I know her!*

Cora frowned, leaning closer to the windowsill. She caught no sight of the unicorn or whoever had caught his attention. *What? Know who?*

The answer dove straight toward her, making her bite back a gasp. With her attention on the ground, she hadn't seen the falcon until it landed on the sill before her.

Cora hopped a step back, barking a yelp of surprise before she could stop herself.

"Highness," her guard called from the other side of the threshold.

"I'm fine," she assured him. She wasn't sure if he could see the window from his post, but at least he knew better than to enter the room. "It's just a bird."

Lowering her voice, she shuffled closer to the falcon. "What are you doing, Berol?"

The falcon's wings were splayed, head bowed. Her posture, along with the long string of chirps she uttered made her seem anxious. Upset. Then Cora noted the scroll of parchment in one talon. The falcon hopped closer, disturbing the line of salt on the sill.

Cora frowned, eying the paper. "Is that...for me?" A spark of hope flitted in her chest. Perhaps Teryn had sent her a sweet letter and, instead of disturbing her with his presence, he'd sent Berol. She extended her hand toward the falcon. Berol uncurled her talon and dropped the scroll onto her inked palm.

Cora quickly unrolled the paper and found it was a short letter. Her eyes dipped to the bottom to find the sender's name. It was from Teryn's brother, King Larylis.

> Teryn,
>
> I hope this note finds you well. Berol delivered me something that looked like a scrap of your shirt, and it worried me. Please send her back with a reply letting me know if you're all right.
>
> —Larylis

Cora cocked her head to the side. "Why didn't you deliver this to Teryn?"

Berol, of course, gave her no answer. Even when she tried to connect with the falcon's mind, it gave her nothing like the connection she could form with Valorre. Instead, all she felt was unease, agitation.

"Highness," came her guard's voice again, edged with a note of urgency. Berol took off from the sill, sending a gust of salt and rosemary in her wake.

Cora tucked the note in her apron pocket and turned toward the door. "Yes?"

A pause. Then, "Something has happened, Princess. Master Arther is here to escort you to speak with the king's council at once."

∼

Cora's heart was in her throat by the time she made it to the bottom of the tower stairwell where Master Arther awaited. After Berol's strange behavior and the letter she'd delivered, Cora couldn't help but think the worst. Something must have happened to Teryn. She hadn't seen him since yesterday morning. Had he returned home without saying goodbye? Had he been hurt or injured on his way? Even so, how had Berol had enough time to make it to Dermaine Palace and back? She supposed falcons were fast, but still...

"What happened?" she asked Master Arther, her voice both sharp and trembling.

The old steward wrung his gloved hands. "It's best you hear it from the council—"

"No, I will not take a single step farther until you tell me what happened."

Arther glanced around, but the hall was empty. Thankfully, the wing beneath the North Tower Library was rarely frequented by anyone but the guards. He released a sigh, and Cora braced herself for the worst.

Please don't say Teryn is...that he's...

"It's about His Majesty the King."

Her mind went blank. "What? Not Prince Teryn?"

Master Arther grimaced. "Well, it's about him too, Highness."

Her pulse hammered, setting her mind back to racing. "Please just tell me at once."

"You really should speak with the king's councilmen—"

"They are not your monarchs," she said, voice rising to a shout. "Tell me or I'll find someone else who will. And another steward while I'm at it."

She was too anxious to feel guilty for her sharp words. While she'd never made such an imperious threat, she was going out of her mind. Her mental shields were already beginning to fray, inviting in Arther's apprehension, and the curiosity of the stairwell guard behind them.

"Very well," he mumbled, folding his hands behind his back. "Highness, His Majesty attacked Prince Teryn. He drew a dagger on the prince inside the Godskeep during one of his..." The steward cleared his throat. "Moments."

Cora pulled her head back, unable to believe his words. "What? How could that...how would he..."

"Lord Kevan will tell you the details. The council has assembled and awaits your presence."

"Where is my brother?"

"He's in his room under guard—"

That was all she needed to hear before she darted from the steward and hurried through the halls toward the keep. The rush of her blood pounded through her ears. She paid no heed to Master Arther's pleading calls behind her, nor the sound of his feet as he shadowed her up the keep steps. She didn't slow, didn't stop, until she reached her brother's closed doors. Two guards stood outside them, men she recognized as members of Dimetreus' personal guard.

"Open the doors," she said, tone filled with cold authority.

"The king is at rest, Highness," one of the guards said, tone dry.

"Open the doors now."

They held their positions. Master Arther caught up with her, cheeks flushed pink, gray hair in disarray. "Highness, please—"

The doors began to open, drawing Cora's attention back to them. But she didn't have the guards to thank; they were opening from the other side. She nearly crumpled with relief at seeing her brother's face. His expression was wan, skin pale, reminding her too much of how he'd looked when he'd been under Morkai's control.

"Aveline," he said, eyes turning down at the corners. "You must have heard."

Cora glanced from her brother to the guards. The latter made no move to usher the king back inside his room or close the doors, which suggested he wasn't being held prisoner. Then again, he didn't invite her inside or cross the threshold into the hall.

She lowered her voice. "Can we speak in private?"

He gave her a solemn smile. "It's better if we speak here."

Her shoulders tensed. "What happened, Dimi?"

"What have you been told?"

She pursed her lips, eyes roving to the guards again, then to the steward.

Dimetreus held up a placating hand. "It's all right, Aveline. My guards saw what happened, and I'm sure Master Arther knows about the incident too. You may speak with candor."

Clenching her jaw, she inched slightly closer to her brother. "Is it true you attacked Prince Teryn in the Godskeep?"

He gave her a rueful nod.

"How, Dimi? Why?"

"It's as everyone feared. My mind…I'm unwell, Aveline."

She shook her head. "I don't understand. What happened?"

His expression turned haunted, eyes distant. "I saw *him*, Aveline. The sorcerer. I heard him, but he wasn't truly there. It seemed so real. Sounded so real…" He shook his head. "I pulled my dagger on the prince and nearly slit his throat. Thank the seven gods my guards were fast enough to stop me. That the prince managed to get through to me, snapping me out of my hallucination."

Cora's stomach turned. She couldn't imagine her brother doing such a thing—

No, that wasn't true. While she couldn't imagine this version of Dimetreus acting so irrationally, she could imagine such a reaction from the man she met two months ago when he was being controlled by the sorcerer. The night Morkai had brought her to meet her brother in the dining hall, the king had been sweet and jovial one moment, then violent and suspicious the next. He'd called her sister, begged to see her dance, then ousted her as an impostor.

Had she been wrong to trust he could overcome the sorcerer's abuse?

"You know what this means, right?" he asked, rousing her from her thoughts.

She met his eyes with a questioning glance.

"My council has officially deemed me unfit to rule. According to the terms of the alliance we agreed to, I must abdicate at once and pass my rule to you and your husband. The peace pact will require it."

The blood drained from her face, making her knees go weak. "No. No, they can't do this. They're wrong—"

"They're not." His voice was so firm, Cora was forced to swallow her words. Stepping closer, he gathered Cora's hands in his. "I can't do this, Aveline. My mind is fraying. I'm in no state to rule this kingdom any longer. Not only that, but..." He shifted his jaw, then dropped his head, bringing his lips close to her ear. "My hallucination...it made me remember something. Something I'm not proud of."

She couldn't bring herself to utter a word, to do so much as breathe loudly.

"I let Morkai take my mind after Linette died. I gave him permission to use me, to warp my thoughts, in exchange for a promise that he could bring her back from the dead."

She pulled back slightly to meet his eyes. A chill ran down her spine. "That's not possible. He was already controlling you when she died. He made you believe that I..."

Her body went rigid. In learning to trust her brother again, she'd forgiven him for condemning her for his wife's death. She'd told herself Morkai had made him believe she could have done such a thing.

What if she was wrong? What if that enraged reaction at having found her in the room with the dead queen...had been genuine?

She forced the question from her mind. No, she remembered the strange sheen over his eyes when he'd ordered her to the dungeon. He hadn't been in his right mind back then, even before his wife's demise.

"It's just the guilt," she said, her voice uneven. "You're letting guilt get to you, brother."

Still holding her hands, he gave them a squeeze. "I'm grateful for your faith in me, but even if you're right, it doesn't matter. I've proven myself unstable."

Cora opened her mouth to argue but her brother spoke first.

"I'm tired, Aveline. So tired."

Her brother's sorrow slammed into her, destroying the last of her shields. She felt his exhaustion. His fear of his own mind. It was so potent, it made her breath catch.

"I thought I was a poor king because of a sorcerer, but the truth is, I am a shell of a man without Linette. Sometimes I wish I'd died on that battlefield. At least then I'd be with her now."

A spike of betrayal pierced her heart. How could he say such a thing? Was their kingdom not important to him? And what about *her*? Wasn't Cora enough to make him cherish being alive? "Don't talk like that."

"You will be the king I cannot be. Marry the prince and take my crown. You will serve this kingdom better than I ever could."

Panic laced her throat as she realized what he was saying; she was expected to marry Teryn *now*. To become queen *now*.

She shook her head. "I was never meant to rule, Dimi. I am here to help *you*. To reclaim your birthright and establish your legacy. I never intended..."

She couldn't finish. How could she admit that she'd seen her role as a temporary one?

Dimetreus' brows knitted into a furrow. "Are you not happy here, Aveline?" When she gave no answer—for what could she even say in such a frazzled state?— he spoke again, his voice barely above a whisper. "I know you could have abandoned me at Centerpointe Rock, but you didn't. That was selfless of you. Should you reject the burden I'm placing upon your head, I won't blame you. Never could I begrudge you a life of freedom if that is what you want."

Cora's chest expanded with a light feeling. He was giving her permission...to say no. To reject her birthright and leave Khero to...

To what? To ruin? To be conquered by King Verdian? With his brothers' positions, it would be easy to accomplish. Was that something Cora could live with? To end the Caelan line just to shrug off the burden of the throne and run free in the woods?

It was selfish to even consider such a thing. She was stronger than fear. Stronger than the weight of a crown.

Dimetreus spoke again. "Whatever you choose, I will support you. But I must make one request—consider love, Aveline. Don't shy away from it if that is what makes you hesitate. You and I have lost much in our lives. Our parents. Linette. But I promise you, love is worth it, even if you lose it in the end."

Cora's mind went to Teryn, to the curse that still stood between them—between the future of her kingdom—should she fail to break it. Everything was happening too fast, too soon, and her heart was struggling to keep up with it.

Regardless of the racing in her heart, the nausea shredding her stomach, she knew what had to be done.

It was time to tell Teryn the truth.

36

When Teryn returned to consciousness, it was to the sound of Cora's voice. It was distant, soft, barely brushing against the edges of his awareness. Yet the sound of it called him from nothingness, and when his surroundings took shape, they weren't the bright light of the crystal or even Emylia's temple bedroom illusion. Instead, he found himself before a door. The door inside his bedroom at Ridine Castle.

Cora's voice echoed from the other side, along with a rumbling knock.

"Teryn, are you there? It's Cora."

Teryn's consciousness sharpened. He connected to his breath, his pulse, the hammering of his heart. The events he last recalled—Morkai tricking Dimetreus into attacking him—surfaced in his mind, but he anchored his focus with the sound of Cora's voice. He was pulled to the melody of her tone, the sensation so strong, he felt it could draw his ethera straight through the door. But as he tried to take a step through the physical matter, he felt a much stronger pull against his back. Glancing behind him, he saw his body resting in his bed. This was as far as his tether to the crystal would let him go.

"Teryn, please. We need to talk."

He whirled back toward the door. Everything inside him begged to answer, but he knew his voice wouldn't travel to reach her. Not from whatever plane of existence his ethera was on. So he pressed his palm to the door, felt the resistance hum. She knocked again, and the vibration rang through him like ripples on smooth water.

"Are you there?"

"I'm here," he said, his voice hollow against the resonance of hers. It didn't matter that she couldn't hear him. He was there. He was there and he'd fix this.

She knocked once more, and he welcomed the reverberation like a caress.

Gods, this was as close as he could get to touching her. To being beside her.

He stayed like that for several long moments, even after he realized she'd left.

"You projected yourself outside the crystal on your own this time," Emylia said, suddenly beside him.

"It was Cora's voice that brought me here."

She released a heavy sigh. "You shouldn't have overexerted your ethera, Highness. It's dangerous to wait until your ethera forces you to rest."

He turned away from the door to face her with narrowed eyes. "Why?"

"Your ethera requires rest and recovery, just like a human body does."

"I know that, but why is it so dangerous for me to be forced to rest after overexertion? What haven't you been telling me?"

She nibbled her bottom lip before answering. "Being forced to rest abruptly severs your connection to your vitale, the same way fear or panic does."

Teryn folded his arms. "And that's a bad thing because..."

"Because it causes your body's functions to begin to shut down."

Teryn blinked at her. So that was why she was always reminding him to focus on his breath, to strengthen his vitale. It had been less about maintaining his strongest connection and more about preserving his body's functions. Did that mean...

"Could that...kill me?"

She nodded.

Anger sparked inside him. "Then why the seven devils didn't you tell me?"

"I didn't want to worry you," she said. "I knew it would only make you panic more." Her voice was brimming with apology, and yet...

He remembered how nervous she'd seemed when they'd followed Morkai into the Godskeep. How she'd tried to get him to rest before Morkai spoke with the king. Had she only been anxious over the prospect of him overhearing something that would cause his fear to spike, tearing him away from his vitale and forcing his ethera to rest? Had her concern been due to precaution...or premeditation?

Teryn's fingers curled into fists. He hated that he was starting to get used to the way the gesture buzzed, the way he was beginning to forget what being made of flesh and blood felt like. "Did you know? When we entered the Godskeep, did you know what Morkai had been planning to do?"

She shrank down, shoulders tense. "I had an inkling, but I didn't want you to panic. You can't focus on what he's doing. You can only focus on regaining control of your cereba."

"So I can remove the crystal from my body and destroy it. Which we still don't have a solution to."

"I have an idea."

Teryn tightened his jaw. "Why the seven devils haven't you told me?"

"Because it's just that—an idea. Actually, it's less of an idea. It's simply...knowledge. I know how Morkai made the crystal unbreakable. A year ago, he wove its fate to a unicorn horn, focusing on the horn's indestructibility. The crystal now has the same properties that a unicorn horn has. It cannot break, burn, or crack."

Teryn was torn between feeling daunted by such facts or elated that he finally had something to work with. There had to be a solution now. He pondered what he knew about unicorn horns, most of which he'd learned from the now-dead Prince Helios. "You said the crystal can't be cracked or broken, but there must be a way. If it has the same properties a unicorn horn has, then it can be cut. Horns can be carved."

She shook her head. "Only severed horns can be carved. The horn Morkai used was still attached to the unicorn when he cast the fate weaving."

"Then what is your idea? How do we use this knowledge to destroy the crystal?"

"To break a curse, spell, or enchantment, one must go through the motions that were placed upon it but in reverse. Morkai used a bastardized version of an ancient Elvyn magic called *weaving*. Elvyn weavers used sky, but Morkai was never able to utilize this magic. Instead, he used blood. He'd draw out blueprints for complex patterns to execute his spells and cast them using blood. Since the crystal and horn were both inanimate objects, he had to use his own blood for that weaving, along with most of the magic he'd currently stored in his Roizan."

Teryn's mind spun with the information. Weaving. Ancient Elvyn magic. The Roizan. Teryn had witnessed the sorcerer utilize blood in such dark ways. He'd even attempted to kill Teryn with that very magic at Centerpointe Rock. The Roizan, however, he only partially understood. During Cora's interrogation, she'd told the inquisitors that the creature he'd known as the Beast had a name. *Roizan.* He'd learned the intel during his own interview. One of many he'd endured to prove Cora's identity. "What exactly is a Roizan?"

"A Roizan is a creature born from death, a sorcery of the forbidden Arts of the sanguina and ethera—blood and spirit. Neither alive nor dead, it becomes a vessel for magic that can be drawn from at will. It amplified Morkai's own magic, allowing him to do things he never could have done on his own. Large feats of magic either empty or destroy the Roizan, but the beasts are essential for doing magic beyond one's means."

"You said to nullify the enchantment that makes the crystal unbreakable, we would need to reverse the spell he'd placed on it. How the seven devils can we do that?"

She gave him an exasperated look. "I don't have all the answers yet, but I'm working on finding a way. One thing we'll need is Morkai's blood—the blood from his original body. He'll have some stored somewhere, and we can count on him to retrieve it himself. There are certain spells he won't be able to cast with the blood from your body alone. He'll need his own. The second thing we'll need..."

She paused, expression falling.

"...is the blueprint for the pattern he used to bind the qualities of the crystal to the unicorn horn."

"Do you have a way of finding this blueprint?"

"Not exactly," she said with a grimace. "He never showed it to me. He has the power to block me from projecting my ethera outside the crystal. It takes constant focus, so he couldn't do it all the time, but he must have been doing so when he drew the blueprint. I watched him weave the spell, but I couldn't see the pattern he used clearly. It was complex. Miniscule from where I stood."

Teryn rubbed his brow. "How are we to reverse a spell with a pattern we don't know? How do we reverse a spell at all? Is that something you have the power to do?"

"No, that is not something I can do. You'll have to be the one to reverse the spell."

Teryn's eyes went wide. "I don't know the first thing about casting magic."

"You don't need to. Blood magic follows rules. Patterns. That's why Morkai relied on it so much. Once we have everything we need, and you've strengthened your connection to your cereba as much as you can, you'll need to take over your body and draw the pattern in reverse using Morkai's blood. On paper, on a stone, it won't matter. You simply must reverse the lines he drew. As for the pattern itself... do you remember how I told you I was a seer when I was alive? I still maintain some of my abilities. I can watch my own memories. I've been trying to study my memory of Morkai casting the spell, watching it from different angles to see if I can untangle his movements. I've also sought the greater Art of seeing, seeking answers from the spiritual plane beyond. I haven't glimpsed the pattern yet, but..." Her eyes unfocused. "I have seen that we must stay the course. Keep doing what we're doing."

"That's all? Stay the course?"

"It's an imperfect Art, especially for someone no longer alive. I don't *see* as strongly as I used to. Even if I do manage to catch glimpses with the sight, when it comes to Morkai, everything is shrouded in these tangled...threads. I don't know what else to call them. All I know is that they're working against him. So when they pull me forward and tell me to stay the course, I listen."

Teryn leaned against the doorframe, felt the energy thrum against his back. Gods, no wonder she hadn't told him this. It didn't help at all. Perhaps Emylia was used to blind trust when it came to magic, but Teryn still felt lost in this world of fate and blood sorcery. There was so much he didn't know. So much he didn't understand. His mind wandered back to the Godskeep, saw Dimetreus draw blood from Teryn's own throat.

His gaze locked on Emylia's. "You said you had an inkling about Morkai's plan in the Godskeep. What were his reasons behind it?"

Emylia held up her hands in a soothing gesture. "If I tell you, you must remember that there's nothing you can do—"

"Just tell me," he ground out.

She folded her hands at her waist. "Morkai's plan was to destabilize the king and prove to the council that he's incapable of ruling. The council has made their decision. You know what happens next."

Teryn's pulse quickened. "Cora will be forced to ascend to the throne."

Emylia nodded. "But first she must marry you. Morkai has spoken to the council in your place and has agreed. I don't know about Cora, but as of now, your marriage contract is set to be signed first thing tomorrow morning."

It took all of Teryn's focus not to lose touch with his breathing, with the rapid thud of his heart. "He's going to marry her...as me. Tomorrow."

"Yes."

His voice came out cold. Sharp. "What happened to *you have time, I promise*?"

"You still do have time. Maybe not as much as you thought, but enough to do what must be done."

"I have until tomorrow morning to regain control over my body before he..." He couldn't say it out loud. No, that would make it too real. Gods, he thought he had a year, not a matter of days. In what world did Emylia consider that enough time?

"He won't attempt to consummate the marriage, if that's what you're worried about. He'll continue to try and maintain his distance for the time being."

"Why is he forcing her to ascend to the throne so soon, to finalize the marriage alliance so suddenly?"

"He wanted to act before Cora could catch on," Emylia explained. "This way, even if she does grow suspicious, he secures his role as king consort while he puts all the other pieces of his plan into place."

"What is his plan? I know he intends to rule Menah, Khero, and Selay as one, and that he wants to use my marriage to Cora to make that happen, but...how?"

"I don't know, but I have a feeling he'll execute it at the signing of the peace pact."

Teryn's heart raced. Seven devils, the signing was to take place at the end of the month—eleven days from now. Larylis and King Verdian might already be on their way. When they arrived, Morkai would have every monarch—every person who stood between him and total rule—under one roof.

He cursed under his breath.

"There's something else he'll be working toward," Emylia said, her voice barely above a whisper.

"What?"

"Once your marriage to Cora is secure, he'll pour all of his focus into making his takeover of your body complete."

Teryn straightened, a chill running through him. "What does he need to make the takeover complete?"

"He needs to forge a fate weaving. To do that, he'll need your blood, his original body's blood, and a Roizan. Your blood will be easy, for he merely needs to cut your flesh. As for his blood, well, I already told you about that; he has vials of it hidden somewhere. He always kept a stash of his own blood, as a precaution against using all the blood he'd stored in his crystal. Since Cora's attempts to energetically clear the crystal emptied it of blood, his hidden store is his only option."

Teryn's mind spun as he worked to keep his breathing steady. "What about the Roizan? How long does it take for him to create one?"

"A Roizan can be forged in a single night, but it normally takes years to strengthen it with magic, to fill it with enough power for a fate weaving."

"That's some relief. I'll be able to reclaim control by then. If not to remove the crystal and destroy it, then to figure out how to work my voice. Tell Cora the truth. She'll see through him—"

Emylia hung her head with so much defeat, he swallowed his words. Her voice came out small. "It may take years for a Roizan to be strong enough to work great magic, but Morkai doesn't have years. Not even a single year. Perhaps not even a month."

Teryn's breaths grew shallow, but he couldn't bring himself to speak.

She lifted her head and met his eyes with a mournful expression. "Being forced to rest your ethera isn't the only thing that deteriorates your body. The mere act of being split like this will slowly wreak havoc upon your inner functions, day by day. There are only two things that can happen. Either Morkai succeeds and makes the takeover complete, or you reclaim your body and force Morkai out. Otherwise... you'll die."

His eyes went wide as dread sank every inch of his incorporeal form. He sagged against the doorframe once more. "Why didn't you tell me this from the start?"

"If I'd told you early on," she said, "you'd have succumbed to your fear. Fear and panic are what detach you from your vitale. Detaching from your vitale harms your bodily functions and prevents you from connecting to your cereba. You must keep that connection strong. Regardless of what you think I should have told you, it doesn't change what must be done. You have one choice. One course of action."

"Reclaim my body. Break the crystal." The words came out flat. Even more hollow than they normally sounded on the spiritual plane.

"You focus on the former. I'll work on solving the latter."

He gave her a pointed look. "You mean the memory you can't clearly see? And the vision that keeps telling you to stay the course?"

"It's the best we have." She gestured toward his sleeping body, dozing upon the bed. "Now is your chance to practice your side of the plan, Highness."

Fueled with a stronger sense of determination—if not a deeper sense of dread too—he made his way toward the bed. He reached the side and glanced down at his sleeping form. A sick feeling coursed through him as he noticed the hollows of his cheeks, the bags under his eyes. And...was that a wisp of silver at his temple? Teryn leaned forward to get a better look at the strand. It was mostly hidden beneath his dark waves, but it was there. It reminded him too much of King Dimetreus' hair, a silver-streaked brown that belied the king's true age of nine-and-twenty.

Whether he had himself to blame for overexerting his ethera or if these physical signs of bodily strain would have begun to show regardless, he knew not. Either way, Emylia was right; his body was deteriorating.

He shifted his gaze to her. "How do you know so much? About Morkai? His plans? About what's happening to my body?"

She gave him a sad smile. "I've been here for a long time. I've seen much of what Morkai does, and you aren't the first soul I've encountered inside this crystal. You ask me why I kept the secrets I kept? Because I've seen this all before. Again and again. I've witnessed the dangers of knowing you're running out of time. The madness that ensues. The futility that follows."

He shuddered. "Has Morkai ever succeeded at fully possessing another body?" If so, then the body he knew as Morkai might not even be his original one.

"No," she said.

Teryn was relieved at that. Yet, as he settled into his body's frame, he realized something; just because Morkai hadn't ever successfully transferred his soul to another body didn't mean the previous souls had survived. More concerning than that was the question of why the sorcerer had ever considered possessing another body when he'd had his own. Before his death, he wouldn't have had any need for a new body. Had he trapped other souls simply as a precaution?

Or was there more Emylia had left unsaid?

37

Cora left Teryn's door, her heart heavy with disappointment. Where was he? This was the second time she'd come to find him that day. A servant had insisted she'd seen him enter his room not long ago, but he hadn't answered when she'd called, just like the first time. He couldn't have been with the physician, for she'd gathered enough intel to learn that his wound had already been tended and hadn't been too deep in the first place. Even so, he may have been given something for the pain after his cut was treated. He could be sleeping. When she'd extended her senses, she'd felt *something* that suggested he was inside, but it was nowhere near as strong of an emotional impression as she normally received. But if he was sleeping, was he going to do so until morning? They didn't have time for that.

Cora was all too aware of the ticking clock.

She'd spent the previous hour talking with the council. Or being talked *at*, to be more accurate. No matter how she'd tried to argue in her brother's defense, the truth was that she and Dimetreus had already agreed to give Dimetreus' council the final say on the king's abdication. These terms had been necessary to forge the alliance with Verdian and would be written into the upcoming peace pact. Cora knew Verdian would refuse to sign it if she tried to go back on her word, and there was no talking the council out of their decision. Especially since the king had wholeheartedly agreed.

All that was left was for Cora to marry Teryn.

But she couldn't do that until they had a chance to talk. She couldn't enter their marriage with the secret of her curse.

She wandered through the halls of the keep, unsure where she intended to go. Returning to work in the tower would be too dangerous in her current state of mind; she knew she couldn't focus on clearing with her head so full of this newest burden. But as she passed the wing that led to her room, she found herself unwilling to turn. No, she couldn't sit idly in her bedroom either. She glanced out one of the windows in the hall and caught a glimpse of the early evening sun. There was still plenty of light left in the day. Perhaps she could sneak out after all...

She turned down a corridor that led to a portion of the keep that had yet to be refurbished, her mind set on entering the servants' passage—

She pulled up short as a figure, hunched at the base of the far wall, came into view. At first, she saw only a curtain of silver hair draped over dark blue silk, but as she took a step back, the woman's face lifted from her hands, revealing Queen Mareleau's tear-filled eyes. Startled, Mareleau bolted upright and pushed to her feet, swiping her cheeks with the backs of her hands.

Sorrow surged against Cora's shields, and she was too fatigued to block it. It swept over her, sinking her heart. Or perhaps it simply rested alongside a heart already sunk. Cora could tell Mareleau was embarrassed at being caught crying, so she dipped into a curtsy and turned to leave.

"I'm pregnant," Mareleau said to Cora's back.

Cora turned back around. "Oh?"

"My moon cycle is overdue. I'd lost track during my travels, but that and the emotions I've been having, not to mention the—" With a grimace, she put a palm to her stomach. "The nausea. I...I think you were right. I'm pregnant."

Cora frowned. Her voice sounded so empty. So resigned. "Did you not know, Majesty? I thought it was merely a well-kept secret, not something you were unaware of."

She crossed her arms and lifted her chin. "Who told you in the first place?"

"Lady Sera," Cora admitted, feeling no guilt about outing her. "She mentioned instructions your mother had given your maids, insisting that you'd conceived on your wedding night, and that they were to forbid you from drinking wine."

"Mother." Mareleau bit out the word like a curse.

The queen's emotions surged against Cora's shields again, a medley of annoyance, guilt, and grief. At least this time Cora's nerves were more at ease, allowing her to connect with the elements and thicken her mental wards. Apparently focusing on someone else's problems were enough to distract her from her own. As much as Cora lacked any sort of friendly feeling toward Mareleau, maybe the distraction was what she needed. And from how the woman had stopped Cora from leaving with her statement that she was with child, perhaps Mareleau needed someone to talk to.

She supposed it wouldn't hurt to be that someone. For now. She took a few steps closer. "If this was something your mother already knew about, then why do you seem so surprised?"

Mareleau narrowed her pale blue eyes, lips pursed tight. Then, with a sigh, she spoke. "I lied."

Cora arched a brow. "About what?"

Mareleau averted her gaze and wandered to the nearest window. Lacing her fingers through her hair, she wove a messy braid as she stared with eyes that didn't seem to see anything beyond the window. "I lied about being with child so that my father would allow me to wed Larylis."

Silence stretched between them in the wake of her confession. Cora could hardly believe what she'd heard.

"No one else knows but Larylis—and Teryn too, now—so don't tell anyone." Her voice was nearly monotone, devoid of the barbed ire Cora expected from her.

Cora moved closer and lowered her voice. "Why are you telling me this?"

"I don't know. Maybe because my lie no longer matters. It's true now."

"And you aren't happy about that?"

Mareleau shook her head, lips curved down in a frown. "I'm not ready. I wanted more time with my husband. More time to...just be a woman in love. My parents kept me and Larylis apart for three years. Now that I have him, I just wanted it to be us for a while." She shifted her gaze to Cora. "You think I'm selfish, don't you?"

Cora could tell her that this new development neither added nor subtracted from her opinion of her. She expected the queen to be selfish. Cold. Haughty. That was all Mareleau had shown of herself so far.

Instead of saying that, she admitted something that hit far closer to home. "At least your position as queen is secure. You've managed to fulfill your singular duty."

"No," Mareleau said, whirling toward Cora with a clenched jaw. "I haven't fulfilled my duty, I've only taken the first step. The first of many exhausting steps, and one I wasn't even ready to take. Do you know what happens next? Next everyone will speculate whether it's a boy. When I birth my child, I'll be praised if it is. If not, I'll be consoled. Then I'll be expected to try again. Again. Again."

For the first time, Cora found herself able to relate to the queen. She too felt the burdens of such a role. But she wasn't ready to express their similarities. "It doesn't need to be a boy. You and I are both women and heirs."

Mareleau snorted a humorless laugh. "Are we though? Are we truly heirs? You know how they judge us. How they see us as less than a male heir."

Cora wasn't sure who Mareleau's use of *they* referred to. The people in general? Her parents? Her uncles? She supposed it didn't matter, for all were likely true.

Mareleau's tone turned sharper. "My father was so afraid of what my uncles would do to me as his heir. According to him, the only way I can keep my throne is if Larylis and I merge our kingdoms upon Father's death. Had I tried to rule as queen with only a consort of a lesser title at my side, my uncles would have fought to take my birthright. He went so far as to suggest they'd kill me for it."

Cora suppressed a shudder. The men she spoke of—Kevan and Ulrich—now had a stranglehold on Khero's council, on her very kingdom. She knew they were overly ambitious men, but were they truly as devious as Mareleau had said?

The queen seemed to be thinking along the same lines. "I wonder if he positioned them as your councilmen for this exact reason. To have them so preoccupied in your kingdom that I might have a fighting chance at keeping mine."

Cora bristled. Mother Goddess, was she right? She hadn't gotten the impression that Verdian thought too highly of his daughter, but what if he'd had more than one motive in appointing his brothers to Dimetreus' council?

Mareleau turned back toward the window. "Whatever the case, it isn't fair. Why must this be all we're worth as royal women? As nothing more than vehicles for our kingdoms' future kings. Why are we not kings ourselves?"

Cora nearly sagged with the weight of her words. With the truth of them. Yet Mareleau had something Cora didn't. "Being with child may not be something you're ready for, and it may be unfair that bearing heirs is expected of you, but what else can you do? At least with an heir, regardless of gender, you hold a weapon against your uncles' claims to your birthright."

Her lips lifted in a sneer. "Children shouldn't be weapons. Or pawns. Or… anything but what they are."

Cora's mouth snapped shut. Again, she found herself agreeing with her. Understanding her. But what was there to do about it? Mareleau was in a position where she could rebel against the norms. She was already queen. Her husband was king. An heir was on the way. How would she feel in Cora's position, if the choice and capability were taken away from her like it had been done to Cora?

Anger heated Cora's blood, and she let it rise. It felt better than feeling lost. Uncertain. Trapped. "You know what? You are selfish. No, children shouldn't be weapons or pawns, but here you are complaining when you could be grateful you can have children at all. Do you know what it's like for royal women with the opposite problem?"

Mareleau scoffed. "No, do you?"

Cora pursed her lips against her own rage, against the truth that scalded her tongue.

The queen suddenly straightened. She must have seen something in Cora's face, for her own paled. "Aveline…are you…"

"I was cursed." The words came out sharp yet trembling. "The sorcerer who once invaded my home—the man who forced my brother to wage war on Menah and Selay—cursed me to die childless."

The same silence that thickened the air after Mareleau's confession now settled in the aftermath of Cora's.

Mareleau's eyes went wide. "So you can't…"

Cora shook her head. "Not unless I can figure out how to break the curse. Which makes me an inadequate heir. And I don't know where you've been all day or what you've heard, but my brother is being forced to abdicate. I'm expected to marry Teryn first thing in the morning and take on the mantle of queen. A queen who may put an end to the bloodline she's expected to further. I haven't even told Teryn yet."

"Why not?"

"I'm afraid he'll value having children more than marrying me." Saying it out loud made her wince. Hearing her words somehow made her fear seem even more unfounded.

"Why would he care? It's not like his kingdom would suffer from lack of heir. Only yours."

Cora gave her a pointed look. "As king consort, Khero *will* be his kingdom."

"Well, fine, I suppose that's true. But all hope isn't lost. You have relatives, don't you?"

Cora shook her head. One of the first things she'd learned during her interrogations was that her nearest relatives—most of whom had served her brother at Ridine before Cora was forced to flee the castle—had died, leaving none alive to corroborate Cora's story. It hadn't been hard to glean why none remained living. "Morkai ensured all contenders to the throne were eliminated."

Mareleau furrowed her brow. "Oh. Well...that doesn't matter either. With your marriage to Teryn, you'll have new family ties. Teryn and Larylis have younger brothers."

Cora had never considered such an option, but appointing the role of heir to the nearest male relative wasn't unheard of.

Mareleau spoke again. "Where do you think my father got his crown? He wasn't born a Harvallis. He wasn't even a prince, which is why my uncles are only lords, despite having a king for a brother. My father was simply the eldest living male blood relative of the former King of Selay. I know a distant relative doesn't have the strongest claim, not nearly as strong as a child. And maybe you can't further the Caelan bloodline, but do you honestly care about bloodline politics?"

Cora's answer came easily. "No, I only care about the safety of my kingdom."

"Then it's settled. You'll tell Teryn about the curse, you'll marry, you'll appoint an heir, and once your reign is strong, you'll crush every last hope my uncles have at gaining more power than they deserve. Meanwhile, I'll do the same from my kingdom."

Cracks began to form in the heavy shroud of Cora's fears. For the first time in days, she felt hope. Hope that remained even if she couldn't break her curse. To think she had Mareleau to thank for such a shift in perspective.

She couldn't stop her mouth from lifting at the corners. "I didn't know you were such an optimist, Your Majesty."

Mareleau lifted her chin. "Apparently all it took to improve my mood was to hear about the dire hand you've been dealt."

Cora rolled her eyes. "I'm glad my plight has brought you such amusement."

The queen stepped closer, her haughty composure back in place. "You know, you aren't horrible. I don't hate you."

"And you are tolerable yourself," Cora said dryly. Then she softened her tone. "I'm glad you don't think children should be pawns. You'll make...an okay mother."

Mareleau smiled back at her. It was probably the first smile she'd ever received from the queen. But her face crumpled so suddenly, Cora hardly knew what was happening. Not until Mareleau did the absolute last thing Cora expected her to do...

She threw her arms around Cora...

And hugged her.

Mareleau was so much taller than Cora that she found her face nearly buried in the other woman's bosom. Still, she was too shocked to move.

The queen heaved with sobs. "I'm sorry," she said, voice strangled by hiccups. "I'm just really...emotional lately and I can't control it. I don't even like hugs."

"Neither do I," Cora muttered. And yet neither broke away. Instead, they stood a little closer, held each other a little tighter. Maybe they both needed an embrace with all they were going through, and they were simply tolerating the comfort of the last person they wanted it from. Or maybe it was more that they'd found an anchor in the other. A mirror. For in this world of cruel games and royal burdens,

Cora and Mareleau were perhaps the two people who understood each other the most.

38

This time, Teryn didn't need all night to make progress. The first hour he lay in the space of his body, he managed to flinch every one of his fingers on both hands. The second hour, he moved his left leg. That had woken Morkai up enough that he'd rolled over and shifted Teryn's body on its side, but Teryn wasn't daunted. Instead, he adjusted his ethera to fit the proper bounds, aligning his hands, feet, torso, shoulders, and face, filling his form the way his soul was meant to.

Now it was time to work on the task he'd come to consider his highest priority: forming speech.

He breathed deeply, feeling his lungs expand, the air moving through his nostrils. His heart beat a steady rhythm while his pulse sang with his blood. He lost touch with the passing of time, focusing instead on the perfect harmony between his ethera and vitale. The singular connection that ensured he was— undoubtedly—still alive. That this body was still his.

Once he was fully settled into this awareness, he poured all his focus into repeating the feat he'd only barely accomplished last time. Shifting the course of his breath, he exhaled out of his mouth. His lips parted to release the warm air, and he breathed again. As the air left his lungs, he felt it tingle against the sides of his throat, the roof of his mouth. A hum of energy rose around him, surging through his blood, merging his body and ethera. The energy was as tangible as the vibrations from a string quartet, a beautiful melody that elucidated Teryn's control. His capabilities. Now all he needed to do was shape that energy into movement and sound.

Teryn.

His name wove through this melody and stitched itself into his consciousness. He didn't let it break his concentration, even as he searched his mind to identify the voice. Was Emylia talking to him? No, she'd returned to the bounds of the crystal and had left him to practice alone. Besides, this voice filled him with warmth. With purpose.

It was Cora.

At the door again.

"Teryn, I know it's the middle of the night but...but that also means you're in there. I know you are."

I am, he thought, but it wasn't enough to think it. He had to speak it.

A new sense of urgency—of need—filled him. Cora was right there, on the other side of his bedroom door. All he had to do was tell her.

"I'm not leaving until you open this door. I'll get Master Arther to unlock it if you won't do so yourself."

Teryn directed his attention to the inside of his mouth, the placement of his tongue. Slowly, his tongue lifted, the back of it connecting with flesh at the roof of his mouth, and his lips formed an *O* shape.

"I don't even know how badly you were hurt." Her voice came out with a quaver, a sound that nearly cleaved Teryn's heart in two. But instead of breaking, he used it as fuel, gathering his pain, his desperation, and sending it out in a surge of energy through his vocal cords.

"Please. I *need* you right now."

"Cora!" The word left Teryn's mouth in a shout. A bit uneven, perhaps, but it was clear.

He'd done it.

But in that same moment, Teryn's body bolted out of bed, and Teryn was no longer in control of it. No matter how he tried not to feel disappointed after such a success—even one so short-lived—it was impossible not to. Especially when Morkai's eyes slid to the door.

"Teryn, I heard you," came Cora's voice. It was oddly more muted now that he was out of his meditation. Somehow, she had sounded so much closer before. Like she'd been speaking directly to his soul. "Please let me in."

Morkai glanced around the room, eyes wild, then stormed over to the door. He gripped the handle...but halted. Doubling back, he retrieved a discarded black jacket from the foot of the bed and hastily shoved his arms through it. He secured the jacket's buttons as well as the laces of his ruffled shirt collar, hiding not only the thin cut at the base of his throat but any sign of the crystal he wore. Only then did Morkai return to the door and fling it open.

Teryn finally moved from the bed. A sense of loss fell over him. In the wake of having regained temporary control of his body, being nothing more than his ethera felt wrong. Broken. How had he forgotten everything he'd been missing as a body?

Those worries fled his mind as soon as he saw Cora's face. She blinked up at Morkai from the doorway, dressed in only a white chemise draped in a floor-length velvet robe of violet and gold. Her expression alternated between relief and anger.

The latter gained dominance over her features. "Where have you been? I looked for you all day. Have you any clue how many times I've knocked on your door? You didn't attend dinner. You forbade servants from entering—"

"I was resting," Morkai said, voice hoarse from sleep but still so much like Teryn's own.

"From your injuries?" Cora's eyes widened as they searched his face. Teryn knew what she saw—the dark circles, his gaunt cheeks. Her expression turned to one of panic. "Teryn, are you all right?"

"I'm fine."

She shook her head. "No, you look...unwell." Stepping in close, she lifted a hand to his cheek—

Morkai caught her wrist so abruptly, Cora froze. Teryn, however, found himself suddenly at Cora's side. Whether he'd run, floated, or simply transported his ethera from one space to another, he knew not. All he knew was the rage that coursed through him at the sight of Morkai's fingers clenched around her wrist like that. He hated that he could do nothing. That he could only watch, only feel his heart race as fear raked claws through him.

Morkai's expression hardened with startled anger, but it lasted only a split second. In the next moment, the look was gone. Had Cora noticed it at all? Her eyes were locked on Morkai's fingers.

With a too-convincing smile, Morkai loosened his grip and brought the back of her hand to his lips. After a brief kiss, he dropped her wrist and took a subtle step back. "I told you I'm fine. Please don't worry about me. We have much bigger things to face in the morning."

Cora narrowed her eyes, her hand still lifted halfway between them. Then she took a deep breath and brushed past him into the room. The breeze she carried vibrated against the edges of Teryn's ethera. She planted herself in the middle of the room, facing away from him. Crossing her arms, she said, "That's what I'm here for. We need to talk."

Morkai's jaw tensed as he glared at her back. Then, with an aggrieved sigh, he closed the door with more force than necessary.

Cora jumped at the sound and whirled toward him. As soon as her eyes landed on his face, Morkai's smile returned.

Teryn's incorporeal form rippled with tension.

"Breathe, Teryn." Emylia appeared at his side. It was the first time he'd seen her since she'd left him to practice. "He won't hurt her. He needs her alive, remember? You need to stay calm."

Teryn couldn't bring himself to reply. Instead, he focused on keeping his breaths steady, his awareness of his vitale strong. Now that he understood the repercussions of overtaxing his vitale, it was more important than ever to take her reminders to heart.

Morkai closed some of the distance between himself and Cora but left ample space, hands clasped behind his back. "I've already agreed to everything the council has asked of me. You don't need to worry. We'll marry in the morning. The peace pact is safe, as is your kingdom."

Cora's brows lowered. "That's not what I mean. There's something else I need to tell you."

"Whatever it is, it can wait," he said, his tone so gentle it made a dismissive mockery of Cora's clearly flustered state.

Her cheeks flushed with restrained anger. "No, it can't. This is important."

"What could be more important than the safety of your kingdom? Is this about *us?* Don't you remember the promise I made? I won't go back on my word. I'll woo you as I said I would. Court you as you deserve. Our marriage contract need not matter when it comes to our hearts. We'll take things slow—"

"I can't have children." The words burst from Cora's lips in an angry shout.

The only movement Morkai made was a mild narrowing of his eyes.

Teryn, on the other hand, felt as if he were being ripped to shreds. Less from the words she'd said and more from the pain behind them.

"That's all right," Morkai said, voice soft. "Truly."

"It's not all right." Tears welled in Cora's eyes, and her voice carried a tremor. "Morkai placed a curse on me. He bound my fate to Queen Linette's using our blood, ensuring I'd die childless like she did."

Morkai's face fell with false sympathy. He took a step forward, and Cora's shoulders sagged. She lifted her hands from her sides as if she expected him to embrace her.

But he didn't. He simply...stopped. His hands remained clasped behind his back.

Teryn's eyes settled on Cora, giving her the attention his body couldn't. Was this what she'd been struggling with the night he'd found her crying in the tower? This...this curse? Grief and rage tore through him. His breaths grew sharp and shallow, threatening him with a wave of panic, but he refused to lose his connection to his vitale.

Morkai tilted his head slightly to the side. "That's what you found so pressing to say? Were you worried I'd reject you?"

"It involves you. It affects the future of my kingdom."

He stepped closer again, slower this time. Still, he made no move to touch her.

She *had* to know this wasn't him. That Teryn would never act so coldly. Would never withhold affection when she so clearly wanted it. *Needed* it.

"There's nothing to worry about, Aveline. I'm here for you. We'll work through this later. Naming an heir isn't something we need to concern ourselves with tonight. Let us get some sleep. Tomorrow is an important day for us." Morkai extended his hand toward the door.

Cora remained rooted in place. Her eyes locked on his face. "Why did you call me Aveline?"

Morkai's expression went blank, but he quickly donned an easy smile. "You're going to be queen. It's time I get used to calling you by your true name."

Fingers curled into fists, Cora strode up to him. Morkai's breath hitched as he took a step back, but Cora closed that space too. Despite their height difference, Cora kept her eyes on his. "What's really going on? This isn't you."

Teryn's heart raced. *No, Cora. It isn't me. Please see that. Please see the truth.*

A tic formed at the corners of Morkai's jaw, but he said nothing.

"You're acting strange," Cora said. "What are you hiding? What is happening to you?"

"Nothing," Morkai said, finally stepping in to fill the space between them. Then, after an agonizing beat of hesitation, he lifted his hands and settled them on Cora's shoulders. It would appear like a gesture of comfort if it wasn't for how stiff Morkai was, as if he were waiting, dreading, poised for the inevitable...

Teryn waited too, waited for Cora to know, to realize, to *feel* what was missing...

She shook her head, lips curving into a frown. "I can't read you."

Morkai's fingers curled ever so slightly on her shoulders. "Why are you trying to read me?"

"Because something isn't right. I can feel that much, but I...I can't feel *you*. Not even when we're close. Not even when you touch me. It's like...it's like you're not really here."

Teryn wanted to believe this was a good thing. Cora could tell something was wrong. But her confession meant Morkai knew that touching her gave her no additional insight. Revealed none of the secrets he was hiding.

Dread wound deep inside Teryn.

Morkai's smile widened with a note of triumph. His posture relaxed as he smoothed out his hands and began running them down her shoulders. "I'm sorry things aren't going the way you hoped. I know we were supposed to have a full year together—"

"That's not it."

"Then what is it? What's wrong?"

"This still doesn't...feel right. Something between us has changed, and I don't understand what it is."

"What can I do to prove everything is going to be all right?"

She stared at him, eyes drifting over his face as if desperate to read the truth written over it. Then her gaze stilled, deepened, locked on Morkai's eyes. Her expression hardened. Lifting her chin, she said, "Kiss me."

Teryn's heart rioted in his chest. *No.*

She stepped in closer, and this time Morkai didn't try to step away. "Kiss me like you did under the tree. Kiss me like you want to be my husband."

Teryn's eyes darted between Cora and Morkai, blood boiling as he saw the smirk twisting Morkai's face, the tilt of his head as he began to lower it toward her uptilted chin. Teryn felt a strange pull, as strong as Cora's voice had been both times he'd heard it on the other side of the bedroom door. This time it was her body, the warmth of her presence calling to his soul, drawing him forward on an invisible tether that seemed to grow straight from the center of his chest. Without another thought, he gave in to the pull and settled into the space of his body.

"Teryn, no!" Emylia's warning barely made it past his awareness, for in the next moment, he felt his flesh against the sleeves of Cora's velvet robe, breathed in the familiar scent of her hair, her skin, felt her with his body, his mind, and his ethera. There was no part of him that wasn't aware of her. So when her lips crushed into his, it was *he* who kissed back. *He* who folded into the embrace of the woman he loved.

39

As soon as their lips met, Cora felt a rush of emotion. She nearly sobbed with relief as it flooded in. Opening her senses and dropping her shields, she welcomed more of the energy that was *his*. His affection. His attraction. His emotion. He'd been acting so strange since the night in the tower, his energy muted and nearly impossible to read. But now it wrapped around her, infusing their kiss with a silent promise. She pressed into him, desperate to erase every inch of space that he'd so stubbornly tried to maintain with her these last couple of days. The way he held her now, one hand cradling the back of her head, the other clutching her body tight against him, stood in contrast to the cold, formal man he'd become. She wound her arms around his neck, wishing he'd lift her off her feet already—

He stumbled back a step, breaking their kiss. She blinked up at him and found his eyes were closed, expression pained. Unlacing her hands from behind his neck, she palmed his cheek. Lightly, she ran her thumb just under the nearly healed cut on his cheekbone. "Teryn, what's wrong?"

"I don't have much time," he said, voice strained. "He's fighting me."

Her thumb stilled. "Who's fighting you?"

His body began to shake. A sheen of sweat coated his forehead. "Morkai," he said through chattering teeth.

Terror ripped through her, muting her sense of his emotions. Or were they growing muted of their own accord? "Teryn, what's happening? I don't understand."

His shoulders heaved with a shudder so violent, Cora was forced to release him. "No," he ground out, eyes still closed. "Touch me again. Keep your hands somewhere on me. I can hold on a little longer if I can feel you. Hear you. Just...say my name."

"Teryn," Cora said, the word laced with panic. She reached for his hand, gripping it as tightly as she dared.

His tremors subsided enough for him to open his eyes. "Morkai has taken over my body using the crystal."

"What do you mean, he's taken over your body? And what crystal?"

He plunged his free hand beneath the collar of his jacket and lifted a leather cord from around his neck. As he withdrew it fully, Cora saw a large amber crystal tied to the end. Memories tugged at the edges of her mind, so potent they nearly overwhelmed her.

The crystal.

The gem that once topped Morkai's cane.

The stone she took from the battlefield.

The object she'd tried—and failed—to clear. To break. To destroy.

Until she was trapped...in a realm of blinding white light...

Before she could remember anything more, he thrust the stone into her hand, closing her fingers around it.

"Take this, but don't look at it. Just...just go now. Keep the crystal in mind and write this all down before it makes you forget. It's been enchanted to be as indestructible as a unicorn horn. You must find a way to break it, but don't let it come within sixteen inches of my body—" His voice cut off in an agonized shout. "Gods, he's fighting me. I can't hold him off much longer."

Cora's heart slammed against her ribs as she tried to take in everything he was saying. It was almost too much to comprehend. And what about Teryn? How the hell had Morkai taken over his body? It didn't make sense. Nothing made sense. And yet she felt the horrible truth of it. Felt the dreadful possibilities hidden in the palm of her hand where the crystal pulsed with that strange energy.

"You have to go," Teryn said, his voice barely above a whisper. He closed his eyes again and stumbled forward.

Her eyes went wide as they fell on a lock of silver hair beside his temple. No, both sides were now shot with a thick streak of white. "Teryn, your hair, it's..."

He lifted his face, teeth bared in a grimace.

Cora's stomach bottomed out as a crimson stream trickled from his nose. "Take this," he said, squeezing his hand around hers and reminding her of the crystal once more. "Run. Write everything down. Find a way to break the stone as soon as you can."

"I can't leave you like this."

His knees buckled, and he slid to the floor. "It's all right. You can. You must. Just go, and know that I—"

He winced again and tugged his hands from around hers, severing their physical connection. "Run."

That was the last thing she heard before his body went motionless, slumped to the side on the floor.

Everything inside her wanted to go to him, to help him, to ensure he was still alive.

But his words rang through her head, echoed by the pulsing warning that blared from her gut. She had to do what he'd said. She had to run.

Biting back an anguished cry, she ran for the door and tugged it open—

The door slammed shut just as fast. She froze, eyes locked on the hand pressed against the door, fingers splayed out, arm trembling either from weakness or rage. A lump rose in her throat, and the back of her neck prickled with fear. She felt the heat of the body caging her in from behind more than she felt any emotional presence. She couldn't turn around. Refused to. There was no way she could bring herself to look into the eyes of the man she loved and find Morkai's hatred—or even his false affection—looking back at her.

"Do you want him to die?" The voice was too close, brushing against the shell of her ear. Worse, it was Teryn's voice. His tone. Yet there was something wrong with it. Something she hadn't heard when the sorcerer had been acting under pretense. He must know now that there was no use pretending anymore.

When she made no reply, Morkai spoke again. "Teryn may think he's found a brilliant plan in getting you to take the crystal away from his body. Distance will certainly tear my soul from Teryn's body and make it impossible for me to control it. But what the prince doesn't understand is that the same goes for him. If I can't reenter Teryn's body due to physical distance, neither can he. Without a soul, the body will die. Teryn will have nothing to come back to even if you manage to break the crystal."

Cora's lungs constricted as she took in this new information. What was she supposed to do? Fight him off? Take the crystal and run, killing Teryn in the process? No answers came, only growing anxiety. She curled her hand so tightly around the crystal, it sent pain radiating up her arm.

Cora! Valorre's voice cut through her fear. *Danger. You're in danger.*

Yes, she sent back, unable to form anything more complex than that.

"Besides," Morkai said, voice deepening as he pressed in closer behind her, "the crystal is unbreakable. You haven't managed to sever a single one of the enchantments I've placed on the crystal, despite your best efforts. You will forget about the crystal as soon as your mind slips down a new train of thought. And when you next lay your eyes on it, it will take your soul instead."

Run away, Valorre said. *Please come here. Now.*

An image shot through her mind, of the castle wall, blanketed in shadows and a sliver of moonlight. Valorre was showing her where he was, just outside the hidden crevice on the other side of the wall.

So badly she wanted to simply *be* there. Without having to fight Morkai off. Without having to rely on running faster than him. Was there anything she could do to get through the wall before Morkai could catch her?

Her palms tingled in answer, not from the crystal she held, but from power surging from her chest, down her arms, and into her hands. It radiated down her legs, her feet. It was soft yet strong, yielding yet powerful.

Turn inward, her magic told her. It was the same feeling she'd gotten when she'd hidden herself and Teryn under the tree not long ago. Then again when she was locked in the dungeon, her magic smothered by her own resentment. And finally, she'd felt it on the battlefield when she'd been trapped under the horse.

Calm moved through her, stilling her thoughts. She focused on the strength of the stone floor beneath her feet, the air that flooded her nostrils, the warmth of the blood rushing through her veins.

"What will it be, Aveline? If you don't play nice, I will make you. I've gone easy on you long enough. Do you recall when I offered you half my heart? I no longer have half to give, and I didn't come this far just to be stopped by you again."

She barely heard him. Barely let herself focus on anything but the elements moving through her, wrapping around her. On the Art that radiated through every inch of her body. Its presence was louder than Morkai's. Stronger.

But what was it asking her to do?

Hide, it had said the first time.

Forgive, it had urged the second.

Stop fighting, it had told her the third. Her mind settled there, on the battlefield at Centerpointe Rock. She recalled how her Art had somehow transported her through space, past physical matter and across a short distance in the blink of an eye. She needed that now. Needed to get to Valorre. To safety.

But how could she repeat that feat? She'd tried to replicate it a few times since that singular incident, but each attempt had been futile. She knew it had to be some form of astral travel, the rare gift witches only talked about but never performed. She knew no one who could do more than astral project—the invisible form of the Art that allowed one to project their souls during meditative states— and it wasn't something she'd ever trained in. So how had she traveled the once?

Feel, her magic told her.

She remembered then.

Emotion had driven her at Centerpointe Rock. She'd moved because she'd had to. Because Teryn's life had been at stake. And then there'd been that time in the council room, where anger had made her feel certain she could take a single step and find herself on the other side of the table, confronting Lord Kevan in all her fiery rage. She'd stopped herself then, had written it off as simply a whim.

But she knew now it hadn't been. It had been her Art.

Morkai gripped her shoulders and whirled her around to face him. "The longer you keep that crystal from me, the more it hurts Teryn's body. The more it ages him. Kills him."

She shuddered but refused to look him in the eye, refused to lose focus. Valorre called out to her again and she latched onto his presence, to his view of the castle wall, to the smell of the earth, to the sound of his hooves beating an anxious rhythm on the forest floor.

"Give me the crystal or I'll take it from you." His hand covered hers. From how feebly he struggled to pry her fingers from around the crystal, she could tell his strength was waning.

If she wanted, she could wrest it from him. She could take the crystal far away, just like Teryn had asked.

And kill him in the process.

Or...

Calm settled over her heart, and she knew there was only one thing she was willing to do.

With a slow exhale, she closed her eyes, fully immersing herself into her connection with Valorre. She could almost feel the earth give way beneath her feet, as if she were standing beside him, could almost sense the mild summer breeze dancing through her hair.

Yes.

She felt it.

Felt everything about the location as if she were already there.

Tugging her hands from Morkai's, she opened her palm, dropped the crystal to the ground, and took a wide step back. Soft earth cradled her heels, rooting her upon moss and soil.

When she opened her eyes, she found herself outside the castle wall, a startled Valorre blinking back at her.

<h1 style="text-align:center">40</h1>

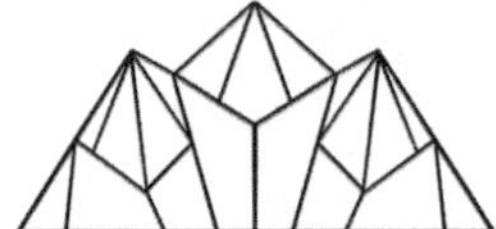

For hours they rode, stopping only when they were far enough away from the castle that Cora felt safe. She didn't think she'd been followed, but she wanted to place distance between herself and the castle nonetheless. The night was still dark when she finally slid down from Valorre's back. She groaned with relief, her legs aching from riding bareback after having spent so much of her recent time indoors. Valorre nudged her shoulder with his muzzle in a comforting gesture, and the sympathy she felt from him nearly brought a sob from her throat. But she refused to cry. She didn't have time to break down, no matter how deep her fatigue.

The sound of running water snagged her attention. A small stream trickled over a narrow rock bed, a soothing melody in contrast to Cora's frantic heartbeat. She crouched before it and gathered a handful of water in her palms. The cool liquid chilled her fingertips and tingled her skin, which served to sharpen her mind. After taking a few sips, she splashed some on her face. It was so cold it was almost painful, but at least it made her feel more awake. More capable of sorting through what had happened. What she'd learned.

Morkai was somehow alive.

In Teryn's body.

She didn't understand how Morkai had taken over Teryn's body, nor did she remember what she'd left behind that had made it possible. She knew there was... something. Some item that escaped her memory the more she tried to think about it. Whatever the case, she understood enough about the situation to guess Morkai had likely regained his strength after Cora left. He could be looking for her. Tracking her.

Which meant she needed a plan. Now.

A familiar presence entered her awareness, and thankfully it wasn't a threatening one. Glancing up, she found a falcon-shaped silhouette circling overhead.

She followed us from the castle, Valorre said, coming up beside her. He lowered his muzzle to drink from the stream while Berol flew down and landed on a nearby rock. Her wings were splayed with agitation, much like they'd been when she'd barged into the tower room with Larylis' letter—

The letter!

After everything that had happened since yesterday, she'd forgotten Larylis' missive. It remained where she'd left it last, in her apron pocket. She remembered the words, though, his inquiry over Teryn's well-being after Berol had brought him a scrap of his shirt.

Her eyes darted to Berol. "You knew it wasn't him, didn't you?"

She let out a sharp, keening cry.

Cora regretted that she couldn't send a letter back. Not that she could fully explain what had happened. What could she even say? *Your brother has been possessed by a sorcerer, but I cannot tell you how or why because some strange magic has made me forget. I promise I'm not crazy. Don't come to Ridine, or your own brother will probably kill you—*

Mother Goddess.

The signing of the peace pact.

Larylis *was* going to Ridine. In fact, he might already be on his way. Verdian too. In a matter of days, Morkai was going to have every monarch who stood in his way in one location. They were falling right into his trap.

She had to warn Larylis.

Cora rose to her feet and tore a scrap of fabric off the bottom of her chemise. Then she scoured the moonlit ground nearby, procuring a thin stick. Finally, she hastily dug beneath the underbrush, turning fresh soil. Gathering a handful of water from the stream, she made a thick paste. Overall, her writing materials were crude at best, but she had no other option. And while blood would serve as better ink than mud, she didn't dare use something of such value. Should Morkai get hold of this, he could use her blood against her.

With trembling hands, she dipped the tip of the stick in the dark paste and brought it to the fabric. She froze, still stuck with the same dilemma regarding what she could say. There was no way she could convey the dangers lurking at Ridine, especially with such limited accommodations. No matter what she said, she couldn't caution him from going to Ridine. His wife was there. She didn't know Larylis well, but if he was anything like Teryn, he'd make haste to reach Mareleau, regardless of the risk to himself.

Instead, she'd have to give him a warning that would allow him to make his own assessment.

Danger at Ridine. Teryn isn't Teryn. Trust no one.
—Cora

It probably wouldn't be enough, but it might at least put Larylis on guard. If anyone could see through Morkai's ruse, it would be Teryn's brother.

After letting the fabric dry for as long as she could stand being idle, she rolled it up and handed it to Berol. Only then did she ponder whether the falcon would heed her directions. Teryn had told her about the creature's intelligence in listening to his directions, but would she understand Cora?

It didn't matter. She had to try.

"To Larylis," she said, handing the fabric to the falcon. Berol gathered it in her talons and flew off at once. Cora watched her until she was swallowed by shadows, hoping beyond hope her letter would serve its purpose.

Warn Larylis.

Maybe save Teryn.

Her chest tightened at the thought, and her mind blared with the weight of her panicked realization.

I left Teryn behind.

Mother Goddess, I left him.

Guilt flooded her, even though she knew she'd had a reason. Yet whatever that reason had been was tangled up in the very thing she kept forgetting. What was that *thing*? Hadn't Teryn asked her to do something with it when he'd spoken to her as himself? And hadn't Morkai threatened Teryn's fate over that same nameless, shapeless, forgotten object?

She bit back a cry as she recalled the blood trailing from Teryn's nose, the streaks of white hair at his temples. It reminded her too much of what had happened to Dimetreus, how he'd aged under Morkai's control. Mother Goddess! She'd left her brother too. And Mareleau. None of them knew...

Cora cursed under her breath, truth dawning.

Her brother *did* know. He'd just suffered too much in his past to trust his own mind. He'd described his interaction with the man he'd thought was Teryn as a hallucination. He'd turned over his crown, his kingdom, all because of *him*. The sorcerer who'd already taken so much from Dimetreus. From Cora.

How much more would he take? How much time did she have?

No answers came, only a hollow dread.

She knew one thing for certain. Whatever Morkai ultimately wanted, it involved dark magic. Which meant there was only one place she could go for help.

"I have to find the Forest People," she said.

Valorre lifted his head from the stream. *Oh, I do like them. They revere me, as they should. As all people should.*

A small smile curled her lips, but it sank into a frown. "How can I face them like this? The last time I sought them out, I brought dark tidings and drew them into a war they wanted nothing to do with. Here I am, once again coming for help."

They are family, Valorre said. *They will understand.*

Family. The word echoed in Cora's mind, warming her chest.

He was right. While she knew there were many who resented her for having hidden her royal identity, there were some who loved her. Salinda. Maiya. Even High Elder Nalia had supported her. No matter how guilty she felt for having chosen her royal family over the Forest People, they'd understand, wouldn't they? They couldn't have expected her to come back with them after the battle at Centerpointe Rock. They'd made it clear Cora could never be a permanent resident amongst the commune again. Her royal identity went against one of their most essential rules—never get involved with royal matters.

But this matter with Morkai was one of magic. The fact that he'd defied death was no small concern. If he was alive in any form, the Arts—both fae magic and witch magic alike—were once again in danger.

Cold certainty stilled her worries. She had to go to them. Now her concern was how. The Forest People would have moved camps just before Litha. That was weeks ago. They could be anywhere now...

No, not anywhere. While the commune rarely ever made camp in the same area twice, they moved according to the fairest weather. In the summer, they chose areas with cooler temperatures, ample shade, and nearby sources of water that weren't at risk of drying out. They'd be near the mountains then. Close to a large river. But that still left too wide a net to cast.

She could try to track them from their previous camp, but that would take too long. She couldn't leave Teryn like that. Couldn't leave her kingdom at Morkai's mercy. She needed to find them *now*.

A ripple of energy ran through her forearms, warming her palms.

"I can astral travel," she whispered. The confession sent a shudder through her. She could no longer pretend the first time had been a fluke. Could no longer make up excuses for having misinterpreted what had happened at Centerpointe Rock.

The thing you did when you startled me out of nowhere, Valorre said.

"Yes, but..."

How could she use that now, when she hadn't a clue where her destination was? Could she travel...to a person? Could she bring Valorre?

When she'd freed herself from under the horse on the battlefield, she'd traveled with everything that had been on her person, everything she'd carried. But not the dead horse. So proximity hadn't been a factor. Was it simply a matter of intent? The horse's body had been something she'd needed to be freed from, a location she'd wanted to leave.

Could she travel with Valorre by touch? Or perhaps through their mental connection?

Valorre left the stream and approached her. Lowering his head in an invitation for her to mount him, he said, *We can try.*

Steeling her resolve, she climbed back onto Valorre's back. A wave of exhaustion crested through her, but she breathed it away. She didn't have time to sleep. She hardly had time to think.

Closing her eyes, she shifted her attention to the elements around her, strengthening her connection to them. She breathed in the mild night air, filling her lungs with the scent of leaves and soil. Pressing her palms to Valorre's shoulders, she let her awareness radiate down his smooth hide, past his legs and hooves to the earth he stood upon. Through him, she rooted her energy to the earth. Next, she shifted her attention to the melodic trickle of the stream. Then tilted her face toward the sky to feel the light of the moon. The warmth of summer infusing the night.

Air. Earth. Water. Fire.

On a deep exhale, she filled her mind with thoughts of Salinda, the woman who'd treated Cora as a daughter. She saw her brown skin, her long black hair, her dark eyes that crinkled at the corners when she smiled. She pictured the slight angle at the tip of her ears, marking her as a Faeryn descendent. Then she imagined the triple moon sigil that marked the tip of her chin, the ink that adorned her neck in complex geometric patterns, the *insigmora* that trailed over every inch of her arms down to her palms.

Cora's own *insigmora* seemed to hum in response, warming her blood, fueling her with the thrum that was her magic. She extended her senses and tried to *feel* for Salinda's presence. Her nearness. Her location.

She got nothing back.

Nothing.

Emotion, she reminded herself. *I need emotion to travel.*

She imagined Maiya next, the girl she loved as dearly as a sister. Her chest felt warm, but her heart felt so clouded with dread. Fear. Fatigue. Her emotions refused to rise past it.

No, I must feel. I must.

She thought of how the Forest People had cared for her. How they'd taken her in and taught her about the Arts. How they'd helped her recognize her clairsentience. Nurture it. Hone it.

Her heart began to lift.

They were my family, she said to herself. *My family. My home.*

Her emotions grew lighter. Richer. More potent.

She shifted her awareness to Valorre, welcoming his mind to connect with hers.

My family. My home. She said it again and again like a mantra, seeking some inkling that could guide her toward the location she sought.

My family. My home.

An invisible tug drew her forward, cleaving through her emotions. She followed it with her mind. Her heart—

My home. The words came not from her mind but Valorre's. Or was it simply a matter of their minds being connected?

I had another home before this.

This time, she couldn't decipher where the thought came from, but the sense of awe that accompanied it was so strong that it pulled her deeper into her emotions, strengthening that tug, that pull toward a place. A vision filled her mind now, a meadow of lush green grass in the most vibrant shade of emerald. Dewdrops glittered rainbow light upon every blade. Flowers in the most spectacular array of color shifted in a playful breeze, creating a susurration more melodic than any stream, any instrument.

It was...breathtaking. Unlike any place Cora had ever been. Was this where the Forest People were now?

Home. The word pulsed through her mind and filled her heart with longing. Another pull. Another tug forward. Everything inside her said to move. To step. To enter this new location.

Valorre shifted beneath her.

He took a step forward.

A flare of warm light kissed the other side of Cora's eyelids. Blinking them open, she greeted daylight. Her mind stumbled under the haze of her meditation, but as her senses sharpened, she realized she and Valorre were in the very meadow she'd seen in her mind. It was even more vibrant than she'd imagined, more stunning.

She dismounted from Valorre's back and fully took in their surroundings. The meadow was surrounded by towering willows, their waterfall leaves swaying in the warm breeze. Yet she saw no tent, not even in the distance. Found no sign that the Forest People were nearby.

Something pulsed inside her. A warning that this was very, very wrong.

Only now did the sudden daylight concern her. No matter where in Khero the Forest People had gone, there should have been no change in time. No hour difference. No way to account for having stepped from night to day. Unless...

Mother Goddess...did she move through time as well as space?

No, that wasn't part of astral travel. Not even astral projection could bypass the present.

I'm sorry.

She frowned, turning back toward Valorre. His muscles quivered, ears twitching in agitation. "What are you sorry for? I...I'm the one who messed this up—"

No. This was my fault. My fault.

Her blood chilled. "What do you mean?"

You thought of home, but I remembered. Remembered my first home.

She swallowed hard. "Are you saying we traveled to *your* home? The place you came from?"

Yes. This...this isn't good for you. I remember now.

Panic laced up Cora's throat. Wherever they were, it was far enough from Khero that it was daytime instead of night. Still, if she brought them here, she could bring them back.

She grabbed hold of his mane in preparation to mount again. "What kingdom are we in? What continent?"

A rush of sound erupted behind her. Cora startled and turned toward it in time to see an enormous sphere of swirling color perched at the edge of the meadow. Three figures strolled out of it as if it were a doorway. As soon as the three were fully outside the strange vortex, it disappeared, leaving Cora to stare at the strangers.

They appeared to be male, and beautiful at that. The one at the center had golden-blond hair the color of honey, fair skin, and piercing blue eyes. The second was shorter than the first, of wide build, and had curly hair in a fiery copper hue. The third was the tallest of the three with umber skin and long black hair laced with gold and silver thread that sparkled in the sunlight. All wore silk britches and an elegant knee-length robe belted with a wide sash. The style was unlike anything she'd seen of current fashions in *any* region. But that wasn't nearly as surprising as the angled tips of their ears. It wasn't a subtle angle either. Not an almost-imperceptible hint like some of the Forest People had. These ears came to a distinct and obvious point.

She couldn't pull her eyes from the three men. Their towering height, their unearthly beauty, their regal style...it was straight from a faerytale. And there was only one word she could think of to suit them.

Elvyn.

An ancient race of High Fae known to be extinct, even more so than the Faeryn.

Cora's heart slammed against her ribs as an impossible truth began to dawn.

We're not in your world at all anymore, Valorre said, finally answering the question he'd left hanging between them. *We're in my world. The fae realm. El'Ara.*

Cora sensed he was keeping himself from saying more. His silence didn't matter; the anger in the three Elvyn figures' eyes was universal enough for her to understand what he'd left unsaid.

She was not supposed to be here.

<h1 style="text-align:center">41</h1>

Teryn did not wake gently. There was no floating in nothingness, no subtle lack of consciousness. There was only an abrupt intake of breath, a startling sense of being alive.

Or...sort of alive.

As he took in his surroundings, he found himself reclined on the floor in the illusion that was Emylia's temple bedroom. She sat beside him on a stack of bright cushions, her expression heavy with concern. Before she could say what he knew she was about to, he tuned in to his vitale and connected with his breaths. They were short and shallow and came with a mild ache in his lungs. His heartbeat and pulse felt more distant than usual.

But that wasn't his primary concern. He settled his attention on Emylia. "What happened to Cora? Did she take the crystal like I told her to?"

The answer was already on her face. "She tried, but...Teryn, there was a reason our plan involved you removing the crystal from your chest and destroying it. I never told you to pass it off to someone else. You were never supposed to remove it in the first place until we were ready to execute our plan."

He pinned her with a hard look. "*Our plan* is nonexistent. I wasn't willing to wait for some hazy future hope."

"Don't you understand? If she'd taken the crystal far from your body and destroyed it, Morkai would have died, but so would you. You are tethered to the crystal, the same as Morkai. Your only link to the world of the living is through your body. And if your ethera is freed from the crystal while your connection to your cereba and vitale is severed...you'd have no hope of being whole again."

Her words sent a chill through him, but he couldn't bring himself to feel regret. Instead, he only felt more vindicated. "I would have been willing to risk my life if it meant destroying the sorcerer once and for all. If it meant keeping Cora safe from him."

Her eyes turned down at the corners. "We'll find a way, I promise."

Teryn bit back his argument. Hadn't she also promised he had more than enough time? "Where is she? Where is Cora now?"

"She got away."

"And where is *he*?"

"He's resting his ethera. He overtaxed himself and was forced to rest shortly after Cora disappeared. However, this is the one time I would caution against practicing with your cereba. Your body...it didn't respond well to what you did. To the two of you fighting for control."

Teryn remembered the blood that had seeped from his nose, the searing pain he'd felt when his body was being wrestled away from him. The only thing that had kept him in place for as long as it had was Cora's presence. That warm tether had remained, pulsing from his chest and anchoring him into his body. Had that been his heart-center? Had it overridden Morkai's?

It had...for a while at least.

Thank the seven gods she'd gotten away after he lost consciousness.

"You shouldn't have done what you did, Teryn."

"I *had* to try. I couldn't let her believe his lies a second longer. Couldn't let him kiss her, comfort her—" He recalled the reason she'd sought comfort in the first place. The reason she'd come to speak to him.

A searing ache pierced his heart.

He slid his gaze to Emylia. "Do you know about the curse Morkai placed on Cora? The one preventing her from bearing children?"

She shrank back slightly, shoulders stiff. Her dark eyes went wide, but she said nothing.

Teryn sat up straighter. "Do. You. Know. About. It."

She gave a sharp nod.

"Tell me."

"It's...it's not something you can change—"

His voice deepened, his fingers curling into fists. "Stop keeping things from me based on whether or not I can change them and just *tell* me, Emylia."

Closing her eyes, she lowered her head. Her voice came out muffled. "I suppose it's well past time for me to be judged for my sins."

Tension radiated through Teryn's ethera.

Slowly, she rose to her feet. Teryn followed, keeping his eyes locked on her hunched form. Her expression was wan, eyes distant.

"It's my fault," she said, voice barely above a whisper. "Everything he's doing. It's because of me."

It took all his restraint to keep his voice level. "Tell me what you know. Please."

"I can't. I'm too much of a coward to confess with words."

"Emylia—"

"But I can show you."

~

The illusion that was Emylia's temple bedroom fell beneath a sheer blanket of fog. When it dissipated, the tapestries and furnishings were left muted in color and clarity, while the light coming in from the windows seemed to shift between midday and early evening, then back again. When Teryn tried to focus on the details of the room—the pattern on the rugs, the designs on the tapestries—they'd change before his eyes. Whatever illusion he saw now, it had the same ephemeral quality as a dream.

"This is my memory," Emylia explained, taking up post against the far wall. Her expression remained hollow, shoulders slumped either with sorrow or resignation. "Or how I remember it playing out, at least. Memories are weaker than illusions, but this is as close to the truth as I can show you."

Teryn stood at her side, tense with trepidation. He had no idea what to expect or how her memories had anything to do with the curse Cora had mentioned.

The bedroom door opened and in walked another version of Emylia. She appeared to be a year or two younger than the Emylia he knew now, but perhaps it was the carefree smile, the sparkle in her eyes, and the buoyancy of her steps that made her seem so youthful. She wore a simple silk shift, belted at the waist with a red braided cord. A similar red cord framed her face, keeping her halo of black curls off her forehead, and ended in a bow at the nape of her neck. Her arms were full of leather-bound books.

Behind the Emylia of memory followed an older woman. She was tall with brown skin and short-cropped black hair. Her state of dress was slightly more elegant, her shift patterned with floral designs, and her braided belt was gold in color.

Neither figure paid any heed to Teryn and his companion. He and Emylia were merely spectators in this memory, not participants.

"He says he's from Syrus," the older woman said. Her voice was soft and slightly muffled, her tone inconstant, as if whatever magic Emylia was using to replicate this memory was unable to properly recall how the woman was supposed to sound. "He seems to be about the same age as you, and with the same fascination with books. For seven days, he's been in our library, asking questions that our archivists don't have answers to."

The younger Emylia set her books next to her bed and turned back toward the woman. "What does this have to do with me, Priestess Calla?"

"The young man is in need of a channel, either an oracle or seer. Moreover, I need him out of our library, and you need to hone your craft."

Emylia's eyes brightened. "You mean I can practice channeling for someone outside of the temple?"

"Yes. I believe you are ready. The man's search is of a nature that will provide you a challenge."

Emylia cocked her head to the side. "What is he asking about?"

"The fae."

Her mouth dropped open, expression falling. "The fae. He seeks answers to... faerytales."

Mother Calla gave her a knowing grin. "I told you it would be a challenge."

Emylia's face wrinkled with disgust. "It's a challenge because the fae aren't real.

A channel is a seeker of truth. How can I act as his seer when the subject is one of myth?"

Mother Calla's mirth slipped from her face. "It is not a temple acolyte's job to judge what is and isn't real. If you are to become a Priestess of Zaras, you must open yourself to new possibilities. You cannot reject a patron based on your preconceived prejudice. You must be willing to seek before you judge, regardless of the subject."

Emylia stiffened, then bowed at the waist. "Forgive me," she said in a rush. "It was wrong for me to judge. Of course I'll channel for this patron."

"You will," Mother Calla said, then closed the distance between them. Placing her finger under Emylia's chin, she urged her to straighten from her bow. The older woman's eyes crinkled with clear fondness. "You're as bold as your mother, and just as stubborn. I believe in you, the same way I believed in her. You'll do her memory proud."

The image stilled. Teryn was about to ask what that memory had to do with Cora, when the fog returned and swept the room away completely. In its place, a new location formed, darkening the edges of Teryn's vision until it formed a cobblestone street bathed in shadow and moonlight. Both sides of the street were lined with narrow townhomes and clustered storefronts.

Teryn caught a glimpse of a hooded figure strolling up to one of the buildings before the image shifted again. The figure was now approaching the door of an inn. Teryn saw Emylia's telltale black curls peeking out from under her hood as the acolyte entered the building. The fog swept the image away once more and formed a small candlelit room. Like the temple bedroom, the room shifted whenever Teryn tried to focus on details, but he was able to make out a narrow cot and a small desk.

Emylia entered the room, tossing back her hood as a young man closed the door behind them. Teryn assessed the man's fair skin, his pale eyes, his shoulder-length black hair. He looked young—perhaps a year younger than Teryn—but there was no denying his resemblance to Morkai. But unlike the duke, this man wasn't impeccably dressed. Instead, he wore plain brown trousers and a cream linen tunic.

The man faced Emylia, frowning as his eyes landed on her face. "*You're* a Priestess of Zaras? You look...young."

She scoffed. "Is that how you greet people in Syrus?"

His expression hardened. "I requested a priestess."

"Well, you got an acolyte. Shall I leave, or are you going to be a gentleman and introduce yourself?"

He ran a hand over his face, then crossed his arms. "Desmond."

Teryn frowned. He'd expected the man to introduce himself as Morkai, based on their striking similarities. Was this truly a younger version of the sorcerer as he'd first assumed, or a close relative? Was Desmond the sorcerer's true name? He glanced at the real Emylia to ask but found her lower lip trembling. A sheen of tears coated her eyes, and her expression sagged with longing.

"Is Desmond your surname?" The Emylia of memory stole his attention back to the scene playing out before him. She arched a brow at the man. "Or are we already on a first-name basis?"

"Desmond is the only name you need to know."

Her jaw shifted side to side. "Fine. Acolyte Emylia."

Desmond's only reply was to extend a hand toward the chair at the desk. "Take a seat and we can get started."

Emylia strode past him, burning him with a sneer on her way. With exaggerated moves, she pulled out the chair and planted herself onto it. Meanwhile, Desmond took a seat at the edge of the bed, elbows perched on his knees. One of his legs began to shake as he watched her. His steely expression cracked, revealing something softer. More anxious perhaps.

Emylia shrugged off her cloak and let it fall over the back of her chair. The candlelight glinted off a crystal she wore around her neck. It was wrapped in gold wire and strung from a chain. Even in the shadowed haze of the memory, Teryn knew this was the very same crystal his ethera was tethered to now.

Removing the chain from around her neck, Emylia set the crystal on the desk and cupped her palms around it.

Desmond's leg stopped shaking as his gaze landed on her hands. "What is that?"

"It helps me channel. It belonged to my mother when she was alive. She was a Priestess of Zaras."

His expression softened further. "Your mother died?"

"My birth killed her," she said stiffly. "Now, what is it you want to know?"

Desmond took a deep breath. "How do I get to the realm of the fae?"

Emylia rolled her eyes, a disbelieving smirk tugging a corner of her lips. Then, with a resigned sigh, she closed her eyes and settled into her seat, her body growing more and more relaxed as she breathed deeply. After several long moments, she spoke, her voice deep and even. "Show me the realm of the fae."

"That's not what I asked."

"I know," she said, tone calm. "Before I can ask how to get there, I must first see that it exists."

Desmond looked like he wanted to argue but remained silent.

Movement fluttered beneath Emylia's closed eyelids.

Desmond leaned closer, and Teryn found himself doing the same. Teryn didn't know much about fae lore, but he'd certainly never heard anyone refer to the fae as having belonged to another realm. Faerytales suggested fae creatures— unicorns, pixies, dragons, sprites—had lived long ago, along with two races of High Fae: the Elvyn and Faeryn. They were said to have inhabited the land once known as Lela—the land that was now divided into Menah, Selay, and Khero. All stories told that every kind of fae went extinct over five hundred years ago.

Teryn hadn't believed there was any truth to such tales. Not until he saw a unicorn with his own eyes. Learned magic was real. Confronted a blood mage who claimed to be an Elvyn prince.

The seer repeated her request. "Show me the realm of the fae."

A weighted silence fell over the room. Teryn folded his arms to keep from fidgeting.

Finally, she spoke again.

"The fae realms are many. They are here but not here. Layered upon this world. Parallel, but on separate planes."

Her eyes flew open, and she dropped her crystal to the surface of the table. "The fae are real," she muttered. Then, shifting in her seat to face Desmond, she said it again. "The fae are *real.*"

His lips curled with the slightest hint of amusement, but he quickly steeled it behind an icy mask. "Yes, but how do I get to their realm?"

Emylia rose from her chair and began pacing the room. "I saw...many realms. There isn't just one. Fae of different races and species exist on parallel planes. I can't ask to see how to get to your particular realm unless I know more about it." She halted before Desmond. "What is the name of the realm you seek?"

He pursed his lips. "I can't say."

She propped her hands on her hips and stared down at him. "I can't be of any help if you keep vital information from me. Honestly, I'm surprised I saw as much as I did, considering my skepticism. But what I'm seeing is taking me in too many different directions. I need to know the name of the realm if I am to see any more answers."

Desmond threw his head back with a frustrated growl. "I can't tell you because I don't know."

She arched a brow. "You don't know?"

He stood and brushed past her toward the desk, planting his hands on its surface. His head hung low, sending his dark hair over his face. "My father sent me. He's the one looking for the fae realm, not me. He's its rightful heir, and I'm simply trying to return him to his throne."

Teryn's eyes widened. Desmond's talk of fae heirs and blood rights reminded him too much of Morkai. Could Desmond's father be...Morkai? While the sorcerer had looked only a handful of years older than Teryn, he was willing to entertain the possibility that he'd been old enough to sire this young man. If Morkai was truly Elvyn, he could have been ageless.

Emylia snorted a laugh. "Your father is the heir to a fae realm?"

His cheeks flushed. "I'm not joking, acolyte."

"Right," she said, trying to hide her amusement and failing miserably. "Open mind. I can do that."

He glared at her for a few moments before speaking again. "He told me the fae realm has a name, but usurpers to the throne cursed him long ago, forcing him to forget. All I know is that it's the realm of the Elvyn and Faeryn."

Emylia nibbled a thumbnail, then gave a nod. She'd managed to rein in her mirth. "All right. I can work with that."

"You can?"

"It might take me days or weeks, but I can continue to channel. I'll seek the realm of the Elvyn and Faeryn and see if I can glean a name. Now that I know it's real..." She met his gaze with a wide smile. "This is actually exciting!"

He blinked at her a few times. Then, ever so slowly, a warm smile melted over his face. "So you'll come back? You'll come back and we'll try again?"

Her expression turned timid. "If you want me to."

"Yes," he said, voice soft, breathless. He reached a tentative hand and brushed his fingers against her wrist. "Thank you."

Emylia bit her lip, eyes locked on his. "Of course."

The image froze, and Teryn cast a glance at the real Emylia. Her expression was still brimming with mournful longing. "I don't see what this has to do with Cora," he said.

"You will," she whispered. "And you will hate me for it." She seemed so small, so defeated, as she turned to face him. "But don't worry. I hate myself for it too."

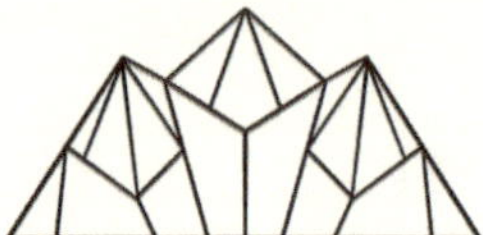

42

The fog flooded the room once again, forming image after image in rapid succession, as if representing the passing of many days. Teryn saw Emylia and Desmond reading in the library, followed by another scene of them sharing a smile from across a long table. Then they were elbowing each other playfully as they walked side by side down the cobblestone street near the inn. Finally, they exchanged a kiss over the desk in Desmond's bedroom.

Teryn didn't know why Emylia was showing him this. These seemed like private moments, not ones meant for great revelations. But as he glanced at the woman beside him, he saw the sad smile curling her lips, the hand she held over her heart. Perhaps she wasn't replaying these intimate memories for Teryn but for herself. Whoever Desmond was—whether he was Morkai himself, or the sorcerer's son—it was clear Emylia had fallen in love with him.

The memory shifted again. Emylia flung open Desmond's bedroom door and found him at his desk inspecting a book. He jumped and slammed the tome shut. Emylia frowned as Desmond shoved the book beneath a stack of papers.

"What are you reading?" she asked.

"Nothing but more boring texts," Desmond said with a wry grin. He ran his hand through his black tresses, revealing a hint of a slightly angled ear. Teryn's breath caught. Had Morkai had ears like that? Teryn couldn't recall. It hadn't been something he'd ever paid attention to. "You, on the other hand, are a far more interesting sight."

Emylia beamed and rushed to Desmond's side, taking his face in her hands. He wrapped his arms around her waist as they met in a passionate kiss. When their lips finally parted, Emylia kept her forehead pressed to his. "I found it," she whispered.

Desmond pulled back. "Found what?"

"I saw it, Des. It's called El'Ara."

His silver-blue eyes went wide. "The name of the fae realm? My father's true home?"

Emylia bounced on the balls of her feet, hardly able to contain her excitement. "Yes."

He bolted upright to stand. "So you can find it now? Find out how to get there?"

"That's why I'm here, aren't I?"

Desmond winked. "I assumed it was because you loved me."

She perched on her toes and planted a kiss on his cheek. "I do, but business first."

Desmond moved from behind the desk and let Emylia take her place in his chair. Like before, she removed her crystal from around her neck and brought it between her palms. This time, instead of perching at the edge of the bed, Desmond kneeled beside the desk.

Emylia settled into her meditative state. After a few deep breaths, she spoke. "Show me how to enter El'Ara."

Her eyelids fluttered, eyes darting side to side beneath them. For several long moments, she said nothing. Then, "I'm seeing something."

Desmond leaned closer to the desk. "What do you see?"

"A...wall. It's a wall of thread, and it's surrounding me, blocking everywhere I try to look."

"Cut the threads."

"They can't be cut, but...I think there's a window. A weakness."

Desmond's fingers curled at his sides.

"I'm getting something," Emylia whispered. "The way in. I see...truth. Someone is speaking from behind this wall of threads."

"What are they saying?"

She shook her head. "I'm a seer, not an oracle. It's harder for me to turn images to words, but...no, I see it."

Another stretch of silence.

"So long as the Veil remains," Emylia said, each word slow and careful, "the Blood of Darius cannot enter El'Ara."

Teryn frowned. Who—or what—was the Blood of Darius?

Desmond, however, wasn't concerned by the name Darius but something else. "The Veil? What is the Veil?"

"A ward woven to keep the Blood of Darius at bay."

"Can the Veil be destroyed?"

"When true Morkara is born, the Veil will be torn, setting into motion the end of the Blood of Darius."

Desmond's voice deepened. "Who is this *true Morkara*? How will they end the Blood of Darius?"

Emylia winced, her eyes darting rapidly now. "The true Morkara is the Blood of Ailan, born under the black mountain. He will unite three crowns and return El'Ara's heart."

"But who is this person? Where can I find the true Morkara?"

Emylia paused, head bobbing slightly side to side. "You will never know him."

Desmond's jaw tightened.

"But...but you may find his mother."

"Who is his mother?"

She winced again, and a sheen of sweat coated her brow. "She too is the Blood of Ailan, but with the beauty of Satsara. She has the blood of the witch, blood of the Elvyn, and blood of the crown. The unicorn will signify her awakening."

"What about this black mountain you mentioned?"

"A black mountain...over a field of violets."

"I've never seen such a place." Shaking his head, he stood and paced before the desk, hands clasped behind his back. "But if I can find it, then...then how do I put an end to the true Morkara?"

"If you end the true Morkara, the Veil will never be torn. The Blood of Darius will forever be barred from El'Ara."

"But if I don't end the true Morkara, he will end the Blood of Darius?"

"Yes," Emylia said.

Teryn's mind reeled to comprehend what he was hearing. *Morkara* sounded so much like Morkai, but he didn't know what it meant. Was it a name? A title? And while Desmond seemed to know who the *Blood of Darius* was, Teryn hadn't a clue. Then there were the other names: Satsara, Ailan.

"There has to be a way," Desmond said. "Tell me a way! Where do I find the black mountain over a field of violets? What is the true Morkara's name? His mother's name? Who are Satsara and Ailan?"

Emylia began to tremble, and her voice came out weak and strained. "Desmond, that's too much. I can't...I can't see any more than that. I need to come out of the channel—"

"No!" His shout made her jump in her seat. He softened his tone. "No, Emy, you're doing great. We can keep going. I'll find a better question." He hung his head and planted his hands at the end of the desk. "It isn't El'Ara my father needs. Not for what he needs to do. It's the power of the Morkaius."

Morkaius. Another word that sounded so much like Morkai.

He returned to Emylia's side and kneeled on the floor again. "Can one claim the power of the Morkaius without entering El'Ara? Can one become Morkaius of *this* world?"

Emylia shifted in her seat, shaking her head. "I don't like this. I'm seeing too much darkness."

"You can do this, Emy. I believe in you. I *need* you to do this."

She shuddered but settled back into her trance. After a deep exhale, her voice regained its steady tone. "To gain the power of the Morkaius, one must first become King of Magic, a crown given, not taken, and reign over El'Ara's abandoned heart."

"What is El'Ara's abandoned heart? Where do I find it?"

"A land left in the wake of the Veil. A heart that once was one, now split by three crowns. One crown rests upon the birthplace of the mother you seek. To become Morkaius of El'Ara's heart, harness the magic that seeps from its center."

Desmond's face broke into a grin. He grabbed paper, ink, and quill from the desk and began to write. "A crown given, not taken. Reign over El'Ara's heart. Harness the magic—"

"He who harnesses the magic will be destroyed by it."

His pen stilled over his paper. "What?"

"El'Ara's magic is too strong to be contained by any man, neither mortal nor fae. It will eat through living flesh and burn living blood. No Morkaius shall survive the harnessing."

His eyes shot to Emylia, and he pursed his lips so tight, they lost color. Then, with a shout, he shot to his feet and swept his arms across the desk, sending books, ink, and paper flying. Emylia opened her eyes and let out a cry, backing away from him, chest heaving.

Silence enveloped the room while the two remained motionless, surrounded by the last of the fluttering papers.

"What's wrong with you?" Emylia finally shouted. "You could have hurt me, forcing me out of a channel like that!"

As his eyes met hers, his face twisted with anguish. He ran to her and gathered her in his arms. "Forgive me, Emylia. Forgive me."

She remained stiff in his arms for several long moments until she softened against him and wrapped her arms around his waist. "I'll try again, Des. We'll find the answers you need."

"I fear what you told me was answer enough," he said, voice muffled as he spoke into her hair. "My father's mission is impossible. And yet, we must find a way. Father must become Morkaius."

She pulled back and glanced up at him. "Why? What does that word even mean?"

"It means High King of Magic, and it's Father's birthright. Becoming Morkaius will give him access to magic beyond what we know."

Emylia frowned. "What kind of magic?"

His expression hardened. "The kind that can bring my mother back."

"Your...mother."

He nodded. "She died, like yours, but not during childbirth. She died of illness."

Emylia's face sank with pity. She brought a gentle hand to his cheek. "Des, no one can bring someone back from the dead."

"The Morkaius can."

"But how can your father become this...this Morkaius? You heard the words. He who harnesses the magic will be destroyed by it."

Desmond shook his head. "Father will find a way. Either that or he will find this mother the prophecy spoke of and end her."

Teryn shuddered at the ice in his tone.

"You can't be talking about...killing someone, Des. That's not what you mean, right? Your father isn't an evil man, is he?"

He smiled down at her but made no attempt to answer her question. "Thank you, Emy. You've helped me so much. I'll return home to Father next week and tell him what you've told me. It has to be enough for him. It will be. Whether in this world or in El'Ara, my father *will* become Morkaius."

Emylia's throat bobbed as something like fear settled in her dark eyes.

The image froze, and Teryn faced the real Emylia. His heart hammered, mind reeling to comprehend everything he'd witnessed. If this was supposed to have been about Cora...

About the reason Morkai cursed her to die childless...

His voice came out with a tremor. "Are you trying to tell me that Cora was supposed to be the mother in this...this prophecy? Are you certain it's truly her?"

Emylia looked even more hollow than she had before, eyes distant. "*Blood of the witch, blood of the Elvyn, blood of the crown.* That means the prophesied mother is part witch, part Elvyn, and royal."

"Cora never said anything about being of Elvyn descent."

She shrugged. "She likely doesn't know. But this clue will convince you. *The unicorn will signify her awakening.*"

Teryn's heart sank. "Valorre."

She nodded. "Her relationship with Valorre is the final piece that makes me certain she's the mother. Yet Morkai acted long before he saw the first sign of a unicorn, long before he even knew who Princess Aveline was. Instead, he followed my prophecy to find the Heart of El'Ara, as it and the mother were connected by the black mountain over the field of violets. It took him years to find the place he sought, but it shouldn't take you nearly as long to figure out."

He closed his eyes, but the closest image he could conjure was the cliff Cora had taken him to. Beneath it, the wildflower meadow stretched out before the Cambron Mountains. If only the flowers were fully purple, then—

"Seven devils," he said, opening his eyes. "It's not a place. It's a sigil."

The vision came to him now—the silhouette of a mountain over a purple background. The symbol of Khero.

"Yes," Emylia said. "Because of the words I spoke, Morkai sought to end Cora's life."

A spike of rage shot through him, but he was too fatigued to hold on to it. "Morkai didn't kill her, though. Why? Why did he curse her instead?"

Emylia rubbed her brow. "Mother Goddess, there's...so much more to tell you, but—" She froze, eyes widening.

"But what?"

She nibbled her lip before answering. "He's awake."

Dread filled every inch of Teryn's ethera. He needed to know the rest of Emylia's tale. Needed to understand the full truth of Desmond, Morkai, and the prophecy.

But just as badly, he wanted to see how Morkai would react now that Cora had escaped his clutches. What would the sorcerer do now that the marriage alliance —his one link to royal power—was compromised? If Teryn's body was beginning to shut down, then Morkai was running out of time.

They both were.

"We follow him," Teryn said, tone resolute, "but as soon as he's asleep once more, you're showing me the rest of your memories."

She gave him a sad smile that almost looked relieved. "And finally my sins will be laid bare."

43

Cora had no time to feel awed over the sight of the three Elvyn males, for the anger on their faces was second only to the rage in their tones. If that wasn't enough, she could *feel* it. Their shock, their ire, their...fear. Or was that her own? Before she could so much as gather her bearings, they charged across the meadow. Her gaze fell on the swords they carried at their hips. Though each had a hand resting upon the hilt, none drew their weapons. Even so, Cora found her hands flinching toward her waist, her shoulder, seeking weapons that weren't there. Only then did she recall what she was wearing—a thin linen shift and velvet robe. She didn't even have her apron and paring knife.

They were nearly upon her now. With every step they took, they shouted at her in a language she couldn't understand. The golden-haired Elvyn at the fore of the group lifted a hand, pressing his thumb to the center of his ring finger and turning his wrist slightly.

Cora didn't know what the gesture meant, but it sparked within her enough urgency to mount Valorre and make an escape.

Only...she found her body frozen.

And it wasn't fear that stilled her, nor any other internal source.

Instead, an invisible force pinned her arms to her sides. Her gaze narrowed on the golden-haired Elvyn's hand, still curled in that strange gesture.

Valorre reared back on his hind legs, kicking out with his front hooves, but the same fae male extended his other hand. With the same gesture, he forced Valorre back to all fours. The unicorn bucked and thrashed, but it was no use. It was as if he'd been harnessed by an invisible bridle.

The other two Elvyn flanked the first. The one with umber skin and dark hair stepped forward and spoke in more words Cora couldn't comprehend. Yet she noted the placating nature of his tone. Unlike the golden-haired fae, whose lips were peeled back in a sneer, blue eyes cast in a glower, or the copper-haired fae who simply looked amused, the dark-haired Elvyn had a much gentler energy. Cora's panic was almost strong enough to drown out the emotions of the three, but she could still bet which of the fae she'd have the best chance of appealing to.

He spoke again, slower this time.

"I don't understand what you're saying," she said, voice edged with hysteria. She tried to focus on deepening her breaths, on rooting herself to the earth beneath her feet, but that only reminded her that she was in another godsdamned *realm*. Whatever the hell that was supposed to mean. And she was still trapped under the unseen force the golden fae was using.

The dark-haired fae released a sigh and lifted a hand. He crossed two of his fingers and slid them through the air in a horizontal line. "What are you?" he said, and this time Cora could understand him.

"Are you human?" asked the golden fae. His words made sense now too, but she realized they didn't match the shape of his lips. Perhaps the dark-haired fae had cast a translation enchantment. Was that something the Elvyn could do? All she knew of Elvyn magic was that they utilized what the Forest People had called the Magic of the Sky. Unlike the Faeryn, who revered the earth and lived in harmony with nature, the Elvyn were said to value beauty, art, music, and luxury. She knew the Elvyn specialized in an Art called weaving—the very magic Morkai tried to emulate with his blood tapestries—but she didn't know what it entailed.

"I'm...I'm human," she finally managed to say.

The copper-haired Elvyn dipped his chin at her lower body. Now that he was near, she could see an array of bronze freckles dotting his tan skin. "What's on her arms?"

The golden fae flicked his wrist, and she found her arm thrust suddenly forward. She winced as the invisible force twisted the limb, yanking it at an uncomfortable angle until her inked forearm showed clearly.

"Fanon," the dark-haired fae said, casting a stern look at the golden fae, "show a little restraint. We don't know if she's guilty."

The word *Fanon* remained untranslated, so she assumed that must be the golden fae's name.

"If she's human, she's guilty," Fanon said. He folded his arms over his chest in a slightly more relaxed posture. The pressure eased from her forearm, returning it to a natural angle. She expected to be freed from his invisible magic altogether, but her arms simply snapped back to her sides. Even though he was no longer actively making that strange gesture, both she and Valorre were still trapped under his magic's influence.

"But those looked like Faeryn *insigmora*," said the stout fae. Belatedly Cora realized his lips had formed the last two words, matching up with what she'd heard.

"She's not Faeryn, Garot," said Fanon.

Despite the disgust and trepidation wafting off the three strangers, Cora saw an opportunity to forge some kind of understanding between them. "You're right, they are Faeryn *insigmora*. Where I'm from, I lived with a group of people who are Faeryn descendants. They took me in—"

"There are Faeryn descendants in your realm?" the copper-haired Garot asked, his green eyes alight with renewed curiosity.

Fanon and the dark-haired fae exchanged a brief look. When Fanon returned his gaze to hers, it was no longer quite so cold. His throat bobbed before he spoke. "Are there any Elvyn survivors in your world? Or...descendants?"

Cora sensed a subtle spark of hope in him. Her heart sank. Why did he have to ask that? She knew her answer would only disappoint him. "I've never met anyone of Elvyn descent."

Fanon's dark glower returned, and with it came a string of clipped words that remained untranslated. Based on his tone, she could only assume they were expletives.

"How did you come here?" the dark-haired fae said. He was now the only one whose name she didn't know. His eyes were a ruby-tinted brown, and the way they crinkled at the corners set her at ease. She got the distinct impression that he was the eldest of the three, despite their equally youthful appearances. Somehow, all appeared to be both young and ancient at the same time, but the dark-haired fae held a weight to his energy, one that bore centuries of life. Of wisdom.

She realized his question still hung between them. She was about to confess what had happened—or at least try to put it into words—when Valorre's voice entered her mind.

Tell them I brought you here. Anxiety rippled from him. *Do not tell them about your magic.*

She glanced at him, saw his muscles quivering against his invisible restraints. *Why?*

Because it was *my fault. I invaded your thoughts with my memory of home. I took a step and brought us here using your traveling magic. But...more than that, I've come to learn the value of a lie. If you do not lie, I fear...something. I don't remember what, but I fear it. They will not like your magic.*

He sounded so uncertain in her mind. So unlike the overly proud creature he normally was.

She returned her gaze to the dark-haired fae. "Valorre brought me."

"What is...Valorre?" Garot asked.

"My unicorn companion."

Fanon scoffed. "The unicorn is your companion?"

"More concerning," said the unnamed Elvyn, "is that she's suggesting he came from her world." Then to Cora, he said, "Please explain."

"Unicorns were considered extinct in my world for five hundred years. Only recently have they reappeared." She tried to keep her voice level. It was easier said than done with the tremors racking her body, coursing with waves of panic over being restrained by a force she couldn't see. Not to mention the fact that she was referring to where she'd come from as *her world.*

Mother Goddess, was this really happening? All her life, she'd thought of the fae as creatures who'd once existed and had simply gone extinct. Now she was supposed to reconcile that they'd come from another world. But how?

"And you befriended this one?" The unnamed male glanced at Valorre.

"Yes," she said, "and we came here by mistake. He accidentally brought me to his home."

Fanon's eyes went wide. He whipped his face toward the dark-haired fae. "What does this mean for the Veil, Etrix?"

Etrix. The final name.

He rubbed his jaw. "It might be torn."

Fanon took a forbidding step closer to Cora, leaving only a foot of space between them. She wanted to flinch back but she still couldn't move. Valorre released a guttural whinny, but he too remained trapped in place. All Cora could do was tilt her head and meet his gaze. She swallowed hard, realizing he was even taller than Teryn. And Teryn was one of the tallest men she'd met. Fanon's build, however, was leaner. That didn't make him any less intimidating.

"Did you cross through the Veil?" he asked with clenched teeth.

"I don't know what the Veil is."

"Then are you a worldwalker?"

Cora was struck with the most potent hatred, and her answer dried in her throat. Similar emotions came from the two fae behind Fanon, but theirs was tangled with far more fear. Fanon's contempt, on the other hand, was too strong to carry much else.

Whatever a worldwalker was, he despised it with a violent passion.

Tell them we came through the Veil, Valorre said.

She shuddered beneath Fanon's icy stare but finally managed to find her words. "I...I think we came through the Veil."

He watched her for a few silent moments, then reached toward his waist. Her heart slammed against her ribs as she expected him to unsheathe his sword—

To her relief, he simply extracted something from inside his robe. Her eyes widened as she took in the strange item. It looked like a large cuff made from two pieces of curved obsidian that ended in tapered points. Like talons. Or claws. A wide gap remained between the sharp tips, and as Fanon tugged on both sides, it widened further on a hinge.

He stepped even closer, bringing the cuff-like object toward her neck.

"What is that?" Cora asked, voice trembling. She struggled against her invisible bonds but they were just as strong as ever. Valorre gave another futile whinny.

"Fanon," Etrix said, his tone brimming with warning. "You don't have to—"

Fanon ignored his companion and proceeded to hook the cuff around her neck. She couldn't see when he closed it, could glimpse no part of it beneath her chin, but as she felt a sharp pain bite into her skin, she realized he hadn't hooked it *around* her neck; he'd hooked the tapered points into her flesh.

Vertigo seized her, first from fear, then from...

A hollow feeling crept upon her awareness. An empty void. An unsettling quiet.

It took her several long moments to realize what was happening.

Her magic...

Her awareness of outside emotion, her connection to the dance of the elements all around her...

It was...gone.

This wasn't the quiet that came from using her mental shields. This was an absence of clairsentience altogether. A rent in her very identity. Frenzied grief rattled her bones, sent her head spinning, lungs tightening, tears springing to her eyes...

"Is this entirely necessary?" Etrix said, striding up to Fanon. With hollow awareness, Cora realized the translation enchantment remained in place. It seemed the strange collar only affected her own use of magic. She cast a glance at Valorre, tried with all her might to convey some silent thought to him.

She didn't know if it worked. Didn't know if he understood the words she couldn't form.

Then she heard a subtle, *I'm here.*

It was simple. Stilted. It reminded her of how they'd begun to communicate when they'd first met. Perhaps their connection was weak when only one of them could use their magic. At least they could converse at all.

Etrix spoke again. "She said she isn't a worldwalker. Even if she was, no worldwalker can move through the Veil. She can't leave, with or without the collar."

"We don't know that," Fanon said, his cruel gaze still on Cora. "The Veil was woven to keep a worldwalker from entering our world; one could still worldwalk out. Besides, if the Veil is torn, who knows what a worldwalker can do? I won't risk letting her escape until we've sorted out the truth."

With that, he turned his back on her and began walking away. He was no more than a few steps ahead before Cora found herself pulled forward by that unseen force. She stumbled to keep her feet beneath her, and when she finally managed to match the pace she was being dragged at, it was too fast. Or was she simply too drained? Too broken in the wake of her stolen magic?

Valorre trotted beside her. Though he too moved against his will, his presence provided some semblance of comfort.

"I'm sorry," Etrix said, keeping pace at her side, "about the collar. I know it hurts, but it's a necessary precaution."

The physical pain she felt biting into the sides of her neck was nothing compared to the absence of her magic. "Where are you taking me?"

"To the Veil," Garot said, grinning over his shoulder like the situation was nothing more than run-of-the-mill amusement to him. He outpaced Fanon and paused at the edge of the meadow. He made a complex gesture with both hands, and the landscape turned to a swirling vortex of green and brown that opened into some sort of tunnel. It was just like what the three males had emerged from when they'd first appeared. Fanon strode straight into it, while Garot waited at its entrance for Cora and Etrix to bypass him.

"Don't worry," Etrix said as they approached the unsettling whirl of color. "So long as you aren't a worldwalker, you have nothing to fear from us."

Cora pursed her lips. She wasn't certain what a worldwalker was, but she could guess. It was a type of human they abhorred, someone who could enter their world at will.

She shuddered.

What if she *did* have something to fear?

What if a worldwalker was exactly what she was?

44

Dawn had risen while Teryn had been watching Emylia's memories. Now morning light streamed through the windows into the halls of Ridine, bathing the flagstones in pink and gold. It would have been a beautiful morning were it not for Teryn's dread. And the fact that he was a disembodied spirit, of course, but that was hardly novel anymore. His feeling of unease grew with every step Morkai took down the quiet halls, mostly empty save for the servants who were already busy at work. The servants bowed when they saw Morkai, recognizing him as Prince Teryn, and Morkai gave them all friendly smiles.

It was his smile—his overly calm demeanor—that chilled Teryn the most.

Having projected their etheras outside the crystal, Teryn and Emylia followed in the sorcerer's wake. Teryn had expected an air of frantic urgency to surround Morkai after having lost the most vital piece of his plan. Instead, Morkai walked with poise. Purpose. Fearlessness.

If that wasn't unsettling enough, the streaks of white running through Morkai's hair—*Teryn's* hair—sent a splinter of panic through him. He hardly dared look too long at the deepening hollows in his cheeks, the purple rimming his eyes. Emylia had warned him that his body hadn't responded well to his fight with Morkai for control. His only solace was that anyone who got close enough to the sorcerer would surely notice these things. The servants hadn't acted like anything was amiss, but they were trained to be polite. Anyone else, though...Master Arther, Mareleau...*someone* would notice there was something seriously wrong with the man pretending to be Teryn. Right?

Finally, Morkai came to the closed door of the king's study. Teryn had been there before. He'd met with Morkai there after the duke had captured Cora and hauled her to Ridine under the pretense of returning her to her place as princess.

That was before Teryn had fully understood what was happening at Ridine. Even then, he'd regretted his betrayal. Hated the duke.

Morkai opened the door to reveal Lord Kevan behind the king's desk, brow furrowed as he read over what appeared to be a contract. At his side stood Lord Ulrich, expression somehow both bored and smug at the same time. Morkai closed the door behind him and approached the desk. Emylia went to the window behind Kevan and stared outside at the blushing sunrise, a note of longing in her face, as if she remained haunted by the memories she'd shown him. Teryn took up post beside the desk where he could see all three men clearly.

Kevan glanced up from the contract. His eyes went wide as they darted up to the top of Morkai's head. "What the seven devils happened to your hair?"

Teryn's pulse quickened. *There.* Someone did notice.

Ulrich huffed a laugh. "Have you slept, Highness? Or were you kept up with premarital jitters?"

Morkai simply smirked at the questions as he lowered himself into a chair at the other side of the desk. "What, you don't like my natural color? Not all of us are skilled at maintaining the façades of ink and dyes." He winked at Ulrich, whose dark bowl cut glittered with gray at the roots. "Perhaps I got tired of hiding. I think it's time we all show candor, don't you?"

Kevan returned his gaze to the contract, already disinterested in the man he thought was Teryn. "Where is Princess Aveline, Highness? The Godspriest will be here any moment. You and the princess—well, I suppose I should call her queen—must sign your marriage contract at once."

Morkai leaned back in his chair, one ankle crossed over his knee, hands interlaced at his waist. It was very much the duke's posture and not Teryn's. "I've already sent a message informing the Godspriest we'll have no need for him this morning."

Kevan's eyes bulged as he looked up from the contract once more. "Why the seven devils—"

"Aveline is gone."

Silence fell over the room. Emylia slowly turned from the window to watch what would happen next.

Ulrich cleared his throat, breaking the quiet. "What do you mean she's gone?"

"She ran away in the middle of the night."

Kevan stood in a rush. "Excuse me?"

"I don't know what drove her away. Perhaps the pressures of the crown were too much for her."

Kevan burned him with a scowl. "Do you jest, Highness?"

Morkai met his stare without falter. "No."

"Verdian will be here within days for the signing of the pact," Kevan said through his teeth. "He entrusted Khero to us. If he sees the kingdom has fallen apart under our watch, he'll—"

"He'll what?" Morkai let out a dark chuckle. "You're councilmen of Khero now. Verdian has no power here."

"On the contrary, Highness, Verdian can usurp Khero in the blink of an eye. That was implied from the start when he and Dimetreus negotiated his and Aveline's freedom."

"Then shouldn't he be grateful to you? Or am I to believe he was being generous in staking such a firm claim on this kingdom? If anything, it seems like he wanted Dimetreus' regime to fail, and the two of you along with it."

Kevan's face burned red, lips pursed tight.

Ulrich took a step forward, teeth bared. "Watch how you speak about King Verdian, Highness."

Morkai shrugged. "I speak only the truth, and I'm going to speak true now. Verdian was right to suspect Princess Aveline and King Dimetreus as incapable of ruling Khero. Dimetreus is a madman and Aveline is both too soft and too volatile for the pressures of the crown."

"That we can agree on," Kevan bit out.

"Which is why," Morkai said, "you should name me King of Khero."

Teryn and Emylia exchanged a startled glance.

Kevan and Ulrich seemed equally as perplexed. "Why the seven devils would we do that?" Ulrich said with a disbelieving laugh.

Morkai slowly rose from his chair and stood before the desk. "Before Dimetreus had his mental fit and tried to kill me, we'd had a candid conversation. He'd confessed that I was just as much his heir as Aveline. And we all know that Aveline's ascension to the throne was entirely dependent upon her marrying me."

Kevan planted his hands on the surface of the desk. He clearly meant to appear intimidating, but with Morkai standing at Teryn's body's full height, the lord seemed more meek than threatening. Especially with how Morkai stared down his nose at the man. "You have no claim to Khero aside from being king consort," Kevan said. "A title which is invalid without the princess."

"And what right does Verdian have?" Morkai shook his head. "You may think I'm out of line for speaking against your dear brother, but we can at least agree that his motives were hardly genuine when he appointed the two of you here."

Kevan said nothing, but Ulrich asked. "How so?"

Morkai spoke with practiced ease. "You went from the heads of Verdian's council in Selay to the heads of council in Khero. I'm sure you were promised new lands and titles upon the signing of the peace treaty, and it seems a lateral move in terms of position. But we know the truth. Verdian's real aim was to get you out of Selay to strengthen his daughter's position as heir. A position she should no longer have now that she's married into a new kingdom. He isn't satisfied with her being Queen of Menah through marriage. No, he wants her to inherit Selay too. Wants to see two kingdoms join as one."

The red seeped from Kevan's face. He maintained his position with his palms on the desk, but Teryn could see the sudden interest that flashed in the man's blue eyes.

Morkai spoke again. "You should be princes, both of you. At the very least, you should be Verdian's heirs. Instead, he's brought you here. And, like you'd begun to suggest, he'll blame you for Khero's current state, for its crazed king and missing princess. If you lose your positions on this council, you know he won't welcome you back onto his. Your places have already been filled. And if he does decide to usurp Khero, he won't keep the two of you in power. He'll only be adding yet another kingdom to his reign. A reign his daughter will inherit."

"You don't know what you're talking about," Kevan said, but his tone held little conviction. "Half of what you say is considered treason."

"Like I said, I speak only truth. Let us not pretend otherwise."

"So you think we should back you as king instead," Ulrich said. His tone was brimming with disbelief, but his eyes were keen. Hungry.

"Dimetreus admitted that I am his heir," Morkai said. "Despite Verdian's lack of respect for his brothers, he did give the two of you ultimate power over accepting the line of succession should Dimetreus fail his duties. Back me as king and I'll give you more than land and titles. Kevan, you should be Verdian's heir, plain and simple. Support my claim, and I'll support you as heir to Selay. We'll work it into the negotiations over the treaty. And you, Ulrich, will be named Duke Calloway. You shall inherit the Calloway lands left by the former Duke Morkai."

Ulrich's eyes flashed with greed and a half smile tugged his lips.

Kevan, on the other hand, dropped into his seat and rubbed his thick brown beard. "There's a reason neither of us were named Verdian's heir," he said, tone infused with a hint of indignation. "We have no royal blood. We are unrelated to the former king and are only related to Verdian through our shared mother. She remarried after the death of Verdian's father, and it was his blood that put Verdian on the throne."

Morkai barked a laugh. "They named a bastard a king. If they can do that, then surely a king's brother can be named heir."

Teryn bristled, hands curling into fists.

Kevan scoffed. "You say *they* like you weren't a part of those negotiations. You abdicated your claim and supported your bastard brother."

Teryn watched closely to see if Morkai showed any surprise, any sign that he was caught off guard by what Kevan had said. Morkai may have gleaned much about Cora, Dimetreus, and the current state of political unrest, but he knew little about Teryn's personal matters.

Morkai, however, was unfazed. He turned a calculating grin on the man. "Just like I'm supporting you. If you must know why I refused my birthright, it was because I would have had to marry Verdian's daughter to keep it. I wasn't willing to do that. On the other hand, I was more than happy to wed Aveline, but she's proven to be as weak as her brother. Now I only want what is best for Khero, and I am certain that is me. And what's best for Selay is you, Kevan."

Ulrich stepped closer. "You think we can get Verdian to agree to these terms? He could refuse."

"He won't refuse," Morkai said. "Refusal can lead to war, and you're only asking for what's fair. Besides, you've taken away a portion of his military. The men who serve under your houses fight for *you*, which means they now fight for Khero. He won't want to go up against that."

Kevan narrowed his eyes. "We are not resorting to war with Verdian."

"These negotiations will be friendly, trust me. We'll hold them during a celebration. A hunt. Instead of signing the pact here, we'll solidify the treaty outdoors, where the environment feels neutral. The three of us will stake out a private place to hold our grand hunt, and when Verdian and Larylis arrive, they will meet us there."

Kevan and Ulrich exchanged a weighted look, one that spoke of greed, desperation, and trepidation.

"Is there a reason you're proposing an isolated location for the meeting?" Ulrich said, brow arched.

Morkai lifted his chin. "Should there be?"

Neither man answered. They exchanged another questioning glance, but this time there was no trepidation. Only hunger. Avarice.

Teryn glanced at Emylia. "Is he using magic right now? A...glamour? Like what he did to Dimetreus?"

She shook her head. "He isn't strong enough to create any lasting glamour. Not without a Roizan. All he's doing is playing into their desires."

Teryn shuddered. It was far more unsettling than if he'd been using magic, for this showed exactly what kind of men Kevan and Ulrich were.

"If you'd rather stand opposite me," Morkai said, "by all means say so at once. But I'd rather have your support, Prince Kevan. And yours, Duke Calloway."

Teryn was tempted to hold his breath for their answer, but he forced himself to keep his breathing steady, drawing air evenly into his lungs.

Kevan finally spoke. "Very well, Your Highness—"

"No. I'll need you to address me as Your Majesty now. I will take my place as king from this moment on. We'll keep it between us until after the pact has been signed. For now, it is enough that my heads of council name me king and show obeisance."

Kevan flushed, jaw tense as if he were about to argue.

Ulrich shared no such hesitation. He fell to one knee, head bowed. "My king."

Morkai nodded. "Duke Calloway."

Kevan's eyes were steely, but he bent into a stiff bow. "Your Majesty, King Teryn."

"Thank you for your support, Prince Kevan." With that, Morkai exited the study, a figurative crown upon his brow. One he'd managed to claim without magic. Without war.

The prophetic words Emylia had spoken in her memory echoed through his head.

To gain the power of the Morkaius, one must first become King of Magic, a crown given, not taken...

The prophecy had said nothing about official coronations or ceremonies. Had given no other stipulations. Which likely meant all Morkai needed was the outward acknowledgment of those qualified to give it. Based on the alliance terms Dimetreus had accepted, Kevan and Ulrich were qualified.

Morkai—with Teryn's name and body—was King of Khero.

The sorcerer had only two crowns left to earn, and he'd make his move during this hunt he'd concocted for the signing of the pact. Teryn couldn't imagine how the sorcerer would succeed without using force that would be considered *taking*, but after what he'd just witnessed, he harbored no hope that Morkai didn't already have a plan.

45

Cora thought she might retch if she was forced to endure the swirling colors of the tunnel much longer. Green, blue, gold, and brown, along with the occasional brighter hue, whirled before her in a horizontal vortex as far as she could see. It looked as if the landscape and sky had warped and spun to form this strange passage. The sensation it created was like riding through the forest at a breakneck pace but significantly more disorienting. While the ground felt smooth and steady beneath her feet, she almost lost her balance several times. With her arms pinned to her sides, she couldn't use them for stability. Instead, the only thing keeping her from falling was the invisible tug that forced her to follow in Fanon's wake.

Cora was about to send a volley of curses at the Elvyn male's back, demanding he slow down or free her from this nauseating place, when the tunnel ceased spinning. The greens and browns spread out like a wave from her feet while the blues and golds formed the sky overhead. They were in a dense forest, the mossy floor the brightest shade of emerald. The tree trunks were thicker than any Cora had seen, their branches towering high overhead. Some held clusters of glowing pink or white mushrooms that were nearly as large as she was, while unfamiliar birdsong filled the air. Tiny insects with jeweled wings flitted in clusters here and there, but none came close enough for Cora to get a good look. Were they pixies? She would have been enchanted by the stunning environment were it not for the current situation. The pain of the collar piercing her neck. The void she felt without her magic.

Fanon rushed on ahead, giving Cora and Valorre no time to adjust to the sudden change of terrain. His magical tether tugged them along, and now Cora had plenty of obstacles to avoid tripping over.

"Fanon," Etrix called, still beside her. "Release the human and unicorn. Let them proceed at their own pace."

"If the Veil is torn, we don't have time to dally," Fanon said.

Yet, despite his words, Cora felt that tug disappear. Though her arms were still pinned, she no longer felt as if she were being dragged. She paused to regain her equilibrium, but she managed only a single breath of relief before the tug returned. She was forced to step forward. This time the pressure disappeared as soon as she began walking on her own. Fanon's unspoken threat was clear: stop walking and he'd resort to dragging her again.

That made any chance of running away impossible. Besides, where would she go? She needed to get back home. Find the Forest People. Return to Ridine. Save Teryn from Morkai. To do any of that, she needed to astral travel. Needed her magic back. Needed to free her arms and get this damn collar off her neck.

She glanced at Etrix, careful not to angle her head too far to the side. Any drastic motion sent a renewed sting of pain where the collar dug into her flesh. At least she felt no trickle of warm blood, which told her the wounds weren't too deep. The Elvyn met her gaze with a tense smile. Whether he kept close to her out of care or caution, she wasn't sure. All she knew was that, so far, he was the only one of the three who'd shown her an ounce of concern. Perhaps he'd help her. First, she needed to better understand her situation.

"What is the Veil?" she asked.

He narrowed his eyes. "You confessed that you entered through the Veil. If that's the case, how do you not know what it is?"

Her mind raced, but she found her answer easily. Keeping secrets and telling lies to cover them was as familiar to her as her own skin. "I know I came through the Veil, but I don't understand what exactly it is."

"You're asking about the Veil?" Cora was startled to find Garot suddenly between her and Valorre. Before now, he'd been walking behind them.

"Garot," Etrix said with the same warning tone he'd used on Fanon.

Garot shrugged. "What? She's clearly not dangerous."

"We've yet to establish—"

"The Veil is like a curtain between your world and ours," Garot said, a smile stretching over his round face. His tone had taken on a whimsical quality, like a bard telling a tale.

That explanation did very little to clarify anything for Cora, but it sounded like a way back to her world. If she couldn't use her magic, then perhaps she and Valorre could escape through the Veil—

Wait. Would Valorre even want to return with her? Her eyes flicked to him, trotting on the other side of Garot. This was his true home. The place he'd come from.

I stay with you, Valorre conveyed in that same clipped style of communication as before. She wondered if it was his magic or the translation enchantment that allowed their connection to remain. It didn't seem like he could speak to the three Elvyn, and they hadn't bothered to address him when they'd inquired about him having come from her world. Once again, her connection with Valorre defied reason. Well, all but one.

The witches amongst the Forest People had kept pets now and then, and some had even claimed an animal as their familiar. She'd always scoffed at the claim. To her, it was another unimpressive quiet magic she hadn't put much value in. But she valued quiet magic now. Very much so.

Which made her wonder...was Valorre her familiar?

You are my home, he said, and she didn't need her magic to glean his conviction. *This is no more home. Sorry I brought us.*

Her heart warmed and broke all at once. *Are you in danger here? Is that why you left?*

Don't remember.

"I'm sorry I couldn't take us any farther by Path," Garot said, stealing her attention. "My *mora* is weaker once the Blight begins, which is why we're proceeding by foot."

Several words stuck out to her. *By Path. The Blight.* But one lingered in her awareness. No, it was...two. When he'd said *mora,* she'd heard two words at once: *mora* and *magic.* His mouth had formed an *O* to suggest the former had been in his language and the latter had been the translation. That was the first time she'd heard two words simultaneously. Did that mean...she *sort of* knew the word in its native tongue?

Insigmora.

Morkai.

Morkaius.

All those words contained *mor* or *mora* in some form, and they'd all come from the fae language, as far as she knew. She recalled that *Morkai* meant *King of Magic* and *Morkaius* meant *High King of Magic.* She'd never been told there was any translation for *insigmora,* but now she understood what part of it meant. Of course her tattoos were named for magic.

Now for her remaining questions. "What did you mean *by Path*? Was that the tunnel we walked through?"

Garot puffed out his chest with a proud nod. "I'm a pathweaver. I can navigate vast distances in a short time by weaving a portal."

Her next question was on the tip of her tongue. She hesitated before speaking, ensuring her tone came out as nonchalant as she could manage. Anxiety still crawled up her throat while grief at losing her magic weighed heavy on her shoulders, but the hope of returning home once she reached this Veil helped her keep her composure. Or at least pretend to. "If I'm unable to return home through the Veil, could you take me by Path—"

"No," Garot said, his grin disappearing. He glanced at Fanon, still leading their party from far up ahead, and lowered his voice. "Traversing worlds is something only a worldwalker can do. And worldwalking is a repulsive, invasive magic."

Damn it. She supposed there was no point appealing to his carefree nature in hopes that he might offer her aid. Still, she appreciated that he was at least answering her questions. "What is *the Blight*?"

"Did you not see it when you entered?" Etrix said from her other side. Though she'd first deemed him the kindest of the three, she was starting to realize he was the keenest too. "If you entered through the Veil, you would have seen it."

"I was asleep on Valorre's back," she rushed to say. "I didn't realize what had happened until I'd woken up and found us in the meadow. That was when Valorre told me he'd accidentally taken me home by crossing the Veil."

He studied her for several beats too long.

"You'll see the Blight for yourself soon enough," Garot said, pointing a finger straight ahead. "We're almost there."

Cora followed his line of sight to where the forest was beginning to thin. Thick tree trunks gave way to slim saplings, then disappeared into a gray fog. Where she stood now, a blue sky shone above the towering canopy of leaves, the sun comfortably warm, but at the edge of the woods, it almost looked like winter lay ahead. As they drew closer, Cora grew more unsettled. The saplings weren't simply small. They were frail. Decaying. And the forest didn't end in a fog; it lost color. Vibrancy. Life.

They emerged from the line of trees and stepped onto a gray path. From here on, there was no more mossy earth or glowing mushrooms. No more birdsong. No insects or pixies. The sky and golden sun were the only sources of color, and they did nothing to brighten the rotting landscape that stretched as far as Cora could see. The smell of rot filled her nostrils, making her wish her arms were free of their invisible restraints, if only to allow her to cover her nose and mouth.

She glanced at Garot. "This is the Blight?"

He gave her a somber nod. "It stretches all around the Veil and spreads farther into El'Ara daily."

A dark shadow passed overhead, blotting out the sun and casting them in momentary darkness. She froze, turning her eyes to the sky. An enormous beast with a long, sinuous body and a wide expanse of wings flew above them. It let out an ear-splitting screech that had Cora's shoulders shooting toward her ears. That, in turn, shifted her collar, causing its sharp tines to tear at her pierced flesh. She forced her shoulders to relax, eyes locked on the flying beast. In a matter of seconds it was far ahead, leaving Cora trembling with awed terror.

Mother Goddess, that was a…a dragon.

Don't like those, Valorre said. *I remember that.*

Did they create this? The Blight? Based on the faerytales Cora had grown up with, she knew dragons could wield flame. That could explain why the land was suddenly devoid of color. Perhaps it had been burned.

Don't think so, Valorre said. *But don't remember.*

Cora cast her gaze back to the path ahead and found Fanon striding on with his hurried pace as if the dragon were no concern. Garot trailed behind him, his steps somewhat less buoyant than before. Only Etrix remained at her side, watching the tiny speck that was the dragon until it was gone entirely.

"I thought perhaps she would come for the unicorn," he said.

"She?"

"Ferrah. The dragon. She's been seen chasing unicorns, especially any wandering through the Blight."

"Why?"

"We aren't certain. The dragons have been restless for months."

Do not like, Valorre said.

Etrix gestured for her and Valorre to proceed. Before she had to suffer one of

Fanon's irritating tugs, she started walking again. She kept her eyes on the sky for several moments, worried the dragon might come back. She had no desire to find out what the creatures did to the unicorns they chased. When she saw no sign of its return, she dropped her gaze to the gray landscape. A wash of color and movement caught her eye.

Half hidden behind a patch of gnarled stumps was a cluster of humanoid figures. They crouched on the ground, palms pressed flat to the colorless earth. They were petite in stature with pointed ears, their skin in every shade of brown and tan, their hair and clothing in the richest earth tones. One was a male with long hair as black as midnight and a tunic of woven moss. Another had hair and eyes in shades of rich green, her leather dress adorned with sparkling beads of morning dew. The nearest figure, a male with hair made from autumn-colored leaves, lifted wide gray eyes to watch them pass. That was when Cora glimpsed the black patterns marking his arms and neck. In fact, all the figures bore such markings on every inch of skin not hidden by clothing. The symbols were more intricate than her own tattoos, but she recognized the *insigmora.*

"Faeryn," Cora said.

"They try to heal the Blight," Etrix said, "but their use of *mora* does little to help. They merely manage to slow the Blight's inevitable course."

"What is the Blight from?"

"The Veil," Etrix said and nothing more. She almost wished Garot was nearby again, for maybe he'd have given a more substantial answer.

She couldn't take her eyes off the Faeryn as they walked by. Unlike the Elvyn, whom she knew little about, she'd heard so much about the Faeryn from the Forest People. The commune's very way of life was dedicated to preserving the Faeryn's ancient ways, their traditions, their harmony with nature. In a way, these figures were like family to her. Not by blood, of course, but an unseen bond.

A sudden spark of hope ignited in her chest. Perhaps if she ran to them, showed them her *insigmora*, and implored them for help, they'd free her from her captors. But as each turned to watch her pass, she caught the ice in their collective gaze, the curl of their lips as they studied her human form. It was enough to tell her they thought no better of her than Fanon did, regardless of the markings on her arms.

She cursed under her breath. It was clear she'd find no allies here, in this realm where humans were feared. Hated. She couldn't fully rely on her own knowledge of the fae either, for the stories the Forest People had told were obviously wrong. The fae weren't extinct. The Elvyn and Faeryn hadn't killed each other in a war five hundred years ago. They were *here.* Alive. Just in another realm.

She could only rely on herself and Valorre, and their primary hope was to get to the Veil and pray to the Mother Goddess there really was a way to cross through.

Only then could she get back home and find some way to save Teryn—and her world—from Morkai.

46

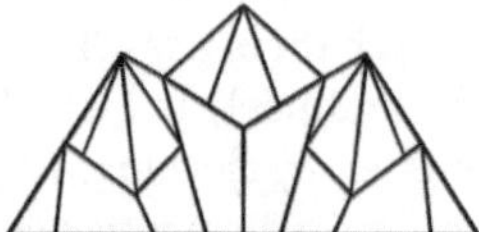

After Morkai left the king's study, Teryn rested his ethera. He had no desire to add more strain to his already failing body. But as soon as he awoke, drifting from his state of floating unconsciousness to bright awareness, he had but one thought. One need.

He opened his eyes and found himself in the illusion of Emylia's temple bedroom. She sat cross-legged at his side, expression resigned as if she knew exactly what he was going to say.

"Show me the rest of your memories."

With a trembling sigh, she nodded.

They rose to their feet. Emylia lifted her hand, and a fog rolled in, covering the floor, walls, and ceiling. When it dispersed, it left behind the muted tones of Desmond's dark room at the inn. Teryn and Emylia stood at the far end while two figures sat at opposite sides of the small desk.

"Are you ready?" the Emylia of memory asked, an edge of excitement in her voice. "We're getting so close, Des. I can feel it."

Desmond nodded, but his expression held a hint of apprehension. "This is our last session before I return home to Syrus to report to my father. I hope what we've learned is enough for him."

"How could it not be? We've done so much work on his behalf, more than he's ever been able to do on his own, right?"

His lips quirked up at one corner. "When did you become such an optimist?"

"Only when it comes to you," she said with a wide smile.

His face fell, voice deepening into a whisper. "I don't know how long I'll be gone, Em. I hate not knowing when I'll be back."

Her smile remained, but it no longer reached her eyes. "Then let's hurry. I don't want to spend our last night together working."

He nodded and anxiously ran his palms over his thighs while Emylia closed her eyes. Desmond kept his voice low and steady. "Where is the mother of the true Morkara now?"

Teryn's breath caught, knowing this man was asking about Cora. The woman he loved.

Emylia, crystal in hand, remained still while her eyelids fluttered. "Unborn."

"When will she be born?"

"The year of the Great Bear."

Teryn was startled to realize how long ago this memory must have been from.

Desmond rubbed his dark brows. "That could be three years from now, thirteen, twenty-three, or more. How many years from now will she be born?"

Emylia remained silent.

Desmond released a frustrated groan. "Fine. What will she look like?"

Again, silence.

He ran his hand through his black hair, sending wayward strands into his pale eyes. His expression brightened. "Wait. She is said to have the beauty of Satsara. What does Satsara look like?"

Emylia tilted her head to show her disbelief. "Just because the mother has the beauty of Satsara doesn't mean they'll look exactly the same. Besides, we don't even know who she is. Every time I've channeled for information on her or Ailan, I get nothing."

"Just try anyway. It could be a helpful clue."

Emylia wore a skeptical frown, but she settled back into her trance. Soon her eyes began to dart behind her closed lids. "I see her," she whispered. "At least...I think I do. She's...beautiful."

"And?" Desmond leaned closer to the desk. "What does she look like?"

"Eyes and hair as black as a raven's wing. Golden skin. She's tall. Slim but powerful. Pointed ears. Mother Goddess, Des! She's Elvyn. A true, beautiful Elvyn." Her voice was rich with awe. "I can't believe I'm seeing one."

Desmond's face melted as he watched her. "She can't be any more stunning than you."

She slowly fluttered her lashes open. "How am I supposed to get any work done when you compliment me like that?"

Desmond rounded the desk and pulled her from her seat. He brushed his hand along her cheek. "We've worked enough. Let's make the rest of tonight about us."

Emylia flung her arms around his neck and they dissolved into tangled limbs and heated kisses.

The true Emylia waved her hand, and the image was swept away in a blanket of fog. When it settled, Teryn found himself on the moonlit cobblestone street outside the inn. The Emylia of memory sprinted past sleeping storefronts, her dark hair flying wild in a mass of bouncing curls. She looked the same age as the true Emylia did now—a year or two older than she'd been in the previous memory. As she reached the door to the inn, she pulled up short. A figure stood just outside the door, back facing her, a long cloak hiding their form. Then the figure turned and revealed Desmond's face beneath the hood. He ran to her and gathered her into his arms.

"I missed you so much," Emylia said, a wide smile stretching her lips. She lifted her eyes to his vacant expression, the sorrow tugging his lips. Her face fell. "What's wrong?"

Desmond took her by the hand and led her inside the inn. They bypassed the dining room and wove through a narrow hall until they arrived at the same small room as before. "Father lied to me," he said as he ushered her inside and closed the door behind them.

The Emylia of memory wrung her hands. Even Teryn could tell this wasn't the reunion she'd been expecting. "About what?"

Desmond unclasped his cloak and tossed it onto the cot. He was dressed in dark slacks and a long black coat buttoned high to his neck. His hair was longer now, reaching several inches past his shoulders, and his cheekbones were sharper. He began to pace the room, hardly sparing Emylia a glance. "He can't bring my mother back, even if he becomes Morkaius. He doesn't have her ethera."

Emylia tilted her head. "Her ethera? Why would he have her ethera in the first place?"

"I've been reading about the magic of the sanguina and ethera, trying to figure out what Father would need to bring my mother back. While there is no clear formula, I do know he would need her ethera. When I asked him about it, he tried to brush me off. But I asked and asked until he told me the truth." He halted his pacing and met her eyes. "He lied to me. He never planned on bringing my mother back when he became Morkaius. He's been using that story this entire time. Using me to find answers to *his* questions, to override the curse that makes him forget his past."

With slow steps, she approached him. "Des, I'm so sorry. I...I did warn you that it wasn't possible—"

His gaze deepened into a glare, but it quickly softened. He closed the remaining distance between them and embraced her. She rested her cheek against his chest, her head tucked beneath his chin. "Yes, you're right, my love. You warned me."

She pulled away just enough to meet his eyes. "What did he say about the information you've gathered for him?"

His jaw shifted side to side. "He said it isn't enough. He told me I have to keep looking until I find the Heart of El'Ara."

"Are you still going to help him, even though you know he lied?"

Desmond shrugged. "I don't know what else to do. He's my father, and this is a matter of his birthright. A birthright that will one day be passed on to me. He can't claim it without me. Not only has he been cursed to forget, but he is physically weak. He can't leave Syrus the way I can, not until he has a clear destination. And that destination is the Heart of El'Ara. Wherever the hell that is, with its black mountain and violet fields. Have you found this place for me yet?"

She shook her head. "I've read up on flower varieties specific to different regions, unique mountain ranges. I've asked foreign visitors. There are several possibilities, but nothing certain."

He closed his eyes, his frustration made clear in the tense line of his jaw.

"I'm sorry, Des. I'll keep trying. You know I'll do anything for you. And if you're determined to continue serving your father, I'll help. Always."

Teryn tried not to wince at the desperation in her tone. How was she so enamored with the man that she didn't see the darkness lurking in his eyes? The very real threat his quest posed? Teryn had seen love make a fool of his father, nearly tearing his country in two, and he'd given up a crown for the love of his brother and for Cora. But this...this was something else. Everything inside Teryn blared with warning.

The real Emylia stared at the floor, a hint of shame coloring her expression. She met his eyes for a moment, nodding as if to confirm his thoughts. That she too regretted this part of her past.

"Is that a promise?" Desmond said, drawing Teryn's attention back to the figures of the memory. He clutched Emylia's cheeks between his palms. "Will you do anything for me?"

Her throat bobbed, but she said, "Anything."

The image faded, then shifted. The two figures were now sitting at the desk on opposite sides. Emylia held her crystal like she always did when preparing to use her sight. Closing her eyes, she said, "What would you like to ask this time, Des?"

His voice came out cold. Firm. "Find my mother."

47

Her eyes flew open at once. "What?"

"I need you to channel my mother's ethera."

She shook her head. "I'm a seer, not a medium. I don't commune with the dead."

"If you can see her, you can draw her forth. I told you; I've been reading about the Art of the ethera and sanguina. I've studied your Art too. You can use the sight to channel my mother."

"Des..."

"You're powerful enough to do this. I know you are. If I'm not going to see her again like Father promised, then I must at least speak to her." He paused, then added, "You said you'd do anything for me."

Emylia pursed her lips, and for a moment Teryn thought she might refuse. Then her expression softened. Her voice came out small. "I'll try."

"Thank you," Desmond said. "Please find her. The spirit of Morgana Solaria."

Her eyes widened. "Morgana Solaria," she echoed. "The Queen of Syrus? You... You're..."

"Prince Desmond Solaria. Son of King Darius Solaria."

A look of hurt crossed her face. "Why didn't you tell me?"

"You loved me for me. I wanted *someone* to love me as I am. For once." Emylia stared back at him, brow furrowed. A tic formed at the corner of Desmond's jaw. "Besides, Father always told me being a royal of this world was nothing when we were the true monarchs of the fae. Now will you find her or not?"

She gave him a curt nod and settled into her meditation.

The room fell under a tense silence as seconds ticked past. Then minutes.

Desmond remained in place at the other side of the desk, hands perched upon his knees. The only sign of his anxiety was the slight jitter of his leg.

"I see her," Emylia whispered.

Desmond sat upright, posture rigid. "You...you do?"

"Yes," she said with a smile. "She looks just like you."

"Make eye contact. Draw her to you."

"I...I don't know—"

"Do it."

Emylia returned to silence. Then, "I made eye contact. She...she doesn't look happy."

"Draw her soul to yours. See yourself connecting with her mind. When she's close, touch her ethera."

Emylia trembled from head to toe. "She...she doesn't want me to touch her."

"Do it, Emylia," Desmond growled. "Do it now."

Emylia let out a strangled cry, then her eyes shot open. Rage darkened her expression. "Desmond," she said, but her voice sounded wrong. Too deep. Too lilting. "What have you done?"

Desmond clasped a hand over his mouth, his expression twisted with emotion. His throat bobbed. Once. Twice. Finally, he lowered his hand and approached Emylia. "I wanted to hear your voice again, Mother. I miss you so much."

His mother's voice hesitated before it emerged from Emylia's mouth again. "I missed you too, my darling, but this isn't right. You should leave me at peace."

"I want you to come back."

"That isn't possible."

"What if it is?" With slow, deliberate movements, Desmond leaned forward. One palm covered Emylia's hands and the crystal within. The other reached for the collar of his jacket and began to loosen the buttons, one at a time.

"What are you doing, Desmond?" his mother's voice asked.

"I want you back, and I'm willing to sacrifice half my heart to get it." He now had the top of his coat unbuttoned. He pulled it back to reveal a strange marking on the white shirt he wore beneath it. It was a complex pattern drawn over his sternum, illustrated with a dark ink Teryn suspected was blood.

"No!" his mother's voice shouted, erupting from Emylia's lips. A cyclone of air spiraled around Emylia, blowing the seer's hair back and sending papers soaring off the desk. "I don't want to come back! Leave me at peace!"

"No, Mother," Desmond said calmly as he lifted Emylia's hands and brought them toward the marking on his shirt. "I need you."

The wind increased, and Desmond struggled to bring her hands the rest of the way to his chest. The lanterns lighting the room flared in a roar of fire, casting it in an orange glow. Emylia's face angled up at Desmond, her lips peeled back from her teeth. "Let. Me. Go."

Teryn wasn't sure whose voice spoke then, for it seemed both Emylia and Desmond's mother cried out in tandem.

Desmond's eyes went wide as he looked down at Emylia, at her twisted expression. He seemed to falter, and the cyclone of wind increased. Desmond stumbled back, breaking contact with Emylia's hands. She, in turn, dropped the crystal and tumbled from her chair.

In the next moment, the wind was gone, the lanterns extinguished save for one. Teryn blinked to adjust to the shift in light.

"Why, Mother?" came Desmond's trembling voice. He stared at the ceiling, blinking back tears, shoulders slumped. "Why didn't you want to come back? Is your love for me so weak?"

Only silence answered.

With a heavy sigh, he lowered his gaze. Teryn saw the motionless heap on the floor before Desmond did.

"Emylia!" Desmond called out, rushing to her side. She was sprawled beside her chair, lips pale, face coated in a sheen of sweat. Her crystal lay a foot away from her empty palm. He fell onto the floor and pulled her into his lap. "Say something. Please!"

She mumbled incoherently as blood trickled from her nose.

"No, please no." He rocked her in his lap, tears streaming from his eyes. "I'm so sorry. Forgive me, Em. I did this. I didn't know this would happen."

"Des," she said, voice weak. She lifted a hand toward his cheek but dropped it before it could make contact. Her face went slack, body limp. Fresh blood trickled over her lips, her chin.

Desmond stared down at her, eyes wide with terror. "No, no, no. Emylia!"

She was silent. Still.

A sob broke from Desmond's throat. He pressed his hands to her cheeks, her neck, her wrist, hands trembling with every move. As he released her wrist, his eyes fell on what lay discarded beside her. The crystal. His trembling ceased. With a chilling calm, he grabbed the amber stone. Then, folding her limp fingers around it, he pressed it to his chest, directly over the blood marking his shirt. As soon as the crystal made contact, Desmond heaved forward with an agonized grunt. He stayed like that for several moments, eyes pinched tight. Then his face relaxed. Slowly, he let Emylia's hand slide from around the crystal, from his chest, to the ground.

He cradled the crystal to him. "I'll make this right, Em," he whispered. "I'll bring you back. I've given up half my heart to do so. It belongs to you now."

He crouched beside Emylia's lifeless body and caressed her brow. "Forget my father. Let him stay cursed." He brought his lips close to her ear. "I'll find the Heart of El'Ara myself. I'll find the mother and make sure she never bears this true Morkara. Then when I am Morkaius, I'll find you a new body and we will rule together."

Teryn felt colder than he ever had before. He no longer held any doubt about who Desmond was. He wasn't Morkai's son, but the sorcerer himself. And he'd trapped Emylia in the crystal out of a dark and treacherous love.

Teryn slowly turned to face her and noted her pursed lips, her empty eyes. "He didn't wait until he was Morkaius," she said, voice hollow.

She waved her hand, and their surroundings shifted. Teryn found himself in a candlelit bedroom he'd never seen before. From the gilded portraits lining the walls and the elegant furnishings, Teryn guessed it was inside a palace or manor. The only thing that belied the room's grandeur was the table that stood at the far end of the room, its surface littered with books, vials, and stacks of paper. It reminded Teryn of the contents in the tower library.

Beside a large four-poster bed stood Morkai—and this time Teryn could see all the signs that he was a slightly older version of Desmond. He had the same ageless grace that the former duke had when he'd been alive, but the tender sorrow he'd glimpsed in the younger man's eyes too. He stared down at the bed. Or, more accurately, the female body that laid upon it.

She was slim with hollow cheeks and black hair streaked with silver. Morkai trembled. "We'll try again, Em."

The image stilled, then shifted. The room stayed the same but there was a new body on the bed. Another young woman. This one thrashed and cried as blood streamed from her eyes and nose. With a sudden lurch, she went still. Morkai threw his head back. "We'll try again."

Another image.

Another body.

Another.

Another.

Teryn watched the images flash before him, each one more gruesome, more heartbreaking, than the last.

Emylia waved a hand and the final scene froze. "Morkai knew there was no hope until he had the power of the Morkaius. Too late, he'd learned that to bring an ethera back to life in another's body, one needed blood from the original body. By now, my body was long since gone. Still he tried."

Teryn swallowed hard before voicing the question he needed an answer to. "You...you tried to do what Morkai is doing to me, didn't you? That's why you know so much. You've not only been in my position, but Morkai's too; the trapped spirit and the invading entity."

She gave a solemn nod. "For the first few attempts, I participated. I was a willing accomplice in trying to take over another's body. He chose women who were unwell. Women who would have died even without our magical interference. It was a mercy, he'd said. But it was clear that what we were doing wreaked havoc on a victim's body. I stopped participating before he moved on to healthy women. By then, he'd also begun sacrificing lives to extend his own. It wasn't his Elvyn blood that made him ageless, but the forbidden Arts. I realized then that the man I'd loved was gone. My refusal to participate in his efforts to bind me to a body made his attempts even more impossible. Years passed before he gave up altogether. Instead, he poured all his focus into finding the Heart of El'Ara and the mother of the true Morkara. He stopped looking for potential candidates for me. At least, for a while he did..."

She waved a hand, and their surroundings shifted yet again. They were now in the tower library at Ridine, the only light coming from the fire blazing in the hearth. Morkai stood beside one of the two chairs facing the hearth, his cane planted beneath him. Cora stood opposite him, in a puddle of spilled tea and broken porcelain. A tea table lay on its side.

Teryn's heart raced as he strode between them. He knew this was only a memory, but he couldn't help wanting to protect her from him.

Morkai stepped closer just the same. "I can give you half my heart."

"Half your heart?" Cora said with a sneer. "Is that what you consider a proper proposal?"

"The other half doesn't belong to me. But you could. I think my heart would like you. It's a jealous heart, but it could come to understand."

Teryn recalled what Morkai had said when he'd first trapped Emylia inside the crystal. How he'd cried out when he'd brought her hand and the stone to the marking on his shirt.

I'll bring you back. I've given up half my heart to do so. It belongs to you now.

"Working with the ethera takes great sacrifice," Emylia said. "To trap me, he had to sacrifice half of his heart-center—the spiritual aspect of his heart. That's what made him colder. Deadlier."

She waved her hand again, but the scene had only slightly changed. Cora was now doubled over, and a shaft of an arrow was protruding from Morkai's ribs.

"I will give you time to choose me," the sorcerer said. "And you will. You will choose one half of my heart willingly, or you will take the other half unwillingly."

The image froze in place.

"Morkai no longer has even half a heart remaining," Emylia said, "for binding his soul to the crystal with his dying breath stole the second half. He is heartless now, both halves trapped in the very crystal that holds our etheras."

Teryn frowned at her, unsure why she was telling him this. Was she trying to make him understand the sorcerer? Pity him? But a far more pressing realization rose to his mind. "He said if she didn't take half his heart willingly, she'd take his other half unwillingly. Does that mean..."

His mind spun. He couldn't bear to say it out loud.

Emylia did so for him. "Yes. With his goals so close to being realized, he'd chosen his next target. He selected Cora to house my soul. Once he has the power of the Morkaius, he'll do to her what he's trying to do to you. With the power he seeks, Cora won't have a fighting chance."

Rage tore through him, boiling his blood, quickening his pulse. It took all his restraint to steady his breaths. "Tell me the truth, Emylia. What do you want? Whose side are you on?"

"Yours," she said, but her voice was empty. Tired. "I don't want to come back, Teryn. I just want to be at rest."

Teryn studied her for a few silent moments. She'd lied to him. Kept vital facts from him. After what she'd shown him, what she'd confessed to doing, he was even less sure he could trust her than he'd been before.

And yet, she was his only hope. He needed her to unravel the weaving in her memories, seek the pattern Morkai had used to strengthen the crystal's density. Only then did they have any chance of getting free.

Unless...

Had Emylia been telling the truth when she'd said her memory had been too hazy? That she'd been too distant to see the pattern clearly?

She narrowed her eyes, and her expression hardened. "Think what you want of me. Hate me if you must. Distrust me. Just please believe that all I want is to be free from my cage and take the monster who trapped me here with me."

Teryn was taken aback by the sudden ferocity in her tone. The rage that rippled through her, strong enough to match his own.

He gave her a curt nod. "Then we continue with our plan."

"We take him down," she said.

To himself Teryn added, *And protect the woman I love, no matter what it takes.*

48

___

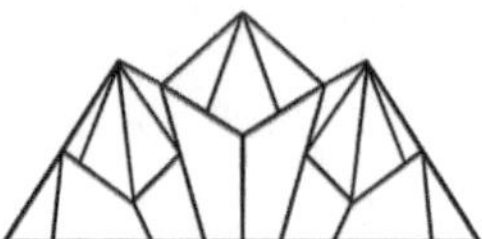

For the first time all day, Mareleau was no longer nauseous. She wanted to believe her calm stomach heralded a finite end to her morning sickness—a misleading term, by the way; she'd thank the seven gods if her roiling gut were relegated to morning—but her relief was likely due to the piece of candied ginger she'd just popped into her mouth. It was a welcome deviation from her constant refills of ginger tea and was all thanks to Ridine's cook. Mareleau had recently learned that if she came to the kitchen to request a refill of her tea in person, the cook would dote on her and hand her a plate of the latest sweet she'd whipped up. The most recent gift being the handkerchief full of candied ginger she now held in her hand.

Mareleau suspected the woman had gleaned the reason behind her constant need for tea, hence the doting. While she'd normally be averse to such babying— she was a queen, after all—she rather liked the woman's attention. And she certainly preferred the candied ginger over the tea.

She meandered away from the kitchen toward the keep but found her feet moving past the correct staircase in favor of a different one. One she'd already visited twice today and was forbade entrance—

She pulled up short once she reached the stairwell in question. It was...empty.

She'd never seen the tower library stairwell unguarded. Not that she'd ever paid much attention to it before this morning. She'd come to call on Princess Aveline, and since the girl hadn't been in her room, she figured she must already be at work in the tower. But when Mareleau inquired with the guard, he'd insisted she wasn't there. Mareleau's anxiety increased after that, right alongside her incessant nausea. She'd been looking for the princess all day to no avail. She tried to tell herself she was simply bored, but after their strangely comforting conversation the day before, she had to admit she wanted to check in on her. Especially since today was the day she and Teryn were to be wed. Had Aveline managed to tell Teryn about the curse? Had she made peace with her sudden marriage? Had their hushed wedding already taken place?

Mareleau knew a thing or two about such matters. Her own wedding had been hurried, but at least she'd been given a feast afterward. Yet it was already nearing sundown and Mareleau hadn't heard a word whispered about the princess' nuptials or her impending rise to queen.

She cast a glance down both ends of the hall, which were empty, and approached the stairwell. A shudder coursed through her as she glanced up the narrow staircase. Her ladies had whispered time and again that this was where Lurel had taken her fall. A pang of grief struck her heart, but she swallowed it down—along with a fresh piece of candied ginger, for good measure. Then, with wary steps, she began to climb.

The door at the top of the stairs was unguarded as well, left open to reveal strands of herbs hanging in the doorway. The waning evening light cast the stairwell in shadow, as well as the room ahead. Perhaps it was only the rumors that sent apprehension crawling up her spine, but whatever it was, it made her want to keep her steps slow. Silent. She lifted her skirts higher, careful not to step on her hem.

She reached the landing and slowly approached the doorway. The scent of rosemary and old smoke wafted into her nostrils. She frowned at the hanging herbs blocking the top of her view and ducked down for a better glimpse of the room. It looked like total chaos, with crowded bookshelves, a cluttered table piled with objects wrapped in cloth, and two large basins beside an empty fireplace. Mareleau had no desire to step inside the room, for she'd surely find herself covered in dust, soot, and whatever the white substance was that lined the threshold. She was about to call out for Aveline when movement caught her eye.

At the far end of the room, near one of the bookcases, a male figure kneeled. She ducked lower, catching sight of brown hair streaked with white, dark trousers, a linen shirt, and a dark blue waistcoat. He was reaching into a hole in the stone floor. She watched as he extracted two small items that looked like glass vials. He pocketed them, then reached for a large object at his side—a square stone—and gingerly set it into the hole. The sound of stone scraping stone set her teeth on edge. When he was done, there was no sign of the hidden compartment.

The man rose to his feet. Mareleau startled and took a step back, reminding herself just in time that she was at the top of a stairwell. She cast a glance behind her and flung out a hand to catch herself against the wall. When she returned her attention to the room, the man was just on the other side of the doorway. But it wasn't just any man. It was Teryn.

Her eyes went wide. "Teryn, your...your hair! What happened?"

"Ah, yes. Everyone wants to know about my hair."

She arched a brow. That did nothing to explain the white streaks. Equally as concerning were the dark circles under his eyes, the pallor of his skin. "Are you unwell?"

"I'm perfectly well, thank you for asking," he said, voice smooth and disinterested. His smile held an edge she didn't understand. Perhaps she wasn't supposed to see him rifling around in here, digging in that hidden hole.

Well, lucky for him, it was Aveline she was concerned with, not him. She couldn't care less about her brother-in-law. Especially if he was going to continue to act so strange. What did Aveline see in him, anyway?

"Where's Aveline?"

He smirked. "You've come to know her on a first-name basis, yet you call her Aveline and not Cora?"

"She hasn't asked me to call her Cora, and I've only decided as of yesterday that I sort of like her." Though now that he mentioned it, she most certainly would start calling her Cora. Even Larylis referred to her as such. And Mareleau was nothing if not at least a little competitive. If anyone would prove to be Aveline's—no, Cora's—closest friend, it would be her. She'd see to it.

But first she had to find the girl.

"So," Mareleau said, giving him a pointed look, "where is she? I've been looking everywhere."

"Why?"

She lifted her hand, showing off the white gold and sapphire bracelet that dangled from her wrist. "I wanted to give her this and tell her she can't keep it."

Teryn gave her a questioning look.

"Something borrowed," she said. "Obviously. It's her wedding day. I thought she could use at least one small tradition." To be honest, the bracelet was merely meant to serve as an excuse to talk to Cora so that she wouldn't have to admit she was concerned for the girl. Mareleau may have decided making friends with someone might not be the worst thing in the world, but she still had her pride.

"Oh, of course," Teryn said.

Yet still he failed to answer her question.

"Are you trying to be evasive or are you just naturally annoying?" she asked, planting her hands on her hips.

Teryn gave her a simpering grin but said nothing.

She pulled her head back. Where was his clever quip? His insult? Mareleau respected people who had the gall to volley her with scalding banter, and if that made her a masochist, so be it. At least she could trust someone who did more than flatter, pander, and praise. Teryn's teasing wit was what had finally endeared him to her, and her unanswered question practically begged for a clever return, but he...said nothing.

Mareleau released an exasperated groan. "Where is she, Teryn? Where the seven devils is Cora?"

He stepped over the threshold to join her on the landing. She descended the next step down to put space between them. "My darling wife will be in seclusion until the signing of the peace pact. We're keeping our marriage a secret for now, and in the meantime, she is taking the time to properly come to terms with her change in status. It's a great responsibility, becoming queen, as you well know."

His words sparked her pride, and she almost answered with an automatic *Of course I know*, but she stopped herself. He still hadn't given her a clear answer.

"She isn't in her room," she said, "and Master Arther claims not to have seen her since last night."

Teryn's mouth tightened, but he quickly donned an easy grin that didn't meet his eyes. "As my wife, she no longer needs to stay in her own room."

She blushed at what he was suggesting, but that didn't change the fact that she'd had Master Arther unlock Teryn's room this morning too, when he hadn't answered his door. Thankfully the steward was amenable to Mareleau's commands, despite being only a visiting queen, but now she was more perplexed than ever. Did Ridine perhaps have a wedding chamber like the one she and Larylis spent their first night in? If so, why would Cora be there all day while Teryn was out here? Alone?

"Surely, she'll accept my visit—" Her words cut off as Teryn handed her an envelope.

"A letter arrived from your husband this morning."

Her heart stuttered as she tore the envelope from his grip and immediately flicked open the seal. Before she could read its contents, she glanced back at Teryn. "Why do you have my letter? Why wasn't it delivered directly to me?"

"Larylis had a letter for me as well, so the messenger delivered them together. I offered to bring you yours."

That was an adequate excuse, she supposed...

"Don't expect too many more before his arrival," he said. "He'll be traveling by now and likely won't have time to write. And you have your own travels to prepare for."

Excitement flooded her. Larylis was on his way! He'd be here soon, and after the pact was signed, she could return home with him. Was that what travels Teryn was referring to? Surely she didn't need to prepare for departure just yet.

"You may not have heard," Teryn said, "but the signing will now take place on a celebratory hunt. In a few days, we'll make camp not too far from here and await the arrival of your husband and father."

Her eyes went wide. "We? As in...me? Going...hunting?" She wrinkled her nose. She'd never been on a hunt before, and she certainly didn't like the sound of camping. Sleeping at shoddy inns on her way to Ridine had been bad enough.

"I want you there. Cora wants you there. As Queen of Menah and heir to Selay, you're an important part of this pact. Besides, it will allow you more time with your beloved husband. He will be going straight there regardless of whether you attend."

Mareleau narrowed her eyes. There was something about the way he'd phrased that last part that almost made it feel like a threat.

Teryn's smile softened. "What will you call it?"

She paled. Was he referring to the baby? Last they'd spoken, she'd confessed to having lied about her condition. Had her newest change of fortune already spread through the castle?

"Your two kingdoms," Teryn clarified, dousing her anxiety. "Once you're queen of both Menah and Selay, what name will give your new land?"

She gave a flippant shrug. "I haven't considered it."

He took a step closer, his feet reaching the edge of the platform. Mareleau descended another step. "You should think about it. You're a powerful woman, Majesty. Power should fill your every thought. I know it fills mine."

She lowered her brows with a dark glower. "Shouldn't your new wife fill your thoughts instead?"

"Oh, she does. It is because of her that I am here. To give her peace of mind, I'll tidy up her work in the tower. It's merely a matter of redecorating. Surely even I can do that."

Then why the hell had he asked *her* to set up his private dinner with Cora a few nights back? Furthermore, the odd clusters of hanging herbs and basins on the floor made it seem like there was something other than redecorating going on. She was about to say as much but thought better of it. Brother or no, she didn't like conversing with him when he was in this strange mood. A mood he'd been in since the dinner they shared, she didn't fail to note.

She left him with no other farewell than an irritated scoff and descended the stairs. Her muscles were coiled with agitation. She still hadn't figured out where Cora was. Nevertheless, she'd find her. Until it came time to leave for this grand hunt she was now expected to attend, she'd have little else to do.

At least she had one source of comfort. She opened her husband's letter and sank into the solace of his words.

Teryn stared down the stairwell, even after Mareleau had gone. He and Emylia had witnessed her exchange with Morkai, and it left Teryn with a hollow pit of dread where his stomach should be. Teryn had realized something when they were talking; Cora wasn't Morkai's final option for getting everything he wanted. Mareleau could provide it in the same way—everything from her two kingdoms to a body he could use for Emylia.

All Morkai would have to do was get Verdian and Larylis out of the way. Force Mareleau to be his bride.

Teryn's lungs felt tight. While he'd managed to protect Cora somewhat, he now needed to find a way to save everyone else. Larylis. Mareleau. King Verdian.

"Teryn." Emylia's voice, pitched with urgency, stole his attention from the empty stairwell. Morkai had now returned to the tower room and was poring over a book on the cluttered table. Emylia stood beside the sorcerer, watching the pages that flipped by.

Teryn made his way inside, eyes locked on the sorcerer's waistcoat pocket. He and Emylia had projected themselves outside the crystal in time to catch him lifting the hidden stone in the floor and extracting the two glass vials. Emylia had been right; Morkai had hidden stores of his original body's blood. A necessary ingredient for Teryn and Emylia's plan. Only one essential remained: the pattern that would allow Teryn to unravel the spell on the crystal.

"What is he doing?" Teryn asked, standing at the other side of the table. His eyes fell on the pages of the book Morkai thumbed through. Each was either scribbled over in an elegant script—one he had a feeling belonged to Morkai himself—or bore intricate patterns rendered in ink. He lifted his gaze to Emylia's.

She gave him an affirming nod. "This is his personal book of spells and blueprints."

"What's he looking for?"

"Probably the weaving he utilizes for his Roizan. Now that he has his blood, that's his next step."

Teryn tried to recall what Emylia had told him about the Roizan. He knew Morkai used it as a vessel for magic, and Emylia had said the creatures were born from death, neither alive nor dead. "How exactly does he create a Roizan? What is it made from?"

"In short, a Roizan is forged from two living creatures who suffer violent deaths during combat with each other, resulting in the two dying at the same moment. Morkai utilizes blood weavings to control the time of death for each animal and prolong the fight."

Teryn's lip curled into a sneer. "He makes them suffer?"

"Pain and violence fuel the forbidden Arts."

Teryn shouldn't have been surprised. This was the sorcerer who'd commanded his bands of hunters to capture and torture unicorns. He cast a dark glower at Morkai, though the mage couldn't see it.

Emylia returned her gaze to the pages Morkai continued to flip through. He paused on one that was filled with notes cramping every spare inch of the margins, scanned it briefly, then turned to the next.

Morkai suddenly went rigid and slammed the book shut with a force that made the table shake. Emylia jumped at the sound and leaped to the side. Morkai's head snapped up, eyes locking on Teryn's. Teryn took a stumbling step back, but Morkai's gaze didn't follow. Instead, it hovered straight ahead.

Teryn released a sigh. Of course he couldn't see them.

Morkai narrowed his eyes to slits. His voice came out cold. Slow. So unlike Teryn's own, it made him shudder. "You're watching, aren't you?"

Teryn's eyes found Emylia's; she looked just as startled as he.

"I know you are," Morkai said. "You're hoping you can fight me. Stop me. Well, I assure you, your hope is futile. Watching me will only make it hurt more when you fail. When you breathe your last breath and I take over your lungs. Your life. Your name. You will be nothing. You'll have nothing."

Teryn's fingers curled at his sides. He was half tempted to step into his body and wrestle control then and there, even if for a short time, out of spite alone. But the edges of his rage cooled as he took in his silver-shot hair, the dull green in his eyes, the hollows in his cheeks. Considering how much damage his single instant of repossession had done to his body, he likely only had one more shot. While he could continue to practice strengthening his connection to his cereba, it would be foolish to fully take control again until they had everything in place.

With a slow exhale, he focused on his breaths, his pulse, his pounding heart.

Morkai's lips curled into a cruel grin. "How about I grant you mercy? Trust me. You don't want to see what happens next." He reached into his waistcoat pocket and extracted one of the vials. With his other hand, he lifted the leather-wrapped crystal from under his shirt and let it rest on top of his waistcoat. Lifting the stopper, he dropped a single drop of ruby liquid onto the tip of his finger and brought it to the surface of the crystal.

Everything went white.

Panic crawled up Teryn's throat as the blinding light surrounded him. He tried to will his ethera outside the crystal, but…he couldn't. No matter how he tried, he remained in place.

"Teryn, it's all right." Emylia's calming tone reached him through the white light. Then, starting with the edges of his vision, the colors dulled. Soon brown, red, and saffron washed over the light, forming Emylia's temple bedroom. The seer stood before him, wringing her hands.

"What happened?" he asked.

"He's blocking us now. Remember how I said he used to block me from projecting my ethera outside the crystal when he wanted to? That's what he's doing to us."

"How long will it last?"

"It's just a simple spell. A temporary seal he created with his blood. He still isn't strong enough to do anything permanent. Not until he has his Roizan."

That wasn't entirely comforting. "What if the seal doesn't break until it's too late? I can't step into my body unless I can project my soul outside the crystal. I can't practice connecting to my cereba if—"

"Teryn."

He frowned, noting the way she continued to wring her hands. He thought it was from anxiety, but now he saw the light dancing in her eyes, the ghost of a smile tugging her lips. "What is it?"

"We have something else to do now."

His pulse quickened. Before he could ask her to elaborate, she waved her hand, sending the temple room scattering in a wash of light. It was replaced with a still image of the tower library, exactly how it had been moments before. Morkai stood at the table, eyes narrowed on a page in his book. If they were unable to project themselves outside the crystal, then this must be from Emylia's memory.

She approached Morkai's side. It was uncanny watching her move through an image while Morkai remained frozen. "Look," she said, beckoning Teryn to stand beside her. She pointed at the page.

Teryn leaned forward, taking in the complex diagram of intersecting lines and loops that marked both pages. The pattern was the same on each page, creating a mirror image. Teryn was about to inquire what significance they held when his eyes fell on the script marking the top of the pages. The left-hand side bore the word *Crystal*, while the right said *Unicorn horn*.

He met Emylia's gaze and she gave him a nod. Her eyes were wide, barely concealing her excitement. "We have it, Teryn. This is the pattern."

He glanced back at the complex markings, feeling both daunted and exhilarated at once. He could barely make heads or tails of the pattern. It would take forever to learn how to replicate it. But…this was it. The final piece of their plan.

"Are you ready to learn how to draw it yourself?"

Teryn swallowed his fear. In its place, he felt relief. A growing sense of determination. That gnawing inertia he'd felt after his father's death had compounded ever since he'd gotten stuck in the crystal. Practicing with his cereba had barely taken the edge off. But now, with such a formidable task at hand, and a clear road ahead to do it, Teryn felt strong. Sure. Tenacious.

"Yes," he said. "Let's unravel this damn spell."

~

King Larylis ached for silence, his wife, and a decent book. Only one was at his disposal, in the form of the empty balcony he stood upon, attached to his borrowed bedroom for the night. Today marked his first day of travel to Ridine Castle, and since he was still in the Kingdom of Menah, his overnight accommodations were provided by an eager lord. Lord Furrowsby's manor was vast, but his hospitality was even more so, which included a musical performance in his grand parlor and a five-course dinner. Larylis had wanted nothing but sleep and solitude when he and his entourage arrived at the manor, but instead he'd been forced to grin and socialize until half past midnight, all while donning the persona of king.

Now that he was finally alone on the spacious balcony, he could let his posture slip, his shoulders slump. He ran a hand through his hair—which was now expertly styled by his valet each morning—loosening it from the stiff gels and waxes that had held it in place all day. He found himself missing the days when no one paid his appearance much heed. Now everything mattered. His hair, his dress, his stride. At least he'd managed to avoid the powdered wigs his valet had suggested. They were popular in Selay, especially with King Verdian. His valet had insisted they'd make him appear more distinguished. Larylis had no desire to don a wig, no matter how fashionable they were, so he'd compromised by subjecting his hair to daily styling.

With a fatigued groan, he leaned over the balcony rail, resting his elbows on the balustrade.

Six more days, he said to himself. Three more days traveling through northeastern Menah, staying at a different lord's house each time, then another three days traveling through Khero. In Khero, he could finally be free from the hospitality of his lords and stay at fine inns instead. When that was all over, he'd reach his destination. Only then would he finally see her again.

Mareleau.

His wife.

His beloved.

What he wouldn't give to shake free from these painfully slow travels. Were he allowed to travel on his own, he'd take a messenger horse and arrive at Ridine in two or three days. Were he allowed to oversee his own schedule, he'd travel with haste and rest only after nightfall, and reach his destination in four days. Instead, his travels had been turned into a political move, a way to engage with his noble subjects.

He understood the reasoning behind it all. He was a king now, and he had responsibilities. Protocols. Impressions to make. Loyalties to secure.

But seven gods, was he tired.

It was safe to say he far preferred reading about kings over being one.

A familiar cadence reached his ears, a soft beat punctuating the quiet night. He stared into the distance, beyond the trees that surrounded Lord Furrowsby's manor, until he saw her. Berol. Moonlight illuminated her wings as she circled over the manor, then made her descent. She landed beside him on the balustrade, one talon curled around something.

Larylis' pulse kicked up. He hadn't received a reply from his brother yet, but the messenger had likely only arrived at Ridine that morning. But Berol would have reached him faster.

He extended his hand toward the falcon. She uncurled her talon and dropped a soft roll of what felt like cloth. Furrowing his brow, he unraveled it, and found a messy scribble of smeared, faded ink. Or was it ink at all? It was too dark to make out the words with moonlight alone, so he rushed inside his temporary bedroom and brought the cloth beside a lantern perched on the bedside table.

His heart leaped into his throat as he read the words. He read it over again. Again. Dread filled his stomach.

Danger at Ridine.

Teryn isn't Teryn.

Trust no one.

What did it mean? It was signed by Cora, but why had she written this message in whatever messy substance marred the cloth? And was the cloth itself...a piece of clothing? It reminded him too much of the blood-splattered scrap Berol had brought him.

None of it made sense. None of it explained anything that was happening. He'd received no other warning. No rushed messages that told of issues at Ridine. His recent letters from Mareleau had contained her usual musings, nothing more.

Larylis bristled with tension. He couldn't wait a week. Couldn't bear to dine and dance when something strange was happening. When his wife could be in danger.

He strode through the room and began to dress in his riding attire. His hands trembled as he laced up his pants, donned his gloves, threw on his coat.

Royal procedure could go to the seven devils. He didn't care if he offended nobles or enraged his guards. He didn't care if leaving now shaved only a few meager days off his travels. If he couldn't act on his instincts, then he was a puppet, not a king.

With hasty steps, he left his room and rapped his knuckles on the next door over. After a few long stretches of silence, a tired face answered the door. But it was the face he trusted most when it came to those who served him—Lord Hardingham. Aside from having been his father's most loyal councilman, he'd always treated Larylis with respect, bastard or no. He'd been at Centerpointe Rock. He'd seen the same terrors Larylis had. Though Hardingham had mourned Arlous' death, he'd stated his support of Larylis' impossible decision, even when the other councilmen continued to question their new king in whispers behind his back.

Only Hardingham would follow Larylis' next demand without question.

"Keep this quiet," Larylis said. "Gather a small selection of guards and meet me in the stables. We make haste for Ridine at once."

Hardingham's only reply was a widening of his eyes, followed by a nod.

Soon Larylis and a modest retinue took off under the blanket of night. His heart raced with fear, the excitement of his rebellion, and a pinch of shame. He knew he could be overreacting. He could be compromising everything.

But with every inch of distance he closed between himself and Ridine, he felt lighter. Freer. He let his thoughts go, lulled by the beat of horse hooves and Berol's wings flapping high overhead.

50

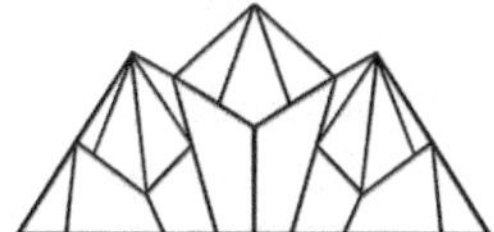

Night had fallen and still Cora and her unwanted companions continued to walk. Her legs ached with fatigue, her neck stiff from trying so hard not to jostle her collar. She'd lost all sense of time, but surely they'd been walking for at least half a day now. Under normal circumstances, a lengthy walk was no problem. She'd traveled on foot plenty during her time stalking Morkai's hunters with Valorre. But this was different. This was walking without rest. Without food. Without any sense of how near or far they were in relation to their destination.

At least the dying landscape of the Blight made for very few obstacles to navigate, but that was of little comfort with the exhaustion that tugged at her bones. She wasn't certain how much time had passed since she'd left Ridine, but she knew she'd been awake for far too long. Thankfully, Etrix had offered her a skin of water—which had been the sweetest, most refreshing water she'd ever tasted—but she wasn't sure how much longer she could go on that alone.

"Can we rest?" she ground out for what felt like the hundredth time.

"No," Fanon said from up ahead. Not once had he fallen back from his position several yards in front of her.

"Then can I ride? If I can just get on Valorre's back, we can travel much faster." She kept her tone pleading and pathetic to hide the truth; if she mounted Valorre, she could outpace all of them and give her and the unicorn a chance to escape through the Veil on their own. If there was a way through, that is.

Fanon glowered over his shoulder. It carried the depth of his ire even with the nighttime shadows muting her vision. "I think not, human."

"I have a name," she said. "It's *Cora*, not *human*."

Fanon had nothing to say to that and simply increased his pace.

"You must forgive Fanon," Etrix said. Both he and Garot strolled at her side. As annoyed as she was with her captors, having the two close by was some comfort.

The Blight was an eerie place. Too vast. Too empty. Too quiet. She constantly expected some faerytale creature to leap from the shadows with pointed fangs and threaten to claw out her eyes. Or perhaps a return of that enormous dragon. Now and then she was certain she could hear its screech in the distance, and she hadn't forgotten what Etrix had said about the dragons chasing unicorns. Thankfully, she'd seen no such creature. In fact, she hadn't seen a single soul aside from her companions since they'd passed the group of Faeryn.

Etrix spoke again. "Acting as Steward of El'Ara is a great burden to bear."

The way Etrix had said *steward* made her think the title was one of respect, and far higher in rank than a castle steward like Master Arther. She frowned at Fanon's back. *He* held a position of power?

"He's no Morkara." A note of sorrow crept into his voice. "We haven't had a true Morkara in a very long time."

The unknown word piqued her curiosity, and she debated asking what it meant. The *mor* portion meant magic, of course, but what about *kara*? It sounded too much like *Morkai* or *Morkaius* to ignore. While she'd kept quiet during most of their walk, focusing only on thoughts of getting home, it occurred to her that her companions might hold vital information about her enemy. Morkai had claimed to be an Elvyn prince, after all. Still, she didn't dare bring him up directly. For all she knew, these three could be the lost prince's most fervent supporters. But she could mine them for knowledge just the same.

"What is a Morkara?" she asked Etrix.

"Morkara is much like a steward, but the burden is given by blood, birth, and *mora*. They hold the highest position in El'Ara and are responsible for directing the flow of *mora* through our entire world. Satsara was the last Morkara we've had, but she died about seventy-five years ago. Fanon has been acting as steward in her place ever since."

"What happened to Satsara?"

A flicker of emotion passed over Etrix's face before he steeled it behind a stoic mask. "Your kind found its way to El'Ara. A human. A worldwalker."

"Oh, let me tell the rest," Garot said, stepping closer to Cora's other side. "You're terrible at telling stories."

"This isn't a *story*, Garot. It's a dark blot in our world's history. Why would you relish telling such a tale?"

Fanon glanced over his shoulder with another scowl. "Why are you bothering to talk with the human at all?"

"I thought she should know the deeds her kind are responsible for," Garot said, but when Fanon faced forward again, he gave Cora an exaggerated wink. She was starting to like the copper-haired Elvyn more and more. Where at first she'd been annoyed by his arrogant amusement over her plight, she'd come to realize his demeanor at least lacked cruelty.

"Fine," Fanon said with a grunt. "Make sure she understands her people's darkest deeds, not just the parts you like to talk about."

Garot puffed his chest and stood tall, and his tone took on the same whimsical quality it had when she'd asked about the Veil. "Morkara Satsara's reign was still new when she met Prince Tristaine, a human lost in El'Ara. He was more than a human, though. More than a prince. He had human magic. A witch, I think your kind call them. And this witch had one of the most dangerous powers we'd ever heard of. One that allowed him to travel anywhere in the blink of an eye."

Cora bristled at hearing him describe a type of magic she held. One the Elvyn considered dangerous. She briefly met Valorre's gaze. *Do you know of this tale? Is that why you told me to lie?*

No. Still don't remember.

Garot continued. "Rumors tell that Prince Tristaine had used scent-based magic to travel. That was how he'd found El'Ara. On Samhain—the day when the barriers between all worlds are at their thinnest—he caught a smell he'd never experienced before and followed it with his magic. That was how he'd crossed worlds for the first time and found himself suddenly in El'Ara. After that, he needed only to recall the scent to return. If you haven't already gleaned, he had the power of a worldwalker."

She gave a sharp nod. His words confirmed everything she'd suspected; a worldwalker was a witch who could astral travel. Not only that, but it sounded like this Prince Tristaine had used clairalience—clear smelling—to do so. Where Cora needed emotion to travel, this worldwalker needed scent.

"You're getting ahead of yourself, Garot," Etrix said, a note of fatigue in his voice.

"Ah, you're right. I was telling you how Satsara first met Tristaine. To explain their first meeting, I must mention the triggers we have woven throughout our land. They alert the Morkara—or the steward, in today's case—of non-fae intruders. On that Samhain eve, when Tristaine first entered El'Ara, a trigger went off and alerted Satsara. As a wardweaver, she took it upon herself to banish the intruder personally. Instead, she met him and fell in love. She didn't weave a ward around the prince to banish him like she was supposed to. No, she wove a secret ward in a forest alcove where she and the prince could meet again. They began an affair, and it continued well after she was forced to marry her Elvyn consort. Satsara eventually found herself the bearer of the human's child. Upon the child's birth, Satsara could no longer keep her secret. She confessed about her human lover to her consort and her tribunal. All agreed that she must banish Tristaine once and for all. So, finally, she met him one last time and wove a ward around his body that would keep him from ever entering El'Ara again. The child, on the other hand, was permitted to remain."

"A mistake," Etrix said. Cora glanced at the dark-haired fae and was surprised to see the deep furrow in his brow, the distant look in his ruby-brown eyes.

"A very grave mistake," Garot agreed. "This half-witch, half-Elvyn child named Darius grew up alongside his Elvyn sister, Ailan."

Cora tried not to let her surprise show at the name Darius. When she'd brought news of Morkai to the Forest People, they'd told her about the Morkaius, a man they'd called the Blood of Darius. She'd never learned who Darius had been, or if he perhaps was Morkai himself.

Garot continued. "Despite Darius' tainted blood, Satsara loved him deeply. It caused her great strife when it came time to name her heir."

"The eldest child of the Morkara is always named heir by blood right," Etrix said, "but as Darius was half human, the tribunal encouraged Satsara to choose the younger, pureblood child."

Garot nodded. "As Darius grew, the wisdom of the tribunal became harder to ignore. The boy was tainted with his father's dark magic. He could worldwalk, just like his father could, and left time and again to the human world. Satsara and her tribunal feared he'd use his power for ill, should he be made Morkara. Eventually, Ailan was named heir instead. In a violent scheme of revenge, Darius tricked Satsara's dragon, Berolla, into wounding his sister, which confirmed everyone's fears about him."

"Berolla?" Cora echoed. She'd heard that name in stories. Faerytales told of a legendary fae queen and her faithful dragon. Even Teryn knew the tale, for he'd named his falcon after her.

"Every Morkara is bonded to a dragon," Garot said, "and Berolla was Satsara's bonded companion. Berolla hadn't meant to hurt Ailan, and Darius' cruel trick nearly ended his sister's life. Because of that, Satsara had no choice but to banish Darius. She had to use the very same wardweaving she'd used on his father years before."

She furrowed her brow. "How many kinds of weavers are there? And what exactly does each power do?"

"There are many," Garot said. "More than I can name. But I'll give you a few examples. As I've said, Satsara was a wardweaver, which meant she specialized in creating barriers infused with a protective purpose. As a pathweaver, I manipulate distance for fast travel. Etrix here is a speechweaver, and he specializes in translation. And Fanon is a skyweaver, which allows him to give shape, form, and pressure to air."

She supposed that accounted for her invisible restraints. A question burned the back of her throat. Her heart hammered as she prepared to voice it. "Is there such a thing as a fateweaver? Or a bloodweaver?"

Garot arched a copper brow. "We have skinweavers who specialize in healing, if that is what you mean by bloodweaver. And we have truthweavers who seek out hidden knowledge about the past, present, and future. Is that what you mean by fateweaver?"

"Not exactly," she said, keeping her tone nonchalant. "Is there any kind of weaver who can change or control another's fate?"

"The Elvyn do nothing of that sort," Etrix said, voice brimming with reproach. "Our magic is neither invasive nor harmful."

She couldn't help but give him a pointed look. If she could move her arms, she'd gesture toward the collar.

Etrix, however, seemed to understand. He gave her an apologetic nod. "Not unless it is out of protection. Like what we're doing to you now. Or like what Satsara did to Darius."

"What she did to Darius was essential indeed," Garot said. "If only her attempt had succeeded. But as she'd begun to weave the ward around her son, Darius realized what was happening. With the power of the worldwalker, he disappeared into the human world before the weaving could take hold."

"Only to return many years later to kill his mother and destroy the balance of El'Ara." Etrix's words came out in a rush.

Garot frowned at him. "That's a terrible way to end the story."

Etrix's throat bobbed before he spoke. "We're here."

Cora looked straight ahead. With the night so dark and the landscape so gnarled and colorless, it took her a moment to see what he was referring to. Then she saw it, a wall of mist and shadow on the horizon. No, it was nearer than that, stretching out from side to side and swallowing the sky above. She shuddered at the sight. "That's the Veil?"

"Yes," Etrix said. "Though it looks like a sheet of dark mist, it is as impenetrable as a wall."

"What happens now?"

Fanon finally came to a halt and turned to face them. "Now we inspect the Veil and see if it's truly been torn. If it has, and we can surmise that you entered on accident with the unicorn, we'll let you go. If the Veil is torn, you'll be the least of our worries. We'll have war on our hands in a matter of weeks, if not days."

"That's a pessimistic take," Garot said with a sideways grin. "You've heard the whispers of the truthweavers. The Veil will only tear when our Morkara returns. If it has been torn, Ailan could be back."

Fanon clenched his jaw. "If Ailan was going to return, she would have done it ages ago."

Garot shrugged. "It's only been seventy-five years."

"Here, yes, but it's been closer to five hundred years for her. Time passes faster in the human realm. If she were able to return at all, she would have by now."

"We don't know what she's been dealing with in the human world all this time."

"She might not even be alive."

"Are you so afraid of hope, Fanon?"

"I'm not afraid..."

The two Elvyn continued to argue, but Cora's mind remained stuck on what Garot had said about the passage of time. Her heart leaped into her throat, sending a question surging from her lips, her tone frantic. "What do you mean time passes faster in the human realm?"

Fanon and Garot ceased their argument, but it was Etrix who answered. "Our two realms experience time differently, in both tangible and intangible ways. We have no exact calculation, but past events have suggested that one day here is equal to approximately one week in the human realm."

A wave of dizziness tore through her, almost strong enough to make her knees buckle. "You're telling me," she said, voice trembling, "that in the time I've been here, walking through the woods and the Blight, watching day turn to night, everyone I know and love has already lived through several days in my absence."

Etrix had the decency to don a sympathetic frown, but Garot only grinned as he said, "Precisely."

This time Cora's knees truly did give out. They crashed into the soft, decaying soil. She sat back on her heels to keep herself from falling forward. "I have to get home," she whispered. Then louder. "I have to get home *now!*"

Fanon sneered at her. "Is that not why we're at the Veil? Like I said, if there's a tear in the Veil, we'll send you home."

She shifted her jaw side to side, burning him with a glare. "And if there isn't?"

His lips curled into a cruel smile. "Then I suppose that would make you a liar."

Mother Goddess, she hoped there really was a tear. Hoped there was a way to cross through. And if not, then she had to find a way to free her hands from Fanon's bonds and remove the collar, all without using her magic.

She glanced at Valorre.

We go, he said.

She gave him a subtle nod, understanding what his clipped words were meant to convey. No matter what it took, no matter what they had to do, she and Valorre were getting out of there.

51

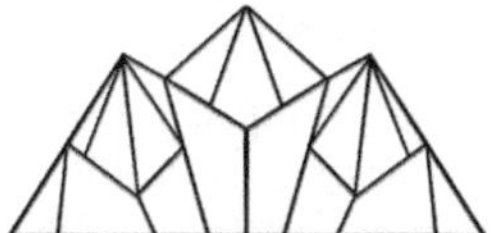

Mareleau hadn't been at the newly erected campsite for more than an hour when she decided she already hated camping. The location was charming, she supposed. She hadn't paid much attention to the scenery on the brief journey here, but now that she'd arrived at her destination, there was little else to do. The wide meadow dotted with bright wildflowers was so lovely, it almost seemed like it had come from a painting. Mountains loomed behind her while a short cliff surrounded by lush forest stood at the other side. The sun was high in the sky, the afternoon warm, but that was where the charm of this supposed hunting expedition ended.

Half of the beautiful meadow and the flowers within it were now crushed by an array of pavilions set up throughout it, leaving only a small area left to wander through. And it was too damn hot for that. Which meant all she could do was sit under the open-air tent that served as a makeshift parlor with her ladies and try not to lose her mind.

Just a few more days, then Larylis will be here, she reminded herself. *Just a few more days after that, and I get to go home with him.*

Mareleau sank deeper into the cushions of the divan she reclined on, grateful she had no one to put on airs for. There were no courtiers in attendance, only servants, and the men were in their own tent at the other side of the meadow, preparing for their hunt. Breah, Ann, and Sera lounged in chairs around her, gossiping with the same ease they always did. How were her ladies so adaptable, regardless of circumstance? Did none of them miss Selay? Verlot Palace? Did none of them yearn for the stability of their new home at Dermaine Palace like she did?

Instead of voicing any of her questions aloud, she filled her mouth with sweets. Reaching across the tea table, she plucked up a lemon cookie and a piece of candied ginger from a porcelain plate. She chose one of each, less out of hunger and more out of boredom. Gods, she was miserable. There was even less to do here than there'd been at the castle. At least at Ridine she could wander alone and find some empty hall to cry in—something her emotions demanded on a whim these days—but here there was nowhere to go beyond this tent or the meadow. Unless she fancied a trip into the woods where she could get eaten by bears, mosquitoes, or both.

At least no one expected her to attend the hunt itself. Teryn, her uncles, and King Dimetreus would depart for the day's adventure any time now. Mareleau cast a glance toward the men's pavilion, and saw only silhouettes as they lounged, drank, and laughed. Around them, servants gathered supplies and readied horses. She was surprised King Dimetreus was here, considering what Cora had said. Dimetreus was technically no longer king. But of course, to abdicate his position, he'd need his sister to take his place.

A sister who was eerily absent.

Mareleau hadn't caught a single glimpse of Cora the last few days, much to her growing dread. Whenever she'd asked Teryn about her whereabouts, he'd insist she was under severe protection and wouldn't publicly show herself until after the peace pact was signed. It made sense, she supposed. If Cora was now queen, she'd need far more protection than when she'd been a princess. But this seemed excessive. Especially considering just how little anyone regarded Mareleau's safety, and she'd been queen for nearly three weeks longer than her new friend.

Breah shifted in her seat and turned toward Mareleau with a wide grin. "Are you comfortable, Majesty? Do you need more tea? More pillows?"

Well, at least *someone* paid attention to her well-being.

Before she could answer, Sera leaped from her seat and began pouring a fresh cup anyway. "You must stay hydrated in this heat. And eat as many sweets as you like." She shoved the plate of cookies a little closer.

Breah scowled at Sera, but the other girl paid her no heed.

Sera batted her lashes. "What else do you need, Majesty?"

Ever since Cora had taken up confinement, Sera had returned to Mareleau's side. It seemed the girl was now desperate to prove she was indispensable. Her efforts, though, bordered on annoying more often than not.

Ann, not wanting to be left out of whatever competition was brewing amongst the queen's ladies, stood from her chair. "How about a bath, Majesty? I saw a tub in one of the wagons. I can boil water for you and scent it with oils. Oh, and wildflowers from the meadow!"

Mareleau didn't want to encourage their petty rivalries, but seven gods, a bath sounded divine. She already felt filthy after this morning's journey, not to mention the sweat caused by the afternoon sun blazing through the open sides of the tent. Additionally, a bath meant privacy. Time alone. Some semblance of peace and purpose in her boredom.

"Very well," she said to Ann, which earned the girl dark glowers from both Breah and Sera, "you may draw me a bath."

~

LARYLIS WAS NOTHING MORE THAN RAW NERVES DRESSED IN HUMAN FLESH AS HE RODE through the forest toward his destination. A page in Lord Kevan's livery led the way, guiding him from Ridine Castle to some undisclosed location in the woods nearby. Apparently, the signing of the peace pact would take place on a royal hunt. Thankfully Larylis wasn't alone, otherwise his imagination might have carried him away to the worst possible scenario. However, it wasn't Lord Hardingham at his side, calming him down with cool logic; it was King Verdian.

Verdian had been the last person Larylis had wanted to meet on the road, but two days ago, Larylis' small entourage had caught up with Verdian's much larger one. Larylis had no choice but to tell his father-in-law of Cora's strange letter to explain why he'd left his retinue. He'd expected a barrage of insults at having acted so recklessly, and Verdian certainly had a few choice words to say, but after reading Cora's fading letter a time or two more, the king had calmed down. He'd still insisted the letter was simply the result of a lovers' quarrel, but his subsequent actions had belied his confident words. Like Larylis had done, Verdian had selected a small group to ride with haste to Ridine.

Thus, Larylis earned his unwanted companion.

He had to admit the king steadied his nerves somewhat. He hoped with all his heart that Verdian was right—that Cora's letter was the culmination of a simple quarrel and nothing more.

"We're here," the young page said, guiding their party into a wide clearing. A sunlit meadow stretched ahead, filled with several pavilions. At the edge of the meadow, a group of men on horseback entered the woods. Larylis thought he could make out the figures of King Dimetreus and Lord Kevan. Closer, another group mounted their horses. Lord Ulrich was amongst them, and...was that Teryn?

Larylis hadn't recognized his brother first, for his back had been facing them. But now that Teryn turned, Larylis saw his face beneath a tricorn hat. Larylis frowned. Since when did Teryn wear tricorns on a hunt? He didn't think he'd ever seen his brother don a hat.

Teryn tugged his horse's reins and faced the approaching party. "Brother. King Verdian. I'm glad to see you've arrived early. We were just about to depart for the day's hunt. Will you be joining us?"

Larylis frowned. That was Teryn's voice, but his tone was too formal. The hat cast Teryn's face in shadow, but Larylis was almost certain his cheeks appeared thinner. Paler.

Verdian said nothing to Teryn and rode straight for Ulrich. Larylis watched as the brothers spoke in hushed tones, their horses side by side. There was something smug about Ulrich's countenance, and he gave only short answers to Verdian's questions, most of which were too quiet for Larylis to hear.

He forced his attention back to Teryn, who remained seated on his horse. Keeping his voice casual, he said, "Are you well, brother?"

"Quite. And you? How were your travels?"

He was too polite. Too stiff. He was acting different, but that didn't suggest anything outright sinister. "We met no trouble on the road. Where is Princess Aveline?"

"She'll be with us shortly." He shifted in his saddle and pointed to the other end of the meadow. "Your wife is in the last tent."

Had that been...a diversion? If so, it worked. Larylis' eyes locked on the elegant pavilion. He recognized Mareleau's lady's maids chatting outside the closed front flap. From the ease of their postures, the animated manners in which they spoke to each other, he sensed nothing amiss. Nothing to suggest Mareleau was in danger.

He returned his gaze to Teryn and saw his brother smiling back at him. It was a familiar grin, as comforting as a warm embrace. Larylis was starting to believe he really had overreacted.

"She's missed you terribly," Teryn said, lowering his voice. His previous air of formality was gone. "I'm sure you already knew that."

Verdian broke away from Ulrich. "I'll see my daughter at once."

"I believe she's bathing, Majesty," Teryn said, prompting a flush of color to rise to the king's cheeks. "At least, that's what I've guessed based on the many buckets of boiled water I saw one of her maids dragging into the tent for the better part of an hour."

Teryn was back to that formal tone again. Was it simply an act he was putting on in front of Verdian?

Larylis glanced back at his wife's pavilion, heart pulsing with longing. While he had many questions to ask Teryn, he needed to see Mareleau. Needed to confirm she truly was safe.

"Why don't you stay here, brother?" Teryn said. "Verdian, you should join us on our hunt. We have much to discuss regarding the peace pact, and what better time to start than now? If we are to take advantage of the daylight, we must leave at once. Dimetreus and Kevan already have a head start." He nodded toward the edge of the woods where the first party was now hidden beyond the trees.

"Very well," Verdian said, giving Larylis a subtle nod. Larylis knew what he was wordlessly trying to convey: Larylis would check on Mareleau while Verdian assessed the situation with Teryn and the others. Verdian ordered two of his guards to remain behind with Larylis while the other two would accompany him on the hunt. Larylis had left Lord Hardingham and his own guards back at Ridine to keep an eye on things there.

"Let's be off then," Teryn said, then cast his smile at Larylis again. "You'll join us on tomorrow's hunt, though, won't you? It will be like old times."

Larylis mirrored his brother's grin. Was he pulling at straws trying to find something malevolent in his brother's eyes? Of course this was Teryn. This was his brother. His best friend. "Like old times."

Only...where was Berol? She'd accompanied Larylis on his journey until he'd met up with Verdian. After that, she'd made an appearance now and then, reminding him she was still following, but her absence struck him now. Why wasn't she perched on Teryn's shoulder, elated to see him? Or at the very least circling overhead?

"Give her this." Verdian's voice roused Larylis from his thoughts. The king pulled his horse up beside Larylis' mount and thrust out a small package.

Larylis took it, brow furrowed.

Verdian's cheeks pinked again. "It's for the baby. My...grandchild," he muttered between his teeth, then pulled his horse away.

Larylis watched after him, a lump caught in his throat. While Larylis knew Mareleau's condition was fabricated, Verdian's gesture moved him. Perhaps he really had come to regret the awful things he'd said to her when they'd last spoken.

Larylis watched the party depart, a sight that made his gut feel heavy, then rode for the other end of the meadow. With Verdian's gift clutched in his hand, he dismounted and made a beeline for Mareleau's tent. Her three ladies caught sight of him and dipped into hasty curtsies.

"Majesty," Breah said, eyes wide, "the queen is inside, but—"

He didn't let her finish. Ignoring their flustered warnings, he charged into the tent, his heart racing with every step.

The air was heavy inside, even warmer than the outdoor summer temperature, infused with jasmine-scented steam. It wafted from a copper basin at the center of the tent. And in it was his wife.

She bolted upright when she saw him, rising from the tub in a rush. "Larylis!"

He pulled up short, eyes falling on her bare torso, taking in the rivulets of water trailing down her neck, her breasts, the planes of her stomach. He'd known she was bathing. Known she'd likely be naked. But seeing her like this, the surprise on her face, followed by the way she immediately sank back into the tub, filled him with an aching sense of self-awareness.

He turned abruptly around. "I'm sorry," he called over his shoulder, not daring to look at her. "I thought you'd be behind a screen."

He heard nothing in reply, only the pounding of his heart.

Seven devils, had he embarrassed her? Offended her?

He'd been too caught in his worry, his passion, his desperation to see her, that he hadn't stopped to consider one important thing: that even though they'd loved each other for years and were now married, their relationship was still new in many ways. They'd been estranged for longer than they'd been lovers and had spent most of their marriage apart. While Larylis was confident when writing love letters, able to bare his soul and express the depths of his heart behind the safety of a quill and paper, he suddenly found himself feeling very much tongue-tied and vulnerable. How was he supposed to act with her in person? Could he voice aloud the things he'd said in his letters?

As for seeing her naked...well, they'd only been wholly intimate once. That hardly granted him permission to barge in on her while she was bathing. What had he been thinking? Still, the memory of their single night of passion surged through him now, mingling with the sight of seeing her in the tub. It sent heat coursing through him that he wasn't sure was entirely appropriate in this moment. Never before had he felt less like a king and more like a fool.

He swallowed hard and took a step forward, prepared to bolt from the tent—

"Larylis." This time Mareleau's voice held no surprise, only softness. "Turn around, you idiot."

The taunting in her tone set his nerves at ease, encouraged his lips to curl up at the corners. Slowly, he shifted back to face her.

She was standing again, but this time her chin was lifted, her shoulders thrown back. Again, he couldn't keep his eyes from wandering down her figure. Now that he had her permission, he let himself savor every inch of her slick skin, her ample curves, the pale hair that framed her shoulders. He lifted his gaze to her eyes, saw hunger in them, as well as a dash of timidity that matched his own. She grinned, biting a corner of her bottom lip.

"Come here." Her words were whispered, but there was command in her tone. "Get in the tub with me."

His stomach tightened, his mind going blissfully empty.

He dropped the gift and shrugged off his jacket and sword belt in quick succession, letting them fall to the floor before he strode straight for his wife. With every step, he loosened a button, discarded one piece of clothing, then the next, until he stood bare before the tub, his lips pressed against hers. She pulled him tight to her, angling her head to deepen the kiss. Her tongue swept against his, and he released a throaty moan.

He no longer felt an ounce of apprehension between them. His fear melted away, as did his self-consciousness. In this moment, he was the confident king he'd been in his letters. Every promise he'd made, every embarrassing poem he'd drafted during their time apart now filled his lips, his tongue, his fingertips, reaffirming his affection for her.

Stepping blindly into the tub, he erased every inch of space that separated them. One hand circled her bottom while the other explored the generous curve of her breast. She arched against him as if she yearned to be even closer than their flush bodies would allow. He breathed in every kiss she gave him like it was air, touched every part of her like he was committing the feel of her to memory. Desire seared his core, coalescing in a hungry roar that pulsed between them, infused their shared kisses and groping hands. He sank into the basin, his fingers tangled in her sodden hair. She followed him into the water, straddling his hips as she lowered herself on top of him.

She pulled her face back slightly, eyes locked on his. "Gods, I missed you, Lare."

He opened his mouth, but she didn't give him a chance to say anything back. Instead, she kissed him again. With a rock of her hips, she lowered herself further onto him, sparking new sensations of pleasure. Larylis forgot his fears, forgot everything but her as they lost themselves in each other's bodies, in their love, and made up for lost time.

52

─────────

Mareleau had never heard a sound more beautiful than Larylis' heartbeat. It thudded against her ear, echoing the pound of her own. They reclined on the pallet that was nestled at the far end of Mareleau's tent, their bodies tangled in blankets and furs. Based on the lack of light streaming through the canvas walls, and the darkening shadows that grew around the single lantern lit inside, it must be night now. Mareleau had lost all sense of time during her impassioned reunion with her husband. The memory of their time in the tub—then on the floor, then again on the pallet where they now lay— flooded her with warmth, and a tingling heat built between her thighs. It seemed her desire for him would never be satiated. Her body, on the other hand, was spent.

She shifted her face to prop her chin on his chest and assessed her husband's countenance. Gods, he was beautiful. His eyes were closed, but she'd drunk in their emerald hue when she'd been astride him earlier, studying his every expression, his every sound, as he'd wrung pleasure from her, and she from him. Their love was both long-standing and new. She was determined to know every angle of him, all the quirks and facets she'd never learned, and any she may have forgotten in their three years apart.

His dark lashes fluttered, and he glanced down at her with a sleepy grin. She lifted a hand and lightly brushed the curve of his bottom lip, then trailed it across the hard edge of his lightly stubbled jaw. His throat bobbed as she brushed the column of his neck, then his collarbone. Her fingers drifted behind his head to where his hair curled slightly, damp with sweat and bathwater. She liked seeing him like this. Undone. Rugged. She liked the way his body tensed as she shifted against him. Lifting herself slightly, she planted a kiss on his lips. His mouth met hers in a tender softness that had been absent between them earlier. With their desires quenched, there was a slowness to their kiss now. A promise.

His hands came to her hips, rounding her curves in a way that had her stomach tightening, her center tingling. Perhaps their desires weren't so quenched after all.

She was about to deepen the kiss, but Larylis pulled away. "I wish we could do this all day."

"Look around, Lare," she said with a chuckle. "We already did."

A furrow formed between his brows. He pulled himself to sitting and glanced around the tent. When his eyes fell on the solitary light glowing from the lantern, a sideways grin took over his lips. He returned his gaze to her. "I suppose you're right. But still..."

She sat upright before him and pushed out her bottom lip in a mock pout. It had the effect she'd been after. His eyes dipped to her mouth. Then to her bare torso.

A groan built in the back of his throat. "You make it very hard—"

"I know." She let her eyes dip to his waist.

"—to talk about anything serious," he said, his words dissolving in a laugh.

"Must we? There are so many better things we could do tonight."

His mirth slowly began to drain from his face. "There...there are some things we should talk about."

She didn't like where that was going. His words almost made her feel like she was in trouble. More than that, they reminded her that she had something very serious to tell him too. Something she hadn't dared confess by way of letter. Her hand went impulsively to her belly, soft and curving in the way it always was, yet too small to reveal the secret growing within. She snatched her hand away and batted her lashes. "Like the gift you brought me?"

Maybe she was a coward for changing the subject, but she wasn't ready to lose the sweetness of their reunion.

"The gift?"

"I saw you carrying a package when you entered. Was it for me?"

His smile returned, but it wasn't as bright as before. "It was, but it wasn't from me. It's from your father."

"My father?" Verdian was an even drearier topic than the one she was trying to avoid. But...had he really gotten her a gift? If so, why did Larylis have it?

Larylis threw back the blankets and left the pallet, making his way across the tent to gather his discarded clothing one piece at a time. Mareleau took the opportunity to admire his lean build, his bare broad shoulders, and the perfect view of his backside. Her shoulders slumped as he hid the latter beneath his trousers, then the former beneath his shirt.

Not wanting to be the only one naked, she retrieved the chemise and robe Ann had left out before her bath. She pulled the chemise over her head and belted the silk robe at her waist. Larylis reached the package he'd left by his jacket and sword belt and brought it back to the pallet with him.

"I crossed paths with your father on my way here," he said, holding the package out to her.

Gingerly, she accepted the gift and lowered herself back onto the pallet. The package was a bundle of brown canvas tied with string. Whatever was inside, it was soft and shapeless.

Larylis planted himself beside her, but there was a tenseness in his posture. "We traveled here together, but when we arrived, he left for the hunt with Teryn, Dimetreus, and your uncles. He asked me to give this to you. But...but I don't know if you want to open it."

She lifted her eyes from the gift to find a grimace on Larylis' face. "Why not?"

"He said it was for the baby. For his grandchild."

Mareleau's heart stuttered. Heat rushed to her cheeks, renewing her panic over what she needed to tell Larylis. But beside her anxiety was something tender. Something laced with guilt and love.

She dropped her gaze back to the package and slowly worked the knots in the string. One by one, they fell away, followed by the canvas wrapping. As it unfolded, it revealed a bundle of cloth. She lifted the item, finding a small blanket made from the softest red velvet on one side and elegant white and gold brocade on the other. The pattern was of vines and roses—white ones to represent Selay's sigil—with woodland creatures weaving through the brambles.

Tears stung her eyes.

Her father had gifted this to her. To the baby. His grandchild.

While she couldn't banish the resentment that constantly burned in her heart, she felt the edges smooth out.

"I think he's sorry," Larylis said, shifting closer to her. "Though I know you'll eventually have to tell him..."

He didn't finish, but Mareleau knew what he was trying to say. Soon she'd have to tell her father that her condition had come to an end. That had been the plan, at least.

With the gift in her lap and the emotions building in her chest, the cruelty of her original scheme struck her like a knife to the chest. Yes, she'd been willing to do whatever it took to be with Larylis, but couldn't she have gone about it another way? She'd been desperate then, fueled by anger and indignation. But she'd lied about a subject that no longer felt like an easy pawn to play with. It felt fragile. Tenuous. Precious. Something that shouldn't be treated like a game. She remembered how Cora had praised her for not wanting to treat children like pawns. The princess had given her far too much credit.

Again her hand went to her belly. She hadn't made peace with her pregnancy and had no clue how Larylis would react. She remembered his bitterness over her lie, but that didn't mean he wanted children any time soon. Yet...something brighter than fear ignited inside her. A fierce and protective fire she'd never felt before. She let it grow. Let it warm her heart and soul.

Her vision blurred beneath a sheen of tears. She felt the pallet shift, then Larylis' arms gathering her to his chest. "It's all right, Mare," he whispered into her hair. "We'll tell him together. I'll support your lie in every way, then we'll never need to speak of it again."

Her pulse sped like hummingbird wings, drawing words to her lips. Once she said them, she couldn't take them back. With a deep breath, she pulled away. He kept his arms around her shoulders, as if he feared she'd fall apart. Maybe she would. Her voice trembled, her tone a whisper. "It isn't a lie. Not anymore."

Larylis blinked at her several times. "What do you mean?"

"It isn't a lie. I...I'm with child."

His eyes went wide.

"At least I think I am," she said in a rush. "I haven't been seen by a physician, but the signs are rather hard to ignore—"

Larylis pulled her back to him again. His embrace was tighter this time, as if he too felt that protective fire. They stayed like that for endless moments, saying nothing, letting their shared tears relay the promises in their hearts.

~

THE EDGES OF TERYN'S CONSCIOUSNESS THREATENED TO FRAY, BUT HE FORCED HIS focus to remain steady, narrowing onto the thin strand of light he drew with the tip of his finger. He didn't know how long he'd been drawing, but the pattern was nearly complete. A rectangle composed of interlocking loops and lines hovered midair beneath his hand. Just a few more lines remained...

Teryn turned his hand, executing a precise loop with the glowing light that trailed his finger like ink. Finally, he made the final mark, a straight line at the very top. With a gasp, he broke away from the pattern. Emylia stood beside him, remaining silent as he connected with his vitale. One breath. Two. He counted his heartbeat, sank into the rhythm of his pulse. Once his nerves had settled, he lifted his gaze to the pattern that hovered before him.

He and Emylia were in her temple bedroom, and the weaving glowed like an apparition in the air. Emylia had taught him how to manipulate the crystal's light, how to use it to cut through her illusions to create markings in the air. It took all of Teryn's concentration to focus on drawing with light, but without a body, much less paper and ink, this was the only way he could practice the pattern.

"It's perfect," she said, stepping closer and studying it from every angle.

Teryn nodded. He already knew it was. This was the seventh time he'd perfectly replicated the markings they'd found in the book from memory alone. Before this, he'd practiced tracing it, then copying the image beside the original. He'd lost count of how many unsuccessful attempts he'd made before his seven perfect ones, but he knew how many days had passed. Five since they'd discovered the pattern. Six since he'd had last seen Cora.

Despite Emylia's insistence that the blood seal would eventually fade, they were still unable to project themselves outside the crystal unless Morkai was sleeping. That wouldn't have been a problem, for Teryn would have an easier time taking over his body while Morkai slept, but the sorcerer was already a step ahead. Each night, he'd begun tying a wrist to the bedpost, and the vials of blood Teryn needed to draw the pattern with were always at the far end of the room. This meant Teryn had to first throw all his efforts into untying the binds around his wrists before he could attempt anything else. Even so, Morkai almost always awoke before Teryn could free his wrist. The one time he'd managed to free himself, he was so fatigued that he hadn't managed more than a single step away from the bed before he lost consciousness.

He hated his own futility. While he'd grown more adept at seizing control over his cereba at night, it still wasn't easy. His moves were uncoordinated, erratic, his limbs too heavy as if they weren't his own. The only time he'd felt somewhat whole was when he'd stepped into his body to kiss Cora.

His heart ached at the thought of her. Where was she? Was she somewhere safe? He had no idea what was happening during the day. What dark deeds had Morkai accomplished in Teryn's absence?

He had no answers. All he could do was practice.

Practice.

Practice.

So that when the time came, he'd be ready to act.

He waved his hand through the weaving and the light dissolved. "Again," he said, and started the drawing all over again, working from the bottom up.

Emylia had shown him the memory of the original weaving. She'd been telling the truth about it being too far away for her to clearly see. The crystal had been resting on a stone in the forest while a pair of hunters held down a gray unicorn with iron chains. Morkai had stood in the shadows far from the crystal—beyond the radius Emylia could project from—while he'd woven his pattern of blood. Unlike Teryn, Morkai didn't use his hands to manipulate blood. Instead, the blood moved on its own above the sorcerer's palm. Still, Teryn had been able to make out one important detail: where the pattern started. It began with a straight line across before weaving downward toward Morkai's hand.

After studying the pattern, Teryn knew it had been forged of a single unbroken line from top to bottom. All Teryn had to do was draw it in reverse. To fully break the spell, he'd need to draw it with the sorcerer's blood, and to do that he'd need to memorize the pattern.

He had one step down. One step that he was determined to repeat over and over—

Teryn's hand froze, his newest drawing only a quarter complete. A sense of pressure eased from around him. It was a sensation he'd only begun to feel since Morkai had blocked him and Emylia from projecting, and he rarely noticed it until it was gone. The only time it dissipated was when Morkai was asleep.

His eyes met Emylia's, and she gave him a nod.

It was time to practice in a more tangible way. Perhaps this time he'd make it across the room to the vials of blood.

But as he and Emylia projected their etheras outside the crystal, it wasn't into the dark bedroom at Ridine Castle. It was a clearing in a dense forest blanketed by night, illuminated under shafts of moonlight that stretched pale claws through the treetops. Teryn's body was hunched on the ground. The sorcerer inhabiting the body curled his fingers, one hand digging into the earth, the other clutching his chest. His head was bent over several pieces of parchment that littered the mossy forest floor. On each page was a pattern inked in red.

Blood weavings.

Morkai's chest heaved, but it was Teryn who felt those breaths, felt the shallow pulses of air that moved inside him. Morkai sat back on his heels and threw his head back, letting the moonlight wash over his face. His lips twisted in a triumphant smile.

Teryn looked from the sorcerer to the bloodstained papers, then to Emylia. "What has he done?"

Her gaze was locked on something farther away.

Teryn followed her line of sight. His breath caught as he saw a hulking form half hidden in shadow. He stepped closer, noting the silhouette of a pair of antlers, an enormous set of paws. The creature shifted on those paws and took a lumbering step toward Morkai. Moonlight shone on brown fur and claws that dug into the earth. Another step revealed a boar-like snout with curving tusks, nostrils flaring over a mouth of serrated teeth. Teryn saw the antlers clearly now, each tine ending in a deadly point. But that wasn't nearly as unsettling as what rested below those antlers; where eyes should be, the creature had four fleshy faces.

Four faces with mouths locked open in a silent scream.

Four faces with hollow gazes.

Four faces Teryn knew.

Four faces that had now become a Roizan.

53

———

The Veil was even more immense up close. Cora stared up at the strange wall, watching it writhe with swirling particles of shadows and mist. When they'd first approached, Fanon had ordered her to walk through the Veil. His smug grin should have been enough to tell her it wouldn't work, but her hope had been too strong. Just when she was certain the Veil would be as yielding as a fog, she'd found herself against something solid. She'd first suspected Fanon's magic, but then she noted her hands were suddenly free, her palms pressed against the invisible wall. As realization had dawned, she'd immediately reached for her collar. But before her fingers could make contact, Fanon used his magic to pin her arms to her sides and fling her several feet back from the wall.

"Well, at least we know the wardweaving remains strong," Fanon had said. After that, he'd approached the Veil, pressed both palms to its swirling surface, and closed his eyes.

Then he'd stood there.

Unmoving.

For hours.

Or had it only been minutes? Now that she knew time moved differently here, she was unable to trust her own estimation. It certainly didn't help that she had nothing to do but stand painfully idle next to Valorre, Etrix, and Garot while Fanon faced the Veil doing...whatever the hell he was doing. Every second that crawled by was like a knife twisting in her heart. Because each of those seconds were minutes for her world. For Teryn. If day broke, they'd be approaching a week.

Mother Goddess, would Teryn last that long? What could Morkai be doing to her kingdom right now?

"I know you must be anxious to return home," Etrix said, stepping closer to her, "but we must give Fanon time. He's extending his skyweaving all along the Veil, seeking the source of a possible tear."

So that was what he was doing. If only Fanon's task took the whole of his attention. She'd tested her abilities to fight her restraints while he was so distracted, tried to approach the wall a few times, but each attempt had resulted in invisible pressure holding her back. She wasn't sure how his skyweaving worked, but his magic was obviously strong.

Garot shifted to face her. "Would you like to hear a story? I find stories relax me, and I never did finish telling you the history of your kind's dark deeds."

She bristled. So far his story had only revealed that a witch had used magic that brought him to El'Ara, and it didn't sound like a *dark deed* so much as an accident that resulted in a love affair. Their child, on the other hand, seemed a bit unhinged, but he wasn't *her kind*. He may have been half witch and a worldwalker, but he was half Elvyn too. After meeting Fanon, it wasn't hard to imagine Darius may have gotten his cruel streak from his Elvyn side.

Of course, there was likely much she still didn't know. Besides, a distraction might make the wait less agonizing. Especially if it provided more answers that could aid her escape.

"Will you tell me more about the Veil?" she asked, trying to sound more bored than desperate. "Has the border between our worlds always been here, or was it created to keep Darius out after he escaped Satsara's first ward?"

"The latter," Garot said, "though the fact that you can see it is proof that the ward is flawed. Had it been properly completed, it would be invisible to us all, and we'd never have to fear anyone crossing into our world again."

"Why wasn't it properly completed?"

Garot's tone took on that whimsical storytelling quality again. "Before I can explain that, I must first tell you of Darius' return. Feeling betrayed by what his mother had tried to do, he now came with invasion in mind. He insisted he was the rightful heir and would claim his place as Morkaius. Not Morkara, mind you, but as the self-proclaimed High King. Where the Morkara is responsible for distributing the *mora* fairly and evenly throughout the land, Darius sought to control it and harness it as he saw fit. War came. He used his worldwalking abilities to bring in human armies wielding weapons of iron. Many, many died."

Cora tried not to let the terrified awe show on her face. Darius was no doubt the first Morkaius Salinda had told her about. She remembered the story, about the illegitimate son of the Elvyn queen, how he'd sought to overthrow his sister as heir. Salinda had said the war ended in a final battle at a palace, and that an explosion had turned the structure into a ruin. She'd surmised that Centerpointe Rock had been that ruin. That was where Morkai had intended to harness fae magic from, after all. It had made sense when she'd believed the fae war had happened in her world, but how was there an Elvyn ruin in the human realm if the war happened in El'Ara?

Garot continued. "Our only hope was Satsara. As Morkara, she had the ability to make a ward stronger than anything any other wardweaver could conjure. So she and her tribunal agreed that she'd weave a ward all around El'Ara. From her seat at the palace, Satsara began weaving her ward, starting at the opposite end of our world, toward her. It took days upon days to weave, but it was almost finished. Only the land surrounding the palace remained when Darius arrived and killed her. In her dying breath, she relinquished the power of the Morkara, officially passing the role onto her heir, Ailan. But not before she secured the edges of the Veil and completed it where it had stopped—around a wide circumference of land surrounding the capital city of Le'Lana. What remained outside the Veil was pushed into your human world."

Cora blinked at him. The capital city of Le'Lana. That...must be the land once known as Lela. The land that was now divided into three portions, one of which was her own kingdom. "So you're saying the place I come from was once fae land?"

Garot nodded, eyes on the Veil. "The Veil surrounds the land that was left behind when Satsara finished her wardweaving too soon. If you came from the land that lies on the other side of this wall, the place we call the Void, then you came from what was once El'Ara's heart."

Cora's mind whirled to reconcile old facts with this new information. The Veil wasn't simply a barrier between two worlds; it was an incomplete ward that surrounded a piece of land that had once existed in another realm. All the tales of the mysterious land that had appeared out of nowhere, suddenly attached to the continent of Risa where once there had only been a beach, made sense now. Those tales hadn't been exaggerated. They'd been true.

And no one...*no one* in her world knew. Not even the Forest People.

Garot continued his story, oblivious to Cora's stunned musings. "The Veil succeeded at locking Darius outside of El'Ara. However, when Satsara had tied off the edges of her wardweaving, she hadn't known Ailan had been at the palace too. Now her heir, our true Morkara, was stuck in the human realm too."

Etrix gave a somber nod. "Which is why Fanon, Ailan's consort, has been acting as steward ever since."

Cora's gaze flew to the golden-haired fae, still standing before the Veil. He was Ailan's consort? While she couldn't forgive him for his rough treatment of her, she could sort of understand his cruel demeanor. His consort was trapped in the human realm because of a war a worldwalker had started. A war with human soldiers wielding iron weapons.

Garot lowered his voice to a whisper. "Not everyone thinks Fanon should have been named steward. Many would have rather followed Etrix."

"Garot," Etrix growled in warning.

"I'm just saying," Garot whispered. "You were Satsara's consort. Had she not relinquished the power of the Morkara before she died, you'd have been steward."

Cora's eyes widened. Etrix had been...*Satsara's* consort? The one Satsara had been forced to marry while carrying on her affair with Prince Tristaine? Cora was surprised Etrix had been able to bear Garot's tale with nothing more than the occasional furrowed brow. Then again, if what they'd said was true, over seventy-five years had passed since Satsara's death. Perhaps Etrix had been able to move on where Fanon could not.

Complicated, Valorre conveyed.

She agreed. It seemed humans weren't the only ones who had complex marriage politics.

Etrix let out a dark chuckle. "You think I want that responsibility? I have enough work on my plate as Head of Tribunal."

"I suppose you're right," Garot said. Then he turned to Cora, including her in the conversation again. "I'm certainly happy to be without Fanon's burdens. Everyone knows he's only a steward and can't direct the *mora*, yet he gets struck by the people's ire over the Blight."

Cora shifted her gaze to the decayed landscape. It struck her as more significant now that she fully understood what the Veil was. "Why is the Blight happening?"

"Another unforeseen circumstance of Satsara's incomplete wardweaving," Etrix said.

"In other words," Garot said, "the Veil is to blame for the Blight, and that is due to how the *mora* moves through El'Ara. It is born at the center of our world, in the heart of our planet's core. From there, it travels to the surface in the fire dunes, the land at the complete opposite end of our world, then travels through veins deep underground. These veins crisscross the land until they join again at the polarity opposite the fire dunes. That polarity was located in the capital city of Le'Lana. The palace of the Morkara was built directly over that polarity, its very structure designed to funnel the *mora* straight from the conjunction of those veins of power. The Morkara has always been in charge of directing the flow of *mora* back into our world, distributing it evenly, fueling light, heat, and technology."

Cora frowned. "You mean it generated flame? Like lanterns and hearths? Can you not produce flame without it?"

"Your technology is different from ours," Etrix explained. "Our light and heat come not from flame but the *mora*."

Garot's mouth quirked in a sly grin. "I once met a truthweaver who insisted the human realm would one day discover something similar. Do you have that yet? Instantaneous light? Means of travel fueled by combustion?"

Cora shook her head, having not a single clue what he was talking about.

"Disappointing," Garot said with a sigh. "I was hoping you could tell me some stories next."

Etrix frowned. "Is it not taboo to show interest in the human realm?"

Garot rolled his eyes, not bothering to answer the question. "Anyhow, because the Veil trapped the Heart of El'Ara—our very source of *mora*—in the human world, balance has been disrupted. The *mora* seeps through the Veil, traveling along those underground veins as if Le'Lana wasn't a world away. Without a Morkara, we have no one to call the *mora* back. No way to return the flow to our land. So the *mora* leaves our world and does not return. That is why the land is dying."

"That isn't the only balance that has been unsettled," Etrix said. "Without any way of directing the flow of *mora*, we have nothing to trade. We are unable to uphold our alliances with the Faeryn, which has made our relationship with them tense. They resent us for the Veil. Blame us for what is happening to the land. We fear war with them. But that's not all. While the Mermyn stick to the seas and the Djyn reside in the fire dunes, they too could pose a threat. The Blight hasn't reached them yet, but if it ever does, they could wreak havoc on our realm. The Mermyn could flood the world, or the Djyn could burn our land to cinders."

Cora was once again startled speechless. The Mermyn and Djyn...were these other types of High Fae? She'd only ever heard of the Faeryn and Elvyn. The fact that there were even more kinds of fae made her head spin. Yet the plight of the land sank her heart. "Is there nothing you can do about the Blight?"

"All we can do is wait for our Morkara," Garot said. "We don't know what happened to Ailan and Darius after the Veil went up. We only have our truth-weavers to rely on. As far as we know, the Veil will tear when we have a true Morkara again. We hope Ailan is alive and will return, but most of our truth-weavers have said our true Morkara will be born from her bloodline."

"Don't say that so loudly," Etrix said, eyes flashing toward Fanon.

Garot pursed his lips, expression abashed. "Right. Fanon doesn't like hearing about this prophesied heir, for it would suggest Ailan's heart has moved on in the human world."

"One's heart and body aren't always aligned," Etrix said. "One can love someone while physically being with another."

Garot gave him a sad smile, and Cora realized Etrix was probably referring to his relationship with Satsara. Had they loved one another, even with their forced pairing and infidelity? Or had he been the one she'd been with physically while loving someone else?

Garot spoke again. "Whether it's Ailan or this child of prophecy, we await the tear in the Veil."

Cora's pulse kicked up as his words triggered dawning realization.

The unicorns. The mother. The child. Who do you think you are in that prophecy?

Cora cursed under her breath.

This child they were waiting for, this heir of Ailan...

Was that...her future child?

The one she'd never have?

The one Morkai had ensured would never be born?

Her stomach bottomed out, adding to the hollow feeling that remained where her magic once filled.

Morkai's curse...

The fate weaving...

If left unbroken, the Elvyn might never have their Morkara again. The Blight could grow. El'Ara could be destroyed.

Panic crawled through her. She had to tell them. They *had* to help her—

"There is no tear." Fanon's voice rang out from near the Veil. Her eyes darted to him. The first blush of sunlight crept up from the horizon, illuminating his dark glower, his blue eyes pinned on her. "The Veil is fully intact, which means you lied. You couldn't have passed through the wardweaving. Worse, it means you're a worldwalker."

54

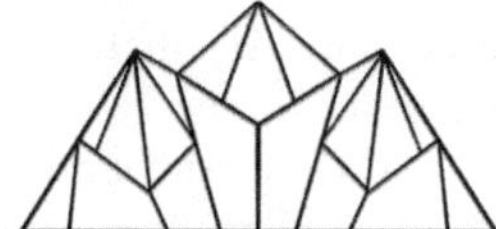

Fanon strode over to Cora, hand on the hilt of his sword. "Tell me how you got here, human."

Lie. Lie. Lie. Valorre's panicked words threaded through her mind.

Her shoulders sank with the weight of her own futility. She was tired of lying. Tired of pretending she was someone she wasn't. Lying about how she'd gotten here hadn't given her a way home. Hadn't gotten her through the Veil.

Beneath that lie was a mountain of others she'd told.

She'd lied to the inquisitors and claimed to know nothing of magic. It had earned her her place as princess, solidified Dimetreus' throne, but where were the fruits of such efforts now? Dimetreus' council still didn't trust her. Or him, for that matter. He'd lost his right to rule, was forced to abdicate according to the terms of an alliance that was supposed to be built on trust.

More recently, she'd lied to Teryn and told him nothing was wrong the night she remembered the curse, and he'd gotten possessed by a dead sorcerer.

She'd lied to Lurel. Told her the tower library wasn't dangerous. The girl was now dead.

She'd lied to the Forest People, kept her royal identity a secret. In later confessing the truth, she'd earned their distrust.

Lies upon lies upon lies.

She used to think they protected her. Saw them as a necessary precaution. But now she found they were circular. Perpetual. Simply a way to delay the inevitable.

Mother Goddess, she was tired of it.

She held Fanon's gaze, matching his glare with one of her own. *I am the very thing you fear.* The confession was perched on the tip of her tongue, moments away from leaving her lips, when Etrix stood between them.

Hands grasping the other Elvyn's shoulders, Etrix forced Fanon back a few steps. "You said the Veil is intact, Fanon. No worldwalker can move through the

Veil. You know this. Even if it had been torn, there was no guarantee a worldwalker could have gotten through."

He pointed a condemning finger at Cora. "Then how is she here?"

Valorre reared back and managed to lift off the ground, hooves flailing, before Fanon's magic brought him crashing back down to all fours. He let out an enraged whinny, but it was drowned out by a piercing screech that shattered the air in the distance.

Cora's blood went cold. She glanced at the sky and saw a familiar shape—the dragon—soaring toward them. Fanon shook loose from Etrix's grip, but instead of rounding on Cora, he faced the oncoming dragon. "Damn it, Ferrah, you unruly beast," he muttered.

"She wants the unicorn," Etrix said.

Valorre thrashed and neighed, but Fanon's restraints refused to give.

The dragon circled overhead, then began her descent.

Cora took a few steps back, angling closer to her unicorn companion. "What does she want with Valorre?"

Etrix's expression turned wary. "Like I told you, she's been seen chasing his kind through the Blight."

He didn't elaborate, but she feared the worst. She doubted the dragons only gave chase.

As the dragon drew nearer to the ground, Cora got a better look at the creature. She was massive, her sinuous body and tail the length of at least ten horses. Her scales were an opalescent white that glinted pink, blue, and purple in the rising sunlight. Her enormous wings were comprised of white feathers. Additional feathers framed her scaly face, and from her snout protruded long, trailing whiskers. Her eyes were a deep shade of violet with black slits for pupils. She landed with an earth-shaking thud several yards away.

Valorre quivered, ears twitching back and forth. *I remember her. Do not like. Not friends.*

The dragon took a darting step forth, but Fanon leaped forward too, hand outstretched. "Ferrah," he said, voice a deep growl. "Stay back."

To Cora's surprise, the dragon obeyed. Or was it Fanon's magic that held Ferrah at bay? The creature swiveled her neck to the side to get a look at Valorre. Her forked tongue flicked out of her mouth, carrying a hiss of steam.

Fanon spoke again, tone firm. "Stay. Back."

"Fanon," Garot said, wide eyes locked on the dragon. "The human said she arrived on the unicorn—"

"Let us not debate the human's lies until we've sent Ferrah back to the caves."

"Yes, but what if this has everything to do with Ferrah? What if the human is telling the truth?"

Fanon kept his gaze on the dragon a few beats more, then slowly shifted his eyes to Garot. He spoke through his teeth. "In what way?"

"What if unicorns can cross the Veil when no other creature can?"

"How is that possible?" Etrix asked.

"We know their horns have the strongest *mora*," Garot said. "Their powers haven't been compromised by the Blight unlike the rest of us. And we know they've been disappearing for the last two months."

"I thought Ferrah was to blame for that," said Fanon, turning his gaze back to the dragon.

"Yes, but what if she hasn't been chasing the unicorns to harm them? What if she's been chasing them through the Veil?"

I remember, Valorre said. *Yes. Ran from dragon.*

Cora's eyes went wide. If unicorns had been disappearing from El'Ara for two months but had been in her world for about a year now...it lined up, considering the time discrepancy between the two worlds.

Etrix frowned. "To what end?"

"The dragons have been restless for months," Garot said. "Particularly Ferrah. They've never been like this before, which means something has changed. What if Berolla's hatchlings sense the impending return of our Morkara? What if they sense Ailan or her heir and have sent the unicorns through the Veil to find them?"

Fanon scoffed. "That's a bit of a reach, isn't it?"

"Perhaps, but..." Garot glanced at Valorre. "We could test the theory. We do have a unicorn."

Etrix furrowed his brow, studying Valorre. "What do you propose?"

"We let the unicorn try to move through the Veil," Garot said. "If the unicorn slips through the wardweaving, we'll know it was the creature's horn that allowed him to pass."

Was my horn, Valorre conveyed to her. *Used your travel magic. But was my horn. It will work.*

Cora's chest sparked with hope. "You'll let us try to leave?"

Garot gave her a warm smile, but before he could utter a word of affirmation, Fanon spoke. "The unicorn can attempt to leave through the Veil, but not with the human. We must test the theory first. If the unicorn returns, we'll know for certain that the girl was telling the truth. Then we'll remove the collar and restraints and let her leave with him."

Her gaze darted to Valorre. Dread sank her stomach. She didn't like the idea of him leaving without her. What if Garot's theory was correct about how the unicorns had left, but not about their ability to come back the same way? Valorre had admitted that his horn had allowed them entrance into El'Ara, but that he'd used her ability to astral travel to get here. What if he couldn't return without her using her magic again?

Valorre voiced an additional worry. *What if Veil makes me forget? What if I don't remember you on the other side? I want to remember. Don't want to forget.*

Her anxiety only grew. Valorre could be right. When she'd met him, he hadn't remembered where he'd come from. Hadn't even been able to recall that he'd lived in another realm.

But this might be her last chance at getting home without engaging in further conflict with the Elvyn. She'd been prepared to tell the truth about her powers when it had seemed she was out of options, but this could really work. There was logic involved.

I'll do it, Valorre said. *Worried. But I'll do it.*

"All right," Cora said, her voice rough. "We'll send Valorre through the Veil, and when he returns, you'll free me and let me go back with him."

Fanon glared at her for a few moments but finally relented. "Very well. Unicorn, approach the Veil."

Valorre started to walk toward the Veil, head lowered. Cora took a step to follow but felt an invisible tug pull her back. She cut a scowl at Fanon, but he simply stared down his nose at her. Behind him, Ferrah shifted her head, tongue flicking as she watched Valorre with hungry interest.

Mother Goddess, Cora hoped Garot was right about his theory. With how the dragon kept her slitted violet eyes on Valorre, she seemed like a predatory beast, not a creature capable of masterminding a scheme to send unicorns through the Veil to find a lost heir.

Cora swallowed hard and returned her attention to Valorre. He was just a few feet from the swirling mass of mist and shadow now. Another step. Another. Now his horn was just inches from the Veil. He paused and swiveled his head toward Cora.

Will remember, he said.

Her throat went dry and burning tears pricked her eyes. She wished she had access to her magic so she could convey the full weight of her feelings—that she loved him. That he was her best friend. Her familiar. That meeting him was a miracle she'd never ever regret, no matter how much hardship had followed. But she couldn't touch her magic. She could only hope his was strong enough to read what was in her heart. With a somber smile, she gave him a nod. *I know you will.*

He held her gaze for several beats more. Then he returned to face the Veil. His next step brought his horn to the misty surface. Then his head. His neck. His shoulders. Then he was...gone.

He'd made it through.

She glanced at her companions, saw the bright awe in Garot's green eyes, the surprise in Etrix's raised brows. Only Fanon looked unimpressed. If anything, he looked annoyed. Ferrah, however, seemed calmer now. She'd settled onto her belly, legs curled up beneath her like an oversized feline. Her tail swished lazily over the colorless earth.

Cora turned back to the Veil and watched where Valorre had disappeared. Any moment now, he'd return. Any second, she'd see his horn pierce the misty wall. But with every breath she took, her sense of foreboding grew. These seconds that passed for her were minutes for him. Her minutes were his hours.

So why wasn't he coming back?

Pain lanced her heart as she considered the possibility that Valorre's fears had come to pass.

He'd...forgotten her.

No. No, even if he had, she...she'd find him again. She must.

Trembling, she faced the three fae. "Your theory was correct. Now you know how I entered your realm. Let me go home now."

"Unless you are a worldwalker, you cannot pass without a unicorn," Fanon said. "We will not send another of ours through the Veil."

Garot gave Fanon a scathing look. "You said she could leave if we proved she'd arrived like she'd said."

"I said the unicorn must return to prove our theory."

Rage simmered in Cora's gut.

"Fanon," Etrix said through his teeth, "we've proven enough. Let us find another unicorn and send her on her way."

"We cannot let her leave. She now holds vital information that will allow anyone to cross. The last thing we need is an army led by Darius charging in on the backs of our missing unicorns."

"You may be steward," Etrix said, "but you cannot decide this on your own. Take her to the tribunal if you must. Let us debate whether to send a unicorn with her so she can leave."

Fanon huffed a humorless laugh. "You know what the tribunal will choose. You may be soft, but the others aren't. They'll demand her head before she can utter a word in her defense. Better I grant her mercy now." With that, he unsheathed his sword and marched toward Cora.

Garot and Etrix tried to pull him back, but Fanon's invisible bonds pulled Cora straight to him. With a flick of his wrist, she was forced to her knees. The edge of his blade glinted in the early morning sun.

Cora's heart leaped into her throat, but she refused to let her fear show. Instead, she held his gaze, dared him to look her in the eye as he condemned her to her fate.

"Believe me, human," Fanon said, and there was a hint of pity in his eyes, "this is mercy."

Garot and Etrix fought to stop him, but he flung them back with his magic.

He lifted his sword.

"Kill me and you kill the blood of Ailan."

Fanon froze. "What?"

"You heard me. I am of Ailan's bloodline. Kill me and you kill any chance at getting your Morkara back."

His lips curled away from his teeth. "Explain."

Cora spoke quickly, every word laced with her rage. "I don't know who Darius is, but there's a man in my world who claims to be an Elvyn prince. He's been working against me most of my life because he knows I am the mother in a prophecy that claims my child would be his enemy. He calls himself Morkai and is trying to become Morkaius of my world. He plans to harness the magic that seeps from a place we call Centerpointe Rock—a ruin that once was the Morkara's palace. He will drain magic from this realm. He could come for you next and tear this entire Veil down."

Etrix and Garot both took stumbling steps forward, suddenly released from Fanon's magic. Etrix stared at her with wide eyes. "You...are of Ailan's blood?"

"Yes." It felt so wrong to say it. So false. Perhaps there was a part of her that still didn't believe it. Or maybe she just didn't want to. Admitting to such a role meant bearing the fate of two worlds. "I wasn't certain until I heard your stories, but now I know. And you can help me stop Morkai. You're stronger than he is, stronger than anyone in my world. If we don't—"

"You're not the blood of Ailan." Fanon's eyes narrowed to slits. "You haven't got a single drop of Elvyn blood in your body."

"You don't know that," Etrix said. "Only Elvyn blood relatives can sense their kin at close proximity."

"Then tell me, Etrix, is she your kin? If she's of Ailan's bloodline, then she's of yours too."

Etrix studied Cora for a few long moments, wrinkles deepening his brow.

Cora's heart racketed. What if she'd been wrong? What if Morkai had been? She held her breath, waiting for Etrix's pronouncement, words that would either condemn her as a liar...or confirm her claims once and for all.

He shook his head. "I don't sense anything—"

"Then she's lying."

"—but we have no precedent for meeting kin from a part-human, diluted bloodline. We don't know how many generations out she is from Ailan."

Fanon scoffed.

Etrix stepped in close to Fanon, brought them face to face. "Don't let your pride get in the way. If this girl truly is Ailan's kin, if she's destined to bear our true Morkara, then we must act rationally."

Fanon didn't balk at Etrix's proximity. "Very well. Let's act rationally. Come, Ferrah. There's one way to know if the human speaks truth."

"What are you doing?" Etrix bit out.

"A test," Fanon said with a smirk, "by dragon."

55

ora was hauled to her feet by Fanon's unseen tethers. The sudden movement piqued the dragon's interest. Her pupils narrowed, and she slowly began to rise from her belly, planting her four slender legs beneath her. She splayed her white feathered wings before folding them onto her back. Her tongue flicked out several times, sending wisps of smoke curling into the air. The sun was climbing higher from the horizon, casting the gray landscape under a glow that did nothing to warm the stark appearance of the Blight. Nor did it thaw the ice in Cora's heart.

"What are you going to do to me?" she asked, voice trembling.

Fanon gestured over his shoulder for the dragon to approach. With slow, slithering moves, Ferrah crept toward them. "Only the Morkara's bloodline can bond with a dragon. Since I am Ailan's consort, I can command them and hope they listen, but I cannot bond with them. If you're truly of Ailan's lineage, you'll have no problem bonding with Ferrah."

"That could work," Garot said, expression brightening.

Etrix didn't share his enthusiasm. "This is reckless."

Fanon shrugged. "It's the only way we'll know for sure."

Cora's eyes darted from the approaching dragon to the three fae. She tossed Etrix a pleading look, but he gave Fanon no further argument.

Ferrah was just behind Fanon now, her slitted eyes locked on Cora. The creature was stunningly beautiful with her opalescent scales, her feathered wings, her long whiskers. She was a faerytale creature come to life. A fae she'd always fantasized about when she and Maiya had visited the hot spring caves. The Forest People's stories insisted dragons had once lived in the caves, and that—over time—the creatures had turned into the bioluminescent worms that now inhabited them. She'd never been sure if she believed those tales, but they had been enchanting. Charming.

The dragon who stood before her now was anything but charming. Beautiful, yes. Terrifying, more so.

Fanon stepped to the side, leaving only empty space between Cora and the dragon. Her muscles seized up as the creature stared down at her.

"Go ahead," Fanon said, a false smile tugging his lips. "Bond."

"What the hell does that mean?" she ground through her teeth.

"She doesn't know how." Etrix shifted his jaw side to side. "All you're doing is frightening her."

"Oh, that's all right," Garot said, tone gentle. He took a step forward but halted in place when Ferrah swiveled her head toward him with a sharp hiss. "Sorry, Ferrah. Allow me to show your new mommy how all of this works."

Cora paled. She didn't want to be this creature's *new mommy*. She already had a familiar.

Ferrah flicked her tongue at Garot a few more times, then took a step back. Cora noted the horrifying length of her claws, along with the deep gouges left in the soil where her talons had just been.

With slow moves, Garot shifted to the side, his gaze on Cora. "First, you're going to bow. Dragons are proud creatures and will refuse to bond with anyone —even someone of the Morkara's bloodline—who doesn't bow first. After that, you're going to hold your body as still as you can. One arm must stay loose at your side, fingers spread to show you hold no weapon. Your other must lift, palm forward, toward Ferrah." He demonstrated but did so away from the dragon.

When Cora failed to mimic him, he gave her an encouraging nod. "Go ahead. It's your turn. Face Ferrah and greet her."

She gave him a pointed look. "I can't move my arms at all."

Something loosened around her, and she found her arms suddenly free. Her muscles ached from disuse. The only time she'd been free since Fanon had trapped her was when he'd forced her to walk into the misty wall. But now...she was truly free. Her fingers flinched, tingling with anticipation. If she wanted, she could reach for the collar, remove it, and access her magic. She could avoid this ridiculous ritual and be back home before she knew it—

"Make any move but those Garot has shown you," Fanon said, "and I'll have your arms pinned in place again. Then you can be Ferrah's snack instead."

It took all her effort to keep herself from reaching for the collar regardless. But she knew removing the collar was only the first obstacle. She'd used her traveling abilities twice, and both times she'd needed time to tune in to her emotions.

"What are you waiting for, human?" Fanon let out a cruel chuckle. "Are you frightened because you lied? If you are the blood of Ailan, then you have nothing to fear."

Her stomach tied itself in knots. She *was* of Ailan's blood. Wasn't she? Morkai had been so certain of who she'd been that he'd cursed her. It was still so much to wrap her mind around. So much to doubt. To fear.

But...

But she had to try.

If this worked, she could earn the Elvyn's respect. Get them on her side.

Encourage them to help her fight Morkai. Beseech them to find a way to reverse the blood weaving he'd placed upon her.

And if it doesn't work, this thing is going to eat me. That she was certain of.

"The dragon or my blade," Fanon said. "Choose which you'd rather greet. Now."

Gritting her teeth, she fully faced Ferrah. Every muscle in her body quivered as she lowered her head into a bow. She held the position for several long seconds before slowly straightening to her full height. She bit back a scream as she found Ferrah's face just a few feet from hers. The dragon studied her, shifting her head from side to side.

"Now lift your hand," Garot called in a too-loud whisper.

She didn't want to move at all, but she feared what would happen if she didn't.

Breathe, she chanted in her mind. *Breathe.*

Air flooded her nostrils, steadying her nerves the slightest bit. The sensation would have brought more comfort if she could feel the familiar magical connection to the air element. Without it, it was just air moving through her lungs. Nothing else. At least it was something. Routine.

Finally, she forced herself to move. With one arm loose at her side, fingers splayed to show her hand was empty, she lifted the other, palm forward.

"Level with her snout," Etrix said, but she couldn't bear to look at him. Of the three, his emotions had proved to be the most rational in any given moment. If his eyes held fear, her terror would grow.

She raised her palm until it was just a foot away from Ferrah's snout. Everything inside her told her to snatch her hand back. She yearned for her magic, yearned to feel the tingle of it surging through her palms. Then perhaps she'd know for sure whether she was doing the right thing.

Or if this was all a terrible mistake.

Ferrah flicked her tongue. Once. Twice. It tickled Cora's palm, while steam wafted over her face.

Cora's heart hammered so hard, she feared it would crack a rib. Her lungs constricted with panic.

Ferrah's throat rumbled with something like a growl. Her scaly lips lifted in a snarl, revealing the pointed tips of her teeth. The breath that brushed Cora's face became unbearably hot.

"It isn't working," Garot said, tone panicked. "Maybe her blood is too diluted. Maybe Ferrah doesn't recognize her as Ailan's kin."

Fanon let out a dark chuckle. "What happened to your theory that the dragons had sensed some great awakening of Ailan's heir? Here's proof that you were wrong."

Ferrah opened her mouth wider, revealing a bright glow at the back of her throat.

Cora stumbled a step back.

"No, Fanon," Etrix said, tone laced with panic. "Maybe it's the collar. It's dulling the *mora* in her blood." Then louder, he shouted at Cora. "Take off the collar!"

"Do not—" Fanon's words ended with hiss as Cora reached for the collar with both hands. Pulling the two sides, she opened the cuff on its hinge and pried the tines from her neck.

Emotion surged through her in a rush. Warmth blazed from her chest, down her arms, filling her palms with a tingling heat. Fear echoed through her—her own mixed with Etrix's and Garot's. From Fanon, she felt anger and vindictive pride. And from the dragon...

Cora met her slitted purple gaze and was struck with the heat of Ferrah's ire. Her annoyance. Her enraged confusion. Ferrah's sinuous neck quivered with another growl, her breath so hot it scalded Cora's face. The glow at the back of her throat grew brighter. Brighter.

It's going to kill me. Cora was certain, whether from common sense or the return of her clairsentience.

To make matters clearer, a warning rang through her, filling her body with urgency. *Run.*

The dragon swung her head back and bellowed a screech.

"Get back!" Etrix yelled. He and Garot dove out of the way. Even Fanon looked panicked as he retreated several steps back. Ferrah lowered her head, but Cora didn't wait to see what happened. Turning around, she kicked up her feet and ran as fast as she could.

The ground trembled behind her, and heat licked her ankles. A bright blaze flashed in her periphery—purple flames—but she forced herself faster. Faster.

She knew what she had to do. And now that she'd removed the collar, she could do it.

With a deep breath, she called the elements to her. Air in her lungs. Earth beneath her feet. Water in her blood. Fire chasing her steps. It wrapped around her, fueling her emotions. Fear. Terror. Worry. She sank into these feelings, affirmed their presence, their legitimacy.

The ground shook faster now, and another screech rang out behind her.

She closed her eyes and sought something lighter than fear. Something warmer than dread. Her thoughts immediately went to Teryn. A spike of worry surged through her, but she kept her thoughts on a softer path. A vision flashed in her mind's eye, of her and Teryn's kiss against the tree. Calm flooded her mind. Her heart. Her soul.

Yes.

That was where she could go.

She continued to run blindly, pumping her legs over the barren earth, trusting herself not to fall, and turned her thoughts over to Teryn. His lips on hers. His hands in her hair.

Her chest warmed. Her heart flitted.

She enveloped those emotions around her and visualized the tree under which they'd kissed. She saw its wide trunk, its bark, its bright green leaves. She saw the grass covering the cliff. Saw the wildflower meadow beneath it.

Every part of her felt like she was there.

Safe.

Home.

Heat scalded her back, but she ignored it, imagining it was sunlight blazing over the cliffside instead.

She sent a surge of magic into her feet...

And took a purpose-fueled step.

As her feet landed, the ground softened, the air shifted. She opened her eyes and flung out her hands, stumbling as she nearly collided with the tree she'd held in her mind's eye. Night surrounded her, as did the scents of the familiar woods. She'd done it. She was here. A cry of relief escaped her throat, and she sank to the base of the trunk, arms curled around her knees as she caught her breath.

She sat like that for minutes on end. Sobs tore from her chest, erupting with the weight of her emotions, the return of her magic, the terror of what had just happened.

Once she could breathe easily again, she unhooked her arms from around her knees and rose to her feet. She brushed out the skirt of her robe, frowning at its singed hem. A tendril of dark hair caught her eye, and she saw it too had been singed. Only then did she note the faint smell of burning in the air. How much hair had she lost? Was the back of her robe intact?

She reached for the lock of hair but realized she still held the collar in one hand. With a glare, she shoved it into her robe pocket with far more force than necessary. Then, stepping toward the edge of the cliff and into the moonlight, she assessed the charred strand. She ran her fingers through her tangled ends, relieved to find most of her hair still there—

Movement caught her eye from beneath the cliff. The moon illuminated the vast meadow below.

Cora bit her lip to smother her shout of alarm.

It wasn't the tents that startled her. Not the makeshift camp that had invaded what she'd once considered her most favorite and sacred location.

It was the monster that emerged from the trees.

56

___

A thunderous roar reverberated through the night. It echoed through the tent, shattering the moment Mareleau and Larylis had been sharing. Sweetness had filled their embrace mere moments ago—mingling with the joy and terror that came with knowing they'd soon be parents—but now they both froze, tensing in each other's arms.

"What was that?" Mareleau whispered.

"A bear, probably," Larylis said, trying to appear composed. Though he'd gone on countless hunts with his brother growing up, he never fully understood its appeal. Hunting prey, delivering killing blows, hearing animalistic screams when a wound missed its mark and caused unnecessary pain...he'd hated all of it. The sound he'd just heard reminded him too much of those screams—an eerie, keening cry of pain.

"A bear?" Mareleau pulled back from him, face ashen. "Bears can't claw through tents, can they?"

He forced a reassuring smile to his lips. "There will be guards on patrol, ready to confront any hungry interlopers." Even as he said it, an unsettling chill fell over him. In the wake of the roar, he heard only silence. He was grateful not to hear a repeat of the sound, but he expected to at least catch strains of commotion coming from the camp. As far as he could tell, the roar had come from nearby in the woods, which meant everyone else would have heard it too.

But...now that he thought about it, he hadn't heard anything to suggest the hunting party had returned from their hunt. The darkness blanketing the tent walls told him it was well past nightfall, so they would have returned hours ago. Of course, it was possible he would have missed the party's return. He had been rather...*distracted*.

Ever since he'd first entered the tent and laid eyes on Mareleau, she'd consumed his every thought. In the hours that followed, he'd been immersed in pleasure, in the joy of their reunion. Then came her confession, which had brought an entirely new set of emotions to contend with.

But in the hollow wake of that roar, he was reminded of all the other reasons he had to feel uneasy.

He pulled farther back and met his wife's eyes. "Mare, I need to ask you some serious questions."

She shrank down a little, pulling the small blanket her father had gifted her to her chest. He knew she'd purposefully changed the subject when he'd first suggested they speak of serious matters, but they'd ended up on one of the most significant topics anyway. Still, he couldn't let her escape his line of questioning this time.

"There was a reason why I left my retinue to make haste to Ridine. That same reason drove your father to join me."

"What reason?"

Anxiety tickled his chest. "Has my brother been acting...odd?"

Some of the tenseness left her composure, replaced with haughty annoyance. "Odd is a word for it."

"How so?" Larylis held his breath, hoping her answer would be something mundane, dismissible.

"In the way he talks, I suppose. For a handful of days, I thought I could come to like him as a brother, but then he got...weird. There's something going on with him. Did you see his hair?"

Larylis frowned. "He was wearing a hat when I saw him."

She barked a laugh. "Of course he was. His hair has gone half white, like an aging old man, but he acts like it's nothing. He looks unwell lately, yet he refuses to acknowledge it."

His mind stumbled over her words. Teryn's hair had gone half white? He was unwell? Larylis didn't know what to think. The hat had hidden Teryn's hair and had cast his face in shadow, so he hadn't noticed anything too odd about his appearance. Then again, he could deem Teryn's sudden inclination for tricorns odd enough. Not to mention that too-formal tone he'd used.

"Did he and Cora quarrel?" he asked. "That you know of, at least? Have you seen her lately?"

Her brows lowered, revealing a hint of concern. "I haven't seen her since the day she found out she had to marry Teryn. She was worried about...about a certain conversation they needed to have before she'd feel comfortable marrying him, but I thought she'd made peace with it. I tried to see her on her wedding day, but Teryn said she'd taken to seclusion for her own protection. He said I wouldn't be able to see her until after the peace pact was signed."

His muscles tensed. He'd already been alarmed when she'd used the words *had to marry Teryn*, for that wasn't right. Teryn had come to propose to her and fulfill the terms of the pact, but he'd never force her into something she didn't want. That, however, wasn't the most troubling thing she'd said. "What do you mean their wedding day?"

"They were supposedly married five days ago."

"Why? The alliance terms should have given them a year."

She pulled her head back. "Has no one told you?"

"Told me what?"

"Dimetreus was deemed incapable of ruling by his council. Cora was forced to take his place and ascend to queen, but the alliance agreement states she must marry Teryn for the council to accept her rule."

A chill ran down his spine. He hadn't heard a word of this, and Verdian hadn't said anything either. He could understand some level of secrecy, but this…

This felt like something else.

He rose from the bed and began to pace. "You said you haven't seen Cora in how long?"

"Six days."

"And how long has Teryn been acting different?"

"A week at least."

He halted in place. He still didn't know what it meant. How could Teryn not be Teryn? And where was Cora? If she was in seclusion for her protection as Mareleau had said, then why had she sent that letter with Berol?

Another roar shattered the air, severing Larylis' train of thought. This time, the sound was closer. It had come from the other side of the meadow, if he had to guess.

Muffled shouts of alarm followed, but far fewer than he'd expect from a full camp. A rhythmic thud like galloping hooves sped by the tent.

Then came a scream.

Larylis charged across the tent, gathering up his sword belt and strapping it around his waist. Mareleau followed after him, panic lacing her voice. "What are you doing? Where are you going?"

"To see what the seven devils is going on out there."

She clung to the front of his shirt. "Don't you dare leave me."

His resolve cracked, along with his heart. But he couldn't hide when people were screaming. When something dark and twisted was happening around him. He pulled Mareleau to his chest, pressing a kiss to her forehead. As they broke apart, he reached for his belt and unsheathed a dagger. He pressed the hilt into her palm. "Stay safe. Hide. I love you."

She was still blinking in confusion at the dagger when he fled the tent. As soon as he stepped outside, he was nearly bowled over by a charging horse—*his* horse. The palfrey paid him no heed as she darted past, disappearing into the trees behind another horse. The first must have been what he'd heard galloping by. He glanced down the other side of the meadow. He expected more chaos than a few fleeing horses. At the very least, he thought others would be out to investigate the sound. But the camp was too quiet. Too empty. He saw no other horses to suggest his brother's party had returned. And where were the guards Verdian had left behind? Who had made the muffled shouts he'd heard? Who'd screamed?

He strained his ears for the slightest sound…

Shuffling movement had him whirling to the side. He reached for his sword, unsheathing it before pointing its tip at the cluster of shadows that hovered by the nearest tent.

A whine keened from the shadows. He blinked into the night, stepping closer, and finally made out the faces of Mareleau's three maids. Relief uncoiled the knots in his stomach. "What are you doing?" he whispered.

The three were shaking, clinging to each other. "We heard that roar," Ann said, voice quavering. "We left our tent to go to our queen, and then...and then we saw a body."

Hair rose on the back of his neck. "A body?"

"A guard, I think," Ann said. "There was...blood."

His heart beat faster, and his sword arm began to tremble. "Do you know if the hunting party returned?"

Breah shook her head. "Not even the servants have come back. Only a few of us were left behind in the first place, but we haven't seen anyone in hours."

Seven devils, none of this was good. He pointed at Mareleau's pavilion and filled his voice with the command of a king. "Hide with the queen. Do not leave until I return."

With hasty nods, they shuffled away.

Larylis proceeded forward, eyes cast over the moonlit meadow. There was no sign of the creature who had made the noise. It would have been a comfort were it not for the missing hunting party and the body Ann claimed to have seen. He crept forth along the row of tents, seeking any sign—

A dark form was sprawled in the grass up ahead, and he suspected it was a body. He took a step forward, but the ground rocked beneath his feet.

One thud rumbled nearby. Then another. It was heavy and rhythmic like footfalls, but far too slow and deep to belong to a human or a horse. He turned in a half circle, trying to ascertain where it was coming from. It sounded like it was somewhere behind the tents. But as he faced the direction of the rumbling beat, a figure emerged from between the nearest pavilions, striding straight for him. The moon illuminated dark hair streaked with white, hollow cheeks, and a face as familiar to him as his own.

Teryn.

He stopped before Larylis. "Greetings, brother. Are you ready to join me on that hunt now?"

❧

Mareleau's eyes darted between the tent flap and the dagger in her hand. What was she supposed to do with a dagger? And why the hell had Larylis left her alone like this? Her legs trembled, torn between running after him and darting under the nearest piece of furniture. With the tent so sparse, the only thing she could hide under was a table.

Before she could do anything, the tent flap flew open. Her heart leaped into her throat, half with panic, half with hope, but neither danger nor salvation entered the pavilion. Instead, Ann, Breah, and Sera charged inside, uttering incoherent words as they closed in around Mareleau.

"Did you hear it?" Sera asked. "The roar?"

Now that her ladies were here, she felt some lessening of her terror. Stronger than her comfort, though, was the urge to contrast their fraying composures. She was queen. She couldn't act like them. Without intending to, she straightened her spine and threw her shoulders back. Tightening her fingers around the hilt of her blade, she lowered the dagger to her side. "Larylis said it's probably just a bear. There's nothing to get worked up about."

"Then what is *that*?" Breah's question hung in the air as a heavy thud shook the ground beneath them. With every trembling pulse, the sound drew nearer. Nearer.

"It could still be a bear," Mareleau said, but there was less conviction in her tone. Why the seven devils should she be comforted about a bear in the first place?

The thudding was so close now, the walls of the tent rippled with every beat. It was coming from the back end of the pavilion.

The three girls crowded around Mareleau, clinging to her arms, her robe. Together they took a step back, then another. The thud stopped just behind the tent. What followed was a distinct snuffling, then something heavy rubbing against the canvas, scraping the other side of the cloth wall with an ear-splitting scratch.

Mareleau flung out the hand holding the dagger, then motioned for her ladies to retreat toward the tent flap.

They took one step back, then another, as the creature continued to rub against the back of the tent.

Something pierced the canvas, a sharp tine that protruded inside.

Sera smothered a scream behind her hand, and Mareleau had to bite the inside of her cheek to keep from crying out as well.

This creature wasn't a bear. A stag then? That wasn't encouraging either. Mareleau had no direct experience with any animals but her mother's lapdogs. When they misbehaved, her mother summoned their trainers. What the hell was she to do with an angry stag?

They stepped back again, careful to keep their steps soft. Only a few feet remained between them and the tent flap. But what then? Could they run? Hide? Based on the snuffling sounds that continued, the beast had a keen sense of smell.

The tine pierced deeper through the canvas. Then, with an echo of the roar she'd heard earlier, the tent wall split as the tine tore a diagonal line across it. An enormous, misshapen head protruded through the gap, followed by paws. Hooves. The light of the lantern illuminated fur, flesh, claws, and horns, too many different characteristics to belong to a single animal.

"Run," Mareleau whispered to the other girls. The demand was meant for her as much as them, but her legs were too wobbly to move. Her hand remained thrust before her, but the dagger looked more like a toy in the presence of her terrifying foe.

Anxiety crawled up her throat, tightening her chest, but it ignited something else inside her too—the same fierce protectiveness she'd felt when she'd confessed the truth to Larylis. It didn't shrink her fear, but it settled beside it, bolstering her legs, her arms. Her fingers closed tighter around the hilt of the dagger.

"Run!" she said again, her voice a shout, and this time her body and her ladies listened. They stumbled through the tent flap and darted toward the other side of the meadow. Breah was fastest, sprinting several feet ahead, but Ann and Sera trailed behind, sobbing with every uneven step. Mareleau glanced over her shoulder in time to see Sera fall. Ann reached for her, hauling her to her feet, but an immense shadow closed in behind, backlit by a sudden leap of flames. The tent lay in tatters and was now being consumed by what must be the remnants of a smashed lantern.

The beast bounded for Ann and Sera, who were still struggling to gain purchase and run. Mareleau glanced at Breah, who was almost to the other end of the meadow now, then back at the two girls. Without a second thought, she bared her teeth and rushed to her ladies, pulling them to their feet with her free hand. With her other, she flourished the dagger at the oncoming beast. Her heart hammered so loud, it drowned out its thundering steps, its roar. She was only aware of the heat of its breath as it closed in on them.

Ann and Sera finally managed to start running again, and she shoved them before her, away from the beast. She kicked up her feet, lifted the hem of her robe, and darted after them.

A flash of fur and flesh skidded before her, blocking her retreat. She thrust out the dagger again, leaping back.

The monster faced her, mouth gaping to reveal unnaturally sharp teeth. She lifted her face, taking in the sight of the creature clearly for the first time. It was larger than a carriage with clawed front paws contrasting rear hooves. Its boarlike snout was framed with tusks. A pair of overlarge antlers sprouted from its head. Its rear ended in a bushy wolflike tail.

But its eyes.

Above its massive snout, it had four sets of eyes from four human faces, skin pulled taut over what should have been the creature's upper skull. Each face was linked to the next, skin fused with what looked like scar tissue, then melting into the more animalistic features—the boar snout, the stag head, the bear neck.

The monster shifted to the side, pinning one distinct pair of eyes on her.

Her breath caught in her throat. The dagger slid from her grip and fell into the grass at her feet.

She knew this gaze, with irises as blue as her own. Eyes lined with creases she'd watched deepen over the years. A brow constantly furrowed in either anger or frustration whenever she was in its presence.

Bile simmered in her gut.

She forced her attention away from the face, but there was nowhere else to look but at these four terrifying visages.

Uncle Ulrich.

Uncle Kevan.

King Dimetreus.

And the one that continued to look at her with its eerie, lifeless stare.

A word left her lips in a cry. "Father."

57

Cora's lungs heaved with trembling breaths, a muffled scream building in the back of her throat. She watched the meadow, vaguely noted the flames, the figures, but her brother's face was all she could see. The sight of it replayed before her eyes like a grotesque tableau, along with one undeniable truth.

Her brother was dead.

There was no way around it. She knew what the creature was. She knew what it meant to see Dimetreus' face protruding from the monster's skull.

Morkai had made her brother into a Roizan.

Along with Kevan, Ulrich, and Verdian.

He hadn't simply murdered those who stood in the way of his goals. He'd violated them. Twisted their bodies with blood magic.

She'd seen the process in the book she'd burned.

Two animals locked in battle.

Two animals dead.

Two animals reborn as one.

What did it mean that this Roizan had four faces? Animal parts from at least four different creatures? Had they all died at the same time, in the same battle, to create this abomination? Or had he created Roizan after Roizan, and pitted them against one another?

It didn't matter.

Nothing mattered.

Dimetreus...was dead.

She'd known the creature that had emerged from the trees was a Roizan, even before she'd caught a clear glimpse. It had plodded toward her cliff, and she'd watched it with bated breath, inching closer and closer to the edge for a better look. As soon as it had passed beneath where she stood, it paused, turning its monstrous face toward her. That was when she'd seen it. The faces. Her brother.

It had let out a bellowing roar then, one that had sent her stumbling back, clutching the nearest tree for stability. When next she dared look at the meadow, it was gone.

Gone.

Dimetreus was gone.

She heard another roar, this one from the other side of the meadow. The sound sent a shudder up her spine, a sensation so violent it sharpened her senses. Cut through her sorrow. Reminded her why she was here.

For Teryn.

If the Roizan was here, so was Morkai. So was Teryn.

She forced herself away from the tree and crawled back to the edge of the cliff. Fire leaped from a mangled tent, and the Roizan now circled a figure. Moonlight glinted off pale hair. Mareleau. The queen had fallen to her knees, eyes empty as the monster with her father's face paced around her.

Cora's heart stuttered at the sound of Teryn's voice. It carried over the sound of crackling flames, but it was spoken with the sorcerer's lilt. "Ah, you've found her. Very good."

She squinted into the dark until she caught sight of Teryn's body stalking toward Mareleau and the Roizan. Another figure trailed behind, steps uneven, hand clutched to his chest.

King Larylis.

Morkai held his hand open to the side, palm facing up. Cora leaned closer to the edge. She couldn't see what he held, but she could guess. Now that Morkai had his Roizan, he could perform far more impressive feats of magic than he'd been able to without it. A ball of blood likely hovered over his hand, and based on how Larylis clutched his chest, it belonged to him.

Larylis doubled over and fell to his knees.

Mareleau let out a cry.

"Now," Morkai said, "it's time for us to come to an agreement."

~

Mareleau didn't know what was worse: her father's lifeless face used as a monster's eyes or her husband's peril. The beast rounded behind her, giving her a clear view of Larylis. His shoulder dripped red, a gash splitting his sleeve. His face was twisted in agony. The way his fingers clawed at his sternum suggested he was fighting some invisible internal affliction.

Rage built alongside her terror, and she shifted her attention to the man who stood before her. He stared down his nose at her, a strange red bead hovering an inch above his open palm. He showed no fear for the beast that circled her, no concern for the flames that steadily burned away more and more of her tent. Pain pierced her heart as she remembered the gift she'd unwrapped not long ago, the beautiful blanket her father had given her, a symbol of his forgiveness and affection, now lost forever to the flames.

"What are you doing, Teryn?" She spoke with a quaver, fueled by equal parts fear and rage.

"He isn't Teryn," Larylis said, voice weak, strangled between his teeth.

Teryn shifted to the side to assess him. An amused grin curled his lips. "No?"

"I don't know how it's possible," Larylis said, "but you're Morkai."

The name echoed in Mareleau's head. It belonged to the duke who'd orchestrated the battle at Centerpointe Rock. The one who'd cursed Cora to never bear children.

She stared at the man who wore Teryn's face. It was impossible. Or it should have been. Aside from the graying hair, the pallor of his skin, and the overall signs of ill health, this *was* Teryn.

But his actions, his words, the subtle changes in his personality over the past week...

Not to mention the monster with four faces. A creation that shouldn't exist.

Larylis was right. He had to be. Somehow, this man was the former Duke Morkai brought back to life.

Larylis pinned Morkai with a scowl. "Where is my brother?"

Morkai patted his chest. "In here. This remains his body somewhat, though it won't be for long."

Larylis shifted, wincing as he tried to get a leg underneath him to stand, but Morkai curled his fingers inward toward the ball of blood. Larylis clutched his chest again and slumped back on his heels.

"Lare!" Mareleau tried to crawl forward but was intercepted by the creature. It pinned her beneath her father's empty gaze and sent her scrambling back. It rounded behind her again, returning her view of Larylis and Morkai. The sorcerer's eyes remained on her husband, that crimson ball still hovering over his hand. Was Morkai using the ball of blood to hurt Larylis somehow? To render him immobile?

Meanwhile, she was unscathed, guarded only by the monster. While the beast was terrifying, she realized something: Morkai didn't see her as a threat. Not the way he saw Larylis.

Of course Morkai wouldn't consider her a threat. He didn't know her. To him, she was just a simpleminded, pampered queen. He couldn't possibly know the full depths of her history. Her viciousness. The people she'd hurt. Lied to. Manipulated.

She could use that. The protective fire rekindled in her chest, her belly, encouraging her. Panic clawed her bones, but she could use that too. She could use all of it.

"What do you want from us?" she asked, letting her voice quaver even more, letting tears trail down her cheeks. Through her terror, she sought her trusty *magic trick*. Where normally she used it to don a confident outer shell, she used it for the opposite effect now.

Weak, she thought. *Frightened. Soft. Desperate.* The façade tugged her shoulders to her ears, raised the pitch of her voice, turned down the corners of her eyes. She hunched over the earth where she kneeled, hands digging into the soil as if she could barely hold herself up.

Morkai took a few steps closer to her. "Do not weep, Your Majesty. With your father's death, you've added yet another kingdom to your reign. Is power not worth celebrating? You are now Queen of Menah and Queen of Selay. I asked you before what you'd call your new kingdom once the two merged as one. Have you decided yet?"

"Why would I even think about such a thing at a time like this?" Her voice edged on hysteria. It was an honest illustration of her current state, but with her mind focused on crafting a weak outer persona, it helped her pretend it wasn't. Helped her detach. Feel like she was in control. "My father is dead. I don't care about what that means for me as queen."

Morkai gestured toward Larylis. "With your marriage, your husband has inherited a new kingdom as well. Your father was ambitious in setting you up as queen of one kingdom while keeping you as heir to another. It isn't unheard of for kingdoms to merge under such arrangements, but I daresay a bastard has never risen so far in such a short time."

Larylis narrowed his eyes, but his face twisted into another wince.

A sob tore from Mareleau's throat. "Stop hurting him!"

"Should Larylis die," Morkai said, "there would be quite a battle over who had the greatest right to the throne."

Terror sparked inside her. She wanted to flee from her fear, but she reminded herself that she needed it. Needed all these dark emotions to craft what she wanted Morkai to see.

She shrank down, cowering. *Weak. Small. No threat at all.*

Morkai spoke again. "As queen of the single entity that is your newly merged kingdom, you could continue to rule as reigning monarch. But without an heir, your claim will be weak. Especially when Prince Teryn still lives, and his blood right to Menah is stronger, regardless of the marital ties that have joined the kingdom to Selay."

She had to force herself not to react to the part about not having an heir. Force herself not to press a palm to her belly. Morkai didn't know. Of course he didn't. She'd told the man she'd thought was Teryn that she'd lied. She made herself sniffle, crafted a miniscule tone of voice. "What are you trying to say? You...you're going to kill my husband?"

"In the unfortunate case that Larylis dies, leaving Menah and Selay in a contest of crowns, the most peaceful solution would be the one that creates the least amount of conflict. One that keeps bloodlines and land rights as they stand, with Menah and Selay as one. Better yet, why not reform Lela? Why not join three kingdoms? Do you understand what I'm suggesting?"

She shook her head.

"Then I'll spell it out for you. For the sake of peace, the best solution would be for you to marry Teryn, the new King of Khero."

Fire boiled her blood, and she didn't have to fake her rage as she shouted at the sorcerer. "I would *never* marry Teryn."

His gaze hardened, and he curled his fingers toward the ball of blood again. Larylis cried out, head falling forward as he clawed at his torso. "I don't have to give you a choice."

"Stop!" She extended a pleading hand. "Please stop hurting him! I take it back. I'll do anything you say. Is it my kingdom you want? Menah? Selay? They're yours. Take them. Take all of it. Just let me and Larylis go."

Morkai scoffed. "You're going to hand over your kingdoms, just like that? I thought you were stronger."

The amusement in his voice said the opposite. This was exactly what he'd expected of her. She was so lost in her fear over Larylis' fate, she wasn't sure if her words had been truth or bluff. Lies had always left her lips easily, but now...now she'd do anything to save her husband. Promise anything and mean it with her whole heart.

"Let us go," she said. "Let Larylis go and our kingdoms are yours."

He barked a laugh. "You don't expect me to—" He laughed again, so abruptly, it had him stumbling forward. He caught himself, hands on his knees. As he heaved again, she realized it wasn't laughter at all but a coughing fit.

Larylis slumped, face easing with relief as he was finally freed from whatever Morkai had been doing to him. Mareleau's eyes bored into her husband, willing him to realize this was his chance. Larylis' eyes locked on the sorcerer, his hand flying to his hip—

His scabbard was empty.

He scrambled to his feet anyway, took a charging step forward.

Morkai righted himself and thrust a palm toward Larylis. Mareleau's heart sank as her husband stumbled back, clutching his chest once more. Streams of red flitted through the air from the gash in his arm, dancing toward the sorcerer's open palm. It became a ball of crimson, like the one he'd held before.

Morkai's chest heaved. He swiped his free hand over his mouth, but when he pulled his palm away, his eyes widened. Mareleau wasn't sure what he saw in his hand, but the blood smeared over his lips made it easy to guess.

He'd coughed up blood.

Whatever was wrong with Morkai—or Teryn's body—it was catching up to him. Something like fear danced in his eyes as his lips curled up in a snarl. "You want to live?"

"Let my wife go," Larylis bit out. "Do what you will with me."

"No!" Mareleau called. "Let *him* go. Please! I'll make any promise."

Morkai's jaw was tense, all prior amusement gone from his face. "Fine. I'll give you a chance to survive, brother."

"Don't call me that. You're not Teryn."

Morkai reached for the sword at his hip and freed it from its scabbard. He tossed it to the side, letting it land in the grass several feet away. "If you can survive a fight with my Roizan, I'll let you and your wife live."

The monster leaped away from Mareleau toward her husband. Morkai turned his palm to the ground, and the bead of blood disappeared. Larylis straightened, freed from the sorcery, but the monster was just a few feet away. Mareleau's heart climbed into her throat as Larylis dove to the side, reaching for the sorcerer's discarded blade.

Morkai shifted before her, blocking her view. "Stay here and watch," he muttered, reaching into his jacket pocket. He extracted a vial with one hand and unsheathed a short knife with the other. She caught sight of him rolling back his sleeve and making a shallow cut in his flesh before he turned around, back facing her.

Of course he turned his back on her.

She'd succeeded in presenting herself as weak. To him, she was just a woman he could manipulate. A queen he could steal from.

She inched backward, lips peeled back in a snarl. Her hand closed over something hard. Glancing down, she saw the hilt of a dagger. It was the one Larylis had given her before he'd left the tent. She'd dropped it when she'd glimpsed her father's face on the monster, but now her fingers curled around it. Chest heaving, she rose to her feet, blade in hand.

58

Teryn tried to step into his body, but it was no use. Morkai's grip on Teryn's cereba was too strong. It was nowhere near as malleable as it was when the sorcerer was asleep. The only time he'd managed to control his body while awake was when he'd intercepted Cora's kiss. He couldn't fathom what was different now, aside from Cora's obvious absence. Perhaps the Roizan was to blame. Already Teryn could tell the sorcerer's magic was stronger. No longer forced to rely on spells cast on paper, he could weave blood through the air like he had before he'd died.

Morkai was doing so now. A pattern formed over his open palm, one intricate line at a time. It was constructed from two strands—one emerging from the vial in his hand, the other from the blood that seeped from the cut in his forearm.

Teryn cast a glance at his brother and found him engaged with the Roizan. They clashed, a flurry of claws and teeth versus the sword Larylis had managed to snatch from the ground. Teryn's eyes flashed back to the weaving Morkai was creating, the strands of blood that danced through the air in complex loops and lines. He knew better than to trust what Morkai had said; there was no way he'd let Larylis live. He knew what his plans for Mareleau were—to provide Emylia a body —but even she would have to die to bring it to fruition. And since Morkai had Teryn's body to blame for all that he did, all that he forced Larylis and Mareleau to sacrifice, he had a workaround over the rule that the crown must be *given not taken*.

Teryn looked back at the fight. It had barely begun, but already Larylis had suffered a slice over his torso. Though Teryn had a feeling the battle was more than one of survival. If Morkai was forging a blood weaving...

"He'll make Larylis part of his Roizan," he said under his breath. With a renewed sense of urgency, he stepped into his body once more, felt the buzzing resistance all around him. His ethera fought against the movements of a physical form not under his control. He aligned his ethera's hands with his body's hands, tried to wrest control, turn his wrist, drop the blood—

"He's not making another Roizan." Emylia appeared before him, gaze locked on Morkai's palm. Her eyes lifted to his, wide with terror. "Creating a Roizan with multiple human lives made it strong enough to do what he needs to do next. Your brother's battle with the Roizan is a distraction. You saw how Morkai coughed up blood. He's running out of time. You both are."

Teryn glanced back at the pattern that continued to weave, studied the two distinct threads of blood that tangled together. Something tugged at the edges of his ethera, an unyielding pressure that grew with every beat of his heart.

"I recognize this pattern," Emylia said. "He's finalizing his possession of your body."

CORA DIDN'T KNOW WHERE TO LOOK, WHAT TO DO. CHAOS FILLED THE MEADOW AS the fire continued to eat away at the tent, its flames now lapping up the sides of the next one over. Larylis was doing his best against the Roizan, focusing on dodging swipes and landing blows on its limbs to slow it down, but it was an unwinnable fight. His only advantage was the creature's bulk and lack of agility. Even so, the Roizan was a monster of magic. She had no doubt it could outlast a human's stamina. All it needed was one fatal swipe of claws. One violent kick of its rear hooves.

Then there was Teryn. She hoped his soul was safe for now, but Morkai was using his body to cast a blood weaving. She had to stop him. She had to do *something*.

Her hands went reflexively to her waist, her back, desperate for her bow or a dagger. The motions were futile; she already knew she'd find no weapon—

Except...there was *something* there.

The hand that clutched her empty hip brushed over a lump in her pocket. She patted it again, making out the curved shape of the collar that had pierced her neck not long ago, rendering her magic null. Calm certainty flooded her as she extracted the device. Her eyes narrowed on Teryn's body. She could cross the distance between them, collar him, and sever Morkai's magic. It wouldn't stop the Roizan from fighting Larylis, as the creature was its own vessel for magic, but she could at least stop Morkai from completing his weaving. It might even return Teryn's soul to its rightful place.

She hoped.

Breathing deeply, she forced her nerves to steady, her mind to clear. She rooted her feet to the earth, gathered lungfuls of smoky air, let the flames dancing in the meadow fuel her fury, let her warm affection for Teryn guide her emotions, calling her to cross the space between them...

Light glinted off steel, and her eyes locked on the blade in Mareleau's hand. Her stomach clenched, threatening to shatter her concentration. She exhaled her panic, focused on Teryn's back, the familiar curve of his neck, the width of his shoulders, the sturdy feel of them beneath her palms.

Mareleau charged forward, thrust the blade toward the bottom of his ribs...

Cora closed her eyes.

Opened the two ends of the collar.

Took a step.

And felt the knife meant for Teryn sink into her shoulder.

Cora ignored the pain that radiated through her back, her arms, and instead focused on snapping the collar shut. Closing on its hinge, the pointed edges dug into Teryn's neck. He went rigid, a cry escaping his lips. From behind him, she pressed her palms to the sides of his face, stood on tiptoe, and whispered his name.

"Teryn."

THE SOUND OF CORA'S VOICE SENT TERYN'S ETHERA SURGING INTO HIS BODY. PAIN erupted at the sides of his neck, and he fell to his knees. Then she was there, rounding to the front of him, her hands framing his face, her voice caressing his ears. Ears that were his. A touch he could feel. Her face filled his vision, her brow knitted with concern.

He was home.

Home.

His body was his own.

"Cora!" Mareleau's voice trembled as she crouched beside them. A dagger shook in her hand before falling to the ground. "Cora, I'm sorry."

Cora's throat bobbed. "Bind my shoulder," she barked at Mareleau. "Hurry."

Teryn blinked a few times, willing his mind to reconcile what was happening, the sensation of being whole again. Something still felt wrong. There remained a pull at the edges of his awareness. He shook the thought from his mind, more concerned with Cora. "Your shoulder," he said, voice far weaker than he wanted. "What happened?"

"Mareleau stabbed me," Cora said, though there was no ire in her tone, only cold logic. Her grimace, however, revealed her pain. Through her teeth, she said, "Luckily, she's lousy with a blade."

"It was meant for him," Mareleau bit out, then pursed her lips as she tore the silk belt from around her robe and began wrapping it around Cora's upper arm. "I...I thought he was Morkai. I thought Teryn was gone."

Teryn swallowed the dryness in his throat and tasted blood. "I wouldn't blame you," he said to Mareleau, "if the blade had met its mark. If it rids us of Morkai—"

"No." Cora's tone was sharp. She lowered the hand that belonged to the same side as her injured shoulder but kept the other on his cheek. Her touch was warm against his flesh. He was grateful for the pressure. It seemed to anchor him into his body. Did she know that? Was that why she wouldn't sever the touch? "You aren't sacrificing yourself, so don't you dare suggest it."

"Cora..." He lifted a hand, his moves slow and heavy, and managed to brush his thumb along her cheek. Even that much movement fatigued him. How long could he keep this up? As he dropped his hand, he felt a renewed surge of pain at the sides of his throat. "What is this?"

"It's a collar that suppresses magic."

He had no idea where she'd come across such an item, but if it was responsible for keeping Morkai at bay, he was grateful for it.

Something tugged on his awareness again. Pressure clawed at his ethera, trying to drag him out of his body. He winced. "He's still fighting me."

"And that thing is still fighting Larylis," Mareleau said, tone frantic. "We have to help him."

Cora whirled to the side, though she kept a hand on his cheek. Teryn frowned as something caught his attention. Hovering in the air above Cora's head, nearly invisible amongst the chaos and commotion, was a tapestry of blood. Two interlocking threads wove tighter and tighter, moving of their own accord.

His pulse quickened. Morkai's blood weaving...was finishing itself, even with the sorcerer no longer in control of Teryn's body. He glanced at the gash in his arm, the hand that had held the vial of blood Morkai had used for the tapestry. Crimson had ceased streaming from his cut, and the glass bottle lay on the ground, its contents seeping into the earth. Yet that didn't stop the tapestry from weaving higher and higher.

He lifted a hand and attempted to swipe his fingers through the pattern. An invisible force blocked him. Cora turned her attention back to him, then at the pattern suspended over her head. She gasped and shrank away from it. He tried again to swipe at it, from a different angle this time, but his fingers stopped an inch away.

The Roizan. It had to be the key, the reason Morkai's magic endured despite the strange collar Cora had put around Teryn's neck. And if the tapestry reached completion before Teryn could break the crystal...

Panic seared his heart, but alongside it was a cold and heavy sense of resolution. "I have to end this now."

CORA'S BROW FURROWED AS TERYN SHRUGGED OFF HIS JACKET AND HIS WAISTCOAT, then undid the buttons of his shirt. "What are you doing, Teryn?"

"I need a reed," he said, voice weak but surprisingly calm.

"A reed?"

"To write with." He reached the middle button of his shirt, revealing something underneath, strung by a leather strap. The nearby flames glinted off the facets of a crystal—

He paused and covered it with his hand. "Don't look at the light."

She averted her gaze, but memories surged through her. The unbreakable stone. The night Teryn had fought through Morkai's possession and told her the truth. The many enchantments that had forced her to forget about the object. She kept her eyes on his as he finished unbuttoning his shirt.

He spread the article on the grass before him and extracted a fresh vial from within his discarded waistcoat. "A reed," he repeated. "Please, Cora."

She jumped into action, plucking a tall slender stalk of grass that hadn't been trampled by the Roizan. "What are you doing?" she repeated, handing it to him.

"Reversing the spell on the crystal so it's no longer unbreakable. Once I finish drawing the pattern, you'll need to take the crystal from around my neck, ensuring it's no longer touching my body—at least sixteen inches away from my chest—and shatter it." He unstoppered the vial and dipped the reed inside. Its tip dripped crimson as he brought it to the bottom hem of the back of the shirt. There he paused, eyes unfocused. Then he lifted his gaze to Cora's, his free hand brushing his collarbone. "You said this device blocks magic?"

She nodded.

He cursed. "This won't work unless we remove it. What I'm about to do is considered blood magic. I may not need to be a witch to draw the pattern, but...we can't risk it not working. This could be our only chance."

Anxiety raced through her. "The collar might be the only thing keeping Morkai at bay. You said he's still fighting you. What if he regains control without it?"

"I'll fight back," he said, but as the words left his lips, a trail of blood began to trickle from his nose.

She crouched beside him again, tone frenzied. "He's already hurting you. Teryn, you're bleeding!"

His face fell, but there was no surprise in his eyes. "I'll do whatever it takes. If he regains control, touch me again and call my name."

Tremors seized her. His battle with Morkai was killing him, that much was clear. The more he fought, the more his body suffered. But what other choice did they have?

"Remove the collar, Cora," he said, tone soft. Mournful. Resolute. "We don't have much time."

She tried not to read too far into his words. Tried not to think what he meant by *we don't have much time.* Tried not to hear the resignation in his tone that told her he was ready to die.

With trembling hands, she reached behind his neck, separated the two sides of the collar, and pulled it away.

He offered her a sad smile.

And began to paint with blood.

59

Larylis wasn't a warrior. He was hardly a king. He'd been trained in the art of the sword alongside his brother, but his strength had always resided in books. Knowledge. He'd read about warriors, survivors, wars, and battles. He understood combat both physically and intellectually, but he didn't consider himself a fighter. There were times when he marveled that he'd survived the battle at Centerpointe Rock at all.

That experience had certainly tested him, though he was convinced the only thing that had kept him on his feet was the incessant numbness he'd felt in the wake of his father's death. He'd felt fear then, yes, but it hadn't been as strong as his guilt. That guilt had allowed him to defy death, to risk everything, uncaring what happened to him.

He didn't have that luxury now.

Gone was his self-loathing, self-hatred. Gone was his desire to be punished for every good thing he'd been given.

I'm sorry, Father. I can no longer bear the burden of your death. I can no longer wish I'd have taken your place.

Because now, more than anything, Larylis wanted to live.

That *need* to survive generated waves of fear. It grew with every swipe of the Roizan's claws. Sent his heart thudding with every kick of the creature's hooves that brought him to the brink of death. He wasn't blanketed in numbness this time, no matter how he wished he could be. Instead, he was plagued by the selfish yearning to breathe another breath. To experience all the joys and pleasures life had in store for him.

Mareleau.

Their unborn child.

Every experience they'd yet to have.

He could tell himself he was fighting for the citizens he was responsible for too, but it wasn't the selfless desires of a king that kept his arms swinging. Kept his legs dodging. Kept his body rolling. Standing. Running. Swiping. Stabbing.

It was *her*. Their future. To hell with everything else.

The Roizan swung a massive paw. Larylis dove to the ground, but pain seared his thigh. He didn't have time to look at the wound, didn't have time to wipe the sweat from his brow. He rolled to the side, climbed to his feet, fighting the pain that screamed in every muscle, every bruise, every torn inch of flesh.

He rounded the creature, darting behind it on aching legs. The beast swung its head, trying to pin him beneath one of its four sets of eyes. With its rear hooves, it kicked out, grazing Larylis' ribs. His vision blackened, but he swung his sword again and again, grunting with the pain that radiated up his arms each time his blade met the thick hide of the Roizan. His next swing sank into the beast's slender leg.

The creature bellowed. It planted the wounded limb on the earth, but the grass had been turned to mud. The Roizan slipped. Fell. Skidded to the ground.

Larylis charged for the injured leg. Gritting his teeth, he swung. Cleaved.

Whatever it took, he'd live.

He *had* to live.

⁓

MARELEAU HAULED CORA TO HER FEET BY HER GOOD ARM, THOUGH CORA WAS certain the girl wasn't being mindful of the wound she'd inflicted. "What are you doing?" Mareleau asked, eyes darting from Cora to Teryn. She gestured toward the field, teeth bared in frustration. "We have to help Larylis."

Cora spotted Larylis scrambling to his feet, moves lethargic. The Roizan hobbled after him, one of its hind legs missing. Larylis must have severed it to slow it down. The beast opened its maw, raking its tusks from side to side as it charged in close. Larylis rolled to the other side and dove to his feet, managing to sink his sword into the monster's neck. The Roizan let out a bellowing roar, then hobbled in for another charge.

Though Larylis fought relentlessly, Cora could see the exhaustion in his limbs, the ashen pallor of his skin. She cast her gaze throughout the meadow, seeking anything she could use to help him. The camp had been made as a base for a hunting excursion, but there were no weapons in sight. The hunting party must have taken them all with them.

Teryn cried out, drawing her attention back to him. His face contorted, and his hand shook as he fought to form the next line of his intricate pattern on the back of the shirt. In the next moment, his face went slack, eyes hard.

A chill shuddered through her.

She knew that look.

Knew it didn't belong to Teryn.

She rushed before him and framed his face with his hands. "Teryn."

His eyes rolled back. The sorcerer's steely gaze disappeared, and Teryn regained control of his body. She moved her hands to his shoulder, ready to inter-vene again if needed. He erupted with a cough, one that sent specks of blood flying from his lips, but he immediately returned to his task, dipping the reed back in the blood, painting a delicate slash of red, then a loop. Higher and higher the pattern climbed. He lifted his eyes, frowned at something in the air, and returned to paint another loop.

Cora squinted into the space above them where Morkai's weaving continued of its own accord. The pattern was more complex than the one Teryn was painting. It was taller too, and she feared that meant it was more complete. From the hasty speed of Teryn's brushstrokes, she got the sense that he was racing against this one. If only she could disrupt the pattern—

Something slammed against her, and she fell to her side. She looked up in time to see Teryn—no, Morkai—standing over her. Mareleau reached for her, dragging her to the side. She bit back a cry as her shoulder screamed in pain. Morkai released a growl of frustration and snapped his fingers. Suddenly, the Roizan turned away from Larylis and hobbled toward Cora and Mareleau, the four grotesque faces inching closer and closer.

Cora threw an arm around Mareleau and tried to focus on...on *somewhere* to use her magic to travel to, but her mind was racing too fast, her emotions too tangled, too panicked.

The Roizan opened its maw...

It froze, a bellowing screech piercing the air. Cora and Mareleau scrambled back. It shook its head as smoke wafted from one of the four faces—Ulrich. In the next moment, the fleshy visage blackened and charred until it sloughed off the creature in a puff of ash.

Morkai muttered a curse. He stood before his tapestry, studying it with intense concentration. The red threads continued to climb, but they were slower now.

The Roizan thrashed, bellowing in rage as the next face began to blacken.

Cora's pulse quickened, but not with fear. Hope bloomed inside her. Morkai's blood weaving must be using too much of the Roizan's magic.

With a deep inhale, she pushed her panic down and focused on the grass near Morkai's feet. On her exhale, she extricated herself from Mareleau, rose to her feet, and took a step through space.

Morkai leaped back at her sudden appearance. Before he could react, she touched his cheek and called Teryn's name.

∼

RETURNING TO HIS BODY FELT LIKE TORTURE, HIS EVERY MUSCLE ACHING, HIS STOMACH turning with bile. Yet Cora's voice cut through these sensations, bolstering him, giving him the strength to fill the space of his body. His hands became his own again, his legs under his command.

Wincing, he kneeled over his unfinished painting. His hands shook as he gathered up the discarded reed, dipped it in the sorcerer's blood, and picked up where he'd left off. His vision blurred, his lips chapped and bleeding. Every move he made grew increasingly heavy. Despite his efforts to deepen his breaths, his lungs felt shallow, uneven. His heartbeat failed to keep a steady rhythm, his pulse slowing with every second.

"You're almost there." Emylia's gentle tone entered his awareness. It sounded wrong to hear her voice with his true ears now that he was back in his body. Or was it still his ethera that heard her? She crouched beside him, the edges of her form wavering as she watched his progress. "You're so close, Teryn. You can do this."

"Why can I hear you?" He spoke the words, but they didn't leave his lips. "Why can I see you?"

Her mouth tugged into a frown. "Morkai's spell is almost complete. With every strand, it fights to sever you from your body, fights to trap you as an ethera for good. Even though you're in your body, you straddle the line between life and death. Your feelings for Cora are all that keep your connection to your cereba intact, linking it to your heart-center."

He felt Cora's hands then, palms against his cheeks, but it wasn't his flesh that felt her touch; it was the buzzing resistance of his ethera. His name left her lips over and over like a mantra.

The Roizan roared again, and Teryn felt a stronger tug, fighting to wrench him from his body.

"Teryn. Teryn. Teryn." Cora's voice kept him in place, while Emylia's urged him to keep painting. Don't lose focus. He was so close.

So close.

Cora said his name again, and this time it ended on a sob. He was vaguely aware of the blood dripping down his chin, tingling the surface of his ethera.

"One last line," Emylia whispered, the sorrow in her tone mingling with Cora's cries.

"Teryn, Teryn, Teryn..." Cora continued to chant, and he felt her lips press against his cheek, felt her cradle his face, her tears mingling with his blood.

With a final surge of intent, he painted the last line and closed the pattern in a slash of red. Then, with all the waning strength he had left, he lifted the leather strap from around his neck and shoved the crystal into Cora's trembling hands.

"I love you," he said, but the words left the lips of his ethera, not his body. "I love you," he repeated, and this time he managed a garbled whisper before his hands slipped from the crystal.

∼

CORA STARED DOWN AT TERYN, LIMP IN THE GRASS BEFORE HER. BLOOD STAINED HIS lower face, trailed down his neck and over the puncture wounds that had been left in the collar's absence. His hair was now entirely silver, skin so pale she could see blue veins beneath it. She didn't dare look at his chest, couldn't bring herself to note if it still rose and fell.

The man she loved was dying, but there was still more work to be done.

She swallowed down her sorrow and turned herself over to logic. Safety. The anchoring element of earth cradling her knees, her legs. Breathing in, she called on the element of air to guide her intellect. The growing flames fueled her resolve. Her strength of will.

The watery realm of grief would have to wait.

"Where is your dagger?" she said to Mareleau, but the other woman's eyes were locked on the Roizan. It had ceased its attack, and now a third face sloughed off into a puddle of ash.

King Verdian.

Mareleau was too distracted to pay Cora's question any heed, but she needed something to break the crystal with. If only she could find the dagger and slam the stone with its hilt. Her eyes flicked to the pattern that was suspended in midair. It continued to slowly weave, which meant they still weren't safe. So long as the crystal was intact, no one was safe from Morkai.

Ignoring the heavy ache in her heart, she slowly inched away from Teryn's side in search of the dagger, a rock—

A curved black tip caught her eye. The collar. She'd dropped it when she'd removed it from Teryn's neck, but now the pointed tines called to her. She scrambled for the cuff and gathered it in her hand. Then, dropping the crystal to the ground, she pressed one sharp tip to the widest facet.

Splinters fissured in a radius around the point...

But it didn't break.

The Roizan bellowed again, tossing its head side to side. It pushed off from the ground, angled its face until its remaining pair of eyes—Dimetreus'—locked on hers. It charged forward, teeth bared. Larylis leaped into its path. Swinging his sword in an arc, he cleaved through the Roizan's front leg, severing its paw. It skidded to the ground, thrashing to rise on its two remaining limbs.

Cora returned her focus to the collar and the crystal, pressing harder. Harder.

Another crack.

White light streamed from the fissures, nearly blinding her.

She closed her eyes against the glaring light and pressed again. Again.

The brightness struck her eyelids, and for a moment she wasn't sure if they remained open or shut.

Gritting her teeth, she forced the tine deeper into the crack. A splintering sound struck her ears, tinkling like a thousand shattering mirrors.

The pressure gave way beneath her, and she felt the sharp tine strike the soil under the crystal. The light disappeared, leaving darkness on the other side of her eyelids.

Fluttering her lashes open, she stared down at the ground.

The crystal lay in two broken halves.

The claw pierced the earth.

When she glanced up at where the blood weaving had been, there was only sky.

60

First Teryn was swallowed by darkness, his consciousness faint and floating in nothingness. No thoughts. No memories. Just a much-needed sleep. A final rest.

Then light bled into the void, splitting it into shards. It burned brighter and brighter until it was all that there was. All Teryn could see. It dimmed at the edges of his vision, shrinking inch by inch until it narrowed into two points of light.

Teryn's mind felt slow, heavy, as he took in his surroundings. They were familiar like a dream, and just as hazy.

A dark meadow bathed in fire and moonlight.

A beautiful woman crouched upon the earth.

Before her were two halves of a broken crystal from which the points of light glowed. The woman moved slowly, as if the passing of time had been reduced to a leisurely crawl. He watched as she gathered up the two halves of the crystal and brought them toward the blazing fire that lapped over the walls of a tent. It was strange seeing flames move so slowly, but even stranger to watch the woman. The longer he looked at her, the more certain he was that he knew her. The feeling only grew as she moved farther away from him. The wider the distance grew between them, the more desperate he was to draw her back.

Something warm and heavy condensed in his chest.

A name formed in his mind.

Cora.

And he remembered.

His memories brought a hollow ache, one that deepened when his eyes fell on a body sprawled in the grass nearby. He hadn't noticed it at first, not with his attention so absorbed by Cora, but now he saw his own slack face, eyes closed. Was he... dead? The world didn't look how it had when he and Emylia projected themselves outside the crystal. There was a haze between him and the plane of existence he watched. A discrepancy between time and space that sent waves of panic through him.

Stark illumination drew his attention away from his body. Even though Cora had taken the broken halves of the crystal to the fire, the two points of light remained on the earth. Beside it, another familiar figure kneeled. This one, however, didn't belong to the living world.

"Emylia," he said. His voice rang hollow, lacking all resonance.

She met his eyes briefly, lips pursed tight. While her form appeared as solid as it had inside the crystal, the edges rippled like smoke. She collected the pieces of light in her palms, as gingerly as one would handle their most fragile treasure. "I must act quickly," she said, voice as hollow as his. "We don't know what he'll become without his heart."

A bolt of alarm shot through him. "What *who* will become?"

It was fruitless to ask; he already knew the answer. A dark shadow drew his gaze to the center of the meadow. It towered twice his height, a shapeless mass of writhing tendrils that lapped out in every direction, fluttering at a violent pace as if on an invisible storm wind.

Emylia strode straight for the shadow, her moves not restricted by the sluggish momentum that had fallen over the plane of the living. Belatedly, Teryn followed her, felt the buzzing pressure between his feet and the earth beneath them. "What are you doing?"

"An ethera without a heart-center becomes a wraith," she said, "but Morkai... he could become something worse. I have to save him."

Teryn hadn't a clue how Emylia planned to save the sorcerer, nor did he think Morkai should be saved at all.

He could become something worse.

Teryn didn't like the sound of that.

His ethera constricted with fear as they approached. The shadow that was Morkai's ethera gave no reaction. It had no face. No eyes. Nothing to suggest it was sentient at all.

Emylia stepped far closer to it than Teryn dared, the two orbs of light cradled in her palms. She stared up at the shadow. A desperate emotion twisted her features, tugged the edges of her lips, turned her eyes down at the corners. Whether it was hope or terror, Teryn knew not.

"You sacrificed the first half of your heart-center to save my soul," she whispered, voice trembling.

The shadow shifted, drawing closer to her as if to hear her better. The undulating tendrils began to contract, shrinking more and more until the shadow was only as tall as Teryn. Little by little, the edges of the shadow became smooth, taking on the semblance of hands, legs, a torso. It resembled a wraith now, its body colorless and semi-transparent. Only its face remained hidden behind the rippling tendrils.

Emylia spoke again. "You sacrificed the second half of your heart-center when you tethered your soul to the crystal. In return, you became heartless."

The wraith lifted a hand and brushed it over his shadowed head. His fingers smoothed the undulating tendrils, leaving gray flesh behind to form Morkai's face.

Teryn tensed, eager to evade Morkai's gaze, but the sorcerer only had eyes for Emylia. Morkai stared down at the seer, expression cold. "Don't you dare condemn me, Emylia. Everything I've done has been for you."

Her brows lowered into a glare. "You didn't do this for me. I never wanted you to do the things you've done. I never wanted you to become Morkaius."

"You were the one who helped me learn how to become Morkaius. You gave me the knowledge I sought. How could I not use it to bring you back?"

"I regret what I channeled for you. I regret it with all my heart."

He bared his teeth. "You told me you loved me. That you'd do anything for me."

"You used me. Manipulated me." Her chest heaved, shoulders tense.

Morkai's throat bobbed. "Is that really how you feel?"

She nodded.

Rage flashed over his face, but it didn't linger. His jaw shifted side to side. When he spoke, his voice quavered with emotion. "I can't apologize. I did what I thought was right. Nothing you say will change that. Hate me now if you must. I will continue to love you as I always have, and I will cling to the love you gave me when you meant it."

Her chin wobbled. Tears glazed her eyes. "I don't hate you, Morkai. I could never hate you. Long ago, you were the man I loved." She stepped closer. Morkai flinched, his ethera going rigid. He recoiled as she lifted a hand but froze as she brought it to his cheek. Shadows rippled beneath her touch. Her lips curled into a sad smile, her eyes mournful. "I loved Desmond and always will."

Morkai's expression softened with a startling tenderness. "Emylia—"

"But you're not him."

With the hand that still cradled the light, she thrust her fist into Morkai's chest. He cried out, stumbling back. Emylia retreated as well, hand now empty.

The points of light glowed from within Morkai's chest, burning brighter and brighter until they merged as one. The light coursed through him, from his chest to his hands, feet, and head. Color spilled over his gray flesh, painting his pale eyes, his dark hair, a simple shirt, and a pair of trousers. Years filled out his cheeks somewhat, until he appeared a slightly younger version of himself. Teryn recognized this manifestation from Emylia's memories—it was Desmond. Though the edges of his form weren't fully solid, he was no longer transparent like a wraith.

He fell to his knees, hand clutched over the center of his torso. "Emylia."

She ran to him, framed his shoulders with her hands. "Des!"

He looked at her as if seeing her for the first time. Elation filled his gaze, tugged his lips into a smile. He trailed his fingertips over the curve of her cheek, her neck—

His hand fell.

Clutching his chest again, he sat back on his heels. "What did you do to me?"

Emylia's brows knitted together. "I gave you back your heart, Des. You won't be a wraith. We can move to the otherlife, side by side."

His face twisted, teeth bared. His voice came out strangled. "Why does it burn?"

Her eyes dropped to Desmond's chest, where white light began to glow through his ethera. "Des, what's happening?"

"It hurts. Gods, it hurts. What have you done?"

The light burned brighter. With a shout, he threw his head back. The white light spilled from his mouth, spiraling over his form. Desmond's limbs flailed, arms fluttering as if made of paper, while the light streamed from his hands and feet. Emylia gripped the edges of his burning ethera, but every part she touched crumbled into ash.

It continued to burn until nothing remained, neither light nor shadow. Not even ash lingered.

Emylia sat before nothing, clutching at air. She trembled, staring at the place Desmond had been a moment before.

Teryn watched, not knowing what to say. What to feel. He wasn't sorry to see all that remained of Morkai burn away. He wasn't sorry Desmond's soul couldn't be saved. Then again, he wasn't happy either.

He was...numb.

The edges of his consciousness began to fade.

Where was he? Where had he been?

Hadn't his heart ached for someone?

Hadn't there been flames?

A field?

"Teryn."

He opened his eyes. When had he closed them?

Emylia stood before him, sorrow etched into the lines of her face. "Don't fade away, Teryn. I couldn't save him, but it's not too late for you. You can still go back."

He blinked a few times, willing his mind to clear, but the haze was growing, eating at his awareness, his memories.

A tingling sensation buzzed over his shoulders, and he found Emylia was shaking him. "Don't fade away! You have to go back." She forced him to turn around, and his eyes landed on something not too far away.

A woman with dark hair bent over a body. Tears filled her eyes as she gently slapped the man's cheeks.

No, not just any man. That was *him*.

And that woman...

"Cora." Her name warmed his ethera as it left his lips.

His mind sharpened again, his memories melting back into place.

"Hurry, Teryn," Emylia said. "Connect to your vitale. Feel your heartbeat, the air filling your lungs—"

"There's nothing." The realization cleared his mind further, this time with fear. Where once he'd felt his blood and breath, there was only a hollow void. His vitale...it was lost to him.

There was no heartbeat.

No breath.

No pulse.

He was...

Teryn.

The sound was felt more than heard. It sent a shudder through him, sent awareness through every inch of his ethera. From somewhere deep inside his soul, a heavy thud echoed.

He glanced at his body, saw Cora's lips beside his ear. Tears trickled down her face. A single drop fell upon his cheek. Something buzzed against the same spot on his ethera.

Teryn.

Another echoing beat. A thud that hammered in his chest.

"There's still so much more for us to do," Cora whispered. "So much more I need to tell you. I'm not done with you yet. Do you hear me? You promised to court me. Remember? I won't let you break that promise."

A thud.

A pulse.

A breath.

"Come back to me, Teryn."

A rushing intake of air.

61

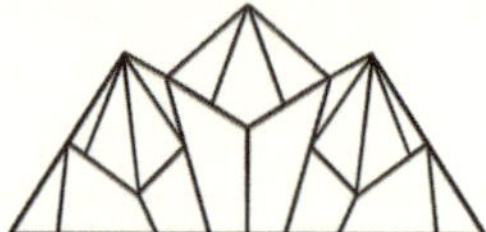

Dawn broke over the horizon, and with it came a summer storm. Cora didn't know if she had fate or magic to thank for the rain. She had prayed for it. Had sought the element of water with all her heart, begging every blade of grass to lend the meadow its dew, begging the clouds to converge if only for a day. Because rain was exactly what they needed.

Rain to stop the flames from devouring more of the tents, more of the meadow, more of the trees.

Rain to drench the earth where a mangled body had long since burned to ash, where two kings, two lords, and four animals had been laid to rest on a makeshift pyre of lantern oil and crushed wildflowers. It was the only dignity Cora and her companions could deliver those who'd died to become a Roizan. At least no one else would have to witness what had been done to them.

From under the shelter of a wide pine where the fire had yet to spread, Cora watched the downpour. Rain devoured the last remnants of the flames, leaving what had once been Cora's favorite location scarred with scorch marks and the skeletons of half-eaten tents.

"This is the best I can do." Larylis' voice pulled her focus from the meadow. She glanced down at where he crouched beside Teryn. He'd constructed a pallet of canvas tied to two beams of wood—materials that had been salvaged from one of the unburned tents.

Her eyes lingered on Teryn's slack face, his hollow cheekbones. It broke her heart to see him this way.

But at least he was alive.

He'd taken a breath in her arms, muttered something she couldn't understand. Since then, his breathing had remained steady, his heartbeat strong. He needed medical attention and rest, but Cora had hope. She'd cling to it. Tether it to her heart and carry it herself if she must.

But she wasn't alone. Larylis carried the hope with her, and she suspected Mareleau did too.

"Are you ready?" Larylis asked, glancing from Cora to Mareleau. The latter sat at the other side of the tree trunk, hugging her knees to her chest. Ann, Sera, and Breah hovered around her. Larylis had found the three ladies not long ago, when Cora and her companions carried Teryn under the tree to keep him out of the rain. They'd been hiding at the base of Cora's favorite cliff, trembling, hardly able to say a word. Now they stared sightlessly ahead, arms linked as if desperate for the comfort of another's flesh.

Larylis rounded the tree and kneeled before his wife. Placing a hand under her chin, he gently lifted her eyes to his. "We must get Teryn back to the castle. We can't wait for your father's retinue to find us."

Mareleau flinched at the mention of her father, her eyes darting toward the charred field. "We're all that's left," she whispered.

Cora's chest tightened. While Cora had been able to smother her pain, tamping it down beneath a cool blanket of logic, Mareleau's composure seemed to be clinging to frayed edges. But Mareleau was right. They were all that was left. Not just of the camp, though that was certainly true. Larylis had scouted the area and found no other survivors. He'd located the bodies of two guards in the meadow, both mutilated by the Roizan. In a nearby clearing, he'd found more signs of slaughter—claw marks in the earth, on trees. Blood. Bones. Empty saddles drenched in gore. When Morkai had created his Roizan, he must have let it feed on the witnesses, the councilmen, servants, and horses he'd brought on the hunt.

But Cora was certain Mareleau meant something else—that Cora, Mareleau, Larylis, and Teryn were all that was left to rule their kingdoms. Verdian was gone. Dimetreus too. King Arlous had been the first to perish, at Centerpointe Rock.

It was daunting to think that Menah, Selay, and Khero now lay in their hands.

Mareleau's eyes were wide and haunted as she reached for Larylis, clinging to the bloodstained collar of his shirt. Cora had bound his wounds as best she could, but he'd need medical attention too. "What will we do?" Mareleau asked.

Larylis lifted a shoulder in a fatigued shrug. "Whatever it takes."

"But...what will we tell people?" Her eyes flicked back to the meadow. "No one will believe what happened here."

Cora took a step closer to them. "We'll tell the truth. Maybe not to the public, but to those we trust."

Larylis furrowed his brow. "Are you sure that's wise? Our council will think we're crazy."

"Then let them," Cora said. "I'm tired of lying about magic. I'm tired of hiding the truth and pretending I'm something I'm not. We defeated a sorcerer. A beast. Magic exists in this world, both dark and light. It's time we stop hiding that."

Mareleau and Larylis didn't seem convinced, but it didn't matter. They could do what they wished, and so would Cora. She was Queen of Khero now. Kevan and Ulrich were no longer around to control her. To tell her what she was and wasn't qualified to do. The peace pact was broken, as were its constraining terms. She didn't need anyone's permission to rule her kingdom.

She owed it to her brother to be queen.

She owed it to herself to be a witch.

She was both, and she wouldn't shy away from either. Not anymore.

Larylis extended a hand to his wife. "Come. We must hurry."

They managed to heft the four corners of the pallet between them. Even Mareleau's three ladies managed to assist, which Cora was grateful for. With her shoulder wounded, she had but one arm to use, and even that pulled on the hastily bound lesion. Their slow pace made Cora's nerves coil tight. Every second that ticked by was one Teryn endured without proper care. She kept her eyes on his face, his chest, thanking the Mother Goddess for every breath that left his lips. Her relentless focus on him prevented her mind from straying to topics she had even less control over.

Like Valorre.

Her heart ached whenever she thought of him. Whenever she recalled how he'd left the Veil, terrified that he'd forget her.

She understood what had been missing now, why he hadn't come back. He'd only needed the magic of his horn to exit the fae realm, just like she'd only needed her magic to leave El'Ara. It was as Fanon had said: the Veil had been woven to keep worldwalkers from entering, not from leaving. But while she and Valorre had been able to leave with their own magic, they'd needed each other to enter. Without his horn paired with her worldwalking ability—a combination the Veil couldn't account for—he hadn't been able to get back in.

Either that or...

He'd forgotten her.

Stupid.

The voice flooded her heart, her mind, sending her pulse speeding. She was so shocked, she nearly dropped her side of the pallet. *Valorre?*

You are stupid to think I would forget you. My memory is mightier than that.

She nearly wept as she felt his presence. She couldn't see him, but she could feel his proximity. He was drawing closer by the second. *How did you get here?*

His smug façade faded away, replaced with genuine concern. *As soon as I crossed the Veil, it disappeared. There was no wall. Only forest in our world. I knew you'd find a way out, so I tried to return home, to where you'd go. I've been running for a day, trying to get here, but I was lost. I didn't know where the Veil had brought me.*

He'd been running for a day. To her, it had only been hours since she'd left El'Ara. *How did you find your way?*

She found me. Led me in the right direction.

She?

In answer, a rhythmic beat pulsed in the air. Cora glanced up in time to see Berol making her descent toward the pallet. Sera squealed, pulling her hands from the pallet as Berol landed on one of the wooden carrying posts.

"There you are," Larylis said. Though he tried to grin, the expression was strained. Empty. "Where have you been?"

Her wings were splayed as she shuffled down the length of the pallet until she reached Teryn's face. She tilted her head side to side, a barrage of frantic chirps erupting from her beak. She hopped from the post to the canvas, then gave Teryn's cheek a tentative peck, right over the fading scar that marred his flesh. There was something apologetic in the way she nipped at him. Had Berol given him that wound? Perhaps after Morkai had taken possession? Cora recalled how the falcon had brought Larylis' letter to her in the tower room instead of Teryn.

She nibbled his cheek again, this time a little harder. Cora was almost of a mind to shoo her away lest she injure him, but a soft smile flicked over Teryn's lips. "Berol." His voice was soft, a creaking whisper.

"He's awake!" Larylis pulled up short, forcing the rest of them to stop as well. Slowly, they lowered the pallet to the ground. The rain had ceased, and the morning sun was just beginning to peek through the clouds.

Cora ran to his side and brushed his silver hair off his forehead. "Teryn."

He caught her hand with his. His grip was loose, but he managed to squeeze her palm. "Cora...I..."

She hushed him. "Just rest. You're safe now. He's gone."

The memory of the broken crystal flashed in her mind. She'd watched it crackle and burn after she'd thrown it in the flames until there was no sign of it left. She had to trust that meant Morkai's soul was no longer able to possess anyone.

He spoke again, brow furrowed, but his words were too quiet to hear. She leaned closer and smoothed her hand over his hair. Berol chirped, nipping his ear. "It's going to be all right. It's over."

He blinked, and his green eyes gained steady focus as they locked on hers. "I...I don't think it's over."

Her hand went still in his hair. "What do you mean? Is Morkai—"

"He's gone, but...but I don't think he was the last threat to us. His father... Darius...Elvyn prince."

The name sent her stomach bottoming out. "Morkai's father was Darius?"

"Who's Darius?" Larylis said, leaning closer, but neither Cora nor Teryn took their gazes from each other.

"King Darius of Syrus," Teryn said. "He's the reason Morkai found Lela. Found you."

"King Darius of Syrus," Cora echoed. She'd heard that name. Her mother had been from the Southern Islands. She'd told Cora tales of Syrus, Zaras, and the other isles, though even if she'd had no personal knowledge of the location, the Southern Islands were hardly a secret. Selay had exclusive trade with them. Cora was certain Syrus' king—Darius Solaria—was still alive. But how did Teryn know about this?

"There's so much more I need to tell you," Teryn said. His face twisted with a wince.

She brushed her hand over his hair again. "Me too. But we have time."

He nodded, lashes fluttering shut, and sank back into slumber.

She exchanged a glance with Larylis, then Mareleau and her ladies. In wordless agreement, they hefted the pallet back up. Berol took off into the sky, soaring toward the castle.

I'm almost there, Valorre said.

She could feel him even closer now, a comfort that mingled with her growing dread.

If what Teryn had said was true, the danger they faced last night—and at Centerpointe Rock before that—might only be the beginning. Her mind whirled over possibilities.

A broken prophecy.

A fae realm, dying without its heart.

A true Morkara who would tear the Veil and make El'Ara whole.

And the mother who would bear this child, this savior...

She was no closer to breaking the spell that had been cast upon her.

Did that mean Morkai had won after all?

She shook her head, focusing instead on the rise and fall of Teryn's chest and the feel of Valorre's growing nearness. It was all she could do to face the crushing pressure as the fate of two worlds settled upon her shoulders.

EL'ARA
THE BLIGHT
THE VOID
THE VEIL

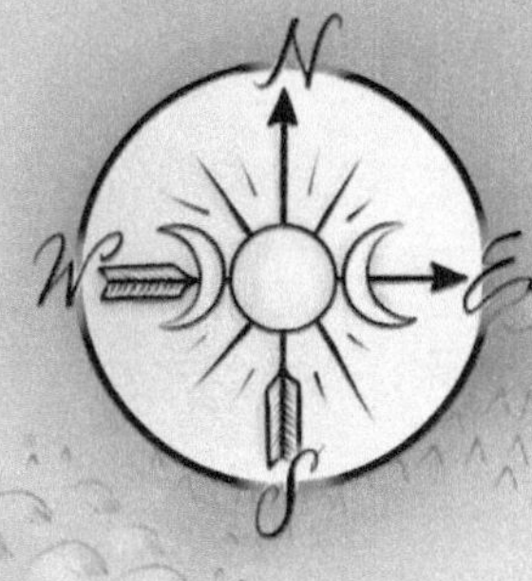

LE'LANA
BEFORE THE VEIL
PALACE OF THE MORKARA
THE MISSING HEART OF EL'ARA
N
W
E
S

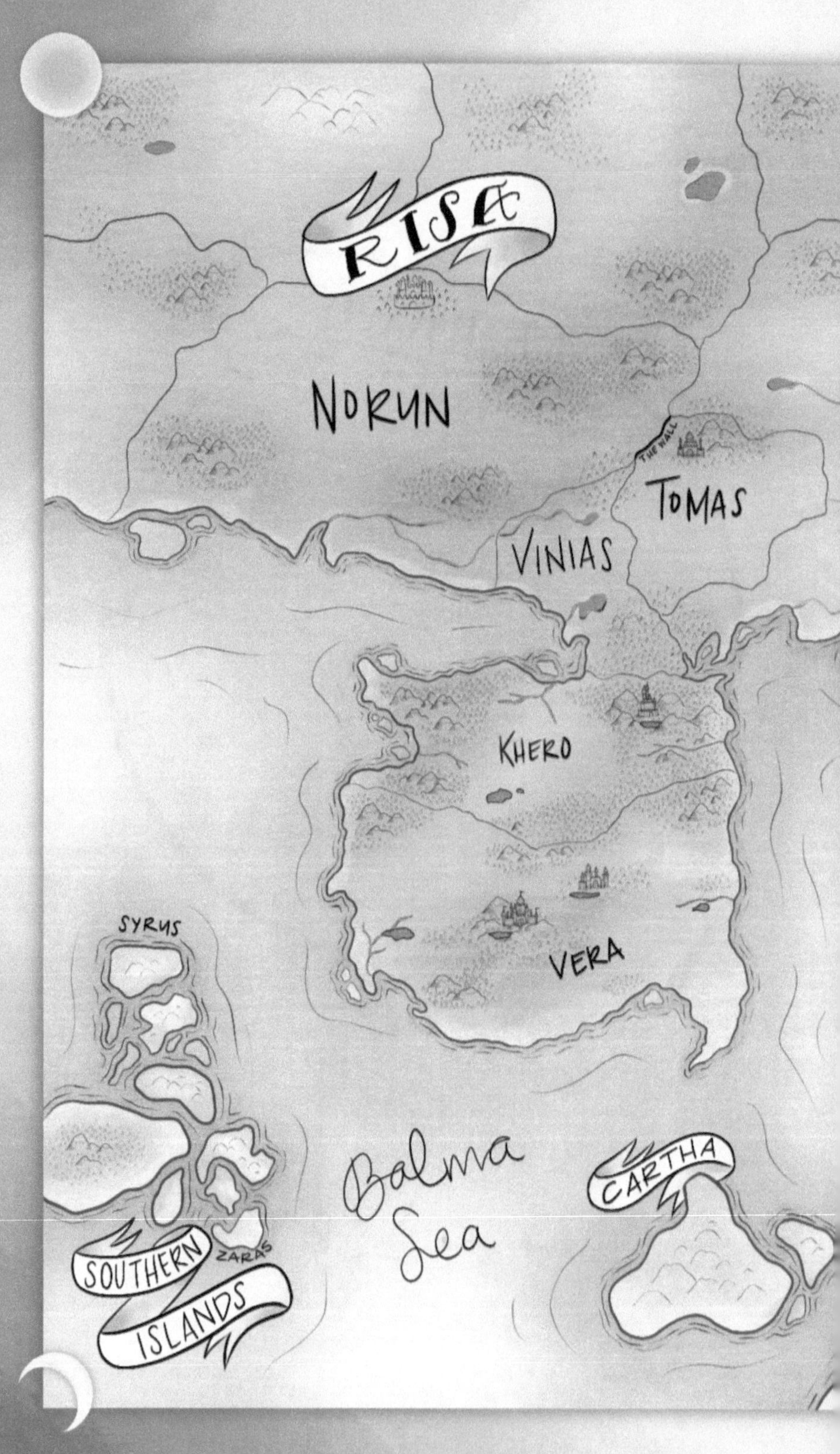

RISA
NORUN
THE WALL
TOMAS
VINIAS
KHERO
VERA
SYRUS
Balma Sea
ZARAS
SOUTHERN ISLANDS
CARTHA

LELA
DELANY
CAMBRON PASS
RIDINE CASTLE
Khero
THE TEAR
ISHVONN WOODS
CENTERPOINTE ROCK
FORMERLY SELAY
DERMAINE PALACE
VERLOT PALACE
Vera
FORMERLY MENAH
BRUSHWOLD
N
W
E
S

A FATE OF FLAME

BOOK THREE

1

veline Corasande Caelan had only one good memory of the dungeon at Ridine Castle. A kiss. It had been delivered with a blend of trickery and desire, and she'd received it with equal parts yearning and rage. It was a strange first kiss between her and Teryn Alante, but it held a special place in her heart.

It was that special place, that steadying warmth, that allowed Cora to keep her nerves from fraying in that same dungeon now. To anchor herself in this moment without letting her mind drift to all the dark memories this place conjured. Cora hated coming to the dungeon, but at least she wasn't a prisoner this time. No, this time she was the captor.

She kept her face impassive as she studied the man tied to the chair at the center of the cell. He was an older man with shaggy gray hair and a build that bordered on frail, but Cora wasn't swayed into sympathy. This man was dangerous.

Captain Alden of Cora's royal guard stepped closer to the captive, one hand on the hilt of her sword. Alden was already an imposing figure with her towering height and scarred left cheek that spoke of her experience in battle, but the way she scowled down at the prisoner, her face lit by the single lantern resting on the ground, made her look downright terrifying. Her golden hair was pulled back in a tight bun that showed off all the hard angles of her face. "Why were you seeking information about Ridine Castle?" she said, voice low and controlled.

To the prisoner's credit, he held Captain Alden's eyes without falter, even though one of his own was nearly swollen shut, and delivered his answer with equal calm. "I was simply doing my job. Every kingdom has its spies. Even yours."

Cora kept her breaths even, her palms open, seeking the truth beneath the prisoner's lies. While her abilities were far from infallible, being a clairsentient witch had its uses. Her magic worked through feeling, both physical sensation and emotion alike. She was familiar enough with her internal nudges to know which sensations meant danger and which meant safety, as well as other varying shades in between. Her emotions fueled her magic and had even allowed her to accomplish strange and unusual feats. The most recent of which was her ability to astral travel. Or, as she'd learned the fae called it, worldwalking.

Now her magic was less focused on her own feelings and more on the prisoner's. Not every clairsentient witch could physically feel the emotions of others, but Cora's magic had always been like this. It was often a burden that required nearly full-time use of mental shields to block outside emotional stimuli, but in this situation her powers were essential.

With her mental wards down, she let the man's emotions flood her. They were dark, heavy, clouded with secrets. Arrogance tinged these sensations, reflected in his smug expression, the way he grinned despite his split lip. But there was something else there too: a dash of fear. Cora wondered if it had anything to do with the muscular gaoler who leaned against the cell wall behind the prisoner. His arms were folded over his chest, hands curled into fists—fists that had caused the spy's current wounds.

Were Cora kinder and softer she'd have felt bad for the old man's condition. But she was neither kind nor soft where spies from Norun were concerned. Not after the unsettling rumors her own spies had uncovered. According to their intel, the Kingdom of Norun had recently formed an alliance with Syrus—the very kingdom she feared more than any other. For Syrus was home to an enemy she hoped she'd never meet—King Darius Solaria, father of Morkai, seeker of the fae realm. A realm she'd been to, just over seven months ago, and now held valuable secrets about.

Captain Alden spoke again. "Why has Norun taken such an interest in Khero?"

The spy scoffed. "Sudden? I'd hardly call it sudden. Norun isn't easy to forgive, and your kingdom is responsible for the death of Prince Helios."

Cora bristled at the accusation. Retorts roared inside her, but she held them back with a tightening of her jaw. She wasn't here to argue with the prisoner, only to gather information. Still, she was losing patience with Norun's insistence that Khero was to blame for Helios Dorsus' death. The prince may have died in her kingdom last spring after being devoured by Morkai's Roizan, but Cora and her allies had gone to great lengths to refute any association with the former duke and denounce every action he'd taken in the name of Khero. Besides, Helios had hardly been innocent. She'd witnessed his demise firsthand and hadn't been sorry to see him go. Helios had been in the process of trying to kill Teryn when the Roizan attacked, and before that, he'd intended to carve a unicorn's horn from its head while it was still alive.

No, Cora felt no remorse where Prince Helios was concerned. She couldn't even muster a flicker of sympathy for his grieving father, King Isvius of Norun. Yet she wanted none of the blame for what had happened to the prince and resented that she bore all of it. Why Norun was only blaming Khero and not Selay was beyond her. Helios had only come to Khero because of Mareleau's Heart's Hunt. Perhaps it was because Khero was the easier target and closer to Norun's borders. Meanwhile, Selay was no longer just *Selay*. It was now Vera, a kingdom forged from Selay's formal merging with Menah. Compared to Vera, Khero was small and vulnerable, without the support of trade allies across the sea and in other continents.

"Does Norun seek retribution on Khero?" Captain Alden asked.

The prisoner shrugged, the move stunted by his bindings. "Like I said, I'm just a spy. I gather specific information and share it with my masters. I'm not privy to Norun's secrets."

The man's emotions contracted inside Cora, tightening like a fist in her gut. They contradicted the nonchalance on the man's face. "He's lying," she said through her teeth. "He knows so much more than he's saying."

The captive's crooked, half-swollen gaze shot toward her. A corner of his bruised mouth flicked up. "Is this by chance the young queen?"

Cora's breath caught. She stood in shadow near the cell door, the hood of a plain gray cloak pulled low over her forehead, yet the spy had surmised her identity. Had it simply been a reckless guess, or was it obvious?

She was suddenly aware of her poise, the lift of her chin, the way she held her arms easily at her sides. They were habits she'd picked up over the last several months since her coronation. Habits she'd developed as a front, a way to radiate the regality she didn't feel. Yet she'd come to don them with ease now, slipping into them like a second skin.

Alden angled her body to intercept the prisoner's stare. "You forget who's doing the questioning."

"Ah, I see. You'll have to forgive me."

His confidence seeped into Cora, sending chills down her spine. He was the fourth Norunian spy who'd been captured on her lands, yet he was by far the boldest. The others had stayed mute through questioning and had ultimately lost their lives. But how many others might have slipped through the cracks? How many spies were crawling across her kingdom without anyone being the wiser? Cora hardly had enough spies of her own, for Khero was still recovering from all it had lost at Morkai's hands, and that included military and staff. She'd been queen for just seven months, and every day she felt the weight of how much was left to rebuild.

It all fell on her shoulders.

Alone.

No, not alone, she reminded herself. She had allies. Queen Mareleau. King Larylis. And soon she'd have Teryn beside her, sharing her burden as king consort. Her husband.

She'd been engaged to him since last summer, and she'd nearly wed him too, after her brother had been forced to step down as king. Marrying Teryn had been a condition her council had demanded, a formal alliance they'd required before they'd recognize her as Dimetreus' heir. Thankfully, she'd escaped the castle before the marriage had been finalized, for if she'd married Teryn then, she'd have wed a false version of him—Morkai possessing Teryn's body. Not that she'd escaped Morkai's treachery unscathed. No one had. He'd murdered her brother, his councilmen, and Mareleau's father. Three kingdoms had been thrown into chaos after a single night's tragedy.

A tragedy Teryn almost hadn't survived.

Panic laced through her when she remembered how he'd looked when he'd departed home with his brother to be tended to by their kingdom's skilled physicians. The kind of physicians her own kingdom lacked. His cheeks had been so gaunt then, his hair fully white. But she reminded herself he *was* alive. Alive and well, and soon he'd come home to her.

Soon he'd marry her.

Soon she could tell him everything she couldn't say while he'd been healing from his wounds.

Calm warmth seeped into her, lessening some of her dread and anchoring her back in the present moment. She locked that warmth in her chest and poured her focus into her magic, narrowing her attention on the prisoner's emotions.

"I'll ask you again," Captain Alden said. "Does Norun seek retribution on Khero? Is your kingdom planning to invade or attack Khero?"

Cora nearly shuddered at the question.

"I haven't a clue," the spy said, and Cora was struck with another tightening of emotion. Another blanket of heaviness.

More lies. Which meant he knew the answer. And if it was an answer he refused to give, that could only mean one thing.

Norun *was* planning some form of retribution. Everyone on the continent knew Norun was famed for its successful war campaigns. In the last decade, they'd conquered two kingdoms—Haldor and Sparda. Would Khero be next?

Cora's knees threatened to buckle, but she took a steadying breath, fighting past the dank stench of the cell to fill her lungs with air.

The gaoler chuckled from his place against the wall. "Perhaps I can loosen 'is tongue. He's a bit more talkative than 'e was before we had our private chat. Just think how much more 'e might say after our next rendezvous."

A flicker of fear shot through the prisoner's emotions.

"Not yet," Alden said. "I have one more question."

The spy turned a contrived look of boredom on the captain.

"Has Norun formally allied with Syrus?" Alden asked.

Surprise ruptured the captive's emotions, and it briefly colored his expression too. Finally, they'd cracked the spy's smooth façade. His surprise quickly faded, however, and he regained his air of indifference. "How should I know?"

Alden raised her voice. "Is Norun planning an attack on Khero *with* Syrus?"

Another stunted shrug. "I know nothing more than what I've told you."

His emotions grew tighter inside Cora, contracting again, but even without her powers it was obvious he was lying. This man was clever, well-spoken, and knew too much.

Captain Alden cast a questioning glance at her queen. Cora gave her a subtle nod, and Alden tipped her head toward the gaoler. "He's all yours."

The gaoler pushed off the wall with a cruel grin, cracking his knuckles as he sauntered toward his captive. Cora turned on her heel and exited the cell. As the door closed behind her, the prisoner's fear lanced her gut, but she breathed it away, banishing the no-longer-needed emotions. She strode down the dimly lit dungeon hall, her steps swift, focusing only on the elements around her—the stale air, the stone beneath her feet, the flickering light from the sparse lamps, the moisture dripping down the walls. Air, earth, fire, water. The substances that fueled her magic. Protected her. Guided her. She drew them closer now, imagining them wrapping around her like a cocoon until she could feel her mental shields snapping into place.

The prisoner's fear no longer prodded her, and she was left with only her own emotions.

She reached the end of the dungeon hall when she heard the first strike of flesh against flesh. A grunt of pain. She shuddered, knowing a man was getting beaten on her order, but she could only summon the slightest pity. The spy knew too much and was harboring important information. Information she needed. She wouldn't let herself regret what had to be done.

Cora was a queen to her people.

A witch at her core.

And if it meant protecting her kingdom, she could be a villain to her enemies too.

2

───────

Fatigue weighed heavy on Cora as she ascended the stairwell leading from the dungeon. Taking on another's emotions did that to her, as did thoughts of war. But there was one thing she could count on to clear her head. Or rather one *creature*.

She paused on the next step and closed her eyes, extending her senses outward, seeking a familiar mind. A wordless greeting responded, carrying a warmth as comforting as a hug. Valorre, her unicorn companion and dearest friend, was close enough that she could feel his presence despite the walls between them. She could almost smell the soil of the forest outside the castle, hear the snapping of twigs beneath his hooves, feel the heat of the sun streaming through the canopy of trees. Her lips stretched into a smile. She opened her eyes and raced the rest of the way up the steps. *I'm going to try to sneak out*, she mentally conveyed.

Even though she was often in the presence of her guards or lady's maids, she could find an excuse to be alone and use her worldwalking ability to reach the forest in the blink of an eye. All she needed was strong emotion to drive her and a clear destination.

She expected Valorre to respond with approval, for it had been weeks since Cora had snuck out for a forest ride. Instead, a ripple of hesitation moved through their energetic link. *I don't think you should.*

She frowned as she pushed open the door at the top of the staircase. *Why not? Well...because—*

"Prince Teryn has arrived." Master Arther, steward of Ridine Castle, practically sprang before the doorway. He wrung his gloved hands as exasperated relief eased the furrow between his brows.

Several emotions shot through Cora one after the other. Shock, panic, excitement. "He...what? He wasn't supposed to be here until tomorrow. When did he arrive?"

"Less than an hour ago, while you were...down *there*." He said the last part in a whisper as he cast a glance at the door Cora had emerged from. Not that there was any reason for secrecy here. No one entered the halls leading to the dungeons aside from Cora, her guards, and approved staff. Now the only other people in the hall besides Cora and Arther were two members of the royal guard who'd stood sentinel outside the door.

Cora shifted her mental focus from her steward to Valorre. *Did you know? Is that what you were about to say?*

Yes, came Valorre's reply.

Why didn't you warn me? He could have. While her guards had been ordered not to interrupt her while she was in the dungeon, Valorre hadn't been given such a restriction.

You were busy, Valorre said. *Didn't want to distract you from scary men in the dark place.*

The dark place was what he called the dungeon. While their connection was strong enough to give each other impressions of their current locations or environments, Valorre didn't always understand the impressions he received.

Cora returned her attention to Arther as she realized he was speaking again. "—King Larylis and Queen Mareleau will be here in just two hours."

She frowned. "Teryn arrived separately from them?"

"Yes, he said he rode ahead."

Her lungs constricted. "Was something wrong? Was there an emergency?"

"No, it seemed more like he grew tired of his retinue's slow pace."

That was a relief. After everything that had happened last spring and summer, Cora's mind was often quick to go to the darkest places when anything seemed out of the ordinary. But Teryn's actions made sense. Mareleau's retinue was moving slowly due to her pregnancy and the precautions required around travel. She couldn't blame him for taking off on his own. If only he'd sent word ahead of time, she'd have been there to greet him.

"Where is he now?" she asked.

"He said he was tired after his ride, so I escorted him to his guest chamber to rest."

She was about to ask why Arther had taken him to a guest room and not her own chambers, but she stopped herself. Even though she and Teryn would share the royal suite once they were wed, they couldn't be seen sharing quarters before their wedding.

A troubling thought occurred to her.

She took a step closer to Arther. "He said he was tired? Did he seem unwell?"

"He seemed...fine," Arther said, brows knit with confusion.

Just fine? Her lungs tightened all over again. She cast the same question at Valorre.

I didn't see his face, he conveyed. *I saw him riding but he wore a head blanket.*

A cloak, Cora corrected. *Then how did you know it was him?*

Smelled like him.

He has a smell?

Like strength and moonbeams.

Cora nearly snorted a laugh. She could have taken comfort in Valorre's insistence that he smelled like strength, but she couldn't take him seriously with the part about moonbeams. Valorre had always had a bit of a crush on Teryn. Of course he'd smell like strength and moonbeams to him.

She shook her head and pulled her consciousness from Valorre's. This was no laughing matter. If Teryn was fatigued after his ride, that might mean he'd pushed his stamina too far. Mother Goddess, why the hell had he ridden ahead of his retinue? His physicians had given him the go-ahead to travel months ago. In fact, he'd been scheduled to arrive last month but had been delayed when an unexpected envoy had arrived from Brushwold, and Teryn had stayed behind to help his brother host them. An extra month of recovery should have aided his health, but just because Teryn was fit to travel didn't mean he was in peak condition. Cora had seen what Morkai's possession had done to his body. He'd nearly died from it. He'd hardly been able to move or speak when she'd last seen him.

Cora's mind spun to the darkest places all over again.

She lifted her chin. "I must see my fiancé at once."

Arther released a long-suffering sigh and spoke with a practiced tone. "It wouldn't be proper, Majesty. You must hold a formal audience and greet him before the court. You know this."

She opened her mouth to argue, but he was right. Seven devils, she was loath to admit it, but now that she was queen, she was bound by rules of royal propriety before the public eye. And Ridine Castle was no longer as private as it used to be, especially with her fast-approaching wedding. Her coronation had been a private affair, a somber necessity after a great tragedy, which meant the royal wedding would mark the first public celebration the castle had hosted in years. As a result, eyes were everywhere.

Yet she didn't have the patience to wait hours to see Teryn. She hadn't seen him in seven months. Seven achingly long months with only letters between them. She was dying to see that he was well with her own eyes. To hear his voice. And to tell him all the things she never had the courage to convey by pen and paper.

Arther softened his tone. "Besides, Majesty, he's likely sleeping by now. He asked to rest. We will move your audience with the king and queen to this evening after they arrive, so you may receive Prince Teryn shortly."

Tension unraveled from her shoulders but not entirely. She *had* to see him. Maybe he was sleeping. Maybe they couldn't have the heartfelt conversation she'd been planning for. She could at least rest her eyes upon his face and know he was well. Only then could she fully relax.

She released a calming breath and gathered her composure. Then, steeling her expression, she delivered her lie. "You're right, Master Arther. I am so grateful for your counsel. I shall return to my quarters at once and ready myself for tonight's audience with our royal guests."

"That is the right choice, Majesty. I will clear the way through the great hall so you may reach the keep without further ado." After a bow, he turned on his heel—but halted midstep. His eyes shot back to her, widening as they took in her ensemble. His nose wrinkled with clear distaste. "Please allow me to take your cloak."

Heat flushed her cheeks. Right. She'd nearly forgotten about the dark cloak she was wearing. Having donned it for secrecy over fashion, it was hardly fit for a queen. And even though Arther would clear the way ahead, courtiers would still see her.

She gave him a thankful grin and undid the clasp at her neck. Underneath the cloak, she wore a mauve brocade gown with a ruffled square neck and an overskirt that parted at the center to reveal layers of ivory lace—a far more regal look. When she passed him a cloak, she added with contrived nonchalance, "Which guest room is my fiancé in?"

Arther's eyes narrowed with suspicion, but he had no reason to hide such information from her. "The Cambron suite, Majesty."

"Thank you, Master Arther."

He bowed once more and strode ahead toward the great hall. Cora hid her smile behind his back.

~

HER HEART WAS A RACING, RIOTING MESS BY THE TIME SHE ENTERED HER BEDROOM IN the royal suite. She'd dismissed her lady's maids, ordering them not to return to ready her for tonight's audience for another hour. She probably didn't need a full hour, considering Teryn was likely dozing by now, but it would ensure no one would enter her chambers and find her missing.

She stood before the mirror, checking her appearance. Turning her face to one side then the other, she studied her golden-tan skin, her dark eyes rimmed with kohl and powdered cosmetics, her black hair pinned in a coronet. As she patted the neat braid that encircled her head, a stray tendril sprang loose, falling onto her cheek. She was about to reach for a hairpin from her vanity but stopped herself. Teryn's voice rang from memory.

I like when it's a mess, he'd once said about her hair.

A giddy grin tugged her lips as she loosened another strand of hair, then another. With her hair properly mussed, she removed her gloves and brushed her tattooed palms over her skirts, smoothing wrinkles that weren't there. Assessing herself once more, she gave her reflection an approving nod, though she wasn't sure why she was going through all the trouble. Teryn probably wouldn't be awake to see her. Still, on the off chance that he wasn't sleeping, she wanted to look her best.

Anxious excitement flooded her heart, sending it thudding even faster. She needed to steady its raging pulse with at least a sliver of sobriety. While she was satisfied with her appearance, she needed to ready herself for the inevitable changes she'd find in him. He may look different from the man she'd fallen in love with. His hair had been sapped of color during his battle over his body and would likely be brittle and gray. He'd be thinner. Weaker. A far cry from the broad-shouldered man who'd once made her blush while dueling shirtless. It might break her heart to see how much he'd changed. How badly his body had been broken.

But she would love him just the same.

And if he was awake, she'd finally get to tell him that. Finally say the words neither had let past their lips despite feeling them pulse between them, despite almost hearing them in mumbled tones when Teryn was barely conscious, despite reading them between the lines of their letters.

She took a steadying breath, filling her lungs with air. Then, rooting her feet beneath her, she connected to the element of earth. Afternoon sunlight streamed through the open windows of her bedroom, linking her to the fire element. Then the emotions flooding her chest, nourishing her very soul, connected her to water.

Closing her eyes, she thought of Teryn. Felt his proximity, his nearness, his presence, just down the hall. She knew how close his room was. The Cambron suite was just two doors away. If she wanted to, she could sneak down the servants' passage, using her magic to extend her senses, cloak herself in shadow, and evade passersby no matter how busy the secret halls had become. But she wouldn't, for she had faster means. Easier means. Quieter means.

She could cross the distance between them in a single step.

Keeping her emotions fixated on Teryn, she pictured the bedroom in the Cambron suite, imagined him lying on the bed, safe beneath the smooth linen sheets and velvet blankets. She imagined the carpeted floors beneath her feet, the bedroom door behind her, the four-poster bed just ahead. Calm settled over her despite the excitement radiating from her chest. Then she took a single step.

She opened her eyes and found the new destination before her, exactly as she'd imagined it. A cream-and-violet patterned carpet cradled her feet while a mahogany bed stood before her.

But Teryn wasn't on that bed.

He was standing mere feet away, half facing her.

Shirtless.

The top button of his trousers undone.

Her breath caught as she took in the low rise of his waistband, the fingers that had been in the process of loosening the next button down, his muscled forearms. She lifted her gaze, drinking in the sculpted V of his lower abdomen, then his rib cage, marred with the puckered scar he'd earned at Centerpointe Rock. She studied his curving biceps, his wide shoulders, his silver hair that fell in tousled waves just above his collarbone.

Mother Goddess, this was not the frail, weak version of Teryn she'd expected. Sure, he was slightly leaner than he'd been before, but he didn't look unwell at all.

He looked…good.

Really, really good.

Her eyes darted to his face and found his familiar green irises sparkling with mischief. A corner of his lips quirked at one corner. "What a pleasant surprise."

3

———

Cora had no thoughts. None. Just shock and lust and...what had he just said? He'd spoken, but she'd been too distracted to hear.

"It's a good thing you didn't arrive a second later," he said. "Unless...an eyeful is what you were going for."

Her eyes dipped back down to the open top button of his trousers and she realized what he was referring to. Had she invaded his room any later...

Her cheeks blazed. What the hell had she been thinking? What had she nearly walked in on? Sure, he could have been undressing for bed, but he also could have been preparing to do...other things.

She clenched her teeth as if she could chew through her mortification. How had she not considered the myriad of situations she could have stumbled upon? She'd been expecting a tired, frail figure asleep on the bed, not a virile young man encased in muscle with a teasing smirk on his lips.

What an idiot she'd been. "I should go," she muttered as she whirled abruptly on her heels—

She stumbled as hands framed her shoulders and tugged her back a step. It took her a moment to realize what she'd almost collided with. Straight ahead was the closed bedroom door that she'd nearly slammed into in her haste to get away. Teryn had pulled her back just in time...and now held her against his chest, every inch of his bare torso pressed against her back. His skin was hot against the bare flesh at the nape of her neck—the only exposed skin that touched his.

His voice rumbled low in her ear, his breath warming its shell. "Is that any way to greet your fiancé?"

Her heart slammed against her ribs and she was certain he could feel its rhythm as he held her close from behind. She opened her mouth but she was too dumbfounded to conjure anything like a clever retort. Or *any* retort.

"Or..." He drew out the word as he took a step back, breaking their too-warm contact, and gently turned her to face him. With his hands still on her shoulders—his hold looser now—he asked, "Are you here to break things off with me? Did you have me travel all the way here just to tell me you've changed your mind about us?"

"No," she managed to blurt out. His lips curled in that devious way again and she realized he was teasing. She let herself smile then, let herself focus on all that was familiar about him. His grin, his emerald eyes, his sharp cheekbones. And his voice. The voice she'd yearned to hear every day for the last several months. She blew out a breath, her nerves unraveling.

But her calm was short-lived, for in the next moment, he closed the distance he'd created and moved his hand from her shoulder to her cheek. Her heart racketed once more, and her eyes dipped to his mouth. Was he going to kiss her? She'd been waiting for this moment for so long, yet none of her fantasies had gone like this. She averted her gaze to his neck, taking in the circular scars on both sides of his throat, twins to her own, caused by the magic-suppressing collar they'd both briefly worn. Her eyes flashed back to his, but she couldn't meet his gaze. So instead, she dragged her attention further down. But that only brought her to...

Muscles.

Naked skin.

And...Mother Goddess, why did he look so good?

Her cheeks burned hot as she wrenched her eyes back to his face and found a furrow between his brows.

Slowly, he let his hand slide from her cheek and stepped back again. "What's wrong? Am I making you uncomfortable?" There was no jest in his tone this time, only genuine concern.

That made her heart sink. Squeezing her eyes shut, she delivered an internal scolding. *Get ahold of yourself, Cora!*

As she opened her eyes, she forced herself to hold his gaze without blushing. Or...tried to. "No," she said, voice level. "I just didn't expect you to be so...so..."

Healthy.

Awake.

Handsome.

He arched a teasing brow. "So...?"

She crossed her arms and lifted her chin. "Shirtless."

He smirked at that. "Well, I was about to take a nap. I rode hard to see you." The words *rode hard* conjured the wrong images in her head. "When Master Arther told me you were preoccupied, I figured I'd get some rest."

"Why were you taking off your pants?" As soon as the question left her lips, she regretted asking. Why the hell did she ask that?

"I don't sleep clothed," he said with a chuckle. "You would have learned that eventually. Sooner rather than later." He winked and sent her stomach flipping.

How the seven devils could he flirt so easily with her, speak to her as if no time had passed, as if a great tragedy hadn't nearly killed him, while she was so flustered? She supposed he'd been prepared to see her exactly as she was. Meanwhile, she'd been picturing a very different version of him.

He squinted, studying her with puzzled amusement. "Why do you seem disappointed?"

"I'm not disappointed. I'm just…I didn't expect…" She waved a hand at his torso. When the gesture failed to deliver her point, she propped her hands on her hips and asked, "Why the hell are you in such good shape?"

"Were you hoping your husband was an invalid?" His tone was teasing again, and it helped ease her nerves.

"No. Just…" Her cheeks blazed like a wildfire. She pursed her lips to hide her embarrassed smile.

"I like seeing you flustered over me for once. It makes me feel like less of an idiot."

She shifted to the side and covered her face in her hands. "I'm being ridiculous, aren't I?"

"What's ridiculous," Teryn said, voice dipped low, "is you haven't let me kiss you yet."

Lifting her face, she glanced at him sidelong, saw the want in his eyes, the serious edge of his jaw. Maybe this wasn't the reunion she'd spent months planning for, but it was the one she'd yearned for. *He* was the one she'd yearned for, no matter what he looked like, no matter his health, his condition, his status. She wanted him. Loved him. And he was finally here. Home.

Steeling her resolve, she fully faced him again. This time she closed the distance between them of her own accord. He was so much taller than her, she had to angle her head back to hold his hungry gaze. When only a few sparse inches separated them, she lifted a hand and rested it over his chest. Her palm thrummed, with magic, with his heartbeat, with the heat of their contact. She rested her other hand at the nape of his neck, beneath his silver-white hair.

"All right," she said, her words trembling. "I'm ready."

Teryn's expression softened, opened, reflecting Cora's vulnerability as he slowly wound his arms around her waist. Then, inch by inch, as if afraid any sudden move might make her flee, he lowered his lips to hers. Their mouths met in a kiss so soft, so tender and sweet, it made Cora want to weep. He kissed her again, the pressure firmer, and all her embarrassment melted away. There was no room for it here, not where their lips met. When he kissed her once more, she pulled him closer, angled her head, and parted her lips. His grip on her waist tightened, and he slid one hand up her spine until it cradled the back of her head. She parted her lips further and his tongue swept against hers, caressing it with needy, probing want.

"Gods, I missed you," he said against her open mouth. The words made her shudder with pleasure. He'd said as much in his letters but hearing those words, as coated as they were in desire, was better than anything she could have imagined.

"Teryn," she whispered.

He stiffened against her, his fingertips digging into the hair at the base of her coronet. His words came out deep, throaty. "Say my name again."

She startled at the demand in his tone, but it was a pleasant kind of shock. Memories blossomed, bringing her back to that dark night last summer, when she'd said his name again and again while he fought to retake his body from Morkai. She expected those memories to dampen her desire, but they didn't. Instead, they reminded her that he'd come back. Time and again, whenever she'd uttered his name, touched his face, he'd come back to her. He'd fought Morkai's possession because of the connection she and Teryn shared.

Her heart opened even more, flooding with warmth. Finally, she gave in to his order and repeated his name. "Teryn."

He devoured the word with another kiss, one hard and unyielding. "Seven devils, I missed the sound of your voice."

She was about to return the sentiment, but before she could, his hands encircled her waist and lifted her with ease. Her bottom hit a hard surface, and she released a grunt of surprise. It took a moment to realize she was now sitting on his dresser. Shock turned to thrill as his lips found hers again, then his hands found her ankles, her calves, her knees. Inch by inch, he lifted her voluminous skirts higher, allowing him to step between her legs. She aided his efforts, dragging her unwanted layers out of the way until she could hook her calves around his waist.

His lips left hers to trail down her neck, then across her collarbone. Slowly, he brushed his mouth over the upper curve of her breast, the flesh raised above the tight bodice of her gown. His hand cupped the other side and she was suddenly desperate to do away with her gown altogether. She arched into him, a fire burning hot in her core. She'd never felt desire so strong, not even when they'd kissed against the tree after Teryn proposed to her. The power of her yearning was terrifying. Addicting. Begging to be quenched.

She pulled him closer, tightening her legs around his waist. His lips left her breast to return to her eager mouth, while his hand slid from her bodice down to her thigh, resting over the hem of her silk stockings. His thumb slowly swept back and forth, and she was desperate to feel his fingers slide beneath her garter, unhook it, and climb higher. Yet his hand did no such thing, remaining on her silk-clad skin. The most delicious frustration surged through her, so she let her hands wander where his did not, sweeping them over his chest, his arms, his back. She slid her palm down the front of his abdomen. His muscles flexed against her palm, and a tremor ran through him.

Mother Goddess, she was drunk on the feel of him and she wanted more. She wanted every inch of his skin, everywhere. She wanted to paint their love with their bodies, their tongues...

The word *love* cooled some of the fire that had taken over her senses.

Right. None of her plans regarding their reunion including lovemaking within the first few minutes of seeing each other. Not that she truly minded, but she'd promised herself she'd express her feelings before they took a single step further in their relationship. Her surprise at seeing him looking so well may have thrown a hitch into some of her preparations, but she was determined to keep the others intact.

With a strangled moan, she pulled her lips from his and leaned slightly back. "Wait," she uttered.

Teryn froze at the word, though his chest heaved with rapid panting.

Silence enveloped them, save for the cadence of their breaths, as Cora cooled her ardor enough to get the next words out. "I need to talk to you about something before we..."

"Before we what?"

"Before we..." She stared down at the nonexistent space between them. "Before we do this."

A corner of his mouth flicked up. "This? What exactly is *this* you speak of?"

She gave him a withering look. "You know what I'm talking about."

His eyes narrowed. "Did you think I was going to take you here and now? That our first time would be on a dresser?"

The way he said that paired with the visuals in her head made her wish she hadn't said a word. She had no qualms about being taken here and now on a dresser.

"You did, didn't you? What a dirty mind you have."

She scoffed. "Me?"

He arched a brow, and she suddenly noticed the placement of her hands. One was still pressed to his chest, but the other...

Her gaze dipped to the thumb and forefinger that were frozen over the button of his trousers. She'd been in the process of loosening it when she'd broken their kiss.

He wasn't the one who'd tried to take things further, *she* was.

She yanked her hand away, but he caught it in his and brought it to his lips. "I'm teasing," he said, then released her, taking a full step back, breaking the circle of her thighs around his waist. "You're right. We should talk first."

She opened her mouth, but how the hell could she speak from the heart and say all the things she wanted to say if her heart wasn't currently in charge?

The flash of heat burning between her thighs reminded her exactly which part of her *was* in charge, and it wasn't interested in conversation. She bit her lip, eyes skating over the sheen of sweat that had just begun to glisten on his chest. Would it really be so bad to just pull him back to her and...save talk for later? She wasn't chaste by any means. She'd enjoyed a few short trysts when she'd lived with the Forest People, experiments devoid of love.

And yet, it was different with Teryn. There *was* love between them, and she needed him to know that. Needed him to know exactly what she wanted from their union. It was more than desire. More than attraction. More than a political alliance for the sake of their kingdoms.

Cora had practiced putting all of this into words, but her lust was chasing it away. She needed to gather her bearings. Reassess. Come back with a clear head.

She swallowed hard and leveled her voice. "Let's talk later."

He grinned. "After dinner then? Come to my room." When she said nothing, he added, "I promise I'll be fully clothed."

A shy smile lifted her lips. "All right. For now, I should go."

With a nod, he held out his hand and helped her down from the dresser. She could barely meet his eyes as she smoothed down her wrinkled skirts. "I'll see you tonight."

"Tonight," he whispered back, his knuckles briefly brushing her forearm.

Everything inside her wanted to fold into his arms with a parting kiss, but she knew better. A parting kiss would turn into so much more. So instead, she turned her back on him. Then, letting her desire fuel her magic, she closed her eyes, pictured her bedroom, and disappeared.

4

The room immediately felt colder after Cora was gone. Teryn stared at the empty space where his fiancée had been just a moment before, awed at how suddenly she'd disappeared. It was the first time she'd used her traveling magic while he was watching her. She'd first used it at the battle at Centerpointe Rock. Then again last summer to escape Morkai's clutches while he'd possessed Teryn's body. Finally, she'd used it to lock a strange magic-suppressing collar around his neck to momentarily free Teryn's body from the mage's control.

It hadn't been until he'd gotten well enough to write to Cora that he'd learned the whole story of what had happened that night. About Cora's newest power. Its strengths and limitations. Where Cora had been before she'd arrived at the meadow. How she'd gotten there. What the collar was and how it had been used against her when she'd unintentionally crossed worlds to enter the fae realm.

Just when he thought she couldn't impress him more, she was always proving just how incredible she was. And now that they'd finally seen each other for the first time in seven months, he was reminded how good she felt. How good she smelled. The sound of her voice. The rhythm of her sighs. Kissing her, touching her, had made him feel so alive. So immersed in his body.

He still had nightmares of what it felt like to be trapped in Morkai's crystal. A disembodied spirit. At night, he often startled awake, panting, shouting into the dark just to hear a voice that was his own, clawing at his skin to ensure he could feel it. During the day, he did whatever he could to feel alive. Walking. Moving. Talking. Writing. Three months ago, he'd been given the go-ahead by his physicians to take up strenuous activity, so he'd thrown himself into training. Sword. Spear. Glaive. Halberd. Anything that would ignite a fire in his muscles and remind him he was the sole operator of his body.

But none of that had made him feel as whole as when his lips had met Cora's, as desire coursed through him like a raging fire when he'd pressed closer to her on that dresser. He smirked at that piece of furniture now. He'd probably come on a touch too strong, but he'd been unable to help himself. He hadn't expected her to show up in his room out of nowhere. It had thrown all his polite, respectful plans out the window. He'd meant to greet her formally, reunite with her softly, and ease them both into the marriage they were about to embark upon.

He barked a laugh. How naive he'd been. There'd been nothing soft, formal, or polite about the way he'd kissed her, nor she him. There certainly hadn't been any of that in the way her hands had roved his chest. The fingertips she'd tucked under his waistband, absently working to free the button of his trousers.

Clenching his jaw, he curled his fists. It was all he could do to keep from taking himself in hand and releasing the aching tension she'd built inside him. Instead, his only release was a heavy exhale, for now was not the time to act on his baser instincts. Not when he had an audience.

Banishing all thoughts of Cora on the dresser, he secured the top button of his trousers and addressed the woman who stood in the corner of his room. "I'd appreciate it if you didn't spy on intimate moments between me and my future wife, Emylia."

The woman's eyes widened. Her form was semi-transparent and devoid of color, but Teryn had known her when they were both spirits—etheras—and had seen her with brown skin, dark eyes, and black curls.

She brought a hand to her mouth, then dropped it. "You...you can see me?"

"I can." He retrieved his discarded riding tunic from the end of his bed and pulled it over his head. There was no point in trying to nap now. He'd been eager for rest after his hasty ride to Ridine Castle, for the activity had strained him. He hadn't anticipated a need to reacquaint his body with riding, thinking his weapons training had been enough to strengthen him overall. But no, every activity Teryn had once enjoyed now required a period of adaptation. He still had endurance to strengthen. Stamina to increase.

At least his surprise visit from Cora had cleared away his fatigue.

With his tunic on, he turned to face Emylia fully. She shrank away from him, as if suddenly afraid. Then, with a shake of her head, she seemed to remember herself.

"I'm sorry," she said. Her voice was soft and lacked the resonance it would have if she were alive, but he could still make out her words. "I had no idea you could see me."

"That's what you're sorry for? Not that you were spying on a clearly private moment? How long were you going to watch?" He'd been vaguely aware of her presence—or at least *some* presence, tickling the back of his neck—ever since Cora had entered his room. Strange presences had become common to him over the last several months, so he'd been able to ignore it and give all his attention to Cora.

Emylia shrugged. "I see a lot of things these days that are considered taboo or private. I suppose I've lost that sense of propriety."

"Why are you here?"

"I heard you'd arrived. I wanted to see that you were well."

"No, why are you *here*? In this plane of existence. Why haven't you moved on?"

Her expression turned mournful. "I tried to move on to the otherlife, but I was blocked."

His breath caught. "Is it Morkai?" He hated saying the name out loud. Hated the way it made his skin crawl and made him fear he was merely a visitor in this body and not its owner.

"No," she said, holding up her hands in a placating gesture. "It's nothing like that."

Relief uncoiled his muscles. The last thing he needed was for Morkai to return in any form, even to torment the dead. The mage had already conquered death once. But Morkai was gone for good. Teryn had witnessed the mage's final death last summer, watched as his soul was burned to ash by flames of white light.

Emylia spoke again. "It's more like...I'm the one who's stopping me. There's too much heaviness here." She placed her hand on her chest.

He frowned. Emylia had told him that an ethera without a heart-center would become a wraith. But she still had her heart-center, and she was nothing like the terrifying, mindless wraiths he'd once fought at Centerpointe Rock, courtesy of Morkai's blood magic. So what was she?

"Are you a ghost?" he asked.

She gave him a wry smile. "I'm an ethera with unfinished business, so I suppose ghost is an adequate term." When Teryn only nodded, she added, "You're taking this rather well. I would have expected more shock."

Teryn debated keeping quiet about the next part but relented. "You're not the only apparition I've seen lately," he quietly confessed.

She moved closer to him. "What do you mean?"

"Ever since I returned to my body, I've been able to see spirits." His eyes unfocused as he recalled his terror in the early days of regaining consciousness. Every now and then he'd catch sight of floating lights, hazy unaware figures who'd wander in through one wall and out another, or colorless specters who seemed keen enough to witness the present—much like Emylia. At first, the visions had caused great distress, sparking fears that he was one of them, or that they were here to drag him back to the spiritual plane. As months went on and none had interacted with him, much less harmed him, his fears lessened. By now, he was used to it.

Emylia's mouth fell open. "How? Why?"

"I don't know. I would guess it has to do with the fact that I was once an ethera. Or perhaps that I nearly died."

Emylia didn't seem to know what to say to that, and Teryn didn't like the pitying look in her eyes.

"Enough about me," he said. "Where have you been all this time? Are you trapped here? Because your ethera was freed nearby?"

"No, I can wander to any location I've been before, but I've chosen to stay at Ridine."

"Is this where you have unfinished business?"

"In a way." Her expression turned mournful again. She drifted toward Teryn, then halted in place. She blinked at him a few times, looking as startled as she'd been when he'd first faced her.

"What is it? Why do you keep looking at me like you're afraid?"

She shook her head as if to clear it. "I don't know. Maybe I'm just not used to seeing you like this. You fully alive, while I'm the only one who's a spirit."

That made sense. It was strange seeing her as a colorless being, and not the bright figure he'd known in the crystal.

She settled upon the closed trunk at the foot of Teryn's bed. "I can't shake my guilt over what I've done. Particularly how my actions have hurt Cora. So I've stayed close by and watched over her."

A bittersweet ache pounded in Teryn's chest. He was glad she'd chosen to watch over Cora, but at the same time, she deserved to move on. Even though she'd used her powers as a seer to channel vital information for Morkai—information that had led to countless tragedies at the mage's hands—she was sorry for her role. Love had driven her actions, a blind and reckless love that Teryn could neither condone nor condemn.

Love was madness. Treacherous and beautiful all at once. It could start wars or end them. Could save a life or destroy it.

Emylia had experienced the darkest kind of love. Because of its invisible scars, even the peaceful embrace of the otherlife eluded her.

"How has Cora been?" he asked. "I know what she's conveyed in her letters, but I worry she might be acting like she's fine when she isn't."

"It has been hard for her," Emylia said. "She doesn't let her pain show around others."

He couldn't imagine how painful the last seven months had been for Cora. He'd been nervous to come back to Ridine, terrified over what memories his return might conjure, what new nightmares might await. Yet Cora had stayed the entire time. Stayed in a castle where a blood mage had terrorized her. Stayed in the last place she'd seen her brother alive.

He'd have stayed too, if the choice to leave for Dermaine Palace hadn't been made for him while he'd been unwell. Ridine had still been in the process of being restaffed back then and hadn't had the medical advancements Dermaine offered. Teryn would have suffered less adequate care if he'd been lucid enough to say so, but neither Cora nor Larylis had given him that choice. His healing had been too important to them. So he and Cora had been separated with nothing to connect them but letters. Cora couldn't even use her special ability to visit him, for she needed to be familiar with a place to travel there. He'd worried she'd been suffering on her own, crowned queen in the wake of her brother's death, surrounded by strangers yet again.

The only good that had come from the situation was that Cora had been able to take her crown on her own merit. Lords Kevan and Ulrich were gone, as was King Verdian, leaving no one to diminish Cora's worth as queen, no one to say she couldn't be her brother's heir until after she'd married Teryn. She'd been sent new councilmen from Vera, ones selected by Larylis—and Teryn, once he'd been of sound mind—particularly for their loyalty and open-mindedness.

Still, it had to have been lonely. Painful. Teryn hated that he hadn't been here. Hated that Cora hadn't allowed him to come sooner.

But at least someone had been here to watch over her.

"Thank you," he said, giving Emylia a deep nod. "Thank you for being here when I could not."

Her lips curved in a sad smile. "I haven't found a way to be helpful, but I hope there's something I can do. Something that will allow me to make up for my sins."

"Like what?"

"I don't know, but perhaps the fact that you can see me will matter. I've already told you nearly everything I know about Darius, but perhaps there are other things I can recall. Other things I can discover."

Teryn stiffened. King Darius was a constant source of dread for him, Cora, Larylis, and Mareleau—for everyone who knew the truth. Once Teryn had been well enough to speak and write, he'd conveyed what he'd learned from Emylia while he'd been trapped in the crystal, and Cora had done the same with what she'd learned in El'Ara. Together they'd painted a frightening landscape of possibilities. Only a handful of their most trusted advisors knew what they knew, but they were all of one mind—Darius was not a threat they could ignore.

"He's still alive," Emylia said. "I can't see him, for I can only wander places I've been myself, either as a living being or as a spirit, but I've devoured all the information Cora has learned and tested it with my own knowledge. King Darius has ruled Syrus for five hundred years. Most assume *Darius* is merely a naming convention passed down through heirs, but I know better than to hope that's the truth. The current King Darius is the same man who sent his son to find information on El'Ara."

Teryn nodded. He and Cora had surmised as much in their correspondence, but anything beyond that was guesswork. "Do you believe Morkai conveyed what he'd learned about Lela? About...Cora?"

Learning what Morkai had done to Cora—cursing her to never bear children during her lifetime—had nearly broken him. Morkai had done it to stop a prophecy from coming to fruition, one that predicted Cora would bear the *true Morkara*, the ruler of the fae realm. Should her child be born, the Veil separating the two worlds would tear, compromising the protective ward that had been forged to keep worldwalkers from entering El'Ara. But somehow, it would also put an end to Darius. According to the memories Emylia had shared with Teryn while they were in the crystal, Morkai had eventually abandoned Darius and had taken his father's mission as his own, long before he uncovered Cora's identity. Was there any hope that Morkai had never shared his later findings with Darius?

"I don't know for certain," Emylia said, "but I assume Morkai told him everything. If not while he was still alive, then upon his death. Even though Morkai abandoned his father after their falling out, I don't think he'd let all his work go to waste."

Teryn couldn't help but agree. Morkai was nothing if not tenacious. If he'd been able to tether his soul to a crystal upon his death, he could have woven a spell that would deliver information to Darius under certain circumstances. And while he and his father sought separate goals—Morkai wanting to utilize fae magic in the human world, Darius aiming to return to El'Ara and rule there—their means were aligned.

Dread sank Teryn's gut. It was too much to hope Darius didn't know about Lela. Syrus' recent dealings with Norun were proof that he was angling to get closer.

His only consolation was something he recalled from Emylia's memories. According to Morkai, Darius was physically weak and couldn't easily leave Syrus. He may be a worldwalker like Cora, but if his magic worked like hers, he couldn't travel to a place he was unfamiliar with. Lela once been part of El'Ara, but after five hundred years, it couldn't possibly resemble the place Darius had once lived. Even if it did, there was another condition Morkai had mentioned in Emylia's memories: Darius was cursed to forget. He hadn't even been capable of recalling the name of the realm he'd come from.

That wasn't enough to make Teryn feel at ease.

"I'm sorry," Emylia said, soundlessly rising to her feet from his trunk. "I shouldn't make you talk about such dire topics."

He shook his head. "It's all right. We need to discuss these things, no matter how dreadful they are. And you will be able to help us. I'm sure of it."

She smiled, and this time it looked genuine. "I must admit, talking to you has reminded me of my humanity. I've gotten too used to being invisible, but now that I know someone can see me, I'll have to mind my manners. I really shouldn't have spied on you and Cora. I won't do it again. Not in...*that* sort of scenario."

"I appreciate that."

"Well, I'll leave you alone for now." Her form began to fade, but not before she gave him a mischievous wink. "I promise to give you ample privacy tonight."

She faded away completely, but her parting words made his stomach tumble as he recalled inviting Cora to return to his room this evening. Though he'd soon see her at the formal audience and at dinner afterward, tonight they'd be alone. Tonight he wouldn't hold back.

Tonight Teryn would bare his heart to the woman he loved.

5

The selfish side of Mareleau Alante resented being back at Ridine Castle. Or perhaps it was her rational side. She had good reasons to dread being here and they had nothing to do with the petty grievances she'd once held against the castle the first time she'd come.

"Gods, what a dreary place," Queen Mother Helena said, glancing around the guest suite. It was a large room, though sparsely furnished. The stone walls were draped with violet tapestries bearing Khero's black mountain sigil. The flagstone floors bore several plush rugs to stave off the late winter chill, and a fire roared in the hearth.

"It's a castle, not a palace, Mother," Mareleau said, irritation lacing her voice as she sat at the edge of the bed, enjoying the relief of rest. Though she'd just left her coach after hours on the road, ascending the stairs of the keep had winded her. She supposed that was normal for a woman three weeks from giving birth.

"I thought the queen would have a better sense for royal decor," Helena muttered.

Mareleau rested a hand on the rounded curve of her belly and tried to focus on the sweet flutter of movement beneath her palm and not the grating sound of her mother's voice. It was all she could do not to order Helena out. They were alone. Her ladies had gone to fetch their queen chocolate from the kitchen, and her midwives awaited her needs in her suite's sitting room. She'd be happier if Helena were gone too, but she refrained from saying so, partially because she was trying not to give in to her sharper instincts anymore. She'd be a mother soon, and the sooner she figured out how to stop resenting the woman who'd birthed her, the sooner she could trust herself to do better than what had been done to her.

Besides, her mother's criticism was only half sincere. Though Helena tried to hide it, she mourned the loss of her husband and buried it beneath layers of trifling complaints and fussing over Mareleau's pregnancy. And it wasn't that Mareleau didn't understand her mother's gripes about Ridine. Half a year ago, she wouldn't have defended the castle. In fact, she'd hurled her share of insults over its shoddy accommodations. But things were different now. She may not have the best memories of Ridine, but this was her friend's home. Cora was doing her best to be a proper queen, and the evidence was all around her. When Mareleau had last been here, only a small selection of rooms had been refurbished. Now the grandest chambers were fit for royalty. Or...fit enough. She wouldn't have minded if the mattress were plusher or the blankets were softer.

"Such an ugly sigil. And it's everywhere!" Helena wrinkled her nose at the purple tapestries. Then, with a shake of her head, she cast an indulgent smile upon her daughter. "I'm relieved you and your husband kept much of Selay's sigil intact when designing Vera's."

Mareleau wanted to argue that she and Larylis hadn't had any say in the design of Vera's sigil—an eagle and rose entwined, their silhouettes white on a gold background—nor had they cared to. They'd had much more pressing matters to attend to. Such as merging two kingdoms into one and supporting Cora as their ally, doing whatever they could to ease the chaos that had befallen Khero. New councils had to be forged in both kingdoms. New titles given. Numerous lies to tell. Burdens to bear...

Mareleau blew out a heavy breath.

She didn't expect her mother to understand, for Helena hadn't been here last summer. The queen mother hadn't witnessed the chilling change in Prince Teryn when he'd been possessed by a scheming mage or seen the horrifying monster with four faces, one of which had been King Verdian's. As much as Helena grieved the loss of her husband, their relationship had never been a love match, and all she knew of his death was what the public knew—that a rabid beast had attacked the royal hunting party while they were at rest, and that a fire had broken out as a result. Helena wasn't haunted by the terrors of that night.

But Mareleau was. She knew the truth. And that truth had shaken her world and shifted her priorities. There were more important things than jewels and palaces and luxury. She now knew that relationships were precious, even the ones that were laced with bitterness and conflict. She knew regret for not making up with someone she loved, despite the friction between them. She knew the pain of never getting to say goodbye.

A gentle kick nudged her palm, and a smile warmed her lips, banishing her unpleasant thoughts, even as a far less gentle kick to her ribs followed. Mareleau had numerous reasons for trying not to push others away like she used to, and her unborn child was the greatest one. She still wasn't confident about becoming a mother, but something fierce had sparked inside her months ago, and it grew brighter every day.

Her eyes landed on the opposite wall. It separated her suite from Larylis' and she wished she could tear it down. He was busy changing and readying himself for their audience with Cora, but he'd be far better company than her mother. And she missed him.

Though they'd journeyed to Ridine together, they'd been given separate rooms by the different nobles who'd offered them their homes and hospitality each night, and her accommodations at Ridine were no different. Not only was it proper to offer a king and queen separate chambers if available, but Mareleau required more space at night than she had before. It seemed every evening she added a new pillow to her bed just to feel comfortable enough to sleep. By now she practically slept in a fortress of pillows, stuffed strategically on every side of her. Which, of course, made her a rather difficult bedfellow.

She angled her body to the side and assessed the pillows at the head of the bed, counting four. That certainly wouldn't be enough. She needed at least six—

Another kick prodded her ribs, and she let out a sharp hiss.

"What is it?" came Helena's frantic voice as she darted for Mareleau and planted herself on the bed beside her. "Is it contractions? Has your water broken?"

"Mother," she ground out between her teeth. How often had she heard those same questions over the last few weeks whenever she so much as frowned?

"I'm serious! Are you all right?"

"For the thousandth time, yes."

Helena tutted. "I knew you shouldn't travel so close to your due date."

"I've told you time and again, I'm not that close to my due date."

Helena pursed her lips and a heavy silence fell between them. Neither had broached the subject of the midwives' calculations versus the lie Mareleau had once told. A lie that had won her permission to marry the man she loved but had left her father furious. Mareleau suspected her mother no longer believed her daughter had conceived during the Heart's Hunt like she'd insisted all those months ago, for if that had been the case, she'd be nearly six weeks overdue. Why Helena had never confronted her daughter about her lie, Mareleau knew not, and she wasn't going to confess. She couldn't bear to admit that her lie had widened the chasm between her and her father. Couldn't bear to admit he'd died with so much animosity left between them, save for the olive branch he'd extended in the form of a child's blanket he'd gifted her. A blanket that had burned to ash before she'd even held it more than once.

No, she couldn't bear that pain, that responsibility.

Perhaps Helena knew that.

When Helena next spoke, her tone was no longer edged with worry. Instead, she was back to her halfhearted griping. "I don't understand why you wanted to travel all the way here just to leave again in a matter of days. We'll have traveled more days than we've visited."

Helena was right but Mareleau didn't care. So long as she could attend Cora's wedding and return home by her due date, she was happy. She was hardly in danger of harming her pregnancy due to travel conditions. Their progress was ridiculously slow and careful, taking ten days when it could easily have taken seven. She knew this, because that was how long it had taken to return to Dermaine Palace when she and Larylis left Ridine last summer. And that had been with an injured Teryn in tow. Mareleau had been babied even more than him, her traveling coach the epitome of luxury. It was so large it might as well have been a cottage on wheels, with a built-in divan and ample room for her ladies and midwives to remain at her side.

"What if you go into early labor?" Helena said. "Seven devils, what if you give birth *here*?"

Mareleau rolled her eyes. "We'll be home just in time."

What did it matter where she gave birth? She had several midwives in attendance night and day, and at least one stood outside her door now, awaiting her needs. Even if she were to go into labor on the road, she could handle it. After surviving a monster, a blood mage, and three straight months of morning sickness, there was little that intimidated her anymore.

"I just don't understand why you want to attend your brother-in-law's wedding so desperately. Larylis could have come without you."

"I'm not here for my brother-in-law," she said with a scoff. Though she didn't hate Teryn nearly as much as she used to, it was true that she wasn't here for him. "I'm here for Queen Aveline."

Helena gave her a patronizing smile. "Dearest, you know she only invited you out of formality. You weren't obligated to come."

Mareleau barked a laugh. If only her mother knew that Cora had specifically asked her *not* to come and to stay home and take care of herself instead. If Cora had wanted her to stay home so badly, she shouldn't have ordered her to stay away, for Mareleau was nothing if not stubborn. Just seeing those words penned in Cora's hand made her want to prove her wrong—that she could take care of herself *and* attend her wedding.

"It's not like Aveline had the decency to attend your wedding feast," Helena muttered.

Mareleau shrugged. "We weren't friends then."

Helena pulled her head back and blinked at her a few times. "Does that mean you consider Queen Aveline your friend now?"

"She's not just a friend. She's my *best* friend." Her cheeks flushed at the confession. She hadn't intended to admit her friendship to her mother. Not that she wanted to hide it either. She just wasn't used to being candid with her mother or talking about emotions. Though she tried not to push Helena away as often as she once did, she still harbored a grudge for how her mother had treated her, how she'd ignored the emotions she'd shared, how she'd refused to take Mareleau's love for Larylis seriously, even going so far as intercepting her letters to him and having a scribe forge her heartfelt words into ones that drove them apart for three years. How Helena had failed to show any sympathy or concern when her unwanted suitors had hurt her.

Recalling that now sent waves of fury through her, but she did her best not to turn herself over to the emotion. Mareleau had made mistakes in the past. She could forgive her mother for hers. Or try to at least.

"I didn't realize," Helena said softly.

"Well, now you do," Mareleau said as she rose from the bed and took a few steps away from her mother, "so please stop insulting her home."

A beat of silence followed, then her mother's footsteps slowly approached. "Dearest," Helena said, a hesitant waver in her voice, "I'm glad you told me, and I'm happy you have a friend. I hope you know you can tell me anything."

Mareleau's chest tightened. She couldn't bring herself to meet her mother's eyes. She was too afraid Helena would see the truth and all her secrets would spill out then and there. How could she voice the shadows in her heart, ones that buried her burdens, her guilt over her father's death? That was a level of vulnerability she wasn't ready for, not with her mother.

So she did what she did best. She lied.

Summoning her *magic trick*, she wrapped an air of indifference around her like a protective shroud. "You never know when a friend might become useful," she said, tone cold. "The closer I keep Aveline, the easier she'll be to use later."

Helena's expression hardened in an instant, closing like a shuttered window, but Mareleau was almost certain she saw disappointment in her mother's eyes.

Mareleau had spent a lifetime disappointing Helena, so that was nothing new, and it was far more comfortable to the alternative—opening up, forgiving, and trusting the person who'd once rent scars upon her heart.

6

Cora fought every urge to fidget as she sat upon her throne before an audience of courtiers flanking a carpeted aisle. Any minute now, her royal guests would arrive. She'd have to receive King Larylis, Queen Mareleau, and Prince Teryn with rehearsed formality, all for the sake of their spectators. She'd have to see Teryn, speak to him in a cold and unwavering tone, and try not to blush. After their heated kiss mere hours ago, she feared it would be easier said than done.

Hence her current urge to fidget.

The discomfort of her ensemble certainly didn't help. Her shoulders were heavy with the weight of her ceremonial cape, a mink-lined monstrosity of purple velvet emblazoned with Khero's black mountain at the lapels. Her dress was nearly as smothering with its layers of heavy brocade, silk, and lace, boasting several shades of purple from lilac to violet. Purple wasn't her favorite hue, yet it represented her kingdom. During formal audiences such as this, it was the most appropriate color to wear.

The stares of the courtiers were almost potent enough to burn, but she kept her gaze fixed on the doorway at the far end of the room, where her guests would soon enter. Her mental shields wavered, threatening to draw in the audience's emotions. To strengthen her wards, she pressed her palms against the smooth, solid arms of her mahogany throne. Her tattooed palms tingled with the strength of the earth element, anchoring her, calming her, smoothing her nerves.

In a small act of boldness, Cora almost always kept her hands and forearms bare, revealing the *insigmora* inked there. The tattoos were a symbol of her magic, geometrical shapes and moon phases that were sacred to the people who had raised her for six years. Her former Head of Council had ordered her not to show off her tattoos, but now that Lord Kevan was dead, she refused to hide them. They were a part of her, as were the Forest People. It didn't matter what rumors circulated about her. If the people surmised she was a witch, so be it. She *was* a witch. While she understood the dangers of outright saying so this early in her tenuous reign, she wouldn't hide it either. Witches—a term hurled at anyone who had uncanny abilities, keen senses, an interest in folk medicine and ancient traditions, or even an overt fondness for nature—would be protected under her rule.

Let them talk. Let them know that ousting such individuals from their towns and homes would not be tolerated. It was the one stance she would not budge on, even if it put her throne at risk. She'd rather lose her crown than ignore the plight of her own kind.

Movement caught her eye from just outside the doorway. Her pulse kicked up, but she kept her expression neutral. The Master of Ceremonies stepped forward and announced the arrival of her royal guests.

"His Majesty Larylis Alante, King of Vera. Her Majesty Mareleau Alante, Queen of Vera."

Two figures crossed the threshold and began their slow procession down the aisle. Cora's eyes met Mareleau's at once, and the other queen gave her a subtle smile. She looked beautiful with her pale blonde hair cascading down her back in neat curls, her silver-blue gown edged with white lace, its high waist sending gathered pleats to cascade down her abdomen, accentuating the curve of her belly.

Gods, Cora wanted to run down the dais and gather the woman in a hug. There were few people Cora felt compelled to greet with such affection, and there'd been a time when she'd vowed that Mareleau would never be one of them. But they'd bonded in an unexpected camaraderie last summer, after Mareleau had shared her vulnerable side and Cora had done the same in turn. Their friendship hadn't ended after Mareleau returned home. They'd struck up a correspondence and sent letters back and forth, almost as often as Cora and Teryn had. Cora had been so fixated on seeing her fiancé for the first time in half a year that she hadn't realized how elated she'd be to see her friend too.

Her gaze left Mareleau to assess the man beside her. She had to smother a laugh at seeing King Larylis, for he looked almost as uncomfortable as Cora felt in his formal garb. He was dressed in a white-and-gold ceremonial coat with a high collar buttoned almost to his chin, and a long gold cape trailing from his shoulders. His dark, copper-brown hair was shorter than she'd last seen it, the sides trimmed while the top was swept away from his brow. Upon his head, a gold crown rested, a simple band compared to Mareleau's silver-and-sapphire tiara.

The pair reached the foot of the dais and dipped their chins in respectful greetings.

Cora returned the gesture and uttered her rehearsed welcome. "Khero gladly receives Your Majesties' presence at Ridine Castle."

Larylis echoed the sentiment back. "Vera is honored by Khero's great welcome."

"We congratulate you on your upcoming nuptials," Mareleau said, her tone melodious and far less stiff than her husband's.

Cora gave a practiced nod. "I accept your congratulations with great thanks."

She clenched her jaw to keep from saying more. So badly Cora wanted to exchange more than dry statements she'd learned by rote, especially with Mareleau. But now wasn't the time. Informal conversation would have to wait until dinner.

Cora's eyes darted back to the doorway, anticipating her next guest. The Master of Ceremonies delivered his announcement.

"Her Majesty, Queen Mother Helena Harvallis. His Royal Highness, Teryn Alante, Prince of Vera, future King Consort of Khero."

Cora gripped her armrests tightly as Teryn escorted Helena through the doorway. Her breath caught at Teryn's warm smile, his gaze immediately locked on hers. She was grateful for their earlier reunion, for if she'd seen him for the first time now—his silver hair tied back from his face, his formal coat in gold and emerald, the latter color bringing out his eyes, the way his trousers hugged his muscled thighs—she might have fallen off her throne.

She could hardly bring herself to cast the queen mother more than a cursory glance, though the woman was dressed almost as elegantly as Mareleau.

Larylis and Mareleau stepped to the side to make room for the new guests. Teryn held her gaze, eyes twinkling with the same mischief they'd shone with earlier, even as he folded into a formal bow. Her heart kicked up as images invaded her mind, of him hefting her onto her dresser, his lips tasting her skin—

She let out a shaky breath and delivered her formal welcome, an almost-word-for-word echo of the one she'd given Larylis and Mareleau. Her mind was so frazzled she couldn't be sure she hadn't stumbled over her words, but the fact that none of the courtiers snickered was a good sign.

Helena offered her expected congratulations, then Teryn spoke next. "I am humbled and deeply honored by our forthcoming nuptials that will bind our houses in health, sickness, celebration, and solidarity." His formal tone was so at odds with the smile quirking his lips.

Oh, those godsforsaken lips.

She forced her eyes back to his. "Yes," she said before she realized that wasn't the response she'd memorized. Steeling her nerves, she delivered the correct lines. "I too am honored by the strength our union will bring and look forward to our nuptials."

Cold. So cold. So lacking.

His gaze finally left hers as he stepped off to the side to allow Cora to give her attention to her next guests. She wasn't sure who else had arrived today, as she was only expecting a few more noble families to attend. How could she focus on anyone else with Teryn so close?

Against her better judgment, she cast him a quick glance. He winked, and she couldn't fight the smile that curved her lips—

"His Royal Highness, Lexington Quil, Crown Prince of Tomas. Her Highness, Lily Quil, Crown Princess of Tomas."

The Master of Ceremonies' announcement had Cora sitting forward on her throne before she could rein in her surprise. A name left her lips. "Lex?"

She would be mortified by her break in composure if it hadn't been mirrored by Teryn and Larylis. The two whirled to face the doorway just as two figures entered.

A man with dark-blond hair and a plump physique sauntered into the room, a ridiculously smug grin between his ruddy cheeks as he escorted a pretty woman beside him. She was almost as short as Cora with curves that rivaled Mareleau's. Her auburn hair was arranged in a braided updo, displaying a rounded face and a disarmingly pleasant smile.

Cora couldn't believe Lex was here. She'd invited him, but she couldn't recall if she'd been informed of his reply. And the woman beside him was...his wife? He hadn't been married when she'd last seen him, which had been at the battle at Centerpointe Rock. He'd come to Verlot Palace when she'd been taken by Verdian as a temporary hostage, but she hadn't been able to bid him farewell before he'd left. While she and Lex hadn't grown nearly as close as she and Teryn had during their travels last spring, she had fond feelings for the man. To her, he was a hero. He'd outwitted Morkai with a lie, pretending to side with the mage, after which he'd fled to Dermaine Palace to warn King Arlous about the sorcerer's plans. He'd even fought in the battle against Morkai's forces.

I know him! Valorre's exclamation invaded Cora's mind.

When did you get here? She hadn't felt his consciousness connect with hers since earlier when he'd insisted Teryn smelled like strength and moonbeams. He was like that these days, coming and going at will, popping into her mind whenever hers drifted somewhere that interested him. Thank the gods he'd left her alone during her reunion with Teryn.

I know him! he repeated. *One time he didn't share his apple with me. Remember that?* A flicker of resentment wove through the unicorn's words, but his statement was otherwise good-humored.

I remember, Cora said and returned her attention to the approaching couple.

Lex and Lily stopped before the dais and gave Cora an exaggerated bow. Before Cora could deliver her formal welcome, Lex turned to the side and waved at Teryn and Larylis. Not a bow. Not a nod. A casual wave.

Whispers broke out from the courtiers at the fore of the audience, gossiping about his lack of decorum.

Leave it to Lex to breach formalities without a care in the world.

A grin split Teryn's face. Then, with an amused roll of his eyes, he strode forward and crushed Lex in a hug. Cora froze in surprise, flushing as more whispers broke out. Teryn stepped away, and to Cora's surprise, Larylis took his brother's place, hugging Lex with only slightly more restraint.

Mareleau arched a brow at the display while Helena looked scandalized. Cora's gaze flicked to the courtiers, then back to the warm reunion before her. She wasn't sure what to do in this situation. Wait idly by? Call for order? Her palms tingled with a flood of calming energy, and she knew what she needed to do. No, what she *wanted* to do.

She rose from her throne and the audience went silent. Lex separated from Larylis, eyes widening when they fell on Cora. "Oh, right! Majesty, thank you for—"

His words cut off as she marched down the dais, her skirts and cape trailing behind her. Lex's expression faltered, as if he only just now considered that he might have made a blunder. He opened his mouth, stammering for words, but

Cora gathered his hands in hers and gave them a firm squeeze. Her lips lifted in an unrestrained smile.

"Lex," she said, tone sincere, "thank you so much for being here. I can't express how much it means to me."

His cheeks reddened and his expression turned bashful.

She released his hands and took up those of the woman beside him. Lily made a startled sound, but her sweet smile remained. "You and I aren't acquainted yet," Cora said, "but I do hope that will change."

"You honor me, Majesty," Lily said, her voice small.

"The two of you honor me." Cora's tone regained some of its formality. She spoke louder, allowing her words to carry to the courtiers. "Lex, you are my kingdom's ally as well as Vera's. You aided us when Duke Morkai tried to destroy us." A collective intake of breath sounded from the audience at the mention of the duke, but Cora continued. "I look forward to furthering our friendship and am grateful for your presence."

Lex bent forward in a bow while Lily dipped in an elegant curtsy.

Cora lowered her voice and adopted a casual tone again as she asked, "You'll join us for dinner, won't you?"

"Of course," Lex said, puffing out his chest.

"Good." With one last smile, Cora left the couple and settled back on her throne with controlled poise. She was pleased to see the courtiers were no longer whispering. Now that their queen had validated what they'd previously deemed unseemly behavior, they had no reason to.

Lex and Lily joined the others and Cora shifted her focus to greet her next guests. Though she continued to deliver her memorized words and welcomed nobles who were no better than strangers, her brief reprieve with her friends was enough to make the rest of the ceremony far more enjoyable.

7

Cora was eager for dinner for more reasons than one. For starters, it would mean the most formal part of her evening was through. Secondly, she was famished. Only now, as she entered the dining hall where aromas of sizzling meats, stews, and fluffy breads infused the air, did she realize she hadn't eaten since breakfast. She'd been too flustered after her kiss with Teryn to take lunch. After the welcoming ceremony, she'd had just enough time to change out of her ceremonial raiment and into a dark blue dinner gown and have her ladies restyle her hair. It now hung over her shoulder in a long braid.

She was grateful that she was the last to arrive—a formality, of course—for it meant the dining hall was loud enough to smother the sounds of her growling stomach. The hall wasn't particularly rowdy, but there was just enough sound from the harpist in the gallery, the shuffling bodies at the tables, and the occasional whisper to keep the room from being dead silent. It didn't stop her from blushing as she climbed the dais at the end of the room and took the empty seat at the head table, between Mareleau and Teryn. Her plate was already laden with the table's ample offerings, eliciting the loudest growl from her stomach yet. She shot a horrified glance at Teryn, but if he heard the sounds roaring out of her, he made no sign of it.

Like her, he'd changed after the ceremony and was now dressed in a dark frock coat over an ivory brocade waistcoat and white silk cravat. She gave him a brief smile but dared not meet his eyes too long, lest she get thoroughly distracted. Dinner may be a less formal affair than the earlier audience she'd held, but she still had duties to perform as queen, and everyone was waiting on her.

Casting a benevolent gaze upon the room at large, she lifted her glass of wine, signaling the start of the meal. The courtiers in attendance raised their glasses, and after the queen took her sip, so did the rest. Relief coursed through her. Now that her guests could begin eating and politely conversing, she and her companions would have some semblance of privacy, for the dais set them apart from the other rows of tables.

Mareleau seemed to have the same train of thought, for she playfully elbowed Cora in the arm. Cora glanced to the side as she took up her fork and met her friend's smile.

"It's really nice to see you again," Mareleau said. Her tone took on a teasing quality. "Your castle isn't nearly as hideous as it was before."

Cora let out a lighthearted scoff. "What high praise."

"You really should have replaced the linens I selected." Mareleau tapped the tablecloth beneath the violet runner. "Don't you recall I selected these with Master Arther out of spite when you wouldn't let me attend the council meeting with you?"

Cora frowned. "What's wrong with the linens? They look fine to me."

Mareleau gave her a patronizing look. One that would have gotten under her skin before they were friends. Now she knew it was cajoling. "Cora, dear, the thread count is offensively low."

Cora rolled her eyes, but the gesture was interrupted by a slight wince from Mareleau. Her hand shot to her belly, a furrow on her brow. Cora opened her mouth to ask if she was all right, but Mareleau gave a subtle shake of her head.

Mareleau leaned in close and whispered, too quiet for anyone else to hear, "I'm fine. I don't want to make either of them fuss over me." She angled her head to the side, and Cora looked down the table. Queen Mother Helena was farther down, engaged in conversation with a visiting marquess. Larylis sat on Mareleau's left, quietly eating his meal. His gaze was so unnaturally fixated on his plate, Cora thought he had to be listening in on their conversation. Then she noticed his attention wasn't on his plate but his lap. More accurately, on the book there, hidden just beneath the edge of the table.

Cora's gaze shot back to Mareleau, eyebrows raised in question. Was reading at the table a usual occurrence for the king? In answer to her silent question, Mareleau mumbled, "Always."

Cora watched her friend for a few beats more, half tempted to extend her senses and ensure she truly was all right. She hadn't wanted Mareleau to travel all the way here in her condition, but of course, she hadn't listened. Still, if Mareleau didn't want people fussing over her, Cora would do her best not to pry.

Instead, she shifted her attention to her plate and brought a bite of almond-crusted lamb to her lips. The meat was so tender, her lashes fluttered shut. It took all her restraint to chew slowly.

A soft touch brushed over the back of her hand. She opened her eyes and found Teryn leaning toward her, his hand propped on the table beside hers, the backs of his fingers caressing the curves of her knuckles, one at a time. It was an oddly sensual touch, and she nearly dropped her fork.

"You're still coming to me tonight, right?" he whispered.

She swallowed her bite of food, her throat suddenly thick. "I am," she said, and a shudder of anticipation tore through her. Mother Goddess, how could she calmly finish her meal knowing she was meeting privately with Teryn afterward? She was looking forward to it with equal parts desire and terror. Would she manage to confess everything she'd been yearning to say? Or would he render her speechless before she got the chance?

Lex's voice cut it on her thoughts. "I'd say I'm surprised, but I'm not."

Cora tore her attention from Teryn's probing stare and faced Lex, who sat on the other side of her fiancé. Lily sat on Lex's right, taking dainty bites of stew.

"About what?" Cora asked before spearing another delectable piece of lamb.

Lex gestured between Cora and Teryn. "About the two of you. It's well past time, if you ask me. And I'm not just talking about the political alliance. I'm talking about...you know." He waggled his brows and gave Teryn a significant look.

Teryn pursed his lips, his expression suddenly abashed.

Cora glanced between the two men, trying to puzzle out what she was missing.

Lex's eyes widened as if Cora and Teryn were daft. "I mean his feelings for you! He's been smitten with you since last spring. You've told her, right?"

Teryn grumbled under his breath, then gave Cora an apologetic look. A strand of silver-white hair fell over his brow, loosened from the leather tie that held the rest back. Cora fought the urge to brush it off his face. "Lex is under the impression that I agreed to rescue unicorns with you because I fancied you."

She nearly barked a laugh but managed to morph it into a soft chuckle. "Is that how you got him to come along on our exploits?" To Lex, she said, "My friend, I'm sorry to say but you've been lied to. His heart was set on a certain bounty, not me."

She gave Teryn a good-humored scowl. She liked that she could joke about the past without resentment. Where once Teryn's betrayal had stung her, now she saw every moment, every circumstance—the good and the bad—that had brought them together as something to be grateful for.

Lex stared open-mouthed as understanding dawned. He uttered an extended, "Oooohh." Then he narrowed his gaze at Teryn. "I don't know why I didn't realize that until now. All this time I thought you were a romantic."

Teryn rubbed his brow. "You weren't entirely wrong."

Lex's expression brightened. "Do say more. Tell me, has this become a love match after all?"

Cora's gaze whipped to Teryn, her cheeks heating furiously. She didn't want him to answer, not here, not publicly. This was the topic of conversation she was hoping to save for tonight. His hand rested over hers, his touch firm yet calming. He gave her a subtle nod, as if to say he understood what she was thinking.

Teryn turned back to Lex. "I'll tell you a secret I've yet to share with my fiancée."

Cora's breath caught and she wondered if she'd misinterpreted the look he'd given her entirely. Maybe he didn't understand her at all. Maybe he was about to confess his feelings for all to hear, when Cora wasn't at all prepared.

"Cora," Teryn said, "was my first crush."

Her mind emptied. That wasn't what she'd expected.

He spoke again. "Princess Aveline Caelan, age six. My first one-sided love. A two-week-long affair, and I daresay she hadn't a clue I existed the entire time."

"What are you talking about?" Cora was halfway between a chuckle and a frown. She couldn't tell if he was making up the story.

He shifted his gaze to hers. "You don't remember at all, do you?"

"Remember what?"

"You visited Dermaine Palace once with your parents. I followed you around like I was your shadow, but tried to evade your notice when you caught sight of me. Whenever you did notice me, you turned your nose up like I was pure scum for existing in your presence."

"I can confirm this is true," Larylis said, leaning forward to speak down the table. "I was quite embarrassed for him."

Something warm and tender flooded her chest. "I don't remember that." It had been so long ago, before the great tragedies that had befallen her—the deaths of her parents, her exile from Ridine. She hadn't even remembered she'd been to Dermaine before.

"I clearly wasn't very memorable," Teryn said.

She realized something else he'd mentioned. That she'd visited with her parents. "So you met my mother and father?"

"I did."

Tears sprang to her eyes. The fact that the man she loved had met her parents —and that they'd met him—meant more to her than she could have imagined. She couldn't bring herself to speak for fear that she'd start sobbing then and there.

"That's a very sweet story," Princess Lily said in her quiet voice.

Cora shook the tender revelations from her mind and poured her attention on the couple next to Teryn. "What about the two of you? How did you come to marry?"

Lex reached beside him and gripped his wife's hand. A proud smile spread across his lips. "Lily is my long-time sweetheart."

Teryn nodded. "I remember you telling me about her during our travels."

Cora opened her mouth, on the verge of asking why Lex had participated in Mareleau's Heart's Hunt if he'd already fancied another woman, but she stopped herself just in time. She couldn't ask such an impertinent question, no matter how her curiosity burned.

Lex leveled a knowing look at her. "I know what you're thinking, and, no, I never had any intention of winning *her* hand," he said with a significant nod toward Mareleau, who in turn nearly choked on her dinner roll. "I only participated in the Heart's Hunt because my father threatened to disinherit me if I didn't at least *try*. I figured I'd give it my worst effort, come home defeated, and then get permission to marry the woman I actually cared for."

"Well, he's a blunt one, isn't he?" Mareleau said under her breath.

Cora's eyes darted to Lily to see if she showed any sign of discomfort at being at the same dinner table as the woman her husband had once been forced to court, but she merely grinned as if thoroughly amused.

Lex went on. "My heart has always been for Lily, and I wouldn't have considered attending that ridiculous Beltane festival if I'd thought I'd had any chance at winning that poetry contest."

"Your poem was terrible," Teryn agreed. "*Your hair is the color of light ale. Your skin a milky pallor.*"

Larylis looked up from his hidden book, a distant look on his face. "*You are graceful like a deer and smart like a fox.*"

"Ah, yes," Lex said with a grimace. "My prize-winning poetry."

Larylis gave Mareleau a crooked grin. "I'd say your words captured my wife's greatest assets rather accurately."

Mareleau burned him with a glare but it was betrayed by the smile pulling her lips.

Lex cleared his throat and shrank down slightly. "His Majesty isn't uncomfortable about..." He lowered his voice and leaned in, ensuring his words wouldn't carry to the lower tables. "You know...that every man at this end of the table has, in some way, courted your wife?"

Mareleau made an indignant squeak and rounded on Lex. "Does it bother *you* that I'm the one who deemed your poem the winner of my contest?"

Lex pulled his head back. "I don't know why, but I feel like I should be offended by that."

Lily patted his shoulder. "There, there, my love."

Cora's chest rumbled with laughter, and Teryn's mirth was so potent, his eyes were crinkled at the corners. She loved seeing her fiancé so amused, so carefree. This was the most lighthearted royal dinner she'd had since being crowned queen. For the first time since taking the throne, her friends were here. Her beloved was here. There were joys to celebrate, matters to laugh about.

Mother Goddess, she wished it could always be this way.

The darker part of her day—overseeing the prisoner's interrogation—threatened to dampen her joy, reminding her of the threats that might await, but she wouldn't give in. Not yet. Not now.

After Teryn sobered from his amusement, he said to Lex, "You never explained why your father was so against your marriage to Lily, other than the fact that she wasn't a princess. How did you convince him to allow your marriage?"

"Well, you see," Lex said, "my Lilylove is the niece of a Norunian rebel."

Mention of Norun made Cora freeze, her glass of wine halfway to her lips.

"Her uncle, Orik Allgrove, is the former King of Haldor," Lex explained, "and has been stirring unrest against King Isvius for many years now in hopes that he'll build a rebellion large enough to take back Haldor."

Cora listened with rapt attention. Isvius was the King of Norun and Prince Helios' father, while Haldor was one of the kingdoms Norun had conquered several years ago. Lex's mention of unrest and potential rebellion could prove useful if Norun resorted to war with Khero like she feared.

Lex spoke again. "As you can imagine, Tomas is not keen on getting conquered by Norun, and my father has gone to great lengths to avoid drawing attention to our kingdom. Save for building the wall between our borders, of course, which my father stands by as a brilliant necessity. So he feared pairing me with the niece of a known rebel would attract Isvius' scorn."

"What changed his mind?" Teryn asked.

"Aromir wool, of course," Lex said with a flourish of his hand and an exaggerated mock bow. "I can't thank you enough for orchestrating Tomas' inclusion into the trade agreement with Brushwold. When Father learned of it, he was willing to reward me. Hence the only reward I could ever want." He patted Lily's hand, who blushed furiously in turn.

Cora hated shattering the lovely mood with her next question, but she had to ask. "Your father's determination to avoid conflict with Norun must mean he keeps abreast of the kingdom's latest moves and developments. Are you by chance aware of any troubling rumors regarding Norun? Anything about them potentially targeting another kingdom? Preparing for conquest?"

Lex exchanged a weighted look with Lily. Cora extended her senses, desperate to know what lingered beneath that look, but all she could read was...excitement.

"Let's just say," Lex said, a sly smirk turning his lips, "that my rise in esteem and Lily's influence as princess have sparked...certain developments."

Her heart quickened. "Like what?"

Another significant look passed between the couple before Lex leaned in closer. His voice was barely above a whisper. "All the Norunian rebels need for a successful rebellion are weapons. The military confiscated all their weapons long ago and forbids all citizens from bearing arms. Yet it just so happens that someone has a wall. A wall from which certain exports leave. And Tomas' primary export to Norun is manure."

Cora frowned, unsure what he was getting at.

Lily kept her voice as quiet as her husband's. "We're smuggling weapons in shit —" Her hand flew to her mouth, though her lovely face maintained its sweet expression. "Pardon my language, Majesty. In *manure*. Soldiers don't bother auditing the manure merchants' carts. You can imagine why."

It took Cora several moments to understand the brilliance of what they were doing. And the daring. Lex was spurring a rebellion!

Teryn seemed equally as impressed. "Do you know when it will take place?"

"At the end of the month," Lex said. "The rebels almost have enough... manure."

Cora's heart sparked with excitement. If the rebels succeeded, Cora might not have to worry about the hostility the prisoner had hinted at. At least not from Norun. Syrus, of course, remained a mysterious threat...

Teryn placed his palm on her thigh, beside her hand that was fisted around the folds of her skirt. She didn't recall having moved her hand there, but she must have in her anxiety and excitement during all the talk about Norun and rebels. Teryn's fingers smoothed her own until she released the fabric of her skirt. Then he entwined their fingers, a gesture that reminded her they would face this together. They would face whatever came next, side by side.

"Will you keep us apprised of developments?" he asked.

"Of course," Lex said. "Anything for my allies."

8

ora was ready.

She *was.*

She really, truly was.

At least, she figured if she kept telling herself that, she might be. Dinner had ended an hour ago. Her maids had already been dismissed after assisting with her bath. The evening was creeping toward midnight, and Cora worried that if she waited too much longer, Teryn would give up on her coming at all.

She couldn't dally. What good was pacing around her room doing? She thought she needed to practice what she wanted to say, but she'd been doing that for months, and when it had finally come time to see Teryn, she hadn't been able to convey any of the things she'd intended to.

It was now or never.

Cora brushed her damp palms over the front of her cream velvet robe. Beneath it, she wore an ivory silk chemise trimmed with lace. She tried not to overthink what it meant that she was about to visit her fiancé in her underclothes, for what else could she do? She couldn't have asked her ladies to lace her back into her dinner gown after her bath. Moreover, to say *certain thoughts* weren't on her mind would be a lie. And after their kiss earlier, after the way he'd demanded she say his name, the way he'd propped her on that dresser, she knew those things were on his mind too. But as long as Teryn didn't pounce on her the second she arrived, she'd have a chance to accomplish her mission before being swept up in desire again.

In the meantime, she tugged the neck of her gown a little closer and tied the sash around her waist a tad tighter. Then, closing her eyes, she thought of Teryn.

When her mind raced forward to how their conversation might go, she drew it back and settled her thoughts in the past, at dinner. She recalled the warmth of his fingers laced with hers, his steady, anchoring touch. She imagined the way his skin felt beneath her palm. As her nerves settled, allowing her to fully focus on her magic, she pictured his bedroom. She imagined it much like it had looked earlier, but this time she envisioned it under a blanket of night. Curtains drawn, the lighting dim, the glow of a single lamp warming the walls. She *felt* like she was there. Felt Teryn's presence, his nearness.

Then she took a step.

Felt the distance between their rooms fold until it was merely a hop away.

And planted her feet firmly in her destination.

She opened her eyes to find she'd succeeded in her travels. Only, it wasn't the dimly lit room she'd pictured. Instead, the bedroom was cast beneath a golden glow, the walls flickering with the light of what appeared to be a hundred candles. She was so startled by this unexpected vision, so distracted by the ivory flame-topped pillars that encroached upon nearly every flat surface, from the dresser to the nightstand to the bureau, that she almost didn't notice Teryn.

He leaned against the far wall, one arm propped on a windowsill, ankles crossed. It seemed he'd kept his promise about wearing a shirt and had even managed to keep it mostly buttoned. He was free of his cravat and dinner jacket, the only other articles left of his evening attire being his trousers and open waistcoat. His pale hair was no longer tied back and hung loose like it had when she'd first invaded his bedroom. She was still struck by that moon-white hair, how it was neither thin nor fraying like she'd expected it to be. How it cascaded around his face in lazy waves. How it somehow suited him just as well as his golden-brown tresses had.

"You came," he said, not moving from his place by the window.

She took a few hesitant steps forward, gaze flicking from him to the candles and back again. "You did all this? For me?"

"It wouldn't be the first time." He pushed off the wall and closed just as much distance as she had. Which was a measly three feet. Perhaps he was allowing her to set the pace between them. She nearly sprinted the rest of the way to him, jumped into his arms, and pressed her lips to that deliciously plump mouth of his, but she held back. She absolutely *had* to express herself through words before she turned herself over to her body.

"What do you mean it wouldn't be the first time?" she asked. Then a sound tugged upon her awareness. "And is that...music?"

"It is music." He angled his head toward the windowsill behind him.

Cora saw nothing but a long wooden box. "What is that?"

"Your wedding gift."

Curiosity overtook her. She swept toward the windowsill, her heart racing with every foot of space she closed between herself and Teryn, then brushed past him. The sound was louder now, a sweet yet tinny melody that emanated from the box. The box itself was a long, narrow rectangle of black lacquered wood decorated with red-and-gold cherry blossoms. A jewelry box, perhaps? Teryn stepped beside her, and the scent of soap and pine filled her senses. He leaned in close and whispered, "Open it."

She met his eyes, his smile, and her heart nearly burst from her chest. She was reluctant to tear her gaze away, but she was still so curious about the box. He'd said it was her wedding gift, and the music box was stunning in itself. But if he wanted her to open it, perhaps her actual gift was inside.

Dragging her attention from Teryn to the box, she brought her hands to the lid. As she lifted it, Teryn said, "I know we already chose rings from our royal collections, so I didn't get you wedding jewelry. Besides, I thought this would suit you better."

The music grew slightly clearer as the box opened on a hinge. Inside was a compartment lined with red velvet, and at the very center lay a stunning dagger. Cora's breath caught at the beautiful steel blade, flickering orange from the undulating candlelight, but that was before she noticed the hilt. It was even more breathtaking, with a crossguard engraved in a floral pattern that continued onto the hilt. At its center was the most moving touch of all—a unicorn rearing back on its hind legs, mane rippling and merging into the floral engraving. Tears glazed her eyes as she ran her fingers over the design, marveling in its craftsmanship.

"You like it?" Teryn's voice was edged with uncertainty.

"I love it," she said, and her heart hammered at the word *love*. Slowly, she slid her gaze from the dagger to him.

"I had it made specially for you," he said. "I wanted it to represent you in every way. Your beauty. Your fierceness. Your connection to Valorre. And...to me."

"You?"

He reached for the box and closed the lid again. "Do you remember the first time you held a blade to my throat?"

She nearly barked a laugh that he had to specify *the first time*, but he was right to. He'd been on the other side of her blade more than once. She recalled their first encounter now, when they'd met by a stream. Teryn had almost thrown a spear at Valorre and Cora had stopped him by shooting an arrow at his neck in warning. It had struck a cherry tree behind him, pink blossoms in full bloom. After that, she'd confronted him with her knife and they'd had a brief altercation.

Laughter tore through her chest. "You dedicated my wedding gift to *that* moment between us?"

"The most important moment." His eyes glittered with mirth as he lifted a hand and softly brushed it against her cheek. Her stomach fluttered, and it was all she could do not to angle her face and press her lips to his palm. She would not kiss him until she'd confessed her heart's deepest longings.

But as she opened her mouth to just say it already, the words wouldn't come. Was she supposed to blurt it out? Pair it with some sweet gesture? Sweet words? If only she were as thoughtful as he was. If only she'd had the foresight to have gotten him a gift that would render him speechless. If only—

"May I have this dance?"

Her mind emptied. She'd been so wrapped up in her thoughts, she hadn't noticed Teryn pull his hand from her cheek or step away. He now held the music box in his hand and was winding the brass key at the back. A cranking sound emanated from the box, but as he set it back down, the melody resumed. Cora shook her head to clear it. "Dance?"

He sketched a bow, a sideways grin pulling his lips. As he straightened, he held out his hand. What else could Cora do but take it? Her nerves settled as she placed her hand in his. He pulled her against him, too close for any kind of dance at a public ball. But here, in the privacy of his room, it was perfect. She kept one hand clasped in his and wound the other arm around his back. Then, turning her face, she nestled her head to his chest, the pound of his heart merging with the rhythm of the music box. Slowly they swayed, saying not a word for minutes on end.

Finally, Teryn gently loosened her arm from around his waist and guided her into a slow spin. When he reeled her in, her back was to his chest. They swayed side to side as he brought his lips close to her ear. "I never answered your earlier question."

She shuddered as his breath rustled her hair. "What question?"

He spun her away from him again, then folded her back into his arms, their chests pressed together once more. Holding her eyes, he said, "When you asked about the candles, and I said this wouldn't be the first time, I meant that I've done this for you before. Or something like it. Twice, in fact."

"When?"

He grinned, and there was a bashful quality to it. "The most recent time was for the dinner we never got to have last summer. I had to coerce Mareleau into helping me organize it, but…"

He didn't need to finish. She knew what had happened that night. She'd been an emotional wreck after remembering the curse Morkai had placed upon her, and Teryn had gotten captured in the mage's crystal. Sometimes she wondered what would have happened if she'd never turned him away that night, if she'd gone to dinner with him instead of sitting alone with her pain, but it was folly to wonder. What was done was done.

"The first time, though," Teryn said, "was when I asked you to come see me in the garden at Verlot Palace."

Her heart sank. "The night I left. When I…when I thought you'd married Mareleau."

He nodded, chuckling to himself. "I had the most ridiculous spectacle prepared for you. A candlelit alcove, a harpist, a table set with wine and sweets."

Regret had never pierced her so hard as it did now. She had no clue he'd done that for her. "I'm so sorry—"

"Don't apologize," he said, and there was only gentleness in his tone. "I'm not telling you this, doing this, to make you feel guilty. I'm doing this because I never want to miss anything between us ever again. Never want to miss any chance, any opportunity. Obstacles have drawn us apart, but I will never let them hold me back." His tone turned serious, as did his expression. A fierceness shone on his face, one that told of the hardships they'd endured, the darkness they'd faced and survived.

The song began to slow, the mechanical melody reaching its end. They stopped their dance but neither stepped away. Cora's heart raced, knowing it was time. She could feel the shift in Teryn's mood as well as her own, something as fierce and sharp as lightning crackling in the air between them. Invisible layers fell away, confessions breaching the frail walls they'd both constructed to hold them in place. It was a mutual shedding. A mutual baring of souls. She knew this. Felt this.

Teryn stepped even closer and framed her cheeks in his hands. His eyes locked on hers, blazing with an emerald fire so heated she couldn't look away. "I almost died, Cora. All of us have danced with death, you, me, Larylis, Mareleau. We don't know what lies ahead and our time as living beings isn't guaranteed. I don't want to waste a single second of this life not loving you. Not showing you, in all that I do, that I deeply and steadfastly love you."

Cora nearly sagged against him at the sound of those words. Her lashes fluttered shut as she let them wash over her. She'd known it in her heart, but hearing him say it—*finally* say it—was different.

"You love me?" Her voice quavered.

"Of course I love you." Restraint edged his voice, as if he wanted to shout the words, declare them for the world to hear. "I've said it to you so many times in my mind, in my heart, but you never heard me. I fought to utter the words when my spirit was barely clinging to my body. I've sung it from the depths of my soul. I know you couldn't hear me, but did you never once at least feel its melody?"

"I did," she breathed. "I even sang it back to you. Just...just never aloud."

He released a slow breath, then pressed his forehead to hers. "I'm still waiting to hear it," he said, and this time there was a note of teasing in his voice.

Her heart slammed against her ribs. Yes, now was the time.

She swallowed hard.

"I love you, Teryn. I'm sorry I'm not as romantic as you. I'm sorry I'm not as brave or eloquent with my words—"

"No," he whispered. Placing his forefinger under her chin, he lifted her face, forcing her to meet his eyes. "You're perfect as you are. I want nothing more from you. Let me spoil you. Let me say the things I couldn't put to pen and paper. Let me make a fool of myself before you. You don't have to do anything in return. Just love me."

"I do. I love you. I can't even tell you how much I do."

He sighed, and it seemed to drag years off his visage, making him look boyish and beautiful and carefree. Mischief worked the corner of his mouth. "Does that mean I've good and properly wooed you?"

Cora remembered the promise he'd once made. That even though they were engaged, he'd court her. That before they lived as true husband and wife, he'd win her heart, no matter how long it took.

She realized there was something else she needed to make clear. Placing her hands on his chest, she gathered the collar of his shirt in her fists and tugged him closer. "I don't need you to court me or woo me anymore, Teryn. I don't need us to take our marriage slow, nor do I want to. Do you understand? I'm already yours."

"You're mine?" She'd never seen such a gorgeous smile. His face lit up with it, with pleasure, with pride.

"And you're mine." She pulled him closer again, their bodies flush. The same fierce quality she'd glimpsed on his face earlier now burned inside her, sparking yearning. Now that she'd said all that she'd wanted to say, her body tingled with the desire she'd been holding at bay. It rushed through her arms, filling her palms.

It coursed down her legs, gathering at her core. Gods, she loved him. Gods, she wanted him.

A look of surprise crossed his face. Then a question. "When you say you don't want to take our marriage slow..."

She answered him with a kiss.

9

Their lips met with a reckless fervor, parting at once. Her tongue swept against his, tasting their mutual confession. Cora trembled at the flood of desire pouring through her, so strong it was as if it had broken a dam. She supposed that was expected after she'd pent it up all afternoon and evening. Now she turned herself over to it, let her body take the lead. Her muscles uncoiled as if breathing a collective sigh, one that said *finally*. Every ounce of tension that left her body collected in a pool of heat at her center, warming her lower belly, burning in a ball of hungry heat between her thighs. Meanwhile, her heart opened, expanded, singing with the glorious revelation, the trust, that Teryn loved her. He well and truly loved her.

And he was *hers*.

Teryn's arms wound around her, one hand weaving through her loose tresses, the other pressing into her back, tugging her closer. She arched against him, desperate to feel more of him, all of him. Her palms burned with her yearning, igniting every line of ink that marked them. She released Teryn's collar and let one hand cradle the back of his head, the other slipping beneath his shirt to smooth over his pectoral, his shoulder. He hissed in a breath at her touch, shuddering beneath her palm. A wicked smile curled her lips, and she drew the other hand away from his neck, down his chest, to the hem of his shirt. Lifting it, she slipped her hand underneath and splayed her palm over his muscled abdomen. A stifled groan left his throat and he took her bottom lip between his teeth. She gasped at the slight pressure he applied, thrilled that her touch had sparked such a reaction in him.

He pulled back suddenly, and for a moment she feared he would ask her to stop, tell her *he* was the one who wanted to take things slow. She'd honor that, of course, but as he looked down at her with half-lidded eyes, lips swollen from the ferocity of their kisses, she desperately wished he wouldn't make such a request.

Thankfully, he merely reached for the collar of his shirt and pulled the article over his head. Though this was her second time seeing him bare-chested today, this time was different. She felt no apprehension. No fraying nerves. Only fascination and desire.

His chest heaved as he stood before her, making no move to return to her arms. As much as she wanted to feel him against her, she wanted this too—a moment to look him over. Admire him. Drink in the sight of the man she loved without any reservations. She lifted a hand and alighted her fingertips upon his ribs, right over the scar that marred his flesh. He tensed as she touched him, tracing the line of puckered skin. Then she trailed her hand up his torso, over his chest, his collarbone, then up his neck. She smoothed her thumb over the small circular scar there.

Finally, he dared to move, lifting a hand to her neck as well. He brushed his fingers softly over her identical scar, then bent forward and caressed it with his lips. He did the same to the scar on the other side, a slow and tender gesture. They both held these twin marks, a permanent reminder of the collar they'd both worn.

When Teryn pulled back, something dark flashed in his eyes. "If I ever meet the man who did that to you..."

She silenced him with her lips. There was no use making idle threats against the Elvyn male who'd trapped her in that collar, stifling her magic. Fanon was a world away, in the fae realm. Cora may hold the secret to entering the realm—her worldwalking magic paired with Valorre's ability to pierce the Veil that protected El'Ara—but she had no intention of returning.

Besides, she didn't want to think about El'Ara, the Veil, or the prophecy her fate was entwined in. The only thing she wanted to be entwined with right now was Teryn. His lips. His arms. His body. His love.

She pulled back slightly and infused her tone with a taunting lilt. "You may want revenge on the male who put me in that collar, but what about what I did to you? I'm the one who collared you. Do you want to punish me?"

A wry grin quirked his mouth. "Do you want to be punished?"

"I do," she whispered.

"How?" His voice came out like a growl.

It reminded her of how he'd sounded when he'd told her to say his name earlier. The demand in his tone had been so thrilling. She wanted to hear it again.

She gave him a coy smile. "I'll let you make one command of me. Tell me one thing to do to make up for my previous misdeeds, and I'll do it now."

"Anything?"

She stepped closer, angled her head higher. "Anything."

His throat bobbed. Silence stretched between them before he managed to speak. "Undress for me."

That same thrill tore through her. All she could manage in reply was a nod.

Slowly, he backed away from her and sat at the edge of the bed. She stood before him, and a flicker of apprehension moved over his face. "Is this all right?" he asked, voice soft. He reached for her, softly touching her arm as if to tell her she didn't *have* to do this.

His hesitation warmed her heart, but it also filled her with the slightest self-consciousness. Still, she *wanted* to do this. Needed to. Her heart thundered in her chest. "Yes."

With a nod, he pulled his hand away and sat back, his posture easing.

With trembling hands, she undid the tie at her waist and let her robe fall open. She watched his face as his eyes wandered over the length of her chemise. His lips parted as she slowly let the robe fall from her shoulders. Then she dragged the top of her chemise down her shoulders, slipping her arms through and freeing them, before baring her breasts. Her moves weren't elegant or seductive, but it didn't matter. Teryn watched her with such rapt attention, his gaze heavy with desire, that she felt like the most beautiful, alluring figure in the world. She tugged her chemise the rest of the way down and let it fall at her feet.

Teryn bit his bottom lip as he looked her over, then his gaze rested on hers. "Can I touch you?"

She shuddered at the question. "Please."

He reached for her with gentle hands, bracketing her hips with his palms. He pulled her closer to where he sat at the edge of the bed until she was standing between his legs. Their heights weren't so different with him sitting, and for once she stood slightly above him. He lifted his chin and she tasted his lips, a slow and languorous kiss. When they separated, he brought his mouth to her neck. Then her upper chest. With his tongue, he explored the arched curve of her breast. She released a soft cry as his tongue skated over her sensitive peak. His hands tightened on her hips at the sound.

Her desire grew tenfold, at the pressure of his palms, the pleasure he painted with his tongue. It made her knees weak. Giving in, she dropped herself into his lap, straddling his hips. Hips that were annoyingly still clothed.

He tensed beneath her, his hands roving along her upper back then drifting down, down, curving around her bottom. She pressed her mouth to his again, and he tugged her tighter to him. Then, in a swift move, he flipped her onto her back. The soft velvet blankets contrasted Teryn's hard angles, the stiff fabric of his trousers. Trousers that were straining against his desire in obvious ways.

"Teryn," she whispered against his mouth. "I want more of you."

"How much more?"

"All of you. I told you, I don't want to wait."

He pulled back slightly, hovering over her. "Are you sure?"

"You don't want to waste a single moment between us. I don't either." With that, she slid her hand down his chest to the waistband of his trousers, tucking her fingertips just beneath the fabric. He groaned, then shifted to the side to undo his trousers' buttons, freeing himself at last. She didn't think her heart could beat any faster, but it nearly shot from her chest as she explored him with her palms. He did the same to her, feeling the parts of her he hadn't touched yet. They held each other's eyes, coaxing sounds from each other, testing which touches made the other shudder, which had them arching into each other for more.

Then finally, when Cora didn't think she could take another second of the beautiful torment they teased each other with, she shifted more firmly beneath him, and let him settle fully over her.

They paused and exchanged a tender kiss. "I love you," Teryn said when their lips parted.

"I love you," Cora echoed back.

Then Teryn seated himself fully inside her. Cora gasped at the fullness, the rightness, the euphoria that thrummed through her as their hips began to move. She'd never felt this before. Sure, she'd taken lovers when she'd lived with the Forest People, but it was nothing like this. Nothing like the connection between her heart and Teryn's. Nothing like the emotion that tore through her as they quickened their pace, reading each other's bodies, movements, signals, as if they were speaking a brand-new language.

Teryn gripped her hand, pressing into the blankets beneath them, an anchor to reality as her euphoria grew. Heat continued to build at her core, growing hotter and hotter, even as the thrust of their hips sated it. She wanted more. More. Again and again.

Finally, she crested the wave of pleasure, feeling it tear through her, coursing through every inch of her body, her soul. Her eyes watered with the force of it. The promise of it.

Teryn pressed his mouth to hers once more. "I love you," he said, voice strangled. "I love you so much, Cora."

The words drove her over the edge, release shuddering through her. Teryn found his next, a wave that chased her own, that danced with it. That rose and calmed with it.

They remained entangled, sweat soaked and spent for minutes on end, neither speaking as they caught their breath, communicating with wordless smiles. Teryn brushed the hair away from her brow. When they finally managed to separate, it was only to rearrange themselves. Teryn reclined on his back while Cora draped herself over him, her head cradled against his chest. She closed her eyes and gave in to a moment of rest, lulled by the sound of his heart.

10

Teryn couldn't stop looking at her, the beautiful woman dozing on his chest, a soft smile on her swollen lips. His body was sated, but his eyes couldn't get enough of her, nor could his hands. He caressed her dark tresses—tangled now, thanks to their activities—and wound his fingers through her hair, memorizing its sheen, its texture. His other hand brushed the dark tan skin of her forearm that was draped across his chest.

How did he get so lucky?

What did he do to deserve this fierce and gorgeous creature?

He studied the side of her face, her bare shoulder, her slender neck. As his eyes settled on her puncture scar, a protective fire burned inside him. He'd felt it when they'd assessed each other's scars earlier. While he felt no bitterness at having worn the collar briefly himself—it had helped him take back his body, after all—seeing hers filled him with rage. In her letters, Cora had told him all that had happened in El'Ara. How she'd been forced to endure that collar for nearly an entire day, how an Elvyn named Fanon had hated her beyond reason, going so far as to pit her against a dragon.

His anger at that Elvyn male was so strong, it overshadowed any sympathy he might feel for those who lived in El'Ara. For the fact that their land was dying, smothered by the Blight that was slowly creeping from the Veil. He was almost glad Cora couldn't fulfill her role as the mother in a prophecy that foretold the fae realm's salvation, if only to spite that single Elvyn. Though he couldn't fully relish it. Not when Cora's inability to birth the prophesied savior had come at such a heartbreaking cost—being cursed by Morkai.

Cora stirred, drawing his mind from his dark thoughts. As she lifted her head from his chest, his stomach sank. He knew what she was going to say before she uttered a word.

A sad smile crept over her mouth. "I should get back to my room."

"Can't you stay?" he asked, running a fingertip over her cheek, her chin.

"I wish I could, but what would my ladies think if they found me missing in the morning?"

She was right. As queen, she granted honors to aristocratic families by appointing their daughters and nieces as her royal lady's maids, or their sisters and wives as ladies-in-waiting. That didn't mean they were women she could trust. As far as Teryn knew from the letters they'd exchanged, she hadn't gotten close to any of them. If they discovered any unsavory gossip about Cora, they could spread it through the castle and beyond in a matter of hours.

He hated that royal women were expected to remain chaste while men were not. He hated that their pure and beautiful love could devolve into a scandal, even though their wedding was a mere few days away. Even so, this wasn't the time to battle such lofty expectations and traditions. Cora's reign was still new.

Yet he couldn't bear to let her go so soon.

"Go back in the morning then, before sunrise," he said.

Her eyes narrowed in consideration. Then suspicion. "I have a feeling we won't get much sleep if I stay the night."

He shifted to the side and rolled her onto her back. Her eyes widened with amused surprise. He nipped at her bottom lip. "Whatever could you mean, Your Formidable Majesty?"

"Hmm, I wonder." She glanced down, arching a brow at the part of him that answered for both of them.

Just when he thought he was sated, his craving for her returned. He angled himself closer to her, let his hand skate up her thigh, her hip, her stomach, until he cupped one of her breasts in his hand. He ran his thumb in a slow circle over her hardened peak, delighting in the way her lashes fluttered shut, the way her lips parted. "What do you say?"

She opened her mouth, either in a gasp or to give her answer, but before he could find out which it was, a rhythmic knock invaded his awareness. It was coming from his sitting room, at his suite's main door. His bedroom door was closed, stifling the sound. He had every intention of ignoring it, even as it sounded again, more insistent this time.

Cora released a heavy sigh. "You should answer that."

Teryn groaned, and it wasn't the pleasurable kind. "Must I?"

She shrugged. "It could be important."

The knock sounded again, an incessant rumble that told him his caller would not relent.

Cora leaned forward and captured his lips in a too-short kiss. "Don't worry. I'll wait until you return before I leave."

His heart fell. That meant she was leaving after all. He wasn't ready to say goodnight, but perhaps if he dealt quickly with their interloper, he could go back to convincing her to stay just a little longer.

With another frustrated groan, he dragged himself away from Cora, donned his shirt and trousers with haste, and marched from his bedroom. He closed the door behind him and strode through the sitting room in darkness, the only light coming from the moon's pale white streaks that shot through the windows. When he reached the door, he flung it open with far more force than necessary.

He opened his mouth, ready to tell his caller to kindly piss off, but held himself back as he saw who was on the other side of his threshold.

Mareleau glowered at him, teeth bared. Without waiting for his permission, she charged inside and closed the door behind her. Crossing her arms, she faced him. "I need to speak with Cora right now."

His mind stuttered before he conjured a reply. "What makes you think she's here?"

She gave him a withering look. "It's five nights before your wedding and you just saw each other for the first time in months. She's not in her room, which means of course she's here. Tell her I need—"

The sound of his bedroom door creeping open silenced her. "Mareleau, what's—"

"Seven devils, Cora," Mareleau said with equal parts relief and frustration. "There you are. I need you."

"Why?" Cora was dressed in her chemise and robe again, though her tangled hair and crooked sash made it obvious what they'd been doing before.

Mareleau glanced from Teryn to Cora, a wild look in her eyes. Finally, her gaze settled on Cora. "Either I've just wet my skirts for the first time in my adult life, or my waters have broken. Gods above." Her voice broke, rippling with a frantic tremor. "I'm going into godsdamned labor."

~

Every inch of bravado Mareleau had ever possessed, all her boasting that she could give birth anywhere and it wouldn't matter, fled the instant she admitted she was going into labor. Here. Now. She'd been brave when she'd thought the grand event was still weeks away, and her midwives had indulged her, assuring her she'd more likely deliver late than early. But this...no, this couldn't be happening.

Cora took a step closer. "You're going into labor? Are you sure?"

"I'm pretty sure the water soaking my skirts says I am." She couldn't stop the panicked edge from creeping into her tone, but at least it helped mask her embarrassment. She didn't want to talk about this in front of her brother-in-law, but it couldn't be helped. She needed Cora. For what, she wasn't entirely sure. All she knew was that she couldn't face her mother or her midwives right now. Her mother would fly into hysteria, which would only heighten Mareleau's own, while her midwives would confirm her fears. That this was happening. She was giving birth.

Her abdomen tightened, a strange and foreign feeling that was somehow coming from inside her, against her will. She'd experienced lesser contractions for days now, ones deemed normal by her midwives, but the ones she'd begun feeling this evening were anything but mild. They'd begun at dinner and hadn't stopped.

She closed her eyes, hand to her belly, and waited for the tightening to pass. When it did, there remained a similar constriction in her chest. "I can't do this."

"Breathe, Mareleau," Cora said, her voice soft and calm. She placed her hands on Mareleau's shoulders. "Tell me slowly. Why are you alone? Where are your ladies?"

"Breah is down the hall." Despite trying her best to speak slowly like Cora had requested, her words still came out rushed and racked with a tremor. "I asked her to keep watch while I came to find you."

"Yes, but why did you come find me? Why not your midwives?"

Mareleau opened her mouth to answer that which she hardly understood herself. She'd awoken after a couple fitful hours of sleep and left her room to pace the halls, choosing Breah to accompany her. Waking up to walk in the middle of the night wasn't unusual for Mareleau, for she often woke due to discomfort and needed to stretch her legs before settling back into her fort of pillows. But tonight, as she'd slowly wandered the corridor outside her suite, waiting for restfulness to settle back in, she'd felt a sudden gush of warm water. She'd frozen in place, her mind whirling. Once she'd been able to form a coherent thought, it had been to find Cora at once.

The reason?

Mareleau shrugged and blurted out the first semi-reasonable thing that came to mind. "I came to you so...so you can stop this."

Cora pulled her head back. "Stop what? Your labor? How the seven devils do you expect me to do that?"

"I don't know. Your...magic."

Cora leveled a look at her that conveyed just how ridiculous Mareleau's words were. Yet she'd already known that as soon as they'd left her mouth. Mareleau had learned many things about Cora over the last few months of their increasing correspondence, particularly about her past, her abilities, and how they related to what had happened that night in the meadow seven months ago. When she thought rationally, she knew Cora could do nothing about her situation.

So why had she come to Cora?

"I just need a friend, all right?" The tightness in her chest eased a little as she settled on this truth. "I need you to be here for me, that's all."

Cora's expression softened. "I'm here. I'll stay by your side through what comes next, but you need to tell your midwives you're going into labor. Your mother and husband too, for that matter."

Teryn voiced his agreement. "Larylis deserves to know."

"I can't tell Larylis," Mareleau said. "Not yet. You know how he gets when he's anxious. He'll start reciting great queens of history who've given birth in unusual situations. If I have to hear about Queen Constantina of Rovana in 56 Year of the Stag one more time, I will scream."

She'd had enough of Queen Constantina, who'd ridden into battle heavily pregnant and gave birth behind a shield wall while arrows rained overhead. Mareleau didn't need that kind of pressure. She wasn't nearly as valiant.

Teryn's jaw shifted back and forth before he released a resigned sigh. "You make a valid point."

"Your mother then," Cora said. "It will be impossible to avoid her anyway. Isn't she staying in your suite with you?"

She was, and Mareleau wouldn't be surprised if her mother was already frantically looking for her. And yet...

"I can't handle her right now. If she finds out I'm going into labor here, she'll only say *I told you so.*"

"And I won't?" Cora removed her hands from Mareleau's shoulders and propped them on her hips. "I told you not to come, Mare. You had to have known this was a possibility."

She had known, and she'd thought she'd been prepared. She'd imagined several scenarios, walked through each one in excruciating detail, per her husband's insistence. So long as she'd agreed to work through the myriad of possibilities they might encounter regarding her pregnancy, he'd support her travels. But in every scenario, she'd been calm. She'd had a plan. She'd dealt with every imagined ordeal with grace.

Reality, however, was proving far different. She hadn't anticipated this all-encompassing shock. This terror. This dreadful feeling that the gods had made a grave mistake in bestowing such a heavy responsibility on her. She wasn't ready. She'd never be ready. Why did she ever have the nerve to consider herself an adult?

Another contraction stuck her abdomen. She closed her eyes and felt a gentle hand smoothing circles over her back.

"I can't do this," Mareleau said, tears leaking from her tightly squeezed eyelids. "I can't be a mother. I'm going to do a terrible job. I'm going to be awful."

"No, you won't," Cora said. "Don't you recall what I said to you, after you first told me about your pregnancy? I said you'll be an okay mother."

The tightness eased, allowing her to scoff. "An okay mother," she echoed. "That's hardly comforting."

"Well, it should be. Because that's all you have to be. You don't need to be perfect. You don't have to do everything right. Was your mother perfect?"

"Hardly."

"Exactly. Look how great you turned out."

Mareleau pried her eyes open but she couldn't see much through her tears. She coughed on a sob before she managed to say, "You think I'm great?"

"You're at the very least tolerable." The teasing in Cora's voice gave Mareleau a sense of calm to cling to. If Cora was taunting her, refusing to give in to her vanity, things couldn't be too dire, right?

Mareleau blinked the tears from her eyes and found her friend's smiling face. She blew out a shaking breath.

Cora rubbed another circle over her back. "Are you ready? Can we go tell your midwives now?"

Ready wasn't the right word, but she had no other choice. With a shaky nod, she said, "Fine. Let's show Queen Constantina who can give birth in a worse environment."

"Aww, you're insulting my castle again," Cora said in a simpering tone. "You must be feeling better already."

Mareleau gave a humorless laugh, then pinned Teryn with a warning look.

"Don't you dare let Larylis in my room until I say so. I don't care if you have to tie him to a chair."

Teryn gave a reluctant nod, then Cora steered Mareleau out the door.

And toward the greatest battlefield she'd ever face.

11

As promised, Cora stayed with Mareleau throughout the entire ordeal. She'd attended numerous births amongst the Forest People and had even assisted with them. But this one was different, for it was her friend on the bed, her friend in pain. She wished she could play a more proactive role in helping her, but between the four midwives, Mareleau's three maids, and Queen Mother Helena, there was little for Cora to do aside from what Mareleau had asked of her: simply being there for her.

Cora held her hand through every contraction. Depending on Mareleau's ever-changing mood, she chanted encouragement or whispered words of soothing. Despite her best efforts, Cora found her mental shields growing weaker as the hours stretched on and on, not a wink of sleep behind her. Delirium took over, and she wasn't sure it belonged more to her or to Mareleau. Their emotions were entwined by morning. Mareleau's pain was Cora's pain. Her fatigue, Cora's fatigue. Her fear, Cora's fear.

There were times the latter emotion grew unbearably strong, dipping into sorrow and panic when Mareleau would mutter that her baby was too early, that this was too arduous, too long, that surely something was wrong. It almost made Cora wish she had the power of the narcuss.

Morkai's power.

She hated that she even thought of it, but if she had his magic, she could impress calmer thoughts upon Mareleau. A narcuss was the inverse of her power. Where Cora could feel the emotions of others, a narcuss could change what another felt and perceived. Particularly in the minds of the weak or fearful.

Cora banished these thoughts whenever they crept upon her, for what good would they do? She wasn't a narcuss. The only one she'd ever met was Morkai, and he was dead. Cora couldn't force Mareleau's pain and fear away, and even if she could, what right did she have? Those emotions belonged to her friend. All she could do was feel them with her. Help her through to the other side.

The other side finally came.

After twelve hours, a baby boy took his first breath in the world, followed by a tiny, wailing cry. It was just past noon. The room remained dim, the curtains drawn shut. After half a day and no sleep from anyone—save Mareleau's three ladies, who'd left to doze in the sitting room hours ago—the blaring light of day was an unwelcome intruder.

The baby's cry filled the room, such a soft yet sharp sound. Such a signal of joy and relief. It was strange how the cry somehow made everything seem quieter. Calmer. Like the entire world had gone to sleep and now orbited that sweet small sound.

Cora sagged against the edge of the bed, knees on the floor, arms draped over the side of the mattress. Her lungs opened wide, allowing her to breathe easier for the first time in twelve hours, but she still felt the haze of delirium.

Mareleau sobbed as a midwife placed the swaddled babe in her arms, and Cora found her eyes glazing as she watched them, watched her friend's lips widen in a smile, watched as Helena sat beside her daughter on the bed, tears streaming down her cheeks.

"He's so tiny," Mareleau said, a tremor in her voice.

"He is small, Majesty," the midwife agreed, "but he's healthy."

Helena leaned closer to her daughter until their foreheads touched. "He's beautiful."

Mareleau's grin widened. "He is."

Cora smiled, watching Mareleau interact with her mother. Despite Mareleau's worries, Helena hadn't harped on her daughter at all. She'd been stunned silent for most of the ordeal. For the first time, Cora had seen the queen mother as timid, as if the woman was desperate not to upset her daughter and make things harder for her.

"Would you like to try to nurse him?" the midwife asked.

Mareleau nodded, equal parts joy and trepidation on her face.

Cora opened her mouth to ask if she should leave, but before she could utter a word, Mareleau whispered, "Stay. Please."

So instead, she rested her head on her arms, closed her eyes, and gave her friend a moment of privacy.

～

Cora woke to the sound of song.

She lifted her head and found the room was no longer dim, the curtains parted over the far window to let in the light of an overcast afternoon sky. She wasn't sure how long she'd slept, but the room had been tidied and the midwives were no longer there. Mareleau and Helena were in almost the same positions they'd been before Cora had closed her eyes, nestled side by side. The music Cora had awoken to was coming from Helena. The queen mother sang a lovely, lilting lullaby, her voice a soothing soprano.

Cora straightened, rubbing sleep from her eyes. Though fatigue still weighed down on her, she found much of her delirium had cleared, enough that she could connect to the elements and strengthen her mental wards again. With her shields in place, she met her friend's eyes.

Mareleau brightened. "You're awake," she whispered over her mother's song.

Cora nodded, and Helena finished her lullaby, her final note ringing out long and sweet. Cora cleared her dry throat before she spoke. "I had no idea you sang so well, Helena."

The queen mother beamed at the compliment. "I've always had a talent for music. When I was younger, I was praised for having perfect pitch."

"Oh, don't get her started on her perfect pitch," Mareleau said with a roll of her eyes, a gesture that was tempered by the smile she wore. It seemed the two were still getting along.

"I played harp and piano," Helena said, sitting a little straighter. "I could perfectly recite any song by ear after hearing it only once. I was such a prodigy, my father used to call me his *Little Siren*."

Mareleau said the last two words in unison with her mother, but in a deep and mocking tone.

Cora chuckled, though she was thoroughly impressed, if the queen mother wasn't exaggerating. Musical talents weren't Cora's forte, but she'd always admired musicians. Especially those amongst the Forest People. She'd known several clairaudient witches who'd expressed their magic through song, using their impressive hearing to compose or replicate beautiful music they would play for the commune. If Helena was as much of a prodigy as she suggested, there was a chance she had a magical gift and didn't even know it. Not every witch came to know their own magic for what it was, for many expressed their abilities in ways that blended seamlessly with societal norms.

Cora held a secret smile. Perhaps she wasn't the only queen who was also a witch.

"Do you want to see him?" Mareleau's question pulled Cora from her thoughts. She angled her head at the empty space beside her, opposite Helena.

"Of course," Cora said with more enthusiasm than she felt. More than anything, she wanted to curl up on a soft surface and go back to sleep. Yet she wanted to enjoy this moment with her friend. Of course she did.

Reluctantly, she dragged herself off the ground, her body aching from her unfortunate sleeping position, and settled in beside Mareleau. She was careful not to get too close lest she wake the sleeping baby in her friend's arms. Perhaps she was a touch anxious too, though she wasn't sure why. She'd been around plenty of infants and children when she'd lived with the Forest People. Even so, she wouldn't call her maternal instincts strong. Maiya, her dear friend and foster sister, had excelled in that regard, scooping up the little ones and swinging them around while Cora kept a modest distance. Then again, Cora had kept nearly everyone in the commune at arm's length.

Mareleau leaned slightly closer to Cora, showing off her bundle. A tiny, wrinkled face was all Cora could see in the swaddling, and though she should say he was beautiful, he looked...less so.

Her maternal instincts were awful indeed.

"He's lovely," Cora said, forcing her voice to sound wistful.

Mareleau furrowed her brow, and for a moment, Cora feared she'd oversold the compliment. But Mareleau's next words held a note of concern. "Is this painful for you? To...to see him? To be in this situation with me?"

Cora's stomach plummeted as she realized what Mareleau was implying. She was concerned for Cora's well-being because of the curse that had been placed upon her. Because this experience was one Cora might never have. To be honest, Cora hadn't given it much thought while she'd been aiding Mareleau through her labor, but now...

The unicorns. The mother. The child. Who do you think you are in that prophecy?

No, she still didn't want to think about it. Didn't want to revisit what Morkai had done to her. Didn't want to reflect on all the information she'd learned from Teryn, pieces of the prophecy that proved, without a doubt, she had been the prophesied mother Morkai had sought.

Blood of the witch, blood of the Elvyn, and blood of the crown. The unicorn will signify her awakening.

More than that, she didn't want to think about what her curse meant for El'Ara. Without their true Morkara, there was no one to command the flow of the *mora*—the fae word for magic—and keep it from seeping out into the human world. No one to stop the Blight that was slowly consuming the realm.

It wasn't sorrow that kept her from these thoughts, nor was it grief.

No, it was something darker.

Something she didn't want to admit.

Apathy.

An emotion that lingered in the wake of her time in El'Ara, when she'd been treated like a criminal by the Elvyn who'd found her. Two of the males, Etrix and Garot, had been kind to her, but Fanon had nearly gotten her killed. Had nearly killed her himself. Even the Faeryn, the race of High Fae the Forest People were descended from, did nothing but eye her with disdain when she'd come across a group of them trying to heal the Blight.

If she looked too close at that apathy, if she recognized even an ounce of truth in it, she'd have to consider that maybe she wasn't such a good person.

Cora forced a smile to her lips. "I'm fine, Mare." Her eyes darted to Helena, who was watching them intently.

Mareleau stiffened, as if only now remembering her mother's presence. She angled her head toward the queen mother, but Helena already seemed to understand. Scooting off the bed, she said, "I should see if your husband is awake yet."

"Thank you, Mother." Mareleau's voice held more gratitude than Cora was used to hearing from her friend. "If he's still asleep, let him stay that way, just a little longer. He was awake all morning."

Helena nodded, then left the bedroom, closing the door softly behind her.

Once they were alone, Mareleau faced Cora again. "I'm sorry. I shouldn't have brought it up in front of Mother. She doesn't know about..."

"My curse," Cora finished for her, voice flat.

Mareleau spoke again. "And I'm sorry that I didn't think of you, that I didn't worry about you until this moment."

Cora let out a long breath, and when she attempted her smile once more, it was genuine. "I can't possibly condemn you for not thinking of me until now. *I* wasn't thinking of myself either."

"Still, I'll ask you again. Is this painful for you?"

"I'm all right," Cora said, not bothering to hide the weary edge in her voice this time.

"Good." Mareleau cast her eyes back to her baby. A light laugh left her lips. "You know, newborn babies aren't quite as cute as we're led to believe, are they?"

Cora snorted a laugh. "I wasn't going to say anything."

"I mean, he is beautiful in my eyes. Completely and utterly beautiful. And yet... he does look a bit like a wrinkly old man. Don't you, Noah?"

Surprise rippled through Cora. "You named him?"

"It's a name Larylis and I both liked for a boy. I suppose I'll find out if my husband still approves of it once he gets here. Speaking of..." She turned toward Cora with a grimace. "How ugly am I?"

Cora leveled a glare at her. "You're never ugly."

"But my hair must look terrible. What about my eyes? Are they red and swollen from crying? Do I look half dead or more like three-quarters? I'm open to the truth."

Cora rolled her eyes. Her friend's hair was admittedly a tangled mess, but this was hardly the time for vanity.

Mareleau sighed. "No, of course you won't tell me. I'd use my magic trick, but Larylis can probably see right through it."

"Magic trick?"

"Oh, it's not real magic. It's this thing I do where I pretend I can change my outer appearance and influence how another perceives me. I used to do it all the time when I was trying to get out of unwanted engagements. It's just a matter of altering my posture and expression, and it doesn't work on everyone."

"What do you mean? Show me?" Cora was both curious and amused.

"I'll try. But remember, it might not work." Mareleau adjusted her son in her arms and sat a little straighter. Then she held still for a few seconds, staring straight ahead, eyes unfocused. Slowly, a soft smile melted over her lips and she angled her face toward Cora. Her countenance was nearly glowing, her sapphire eyes as bright as the sea, the apples of her cheeks perfectly rosy. She didn't look at all like someone who hadn't slept—

Mareleau shook her head, averting her gaze. "Ah, I'm too tired. I can't do it."

Cora blinked at her, at her profile, at cheeks that had held such a rosy hue for all of a second. At eyes that had momentarily lost their puffiness and the dark circles that hung beneath them.

Had Cora merely hallucinated? Was she so fatigued that her mind had played along with Mareleau's game?

That was when she felt the tingle in her palms, sparking every inked line of her *insigmora*. Was Cora sensing...magic? A heavy warmth settled in her stomach, followed by a lifting sensation in her chest—a medley of clairsentient feeling that said *truth*.

Mareleau...had magic.

Again that feeling in her stomach, her chest.

Truth.

Mareleau could cast a glamour.

Truth.

Mareleau was a witch.

Truth.

12

Maybe it shouldn't have surprised Cora that Mareleau could use magic. She'd entertained the idea that Helena might be clairaudient. Why did it send such a chill down her spine to consider Mareleau might be a witch too?

Another heavy feeling settled in her stomach, but this one was sharper than the one that said *truth*. It said *pay attention*.

She wasn't sure what she was supposed to pay attention to, but she realized she was doing the opposite when Mareleau asked, "Were you listening?"

"No, I'm sorry." Cora shook the thoughts from her head and gave her friend an apologetic smile.

"I said, I'd like to name you Noah's godmother."

Something soft melted in Cora's heart. "You want me to be his godmother?"

"I do." Mareleau's expression turned hesitant. "Is that all right? Do you want that? Or is that incredibly rude of me to even ask, considering your—"

"It's lovely," Cora cut in before Mareleau could mention her curse again. "I'd be honored to be Noah's godmother."

"You know," Mareleau said, drawing the words out slowly, "you could name him your heir." When Cora didn't reply, she rushed to add, "Temporarily if you wanted. Your husband's nephew would make a suitable heir, don't you think?"

Cora glanced down at the sleeping babe. Son of her friend. Nephew of the man she loved. She supposed he would make for a worthy heir. Yet, as the first son of Mareleau and Larylis, he was already heir to Vera. Did that mean...

She shifted her gaze back to her friend, who seemed to already know what was on her mind.

"I promise, I'm not saying this because I want Noah to inherit your kingdom. I don't share my father's obsession with legacy. All I'm saying is that naming him your heir for now could secure Khero's standing even more than your marriage to Teryn will."

Cora huffed a laugh. "When did you become such a persuasive politician?"

"Probably when I was forced to become the queen of two kingdoms before I'd even gotten used to reigning over one."

"Well, you make quite a convincing case."

"Then I'll add one more thing. Merging Menah and Selay into Vera has been beneficial for our kingdoms. Uniting our resources, pooling our assets...I've seen nothing but good come of this. Our kingdoms were small, so merging the two hasn't stretched us thin or made it difficult to serve our people. So if you ended up...you know, keeping Noah as your heir, and Khero merged with Vera at the end of your reign..." Her expression turned hesitant again. "I'm just saying it wouldn't be the worst thing."

Cora pondered her words. While a stubborn, prideful part of her rebelled at the thought of turning her crown over to someone else—someone not of her blood, her family—she recognized this as only a small part of her. The greater part saw wisdom in Mareleau's words. If the curse Morkai placed on Cora never lifted, if she lived the rest of her life without ever bearing her own heirs, Mareleau's suggestion could be the solution she'd been looking for all along. She'd never been overly fond of bloodline politics in the first place, and what she really cared about was the safety of her kingdom. She cared that her people thrived, both during and after her rule. Handing her crown to Noah, to Cora's newly named godson, to a child who might very well come to feel like family soon...

"You're right," Cora said. "It wouldn't be the worst thing."

"See? I knew it was a good idea." Mareleau's expression turned thoughtful. "Three kingdoms united. I wonder why they ever divided Lela in the first place."

A shudder ripped through Cora. Was it relief over having a possible heir? In answer, that earlier feeling returned, sharpening in her gut. *Pay attention.*

To what? Cora wondered.

Then Mareleau's words echoed in her mind, unraveling something...

Something about three kingdoms...

No, three crowns...

And Lela...

He will unite three crowns and return El'Ara's heart.

Cora nearly choked on a sharp intake of breath as the words of Emylia's prophecy invaded her consciousness. Teryn had conveyed everything he'd learned, and she'd done the same with what she'd discovered in El'Ara. Together, in the letters they'd exchanged, they'd merged their knowledge. Even though Cora's place in the prophecy had been thwarted, they'd figured the information might prove useful in dealing with Darius. In understanding him, predicting his aims. Not that it had helped them yet.

So why was this piece of the broken prophecy striking her so fiercely right now? Was she merely being reminded of what might have been? What could have been, were she in Mareleau's place? The promised Morkara in Cora's arms, instead of Noah in Mareleau's?

Or...

Could it be...

Blood of the witch, blood of the Elvyn, and blood of the crown.

Cora stared at Mareleau, assessing her under a chilling new light. After witnessing the glamour Mareleau had cast, she could believe Mareleau was a witch. But did she have Elvyn blood? Cora had never been able to answer that question for herself, ever since she'd learned of this part of the prophecy.

The Elvyn had died long ago. Now that Cora knew of El'Ara's history, she understood that the only fae who had ever lived in Lela were those who'd been trapped outside the Veil. While the Faeryn descendants lived on as the Forest People, there were no records of any Elvyn bloodlines that remained. No way to know if Cora had Elvyn blood in her family tree. Her mother was from the Southern Islands, and the only Elvyn there was Darius. Cora didn't want to consider any blood relation to him. Besides, wouldn't Morkai have known if they were so closely related? Furthermore, it wasn't just *any* Elvyn blood that qualified the prophesied mother. It was Ailan's blood. While Darius and Ailan shared their mother's blood, a descendant of Darius would not be the Blood of Ailan.

That left Cora's father. His ancestry was local to the continent of Risa, so he could have been a descendant of Ailan.

But the same could be said for Mareleau.

When will she be born?

The year of the Great Bear.

Mother Goddess, Cora and Mareleau were the same age. They'd been born the same year. Yet the prophesied mother was supposed to have been born in Khero—

No.

Not the mother.

The true Morkara is the Blood of Ailan, born under the black mountain.

Born *under*, not *to*. Cora pulled back from her friend slightly, heart racing. Mareleau was so enchanted by her sleeping son, whose tiny hand was now curled around her forefinger, that she didn't notice Cora's startled scrutiny. Cora's gaze lifted to the walls, to the purple tapestries lining them, boasting Khero's sigil.

A black mountain over a field of violets.

Cora's breaths grew sharp. Could...Mareleau be the mother? Not Cora? Could Noah be the true Morkara?

There was still one final piece of the prophecy. The line that had been the most convincing of all, proving Cora was the prophesied mother.

The unicorn will signify her awakening.

The unicorn. Valorre. Cora's familiar. After he'd come into her life, everything had changed. She'd awakened to truths she'd never known were missing. Her magic had grown tenfold.

At the thought of him, he entered her consciousness.

You're distressed, he said.

Distress. Was that what she was feeling? She wasn't sure what to call it, the tremor that had taken over, the thundering of her heart, the tightness in her chest. Perhaps distress was the right word for it, but she was more desperate than anything. Desperate for the truth. For the final piece of the puzzle to click into place, either confirming or dismissing her suspicions.

Valorre, she conveyed, *when we were in El'Ara, you remembered some things. You said you recalled running from dragons—*

I remember everything. Cora felt his surprise as if it were her own. *I...I remember it all now.*

The dragons chased you from El'Ara. Through the Veil.

Yes, they knew my horn would let me leave.

Why did they chase you?

They...they felt her.

Cora swallowed hard. He'd said *her* not *you*.

Who did they feel? she asked.

The Blood of Ailan. They felt her mora.

Magic. They felt the prophesied mother's magic.

"Mare," she said, turning to her friend. Cora could feel the quaver in her voice, but Mareleau didn't seem to notice. She merely cast a questioning glance at her. Cora worked the dryness from her throat before she spoke again. "When did you start using your magic trick?"

Mareleau shrugged. "I've always used it in some form or another. It serves as a sort of protection. A way for me to feel like I'm someone else on the outside."

"Was there ever a time when you felt like...like people started reacting to your magic trick?"

"The suitors I got rid of certainly reacted strongly," she said with a wry grin.

"When was that? When did you first drive away an unwanted suitor with this trick?"

Her expression turned thoughtful. "About a year ago? No, a little longer than that. Maybe a year-and-a-half ago?"

Cora's heart fell. A year-and-a-half ago. When the first unicorn was spotted in the human world.

Mareleau frowned. "Why do you ask?"

Cora couldn't answer. She couldn't form a single word, and thankfully she was saved from needing to as Mareleau's door opened. Larylis and Helena rushed inside. Cora felt detached from her body as she slid from the bed, allowing Larylis to take her place and meet his son for the first time. She wanted to be moved by the tears in Larylis' eyes, by the joy in her friend's face, but she felt none of that. Felt nothing and everything at once as she excused herself and left the room.

Her lungs constricted as she swept from the suite and into the hall. The corridor was blessedly empty, so she let herself lean against the wall, let herself gather in lungfuls of air even as her chest continued to tighten. She tried to root her feet to the floor, to connect with the steadying earth energy, but her mind spun too fast, her thoughts and heart in disharmony as both fought for an anchor.

Mother Goddess, why did she feel this way? Why did she feel like her world had just been upended? Surely this wasn't the right response. Yet she couldn't name her emotions at all.

Was this simply the shock of discovering the prophecy remained?

No, this was more than that.

It was never me, she said to herself.

She waited for relief to follow. Relief was what she should feel. That was what her frail hold on logic told her, anyway. She'd never wanted to be the central figure in some ancient prophecy meant to save a people who didn't even care for her. She didn't want to save or condemn El'Ara. She didn't want any of this. Shouldn't she be glad the burden was no longer hers to bear?

Yet that...

That was the source of her unnamed emotions.

The burden wasn't hers to bear.

It never had been.

But she had already borne the brunt of it. She'd been targeted by a blood mage. Cursed by dark magic. Her childhood destroyed. Her future tampered with.

She'd.

Already.

Suffered.

She named it then, that dark and swirling vortex of emotion that tore through her, growing, releasing, spilling from her eyes in the form of tears.

It was rage.

Rage.

Violent and bottomless, so vast she wanted to scream.

"It was never me," she said through her teeth. A strangled sob caught her voice, and she dropped her face to her hands, her fingers curled, digging into her skin. "It was *never* meant to be me."

All she heard were her sobs. All she felt were the trails of her tears, the heaving of her shoulders.

Then strong arms folded around her, bringing with them the scent of soap and pine. And a voice, deep and mellow, whispering her name, weaving through the chaos of her rage. It was Teryn. Her anchor. She melted into his arms and buried her face in his chest. She cried, screamed, and shouted until the anger left her breath.

Until her fury got its fill.

13

It tore Teryn up something fierce to find Cora crying like this. His soul felt as if it were being ripped from his body all over again. His first thought upon finding her sobbing in the hall was that some great tragedy had befallen Mareleau or the child. But how? It had only been minutes since he and Larylis had awoken from where they'd haphazardly dozed on the furniture in Teryn's suite to the news that Larylis was officially a father. Larylis had left with Helena and must already be inside. Could something have happened in those few extra minutes he'd given his brother to meet his son in private?

As he wrapped his arms around Cora, he understood that wasn't the case. The way his fiancée trembled in his arms, teeth gritted, hands curled around the fabric of his jacket, told him this was not a shared grief but a personal one. And the way she wailed "It was never me" over and over sent a chill down his spine.

Once she calmed enough to separate from him, he ushered her swiftly down the hall to her quarters. Everything inside him wanted to scoop her up and carry her into her room, but she was the queen of this castle. He would not cause a spectacle if he could avoid it. Where he couldn't draw the line, however, was at being alone with her. Propriety could go to the seven devils, as could the bewildered maid who tried to argue as he ordered her out of Cora's suite.

With the door slammed shut and privacy secured, Teryn led Cora to the wingback chair before the roaring hearth. It was afternoon, but the late winter chill was prevalent. He hoped the heat would ease her tremors, though he knew better than to think they were due to the cold. Regardless, she had to be at least somewhat chilly, as she was still dressed in the same ensemble he'd last seen her in—the same robe and chemise that had graced his bedroom floor last night.

No longer racked with sobs, Cora settled into the chair, eyes unfocused. Teryn's chest tightened at the sight of her, at her empty expression, her red-rimmed eyes.

He wanted to comfort her, assure her, hold her, but he didn't know what kind of comfort she needed right now. There was a chance she wanted to be alone. It wouldn't be the first time. The last time he'd found her crying, she'd asked for exactly that, and he'd acquiesced against his every instinct. If she pushed him away now, would he have the strength to grant that request?

Daring neither to get too close nor pull away too far, he settled for kneeling before the chair, his hand softly covering hers. "Cora," he whispered, eyes searching her dark, empty irises. "What happened?"

She said nothing for several long moments, but that was better than her asking him to leave. Finally, her gaze sharpened and focused on Teryn. Her lower lip quivered, sending a spear of pain through his chest.

"I'm not..." She cleared her throat, blinked away fresh tears, and tried again. "I'm not the mother from Emylia's prophecy."

Silence.

Such agonizing silence.

But he didn't dare speak yet. She wasn't finished with her tale, and she needed the freedom to express her pain on her own terms. In her own time.

Cora's throat bobbed before she spoke again. "Mareleau is. She always was. It was never me."

Questions surged through his mind, but he tightened his jaw to keep them at bay. Not yet. He couldn't hound her with questions yet.

Instead, he gave her hand a soft squeeze. With the other, he slowly lifted his fingertips to her cheek and wiped away the trail of tears glinting in the firelight. Keeping his voice steady, he asked, "Do you want to talk about it?"

Her gaze went distant again, but she eventually gave a nod. "Yes. I need logic right now."

She stood and approached the fireplace. Teryn rose to his feet and followed, leaning against the wall beside the hearth, his arm propped on the mantle. Then she told him. She explained what had happened in Mareleau's room and the revelations she'd had. She told him all the reasons she believed Mareleau to be the true prophesied mother. Mareleau was very likely a witch, and it made sense for her to be the Blood of Ailan too. More sense than Cora, at least.

Teryn could see why she thought that. Cora had been forced to try to bond with a dragon in El'Ara, something only those of the Morkara's bloodline could do. The attempt had failed miserably. Though there had been reasons to explain it— she'd removed the collar too late, her Elvyn blood was too diluted—it made the most sense that she simply wasn't of Ailan's lineage.

"Every time I stated that I was descended from Ailan," Cora said, voice hollow as she watched the dancing flames, "it always felt wrong. It always felt like a lie. I'd thought it was because I wasn't confident in claiming such a significant role in the prophecy, but the truth is that...it wasn't me."

Teryn reached out and brushed his knuckles against hers, a silent reminder that he was here. He was listening.

She spoke again. "As for Valorre, he was chased from El'Ara by the dragons who'd sensed Mareleau's awakening magic. Valorre was able to pierce the Veil with his horn, but when he reached the other side, his memories were compromised."

Something flickered across her expression. Hurt or rage, he wasn't sure, but this had to pain her. Valorre was her best friend and familiar. Meeting him must have felt like fate, the one solace that came from being entangled in the web of prophecy.

Yet now she had no place in that prophecy. She'd only met Valorre because he'd unwittingly been looking for someone else. Worse was that which she'd yet to say.

That she'd been cursed in Mareleau's place.

She, who had no part in the prophecy, had been hurt and abused because of Morkai's misinterpretation of Emylia's words. Not that he could wish Cora's fate on Mareleau. She was his sister-in-law, the woman Larylis loved. She was Cora's friend.

But to say he didn't feel the slightest bit of resentment that she'd been granted the safety of a coddled childhood while Cora had been running for her gods-damned life would be a lie.

"This is my fault." The voice startled him, for it didn't belong to Cora. He straightened and found Emylia beside him, between him and Cora. Her eyes were on his fiancée, her semi-transparent form rippling with tremors. "I did this."

Cora shook her head and faced Teryn, oblivious to the apparition standing beside her. "Valorre has all his memories back. It happened suddenly—"

"I'm so sorry," Emylia's voice cut over Cora's, and Teryn tried to tune it out. He couldn't acknowledge her presence, for Cora didn't know about Teryn's uncanny new ability.

"—which makes me wonder if the Veil has torn."

"This is why I can't move on," Emylia wailed.

"What do you think?" asked Cora.

Teryn opened his mouth, but Emylia spoke first. "This is why I'm plagued with guilt."

"Emylia," he barked, unable to ignore her a second longer.

Both Cora and the spirit stiffened. Cora frowned. "What about Emylia?"

Closing his eyes, he rubbed his brow.

"I'm sorry, Teryn," Emylia whispered. "I didn't mean to intrude. I didn't realize you could see me again."

"Well, I can, and you are intruding. This is a private conversation."

"Wait..." Cora's voice had him opening his eyes with a resigned sigh. "Are you... talking to Emylia *right now*?"

He supposed there was no better time to tell her. "Yes."

"How?"

"Ever since I returned to my body last summer," he explained, "I've been able to see spirits. Emylia is the only one who has communicated with me. She's been watching over you."

Emylia clasped her hands to her chest. "Tell her I'm sorry."

"She says she's sorry."

"Tell her this is all my fault. Tell her I don't know how I'll make up for what I've done. Tell her I—"

"Emylia," he said, a warning in his tone, "I get it." Then to Cora, he said, "She feels incredible guilt for her part in channeling the prophecy. She hasn't been able to move on to the otherlife and hopes she can atone."

Cora's expression hardened, and he didn't miss the way her fingers curled into fists at her sides. Then she averted her gaze to the fire and folded her arms over her chest. "It was a mistake, but I can't hold it against her. Nor can she be blamed for the actions Morkai took based on the conclusions he came to."

Her voice sounded dry and rehearsed but it seemed to appease Emylia. Her form ceased its trembling. "If there's anything I can do to help, please tell me," Emylia said.

"She wants to help," Teryn conveyed.

"Has she learned anything useful as a spirit, now that she's been freed from the crystal?" Cora asked.

"She confirmed that the current King Darius Solaria of Syrus is indeed Morkai's father."

"That's hardly news," Cora countered, though her words lacked bite. "We already guessed as much. Does she know what his plans are? Is he using Norun to wage war on Khero?"

Emylia shook her head. "I don't know about his current plans. All I know is that he sought El'Ara and likely still seeks it. If he's learned what Morkai discovered—that Lela is the Heart of El'Ara—he might seek to invade Khero to gain access to the Veil, with the goal of finding a way to cross it. Since the Veil surrounds the entirety of Lela, he might not stop at targeting Khero either. He might try to conquer Vera too, just to ensure he can freely search every inch of the Veil."

Teryn conveyed Emylia's words, then added to Cora, "At least we know he's physically weak. And that he doesn't know what you know—that unicorns can pierce the Veil and that a worldwalker can use them to enter El'Ara."

"Yes, but there is an additional concern," Cora said. "The prophecy stated that the Veil would tear when the true Morkara was born. The latter has happened, so we must assume the former has too. Valorre suddenly got all his memories back this morning—"

Her words cut off, and Teryn was certain they were thinking the same thing. "Darius might have his memories back too." He looked at Emylia for confirmation.

She shrugged. "Morkai said his father had been cursed to forget El'Ara, but he didn't say how or why. It could have been the Veil that had made him forget."

"Which means a tear in the Veil could return his lost memories," Teryn said. Seven devils, if Darius had his memories back, if he could recall the land he'd once left, the land that had once been a piece of El'Ara, could he worldwalk straight here? Cora had told Teryn about the war she'd learned of in El'Ara, and how Darius had used his power to bring in human armies. Did that mean he could worldwalk with multiple people in tow? Did he even need to ally with Norun to accomplish his goals?

Cora took in a sharp breath. "What if the Veil was also the cause of Darius' physical weakness? What if..."

A chill shot through him. She didn't need to finish. If Darius was no longer weak, they might soon face a formidable foe.

"What does this mean for us?" Cora asked. "What's going to happen?"

"I don't know." They locked eyes, and his shoulders grew heavy. There were still so many unanswered questions. Some Teryn wasn't ready to voice; primarily, if they had to choose between war with Darius or complying with him, would it be better to simply give him access to the Veil? Would it really be so wrong to condemn El'Ara, if it rid the human world of such a great threat? Or was Darius as ambitious as his son? Would he use his power as Morkaius of El'Ara to harm the human world too? Teryn knew one thing; there wouldn't be any easy answers.

"At least we hold intel he doesn't have." Cora kept her voice low as if she feared the very walls would carry her secrets to their enemy. "He doesn't know about Mareleau and Noah. He doesn't know about my and Valorre's ability to cross the Veil."

Teryn nodded. "We should do whatever we can to stop word of Noah's birth from spreading. If Darius finds out a royal child was born *under the black mountain,* that could be all he needs to put the pieces together."

"You're right," Cora said. "We need to keep his birth a secret. Hopefully we can stop rumors from spreading before it's too late." She turned on her heel and marched toward the door.

Teryn caught her hand in his, halting her. "Where are you going?"

"I need to tell Helena not to announce Noah's birth. And...and I need to tell Mareleau the truth."

He took a step closer. "You've been awake for over a day. Rest. I can speak to Helena and Larylis. He can tell Mareleau."

She pursed her lips, and the fatigue tugging at her features made it clear she was at least tempted by his offer. She shook her head. "No, I should be the one to tell Mareleau. I want to be there for her." Her jaw tightened when she said the last part, but he didn't comment on it.

"Let me at least deal with Helena then. Let me bear this burden with you."

Her shoulders dropped and a sad smile worked the corners of her lips. "All right."

He gathered her face in his hands and forced her to hold his eyes. "Sleep as soon as you've spoken to Mareleau. Promise me."

She nodded. Then, with a parting kiss, he let her go.

His chest tightened as she left the room. It had pained him to see Cora cry earlier, but it pained him just as badly to see her so composed. So determined. She must be smothering her grief. Burying it. Yet he could relate. After his father had died, he'd buried his emotions in a flurry of activity and constant motion. How could he tell her not to do the same?

"I'll go home to Zaras," Emylia said, reminding him of her presence. He found her colorless form bent before the fireplace, staring longingly at the undulating flames. He wondered if she yearned to feel their heat. "It's the closest I can get to Syrus. Perhaps I can uncover some useful information about Darius."

"Thank you," Teryn said.

Her face crumpled as she straightened and faced Teryn. "I really am sorry. I've caused her so much pain."

"I know."

With that, Emylia's form rippled and dispersed until nothing of her remained.

Teryn blew out a heavy breath, steeled his nerves, and left Cora's room to nip a rumor in the bud. Hopefully he could cut it down before it had a chance to take root outside these walls.

14

Larylis had read every book he could find about pregnancy, childbirth, and parenting, his sources ranging from medical texts to fiction. He'd been startled to find just how quickly he'd run out of reading material. And it wasn't because he'd read through them so quickly. It was because the royal libraries at both Dermaine and Verlot were severely lacking in the subject. Especially where parenting was concerned or any of the myriad of other facets of becoming a new father.

So when he met his son for the first time, he found not a page of reading had been adequate in preparing him. The emotions welling up inside him at the sight of his wife holding their tiny child were stronger than anything he'd felt before. Stronger than grief or mourning. Stronger than desire or betrayal.

Mareleau's joy mirrored his own as he settled onto the bed beside her. He let that joy wash over him. Let it sweep away the last vestiges of the anxiety he'd carried around all morning. The last twelve hours had been hell on his nerves. Mareleau hadn't wanted him in her room while she labored, and he'd respected that. Respected it yet went half out of his mind pacing Teryn's room. His only comfort was reciting all the great queens of history who'd delivered early babies or experienced surprising births. Teryn had tolerated this madness with stoic calm and had stayed by his side all night and morning until both had fallen into fitful rest.

When a knock had sounded at Teryn's suite door, Larylis had bolted awake at once, shooting to his feet from the divan he'd been dozing on. His heart had nearly leaped from his chest when his mother-in-law announced that Mareleau was ready for him to see her.

He'd rushed down the hall to his wife's room at once, fearing his heart might stop before he made it.

But it hadn't. Instead, his heart had been shattered and soothed all at once.

And now it was calm.

Calm.

A feeling he wished would last forever.

He could hardly tear his eyes from his son—from Noah—but he managed to shift his gaze to his wife. His brave, beautiful wife. She caught him looking at her and gave him a warm yet tired smile.

"You did well," he said.

Her expression faltered a bit at that. "Yes, I secured our heir."

"You know I didn't mean it like that."

She blinked a few times as if realizing she did in fact know. She shook her head. "No, of course you didn't. I suppose I'm already on edge waiting for all the congratulatory sentiments. Congratulating not me for being a mother, and not Noah for being born, but our legacy. That we've finally secured our throne. As if simply being crowned isn't enough. To be honest, I almost wanted him to be born a girl, just to spite their expectations. And yet..." She released a heavy sigh. "Birthing male heirs is what is expected of me as queen, so I better steel myself for all the congratulations."

Larylis draped his arm behind her and hugged her close to his side without disrupting her seated position or the sleeping babe in her arms. "It's not what I expect of you. If we'd had a girl, I'd have been just as pleased. I'd have named her our heir without any reservations. I would have empowered her as she grew up. I wouldn't belittle her or make her feel inferior in my attempts to protect her."

She winced at his words, reminding Larylis of the guilt she harbored over her father's death, particularly over their lack of reconciliation. But it hadn't been her fault, and his tragic death didn't mean they had to overlook his flaws. Verdian had been a great king but an imperfect father, just as Larylis' own father had been a great king yet a flawed husband to Teryn's mother.

Larylis wouldn't be like either of them. He would honor their lives, mourn their deaths, and learn from their mistakes—the same way he learned from textbooks and historical records.

"You are right, though," he said. "We have our first child, a male heir, which means we are going to be inundated with mildly offensive and outdated platitudes."

She smirked at that. "At least we have Cora and Teryn's wedding to overshadow our big news. We'll have some respite before the attention shifts to us."

"We'll be expected to host a grand party," he said with a grimace.

"Does that mean I can coerce you to dance?"

He made an exaggerated look of displeasure. "I suppose I can tolerate a single dance."

Her smile grew brighter, sweeter. She angled her face toward him and lifted her chin. "I love you, Larylis."

His heart stuttered. They'd been married for over eight months now, and he still wasn't used to those words.

"I love you too," he whispered back, then brushed his lips against hers. He didn't dare kiss her any deeper, for she was fatigued. He'd claim her love, not her attention. Not until she was rested and ready to divert any focus from Noah to

Larylis. He didn't care if it took weeks. Months. Years, even. He'd gleaned enough from his many hours of reading to expect things to be different between them for a while. They'd find a new rhythm. A new way of life. A new way to love one another, even as their hearts had now split into three.

He pulled his lips from hers, but their eyes remained locked. Gods, she was beautiful. Even more so now, with her hair mussed and her eyes shadowed with dark circles. He was so enchanted by her that he didn't notice they had a visitor until a throat cleared.

He turned his gaze to the door, expecting to find Helena, for she'd stepped out to give them privacy when Larylis had arrived. But it wasn't his mother-in-law standing in the doorway. It was Cora.

The darkness in her eyes, the grief in her expression, should have been enough to warn Larylis that his world was about to be upended.

~

CORA HATED BEING THE BEARER OF SUCH TIDINGS. IT BROUGHT HER NO SATISFACTION to see her friends' happy faces cloud over. She'd almost lost her nerve and kept quiet but that would have been even more unbearable. Cora was done lying to the people she loved, especially where magic was concerned. She'd seen negative repercussions both from telling the truth and keeping secrets, but the latter had always burdened her more. More than anything, Mareleau deserved to know the truth. As did Larylis.

So she told them.

She sat at the foot of the bed, not wanting to close the distance lest the proximity of her friends' emotions test her mental wards. Halfway through, Teryn joined her, sitting silently at her side, her hand in his. He must have spoken to Helena already. Cora wasn't sure what he'd told her to ensure she kept Mareleau's midwives and maids silent. Helena had been left in the dark about magic and only knew what had been made public. So Teryn had either given her an ominous warning or made something up. Whatever it was, Cora trusted him. He'd asked to share her burden so she would let him.

Silence fell after she relayed what she'd come to say. Mareleau spoke first, her voice trembling. "You think I'm a witch."

Cora nodded.

"That I have Elvyn blood."

Another nod.

"You think Noah is...is..." She stared down at her son, her face twisted either with shock or confusion. "You think he's some prophesied fae king?"

"Yes," Cora said.

Mareleau's shoulders sank. If she hadn't already looked exhausted, she looked practically lifeless now.

Larylis too looked drained, his face pale. His voice was hoarse as he said, "What does this truly mean? In a practical sense."

"We don't know," Teryn said. "All we need to worry about now is keeping

Noah's birth a secret. We'll spread word that Mareleau left. That she was too uneasy being here so close to her due date."

Mareleau scoffed. "I came here for your wedding."

Cora gave her a pitying glance. "You can't be there, Mare. Not unless you can hide that you've given birth."

"So you're telling me," Mareleau said, her tone sharp, "that I came here for a wedding I can't attend. And that my very presence *for* your wedding is what made the prophecy come true. What would have happened if I'd stayed home? Would that have broken the prophecy? And would that have been good or bad? Is this really all on me and my actions?"

A flicker of panic-laced guilt shot through Cora, but it wasn't her own. Mareleau's spike of emotion battered Cora's shields. Cora shifted on the edge of the bed, pressing one of her feet more firmly on the floor to ground her energy and strengthen her wards.

"What exactly is Noah meant to do anyway?" Mareleau said. "He's a gods-damned baby. And what clue do we have from the prophecy? *He will unite three crowns and return El'Ara's heart*. The prophecy said a whole lot about me, but not much about their true Morkara. Are we supposed to fend off King Darius until Noah comes of age and becomes some fated warrior that will destroy him?"

Cora had no answers to give. She glanced at Teryn, wondering if there was more Emylia could tell them. As far as Cora knew, she'd been a seer—a witch with strong clairvoyance—which meant she'd channeled the prophecy from images and put them into words. Had she seen how Noah would unite three crowns? What it meant for him to return El'Ara's heart? There were so many ways those words could be interpreted. Uniting three crowns may already have happened when Cora considered naming him her heir. Or would her marriage to Teryn bring that about, as her husband's nephew would surely link Khero to Vera, regardless of who was named heir? The three crowns themselves could refer to the two kingdoms Mareleau inherited plus Khero. Or it could refer to Vera, Khero, and El'Ara, united by his birth. Returning El'Ara's heart could simply mean reforging Lela into a single kingdom. Or it could mean drawing the land back to El'Ara.

Cora's mind spun with possibilities.

Mareleau spoke again, and this time her voice cracked. "What about the future? Is Noah supposed to grow up just to leave me to rule the fae realm?"

Cora met her friend's tear-glazed eyes. "We don't know, and we can't worry about that now."

"How can I not worry? This is unfair."

Unfair.

The word lanced her chest, and she flinched.

Mareleau spoke again. "I never asked to be part of this prophecy. For my newborn son to be burdened with this responsibility. I never asked—"

Mareleau's voice cut off, her eyes wide as they locked on Cora's. It was then Cora became aware of her own expression. Of the tightness of her jaw. The narrowing of her eyes. She hadn't meant to glare at Mareleau. Hadn't meant to react so sharply to her friend's tirade.

Mareleau averted her gaze from Cora's. "I'm sorry. I didn't ask for this but neither had you."

Cora said nothing, for what could she say to that? To the reminder that Mareleau may bear the true responsibility as the prophesied mother, but Cora had already been punished for it?

Cora hated the flicker of resentment that sparked in her heart. Hated the anger that continued to simmer.

A soft cry shattered the air, and all eyes fell on Noah.

"I need to nurse him," Mareleau said, tone flustered.

"We'll give you privacy," Cora said, and she and Teryn rose from the bed.

Larylis gave his wife a questioning glance, but she whispered, "Stay."

Cora's chest tightened as she and Teryn headed for the door. She couldn't help but feel anxious after that tense exchange she'd had with Mareleau. Desperate to mend the rift, she stopped at the doorway and turned a hopeful look to her friend. "I'll come back later, all right?"

Mareleau met her eyes and gave her a soft yet tired smile. "All right."

Cora let that smooth the edges of her nerves as she and Teryn left the room, his hand clasped comfortingly around hers.

15

Flames simmered around Cora. She could feel them more than see them, their heat scalding her hands, her cheeks. As for where she was, she didn't know. A smoky haze clouded her vision, smothering her senses. Finally, a pinprick of darkness stood stark within her murky surroundings. She darted toward it. It grew with every step she took until it widened around her, forming a hallway. The smoke cleared, but the flames remained. Still, it was just the heat of them. A hint of gold flickering up the walls. No matter how she tried to focus on those flames, all she saw was reflected light.

Sweat beaded her brow and dampened her nightdress. She rushed farther down the hall, turning her attention right and left for any sign of where she was.

Then she felt it. A sickening unease. A deep and hollow knowing that something wasn't right. She'd felt this way before, night after night, haunted by dark hallways. That was when she recognized the walls around her. Walls that had graced countless nightmares. Her dreams of Ridine, of the night she'd been condemned by her brother and banished from the castle by Morkai, had once been so pervasive she'd needed a sleeping tonic. That dream had run its course after she'd returned to Ridine and reclaimed her role as princess. Yet nightmares hadn't ceased plaguing her. After last summer, her mind had gained new fuel for dark tableaus. Her brother's visage fused with the body of a Roizan had visited her darkest dreams regularly.

While her nightmares always wrenched her heart, they no longer terrified her as badly as they once had. She could recognize that she was dreaming far faster, detach herself from her fear.

She halted her steps, acknowledging that this too was just a dream. A new manifestation but a dream nonetheless. Releasing a slow sigh, she closed her eyes and tried to focus on her true body, on the bed she was nestled in. The heat of the flames distracted her, pulling her mind back into the realm of the nightmare.

Then a voice.

"We meet again, Aveline."

Cora clenched her jaw, hatred boiling her blood. She opened her eyes. Duke Morkai stood before her, hands in his pockets, posture at ease despite the light of the flames still dancing up the walls. They turned his dark suit a flickering orange, illuminated the underside of his jaw.

Her fury continued to rise at the sight of him, but she felt no fear. Even here, in the bounds of this nightmare, she knew Morkai was dead. Teryn had witnessed the mage's soul being consumed by light. It had devoured all that was left of him.

This was merely a facet of Cora's mind, nothing more.

This she could face.

"If only we could meet again," she said through her teeth, "just so I could see your expression when I told you you were wrong."

"Wrong?" He arched his brow.

"You were too confident in your own findings. You didn't even question them when the answer was a kingdom away. You chose the wrong girl. Tormented the wrong girl. You failed in every way."

His lips widened into a cruel grin. "Did I?"

In a flash of movement, Morkai's arm shot out to the side, toward one of the shadowed walls. As he drew the arm back to him, he pulled a figure along with him.

Mareleau.

It was like he'd dragged her from the shadows. He shoved her forward, and she stumbled to the ground at Morkai's feet. As she lifted her head, her eyes found Cora's. She reached for Cora, but the sorcerer's hand closed around her throat from behind. He hauled her roughly toward him until her back slammed into his front. He wound his arm over her middle, caging her against him.

"Did I torment the wrong girl, Aveline?" Morkai taunted. "Perhaps I should remedy that."

Mareleau's eyes were wide and frightened, pleading with Cora. "Help me," she got out before his fingers, impossibly long now, tightened further around her throat.

Cora let out a strangled cry. She may have escaped her fear before, but now it grew tenfold, spiking her pulse at the sight of her friend. She tried to remind herself this was a dream, but this was the first time someone other than her—someone alive, someone she cared for—was in danger in one of her nightmares. It battled reason and logic until all that was left was terror.

"Let her go!" Cora shouted.

"Will you take her place then?" Morkai asked. "Will you suffer what she suffers? Will you allow me the pleasure of strangling the life from your lungs in her stead?"

Cora opened her mouth but couldn't make a sound. The answer should be yes. The answer should be...

It should be...

"You said I chose the wrong girl." Morkai thrust Mareleau away from him, closer to Cora, but his fingers remained around her throat, ever extending until they took the shape of claws. One pointed tip dug into the flesh at the base of her throat, drawing a line of blood.

"Stop," Cora said.

"Make up your mind, Aveline. Who should I have targeted? Who should I have hurt? Her? Or you?"

"Neither."

"Oh, but you must choose. Which of you shall burn?"

The scent of burning hair flooded her nostrils, and Cora noticed the ends of Mareleau's pale strands blackening. The light of the flames grew higher, their heat almost unbearable, but still she couldn't see them.

Another claw sank into Mareleau's neck. She whimpered, fighting against his hold. "Should it have been her all along?" Morkai said. "Should I have cursed her? Framed her for murder? Drove her into the forest?"

"No!" Cora shouted.

"Would you trade places with her then? Here? Now?"

Again, Cora couldn't bring herself to take Mareleau's place. Why? Why couldn't she do the right thing?

But...was it the right thing?

The dark resentment she'd felt earlier sparked in her chest.

I don't need to suffer in her place.

I never deserved to.

"Say it out loud," Morkai said, his voice a taunting hiss. "Confess the darkness in your heart or it will burn you from the inside."

"No," she said through her teeth. "That's not me. Those thoughts aren't mine. I would never wish my pain on someone else."

"Then why won't you take her pain away? Why won't you willingly take her place?"

"That's different. This isn't real. You aren't real."

"I am the shadow you won't acknowledge. I am the ember you wish you could smother."

"I don't care what you think you are. Just let her go."

Morkai's gaze darkened into a glare. "I'm disappointed in you." With that he released Mareleau's throat and thrust her into Cora. Cora pulled her friend close, lungs heaving with relief, but as her arms closed around Mareleau, the other woman collapsed into ash. Tremors racked Cora's body as she stared at her soot-covered hands. At the pile of ash that was once her friend.

Finally, she saw the source of the flames.

They were coming from her all along.

～

CORA WOKE WITH A SHARP CRY BUT STIFLED THE SOUND AS SHE BLINKED INTO darkness. Her chilly room was a balm on her sweat-soaked skin, and for several long moments she simply lay there, listening to the beat of her heart, the pulse of her breaths, until both settled to a more natural rhythm. Once she could rise from her bed without shaking, she crossed the floor to her window. Pulling back the long velvet drape, she found an inky night sky muted by the frost coating the window.

As she stared out at the dark scenery, she willed her mind to sharpen, to fully separate from the dream. Once it did, she realized what day it was. Or soon would be.

The day of her wedding.

That calmed her down, aided in clearing her mind.

She couldn't have been asleep for long, considering the lack of light on the horizon, paired with how late she'd gone to bed. She should get back to sleep if she wanted to be rested for the grand event. She was already sleep-deprived as it was. Over the last few days, sleep had become second to spending time with Mareleau and Noah. Though her friend had Larylis and Helena to support her and give her chances to rest amidst the chaos of having a newborn, Cora wanted to be there too. Since Mareleau was rumored to have left Ridine, she was forced to remain in her suite, something that drove her half out of her mind. The least Cora could do was spend time with her.

Images from her nightmare shot through her mind. Of Mareleau's horrified expression. Of the blood trailing down her throat as the sorcerer dug claws into her neck.

Are you all right? Valorre's question cut through the memories, dispersing them.

She calmed once more as she connected to her unicorn friend's consciousness. He wasn't as near as he normally was, but he was still within range to communicate. *Yes,* she conveyed back to him.

The blood mage can't hurt you, Valorre reminded her. *He's gone. He'll never come back.*

I know, she said. He was right, yet she hated that Morkai could still haunt her like this. Worse was the dread that was her constant companion—the knowledge that while Morkai may be gone, his father remained. Everything that had happened to Cora, to her friends, to her kingdom, Darius had begun. He may not have asked his son to try to harness fae magic in the human realm, but he'd sent him on a mission to find El'Ara. That mission had led to all the knowledge had Morkai discovered. To Emylia. To the prophecy. To Lela.

To Cora.

Fiery rage burned in her heart. It reminded her too much of her dream, but she wouldn't give in to those terrible visions again. Sleep called to her, but she dreaded returning to the nightmare. And there was one place she could count on to make her feel bold. Brave. Accomplished. To remind her of just how strong she was. With resolve in her heart, she donned her robe and strode from her room. The halls were empty this late at night, save for the guards patrolling them. They acknowledged her with deep bows as she brushed past.

She left the keep and entered the wing of the castle she sought. One that rarely saw visitors. Then up a dim staircase she climbed, to a tower that once held so much darkness. Moonlight greeted her as she entered the North Tower Library, bathing the circular room in a pale glow. It fell upon the clean flagstone floor, the freshly polished tables, the bundles of herbs and flowers that hung to dry from the rafters.

Satisfaction flooded Cora. This room had belonged to Morkai, but no longer held an ounce of his influence. Cleaning the library had taken much of her focus over the last several months, as every item had to be energetically purified before it could be burned or buried. Just weeks ago, her task had been completed at last. The room belonged to her now.

She could have sealed it off and never set foot in it again, but she'd decided to do the opposite, invading it with her own energy. Her own magic. Here she could fully be a witch, honoring the practices the Forest People had instilled in her. Not that she had many chances to truly practice magic these days. Yet taking over this room, using it to dry herbs, to collect stones, leaves, sticks—anything that caught her fancy while out on forest rides with Valorre—was enough. It was proof that she'd bested Morkai, in life, in death, and after.

She breathed in deeply, allowing her pride to grow. "I defeated you," she said to the room, her voice devoid of quaver. "You may haunt my dreams, but you're gone."

No darkness echoed back. No shadows flickered in reply. There was merely peace here.

Her muscles uncoiled and she strolled along the perimeter of the room. She'd had it fully refurbished with a new couch, a single bookcase, and a few small tables and nightstands. She stopped at the nearest nightstand, its surface decorated with an array of crystals she'd found by a stream nearby. They were arranged in a circular pattern around several crisscrossed sticks. Together they formed a talisman for protection. She smiled down at her work, but her grin faltered as her gaze fell just beneath the tabletop, to the narrow drawer there. Gingerly, she slid it open.

Moonlight glinted off a cuff made from two elongated talons, as dark as obsidian. It was the magic-suppressing collar. She hadn't known what to do with it after she'd found it in her pocket upon returning from the meadow last summer. It was a dangerous object, one the Elvyn had used to stifle her magic. Yet it had also saved her and her friends in a couple of ways. When she'd used it on Teryn, he'd been able to temporarily wrest control of his body from Morkai. When she'd used it on the crystal, she'd been able to break the stone, freeing Teryn's ethera. Unlike Morkai's belongings, it didn't hold any dark energy, so she couldn't bear to destroy it.

Instead, she kept it here, hidden yet revered. Hated yet treasured.

Beneath it lay the only thing of Morkai's she hadn't destroyed.

His book of blood weavings.

It was perhaps the most dangerous item of all, yet she'd never found a way to burn it. She'd cleared its residual energy, but the horrific tapestries and spells remained. At least they were only blueprints. The only active blood weaving—the one that had killed Lurel—had already run its course.

There was one more reason she'd kept the book instead of burying it with the other dangerous, undestroyable items: the niggling sense that maybe one day they'd need the information in that book.

It had already come in handy once, when Teryn had glimpsed the blueprint that had rendered Morkai's crystal unbreakable. Teryn had reversed that tapestry, gaining freedom for himself and Emylia. He'd used blood magic, a forbidden Art, but he'd done it for good.

Maybe that was where Cora's most secret motivation lay.

In hopes that someday they might figure out how to reverse the blood weaving Morkai had used to curse her.

Slamming the drawer shut, she lifted her chin and reminded herself all she'd survived. All she'd conquered. And all she still had to look forward to.

Her wedding.

Teryn.

Once the sun rose, it would finally be time to marry the man she loved. She'd been waiting months for their reunion, yet she'd hardly seen her fiancé lately. They'd opened their hearts, shared their love, taken pleasure in each other's bodies for the first time...and then their lives had been interrupted by Noah's birth. They'd slept separately ever since, following the rules of propriety and honoring Cora's own fatigue.

After her wedding, that would change. She'd done enough for Mareleau. Gods, she'd done enough for her kingdom too.

It was time to focus on herself.

She deserved that.

She wouldn't let the prophecy or her nightmares cast shadows upon the day she'd been eagerly awaiting. She wouldn't let guilt or resentment or selflessness keep her from enjoying the one bright spark in her life.

The future may be uncertain, and her foes may be closer than she liked.

But here, now, she'd enjoy the present. The peace, the love, the excitement that awaited her.

For as long as it could last.

16

Teryn didn't have the best memories of the Godskeep at Ridine Castle, but he was hoping to make new ones today. If anything could help him forget what had happened the last time he'd been here, when he'd been helpless as Morkai used his body to undermine King Dimetreus, it was his wedding.

If his bride ever showed up.

He wasn't sure if she was late or if time had slowed to a crawl simply because he was the sole focus of every pair of eyes in the nave. The aging Godspriest stood behind the altar in white robes and seven beaded necklaces, each to represent a different deity, but being the groom, Teryn made for a far more interesting sight.

Most of those in attendance were strangers, esteemed nobles or representatives of Khero's great houses, though there were a few familiar figures in the front row. Larylis sat beside Lex and Lily, a trio of comforting faces. Mareleau and Helena were absent, as they were now rumored to have departed early for the queen's well-being. Thankfully, it seemed they'd fully managed to smother the rumor of Noah's birth before it had spread beyond Mareleau's bedchamber.

He flicked his gaze up to the rafters and found Berol's telltale silhouette. He wasn't sure how or when his peregrine falcon had snuck into the Godskeep, as she normally kept to the forest surrounding the castle, but it seemed she was determined to attend his wedding. He wondered how Valorre felt about being excluded.

As he lowered his eyes back to the audience, Larylis gave him a reassuring nod while Lex winked at him. It was enough to bolster his nerves, and he focused his attention at the end of the aisle. The closed door. Where soon his bride would enter and she'd fully be his—and he hers—at last.

He hadn't expected to be this nervous. It took great control to resist the urge to fidget, to tug the smothering collar of his ceremonial coat, a burden of white-and-gold brocade with a ridiculously high-buttoned neck, affixed with a golden cape. It was almost identical to the raiment his brother had worn to the formal audience with Cora, and now it was Teryn's turn to represent Vera's sigil and colors. This entire ceremony was more for the benefit of the people than anything else, so Teryn's attire was meant to demonstrate his side of the formal union between Vera and Khero.

The tune from the pipe organ shifted to a more distinct melody, one that had Teryn straightening. He knew what that meant.

It was time.

The doors at the end of the nave slowly opened. His breath caught as Cora filled his vision. She was dressed in an ivory gown with a square neckline, ruffled sleeves that opened at her elbows, and delicate lacework down the front of her skirt. The back trailed behind her with more lace, as did the violet cape that hung from her shoulders. Her neck was adorned with a gold necklace beset with amethyst stones, and her simple gold crown rested upon her head. Her dark tresses had been braided into a complex updo. She wore ivory lace gloves that ended at the wrist so as not to hide her tattooed forearms.

His grin was automatic, but as his eyes met hers, he couldn't help the teasing tilt that angled one corner of his lips. Not when he could see just how uncomfortable she was. She'd already complained by letter about her ostentatious wedding gown, and she had to be wincing at all the attention she was now receiving. Teryn's eyes weren't the only ones on her. The audience had risen to their feet and watched as she made her slow procession down the aisle, trailed by her maids.

Teryn held her eyes with every step, and she did the same with his. The nearer she came, her expression grew more relaxed, her smile wider. As she approached the dais, his attention snagged on her waist. At first he hadn't noticed the ivory silk belt she wore there, but now he did, for upon it hung the dagger he'd gifted her, half hidden in the folds of her skirt.

His heart tumbled and melted all at once, and his smile grew wider yet. "Perfect," he whispered as she took her place beside him. She let out a shaky breath, giving him one more gorgeous smile before facing the altar.

Gods, she was beautiful, just like the blade he'd given her. He was honored she'd paired it with her gown. It suited her more than all the lace and silk and jewels. It suited *them*.

The Godspriest began his speech, which meant Teryn had to wrench his eyes away from his beloved. The inches of space between them were proper yet agonizing. He wanted to reach for her palm and pull her closer. Instead, he clasped his gloved hands at his waist and forced himself to focus on the Godspriest. The man's words were drowned out by the racing of his heart, the anticipation rushing through his blood.

Finally, the Godspriest directed him and Cora to face each other. They did as told, and Teryn was rewarded with the sweetest, most timid smile he'd ever seen grace Cora's lips. He'd seen her naked. He'd touched every bare part of her. He'd felt her tremble with release. Yet this was a new level of intimacy. Vulnerability. And he was glad of it. Glad that this ceremony could still feel so deeply personal, even though they were merely performing a ritual countless others had done before.

Upon the Godspriest's instruction, he and Cora clasped hands. Even through their gloves, he could feel the warmth of her. He held Cora's eyes, lost in them, in her, as the Godspriest performed the next part of the ritual.

One by one, he removed a strand of beads from around his neck and draped them over the couple's clasped hands.

Red beads for the Goddess of War.

Blue for the Goddess of the Sea.

Green for the God of Mercy.

Gold for the God of Justice.

Black for the Goddess of Death.

White for the God of Creation.

And finally, pink for the Goddess of Love.

Then came the ceremonial words. Cora went first, repeating the dry and feelingless statements to Teryn. When it was Teryn's turn, he held her palm tighter, desperate to convey that which was in his heart. Not the words he had to repeat. But the ones in his mind.

Open your senses to me, he silently begged of her as he gently tightened his grip once more in a single, deliberate pulse. *Feel what I truly mean to convey.*

Out loud he said, "I, Teryn Alante, Prince of Vera, take you to be my wedded wife."

I, Teryn, ask you to have me, exactly as I am.

"In doing so, I bind our houses..."

I bind my heart to yours.

"...uniting Vera with Khero."

Uniting our souls.

"I honor you for better or worse, for fairer or fouler, in sickness and health..."

I honor you in all things. I am here for you always.

"...to love and cherish 'til death do we part..."

I love you. I've already loved you beyond death. I fought death for you and I will fight death again if it means coming back to you.

"...in accordance with the law of the seven gods."

This is what I want. What I choose. I choose you. I will always choose you.

Cora's eyes glazed with tears, and he wondered if she'd understood. If she'd opened herself to his emotions to at least feel what he'd woven between his words. She squeezed his hand back in answer. She knew what was in his heart.

The Godspriest removed the beads from their hands, granting blessings from each of the gods. Then, finally, their hands no longer burdened with the strands, the man announced them husband and wife.

Teryn's heart thundered against his ribs as he reached for Cora. He wasn't even certain the Godspriest had stated they could kiss, but he didn't care. He framed her face in his hands, and her arms wound around his waist. Their lips met in a firm yet tender kiss. How badly he wanted to deepen it, to sweep his tongue against hers, to steal her breath and give her his in return, but he settled on a prolonged meeting of their mouths. A silent reiteration of everything he'd conveyed in his vows.

When they eventually pulled apart, he found Cora's cheeks were wet and her smile was wide. "I love you," she whispered, the sound drowned by the audience's applause.

Those words would wreck him until the end of time. He'd never tire of hearing them. He nearly bent in for another kiss when a shadow fell over Cora's face. Cora froze, and the Godskeep fully darkened. The room was already dim enough, lit only by the few narrow windows lining the nave, but it was as if the curtains had been closed over them all at once.

Just as fast as the shadow had fallen, it was gone. Silence echoed in the room, punctuated by startled gasps. Teryn and Cora exchanged a questioning glance. That hadn't seemed like a natural shadow. It had moved too fast to be a cloud covering the sun, and the sky had been overcast when he'd entered the Godskeep earlier. What the seven devils had caused that shadow?

In answer came a piercing screech that shattered the air.

17

Mareleau jolted awake at...something. Had it been a sound? Had Noah cried? A glance at the bassinet beside her bed told her he was still asleep. With a sigh, she rolled back onto her pillows. She hadn't been dozing for long, as she'd only begun her nap after Noah had fallen asleep. Now that she was awake, a plethora of unwelcome feelings settled over her. Unending fatigue. Bitterness at being excluded from her best friend's wedding. Ever-darkening resentment over the prophecy. Anger at not being able to leave her room.

"Did you hear that?" her mother asked as she swept into her bedroom from the sitting room.

"Hear what?"

Brow furrowed, Helena approached one of the windows and peered out. "I thought I heard something. An animal, perhaps."

Now that she thought about it, she had startled awake at something. "It was probably just a bear in the woods."

The words dried on her tongue as soon as she said them. They reminded her too much of when she'd said nearly the same thing before she came face to face with Morkai's monstrous Roizan. A creature that wore her father's face...

"This place isn't suitable for you and Noah," Helena said, scowling at the landscape.

Mareleau said nothing in Ridine's defense. After being stuck in her suite over the last few days, she was starting to regret every kind word she'd said about the castle, every way in which she'd defended it to her mother. It was starting to look much like it had when she'd arrived last summer, dreary and sinister despite its new furnishings. Even her emotions harkened back to how she'd felt then.

Useless.

Helpless.

A pawn on a game board.

This time, instead of her father moving the pieces, it was fate.

Destiny.

Her faceless nemesis.

She clenched her jaw at her own futility. If only she had someone corporeal to rail at, to rebel against, then perhaps she wouldn't feel this crushing weight on her chest—

A soft cry emptied her mind. Tenderness softened her edges as she rose from the bed and greeted her awakening son. Just looking at him reminded her she wasn't useless. She had a purpose. Fate be damned, her purpose was to raise her son.

For what? For whom? some part of her taunted, forcing her to confront the fact that the prophecy wanted Noah to be some destined king of the Elvyn. Their Morkara.

She internally scoffed. If fate wanted her son, it would have to go through her first. It would have to greet her face to face and drag her and Noah onto their destined path.

Mareleau would not be weak. She would not give in to her darker emotions or the ones that made her feel small. She'd stand tall and proud and remember that she'd gotten everything she'd wanted through her own means, and she'd do it again.

A smile curled her lips as she lifted her son from his bassinet. At the feel of him in her arms, a warm yet tender fire filled every part of her. It was enough to burn away the dregs of jealousy over Larylis attending the wedding without her. At least they could leave once it was over and all the guests had departed.

She bounced Noah in her arms and brought her face close to his. "I can't wait to bring you home," she said in a sing-song voice. A tone she never would have imagined using in the past.

"I still don't understand why we didn't leave with your ladies and midwives," Helena said, eying Mareleau with a questioning glance. "If there's a spy here, wouldn't it be safest if we'd left?"

Mareleau pursed her lips. Teryn had come up with a lie to keep Helena quiet, telling her they suspected a spy from Norun may have infiltrated the castle with one of their guests to attend the ceremony. According to his story, it wouldn't be safe to admit Noah had been born here, in case the spy sought revenge on Vera for the death of Prince Helios. Mareleau had done nothing to refute Teryn's tale, for only the truth would suffice, and she wasn't ready to give it.

"You know why," Mareleau said, keeping her voice level. "The coach with my ladies will serve as a decoy. Once they send word that they've arrived at Dermaine, we'll know Teryn's suspicions were unfounded. It's merely a precaution."

Helena made a flustered sound and turned back to the window. "To think Norun could seek to target us at all."

It was an unsettling thought, and it wasn't far from the truth. She'd learned about the threats Cora had uncovered. Even though Norun's attention seemed fixed more on Khero than Vera, that didn't mean they held Vera blameless. And that was without considering the alliance Norun was forging with Syrus—an island kingdom not too far across the Balma Sea. If King Darius sought to invade, he could do so by sea, and the nearest shore he'd find belonged to her kingdom.

A shudder rippled through her, but she tore her thoughts from such troubling matters and focused all her attention on her son once more. He'd ceased crying and was blinking his tiny eyelids. Her smile grew wide as she watched the little furrow on his brow, one he always seemed to get when he was looking up at her. Or whatever he could see of her. She brought her face closer and kissed his soft forehead. Breathing deep, she inhaled the sweet scent of him, and peaceful joy settled over her.

This was love. This was happiness. This was the culmination of everything she'd fought for, without even knowing it.

"You're so good with him." Helena's voice stole her attention. There was a wistful note to it. Helena's expression was soft and open, something Mareleau rarely got to see, and when Mareleau met her mother's eyes, they were glazed with tears. "You're better than I was with you. You're more attentive. More involved."

Mareleau wasn't sure what to say to that. Helena had tried—and failed—to convince her to employ a wet nurse. She'd pressed the matter for months during Mareleau's pregnancy, insisting it was proper for a queen, that royal women didn't nurse their own children, and some didn't even see their children more than once or twice a day. Mareleau had only grown angrier and angrier, and Helena had eventually given up. It was strange that Helena was now praising the actions she'd once deemed unqueenly.

"I don't know if I've said it out loud," Helena said, "but I think you're going to be a wonderful mother. You're already a wonderful queen and...and a wonderful daughter."

The tenderness in her voice cracked Mareleau's heart. It weakened her, speared her with guilt over the lies she kept. She'd been determined to have a somewhat less volatile relationship with her mother, but they still had many broken bridges to mend before they could have anything like a true mother-daughter bond. Yet her mother's words closed some of that distance, bound some of what had been broken. Helena was taking the first step. Was it time for Mareleau to take the next? There was only one thing she could think to close her end of the chasm.

Tell the truth.

About her lie.

About her guilt in her father's death.

About the prophecy.

It terrified her to state even a word of confession regarding any of these subjects. And yet...

She could start with one small truth, couldn't she?

"Mother, I..."

Helena took a step closer. "Yes, dearest?"

Mareleau took a trembling breath. "I didn't conceive during the Heart's Hunt."

Her mother gave her a sad smile. "I know. I can do math as well as your midwives can. You did what you had to do. I understand that now."

Relief coursed through her. That wasn't so bad. In fact...it was sort of good.

Could she confess even more? Put her guilt to words? Tell Helena the truth about how King Verdian had died?

She took another deep breath. "When Father came here for the signing of the peace pact—"

Her words were swallowed by a sharp sound, one that made both women jump. A shadow fell over the room, there one moment and gone the next.

"That's the same sound," Helena said, whirling back to the window. "What in the seven devils was that?"

Mareleau cradled Noah close to her chest and approached the window beside her mother. The sound echoed through her ears, a chilling screech she'd never heard before. It wasn't the roar of a bear. It wasn't even the bellowing cry of the Roizan. It was louder. Sharper. And so very wrong.

A rhythmic sound reached her ears next, a pulsing thud from overhead. It drew closer. Louder. The room seemed to shake with the beat.

Then another shadow darkened the room, and this time they saw its source.

A winged creature soared over the castle, far too large for anything that should be airborne. Far too terrifying to even exist. Its body was long and sinuous, covered in pale, opalescent scales. Its wings were comprised of white feathers. So fast it flew past, becoming a pinprick in the distance in a matter of seconds.

Mareleau swallowed hard, hoping that was the last she'd see of it.

Yet that hope was futile, for the creature drew near once more, from a speck to a distinct shape, soaring straight toward the keep. She saw its face then, a massive scaly thing framed by more white feathers, its terrifying snout trailing long whiskers. It flew by the window, and Mareleau and Helena leaped back.

Helena released a yelp of alarm. "That thing...was that a..."

Mareleau knew the word her mother was trying to find. It seared her throat as she finished for her. "A dragon."

18

Outside the Godskeep, Cora's stomach dropped into a hollow pit as she stared at the creature circling in the sky overhead. Chill after chill shot through her as she took in those white scales, those feathered wings. There was no doubt what this creature was. *Who* this creature was.

It was Ferrah. The white dragon she'd met in El'Ara. Cora couldn't help but remember the heat of Ferrah's flames as she'd chased Cora in a rage.

Even more chilling was her next realization: this was irrefutable proof that Cora had been right, that Noah was indeed the true Morkara. If dragons were in her world, the Veil was torn.

Teryn placed a comforting hand on her lower back, but she could feel the tension radiating from his palm. The same tension etched the lines of his face. His jaw was slack, eyes haunted, as he stared at the creature. He hardly seemed to notice Berol flapping frantically over his shoulder, unable to land for the absence of the leather pad he normally wore when outdoors. Finding no good perch, she flew to the Godskeep roof instead. Teryn let out a shaky breath ending with, "Seven devils."

The sentiment was echoed by those around them, muttered in gasps, whimpers, and startled cries. After the piercing screech had sounded, she, Teryn, and Larylis had left the Godskeep with a handful of guards and ordered their guests to remain inside. But when the second screech had rumbled the entire building, the others came rushing out. Master Arther had tried to calm the guests down, but he now stood silent, his eyes turned to the heavens as Ferrah swooped across the overcast sky and disappeared into the heavy clouds.

"Mareleau," Larylis said, his voice strangled. "Noah." As he rushed into the castle, Cora had her next revelation. Not only was the Veil torn, but Ferrah was here for the same reason she'd chased unicorns through the Veil and into the human world.

She was here for Ailan's heir. The true Morkara. Mareleau and Noah.

The question was, what did she want with them? Was it enough to merely find them? She couldn't imagine the dragon sought to harm them. Dragons were supposedly connected to the Morkara's bloodline. Cora had drawn Ferrah's wrath when Fanon had forced her to try to bond with the dragon, but...she had to believe Ferrah would react far less violently to El'Ara's promised savior.

That was her hope, at least.

"You've got to be godsdamned kidding me," came Lex's voice. He and Lily came up beside them. "Was that a bloody dragon?"

Teryn gave a tight nod.

Lily turned pale as she glanced at her husband. "I thought your tale of unicorns and wraiths was strange enough."

Captain Alden approached her queen with a bow. "Orders, Majesty?" Her voice held no quaver, but her composure was betrayed by her ashen face, the haunted look in her blue eyes. Cora had appointed Captain Alden to her royal guard for her battle experience. She'd fought for King Arlous at Centerpointe Rock and bore the scar on her cheek to prove it. She'd witnessed the horrors on that battlefield, beheld wraiths, the Roizan, and deadly vines wielded by magic. When Cora had taken the crown and worked with Larylis, Teryn, and Mareleau to staff her castle, Alden had been one of the first to gain a position. Yet even after all the captain had seen, she was clearly shaken.

Cora opened her mouth, but she didn't know what to say.

"Shall I post archers?" Alden asked.

Archers. What the hell could archers do against a dragon? Arrows couldn't combat fire, and she suspected they couldn't pierce dragon scales either. Besides, Ferrah hadn't attacked. Not yet, at least.

Memories of the dragon's searing flames chasing her heels flooded her mind.

"Post them," Cora said, and her voice wasn't nearly as steady as Alden's. "Defensive positions only. Shoot only if she attacks. Do not provoke her."

Alden bowed, then rushed into the castle.

Cora wanted to feel comforted by the protection of the royal guards who remained behind, as well as the archers Alden would post, but her stomach only sank further. Dread filled every inch of her, blaring a warning.

Her mind went to her unicorn friend.

Valorre! She mentally reached out to him. He'd been out of range all morning. She suspected he was sore about being excluded from her wedding and had chosen to entertain himself far away. Still, she had to ensure he was all right. She remembered how frightened he'd been of Ferrah in El'Ara. *Valorre, are you near?*

Fornication! Yes, I'm near.

His mental reply brought her equal parts relief and confusion. The first word was entirely out of place. *Are you all right? Are you safe from her?*

I'm safe. They aren't paying attention to me.

Cora's blood went cold. *They? There's more than one?*

I saw two. Excrement, this is bad.

She frowned at yet another out-of-place word. Fornication. Excrement. Since when did he randomly state such crass words? *Valorre, are you trying to curse?*

I would never place a curse on someone, even if I knew how.

No, I mean...is that your attempt at using expletives?

His only reply was a ripple of puzzlement.

If the situation weren't so dire, she'd be amused, but this situation was far from amusing. According to Valorre, Ferrah wasn't the only dragon here. She rushed to the other side of the courtyard outside the Godskeep, eyes to the sky, seeking any sign of wings among the clouds.

Teryn shadowed her steps, hand protectively on her lower back. Just minutes ago he'd touched her for far more pleasant reasons. The sealing of their marriage, their kiss. Everything had been perfect.

Then it had been shattered.

Resentment tightened her chest.

Teryn sucked in a breath. "Fire."

Cora followed his line of sight to a column of gray smoke wafting into the air in the distance. Mother Goddess, she hoped that wasn't a village. She blinked a few times, orienting herself with nearby geography. Her only solace was that there were no surrounding villages in that direction. There was, however, vast farmland.

The column grew denser, rising higher into the clouds.

Then a dark shape emerged above the trees. Cora made out the distinct silhouette of wings lifting a sinuous body into the sky.

Too fast the dragon approached, crossing the distance in a matter of wingbeats. And it didn't take long for Cora to realize it wasn't Ferrah. This dragon was probably twice as large with midnight-black scales and leathery wings instead of feathered ones. It flew over the courtyard, lower than Ferrah had dared to fly, eliciting cries of terror from the wedding guests.

Cora stepped back, pressing herself into Teryn. She flung out her hand and he grasped it tightly in his. Her heart pounded so hard she feared it would shatter her rib cage.

She held her breath as it flew past the castle, praying it would fully leave. Yet instead of soaring into the distance, the dragon circled around Ridine and made its descent. Its enormous wings pulsed through the air in heavy beats, slowing its momentum until it landed on one of the battlements. A funnel of air rushed over the courtyard, snatching a tendril of hair from Cora's previously perfect updo.

No cries erupted from the battlements. No arrows shot through the sky. Captain Alden would still be readying the archers. Thankfully, the dragon didn't attack. It merely perched upon the battlement like it was its nest. But what would happen once the archers arrived?

"Go. Just go," Cora whispered, wishing she could use her magic to convince the creature to leave Ridine.

Another pair of wingbeats sounded overhead. Ferrah had returned. Following the black dragon's lead, she circled over the castle before descending toward it. To Cora's terror, she landed not on another one of the battlements, but directly upon the keep. And she didn't nestle upon the roof like her companion. Instead, she gripped the crenellations and leaned over the edge, stretching her long neck until her head was level with the top row of windows.

Ferrah was looking for something. No, someone.

Cora knew exactly who. She'd known as soon as Larylis had uttered their names and charged into the castle. Was he with them already? Mareleau must be terrified either way.

A screech shattered the air, louder than anything she'd heard yet. Cora's gaze whipped toward the black dragon. Its head was reared back, its attention locked on the next battlement over. Cora couldn't see it from here, but she guessed Alden's forces had arrived and that the dragon had noticed them. A red glow blazed between the scales on the dragon's throat. Cora's shout was drowned out by those around her as a burst of crimson flame shot from the dragon's mouth.

Urgency propelled Cora toward the castle, though she didn't know what she was doing. What the seven devils could she do? Perhaps the dragons weren't here to harm Mareleau and Noah, but they were a danger to everyone else. To her archers. Her wedding guests. Her castle.

Her guards marched after her, as did Teryn.

"Orders, Majesty?" called the guards.

"Where are you going?" Teryn asked, taking her arm and pulling her to face him.

Panic raked claws down her throat. She didn't know what orders to give. She'd asked Alden to post archers on the battlements and now they...

Mother Goddess, they might all be dead now.

What could she do?

What the bloody hell could *any* of them do?

Teryn gently grasped her shoulders in his hands. "We need to get the dragons away from Ridine," he said, his voice deep and calming, serving as an anchor. Her tether to logic. "Is there anything we can do to aid that? Anything that will lessen the casualties? Anything *you* can do?"

He said the last part in a lower tone, though he needn't have bothered. He was referring to her magic, but the guests in the courtyard were far too frightened to pay them any heed. And those of her royal guard knew of her magic. Or, at the very least, she'd never hidden it from them.

The question cleared some of her panic. She may not have the answers, but perhaps she could find them through her Art. The last thing she wanted to do was relax and turn inward, but she'd long ago learned the value of doing so.

Closing her eyes, she let out a slow exhale and rifled through her flurry of anxious emotions until she found the steady ones lurking beneath. She shifted her stance, feeling solid earth beneath the soles of her silk wedding slippers.

A line from the prophecy wended its way through her consciousness.

The unicorn will signify her awakening.

She frowned, unsure of what that had to do with this situation. Then she remembered. The dragons had sensed Mareleau's awakening magic and had sent unicorns through the Veil to find her. Now that the dragons could enter the human world of their own accord, they could find Ailan's heir themselves. That was why they were here.

She'd already gleaned as much.

Yet there was something she hadn't touched on.

If the reason they could find Mareleau was her magic...

Cora's eyes shot open as the solution dawned on her. It was a risk. There was a chance it might not work.

And she'd have to hurt Mareleau to do it.

19

Mareleau had never seen anything so large or imposing as the black dragon that had passed over the keep moments before. She'd thought the white dragon had been terrifying, but this new one was positively monstrous. Her heart beat a frantic rhythm as she and Helena stood beside the window, alternating between peering out it for any sign of the beast and hiding out of view. There was no sign of either dragon now, just the pillar of smoke in the distance. Mareleau could only pray to the seven gods that Ridine wouldn't soon share the same fate as whatever now burned.

Noah began to whimper in her arms. He was probably hungry, but she couldn't nurse him now. Not when dragons were swarming the sky. She shushed and rocked him, though how could she calm him when she couldn't even calm herself?

The floor rumbled beneath her feet. Or was that the ceiling?

"Oh, gods." Helena clutched her hand to her chest. "What the hell is happening? How is this possible? How are these creatures..."

The room rumbled again, and there was a distinct tapping that sounded above the ceiling.

Devils below...was one of the dragons on top of the keep?

A shadow darkened the window, and Mareleau leaped back. There was certainly something above the roof. She lowered her voice to a whisper. "Maybe we should get away from the windows—"

"Mare!" Larylis' voice had her jumping out of her skin, but as she whirled to find him charging into her room, her nerves settled by at least half.

She heaved a sob as she ran to him, letting him fold her and Noah into a hug.

"What's happening out there?" Helena asked.

"There are two dragons—"

Larylis' voice was cut off by a screech that pierced the air, the sound far too close and loud for comfort. It was coming from directly above her room. Human shouts followed, though these were more distant.

"The archers must have attacked," Larylis said, then gently loosened Mareleau from his embrace. Placing a hand at her back instead, he ushered her toward the door. "Come, we need to get you—"

Another screech, then a wall-rattling thud. Mareleau looked over her shoulder just in time to see something long, white, and scaled—a dragon's tail—slam against her bedroom wall from outside. The windows shattered from the impact, sending shards of glass surging into the room. Mareleau uttered a cry, ducking her head just as Larylis angled her behind him. Helena clung to her daughter's side, either shielding her or simply cowering.

Together they rushed from the bedroom, heads low to avoid shards of glass to their faces, and entered the sitting room. Thankfully, they'd already been near the door when the windows had shattered, so most of the splinters hadn't reached them. Mareleau's breaths came out in jagged sobs. Her feet didn't stop moving. She was desperate to be out of her suite, out of the keep. There were fewer windows in the sitting room but that didn't mean they were safe.

Was anywhere in Ridine safe when there were two dragons?

They left the suite and entered the hall. It was empty, as all the guests had been at the wedding, yet screams could be heard deeper in the castle. Perhaps from servants.

Larylis led Mareleau down the hall at a swift pace, Helena marching at their side, keeping as close to her daughter as she could. They halted at the next intersection. Larylis looked down one way, then another. Mareleau caught sight of the row of windows that lined one of the halls. Her heart climbed into her throat at the view. Upon one of the battlements the black dragon perched. Shouts rang out, probably from soldiers or archers, and a lick of red flame shot into the sky.

Larylis ushered her down the opposite end of the hall instead. "Seven devils," he said under his breath. "Where do I take you? Where might they be unable to sense you?"

"Sense me?" she echoed.

Larylis said nothing, simply stared ahead, brow furrowed as he frantically guided their party toward the stairs that led out of the keep. That was when Mareleau realized something she hadn't considered until then.

The dragons were here for *her*.

Or perhaps it was Noah.

Either way, this...all of this...

Was her fault.

She rooted her feet in place, her lungs constricting. Noah let out a wail that shattered her heart and clashed against her ever-growing fear.

"Mare," Larylis said, whirling to face her, "we have to keep going. I'll take you somewhere safe."

"Where? Where can you take me that will keep us safe from dragons?"

"I...I don't know. They may only be attacking because they were provoked by the archers, and I doubt they're here to hurt you. Not if what Cora learned in

El'Ara is true. If I can at least take you somewhere the dragons can't sense you..."
His expression fell, shoulders drooping.

That told her enough to realize where his mind had gone. She voiced it. "The dungeon."

Helena gasped. "You can't take her to the dungeon."

Larylis rubbed his brow. His voice came out laced with fatigue and regret. "Just until the dragons leave. *If* they'll leave. It's the deepest level of Ridine. I'll stay too, I'll—"

"Yes." The word flew from her lips even as it sank her heart. The last place she wanted to be was in a godsdamned dungeon. But if it kept her and Noah safe...if it kept Ridine safe, her friends safe, and everyone else who was here...

She lifted her chin, portraying a queenly aura she didn't feel. "It must be done."

Larylis' expression grew even more tortured. He opened his mouth, but before he could say a word, a figure bounded up the stairs. Mareleau's eyes grew wide at the sight of Cora, her hair spilling from its updo, the delicate lace at the hem of her ivory gown torn and stained, even though she had half of it gathered in her arms to assist her climb. Their eyes met, and Cora's countenance turned apprehensive. Still, she rushed straight for Mareleau.

"I'm sorry," Cora said, voice strained as she reached for Mareleau. Mareleau froze, expecting an embrace. But her friend wasn't here to comfort or hug her.

A sharp pain erupted from the sides of her neck. Then came the weight of something resting against her clavicle.

Cora took a step back, eyes glazed with tears. "I'm so, so sorry, Mare."

Mareleau shifted Noah's weight to one arm and lifted her free hand to her neck. Her fingers met a smooth, hard surface. She realized then what this was.

Cora had collared her.

20

Teryn's first day as king consort had thoroughly gone to shit. Thankfully, Cora's gamble with the collar had paid off. The dragons had disappeared hours ago, but only after leaving a dozen shattered windows, a crumbling keep roof, a charred battlement, and a few casualties in their wake. Teryn hadn't seen what had sparked the fight between the archers and the black dragon, but Captain Alden's report stated the dragon had grown hostile as soon as it had spotted the armed soldiers. Their arrows had done nothing to the creature, and they'd had no defense against its flames, hence the casualties.

Now those lives hung heavy on Teryn's shoulders, if only because they weighed on Cora's. She'd given the order for the archers to take their posts. He wouldn't let her bear that alone.

He eyed her across the council table; she was seated at the head while he occupied the foot. She didn't bother maintaining a regal posture as she sank deep in her chair. It was evening now, and their formal council meeting had ended. They'd come up with very few solutions regarding the dragons, only addressed reports of burned farmland, missing livestock, and the overall terror of the people who'd spotted the dragons in person. The wedding guests had been desperate to leave Ridine at once, and Cora and Teryn had decided to let them. There wasn't much they could do to protect them, whether they were at Ridine, on the road, or in their homes, so if it made them feel safer to flee the castle, so be it. Only those who'd come from north of Khero were cautioned to stay until a scouting party could be sent ahead. Which, thankfully, was just one retinue.

Lex and Lily entered the room with hesitant expressions. A hazy figure swept in along with them, one only Teryn could see. The ghost was female, and from the look of her simple yet dated attire, she must have been a servant who'd died at Ridine decades ago. She swept down the length of the table, hardly noticing its occupants. But as soon as she approached Teryn's end, her eyes locked on him.

She launched a floating step away, muttering to herself. "No, not you. No, no, no, no. Not that one." Then she left almost as quickly as she'd come, disappearing into the nearest wall. That was the fourth spirit Teryn had spotted since entering the council room, but the first that had come so close. Not to mention her strange reaction. It reminded him of Emylia's startled responses when she'd first learned he could see her as a ghost.

Thoughts of Emylia made him wonder if she'd made it to Zaras. If so, had she managed to gather any intel on Syrus? He wasn't sure how fast a spirit could traverse great distances, but now that Emylia was no longer tethered to the crystal, he supposed many things were possible.

Cora brightened somewhat when she saw Lex and Lily, though the look held a fatigued edge. "Come," she said, extending a hand to the empty chairs.

Now that the formal council meeting had ended, only two figures aside from Teryn and Cora occupied places at the table: Captain Alden and Lord Hardingham. The latter was a middle-aged man with neatly trimmed auburn hair, a short beard, and kind brown eyes. He was previously Larylis' councilman—and his father's before that—and was now Cora's Head of Council. After Cora had lost her brother's councilmen to Duke Morkai's slaughter last summer, she'd been left with no one to fill the roles. So Larylis and Mareleau had strategically staffed her council with the most trustworthy men and women they could spare. Hardingham had been at the top of that list.

"Thank you for agreeing to meet with us," Cora said as Lex and Lily claimed seats at Cora's end of the table.

Lex blushed. "Thank you for including us in...whatever this is about. I hope we're talking about those bloody dragons."

"Yes," Teryn said, giving him a halfhearted grin, "we are talking about those bloody dragons."

The council room door opened again, and in walked Larylis and Mareleau. Larylis looked as exhausted as Teryn felt, dark circles shadowing his eyes. Mareleau, on the other hand, walked with her head held high despite the collar piercing both sides of her neck. Her skin was red and inflamed around the punctures, but she wore the object as if it were a necklace. Teryn had been too distracted, too detached from his body, to recall how it had felt to wear the collar. And he hadn't been burdened by it for long. Whereas Cora had been forced to wear it for hours.

Cora paled as soon as her eyes landed on her friend. She rose from her chair and rushed to her. As she reached Mareleau, she fluttered her hands as if she couldn't decide whether to give her a consoling touch or not touch her at all lest she cause pain. "Are you all right? Does it hurt?"

Mareleau waved her off, but there was no malice in the gesture. "Don't baby me, Cora, I'm fine."

Cora bit her lip before forcing a smile. "I'm glad you're all right." She returned to her seat, and Mareleau and Larylis claimed chairs near Teryn's end of the table. Larylis and Lord Hardingham exchanged warm greetings.

"Where's Noah?" Teryn asked.

"He's sleeping," Larylis said. "Helena is with him."

"She won't be attending?"

Mareleau answered with a decisive, "No."

Teryn figured that meant Helena was still in the dark about most things. He and Cora had organized this less formal meeting to discuss the topics they couldn't —or weren't ready to—share with the council.

A dark shape dove from the rafters, eliciting a squeal from Lily. But it was only Berol, so no one else was startled. She hadn't wanted to let Teryn out of her sight after the appearance of the dragons and had followed him inside the castle afterward. Now she alternated between haunting the rafters and crowding his personal space. He'd had the presence of mind to don his shoulder pad, upon which she landed now. Absently, he extracted a strip of duck from his waistcoat pocket and fed it to his falcon.

"If that's all of us," Cora said, "I'll begin. Lex and Lily, I'll address what concerns you first so you needn't feel obligated to remain if you'd rather not linger on the dark topics we're about to discuss."

Lex and Lily exchanged a worried glance, then returned their attention to Cora.

Cora took a deep breath. Teryn wished he was sitting beside her so he could hold her hand. Remind her he was here. She wasn't alone. Her eyes flicked to his as if she'd been of the same mind. With the warmest smile he could muster, he gave her an encouraging nod.

She nodded back and angled herself toward Lex and Lily. "If you're wondering why we've requested that you follow a scouting party home to Tomas, instead of departing at once, it's because the border north of Khero may be unsafe. Now, humor me while I explain the next part, for I know it will come across as fiction. Something called the Veil surrounds the kingdoms of Khero and Vera, the land once known as Lela. The Veil is like a curtain between our world and...well, the fae realm."

She paused, waiting for their reaction.

Lex frowned, his mouth curling halfway toward a grin. But as he met Teryn's gaze and found there was no mirth on his face, he paled. Facing Cora again, he said, "Fae realm. Right. I've seen unicorns, a man-and-unicorn-eating monster, and now dragons. A magic curtain to the fae realm shouldn't be impossible to accept."

Lily gave an awkward laugh but it was tinged with hysteria. "Right," she said in her small voice.

Cora continued. "Until recently, only unicorns had been able to cross the Veil, and only to leave the fae realm—El'Ara—which is why they only recently appeared in our world. The appearance of dragons tells us the Veil has been torn. In other words, there's an opening somewhere in that curtain that separates our worlds. We don't know where the tear is or what would happen if people accidentally crossed it. Nor do we know what other creatures may emerge from it."

"It could be anywhere," Teryn said. "Or everywhere. We don't yet know if the tear is a single location in the Veil, or if it merely means the entire Veil is weakened."

Cora stood from her chair and pointed at a map that had been laid out upon the table from the previous meeting. She tapped the stretch of land between northern Khero and southern Vinias—the kingdom that lay between Khero and

Tomas. "Since the Veil surrounds Lela, it exists here too. You can't reach Tomas without crossing it."

"Even if you go by sea," Teryn added, "you'd still have to cross the Veil. You are, of course, welcome to do whatever you choose, but as you are our friends and allies, we suggest you let our scouting party test it first."

"Oh, I very much agree," Lex said. "I'll trust your scouts to assess the border. No questions asked."

Cora turned her attention to Captain Alden. "When will the scouting party be ready to depart?"

"Majesty," the captain said, "Lieutenant Carlson will be ready to depart for the Khero-Vinias border at first light."

"Thank you, Captain Alden," Cora said with a gracious nod. "Any other updates?"

Alden cast a hesitant glance at Lex and Lily before answering. "Yes, Majesty. I have one pressing update that I didn't bring up during the formal meeting, for it is a private matter of state regarding a subject not all council members are apprised of. Do I have your permission to speak on this subject now, Majesty?"

"You do."

"We've gotten more intel from the Norunian spy in our captivity."

Teryn straightened. Cora had told him about the man being held in the dungeon, as well as the overall influx of spies from Norun. "What did the spy say?"

"He admitted to Norun's formal alliance with Syrus and confessed King Darius is in southern Norun at this time, near the Norun-Vinias border. While he wouldn't outright confess that Syrus and Norun seek to wage war on Khero, he admitted that Darius has recently summoned a fleet of warships from Syrus to make landfall in southwestern Vera."

Larylis cursed under his breath.

Cora and Teryn locked eyes across the table. Even though they'd suspected Norun and Syrus were allying to target Khero, this was the first outright confession they'd gotten that it was so. Not only that, but Khero wasn't the only target. If the warships were landing in Vera, King Darius sought Larylis' kingdom too.

If Darius had already launched the warships before the spy had been captured, he'd made the decision long before the appearance of dragons.

Before irrefutable proof that the Veil had been torn.

Before proof that the true Morkara was born.

How would Darius proceed once he learned of today's developments? It would be impossible to keep word of the dragons from spreading. For all they knew, they could have flown over the entire continent of Risa by now, and beyond. Worse was the fact that Darius had already launched his fleet. It didn't take more than two weeks to cross the channel between the Southern Islands and southwest Vera. The fleet could already have made landfall.

Teryn's mind reeled. So badly he wanted to say something comforting. Something hopeful—

"I know nothing about the naval fleet." The voice came unexpectedly from his side. Teryn bit back a curse, nearly leaping out of his skin as he found Emylia occupying one of the vacant seats at his left. His sudden jolt had Berol launching off his shoulder in favor of his chair's backrest.

"Don't do that," he said to Emylia under his breath. Luckily, his voice didn't reach the others at the table, for Lord Hardingham had everyone else's attention now, reading the report of dragon sightings he'd shared at the council meeting.

"Sorry," Emylia said. "I thought you would have noticed my arrival. Anyhow, like I said, I can't confirm anything about the naval fleet, but I've managed to gather that Darius has been away from Syrus for at least a month, and half his military force is currently out of the kingdom."

Teryn assessed her information. It gave weight to the spy's confession about Darius being physically present in Norun, and potentially accounted for the warships too. If half his military force was gone, they had to be on those ships. He pursed his lips, not daring to share what he'd learned with those at the table. Cora was the only one who knew about his strange new ability to see spirits, and he wasn't in the mood to explain it to anyone else. He'd tell her after the meeting.

Lord Hardingham set down his report and looked to his queen for further discussion.

Cora's eyes were distant, her countenance falling with every second. She looked so empty. So defeated. Teryn curled his hands over his armrests. It took all his restraint not to run to her. He wanted to soothe her, touch her, but he kept his seat. His wife wasn't weak. She was stronger than anyone knew, and he'd never undermine that, even at an informal meeting like this. He'd save comforting caresses and calming words for behind closed doors.

"What do we do?" came Mareleau's voice. Finally, her cool façade cracked. Her voice trembled, with what sounded like fear at first. But as she spoke again, her tone was colored by rage. "What the seven devils do we do? This collar may keep the dragons from Ridine Castle now, but I can't wear it forever. And it won't stop the beasts from burning land and crops and devouring livestock. It won't stop Darius from knowing..." Her throat bobbed and angry tears glazed her eyes. Larylis reached for his wife's hand, gathering it in his. Mareleau's jaw shifted side to side before she finished what she'd been trying to say. "It won't keep him from knowing my son—his prophesied enemy—has been born. What the hell do we do?"

Cora sank deeper into her chair and rubbed her brow. "I...I don't know. There's so little we can do right now. I have one idea. I don't know if it will help, but I think it will be worth trying."

Teryn leaned forward, propping his elbows on the table and steepling his fingers. "What's your idea?"

She blew out a heavy breath. "Mareleau, Noah, and I will go to the Forest People."

21

Cora's suggestion was followed by dull silence. She didn't blame those around her for their shock. Even she found the idea she was about to propose daunting. Locating the Forest People might be impossible. They might not welcome her back, even as a visitor. Not all members of the commune had agreed with the elders' decision to involve themselves with the battle at Centerpointe Rock, and Cora's very existence defied the Forest People's primary rule: never get involved with royals or royal matters.

Still, she could think of no better way to find at least some answers. Solutions too, if they were lucky.

Mareleau finally broke the silence. "What do you mean we'll go to the Forest People?"

"Who..." Lily's soft voice was barely audible, but she cleared her throat and tried again. "Who are the Forest People, if you don't mind me asking? Um... Majesty?"

Cora offered Lily a gentle smile. "Don't worry about calling me Majesty here. To answer your question, the Forest People are a commune of witches and Faeryn descendants. They raised me for six years when I was living in exile from Ridine Castle."

Cora's gaze flashed to Alden and Hardingham, who revealed no discomfort at her explanation. They already knew the truth about her past, about Morkai and magic, but she was still getting used to speaking so freely about such subjects with her closest allies. Part of her expected to be condemned for daring to voice the truth, much like Lords Kevan and Ulrich had done, devils take their souls.

"The Forest People know about the prophecy," Cora said. "I've heard them speak about it before, but I didn't have enough context to understand what they were saying. If anyone could give us a clue about how to deal with the dragons, it's them."

She'd been so shocked when the Forest People elders had spoken about the prophecy. It was the first time she realized the elders held vast knowledge they didn't share with the rest of the commune. If anyone knew the most, it would be Salinda, the commune's Keeper of Histories and Cora's former foster mother.

"You've lost me," Lex said. "I don't know a damn thing about this prophecy."

"I'll fill you in before you leave," Teryn said.

Cora continued. "Furthermore, there's still the mystery of Ailan. Darius and Ailan were trapped outside the Veil together. If Darius is still alive, Ailan might be too. She might be our key to sorting this all out, and the Forest People might have some clue as to how or where we could find her."

"I still don't understand," Mareleau said, an icy edge to her tone. "Why would Noah and I come with you to find them?"

"They may know how to suppress your magic without the collar," Cora said. It was the only reason she sought to bring Mareleau with her. "I know how to draw mental wards around my own magic, but I haven't a clue how to teach you to do it, nor how to do it for you. The Forest People have witches skilled in protective wards."

Larylis spoke next. His voice was slow and controlled, but his rigid posture betrayed his composure. "Couldn't you find the Forest People first and bring someone back to aid her?"

Cora sighed. "I doubt I could convince any of them to leave the commune, much less set foot on royal land. The Forest People take great lengths to stay out of royal matters."

"So they might not help me anyway," Mareleau said.

"I think if we go to them, they will. I know at least some will be open to it. We have to try. You said it yourself, you can't keep that collar on forever."

"I take it you intend to bring Mareleau and Noah alone," Larylis said, and this time his tone was far from controlled, "as you've said nothing about me. Or Teryn. From this, I must surmise you intend for me to be separated from my wife and newborn son."

She swallowed hard and forced herself to meet his eyes. Her fatigue was growing by the minute, which made for weak mental shields. Already the emotions of her companions were invading her senses. Larylis' anxiety slammed into her, tinged with fear, grief, and anger. She wished she could allay those feelings, but she couldn't. She could only add to them. "A naval fleet is heading for Vera's shores. I can't tell you what to do, but I'm certain you already know the necessary course of action."

He cursed under his breath, his hand curling into a fist over his armrest. "I must ready Vera's defenses," he said through his teeth.

Cora took a fortifying breath before shifting her gaze to Teryn. His eyes were distant. He sat sideways in his seat, elbow on his armrest, jaw propped on his palm. He rubbed his brow with his free hand. "And I must stay here to act as Khero's ruler while you're gone. The queen and her consort can't both be absent at such a tumultuous time."

Cora's heart cracked. He was taking this decision better than she expected, but that was only on the outside. Inside, his emotions were just as frayed and raw as

Larylis' were. She hated doing this to him. Hated that this was her idea and that she'd leave him so soon after their wedding. Berol nipped at his cheek from her place on the back of his chair. He gave the falcon a sad smile and scritched her feathered chest.

"Well, it's lovely that everyone else seems resigned to this absolutely ridiculous plan," Mareleau said, not bothering to hide her ire, "but I still have several questions. How the devils are we supposed to find the Forest People?"

Cora winced. She'd told Mareleau about her past in one of the many letters she'd written to her friend over the last several months, which meant she knew the commune was nomadic. They moved camps every season, ensuring they were never in any place long enough to draw local attention, as well as to follow the most favorable weather. Yet Cora knew the general area the commune would be in. As it was still winter, they would be in southwest Khero. Though that wouldn't last for long. The commune would move again by Ostara, which was two weeks away.

That left only one option.

She'd have to locate them with her magic and use her worldwalking abilities to travel directly to them. She hadn't a clue if she could accomplish the first task—

If you can feel them, we can find them, came Valorre's voice.

She relaxed slightly. He'd checked in with her frequently throughout the day to assure her he was in no danger from the dragons. Knowing he was still safe was enough to smooth the edges of her nerves. Yet his words did little to bolster her confidence.

You said that before and things didn't work out so well, she reminded him. It was how they'd ended up in El'Ara. Cora had been in the process of feeling her way to the Forest People—or trying to, at least—when Valorre had somehow overridden her focus with visions of his own. Of his original home. He'd taken the step that was required to initiate Cora's abilities, and they'd found themselves in the fae realm.

That was my fault, Valorre said. *I won't do that again.*

I still don't know if it's possible.

I think it is. I believe we can do it together. I'm your familiar, remember?

She relaxed even more. Valorre was indeed her familiar. She used to scoff at the concept of familiars, seeing them only as a witch's pet devoid of a magical bond. But now she understood it was more than that. As her familiar, Valorre strengthened her magic. She never could have entered El'Ara without him, without his visions, memories, and his horn's ability to pierce the Veil. But would they be able to find a place neither of them had physically been?

We can find the Forest People. I'm sure of it.

She hoped he was right. She *needed* him to be right. Otherwise, they'd be searching forever.

She voiced her idea aloud and received another long stretch of silence.

Then Mareleau barked a laugh. "You're going to use magic to find them. And you're somehow going to do it with me and Noah in tow."

"That's too dangerous," Larylis said. "Have you ever used your abilities with another person before?"

"With Valorre, but not with another human being. I'll practice first." She didn't bother feigning confidence. She knew this was madness. Yet they had to try. Her one consolation was that she suspected it was possible. The Elvyn had told her how Darius had used his abilities to bring in human armies to attack El'Ara with iron weapons. That meant he'd been able to travel with multiple people at once. Cora hated comparing herself to him, but if it meant her goal was viable...

"I'll practice with Teryn," she said, "if he'll let me."

"Of course," he said at once. "With Berol too."

"Berol?"

He offered the falcon a strip of meat and she hopped from his backrest to his shoulder pad. "You're taking her with you. As soon as you find the Forest People, send her back to me so I know it worked."

It was a risk adding another being to her travels. She'd already have to world-walk with Valorre, Mareleau, and Noah. Now Berol too. And that was only if she managed to locate the commune. "We'll all do our best to rest tonight, and I'll practice in the morning. As soon as I'm certain I can accomplish this feat, we'll depart."

"You'll depart," Larylis echoed, "as early as tomorrow?"

"Yes. Likewise, I assume you'll want to leave for Vera at once." She hated that every word deepened the agonized look in his eyes. There was only one concession she could offer. "After I find the Forest People and they've helped Mareleau suppress her magic without the collar, I'll bring her and Noah straight to Verlot Palace. I've physically been there, so it won't be a challenge for me to worldwalk there."

That eased some of the pain on his face but he said nothing.

Cora shifted her gaze to Mareleau, awaiting her next objection. She didn't blame her friend for her qualms. No, she fully understood them. If Mareleau decided not to come with Cora to speak to the Forest People, she'd accept her decision. But she was confident they could help mask her magic and render the collar unnecessary. Cora couldn't stand the thought of her wearing it a second longer, and that was only considering her friend's pain. There were other possible complications, like infection.

To her surprise, some of the fire seemed to go out of Mareleau. She shrank down, as if sinking into her own resignation. Her voice came out hollow as she spoke. "You said the Forest People might have answers about the prophecy. They might know more about Noah's role in it. About...my role."

Cora could only nod. A bitter ache flashed through her, a reminder of how she'd been targeted for that very role. A role that was never hers to play.

"And they are firmly against Darius," Mareleau said, "who we know sees us as his enemy."

Another nod.

Her eyes grew distant. "Then they very well may be the only ones who can help."

"I think they're our best chance at understanding the situation we're in," Cora said.

"Fine." Mareleau rose from her chair in a rush. The chair legs screeched against the flagstones as she shoved the piece of furniture back, then promptly swept from the room without another word.

Larylis was much slower to rise, and he lingered at the table for several long moments before he spoke. "I don't like it. I don't like any of this. But I understand the necessity of this plan."

That was all Cora could have hoped for. None of them liked the situation they were in, but if everyone understood and accepted how they must proceed, Cora could be satisfied.

Larylis followed his wife. Alden and Hardingham exited the council room next. That left only Lex and Lily.

Lex gave them a wary grimace. "I only understood a solid half of what we talked about just now, and I sure don't envy you. I almost feel guilty for leaving tomorrow, but this isn't exactly my circus or my monkeys."

Cora frowned. "Did you just call my kingdom a circus?"

Lily placed a hand on her husband's forearm. "What he means is, even though we must return to our own kingdom, we will do whatever we can to help."

"That's exactly what I meant!" Lex beamed. "You can count on us to pass on any intel about the King of Syrus. If he's in southern Norun near Vinias, we'll hear about it while we journey home to Tomas. Vinias is a neutral kingdom, and they aren't known for discretion when it comes to other kingdoms' affairs. Then again, it also makes them a shit ally when they're all that stands between you and a kingdom that seeks to—"

Lily elbowed him. "As promised, we'll keep you apprised of rebel activity in Norun too. The rebels may not be able to keep King Darius at bay, but if they succeed at stirring chaos in Norun—or, as we hope, taking Haldor and Sparda back—he won't be able to depend on Norun's military forces to aid him."

That sparked something like hope in Cora's chest. "Thank you."

Once Lex and Lily exited the room, leaving Cora and Teryn alone at last, Cora swept over to her husband. He was still slumped sideways in his chair, and when she kneeled before his legs, Berol launched from his shoulder to the rafters. Teryn gave her a sorrowful smile. She returned it and scooted closer on the floor, resting her head on his thigh. There was something comforting about sitting like this, with him in the chair, her on the floor, his leg a firm pillow. It made her feel—at least for now—like she didn't have to be the one in charge. The queen responsible for weighty decisions. Like this, she could be small and afraid, soothed by the man she loved.

He extended a hand and ran his fingers over her smooth tresses. She wore a simple day dress beneath her more formal robe, her hair in a long braid. They stayed like that for several quiet and contented moments.

Then Cora angled her face until their eyes locked. "This isn't how I wanted to spend the first day of our marriage."

His hand left her hair to brush her cheek. "Nor I. If someone had told me I'd have my new wife on her knees before me on my wedding night, I'd have had a much different picture in mind."

She was too tired to even blush at his words, though she appreciated his attempt at levity. So badly she wanted to believe their night could be salvaged.

She'd been looking forward to an encore of the passion they'd explored the night he'd arrived. But now, with the lost lives of the archers weighing on her heart, as well as her anxiety over what was to come, this wasn't the time for desire.

Teryn knew it too, for he did nothing to take advantage of their current position, despite his teasing words. Instead, he continued to caress her cheek, her hair, while she nestled against his leg, breathing in the scent of him, letting his stoic calm—however feigned—forge a moment of peace in this godsforsaken day.

22

Larylis had never hated being king more than he did now. He understood what Mareleau needed to do. Understood the importance of his duties in defending Vera's shores. But why did necessity and duty have to stand in such stark contrast with his heart? Why was the best solution to be separated—however briefly—from his wife and child?

He climbed the stairs to the keep, his pace brisk to catch up with Mareleau. Then he found her. Gone was her haughty anger, her fierce demeanor. Instead, she sat slumped on the top step, shoulders hunched, head lowered. He rushed the rest of the way up and crouched on the step below her, bringing them face to face.

"Mare, what's wrong?" He winced at the question, for he knew what was wrong—everything. *Everything* was wrong.

She lifted her face, her cheeks wet with tears. When she spoke, her voice was small. "My neck hurts."

His eyes darted down to the collar. The skin around the puncture was red and inflamed. His heart fissured at the sight of it, but where cracks had formed, tenderness flooded in. It left no room for bitterness or anger. Only love and logic. The two things he treasured most.

"The Forest People will help you," he said, and he hoped it was true. It had to be. He'd seen them wielding vines as weapons at Centerpointe Rock. Stifling Mareleau's magic or teaching her how to build magical wards around her powers had to be possible.

Being separated from Mareleau and Noah no longer seemed like something to rail against. It still tore him up to think of being away from them, of Noah experiencing a single day where his father wasn't present or involved, but he could accept it now. He could let her go, knowing she'd find physical relief from her current pain. He could return to Vera and rally his forces, knowing he was defending their home. Noah's future.

His heart, necessity, and duty were aligned after all.

She sniffled and attempted to dry her eyes. "I hope so."

He shifted onto the step beside her and put his arm around her shoulders. She started to lean toward him but released a hiss of pain.

"I can't even lean into you," she said, and that brought on a renewed flood of tears.

Larylis folded himself around her as best he could without disrupting the collar, caressing her back, stroking her hair. For several long moments, she simply cried. He was grateful for the late hour and the fact that most—if not all—the wedding guests had already departed. Mareleau would be embarrassed if anyone else saw her this way. She always put on such a proud façade around others. She'd even done so with him, acting cold and haughty whenever they'd been forced to interact during their three-year estrangement. He'd witnessed firsthand just how readily she wielded her outer composure as a shield.

But shields could break, and hers had borne its brunt of emotional warfare the last few days. She needed this release of tears, this moment where she could safely crumble. He was determined to give it to her. To make it last as long as she needed. And if anyone dared intrude, if someone so much as stepped foot at the base of the stairs, he'd impale them with a glare so dark they'd leave in an instant.

Luckily, no unwanted interlopers found them, and soon Mareleau had cried her fill. He was about to extend his hand and offer to escort her to her suite when she blurted out a question that had him rooted in place.

"Did I force you to fall in love with me?"

He blinked at her, unable to find any strand of logic or reason in her question. Her cheeks were dry now but her eyes were distant, and she pointedly refused to meet his gaze. "What do you mean?" he asked.

She pursed her lips before answering. "I mean my magic. Did I use my magic on you to make you fall in love with me? Did I...conjure a glamour that made me desirable?"

He remained dumbfounded. How could she consider such a thing?

She spoke again, her words becoming increasingly rushed. "Now that Cora has told me that my...my *magic trick* is real, I can't help but wonder if I've used it in ways I wasn't aware of. I've ended unwanted engagements with it. I've made men think I was ugly, clingy, or annoying—whatever would cast me in an unfavorable light—which I always thought was just me acting. But it wasn't just acting. It was a glamour. And if I can create a glamour to make men dislike me, then I can—"

"Don't you dare finish that sentence," he said, his tone firm. He returned to his previous position, facing her on the step below. He wouldn't make her turn her head just to meet his eyes. Instead, he gave her no other place to look, filling her vision as he crouched before her. Tenderly, he gathered her hands in his. "You didn't cast a glamour to make me fall in love with you."

Tears glazed her eyes. "How do you know?"

"Because," he said, allowing his lips to tilt at one side, "if you recall, I didn't like you at all when we met. We bickered all the time. I insulted you in ways I'm embarrassed to recall all these years later."

She emitted a shaky laugh that was half tangled in a sob. "I insulted you worse."

He returned the laugh. "Yes, the flirtations of fifteen-year-olds leave much to be desired. Yet isn't that proof enough? Our first kiss was in the middle of an argument. Would I have pressed my lips to yours while you were hurling insults at me if I hadn't been completely and utterly smitten with you?"

"That sounds like proof that I *did* use magic on you," she said, yet there was humor in her tone. "Who in their right mind would have kissed a prickly woman like me?"

"Someone who loved you, petals, thorns, and all."

She chuckled. "Of all the men who've ever had the nerve to compare me to a flower, I never expected you to be one of them."

"Honestly, I saw your thorns long before I saw your petals. Before and after that sweet stretch of time when we first fell in love, you only showed me those thorns."

It harkened back to the nickname he and Teryn once gave her: Thorn Princess. Larylis had uttered the moniker disparagingly on many occasions, but in his secret heart of hearts, he'd carried a feeble hope he'd feel even the slightest prick of her ire. If that was all he'd ever get from her, he'd take it.

"I loved those thorns," he whispered.

Her expression softened. She shifted her hands, no longer limp beneath his, and clasped his palms.

"I've only ever seen you," Larylis said. "You, exactly as you are. Wicked and beautiful. Brave and cruel. Sensitive, sweet, and kind. Fierce, fiery, and bold. I've seen what you hide and what you present to the world. I've seen your love and loyalty. Your bitterness and rage. If you've ever cast a glamour, I've never seen it, Mare. Just you."

Her face crumpled, returning to tears. "It's so unfair," she wailed, gesturing to the collar. "I would have kissed you just now, but I can't lean—"

Larylis cut her off with a press of his lips. It was a soft kiss, just a tender brush lest anything firmer make her jostle the collar, but it was what they both needed. A gentle reminder of their love. The sweetness that was forever between them, even on the darkest of days. Their relationship had seen its share of challenges, and they'd come out stronger after each one. They would get through this too.

～

Mareleau felt empty as she entered her quarters, but it wasn't the bad sort of emptiness. It was a refreshing kind. She'd released so much with her tears, shed layers of frustration, bared doubts that had haunted her these last few days. Larylis' loving words had placed a balm on her soul. She could still feel the warmth of his hands, even though he was no longer holding them.

He'd left after escorting her to her suite, for he now had travel plans to organize for his return to Vera, but he would be back tonight, to spend what may be their final evening together before they had to part ways.

She hated the thought of being away from him, but she hated the collar more. She'd do whatever it took to rid herself of the device. Even if it meant traveling by magic to plead for the aid of strangers. Strangers who had magic. Strangers who might know more about her and Noah's role in the prophecy.

Her confidence flared as she opened the door to her bedroom, and she was able to greet her mother without betraying a hint of the emotions she'd succumbed to in the stairwell. Helena sat in a chair by the window, staring out at the night sky while Noah dozed in his bassinet, set upon a mahogany stand. Mareleau's heart softened further as she approached the bassinet and took in her son's peaceful face. The sight of him swept away the remnants of her woes and replaced them with a tingling warmth. She wanted to gather him in her arms and hug him to her chest, but she resisted, not wanting to wake him. He'd likely wake to nurse shortly anyway.

She approached the window and assessed the inky sky spread above the dark silhouette of mountains. "Any sign of dragons?"

Helena finally tore her gaze from the window. "No, not since they departed earlier." Her eyes drifted down to Mareleau's neck, narrowing on the collar.

Mareleau braced herself for the questions she knew were coming. Her mother had begged her to explain what was going on, why she wore the strange collar, why she no longer needed to stay cooped up in her room. Mareleau had given her only curt answers, mostly consisting of halfhearted promises of *later*, and she'd eventually need to make good on that. Yet all the bracing in the world couldn't prepare her for the words that left her mother's lips.

"Were you present the night your father died?"

Mareleau stiffened, her chest tightening. She swallowed the dryness in her throat and forced a casual tone. "You know I was at the camp for the signing of the peace pact."

"Yet you were not with those who were attacked. You, Larylis, Teryn, Aveline, and your ladies were the only survivors."

"We were the only ones who'd stayed behind while the others went out on the hunt." Despite her attempts to sound nonchalant, a tremor racked her voice.

"So you didn't see the rabid beast that attacked the party."

A shudder tore through her as visions of flame and monstrous flesh entered her mind. She couldn't bring herself to say no. Couldn't carry on with the same story she'd allowed her mother to believe. The same story that had been released to the public. "Why do you ask?"

Helena exhaled a slow sigh, her attention drifting back to the window. "Now that I've witnessed dragons, creatures that shouldn't exist, I can't help but think of the rumors. Ones of wraiths and monsters during the battle at Centerpointe Rock. And it makes me wonder about what happened to your father. Makes me question if it hadn't been a rabid beast at all, but something...something more like..."

Helena trailed off, jaw going slack. She looked so worn, the furrow on her brow deepening all the other lines in her face. Her skin, while normally radiant, was dull and pale. Her gray-brown hair hung long and limp around her shoulders.

Mareleau had been so distracted by Noah, by the stresses and novelty of being a new mother, by the revelations regarding the prophecy, at the unfairness of being cloistered in her room, that she hadn't given her mother much thought. Now she realized this was one of the first times she'd seen Helena without her signature extravagant state of dress. Ever since Noah was born, she'd stayed with Mareleau, refusing to join the others when Mareleau took to seclusion in her room. She'd donned simple clothing, didn't complain about their lack of maids, and aided Mareleau into her nursing gown each day as if she were the maid. Over the last few days, Helena hadn't acted as the esteemed queen mother. Just...Mareleau's mother.

A pang of guilt struck her heart.

Helena shook her head and faced Mareleau once more. "I know I haven't been the best mother to you, and I know I've given you reasons not to trust me. I betrayed your love when I intercepted your letters with Larylis and had new ones forged. I abandoned you to your suitors and didn't apologize when they hurt you or made unwanted advances. I know I don't deserve your trust, but I'm asking you to try to let me earn it. To please not shut me out. If there's something going on, some burden you're carrying, something you're not telling me...please invite me in."

Her mother's expression was so vulnerable, so sincere, it tore down her defenses.

It was time to tell the truth.

With a sad smile on her lips, she perched upon the bed.

"Come," Mareleau said, patting the spot beside her. "There is much I need to explain."

23

The next morning, Cora and Teryn stood hand in hand, Berol upon her husband's shoulder, in the middle of their bedroom. Should anyone stumble upon them, holding stock still and silent, eyes closed, dressed in their most basic and un-regal daytime attire, they'd have made an odd sight indeed. Thankfully it was early, just after dawn, and all the servants knew better than to disturb a new couple after their wedding night. Not that they'd had one in the newlywed sense.

They'd spent the night in Cora's bedroom—*their* bedroom now—nestled in each other's arms. But they only touched as an extension of the comfort they'd sought in each other in the council room the night before. Their hearts had still been too heavy when they'd gone to bed. That heaviness hadn't dissipated with daybreak, and now that it was morning, there was work to be done.

Cora breathed deeply, filling her lungs with air, inviting the element in and around her. She shifted her stance, feeling the firmness of the floor beneath the soles of her shoes, anchoring herself with the earth element. A squeeze from Teryn's hand did the same, and as she pressed his palm in return, her heart flooded with warmth. She focused on it, letting her love for Teryn grow, to fill her chest, to lift her mood. That was the element of water, which echoed the blood surging through her, the moisture on her lips. She breathed deeply again, and this time she focused on the gentle sunlight kissing her eyelids as it streamed through the windows. It resonated with her strength of will, her determination. The element of fire.

With her connection to the elements secure, she shifted her focus back to Teryn, to the warmth of his hand, to her awareness of his presence. Then to Berol's. She was prepared to test not only her ability to worldwalk with another person but Berol too. Furthermore, she would determine if she needed to be touching both of them, or if it was enough that Teryn and Berol were touching, and that Cora *intended* to bring both along.

She opened her consciousness, allowing her mental wards to come down as she took in the emotions of her two companions. She sensed them, felt a flicker of Teryn's nervousness and Berol's far more neutral curiosity. She sank into those feelings for several breaths until the connection felt effortless. After that, she filled her mind's eye with a vision of a particular place in the woods, not too far from the castle's outer walls. It was where she often met with Valorre for one of their carefree rides whenever she could steal away from her queenly duties, and she'd grown accustomed to worldwalking there.

She envisioned the space, a small clearing with a wide oak tree. Behind it was a large shrub, and Cora knew her bow and quiver of arrows were stashed there. Practicing archery had become another component of her secret rides with Valorre. She could practice in the armory whenever she wanted, but doing so outdoors was more satisfying than shooting in the training room, watched by guards and attendants. Practicing in the forest made her feel so much like her old self—or more like her two selves combined. The witch and the queen. Daughter of the Forest People. Daughter of the crown.

The thought curled the corners of her lips, and her connection to the space strengthened. In turn, her vision of the clearing sharpened. She imagined the scent of earth and frost, pictured the rising sun slowly illuminating the space more and more. Shifting her feet again, she imagined how the earth would feel, hard after a chilly night but just beginning to give way beneath the morning thaw.

She focused on Teryn's hand again and found her connection to him had remained intact. All that was left was to take a step.

With one more deep breath...

She honed her focus on that clearing...

Lifted her foot...

And settled it onto firm soil.

She opened her eyes with a gasp as the chilly morning air brushed her cheeks, her hands. Her gasp was echoed by Teryn, whose eyelids had flown open as well. And there, upon his shoulder, perched Berol. With her hand still clasped around Teryn's, Cora whirled toward him with a wide smile.

"You did it." He shook his head as if he could hardly believe what he was seeing. Berol flapped her wings and launched off his shoulder to one of the oak's lower boughs. Teryn faced Cora and softly laid his free hand on her cheek. "You're godsdamned incredible."

His praise flooded her chest. She had to admit she was impressed with herself too. She'd been fairly confident she could accomplish the feat of traveling with others, but thinking it and doing it were two different things. Now that she'd proven it was possible, her pride swelled. It was enough to help her forget the darkest aspects of their situation, if only for a moment.

She lifted her chin and Teryn met her halfway in a tender kiss. His lips were warm, a welcome thing in their frigid environment, and as he pulled her ever closer, a spark of passion ignited. She angled her head, parting her lips for the sweep of his tongue. Perhaps she was merely riding the high of her accomplishment, but she suddenly wished she'd tried a little harder to enjoy her wedding night. Perhaps it wasn't too late—

I'm here, I'm here!

She froze at Valorre's words. His presence filled her awareness, and she could sense him trotting toward them from not too far away. With a sigh, she reluctantly broke their kiss and gave Teryn an apologetic smile.

His lips curved in a lopsided grin that had her stomach tightening. "Let me guess. Valorre's here?"

"He is. I told him to meet us if he felt my presence enter the woods."

"What stellar timing that unicorn has." He gave her one more kiss, on the cheek this time.

Cora sensed Valorre's excitement growing with every step he drew nearer. He must be excited to see Teryn, for it was a greater level of anticipation than he usually reserved for her. It made sense considering the unicorn hadn't seen Teryn since the battle at Centerpointe Rock. Unless she counted when Valorre had supposedly glimpsed him riding toward Ridine from afar. But he'd smelled him more than seen him, if his talk about the scent of strength and moonbeams was true. Even before that, when Teryn had come to Ridine last summer, the two hadn't met face to face. By the time Valorre had reunited with Cora after they were separated in El'Ara, Teryn had been unconscious and recovering from his wounds.

Finally, Valorre trotted into the clearing, pulling up short as he saw them. His body stilled, head straightening, ears perking up. His emotions flared inside Cora, and what she first took as joyful surprise shifted into something she didn't fully understand.

"Hi, old pal," Teryn said, offering a wave.

Valorre gave a snort, then skipped back a step. His nostrils flared, his posture stiffening.

Cora frowned. "What's wrong, Valorre?"

He stomped a hoof, snorting again. His emotions flared once more, and this time Cora could make out a distinct thread of indignation. *How...how dare he get more handsome!*

She leveled a glare at him. "That's what you're upset about?"

Teryn glanced between Cora and Valorre, only able to hear one side of the conversation.

That's my *look!* Valorre said, scraping the earth with his front hoof. *I'm the one with a mane like moonlight. Why does he have one now? And why does it make his eyes glitter like emeralds? Fornication, I'm so embarrassed. Why didn't you warn me?*

Cora pursed her lips to keep from laughing. This was a serious matter for Valorre.

It's insulting that he must try to look more beautiful than me. I am not pleased. Not pleased at all. With that, Valorre trotted back in the direction he'd come.

Teryn turned to Cora with an arched brow. "What just happened?"

She stepped close to him and reached for one of his silver-white strands. "He likes your hair."

Teryn gave her a wry grin. "That didn't seem like admiration."

"Trust me, it was." Cora shifted her fingers to the pale tresses near his brow and brushed a strand off his forehead. "I don't know if I've mentioned it, but I like it too—"

No, no. Valorre charged back into the clearing and made a beeline straight between Cora and Teryn, forcing them to step apart. He sidled into Cora, herding her away from Teryn. *We have work to do.*

With a roll of her eyes, she mouthed *sorry* at Teryn, who merely chuckled at Valorre's odd behavior.

Come, Valorre said, stopping only once they'd reached the other side of the clearing. *Let's find your Forest People.*

Cora was about to settle in and focus on her next test when Valorre let out yet another snort. Shaking his mane, he said, *I am still much taller than him.*

THE MORNING SUN HAD FULLY RISEN OVER THE CAMBRON MOUNTAINS BY THE TIME Valorre settled down enough for Cora to concentrate. He'd asked about a dozen times whether Teryn could see him blushing, to which she'd reply that he couldn't blush. To that, Valorre just had to know if she was *certainly sure* he couldn't. She was almost of a mind to find the Forest People without Valorre, but the threat of her not needing his aid was enough to get him to relax.

After reconnecting with all the elements, she placed her hand on Valorre's soft hide. Her palm thrummed in response, sending warmth radiating down every line of her *insigmora.* She glanced briefly at her forearm, where the geometric shapes spanned from her palm to just below her bicep. Her gaze settled upon the spiral that marked the skin above her elbow crease. Beside it, new shapes had taken form, a crescent moon, a few small triangles. She recalled when she'd noticed the spiral. It had been the first tattoo that hadn't been physically marked upon her. Instead, it had formed on its own, something that had surprised her but not Salinda. Ever since, more tattoos had grown, particularly after the tragic night last summer.

Despite being a Faeryn tradition, her *insigmora* had taken on a life of its own. Cora now knew she had no fae blood, neither Elvyn nor Faeryn, yet her tattoos continued to grow with her magic, just like they did for the other Forest People. Even apart from them, Cora's body, her magic, remained entwined with those who'd trained her. They were family. They were a piece of her heart and soul. She could find them.

She let this confidence wash over her as she closed her eyes and settled her attention on her heart, drawing on her love for Salinda and Maiya. She pictured their smiling faces, felt their warm hugs, heard their encouraging words. Doubts shot through these imaginings, bringing questions of whether they'd be happy to see her again or if they'd condemn her for not visiting sooner. Or if they'd be upset that she came back at all, because of their rules about royals.

They are family, Valorre said. *You don't need to doubt them.*

She let his words bolster her confidence, and she breathed her doubts away. Returning to thoughts of Salinda and Maiya, she settled deeper into her affection for them. For the strong guidance of a mother. The love of a sister. The loyalty of family. She lingered here, fueling her magic with emotion. Then she let her mind drift from her foster family to the camp in general. She sought the scents of woodsmoke and herbs, imagined the sounds of those waking from slumber. Memories of whispered voices, hushed steps, and the comforting clatter of cookware flooded her consciousness. The memories were so vivid, it was like she was there. Truly *there*.

Whether it was just a memory or a glimpse at their location, she knew not, but an internal nudge told her she was on the right track. This was how to find them. How to feel them.

She let her memories sharpen yet turn yielding at the same time. She opened herself to alterations, to imagine the camp's surroundings without shaping the location from physical recollection. All the while she kept her heart tethered to her love for the commune that had raised her, for Salinda and Maiya, for her other friends and acquaintances, for how they'd taught her to be the witch she was today.

Something warm and heavy pulsed in her chest, blooming outward and flooding her arms, her palms, tingling her *insigmora*. It pulsed back at her from her connection to Valorre, from his soft flank to her palm, up her forearms, and back to her heart. The circuit continued, a pulse of loving energy.

I can feel them too, Valorre said. *I feel the camp. I hear it. Smell it.*

Excitement rushed through her, but they needed to see something too, if they wanted to travel there. Preferably something outside the camp, so they didn't show up out of nowhere like apparitions.

There's a lake, Valorre said. *My brethren have seen it. They've passed the lake and the camp. The two locations are close.*

Cora's concentration nearly faltered at that. Valorre could sense fellow unicorns when they were nearby, but if the Forest People were in the region of Khero she expected them to be, he was sensing his brethren from a much farther distance than usual. And...communicating with them? But how? Was this a side effect of the tear in the Veil?

Yes, Valorre said. *I remember now. I have always sensed my kin when nearby, like all fae can.*

Cora recalled Etrix saying something similar, that the Elvyn could sense their kin. But for Valorre...

All unicorns are connected. Brethren. Kin. And now I can sense them easier than I could before.

That's...amazing, Cora said.

There would be more time to marvel at such a connection, but for now she pushed her awe aside and settled back into her meditative state. His vision of the lake filled her mind. Frost marked the shore while the lake's glossy surface reflected a cloudless sky. She couldn't be sure how long ago this vision was from, but that didn't matter. The location was important. Keeping her heart wrapped around her warmest emotions, she poured all her attention into that image. She imagined how the earth would feel beneath her feet, how the water would sound as it lapped upon the shore. Valorre did the same, his concentration strengthening her own, until the location felt real enough to touch.

Real enough to step into.

With a deep breath, she took a step...

And rooted herself at the edge of the lake.

Awe fell over her, but it was interrupted by an icy breeze that bit her cheeks, much sharper without the protection of the woods. She glanced at Valorre, who seemed far less surprised as he looked out at their change of location.

"We did it," she said.

Of course we did, came his smug reply. *I am quite talented.*

She couldn't stop the grin from forming on her lips, but there was still one thing left to do to ensure their task had worked as intended. A wave of fatigue swept over her and attempted to fray her concentration, but she breathed deeply, strengthening her connection to the elements once more. Then, extending her senses, she sought familiar strains of consciousness. At first, she got nothing back, felt nothing in her quiet surroundings. She pushed further, extending her reach wider. Valorre sidled into her, as if to remind her to utilize his strength as well. She reached for him again, pressed her palm to his hide...

She felt them.

It was a small spark, but it was there.

Salinda.

Maiya.

She'd found the Forest People.

24

Teryn paced the clearing, feeling as if he were going out of his mind. A chill had crept down his spine when he'd witnessed Cora and Valorre disappear, and it hadn't left since. He stared at the empty space she'd occupied. The plan had been for her to try to find the Forest People, travel there, and return at once.

"Shouldn't she be back already?" he voiced aloud.

Berol gave him no answer. She seemed fully unperturbed as she preened on the oak branch.

He shook his head. Had it been five minutes? Ten? Thirty? Or had it merely been seconds that felt like hours—

Sound and motion filled the clearing. He halted his pacing and found Cora and Valorre in nearly the same place they'd vacated. His heart leaped into his throat, half with relief, half with surprise. Even though he'd been expecting her, he wasn't sure he could ever get used to seeing someone appear from thin air. Berol too had lost her composure and was rapidly flapping her wings, squawking at the newcomers.

Teryn rushed to Cora and framed her face with his hands. She looked slightly pale and unsteady on her feet. "Are you all right? Did something happen?"

Despite her pallor, she grinned, and the sight set him at ease. "I'm a little tired, but everything went fine. I found them. I truly found them. Now Valorre and I both have a clear image of the location. That will greatly aid my efforts when I return with Mareleau and Noah in tow."

"And Berol," he reminded her. It would be even harder waiting for his falcon to return with word that their party had made it and had physically reached the camp, but at least it would be something.

She rolled her eyes. "Yes, and Berol."

He let out a heavy breath and folded his wife in his arms. Perhaps he was being overprotective, but soon they'd part ways and he wouldn't be there to protect her at all. If this was his last chance to fuss over her, he'd take it. He planted a kiss on the top of her head. "You have no idea how tormenting it was to watch you disappear."

"I have some idea," she said, and the serious note in her voice reminded him that she had witnessed similar terrors. Not with him turning fully invisible, but his soul leaving his body. A blood mage taking over. Or when Teryn had nearly died.

They stepped apart and Valorre tossed his mane with a snort.

Cora's smile turned wry. "Valorre wants to know if it was torment watching him disappear too."

He wanted to laugh, but Valorre's earlier tantrum had him steeling his expression. "Oh, very."

Valorre must have been pleased by that because he seemed to stand a little taller as he shook out his mane.

"We should return." Cora strode over to the oak tree and extracted a bow and quiver from behind it. Shouldering her weapons, she said, "I might need these for our travels."

That of course had his protectiveness flaring yet again. The thought of her being in any sort of danger made him want to discard his duties as king consort and insist on coming with her. But he knew better. Not only could his wife protect herself, but with her absent, he was the only one who could protect Khero and Ridine Castle. Staying behind *was* his way of protecting her. His eyes flicked to her waist where the dagger he'd gifted her hung from her belt. That eased his panic even more, for he was fully aware of her skills with a dagger.

"I'll be fine," she said, as if she could read his mind. "Besides, I'm not leaving just yet. We have some time."

He nodded, but his mind lingered on the last word. They hadn't fully set a time for Cora, Mareleau, and Noah to leave. They hadn't even determined if it would be today or if they'd wait for the following morning. He supposed it would depend on the severity of Mareleau's discomfort with the collar as well as how dire the situation with the dragons had become overnight. He hadn't heard a single roar or wingbeat while they'd been in the woods. If they were lucky, the creatures could have fled back through the Veil, unable to sense Mareleau's magic.

Teryn's hope was short-lived. After Cora worldwalked them back to their suite, a missive from Lord Hardingham awaited outside their bedroom door. A council meeting would commence at once to address the latest developments with the dragons. Teryn and Cora rushed to get ready, not even bothering to call upon their servants to aid them, and hurried to the council room.

There they got their answer for how dire the situation had become.

The first report stated more crops had burned. The second reported dragon sightings all over the kingdom and beyond. The final, however, detailed the burning of a farmhouse. The family of four that lived there. And the father who had died in the flames.

Teryn's stomach dropped to his feet. He and Cora didn't have time after all.

Only for goodbye.

～

Four innocuous words were now the most hated in Mareleau's vocabulary: *it's time to go*. Cora brought these words to her door, and as much as she wanted to argue, she didn't dare. She'd heard the report too. Larylis had told her after she'd insisted on his honest summary of the council meeting he'd attended with Cora and Teryn. After that, she'd known it was only a matter of time before Cora came to give the official word that they had to leave.

At least Mareleau was—hopefully—closer to comfort. Sleeping in the collar had been even more uncomfortable than sleeping while pregnant. If leaving now meant she could soon forgo the godsforsaken device, then she at least had one bright side to look forward to.

She forced herself to focus on that alone as she prepared for her journey with shaking hands. Larylis was gathering his party for his own travels, and Noah was sleeping in his bassinet. Mareleau was left on her own in her bedroom to pack for a journey she still struggled to reconcile. She'd never traveled without a retinue. Without maids and a coach. What the hell was she supposed to bring for a magical trek to visit a mystical commune in the woods? How the seven devils was she supposed to prepare—

A gentle hand fell over hers, stilling her trembling fingers as she fumbled with the chemise she was stuffing into the leather traveling bag.

Helena spoke in a calm tone. "Allow me."

Right. Mareleau wasn't fully alone. Her mother was here too. She faced Helena, blinking back tears. Helena made no mention of Mareleau's undignified crying nor the sheer number of small, tangled braids that wove through her tresses, courtesy of Mareleau's habit to braid when she was anxious. Instead, she simply smiled and gestured for Mareleau to step aside.

Despite Helena's kind expression, her eyes were shadowed with dark circles. They'd spoken for a long while last night, shedding tears as Mareleau finally confessed all the truths she'd been hiding. Helena now knew how her husband had died. How the last contact Mareleau had had with her father was a gifted blanket that she'd later lost to the fire. Something had changed between them ever since. Something small and fragile existed where there once had been a wall of thorns. It wasn't perfect, and it wasn't exactly warm, but it was open. That was enough.

She stepped back and allowed Helena to take her place before the bag that was perched at the foot of Mareleau's bed.

Helena moved slowly, calmly, extracting everything Mareleau had packed, then sifting through each item. In the past, Mareleau would have railed at her mother for inserting herself into her business, but this didn't feel like nitpicking, nor a way for Helena to demonstrate superiority. This felt like care. This felt like something a mother would do.

"Queen Aveline said you wouldn't need much," Helena said, "as the people you are visiting will have plenty of resources for you and Noah. Let's pack a spare nursing gown, underclothes, and swaddling. That will be enough."

Mareleau's throat constricted as she watched her mother pack the bag. Something Helena had likely never had to do for herself.

Yes, something had changed between them indeed. Mareleau hoped it would continue to grow when she returned.

Once Helena finished packing the bag and faced her daughter with a proud look, Mareleau did something she rarely felt inclined to do.

She hugged her mother.

As soon as the sun had set, Larylis walked with Mareleau to Ridine's stables, his wife's bag slung over his shoulder and his son in his arms. He tried to memorize the precious shape and weight cradled against his chest. Noah was so small. So light, even in the layers of swaddling he was wrapped in. It was agonizing that Larylis even felt the need to treasure this moment, to treat holding his son as a last memory. Yet it would be a final moment, for a short time at least.

The seven gods were cruel to separate them like this. He only hoped that when Cora worldwalked Mareleau and Noah home to Verlot Palace after they accomplished their task with the Forest People, he'd be there too. And not fighting on Vera's shores against King Darius' army.

That gave him an unwanted chill. He'd hardly slept a wink last night and probably wouldn't until he received confirmation about Darius' fleet. He'd received no word that it had been spotted yet. Of course, the ships could already be approaching Vera's shores. The news would be delayed by the rate a messenger horse could travel. It was the worst kind of anticipation, like being poised barefoot on shattered glass, waiting to feel the sting of the cut.

He shook the thoughts from his mind and refocused on Noah in his arms. His son was content, freshly nursed, and awake. The last light of the setting sun painted his chubby cheeks pink, the only part of him visible from his swaddling. Larylis was grateful that the night was decently comfortable for the end of winter, absent of icy wind or torrents of rain. A small consolation.

Too soon they reached the closed doors to the stables. Captain Alden stood outside—the only other person they'd come across on their way here. Cora had arranged things so they could leave privately, without stirring too much gossip or concern. They hadn't refuted the story that Mareleau had already returned to Vera, and the official statement regarding Cora's upcoming absence was that she would lead another scouting party to the Khero-Vinias border. Easy-to-digest lies for the councilmen and allies who weren't privy to the full truth.

Alden nodded and stood aside, granting them entry. As they paused before the doors, Larylis glanced at Mareleau. She lifted her chin and threw back her shoulders, despite that awful device she still wore, then let out a shaky breath.

"Are you ready?" he asked, shifting Noah's weight to one arm so he could brush his fingertips against hers.

Her shoulders dropped and she gave him a sad smile. "No. But...yes.

They found Teryn and Cora already inside. Teryn greeted them with a nod. Berol, perched upon Teryn's shoulder, chirped at seeing Larylis. Exhaustion etched the lines of Teryn's face, and Larylis knew then that there was one person who felt like he did. Yet even they couldn't find comfort in each other's company for long. Come morning, Larylis would depart with his retinue.

Larylis' gaze shifted to Cora, who was busy saddling a horse.

Only...it wasn't a horse. It was Valorre.

A unicorn.

Getting saddled.

Now he understood another reason why Cora had demanded such secrecy and had wanted to wait until just after nightfall. She'd smuggled a unicorn onto castle grounds. While the existence of unicorns had become somewhat accepted by the greater public over the last several months, most citizens had never seen one. It would certainly cause quite a stir if any of the servants spotted Valorre.

Larylis couldn't help feeling awed at his proximity to the creature. He'd seen the unicorn charging through the battlefield at Centerpointe Rock, but he hadn't met him face to face. If his heart weren't so heavy, he'd be amused at the sight of the majestic fae animal with a saddle on his back.

"There's a unicorn," Mareleau said, pulling up short.

Right. She must be shocked. While Larylis had at least glimpsed Valorre with his own eyes, Mareleau had never seen a unicorn in person.

Cora lifted her gaze from the saddle's buckle. "Mareleau, please meet Valorre." Her words were kind yet edged with impatience or fatigue. Then she added, "Yes, Valorre, you look incredibly fashionable."

Valorre tossed his mane then shifted his head toward Teryn.

Cora rolled her eyes and addressed Teryn. "Valorre wants to know if *you* think he's fashionable."

Teryn extended a hand and patted the side of the creature's neck. "Oh, I think you look incredibly dashing."

Valorre whinnied as if Teryn's praise pleased him, while Berol nipped Teryn's cheek from her place on his shoulder. He idly scritched her feathers to placate her too.

"You're saddling him," Mareleau said. "A unicorn."

Cora tugged on the buckle, testing that it was secure, then straightened and brushed her hands on her gray wool cloak. Beneath it, she wore a simple wool skirt and matching top. Mareleau too had chosen her plainest nursing gown for her travels, though her fur-lined Aromir wool cloak betrayed her status.

"I figured this would be the easiest way to use my abilities with all of us," Cora said, retrieving a quiver of arrows from the stable floor and securing it to the saddle. "You will mount Valorre with Noah, Berol will perch on the pommel, and I'll worldwalk while touching Valorre's side. That should bring us all to our destination."

Mareleau scoffed. "*Should*? That word doesn't inspire my confidence, Cora. And I'm supposed to mount a...unicorn? Sit in a saddle holding my infant son?"

Larylis shared her reservations. Panic flared sharply inside him, but he reminded himself that Queen Constantina of Rovana had led her army to victory with her newborn son in one arm and her sword in the other, dripping with the blood of her enemies. Not that he wanted Mareleau doing anything as reckless as Queen Constantina. At least Cora had cushioned the saddle in blankets and furs.

Cora grimaced. "It's sidesaddle. I figured you'd prefer that."

Mareleau threw her arms in the air. "Yes, well, it doesn't negate that my lower bits were stretched to oblivion mere days ago."

"It's just while I'm using my abilities," Cora said. "We can walk the rest of the way as soon as we get to our destination. And...if you really don't want to come, you don't have to, Mare."

Larylis' breath snagged on an ember of hope.

Yet did he truly hope she'd stay behind? Remain in that painful collar for even a second longer than necessary? The ember cooled, and he realized it hadn't been hope at all, merely selfishness.

Mareleau finally replied, "Fine, I'll mount the unicorn."

Valorre snorted and scraped a hoof on the floor. Cora released a long-suffering sigh before turning a pleading look at Mareleau. "He wants to know if you think he looks fashionable too."

That seemed to drain Mareleau of her ire. Her expression went slack before a slight smile curved her lips. "I think he's beautiful."

After Cora finished preparing Valorre's saddle with all their belongings, Teryn retrieved a mounting block. Mareleau marched up the block and climbed into the saddle with practiced ease, wincing only slightly as she shifted in her seat. Now it was time for Larylis to release the bundle in his arms.

His eyes burned as he approached his wife. He stared down at Noah's face one last time, studying his eyelids that had fluttered closed, the sweet, furrowed look on his face as he slumbered. Gods, his heart ached. He hated this wordless good-bye. Hated the way his heart was being cleaved in two as he climbed the mounting block and gently transferred Noah into Mareleau's arms. Tears trailed down his wife's cheeks. He leaned forward and met her lips with a brush of his own.

"I love you," he whispered.

"And I you," she replied, voice trembling.

He slowly stepped down from the mounting block, feeling colder with every inch of space he placed between him and the two people he loved most. From the corner of his eye, he saw Cora step out of Teryn's arms, caught Teryn swiping a hand over his cheeks. Berol launched from Teryn's shoulder and landed on the saddle's pommel.

"There's one last thing to do," Cora said, tone wary. "We need to remove the collar. Otherwise, it could interfere with my abilities."

Larylis' heart leaped into his throat. "Is that safe?"

Cora angled her head toward him. "The dragons might sense her magic, but we'll be gone before they can locate her here. And when we get to where we're going, I can put it back on."

Mareleau's expression sagged as if she dreaded both having it removed and replaced. "Do it," she said through her teeth. "Let's get this over with."

Cora climbed the mounting block and reached for the collar with both hands. The cuff opened on its hinge. Larylis' gaze locked on the twin lines of blood that trailed down his wife's neck, but Cora wrapped a strip of gauze loosely around where the collar had been. He had to grit his teeth to keep from interfering, to stop himself from begging her to stay.

He was half in a daze as Cora pocketed the collar, stepped down from the mounting block, and placed her hand on Valorre's flank.

Larylis watched, hardly breathing, not daring to blink.

One second.

Two.

Cora took a subtle step forward.

Then they were gone.

Gone.

And Larylis felt as if all the warmth and light had been leached from the world.

25

Cora planted her feet on the lakeshore. Opening her eyes, she saw the lake blanketed in night, a crescent moon reflected on its surface. She shifted her gaze to Valorre's back and released a slow exhale as she found all her companions intact upon the saddle—Mareleau, Noah, and a mildly flustered Berol, who flapped her wings before readjusting her position on the saddle's pommel.

Mareleau blinked at their new surroundings, though Cora couldn't be sure she wasn't blinking tears from her eyes. This couldn't be easy for her. It wasn't even easy for Cora, and she was somewhat used to the jarring effect of instantaneous travel by now. Neither of them could be expected to get used to leaving the people they loved.

I told you it would be easy to get here. Valorre's boastful voice interrupted her thoughts. *I am incredibly helpful.*

You are, Cora replied. His arrogance wasn't unfounded; because of him, it had been much easier to reach the lake this time than the first, even with her extra travelers. Since both she and Valorre had the image of their destination in mind, she hadn't needed to focus quite as hard. Instead, Valorre had held the image while she'd sensed her companions.

Mareleau sniffled, drawing Cora's attention back to her.

"Are you all right?" Cora asked.

"Fine," she bit out, but her shoulders were visibly shaking. She looked pale too, though it was hard to tell for certain in the moonlight.

Cora glanced at the gauze around Mareleau's throat. There were two dark spots on each side, but the material wasn't soaked through. That gave Cora some semblance of relief. If her friend was pale, at least it wasn't from blood loss. Her relief was short-lived, for she knew what she had to do next. She reached inside her cloak pocket until her fingertips brushed the sleek tines of the collar.

"Don't." Mareleau's voice trembled as she spoke the word, her eyes locked on Cora's pocket. "Please don't replace it just yet. I know it's selfish of me to ask—"

"I understand." Cora withdrew her hand and left the collar where it was. She was half relieved, for she wasn't sure she had the strength of will to exacerbate her friend's wounds if she could help it. "Perhaps we can reach the Forest People and get aid before the dragons sense you."

"Thank you," Mareleau said, her expression easing. "If we hear a single wing-beat...do what must be done."

Cora nodded.

"Where are we?" Mareleau rushed to ask, as if eager to change the subject.

"We're in southwest Khero. I believe this is Lake Sarrolin, which means the nearest village is Brekan. Now I need to find out which direction the Forest People are."

Cora closed her eyes and extended her senses. A wave of fatigue washed over her, much like it had the first time she'd come here. This time, it must be due to the feat of traveling with so many. She was tempted to take a moment to rest, but she didn't want to risk staying in place too long, lest they attract the dragons. Breathing deeply, she pushed past her exhaustion, seeking nearby emotion. Valorre snorted, reminding her to utilize him. She pressed her palm to his neck. Her fatigue lessened and her awareness increased. Familiar energies brightened at the edge of her consciousness. She shifted side to side, seeking direction. Her heart pulsed as she faced the opposite end of the lake.

That was where she would find them. "Let's go."

～

SALINDA WAS ALREADY WAITING FOR HER.

Cora felt her proximity before she saw her, half hidden in the shadows of a cedar tree. As they approached, Salinda stepped forward, eyes crinkling at the corners. Moonlight shone on the woman's dark hair, her simple wool dress, the tattooed skin visible on her forearms, chest, and neck. As well as the single tattoo that marked her as an elder: the triple moon at the tip of her chin.

Cora's heart lifted, both at the familiar loving face and the tangible proof that stood before her. She'd already known she'd succeeded in finding the Forest People. She'd been able to *feel* them. But now Salinda was there, serving as irrefutable evidence that Cora had used her clairsentience to worldwalk to a place she'd never physically been.

You had my help, Valorre reminded her.

You're right. She couldn't have done it without him. Without their connection. Without his link to his unicorn brethren and the image of the lake they'd helped him form.

Still, she wanted to take a little credit for herself.

Cora rushed the rest of the way to Salinda, and they met in a tight embrace. The smell of rosemary filled her senses, such a beloved aroma that always reminded her of her foster mother.

"Maiya knew you'd come tonight," Salinda said, squeezing Cora tighter.

When they released each other, Cora scanned the trees around them. "Is Maiya..."

"She stayed back at camp."

Cora's heart sank. She still wasn't sure her party would be permitted to enter the camp, but she hoped she'd at least get to see Maiya. Regardless, it was impressive that her friend's claircognizance had grown so strong. She'd predicted Cora's arrival the last time she'd come too.

"She knew exactly where you'd be this time. South end of camp, toward the lake." Salinda's eyes left Cora to land on the figures lingering slightly behind. Some of the mirth left her expression, and her voice took on a subtle edge. "She also mentioned you'd be bringing friends."

Cora understood the woman's apprehension. Doing what she was doing—bringing strangers to the commune—would have been against the rules when she'd been considered one of them. It was so much worse now that she was an outsider. A royal. "I did," she said, masking her grimace. "Please allow me to introduce you to Mareleau and her son, Noah. Mareleau, this is Salinda. The woman who raised me for six years."

Mareleau tipped her chin in greeting. It must have rankled her pride to be introduced as simply Mareleau and not her full title as queen, but they were all better off if they spoke as little of royal matters as they could. For now, at least.

"And you remember Valorre," Cora said. Some of the Forest People had met him when they came to fight at Centerpointe Rock, and he'd basked in the reverence they'd shown him. He tossed his mane, eager to draw Salinda's attention. Cora didn't mention Berol, for the falcon had already taken to the skies on their way here. She didn't thrive off meeting people the way Valorre did.

"It's lovely to see you again," Salinda said to Valorre, offering him a respectful nod.

Valorre's emotions flared with pride. *Ask her if she thinks I look fashionable—*

I'm not asking her that right now, Cora mentally conveyed, then spoke to Salinda out loud. "This may sound like a strange request, but we desperately need someone's aid in suppressing Mareleau's magic."

Salinda squinted, studying Mareleau. "Bernice is our most skilled warder now. She took Druchan's place as an elder witch."

Cora's breath caught at the mention of Druchan. He hadn't been fond of Cora after she'd returned to the commune with tidings of war, but he'd fought at Centerpointe Rock anyway. And died. She couldn't help but feel responsible for that.

Salinda continued. "Bernice can create a lasting ward around another's magic, but...I'll need to see if I can convince her to leave Nalia."

A spike of emotion slammed into Cora. She'd kept her mental shields down to sense her proximity to the camp, and now she felt a hollow grief that wasn't her own. She spoke through the secondhand pain. "Is something wrong with the High Elder?"

"She's been unwell for days," Salinda said. "She'll only allow Bernice to tend to her. We think she's..."

Salinda didn't need to finish. High Elder Nalia was dying.

"I'm so sorry," Cora said, and this time her own grief mingled with her foster mother's. Nalia was beloved by everyone in the commune. She'd been one of the few people who'd supported Cora when she'd confessed the truth of her history and identity. She'd always been old, wrinkled, and hunched. Yet fierce too. When Cora had last seen her, she'd seemed as healthy as ever.

"She's had a full and long life," Salinda said, her voice rich with emotion. "There isn't a single person alive who hasn't known her from birth. We knew she'd eventually leave us. Now, come. Let's get you and your friend to my tent without drawing too much attention."

~

The witch named Bernice sat before Mareleau in Salinda's tent, burning a bundle of fragrant herbs in a clay pot. Cora had never been personally acquainted with the witch when she'd lived in the commune, but she recognized her curly red hair and her wide build. Bernice was clairalient and used scents to cast wards. Both Bernice and Mareleau kept their eyes closed while they sat on Salinda's cot. Meanwhile, Salinda rocked Noah in her arms. He'd woken after Mareleau had dismounted Valorre—who was now wandering the woods nearby—and, after being nursed, was content enough to be held by a stranger.

The tent grew hazy with the smoke, but it was a comforting aroma. The blend of sage, rosemary, frankincense, and mugwort was commonly used for wards and protection. Cora could have selected them on her own, but she knew better than to think she could do what Bernice was doing. Cora could protect a physical space with herbs but she had no experience in shielding someone else's magic. And Bernice was doing exactly that. The magic sizzled in the air, thickening around Mareleau as the witch guided the smoke around her. The Forest People called it quiet magic, and it was the kind Cora used to dismiss as unimpressive. Now quiet magic had become ingrained in Cora's soul.

Bernice released a slow exhale. "It is done. It should hold until morning. After sunrise, I'll cast it again if you're still here."

Mareleau opened her eyes. "Thank you," she said, voice tight. Mareleau wasn't used to interacting so freely with strangers, especially with those so far beneath her station. Yet she was being respectful. Or perhaps just quiet. She hadn't said much since they'd arrived.

Salinda returned Noah to his mother's arms and faced Bernice. "How is Nalia?"

Bernice rose from the cot, not meeting Salinda's eyes. "The High Elder has asked me not to speak on her condition, so I won't."

Cora frowned, studying Bernice's pursed lips, her suddenly tense shoulders. She expected to sense the same sorrow Salinda emitted, but Bernice seemed more annoyed than anything. Salinda gave the witch a sympathetic smile but didn't press for more.

Bernice left the tent before Cora could make sense of the exchange.

"Now that we've taken care of your friend," Salinda said, "will you tell me why you're here?" If the edge in her tone wasn't evidence enough of her apprehension, it flowed from her in waves. Gone was the joy of their reunion. Not that Salinda was angry. She was more wary, as she had a right to be. Cora was clearly not here for a casual chat.

Salinda settled on a pile of furs near a makeshift writing desk, upon which quills, ink pots, and dozens of loose papers were messily strewn. She gestured for Cora to take a seat on the cot next to Mareleau.

Cora did so, exchanging a hesitant glance with her friend before saying, "One of the reasons for my visit is as you already know; we need to mask Mareleau's magic. She only recently discovered she's a witch, and there have been...unfortunate consequences. We are grateful for Bernice's help, but we were hoping someone can teach her to ward herself."

"I see. And what are these unfortunate consequences?"

Cora swallowed hard. "That's the second matter we've come here for. Has anyone in the commune reported dragon sightings?"

"So you've seen them too? A pair flew overhead yesterday morning. We could hardly believe what we were seeing." She shook her head, expression bemused. "Though I suppose if unicorns can return from extinction, dragons can too."

Cora pursed her lips. She needed to tell Salinda the truth about where the fae creatures had come from, that they'd emerged not from extinction but a different world. But there was so much more to explain before she could touch on that.

Salinda's eyes narrowed, and her bewildered look turned to concern. "Are you suggesting the dragons are the unfortunate consequences of your friend's magic?"

"In a way," she confessed, and the weight of her tale settled all around her, lacing her bones with another wave of fatigue. She pushed past it and went on to explain what she could, starting with her unintentional visit to El'Ara and all she'd learned there. About Satsara, Darius, and Ailan. About the Veil and the Blight. How and why the unicorns had entered the human world, chased by dragons to find Ailan or her kin. Then—after casting a questioning look at Mareleau and receiving a subtle nod in return—she confessed to her companions' identities. Not only was Mareleau the Queen of Vera, she was also the prophesied mother. The Blood of Ailan. And Noah was the true Morkara of El'Ara.

Salinda leaned back in her pile of furs, eyes distant. "That's a lot to take in. None of us had ever surmised that Lela was a land from another realm. We thought our ancestors were from another time, not another place. We knew about the prophecy and the first Morkaius, but not in such detail. The Blood of Darius is a term known to us, but we've never heard the names Satsara or Ailan. And we hadn't a clue Darius referred to a living king."

Cora's stomach dropped. She'd hoped Salinda would have more to share. That she'd admit that she knew everything Cora knew—and beyond—and that the elders had simply chosen to keep these historical facts a secret. She clung to one last strand of hope. "Are you sure there's nothing else you know? When we spoke about Duke Morkai last spring, the elders seemed to know so much. Do you at least know where any of the Elvyn may have settled after the Veil was formed? The Faeryn became the Forest People, but where did the Elvyn go? If Darius is still alive, his sister might be too. If we can find her..."

"I'm sorry, Cora," Salinda said, lips curled down at the corners. "At this point, it's safe to say you know far more—"

Her words were drowned out by a distant shout.

Then another.

Salinda bolted upright and rushed from the tent. Cora scrambled after her, but she froze in place as she reached the tent flap.

That was when she felt it.

The clairsentient warning ringing through her blood.

That was when she heard it.

The rhythmic beat of wings.

26

The shouts from the camp rose to a crescendo, mingling with wingbeats and a distant, ear-splitting screech. Cora rushed the rest of the way through the tent flap, just as a gust of wind slammed against her, blowing her braided hair back. She turned her face to the sky as an enormous silhouette passed overhead. Then another shape, at the other end of camp near the common area. There, the white dragon—Ferrah—began to descend. Her feathered wings beat the air, extinguishing the cookfires and sending startled diners scrambling back, dropping clay bowls in their haste.

Salinda had stopped several paces ahead. She abruptly whirled toward Cora with accusation in her eyes. It was a look devoid of malice. Only fact.

Cora had brought this upon them.

Her legs nearly gave out at the realization. Bernice had said the ward would last until morning, but it apparently hadn't been strong enough to mask Mareleau's magic from the dragons. Guilt struck her chest, and with her mental shields still down, she felt the fear of the commune. It blanketed her mind, drowning out her sense of self.

Ferrah descended fully to the ground. Archers and spearmen surrounded her. Cora wanted to shout that the weapons wouldn't work against the dragon and would only make her angry, but she couldn't form a word, not with so much secondhand fear clouding her senses. Besides, her voice would never carry over the cacophony. The screams. The wingbeats. A second dragon—the black dragon —began to descend. The archers fell back.

Aimed.

Shot their arrows.

The arrowheads glanced off scales.

A violet glow emanated from the base of Ferrah's throat, illuminated behind her opalescent scales. Then a red glow from the creature still mid-descent.

Cora! Valorre's voice shattered the noise, broke through the outside emotions, and gave her something to cling to. She breathed deeply, steadying her feet, regaining control. With an exhale, she forced the outer emotions away and slammed a makeshift ward in place. It was enough to sharpen her mind and remind her of the solution she carried.

She plunged her hand into her cloak pocket.

"Do it," came Mareleau's voice.

Cora spun around to find her friend outside the tent, Noah in her arms. The gauze was gone, exposing the inflamed wounds on her neck. Cora's stomach churned but they had no other choice. Regardless of their efforts, they'd failed. The Forest People couldn't help them. Not with Mareleau. Not with the prophecy, the dragons, or the threat of Darius.

They'd fully failed.

Gritting her teeth, she extracted the collar from her pocket and charged for Mareleau. "I'm so sorry," she said as she prepared to clamp it around her neck—

"Ferrah!" The female voice rang through the camp, rising above all the other sounds.

Cora was dumbstruck at hearing the dragon's name. Who else would know it but her? She halted, the collar mere inches from Mareleau's neck, and cast a look over her shoulder. Ferrah snapped her maw shut, closing her teeth over a flicker of purple flame, extinguishing it in a puff of smoke.

The voice called out again. "Hold your weapons! Fall back."

The archers and spearmen hesitated.

Cora scanned the crowd, seeking the speaker, but it was too dark to make out a single figure amongst the chaos. Only one cookfire remained burning, the cauldron that had hung over it now toppled on its side, its contents spilling onto the soil.

The black dragon landed beside Ferrah, sending the ground rumbling.

"Fall back!" the voice repeated, and the fighters lowered their weapons and scrambled away from the two creatures.

Finally, Cora could make out the speaker. A tall, slender female strolled toward the clearing, hand outstretched toward the dragons. She made a shushing sound, and the dragons seemed to calm.

Ferrah folded her wings down her back and shuffled a few steps away, head low. The black dragon, however, took a step closer. But not to attack. Instead, it lowered its head, crouched down, and touched its massive snout to the woman's outstretched palm. Its sinuous black neck trembled, and a soft rumbling emanated from its chest. A sound somewhere between a chirp and a cry left its mouth as it nuzzled the woman's hand. The creature was so much larger than the figure, it could have knocked her over with a single breath. Yet all it did was gently nudge her hand, eyes closed.

Cora's feet moved before she knew what she was doing, drawing her closer to the clearing. The dragons. The woman.

"I'm here," the woman said. "I'm here, Uziel."

Silence fell over the camp, though it was punctuated with whispers and muffled cries.

Cora stopped moving once she reached Salinda's side. She was much closer to the clearing now, but she still didn't recognize the woman from behind. Long black hair trailed down her back and her brown skin was unadorned with tattoos. The brown bodice and patchwork petticoats she wore seemed slightly too big in places and too small in others. Her bodice was loose and seemed to ride high on her midriff, while the hem of her skirt was well above her calves. A style inappropriate for winter.

"Who is she?" Cora asked, but Salinda only shook her head.

The woman stepped closer to the dragon and pressed her forehead to the creature's snout. It let out another string of chirps. Then the woman spoke.

The words sent a chill down Cora's spine. Not because she understood them, but because she *couldn't*.

Couldn't, yet she recognized their cadence. The way they rang with a strange sense of familiarity.

She was speaking the language of the ancient fae.

A language the Forest People rarely spoke, aside from sparse words and partial phrases. Yet this woman spoke with ease and clarity...like the Elvyn had in El'Ara. Though their words had been translated by magic, she'd heard them speak before Etrix had woven his translation enchantment.

The dragon named Uziel kept its head lowered and backed away from the woman's hand. Then, extending its leathery wings, it beat the air. Once. Twice. The first gust of wind sent the woman's long black hair blowing away from her face, revealing the pointed tip of an ear. The second gust rushed over the camp, and Cora had to shield her eyes as clouds of dirt funneled into her. By the time the wind subsided, the dragons were no longer on the ground but soaring high overhead.

Then they were gone.

Relief uncoiled inside her, and she realized much of it wasn't her own. She hadn't been able to make out Valorre's voice since he'd called her name, but she felt his proximity, their mental link.

You're all right? he asked, his voice finally cutting through the disorder in her mind.

I am, she said, but she couldn't focus on herself right now, or even Valorre.

Her gaze locked on the woman, still facing away from her. Cora knew who she was. There was only one person she could be.

Finally, the woman turned around.

A pair of familiar eyes met hers, and Cora realized there wasn't only *one* person this figure could be.

She extended her senses beyond the thin walls of her temporary shields. The energy that pulsed back was as familiar as those dark irises. Her body was unrecognizable aside from the shape of her eyes, the kind expression in them. Gone were the crow's feet that once lined them, the wrinkles that had dug deep furrows in the woman's face. Gone was her hunched posture, her aged frame.

Salinda seemed to realize the same thing. She took a step toward the woman. Her voice was strangled as she uttered the name. "Nalia?"

It shouldn't have been possible. Nalia was supposed to be dying. She was supposed to be the oldest woman in the tribe, not the tall and youthful beauty who strode toward them now, drawing the eyes of the frightened and confused spectators. But this woman bore the High Elder's energy. Despite outward appearances, this was her.

The woman stopped before Cora and Salinda. She gave the latter a sad smile, which revealed the ghost of the wrinkles that used to frame her eyes. "Yes," Nalia said. "It's me."

But that wasn't her only moniker. It struck Cora that the answer had been here all along. Hidden in the High Elder's name itself. She spoke it out loud, reversing the letters, and marked this woman as the one she'd needed to find.

"Ailan."

The woman with two names released a heavy sigh and met Cora's eyes. "Yes. I am she."

Whispers broke out from those nearby.

"Who is she?"

"Did she say she's Nalia?"

"Did she just speak to the dragons?"

"Is that...Cora?"

"Who is the stranger beside her?"

Cora's skin prickled as several sets of eyes fixed on her and Mareleau. Mareleau edged closer and Noah let out a small cry, drawing more eyes their way.

Ailan—or Nalia, or whatever the hell Cora was supposed to call her—whirled toward them. Voice low, she said, "Go to my wagon. I know the two of you have questions."

"They aren't the only ones with questions," Salinda said, marching up beside Ailan. "You owe us all an explanation. The elders especially."

"I know. And I will give them one. First, let us get our guests some privacy while we set everyone at ease."

"We?" Salinda pulled her head back. Their argument was drawing even more nearby spectators. "You want me to help you put everyone's minds at ease? I don't even know if they *should* be at ease. I don't know who you are—"

"You know me." Her words were firm yet kind and sounded so much like the High Elder. "Please, take my side for now. Once I've spoken with our guests, then with the elders, you can make your own decision."

Salinda's jaw shifted side to side. "Fine."

Ailan gave her a tight smile, then faced Cora and Mareleau again. "Go to my wagon. I'll be with you shortly."

Cora was happy enough to oblige. With her mind still reeling, she could use a few quiet moments to collect her thoughts. Cora led Mareleau to the center of camp toward the High Elder's wagon. In the winter months, Nalia spent her nights in an enclosed living wagon as opposed to a tent like most of the others. Cora kept her head down, and Mareleau shuffled close at her side, but most of the commune was too distracted to pay them much heed, especially under the blanket of night.

Soon they reached the wagon and climbed up the short steps to the ornate door, painted in a green, yellow, and red floral motif. The inside glowed with lantern light, illuminating the rounded ceiling, the brightly painted walls, the ornate blankets, the cramped furniture. The tiny space somehow managed to host a bed built atop a cabinet, a small nightstand, two long benches, and even a stove and countertop. More of Bernice's herbs clouded the air, so it must be true that the witch had been tending to the High Elder. But why? The woman hadn't been dying like everyone thought.

Cora and Mareleau sat on one of the cushioned benches. Noah hadn't stopped fussing since he'd let out his attention-drawing cry, so Mareleau set about undoing the top of her nursing gown to feed him. Cora nestled into the corner of the bench and drew her knees to her chest. That was when she realized she was still clutching the collar. Thanks to whatever Ailan had said to the dragons, she no longer needed to use it on Mareleau. For now, at least. She stuffed it back in her pocket.

"Well, this certainly could have gone better," Mareleau said. Her dry tone gave Cora some sense of normalcy to cling to. "You truly had no idea?"

"That our High Elder, who we all assumed was a Faeryn descendent, was living a double life as a legendary Elvyn royal? Not a clue."

Mareleau huffed a cold laugh. "I can't tell if the whole name reversal is utter brilliance or the stupidest thing I've ever heard."

Cora heartily agreed.

Mareleau's eyes wandered the inside of the wagon as she nursed her son. "So... this is how you lived for six years?"

"No, this is luxury," Cora said. "I lived in a tent."

"A tent? Like the first one we entered, with the messy furs and lack of furniture?"

"Salinda is renowned for her disorderliness. But yes, I lived in a tent like that. With Salinda's daughter, Maiya." Her chest squeezed at the name. She hadn't seen Maiya in the crowd earlier, but it would have been nearly impossible to notice her in the chaos anyway.

"How did you do it? How did you go from being a princess to a runaway living in the woods without losing your mind?"

Cora shook her head. "I didn't have much of a choice. Morkai released me from Ridine's dungeon and sent his Roizan after me. The woods were my only option. I'm lucky the Forest People found me, otherwise..." She shuddered to think of what might have happened. She'd have starved or perhaps been eaten by some wild creature. She'd always been grateful that the Forest People had happened upon her when she'd been aimlessly wandering, but only now did she grasp just how miraculous it was. At twelve, she hadn't known how large her kingdom was, or how vast and unpopulated the forests. She'd had no reason to believe there weren't dozens of communes like the one that had found her.

Yet now she knew there was only one. And it had found her before any dangers had.

Another shudder ripped through her, but this time it carried a feeling that was somehow both heavy and light at the same time. It prickled her skin like a thousand tiny threads brushing over her, radiating with some potent energy—

"Did you like it here?" Mareleau's question pulled Cora from her thoughts.

She shook the strange feeling away. "I did. I loved it. No matter how much I love my kingdom, my castle, and Teryn, the Forest People will always feel like another home to me."

They sat in silence for a while longer. Or something like silence. Outside the camp, voices could still be heard. Footsteps. Commotion. She was glad not to be part of it, not because she didn't want to help, but because it wouldn't be welcomed or needed. The Forest People may be her second home, but very few considered her family anymore.

The door finally opened and Ailan marched up the steps into the wagon, followed by Salinda and Bernice. "Thank you for waiting for me," Ailan said to Cora and Mareleau as she settled upon her bed. Salinda and Bernice claimed the other long bench, both wearing disgruntled expressions.

Mareleau had finished nursing Noah—who was now awake yet content—and shifted closer to Cora as if she wanted to be as far away from the Elvyn woman as possible.

"I still think this conversation should happen in the presence of the elders," Bernice said.

"And I insist that I speak separately with them," Ailan said. "Otherwise, we'll spend an hour arguing over whether Cora should be here. Besides, we'll have a much fuller picture to share once we address the reason she and her friend have come."

"They came here to find you, *Ailan*." Salinda said the name with no small amount of ire. She shook her head. "I don't even know what to call you."

"Call me Ailan or Nalia. The latter has been my name for five hundred years. Longer than I was called Ailan."

"Why did you choose that name anyway?" Cora said, her voice coming out smaller than she wanted.

"If you know who I am, then I take it you know about my history? The battle with my brother? The Veil my mother wove to lock him out of El'Ara?"

Cora nodded.

"Then you know that Lela was once a piece of El'Ara," Ailan said. "When Satsara sealed off her unfinished Veil, it pushed the remaining, unwarded land into the human world. My brother and I were henceforth trapped here. Darius used his worldwalking abilities to return to his father's island kingdom, Syrus, while I remained here. Yet soon I realized the Veil was affecting my memories. I began to lose them. This was a good thing where my brother was concerned, for it seemed he'd forgotten even sooner than I had, losing even his memory of Lela's existence.

"For me, forgetting was a tragedy. I didn't want to forget lest I was still needed in El'Ara. Lest there was any way I could figure out how to return to my home. Still, the memories slipped away. I forgot the name of the fae realm. I forgot that I'd come from another realm at all. I did my best to record what I did recall, and I passed that on to the Faeryn who'd been trapped outside the Veil, and later to their descendants. After a brief sojourn in human society, I settled with the Forest People for good, and they accepted me as one of their own. By then, I couldn't remember much, but I knew we needed to protect this piece of land called Lela. I chose a moniker that would allow me to keep some semblance of my former self intact."

"Why do you look like this?" Bernice asked, eying Ailan through slitted lids. "You asked me to suppress your magic over the last several days, and each day you've appeared younger. I held my questions upon your order, but if this is a time for answers, I'd like to know why you've had me keeping secrets from the rest of the commune."

"This is my true appearance," Ailan explained. "High Fae cease aging when they reach maturity and can maintain the same appearance until they take Last Breath."

Cora puzzled over the last two words. She stated them like they were a specific title, though the meaning felt like *death*. Was Last Breath the Elvyn term for dying?

Ailan spoke again. "My aging was another effect of the Veil. With only a slight connection to the magic that fuels my immortal life—the magic that seeps from El'Ara—I aged like a human. And yet, the small amount of magic I receive has been enough to allow me to continue living. Then five days ago, I felt a surge of magic. An increase of *mora* pouring through the Veil, unlike anything I've felt since living on this side of the ward."

Cora's muscles stiffened. "The tear in the Veil."

Ailan nodded. "Not only did my memories return, but I began to age in reverse. I kept to my wagon, unsure how to address what was happening—"

"You hid from us," Salinda said.

"Call it what you like, but I did what I felt was necessary. My whispers told me to wait."

Salinda pulled her head back. "What do you mean by *your whispers*?"

"I'm a truthweaver," Ailan said. "That's my Elvyn ability. Like a witch who's an oracle or seer, I weave threads that seek truth and receive guidance in return. The whispers of my weavings told me to stay. Wait. But then the dragons came."

Cora's eyes darted from Ailan to Bernice. "Is that why you had Bernice suppress your magic? To hide from them?"

"I wasn't ready for them to find me."

Anger heated Cora's blood. She sat forward on the bench and spoke through her teeth. "Instead, you let them find her." She gestured toward Mareleau. "Instead, you let them attack my castle. My people. You let them burn crops and... and let their flames take lives."

Ailan's face fell but she said nothing.

Cora spoke again. "You spoke to them tonight. You made them leave the camp. Does that mean you could have sent them away from the start? Could you have sent them back to El'Ara if you hadn't been hiding from them?"

"I didn't send them back to El'Ara. I ordered them to wait for me until morning. To find a safe place to nest away from people. Uziel is my bonded dragon. Now that he's found me, he won't leave my side. And Ferrah is young and reckless. Neither will return to El'Ara until I do. Which I will soon."

"Why did you wait? If you can return to El'Ara, you should have done so as soon as you knew the dragons were looking for you."

"I told you," Ailan said. "My whispers said to wait—"

"Your whispers are flawed."

"They never speak without reason."

Cora scoffed. "What reason could your whispers have had for allowing dragons to wreak havoc on my kingdom? Or do they only care for the fae realm?"

Ailan lifted her chin, refusing to be cowed by Cora's growing rage. "I see three reasons sitting before me now. Three people they clearly wanted me to join before my return."

Cora's eyes widened as she realized Ailan was referring to her, Mareleau, and Noah. The latter two she could understand, but why had she included Cora? She'd lost her place in the prophecy—no, she'd never had a place.

"What do my son and I have to do with this?" Mareleau said. "What is his role in this ridiculous prophecy? You do see he's a baby, right? Yet your brother is targeting Khero and Vera *now*. What can Noah do to stop the Blood of Darius, or whatever the prophecy says?"

Ailan's expression softened, as did her tone. "Blood of my blood, I wish I had all the answers. Time and again, I've cast truthweavings, yet my whispers tell me the same things every time. Things I'm sure you already know. I've even shared these whispers—what you call the *prophecy*—with the elders, as it was the one way I could try to protect this land should I perish before my brother. I don't know much more about the prophecy than you likely do, but without a doubt, you are my kin, and he is my heir. He is the true Morkara of El'Ara."

Mareleau pulled Noah closer to her chest. "But what does that mean? What do you expect him to do? The prophecy states that Noah will unite three crowns and return El'Ara's heart. That he will end the Blood of Darius. Does that not refer to him coming of age and inheriting three kingdoms? Facing Darius?"

Ailan furrowed her brow. "Inheriting three kingdoms?"

"Noah is the heir to Vera," Cora explained, "which was merged from two king-doms already. And I...I considered naming him my heir as well, as he's my husband's nephew." She pursed her lips before she could say a word more. Before she could admit that she couldn't have an heir of her own because of the curse Morkai had placed upon her.

Ailan's eyes went unfocused as she considered. "I can see your reasoning for interpreting it that way, but it could mean many things. Prophecies are never infal-lible. They are merely whispers of one's weaving, open to interpretation. Their very nature makes them deceptive, which is why they often come to fruition in unexpected ways, even when one tries to stop them."

A flicker of anger ignited in Cora's chest. She knew plenty about that. She was the victim of such misguided interpretation.

Ailan continued. "First of all, my whispers never said Noah would face Darius, only that his birth would tear the Veil and set into motion Darius' end. That has already begun. As for uniting three crowns, it could refer to uniting the three king-doms of Lela like you've surmised, or it could refer to uniting two human king-doms with El'Ara. Returning El'Ara's heart...well, that part is both essential and inevitable, but it doesn't mean he'll physically do it himself. You, however," she said, shifting her gaze to Cora. "I'm uncertain of your role."

Cora bristled. "My role? I have no place in this prophecy. Morkai thought I was the mother, and many of his actions revolved around that assumption. But he was wrong. He focused so much on me, he never guessed the true mother was meant to be Mareleau." Every word burned like fire on her tongue, but she kept her expression steady.

"You may not have been named in the prophecy, but you have been drawn in nonetheless. Maybe you were always meant to protect Mareleau. To serve as a decoy for my kin." She smiled indulgently, like she was bestowing some great honor upon Cora.

"Decoy," Cora echoed, voice cold. All the anger she'd tried to hold back now flooded her, sending her fingers curling into her palms. "Do you know what Morkai did to me as a *decoy*?"

Ailan's eyes went wide but she gave no reply.

"Are you saying that I suffered for some grand purpose? That I was cursed in her place by design? That I was toyed with all so I could protect *her*—" The bitter tang that coated the last word silenced her. Fire filled her vision, reminding her of the nightmare she'd had the night before her wedding, when Morkai had taunted her using Mareleau's life.

Should it have been her?

Devils, no, of course it shouldn't have been Mareleau. Morkai shouldn't have cursed either of them.

Flames danced in her mind again, and she saw another flash from that dream, how even though she'd saved her friend from the duke's clutches, Mareleau had burned to ash as soon as Cora had touched her.

I am the shadow you won't acknowledge. I am the ember you wish you could smother.

She forced the echoes from the nightmare away until the tightness in her chest eased. Reluctantly, she met Mareleau's gaze. Her friend had gone a shade paler.

Cora shrank back. "I'm sorry. I didn't mean it like that."

Mareleau gave her a sad smile. "You're allowed to mean it like that. I wouldn't blame you for resenting me for what was done to you."

Tears glazed her eyes. "I don't, Mare. You're my friend. I could never resent you. That...that isn't me."

Salinda leaned forward and patted Cora's knee. While she appreciated the woman's attempt at consolation, the pity that clouded the wagon was potent enough to smother her.

She forced herself to sit taller, burying her unpleasant emotions until she could speak with calm. "I don't have a place in this prophecy."

"You do," Ailan said, not bothering to add to the sympathy that poured from the others. In that moment, Cora was grateful to the woman. Ailan's perspective may enrage Cora, but at least the Elvyn wasn't going to pander to her. "Whether you like it or not, you have become a part of this. I can feel the threads woven around you, linking you to my kin, to me. I never felt them when you lived in the commune before, but maybe I hadn't been looking then. Even so, my whispers drew me to you from the start, long before I knew why."

Cora remembered how she'd shivered at the imagined feeling of threads brushing her skin earlier. She'd been recalling how the Forest People had found her and realizing how miraculous that was. Had Ailan been the reason they'd crossed paths in the first place? Had she been following her whispers the day they'd found her stumbling through the woods?

Another shiver prickled her flesh, along with that strange brush of threads again.

"Maybe you're more than just a decoy," Ailan said, again without warmth. Without pity. "Maybe you have a more proactive role to play. Whatever the case, I don't think we are meant to wait for Noah to come of age and act on his own. The whispers tell me the time is now."

"Now...what?" Mareleau asked.

"Now," Ailan said, "we find the tear in the Veil. Lead the dragons. And return to El'Ara. Together."

28

This was the second time in two days that someone had suggested Mareleau go somewhere she didn't want to go. She stared at the woman with two names. The woman who was a stranger yet somehow also her distant kin. "Why the seven devils would I go to El'Ara with you?"

"Because," Ailan said, "it's the safest place for your son."

"The safest place for him is..." She bit off her words. She was about to say the safest place for Noah was wherever Mareleau and Larylis were, but was that true? Larylis was preparing to face King Darius' navy. War could swarm Vera and Khero any day now. Where *would* the safest place for Noah be?

She stared down at him in her arms, took in his peaceful dozing face. She would do anything to protect him. Anything.

Yet that didn't mean she trusted Ailan. At least she wasn't alone in that. Cora didn't seem any more trusting of the Elvyn, and the other two women in the wagon —Salinda and Bernice—regarded Ailan with unveiled apprehension. Maybe even hostility.

"My brother is coming," Ailan said. "The fact that I have my memories and youth back means the same will be true for him. He will know it means the Veil has torn, that the *mora* is pouring through the tear. And, because of his son's efforts, he will know the reason the Veil has torn—that the true Morkara has been born."

"Morkai knew all about the prophecy," Cora said, sending a spear of betrayal through Mareleau's chest. It wasn't like Cora was necessarily agreeing with Ailan, but she was supporting the woman's case, if only slightly. "He channeled it through a seer named Emylia, and he reported his findings to his father. Darius was the one who had sent Morkai to find information on El'Ara in the first place. There's no doubt Darius knows everything now, as he's already begun targeting our kingdoms —and he did so even before the Veil was torn."

"Then he's even more dangerous now," Ailan said. "He will invade to gain access to the Veil and seek the tear. He's always wanted complete control over El'Ara, and he will stop at nothing to get it."

"Then how," Mareleau said, "do you figure it's safe for Noah to enter the very realm your brother seeks to attack? Wouldn't it make more sense for me and Noah to stay out of El'Ara entirely? If he'll be so fixated on the Veil, he won't have time to consider some prophesied baby that might one day be his doom."

"Noah poses a danger to Darius in the present, simply for being the true Morkara. The *mora* has chosen him, and Darius will be forced to act."

"What do you mean the *mora* has chosen him?" Cora asked. "Isn't the title of Morkara passed down through named heirs? You were named Satsara's heir, which would make you the Morkara."

"Yes, I am Satsara's heir." Ailan frowned as if she was surprised Cora knew that. "Yet there are other ways for a Morkara to name their heir, and there are ways other than death to pass the title on. My mother named me heir, overriding Darius' birthright as eldest, which sparked the war with my brother. He sought to kill both me and my mother, for the *mora* will still recognize bloodline inheritance, if the Morkara and their named heir die before a new heir is named. When he murdered Satsara, I inherited her role as Morkara.

"When Darius realized we were trapped in the human world, he tried to defeat me. If he'd managed to kill me, he would have inherited my newly given title. And he almost did. Before he could land the killing blow, I thwarted him in a similar way my mother had; I relinquished my title. But not to my named heir, for I had no children yet. Instead, I passed the title to my unnamed heir."

"What does that mean?" Cora asked.

"Passing the title of Morkara to one's unnamed heir gives agency to the *mora*, allowing it to choose someone from the Morkara's bloodline. It isn't always the nextborn, either. It can be kin further down the bloodline. Anyone. Unless the Morkara names another, the *mora* is free to choose, however long it takes. This protected me from Darius, for he could no longer end my life without risking his place in bloodline succession. If I'd died before furthering my bloodline, the *mora's* search for my heir would have stalled, and it would have been forced to forge a new path. Yes, there was a chance it would simply have worked in reverse and chosen Darius as my heir, but it also could have chosen a new bloodline entirely.

"He knew the *mora* wouldn't choose him willingly, not unless he was a last resort. It would sooner choose a new bloodline to carry the role of Morkara. Thwarted, he fled to Syrus and left me alive, knowing he wouldn't get another chance at taking the title he so greatly coveted until the next Morkara was chosen from my bloodline.

"Noah has been chosen. He *is* the Morkara. If Darius meets your son face to face, he will know it as well. The Elvyn—even half Elvyn like Darius—can sense their kin when in their immediate proximity. Since Darius and I share Satsara's blood, he will sense that blood in Mareleau and Noah. There will be no fooling him. He will seek to end Noah's life and mine, to follow the reversal of the succession until it's back in his hands."

"Follow the reversal..." Cora tilted her head. "Doesn't that mean he has to kill every person in your bloodline in order to be next in line?"

"No. In the rare cases where the *mora* was given agency to choose an heir, it doesn't consider the generations that lie between the new Morkara and the previous one as contenders for the title. Instead, it considers only the chosen heir, the previous Morkara, the children of the previous Morkara, and so on. I was briefly Morkara, before I passed the title to my unnamed heir, so at one point, my children counted. But as none are still alive, no contenders lie between me and Noah. We are the only living contenders aside from Darius."

Anger simmered in Mareleau's gut. "You drew a target on my son's back. You passed on this burden to some future kin just to prolong your life. Wouldn't it have been better if the title had passed on to a new bloodline? To someone inside the Veil and not in the human world?"

Ailan's face fell. "I considered taking Last Breath and letting the role of the Morkara leave my bloodline. Had my memories not faded shortly after, I may have eventually done so. But all I had by then were my whispers, and they told me to wait. That the true Morkara would be born from my blood and that Darius would be defeated at last."

"What purpose would your so-called whispers have had for waiting? For passing this burden on to my son?"

"I can't say. There's no way to know what alternate future there could have been. Darius would likely have continued to seek El'Ara despite being thwarted. He'd likely still have fathered Morkai and sent him to find information on the fae realm. Maybe you'd all have been safe from his machinations, but maybe he'd have gotten his way instead. Maybe he'd have succeeded at becoming Morkaius of the human realm without having made an enemy of Cora."

That sent her mind reeling. She hated that Ailan was right. There really was no way to know whether things would be better or worse if Ailan had made a different choice.

She shook her head. "You still haven't given me any reason to believe Noah would be safer in El'Ara than here."

"He's safer on the other side of the Veil because there's still only one way for Darius to enter El'Ara: through the tear, and that is somewhere we can defend, if we can get there first."

Cora spoke. "Does that mean you believe the tear to be a singular location and not a general weakening of the Veil?"

"Yes, the tear represents a single location. One mere split in the Veil. I can feel it like a sliver in the *mora* that flows to me, and it's close. As of now, Darius doesn't know where the tear is. It won't be easy for him to find either, for he's not as strong as he believes. His connection to fae magic is weaker than mine. He relies on his powers as a witch and a worldwalker, but he has no abilities as a weaver. No way to find the tear in the Veil quickly."

Salinda arched her brow. "And you can?"

"Yes, for I have something he doesn't," Ailan said, her lips curling slightly at the corners. "A dragon. Two, actually."

"The dragons can sense the tear?" Cora asked.

Ailan nodded. "Fae creatures have the strongest connection to the *mora*. Uziel and Ferrah will guide us to it. And that includes you, Cora. I need you to come with us."

Cora stiffened. "Why the hell would I come? Why do you keep including me in this?"

"You are Queen of Khero," Ailan said, voice firm. "You speak for your kingdom, and you've already admitted Khero is being targeted by Darius. We're in this situation together whether we like it or not. If we have any hope of defeating my brother, we must stand united and forge an alliance. I want you with me when I return to El'Ara and speak to the tribunal."

"I've already been to El'Ara," Cora said, voice low. "I was neither well received nor well departed."

Salinda and Bernice turned wide eyes to Cora. While Cora had given Salinda a summary of last summer's events, she hadn't gone into much detail.

Ailan's posture went rigid. "You entered El'Ara? Before the Veil was torn?"

Cora thinned her lips, reluctance written across her face. Mareleau knew what she was keeping unsaid. That she was a worldwalker. Salinda had taken the confession in stride, praising Cora for her growing magic, but admitting as much to Ailan was different. The Elvyn viewed her abilities as a threat. Would Ailan see Cora the same way?

"I..." Cora began. "I...apparently...am a worldwalker."

Ailan's eyes widened, her dark irises flashing with something like fear.

Cora spoke again, calmer this time, as if emboldened by Ailan's reaction. "I can use my clairsentience to astral travel to any place I can form a clear image of. I unwittingly did so with Valorre, when he filled my mind with a memory of his home."

Ailan cursed under her breath, shoulders sagging. "The unicorns. It makes sense now. I didn't understand why or how the unicorns first began to appear here, as my memories were compromised. But now...yes, of course their horns can pierce the Veil."

"The unicorns' memories were compromised too, so they weren't able to return to El'Ara," Cora said.

"Now they might remember." Ailan's gaze locked on Cora's. "We must go. We must protect the tear. My brother cannot find out about what the unicorns can do. What *he* could do with them."

"I'm not going back," Cora said. "Your people hate humans. Your consort nearly had me killed."

Ailan sucked in a breath. "You met Fanon?"

"I did. I met Ferrah too, and she tried to burn me alive."

Ailan's throat bobbed. "I'm sorry for how you were treated, Cora. I will not let them treat you like that again. When I return, I will have the authority to keep you safe. I may not be Morkara, but I am something like a regent until Noah comes of age."

"How dare you talk about Noah coming of age, like you have any say in his future," Mareleau hissed through her teeth. It took all her restraint not to shout, lest she wake Noah. "I am his mother."

"In El'Ara you will be respected as Edel Morkara'Elle. That is like a queen mother—"

"I am more than that already. I am a queen in this world. I don't care what I am in your fae realm, or what Noah is."

"It is his birthright, and he's already claimed it just by being born. Unless he chooses to pass the role to someone else when he comes of age, none of us can change that."

"I can refuse. You can't take him from me."

Ailan released a trembling sigh. "No, I won't take him from you, nor will I force you to come. Instead, I will trust that you will do the right thing. That you will put his safety ahead of your personal ambitions."

Mareleau's jaw went slack. The words stung more than Ailan likely intended, for although she hadn't used the word *selfish*, that was all Mareleau had heard. Mareleau had been called selfish numerous times, but only in the last several months did she start to feel it was true. She'd done terrible things to get what she wanted. Lied. Schemed. Hurt people she loved. Was she acting selfishly again? Was refusing to take Noah to El'Ara truly selfish? Would he be safe there?

Her lungs tightened as the weight of this choice squeezed her from every side. She'd made poor choices before. Like when she'd given her cousin Lurel to Cora as her lady's maid—a choice that ultimately resulted in the girl's death. Or when she'd lied to her father about being pregnant, driving a wedge between them. How he'd died before they'd gotten the chance to reconcile.

Ailan's tone softened. "The *mora* chose him, Mareleau. While I believe you and Cora are more important to the prophecy than the whispers have made it seem, there are still reasons it chose him. The *mora* has seen something in him, something El'Ara needs, that no one who has come before him has been able to provide. Fate has seen a future for him in the fae realm, and that same future can be yours. Being the mother of the Morkara is no small thing in El'Ara, and should anything happen to me before Noah comes of age, the *mora* will recognize you as regent over the magic instead.

"I know you love your kingdom, and I understand how much it burns you up to think of leaving it. But El'Ara is vaster than just a kingdom. It's an entire world. A world made up of more than the Elvyn. More than the Faeryn. The Morkara is responsible for redistributing magic to the farthest reaches of the world, over the seas of the Mermyn, down to the fire dunes of the Djyn. There are fae creatures besides unicorns and dragons, homes and communities across the world, innocent beings who depend on El'Ara's magic for survival. They need their Morkara in order to thrive."

Mareleau couldn't help but be moved by the portrait she painted with her words. True, all she'd seen of the fae so far had given her reasons to fear and resent El'Ara. But there was an entire world beyond the Veil that she truly knew nothing about.

A world her son had been chosen to rule.

"Even if you only want to consider your world," Ailan said, "there are additional reasons you must come with me. While I can guide the dragons back to El'Ara, if you and I are separated again, the dragons will sense my blood in you through your magic. They will find you. Stifling your magic with wards may keep them from locating you, but that doesn't mean they won't enter the human world to look."

"Can't you seal the tear in the Veil once you're on the other side?" Cora asked.

"The Veil is more complicated than that. Sealing the tear won't bring El'Ara's heart back. That's a problem we will need to solve after we defeat Darius." She turned her attention back to Mareleau. "You don't have to promise to make El'Ara your home just yet. We will figure out the future later. Together. For now, we need to defend two worlds. You won't have a kingdom to rule if we don't work together to keep Lela and El'Ara out of Darius' hands. And for now, Noah is safer behind the Veil. Trust me in this."

Her lungs constricted further. She didn't want this burden on her shoulders. She wanted someone else to choose for her, yet at the same time, she railed at the thought of being ordered around or putting her fate in someone else's hands.

She had to make this choice.

For herself.

For Noah.

For whatever consequences awaited.

She was nearly dizzy with the responsibility, yet she managed to form the words, "When will we leave?"

Ailan didn't answer at first. Instead, she closed her eyes, lifted her hands, and linked her forefingers together. Then, angling her palms, she laced the rest of her fingers and pressed the tips of her thumbs to her chest. Mareleau had never seen such a strange gesture. The silence that followed told her Ailan was focusing. Or... listening? She had droned on about her precious whispers.

With a slow exhale, Ailan opened her eyes and slowly unlinked her fingers. "Tomorrow by midday," she said. "We'll take the wagon and find the tear in the Veil before Darius sets foot on this land."

Gods above, she hoped Ailan was right. More than anything, she hoped she was making a choice she wouldn't soon regret.

29

Cora had forgotten the quiet melody of dawn so deep in the forest. It had been too long since she'd experienced the soft hum of awakening activity in the commune, the scent of the morning cookfires, the peaceful silence of those still sleeping. It seemed not even the chaos of last night could disrupt the Forest People's daily routine. The only differences were the extra figures tending to the destroyed common area, lighting new cookfires, raking the earth, and rearranging the stones and logs that served as seats.

She pulled the hood of her cloak lower, hurrying her steps as she passed the bustle of activity. She was determined not to be noticed by the others on her way to find Valorre. Though Ailan had spoken with the elders last night—after offering Cora and Mareleau her wagon to sleep in—she didn't know how that meeting had gone. Cora hadn't seen the High Elder since she'd left with Salinda and Bernice.

Cora still wasn't sure how to feel about Ailan. About all of this. Ailan was so different from the Nalia she'd thought she'd known, yet similar at the same time. She still held the same air of authority. The same kind eyes. At least one thing was certain: Ailan wanted to defeat Darius as much as Cora did.

It was that determination that propelled her feet toward the edge of camp, two sets of letters rolled together and clenched in her fist. She found Valorre not too far away. She hadn't had time to unsaddle him last night, and something was perched upon his pommel—Berol. She paused her preening to eye Cora, then went right back to it.

"I'm glad you were easy to find," Cora said. She hadn't seen the falcon since she'd taken to the skies on their way from the lake.

She's been with me ever since the dragons appeared, Valorre said, tossing his mane in greeting.

"With you?"

We're friends. She came to me for protection. She knows how brave I am.

Cora snorted a laugh. So Berol was a bit of a coward when Teryn wasn't around. Had he been here when the dragons had landed, the falcon would have dove in without hesitation, doing whatever she could to keep them away from Teryn.

"I see where your loyalties lie," Cora said, humor in her tone. "It's obviously not with me. That's all for the better. I suppose it means you'll reach him quickly."

Her heart sank as she approached Valorre's side and extended the hand with the two letters. She hadn't read the second letter, but she could guess at its contents. It had probably been even more painful to write than Cora's. Mareleau's letter would eventually reach Larylis and would convey their newest developments. Particularly the fact that Mareleau would not be returning home after all and would seek refuge in El'Ara. If refuge was truly what they'd find.

Cora's letter was of a similar nature, informing Teryn that she was taking a detour before coming home. At least she had a solid plan *to* come home. Ailan wanted Cora there for the meeting with the tribunal so they could begin negotiating an alliance to face Darius together. Mareleau, on the other hand, only had a vague idea of her stay there. A vague promise of protection.

Cora could at least carry the comfort of a failsafe, one she'd relayed to Mareleau after Ailan and the others had left the wagon: if things in El'Ara took a turn for the worse, if Mareleau and Noah seemed to be in any danger, if they faced even an ounce of scorn from the Elvyn, Cora would take them and worldwalk the hell out of there. She would steal their Morkara and damn them all if it came down to it.

Berol extended her talon at the sight of the scroll.

With a resigned sigh, Cora turned it over to the falcon. "To Teryn."

She expected Berol to fly off at once. Instead, she froze on Valorre's back, beady eyes pinned on Cora. As she released an aggrieved chirp, Cora realized what the falcon was waiting for. "Oh! I...I don't have any treats. I'm sorry."

She is not impressed, Valorre said.

"Teryn will give you extra for me," Cora said with a grimace. Berol abruptly pivoted away from her—a cold shoulder if she'd ever seen one—before launching into the sky with the scroll of letters curled in her talon.

~

Cora had one more visit to make before returning to Ailan's wagon. She wove through the tents, seeking the one that belonged to Maiya. The tents looked similar to one another, especially in the winter season, with their rounded walls and pointed roofs. While the Forest People dressed the reed-and-willow frames of their tents in thinner fabrics in the summer, allowing them to show off bright colors, patterns, and other personal touches, in the winter the tents were comprised of oiled hides and felted wool. As a result, the camp was a sea of brown and tan.

On an exhale, she pried a hole through her mental wards, extended her senses, and searched for a familiar echo. She was struck with a barrage of recognizable energies, so potent they filled her with a bittersweet ache. Of course that would happen; she should have expected it. She may have kept most of the commune at arm's length when she'd lived here, but she'd still been physically close. She'd gotten used to their energies and emotions, and now that she was among them, it was hard to pick out a specific one. Yet there was one set of emotions that tugged on her more than all the rest. She narrowed her focus to it, followed it, and was rewarded with the sight of a figure she'd recognize anywhere.

Maiya stood outside a tent not too far from Salinda's. Her long black hair hung loose down her back. She was dressed in layers of patterned skirts, a long-sleeved top with fur-lined cuffs, and a thick red vest. In her arms was a bundle of firewood.

Cora quickened her pace, desperate to reach her friend before she disappeared into the tent. Maiya paused just as she reached the tent flap and whirled toward Cora. Cora's lips stretched into a wide smile as she closed the remaining distance.

"Cora!" Maiya's grin mirrored hers, though she didn't set down the firewood or embrace her friend. Instead, she cast a furtive glance around the camp and nodded at Cora to follow her inside.

Cora tempered some of her excitement and quietly entered the tent after her friend. She pulled up short at the sight of the interior. The last time she'd been inside Maiya's tent, all of Cora's belongings had remained exactly as she'd left them. They'd always shared a tent since the day Cora had joined the commune. She hadn't expected Maiya to carry around Cora's things and maintain an unused space as if she'd never left, yet seeing proof of her own absence was more startling than she'd anticipated.

That wasn't the only change either. The tent was larger overall with more furnishings, finer rugs, and a much wider bed. This was a married couple's tent.

She faced her friend with wide eyes. "You and Roije…"

Maiya crouched before the small stove and placed one of the logs inside. She grinned over her shoulder. "We were handfasted in the fall."

"I'm so happy for you." The warmth in her heart washed away the bitter ache at having seen her things replaced. Maiya had loved Roije for a long time yet had always been too shy to make a move. When Cora had returned to the Forest People last spring, her friend and Roije had just begun courting. And now they were wed, bound by ritual handfasting. She wished she could have been there, could have seen their ceremony. Maiya must have looked radiant, and Roije—

The blood left Cora's face. Shame replaced her joy as she recalled something about Roije she never should have forgotten.

"Roije…his arm…" Cora swallowed hard, working the words from her throat. "Did he heal well?"

Maiya's expression fell, and she quickly turned back toward the stove, busying her hands with a kettle. "He did."

Cora didn't miss the curt edge to Maiya's words. Did she blame Cora for what had happened to her husband? Roije had fought at Centerpointe Rock and had faced Morkai directly. He'd lost an arm for it. Mother Goddess, she'd thought about his fate several times since then, yet she hadn't considered it since stepping foot into the camp. Not until now.

"I'm sorry," Cora said, voice trembling. "That should have been the first thing I asked—"

"And you?" Maiya faced her again, this time with two mugs of fragrant tea in her hands. "How have you been?"

Cora blinked at her a few times, surprised by Maiya's deliberate change of subject. Her lips were pulled wide but the smile no longer reached her eyes. Cora shook her head, accepting one of the mugs her friend offered. "I...I'm as well as I can be, considering current circumstances."

Maiya sipped her tea. "You're a queen now, if the news from the villages is to be believed."

"I am."

"You still don't mind if I call you Cora and not Highness or Majesty?"

Cora's shoulders slumped. "I always want to be Cora to you. To everyone here."

Maiya's jaw tightened, and Cora was struck with a spear of anger that wasn't her own. Still, her friend's grin remained on her lips and she kept her tone light. "I don't think you can be *just* Cora anymore. Not to the commune at large."

"Why do you say that?"

Maiya gave an easy shrug and took another sip of her tea. "Twice you've returned since leaving us, and twice you've brought terrifying news. Last time, you took some of our people to war. This time, you're taking our High Elder."

"That's not...I don't mean to be a harbinger of doom, but—"

"I'm just telling you how it seems to the commune." Maiya's tone took on a sharper edge. She was so unlike the sweet shy girl she'd been not even a year ago. "I'm explaining why you can't expect to be received as Cora anymore. To the commune, you are Her Majesty Aveline, Queen of Khero."

"And you? You said the commune sees me this way, but how do you see me?"

Maiya let out a long breath, her expression softening. "I see you as a treasured friend whom I'm looking at for the last time."

The weight of that statement pressed hard upon her chest. She wasn't sure how to take those words. Was she saying she never wanted to see Cora again? Warning her to stay away? Or was this a claircognizant *knowing*?

"It doesn't mean I don't wish it were otherwise." Maiya's voice came out soft, strained. "You were my sister, Cora. But...but now you're a queen. You can't just show up when you need something. It makes a mockery of our core principles. The very rule that allows our commune to live in peace."

Mother Goddess, she was right. Cora knew she was right. Fate may have wanted Cora to come here, to meet Ailan, to walk the path her threads had woven, but after this...

She needed to let the Forest People go. Not from her heart. Never from her heart. But she could not use them as her political allies ever again. Even asking them to teach Mareleau magic had been offensive enough. At the time, it had seemed like the only recourse. Yet she couldn't use them as a recourse. A last resort.

"You're right," Cora said, voice trembling. "I can't do this again. I won't do it again. Yet I will keep you and everyone else in my heart. I will protect you in whatever way I can, even if it means never coming to find you again."

Maiya set down her mug of tea and sank onto the foot of her bed. Cora did the same, having no sense of thirst with such a heavy conversation. She kept her distance from the other girl, sitting a few feet away.

"How will you protect us from the newest magic war that's about to clash on our land?"

Cora shook her head. "I don't know yet. Did your mother tell you about it?"

"She told me and Roije late last night. Neither of us could sleep after seeing the dragons, not to mention all the rumors that were circulating camp."

"Ailan—Nalia—is taking us to find the tear in the Veil. We're leaving today, and none of us are asking the Forest People to fight this time."

Maiya stared down at her hands, idly picking her nails. She lowered her voice to just above a whisper. "Have you thought about giving him what he wants?"

"What...who wants?"

"The King of Syrus."

Cora blinked at her. "You mean...give him Noah?"

"No!" Maiya lifted her head and met Cora's eyes. "No, I don't mean giving him the child. What I mean is...as queen, you are in a position to negotiate with him as a fellow monarch. You can give him what he truly wants—access to the Veil. El'Ara. In exchange for leaving Lela alone."

Cora would be lying if she said she hadn't considered it. The Elvyn weren't exactly her friends, and even the Faeryn she'd come across in El'Ara hadn't treated her any better, but that didn't mean they deserved destruction. And what about the other fae? The Djyn, Mermyn, and all the fae creatures like Valorre and the dragons. What would happen to them if Darius took control of El'Ara?

Furthermore, he was a worldwalker. Giving him access to El'Ara wouldn't keep him out of the human world, and she couldn't trust the fae realm was all he wanted. She had to remember Darius was the one to first use the term Morkaius, not his son. He didn't want to simply manage the flow of magic throughout El'Ara like the Morkara was meant to. He wanted to be High King of Magic. He wanted to control and take. If he wasn't content with all he'd gained there, he could take his new powers and turn them against the human world. Even if Cora negotiated an alliance for the safety of her people, could she bear the burden of what else he might do to other kingdoms? Other people?

Darius could never have what he truly wanted unless Noah was dead.

"No," Cora said. "The only way to truly protect our world is to stop Darius entirely."

"What happens after you stop him?" Maiya asked. "Mother said Lela is a piece of El'Ara. That it is the heart of the fae realm. What happens to this land after you defeat Darius? Will the Elvyn seal the tear and leave us alone? Or will they fight to take Lela away from us?"

Cora's breath caught. That was a question she hadn't considered. "I don't know. But I promise you, I will do whatever I can to protect this kingdom and this land."

Maiya held her gaze, but there was no hope in her eyes. Doubt rolled off her in waves. Cora could see herself the way her friend saw her now—young, small, and very much in over her head. Maiya had always believed in her, always encouraged her, but what she was facing went beyond Cora's capabilities. She knew that. But Cora wasn't alone. She had Teryn. Mareleau and Larylis. Even Lex and the

Norunian rebels he was supporting. She had alliances she could count on, and she was about to forge a new one with the Elvyn. It was daunting. Maybe even impossible.

But she would give it her all.

Maiya's face crumpled, and her chest heaved with a sob. "I really am happy to see you. You will always be a sister in my heart. Please believe me. I didn't want to have this conversation. I never wanted it to be like this. It's just—"

"I know, Maiya." She reached for her friend and pulled her into an embrace. "I know. You don't have to explain."

She didn't need Maiya to say another word. She understood fully. It was time for a final goodbye. Time to close the door on six years of her life and the people who made her the witch she was today.

Maiya sobbed onto Cora's shoulder, but Cora kept her eyes dry, refusing to add her own emotions to the medley filling the tent. Instead, she opened herself to her friend's grief, her fear, her hopes, and memorized every painful inch of it. That way she could carry it with her. That way she could remember, as she faced the inevitable challenges that lay ahead, what she was fighting for.

30

Mareleau hoped she was at the right tent. She stood before the leather flap that served as a door, Noah cradled in one arm, her free hand raised in a fist, only to realize there was no point in knocking on such a soft material. And she couldn't very well barge in, for there was still the question of whether this *was* the right tent. It should have been easy to find. Not only was it the same tent Salinda had brought them to upon arriving last night, but Cora had pointed it out from the wagon that morning, before she'd left to find Valorre and Berol.

She hated feeling awkward like this, but she was fully out of her element. Here it hindered more than helped that she was queen. Here she couldn't rely on being waited upon. She'd spent the night in a godsforsaken wagon, after all, on a cramped bed. The accommodations had been smaller than the traveling coach she'd ridden to Ridine in, yet Ailan had offered it to her and Cora like it was some high honor.

Mareleau shook the thoughts from her head, reminding herself that if anything would serve her around the Forest People, it was humility.

So she cleared her throat and adopted as pleasant a tone as she could. "Salinda? Are you—"

"Come in," came the woman's voice from inside.

She hesitated. This was normally the part where someone else would open the door for her. But no, of course that wouldn't happen here. She lifted the tent flap and awkwardly shuffled inside.

"Mareleau." Salinda greeted her with a warm smile. It was strange being on a first-name basis with a stranger, but of the few Forest People she'd met, she liked Salinda best. The woman's grin looked tired as she gestured for her to take a seat on her pile of furs. Mareleau accepted the seat, finding it far more comfortable than she expected.

Salinda strolled to the bed where she was packing items into a bag. "I was just getting some things ready for you. Extra swaddling, absorbent moss, a carrying sling, and lactation herbs."

Her mouth fell open. "Oh...that bag is for me?"

"I figured we might have some items you wouldn't have had where you're from."

She was right about that. She hadn't heard of the latter three items. "Thank you. That's...rather kind of you."

Salinda smiled over her shoulder. "You may be a queen and part of some great prophecy, but you are still a mother. And he, whether the heir to a human kingdom or the Morkara of the fae realm, is still just a baby."

For some reason, those words warmed Mareleau's heart. She hadn't realized how badly she needed to be reminded that she was more than the subject of a prophecy. More than a royal. Her identity was her own.

Salinda put the last item in the bag and sat at the edge of her bed. "But that isn't why you came here, is it?"

"No." Mareleau shifted in her seat and Noah began to fuss.

"May I?" Salinda leaned forward, extending her heavily tattooed arms.

Mareleau didn't love when other people held Noah, but she also could use a break. She hadn't had one since Salinda held him last night. Carefully she transferred her son to Salinda, then nestled back into the furs. Salinda began bouncing and speaking to him in a sing-song voice, which halted his mewling protestations.

"I was hoping," Mareleau said, "you could teach me about casting wards with my magic."

Salinda cocked her head. "Now that the dragons are being dealt with, you don't need to learn warding as urgently."

"I may not need to cast wards around my own magic, but I'd like to learn how to cast them in general. I want to protect Noah."

"There is very little I could teach you before you leave. Besides, even though I have both witch and Faeryn blood, my magic favors my Faeryn heritage. Faeryn magic works with the Magic of the Soil. Earth magic. You have Elvyn blood, which utilizes the Magic of the Sky. Weaving, in other words, like Ailan does. You'd have better luck talking to her."

"I don't want to talk to her yet." Mareleau winced at her petulant tone. She simply didn't like or trust Ailan, though that was mostly because Mareleau couldn't help blaming her for everything that was happening now. "I'd at least like to know what kind of witch I might be. Cora uses emotion, and she believes my mother uses sound. I'd like to know which of the six senses my magic favors."

"I suppose I can help with that," she said, tone kind. "So tell me about your magic. Cora mentioned last night that she discovered you were a witch because you'd cast a glamour."

Mareleau nodded. "I never knew that's what I was doing. I've always called it my magic trick, but I didn't think it was real magic."

"Tell me more about it."

She did, explaining how she'd always had a knack for donning a façade to appear a certain way to others. Most often, she used it to seem composed and regal. To gain respect. Then she explained how she'd honed that talent into something else, to rid herself of unwanted suitors. That was when she'd begun using the term *magic trick*, for it had worked splendidly. Miraculously.

"All I needed to know," Mareleau said, "was what my suitor wanted to see and what they feared to see."

"How did you find out?"

"I just...knew. It didn't take many conversations or encounters with my suitors to figure it out. I knew from what they talked about and what they didn't talk about. I knew from how they acted and reacted."

"That sounds like claircognizance—clear knowing. My daughter has that gift. She's honing her Art for dream divination. Someone will tell her about their dream, and she simply knows its meaning. Other times, she suddenly knows something will or won't happen. Like how she knew Cora would come yesterday."

"I've never done anything nearly as impressive as that."

"Explain more about what you have done then. How have you used what you know to craft a glamour?"

Mareleau shrugged. "In the past, I've simply portrayed the traits my suitors disliked or expressed myself in a way that countered what they did like. I'd make a suitor who wanted a cold and distant wife see me as clingy and smothering. I'd make a suitor who wanted a vapid, easy, and beautiful wife see me as cunning, difficult, and ugly."

She'd crafted the latter glamour on the last suitor her parents had tried to pair her with before they'd agreed to let her host the Heart's Hunt. Frederick had nearly won her over. Not her heart, of course, for that had always belonged to Larylis, even when she'd been tricked into thinking he'd abandoned her. Yet Frederick had almost won her hand, a marriage alliance built on common interests. That was before she'd discovered he'd been dallying with her best friend and lady's maid, Katra, and had even promised to make the girl his mistress. She'd delighted in using her magic trick on him then, watching his face turn pale as she'd let her posture sag, let her expression shift into something hideous. Even now, the corners of her lips curled up, vindictive pride igniting in her chest.

Salinda narrowed her eyes. "Have you always cast glamours—or used this magic trick, as you call it—for personal gain?"

"I suppose so." Why did she feel like she was admitting to a bad thing? Who wouldn't use whatever was at their disposal for personal gain? Perhaps she delighted a little too much in tormenting the people who'd hurt her, but...well, she certainly wasn't going to admit that.

Salinda's brows knit together as she absently rocked a now-sleeping Noah. "Your mother is likely a clairaudient witch, and we know you inherited Ailan's Elvyn blood from one of your parents. We can assume it was through your father."

"Is that significant?"

"Elvyn-witch hybrids are rare, considering there are no living Elvyn aside from Ailan. That we know of, at least. It may be possible..."

"What's possible?"

"I believe you're a narcuss. It's a rare Art, so we know very little about it. I've always believed a narcuss to be the shadow of the empath, projecting emotions outward instead of taking others' emotions in. But you seem to utilize claircognizance to project the outcome you want. You change what a person sees and knows about you, forcing an impression."

Mareleau's stomach sank. The way Salinda described a narcuss left little to be desired. Forcing an impression? Projecting an outcome she wanted? Those terms made her seem more like a villain than a witch. "Aren't there other kinds of witches who do something similar, other than...whatever a narcuss is?"

"Somewhat, but the reason I believe you're a narcuss is because the last witch who we know for certain had that power was also an Elvyn-witch hybrid. It could be that the Art of the narcuss is exclusive to that combination."

Mareleau sat forward eagerly. "You know another narcuss?"

"I wouldn't say I ever knew him personally." Her tone held a wary note.

That was enough for Mareleau to put the pieces together. "You're talking about Morkai, aren't you?"

Salinda's nod of confirmation sent Mareleau's stomach roiling.

"I...have the same magic as *Morkai*?"

"It doesn't have to be a bad thing," Salinda said, softening her expression. "I didn't mean to make it seem that way. We just don't have many examples of one using that magic for good. But you can choose how you use it. You may have used it for personal gain before, but there is nothing inherently wrong with that. And as you overcome your personal challenge, you'll find other ways to use your Art, and your magic will grow stronger."

"What do you mean by personal challenge?"

"Every witch grows their magic by overcoming challenges that are personal to them and their Art. Most often, a witch is confronted with the option of doing what feels easiest versus what feels most difficult, what goes against their base instincts. Only you will know what that challenge is, but it very well may be using your Art in a way that feels unnatural. Using it to help others instead of for personal gain."

"Like how I want to learn magic to protect Noah? Isn't that counter to what a narcuss would do?"

"Perhaps," Salinda said. "Yet always question such lines of thinking. As a narcuss, it will be easy to convince yourself that what you do for personal gain is for another's sake. I'm sure Morkai justified all his actions that way."

Her gut turned again. Seven devils, she was right. Teryn had discovered exactly that while trapped in the crystal. How Morkai—Desmond, as he was called before he took on the new name—had originally sought answers for his father, all in the hopes that Darius would resurrect his dead mother. After Emylia died, he'd sought the power of the Morkaius so that he could eventually bring her back. Morkai had believed his dark intentions were selfless.

But...but Mareleau wasn't like that. Was she?

"Am I being selfish for wanting to protect my son? All I want is for him to be safe."

"Why?"

"Why? What do you mean *why*? Because I love him, that's why. Because I want him to live a long, healthy life. Because I want to see him grow up and experience being his mother—" The words caught in her throat.

"Because *you* want to experience that."

Mareleau thought she might be sick. Even her desire to protect her son ultimately came back to how it served her. Had she always been this way? Had every good feeling, every wish, every hope, been some desire born from her selfish, dark heart—

"There is nothing wrong with wanting those things for yourself." Salinda's voice came out firm. "I didn't say any of that to condemn you, only to demonstrate just how great your challenge might be. Just how subtle the divide between what you do for others and what you do for yourself. Being a narcuss does not make you evil."

Her shoulders sank nonetheless. "What do I do then? How do I ensure I don't end up like...like *him*?"

"Seek the truth inside yourself. Question what you think you know. If you meet darkness, simply bring it to light. Acknowledge it. When you feel those selfish undercurrents running through you, admit them, then let them be. You need not outrun your nature. Just don't let it control you. When you feel a challenge to counter your base instincts, face it. If you fail, forgive yourself and move on."

"You make it sound easy."

"It isn't easy, but you're not alone. A narcuss isn't the only one who faces their darkest side. We all do."

"Even you?"

"Especially me. You saw how quickly I turned my heart against someone I've loved my whole life."

"You mean Ailan? That's understandable. She lied to you. She pretended to be dying to avoid confronting the truth." A cloud of guilt reflected back, reminding her that she could relate to Ailan's actions. She'd pretended to be pregnant, after all.

"Perhaps, perhaps not. What matters is I saw my dark feelings, my hate, my anger, and I called them into the light. I revealed them and released them. I'm still angry and confused. I'm also hopeful that I can forgive her. It is a choice to follow the path of hope and love, even when dark feelings remain. Strength isn't being good or perfect. It's meeting your darkness face to face and moving forward instead of sinking into it. No matter what you find in those shadows, it is important that you love yourself."

Love herself? She'd never had a problem putting herself first, but had she ever truly loved herself? Not especially. She was flawed and had done terrible things in the past, but...could she love those sides of her? Truly love them?

Larylis' voice echoed through her head, warming her heart.

Someone who loved you, petals, thorns, and all.

Well, if he could love her through all her lies, schemes, and manipulations, maybe she could do the same.

She released a slow sigh. "I'll try."

"That's all you ever have to do. Just try."

Mareleau gathered Noah back into her arms and left Salinda's tent. She hadn't gotten the answers she'd wanted. She hadn't learned a stitch of magic.

Yet she'd learned a little more about herself, a side she'd never known. Maybe that side of her—the side she shared with a villain she despised—could somehow prove useful in facing the villain that lay ahead.

31

Teryn hated how quickly relief could turn to dread.

He scanned the letter in his hands three times over, his stomach sinking deeper with each repetition. He'd been so elated to see Berol. She'd caught his eye while he'd been meeting with Master Arther and Ridine's head mason regarding repairs on the keep roof and destroyed battlement. He'd hardly been able to focus on inspecting the parapets and discussing repairs when all he'd wanted was the letter curled in Berol's talon. Yet she'd kept her distance until Teryn's guests had left and he was alone on the battlement.

Now the wind cut his cheeks, threatening to tear the letter from his fingertips, as he read the note once more. Then, with a sigh, he pocketed the letter and leaned over the parapet wall, elbows propped upon the chest-high crenel before him. Berol hopped down from one of the merlons and nipped at his arm. Absently, he fed her a strip of dried venison.

Cora's letter contained good news. They'd found the Forest People as planned. Mareleau was no longer targeted by the dragons. They'd found a solution to return the dragons to where they'd come from and had even found Ailan.

At least that's what he'd determined from the sparse details her letter contained.

We found who we've been looking for. Not just the many I sought, but the one. She has promised to keep her kin safe and has control over the troublesome beasts. I will attend a meeting with her people to form an alliance and will come home as soon as I can.

Those were the lines that had required the most repetition. From the way she'd avoided stating names and locations, she was being cautious in case Berol was intercepted by the enemy. It was a practical choice yet a maddening one. He wished she'd simply spelled it all out so that he didn't have to guess. But what other conclusion could he come to? They'd found Ailan and would next find the tear and bring the dragons back through it. Mareleau and Noah would be protected behind the Veil, and Cora would try to forge an alliance with the Elvyn.

There was hope in her letter. A miraculous hope at that. Finding Ailan hadn't been part of the plan, only a feeble wish. Yet somehow Cora had found her amongst the Forest People. And an alliance with the Elvyn could be exactly what they needed to defeat Darius. He had two armies, after all—the naval forces he'd launched from Syrus and the forces he'd gained from his alliance with Norun. To defeat him, they needed more soldiers than he had. More strength.

Yet that hope led to dread, for it meant Cora was going farther away. It meant he had even less of an idea where she was, if she was safe, or when she'd return.

I miss you. I love you. I'll return.

That was how the letter ended. He'd trust those words, even if they did nothing to lift the heaviness in his heart.

"You should have gone with Cora."

Berol cocked her head, but Teryn hadn't been talking to her.

A faint figure had formed beside him.

Emylia crossed her arms and leaned against the parapet. "You wanted me to act as your messenger bird as well?"

"Now that I'm reminded how practical and cautious my darling wife can be in writing, I realize you would have served as a better way to glean solid information."

"At least you know she's safe."

Neither of them said what lingered unspoken. That she was safe...*for now*. And now that Berol had left Cora's side, he wasn't sure when he'd get another update.

Berol nipped his arm again. At first he thought she was asking for more treats. While that may be the case, it reminded him of the second letter that had been rolled up with the first. He hadn't dared read it, for it had been addressed to Larylis. That isn't to say he wasn't tempted, for there was a chance Mareleau hadn't been as careful with her words and information as Cora had. She may have shared more details that would give Teryn a clearer idea of their situation. And yet, whatever she wrote was meant for his brother. He wouldn't cross that boundary.

With great reluctance, he turned the scroll over to Berol, along with another strip of meat.

"To Larylis." He didn't mention where to find him, for he was likely still on the road. Berol had demonstrated a remarkable knack for finding those she was familiar with no matter where they were. He trusted she'd find Larylis too.

Berol took the letter and flew off the battlement. He watched as she quickly turned into a speck in the distance.

"Cora will be fine," Emylia said. "You know how strong she is."

He did know, but seven devils, this situation was devolving into unknown territory. Quite literally, in some respects. There was so much they still didn't know. So much they couldn't plan for. Cora's vague details only contributed to that untethered feeling.

His gaze drifted from the sky—Berol no longer in sight—to the landscape. Thankfully it was free of smoke and the shadows of wings and had been since the night before. No wonder he hadn't gotten any new reports of fiery destruction or dragon sightings. If Cora had found Ailan, and Ailan had control over the dragons, that was one less problem he had to address.

Though addressing problems was something he thrived on. Planning for repairs, holding audiences, offering reparations to those who'd lost their homes and crops to dragon fire...he'd been trained for these things his whole life. As troublesome as these matters were, staying busy kept the edge off his restlessness. Moving, acting, problem-solving—serving as king consort while Cora was away—gave him purpose. Robbed him of opportunities to panic.

Something moved far below in his periphery, drawing his gaze to the charred field that marred the castle lawn. There a pale semi-transparent figure wandered across the dead earth. At first he thought Emylia had transported herself there, but no, she was still at his side.

He narrowed his eyes until he could make out the distinct shape of the wraith, a ghostly sword at its side. Its eyes were hollow holes.

He cast a questioning look at Emylia. "Is that..."

"One of Morkai's warrior wraiths?" She nodded. "I think so."

He didn't like to recall how aggressively the wraiths had fought at Centerpointe Rock. Before that, Morkai had demonstrated his ghastly army's capabilities on the very charred field the wraith wandered over now. Proved how deadly they could be when he forced a servant to face his hoard.

"How did he get the wraiths to follow him?" Teryn asked.

"He did what he'd always done. He used a blood weaving. He burned the castle garden to ash, offering death for life."

"And that's all they needed to fall under his command?"

"No, it was more complicated than that. He shared a connection to those wraiths, through his father. The wraiths he called to him were the souls of those who'd fought in El'Ara for Darius."

Teryn remembered what Morkai had said about the wraiths during his demonstration.

Spirits from a nearly forgotten war.

They died trapped between two realms...

Now they serve me.

"They died in the fae realm," Emylia said, "yet their souls were tethered to the human realm. Their heart-centers were torn from them, leaving them as empty, hollow spirits, unable to cross to the otherlife. Without one's heart-center, they have no attachment to the otherlife, no reason to go home. Yet without a heart-center, they remain forever hungry. Lost. That is where tales of vengeful and violent spirits come from."

So that was why wraiths were so different from ghosts. Ghosts had unfinished business like Emylia or were desperate to cling to the lives they'd had like some of the ones he'd seen in the castle. Wraiths, on the other hand, had lost the very thing that made them want anything. They were hungry but didn't even know what for.

Emylia spoke again. "He used that hunger to his advantage. With his own blood, he wove an attraction enchantment that called the wraiths to Ridine. The wraiths were drawn to his blood because they sensed their former master's in it—Darius, the king they'd served and fought for, the man who'd fueled their sense of purpose when they'd been alive.

"Once Morkai drew the wraiths to the castle grounds, he sacrificed the garden and gave them sentience, and the ability to act as if they were alive, able to wield their weapons and end lives. After that, they chose to follow him. He gave them what every wraith craves—a purpose. He promised them a battle that would help them atone for the mission they'd failed to complete for their former master. Furthermore, he'd end their wandering torment by giving them the peace they couldn't find on their own. Once he had the power of the Morkaius, he would lay their etheras to rest.

"Lay them to rest? How would he do that?"

"Magic can exorcise spirits, though I don't know if Morkai had truly cared enough about their fate to plan that far ahead."

"That's really all it took for him to gain an army of souls? Spill his blood, give them a purpose that harkened back to their former lives, and promise an end to their wandering?"

"No, there was more to it than that. His army was flawed at first. They could only maintain sentience for short stints once they began fighting, and if they were defeated in combat, that would often be enough to end their bloodlust. That was when he forged a connection between them and his Roizan. It allowed them to reanimate again and again, never tiring."

He stared down at the wraith, watching as it wandered aimlessly over the charred field. "Are the wraiths still dangerous? If he sacrificed the garden to give them sentience, do they still have it? Can they still kill, or can they only wander the field that gave them life?"

"Maybe they could be dangerous if they had a purpose again, but that died with Morkai." Emylia frowned, turning narrowed eyes to him. "Why are you so interested?"

Something dark echoed in his chest, and he realized he wasn't questioning Morkai's actions out of idle curiosity. There was a part of him that wanted to figure out what he'd done, to study it from every angle. And a much smaller, quieter part of him that wondered if he could do it too.

He'd already painted with blood. He'd worked blood magic and now knew how simple it was. Not easy, but simple. Just a pattern. A formula.

"Do not lust after blood magic," Emylia said. "There's a reason it's forbidden. There are repercussions."

She was right, and he shuddered at his own thoughts. At how alluring they were, despite knowing he shouldn't have them. Yet something in him had changed last summer, as subtle a change as it was. He'd greeted death. Had danced with it. Defeated it. It didn't repulse him the way it once had, and there was a faint piece of it that stayed with him still, evident in his ability to see spirits. Was that one of the repercussions Emylia was referring to?

He glanced at the warrior wraith again. It walked in slow, hapless circles at the center of the field.

Then it halted.

Turned around.

And lifted its hollow, eyeless gaze to Teryn.

His breath caught as he was struck with a sudden yearning for...

For what?

He didn't know, nor was he sure the yearning was coming from him. It almost felt as if it was coming from the wraith.

Teryn took a step away from the parapet.

The wraith blinked, then averted its gaze. After a few moments of stillness, it proceeded to cross the field and disappeared at the end of it.

Teryn's heart slammed against his ribs. Most spirits avoided him, or at the very least ignored him. But that one...

What was the yearning he'd felt?

"What's happened to me?" he said under his breath. "Why can I see spirits? Why has death chosen to cling to me?"

And if it hadn't chosen to cling to him...then had he chosen to cling to it?

"I don't know." Emylia nibbled her lip. Her wary expression reminded him of when they were locked in the crystal together and she'd hidden information from him.

He fully faced her and took a step closer. She launched a step back, her expression wild with sudden fear.

That wasn't the first time she'd reacted like that.

It reminded him of the ghost in the council room the other day. The one who'd fled after she'd gotten close to him.

He narrowed his eyes. "What aren't you telling me? Why have you been afraid of me?"

She wrung her semi-transparent hands. "It's just...when I get close to you, I feel...I don't know what I feel. It's just this sense that...that I'll cease to exist."

"What does that mean—" His words cut off as approaching footsteps interrupted their unsettling conversation.

"I don't know," Emylia whispered and disappeared before him.

He turned to find Captain Alden striding across the battlement. A small ember of hope ignited in his chest. He'd tasked her with questioning the spy again to see if they could get any more information. If they could just get a little more insight into Darius' plans...

Alden stopped before him with a bow, but when she straightened, her face was pale.

"Report," Teryn said.

"It's...the spy, Majesty."

"Have you gotten more intel from—"

"He's dead. The spy is dead, and it wasn't an accident."

Teryn's mind went blank and he nearly huffed a laugh. He'd been foolish to hope. The last of it drained from his body as Alden finished her report, detailing how they'd found the spy's body in his cell, how his face had been beaten nearly to a pulp.

Teryn replied with a calm he didn't feel, agreed with her conclusion that the spy had been purposefully silenced after revealing information about the naval fleet. When she left, he faced the parapet once more and pounded a fist upon the stone crenel.

He was supposed to solve problems. He was supposed to protect Ridine while Cora was away. Instead, he'd lost their only asset to help them gain intel on the enemy. And worst of all, if the spy had been silenced in the dungeon, that meant something far worse.

There was a traitor somewhere in the castle.

32

For three days, Cora and her companions searched for the tear, traveling mostly at night. This, of course, was to limit the possibility of dragon sightings. There was no way to know if Darius didn't already have eyes in Khero, seeking signs of the tear. He already had spies in her kingdom, or at least his Norunian allies did. And now that a third dragon had joined Ferrah and Uziel—proof that the creatures would continue to pour out of El'Ara in search of Ailan and Mareleau—it was even more imperative that they return them to the Veil.

The road was cloaked in predawn shadows and a faint wash of moonlight as Cora rode beside Ailan's wagon. The wagon was pulled by a pair of the Forest People's horses while Valorre served as Cora's mount—his idea, for he seemed to have taken a liking to his fashionable saddle. Or perhaps he was jealous of the new horses.

When they'd set out for tonight's journey, Ailan had insisted they'd find the tear before sunrise. Cora was surprised that the Veil had torn so close to Ailan and not closer to Ridine where Noah had been born. When Cora had asked her about this, Ailan had explained that even though Noah's birth had caused the surge of *mora* that split the Veil, Ailan was still regent over El'Ara's magic and would be until he came of age. The *mora* was just as desperate to reach her as it was to find its Morkara.

Wings beat the starlit sky overhead, and a dark silhouette rose above the tree line. Cora's hands flinched, one toward the bow at her back, the other toward the quiver of arrows attached to the saddle. She smothered her defensive instincts to draw her weapons and settled for grasping the hilt of her dagger—the beautiful gift Teryn had given her—as she watched the dragon carry off some unfortunate creature in its talons. From the dragon's massive size, it was Uziel. He flew over the road to the other side, where the landscape ended in a steep cliffside. His silhouette dipped beyond the cliff, likely to devour his prey upon the beach far below.

Ailan had promised the dragons would cease burning crops and stealing livestock, upon her order, but they still needed to feed. Thankfully, they did so out of sight.

I still don't like them much, Valorre conveyed. *Now that I have my memories, I recall my kind has never gotten along with theirs. Too unrefined.*

Is that so? Cora stifled a laugh and wondered if all unicorns were as arrogant as Valorre.

What the fornication is he even eating? His prey was almost as large as me.

What I'd like to know, Cora said, *is where you got these strange expletives from.*

Strange? How are they strange? The sentinels at the castle walls use them all the time in conversation.

Is that what you do when I'm not around? Wander the perimeter and listen in on the sentinels' private gossip? Cora chuckled. *Regardless, I think you've misunderstood. The words you use aren't quite the same as theirs.*

Yes, well, I could hardly comprehend what the sentinels' words meant at first. Once I gleaned their meaning, I decided to use far more concise variations. I'll have you know that makes me more refined and more creative. I can use better words than shit, crap, devils, and fu—

I get it. You're oh so clever and refined with your foul language.

Thank you. I knew you'd agree.

Cora rolled her eyes.

I'm nothing like these fatherless sons, he said with a huff at the two horses pulling the wagon, Ailan at the reins. *They haven't a thought in their heads. Look how much taller I am! Look how much faster I can trot!*

"No you don't," Cora said out loud, tone sharp. "I know you're faster, larger, and smarter, but you don't need to show off."

Valorre mentally scoffed but resisted his urge to race ahead.

Ailan released a soft chuckle from the box seat. "You have a strong relationship with him, don't you? He's your familiar."

"Yes, he is." Some of her mirth died down. Even after traveling with Ailan for three days, she still hadn't fully warmed to her. The same went for Mareleau, who often treated the woman with downright coldness. She couldn't blame her.

Cora cast a glance down the length of the wagon, finding all the shutters closed with no sign of light behind them. Mareleau and Noah must be asleep.

Ailan spoke again. "I imagine it is like my bond with Uziel. The Elvyn don't call them familiars, as that term belongs to witches, but the connection is the same."

Cora was caught between curiosity and her steady apprehension of Ailan. She fought past the latter and gave in to the former. "Do Elvyn bond with other creatures besides dragons?"

"No, only dragons, and only the Morkara and their descendants can bond with them. Even so, the dragons can refuse to bond with certain people, regardless of bloodline. That was what happened with Darius. It very well might be what set everything into motion."

Cora nudged Valorre's side to bring him closer to the wagon. The road was plenty wide, but Cora's curiosity made her want to draw nearer. "What do you mean?"

She opened her mouth but didn't utter a word. Maybe she didn't know where to start. When she did manage to speak, her eyes were distant, her gaze hovering over the star-dappled sea that stretched beyond the cliffside. "My brother's jealousy knew no bounds. He hated me from the moment I was born. You know about my brother's father? The prince who worldwalked into El'Ara and stole my mother's heart?"

"Tristaine," Cora said. "I learned about him in El'Ara. How Satsara was sent to weave a ward around him that would banish him from the fae realm, but she fell in love with him instead."

Ailan nodded. "Shortly after Darius was born, she relayed the truth of his parentage to her consort and tribunal."

"Her consort..." Cora was reminded of something she'd yet to mention. "Etrix. He was Satsara's consort and...and your father, right?"

Ailan's gaze sharpened as she whipped her face toward Cora. "Yes. How did you—"

"I met him. He, Fanon, and an Elvyn named Garot were the ones who found me."

"You met my father."

"He and Garot were...relatively kind to me."

Ailan's lips turned down. "I'm sorry Fanon was unkind. I...I can't imagine how the years have felt for him. I've had over five hundred years away from him, but it hasn't been nearly so long for him. More like seventy-five years, based on the discrepancy in the passage of time between here and El'Ara. He must still cling to hope that I'll return, yet at the same time, the truthweavers must have heard the same whispers that have spoken to me. He will know I've furthered my bloodline in the human world. Essentially moving on from him."

"Were the two of you in love?" Maybe it was a silly question. In the human world, political alliances were often loveless, and Satsara's affair with Tristaine suggested her relationship with Etrix may have been the same. But just like Cora had been blessed with a marriage to a man she loved, maybe the same happened in El'Ara.

"We were," Ailan said, her expression turning distant once more. "I didn't expect to love him, but I did, and he loved me fiercely in return. It surprised us both. The Morkara and their heirs are paired strategically with their consorts to grant honors to great Elvyn families, much like human royal marriages. Neither of us expected love."

"What about Satsara and Etrix?"

"Ah, that brings me back to what I'd been trying to explain. Their pairing had been far colder than mine and Fanon's was. They both had lovers, as that is commonplace for many Elvyn. And unlike human rules of succession, only the Morkara's bloodline counts when passing the role to their heirs. The Morkara's heir can be born from any partner they choose. So when my mother conceived Tristaine's child, the only alarming thing about it was that the child was half human. By then, Satsara and Etrix had begun to form a warm relationship, a love born from friendship and honesty. She admitted to her newborn son's origins and that she'd never banished the human she'd been sent to exile years ago. The tribunal agreed to treat her son with the same respect a pureblood Elvyn heir would receive, so long as she banished Tristaine once and for all. She agreed and raised Darius as her precious prince.

"After several years, Satsara and Etrix grew closer, eventually developing a physical relationship and bringing me into the world. Naturally, the tribunal favored me over Darius, for even though they treated Darius with the reverence required, they remained suspicious at heart. Their misgivings only solidified as he grew older and discovered his ability to worldwalk. What started as simple pranks —startling the servants, sneaking into places he shouldn't go—evolved into dangerous acts. He managed to worldwalk to his father in Syrus somehow, which opened his ability to travel to the human world. From there he'd bring in human captives, sometimes for pleasure, but other times for trickery and torment, abandoning them in the woods and watching how they fared or setting fae creatures upon them."

Cora's stomach turned. All the childhood faerytales that described vicious fae and deadly tricks now seemed chillingly real. But there was something that left her even more unsettled.

"How did Darius worldwalk to Syrus? Had Satsara allowed Tristaine to take him there before she'd banished him, or do his abilities work differently from mine?"

"His abilities work like yours," Ailan said. "He only ever worldwalked to places he'd been before. I never learned how he'd managed to worldwalk to Syrus the first time. Tristaine first found El'Ara unintentionally. Maybe Darius' journey was accidental too."

Ailan was right about Tristaine. He was a clairalient witch who'd first found the fae realm by following a scent. If she remembered Garot's tale correctly, that had been on Samhain, when the veils between worlds were thinnest. Perhaps the same phenomenon had allowed Darius to find his father.

Ailan continued. "As much as my mother doted on her son, not even she could deny how dangerous he was becoming. He'd already reached maturity, and I was approaching it myself. The tribunal urged her to wait to choose her heir until I came of age, just to give us an equal chance at proving our worth. Mother clung to her hope that Darius would change, clung to the child that represented her first love.

"Then came the turning point. I reached maturity and was allowed to try to bond a dragon. Darius had been rejected four times, and the tribunal was beginning to worry Berolla's hatchlings were too wild for bonding. But I was deeply drawn to the eldest and largest of Berolla's progeny—Uziel. We bonded almost as soon as I'd begun the ritual."

Cora couldn't help the grimace that tugged her lips. She'd been forced to attempt that ritual herself with Ferrah and had nearly been burned to a crisp.

Ailan's face fell. "Darius was jealous. He sought to disrupt the ritual by startling my mother's dragon. He worldwalked in front of me and lifted his chin at Berolla— a disrespectful gesture one should never make to a dragon one has not gained the approval of. Berolla swiped out in a rage but Darius disappeared just in time, leaving me to bear the slash of her talons. Uziel swept me aside before the gash turned fatal, but I was still badly wounded.

"Darius wept pitiful tears, begging for my forgiveness, insisting it had only been a prank to test my bond with Uziel. But the tribunal turned firmly against him once and for all. My mother was finally forced to admit that her son was far more treacherous than she wanted to believe. Giving in to the wisdom of everyone around her, and her love for me, she named me heir and prepared to banish her beloved son, the same way she'd exiled Tristaine."

Cora remembered Garot explaining Satsara's attempt. An attempt that failed when Darius realized his mother was trying to weave a ward around him. "He escaped."

"He did," Ailan said. "He used his powers to escape to Syrus before her ward was completed. I'm sure you know the rest. Years later he returned to El'Ara, waging war upon the realm to claim his place as Morkaius of El'Ara. He had Syrus' military strength by then and used his abilities plus the discrepancy of time to constantly barrage our forces. He could worldwalk with entire groups of soldiers at once, then leave and return with more in the blink of an eye. When he needed to retreat and regroup, he could take a week to recover while we had only a day. He was relentless, and his men were armed with iron—the deadliest metal to faekind. Even superficial wounds with iron could be lethal for our fighters, where normally only excessive blood loss, beheading, or voluntary Last Breath could end our lives."

Cora couldn't imagine the terror of constant war, yet it did help her understand —at least somewhat—the disdain Fanon had treated her with. Darius had used his abilities in horrifying ways, even before he'd resorted to war. Playing vicious pranks, taking human captives for his own amusement. He certainly wasn't a glowing endorsement for witches. While she still resented having been treated so cruelly, the Elvyn had no other example to go by. No reason to trust humans or witches when the only ones they'd met had caused harm.

"I'm surprised you don't blame witches like those in El'Ara do," Cora said. "You lived alongside them. Welcomed them into the commune. Appointed them as elders to sit beside you. Or was that only because you'd lost your memories?"

"It is true I forgot many details regarding myself and Darius, but I don't think I could have resented all witches, even if I'd remembered. Witches, fae, non-magical humans...we're all the same. There is good and evil in all of us, and I don't think Darius' heritage as a witch is the reason for his darkness. Maybe my mother was too naive and didn't try to guide him away from his darker instincts. Maybe Tristaine was responsible for filling his head with blood and violence. Whatever the case, I do hope to change the minds of Fanon and those who share his prejudices. They will need to change if we are to ally our peoples and stand against Darius."

"Are you anxious about seeing Fanon again?" Cora asked, only to realize what a personal question that was. She continued to cling to a rebellious fire that kept her from wanting to get too close to Ailan. At the same time, she had loved Nalia, and the more they talked, the more Cora was beginning to merge the two identities in her mind.

"I am," Ailan confessed. "Romantic relationships are hardly my priority, but I can't help wondering if there's a future for us. After our most pressing matters are taken care of."

Cora's heart softened. "Will he really be so angry that you moved on? He knows it's been five hundred years for you."

She shook her head. "He's a stubborn creature, and he's always wanted me all to himself. He never liked the idea of taking lovers or treating our relationship like anything but a committed union between us. I felt the same, of course, but things changed when I was trapped in the human world. Not only were my memories of Fanon disappearing, but I had only the whispers of my weavings to guide me. Once humans discovered the new land that had sprouted from the southern edge of Risa, my whispers urged me to integrate with society and bear heirs. I didn't experience love again, not like I had with Fanon, but I did start a family."

Cora knew Ailan had had children, but Cora hadn't pictured Ailan with a family. A husband. Sons and daughters. "How long did you live in human society before you settled with the Forest People?"

"Once my children and grandchildren died, I felt the whispers calling me away. I met my great-grandchildren, but they didn't cling to me the way my closer kin had, for they had many other relatives. Besides, I couldn't appear to live forever, even with how my appearance had aged."

"Were none of your children immortal, even with the Elvyn blood they'd inherited from you?"

She shook her head. "They aged the same as any human."

"Then how is Darius still alive? Morkai used blood magic to extend his life, but from what you've said about Darius, he's as immortal as you are. Can he even be killed?"

"He can be killed just like the rest of my kind—beheading or excessive blood loss. He heals relatively fast, so a minor wound won't do. Even running him through with a sword won't do much, for he merely disappears, removes the weapon, and heals. But he can be killed so long as he can be outsmarted. And as for your first question, I believe his immortality is due to being born in El'Ara and remaining in the line of succession. If Noah or I perish, Darius still has a chance to claim rule. Until my brother dies, the *mora* will recognize that and fuel his life."

When she put it that way, Cora couldn't help but question Ailan's choices. If she'd died without any heirs, the *mora* could have chosen a new bloodline from someone still behind the Veil in El'Ara. But like Ailan had said then, there was no way to know what the repercussions would have been. Would the new Morkara have been able to fix the Veil and return El'Ara's heart? Would Morkai still have been born to wreak havoc on the human world?

None of them had the answers to *what if*. Yet it did bring to mind a question she'd yet to ask. One Maiya had voiced. Since then, it had clouded Cora's heart.

"What happens to Lela after we defeat Darius? When I asked if you could seal the tear in the Veil, you said it was more complicated than that, because sealing the tear wouldn't bring El'Ara's heart back. So what will you do instead?"

Ailan met Cora's gaze, lips pursed. "I don't know yet, and neither of us may like the answer when we find it."

A chill ran down Cora's spine. She opened her mouth to ask her to elaborate when Ailan tugged the reins and brought her wagon to an abrupt stop. Cora halted Valorre beside it. "What is it?"

Ailan's gaze was fixed at the edge of the cliffside. "It's here," Ailan said, voice breathless. "We've found the tear."

33

Cora dismounted Valorre and watched from the road as Ailan approached the edge of the cliff. The dark sea stretched out toward the horizon while the first blush of dawn slowly crept from behind the mountains in the east. Cora's heart climbed higher into her throat with every step Ailan took toward the cliff's edge. It triggered her instinctual terror to witness something so outwardly dangerous. But according to Ailan, the tear lay at the very edge.

Don't fear for her, Valorre said, nuzzling her shoulder. *She's right. I can feel the tear just ahead.*

Uziel shot up from the other side of the cliff, finished with whatever beast he'd taken to the beach to consume. He landed with a thud down the road. The rustling in the woods behind Cora told her Ferrah and the third dragon were nearby too.

The wagon door swung open and Mareleau emerged with Noah in her arms. Her eyelids were heavy with sleep and her silvery tresses were plaited in a messy braid down her back. "What's happened? Did we—oh, devils."

Mareleau's gaze caught Ailan's figure at the edge of the cliff. The woman stood with her hand outstretched, her patchwork petticoats billowing behind her on the early morning breeze.

Mareleau's shoulders fell. "Don't tell me…"

"Yep. The tear is inconveniently located at the edge of a godsdamned cliff."

Not a fan of cliffs, Valorre added.

Ailan continued to reach into the air before her as she took another step closer to the edge, then to the left. She leaned slightly forward…

Her fingertips disappeared.

She whirled toward them with a wide smile. "It's here. We can step through it."

"Or maybe plummet to our deaths," Mareleau said under her breath.

Valorre conveyed his agreement. *Not a fan of plummeting to my death.*

Ailan faced Uziel, who eagerly padded over to her, head low like an obedient puppy despite his massive size. She whispered something in the fae language to him, then stepped aside. The black dragon took her place at the edge of the cliff and charged forward without a hint of hesitation. His head disappeared first, then his sinuous neck. His enormous belly and hindquarters followed, then finally his tail. Now there was only sky. Ailan continued to watch the space until a black scaled snout protruded from nothingness. Uziel flicked his tongue and disappeared once more.

Ailan gave a satisfied nod. Then, angling her head over her shoulder, she spoke in her ancient language again. Ferrah darted from the forest toward the cliff in a blur of opalescent white, and a slightly smaller green dragon raced after her. Showing the same confidence Uziel had, they sprang off the cliff and disappeared beyond the Veil.

With the dragons gone, Ailan approached the wagon, lips curved in a frown. "There's no way we'll get the horses to step off a cliff. We'll have to hide the wagon somewhere off the road and set the horses free. Considering the difference in the passage of time, it would be inhumane to tether them, not knowing when any of us will be back."

Cora could agree with that, but...

"What about Mareleau?" she said. "We're going to make her walk with Noah through El'Ara?"

There was one solution, of course. Once they were on the other side of the Veil, Cora could try to worldwalk her companions to the meadow she and Valorre had accidentally traveled to last summer. Now that they'd accomplished their goal of locating the tear, it was no longer necessary to travel by traditional means. Still, she resisted bringing the option up. If there was one way to make her return to El'Ara even more unwelcome, it would be to worldwalk there.

"I do have legs, you know," Mareleau said with a withering stare.

Cora returned the look. "You also recently had a baby."

"I can still manage to walk."

I have a saddle. Valorre rippled with indignation. *And I'm quite comfortable to ride. Everyone knows this.*

"We won't need to walk far," Ailan said. "The Elvyn have woven triggers throughout the land that are set off by human intruders. A pathweaver will come straight to us."

That made sense, for that was exactly how the Elvyn had found her and Valorre when they'd entered El'Ara the first time. But Garot had been unable to use his pathweaving in the Blight—

The blood left Cora's face as she realized there was another thing she hadn't discussed with Ailan. She'd assumed her whispers had told her, but...

"Ailan, do...do you know about the Blight?"

A furrow formed between her brows.

Mother Goddess, she didn't know. Cora desperately did not want to be the one to tell her, and she'd find out for herself soon enough. But didn't Ailan deserve a warning at least?

"The land around the Veil is dying," Cora confessed. "It's a consequence of the *mora* pouring from El'Ara into the human world and being unable to return. Your people call the dying land the Blight. Pathweavers can't use their magic to traverse that part of El'Ara. The triggers may not work there either."

Ailan paled with every word. "I didn't know. Though I should have. Of course there would be consequences to losing El'Ara's heart."

"Having to walk sounds like the least of our worries," Mareleau said in a dry tone that somehow alleviated Cora's guilt. Not that the Blight was in any way Cora's fault, yet she wished she'd have told Ailan sooner. Even Cora had been saddened to see the dead, colorless land of the Blight. She couldn't imagine how much worse it would be for someone who loved that land.

Ailan steeled her expression. "It changes nothing where our plans are concerned. Let's proceed."

~

THEY LEFT THE WAGON DEEP IN THE WOODS AWAY FROM THE ROAD AND SET THE TWO horses free. Valorre was rather smug about this, but Cora hoped the horses were intelligent enough to make their way back to the Forest People. The wagon itself would have to remain where it was. Thankfully, it posed little threat as evidence. There was nothing inside that would reveal it was ever home to Ailan, only that it belonged to a nomad. Anyone who stumbled upon it would likely assume the owner had met an ill fate while camped there.

Ailan shouldered Mareleau's bag of belongings while Cora touched each of her weapons in turn—bow, quiver, dagger. A comforting routine in preparation to step off a cliff and return to a realm she wasn't welcome in. Noah was nestled close to his mother's chest in the carrying sling Salinda had gifted Mareleau. Together the party left the woods and approached the road. Dawn was spilling farther over the landscape with every minute, requiring more caution as they crossed over to the cliffside. Cora's gaze darted left and right, her mental shields down, senses extended in case anyone approached. They were still alone. Still safe.

Ailan stepped to the edge and reached into the sky. Her hand disappeared at once. "Cora, do you want to go first?"

Devils, no, but what choice did she have? If Ailan went first, Cora and Mareleau would be left to find the tear on their own. And she wasn't going to make Mareleau go first.

Swallowing her fear, she took a step—

I think not, Valorre said darting in front of her. *I will test the safety of the tear. We can't rely on those inelegant dragons, after all.* With his head held high, he trotted toward Ailan's half-invisible hand. In a matter of heartbeats, he was gone.

Cora had to admit, her arrogant friend had emboldened her. With a fortifying breath, she stepped to the edge of the cliff and extended her hand near Ailan's until it plunged into nothingness. She paused, releasing her breath in a trembling exhale.

Then she stepped off the cliff...

And stepped onto colorless earth. The Blight was blindingly bright after the dim light of dawn, invading her senses with shades of gray. The only color was the cloud-speckled blue sky overhead.

Valorre stood before her, tossing his mane. Despite his earlier confidence, he radiated relief at seeing her hale and whole on this side of the Veil. Cora stepped out of the way to give room to her companions. The Veil was nothing more than a wall of swirling particles of pale mist. Even though it looked like something soft and insubstantial, she knew firsthand that it would feel as firm as a wall should she try to touch it. Aside from the tear, she supposed.

A hand shot through the mist, quickly followed by a body. Mareleau planted both feet before the Veil, her eyes squeezed tight, her arms wrapped protectively around Noah in his sling.

Cora put a hand on her shoulder. "You're all right, Mare. You made it."

Mareleau forced her eyes open and stumbled toward Cora. "That was terrifying."

A second later, Ailan followed, emerging from the mist with far more grace. But as her eyes darted across the landscape, her expression crumpled. Her hand flung to her lips, and she widened her stance as if to keep steady. "This is so much worse than I expected."

All around them was parched soil and the gnarled stumps of long-dead trees. There was no sign of the jewel-toned forests, groves, and meadows Cora had seen on her way to the Blight the first time she'd come here.

Tears glazed Ailan's eyes as she turned back toward the Veil. Extending a hand, she pressed her palm to the swirling particles. Cora watched with rapt attention. Did she know of a way to call the *mora* back? She had claimed to be regent over fae magic until Noah came of age.

With a frustrated groan, Ailan dropped her hand, her fingers curling into a fist. "The *mora* can be called back to the land, but the tear is too thin. It's like pulling it through the finest sieve. The effort to complete such a task...I don't even want to estimate how long it would take."

A shadow fell over them, bringing with it the beat of wings. A gust of wind sent gray soil swirling about as Uziel landed. Cora, Mareleau, and Valorre backed away as the dragon nuzzled Ailan's shoulder. It was similar enough to how Valorre comforted Cora that she could almost find it cute.

Almost.

Ailan's posture relaxed. She turned her gaze to Cora. "Does your magic work here?"

Cora nodded. She'd escaped El'Ara with her abilities before. Her magic hadn't been hampered by the Blight, nor had Fanon's or Etrix's. Fanon had still been able to use his invisible restraints while Etrix's translation weaving had remained. Only Garot seemed unable to weave in the Blight. The only thing that had held Cora back had been the collar she'd been burdened with.

Her skin crawled, remembering its tines piercing her neck, the empty void where her magic had been. She resisted the urge to tuck her hand in her cloak pocket, where the collar remained hidden. She hated carrying it on her person, bringing it to the very place where it had been used against her. But she couldn't have left it in the wagon. Not if she wanted to avoid leaving evidence behind.

"Will you use it?" Ailan said, stepping away from Uziel. "Will you take us somewhere beyond the Blight? Somewhere a pathweaver can reach us quickly?"

Cora's stomach turned. "Are you sure? My magic is hated here. Fanon will be enraged—"

"I don't care." Her voice was so tired. So empty. "I don't want to look at this dying land a second longer than I must. If anyone tries to condemn you for doing what I asked of you, they can take it up with me."

Cora gave a reluctant nod. "I'll try. Gather around me and Valorre."

At a word from Ailan, Uziel launched into the sky. Ailan and Mareleau followed Cora's directions, crowding in close. "We need to make physical contact, and I need to be touching Valorre. Do not break contact, even if I move."

She pressed a palm to Valorre's hide, then clasped Mareleau's palm with her free hand. Ailan settled her hand on Cora's shoulder. Closing her eyes, Cora focused on each point of contact in turn, then envisioned the meadow she and Valorre had traveled to. The image came to mind easily, courtesy of Valorre's clear memory. She shifted her stance, felt the dry earth beneath her shoes, and imagined the plush grass of the meadow. Instead of rot filling her senses, she imagined crisp air and fresh greenery. After acknowledging her companions once more— Mareleau's hand in hers, Noah's sleeping presence in his sling, Ailan's palm on her shoulder, then Valorre's warm hide—she took a small step forward.

She smelled the change of air before she opened her eyes. Heard hollow silence turn to birdsong. As she blinked into warm sunlight, she found the green meadow all around, her companions beside her. They stepped apart and a wave of dizziness washed over her, reminding her of the toll worldwalking with others took on her.

Then they waited.

But it didn't take long.

A swirling vortex of green and brown warped the air at the edge of the meadow until it was as wide as a doorway. Three familiar figures strode through it, one with dark hair, one with copper tresses, and one with honeyed locks and sharp blue eyes. Etrix, Garot, and Fanon. The vortex disappeared as soon as all three were outside it.

Fanon's lips peeled back from his teeth, his eyes widening as they landed on Cora.

Ailan stepped forward, arms spread, commanding the attention of the Elvyn males.

The three pulled up short.

Fanon's chest heaved as if he'd been struck by an invisible blow. He staggered back, but his legs gave out beneath him. He sank to his knees. "Ailan."

With a slow and careful stride, she approached Fanon, then softly laid a hand on his shoulder. "Hello, Fanon dear," she said, voice quavering. "It's been a long time."

34

Mareleau's cheeks heated. The reunion before her was chaste in every way, yet she could see the passion, yearning, and agony that filled the blond Elvyn's eyes. Tears streamed down his cheeks as he tipped his head back and whispered something Mareleau couldn't understand. She'd be more moved by the couple's reunion if she didn't know exactly who the blond was —Fanon, the Elvyn who'd been cruel to Cora.

Her gaze swept to the other two figures. They must be Etrix and Garot, the other two males Cora had told her about. Etrix was the tallest with umber skin and black hair braided with gold and silver thread. Garot was the shortest and widest of the three and had fiery hair, tan skin spattered with bronze freckles, and green eyes. All three appeared no more than ten years her senior, but there was something about them that made them seem ancient and ageless at the same time. Etrix carried himself in a way that made Mareleau think he was the eldest. All had pointed ears like Ailan and were dressed in silk trousers and matching robes belted with a wide sash. She didn't miss the sword each carried at their hips either.

Tightening her hold around Noah in his sling, she sidled closer to Cora and Valorre. She was grateful the attention was fully on Ailan and not them, but it didn't soothe her nerves. All around her was evidence of just how far from home she truly was. The meadow they stood in rippled with blades of grass as high as her calves and as green as the brightest emerald. Willow trees danced in the breeze, their long branches swaying with more motion than a tree should ever have. Butterflies alighted on rainbow-hued dewdrops and carried them away, but their wings were far too vibrant for a regular butterfly. And too plentiful; some had as many wings as a rose had petals. The birdsong that filled the air was melodic but unlike anything she'd heard. It was lovely and terrifying all at once. She wasn't sure whether she wanted to keep looking around the meadow in search of new surprises...or force her eyes to remain only on the familiar.

Ailan stepped away from Fanon. Her fingers lingered on Fanon's cheek for several long moments as she turned to face the other two.

Garot bent in a formal bow and said something in Elvyn. Ailan acknowledged the gesture with a hand to his shoulder. He beamed as he straightened. She approached Etrix next. His dark eyes were turned down at the corners and glazed with tears, yet his posture was stiff. He seemed uncertain how to greet her. Then Ailan folded against his chest, arms around his waist. He in turn wrapped his arms around her and rested his cheek against the top of her head.

Cora leaned in and whispered, "Etrix is Ailan's father."

That caught Fanon's attention. He'd risen to his feet and now shot cold blue eyes their way. While the snarl he'd first worn was gone, there was no warmth in his expression.

Mareleau's first instinct was to shrink beneath that open hostility, but she wasn't made for shrinking. Instead, she lifted her chin and held his gaze right back with an equally cold stare, eyes narrowing until he finally looked away. She resisted the urge to laugh. That had been too easy. She hadn't even employed her magic trick. Or her Art, as Cora and Salinda called it. Either way, the Elvyn were mistaken if they thought they could beat her at a glaring contest. If anyone could destroy a man with a look alone, it was Mareleau.

Ailan released Etrix from her embrace and asked him something in that same incomprehensible language. With a nod, Etrix took a step back and lifted a hand. Then, crossing two of his fingers, he slid them through the air in a horizontal line.

"Translation enchantment," Cora explained, but she hadn't needed to, for when Fanon spoke next, Mareleau understood him.

"Will you tell us why *they're* here?"

With a smile, Ailan gestured toward Cora. "This is my dear friend and ally, Cora. Formally, she is Aveline Caelan, Queen of Khero."

"So we meet again," Garot said, his face splitting with an easy grin. His gaze shifted to Valorre. "Your friend as well. What a dashing little vest he's wearing. A bit clunky, but—"

"Do you know what she is?" Fanon jutted his chin toward Cora, a motion that carried as much violence as a raised blade. "Do you know she's a witch? A world-walker? And what in the *mora's* name is that unicorn wearing?"

Mareleau had forgotten how strange it might be to see a unicorn in a saddle, but she was used to the sight by now.

Valorre snorted in response, a derisive sound even to her ears.

"I know exactly what and who she is," Ailan said, ignoring the jibe at Valorre. "I have known her for many years. And based on what she's told me, I am not pleased by how you've treated her in the past."

Fanon paled but said nothing in his defense.

"If you're done making my ally feel unwelcome," Ailan said, "I have someone else I'd like you to meet. Pray you get your salutations right this time around."

She left the three Elvyn to stand at Mareleau's side, then placed a gentle hand on her shoulder. "This is the blood of my blood, Mareleau Alante, Queen of Vera."

"*Khero* and *Vera* mean nothing to us," Etrix said. There was no reproach in his tone, only truth.

"Khero and Vera are the two kingdoms that comprise the land on the other side of the Veil," Ailan said. "The land we once called Le'Lana."

"The land the humans stole," Fanon said with a scoff.

Ailan ignored him. "There's one more I want to introduce you to."

Keeping one hand on Mareleau's shoulder, Ailan rested the other on the outside of the carrying sling. Mareleau resisted the urge to flinch away. She wasn't fond of unwarranted touch, but there was something comforting about Ailan's gesture. She was claiming Mareleau and Noah as her own. In this situation, it was a welcome protection.

"Please meet Noah, blood of my blood and Morkara of El'Ara."

Etrix bent a knee first, folding into a formal display of obeisance. Garot followed.

Only Fanon hesitated. "Our...Morkara. Not *future* Morkara, not merely your heir."

"Yes."

"You relinquished your title to a...a baby."

"I had my reasons." She held his gaze with unwavering authority, much like Mareleau had done, until Fanon bent his knee like the others. For the first time, Mareleau felt a kinship with the woman. Perhaps breaking men with fierce looks had been passed down through bloodline.

"Rise," Ailan said after a few long moments.

The three rose to their feet. Garot spoke with palpable excitement. "We have a Morkara again. This is a moment for future stories! A heroic return to tell for ages, and I'm here to witness it. I can hardly believe my luck."

Etrix spoke with far more sobriety. "Can we stop the Blight? As regent, you can move the *mora* on the Morkara's behalf. You can finish Satsara's Veil—"

"There's much more we must discuss before we take action," Ailan said. "Everything we do will have vast consequences. Calling the *mora* back is no small feat. Even if I called back enough to strengthen a team of our greatest ward-weavers, it would take time to untie the edges of my mother's ward and finish where she left off. And that's without considering that Darius will try to invade before we can finish the Veil, or the thousands upon thousands of humans who inhabit Lela."

"What happens to the humans is beneath our concern," Fanon said.

"What happens to the humans is of *my* concern," Ailan said, "which makes it yours. Your duties as steward have been fulfilled. I am here now, so you will heed my word."

There was no room for argument with the edge infusing her tone.

"As you wish, regent." Fanon spoke through his teeth, but there was a softening around his eyes that harkened back to their bittersweet reunion.

She returned that look, then addressed the others. "The situation may be complex, but I agree it is one we must address at once. Garot, please weave us a path to..."

Etrix finished for her. "Alles'Taria Palace. We kept the name of the original seat of the Morkara, to honor the palace that was lost in El'Ara's heart."

The palace that was lost...

Centerpointe Rock.

Cora had told Mareleau about the rock's origins. While she'd never seen it, only heard about it from Larylis and Cora, the thought that an entire palace could be whittled down to a single ruin like that was chilling.

"To Alles'Taria Palace, then," Ailan said. "Once we reach it, weave a secondary path to take Cora and Mareleau straight to a private room. I don't want anyone gawking at our guests, or even knowing they're here until we've spoken with the tribunal."

Garot strolled to the edge of the meadow and gestured with a complex wave of his fingers. The swirling vortex they'd emerged from opened once more. "Right this way."

Ailan gave an encouraging nod for Cora and Mareleau to follow. Valorre tossed his mane, clearly as reluctant as Mareleau was. Yet she followed nonetheless, stomach turning with every step she took toward the three Elvyn and the strange tunnel. She nearly lost her footing as they entered the Vortex. While the ground remained solid beneath her feet, the swirling colors of green and brown made it impossible to keep her bearings. So she fixed her gaze on Ailan's back instead. The Elvyn closed in behind them.

She cast a squinted look at Cora. Her friend's grimace told her she was tolerating the nauseating tunnel just as poorly. Mareleau leaned in close. "Yet another situation that could have gone better."

"To be honest," Cora whispered back, "I think it could have gone far, far worse."

An ominous statement, yet Cora would know. The collar she carried was proof enough of just how bad a human could fare in El'Ara. That made the back of her neck prickle as they walked on down the dizzying path with no end in sight. But worse than her fear of what lay ahead was the dread that swelled inside her, growing with every breath, every heartbeat. It reminded her that every minute here was hours back home. Hours were days. A single day was a week.

Being away from Larylis this long was already torment enough.

How much harder would it be for him?

35

It had been four days since Larylis had last seen his wife and held his son in his arms, and every minute was like a spear to the chest. Not even the letter Berol had delivered three nights ago had alleviated the pain. If anything, it had only made it worse. For now, he knew his wife and child were going far beyond his reach.

At least they'd be safe.

He stared out the window in Verlot Palace's Royal Study at the mountains and forest awash with sunset hues. Instead of the pink-kissed green that comprised his view, he wished he could cast his gaze over the Balma Sea and pinpoint the enemy. But not even reports from the southwest lighthouses had caught sight of the fleet.

He'd arrived at Verlot that morning after maintaining a breakneck pace with only the closest members of his retinue. He'd already met with his council and analyzed the updates from the scouts.

No reports of enemy activity. No reports of unexpected ships approaching Vera's shores.

It was too early to expect much as far as his scouts' efforts were concerned, for he'd only dispatched them by land and sea days ago. Yet shouldn't he have received *something*? Some word that the prisoner's warning was true?

He'd done the calculations a thousand times in his head, and on paper a thousand times more, assessing different routes, different ports, different hidden harbors. No matter how many times he tried to come to a new conclusion, he couldn't. Because if Darius had launched his fleet *before* the prisoner had left to spy in Khero, even if only days before the man had gotten caught and taken into custody, it didn't change that the ships should already be here. They should at least be in sight. If they were staying in the channel, waiting to make the rest of the journey at some later date, merchant ships would have passed, giving scouts some information to glean from talk at the ports.

More troubling was Teryn's newest update, delivered by Berol mere hours ago. Ever since Berol had brought Mareleau's letter, he and Teryn had utilized her to exchange daily updates. Unlike messenger horses, the falcon could fly between the two castles, one direction and back again, in less than a day. So far every update from Teryn had been the same. No news. No updates. Then today…

The prisoner has been killed.

Larylis planted his hands on the windowsill, squinting at the mountain range in the distance but not truly seeing it. He assessed the facts. The prisoner had confessed to Darius being in southern Norun, and that he'd summoned his fleet to make landfall in southwest Vera. Within days, the spy had been found dead in his cell. He'd clearly been punished and silenced, and from someone inside Ridine at that.

And yet…

Larylis pushed off the windowsill and paced before the desk. He couldn't shake the feeling that something was wrong. He may not have emotion magic like Cora, nor was he a seer like Emylia, but the last time he'd had this horrible feeling—when he'd feared his wife was in danger at Ridine last summer—he'd been right. He'd received a warning from Cora back then, and he could have dismissed it, yet his instincts had picked up on a danger he had no explanation for.

And it was happening again.

He knew why. Knew which piece of the puzzle disturbed him the most.

If there was a traitor in the castle, someone who could enter the cell and kill a man without getting caught by the guards or gaoler, they could have silenced the prisoner sooner. Or freed him. Why act only after he'd talked?

The skin at the back of his neck prickled, and he recalled an echo from history. He strode over to one of the many bookshelves lining the study walls. The massive collection of historical records and tales were a new addition after Larylis and Mareleau had inherited Verlot Palace as their secondary residence. Larylis could always think better and clearer when surrounded by books, and with every step he took toward the shelf, the sharper his mind became.

He picked up the book he was looking for and opened it toward the back. Flipping pages, he scanned the text until his gaze landed on the name and date he sought.

King Samuel. The Battle of San Dohrinas. Year 159 of the Eagle.

He read the brief record of the battle, pausing when he found the paragraph he was most interested in.

After days of withstanding torture, the spy in King Samuel's custody revealed where Borfian's forces would invade and gave three locations that they would attack. King Samuel divided his army and sent forces to each location, leaving only a small garrison in San Dohrinas. The city proved to be the true object of Borfian's attack, and the fortress fell in a fortnight.

Larylis closed the book and returned it to the shelf. The case he'd just read about wasn't the first or last of its kind, but it was the most recent he'd studied. The king had done his due diligence to ensure the spy's information was correct.

Enemy forces had been spotted in two of the locations, so he'd trusted the third would soon follow. Yet in the end, the two forces had been a bluff and the third hadn't existed at all. The prisoner had gotten captured and tortured on purpose, all to misdirect the king. And even though King Samuel hadn't fully abandoned the city, he'd divided his numbers enough to give Borfian the win.

That was what *this* felt like now. Like they were being toyed with. Divided. On purpose.

The spy had given three pieces of intel: that Syrus and Norun had allied, that Darius was physically present in Norun, and that he'd summoned a fleet from Syrus. The first could be easily confirmed. They'd already suspected the alliance between Syrus and Norun. The second could soon be confirmed as well. As for the last...

Well, the fact that the prisoner had been silenced was proof enough that what he'd said was true.

But what if it wasn't?

Larylis gritted his teeth. The whole situation felt like a mind game. A battle of facts versus instinct. He couldn't call off his scouts. He couldn't ignore the potential that the fleet truly was coming. But he wouldn't sit around and wait to be made a fool of either.

~

"THE CORPSE AND THE PRISONER ARE NOT THE SAME MAN," THE GAOLER SAID, gesturing toward the cloth-draped body inside the cell. The burlap covering did nothing to hide the smell.

Teryn breathed through his mouth, desperate to get this meeting over with so he could leave the dungeon. He'd been in one of these cells before, and his stay had been anything but pleasant. Though at least there hadn't been a rotting corpse back then.

"I'm not supposed to be here," said a frail voice. Teryn did his best to ignore it, for it was coming from the pale apparition that hovered over the dead body. It locked hollow, pleading eyes on Teryn. "Please. I'm not supposed to be here."

Teryn averted his gaze to the gaoler. The man was an inch taller than Teryn, which was saying something, for Teryn was used to being the tallest in most crowds. His arms were roped with muscle and scars, and his deep-set eyes were lined with creases. His lips were thin yet wide and he had a head of shaggy brown hair that reached his shoulders. Though Teryn hadn't interacted with many a gaoler before, he looked exactly like a man who chained and beat people for a living.

He'd also been Teryn's primary suspect for murdering the prisoner. *Had been* being the key, for the gaoler had an alibi. Everyone, it seemed, had a damn alibi, from the guards to the cooks to the dungeon sweepers.

"That's not the same man, Majesty," the gaoler said again. "I've beaten the living piss out of the prisoner. I'd know him if I'd seen 'im. *He* is not the same."

Teryn shifted his gaze from the gaoler to Captain Alden, who stood off to the side. She shook her head. "He looked like the same man to me. I only saw him with bruises on his face."

The gaoler nodded eagerly. "I put them bruises there. But not those ones. They ain't even in the right places. Whoever put 'em there wanted the bastard unrecognizable."

"I'm not supposed to be here," the ghost lamented, stepping away from the body.

Teryn assessed the semi-transparent figure before asking the gaoler, "What did the prisoner look like before you, uh, beat the living piss out of him?"

"Older man. Gray hair. Slender. A real wily bastard. Bad attitude. Thinks e's cleverer then 'e is."

Teryn's gaze flashed to the ghost. He could only assume the spirit belonged to the corpse, and even though Teryn couldn't be sure the man's hair was gray, for the apparition was colorless, he matched the physical description enough.

"I'm tellin' ye, Majesty." The gaoler crossed his enormous arms over his chest. "Not the same man."

"Thank you for your time," Teryn said. "You may go."

The gaoler gave a clumsy bow and left Teryn and Captain Alden alone before the cell.

Teryn arched a brow and lowered his voice. "We're sure he's not our man?"

"He was off duty at the time the prisoner was murdered," Alden said. "His wife confirmed it, as did the guards. The guards themselves patrolled in pairs, and each soldier has confirmed their partner's presence. None saw any suspicious characters leave or enter the dungeon hall."

Teryn had already been told as much. No one had seen anything strange. No unfamiliar servants. No delayed guard rotations. He had to acknowledge that much of the castle's staff was relatively new and more positions were constantly being filled as the crown regained its wealth and stability. So could he truly trust that there hadn't been a suspicious soul in sight during that time?

"I'm not supposed to be here." The ghost approached the open cell door. Well, Teryn supposed there was one suspicious soul after all.

"Will you give me a moment, Captain?"

Alden's brows knit, but she folded into an obedient bow.

Once alone, Teryn faced the ghost. "Who are you?" he whispered.

"You...you can see me. I knew you could." His voice trembled, as thin and frail as a fallen leaf.

Teryn reworded his question. "What is your name?"

"John McMullighan, sir. Or...Majesty."

That wasn't the name on record for the prisoner. Not that anyone believed the name the spy had given. Vlad Samarus. The surname was one of the most common in Norun and practically screamed *fake*.

"Where are you from?" Teryn asked.

"I'm from northern Khero, Majesty. Greenfair Village."

Teryn pondered the village name. It was north of Ridine Castle. "How did you come to be in this cell?"

The ghost's voice turned pleading again. "I don't know. I was at the tavern after a hard week's work, same as usual. I headed home after a few pints, and then...I have no memories of what happened. Next thing I know, I...I'm looking at my body."

If the ghost's tale was true, perhaps the gaoler was right after all. That was, of course, even more troubling. It meant the prisoner hadn't been murdered for giving away intel. Instead, he'd been freed and replaced with a decoy.

Seven devils...

The prisoner was free. He'd left them with key information about the enemy, but what could he have gleaned in exchange? What had he learned that he could now use against them? And most pressing of all, who the hell had freed the man? Who was the traitor?

Teryn rubbed his jaw. This was bad.

"Take me home." The ghost reached for Teryn's hand, making Teryn launch a step back.

Yearning struck him then, the same he'd felt when the warrior wraith had looked at him from the charred field. "What do you mean, take you home?"

"I don't want to be here. I'm not supposed to be here. I...I want to go back. I have a home, a family. You must take me home."

Pity tightened Teryn's chest. "You can't go home. Your body is dead."

The ghost stepped forward again. "You can take me home. You can make this end."

"I don't know what you mean."

The spirit's tone took on an eerie quality, edged with desperation. The yearning sensation grew, multiplied tenfold. "You are a black flame, burning like the embrace of a cruel mother. As final as death. As comforting as home. Take me home. Take me home. TAKE ME HOME."

"Fine," he rushed to say. He didn't know what he was agreeing to, only that he wanted to stop the specter's frantic wailing. The ghost reached for Teryn's hand again, and this time he didn't flinch away. This time, he extended his palm.

Fingers he couldn't feel closed around his hand. The spirit's expression shifted from agonized to peaceful in the blink of an eye.

Then he was gone.

So was the yearning.

Teryn stared at the place the spirit had been, then down at his hand. There was nothing to explain what had happened, only the ghost's desperate final words.

Emylia's too.

...if I get too close, I'll cease to exist.

Did Teryn have the ability...to send wandering spirits to the otherlife? Was that yearning coming from the dead, from their craving for oblivion?

His breaths pulsed sharp and shallow as his mind reeled to comprehend what all of this meant. His connection to ghosts wasn't an Art of the six senses, nor was it an earthly power like the Faeryn wielded. He wasn't a witch, an Elvyn weaver, or a Faeryn descendant.

Which left one question.

What am I?

36

Elvyn baths were disturbing. Not that they were unpleasant. Quite the opposite, in fact. Cora reclined in a tub that was nestled in a private, dimly lit room attached to the borrowed bedroom Garot had brought her and Mareleau to via pathweaving. Crystalline sconces lined the walls, lit with a faint luminescence that glowed too unwaveringly to be a flame. The floor was a gold-veined white marble, and the walls were a pale blue crystal, giving the impression that one was walking on clouds. The adjoining bedroom looked the same but with arched windows covered in gold filigree shutters.

The basin she soaked in was larger than anything she'd used at Ridine, twice as wide as her body. It was carved from the same blue crystal as the walls and was perched upon gilded feet. There was no need to wait for servants to haul in buckets of boiled water, for warm liquid poured from a tap at the turn of a handle. It was an impossible magic that Garot had explained as if it were commonplace. That was the disturbing part. For a land that utilized magic that was supposedly weakened by the Veil, this bath was nothing short of a miracle. What greater miracles were the Elvyn capable of when the *mora* was at full strength?

These were Cora's musings as she soaked in the tub, submerged to her neck in lilac-scented water. Her muscles uncoiled with every breath, though she couldn't fully relinquish her anxiety. At the back of her mind remained the constant chiming of an imaginary clock, one that ticked the hours that were passing in the human world. Hours where anything could be happening. Hours she'd never get back. There was nothing she could do, of course. Until the tribunal meeting was over and she had some form of an alliance to bring back to her people, all she could do was wait.

And there were, admittedly, more unbearable ways to wait than in a comfortable bath.

Ah, so you aren't being tortured, came Valorre's mental voice. *That is good to know.*

Another layer of relief unraveled at the feel of his not-too-distant presence. *It seems you aren't either.*

They'd parted in the woods outside the palace before Garot had taken her and Mareleau to their room. She hadn't wanted to separate from him, especially when he still wore the saddle laden with Cora's belongings—her bow and quiver, especially, which Ailan had requested she not bring inside the palace. She feared Valorre may be subjected to the same disdain Fanon had shown. Perhaps even from his own kind, should he cross paths with other unicorns. Yet now, as she connected with her unicorn companion, she got the distinct sense of carefree frolicking.

You must be having fun, she said.

I'm only tolerating my surroundings. There just so happens to be a rather nice meadow outside the palace.

She chuckled. *And I'm only tolerating this bath.*

You see, we are of the same mind.

She wanted to tell him it was all right if he liked this place. El'Ara was once his home, after all. But she held her tongue, for it would only offend him. He was feigning dislike of El'Ara out of solidarity, and if she wanted to confront that, she might have to confront something far more unpleasant.

That maybe this was where he belonged.

Cora soaked until the water began to cool. Only then did she force herself from the tub. She felt bad for having left Mareleau alone for so long, but her friend had been curt and pensive after Garot had departed, and the tangled emotions that seeped into Cora made her think Mareleau might have wanted some time alone. Cora had felt the same. They had so many uncertainties and very few answers. There was much to process and little that could be helped with sympathy or discussion. Not until after the meeting. Which would—hopefully—commence soon.

Outside the tub, she found a bath sheet so plush it almost felt criminal to dry herself off on it. Yet dry herself she did, marveling all the while at its softness and absorbency. Next, she turned her attention to the clothing Garot had left behind along with his suggestion that she dress in traditional Elvyn attire for the meeting. She inspected each article, finding flowing silk trousers, a matching robe, and a gold sash. The silk was the finest quality and a shade of indigo so deep it was almost black. Gold lace and delicate embroidery lined the robe's hems while stars and moon phases decorated the skirt and bodice. She could tell at a glance that the robe was not meant to be worn with a corset. That was all for the better, as the clothing and undergarments she'd arrived in were in grave need of laundering.

Despite the ensemble's simplistic design, once she was dressed, she felt as elegant as she'd be in a ballgown. More than that, she was supremely comfortable. She hated to admit it, but the Elvyn may be onto something in terms of fashion.

She strode to her pile of clothing and extracted two items hidden beneath—the magic-suppressing collar and her beautiful dagger. The first item she tucked into one of her robe's pockets. The latter, she hid behind her back in the folds of her sash. That filled her with a sense of calm. Control. A reminder that she wasn't defenseless in this place where most considered her an enemy.

As she left the bathroom, voices reached her ears. She entered the bedroom and found Mareleau wasn't alone. Her friend sat at the edge of the massive four-poster bed, dressed in a pale blue version of Cora's new attire, bouncing a silk-swaddled Noah in her arms. An anxious expression twisted her features, and several messy braids hung from her freshly brushed tresses. Beside her stood Ailan and Garot.

Garot greeted Cora with a grin. His presence suggested he would take them directly to the meeting and not through the halls of the palace. That made Cora's anxiety flare with a sharp pinch. She'd hardly glimpsed more than a few towering white spires over the treetops before Garot had whisked her and Mareleau directly to their room. The view outside the arched windows in the bedroom revealed sky, forest, distant mountains, and a dizzying view of the landscape far below. Not having a clearer visual of the palace itself made her feel like a prisoner. It reminded her too much of when she'd been stuck in her beautiful room at Verlot Palace while King Verdian questioned her identity for weeks on end.

She swallowed her panic and brushed her fingertips over the back of her sash, taking comfort in the firm lines of her hidden dagger. "Is it time?" she asked as she approached the others.

Ailan nodded. She too had bathed and changed since they'd parted ways outside the palace. The bottom half of her long black hair flowed freely around her shoulders while the top was arranged in several intertwining braids around the crown of her head. Her robe was even more stunning than Cora's, in shades of crimson, saffron, and persimmon, patterned with botanicals Cora had no name for. Her sleeves trailed nearly to the floor while her sash glittered with multihued jewels. She looked every inch a royal.

"We've gathered the tribunal," Ailan said. "I've spoken to them on my own and discussed all that can be discussed without you present."

Cora hadn't been aware that any portion of the meeting would be held without them, but she wasn't disappointed to have missed anything. She was here to forge an alliance and nothing more.

Ailan spoke again. "I've secured a binding vow from every member on the tribunal that they accept, honor, and protect Noah as their Morkara, despite his human blood. There was very little they could do to contest it, but it didn't stop them from arguing over his origins for the better part of an hour."

Cora winced. She was indeed glad to have missed that in favor of her overlong soak in the tub. But something snagged her attention. "What do you mean by a binding vow?"

"The High Fae are bound by vows, bargains, and promises when stated with certain words. Breaking them results in immediate Last Breath."

Cora's eyes widened. Faerytales often spoke of fae bargains but this was the first time she'd heard confirmation of the tales' validity. The same tales also claimed fae couldn't lie, which Valorre had demonstrated to be false numerous times. And Ailan had convinced the Forest People she was dying.

Mareleau narrowed her eyes. "You said you discussed all you can without us present. What exactly are we needed there for? Will we only be talking about the alliance?"

Ailan's expression turned wary. "There are certain formalities we need to proceed with. I may have final say as regent, but the tribunal ensures the Elvyn people get a voice in every decision we make. They would like to discuss...you and Cora. Your human heritage forbids you from being here, which means we need to establish new rules regarding your presence."

Her words had Cora's muscles tensing. "You're putting us on trial."

"I'm not going to lie," Ailan said. "It may feel like that. But they *will* accept you. They may request a demonstration of trust. From Cora in particular. A guarantee that you won't use your magic against them."

Her blood went cold. The collar tucked in the pocket of her robe suddenly felt heavier. She could guess what a guarantee of protection would look like to the Elvyn.

Ailan sighed. "I know it sounds offensive. You've done nothing wrong. Yet our people establish trust through binding vows, and those with human blood cannot make them. The Elvyn people learned the hard way with Darius."

The edges of Cora's indignation softened slightly. Tristaine and Darius were the only humans the Elvyn had ever dealt with, and neither painted a pleasant picture for her kind. As much as she hated bearing such cold suspicion, she could almost understand it.

Even as it boiled her blood.

"Fine," she bit out. "I'll establish trust however I can."

It was for the alliance. Her people *needed* this alliance. They needed any advantage they could get to face Darius when he inevitably came. Yet as Garot opened his swirling tunnel and ushered Cora and her companions inside, she was left to ponder: how could she establish trust with people who saw her as a villain?

37

The tunnel ceased its spinning in a matter of seconds. The whirling colors of ivory, blue, and gold melted outward to form a hallway featuring the same gold-veined marble floors as the bedroom and bathroom, the same blue crystalline walls. At the end of the hall was a pair of white doors painted with intricate gold vines. Etrix stood before them and greeted his daughter with a formal bow.

"We're ready, regent," he said as he straightened. The fact that Cora understood his words told her he'd already woven his translation enchantment.

However, Cora wasn't sure *she* was ready, and from the way Mareleau edged closer to her, arms cradling her son tightly to her chest, her friend was equally as apprehensive. Cora had been to plenty of council meetings now that she was queen, but was an Elvyn tribunal the same as a council?

They weren't given long to ponder, for Etrix pushed open the doors and led the way inside. The room beyond was a wide, circular shape and darker than the hall had been. The sconces that lined the walls offered only a faint glow. The rest of the light came from overhead, where dazzling flashes of illumination darted beneath a domed ceiling. Cora blinked up at the lights; they came from glowing wings. Were they...butterflies? They cast the room in shades of blue and green. But as she stepped farther into the room, their wings glowed brighter, shifting to yellow and orange. Some deepened to a fiery red.

"Hold out your hand," Etrix said. Cora stopped in place and dragged her eyes from the ceiling to find her companions had halted too. Ailan stood beside Etrix. A butterfly hovered over each of their heads; Etrix's was blue while Ailan's flickered between green and yellow. She didn't see Garot until she noticed him settling into a chair nearby, a blue butterfly over his head. That drew her attention to the circular perimeter of the room and the three tiers of seating that lined the walls, the highest tier being the closest to the walls while the lowest circled the floor at the very center of the room. An Elvyn figure occupied almost every chair, leaving a few empty at the innermost tier.

Remembering what Etrix had said, she turned her gaze back to him and lifted her hand. A butterfly fluttered down from the ceiling and alighted on the back of her hand. Up close, she saw it had a total of eight delicate wings, all of which glowed a cloudy yellow-green. Just as quickly as it had touched down, it launched back into the air. This time, it hovered over her head and remained there, much like the ones floating above Etrix, Ailan, and Garot. Another glance at the dome showed most of the butterflies had dispersed and now fluttered above individual Elvyn figures. The light from their wings illuminated harsh stares as well as some curious expressions like Garot wore. Her eyes fell on another familiar face—Fanon—flickering orange beneath the glow of his butterfly. His eyes narrowed slightly as he met Cora's gaze, and she turned her attention to Mareleau.

It was her turn to claim a butterfly. Mareleau's eyes danced, expression enchanted, as the winged creature perched upon her hand shifted to a blue glow before hovering above her head.

"Their colors match our moods and emotions," Ailan explained, voice low. "They ensure no one hides their true feelings from the rest of the tribunal. They also allow us to wordlessly demonstrate our choices when voting on a decision."

That drained the pleasant aspects of Cora's fascination. Now she felt naked. She was used to experiencing others' emotions, but to have hers bared for others...

The light above her head shifted to orange. If the Elvyn associated color with emotions the same way the Forest People did—especially the more artistically inclined—blue would represent baseline calm, progressing into deeper emotions with teal, green, and yellow, then ending with more heated emotions represented by orange and red. White and violet were often used to express pure or spiritual aspects of magic.

The orange wings overhead made her annoyance clear for all to see. She gritted her teeth.

"Come," Etrix said, gesturing toward the empty chairs at the innermost tier, "take a seat."

Cora and Mareleau exchanged a wary glance before following him to the center of the room, then to the velvet-upholstered wingback chairs. They were about to sit down when shuffling movement had them halting in place. The Elvyn rose from their seats to kneel beside their chairs, heads bowed low. A murmur of *Morkara* rumbled through the room. Cora's eyes darted from the bowed heads to Ailan, only to find her kneeling beside Etrix.

Right. Ailan wasn't Morkara. Noah was.

Mareleau noticed at the same time, her cheeks flushing at the attention her son was receiving. Finally, the figures rose and returned to their seats. Cora and Mareleau did the same.

Ailan sat between Mareleau and Fanon, while Etrix stood at the center of the room. Cora recalled from her first time in El'Ara that Etrix was Head of Tribunal. "Now that we've had our brief recess, we can discuss the last of our topics."

"We should address the criminal offense first," one of the Elvyn seated on the second tier said. A red butterfly cast his cold expression, his pursed lips, his angled ears beneath short dark hair, in a crimson glow.

Cora bristled, knowing she was the so-called criminal in question.

"No," Ailan said, "I already have our first topic prepared. I want a binding vow stated before Queen Mareleau, mother of our Morkara, that you welcome, accept, and protect her, same as her son whom you've already sworn to honor."

A rumble of disagreement spread throughout the room. As more voices added their dissent, Etrix's translation enchantment lost its effectiveness. Too many Elvyn spoke out, and thanks to the butterflies' orange and red hues, Cora didn't need to understand what they were saying to glean the gist of it. They didn't want Mareleau here.

Fury burned in Mareleau's eyes, matched by the red butterfly overhead. Cora reached across her armrest to lay a comforting hand on her friend's shoulder. She hoped it conveyed her wordless promise—that if worst came to worst, she'd world-walk her and Noah out of there at once.

Mareleau gave Cora a knowing nod, and her butterfly cooled to orange.

Etrix raised a hand, and the arguing ceased. When he spoke, his words were clear, his translation weaving back in place. "We are not here to discuss all humans or witches. Just the two human queens in question. Only one is up for discussion now."

"Mareleau is the blood of my blood," Ailan said. "Should I die before Noah comes of age, the *mora* will recognize her as regent, and there is nothing you can do about that. She must be allowed to stay here with him, even if only for the sake of the flow and control of *mora*."

"Allowed," Mareleau muttered through her teeth, quiet enough so only Cora could hear. "As if they can keep him from me. As if he belongs to *them* and not me."

Cora wasn't sure if the rage she felt was Mareleau's or her own. She was angry on her friend's behalf. On Noah's. Mareleau had only agreed to come to El'Ara for her son's protection, and to keep the dragons from seeking her in the human world. She hadn't even begun to discuss whether she and Noah would live here. Ailan had promised her time to save such choices for later, that they'd figure out the future together after they'd defeated Darius.

Ailan continued. "She brought her son here to honor his position as Morkara of El'Ara. In return, you must honor her as Edel Morkara'Elle."

The last few words remained untranslated, but they were vaguely familiar. Ailan had once said they meant something like a queen mother.

"You've already accepted the *mora's* choice to deem Noah your Morkara," Ailan said. "You've accepted him despite his human blood."

"If we accept her," said the same dark-haired Elvyn from the second tier, "are we to simply accept all other humans in the future? What if she bears other children? What of the Morkara's children? Are we to accept a diminishing bloodline, accept that our people may one day cease to be should the humans proliferate faster?"

A few Elvyn voiced their agreement, but Etrix spoke. "I've already stated that we are not discussing all humans. Nor are we discussing the distant future. Your fears are valid, and they will be addressed in due time, but today we discuss only the most pressing topics. Do you vow to honor, protect, and accept our Morkara's human mother, Mareleau, as Edel Morkara'Elle?"

Another murmur of dissent hummed around the room, but the voices ceased when Etrix bent his knee.

"Then I shall be the first," he said. His butterfly adopted a violet glow. "Edel Morkara'Elle Mareleau, I state my binding vow that I honor, protect, and accept you as the mother of my Morkara and a citizen of El'Ara."

Garot quickly followed suit, kneeling beside his chair like everyone had done for Noah earlier. Ailan followed next, then—to Cora's surprise—Fanon. After that, the other Elvyn bent their knees in turn until every head was bowed. Beneath the violet hue of their ever-fluttering butterflies, they stated their vows.

When they rose and returned to their seats, the colors shifted mostly back to shades of orange, though some had cooled to green or blue.

Mareleau released a slow exhale. Her relief was so palpable, it made it past Cora's wards. Cora offered her a reassuring smile, but it left her face at Etrix's next words.

"We will now discuss the other human queen, Aveline Caelan."

Cora's heart kicked up, and her butterfly flashed red before she forced her breaths to even out, her emotions to calm. Everything had turned out well for Mareleau. Perhaps it would go well for her too.

Of course it was easy for Mareleau, sniped some dark part of her mind. *Everything is easy for Mareleau. You're just her decoy, remember?*

Resentment speared her chest. It was so sudden, so violent, she nearly gasped out loud. What the hell was that about? Those hadn't been her thoughts. She could never think that about Mareleau! Yet...they'd come from inside her, not outside. No, that was impossible.

"She was condemned by our former steward," said one of the Elvyn, tone brimming with disgust. Cora was grateful for the distraction. The resentment faded from her heart as she found a new target for bitter feelings. "Fanon sentenced her to death—"

"A sentence that was supported neither by me nor the rest of the tribunal, mind you," Etrix said. "Furthermore, Queen Aveline has been pardoned by our regent. She is a close ally of our regent, our Morkara, and our Edel Morkara'Elle. Her guilt or innocence in breaking our laws is not up for debate. We are here to establish new rules to accommodate the alliance our regent would like to propose to the humans."

"She's a worldwalker," the same Elvyn said. "She entered our world with her magic and left the same way. She should be punished before we can even consider allying with her."

Etrix's butterfly darkened to a shade of teal, the only sign he was growing impatient. "It remains impossible for a worldwalker to utilize their magic to cross the Veil *into* El'Ara. As Ailan already explained, the human queen's actions were accidental. It was only her connection to a unicorn—and his horn's ability to pierce the Veil—that allowed her to enter our world last month."

Last month! Mother Goddess, that's right. To the Elvyn, it had only been a month since last summer's events.

Etrix went on. "Preventing a worldwalker from exiting El'Ara through magical means was never woven into Satsara's wardweaving. She left El'Ara for fear of her life after being targeted by the dragon Ferrah."

"She has crucial information," said another Elvyn, this one seated on the third tier. He gestured toward Cora. "Should she give this information to Darius, share how he could utilize a unicorn to cross the Veil, we'll be done for."

"Which is why we're forging an alliance," Ailan said, her butterfly flickering between orange and red.

"How can we trust her?" said another voice.

Then another. "She's human! She can't make a binding vow."

And another. "I still say she should be punished."

The voices overlapped, compromising Etrix's translation magic once more.

Anger simmered in Cora's gut, melding with the enraged emotions clawing their way past her shields. It sent a piercing ache to her temples.

"I want to hear what Fanon has to say," said Garot.

Cora shot him a glare across the room. Of all the people to make such a suggestion! And she'd thought he was on her side. Was he simply obtuse?

Fanon's jaw shifted side to side. His butterfly glowed a deep orange, and he slouched in his chair like he wanted to be anywhere else. Cora braced herself for whatever hatred he was about to spew.

His voice came out tight. "Whatever I have said or done as steward is no longer relevant. We have our Morkara now, and our regent. I condemned the human queen as I saw fit when the authority was mine, but our regent has condemned those actions in turn. We have Ailan's judgment now. You need not mine."

Cora blinked a few times, surprised by his words. She wasn't the only one. While his statement moved some to silence, it outraged others.

"We still can't trust her!"

"How can we trust an alliance with a worldwalker?"

"She must demonstrate her worth as our ally."

"She could use her magic at any time."

Another ache pierced Cora's temples as the arguments dissolved back into chaos. Devils below, she felt like she was in the council room with Lords Kevan and Ulrich, the target of their ire and suspicion. She never had managed to earn their trust or respect before they'd met their demise, but she had gotten her way a few times with a blend of truth and lies. She tried to think of some way to utilize those same lessons now, but she had just one idea. One that weighed heavy against her thigh and sent a memory of pain through her neck.

Breathing out a slow exhale, she rose to her feet. "Can I speak?"

The arguing voices went silent.

Ailan sat up straighter, brow furrowed. Etrix turned to her, head tilted slightly to the side. His butterfly flickered a deep green, then softened back to blue. "Yes, Queen Aveline. You may speak."

"Your regent has already spoken on my behalf," Cora said to the room at large, not bothering to hide the irritation in her voice, "so I will not repeat what has already been said. No, I cannot make a binding vow, and I know a human's promise means nothing to you without one. All I can offer you is this."

Cora extracted the collar from inside her robe. Her stomach turned just to hold it. She lifted it for all to see. "If you can't trust my magic, then collar me until it's time for me to return to my people. That's all I can offer you."

She held her breath, waiting for more arguments, or for one of the Elvyn to act and snap the device around her neck.

But Ailan spoke first. "Where...where did you get that? Why do you have it?"

Cora faced the regent as Ailan rose from her chair to stand beside Cora. The Elvyn woman's eyes were wide as they locked on the item in Cora's hand.

Cora was surprised by her reaction. While it was true she hadn't mentioned the collar when she'd talked about her time in El'Ara, she'd had no reason to believe Ailan would be so shocked by it. "Fanon used this on me. It suppressed my magic."

Ailan shot a fiery gaze at Fanon, her butterfly darkening to blood-red. She pointed at the device. "That was made for one individual."

Fanon shifted uncomfortably in his seat. "It was made for a worldwalker. I brought it with us to investigate the trigger that had alerted us of an unwelcome intruder."

"You shouldn't have used it on her."

He opened his mouth but quickly snapped it shut. His butterfly was almost as deep-red as hers now. "As you say, regent."

Ailan marched up to Cora and snatched the collar from her hands. "No one will use this on her, or any of my human allies. This was reserved for Darius, and for him alone it will remain."

Disgruntled murmurs sounded throughout the room, but Ailan spoke over them.

"Don't you see now? The human queen has demonstrated trust in the only way she can. She offered to let us collar her, and we will let that be enough. She returned a priceless, irreplaceable item to where it belongs. It is perhaps the only thing that will give us a chance to defeat Darius."

Another ripple of surprise moved through her. Cora had assumed the collar was a common piece of Elvyn technology, not a one-of-a-kind artifact.

"It didn't work before," one of the Elvyn said. Her expression was neutral beneath the glow of her yellow-green butterfly.

"That doesn't mean it isn't an advantage," Ailan said. "Now, enough with this back and forth about Queen Aveline. She is my ally, and she has demonstrated trust like you demanded."

When no one stated a word of reproach, Ailan returned to her chair. Cora did the same and was relieved to feel somewhat lighter. She hadn't realized how much she'd dreaded wearing the collar again until it was taken from her hands. Ailan now held it in her lap, gingerly, as if it were precious.

Cora couldn't help but wonder about it. Why was it so irreplaceable? What had the Elvyn female meant when she'd said it hadn't worked before? Had they tried to use it on Darius? Had it been part of Satsara's attempted wardweaving?

There was a story there, and Cora needed to know more.

"Now," Etrix said, drawing her attention away from the collar, "let us discuss the alliance."

<h1 style="text-align:center">38</h1>

The meeting was tedious. Mareleau was willing to bet the tribunal spoke less about the alliance itself and more about placing restrictions on Cora. She could leave El'Ara via worldwalking, but only with express permission, and in the presence of at least two witnesses from the tribunal. She could not use her connection to Valorre to cross the Veil ever again. She could enter through the tear to report back about her side of the alliance, but there were layers of protocol she'd have to endure.

Mareleau would have felt more indignation on her friend's behalf if her mind weren't swarming with a thousand unanswered questions. They burned her tongue as she and Cora followed Ailan and Fanon out of the meeting room and into another one of Garot's swirling tunnels. Now that the meeting was over, Cora was eager to return to Ridine Castle. Their party was on their way to reconvene with Valorre in preparation for Cora to worldwalk home.

Home. Such a lovely word.

So badly Mareleau wished she and Noah were going home too.

Mareleau hurried to Ailan's side, unable to hold her questions back any longer. "What about my husband?"

Ailan met her gaze with a furrowed brow. Fanon's expression flashed with annoyance before he marched on ahead. Ailan fell back to keep pace at Mareleau's side. "Your husband?"

Mareleau did everything she could to keep her voice steady despite the suppressed rage that tightened her lungs. "You've already made plans for me and Noah under the assumption that we'll be citizens here. That I'll relinquish my kingdom and my role as queen in the human realm and live in El'Ara instead. Need I remind you I've agreed to nothing of the sort?"

Ailan gave her a tired smile. "I know, blood of my blood. I spoke as I did for the tribunal's sake, for I needed to secure their binding vow. But I haven't forgotten what I said to you before. I meant it when I told you we'd figure out the future together. Defeating Darius takes precedence before all else, as does protecting you and Noah."

The swirling colors of the tunnel shifted from the pale hues of the palace to the greens and browns of the outdoors.

"What about my husband?" she said again, her tone edged with impatience. "I want the same protection for him. The same guarantee that he'll be granted respect and citizenship should we decide..."

She couldn't bring herself to finish. She wasn't ready to imagine a future in El'Ara. Noah was a prince of Vera, and she was its queen. Yet Noah's connection to El'Ara transcended bloodline politics and involved an entire world, not just a kingdom. It was a matter of magic and fate. Something she wasn't sure she could fight.

"She's right to ask," Cora said.

Ailan stopped in place just as the blues and greens went still and spread outward to form a moonlit forest. Garot lowered his hands, his pathweaving complete. Fanon leaned lazily against a nearby tree trunk. Mareleau glanced overhead where dark trees stretched toward an inky starlit sky. Were Mareleau in a better mood, she may have found the quiet woods charming, but now they felt sinister.

Cora spoke again. "I want to know the answer too. Not just about Larylis, but all the citizens of Lela. You may not want to discuss the future with your tribunal just yet, but we deserve to know what's in store for us. I've agreed to forge an alliance between our people so we can fight Darius together, but what exactly are my people fighting for? What future awaits when Darius is gone and all that remains is sealing the tear? What happens to the people of Lela when you reclaim El'Ara's heart?"

"I already told you. I don't know the answer yet."

"Give us something," Mareleau said, voice quavering. "Give us some idea of what our futures could look like. Give me a reason to believe your protection is worth a damn."

Ailan's posture tensed, and she heaved a sigh. "I...I have some ideas for how we could work together. I know you value your kingdom. Perhaps...perhaps we can wait to seal the tear and complete the Veil until you and your husband have lived full lives. Once we defeat Darius, we'll need only worry about healing the Blight. Fifty years in the human world is just over seven in El'Ara. We can hold off the Blight that long, and it will give us time to prepare for what happens next."

The edges of Mareleau's anxiety began to smooth. That didn't sound terrible. She and Larylis could continue to rule Vera and live full lives with their son. Noah could be a prince of two worlds until then.

"If we wait to complete the Veil," Ailan said, "that will give your people time to prepare for Lela's return to El'Ara. They will have time to find new homes, new kingdoms—"

"Exile," Cora said. "The future you see for my people is exile."

Mareleau's blood went cold at the word.

"Or citizenship of El'Ara," Ailan rushed to say. "I know both options are unthinkable right now, but we *can* work together. That's what our alliance is about. Defeating Darius and forging a future beyond that."

Fanon snorted a laugh.

Mareleau furrowed her brow. Etrix wasn't there to weave his translation magic, so Fanon shouldn't have been able to understand Ailan's words.

He pushed off the tree he'd been leaning on and strode closer to them. With a shake of his head, he said something in the Elvyn language.

"Fanon," Ailan hissed through her teeth.

He spoke again, his tone barbed. Garot nodded in agreement, though his words were lost to lack of translation as well.

"What are they saying?" Mareleau asked.

Fanon sauntered up to her, extending a closed fist. She flinched back, arms going protectively around Noah's sling. He said something with a nod at his fist, and when she made no move, he wrested one of her hands away from Noah and forced something into her palm.

She nearly dropped it before she noticed a delicate silver chain, just long enough to be a bracelet, strung with a small onyx orb.

"Gift from Etrix and one of our charmweavers," Fanon said with no small amount of irritation. Her eyes widened as she realized she could understand him. "And what I said is that my lovely consort is too optimistic."

Ailan glared daggers at him as he moved to Cora next, dropping a bracelet in her hand. Ailan hissed his name again, but he paid her no heed.

"The tribunal will never agree to let humans live in El'Ara," he said. "Nor will they agree to wait a year, much less seven, to seal the tear and complete the Veil."

"You don't know that," Ailan said, then turned her gaze to Mareleau and Cora. "He doesn't know that. I'll do everything in my power to get them to agree to a solution that benefits everyone. Don't listen to him."

"Why not?" Fanon said with a scoff. "I'm the only one telling them the truth. And here's a truth for you, my love. The tear has increased the Blight's growth tenfold."

She paled, her jaw slack. Then she spoke under her breath. "Do you want this alliance or not?"

Fanon said nothing but Garot raised his hand. "I do, but Fanon is right. The tribunal will never agree to let humans live in El'Ara. Well, aside from the Edel Morkara'Elle, but we saw how well that discussion went."

"So, exile," Cora said, tone empty. Movement rustled the underbrush, and moonlight caught on white fur. Valorre emerged from between the trees and gently nudged Cora's shoulder with his muzzle. "I'm forging an alliance for the eventual exile of my people."

Ailan's shoulders fell. "I'll give you time. That I can promise you. As regent, I can hold off the Blight long enough to sort everything out."

Mareleau's heart sank to her feet. The promise of time was meaningless when she couldn't guarantee exactly how much they'd be given. She met Cora's gaze and they exchanged a defeated look.

"I need to get back," Cora said, absently stroking Valorre's neck.

Mareleau didn't want Cora to leave. She was her only friend in this strange place. The only person here who was truly on her side. Once she left, it would just be her and Noah.

Alone.

The future uncertain.

She swallowed the tightness in her throat and reached into the pocket of her robe. She extracted a wrinkled piece of parchment and held it out for Cora. "See that this gets to Lare." She hated that her only communication with her husband could be a one-way letter. For now. She wouldn't give up on getting what she wanted. What she needed.

Cora clasped her fingers around the paper, but she didn't pull away. She gave Mareleau a weighted look, one that spoke of last resorts. Mareleau glanced at Cora's hands, one connected to the paper they both held, the other pressed to Valorre's neck. Realization dawned. All Mareleau needed to do was give the slightest sign, the subtlest nod, and Cora could worldwalk them away. Mareleau would be free of this place where she might as well be a prisoner. She could see her husband again. She could go home.

Home.

Home.

It was a tantalizing offer that sparked every selfish instinct she harbored. But on the other side were the repercussions of that choice. Should she run away like that, they'd forfeit the alliance and make an enemy of the Elvyn people. The dragons would return to the human world to seek her out. Even if she learned to ward her magic, the dragons would likely still search for her and destroy crops, homes, and lives in the process. And she wouldn't put it past the Elvyn to hunt her down themselves and take their Morkara back by force.

Mareleau may be determined to get her way, but her decisions carried weight. Consequences. Ones that could become burdens she might never fully shrug off.

She'd find a better way to fight for what she wanted.

For now...she could only let go.

With a slow sigh, she released her hold on the letter and took a step back.

Cora gave her a relieved nod, as if she was of the same mind. Then she turned her back on Mareleau and fully faced Valorre.

In the blink of an eye, her friend was gone.

Leaving Mareleau and Noah behind, an entire world away.

39

Evening greeted Cora as she planted her feet in the forest outside Ridine. After removing Valorre's saddle and stashing it in the underbrush for the time being, she bid him farewell and worldwalked straight to her bedroom. The room was blessedly empty of servants, but it was empty of Teryn too. A wave of vertigo washed over her, and she sank onto the edge of her bed. She had half a mind to curl up under the covers and sleep, but she shook the thought from her head. How many hours had it been since she'd last slept? The time discrepancy between the two realms made it impossible to calculate.

Whatever the case, she reasoned her fatigue was mostly due to worldwalking to different locations in such quick succession. At least that's what she told herself. In truth, she hadn't expected to feel so exhausted now that she was no longer traveling with multiple companions in tow. Maybe moving between worlds took an additional toll.

Then how had Darius been able to worldwalk so frequently with multiple soldiers during his attack on El'Ara? Had he rested in between? Or were her abilities weaker than his? True, she'd only learned of her traveling magic last year. Yet the fatigue that weighed down her muscles now begged the question—was her magic growing weaker in general?

Her magic had weakened before, when she'd been trapped in the dungeon with Teryn. She'd been convinced Morkai had suppressed her magic, leaving her connection to it frail. But when she'd searched for the source that had stifled her, she'd found it inside herself. It had stemmed from resentment she'd been carrying over Teryn's betrayal.

Something pulsed in her heart.

A feeling that said *truth*.

She placed a hand to her chest, and her palms thrummed in echo of her heartbeat. Did that mean...was she stifling her own magic again?

A leaden weight filled her stomach, and it spoke of her resistance to investigate the source. But why was she resisting? If another challenge was trying to present itself, she had to face it. It was how witches grew their magic, and she needed to be at her strongest. Yet as soon as she tried to soften and yield to look into the dark pull, she saw only flames. Felt only a burning resentment that made her skin crawl, blistering beneath that imagined fire.

She rose to her feet, detaching herself from those thoughts. Investigations into her magic could wait.

Right now, she needed to find her husband.

TERYN THRUST HIS SPEAR, RELISHING THE STRETCH OF HIS LIMBS, THE BURN OF HIS muscles. He pivoted, evading his imaginary opponent's attack, and slashed down to parry. Another pivot. A longer thrust of his spear. His entire body moved in concert, his stance shifting in precise yet fluid motions, his spear an extension of his arm. He repeated the drill again and again, his only witnesses being the empty suits of armor and racks of weapons that lined the perimeter of the armory.

Ridine's armory was a windowless hall of mahogany and flagstone with a training floor at its center. This was the only place he could think to go after the latest missive he'd received. The only place he could think to release the anxiety and rage crawling through his body.

King Darius had made his first direct contact with Khero, and it had come in a written demand for surrender. In three weeks, Darius and five thousand men would arrive at a specified location on the Khero-Vinias border. If Khero refused to surrender, they would then proceed to discuss terms for war.

It reminded Teryn too much of Morkai.

The mage's demands for surrender.

The meeting at Centerpointe Rock.

King Arlous' resulting death.

Teryn repeated his drill—thrust, slash, thrust—taking pleasure in how it felt to move. To be alive. To not be a hostage this time.

Yet that solace was short-lived. King Darius was now a concrete enemy, not just a man from myth and rumor. There was no denying that he was coming or what he wanted. There was no taking comfort in doubt, in the sliver of possibility that Darius wasn't a threat like Morkai was, that his alliance with Norun had nothing to do with Khero.

That was the most terrifying part—Darius' threat didn't involve him alone. Half his force of five thousand men belonged to Norun. Furthermore, a legion of twelve thousand Norunian soldiers were already marching from the capital and would join Darius should Khero refuse to surrender. Meanwhile, Khero had only four thousand soldiers.

Seven devils, those odds were terrible.

There had been no mention of Darius' naval fleet, but that was a matter for Vera, not Khero. Teryn was starting to suspect his brother was right. Larylis had posed a theory in a letter he'd sent back with Berol a few days ago. That the prisoner's words had been a bluff meant to draw Vera's attention toward a threat that would never come and leave Khero vulnerable.

Not that it mattered much. Even with their combined armies, they would still be outnumbered. Even if Vera supported the fight against Darius, Larylis couldn't fully dismiss what the prisoner had said. It could have been a lesser misdirection—that the fleet was still coming, but not making landfall in southwest Vera. Which meant Larylis needed to keep some of his soldiers ready in the south.

There was hope in the alliance Cora was forging, but she'd been gone from Ridine for ten days now. It had been nine days since he'd received her letter about going to El'Ara.

Was she still there? Had they found the tear yet?

At least he had some additional intel. He'd been right about Mareleau's letter to Larylis; she hadn't been nearly as sparse with details as Cora had been. Larylis had relayed what her letter had included—that the Forest People's camp had been outside Lake Sarrolin near the village of Brekan. And that they would begin their search for the tear on the western coast.

Teryn would have been livid that she'd divulged so much information during such tumultuous times if it hadn't provided him such relief. Just knowing vaguely where Cora was had carved leagues of stress from his bones. Besides, he couldn't give in to the fear that Berol's letters could be intercepted. That would only lead to madness.

Sweat prickled his forehead as he continued his drill, his mind reeling to come up with countermeasures. Surrender was out of the question, and if Cora didn't come home soon, he couldn't count on Elvyn reinforcements.

No, the best scenario was to face Darius' smaller force. And there was a chance for that. Darius' letter wasn't the only one he'd received today. A messenger had also arrived with a brief note from Lex.

It begins on the thirtieth day. Those who've been robbed will take back what they've lost.

That was all the note had said. It was so carefully yet cleverly worded, Teryn suspected Lily had penned it for her husband. Those two sentences told him everything he needed to know: the Norunian rebels would launch their rebellion on the thirtieth of this month—less than two weeks from now. They would fight to take back Haldor and Sparda, the two kingdoms Norun had conquered. The rebellion would wreak havoc on Norun and delay the progress of Darius' reinforcements. The King of Syrus would be isolated with only his five thousand men.

With some additional men from Vera, they could be evenly matched.

But Teryn didn't want even.

He wanted—needed—to win.

Dark thoughts clouded his mind, taking him back to Centerpointe Rock. To Morkai's dishonorable actions during the meeting. How he'd signaled battle without giving them a chance to negotiate the terms for war. What he'd done made Teryn sick with rage.

Yet as he thrust his spear and imagined his faceless enemy on the other side, he didn't feel nearly as sick when he considered doing something similar himself.

Darius' threat was a matter of power, magic, and desperation.

Maybe only equal measures of power, magic, and desperation could lead to victory.

And Teryn had one idea that might allow him to catch Darius unawares. To end the battle before it had begun.

He wasn't sure he could even do it.

It might damn him to the seven hells.

But if it saved Khero's future, he'd risk the stain on his soul.

40

Cora found Teryn in the armory. The shuffling of his feet and the sound of his heavy breaths reached her ears just before she rounded the corner. He didn't notice her approach. She kept her feet silent so as not to disturb his practice and leaned against the wall just past the threshold.

His pale hair was tied back, revealing a determined look on his face. He wore only trousers, his nightshirt draped over a rack of polearms. Sweat glistened over his taut muscles, a sight that wasn't at all unpleasant. She studied the contraction of his abdomen as he pivoted and slashed, the bulge of his biceps as he thrusted. She'd seen him train with a sword and hunt with a spear, but she hadn't watched him train quite like this—with focus and zeal and a deadly skill that was a bit terrifying yet...strangely erotic.

She folded her arms and leaned her head against the wall, her gaze sweeping over the length of him. Mother Goddess, she was lucky this man was hers. Not that she'd gotten a chance to enjoy her husband quite yet. They'd had their night of passion before their wedding, but they still hadn't had a true wedding night. As she watched him move gracefully over the training floor, she realized just how unfair that was. Here Teryn was practicing for a battle they couldn't avoid while she'd spent...however long she'd been gone establishing an alliance. They should have been wrapped in each other's arms, enjoying the life of newlyweds, not facing war.

"Are you going to keep staring?" Teryn said, startling her. His gaze was fixed on his imaginary enemy as he sidestepped, then thrust. After a final slash and thrust, he angled his body to face her and planted the butt of his spear on the ground. A corner of his mouth lifted. "Or are you going to kiss me?"

A thrilling warmth ignited in her chest at the challenge in his eyes, the taunting in his voice. If he could still make her feel like that amidst everything that was going on, maybe there was hope for them yet. For them to enjoy some semblance of newlywed life.

She raced over to him and he met her halfway, grasping her around the waist with his free arm and pressing his lips to hers. Her palm rested over the slick skin of his pectoral. Just as quickly as he'd kissed her, he pulled away.

His expression turned bashful, but he held her eyes. "Sorry. I'm sweaty, aren't I?"

"I don't entirely mind," she said with a coy look, though she had to admit, her lips tasted like salt.

He released her waist and strode to the rack of polearms, exchanging his spear for the shirt he'd hung there. She was almost disappointed until she realized he was simply drying off. A wicked smile curved her lips. She wanted to look at him like this a little longer. Extend the playful mood he'd begun.

She swept closer to him, evading his detection while he was drying his face with his shirt. As he brought the linen article down and found her standing so close, his eyes went wide. She blinked up at him, an innocent expression as she reached for the hilt hidden behind her back.

He opened his mouth to speak, but she pulled the dagger from her golden sash and flicked it to his neck. He flinched only slightly but otherwise held perfectly still.

"Don't let me interrupt your training, love of mine," she said.

His eyes simmered, whether with challenge or desire she knew not. All she knew was how it tightened her belly. His lips tugged into a wry grin and he dropped his shirt to the floor. Then, in a flash of movement, he whirled away and retrieved a wooden training dagger from a nearby stand.

They circled each other, and Cora considered whether she should dive for a training blade too. But they were both skilled enough to defend themselves and know when to hold back. She made the first move, striking with her dagger, and he parried her blade with ease. Swiveling to the side, she aimed for his ribs. He caught her wrist in his hand, angled her arm behind her, and twisted her around until her back was to his chest, her knife hand between them. He pressed his practice blade beneath her chin.

"There's something familiar about this position," Teryn said, bringing his lips close to her ear.

She shuddered at the sound and recalled a moment from their first meeting. He'd wrenched her arm behind her that time too, pulling her against his chest, and asked her to stop trying to stab him. The closeness of his voice had caught her off guard then, but now it made her want to get even closer.

She tried to get free the same way she had then, by striking his instep with her heel. Predicting her move, he widened his stance, but he loosened his hold enough to allow her to wrench her knife hand from his grip. She whirled to face him again, striking. He parried, shifted, parried again. At her next strike, he caught her wrist and pulled her to him once more. This time, her dagger wasn't between them, leaving her back flush to his chest. He held her wrist in place while securing his forearm over her middle. His grip was firm enough to hold her still yet soft enough to feel more like an embrace.

She didn't struggle as he brought his lips to the lobe of her ear. Instead, she angled her head, daring him to land a blow with either his mouth or his wooden blade. Instead, he whispered, "What are you wearing, by the way?"

"You only now noticed?" To be honest, she'd only remembered her state of dress when she'd neared the hall leading to the armory. By then, she'd sensed Teryn's proximity and hadn't felt like changing. It was after midnight now, and Cora hadn't come across any servants on her way to find Teryn, only her husband's guards, who were posted outside the hall.

"Oh, I noticed. Also…" His forearm froze against her midsection. Then, angling the hand that held her wrist, he spun her away from him, and for a moment it felt more like they were dancing. He didn't release her wrist. Instead, he angled her arm overhead, bent at the elbow, and stepped in close. His eyes swept over her form, lingering on the deep V-shaped neck of her robe. His throat bobbed. "You aren't wearing a corset."

She lifted her chin, her chest, letting the lay of the thin silk and the peaks it accentuated speak volumes. "I'm not."

That surprised him enough to allow her to catch him off guard. She freed her wrist and darted a step back.

"How about this?" she said. "For every blow you land, I'll remove an article of clothing."

He bit his bottom lip. When he spoke, his voice came out thick. "And what if you land a—"

Before he could finish, she lunged forward and slapped his thigh with the flat of her blade. Just as quickly, she leaped back, a victorious grin on her lips. "If I land a blow, you have to do the same."

His mouth fell open. "Did that one count?"

"It counted." She dropped her gaze to his waistband, then fluttered her lashes at him. "So go on."

With exaggerated reluctance, he brought the fingers of his free hand to the top button of his fly.

Cora watched with greedy anticipation—

Before she knew what was happening, he lunged forward and slapped her lightly with his wooden dagger, in the same place she'd struck him.

She squeaked in surprise, her defenses thoroughly shaken. She debated striking back, but he was already retreating.

"Looks like we've both landed a blow," he said as he worked his buttons in earnest this time. Then, in a taunting tone, he echoed her earlier words. "So go on."

With a huff, she reached under the skirt of her robe with one hand, not daring to drop her dagger, and slid her trousers down. Teryn stepped out of his bottoms, and she was disappointed to see he wore linen undershorts. Devils take those undershorts. Meanwhile, she had no underclothes at all, for Garot had only left her the robe, sash, and trousers. At least the plentiful folds of her robe's skirt hid her bottom half, which meant she still had the more exciting view.

She charged forward, thrusting her dagger, but he parried it. She charged again. Again. His defenses had grown sharper, fiercer. It seemed he was determined to get her out of another article of clothing. Well, she wouldn't go easy on him. She was equally as—

With a yelp, she tumbled back. She'd been so focused on striking Teryn's wrist with the edge of her free hand, she hadn't anticipated him sweeping out her feet. While she'd managed to force him to release his weapon, she'd lost her chance to land a blow with hers.

He caught her before she could fully lose her balance and guided her fall to the floor. Pinning her hands over her head, he lowered his body over hers, careful not to crush her with his full weight.

Heat burned deep in her core, tingling at the thrill of him being on top of her. Yet they were at an impasse. His training dagger was off to the side, but she still held hers. As soon as he released her arms, she could land a winning blow. Now all she needed to do was get him to release her.

With a wicked grin, she wiggled her hips slightly. "This brings back memories too."

"I woke you up from a nightmare much like this."

She spread her legs slightly, letting him settle more firmly against her. She hooked a leg around his hip, making his eyes widen. "I seem to recall you promising me pleasure."

"Is that how you remember it?"

She arched her brow. "Am I wrong?"

"What I said back then was if I took pleasure in touching you, you would experience pleasure too."

"And are you, Teryn? Are you taking pleasure in touching me?"

He rocked his hips slightly, and she could feel proof that he was, in fact, taking great pleasure from this. His grip slackened.

That was all she needed.

Clamping her legs around his hips, she shifted her weight and rolled him onto his back, she on top now. He lost hold of her wrists but flung his hand out toward his wooden dagger. Just as he touched it to her side, she brought her very real blade to his throat.

"I win," she said through panting breaths.

"We both landed a blow," he said.

"Yes, but you only have one more item to take off."

"Don't you too?"

Holding his eyes with a triumphant smile, she reached with her free hand for the sash around her waist. She tugged the tie, and it fell from around her robe.

His expression fell. "Damn that sash."

"Now you know how I felt when I saw your undershorts. Which you will now remove. With both hands. I've won, so drop your dagger and take them off."

Desire darkened his irises at the demand in her tone. He did as told, releasing the dagger and reaching for his waistband. She rose to her knees, still straddling him, and kept her blade to his throat. She accommodated his moves, easing her blade away to allow him to fully slide his shorts down. He held her eyes all the while, which only made the heat between her legs grow to an insatiable, pulsing throb.

Fully nude, he reclined back down, and she lowered herself onto him once more, spreading the folds of her skirt around her so nothing lay between their bare flesh. His hardness dug against her thigh, even as she continued to hold her knife's edge to his throat. She wasn't sure why she kept it there, only that it deepened the thrill, the desire that coursed through her. And from the way he watched her, jaw slack, eyes roving the sliver of naked skin her robe revealed, he felt the same.

"Do you want me like this?" she asked, voice barely above a whisper.

"You mean with murder in your eyes and a knife between us? Gods, Cora." He uttered her name through his teeth. "I want you in every way you'll have me."

She shifted her hips, rocked them, and he moaned with want. His hands caged her hips, fingers clamped around the silk folds of her skirt with an intensity that spoke of either pleasure or frustration. Her dagger's position left him with little range of motion.

He spoke again, echoing her question back to her. "Do you want me like this?"

In answer, she slid over him, holding his gaze as she guided him inside her. She seated herself fully over him and gasped at the feeling, the fullness. Teryn cursed, his eyes fluttering shut.

She tapped the underside of his chin with the flat of her blade. "Keep your eyes open and watch me."

"Devils," he groaned as his eyes locked on hers again, lips quirked in a devious smile. She moved then, sliding up and down his length, igniting pleasurable sensations that burned hotter with every thrust. Just when she thought she could quench that need, her desire only grew. Teryn's expression, the clear yearning in his eyes, the sounds he made, the way he made no move to make her drop her blade, the way he watched her just like she'd demanded, only increased that feeling.

She never imagined she'd want something like this, that she'd take pleasure with a blade in her hand. But gods, it was a thrill. And yet, even as her passion burned, the thrill gave way to more want, and she couldn't take another moment without his hands on her. She tossed her blade to the side.

Teryn moved at once, lifting his upper body to meet her in a crushing kiss, a violent dance of teeth and tongues. His hands roved everywhere he hadn't been able to touch before, tangling in her hair, caressing the column of her neck, then down the length of skin visible through her open robe. He pulled back slightly and parted the robe further, baring her breasts, her stomach, and the meeting of their bodies.

They watched the way they moved together for several beats, then his mouth closed over her breast. She threw her head back at the caress of his tongue over her hardened peak, and let her robe slip fully from her shoulders. Moans left her lips, ones she didn't care enough to stifle. The guards weren't close enough to hear them, and even if they were, she didn't care. There was a boldness to what they were doing that made her euphoric and a roughness between them that hadn't been there the first night they'd made love. Through it all wove a softness in her heart that made her feel safe. Loved. Cherished. Even as Teryn's teeth grazed her skin. Even as she dug her nails into his back.

Release began to unravel inside her, and she rode that cresting wave. Teryn aided it with his fingertips, circling over her most sensitive spot as he continued to move inside her. Then finally, the sweetest, fiercest pleasure erupted from her, one that sent stars to her eyes and whimpers from her lips. Teryn found his release next, and he guided her hips through every wave and valley until they both were thoroughly sated.

As they fell back, out of breath, and stared at the armory ceiling, Teryn spoke through trembling breaths. "Say whatever you want, but I think I won that battle."

41

As Cora and Teryn left the armory, their clothing haphazardly replaced, Cora wondered if maybe they had been too loud after all. Not that the guards gave any indication as the king and queen emerged from the armory hall, but they were well-trained in keeping their composure. It was the silence of the sleeping castle that brought heat to Cora's cheeks, strikingly still and quiet as they strode up the steps to the keep. Even their footsteps were too loud.

That was also when the mood between Cora and Teryn began to change. It wasn't awkwardness. Teryn held her hand with the same warmth and attention he'd given her body in the armory, and his posture was easy. Instead, the strain came from an inevitable fall back to reality in the wake of their euphoria.

Teryn was the first to voice it, leaning in close and lowering his voice to the quietest of whispers. "King Darius made his first direct contact with us today."

She nearly stumbled up the next step, but Teryn's grip on her hand helped her regain her balance. "He did?"

"He issued a demand for our surrender and detailed the forces that await us should we decline." He relayed those numbers now, told her about the meeting Darius had set at the Khero-Vinias border, and the legion of reinforcements already heading their way.

Cora's head swam at those numbers, but before her dread could grow, Teryn handed her a slip of paper. They reached the top of the staircase, and she read the sparse words scrawled across the paper, illuminated by the dim lamps lining the halls of the keep. It was a short, coded message, but...

"Does this mean what I think it means?"

Teryn gave a nod, and she returned the paper to him. Hope filled her chest as she analyzed the words in her head again and again. It could only mean one thing. The rebellion in Norun was set to strike soon. Darius wouldn't likely get those reinforcements.

Teryn's secrecy made her wonder who else knew. Perhaps no one.

Good. That meant it was truly an advantage.

"There's a traitor in the castle," Teryn whispered. "The Norunian spy you'd imprisoned was murdered after he divulged the information about the naval fleet. At least, that's how it was supposed to seem. In truth, the dead man that was left in the cell was someone else entirely. I know because...because I spoke to the corpse's spirit."

"You *spoke* to a spirit?" She went to great lengths to keep her voice down despite her shock. She knew about his ability to see spirits and that he could communicate with Emylia, but speaking to the ghost of a dead stranger...well, that was only half as alarming as what he said next.

"I learned that I can aid a spirit's progression to the otherlife through touch." Teryn's expression turned wary, as if he hadn't fully come to terms with this new information either. "I spoke to the spirit. He remembered nothing after heading home from a tavern in Greenfair Village. After he told me what he could, he grew hysterical. He begged me to send him on, so I did."

Her mind reeled. And not just over Teryn's strange new power. Setting that shocking revelation aside, she pored over what he'd said before that. The prisoner was found dead in his cell after making his confession. But the body—and its spirit—had belonged to a stranger.

Her pulse quickened. "Someone helped the prisoner escape and left a decoy corpse in his place?"

"Yes. It was supposed to look like he'd been silenced on purpose as punishment for divulging key information. Larylis believes it was all a ruse to get us to separate our forces."

Damn. If he was right, they'd played right into that scheme.

They turned down the hall toward their suite.

"Any leads on who may have helped the prisoner escape?" Cora asked.

Teryn shook his head. "None."

She cast her gaze around the dark halls with fresh eyes, seeing sinister shadows and imagining hidden enemies. Even so, this was probably the safest place to talk —while walking, when there was no one close enough to hear their words, no way for someone to lie in wait and overhear their secrets. Even the guards trailed too far behind to hear them. That was some comfort at least.

They reached their suite, and the guards took their posts on each side of the door. The sitting room held a chill as they entered, but their bedroom boasted the embers of the hearth fire. Teryn retrieved a fresh nightshirt from his dresser and pulled it over his head before he went to stoke the flames. Cora freshened up with the ewer of wash water—cold, unfortunately—and changed into a chemise and thick velvet robe.

With the fire roaring and the room growing toasty, Cora wanted nothing more than to crawl into bed. She was about to do just that when Teryn's snort of laughter had her gaze flying to him.

His eyes crinkled at the corners. "Your hair, my love. Bring me your brush."

Her cheeks heated. After their time in the armory, her hair was probably a disaster. She did as asked, and when she returned to the bed, she found him seated upon it, his back propped against the pillows. His hair had come loose from its tie during their...activities...and now hung around his jaw, a few wayward strands strewn over his forehead. How the hell did he look so dashing with mussed hair?

He patted the space on the bed before him, and she crawled upon the mattress and settled between his legs. She handed him the brush.

"Tell me if this hurts," he said, bringing the bristles to the ends of her hair. His tone and hands were so gentle, a contrast to the firm grip he'd had on her hips, the way he'd palmed her body as she'd ridden him.

That sent a tingle of heat low in her belly, and it took no small amount of self-control not to turn around and initiate an encore. Instead, she kept perfectly still. There was pleasure enough in simply feeling him run the brush through her hair. It was a strangely intimate situation, even though maids brushed her hair daily. Having Teryn do it while they were alone in their shared bed was entirely different.

"What about you?" he asked, his voice deep and rumbling. "What happened in El'Ara? Do we have an alliance with the Elvyn?"

"The beginnings of one. They haven't offered anything concrete, but by now they will have stationed soldiers within the tear on the fae side of the Veil. They want us to provide two thousand soldiers to guard the human side. We would have to be discreet, otherwise we'll draw attention straight to the tear's location."

"We could close the roads on either side," Teryn said. "Feign a landslide and guard a wide perimeter around the area."

"The tear is at the edge of a cliff, so a landslide would stand to reason. And we could hide our forces in the woods. Still...two thousand men. They've said nothing about how they intend to help us in exchange."

"And that's half our military. We need those soldiers with us when we meet Darius in three weeks. If we can gain Elvyn soldiers to bolster our numbers and face him with just his force of five thousand, we have a chance at winning."

Cora agreed. So long as the rebellion began as planned, they could isolate Darius with his current soldiers.

"It would benefit the Elvyn too," Teryn said. "If we defeat Darius at the Khero-Vinias border, we won't need to guard the tear. Keeping Darius from setting foot in Lela should be our priority."

"I'm supposed to return soon with our requests for the terms of the alliance," Cora said. "I can demand they provide forces for our confrontation with Darius. We can make a plan with the Elvyn to defeat him." She remembered the collar, how Ailan had called it their one chance to defeat her brother. "In the meantime, I can offer a smaller force to guard the human side of the tear, as a show of good faith until the terms have been finalized."

"Larylis can do that," Teryn said. "He's on a ship patrolling Khero's west coast now."

Cora angled her head to meet his eyes. "He's on a ship? Not in Vera?"

Teryn paused brushing. "After he suspected that the naval fleet threat was a ruse, he left on an unmarked schooner with fifty soldiers to investigate by sea. More than that, I think he wanted to be close to Mareleau. She wasn't quite as discreet as you were in her letter."

With a roll of her eyes, she faced forward again. "Of course she wasn't." She meant to say it in good humor, but it came out with a bitter edge. What was wrong with her lately?

"He and I communicate daily through Berol," Teryn said as he resumed brushing. "He left his generals in charge of watching Vera's shores in case the naval fleet threat was real, but he'll come to our aid in allying with El'Ara. I'm certain he'd prefer to oversee the soldiers stationed there."

Cora pursed her lips. It was a bit reckless of Larylis to leave Vera at a time like this, but she understood too. He'd never truly wanted to be king. He'd only wanted to be with Mareleau.

Of course he did. Everyone loves Mareleau. Your own husband wanted to be with her at one time. Remember?

Her hands curled into fists at the bitter words. The last part wasn't even true. *Stop it! Stop thinking like that. Mareleau is my friend. These feelings aren't mine.*

"When will you need to return?" Teryn asked. "If we're going to march Elvyn soldiers from where I imagine the tear is…"

Cora still hadn't dared state its location out loud. She would save that for the council meeting they'd have tomorrow. When they could post guards around the room and destroy evidence afterward. Even though they continued to whisper, Cora couldn't shake the fear of having a traitor in the castle.

"I'll need to leave soon," she said. "It will take at least two weeks to march soldiers to the border."

There was still so much more to discuss. Most could wait for the council meeting, but there was something she wanted to get off her chest. Something that filled her with a hollow dread. She wasn't sure she could share it with anyone but Teryn.

As if sensing her turmoil, Teryn paused his ministrations and set the brush on the bed beside them.

She angled herself around to face him. "The worst part about allying with the Elvyn…" The words dried on her tongue. She swallowed hard and tried again. "Is that we'll be fighting for our eventual exile from Lela."

Teryn paled. He opened his mouth, but it wasn't he who spoke next.

"Not if you ally with me."

42

Cora's heart shot into her throat as she whirled to face the stranger in their room. Teryn leaped off the bed at once, pulling Cora with him and positioning her behind him. She reached for her waist, but her hands met only air. Seven devils, she'd left her dagger in the armory. Teryn at least had the good sense to lunge for the fireplace poker and brandished it toward the intruder.

The man made no move aside from tilting his lips in an amused grin.

He was on the late end of middle-aged, tall and slender, his posture somehow dignified as he leaned against the far wall, ankles crossed. His salt-and-pepper hair was swept away from his brow to reveal a strong nose and silver-blue eyes that bore an unmistakable intensity. He was dressed in all black from his trousers to the military-style coat he wore. There was nothing familiar about the coat's design to distinguish which military he represented.

Everything about his presence screamed *wrong*, even before she noticed the knife he toyed with.

"I'm glad to see you've finished," the man said. There was something familiar about his voice. "The stamina you young people have."

Stamina. What was he talking about? Had he...

"Who are you?" Teryn asked, voice deadly calm.

"I'm not surprised you don't recognize me, but surely Her Majesty would. No? Ah, it's the absence of bruises, isn't it? You should pay better attention to the people you have beaten at your command."

Understanding clicked into place. "You're...the Norunian spy."

It shouldn't have been possible. Even without the bruises, there was little to link them by appearances alone. He seemed taller, and far less rough around the edges. But that voice. It held a more distinguished quality, but he was just as well-spoken as the man she'd interrogated in the dungeon. With a deep breath, she opened her senses.

His energy was one and the same.

This was the prisoner who'd faked his own death. Freed by someone in the castle and replaced with a decoy body. And from what he'd said...

The stamina you young people have.

Nausea turned her stomach. Had he been...watching them? Their most private moment? It was one thing to enjoy the thrill of getting caught by people she trusted. Enemies were different. There was nothing thrilling about that. It was simply violating.

Had he been inside her castle all this time, lurking in the shadows?

Teryn shifted to the side, deepening his defensive stance. He opened his mouth and gathered in a sharp breath, as if prepared to shout, but the spy spoke first.

"Don't call for your guards." He flipped his knife and caught the hilt with ease. "I can cross the space between us in a heartbeat and shove this through your throat before you've had a chance to blink."

His words pulsed in her mind.

He could...cross the space between them.

In a heartbeat.

She assessed the floor, the bed between them, the wardrobe he'd have to skirt around. The answer was so crushing, she almost couldn't voice it.

"You're Darius," she managed to say.

"Majesty, I wasn't aware we were on a first-name basis," he said, tone mocking.

That was when she noticed something about his eyes; they were so like Morkai's had been, with that same pale blue color. She tried to find similarities to Ailan, but there were none. His complexion was tan but much paler than Ailan's. His hair was gray where hers was black. But as her eyes fell upon his ears, she saw their subtly pointed tips. They weren't as angled as Ailan's but were more so than Morkai's. Surely she or the gaoler would have noticed pointed ears on their prisoner...wouldn't they? His hair had been shaggy enough to cover them, but—

Another realization formed in her mind.

The only time she'd seen him had been before the Veil had torn.

Any differences in his appearance could be attributed to that. Though his aging hadn't reversed nearly as drastically as Ailan's had, it had darkened his hair, straightened his posture, and elongated his ears.

Terror tore through her. Darius...her enemy...was in her castle.

He was *here*.

Standing before her.

Teryn shifted his stance again, teeth bared in a sneer.

Darius raised his empty palm while sheathing the knife at his waist. When both hands were empty, he said, "I'm not here for violence. I'm here to talk."

"Then talk," Teryn said through his teeth.

"Lower your weapon and I will."

Teryn held still for a long beat, then lowered the poker to his side. He kept it firmly in his grip, however, his posture defensive, still half blocking Cora.

"Right," Darius said. "Now, I'm sure you have questions—"

"It was you all along," Cora said, her mind still reeling. With every breath, more of the pieces were clicking into place. "You were never a spy. You got caught on purpose."

And the prisoner hadn't been freed by a traitor. Sure, he could have had an accomplice, but it wouldn't have been necessary. Because if this was Darius Solaria, King of Syrus, all he'd needed to do was worldwalk out of the cell.

Then worldwalk back with a decoy corpse.

Gods, what a fool she'd been. All this time, she'd thought her best defense against him was to keep him from ever stepping foot in Khero, preventing him from familiarizing himself with key locations and securing places to worldwalk to.

Yet he'd been here all along. He'd waltzed straight into her kingdom and into her castle as if he'd been invited.

He arched a brow. "Was that a question?"

"Why did you do it?"

"I wanted to meet you, and getting captured as a Norunian spy was my best bet."

Teryn scoffed. "You could have sent a formal request for an audience. Or negotiated a meeting on neutral ground."

"Yes, but would you have faced me with an open mind? That's what I came to discover. I wanted to gauge my chances at peaceful relations between us, or see if your preconceived notions were too strong."

"You make it sound like you came for tea," Cora said, "but what you really did was invade my castle under a false pretense and a false name and lie to us. If you wanted peaceful relations, you should have tried something else. Pretending to be a prisoner, feeding us false information, and faking your death was a sure way to turn us against you."

"No, you were already turned against me." His voice took on a cold edge. "Thanks to my idiot son. Foolish Desmond, parading around as Duke Morkai. What a ridiculous moniker. As if calling himself *King of Magic* in the fae language would help him become Morkaius."

Cora stiffened at the mention of Morkai. Or Desmond, as was his birth name. Did Darius know his son was dead? Did he blame Cora for his death? Was he here for revenge? Questions burned Cora's mind, but she didn't want to give anything away by asking the wrong one. She couldn't be sure what Darius did or didn't know already, or what Morkai may have told him.

She shifted her feet, rooting herself to the stone floor, and sought logic over fear. His presence was terrifying and didn't bode well for the safety of her castle. Yet she could learn what she could, starting with the facts they'd already exchanged. "When you pretended to be a Norunian spy, you claimed Norun was targeting us over the death of Prince Helios. Was any of that true?"

"Oh, it was true. Before Desmond met his end at Centerpointe Rock, he detailed the prince's death to King Isvius, attempting to paint Selay as the enemy and potentially gain an ally. But when Desmond couldn't follow up to fan the flames of hatred and control their direction, the King of Norun turned his ire upon Khero instead. Norun made for an easy ally when I began correspondence with Isvius and mentioned my plans to invade Khero."

So Darius did know about Morkai's death. And his alliance with Norun was real.

"Why are you targeting Khero?"

He gave her a pointed look. "You know why. I know all about the Veil and Lela and the prophecy. Even before I got my memories back, I knew. Desmond was useful in one thing at least, and that was dying. His death triggered an enchantment he'd forged as a safeguard, ensuring his hard work wouldn't be lost if he failed. The enchantment materialized in a veritable tome of information that landed on my study desk in Syrus. Despite our many decades of estrangement, he'd continued to detail his discoveries and actions. The report told me everything he'd hidden from me after our falling out. It was quite illuminating."

Mother Goddess, was there anything he didn't know?

"I hope you see what's at stake now," he said. "The missive you received from me this morning spoke only truth. In three weeks, we will meet at the Khero-Vinias border, and I will demand Khero's surrender. If you refuse, my Norunian reinforcements will follow and lay waste to your kingdom. Moreover, if I wanted to act sooner, I could. Ever since I left your dungeon, I've spent time orienting myself with certain locations in the castle. It would be easy to claim Ridine. I could have control of it by morning."

Tremors racked Cora's body at his words. At the very real picture they painted. She couldn't keep the quaver from her voice, but at least she had enough rage to hide her fear. "Then why are you here chatting with us?"

"Unlike my son, who used war negotiations as bait for battle, I truly want to avoid war. I'll resort to it if I must, plan for it, but I don't want you to be my enemy." He stepped away from the wall, hands clasped behind his back. "Besides, there is an alternative to surrender."

Cora remembered what he'd said when he'd first arrived.

"You want us to ally with you," Teryn said.

"Yes, but instead of talking in circles about it, I want to extend a personal invitation for Queen Aveline to speak with me in private. And no, the invitation is for one, not two. Aveline will come with me alone."

"Come with you...to where?" Cora asked.

"To Syrus."

She barked a disbelieving laugh. "You want me to go to Syrus with you."

"I can walk us there and back in no more than an hour."

He used the term *walk*, but he didn't mean by foot. "Why do you want to meet with me in Syrus?"

"To show you what the kingdom of an *evil immortal tyrant* looks like." He said it with such jest, but there was nothing funny about this situation.

Cora and Teryn said nothing, which made Darius' expression darken.

"I've called it an invitation, but—" He stepped forward again and disappeared at once.

"—it's not—" he said, appearing on the opposite side of the bed.

"—really—" Now by the wardrobe.

"—a request." He reappeared where he'd first stood. He'd moved so fast, they'd hardly had time to react beyond a flinch. He'd worldwalked with ease, as if he'd been taking a leisurely stroll, hopping from one location to the next with each step he'd taken.

Cora wasn't that powerful. She couldn't activate her abilities that fast.

"I don't want to take you by force," Darius said, "but I can. I can cross this space and take your hand before either of you can react."

"Is that how you intend to get us to trust you?" Teryn said, edging closer to Cora, his poker raised once more. "With threats?"

"What else do you want from me?" Darius said with a sneer. "We're enemies until we agree otherwise. I can't make unbreakable vows like pureblood Elvyn can, but I will still state it out loud. I swear not to harm Queen Aveline Caelan at any time while she is in Syrus."

Cora shook her head. "Your word means nothing."

"What matters to you, then? Blood? Well, then let me tell you this. I have a vested interest in you. A reason why I'd rather not kill you, and it has to do with your bloodline."

"What...what do you mean?"

His lips curved in a cruel grin. "You, Aveline, are my kin."

43

Darius' words rattled around in her mind, but she couldn't make sense of them. "What do you mean I'm your kin?"

"You share my blood," Darius said. "Well, not *my* blood exactly. We both share my father's blood, the blood of King Tristaine Solaria. Your relation to him is diluted over many generations, but I can still sense it when I stand before you. The same way my son thought he sensed the weight of prophecy on you. That's what his report had said. That the moment he saw you as a child, he felt a connection and knew you were the prophesied mother. Can you imagine how embarrassed he'd be to discover just how wrong he was? What he felt wasn't the magical tug of prophecy, but the connection fae feel to their kin. Had he been humble enough to harbor at least a shred of doubt, he'd have done his due diligence to follow your family tree. He'd have followed your mother's ancestry to the Southern Islands, then several generations back to King Tristaine of Syrus, his grandfather."

Cora didn't know what to think. What to feel. She was distantly related to Morkai. He'd targeted her, hurt her, cursed her all because of a prophecy and a sense of connection he hadn't understood.

He'd been wrong.

So recklessly and foolishly wrong.

Every conclusion he'd come to about Cora had been the result of his mistakes.

Everything she'd suffered.

Every loss she'd been forced to bear.

Rage boiled inside her, curling her fingers into fists. Flames filled her mind's eye as a dark weight fell over her, smothering her.

Then a whispered voice. *Should it have been her?*

A thorn of guilt shattered her anger. She forced the dark thoughts from her mind, forced her fury to cool enough to maintain her tether to the present.

Darius spoke again. "I truly mean it when I say I don't want us to be enemies. All I ask is for one hour of your time. Just see what Syrus is like. See what kind of king I truly am. Hear me out, and I'll answer any questions you have."

She breathed deeply, opening her senses to him, to his energy.

"I will not hurt you," he said, "nor will I demand an answer about our alliance today. I will give you time to decide."

She tested the flow of his energy, its lack of constriction. His words didn't feel like a lie.

While she couldn't imagine anything that could convince her to ally with him, this could give her a chance to learn more. And she had one advantage.

She could worldwalk.

Darius had made no mention of her abilities yet, and he couldn't have learned about them from his son's report. Morkai would have relayed details about Cora's clairsentience, but he'd never learned about her worldwalking powers while he'd been alive. It was possible Darius suspected she was a worldwalker based on their shared bloodline with Tristaine, but the ability obviously wasn't gifted to all his descendants. Morkai hadn't been able to worldwalk. Cora's mother hadn't shown even the slightest inclination toward magic.

As far as Darius knew, she was just a clairsentient witch, still learning her magic.

Her abilities may not be as impressive as Darius' were, but if she sensed danger, she could disappear in a heartbeat, just like him. And maybe, if she could catch him unaware, if she could get hold of a weapon, even just a knife...

She could end his life.

But what had Ailan said about killing him?

He can be killed just like the rest of my kind—beheading or excessive blood loss.

He can be killed so long as he can be outsmarted.

She wasn't sure she could behead or force excessive blood loss while outsmarting him, but there was at least a chance.

And if he could take her away by force anyway...

She sidled closer to Teryn. They kept their gazes on Darius for several long beats before exchanging a quick glance. Cora gave him a subtle nod, which made his jaw tighten. Just as quickly, they returned their attention to Darius.

Cora opened her mouth to accept his terms, but Teryn spoke first.

"I want a blood oath. That's how humans secured vows in ancient times, predating written contracts."

Darius smirked. "Yes, I know how history books work."

"Then cut your palm and state the promise you made earlier. That you will escort Queen Aveline safely to and from Syrus, and that you will take her from Ridine for no longer than an hour, and that neither you nor anyone else will cause her harm."

Darius narrowed his eyes. "When I asked if blood mattered to you, this wasn't what I'd had in mind. Are you like my son, then? Dabbling in blood magic because you're not strong enough to do anything else?"

Cora couldn't help the furrow that formed between her brows. Why *did* Teryn want a blood pact from Darius? She'd never known him to value such old-fash-ioned traditions.

Teryn shrugged. "You're about to abduct my wife. If you fear I'll use your blood for nefarious purposes, then I'd say it makes the terms of our agreement almost even."

"Only almost?"

"My wife's safety is priceless. There's nothing you could give me but your life that could balance the scales. So I'll ask for your blood."

Darius continued to eye Teryn, but he drew his knife nevertheless. "Very well," he said with clear reluctance. Holding out his hand, he sliced the blade across his palm. A red line appeared, and as he squeezed his fingers into a fist, a drop of blood fell to the stones. Then another. "I, Darius Solaria, hereby promise that I will escort Queen Aveline, by way of worldwalking, safely to and from Syrus, and that we will stray to no other kingdom. I vow that I will return her to Ridine by the end of an hour *or* allow her to leave on her own at any time. Furthermore, I vow that neither I nor anyone else will cause her harm at any time during the course of our agreement."

Cora analyzed his words, seeking loopholes. Not that it mattered. Like he'd already admitted, this wasn't a magically binding vow, just an old tradition based on superstition. Maybe what Teryn had said was the important part. Instilling a hint of fear in Darius could make him keep his word.

She breathed deeply, connecting to all the elements and sought any sign that this was wrong. Dread pulsed back, as did anxiety, but she felt no clairsentient warning. No inkling that this might be a trap.

"All right," she said, voice thick. On trembling legs, she strode out from behind Teryn. He grasped her hand as she passed him, squeezing it. She squeezed it back in wordless reassurance. Her lungs tightened as she released his palm, felt his fingers slip from hers. She took another step. "I'm ready."

In the next breath, Darius stood before her. He placed a hand on her shoulder, then—

Cora was gone. Teryn hadn't been prepared. Hadn't even seen Darius move. He and Cora had come to the same conclusion—that they didn't have much of a choice but to humor him. Not when Darius held Ridine at his mercy. Not when he could come back at any time, fill their castle with countless soldiers, and claim victory by morning.

Either Darius was less capable than he'd made himself seem or he truly was desperate for an alliance with them.

They needed to find out which was true.

And how to exploit it.

That didn't lessen his terror at having witnessed him taking her like that. His rage at knowing he'd agreed to *let* him take her.

Hatred burned hot in his chest as he narrowed his eyes at the three spots of blood on the stones. Without a second thought, he marched into his sitting room, extracted a piece of parchment from the bureau, and placed the paper over the blood until crimson bloomed over it.

"What are you doing?" Emylia's voice came from beside him. She was as semi-transparent as always, outfitted in an equally hazy loose dress that billowed on a nonexistent breeze.

"Were you here the whole time?" he asked, his tone low and controlled. If she'd been there before, he hadn't noticed her. He'd been too focused on Darius and Cora. "Did you enjoy the show? Did you just stand there mute and watch him take her?"

"What could I have done?"

He was being unfair in taking his frustration out on her, but she'd been avoiding him ever since their last conversation on the battlement. When she'd refused to explain what she'd meant about feeling like she'd disappear if she came too close to him. He understood exactly why now. Because touching her ethera would force her to move on to the otherlife. To claim the peace she'd said she'd wanted but hadn't been able to receive. Peace she'd only find after taking care of her unfinished business.

He knew the truth.

She didn't *want* to move on yet.

And he didn't want her hypocrisy right now.

Teryn finished soaking the blood into the paper and folded it. As he rose, he met Emylia's accusing gaze.

"Don't tell me you're going to do what I think you are," she said.

"What is it you think I'm doing?"

Her lower lip wobbled as her fingers curled into fists. "Let me ask you a question. Why have you been going to that tower room? Why have you been reading that book? You know it's dangerous. You know what that book has done."

He did know, but it didn't shake his resolve, even though she was right in every way. He had no right going into the North Tower Library, reading the book Cora had left stashed inside a nightstand drawer. Seeking answers to the question that had plagued his mind over the past week.

In truth, he hadn't learned anything new, but he had confirmed what Emylia had told him when they'd last spoken. It had all been there, just like she'd described.

"Why, Teryn? Why are you doing this?"

"Because I want Morkai's army of souls."

Her disappointment in him was plain, written in the downward curve of her mouth, the slump of her shoulders.

He shared some of that disappointment too. He'd wanted to wait until he could talk to Cora about it, but now he didn't have time. He needed to act. If Darius returned to attack the castle, he'd be ready. He wouldn't let him win. Whether now, later, or at the meeting at the border, he'd use this advantage.

"There must be a reason why I have this ability," he said. "This connection to death."

"Reason?" She released an angry huff. "What are you talking about? Do you think you're part of the prophecy? You're not. There is no special reason for what has happened to you, just a logical one. Blood magic comes with consequences, just like I've told you. You completed a blood weaving while you straddled the line between life and death. You forged a magical connection *with* death. It's as simple as that."

"Why, though? Why *this* consequence? Why does my touch send etheras to the otherlife?"

She flinched back at his words, demonstrating just how afraid she was of that very power. Then she shook her head. "We might never know. Maybe it's because you succeeded at severing another ethera's ties to your body—Morkai's tie to the mortal world. Now you're gifted and burdened with the ability to do the same for other spirits. To sever the chains that bind them here and free them."

He clenched his jaw. "Then why can't I use it for good?"

"*Are* you trying to use it for good? Or are you lusting after blood magic for revenge?" When he said nothing, she closed her eyes. Finally, her expression softened. She turned a pleading look to him. "Just...take a moment, Teryn, please. Breathe. Connect to your heart. Don't work blood magic on an impulse."

He wasn't acting on impulse. He'd been considering this for a week, weighing possibilities. Still, she was right about blood magic and its consequences. She knew better than anyone that what he wanted to do was wrong. Dark. Forbidden.

Reluctantly, he gave in and closed his eyes. Just like when he'd been trapped as a disembodied ethera, he connected to his breaths, his heartbeat, the rush of his blood, the pound of his pulse. Slowly, he began to relax. His muscles uncoiled, his heartbeat slowed, and the most delicious euphoria struck him. The euphoria of being alive. In his body. In control. It wasn't an impassioned or impulsive feeling. It was real and steady.

He shifted his thoughts to what he'd been considering.

No doubts stood in his way. No guilt. No fear. No remorse.

"I'm doing it, Emylia."

～

TERYN DIDN'T WAIT TO SEE IF SHE FOLLOWED HIM OUT OF THE CASTLE TO THE charred field, the folded piece of paper stained with Darius' blood in his hand. Maintaining the same calm he'd felt after sinking into his bodily sensations, he crouched at the edge of the dead field, just like he'd witnessed Morkai doing the day he demonstrated the abilities of his wraiths. He'd been summoning his Roizan then, but Teryn did it for a different reason now.

He unfolded the bloodstained paper and pressed it against the charred soil. Then he watched and waited. There was, of course, a chance that this wouldn't work. He couldn't perform Morkai's ritual exactly, only use it to inform his own actions. He didn't have any leftover vials of Morkai's blood, just this crimson parchment.

Yet soon a rippling fog crept over the field, much like it had when Teryn had first met the wraiths. Body parts began to materialize—arms, legs, heads, torsos—until the field was filled with hazy soldiers with empty pits for eyes.

Slowly, Teryn rose to his feet and faced the army. Their forms undulated, as if they struggled to maintain their hold on sentience. There was no ferocity in them, none of the violence they'd shown when Morkai had ordered them to fight.

Teryn would have to stir that ferocity himself.

"You lost your lives fighting for King Darius," he said, his voice carrying over the field. He internally winced, hoping none of the castle residents or staff woke up to his voice only to find him talking to himself. Or would they be able to see the wraiths too?

He continued. "You died trapped between worlds, and because of that, you lost your heart-centers. Your connection to life and the otherlife. Morkai gave you a second chance at your lives as great warriors and promised peace when he'd accomplished his goals. Yet he too left you behind."

Some of the wraiths' forms ceased wavering and began to sharpen. Their empty eye sockets seemed to lock onto him, craving more of his words.

"Your former masters may have abandoned you, but I will not. Unlike those you served before, I can make good on a promise of peace. You feel it, don't you? That yearning."

Even more of their forms sharpened, and he tasted their yearning in turn. It grew ravenous. Palpable. The entire field radiated with it.

He was suddenly aware of the danger he was in and how quickly this situation could turn. Should the wraiths want, they could swarm him. They could claim their own oblivion or cut him with their blades.

Clearing his throat, he spoke again. "I can give you purpose and peace. I can give you revenge for being so cruelly abandoned."

His words were manipulative, he knew that. Neither master had meant to abandon them, but soft words wouldn't instill purpose in an undead warrior.

"I won't force you to fight again and again, driving your reanimation through blood magic." The truth was, he couldn't make them reanimate. Not without a blood weaving, and Teryn wasn't willing to do that. And based on what Emylia had said on the battlement, Morkai had been able to secure the wraiths' loyalty through promises alone, but being defeated in battle would end their bloodlust. Which meant Teryn was limited to how long he could use them. And he only intended to use them once. Whether it ended up being in defense of the castle or to defeat Darius at the border meeting, he'd only do this one time.

He continued. "I won't make you wait for some far-off goal before I make good on what I offer you. All I ask is for one final battle. One last act of noble violence."

He reached for the letter opener he'd taken from the bureau before coming to the field. Digging its tip into his forearm, he made a shallow cut. He held out his arm and let his blood drip onto the black soil. "This is my blood. This is the blood you will follow when next I call for you, to fight one last time. This is the blood that will end your hunger and lay your souls to rest."

His heart hammered against his ribs as he waited for their reaction.

Then, as one, the wraiths bent to the earth on one knee and bowed their heads.

Seven devils, it worked. He'd earned their loyalty, just like Morkai.

He heaved a relieved breath.

"That wasn't truly blood magic." Emylia appeared beside him. Or had she been there all along?

"No," he said, "just a blood vow. A promise I can fulfill."

44

Oppressive heat filled Cora's lungs, pressing in all around her, as if the air itself had grown heavy. With a gasp, she tore away from Darius. He released her, and she launched a few steps back. She hadn't been prepared for him to take her so quickly, and the surprise sent shock waves through her legs.

She kept her eyes locked on Darius, who merely straightened the sleeves of his coat.

"Don't look at me with such suspicion," he said. "I've done nothing but take you to Syrus like we agreed."

Her breaths began to calm, and she dared to look away from him. They stood on a cobblestone walkway on a quiet street. Sleeping storefronts lined one side while a stone wall rose waist high on the other. A soft breeze blew across her cheeks, carrying with it more of that smothering heat.

It wasn't an unnatural kind.

It was merely the temperature of her surroundings.

The Southern Islands were known for their balmy climates, even in the winter. Which must mean they truly were in Syrus. She hazarded a glance at Darius again, but he kept his distance, posture straight, hands clasped at his waist.

"Welcome to my hellish domain," he said. "Please, look around. See what a dark and miserable prison I've subjected my citizens to."

His mocking tone grated on her nerves, but she studied her surroundings. They were dark indeed, but that was only because it was evening. The Southern Islands were a few hours behind Khero, so it was sometime before midnight. As for miserable, there was nothing to suggest an ounce of misery. Strains of conversation and laughter floated on the air, while light streamed from homes, terraces, and nearby buildings.

She stepped closer to the stone wall and found a sloping, layered hillside beyond it, edged with streets like the one they stood on, and tall blocky buildings made from colorful stucco. It was too dark to see the hues clearly, but she caught hints of orange, tan, blue, and pink. Some of the rooftops were flat while others boasted terracotta shingles. She even spotted an ornate domed building far below.

The bottom of the hill cut off in a steep cliff, where the first rows of houses appeared to be carved straight from the stone. Beneath that stretched an endless sea dancing with starlight and the lamps of fishing boats.

Gods, she hated to admit it, but her enemy's island kingdom was beautiful.

She did her best to mask her awe as she faced Darius again.

"Come along," he said, starting off down the street.

"To where?"

"I want to give you a closer look at my people."

"Meaning..."

He paused and glanced over his shoulder at her. "We're going to a public house. Having a few drinks."

She pulled her head back. "A public house?"

"What, surprised a king would deign to interact with his own people? Don't think too highly of me. My people haven't seen me looking this healthy before. No one will recognize me as their beloved monarch. To them, I'll be just an old soldier out for a drink."

Annoyance prickled her skin. "I wasn't thinking about you at all. I was more concerned with the fact that I'm dressed in a night robe."

He wrinkled his nose as he studied her, as if he hadn't truly looked at her until now. "Worry not. You'll do. People from all around come to Syrus, either to visit or take up residence. I offer my citizens a way of life not often found elsewhere—but you'll see for yourself. The point is there are no standards of fashion here, with so many outside influences. No one will look twice at your clothes."

With that, he proceeded again.

Gritting her teeth, she followed him. She was barefoot too, but the streets were surprisingly clean, and the cobblestones were well-maintained. Besides, being barefoot outside wasn't an oddity for her. The Forest People valued physical connections with nature and relished any opportunity to set their shoeless soles on soil.

As they navigated the narrow, winding street that lined the sloping cliff, Cora cast her attention up the hill this time, taking in the ever-climbing incline. More rows of buildings stretched above her, and at the very top stood a bell tower beside a crenellated wall. Behind that rose an enormous white dome. The entire structure was illuminated with lanterns, making it a beacon of beauty. She wondered if that was Darius' palace.

She looked from the bell tower above to the sea below and determined they were only midway up the hill. She couldn't imagine how breathtaking the view might be from the top. As much as she craved such a sight, she was grateful they kept to the outer street that ran horizontally across the hill and not one of the streets that led to the higher levels. She was in no mood for a hike.

Sounds of raucous laughter and the clink of plates and glasses grew louder, as did the frequency of light streaming from the windows. Crowds filled the streets ahead, either from groups of men chatting or couples dining at the small tables set beside the wall. Cora hadn't had many experiences in cities, as she'd often stayed behind with the commune when the Forest People had gone to trade in nearby villages. To see so many figures gathered around so late at night, so animated, so energetic...it was a bit overwhelming.

That reminded her to reconnect with the elements and strengthen her mental shields. She wanted to keep a close read on Darius' energy, but that could wait until they'd settled in at their destination.

She wove through the crowded sidewalk. He was right about no one noticing him as their king. In fact, the people barely noticed either of them. Finally, Darius paused outside a building of pink stucco. More sounds of chatter and laughter echoed from behind the heavy wooden door, above which hung a sign.

The Dragon's Arms Public House.

"Here we are." Darius pushed open the door and strode inside.

Cora followed, anxiety fraying the edges of her mental wards. The pub was packed with patrons filling nearly every table in the room. Ale and smoke infused the air, making the dimly lit room seem even darker. The walls were a cream plaster, recessed with small alcoves that held decorative bottles or oil lamps. The red tile floor was sticky beneath her bare feet.

Darius swept through the crowd with ease, while Cora shuffled in his wake, her heart racing as she skirted around the busy tables. A trio of men rose from their table at the same time, chatting as they closed in toward her, paying her not a lick of heed. She was forced to go around and lost sight of Darius. She shuffled this way and that, then finally spotted him at a small table at the back of the room.

With a weighted glare, she rushed the rest of the way there and planted herself in the empty seat, making an effort to pull it as far away from him as space allowed. She fought to catch her breath, seething at being put in such a position.

Darius leaned back in his chair, as if the pub were his home and not a loud room filled with inebriated strangers. His ease mocked her, making her want to hide her discomfort. If she admitted how flustered she was, she'd have to confess she'd never done this before. Never entered a public house or dined with commoners.

She'd never considered herself a sheltered person. Her early hardships had matured her in many ways, while life with the Forest People had given her the sense that she was self-sufficient and well-traveled. Only now did she realize how few of life's mundane experiences she'd had. How truly sheltered she was. How little she could relate to the average citizen.

She was a terrible queen.

True, she'd only been queen for a matter of months, and before that, she'd lived with a secretive commune. Guilt plagued her nonetheless.

A willowy serving woman approached their table, dressed in a floral-patterned skirt and white top that hung off her shoulders. A red kerchief tied back auburn hair to display a sun-browned face adorned with freckles. Her eyes dipped to Darius' black coat, with its high collar and stiff shoulders. Now that Cora was closer, she noted the gold pins at his lapels, showcasing a dragon in a circle of flame. That must be Syrus' sigil. A strange sigil for a king who was rejected by every dragon he'd tried to bond. Did he still hold out hope he'd gain their approval after he became Morkaius?

Something brightened in the serving woman's expression. "Welcome, esteemed soldier. You honor us with your great presence. What can I get for you this evening?"

"Zaran wine, 170 Year of the Eagle," he answered with a charming grin.

The woman arched a brow at Cora.

"Nothing for me."

"Ale for her," Darius said.

The woman flounced off, slapping a patron upside the head when he pinched her backside.

"Lively, happy, healthy." Darius gestured toward the nearby tables. "No one has been beheaded in the streets or drawn and quartered by moonlight. Who would have thought?"

She maintained a stony expression at his continued attempt at sarcasm. "Just because I don't trust you doesn't mean I assumed you were a bloodthirsty king."

Though she had imagined something like it. How could she not when he'd produced such progeny as Morkai? The mage's takeover of Ridine had resulted in an understaffed castle, dusty halls, and countless soldiers who'd been compelled to obey him by blood magic. She'd imagined Syrus would be like that too. Unkempt. Lifeless. Filled with cowed citizens with glazed eyes.

Nothing suggested the pub patrons were enjoying themselves by force. They drank. They laughed. Some even sang bawdy tunes. There was an array of people in different states of dress, different fashions, though all shared an aura of informality.

The serving woman returned with their drinks. Darius accepted his glass of wine with one hand and passed a couple of coins to the woman with the other. Cora's eyes locked on his palm as he withdrew it. All she could see of the cut he'd made the blood promise with was a smear of dried blood. Not a gash or scar to be found. So he truly did have rapid healing.

She leaned back in her chair, arms crossed, not daring to drink the ale before her. "So, you've shown me Syrus. Why else are we here?"

"Yes, I've shown you Syrus, but you'll look at neither me nor my kingdom with unclouded eyes until you have good reason to discard your prejudices. You have questions for me. Ask them. I'll answer with honesty." He took a long pull of his wine.

She did have questions, though she still needed to be careful how she asked them so as not to give too much away. Regardless, she'd take advantage of his offer.

Breathing deep, she pried the smallest hole in her mental shields and focused on his energy as she asked, "How long were you in Khero before you got caught as a pretend spy?"

"Not long," he said, and his energy remained steady. "I'd learned about the spies from Norun who'd been caught in your kingdom so I made the same mistakes they did. Spoke to the same traitorous informants. Asked too many obvious questions. I was caught within a week. But I know what you're really asking, and no, I didn't tour all over your kingdom to secure key locations to world-walk to. I only did that at your castle."

"How long were you wandering around Ridine? Did you worldwalk out of your cell from the start? Where have you been hiding since you faked your death?"

"I haven't been hiding in your castle, cousin."

She bristled at the nickname. They may be distantly related, but they weren't cousins. Allied monarchs often called each other *cousin*, but she and Darius weren't allies either.

He continued. "First of all, I stayed in my cell like a good little prisoner until I was ready to leave. I only left to retrieve a replacement body, and after I planted the decoy, I returned to my soldiers in Norun. I've hardly set foot in Ridine since, aside from the last few days when I was getting the lay of the castle and trying my luck to meet with you."

His energy continued to pulse with the steady hum of truth, but the last part tingled with something sharp and jagged. Maybe there was a lie hidden there, or more to what he was saying. She hoped it didn't mean he suspected where she'd been on the nights he hadn't been able to find her.

"I was lucky to finally find you this evening," he said.

She gave him a pointed look. "In the middle of the night."

"Yes, well, I prefer to avoid witnesses."

"As do I," she said through her teeth.

"Are you embarrassed about my *stamina* comment? Ah, I see you are." He took an annoyingly long sip of wine, an obvious test of her patience. "I didn't lurk and watch, if that's what you're wondering. Yes, I first worldwalked to your castle this evening at an inopportune time and chose to attempt my visit later when I thought you'd be more amenable to a chat. I made my presence known almost as soon as I appeared in your bedroom, so don't paint me as a pervert." He said the last part with a chuckle.

She thinned her lips to show just how little amusement she found in this. "Pervert or no, the fact that you worldwalked straight to my bedroom proves you've been there before. Maybe you didn't spend weeks wandering my castle, but you spent enough time there to orient yourself, as you've already admitted, and one of those locations was my most private space."

With a cold grin, he leaned forward, elbows propped on the table, and laced his fingers. "You really are a worldwalker. You know exactly how my magic works."

She sucked in a breath but tried to keep her expression even. Damn, even with her precautions, she'd given too much away. "Just because I know how your magic works doesn't mean I'm the same as you."

He perched his chin on his laced hands and stared at her with unblinking silver-blue eyes. "Then why is your heart beating so fast?"

What...

What the hell did that mean? Sounds of the busy pub continued to blare around them. There was no way he could hear her heartbeat in such a loud room. Unless...

Was he...clairaudient?

He was half witch, which meant he had a sensory affinity of some sort. Could it be that while she'd been sensing truth and lies from his energy fluctuations, he was doing the same, but with her pulse?

Darius leaned back from the table and swirled his glass. "How is Ailan?"

Cora's heart lurched before she could steel herself.

He snorted a laugh. "That reaction tells me you have met my sister indeed. I won't ask where she'd been hiding, for I haven't given you enough reasons to trust me yet. And I assume she is behind the Veil by now. Does she look younger than me? I imagine aging has been far gentler on her than it has on me, if she's stayed in Lela this whole time."

She refused to address Ailan. Refused to admit any affiliation with her. Instead, she trained her voice to speak with level curiosity. "You aged poorly because you lived in Syrus?"

"Yes," he said, making no comment on her change of subject. "Living in Syrus, so far from El'Ara's heart, aged me horribly, yet my body refused to die. As soon as I set foot across the Khero-Vinias border, though, I felt healthier than I had in centuries. I didn't fully understand what was happening, but I'd learned enough from Desmond's report to understand that the *mora*—my birthright—was healing me. Then the Veil tore and my aging began to reverse—just the slightest bit—and pieces of memories slowly snapped into place. My magic grew stronger. I believe I'll regain the rest of my youth once I become Morkaius."

Cora couldn't keep the glare from her eyes.

"Ah, of course. You still don't believe I deserve to be Morkaius. To you I'm still an evil Elvyn overlord who murdered his mother and seeks vengeance on his sister. So let's face these misbeliefs head-on and start with where it all began. Let's talk about my darling mother."

45

As much as Cora wanted to avoid listening to Darius drone on about his mother issues, she couldn't deny her curiosity. She'd heard Ailan's side of what had happened, as well as Garot's tale. But how did Darius see those same events? The fact that he used a dragon as his kingdom's sigil, despite never succeeding in bonding with one, suggested his perspective may be far different.

Perhaps the perspective of her enemy could give her an advantage.

Cora released a bored sigh so as not to appear too eager. "Fine, justify your actions. Let's hear it."

He smirked, and his expression held something like admiration. "I'm confident you'll feel differently once you've heard my side."

"Do tell."

He swirled his glass, drained its dregs, then lifted the empty cup. Yet another test of her patience as he waited for the serving woman to return. Cora still hadn't sipped her ale and had no intention of doing so. Her arms remained folded over her chest, her jaw tight.

Finally, the serving woman filled his glass and Darius took a sip, a satisfied look on his face. "The Dragon's Arms is the highest value public house in Syrus under the principles of leisure, liberation, and inebriation. Should the pub stand for other values, such as quietude, relaxation, and propriety, The Dragon's Arms would be a low-value establishment. Whereas the Golden Shore Inn, a few streets down, exemplifies those values to the highest standard."

Cora frowned, unsure of what this had to do with his mother.

He continued. "When stripped of principle, neither establishment is better or worse than the other, just different. You can see that, right? Take your personal preferences away and simply see each of those public houses for what they are. Under its own set of principles, each establishment is considered high value. Given the opportunity to demonstrate those principles to clientele who seek the same, each business is allowed to thrive. That is what the Kingdom of Syrus stands for. No one is limited by birth, bloodline, or social class. Instead, everyone is judged by merit and how they serve certain values."

"Syrus is a meritocracy?"

He nodded. "That was all I ever wanted for El'Ara. And the first person who ever put that idea in my head was my mother, Satsara. From as early as I can remember, she'd whisper stories about my father, who was no longer a prince but the King of Syrus by then. She told me I was a prince of two worlds, and an heir to two kinds of magic. She marveled over my abilities as a worldwalker and filled my mind with visions of the future. One day I would be Morkara, and the most unique one El'Ara had ever had—one with the blood of human royalty and the power of a witch, as well as all the powers that came with directing the *mora*. I could bring advancement to the fae realm, find ways to utilize my witch magic to blend with the *mora*.

"Satsara was the first person to use the term Morkaius. *My little Morkaius*, she'd call me. It was supposed to be a secret name, one I'd never speak aloud, but it filled me with so much pride. I wanted to be High King of Magic. I wanted to fulfill the vision she had for me, be the grand king she said my father was. She supported me. Continued to whisper stories about my father, telling me how much she missed him despite having woven the ward that had banished him from El'Ara for good. 'At least I have you,' she'd say. Her pride and joy. Her little High King of Magic."

His expression turned to a grimace and he took a long swallow of wine. "Then my sister was born. She told stories about my father less and less and turned more of her attention to her consort and pureblood child. By then, I was old enough to understand the prejudices the Elvyn held against me. Etrix, the tribunal, and everyone but my mother eyed me with disgust, even as they bowed. Soon my mother's eyes began to dull when she looked at me too."

"Did you give her any reason to doubt you?" She remembered what Ailan had said about the pranks he'd pulled, the way he'd snuck humans into El'Ara for pleasure and amusement, often to their demise.

He huffed a cold laugh. "Mother was easily swayed by those around her. Once the tribunal no longer had to pretend to pin their hopes for the future on me, they shifted their glowing approval to Ailan. The perfect pureblood they'd wanted all along. They urged her to name Ailan heir, or at least wait until she came of age before making her final decision. I was patient. I waited, confident that when Ailan reached maturity, Mother and the tribunal would see that she could offer only a fraction of the value that I could. Mother's words still rang in my head, after all. I knew how much I could do for El'Ara. Knew I could be a Morkara unlike any other.

"Yet it didn't turn out the way I expected. Ailan was named heir and I was set aside. I was crushed, enraged, heartbroken. Then the unthinkable happened. Mother tried to banish me from El'Ara. Do you want to know how it happened?"

She said nothing, for he'd surely tell her anyway. It didn't escape her that he'd avoided mentioning anything about the prank he'd pulled on Berolla and the injury that had almost killed Ailan. A convenient omission.

After another long sip, his eyes grew distant. His voice fell, and she had to lean forward to hear what he said next over the noise of the pub. "She hugged me. Mother took me to the grove she'd once kept as a sanctuary to meet my father in. She showed me the trees, recounted her fond memories. Then she faced me, told me she loved me, how proud of me she was, and hugged me. It was the first time in a long while that I felt loved by her, and it softened the hurt I'd felt after she'd chosen Ailan as her heir. I hugged her back, reveling in the warmth, in the hope that maybe Mother would change her mind. Then I heard it."

His expression darkened.

Cora was still leaning forward, unable to hide her curiosity. "Heard what?"

"The sound of magic weaving around me."

She arched her brow. Wait, did that mean...

"I'm clairaudient," he said, confirming her earlier suspicions. "My magic is fueled by sound, just like my father's was fueled by scent. That's how I worldwalk. I can travel to any place I can visualize, either from memory or physical sight. I activate my magic by forging a sound connection and control the distance by imagining the sound of my destination as near or far. Just like Father, the first time I worldwalked was by accident. I traveled to him the same way he accidentally stumbled upon El'Ara."

His demeanor eased a little at that, a sad smile forming on his lips.

"Did you travel on Samhain too?" Too late she realized she'd given something away, admitting that she knew about his history.

He didn't seem surprised, however, and just continued to grin at his memory. "No, it wasn't the thinning of the veils between worlds that brought me to him, but a memory of waves. Before Mother banished Tristaine, she let him take me to Syrus. I didn't consciously remember being there, but one day, when I was still just a boy, I unexpectedly recalled the sound of waves, ones so different from the lakes and oceans in El'Ara. Suddenly, I could visualize where I'd been when I'd heard those waves. I was so startled, so overwhelmed, that my magic took over. The next thing I knew, I was standing before an old man in a palace on a sunny hillside, the sound of waves crashing far below."

Cora was relieved at his explanation, for it further confirmed that their magic worked the same way. She too had worldwalked unexpectedly the first time, her magic taking over before she knew what had happened. His magic may be more powerful than hers, but at least she understood its strengths and limitations.

He shook his head, the mirth fading from his face. "I always thought my similarities to my father were what endeared me to my mother, but just like him, I lost her admiration. As soon as I heard the telltale sound of Mother's magic wrapping around me in that grove, I knew what was happening. She was trying to banish me from El'Ara. Not just that, but she was attempting it in the exact same place she'd banished my father in, and in the exact same way. With a hug."

A bitter ache struck her, and for a single breath, his pain was hers. She could almost feel the shock of betrayal he must have felt when his mother hugged him, made him feel loved...and then wove magic to expel him from his home.

Yet she knew the other side. She knew what he'd done. The dangers he'd posed to not only Ailan, but El'Ara as a whole. Cora may not know Satsara, but both

Darius' and Ailan's descriptions made it seem like she loved him deeply. Perhaps too much. It must have killed her inside to banish her son, no matter how dangerous he was.

But of course Darius didn't see it that way. To him, he was the sole victim.

He continued. "I worldwalked to Syrus before she could finish her ward, but by then, my father had died. There was no home for me there, and I soon learned that the human realm was just as flawed as El'Ara. It was yet another domain ruled by blood, not merit. Yet another place where I was considered impure. The new King of Syrus—one of my half brothers—called me a bastard. A monster. An abomination. Had either realm judged me for my merit, they would have seen that *I* was the most capable. I could bring the most value as a ruler. I could do more, be more, create more."

"Under the assumption that their values were wrong and yours were right," Cora said flatly.

He narrowed his eyes. "Don't pretend you can't relate. Have you ever questioned the values of your kingdom? Its principles? Its expectations?"

She couldn't deny that. Time and again she'd faced outdated notions. Prejudice. Scorn. Much of a queen's value lay in her husband and—even more importantly—her ability to bear heirs. Even as the monarch of her kingdom, Cora bore the skepticism of certain nobles who'd rather see a man on the throne.

The mere thought boiled her blood.

Yet just because Darius claimed to be better didn't mean he was. His kingdom seemed idyllic, but there were always shadows lurking behind the brightest corners. Even now, she sensed an undercurrent of unrest weaving through the boisterous atmosphere of the public house. As narrow as a splinter, yet strong enough to feel as if it were buried in her side. She hadn't been conscious of it until now, as she'd been more focused on Darius' tale. With every breath, it was growing. Deepening. Creating fissures in the too-perfect cheer filling the room.

The fissure widened. Cracked.

Cora angled her head toward the source of the anomaly.

"Don't you dare report me!" A panicked male voice contrasted the joyful strains of conversation. Cora couldn't see the speaker through the crowd, but she sensed him strongly now. He lowered his voice, but she could still make out his muttered words. "I can't take another demerit this month. You know this."

A deeper tension constricted the energy of the room—a dark and scornful glee at the man's plight. It was coming from those closest to the man and spread farther and farther, from patron to patron, even cutting off some of the conversations—

Darius rose from his chair and set his empty wine glass on the table. "Come, I grow weary of this place. You make for a poor drinking companion."

She opened her mouth, but before she could speak, he grasped her shoulder. Vertigo seized her, and she found herself stumbling over her feet. Sound cut off, as did the stench of smoke and ale. Darius released her, and she managed to regain her balance, but as the dizziness cleared from her eyes, she found their surroundings had changed.

Her bare feet rested on the smooth white marble of a long rectangular balcony. Behind her was an enormous open-air space with several seating areas, potted plants, and ornate rugs. Before her was an elegant balustrade interrupted by thick marble columns.

Darius stood before the rail, as unflustered as ever, gathering lungfuls of air. Cora glanced beyond the balustrade and found they were high above the sloping hillside, with a full view of the multi-layered city beneath them. She must have been right about the opulent building she'd glimpsed on their way to the pub; this must be Darius' palace. There were no guards or servants near the balcony, no nearby strains of emotion to suggest anyone was close by. It made sense that his palace would be so quiet at present, considering the king was supposed to be in Norun.

"Look around," Darius said. "My kingdom is beautiful. What I've created is fair. Syrus flourishes even when its king is not at home. You can see that with your own eyes."

She scoffed. "If it's so beautiful, why didn't you want me to hear more of what that man was saying?"

"He's none of my concern. His peers and the principles of his chosen establishment determine his value. If he's so worried about being reported for a demerit, he should have worked harder to prove his worth."

"You let your people police each other?"

"I give them the authority all citizens should have."

"You encourage a mob mentality. What happens to those who receive demerits? What happens to those you and your society deem of low value? What happens to those born without able bodies or minds?"

"And you're back to clinging to your prejudices. Look with your eyes, Aveline. Look at this peaceful city. *This* is all I wanted to bring to El'Ara." He gestured toward the sloping hillside. "I succeeded in Syrus, after I won the throne from my brother, and this is all I wanted for the fae realm too. Yet the elite—the Elvyn—wouldn't see reason. Just like you refuse to see reason."

"The Elvyn refused to see reason, as you call it, because you invaded their realm." Wind blew over her cheeks, colder than it had been farther down the hill.

"Such is the way of war and progress," he said. "It is a dark and treacherous thing, and not something to take lightly. You don't want war, do you?"

"Of course I don't."

"Nor do I. I value the lives of my people. I want to see a bright future for all of them. As monarchs, we should do whatever we can to ensure the least number of casualties, don't you think?"

"This is where you propose an alliance between us, isn't it?"

He turned away from the balustrade and faced her fully. "I'm not coming to you empty-handed. I will offer you the very thing the Elvyn want to take away."

"What's that?"

A confident grin stretched his lips. "Lela."

She blinked a few times. "What are you saying?"

"You, Aveline Corasande Caelan, will be Queen of Lela."

46

Her mind emptied.
Queen of Lela.
She...she didn't want that.
Did she?

"El'Ara needs its heart before it can be whole again," Darius said. "The *mora* seeping into this world must hold terrible consequences for the fae realm. Before the Veil, the *mora* traveled through the veins of magic that wove through the land and met at the heart of the world, at the Morkara's palace in the Elvyn city of Le'Lana. The Morkara would direct the flow of *mora* from there to wherever they sought to send it. But the Veil must have compromised that.

"First, there was no Morkara in either world to direct the magic, thanks to Ailan's idiotic plan to pass on her legacy to an unnamed heir." His tone took on a sardonic quality. "Yes, I remember all of that now that I have my memories again. But now the Veil has torn, which, according to Desmond's report, means we have a Morkara again. Goody. Yet still, the *mora* cannot flow like it could before, for the Veil blocks its return. Not even the tear can allow enough magic to bring the *mora* back into balance. No, there are only two solutions: either the Veil must come down completely, or it must be completed to incorporate Lela. The Elvyn will obviously choose the latter, for who knows what repercussions could arise should the Veil be fully erased while the fae and human realms are connected through Lela. Our worlds could collide. Yet as a result of completing the Veil, Lela will return to El'Ara and every human on this land will cease to have a home."

She hated that he was voicing her greatest fear—that everything she was preparing to fight for would result in her people's exile. Ailan had all but confirmed it.

He continued. "The Elvyn will never agree to let humans live in El'Ara. Even if they did, the humans would be considered low-value members of society due to their blood. Because—as I've already stated—the Elvyn cling to principles that only benefit themselves. Yet there is another option that will require neither exile nor subjugation. The answer is written in the prophecy. And that is where you come in."

Impatience tightened her chest. Or was it curiosity? Excitement, even? Whatever the case, she needed to know what the hell he was getting at. It took no small effort to maintain an air of nonchalance. "You mean as Queen of Lela?"

"Exactly. My son abandoned his mission to find El'Ara for me and sought to become Morkaius of the human world instead. I never would have approved, for his success would have meant the end of the fae realm. Drawing on that much magic—claiming it, using it in the human world—would have drained El'Ara. As much as I resent the Elvyn for their closed-minded ways, I treasure the fae realm. So believe me when I say I don't condone anything my son did in his efforts to control fae magic for his own selfish aims."

"And that matters to me why?"

He smirked. "It matters because it will allow you to give me the benefit of the doubt when I say this next part. You will take on a role similar to the Morkaius of Lela. No, hear me out. Your husband remains in the line of succession for Vera, and should he inherit the kingdom, the two of you could reforge Lela and rule the land as a whole."

Cora's pulse kicked up, but she hoped he was too busy talking to notice. It was true that Teryn remained in the line of succession for Vera. As Larylis' brother, Teryn had a claim to the throne. A weaker one compared to Noah, but a claim nonetheless. But Darius hadn't mentioned Noah. Or Mareleau, for that matter. Had he not learned their significance? He knew the Morkara had been born, but had he not figured out who that was?

Hope sparked inside her. They'd kept Noah's birth a secret and had spread the rumor that Mareleau had returned home before Cora's wedding. In truth, Darius, Mareleau, and Noah had all been under the same roof for a handful of days. Did he not know?

Of course he didn't.

If he'd known, her friend would be dead, and her newborn son too.

Unless...

Unless Darius wasn't the monster he'd been painted as.

A heavy weight settled over her chest—a clairsentient warning not to give in to that line of reasoning just yet.

Darius spoke again. "You will fulfill every condition to become the Morkaius, the very conditions my son had tried to fulfill. You'll rule over Lela, a crown given not taken. As monarch of El'Ara's heart, the *mora* will flow to you. Should you want, you could harness it."

She barked a cold laugh. "Are you trying to get me killed? I know what the prophecy said about becoming Morkaius of this world. *He who harnesses the magic will be destroyed by it.*"

His face split with a wide smile, too maniacal to be comforting. "Yes, but you won't harness the *mora*. You are going to push it back into El'Ara. And I, as Morkaius of El'Ara, will tear down the Veil, but only after you've returned the *mora* to El'Ara. Without the forced connection between our worlds caused by the *mora* and the Veil, our worlds will separate once more. Do you see? It isn't the land itself that is El'Ara's heart; it's the *mora*. The convergence of those magic veins. Once inside the Veil, they will collide once more and forge a new heart."

She tried to imagine it, tried to picture what he was explaining. If the true Heart of El'Ara was the magic and not simply the land, the fae realm would have a new heart should the lines of *mora* be forced to recede behind the Veil.

And yet...

"I don't understand," she said. "If I don't harness the *mora*, then how will I have the ability to push it back?"

"Like I said, it's written in the prophecy itself. By becoming Lela's monarch, you become *Morkai*, King of Magic. You will have access to the *mora*, and it will flow to you. Yet you aren't going to keep it or harness it or do anything that will make you the Morkaius."

Was he correct?

She fought to recall everything Emylia had channeled. Everything Teryn had learned from her.

To gain the power of the Morkaius, one must first become King of Magic, a crown given, not taken, and reign over El'Ara's abandoned heart.

To become Morkaius of El'Ara's heart, harness the magic that seeps from its center.

Mother Goddess, it really was hidden in the lines of the prophecy. One didn't become Morkaius unless they tried to harness the magic. The prophecy didn't say what one could do with the *mora* simply by being King of Magic—or Queen of Lela, in her case—but what he was saying might be possible.

"You see?" His voice quavered with fervor. "We'll work together, and we'll both get what we want. You'll protect your people and keep the land that has become their home. I'll rule El'Ara and make it a better place."

A better place...by his standards.

Cora hated how prejudiced the Elvyn were toward humans, but did that give Darius the right to change them? Just because he decided their morals were wrong? Did anyone have the right to override another society's values, just because they thought they knew better? To conquer them, change them, all for that people's supposed *own good*? It was a question that had plagued humanity for centuries. Those who answered yes often used such convictions to justify the subjugation of people under the banner of *civilization*. She'd seen hints of it in her own kingdom when her former council members had wanted to hunt down the Forest People and force them to integrate with society.

She couldn't condone that.

She could *never* condone that.

Darius stepped closer. "What I've created in Syrus—a fair kingdom that values one's merit, not their bloodline—can happen in El'Ara too."

"And what of Syrus?" she asked. "Will you just abandon it for El'Ara?"

"Of course not. After I tear down the Veil, I will once again be able to walk between worlds. The human and fae realms will no longer be conjoined, but that doesn't mean we can't continue to benefit one another. Just think what the future could hold. What advancements we could see on both sides. Humans and fae have so much they can learn from one another."

She breathed deeply, sensing his energy. It radiated with hope, with joy, with excitement, almost too potent for her to bear. He truly believed in what he was saying. Even she could see the potential he imagined. The possibilities of sharing resources with another realm.

Yet there remained that steady sinking in her gut. One that told her this wasn't quite right. Just because someone believed in their own principles didn't mean they weren't flawed.

"You want an alliance with me," Cora said, keeping her tone neutral so as not to reveal that she'd already made up her mind, "and you've shown me how we can help each other once you've conquered El'Ara. Yet what would you have me do *before* you've won? How do you expect me to aid you during your campaign?"

He sobered from his excitement, adopting as level a tone as hers. "I will ask only what is fair. Soldiers, access to your lands, and the location of the tear."

Her pulse jumped, and from his nod, she knew he'd heard it.

"Yes, you know where it is, but I won't try to get the information from you now. I will demonstrate my trustworthiness and allow you to consider your options. Alliance, surrender, or war. Either way, this can only end in my success. I will find the tear with or without you, and I will find my sister too. I won't ask you to take any lives for me. Ailan, Mareleau, and Noah will die by my hand only."

Cora couldn't keep her reaction at bay, couldn't hold in her gasp as she heard him speak Mareleau and Noah's names.

"I know about them too," he said, "though I regret that I learned about them too late. If I can claim one flaw, it's that I didn't value the prophecy Desmond was so invested in, aside from what it said about El'Ara. I used logic to test my son's conclusion about you and found it flawed. Since I knew you weren't the prophesied mother, I deduced she simply hadn't been born yet, and so long as she didn't exist, I didn't care about her.

"Before my memories returned, I had no interest in the mother, only reaching the Veil and finding a way inside. Then it tore while I was imprisoned. My mind was befuddled for days as I struggled to process all these new memories, comparing them to the assumptions I'd made, some of which had been incorrect. By the time my mind cleared and I realized the full truth of what had happened— that Ailan's heir had been born *under the black mountain*, in the very castle I'd been imprisoned in—it was too late. Queen Mareleau was gone. As were you."

The pointed look he gave her chilled her to the bone. Did he suspect she and Mareleau had left Ridine together? Even more chilling was the realization of just how close Darius had been to getting his way. For three days, he'd been imprisoned at Ridine while Mareleau and Noah were just floors overhead.

Thank the Mother Goddess his mind hadn't cleared a moment too soon.

"My promises aren't empty," Darius said, "but neither are my threats. My soldiers are in Vinias. Reinforcements from Norun are already on their way from the capital. Only I can stop them. If you're ready to forge an alliance with me, I can end the conflict between Khero and Norun. All they want is Prince Helios' body. I can convince them I've retrieved it. I can halt Norun's progress and stop them from setting foot on your kingdom's soil. Otherwise, they will come for blood and you will be outnumbered."

Breathe in. Breathe out. Don't react.

He didn't know about the rebels. He had no clue that between now and the meeting at the border, his promised reinforcements would get caught in the rebellion. Without them, Darius only had five thousand men. With Khero's forces allied with soldiers from Vera and El'Ara, they could face him with better odds.

"I need more time," she said. "I can't take this alliance lightly. If you want me to trust you, I need more proof. Give me the full three weeks to determine if you're worth my trust and I will meet you at the border as planned with my answer."

His eyes narrowed to a squint. Did he see through her ruse? Did he suspect what she kept hidden? The tic deepened in his jaw and his fingers curled tightly at his sides. Then he whirled back toward the balustrade and propped his elbows upon the rail. His energy flared with frustration.

"Is it the other queen?" he asked, voice low. "Is she the reason you hesitate?"

"You seek to end her life." Emotion crept into her voice, but she didn't bother masking it. "What kind of person would I be if I didn't hesitate?"

"She and her son are two people. *Two.* In exchange for their deaths, thousands of lives could be saved. Are those two lives more valuable than those that would be lost during war? Is it not your duty to put the lives of your people first?" Slamming his fist on the balustrade, he faced her again. "You should *hate* her."

She sucked in a sharp breath.

"My son mistook you for her." He took a forbidding step closer, temples pulsing. "He cursed you to die childless. Destroyed your brother's mind. Tried to start a war in your kingdom's name. You were banished from your own castle, forced to flee, all because you were the wrong girl."

Memories of flames flashed in her mind's eye, the terror of her nightmare echoing in the beat of her heart.

"You've borne the brunt of torment that had been meant for her all along. Does that make you feel noble? Do you fancy yourself a hero, Queen Aveline?" He closed in another step.

She launched back, her knees quavering.

Should it have been her? asked the taunting voice from her nightmare.

Darius continued, tone edged with malice. "Do you take pride in the protection you've provided? Do you enjoy watching her with her newborn baby, flaunting the joy of motherhood that you'll never have? Are you glad you gave up your youth so that she could be coddled? Have you never wondered what your life would have been like had Desmond targeted her instead of you? Have you never wished for it?"

Darkness flared inside her, a dangerous pulse. She tried to smother it down, but it begged her to look at it. Begged to swarm around her. But she couldn't. No, she couldn't. That wasn't her. That darkness didn't belong to her.

He stepped closer once more, towering over her. "Do you deserve the punishment you've been given? Do you delight in the sacrifices you made? Or...do you wish the burden had been given to the one who'd deserved it all along?"

"Stop," she bit out, shoulders trembling. The flames of memory grew brighter.

The darkness in her chest grew tighter. It screamed at her, clawed at her, fought to emerge from the prison that was her heart.

Darius lowered his voice to a whispered hiss. "Should that curse truly have been placed upon you, an innocent child? Born in the wrong place at the wrong time? Or should it have been her? Do you wish it had been *her*?"

"Yes!"

Silence echoed in the wake of that word.

She'd meant to stay *stop*.

Meant to refuse.

Meant to say anything but that horrible, condemning word.

Her body shuddered with a sob. Something wet splashed on her collarbone, soaking the neck of her robe. Only then did she realize tears were streaming from her cheeks.

Her chest squeezed...

Then released.

The sob turned into a breath of relief.

And the darkness inside her left its cage.

47

A witch's challenge was a beautiful and treacherous thing. Beautiful in how much it could grow one's magic. Treacherous in how the means of one's challenge only seemed obvious in hindsight. If Cora had acknowledged the darkness in her heart for what it was the first time it had begged her to look at it, she could have grown her magic days ago.

But that was the nature of challenges.

The way of the witch.

It wasn't meant to be easy.

Now that she'd broken that dam inside her, there was no stifling the darkness. She whispered the lullaby of truth it had wanted to hear all along. "It should have been her."

Anger rose inside her, and she didn't tamp it down. She let it strengthen her voice to a shout. Let her fury pour out of her and burst from her lungs, her heart, her lips. "It never should have been me! I hate that I suffered in her place!"

Darius nodded. "As you should."

More and more of the darkness leaked from her chest, eased from her soul. Her mind spun with the euphoria of its release. How long had she been carrying it? How had it burrowed so deeply—yet so subtly—inside her that she hadn't noticed its unbearable weight? Now that she'd given it freedom, she felt lighter than ever. Her mind too felt clearer. Sharper.

And her magic...

Mother Goddess, her magic felt stronger.

It surged through her body, filling every crevice the darkness had occupied. Her magic tingled the lines of her *insigmora*, burning her palms, radiating through her blood.

The blockage was finally gone—the fatigue that had overtaken her when she'd worldwalked. The solution had been there all along, buried in the darkness she wouldn't confront.

But she confronted it now, watching it, acknowledging it, even as it broke her heart again and again, even as it healed each jagged cut it made.

What a cruel and lovely thing it was.

"I knew you were like me," Darius said, voice quavering with fervor once more. "I knew we were of the same mind. You've felt what it's like when someone under-values you. Or misplaces your value. You feel the same rage that I do. The same sense of justice."

Gods, she wanted to laugh.

She and Darius weren't the same.

He was a fool to think bringing her darkness to light meant she agreed with him.

Everything she'd confessed was true. Every word she'd shouted had come from her heart. But truth wasn't always one-dimensional. Hers was multifaceted.

She wished Mareleau had been cursed in her stead.

She was glad Mareleau hadn't suffered the way she had.

She hated that she'd borne a punishment meant for someone else.

She wouldn't wish the terrors of her past on anyone else, least of all Mareleau.

Yes, that darkness belonged to Cora, a small and vulnerable side of her that she'd tried to ignore. Tried to smother and bury. But that wasn't all Cora possessed. There was a bigger, brighter part of her that could exist beside the darkness. A side that understood her tiny, scared, bitter counterpart for what it was. Not something to be ignored but to be held. Listened to. Freed. Only then could the brighter side truly shine.

Darius remained oblivious and continued to grin at her in triumph. "Now do you see—"

"I still need more time." Her words came out calm. "I will not ally with you until you've proven your merit. That's what you stand for, isn't it? You're asking me to compromise on my principles and allow you to take innocent lives—"

"One of those lives belongs to someone you resent. Taking it would save thou-sands more. It would end a war before it can begin."

"Yet it's a life nonetheless. I don't take that lightly. Give me the full three weeks, and you'll have your answer when we meet at the border. In the meantime, stay out of Khero, stay out of Ridine, and prove you're someone worth trusting."

Irritation flared in his eyes, but he made no argument. His fingers curled and uncurled at his sides until he released an aggrieved sigh. "As you wish. Just don't forget what I told you. You will be outnumbered at the border, should you refuse to either surrender or ally with me."

"I'll have to take that risk."

He extended a stiff hand. "Shall I escort you back—"

"There's no need." She took a step to the side, a vision of the moonlit forest just outside Ridine in her mind, and planted her feet on cold grass. Icy air filled her lungs where mild heat had been before. Darius' palace was gone, replaced with dense forest and a glimpse of the castle walls just ahead.

She took a moment to breathe, to marvel at how easy it had been to worldwalk here compared to all her recent attempts. She hadn't needed minutes to sink into her destination. Just a vision. Intent. A feeling. And here she was. She may not be as strong of a worldwalker as Darius was, but it was enough that her magic had grown.

Where the purgatory have you been? Valorre's frantic voice filled her mind. He was close enough that she heard the pound of his hooves on the forest floor. In a matter of heartbeats, he reached her. *You disappeared. You disappeared!*

"I'm all right," she assured him as she caressed his silky neck.

His panic lessened only the slightest bit. *I kept my distance and gave you privacy while you were mashing bodies with Teryn, and then...and then you were gone. You were just gone.*

If her poor familiar wasn't so upset, she'd be more amused by his *mashing bodies* comment. Or perhaps more embarrassed.

"I know. I'm sorry to have worried you. That's why I came here first."

Although Valorre's worry was great, there was someone else who was probably equally as frantic.

Valorre's emotions flared with jealousy, which he demonstrated by scraping his hoof in the soil. He nuzzled her shoulder several more times, a tad more aggressively than usual, before he finally relented. *Go on, then. You should tell him you're not dead. He...was doing something strange earlier.*

She pulled back. "What do you mean something strange?"

Valorre gave the emotional equivalent of a shrug. *Something with dead people.*

That was enough to leave her equal parts perplexed and concerned. She gave Valorre a final conciliatory pat before worldwalking straight to her bedroom.

She caught Teryn pacing before their bed, his thumbnail between his teeth. He jumped upon seeing her, blinking several times as if he wasn't sure she was real. His eyes were wild, his hair more mussed than before.

"I'm safe," she said.

Her words broke the spell on his surprise, and his expression eased. He rushed to her and folded her against his chest. "Thank the gods. I was about six seconds away from waging war on Syrus myself."

The comfort of his arms, the scent of his skin, the cadence of his heartbeat against her ear, soothed all the fraying edges of Cora's anxiety. She wished the moment could last. Wished they didn't have to talk about what had happened or what would come next.

But she couldn't put it off.

They didn't have time for that.

She pulled slightly away and locked her eyes with his. His energy constricted. The furrow between his brow hinted at a worry he was desperate to voice. Did it have something to do with what Valorre had mentioned?

"What is it?" she asked.

He framed her face with his hands as if he couldn't bear to release her. His throat bobbed. Once. Twice. His voice came out strained. "I...I need to tell you something. Something I've done. My means were questionable, but I think it can help us."

"I'll listen," she whispered back. "Afterward, I have something to tell you too. I have a plan. Or...the beginnings of one. It might make the Elvyn hate me, but it's the only way to truly protect the people of Lela."

Conviction flared in her chest. She knew what she had to do.

Darius may have been wrong about her in many ways. They were nothing alike. Freeing her darkness hadn't filled her with hatred. Bitterness didn't compromise her ability to love.

But he'd been right about one thing.

Lela belonged to her.

48

For the first time in Mareleau's life, there was such a thing as too many sweets. And too many gifts. They filled nearly every surface of her bedroom, from the dressing table to the nightstand and a good portion of the floor. Two marble dress forms boasted bejeweled robes in the Elvyn fashion, which were so heavy and ornate they had to be hauled in by a trio of servants. Decanters of wine, kettles of tea, and plates upon plates of desserts and confections in bold flavors unlike anything she'd tasted were clustered upon the tea table.

After the tribunal's begrudging acceptance of her, she hadn't expected much from her interactions with the Elvyn people, but within an hour, visitors had begun to call. It turned out not everyone was as curmudgeonly as those who'd attended the meeting. Thanks to the translation charm on the bracelet Fanon had given her and Cora, she could easily communicate with them. Her servants and palace staff rarely said much other than to pay their respects, but they always bowed at the waist or bent at the knee in her presence.

Edel Morkara'Elle.

She'd heard that title so many times since the meeting ended.

Perhaps being the mother of the Morkara wasn't too much of a step down from being queen. It certainly came with perks.

And a very full belly.

Yet as full as she was, she was completely unsatisfied. How could she be content when the future was so unclear? Would Ailan keep the tear open long enough to allow Mareleau and Larylis to live out their lives in the human world with their son? And if not, would Mareleau learn to consider this place her home? Would the Elvyn accept Larylis? What would happen to Vera? Who would take care of her kingdom?

She hated those questions, and she likely wouldn't get answers any time soon. They had a war to win, an enemy to kill.

Meanwhile, all she could do was sit in her pretty room and gorge herself on Elvyn sweets.

That and protect her son, of course.

She stared down at Noah with a grin. He lay beside her at the center of a cushioned velvet mat on the floor, staring at the glittering, swaying mobile—a gift from one of his new Elvyn admirers, of course. He was starting to look less like a wrinkled old man and more like a chubby baby. How old was he now? Just over two weeks? It had been so hard to keep track of time, especially when trying to track the passage of days in the human world too. Were she at home without war on the horizon, she'd have celebrated each week since his birth, marked each milestone with gifts and cake.

Gifts and cake were all around them now, but it wasn't for quite the same reason.

Bitterness sank her chest, edged with impatience. She hated feeling useless. Hated waiting. Hated being surrounded by luxury yet impoverished at heart.

Maybe...

If she could only...

She scooted closer to Noah and extended her hands, palms toward him. Closing her eyes, she tried to sense a tingling buzz of magic, tried to feel a ripple of some hidden strength. Instead, she felt nothing. Yet...wasn't she going about this wrong in the first place? She was—*supposedly*—claircognizant, not clairsentient. Her sensory affinity was keen knowing, but here she was trying to *feel* like Cora could.

How could she truly protect her son and make her magic count if she didn't know how to make proper use of her abilities? Clenching her jaw, she opened her eyes. Noah's gaze was on her hands now as he gummed his tiny fist.

Her heart melted at the sight, taking the edge off her annoyance. "I just wish I could protect you."

If she could at least cast a protective ward around him, she'd feel useful. Salinda had helped her understand her magic when they'd spoken in her tent, but she hadn't taught her how to use that understanding for what Mareleau wanted to do most. It was hard to take her magic seriously when she hadn't a clue how to accomplish her goals.

She adopted a playful tone and wiggled her fingers. "You, little Noah, are hereby protected. No? Nothing? Huh."

A soft knock came from the other side of her bedroom door. Ailan swept in.

Mareleau angled her head to face her. "Has Cora returned?"

"Not yet," Ailan said.

It had only been a matter of hours since Cora left El'Ara, but in the human world, more than a full day had passed. Would it take several days to sort out her side of the terms for the alliance? Weeks? Mareleau would lose her mind if that ended up being the case. The sooner Cora returned, the sooner she might have a chance of getting another letter to or from Larylis.

Ailan approached her and Noah. "What are you doing there?"

Mareleau frowned, unsure of what she was inquiring about until she glanced at her hands. They were still extended over Noah. She snatched them back. "Oh, that. I was..."

Why was she embarrassed to admit it? She had no reason to feel ashamed.

She lifted her chin and feigned confidence. "I was practicing casting a protective ward around Noah."

Ailan settled on the floor beside them. "Did it work?"

"Not yet." She didn't mean to sound so defensive. "That's why I'm practicing."

"Is that what kind of magic you hope to have? Wardweaving?"

"Is that an option?" Mareleau hadn't considered whether she might have access to Elvyn magic.

"Perhaps. I know Salinda helped you understand your witch magic, but exploring your Elvyn side may help too. Your magic is a combination of both. And while a weaver's *mora* doesn't always manifest in the ways we want, it's possible you're drawn to wardweaving because it's your specialty. I'm a truthweaver through and through, without a stitch of talent for wardweaving. My wards are weak when I attempt them. Still, I can teach you the gesture for casting them."

Excitement bubbled in her chest. Was she about to learn how to do something useful with magic at last?

"Even if wardweaving isn't your talent," Ailan said, "a gesture may help guide your witch magic. Sometimes external action can aid its flow, for it gives you something outside yourself to trust in."

Ailan extended her palms, and Mareleau mirrored her. She touched her thumbs to her ring fingers, angled her hands, and then linked the pairs of touching fingers together. Angling her hands again, she touched her pinkies, then her middle fingers, then her index. The motions stretched Mareleau's digits in strange and unfamiliar ways, but the challenge made her feel accomplished. Ailan moved her hands again, this time lacing all five fingers together before separating them.

"You end by encompassing the subject you'd like to ward with your hands," Ailan explained. "It may help to imagine an invisible blanket between your fingers, settling over your subject. For large subjects, you may need to repeat the gesture several times and in several different areas until it's completely covered."

Following her instruction, Mareleau envisioned a protective blanket falling from her hands over Noah.

And then...

She cast a hopeful look at Ailan. "Did that work?"

Ailan chuckled. "The Forest People call it quiet magic, and Elvyn magic operates in a similarly quiet way. Wards are particularly hard to test, for that would require an attempt to break through them. But don't be discouraged. With or without this gesture, you're still a witch. You still have a sensory affinity you can work with."

"Claircognizance."

Ailan nodded. "Since knowing is your strength, you must build your trust in your abilities. When you cast your ward, you must *know* it works."

Her heart sank. How could she know when she...didn't? How could she have confidence in something she couldn't see or feel? It had been easy to trust her glamours because she hadn't taken them seriously. She'd brushed them off as a logic-based skill, something she'd assumed anyone could do if they'd tried.

"You've tried warding Noah," Ailan said, "but have you tried warding yourself?"

"I don't care about warding myself." It was an immediate response, but it wasn't fully true. "Or...it's more that Salinda said witch magic grows through challenge. So I'm trying to do the opposite of what my instincts want. It's easy to be selfish, so I'm trying not to focus on myself at all."

Ailan frowned. "Is it easy to be selfish? To me, it looks like your resistance to focusing on yourself is stronger."

"Yes because of the challenge—"

"That's not quite how it works." Ailan shook her head. "I may be Elvyn, but I lived with the Forest People for centuries. I've watched witches flourish and grow. You can't challenge your magic; you must wait for it to challenge you. In the meantime, you grow it by working within your nature. Keep performing feats of magic the way you always have—"

"Casting glamours over myself isn't going to keep Noah safe. I want to create a shield around him or make him invisible to any who would cause him harm."

Ailan released a weighted sigh. "I remember those feelings. That need to protect the fragile being you brought into this world. It's been so long since I've felt that."

"Then you understand why I need to protect him. You claim he's safe behind the Veil, but if your brother finds his way here..."

"I know." Ailan set a comforting hand on her shoulder. Mareleau was surprised that she felt no instinct to flinch away. When had she begun to grow used to this woman? Ailan spoke again. "Why don't you try holding Noah and casting magic around the two of you? See if you can evade the notice of the servants who bring you dinner. Or perhaps convince them you have pointed ears, some feature you can get outside confirmation on. Start with a glamour before you try warding. Start with yourself before you try shifting your magic to others."

Her shoulders fell. That sounded like a tediously slow process, but if it gave her something to work on, she supposed she should be grateful. "All right."

Ailan must have heard the dejected note in her voice, for she rose to her feet with a warm smile. "Come, there's someone I want you to formally meet."

49

Mareleau couldn't imagine who Ailan was referring to, but curiosity got the better of her. Ailan headed for the door while Mareleau rose to her feet and gathered Noah from his playmat. She retrieved her carrying sling from the end of her bed and tucked Noah into it as she strode out of her room. Ailan was waiting in the hall.

"Who am I meeting?"

Ailan gave her a sly grin. "You'll see. I'm not sure you'd come if I told you."

That wasn't at all comforting.

Yet her interest was thoroughly piqued as Ailan led her through the palace halls. She was so distracted with trying to puzzle out their destination that she forgot to marvel at her surroundings until they were three floors down. Mareleau hadn't left her room much since arriving at the palace, save for the tribunal meeting. Now that she'd earned the tribunal's binding vow of respect and protection, she was allowed to explore the palace, but it was an unfamiliar place filled with strange people. She'd felt safest in her room.

They reached the bottom floor of the palace, where the ceilings rose four times as high as the ones in the upper halls. Elegant chandeliers sparkled with pale blue and white crystals that caught rays of sunlight and sent shards of glittering illumination upon the walls. Guards dressed in silver armor over white silk robes lined the hall ahead. They bowed as the trio passed. A pair of Elvyn footmen in blue-and-ivory robes opened the ornate double doors ahead.

Sunlight streamed through the doorway as Ailan led the way. A white marble staircase stretched out before them, leading to a large courtyard. Once they reached the bottom of the stairs, Mareleau glanced behind her, taking in the exterior of the palace for the first time. Her jaw hung on its hinge as she assessed the towering ivory turrets, the gilded balconies, and the pale blue crystalline walls that comprised the lower portions of the structure. She hadn't been able to see much of the castle from her bedroom or any of the halls she'd walked through, but this...

This made her realize just how massive Alles'Taria Palace truly was. It was twice as large as Verlot.

"It's beautiful, isn't it?" Ailan's voice startled her from her awe. She stood beside Mareleau, a wistful expression in her eyes as she admired the structure. There was something almost sad about the look. "Alles'Taria was named and modeled after the original seat of the Morkara, the palace that had been built over El'Ara's heart."

"What happened?" Mareleau asked. "I know five hundred years is a long time, but all that's left of the palace is a rock. At least, that's what I've heard."

"Centerpointe Rock," Ailan said with a nod. "I've seen it once, during the battle last spring. With my memories compromised, I didn't recognize it for what it was. I knew it marked an invisible well of fae magic, but I didn't understand how or why. Now I remember."

Ailan's expression darkened. She turned her gaze away from the spires and started off toward one of the many gardens that surrounded the courtyard. This garden contained tiny trees in myriad shapes and varieties, stone gardens marked with impossibly high cairns, as well as several ponds. Mareleau could only half focus on the beauty. The rest of her attention lingered on the subject they'd left behind.

She knew roughly how Ailan's battle with Darius had ended—he'd killed his mother before Satsara had managed to finish her ward. Then he and Ailan were trapped in the human world. But what had their plan been, and how had Darius thwarted it?

"I was supposed to lure Darius far from the palace," Ailan said as they wove through a grove of waist-high trees with vibrant needle-like leaves and twisting, twining trunks. "My army was meant to keep his attention off what my mother was doing. Her dragon was with my forces too, to convince him Satsara was among us. It was imperative that we keep him fighting until my mother's wardweaving was finished. That meant we couldn't overwhelm his army, for that would only make him worldwalk back to the human world for reinforcements. Upon his return, if he tried to worldwalk to any location already covered by the Veil, he'd find himself blocked and know what my mother was up to.

"So we held back, sacrificing our soldiers so he'd keep fighting us, keep thinking he was seconds away from victory. Only once the Veil was complete would we give it our all and either kill him or obliterate his army enough that he'd worldwalk away. If the Veil was finished, he'd never be able to reenter El'Ara again.

"But he was smarter than that. Or, at the very least, he suspected we were holding back. He and I were fighting one-on-one when the truth dawned on him. He hissed our mother's name, and I knew it was over. I reached for him, latched onto his arm right as he worldwalked away, forcing him to take me with him. Next thing I knew, we were in the forest north of the palace. In another heartbeat, he was gone. He'd left me behind on purpose. Either he'd anticipated I'd try to grab him or he realized it as soon as I touched him and altered his destination.

"I ran to the palace as fast as I could, but Mother was already dead and the palace was destroyed. It may have been the force of Satsara tying off the edges of her Veil so suddenly, or the pressure of forcing El'Ara into the human world, but Alles'Taria Palace was obliterated when I got there. The guards were dead, crushed in the rubble or murdered by my brother. He was killing those who remained as I arrived, popping in and out of thin air to behead the survivors before they even had a chance to defend themselves.

"He came for me next, taunting me about how he'd ended our mother's life while hugging her. While telling her he loved her. He'd slit her throat right after she'd smiled up at him and said she loved him too. He didn't yet know that she'd also tied off her wardweaving, blocking him from El'Ara thereafter, but once he did, he tried to kill me in earnest. No more taunting. No more games. So I did what I thought I should in that split second before he tried to behead me; I relinquished my title as Morkara to my unnamed heir."

Mareleau's stomach sank with guilt. She'd condemned Ailan for having made such a reckless choice back then, but could she blame her? She hadn't had much time for rational thought when her enemy could appear from thin air to surprise her with a blade through her neck at any moment.

They reached the far end of the garden where an arch in a tall hedge wall opened to a sloping hillside behind the palace. Rocky steps led down to where the crystalline palace walls gave way to natural stone. There daylight melted to shadow, the sunlight obscured by the turrets.

"Where are we going?" Mareleau asked, her curiosity now tinged with apprehension.

"To the dragon caves beneath the palace," Ailan said. "Ferrah, Uziel, and the hatchlings live there."

"Wait...don't tell me..."

"I want you to meet the dragons."

The blood left her face and she hugged Noah close to her, though he was already as close as he could be in his sling. She glanced down at his sleeping face, then back at Ailan. "Why?"

"You want an asset that will make you feel safe? If you earn the dragons' respect, they will listen to you."

Mareleau blinked at her. "Safe? You think being around a dragon will make me feel safe? You do realize Ferrah shattered the windows of my bedroom at Ridine Castle and nearly had me skewered with glass. And now you want me to take Noah into a cave full of the creatures?"

"They will not harm him."

"Are you certain?"

"Yes." There was no hesitation in Ailan's voice, only warmth. "He is their Morkara. They would no sooner hurt him than me. Besides, Ferrah didn't mean to hurt or alarm you at Ridine. She'd been looking for you. According to Uziel, he and Ferrah acted against the archers in your defense. They saw a threat to you, not them."

"According to Uziel," she echoed. "As in...you can talk to him?"

"I can communicate with him. It's almost like talking. Should you ever grow close enough to one of the dragons to bond with one, you'll learn what I mean."

Mareleau pulled her head back. "That...that's an option for me? To bond with a dragon?"

"Maybe not today, but someday, perhaps. For now, I am confident you can earn enough of their respect to get them to listen to you, the same way they listen to my consort. That way, even if I am not here, you can take comfort in commanding them to protect you."

This was madness. Mareleau should refuse to take a step further. She should run.

But she didn't.

Instead, a strange thrill buzzed through her. Whether it was out of a need to protect her son or simply her ego wanting to be important enough to command a dragon, she knew not. All she knew was that as Ailan continued to descend farther and farther down the hill, toward the craggy base of the castle, her feet followed. Even as her heart raced. Even as sweat pooled beneath her armpits.

They reached the base of the palace where a dark maw split the stone. There really were caves beneath the palace. Dragons lurking floors beneath her bedroom. Who would have thought?

"Being formally introduced to a dragon...is it dangerous?" she asked. It had almost been deadly for Cora, after all.

"It won't be dangerous for you, I promise." Ailan led the way inside the cave opening. Darkness enveloped them at once, and Mareleau threw out her hands for guidance. One palm met a stony wall. She was about to call out for Ailan to wait when a spark of light blinked just ahead. Then another.

Mareleau took a few hesitant steps. Each one sparked more and more tiny pinpricks of blue-green light. After a few more steps, the walls and ceiling lit up like starlight, casting her, Noah, and Ailan in an aqua glow.

"Dragon flame reacts with the minerals in these caves and leaves these residuals. They get denser and denser the deeper we go."

Ailan was right. As they wove deeper into the tunnels, more of the light painted the walls until she could see everything from the ground to the curving, rocky walls, to the towering ceilings dripping glowing stalactites. It was one of the most beautiful yet eerie sights she'd ever seen. If only Larylis were here. If only Noah was awake and old enough to appreciate such splendor.

If this were your home...

Longing and guilt clashed in her heart. What a traitorous thought that was, when she was already Queen of Vera.

But El'Ara is an entire world. A world like this. A world with magic and miracles I've yet to see.

She shook the thoughts from her head.

"My bonding ritual with Uziel ended in danger," Ailan said, "but that was only because of my brother. He disrespected my mother's dragon, and Berolla meant to punish him, not me. Two of her talons raked through my chest, nearly puncturing my heart, but Uziel intervened just in time. Berolla was so distraught over what she'd been tricked into doing that she atoned by sacrificing the two very talons that had cut me."

"What do you mean she sacrificed her talons?"

"She voluntarily severed two claws from her toes. That collar Cora had was made from those talons. It took us months to understand the magic Berolla had infused them with. No, that isn't accurate. My mother knew, for Berolla had told her, but Satsara had hidden the talons' true purpose from us. It wasn't until we were close to losing the fight with my brother that Mother finally told us what we could do with the claws. That we could stop Darius from worldwalking by puncturing his flesh with them."

"The war with Darius raged for multiple *months*?" Shame sank her stomach as soon as the naive words left her mouth. Of course they'd fought for months. War could last years. Decades, even. Some queen she was. She changed the subject. "You said Berolla infused the talons with magic. Do all dragon talons contain different kinds of magic?"

Ailan shook her head. "Talon magic is rare. Like unicorn horns, talons disappear into ash after the dragon dies. Only a talon gifted from a live dragon contains magic, and it is up to that dragon to decide how to infuse it. No Elvyn would ever ask of such a sacrifice from a dragon. We're lucky Darius never learned of this ability, or he would have found a way to exploit this gift from them."

Nausea turned her gut, along with another pang of guilt. She'd once ordered three princes to hunt unicorns and bring her a pelt, a pet, and a magical horn. Little had she known, the process for taking a horn was nothing short of torture. Yet another choice she regretted making.

The illumination painting the cave walls brightened, drawing Mareleau's eyes to the view ahead. An enormous cavern spread before them, the ceiling twice as tall as it had been before. Tiny pools of flame flickered over the cavern floor in a multitude of colors—red, green, orange, purple. A hulking shape rested at the center of the floor, its silhouette rising and falling like a breathing mountain. Then, with a grumble that shook the ground beneath Mareleau's feet, the shape moved, stretched, lengthened, until it unraveled as Uziel. His enormous dark head lifted from beside his body. His tail swished across the floor as he flicked his tongue toward Ailan.

Another shape stirred behind Uziel, which launched a swarm of tiny, winged creatures—baby dragons?—into the air. They flew off to perch on stalactites and stalagmites, circling the structures with wary looks at the intruders.

Mareleau shrank back. The baby dragons were only the size of a small dog, but they moved so quickly, stared so suspiciously.

Her eyes darted back to Uziel as the creature behind him fully awakened. The aqua glow of the walls glinted off opalescent scales and white feathered wings. After a stretch like Uziel had made, Ferrah bounded over the black dragon, as agile as a cat, and sat back on her haunches. Her sinuous back curved in an arch while her tail lazily coiled and uncoiled beside her. Long white whiskers draped from her maw—a rather toothy maw that was on full display as she yawned.

Uziel slithered over to Ailan, something like a purr rumbling in his throat. Ailan absently stroked his enormous snout as she spoke. "Uziel has agreed to listen to you. The others don't seem interested in meeting you at this time, but Ferrah seems curious enough."

"Others—" Just then, Mareleau noticed the other hulking shapes that she'd first taken for boulders. There were at least half a dozen other dragons asleep in the cave, though all were slightly smaller than Ferrah.

Mareleau's gaze moved to the white dragon, who watched Mareleau like she was a fascinating jewel.

Or a snack.

She tightened her arms around Noah's sleeping form.

"Would you like to introduce yourself to her?" Ailan's expression was so hopeful, contrasting the churning in Mareleau's gut.

She wanted to say no, to flee, to never look back, but beneath her anxiety, that bold thrill remained.

Not waiting for Mareleau's answer, Ailan stepped closer to Ferrah, gesturing for Mareleau to follow.

Her legs trembled, but she found herself moving before she could think better of it.

Ferrah's tongue flicked out but she didn't startle, didn't hiss, didn't do any of the things Mareleau feared she'd do.

"Bow to her," Ailan instructed. "Keep your moves slow and steady."

Mareleau could barely hear her through the blood roaring in her ears. Her heart hammered so hard it felt as if it would climb from her throat. Yet bow she did, as smoothly as she dared. As she straightened, Ailan instructed her in what to do with her hands. She kept one loose and open at her side—which meant she had to fully turn Noah's weight over to his sling—while she extended the other toward the dragon.

Seven devils, a dragon. I'm greeting a godsforsaken dragon. What if she eats my hand? What if she eats my baby? What if she eats me?

Her panic rose to a crescendo, but she managed to perform the correct movements. Palm toward Ferrah. Hold still. Then breathe.

Breathe.

Breathe.

Ferrah rose from her haunches and took a step toward her.

Mareleau nearly lost her nerve and leaped back, but Ailan warned her to hold her position.

Ferrah stepped closer again. Then again. Her tongue flicked in and out with every step until it glanced over Mareleau's palm. She shuddered as it tickled her skin.

Gods, those teeth were close.

Too close.

Ferrah held her gaze for several uncomfortable moments.

Then, with a ground-shaking huff, Ferrah bounded off, feathered wings pressed close to her sides.

Mareleau's gaze whipped to Ailan. She expected to see disappointment on the other woman's face, but instead she wore a wide grin.

"You see?" Ailan said with a chuckle as Uziel sniffed the side of her head, his breath blowing Ailan's black hair in messy streams. "You've earned her respect."

"*That* was earning her respect?"

"That was more than my brother ever managed. She'll listen to you now. Somewhat."

She couldn't help but feel a pang of disappointment. A secret side of her had hoped she'd earn more than just Ferrah's respect. She'd hoped maybe she'd bond with the creature too. Succeed at what Darius had failed.

"You'll have plenty of chances to bond with a dragon in the future," Ailan said, as if she could read Mareleau's thoughts.

Mareleau opened her mouth to deny such hopes when movement rippled at the mouth of the cavern. The telltale swirl of color warping the air foretold Garot's arrival. He stepped out of his vortex and folded into a bow at once, hands open at his sides. "Forgive my intrusion, most honored ones."

Mareleau thought the gesture was for her, Ailan, and Noah, but when he stood, his gaze darted from Uziel to the little beasts who hissed at him from their perches.

Finally, he faced Ailan. "I have an urgent update. Cora has returned, and she's asked to speak to you at once."

50

ora waited in the empty tribunal room, where Garot had brought her. The room was even darker than it had been the last time she was here, as the brightly hued butterflies were nowhere to be seen. The only light came from the dim sconces that lined the curved walls. She wandered the circular floor, her muscles tense. Every minute she was here were several lost in the human world, and she'd already lost close to an hour.

She'd followed the agreed-upon protocol, entering El'Ara discreetly through the tear. There she'd been greeted by the drawn blades of the soldiers who now patrolled the fae side of the tear. After that, she argued over the urgency of her visit, which had been a headache even with the translation charm on the bracelet Fanon had given her. In the end, she'd worldwalked straight to the woods outside the palace, where Garot intercepted her.

She still didn't know exactly how Garot could locate her so easily. The first time she'd come to El'Ara, he'd told her about the triggers that were woven throughout the land, explaining that was how Satsara had come to meet Tristaine. Yet Cora hadn't learned more details than that. How did the triggers alert the Elvyn? How did they know the exact location where the trigger had been set off? It was yet more confusing fae technology, much like the impressive bathtub with its drains and faucets.

The door opened to reveal Ailan. And then...

"Mareleau." Cora hadn't expected Ailan to bring her, for she'd requested to speak with Ailan alone. Nightmare flames emerged from her memory at the sight of her friend, along with a burning well of guilt, shame, and bitter rage. Her confession echoed in her head.

It should have been her.

She breathed deeply, neither burying the emotions nor trying to push them away. Instead, she let all those feelings move through her without judgment.

When they passed, her body felt lighter.

Mareleau's expression brightened with a grin, and she met Cora in a one-armed hug. The other arm cradled Noah's sling. Cora sank into the embrace.

She may harbor resentment for Mareleau, but their friendship was stronger. So much stronger. She hoped Mareleau understood that. Hoped she wouldn't hate her for what she needed to do next.

"Come," Ailan said with a gentle squeeze to Cora's shoulder. She proceeded to the other side of the meeting room and opened an almost imperceptible door. Light flooded from behind it, and Ailan beckoned them to follow her inside.

As soon as Cora crossed the threshold, humid air filled her lungs, much like it had in Syrus. The scent of unfamiliar flowers flooded her nostrils. Glass walls comprised three sides of the small room, inviting in the glow of the setting sun. Potted plants and flowers in every color imaginable cluttered the floor and tables while vines crawled up trellises.

Among all the greenery fluttered the glowing butterflies from the tribunal meeting. They emitted a calming blue light.

"They're beautiful," Mareleau said, tone brimming with awe. She strolled to one of the long walls of windows and stared out at the scenery.

Cora, meanwhile, kept close to Ailan, posture stiff. She wasn't here for a leisurely chat, and a part of her dreaded disappointing Ailan. The woman may look different now, but deep inside Cora still recognized her as Nalia, the High Elder she'd looked up to for six years. A figure whose approval she'd sought.

But Ailan's approval was not her priority.

Her people were.

A butterfly flew over Cora's head, its color flashing a yellow-green.

Ailan frowned at the butterfly until it flew away from Cora, its hue returning to blue. She picked up a glass bottle fitted with a pump and nozzle and began to spray the leaves of a climbing vine bedecked with violet flowers. "Did you have any trouble entering the tear? Or getting to the palace?"

"No." It wasn't entirely true, but it wasn't what she'd come to discuss.

"You saw how many guards I've posted at the tear? I have more soldiers stationed throughout the Blight. Did you bring your soldiers to guard the human side?"

Cora's eyes flashed toward Mareleau. "King Larylis is in a ship nearby with fifty soldiers. I'll send word to him to discreetly patrol the area around the tear."

Mareleau whirled away from the window, eyes bright. "Larylis is close by? Can you get a letter to him?"

Cora opened her mouth to answer, but Ailan spoke first.

"Fifty soldiers," she said, brows furrowed. "That's not what we agreed to. I asked for—"

"We didn't agree to anything yet. The situation has changed. I'm taking charge of our alliance. The Elvyn will agree to all my terms or they will forfeit the alliance altogether."

Ailan paused spraying. "What happened?"

"I met your brother. He took me to Syrus and offered me something I can't refuse."

"You're allying with *him*?"

"No. He's given me the options of war, surrender, or alliance, and I am choosing none of those. Instead, you and I are going to make a plan to work against him, and you are going to give me what Darius offered."

Ailan's throat bobbed, and the butterflies closest to her flickered orange. She resumed spraying the plant. "What did he offer you?"

She swallowed hard. "Lela."

Another pause. Another flicker of orange. "Lela? You want me to...what? Leave El'Ara's heart in the human world?"

"Yes." Anxiety bubbled inside her, reflected in the spike of yellow on the nearest butterflies' wings. To calm herself, she turned her attention to the plant life around her. She circled a potted tree, its base consisting of five slender, inter-twining trunks. Its leaves were wide, flat, and bright pink.

"You know I can't give you that," Ailan said. "El'Ara needs its heart."

Cora continued to circle the plant, steeling herself to explain the next part. "I know El'Ara needs its heart, and you will have it. The heart isn't the land itself but the *mora*. As Queen of Lela—"

"What do you mean Queen of Lela?" Mareleau marched toward Cora. "Are you...stealing my kingdom?"

Cora couldn't bring herself to meet her friend's eyes. "I'm not stealing your kingdom. I'm inheriting it. You and Larylis are going to abdicate. Teryn will inherit Vera, and we'll merge our kingdoms into one. Furthermore, I demand Larylis and Queen Mother Helena live in El'Ara."

Silence echoed back.

Finally, Cora forced herself to meet Mareleau's gaze. She expected to find red butterflies all around her in a halo of rage, but instead, they only flashed yellow. With a deep breath, Cora opened herself to her friend's emotions, sensing shock, confusion, and...

The emotions lifted.

Dispersed.

The butterflies deepened to a bold shade of green.

A bark of laughter escaped Mareleau's lips. "You're claiming Vera as your own and demanding that the Elvyn accept my husband and mother as citizens."

"I am, and I will brook no debate on the matter. No one can remain in the human world who can contest my rule. Lela is mine."

Mareleau blinked at her a few times. Then her lips curled into a trembling smile, and her emotions swelled with an unexpected warmth. Cora knew then that Mareleau had seen through her demand to her true intentions. Although Cora would be making this choice even if Mareleau hated her for it, she was determined that Mareleau and Noah wouldn't be separated from Larylis and Helena.

Ailan wasn't quite so moved. "You aren't giving your friend a say in the matter? She hasn't decided if she wants to live here yet."

Cora lifted her chin. "No, I'm not giving her a choice, or you, and I have my reasons."

"Explain them then."

"As Queen of Lela," Cora said, "I will have access to the magic that seeps from Centerpointe Rock into the human world. I'm going to utilize it."

Ailan's nostrils flared. "You can't harness the magic."

"I won't. I'll push it back." She shared what Darius had told her, about the loophole he'd found in the prophecy. "One only becomes Morkaius after they harness the magic. So I won't. I'll go to Centerpointe Rock and use whatever temporary power I'm granted as Queen of Magic and push the *mora* back through the tear. With the veins of magic on this side of the Veil where they belong, you—or your strongest wardweavers—will seal the tear. Once it's sealed, a new heart will be forged, and your mother's wardweaving will no longer be incomplete."

Ailan's expression went blank, demonstrating her awe-laced shock. Then she shook her head. "I can see that as a possibility, but my people will never agree. You're asking us to position you as Morkaius of the human world. Someone who could take everything from El'Ara."

"I can't take everything without harnessing the magic, which would destroy me. Pushing the *mora* back to El'Ara is my only choice if I want to survive."

"My people won't—"

"They will," Cora said, tone firm. "You will make them agree. Tell them anything, I don't care what it is. Tell them I'm exactly what they fear me to be, an evil witch bent on taking Lela for her own. Tell them I'm a bloodthirsty worldwalker, and the only way to keep the peace with me and defeat your brother is to give me what I want."

Ailan set down the spray bottle and folded her arms. She paced before the climbing vines before she spoke again. "I can get the tribunal to agree if you proceed with your plan to push the *mora* back to us at once. You will secure Mareleau and Larylis' word of abdication—"

"So soon?" Mareleau straightened. "That's all it would take? Just a word of abdication, no formal process? No coronation? Just like that, she's Queen of Lela?" There was no ire in her tone, only curiosity.

"This is a matter of the *mora*," Ailan said. "Fae magic. While it will likely take more work to formalize Cora's position in terms of human politics, the magic will recognize her role once you and your husband state your abdication, just like the role of the Morkara can be relinquished upon a single verbal statement."

"That may be true," Cora said, drawing Ailan's attention back to her, "but I am not going to push the *mora* to El'Ara while Darius still lives. That would trap him in the human world and leave us to deal with him."

Ailan arched a brow. "Then what exactly are you proposing?"

"You said we need to outsmart Darius to defeat him, so we will. All he truly wants from me is the location of the tear. So I'll give him a false location. I'll lead him to a predetermined place where we will ambush him."

"You're forgetting he has no reason to stay and fight once he discovers he's being ambushed. He can worldwalk away before anyone can lay a finger on him."

"He will have a reason to stay if you're there."

Ailan's eyes widened. "You want me to serve as bait."

"I'm acting as bait myself by bringing him to the ambush site. The least you can do is face him. You have the one thing that can stop him, don't you?"

Ailan thinned her lips as she reached into the folds of her flowing robe and extracted the magic-suppressing collar. "Yes, though I failed the last time I tried to trap him with it. I got only a single talon hooked into his skin, but he merely tore it out, tossed it aside, and worldwalked away."

"Then you'll have to try harder this time. Unless...there's more of those?"

"No, this collar is one of a kind. Berolla sacrificed two talons to create it, and it can't be replicated, even if she were still alive." At Cora's questioning look, she went on to explain. "She was trapped on this side of the Veil when my mother died. According to Fanon, she took Last Breath shortly after."

Damn. There went the possibility for more magic-suppressing weapons.

"This," Ailan said, holding up the collar, "is our best hope. Our best chance at preventing Darius from worldwalking while I land a killing blow. And you're right; he won't resist the opportunity to face me if I confront him. But that doesn't mean he won't first worldwalk away to bring an army."

"So we'll station troops from our human and Elvyn forces that will be ready to fight," Cora said. "How many soldiers can Darius travel with?"

"During the war, he often brought in upwards of two dozen men at a time."

Cora's mouth fell open. "*Two dozen?* At once?"

Ailan nodded.

She couldn't imagine worldwalking with that many people in tow. Still, even with those numbers, it would take far too long to bring his entire army. "He'll be eager enough to face you that he won't risk your retreat. He'll only bring in enough soldiers to even the odds."

"Perhaps." Ailan rubbed her brow. "When do you expect this confrontation to take place?"

"He agreed to wait three weeks to hear my answer to his offer of alliance. I can pretend to agree to his terms and take him to a false tear location. But we can't rely on that timeline or that circumstance. In less than two weeks, a rebellion in Norun will cut off his reinforcements, leaving him with fewer soldiers to face Khero with. He might grow desperate to act, or suspect Khero's involvement with the rebellion. If that happens, he may revoke his offer of alliance and use threats against me until I take him to the tear. Our plan will remain the same."

"Based on the passage of time in El'Ara, we have at most three days," Ailan said, voice tinged with panic. She resumed pacing, the butterflies fluttering over her head flashing between yellow and orange. "There's still so much more to figure out. We'll need to establish a location, a way to communicate while we secure our plans, and a signal to alert my people that the ambush must begin..."

Cora had ideas for the latter. Berol had already been passing letters between Larylis and Teryn over the last couple of weeks. The falcon was small enough to fly through the tear without attracting the attention of potential spies. Moreover, Cora suspected the Elvyn would have less qualms about using an animal to relay communications as opposed to a human.

Ailan halted and faced Cora once more. "I have one final condition. I will convince the tribunal to accept your terms to keep Lela in the human world, but you must proceed with pushing the *mora* through the tear as soon as the ambush begins. I'll station wardweavers inside the tear who can get to work sealing it as soon as they feel the return of *mora*. That way you have our aid in fighting Darius, but we can take comfort in sealing him out while he's distracted."

"And if you fail," Cora said, leveling a pointed look at her, "the human world will be left to clean up your mess."

"If I fail, it means I'm either dead or he's made his way inside the Veil. Either way, you and I will have done our parts."

"Darius...inside the Veil," Mareleau echoed, shaking her head. "No, that can't be an option. You said El'Ara was the safest place for Noah."

"It is," Ailan said. "I will do everything I can to stop Darius. However, if he does make it inside the tear, the triggers will warn Garot, and you must get to the dragon caves at once. Darius may be fast enough to evade the swing of a sword, and he may heal quickly from most wounds. But there's only so much dragon fire he can withstand, even with his fae healing. Ferrah and the other dragons will defend you. Uziel will face Darius with me. If I can collar my brother, Uziel can burn him. I'll burn with him if I must. If that's what it takes to keep him from worldwalking away."

Cora's stomach turned at that. At the resignation darkening Ailan's tone. She seemed very un-Nalia-like in that moment, and every inch the Elvyn warrior.

Mareleau's throat bobbed. "What about my husband and mother? If the ward-weavers seal the tear before—" She snapped her mouth shut and shifted her gaze to Cora. "Oh, right. You can still worldwalk through the Veil, so long as you have Valorre."

"It may take some time," Cora said, "but I can return everyone to their proper places once the tear has been sealed."

"So...this isn't goodbye between us yet?"

Cora gave her a sad smile. "Not yet."

"Does that mean you agree?" Ailan asked. She certainly wasn't keen on sentiment.

Cora had been determined not to budge on her terms, but Ailan's proposed condition was fair. The humans and Elvyn would work together to ambush Darius. If Cora succeeded in pushing the *mora* back, and the wardweavers sealed the tear while Darius was fighting Ailan, at the very least Mareleau and Noah would be safe. Forever. Darius would never be able to cross the Veil.

All she had to do was trust Ailan to end him.

Her muscles tensed at the thought of leaving the ambush in the hands of others while she played her role at Centerpointe Rock. But this battle wasn't hers. It was Ailan's to finish.

And Lela was Cora's to protect.

She blew out a shaky breath. "I agree."

51

With a slash of ink on paper and the press of his royal seal, Larylis was no longer King of Vera. His latest correspondence from Teryn had demanded his abdication, and Larylis hadn't balked. He obeyed his brother's wishes, rolled up his formal decree of abdication, and handed it to Berol.

With his palms planted on the bulwark of his ship, he lifted his gaze to follow her flight path high overhead, the warm hues of the setting sun gilding her feathers. Not a pang of regret plagued him as he watched his last ties to the throne disappear from sight.

Why should he regret relinquishing his crown? He'd never wanted it anyway. He'd only ever wanted *her*.

His wife's recent letter, also delivered by Berol, had explained everything, so he'd been prepared. How badly he wished he could see Mareleau now. To soothe her fears and beg her to revoke her apologies.

I'm so sorry to ask this of you, her letter had said, *after everything you've fought for. I'm sorry you have to give it all up now.*

He released a sigh. How did she not understand? Rising from bastard to king was nothing compared to earning her love. If abdicating was what it took to be with his wife and child, so be it. There was no sacrifice he wouldn't make for them.

A crown and kingdom were small in comparison.

With Berol no longer in sight, he lowered his gaze to the sunlit cove straight ahead. Upon one of those bluffs lay the entrance to El'Ara. As much as Larylis wanted to be there, to guard the exact location of the tear, this was as close as he dared get by sea. After nightfall, he and his men would disembark and take up posts surrounding the bluff.

Watching.

Waiting.

Preparing.

Protecting.

There was still much to plan for. Much to organize with Teryn and Cora. There were still so many uncertainties and risks. But for the first time since Larylis' world had been shaken by prophecy, dragons, and threats of war, he was certain of his role, even as his title had been stripped away. He knew with all his heart that he was in the right place at the right time.

Soon an ambush would begin.

And Larylis would stake his life on protecting the two people he loved most.

~

LEXINGTON QUIL, CROWN PRINCE OF TOMAS WAS A GENUINE, CERTIFIED revolutionary.

A godsdamned hero, if you will.

And not just to the rebels in Norun but his friends in Khero too. Today the final shipment of weapons had been smuggled to the rebel forces in the southeastern cities of Norun, and tomorrow the battle would begin. Lex's spies had relayed that King Darius' reinforcements were just north of where the rebels would attack, which meant they'd never make it to Khero.

In one fell swoop, Lex would practically save the whole damn world. He wouldn't be surprised if his portrait ended up in one of those fancy textbooks Larylis was always reading. If so, he'd be sure to send him one, just to boast.

He puffed his chest as he grinned at the small crowd gathered on the battlement atop the wall that marked the border between Norun and Tomas. He used to hate this bloody wall. Not because it wasn't effective; it was. Up until now, his kingdom had avoided all conflict with Norun. Tomas was known as a kingdom of cowards, ruled by a monarch who'd rather hide behind a wall than engage in any form of violence. Lex's kingdom was so unremarkable that Isvius Dorsus, King of Norun, hadn't shown an ounce of interest in conquering it.

Which meant he wouldn't expect what was coming for him tomorrow.

Lex's father, Carrington Quil, the renowned coward king himself, had agreed to send a battalion to aid the fights closest to the border. See? Not so much a coward now, thanks to Lex being utterly bloody brilliant. So what if all Lex had done was secure a trade agreement for Aromir wool? It had been enough to get Carrington to stop fawning over Lex's crybaby brother, who only fed their father's fear of conflict. That little slip of paper promising Tomas inclusion into one of the most coveted trade agreements on the continent was exactly what Carrington had needed to bolster his confidence and convince him to finally aid the rebellion of his former neighbors.

Now those soldiers stared up at the person giving them their pre-battle pep talk, moved to tears by the speaker's words.

That speaker was not Lex.

It was his wife.

His tiny spitfire. His sweet little hellion. His beautiful demon with the voice of an angel. The true hero of the rebellion and savior of the world.

Yeah, Lex couldn't take any of that credit. It belonged fully to her.

Lily wore partial armor and a billowing white gown, the epitome of a warrior angel. Her auburn hair was curled in an elegant updo that put her round cheeks on full display. The softness of her form and the sweetness of her looks paired with her vicious words were an oddly alluring contrast.

"Tomorrow, we will fight to take back the kingdoms of Haldor and Sparda," she shouted. She may be quiet most of the time, but gods above, she could project when she wanted. Her uncle, the former King of Sparda, stood beside her and proudly nodded. Lex, standing on her other side, nodded even prouder. "We will punish Norun for underestimating those they perceive as weak. We will show them that even the smallest rodents bear formidable teeth."

A cheer went through the crowd of soldiers, and Lex tried his best not to swoon. Gods, his wife was adorable. She looked so much like she had when they'd reunited after the Heart's Hunt. Lily hadn't wanted to speak to him back then, for there was that whole bit about him competing for another woman's hand, but he'd had a valid explanation. He'd just needed to find her first. Which he had. Standing behind a podium at a secret rally, giving a speech much like this one, encouraging the rebels to maintain hope. That their time would soon come. All they'd needed were weapons.

Lex had fallen in love with her thrice over while he'd listened to her speech, and after he'd managed to convince her he wasn't pure swine for having participated in the Heart's Hunt, he'd promised to bring her vision to life.

He was honored that the time had come.

She raised her voice and pounded a fist against her breastplate. "Tomorrow, we will stand upon the corpses of our enemies and bathe in their blood!"

Another cheer rose from the crowd, its pitch near deafening.

Lily blushed and grinned from ear to ear like the wicked little cherub she was.

Seven devils, he'd never loved her more.

Cora greeted the North Tower Library not with the affection of a friend but the respect of an old enemy. She stepped inside the circular space and found it just as impotent as ever. It was merely a dim, moonlit room, clean enough to prove it was well maintained but with a staleness that spoke of having very few visitors.

She slowly stalked the perimeter of the room with her head held high, not bothering to skirt away from the shadows that gathered in the darkest corners. She swept past pools of moonlight and shadow, as if they were one and the same, and remembered how far she'd come. Just like she'd done the night before her wedding, when she'd awoken from that fiery nightmare, she was here to remind herself of the enemy she'd already defeated. Of the dark energy she'd banished from every object in this room.

Morkai was gone.

Soon Darius would be too.

She'd returned from El'Ara ten days ago, her alliance with the Elvyn secured along with a plan for their ambush. By now, all the pieces should be in place. Larylis and his soldiers were posted in the woods, some near the ambush location, others ready to defend the real tear. Ailan should have sent some of her Elvyn soldiers to join them. Ailan herself would be waiting in the Blight near the tear for the signal that it was time for her to face Darius. The rebellion in Norun should have begun. Cora and Teryn had sent a battalion north to defend the border, should Darius' forces suddenly invade. In two days, Cora and Teryn would ride to join them and prepare for the meeting with Darius. Meanwhile, Ridine's garrison was prepared to defend the castle should Darius appear at any time.

Her mind reeled to keep all the plans organized in her mind, as well as to measure the time discrepancy between the human world and El'Ara. She wasn't sure whether it was a blessing or a curse that time went by so much slower here.

For Ailan and Mareleau, just over a day had passed since Cora had left. They would experience a flurry of activity from dawn to dusk until the battle began.

Even Valorre had a job to do. For the last week, he'd been seeking out all his remaining unicorn brethren, and perhaps any other fae creatures who may have come through the Veil. Most of the unicorns had figured out how to return through the Veil on their own after they'd gotten their memories back. But there were still some who hadn't left, and she didn't want them trapped here when she pushed the *mora* back. Cora ached at the silence that had once been filled by Valorre's presence, and it was only made worse knowing she wouldn't see him again until they reconvened at Centerpointe Rock. He may be there already, but she wouldn't know until she arrived.

In the meantime, Cora could only wait. Prepare. Plan for numerous scenarios.

She blew out an anxious breath and circled the room once more. This time, she paused at the nightstand upon which her talisman of twigs and crystals rested. This was the only surface that gathered dust in the room, for the servants knew better than to disrupt this design. Only Cora tended to it.

With tender care, she removed each twig, each crystal, with careful reverence, then dusted the table with a silk handkerchief she'd tucked into the front of her chemise. Once clean, she replaced the items one at a time, crossing each stick with precision until it formed something like a star, then arranged the crystals around it. With her protection talisman back in place, she gave the nightstand an approving nod. She stepped away, but not before her eyes fell on the nightstand drawer. That was where she'd previously stashed the talon collar, right next to Morkai's book of blood weaving blueprints.

A book Cora now knew Teryn had read.

He'd told her all about what he'd done with the blood Darius had left behind before he'd taken Cora to Syrus. Told her how he'd made a bond with Morkai's warrior wraiths, earning their loyalty for one final battle, before he'd give them eternal rest. All Teryn had to do to summon them was offer his blood.

She'd been chilled to learn of what he'd done, yet she hadn't felt an ounce of fear. It was more...awe. Relief. They now had a way to bolster their numbers without their enemy being any the wiser.

As for their enemy...

He could act at any time.

Cora sensed Teryn's approach before his footsteps sounded on the stairs. She glanced over her shoulder to greet him with a tired grin.

He was dressed down to his shirtsleeves and trousers, his silver hair hanging in waves around his face. In a few slow strides, he came up behind her and wrapped his arms around her waist. He nestled his face into the crook of her neck. "Couldn't sleep?"

"No," she said. "Besides, I wanted to wait for you."

He'd been in the study all evening, arranging correspondences with the trusted few who knew about Larylis' formal abdication. They were keeping it a secret for now, so as not to alert Darius of their intentions, but they still needed to set some things in motion so as not to throw Lela into chaos once all was said and done.

They stayed like that for several long, quiet moments. These were the moments Cora treasured lately. The calm before the storm.

Too soon, Teryn pulled away. She turned to face him, lacing her hands behind his neck. He frowned, then ran a hand down her bare arm. "Aren't you cold?"

She hadn't noticed the cold until now, but dressed in only her chemise so late in the evening, and in a room without a fire, she had to admit she was chilly. "A little."

He smiled down at her and rubbed both of her gooseflesh-covered arms, pausing as one of his hands brushed over her bicep. He stroked the skin with his thumb, eliciting a shiver from her. "Your tattoos have grown again."

Brow furrowed, she slid her hands from behind his neck, resting one palm on his chest while she inspected the other arm. Sure enough, on the inside of her bicep were more geometric shapes that hadn't been inked with a needle. "Oh, you're right."

She hadn't noticed before now, as it wasn't a part of her body she regularly inspected, nor was it an area that drew her attention in the mirror. Yet as surprised as she was to see the new designs, she'd experienced a similar phenomenon last year, when a spiral appeared on her inner elbow. Salinda had explained that Cora wasn't the only one whose *insigmora* had taken on a life of their own. The tattoos themselves were a Faeryn tradition, passed down to the Forest People—Faeryn descendants and witches alike. Now that she knew more about Lela's history, she wondered if it was the influence of *mora* that made the tattoos grow on their own.

Furthermore...what would it be like once fae magic was properly sealed behind the Veil?

Would her *insigmora* cease growing without the aid of ink and needle?

Would the Faeryn descendants who lived among the Forest People cease being able to use the Magic of the Soil? Would they never again wield roots and vines like they had during the battle at Centerpointe Rock? Would only witch magic be left in the world?

Her questions left her with a pang of guilt, for she hated to think she might be condemning some of the Forest People to a magicless life. Yet it was impossible to know the answers, and she'd already made her choice. She knew what she had to do. She'd deal with the consequences after the *mora* was sealed and Lela was safely hers.

Teryn ran his hand over her arm again from bicep to wrist, then lifted the back of her hand to his lips. "We should get to bed."

She stepped closer to him and heaved a sigh. "Must we?" She'd spoken out of anxiety, for she dreaded sleep these days, fearing all the ways things could go wrong during slumber. But the way his eyes dipped to her mouth made her reconsider her motivations behind the statement.

Teryn lifted his eyes back to hers, holding them with passionate intensity. Her palm was still pressed to his chest, her other hand still resting in his. Slowly, he lowered his lips to hers and caressed them with the softest, sweetest kiss. It was a balm on her soul, a blanket for all her frayed nerves. She melted against him, angled her head, and let him deepen the kiss.

Mother Goddess, she loved him so much. Loved how a single kiss could make her forget her fears. Her worries. The risks they'd soon face.

Yet Teryn's kisses could only do so much.

They couldn't drown out the clamor of bells that shattered the night.

Cora's heart hammered against her ribs as they raced down the stairs and through the main hall. Captain Alden and several members of the royal guard intercepted them.

"What happened?" Cora asked, though she expected she already knew the gist of it.

"Heavily armored soldiers are appearing within the perimeter wall," Alden said, her blue eyes wide with terror. "Two dozen at a time, surrounding the castle. I've sent archers to the wall, but the invading army hasn't attacked. They're waiting beneath a shield wall."

Cora's stomach turned. Darius was here. He wasn't going to wait for the border meeting after all. She breathed past her fear, reminding herself that they were prepared for this scenario. Even her guards were ready, as demonstrated by the clothing, weapons, and armor they carried. One guard passed Cora a pair of trousers, a leather gambeson, and a breastplate while another handed similar items to Teryn. With no time for modesty, Cora and Teryn dressed in the proffered raiment with haste, then donned their weapons—Teryn's sword and Cora's dagger.

After they were fully dressed, the party proceeded to the nearest battlement. Once at the parapet, Cora glanced down at the castle grounds. Just like Captain Alden had explained, soldiers gathered in clusters of two dozen all around the castle.

"Seven devils," Teryn cursed from beside her, his hands gripping the edge of the crenellated wall so hard his knuckles turned white.

"There's at least one hundred soldiers," Captain Alden said under her breath. Then, "No, one hundred and fifty. And more keep appearing."

Cora swallowed hard. Their garrison boasted three hundred, but that wasn't enough when the enemy was already inside the gates. Darius had memorized locations inside the keep itself; soldiers could already be surging through the halls...

Despite the fear tightening her chest, she anchored her soles to the floor, flooded her nostrils with cold night air, and connected to the elements. Earth beneath her feet. Breath in her lungs. The mist in the air. The light of the moon. The fire of her rage. Then, lowering her shields, she sought a specific strain of energy.

It sparked in her periphery, on the distant ground, then was gone the next moment. She whirled toward where she'd sensed him and saw a group of soldiers where there had been none a moment ago.

Then his energy returned, closer this time.

Then closer again.

She and Teryn turned away from the parapet just in time to see Darius appear on the battlement.

"There you are," Darius said with a smirk. He was dressed in his same dark military-style ensemble as before, his gray hair swept back from his severe brow, but with a cuirass and gauntlets.

Captain Alden raised her sword, as did the rest of the royal guard, but Darius disappeared in the next breath. His absence did nothing to relieve Cora's fear, and in another heartbeat, Darius was back, a dozen soldiers behind him. His arms were linked with two of his soldiers, and theirs were linked to their comrades, forming a clustered chain of sorts. Cora's eyes widened at the sight. He could travel with that many companions simply by linking a group together and only making physical contact with two of them.

Darius' soldiers dropped each other's arms and withdrew their swords, taking up defensive stances.

"Majesty," Alden said, her eyes narrowed on Darius. "Orders?"

"Hold positions," Cora said, infusing her voice with as much calm as she could muster. Her fingers begged to unsheathe her dagger, yearned to flinch toward the bow and quiver that weren't there. Yet she kept her arms at her sides as she and Teryn stepped forward, flanked by Alden and another guard. Darius' men held their positions while their king mirrored the step toward the other party. He stood tall, his sword fully sheathed at his hip, hands clasped behind his back as if he had no reason to fear the blades pointed at him.

Why should he fear when he could worldwalk out of harm's way in the blink of an eye?

"What is the meaning of this?" Teryn asked. Cora could feel the fear rippling off her husband, but he too was putting on a good show of keeping his composure. "You agreed to give us three weeks to make our decision—"

"Yes, but that was before my reinforcements were stalled." Darius narrowed his eyes. "Did you have anything to do with that? Aiding your friends in Tomas?"

"We were not involved," Cora said, holding his gaze without falter.

"Ah, but you knew about it, didn't you? When you asked for more time to consider my offer, you knew about the rebellion, right?"

"You threatened us with war. Why wouldn't I use any advantage to protect my kingdom? You're the one who broke my trust. You assured me you'd prove your merit—"

"Don't bother with that," Darius said, a dark chuckle coloring his words. "You never intended to consider my offer of alliance, did you?"

"I suppose you'll never know now. What you're doing—showing up at my castle with an army—is unforgivable."

He took another step forward, pausing only when Cora's guards did the same. Still, he kept his gaze locked on Cora's. "I told you my threats weren't empty, and I was tired of waiting while I knew I was being toyed with. You seem to have forgotten what I said about Ridine. That I could and would take it in a single night, should you give me a reason to."

"So you're here to fight us?" Teryn asked.

"I'm here," Darius said, "to give you one last chance to make a reasonable choice. You've forfeited your option of alliance, but I will still accept surrender. Take me to the tear at once, or Ridine is mine."

53

Cora didn't bother trying to mask the pound of her heart. Let him hear it. Let him think she was afraid. So long as he couldn't distinguish the cadence of fear from the pound of anticipation, it didn't matter if he noticed the spike in her pulse.

The key was masking her eagerness.

"How do you know I'm even apprised of the tear's location?"

He gave her a withering look. "I know, trust me. And don't bother deceiving me. I learned enough during my few jaunts to Ridine to understand the general location. Somewhere west of Lake Sarrolin, am I right? On the coast?"

Cora pursed her lips. Yet another reaction she didn't have to hide. She never should have let Mareleau send letters to Larylis through her and Berol without looking over them first. Then again, back when Mareleau had penned the letter, they'd had no reason to believe there was a spy freely wandering Ridine. The intel had only made it back to the castle because Larylis had shared it with Teryn. Darius must have either overheard one of Teryn's meetings with their trusted few allies or snuck into the royal study and found his correspondence.

Either way, Darius would not be fooled by taking him far from where he expected her to.

Thank the Mother Goddess she had no plans to.

Darius' expression darkened. "It isn't up for debate. You will take me to the tear. If you comply, I will accept your surrender and return to remove my soldiers from your premises. If you deceive or fail me in any way, my men will take Ridine. You have ten minutes before they will act on their own. We can spend that time debating and end this chat in bloodshed, or you can take me to the tear and save your castle. You may have forfeited an alliance with me, but we can still forge favorable terms for your surrender."

Cora and Teryn exchanged a glance. Her husband's throat bobbed, worry etched in his expression. He didn't have to feign that. They may have a plan, but that didn't mean it was infallible. So much could go wrong.

Teryn reached for her hand and squeezed her fingertips. She squeezed his back in wordless reassurance.

Darius' sharp tone invaded their moment. "What's it going to be?"

Cora stepped forward, releasing Teryn's hand with great reluctance. She burned Darius with a glare and spoke through her teeth. "I'll take you."

"Good," he said, voice tight. He extended his arm. "You can travel with a companion, I presume?"

"I can." Her gaze dipped to the proffered arm, hating that she had to touch him at all. But touch him she must, if she wanted to take him where he was meant to go. With a deep breath, she closed the distance between them, linked her arm through his, and closed her eyes.

She pictured a cliff's edge, waves battering the beach far below. She imagined salty wind against her cheeks, the soft give of the grass beneath her feet.

Then she took a step.

And planted her feet in their destination.

She released Darius' arm at once and leaped a step back. One hand remained open at her side, ready to unsheathe her dagger should he round on her. "Well?" she said, raising her voice over the crash of waves far below and the rioting wind tearing loose tendrils of hair from her braid. "We're here. I've done what you asked, now remove your men from my castle."

He assessed her through slitted lids. "How do I know you took me to the correct location?"

Her lips peeled into a sneer. "I thought you could sense the tear, being the *mora's* rightful ruler and all. Oh...can you not? Ailan could."

A tic pulsed at the corner of his jaw. "Show me where it is."

Cora scoffed. "That's a bad idea. You'll be torn to shreds as soon as you enter."

"Then you have nothing to fear. Show me."

She uttered curses under her breath. "If you insist." She kept her gaze on him as she skirted past toward the edge of the cliff. The sound of waves grew louder. She halted just before the edge. "I won't turn my back on you until you provide me some space."

"You think I'm going to shove you off the edge?"

"Yes, and I'd rather you didn't."

He bared his teeth to show his displeasure but extended his arms and walked backward. She waited until he was several feet away before she turned her back to him. Her shields, however, remained down. Sensing.

Extending a hand, she stepped closer to the cliff's edge and reached into the air like Ailan had done when she'd searched for the tear. Cora shifted her feet to the side, reached farther ahead.

Then she closed her eyes.

Pictured her destination in her mind.

And stepped off the edge of the cliff.

For the second time in two weeks, Teryn was forced to watch the woman he loved disappear with his enemy. He let every ounce of his rage show as he eyed the soldiers Darius had left on the battlement. They wore full armor and helms, obscuring their features. He couldn't make out their expressions, see if they were terrified or angry, determine whether they were acting out of fierce loyalty or magical compulsion like many of Morkai's men had.

It didn't matter, though.

Whether they were wicked enemies or innocent souls with families and loved ones, they'd come to his castle. Threatened his home. His kingdom. His wife.

Soldiers were essential tools for war.

But Darius' men would die tonight.

Teryn turned away from the enemy squad.

"Don't move," called one of the men.

Teryn paused but didn't bother turning around. "Your king has my wife. You think I'm going to act against him now? Besides, he didn't leave any orders for me. What harm can I do?"

Only silence answered, so he proceeded once more, past his guards who remained at the ready, swords drawn, eyes locked on the other squad. He stopped only once he reached the wall. Moonlight glinted off the shields hiding the hundreds of bodies filling the castle grounds, illuminating the archers who stood on the wall, awaiting orders to defend or attack.

He breathed deeply and unsheathed the dagger at his hip. Shuffling footsteps and the creak of armor sounded behind him, followed by one of the enemy soldier's voices. "What is he doing?"

Teryn brought the blade to his palm, laying the flat of it over its center.

"I have the means to signal our attack," the same man said. "We don't need to wait the full ten minutes for our king to return. One wrong move, and you'll lose any chance at escaping this alive."

"Your king isn't returning," Teryn said. Even if Darius did, even if everything went wrong and the King of Syrus returned triumphant, Teryn was determined to greet him with a massacre. A tableau of death.

"Is that a threat?" the soldier said. "Or do you not trust His Majesty to honor his word?"

"It doesn't matter if he honors his word. My wife won't be honoring hers." He angled his head over his shoulder, his lips peeling into a wicked grin.

The soldier huffed a dark laugh. "If that proves true, your reign is at an end."

"We'll see." With that, Teryn turned the blade, slashed its edge over his palm, and closed his fist. Blood dripped from his hand as he thrust his fist toward the wall and the grounds beyond. Then, with a whisper, he said, "My blood. My command. Your final fight begins."

<h1 style="text-align:center">54</h1>

ora's steps were more precise than any dance.

She left the cliff's edge and planted her feet on soil. The sound of waves was muted by half, though Darius remained in sight. She was behind him now, at the edge of the woods that lined the coastal road. It was as similar a location to the real tear as she could get without positioning him too close to it.

Her hands moved with practiced ease. Even in the dark, in the shadows of the trees that stood behind her, she knew what to do. She kept her eyes locked on her target—Darius standing at the edge of the cliff, in the space Cora had vacated, feeling through the air as Cora had done—as she reached into the underbrush and extracted her bow and quiver. She didn't bother shouldering her quiver, simply plucked out an arrow, nocked it in place, and pulled the bowstring to her cheek.

She'd practiced this shot numerous times over the past week.

Practiced shooting from this distance.

Imagined her enemy standing exactly where he stood now.

She released the arrow, watched it soar straight for Darius' neck, just above the back of his cuirass—

Before the arrow could meet its mark, Darius stepped to the side and whirled toward her. The arrow whizzed past him, over the cliff's edge, and to the beach beyond. A small, winged silhouette shot into the sky, as if startled by the rogue arrow, and flew away.

Cora forced herself not to follow the shadow with her eyes lest she give away Berol's importance. She couldn't let Darius see the place the falcon now dove to, at another cliff's edge much like this one, far in the distance where the coastline curved toward the east.

Darius, oblivious or uncaring of the startled bird, took a step forward. In the next breath, he was before her, tearing her bow from her grip. She took a breath, a step, and used her abilities to travel several feet away, to the center of the road. Unsheathing her dagger, she brandished it at him, ready to strike should he get too close.

But he didn't draw his sword, nor did he close more than a few feet of space between them. The unveiled disdain in his eyes was sharp enough. "Did you think the crashing waves would be loud enough to mask your presence? To stifle the sound of your bowstring? You tried to fool me, and you failed. That makes you the fool."

She said nothing. Perhaps she should look more disappointed. In truth she was, though she'd never counted on her arrow reaching its target. It would have been satisfying, but Ailan had told her how difficult he was to kill. How he could heal from many wounds a regular human could not. Not only that, but he could worldwalk while injured, flee to safety until he healed.

There was only one weapon that could stop him long enough to land a fatal blow, and Cora was not in possession of it.

Darius stepped to the side, and Cora did the same until they were circling each other. He shook his head. "You've truly disappointed me, Aveline. I respected you as my kin. Admired you as a fellow witch and worldwalker. You've made a terrible blunder in trying to deceive me. Ridine is now mine. My men will attack and everyone in your castle will suffer for it. I'll torture those most loyal to you. Strip their flesh from their bones. Place everyone else's head on a pike."

He said those chilling words with a calm that made them that much more terrifying. All she had to counter her fear was a hope that Teryn's plan would work. That his wraiths were enough to protect Ridine.

Darius halted his circling and narrowed his eyes. "I hear the others too. How many are there in the woods? Fifty? One hundred? I take it this is an ambush. What are they waiting for?"

"I haven't a clue what you mean," she said flatly.

He *tsked*. "Did you think you could isolate me here? That I wouldn't stand a chance against your little soldiers? What you fail to realize is I don't have to stay to watch this pathetic ambush unfold. I have better uses for my time—"

He snapped his mouth shut, hearing the wingbeats before she did. It was the hulking shadow darkening the sky that had first alerted Cora that the time had come. Now the pound of Uziel's wings rose over the crash of waves.

Darius whirled around.

Uziel landed on the coastal road, a red glow burning deep in this onyx throat. Upon his back, at the base of his shoulders, sat Ailan.

With a huff of laughter, Darius drew his sword. "I see. I have a reason to stay after all."

Uziel lowered his head, and Ailan climbed down his leg, as easily as if she were exiting a coach. She was dressed in form-fitting trousers, a knee-length robe, and scaled armor over her chest, shoulders, and forearms. She unsheathed a sword with one hand and raised a double-bladed weapon in the other.

Only it wasn't a double-bladed weapon. Not exactly. It was the collar. The one thing that could stop Darius from worldwalking away.

"It's been a long time, sister dear," Darius said, tone mocking.

"Face me," Ailan said through her teeth, "and we can end this rivalry of ours at last."

"I'll face you, but I'd prefer to even the odds first." In the next blink, he disappeared.

Cora used that moment to focus on the space beside Ailan. She stepped across the distance, appearing at the Elvyn's side. "Has Mareleau been alerted that the battle has begun?"

"I sent Ferrah to her as soon as Berol entered the tear," Ailan said. "She'll be prepared for the worst-case scenario."

Cora hated that there even was a worst-case scenario. Which was why her role was so important. She needed to ensure the Elvyn could seal the tear before Darius discovered its location. "Are your wardweavers ready?"

"Yes. They await within the tear. They will weave as soon as the *mora* surges back to El'Ara and their powers strengthen."

Just then, two dozen soldiers appeared, the same way they had at Ridine. These men, however, weren't waiting under their shields. Instead, they surged forward at once.

"Now!" Ailan shouted.

Uziel opened his maw and shot a volley of flame at the men. Those who acted fast enough raised their shields, but at least half screamed as they fell to the blaze.

Another group of soldiers appeared. Then another. Luckily, Uziel's flame wasn't their sole defense. The flash of light had triggered motion from the woods. Now human and Elvyn soldiers ran forth to meet the enemy forces, even as they grew in number. Uziel roared and snapped but could no longer risk his blasts of fire, lest he harm their allies. The allied troops kept the space around Ailan, Uziel, and Cora clear, funneling the enemy soldiers away. Yet Darius made no attempt to drop his fighters near them. He wanted to face Ailan alone.

The sound of steel against steel drowned out the waves, rose above the wind. Would Darius ever stop bringing his soldiers? Had Cora been wrong—

Darius appeared before them, far too close for comfort. Uziel growled, but he couldn't blast Darius without risking harm to Ailan and Cora. He curved his body around them, but Darius only worldwalked to the side, keeping Ailan in view.

"Go," Ailan muttered to Cora as Uziel tried to hide them again.

Cora blew out a shaky breath. As much as she wanted to ensure her allies weren't outnumbered, that they truly could defeat their enemies, she'd already done her part here. She'd lured Darius, and now he'd fight Ailan.

Meanwhile, Cora had another mission to complete.

Ailan stepped forward, leaving the safety of Uziel's proximity.

With a grin, Darius disappeared and reappeared directly behind her.

Cora's heart leaped into her throat—

Ailan parried his sword just in time, moving as swift and as smooth as the night breeze.

Never had Ailan looked so unlike the elderly Nalia Cora had known.

She could trust this warrior to hold her own.

Cora had a job to do. People to protect. And an entire world to seal away.

With a deep breath, she closed her eyes and left the fray behind.

~

THE HAIR ROSE ON THE BACK OF LARYLIS' NECK AS SOUNDS OF BATTLE CLASHED farther down the coast. The clang of steel was too loud, too near the most precious location of all. The hidden tear just north of his post. Mere minutes ago, he'd witnessed an enormous black dragon—the same that had attacked Ridine—appear out of nowhere at the edge of the cliff with a rider on his back.

The blond-haired Elvyn stationed at Larylis' side had tensed at the pair's appearance, his fingers curling around the hilt of his sword. Not in fear of the dragon or its rider but yearning. Frustration. Impatience.

Fanon wanted to defend that rider. Ailan. The Elvyn who was his consort.

Though Larylis and Fanon could communicate, courtesy of the charm hanging from one of his gauntleted wrists, the Elvyn had said very little to Larylis since they'd taken their positions. Yet even without words, Larylis understood him, could read the terror etched on his face as he watched Ailan in the distance. She and the gray-haired man had been locked in combat for several minutes now, the latter's moves impossibly fast. Fanon's tense posture mirrored Larylis' own. They both wished they could be elsewhere—Fanon defending Ailan, Larylis defending Mareleau—yet both had taken up the duty to protect the location of the tear and intercept anyone who got too close.

Already the battle was creeping this way.

Soon they would need to act. Fight. Protect.

Larylis could hardly believe this was happening. No textbook had ever described anything close to this. There were no kings he could emulate, no warriors he could try to embody. Never had he read about a bastard who'd become king, only to relinquish his crown to save two worlds and be with the people he loved. Never had humans fought alongside Elvyn warriors to protect fae magic.

The nearest fighters continued to clash, though the enemy troops soon outnumbered the allies. Larylis' squad could no longer remain in waiting, nor could Fanon's.

"We join," Fanon said, his words translated through the charm.

Larylis tightened his jaw and forgot every great king he'd ever admired. Every line of text he'd ever used to construct an ideal version of himself—a standard he could never reach. Instead, he thought of Mareleau, Noah, and everything he held dear.

All he could be was himself.

That was enough.

Larylis Alante, battle on Khero's western coast, Year 171 of the Dragon. Loved his family more than life. Destroyed their enemies until victory was his.

He lifted his hand and signaled his soldiers to charge.

55

Cora returned to the battlement she'd left not long ago, though now it stood empty. Teryn, his guards, and the enemy squad were nowhere to be seen. Yet sounds of fighting blared all around; she'd traded one active battlefield for another. Even though her destination lay at Centerpointe Rock, she needed to ensure Ridine was safe. That, and she'd promised to take Teryn with her when the time came to push the *mora* from the human world. It could be too dangerous for her to attempt the feat alone. If anything went sideways, if the *mora* overwhelmed her or she began to harness it when she was supposed to push it back, she could depend on Teryn to anchor her.

She peered over the parapet to find a sea of mist and blood. The mist came from the hazy figures of the warrior wraiths that swarmed the grounds, hacking down Darius' fighters, their semi-transparent weapons making muted thuds against their opponents' swords and armor.

Her archers shot arrows into the melee, picking off more of the enemy fighters one by one. The vicious, bloody fight turned her stomach, but she couldn't bring herself to feel remorse. Not when the tides were in her favor.

Not when the win was hers.

Teryn had made the right call in choosing this battle as the wraiths' final fight. With Darius' men already inside the castle walls, Khero's chances of victory would have been slim without them.

She hurried away from the parapet and entered the stairwell leading down from the battlement. Opening her senses, she sought Teryn's location. To her relief, his energy pulsed back, not too far from where she was now. As she exited the stairwell, the clang of steel met her ears. She unsheathed her dagger—the only weapon on her person now that Darius had wrested her bow from her—and crept toward Teryn's energy as well as the sounds of conflict.

She fled down the hall, noting bodies strewn here and there. Most of them belonged to the enemy squad, but one corpse at the end of the hall was a member of her royal guard.

Her heart clenched.

She rounded the corner at the end of the next corridor and finally caught sight of motion. Captain Alden was engaged in combat with one of Darius' men, as were several more of her guards. Another bout took place down the next stairwell, the only sign being the clash of blades and the sway of the fighters' shadows against the stone wall, cast by the light burning in the sconces.

Teryn's energy pulsed from that direction.

Cora's heart thundered as she rushed toward the stairwell, keeping close to the wall to evade the notice of the other fighters. Not that any were unoccupied enough to pay her much heed. She reached the top of the stairs, her dagger at the ready, and proceeded down on quick feet. She pulled up short at the sight of Teryn. He and one of Darius' men were locked in armed combat. Blood covered one of Teryn's shoulders, his gambeson split open to reveal crimson soaking the linen of his shirt. His left hand was wrapped in what looked like a torn piece of cloth.

Yet the enemy soldier bore wounds too. One eye was slashed and swollen, a gash on his cheek just beneath it. His helm was gone, as were several other pieces of his armor, but he fought relentlessly. Teryn had the high ground and pursued the man farther and farther down the stairs, but with Teryn standing between her and his opponent, his back facing her, there was nothing she could do to help—

No, that wasn't true at all.

She released a slow breath, anchored her feet on the stone beneath her, and poured her focus onto the blood-splattered stair behind the enemy. Without even bothering to close her eyes, she lifted a foot, leaned forward...

And planted her soles on the intended step.

Teryn's eyes widened slightly when he spotted her, but he didn't falter. He kept the man's full attention as Cora swiped out with her dagger and slashed the backs of the man's knees. With a grunt, his legs buckled. Cora retreated down a few steps and Teryn plunged his sword into the man's throat.

Cora's chest heaved as she watched the tip of the blade protrude from the back of the man's neck. Teryn withdrew his sword, and the enemy crumpled onto the stairwell. Cora kept her eyes locked on Teryn, not the dying man or the pool of blood quickly slicking the stairs. Instead, she took in his face, the spatter of blood flecked over his skin, the wounds he'd sustained on his arms.

She sagged with relief to see him devoid of life-threatening injuries.

He assessed her with the same relieved intensity. Her name left his lips as he sheathed his sword. "Cora."

She ran the rest of the way up the stairs to him, skirting around the man and the blood, until she collided with his chest, his arms around her. The discomfort of his hard breastplate against her cheek didn't matter. Only he did.

He pressed a kiss to the top of her head and spoke into her hair. "This is the last of the soldiers who got inside the halls."

She pulled away, knowing they didn't have much time to waste. "The ambush has begun."

"Majesty." Alden appeared at the top of the stairs, followed by more of the royal guard.

It was then Cora heard the relative silence. The conflicts in the hallway above had ceased.

Alden gave her a knowing look. "Is it time?"

Captain Alden and the royal guard knew what came next. Knew what Cora had promised to do. Cora gave her a solemn nod. As much as Cora wanted to wait until every enemy fighter was felled, she couldn't linger. Not if she wanted to fulfill her vow to Ailan and lock Darius out of El'Ara.

"Our victory is secure," Alden said, tone brimming with confidence. "We will finish this."

Teryn and Cora exchanged a glance. If they left now, Teryn would need to call off the wraiths. They couldn't risk leaving them to fight without Teryn's guidance. When they'd served Morkai, they hadn't seemed to care who they killed, only that they fought.

"You can depend on us," Alden said.

"Let's go, then." Teryn sheathed his sword and extended his uninjured palm toward Cora.

She grasped his hand, gave it a squeeze, and worldwalked them back to the battlement. The conflict was quieter now, and as they looked over the wall at the castle grounds, they found only a few groups engaged in combat, some with soldiers from the garrison, others with the wraiths. Misty white continued to fill the field, but most of the wraiths had ceased fighting. Those who'd already been felled were unable to reanimate and had returned to their mindless meandering.

Regardless, Alden was right. The victory was already theirs; Cora could trust her soldiers to end this.

Teryn stepped closer to the parapet and unwrapped the bandage from around his palm. An angry red line marred his skin, but it wasn't actively bleeding. He held his hand out, palm to the air, and whispered, "At ease. Your battle is won. Your vengeance secure."

The wraiths stilled on the field. Some disappeared at once, while others simply lost their bloodlust and proceeded to slowly wander.

"When I call you next," Teryn said, "it will be to send you home."

He faced her then, nodding. This was all they could do for Ridine right now. Their next task lay at Centerpointe Rock.

Again, Cora took his hand. Closing her eyes, she pictured a large flat stone amidst a sea of green.

～

EVEN AFTER FIVE HUNDRED YEARS, AILAN'S BODY REMEMBERED HOW TO FIGHT. HER limbs moved in fluid motions, even as her muscles screamed. The rhythm of battle was ingrained in her bones, and with the return of her youth and memories came everything she'd ever learned long ago.

Warfare and violence weren't the most treasured arts amongst the Elvyn, but they were necessary for a future Morkara to learn. And learn she did, her training thorough. It had come to good use during the war with her brother so many centuries ago.

Unfortunately, what was true for her was true for Darius too.

He fought like death incarnate, with the advantage of unfamiliar human combat techniques paired with his worldwalking abilities. He was always escaping the swing of her sword, evading lethal blows and exchanging them for shallow wounds, if any. His lips remained peeled in a taunting grin as they dueled, his attacks unwavering.

But she didn't give up, even as her body grew weary. She kept her mind sharp, attuned to the whispers of her weavings. While she'd waited inside the Veil for the signal that Darius had arrived, she'd constructed a truthweaving, seeking guidance for success.

She hadn't heard a thing in response until the battle with Darius had begun.

Now they whispered to her.

Told her where to turn.

Alerted her of Darius' next move.

Even so, the battle felt endless.

When would her whispers guide her to land a killing blow? When would they shout, teasing out a weakness in Darius' defenses? When would she have the ideal opportunity to end him?

Sweat slicked her brow and dripped into her eyes as the softest, quietest whisper answered her question.

You won't.

You won't.

You won't.

It should have filled her with dread. It should have frozen her under a blanket of foreboding.

But it didn't.

She'd suspected for a while now that she wasn't meant to be the hero in this war with Darius. The prophecy had said so little about her, after all, and every truthweaving she'd cast about El'Ara's future had been about other people.

Noah, the Morkara.

Mareleau, the Edel Morkara'Elle.

She may not be the hero, but she was meant to fight. Destined to face her brother like this.

Gritting her teeth, she sliced out with her sword, thrust with the talons of the collar that she wielded like a dagger. One of the claws hooked into Darius' inner elbow, just above his gauntlet. He stumbled, his eyes going wide as he realized he couldn't worldwalk away.

This was her chance.

She lunged back and swung with her sword. He arched away in time to avoid a deeper cut, earning only a thin slash across his throat. It was too shallow of a wound to slow him down. Her only reward was the sight of his blood running down his throat. Still, she didn't give up. She shifted her stance, swiveled her arms, and slammed the edge of her blade against his abdomen. He released a grunt as the metal armor crumpled inward, her blade sinking into his skin. But at the same time, he tore the talon from his inner elbow and tossed it aside. Ailan ducked and rolled toward it, gathering it in her hand before leaping to her feet.

Darius now stood several feet away, blood trailing from the corner of his lips as he fiddled with the buckles and straps securing the front of his cuirass.

She gave him a wicked grin.

He may have the advantage of iron weapons, which delivered excruciating pain to pureblood fae, but his armor was human-made. Nothing better than garbage compared to the strength of Elvyn craftsmanship and armor harvested from the shedded scales of dragons.

Darius sneered back at her as he loosened a buckle.

Uziel took the chance to blast him with a ball of red flame.

Darius worldwalked away just in time and reappeared closer to Ailan—too near for Uziel to risk using his flame. He released the final buckle and tore his ruined cuirass off his chest. Blood seeped from his wound, but Ailan knew better than to expect enough blood loss to end his life. No, that blow hadn't been a fatal one.

But it had made his vital organs more vulnerable.

As if the blow had been nothing more than an inconvenient jab, he charged for her, swinging his sword. She dodged. Parried. He disappeared.

Her whispers guided her to the left.

She turned.

Met his blade.

Again.

Again.

It was never-ending, and the sounds of battle around them didn't cease either.

She needed the upper hand.

Needed to find his weakness.

She parried his blade, slashed out, and pivoted in time to meet his next blow. Her eyes dipped to the symbol at his lapels: a dragon encircled in a ball of flame.

She smirked. "Interesting sigil, considering no dragon would have you."

He bared his teeth in a dark grin. "Every dragon in El'Ara will heed my commands once I'm Morkaius. They won't be subject to the prejudices of their former masters."

"The fact that you call a dragon's bonded counterpart their *master* shows just how little you know about dragons in the first place. They would never respect you."

He disappeared.

Reappeared to her right. She met his blade with hers.

"Because I'm impure?" he said through his teeth. "A half-blood? An imperfect specimen, a stain on your precious, stagnant way of life?"

"No," Ailan said with a smirk. "Turns out, dragons don't have a problem with humans."

His expression faltered.

She swung her blade, feinted left, then thrust with one of the talons.

He disappeared before it could do more than slice his torso.

Ailan whirled around just as he reappeared behind her. They exchanged blows, their swords clanging, the sound ringing through her ears.

"They've accepted her," she said, her smirk widening, darkening. "She has already succeeded at more than you ever have. More than you ever could."

He scoffed. "Are you talking about the human mother?"

"You complain about being judged for your human blood, but do you even hear the way you speak about your own kind? You don't respect humans any more than most of the Elvyn do. How does it feel to hate everything you are? To hate both sides of your bloodline so fiercely?"

"It feels like power," he said, slashing his sword against her breastplate.

Unlike his, her armor didn't crumple. It did, however, make her stumble back at the force. She regained her footing and took up a defensive stance.

He spoke again. "I am better than both sides of my bloodline. I am the future of two worlds. Do not mistake my confidence for self-hatred, for I know my worth. You're the one who has always underestimated me. Undervalued me."

"You never once gave me a reason to hold in you any regard."

"And that shall be your downfall. You say the human mother has bonded a dragon?"

Ailan pursed her lips. Mareleau hadn't exactly *bonded* a dragon yet, but she had earned Ferrah's respect. Not that Darius needed to know that.

He chuckled. "I know she's safe behind the Veil with her son—my true enemy, second to you. And if I'm not mistaken..." His eyes narrowed to slits as he inched closer. Ailan stepped back, maintaining a safe distance from him, matching his steps as he began to circle her. "I'll find them in the dragon caves, then?"

Ailan's heart leaped into her throat.

Darius nodded. "Your fear has confirmed it. As for the tear..."

Ailan charged for him as he cast his gaze to the north.

He met her eyes with a wicked grin before disappearing.

Her blade met only air.

56

Silence replaced the sounds of the waning battle as Cora and Teryn found themselves on Centerpointe Rock. The wide plane of weathered stone stood at the center of a vast valley. Outside the valley slumbered the silhouettes of hulking hillsides.

The night was even darker here than it had been at the castle. Cora blinked to adjust to the change in light. She had only a moment to orient herself before she was barraged with irritated relief that wasn't her own.

You're here! I can't believe you made me stay away. Valorre darted down one of the hills and onto the field, practically bowling her over as he leaped upon the rock.

"I'm sorry," she said, caressing his neck, not bothering to mention that he was the one who'd insisted he be at Centerpointe Rock when she attempted her feat.

Just like Teryn, Valorre had feared her being alone during this endeavor. Yet, without knowing exactly when the ambush would begin, it would have been impossible to guarantee Cora could reconvene with Valorre before worldwalking to the rock. So they'd decided he'd come here and wait for her as soon as he'd accomplished his important duties.

"Are your brethren safely back home now?" she asked.

He tossed his mane, radiating arrogance. *Of course they are. I'm highly capable. I guided the last pair of unicorns through the Veil yesterday morning. I've been waiting ever since. Do you know how worried I was about you?*

"I have some idea," she said, giving his neck a final pat. As much as she wanted to enjoy her reunion with her companion, she didn't have time to waste.

Teryn squeezed her hand. "Are you ready?"

"I have to be," she whispered back. With a trembling breath, she sank to her knees and pressed her hands to the surface of the rock. Her *insigmora* thrummed from her palms to her biceps, tingling every line of ink. Her magic rose like a tide in her blood, echoing the pound of fae magic that sang back.

She felt the *mora* pouring from the rock, sensed the well of magic that was available to her.

It was vast.

Terrifying.

Everything inside her told her this magic could destroy her. Could flay the skin from her bones should she try to harness it.

When last she was here, during the battle, she hadn't sensed anything like this. But she hadn't been Queen of Lela then. Now she was.

She swallowed hard, feeling deeper and deeper into that magic.

A gentle hand fell on her shoulder. Teryn crouched beside her. "I may not have the kind of magic you do, but use me."

"What do you mean?"

"Let me anchor you. Let me help. You are Queen of Lela and I am its king. I may not have what it takes to push the *mora* back, but I too have fulfilled every qualification necessary to be King of Magic. We can do this together."

She nibbled her lip, hating the thought of involving Teryn in this.

I may not be a Roizan, Valorre said, scraping a hoof on the rock, *so I cannot act as a vessel to harness the* mora. *But use me too. If it feels like too much, send at least some to me. Let me take some of the burden while you work.*

Between the warmth of Teryn's palm and her connection with Valorre, some of her terror eased. The strength of the *mora* felt less like a thrashing, cresting wave, and more like an unfathomable yet tepid sea. She could do this. She could lean on those she loved.

"All right," she said.

Then, refocusing on the thrum of magic against her palms, she spoke to the *mora*. "I am Aveline Corasande Caelan, Queen of Lela, Queen of Magic. Heed my edict. Move at my command."

∼

AILAN WHIRLED THIS WAY AND THAT, WAITING FOR DARIUS TO REAPPEAR.

He didn't.

Her stomach sank, telling her everything she needed to know before her whispers confirmed it.

North.

Look north.

There he was, the lone figure upon the farthest cliff she could see. Fanon's squad had kept the fighting relegated south of that point, as was his directive. With his abilities as a skyweaver—giving shape, form, and pressure to air—he could forcibly push back anyone who tried to get too close. Yet she couldn't see any sign of her consort in the fray, and now the one person they needed to keep off that cliff was there.

Alone.

His stillness told her he was waiting for her.

With no other option, she gestured for Uziel and climbed back upon his shoulders. She didn't take her eyes off her brother as her dragon flew her to him, landing on the coastal road not far from the nearest skirmish. From the buzz of *mora* humming through her, she knew Cora had yet to send the magic back through the Veil. However, she sensed…something. The *mora* wasn't moving in reverse yet, but it was reacting.

She had to keep her brother distracted long enough.

She dismounted her dragon, chest heaving with rage, and closed the distance between her and Darius.

He met her blade with a speed and fury he'd kept at bay until now. "Always, you underestimate me. Did you truly believe I couldn't sense the *mora*? You think you're that much stronger than me? You've always thought too highly of yourself."

It took all her strength to parry his strikes, to knock back his blade, to whirl to face him whenever he moved through space. Even with the tear so close, even with the tingle of the *mora* fueling her, fatigue was settling into her bones.

Or was it the crushing whisper that foretold of her defeat?

She pushed through the heaviness in her limbs, the tightness in her chest. She'd succeeded in getting under Darius' skin with her comment about Mareleau and Ferrah. Before that, her blow to his breastplate had made him vulnerable. All she needed was one chance. Just a moment to plunge one of the collar's talons into his skin and sever his head from his neck.

That was all it would take.

Then it would be over.

She would win.

You won't.

You won't.

You won't.

Her whispers didn't taunt, they caressed. Like a mother laying a child to sleep.

She swung her blade.

Darius disappeared.

Reappeared behind her.

But she was too slow.

His blade slashed open her thigh.

She cried out as she lost her footing. With a weapon in both hands, she struggled to catch herself as she fell to the slick grass. She planted her good leg beneath her, fought to rise to her feet, but Darius was there.

His blade soaring toward her throat—

It stopped mere inches away.

Ailan's gaze darted to the most welcome face she could ever hope to see.

Fanon.

Her consort.

The love of her life.

Fury twisted his features as he marched toward them, his invisible restraints freezing Darius in place.

But her brother's surprise wouldn't last long. He could worldwalk free in the blink of an eye.

Ailan took her chance and threw herself at her brother, hooking one edge of the talon into his calf before closing the collar on its hinge.

Darius' eyes went wide. He blinked. Once. Twice.

With a thrust of her sword, she pierced Darius' abdomen, pulling it free just as Fanon dropped his skyweaving in exchange for a swing of his own blade. It arced toward Darius' neck, aiming for a clean and decisive beheading...

Freed from Fanon's restraints, Darius could now reach for the collar.

It didn't matter, for it would be too late.

Fanon's blade would strike before Darius' fingers even met the tines...

Yet it wasn't the tines of the collar Darius sought. Instead, he whirled around, closing the distance between him and Fanon. He pivoted, swung his blade...

And cut Fanon's hands off at the wrists.

His blade fell impotent to the grass below.

Ailan called out her consort's name, the agony in her voice like razors in her throat.

She was too distraught.

Too distracted.

Too haunted by the blood pouring from the ends of her consort's blunted wrists...

That she didn't see when Darius removed the collar from his calf.

Didn't see when he disappeared.

Or sense when he reappeared, just behind her.

She didn't even feel the slice of his blade.

Her whispers soothed her with a final caress.

Last Breath has come at last.

57

The *mora* surged toward Cora, the force of it nearly pushing her off the rock. It washed over her, through her, fluttering past. She sensed its journey then, the way it flowed through the Veil on unseen, underground webs of magic, bypassing the wardweaving that stopped everything else. Everything weaker. The strongest vein pulsed from a singular direction to the northwest —the tear. The *mora* was concentrated there, flowing faster, easier. All the lines met beneath her palms, flooding the rock, filling it, and then spilling over the top of the land like an invisible spring.

Now she fully understood why the *mora* couldn't return to El'Ara. She'd understood it intellectually before, after Garot had explained the Blight, but this time she could *feel* it. The way it flowed so confidently toward the rock before stalling and drifting outward in haphazard, sometimes violent waves. Its exit was unhampered by the Veil, but its return wasn't. The *mora* sought direction here at the junction of those veins, but it had no guidance, and it was lost without it. *This* was the importance of the Morkara's duties.

A duty she could mimic now.

As Queen of Magic, the *mora* saw her as someone it could obey.

Whether it *would* was the question.

Like an unruly child, the magic surged again, as if testing her resolve, her strength. It seared her palms, sent chills down her spine.

She focused on the coolness of the stone beneath her hands, the air in her lungs, the dew drops dotting the field, the moonlight streaming overhead. The elements were hers, reflecting the similar-yet-different ones that made up fae *mora*. The magic surged once more, battering her body inside and out. She focused on Teryn's steady touch, Valorre's comforting presence.

Her loved ones.

Her anchors.

She sent her intention back to the *mora*. It funneled from her heart, down her arms, into her palms, flooding the rock beneath her. It spoke to the pulsing *mora* in a silent demand.

Reverse.

Reverse.

Reverse.

The *mora* stilled. Its flow grew calm. And it opened itself to her will.

Possibilities spread before her as she felt the weight of *mora* settle over her. Its strength was somehow crushing and uplifting at the same time. A blanket of lead and light. A blazing, deadly inferno and a gentle ray of sunshine.

It was both. It offered everything. Nothing.

It was unyielding. It was pliant.

She could shape it in her hands even as it burned her.

Yes...she could shape it.

Visions flooded her mind, of all the *mora* offered. The power it could give her. The enemies it could vanquish. The wars it could end. The curses it could break...

Curses.

She was still cursed to die childless, wasn't she? She never had found a way to rid herself of Morkai's most wretched punishment.

Darkness filled her heart, a companion she no longer tried to hide. Yet now that it was here...

It would be a shame not to use the *mora*. At least a little. She could use it without harnessing it. She could keep some for herself, couldn't she? Why shouldn't she be rewarded for all her hard work? Why shouldn't she wield what was freely offered? Why should she send the *mora* back at all? She could be Queen of Lela, Queen of Magic, and do *anything* in this world. She could stitch the tear from here and keep the flow of magic exactly as it was, keep siphoning all of El'Ara's power, lock the fae away and let the Blight take them while she used the magic as she saw fit. She could end Darius in a single flick of her wrist and ensure none of her people ever had to suffer. She could obliterate enemy forces without risking any of her soldiers. She could fortify her body, her soul, and—

"Cora!"

The voice tore through her raging, swirling thoughts.

Then another. *Cora!*

The two voices called her name, one inside her mind, the other ringing through her ears.

She was aware of Teryn's touch then, the hands that framed her shoulders, bracing her like she might drift away. Then she noticed the soft muzzle that bumped her cheek, the breath that blew across her face.

She forced her attention to narrow on that warm breath, those warm hands.

Only then did she realize her palms were no longer pressed to the rock. Instead, she'd risen to her knees, her spine rigid, her head tipped back. The *mora* radiated through her, howling in her veins like a vicious storm.

"You don't need it, my love," Teryn said, his hand moving to her cheek.

She opened her eyes. Her vision was blurry at first, but soon it cleared to show his face. He was pale, expression twisted with worry. Valorre's head was lowered beside him, staring at her with his wide russet eyes.

Teryn spoke again. "You don't need to harness it. You are enough as you are."

She sagged at his words. Fatigue tugged her bones, and she was desperate to collapse. To sleep. But she couldn't quit yet. Her duty had only just begun.

With a trembling sigh, she settled back into the feel of Teryn's hands and the vibrant energy that was Valorre's presence. That's right. She could lean on them. Turn over some of the burden.

"Cora." Teryn stroked her cheek with his thumb, his voice pitched with worry.

"I'm all right," she managed to croak. "I wasn't prepared for the temptation to harness it. I...I'm ready now. This time I'll rely on the two of you."

Teryn nodded. "Don't do this alone. You don't need to."

He was right. She wasn't alone. She could share this.

Teryn moved aside, giving her space to press her palms to the stone again. He moved his hands to her back, his touch both firm and comforting. Valorre kept his muzzle near her shoulder, bumping her with it, blowing hot breaths against her cheek again.

She wouldn't forget them this time.

Gritting her teeth, she faced the *mora* again, but she didn't turn herself over to it. *Reverse*, she demanded, pushing back with her resolve. Fighting its flow. Urging it back underground.

Are you certain? it asked. It pulsed through her, infusing her mind with visions again.

Yes. Cora breathed the temptation away, let the *mora* swirl around her, through her, and into her companions, taking some of the weight off her chest.

You wouldn't rather wield it? Harness it? Take it?

NO. She pushed back even harder, shared more of her burden with Teryn and Valorre. *I am Queen of Lela, Queen of Magic. You yield when I tell you to yield. You move when I tell you to move. Now GO! RETURN.*

Teryn held her tighter.

Valorre's presence grew warmer.

The *mora* cycled through the three figures, then radiated down Cora's hands.

Through her palms.

Back into the rock.

And finally, its flow reversed.

~

MARELEAU HAD PRACTICED THE WARDING GESTURE AILAN HAD TAUGHT HER DOZENS of times by now, and she still wasn't certain if it worked. Noah lay on her bed, wrapped in lavender silk swaddling embroidered with a gold dragon-scale pattern. She sat beside him and performed every move that her hands had already memorized. She pressed her thumbs to her ring fingers, angled her wrists, then linked her fingers together. Another turn of her wrists, and she pressed the tips of her remaining fingers together. She held the gesture for a few breaths, then laced all fingers before spreading them over Noah like she was covering him in an invisible blanket.

She stared down at her results. Like always she could see nothing out of the ordinary. How could she ever know it worked?

Remembering what Ailan had told her about practicing on herself first, she strode to the mirror and repeated the same gesture but for her own body. She tried to perceive *something*, some clue that it had worked, but neither her eyes nor her claircognizance told her a damn thing. Clenching her jaw, she whirled away from the mirror. She didn't have time to practice or wonder. Ferrah had returned from the tear not long ago, which was the signal that the ambush had begun.

How long ago had that been? Ten minutes? Twenty? Was it evening on the other side of the Veil, or daytime like it was here? She tried to estimate the hour, but math had never been her strength. Besides, the discrepancy of time between the two realms was an estimate, not an exact science.

Still, it chilled her to think that even though it had only been minutes for her, hours of battle may have already passed. Hours that Larylis could be fighting. Struggling. Or...

No, she wouldn't think of anything worse than that.

A knock sounded at her door, and Garot entered without waiting for her to answer. "Are you ready? We must make haste to the dragon caves as a precaution."

Mareleau wasn't overly fond of the idea of hiding in dark caves with a horde of feisty dragons, but Ailan had assured her it would be the safest place for her and Noah. That the dragons would protect them if the worst happened.

"I'm as ready as I'll ever be, I suppose." She returned to the bed and scooped up her son, cradling him close to her. She shouldered his carrying sling as well in case she needed it. She'd come to rely on the convenient item and couldn't imagine these early days of motherhood without it.

She joined Garot outside her bedroom and found Etrix in the hall. Both had stayed behind to guard her and Noah. Garot led the way, though not with his swirling tunnel. Instead, they made haste through the halls on foot. The cheery sunlight streaming through the arched windows made it hard to imagine a deadly battle was taking place at that very moment.

They reached the stairwell that led down to the next floor—

Mareleau sucked in a sharp breath as threads of invisible energy poured over her, tingling her scalp, filling her throat, her chest, her stomach. Garot, already a step down, whirled to face her, brow raised in question.

Etrix placed a hand on her shoulder. "Are you all right?"

She opened her mouth but no words came out. The tingling force continued to wash through her, an ice-cold thrum so soft and foreign she couldn't make sense of it. Her mind spun, eyelashes fluttering as the energy flowed down her legs, her feet, then rose again.

Noah stirred in her arms, and the tingle lessened by half.

The sensation remained, but it was subtler now. Quieter. And it was pulsing between her and Noah.

"What..." She swallowed the dryness in her throat. "What was that? Did you feel it?"

Etrix furrowed his brow, head tilting to the side.

"We must—" Garot's words cut off as he reached into the pocket of his teal robe. He extracted a strange green orb, one that glowed with a pulsing emerald light. His tan, freckled face paled, his eyes shooting wide. "No."

Etrix rounded on the Elvyn. "One of the triggers was tripped? Where?"

"Not just one," Garot muttered as he reached for the top of the glowing orb with his thumb and forefinger. Gingerly, he tugged until something like a petal spread down. He peeled another, then another, until the orb flattened out into what looked like a multilayered map. If a map could be made from an unusual flower bud. She could hardly comprehend what she was seeing as Garot lifted one petal, then the other, flipping them and rearranging them like pages in the most oddly constructed book in existence. Finally, he paused on one petal. Darker green veins patterned its surface, which Mareleau soon realized weren't random or organic markings, but shapes of landmarks—lakes, forests, and mountains. It really was a map. And beneath one of the mountains marking the petal pulsed a small red light.

"The dragon caves in Bel'Dawn," Etrix said, brow knitting deeper.

Just as quickly as the red light flashed, it disappeared. Garot flipped through the petals with haste until he found the light again. "Now the Lo'Sel Mountains."

"What's happening?" Mareleau asked, her voice strained. She understood enough to know this map must be what alerted the Elvyn of non-fae trespassers. It was how they'd found Cora the first time she'd worldwalked here, as well as how they'd reached Mareleau's group when they'd arrived with Ailan.

Etrix and Garot exchanged a weighted glance.

Etrix's throat bobbed. "He's here. And he's worldwalking from cave to cave, locations he recalls from when he lived in El'Ara. He's figured out where they'll be hiding."

"That can only mean..." Garot's shoulders visibly shrank, his expression empty as his lips flattened into a tight line. Mareleau had never seen him without a jovial smile on his face. Never heard him at a loss for words. Even Etrix, who always maintained a neutral, stoic air, crumpled, his eyes glazing with tears as he flung his palm over his heart, as if smothering a piercing ache.

Even without their reactions, she understood what had happened. It had been written in that strange tingle of energy she'd felt. The energy that continued to pulse between her and Noah even now.

Ailan was dead.

Mareleau was regent.

And Darius was coming for her and her son.

58

Larylis had witnessed the death of hope and hadn't been able to stop it. He'd been locked in combat with his own opponent, but the glimpses he'd stolen had shown Fanon and Ailan securing their win.

Yet by the time Larylis had pulled his sword from his opponent's belly, Darius was gone. And Ailan and Fanon...

He ran to them now, his heart in his throat. Both lay on the ground, Ailan motionless and Fanon half crawling, half dragging himself toward his consort on his elbows.

Because his hands.

Gods, his hands.

They were gone.

The black dragon roared and thrashed, a piercing, keening cry rumbling in his throat. He circled the two figures, wings splayed, a red glow burning behind the scales of his neck.

Larylis slowed his approach as he neared, which gave him just enough time to roll out of the way of the dragon's sudden blast of flame. The creature snapped his teeth, then charged—

"Uziel, stop!" The male voice was an agonized rasp, but the dragon obeyed nonetheless. "Drop your sword and bow to him, human fool!"

It took Larylis a moment to realize Fanon was speaking to him, but he did as told, dropping his sword to the ground and folding into a bow. Uziel released a hiss, then an agitated rumble, but from the corner of Larylis' eye, he watched the dragon take a grudging step back.

"Leave him be, Uziel." Fanon's voice was even weaker now.

Larylis risked rising from his bow. He cast a wary look at the dragon, who continued to hiss at him but made no move to roast him alive. Taking that as permission, he jogged the rest of the way to Fanon and Ailan. The latter was motionless, her neck severed, the sight too gruesome for Larylis to study. He turned his attention to Fanon, who was at least still alive, though losing blood quickly. He'd ceased dragging himself across the grass and now lay supine beside his consort at a haphazard angle.

Larylis crouched before him. "I'll tie a tourniquet—"

"I can't understand you," Fanon said through his teeth. Seven devils, of course he couldn't. He'd had the same translation charm around his wrist that Larylis wore now. A charm that had obviously been lost with his hands. Steeling his nerve, he sought any sign of the missing appendages, but Fanon halted him with a stern tone. "Don't you dare tend to me. Take the collar and go."

Larylis returned his gaze to Fanon. The Elvyn jerked his chin toward the other side of Ailan's body. Larylis saw nothing in the grass but heavy gouges and pools of blood—

No, there was something. Half hidden in the blood-soaked grass was a talon. Larylis rushed to retrieve it and found not one talon but two. It was the collar that had once adorned his wife's neck.

"Take it and enter the tear," Fanon said. "He's already inside."

Larylis' blood went cold. Darius...had entered the tear?

Fanon spoke again. "Uziel, take him."

"What do you mean, take me?" Larylis asked, but the sound was drowned out by Uziel's roar. The dragon slammed his tail on the ground in protest, setting the cliff rattling.

"Do you want to avenge her?" Fanon's voice was growing weaker by the second.

Uziel ceased thrashing and released a series of piercing chirps. Larylis didn't need to understand the language of dragons to know the creature was grieving.

"Then take him to the Edel Morkara'Elle. She and our Morkara are all we have left of Ailan. Do you understand? Do not fail her, Uziel."

Uziel swiveled his head and pinned Larylis with a forbidding look. He gnashed his teeth, his tongue flicking outward, sending small licks of flame into the air.

"And you, human," Fanon said. He closed his eyes, his chest pulsing with shallow breaths. "Do you want to save the woman you love? Do you want to succeed where I have failed?"

Larylis tightened his fist around the collar. "With everything I have."

"Mount the dragon," Fanon said, understanding his conviction even without a translation. "Enter the tear. Stop him before it's too late."

TEARS OF FEAR AND GRIEF AND RAGE STUNG MARELEAU'S EYES AS SHE, ETRIX, AND Garot rushed from the palace toward the dragon caves. They'd accumulated a squad of guards who now brought up the rear. She wove her arms protectively around her son as she hurried along the same path Ailan had taken her down two days ago.

Ailan.

She was...gone.

Mareleau hadn't fully warmed to the woman, but it would be a lie to say she hadn't grown at least somewhat comfortable with her. Ailan may have stolen her and her son from the lives they'd known and loved…

But she'd treated Mareleau with respect. Fought to position her as a person of high esteem amongst the Elvyn, despite her human blood. She'd taught her the motions for wardweaving and encouraged her to work with the magic she already possessed without undermining her goals.

Just like that, she was gone.

Mareleau would never get to say goodbye.

Could never rely on the woman to protect and advocate for her.

Ailan had been their greatest hope in defeating Darius, and she was gone. Darius was coming for Mareleau and Noah next. Would they die just as easily? Would everything she and her friends and allies had fought for come to nothing?

A tremor ran through her, but it wasn't one of fear. Instead, fury burned her blood, weighing down her feet with every inch she closed toward the caves. The fire blossomed and grew into a wrath so hungry it begged her to fight. *Fight*, not hide.

But what the hell could she do? She wasn't a warrior. She couldn't even weave a damn protection ward. She was a selfish beast, born and raised, and now she was paying the price. There was only one thing she excelled at, and that was looking out for herself. Hiding was all she could do.

If only she weren't a narcuss. If only her magic were better, stronger. If only *she* were better and stronger.

No matter what you find in those shadows, came a voice from memory, *it is important that you love yourself.*

Salinda had said those words when Mareleau had sunk into self-hatred after discovering what she was. Well, a lot of good that did her now. She needed to protect others, not herself. What did *she* matter when she had someone so important to protect?

Is it easy to be selfish? This time it was Ailan's voice that rang in her head. *To me, it looks like your resistance to focusing on yourself is stronger.*

Yes, well…she'd been right.

Mareleau hadn't been able to shift her attention to her own well-being. Every time she'd practiced warding on herself or on her and Noah together, she'd burn with impatience. It had seemed like such a waste of time and magic when she'd rather grow her abilities for others. She needed to overcome her insipid magic challenge already so she could…

Her mind emptied.

Again, Ailan's voice spoke from memory.

You can't challenge your magic; you must wait for it to challenge you.

Calm knowing settled over her as a new awareness began to bloom, rising alongside the furious fire that still burned within. She didn't fully understand it yet, but something was starting to take shape.

The mouth of the cave came into view at last, the afternoon sun dimmed by the towering heights of the palace above. Ferrah was just outside the cave, slithering in anxious circles, then shifting from foot to foot, her feathered wings bristled. As soon as they approached the cave mouth, Ferrah slithered inside. The guards fanned out, creating a half circle around the entrance. Garot gestured for Mareleau to follow the dragon. Just as she was about to enter the dark maw, wingbeats sounded overhead.

The guards' hands flew to the hilts of their swords, but they didn't draw them. For the creature that descended was a familiar one. Uziel landed just beyond the ring of guards, bellowing a string of high-pitched chirps, too eerie to be sounds of joy. No, they were sounds of lament.

If that was the case, who was the rider on his—

Her heart nearly tumbled from her chest as the figure all but leaped off the beast's shoulders and raced for her. A sob broke out of her throat as his arms went around her from the side, careful of their son between them.

"Thank the gods," Larylis whispered into her hair. "You're here. You're safe."

She pulled back and assessed her husband through glazed eyes. His dark copper-tinged hair was mussed, his face splattered with dirt and blood. His armor was dented in places, his padded leather jacket ripped open and dripping blood. But he was alive. He was here and alive and that was all that mattered.

"You must be our Morkara's father," Etrix said, his tone flat. Worry and grief still dominated his expression.

"We can't dally," Garot said, his eyes on his petal-map. Where before only one red light flashed, now there were two.

Some small part of her had hoped Larylis' sudden arrival meant he'd been the one to trigger the alert, but that had been too much to wish for.

Garot spoke again. "We must get inside. Darius is moving from cave to cave, starting with those surrounding the Blight. We built Alles'Taria Palace over an existing cave system. He may not know the palace exists, but he may remember these caves. Even if he doesn't, he could find other fae to torture information from. If he comes across any Faeryn...with the discord between our two races, they may not hesitate to share intel."

Larylis angled slightly away from Mareleau and reached for something tucked under his jacket. He withdrew the two-taloned collar. "I'll fight him. I have this."

Etrix' eyes widened. "If you have that, then Ailan truly is..."

"I'm sorry," Larylis said. He may not have met Etrix before but even he could tell Ailan had been important to him. Now whatever frail hope Etrix had clung to was gone.

Gods, Mareleau couldn't imagine the depths of his grief.

"Fanon urged Uziel to take me here," Larylis said, "and for me to bring the collar."

"What of the soldiers inside the tear?" Garot asked. "The wardweavers?"

Larylis' face paled. "All I saw upon entering were bodies."

Etrix uttered a string of words the charm on her bracelet failed to translate. He faced Garot. "He's probably killed the wardweavers. There's no one to seal the tear once the human queen sends the *mora* back to us."

"*If* she sends it back," Garot said.

There was no condemnation in his tone, but Mareleau bristled nevertheless. "She will send it back. She's probably already trying. But if there's no one at the tear to seal it, she can't complete her mission, right? She can't simply push it back forever with nothing to contain it."

"She's right," Etrix said, already retreating. "I'll take Uziel back to the tear with three more wardweavers. We can't lose this chance."

He strode toward the black dragon, who continued to keen and bellow. Uziel gnashed his teeth at the dark-haired Elvyn but let him mount him anyway. Then, in a matter of several pulses of those leathery wings, they were high in the sky.

"Will he get there in time?" Mareleau asked.

"Faster than I would," Garot said, his eyes still fixed on the map. "My pathweaving doesn't work in the Blight, but Uziel can reach the tear quickly. If he'll listen to Etrix, that is."

Noah began to fuss and squirm, reflecting the panic tightening Mareleau's chest. She hushed and soothed him, bouncing him in her arms. He probably needed to be nursed or changed, but this wasn't the best time. They still needed to hide.

A sharp tapping echoed from behind her, and she spun to find Ferrah waiting inside the cave, her talons beating impatiently on the stone beneath her.

"On we go," Garot said. "Our best hope is to hide deep in these caves. Darius can worldwalk to this location if he has any memories of it, but unless he has distinct recollections of the cave interior, he'll need to traverse the tunnels on foot. And I don't suspect he's alone. My map doesn't show how many people set off the triggers if they are together in a group, and I doubt he'd be foolish enough to enter dragon caves by himself."

Larylis nodded. "I'll wait outside with the guards and halt him with this." He lifted the collar again.

Garot shook his head. "We should give it to your wife to use as a last resort. If Ailan wasn't able to stop him with it, I doubt a human like you could. No offense. If Etrix succeeds at bringing a new trio of wardweavers to the tear, and your friend succeeds at pushing the *mora* to us, we can hope to trick Darius into worldwalking back to the human world. He'll need reinforcements to take down our guards, won't he? If he leaves after the tear is sealed, we'll be safe from him."

Mareleau frowned. "You mean...lock him out and leave him as a problem for the human world."

"Better there than here." His tone was so empty. So tired.

Mareleau understood his apathy in the face of such grave odds, yet she couldn't stand the thought of hiding when their goal was to leave Darius in Lela. For Cora and Teryn to deal with. *If* they could deal with him.

It wasn't that she didn't trust their abilities.

Hell, they were all stronger and more capable than she was.

It was more that she railed at the thought of passing this off on them. Staying safe. Small. Hiding. While they continued to fight for their lives.

"Protect our Morkara," Garot said, his gaze locked on the red light on his map as it disappeared and reappeared on a different petal. "That is your strength and your duty as Edel Morkara'Elle."

All this time, she'd wanted to believe exactly that. That protecting Noah was her strength. Her duty. Her guiding light. That her magic would bloom and unfurl once she'd learned how to use it the way she yearned to.

Yet that fury continued to burn in her chest. Wrath, rage, and rebellion in one.

Was it her selfish side that hated being told what to do?

Was it her prideful side that always wanted to prove others wrong when they claimed to know who she was? What she was meant for? What she was worth?

Yes. Yes, it was. And the confession came as such a relief that she nearly wept.

She understood her challenge now. It wasn't figuring out how to protect Noah. It wasn't refusing to leave his side. It certainly wasn't turning away from herself. It was *trusting* herself. Putting all her faith in her own abilities. Not the abilities she wanted to have, but the ones she already possessed. She didn't need to go against her nature; she needed to dig deeper into it and use it for all it was worth. Salinda and Ailan had been right all along, but only now did she see the truth.

Mareleau was a scheming liar.

A breaker of hearts.

A destroyer of men.

She'd pull off her greatest, most devastating lie yet.

She dropped her gaze to the collar in Larylis' hand. Placing her fingers over his, she squeezed his palm. Wordlessly, he released the collar into her care.

She held his gaze and asked, "Do you trust me?"

His eyes searched hers, swimming with fear. Then he steeled his expression and gave her a nod. "With my life, my death, and everything in between."

Her throat tightened. "Do you trust me with *my* life, death, and everything in between?"

Another flash of fear. Then a sheen of sorrow. But again, he gave her a solemn nod. "Yes."

59

Larylis didn't know the full details of what his wife was planning, but he had to trust her. He did, with his whole heart, even as he feared where that trust would lead. Despite his reservations, this was not the time to balk. Their enemy was near. He could arrive at any second. If Mareleau knew how to stop Darius, who was he to doubt her? Who was he but the other half of her heart? They would beat in tandem until the end.

He stood inside the cave, not far from its entrance, where the only light came from the blue-green luminescence coating the walls. Mareleau was deeper inside the cave system, and her distance somehow felt too near and too far at once. There wasn't a depth she could go to that would ease his worry over her safety. Yet he hated that he wasn't by her side. He hoped the semi-darkness would hamper Darius' ability to visualize locations ahead to worldwalk to, but that was only a gamble. Did Darius' half-Elvyn heritage give him better eyesight? The communications Larylis had received from Teryn and Cora detailed his keen hearing.

Larylis rolled his shoulders and his neck, his muscles screaming in protest. Now that he was standing still, every wound and strain blared, every limb begged to lock up. He shifted his feet and splayed his hands, one then the other, refusing to succumb to inertia.

Then the shouts began.

From just outside the mouth of the cave, a clash of steel rang out. Garot had been right. Darius hadn't come alone. Larylis unsheathed his sword, his pulse quickening. In his mind, he began to recite famous kings of history who'd found victory during great fatigue, but he stopped himself. He didn't need to rely on those great kings anymore. He had himself. He had this moment. He would do this.

Larylis, the bastard.

Larylis, the crownless king.

Larylis, the husband and father.

Larylis, the man who preferred silence and books over parties and warfare.

He would do this.

He would help take down a tyrant.

The sounds of fighting cut off by half, but they continued to ring from outside. Then came footsteps. The aqua glow dappling the walls reflected off a trio of figures approaching. At the center was Darius, whom he'd only seen from afar until now. Even though his form was cast in shades of teal and shadow, Larylis could tell he was coated in blood. It slicked his hair, dripped from the cut on his cheek, painted his clothing and what little remained of his armor.

Yet despite the wounds he'd sustained, Darius was still standing. Still walking with ease and poise.

His fae healing was enviable.

Darius' expression darkened as he spotted Larylis. He motioned for his two guards to charge forward. They were much worse for wear than their master, both devoid of helms. One had a cut across his forehead while the other had use of only one eye, the other swollen shut. They charged past Darius, but before they could reach Larylis, a yellow dragon—half the size of Ferrah—slithered from a cavity in the wall and blasted a ball of golden flame at their legs. Two more dragons, these ones merely the size of large canines, climbed down the stalactites, gnashing their small yet terrifying teeth. Thankfully, none had eyes for Larylis, just the three intruders.

Or...not three.

Only two.

Larylis whirled around to see Darius already several steps ahead. There went Larylis' hope that he wouldn't be able to see well enough to worldwalk. He paid no heed to Larylis, as if he wasn't worth his time. Larylis clenched his jaw and charged after him.

"Stay away from my wife and child."

That got his attention. Darius halted and pivoted on his heel. "Your wife and child, you say? You must be the father of the great infant Morkara."

Larylis crept closer, sword raised.

Darius held his own sword, but its tip was lowered. He still didn't see Larylis as a worthy opponent. From the way he'd abandoned his soldiers to fight the dragons, he didn't value his own men much either.

"Fight me," Larylis said through his teeth.

"Why fight at all? What have I done to deserve your ire?"

"Do you truly need to ask? You seek to end the lives of my wife and son."

Darius ran a hand over his face, wincing at the still-bleeding cut on his cheek. He frowned, as if he hadn't expected the wound to be there. Was his rate of healing slowing down? Was there an end to his power? Was fatigue finally fraying his magic?

"It doesn't have to be that way," Darius said, tone clipped with impatience. His easy arrogance was gone. He *was* worried about something. "You and your wife can surrender to me."

Larylis scoffed. "And sacrifice our son?"

"No. Your wife can relinquish her role as regent and turn it over to me. I will oversee the boy's reign as Morkara and give you and his mother positions in my new government. You will be like a duke and duchess of the human world, second only to me and your son. It's better than any treatment you'll get from the Elvyn."

Larylis said nothing, simply appraised Darius through slitted lids.

"You know I'm right," Darius said.

"I know I can't trust you." Larylis' gaze flicked deeper down the tunnel where slithering motion approached. An orange light began to grow, shifting the aqua hues around them. Larylis pressed himself close to the cave wall just as the dragon released a blast of flame toward Darius. Larylis squeezed his eyes shut as heat seared his face.

The flame cut off.

Larylis opened his eyes to find Darius down the tunnel, his sword dripping blood. The dragon's body slumped to the cave floor, his detached head a few feet away. Tiny dragons crawled up and down the walls, hissing and screeching, but they made no move to get any closer to Darius.

"That's unfortunate," Darius muttered. "I have no intention of making an enemy of the dragons, as I'll soon be their master. I doubt the Morkara's mother wants to see me kill more of them either." He raised his voice at the last part, letting it carry down the tunnels.

Larylis pushed off the wall and charged forward—

Darius disappeared.

Then his voice, too close to Larylis.

"I'll have to try something else," Darius said from behind him. He sliced open Larylis' forearm, forcing him to drop his sword. Before he could retrieve it or launch away, Darius' blade came to Larylis' throat. Still behind him, Darius gripped his shoulder tightly. "Don't move."

Larylis froze.

One of Darius' soldiers emerged from the rear tunnel—the man with the swollen eye. He now had a singed left arm and burns up one side of his neck. Yet his other arm still held a sword. He exchanged a stiff nod with his master.

"Walk," Darius demanded of Larylis.

Larylis kept his upper body still as the three started off. They took only a few steps before their surroundings changed slightly. In a single heartbeat, they were farther down the tunnel, the aqua bioluminescence brighter and more condensed.

"I have your husband, Queen Mareleau," Darius said. There was a slight quaver in his voice that suggested Larylis had been right. His strength was waning. He was growing desperate. "I will give your husband just a few more breaths before I cleave his head from his body. After that, I'll do the same to every dragon in these godsforsaken caves—"

"Don't!" Mareleau's voice rang out from a short distance away. The panic in her tone was like a knife to Larylis' heart. "Don't hurt him, please!"

Darius and the soldier exchanged another nod, and the other man took Darius' place as Larylis' captor. It took all Larylis' restraint not to act. Not to tilt his head and slam it into the soldier's nose before taking his sword. The man was wounded enough to give Larylis a fighting chance.

But that hadn't been part of Mareleau's plan. Not that getting captured had been either...

"Then come to me now," Darius said. "Surrender to me and you, your husband, and your son can live."

"Don't believe him!" Larylis ground out.

Silence echoed back. Then footsteps. They grew nearer and nearer with every thundering beat of Larylis' heart.

"Don't, Mare," Larylis called. "Go back!"

She didn't pay his words any heed. Instead, she emerged from the cavern just ahead, Ferrah behind her, their son in her arms. She trembled from head to toe. "I surrender."

TEARS POURED DOWN MARELEAU'S CHEEKS AS SHE APPROACHED HER ENEMY. SHE'D never seen him before, but she knew the gray-haired man was Darius. Her nemesis. Larylis was at the mercy of another man's blade.

Her shoulders quivered, arms convulsing as she wrapped them tighter around Noah's sling. A sob broke from her lips. "Don't hurt him, please! I'll do anything."

Darius' face broke into a grin that bore equal parts cruelty and amusement. She was everything he'd expected her to be. Weak. Trembling. Embarrassingly feeble.

It was exactly how Mareleau wanted to be seen right now.

Pride flared inside her, but she didn't let it show. She kept it burning in her heart and poured more and more of her intent, her *knowing*, into her glamour.

Her trusty, unfailing magic trick.

She'd never felt stronger. Never been more certain of her abilities.

Even before she'd laid her eyes on Darius, she'd understood his character. What he wanted to see in her and what he most feared to see. That impression grew now as she met his gaze. Despite his belief that the Elvyn hated him for his human blood, he didn't think any better of his bloodline. He considered everyone to be beneath him. He certainly had no respect for a pampered princess-turned-queen who'd been given a life of luxury.

Now he saw what he'd expected all along, and she played into that.

She wore a mask of frail obedience as she stepped closer and closer to him.

"Stop," he said. "Order the dragon to stay back."

Of course he would make that demand. So long as Ferrah kept her distance, she couldn't harm Darius without risking Mareleau and Noah too. With a sniffle, she faced the opalescent dragon. "It's all right," she said, tone simpering. "Stay where you are."

Ferrah splayed her wings but obeyed.

Good. That meant the dragon would listen to her after all.

You understand the next part too, right? she conveyed, but she received no answer. She and Ferrah weren't bonded like Cora and Valorre. Even though she'd explained what she needed Ferrah to do for her, she could only hope her instructions had made it through.

Darius' lips spread wider as Mareleau proceeded closer to him. She was halfway there when she stopped, her knees trembling. His expression darkened. "Come the rest of the way. Give me the child and relinquish your role as regent."

She fell to her knees, unable to hold herself up anymore.

At least, that was what her glamour displayed. Gods, for once in her life it felt good to be underestimated.

Weak. She poured her intent into her glamour. *Feeble. No one to fear. The most pathetic creature you've ever seen.*

"Give me the child." His voice was chillingly gentle.

She heaved another body-shaking sob and extended an empty, pleading hand.

Slowly, he closed the distance between them, then crouched before her. She cradled Noah's sling tighter to her as she met Darius' eyes. A soft smile lifted his lips but it didn't meet his eyes. "Hush, hush, Your Majesty. It will be all right."

More tears gushed from her eyes. Her empty hand found his coat collar. She grasped it like a woman devoured by grief, seeking anything to steady her. He extended his hands toward the bundle she cradled so tightly, so lovingly.

Her lower lip wobbled, eyes turned down at the corners as she held his gaze with a pleading look. "Promise me," she whispered.

He nodded, impatience tightening his false smile. "Anything," he said through his teeth, one hand clawing at the lavender swaddling inside the sling.

"Promise me..." she said again as she aided his efforts, lifting the bundle from inside.

Her fingers clenched his collar tighter while her other hand emerged from the sling. With her fist wrapped tightly around one of the hidden talons, she plunged the weapon into his gut. His eyes went wide as the tine sank into his flesh. She pushed harder, deeper. He finally had the sense to try to dislodge her, but she clung with all her might to his coat, their bodies almost flush.

"Promise me," she said, her glamour falling away, her sorrow twisting into monstrous, bottomless, victorious rage, "that my face will be the only thing you see when you rot in eternal hell, you arrogant piece of shit."

She twisted the talon, then shouted her final command.

"Ferrah!"

With a piercing screech, heat encircled them in a violet blaze. Mareleau kept her eyes open, drinking in the terror that contorted the face before her. It was a beautiful sight, in all its repulsive, savage glory.

If this was the last thing she ever saw, she'd be satisfied with that.

She watched his skin boil and char, his eyes melt from their sockets. Until the purple flame pulsed too bright. Too hot. Until her mind grew hazy, her breaths short and sharp.

Only then did she release her enemy.

Only then did she succumb to death.

<h1 style="text-align:center">60</h1>

Death hurt a lot more than Mareleau had expected.

It was louder too. So loud.

She tried to ignore the sounds, waited for the pain to end. Soon she'd find herself in the otherlife, whatever that meant. Would she find a field of flowers? A tranquil ocean? An eternal banquet with an endless supply of chocolate? How long would she have to wait for everyone else she loved to join her? Hopefully a good long while.

She tried to envision what kinds of chocolate the otherlife might provide, but even as she pictured the most decadent truffles and a cake with ten tiers, that nagging sound interrupted her. It was...a word. No...a chirp? A screech? Why was death so godsdamned loud? Surely her heroic final act had earned her peace and not one of the seven hells instead. Well, if the latter was the case, she'd have to hunt down Darius and plague him in death. She wasn't above becoming a devil if that was her best option.

But no, she wanted chocolate cake, not—

There was that sound again. Why was there sound? Why was it so sharp and loud when she just wanted to sleep?

Sleep.

"Just let me sleep."

"She's alive. Gods, she's alive." The voice was even louder now, but it no longer grated on her nerves. It was familiar to her. Treasured. Why would she ever choose chocolate cake over *that*? Only now did she realize what the sound had been. Her name. Over and over. The word left Larylis' lips yet again, like a chant meant to tether her to the plane of the living.

Another sound shattered the haze in her mind. A sweet small cry.

Her heart pulsed in response, warming, spreading. She jolted, and pain shot through every inch of her.

Oh, right. Death was painful.

No, not death.

Life.

Life was...gods, it was agonizing.

Again that tiny cry reached her ears, and she opened her eyes. Smoke clouded her vision, but she blinked it away. Two faces stared down at her, one bronze, the other...

"Lare." Her voice came out a tired rasp. His cheeks were wet with tears and soot.

She tried to sit but every part of her revolted at the motion.

"Don't try to move," Larylis said. "You're hurt."

"But she's healing." Garot stared down at her with wide eyes. That was when she noticed him bouncing a still-crying Noah in his arms. Noah was no longer wrapped in his lavender swaddling, but the lighter linen layer he'd worn underneath. She'd turned her son's protection over to Garot before her confrontation with Darius. Now all she wanted was to hold her baby.

If only her arms would let her. They remained limp and aching at her sides. "What happened? Why aren't I dead?"

Larylis' eyes bulged. "You intended to die with that gambit?"

"Well, I hoped I wouldn't, but..." She winced, the corners of her lips cracking and stinging.

"You warded yourself today, didn't you?" Garot asked.

"Yes," she said, recalling how she'd cast the wardweaving before her bedroom mirror earlier. Even though she'd hoped the ward had worked, she hadn't been certain. Nor could she have known it would stop dragon flame.

Her magic had felt stronger than ever when she'd faced Darius, but she hadn't been focusing on protective wards. Every ounce of her attention had been reserved for her glamour. She'd been willing to do what needed to be done regardless of the result, even if it ended in death. Her intention hadn't been to undervalue herself to protect others like she had before. Instead, she'd performed her bold act because she knew without a shred of doubt that she'd succeed. That she was strong enough, clever enough, devious enough. Her death or survival simply hadn't factored into her plans.

"What about Darius?" she asked.

"He didn't fare nearly as well as you," Larylis said.

She needed to see for herself. Clenching her jaw, she tried to sit again, and this time she managed to lift herself on her forearms. Larylis braced her back and raised her to sitting. Several feet away, she found a charred husk that must be Darius. A sword lay between his shoulders and severed head.

"For good measure," Larylis explained.

Not far from the body, the soldier who'd held Larylis captive had also been relegated to a corpse, his sword stolen. She hadn't had to feign her terror at seeing Larylis with a sword at his throat. They hadn't anticipated him getting captured. They'd only discussed him holding back just enough to give Mareleau an opportunity to pretend to surrender. It could have gone wrong a thousand different ways, yet Larylis had played his role and she hers. She wasn't the only one who'd risked their life.

Mareleau shifted her attention from the dead to the living—herself. She stared down at her arms, finding them red and raw. Her robe's hem had been fully burned away and what little remained was charred. Every inch of flesh she could see was as red as her arms. Yet just like Garot had said, there were signs of healing too. She frowned. She didn't have fae blood, so she shouldn't be armed with rapid healing. Her glamour and protective wardweaving couldn't be responsible for the feat either.

In that case...

She turned her attention inward and felt the same tingle of magic she'd sensed after Ailan's death. It was stronger now, pulsing between her and Noah, who'd finally ceased crying in Garot's arms. "The *mora*," she said. "It's stronger now, isn't it?"

Garot nodded. "Even without using my pathweaving, I can feel my abilities have been fortified."

"Did the wardweavers make it to the tear?" Larylis asked. "Did they seal it?"

Garot had no answer. None of them could know for sure, not until Etrix returned. But Mareleau didn't want to wait. With a pained groan, she attempted to stand. Larylis aided her efforts, though his expression told her he'd rather she kept still. Someone else helped her rise—a solid force that nudged her other side, as if to help her keep her balance while she clung to Larylis.

Brow furrowed, Mareleau glanced beside her. An enormous head of white feathers and scales braced her ribcage. She bit back a yelp but managed to keep from flinching away.

Ferrah, however, seemed to sense her reaction. She pulled back slightly, her throat vibrating with a high-pitched chirp as she stared at Mareleau with slitted purple eyes. Wait...that chirping. Was it one of the sounds that had awoken her? It made more sense that she would have been perturbed by the strange hum of chirps than her husband's voice.

"She's been like that ever since she cut off her flame," Garot said.

"You mean, you didn't enjoy trying to burn me to a crisp?" Mareleau muttered. "I thought you'd be pleased."

Ferrah flicked her tongue and nudged Mareleau's shoulder, bumping her tender flesh with far more force than necessary. She made to push the creature away, but Ferrah nuzzled her palm, eyes closed, her humming chirps softening to a slightly more melodic tune.

"Oh," Garot said, pulling his head back. He blinked a few times. "Ooooh. Interesting."

"What's interesting?" Mareleau wasn't sure whether to try to push the dragon away again or if she should hold still lest Ferrah chomp her wrist.

"She's bonded to you."

"Bonded," Mareleau and Larylis echoed in unison.

Mareleau reassessed the dragon, who continued to nuzzle her hand, with new eyes. "You mean...nearly killing me endeared me to you?"

Sorry. The word entered her awareness. Not through sound but *knowing.* Mareleau sucked in a sharp breath, not daring to believe that word had come from Ferrah. *You insult me. You think I wanted to burn you? I trusted you to cast a better wardweaving. I didn't think you'd get hurt.*

With every word, the voice grew clearer in her mind, taking on a feminine lilt with an unmistakable edge of chagrin.

Ferrah finally pulled away and removed her face from Mareleau's palm. *I expect better of my mistress and her magic in the future.* With that, Ferrah slithered down the cave and out of sight.

Mareleau stared after her, dumbstruck. After a few bewildered moments, she recalled why she'd wanted to stand in the first place. "We should get to the tear at once and confirm that it's been sealed. Garot, will you weave us—"

"Not *us*," Garot said. He passed Noah to Larylis, who in turn cradled his son against his chest with the tenderest care. "I will go myself. You're regent now, and I'll not have you making such a poor spectacle of yourself until you've healed, washed, changed, and...and done something about your hair."

Her pulse quickened at the last part. She reached for her shoulders, then her neck. It wasn't until she touched her nape that she felt even a hint of singed tresses. Her throat tightened, and she wasn't ashamed of the sorrow that filled her. Maybe it was vain to mourn her long pale locks, but she was only a hero, not a saint. And she wasn't even a real hero. Real heroes wouldn't relish watching their enemy burn.

"Fine," she said, voice quavering. "Please see that the wardweavers have succeeded and report back at once."

Garot gave her a tired smile, looking almost like his carefree self again. "You didn't waste any time settling into your new position, did you?"

She gave him a haughty shrug, ignoring the scream of her muscles. She didn't exactly delight in her role as regent, for it had come at the cost of many lives. Most of all, Ailan's. And many more goodbyes would soon follow. But Mareleau was born to be queen. Born to rule. Born to scheme and lie and deceive. She'd convince this world she was the best regent, the best Edel Morkara'Elle, they'd ever know. She'd make a life for herself, her husband, and her son. Not just any life. A happy one. A fulfilling one.

She wouldn't settle for anything less.

⁓

CORA DIDN'T KNOW HOW MUCH TIME HAD PASSED. SHE SANK INTO A TRANCE AS SHE, Teryn, and Valorre continued to urge the *mora* back. At first, Cora could tell there was something wrong. She pushed and pushed and pushed, but there was no relief. Nothing to aid her efforts at their destination. The strongest vein of *mora* that led to and from the tear remained as strong as ever.

The wardweavers...

They were gone.

Her magic nearly faltered then, but she refused to crumple under the realization. She had to trust her allies. They would come through. They would do their part.

So she pushed. On and on, she fought the flow of *mora*, resisted the temptation to harness it. She shared the burden with her companions, leaned on them more when her strength began to wane, then took back control when she recovered. At times, the cycle seemed endless. Like decades had passed. Centuries. She was convinced she'd become one with the rock and no longer held a purpose or identity. When this happened, Teryn always seemed to know. He'd hold her tighter, speak her name, and call her back to reality, just like she'd done for him all those months ago when he'd fought death.

Just when she thought she might be at the end of her reserves, relief came to her. It was small at first, just a stitch in a gaping chasm, but little by little her efforts were aided. She could almost feel the closing of the tear as it slowly lightened her load.

Her mind sharpened.

She opened her eyes for what might have been the first time in hours. Dawn was on the horizon, just barely touching the tops of the hills around the valley. Her palms remained pressed to the rock, Valorre's soft muzzle beneath her chin, Teryn's arms wrapped around her middle, his face pressed to her shoulder. He whispered encouraging words as she pushed harder, keeping the magic at bay while the tear grew smaller and smaller. Now that her mind was beginning to clear, the process felt achingly slow. Whatever time was passing in El'Ara, it was crawling here. One minute there was several here.

Yet she'd hold out.

They were so close.

And then...

The *mora* cut off.

She sagged as the resistance disappeared. The magic no longer hummed beneath her hands, no longer called to her with tempting visions. Body stiff, she sat back on numb legs. Teryn rolled onto his back, his forearm thrown over his eyes. Valorre settled at the base of the rock, looking dazed.

Cora felt...empty.

She'd only commanded that well of magic for a brief time, but in its wake was a hollow lightness. Glorious relief. She turned herself over to it, closed her eyes, and let sleep take her.

～

Teryn woke to birdsong and midday sun blazing on the other side of his eyelids. Then a peck on his cheek. He pried his eyes open and found Berol's face backlit by the warm sunlight. His arm felt limp and heavy as he lifted it to scritch her feathers. She chirped and nipped his cheek again.

"I'm all right," he said. He was glad to see she was too. She'd fulfilled her mission at the tear, alerting the Elvyn of Darius' arrival. He wasn't sure if her presence meant the battle had ended or if she'd flown here immediately after. She may have been here the entire time he'd held onto Cora.

He rose to sitting, and there wasn't a part of his body that didn't ache from the movement. Berol immediately rose into the air to land on his shoulder—his uninjured one, thankfully. Her weight wasn't exactly welcome, what with the gash he'd sustained on the other side, not to mention his myriad of other wounds, but he didn't have the heart to brush her off.

He shifted to glance where Cora had last been on the rock. His heart stuttered to find her no longer beside him, but as he cast his gaze to the base of the rock, he found Valorre sleeping there, Cora curled up with him, her head propped on his belly.

He calmed at the sight. Their duties weren't exactly over. There were still the wraiths to set free, the aftermath of battle to deal with, both at Ridine and on the human side of the tear, and a final trip to El'Ara—a first trip for Teryn—to say goodbye to those they'd never see again.

Even though he was anxious to set everything to rights, he figured he'd let Cora and Valorre sleep a while longer. Instead, he focused on the one thing he could do alone.

Stepping away from Centerpointe Rock, he unsheathed his dagger and reopened the wound on his palm. Berol let out a string of anxious chirps. The lesion was already red and angry and certainly didn't like being opened again, but he needed fresh blood to call the wraiths to him. As soon as a crimson well filled his palm, he let it drip onto the grass. "Come. It's time to go home."

Silently, the field fell under a misty fog. The haze soon materialized into figures. The wraiths' forms undulated, their eyes empty and unseeing.

"You did well," Teryn whispered. "You helped thwart the man who once ordered you to fight and die for nothing. Instead, you fought for the future of the land you were left to wander in. As promised, I have not abandoned you. As promised, I offer you an end."

He held out his hand but didn't move. He wouldn't hunt the spirits down and force oblivion upon them. He'd let them crave it. Let them come to him for their final rest.

One of the nearest wraiths swept toward him and paused a few feet away.

Teryn kept his hand open, his arm relaxed.

The wraith's form rippled, as if deliberating. Then it closed the final distance, placed his hazy, wavering hand over Teryn's...

The wraith disappeared.

Hunger and yearning filled some of the next closest specters, as if the end they'd witnessed had filled them with craving. One by one, more came forward. One by one, Teryn set them free. One by one, as midday crept on and the sun moved toward the horizon, Teryn fulfilled his oath.

He was practically delirious yet again by the time the final wraith approached. But as his gaze took in the spirit before him, his mind sharpened.

It wasn't one of the warrior wraiths. It was Emylia.

She gave him a sad smile. "Did I do enough to deserve peace?"

He met her eyes with a solemn yet earnest look. "You don't have to do anything to earn your rest, Emylia. You never did. You chose to wander. You can choose to go home."

Her lower lip wobbled. "I don't feel like I did enough. All I did was cause trouble in my life, and in my death...I didn't trust you. I tried to stop you from summoning the wraiths, but you set them free. You didn't succumb to the allure of dark magic."

"Not yet." He let a corner of his mouth lift.

She sighed. "You won't. I know it now. You've become something new. A human with a type of magic I've never seen before. A reaper of souls. I was so afraid when I first realized what you were."

"And now?"

"I'm not afraid anymore, just...ashamed."

"You don't have to be ashamed," Teryn said. He wanted to reach out and comfort her, but he knew what his touch would do. Just like with the wraiths, he wouldn't force peace on her.

"Tell her I forgive her."

Teryn startled at the sound of Cora's voice. He turned and found her sitting on the rock, caressing Valorre's neck. He wasn't sure how long she'd been awake. Had she been watching him while he'd sent the wraiths home? She'd at least been present long enough to hear him say Emylia's name, and the rest of Teryn's side of their conversation.

Cora spoke again, tone gentle. "Tell her she has nothing left to atone for. She never did."

He faced Emylia once more. The spirit sagged, either with relief or sorrow. "I'm so sorry," she said. "Tell her that. Tell her I'm so sorry for what my words led Morkai to do."

"She knows," Teryn said, but he conveyed her message anyway.

Emylia spoke again, and this time her voice took on a fierce edge. "And tell her...tell her she's stronger than she knows. She's stronger than anyone who has ever underestimated her. She's stronger than everything that could ever seek to tie her, trap her, or smother her. She's stronger than any shadow, any darkness, any curse. Tell her that."

A chill ran down Teryn's spine. What did Emylia mean by that? That Cora was stronger than any curse? Was it merely wishful thinking, a desire to make things right, or was it a sign of Emylia's magic? She'd been a seer when she'd been alive. Had she seen an end to the curse Morkai had placed upon Cora?

He shook the questions from his mind. Her words sparked a beautiful hope, but that hope was theirs regardless of the outcome. For it mattered not whether they had children of their own bloodline or chose heirs from another. Whether they ruled like their predecessors or started a revolution. He and Cora would forge their own future together. Royal politics and outdated traditions could go to the seven hells. A witch and a reaper were Lela's queen and king. They were already breaking rules and starting anew.

Still, he conveyed Emylia's words to Cora.

Emylia heaved another sigh, and her form sharpened slightly. Then, with a nod, she stepped closer to Teryn and held out her hand.

"I'm ready to go home," she said, voice quavering.

Teryn's chest tightened. He and Emylia hadn't always seen eye to eye, but she'd helped him through one of the greatest challenges he'd faced. Taught him how to fight Morkai and reclaim his body.

She'd died for love. Fought for love. Grieved for love.

She deserved so much better.

He didn't know a damn thing about the otherlife. Who could truly claim to know? But he hoped it would treat her well. Hoped she'd find the rest her soul so deeply deserved.

He reached for her hand. "Thank you, friend."

She grasped his palm in a handshake he couldn't feel.

Her soul disappeared.

61

It was surreal to stand at the center of the Blight without a wall of mist anywhere to be seen. The colorless earth warped and puckered in a spiral pattern, meeting at a distinct point. Mareleau shuddered at the pulse of *mora* that flowed from that point, moving through the land, through her body. A tether of magic remained forever between her and Noah, a circuit she sensed no matter where he was. Larylis held him, several feet from where Mareleau stood, and still the pulse connected them as strongly as if he was in her arms. She supposed she'd feel it until the day Noah came of age and her role as regent became obsolete.

It was a bittersweet prospect. The day her child would no longer need her. She hoped she wouldn't be too disappointed to give up this power when the time came.

Etrix came up beside her. "We'll need to build a temporary shelter here until an official palace can be constructed. And you'll need to train in how to move the *mora* at once. Our priority is healing the Blight."

She met his ruby-brown eyes and found lines of fatigue on his ageless face. Even though he spoke in a diplomatic tone, he was grieving. His daughter had died only yesterday. It didn't matter that they'd been separated for decades, or that Etrix hadn't even known if she'd been alive in the human world before they'd recently reunited. A loss was a loss, and his was still fresh. A full week had passed in the human world, but here it had only been a day. Luckily, Cora had retrieved Ailan's body and brought it back, along with all the other Elvyn soldiers—the hale, the dead, and the wounded alike.

It must have been exhausting work for Cora, constantly worldwalking back and forth over the past week, often with multiple companions in tow. With the tear fully sealed, the only way Cora could enter El'Ara was with Valorre. Cora had sent word an hour ago—El'Ara time—that her mission was complete. All that remained was escorting Helena to El'Ara.

After that...

Mareleau would never see Cora again. She'd worldwalk away for the last time. Her throat constricted just thinking about it.

Making friends, losing friends.

Yet another bittersweet eventuality.

If you're building a new palace, came a voice in her mind, *I demand ample caves nearby.*

Mareleau glanced skyward and found the opalescent creature soaring overhead. She still wasn't used to her bonded dragon. Especially since Ferrah wasn't the warmest companion. She'd demonstrated a few short-lived bouts of neediness, approaching Mareleau at random times to head-butt her hand with the vigor of a beast who didn't understand her own strength. Ferrah otherwise remained cold and independent.

Like a cat, Mareleau supposed.

I resent that. I don't know what that is.

You don't have felines here? Mareleau thought back. She was amazed that that was all it took to communicate with her. *Small bodies, pointed ears, soft fur.*

You mean the Elvyn?

I said soft fur.

Isn't that what's on their heads? I suppose you wouldn't know. Ferrah said the last part with what Mareleau imagined was a smirk, before flying off and out of sight.

Mareleau touched the ends of her chin-length hair. She'd cried when she'd seen her reflection in the mirror yesterday, but today she wasn't feeling nearly as self-conscious. Her short locks suited her fine, now that one of her maids had taken a pair of shears to them and styled them in loose waves. It left her with nothing to braid when she was anxious, but that was probably a habit she should discard already. She was regent of El'Ara, after all.

"So...this will one day be our home?" Larylis said, coming up beside her with Noah in his arms. She frowned, puzzled by his words until she realized he was referring to the palace Etrix had mentioned. The Elvyn now stood several yards away, staring up at the sky as if mentally constructing their future palace. Mareleau imagined they had Elvyn specialists who designed and constructed their impressive feats of architecture, but if it distracted Etrix from the loss of his daughter, who was she to judge?

"Yes," Mareleau said, meeting his lips with a soft kiss before placing an even softer one on her sleeping son's forehead. She met her husband's eyes again. "Are you all right with all this? I know it's happening so fast. Everything we thought we knew about our lives and our roles has changed."

"I admit, this is nothing like the future I imagined for us," he said, his gaze scanning the barren landscape of the Blight.

Her heart sank. Gods, he'd lost so much. Before she could open her mouth to apologize, he pinned her with a knowing look.

"Don't you dare, Mare." His tone was gentle, his lips tilted in a smile. "Don't tell me I've lost everything, because it's far from the truth. I will ache for the human world and the people we'll have to leave behind. But don't forget who I am at my heart. I wasn't born to be a king, but a lover and a scholar. I have my wife and child.

And now I have an entire world to satisfy my intellectual curiosity. This place is a storybook legend come to life."

That was so like him, and it lifted her heart to the heavens. She wasn't sure how much of his words were meant to placate her, but they served to remind her that they could thrive here. They *would*. And they would do it together.

She pressed her lips to his again, and as she pulled away, movement caught her eye. She and Larylis turned to find the colorless landscape warping and swirling midair not too far away. Mareleau's heart leaped in anticipation. Etrix turned toward the vortex too. It spread wider to create a large opening.

Garot stepped out first. "Look how brilliantly the *mora* has improved my abilities! My Path works through the Blight now."

Fanon followed next, far less jovial. His complexion was wan, and dark circles shadowed his eyes. Mareleau's gaze dropped to the silk bandages wrapping his blunted wrists. She'd heard about the injuries he'd sustained, heard he might not even recover. But there he was. She wasn't his greatest fan, but he'd supported Ailan's wishes where Mareleau and Noah were concerned. So long as his loyalty outlasted his consort's life, Fanon might be an essential advocate in the coming days, second only to Etrix. She needed their support and influence on the tribunal to ensure the Elvyn continued to honor their vows.

Garot and Fanon stepped aside, revealing the faces of those Mareleau had been most excited to see: Cora, Teryn, Valorre, and...

"Mother!" Mareleau took off running. She hadn't expected to feel this relief, this sharp piercing love, this overwhelming comfort. Not for Helena.

But she did, and as she collided into her mother's arms, she knew Helena felt it too. Cora had been right to include Helena in her terms for the alliance. Mareleau needed her mother. Sure, they would likely fight again like they used to, and they would certainly say cruel things to each other when at their wit's end. But they'd mended a gap between them that neither would ever dare widen again.

∾

CORA WATCHED THE REUNION WITH TEARY EYES. LARYLIS AND TERYN MET NEXT, bracing each other's forearms. She gave them a few long moments alone before approaching them and addressing Larylis. "I'm sorry I couldn't bring your mother or brothers."

"It's all right," Larylis said, and there seemed to be only a hint of regret in his tone. He may not be close to Annabel Seralla or his young half brothers, but it must have hurt at least somewhat to know he'd never see them again. Regardless, the Elvyn wouldn't permit it, as it hadn't been part of Ailan's negotiations with the tribunal. Ailan had secured a binding vow from them, granting Larylis and Helena protection, respect, and citizenship in exchange for the terms Cora had promised.

She'd fulfilled every term of her end over the past week, worldwalking the Elvyn soldiers who'd fought alongside the humans. The battle near the tear had been close, but as soon as Darius had disappeared beyond the Veil, many of his soldiers thought him defeated. The tide had turned after that, and the human-

Elvyn alliance ended victorious. Still, there had been many casualties. Yet more lives Cora would mourn as queen. More deaths she bore the weight of.

Meanwhile, Teryn had overseen the aftermath of the battle at Ridine, which had far fewer casualties on their side. The wraiths had truly saved them that night. Shortly after Cora and Teryn had left for Centerpointe Rock, the battle had ended. The survivors had surrendered or fled. Captain Alden had chosen not to give chase to those who ran, and Cora agreed with that decision. Let them run. Let them tell the tale of terror that had befallen them. Let them strike fear into the hearts of anyone who would seek to come for Lela next.

"Thank you for everything you've done," Larylis said, bringing her back to the present. "For ensuring my place here."

"You're welcome," Cora said, then glanced down at Noah. She hadn't paid him much attention since birth, hadn't ever asked to hold him or rock him. Now she knew why—she'd been afraid. Too afraid that the bitterness that had clogged her heart would rear its head and force her to confront it. But she had confronted it. She cast a questioning look at Larylis. "Can...can I hold him?"

"Of course." His answer came so easily. He had no idea how hard it had been for her to utter those words.

Her heart beat a little heavier as he passed the child to her. She looked down at the sleepy, pudgy-cheeked baby, her senses open to whatever reaction she might have. If she felt a bitter pang, she'd accept it. If she felt hurt, or rage, or tears, she'd let it come. And yet...only warmth filled her heart as she held the child for the first and last time. "I wish I could watch you grow up, little nephew," she said, and she meant every word.

"I wish you could too." Mareleau stood before her now, her eyes red from crying during her reunion with her mother.

Cora pressed a gentle kiss to Noah's downy head and passed him back to Larylis. Then she and Mareleau collided in a hug. More warmth filled her, every ounce of resentment gone. Free. She fully sank into the sorrow of the moment, the beauty of this goodbye. She'd hated Mareleau when they'd first met, considered her a rival. The kind of woman Cora could never get along with.

But they'd found camaraderie in darkness. They were different in many ways, but similar too. Stubborn. Bold. Unafraid of violence and cunning if it helped them reach their goals. They both railed against the societal standards that demeaned them.

Two queens.

Two friends.

Two women who would do whatever they could to influence their two separate worlds for the better.

They pulled apart, their cheeks glistening with tears.

"Goodbye, Cora," Mareleau said, voice trembling.

"Goodbye, Mare."

Cora and Teryn stepped back, and Mareleau, Larylis, and Helena huddled close. Valorre nudged Cora's shoulder. It was time for them to go home. Cora took Teryn's hand in hers and placed her free palm on Valorre's neck. She gave one last smile to the people she loved—

"Come, unicorn," Garot said, tone jovial. "I know you'll miss your friend, but it's time for them to leave."

The blood drained from Cora's face, and she sensed the same shock radiating from Valorre. "What are you..."

Mother Goddess, it all became so sorrowfully clear. The Elvyn intended for Valorre to stay behind.

"He's a fae creature," Etrix said. "He belongs here with his own kind. There is no more fae magic in the human world. If he returns to Lela, he will eventually lose his magic."

"He'll become a horse," Garot said. "That's what you call a hornless unicorn in your world, isn't it?"

Cora blinked, struck silent. Even Valorre was mute for once. "No," she finally managed to say. "He...he's my friend. My familiar."

"What they say is true," Fanon said. His tone lacked all the sharpness it used to contain. Instead, it was deeper, laced with grief and exhaustion. "Even more pressing is that we made a binding vow to Ailan. Everyone on the tribunal did, and it outlasts her death. We would accept these few humans as citizens in El'Ara, but none of our kind will be left in Lela."

Ailan had told her as much, but she'd imagined the Elvyn soldiers, not Valorre. Yet...a part of her had understood those terms extended to the unicorns. It was why Valorre had worked so hard to escort his brethren through the Veil before she pushed the *mora* back.

Even so, not once had she imagined Valorre being left in El'Ara when all was said and done.

"We cannot let you leave with him," Fanon said, tone surprisingly gentle. "Doing so would break our oath. And if you leave with him against our will, your actions will void what we agreed to. The tribunal will no longer be beholden to keep their vows."

Cora's stomach turned. She could imagine what that would mean. They could take it out on Mareleau, Larylis, and Helena.

He's right. Valorre spoke into her mind, his tone resigned. *I cannot leave with you if you want your friends to stay safe.*

Cora's heart cracked.

Then his voice took on a cheery tone. *So I'll just come back to you later!*

What do you mean? Her heart thudded with hope. Did she dare hope?

You heard him, Valorre said. *They cannot let you leave with me, nor can you take me with you against their will. But there's nothing in their vow that forbids me from leaving El'Ara of my own accord later for a fully unrelated reason.*

She puzzled over his words. *Your horn may have the ability to pierce the Veil, but our worlds are no longer connected in such a tangible way. The Veil is invisible now. There's no wall of mist to walk through.*

Our worlds still rest side by side. I'll find a way.

You're no worldwalker.

But you are, and we're connected. We always will be.

He was so confident, so assured. She wanted to believe him, but...

Do not doubt me, he said, tossing his mane. *I am a superior being among my kind.*

No unicorn has bonded a human before and none will ever again. I am the smartest and handsomest of all fae creatures. Surely I can find my way to your world.

She couldn't help but smile at that. *Even if it means losing your magic and becoming a horse?*

He internally scoffed. *I'll still be the largest, fastest, and smartest horse on your planet. Don't lump me in with those brainless fornicators.*

Tears rolled down her cheeks, but her heart felt lighter. It was still breaking, and maybe it would never heal. She couldn't rely on the future he hoped for, but she could share his dream.

Maybe someday they'd meet again.

But for now...this was goodbye.

She pressed her face into his neck, memorizing the softness of his coat, the hum of his energy all around her. Teryn joined her, one hand on her shoulder, the other stroking Valorre's mane.

Tell Teryn not to look at a single horse while I'm gone, Valorre said, tone somber.

That's kind of a lot to ask.

Well, tell him not to look at a single one with affection. *He better keep those dazzling eyes to himself. And when he looks at his reflection and sees that stupid moonlight hair, he better think of me.*

Cora chuckled. *We both will. I promise.*

With her lungs still tight enough to burst, she forced herself to pull away from her unicorn companion, her best friend, and the creature who had set everything currently in her life into motion. He was the reason she'd left the Forest People. He was the reason she'd crossed paths with Teryn. He'd changed her life. She couldn't imagine the unbearable silence she'd endure once he was no longer in it.

I'll find you, he said, more certain than ever. *I'll cross worlds forever if I must. You'll see.*

See you soon, then.

She blinked tears from her eyes so she could memorize this final image. Mareleau, Larylis, Noah, and Helena huddled together. Etrix and Garot waving goodbye. Fanon offering a single nod of farewell. Valorre at the center, his head held high, sunlight glinting off his pale fur.

Teryn squeezed her hand, and she returned the gesture. Then she inhaled a deep breath and closed her eyes.

Took a step.

And left a piece of her behind.

EPILOGUE

ONE YEAR LATER – HUMAN REALM

The Reaper King and the Witch Queen lorded over Lela in a bloody iron-fisted reign, striking terror into the hearts of all.

At least, that was what some stories claimed, as told by their enemies. Not that they had many now. A year had passed since the fateful battle, and not once had Norun renewed hostility toward Khero. The kingdom had plenty to deal with after fighting a six-month-long rebellion before ceding Haldor and Sparda back to their former kings. Now Khero had two more allies standing between them and a much smaller enemy kingdom. Cora was certain she could eventually convince King Isvius to forge an official peace pact between Norun and Lela.

Syrus had been more than eager to do so. Once Darius' heir—a wealthy duke who'd boasted the highest merit rating on the island kingdom—took his new post as king, he was quick to disassociate himself from the former king's actions. It was a smart choice on his part, considering Syrus bore the responsibility for the deaths of King Larylis and Queen Mareleau.

The lie grated on Cora's nerves—and her heart—but it was essential. Hardly anyone would believe the truth. She may have claimed rule over the land by right of magic, but if she wanted to keep her crown in the eyes of the people, it was best she didn't spout tales of faerie portals and wars with ancient Elvyn princes. As much as she hated pretending her dear friends were deceased, it was much more believable than them living in a parallel realm inhabited by fae.

Besides, the lie had encouraged peace with Syrus' new king. Cora burned with curiosity to discover what would come of the kingdom without their ageless, five-hundred-year-old king. Would his meritocracy last? Or crumble?

Only time would tell—

"Are you thinking about work, my love?"

Cora shook her head and lifted her gaze to Teryn's. Her cheeks heated, giving her away. Damn. She'd been caught.

"Perhaps," she said sheepishly.

Teryn was half reclined on the blanket they'd laid out in the shade of a cherry tree. His silver hair was longer now, falling just below his shoulders. He was dressed in trousers, a linen shirt, and an open black waistcoat. It was a warm spring day, perfect for a picnic under pink blossoms that drifted from the branches like snow. They had a spread of bread, fruit, and tea sandwiches before them. The sun was bright, the air was fresh, and this was one of their first calm days to themselves in an entire year...

And here Cora was thinking about work and politics. Again.

"We do deserve a day off, you know," Teryn said, lips quirked in a sideways grin.

He was right. After everything they'd worked toward this past year—forging peace, merging Vera with Khero, strengthening their position as king and queen, recovering from physical and emotional wounds—they truly did deserve some time to just be themselves. Teryn and Cora. The reaper and the witch. Two young people in love.

She scooted closer to Teryn, and he fully reclined the rest of the way, angling his body until he was resting his head in her lap. She adjusted the skirts of her cream day dress, arranging it in pools of lace around them. "I'm sorry," she said with a wry grin. "I'll pay attention to you now. I promise."

He grinned up at her, his face dappled by sunlight and the shadows of the cherry blossoms. Cora tilted her head back and found Berol on one of the branches, preening. A gust of wind rattled the blossoms, forcing Berol to splay her wings. In its wake, a flurry of pink petals rained down over them. Cora grinned wide and extended her hand, trying to catch them as they fell. She managed to snatch three before the flurry settled. She opened her tattooed palm and let the petals drift onto their picnic blanket.

Her attention then drifted to her *insigmora*. Her tattoos had ceased growing on their own. It truly must have been the influence of fae *mora* that had made them take on a life of their own in the first place. Still, she didn't need them to grow or change. She treasured her tattoos exactly as they were, a symbol of what she was. A memory of everything she'd experienced, inked on her body.

At least the absence of *mora* hadn't hampered her witch magic. Her abilities continued to grow with every day. Six months ago, she'd managed to dissolve Morkai's previously indestructible book. With a single touch, it had melted to ash. The last visible trace of him was gone.

Teryn's magic remained unchanged. He'd grown used to seeing spirits and would give final rest to the rare few souls who sought him out for it. They hadn't come across any dangerous entities yet, but if they ever did, Teryn was prepared to dispose of them by force.

Teryn's fingertips brushed her cheek, and she shifted her gaze back to him. He grinned up at her from her lap. She ran a hand through his pale tresses, brushing a few errant strands from his brow.

His lashes fluttered shut. "I like the location you chose for our picnic."

"Did you only just now notice?"

"No, I noticed from the start. What a sentimental woman you are."

She snorted a laugh. Though he was right. She'd chosen their location with great fondness. The tree they sat under now was the very same Cora had once shot an arrow into the day she met Teryn. The stream rushed by their blanket in a soothing rhythm.

Teryn wasn't the only person this location reminded her of.

It reminded her of Valorre too.

A heavy sensation struck her chest, and she winced.

Teryn's eyes flew open, brows furrowed. "What's wrong?"

Cora rubbed her breastbone, but the pressure remained. "It's...I don't know. I keep feeling this...ache. Almost like my lungs are inflating, but not my actual lungs. More like...a flare of magic?"

Teryn lifted himself from her lap and faced her. "You don't think something's wrong?"

The sensation passed, and she donned a reassuring grin. "I'm fine. It's probably just my magic growing in a new way."

He didn't look convinced so she leaned forward and pressed a kiss to his lips. He returned it with tender care.

The ache sparked in her chest again.

She pulled back with a grimace she couldn't hide. This time there was more than that heavy feeling. There was a tingle of energy with it, a familiar strain...

A chill ran through her.

It couldn't be.

The energy grew closer, brighter, almost painful in its resonance. Emotions that were hers—yet somehow not hers—flooded her. Anticipation, anxiety, impatience, excitement. It was so overwhelming, it sparked tears in her eyes.

She rose to her feet before she realized she'd moved—

Just as a flash of white emerged from the dense foliage downstream.

A gasp left Cora's lips.

The white unicorn froze in place, ears erect, muscles quivering. Then all three were moving—Teryn, Cora, and Valorre.

I found you! Valorre's voice filled Cora's mind, the most welcome sound she could imagine. *I found you! Do you know how long I've been looking?*

Valorre could hardly hold still as Cora reached him and threw her arms around his thick neck. He tossed his mane, kicked his hooves, and nuzzled Cora with almost enough force to knock her over. She didn't care. Laughter left her lips as happy tears streamed down her cheeks. Even Teryn was moved, his eyes glazed and crinkled at the corners as he patted the unicorn from the other side. Berol must have flown with them when they ran, for she now perched on Teryn's shoulder, chirping and attempting to nip Valorre while Teryn petted him.

Once their excitement cooled to a simmer, allowing Cora to form words, she asked, "How did you manage it? How did you find us?"

I don't know, he said, equal parts innocent and excited. *I followed my heart and thoughts of you. And Teryn too! I tried to do the same thing we did when we worldwalked together. It was much harder without you, but...*

He tossed his mane, and his tone changed at once.

But I am exceedingly capable, as you well know. I had no doubts that I would figure it out, and I did. Looks like I can use your magic just fine.

Was that what that strange sensation had been? Valorre using her magic? She'd begun feeling it more and more the past week. She pressed her face to his soft coat. "I never doubted you."

I've seen some very strange things, Valorre said, abandoning his boastful demeanor. *I saw a world without trees, only tall rectangular castles and horseless metal carriages that swarmed the ground. Humans cluttered the naked, treeless streets. Then I saw a world inhabited only by dragons. That was my least favorite. I also saw a world of eternal snow and a world of eternal night. I rather liked the world of eternal spring. There were these tasty apples...but they did something strange to me. I think I walked on a rainbow? And maybe I frolicked around a bonfire with wolves? The next day, I couldn't feel my tongue or my legs.*

Cora could hardly comprehend his words. He'd traveled to multiple worlds on the way here? And was poisoned by an apple? That was troubling. Mother Goddess, he was lucky to be alive.

She refused to let panic overwhelm her and took comfort in his presence. He was here. He was safe.

"Well, aren't you the world traveler," she said. "Or...multi-world traveler? Whatever the case, will you stay now that you've found us?"

He huffed a breath. *Obviously.*

She wrapped her arms around him again. "I'm really glad you're home."

I am too. A sweet silence fell between them until it was broken by, *Is Teryn glad I'm home?*

With a roll of her eyes, she pulled away from Valorre and conveyed the question to Teryn.

Teryn spoke with unwavering sincerity. "Val, I couldn't be happier."

Valorre tossed his mane with finesse, ensuring it rippled extra elegantly for Teryn's sake.

Teryn extended his hand toward their picnic blanket under the cherry tree. "Would you like to join us?"

Oh, a food blanket!

"A picnic," Cora corrected.

Are there apples?

"You want apples after everything that happened in...where was it? Eternal spring?"

Teryn frowned. "What's this about eternal spring?"

"I'll fill you in," Cora muttered.

At the same time, Valorre gleefully conveyed, *I always want apples!*

They reached the blanket, which sure enough had three very non-poisonous apples, one of which Teryn handed to Valorre.

Valorre internally sighed, then took the apple from Teryn's palm, munching away at once. *He really is the best of men, isn't he?*

Cora chuckled as she and Teryn settled back onto the blanket. "All right, Valorre. You've got some explaining to do. Tell us more about your travels."

~

SEVEN YEARS LATER – FAE REALM

Once upon a time, Mareleau had considered herself to be a woman without a heart. Or, if she'd had one at all, it was surely a shriveled thing, smothered by brambles and thorns. She now knew that had never been the case. She'd always had a heart; she'd simply kept it closed off for too many years. But love had helped break down her walls, and not just love for her husband. He'd been the first to breach them, but even Teryn had helped weaken them when she accepted him as her brother. Cora had shattered them the rest of the way, barreling into her heart despite neither of them wanting her to be there.

After that, it had been easy to love. Or...*easier*.

She'd repaired the burned bridges between her and her mother.

And she became a mother herself.

Now she knew what it was like to have a piece of her heart exist outside her body. First, it had cried, then it had crawled. It was most frightening when the piece of her heart had learned to toddle. She'd soothed many bruises and falls then, but just like the organ that beat in her chest, the child that represented her external heart recovered from every spill.

Noah was seven years old now, perched on a stool beside his father. Mareleau grinned as she watched the pair peering into a crystal cylinder that gave them a view of the stars overhead. They were outside on the rooftop terrace above their suite at Ailana'Auro Palace. The grand home of the Morkara had finished construction a year after the tear was sealed. Mareleau reclined on a cushioned divan, sipping Faeryn honey wine, while Ferrah dozed peacefully beside her, taking up a good half of the terrace.

The night was dark yet the stars glittered like rainbow shards, more brilliantly than they ever did in the human world. Larylis pointed out a constellation, conveying lore and facts about the stars that comprised it. Her husband had been right; El'Ara had provided ample interest for him. He relished learning all he could about the world. He'd become fluent in the fae language a year before she had, and now worked with Garot to record human history. Or as much of it that Larylis knew and could recall. Which was substantial, to be honest. Garot still served as the chief pathweaver in service of the Morkara, but his work with Larylis allowed him to explore his love for stories. Even taboo ones, like human history.

Mareleau took another sip of wine and turned her gaze to the heavens. The stars looked so different from how they had back home. Well, back at her previous home. This was her home now, and she, Noah, and Larylis had important roles here. Even Helena had adapted, and was now a member of Elvyn high society, mingling with the other esteemed mothers.

Regardless, the differences between El'Ara and the human world begged the questions...what exactly were parallel worlds? Were the two realms on different planets? Different planes of existence? Several prominent truthweavers had their own theories, but it seemed not all of them agreed. The whispers of their weavings often conveyed ideas that conflicted with one another's findings.

Those conversations always made Mareleau smile. She knew firsthand just how flawed prophecies and truthweavings could be. The prophecy that had tangled her life had made it seem like her son would be front and center, a chosen one born to battle darkness and save the world. In truth, Mareleau and Cora had played the most significant roles. Yes, Noah's birth had set everything into motion, but he hadn't physically performed any of the feats the prophecy had spoken of.

Which was exactly what had brought the prophecy to fruition.

Mareleau and Cora, two women Darius had underestimated, had defeated him in different ways. Cora took control of Lela using intel he'd given her. Mareleau took his life.

Mareleau's sense of victory, however, was always clouded with a pang of longing. She missed her friend terribly.

Noah giggled at something Larylis had said, then turned the crystal cylinder for a change of view. Their son was aging as normal human children aged, which was supposedly somewhat faster than the Elvyn did. He was growing so quickly, his looks already taking after Larylis'. His hair was several shades lighter than his father's, a rosy gold to Larylis' dark copper. Meanwhile, Larylis' tresses reached his nape in loose waves and a short beard graced his chin. It suited him well, giving him a roguish-yet-scholarly look.

Noah averted his gaze from the cylinder, and his shoulders sank. Mareleau was immediately on alert, attuned to his moods like the admittedly overprotective mother she was.

Larylis noticed too, pushing the cylinder aside to face his son. "What's wrong?"

Noah glanced from Larylis to Mareleau.

She was already on her feet and tried her best to keep her composure as she closed the distance between them. Crouching beside them with a gentle smile, she asked, "What is it, my love?"

Noah dropped his blue-green eyes. "Aribella told me that I'm...I'm a witch, an Elvyn, and a human all in one."

Mareleau clenched her jaw. Aribella was a spoiled brat. Yet she was also the daughter of one of the most respected tribunal members and one of Noah's classmates. Keeping her tone even, she said, "Yes, that's true. You know this, darling."

"Yes, but..." He met her gaze. "She said I'm destined to be evil. That the last person like me tried to destroy the world."

She forced her lips into a reassuring smile. "Noah, I too have the blood of witches, humans, and Elvyn. Do you think I'm evil?"

"You can be scary sometimes, Mum," he said with unabashed candor.

It was all she could do not to laugh. "Yes, well, being scary isn't exactly evil, is it?"

He shifted from foot to foot. "What if I become like him? What if, once I'm old enough that you're not regent anymore, I...do bad things with the *mora*?"

Her first instinct was to insist that would never happen. In her heart of hearts, she knew it was true. But she wouldn't be like Satsara. She wouldn't brush aside serious topics and put her son on a pedestal.

"Here's the thing," she said. "Every person, whether human or fae, has aspects of darkness and light. I was once afraid of my darkest side, afraid of what it meant to be a narcuss. And it's true that all forms of magic require respect and temperance. But you can notice shadows in your heart without letting them take over."

"How can I be sure I don't let them take over?"

"A very wise woman once told me," she said, recalling her conversation with Salinda so many years ago, "that it's a choice to follow the path of hope and love, even when you have dark feelings. Strength isn't being good or perfect but meeting your darkness face to face and moving forward instead of sinking into it. No matter what you find in those shadows, it is important that you love yourself."

Gently, she tapped his chest, right over his heart.

He puckered his lips, shifting them side to side as he pondered her words. "I don't get it."

She and Larylis laughed in unison. Larylis ruffled Noah's hair. "You don't have to understand it yet, but do remember your mother's words. She's a very intelligent woman."

Noah turned a wide-eyed look to Mareleau. "I thought Pa was the smart one."

Gods, even his unintentional insults were adorable. "He is, but I'm quite smart too. And so are you. Thank you for coming to us with such a heavy question." She hugged her son tight. "And if Aribella ever says something like that again, you tell her I'll—"

"Let's not threaten his classmates, love," Larylis said with a laugh.

"I told you," Noah said as Mareleau released him from her embrace. "Everyone says she's scary."

"I'll take that as a compliment," she mumbled.

You know, came Ferrah's lazy voice in her mind, *I could always create a...little accident for this small rude Elvyn who has filled our dear Morkara's head with such somber thoughts. If necessary.*

Mareleau shot her gaze toward the creature and found the dragon still dozing on the terrace. Or pretending to doze. *We are not murdering children. Not even brats like Aribella.*

Just a scare.

Mareleau glared at the dragon until the creature cracked open one violet eye. She understood Ferrah's teasing mirth then. *You're a real feisty beast, you know that?*

Likewise. Ferrah closed her eye and settled back into slumber.

Mareleau shook her head, lips stretched in a wide grin, and settled in between the two loves of her life. With one arm wrapped around each of them, she said, "Show your scary mum your favorite constellation."

~

ALSO BY TESSONJA ODETTE

ABOUT THE AUTHOR

Tessonja Odette is a fantasy author living in Seattle with her family, her pets, and ample amounts of chocolate. When she isn't writing, she's watching cat videos, petting dogs, having dance parties in the kitchen with her daughter, or pursuing her many creative hobbies. Read more about Tessonja at www.tessonjaodette.com

instagram.com/tessonja
facebook.com/tessonjaodette
tiktok.com/@tessonja
x.com/tessonjaodette